THE INSTRUCTIONS

Adam Levin

McSWEENEY'S RECTANGULARS
SAN FRANCISCO

www.mcsweeneys.net

McSweeney's and colophon are registered trademarks of McSweeney's,
a privately held company with wildly fluctuating resources.

ISBN: 978-1-934781-82-1

For my parents, Lanny and Atara Levin

It is a curious enigma that so great a mind would question the most obvious realities and object even to things scientifically demonstrated... while believing absolutely in his own fantastic explanations of the same phenomena.

—FLANN O'BRIEN, *THE THIRD POLICEMAN*

THE INSTRUCTIONS

Gurion ben-Judah Maccabee

Translated and re-translated
from the Hebrew and the English
by Eliyahu of Brooklyn and Emmanuel Liebman

In light of the controversy surrounding our decision to publish *The Instructions*, we wish to clarify the following, once and for all: Gurion Maccabee has received no financial remuneration from us, nor will he ever. In purchasing this book, we paid an advance against royalties directly to the Scholars Fund, and we will continue to pay any and all future royalties to the Scholars Fund after Maccabee reaches the age of majority in June of next year, and regardless of whether the U.S. government ultimately convicts, acquits, or fails to prosecute him for crimes relating to "the Damage Proper," "the 11/17 Miracle," or any other event pertaining to "the Gurionic War." Furthermore, a recent investigation conducted by the National Security Agency has determined that the Scholars Fund, though indeed managed by associates of Maccabee's translators, is neither a terrorist organization nor a sponsor of terrorist organizations.

Conscientious readers need not be troubled.

—David Feldman, Publisher
December 2013

CONTENTS

CODA

There is damage. There was always damage and there will be more damage, but not always. Were there always to be more damage, damage would be an aspect of perfection. We would all be angels, one-legged and faceless, seething with endless, hopeless praise.

Bless Adonai for making us better than angels. Blessed is Adonai for making us human.

Some damage is but destructive, and other damage, through destruction, repairs. It is often impossible, especially while the damage is being brought, to distinguish between the one kind and the other, but because You've made scholars who know of the distinction, we fight to forgive You. Because You know that Your mistakes, though a part of You, are nonetheless mistakes, we accept that Your mistakes, though Yours, are ours to repair.

Blessed are You, Adonai, our God, King of the Universe, Who selected us from all the scholars and gave us *The Instructions* and the Gurionic War. Bless You, Adonai, Giver of the second kind of damage. We want only to fix You.

So let us mistake destruction for reparation with no greater frequency than we would blood for loyalty, loyalty for love, or books for weapons. Help us to be more scholarly. Help us damage Your mistakes. Show us, Adonai, when to set aside our books for weapons, for sometimes scholars must become soldiers, Adonai, for sometimes only soldiers can fix You, Adonai, and only while fixing can we forgive You, Adonai, for those times when only soldiers can fix You, Adonai.

(Amen)

The Side of Damage

Verbosity is like the iniquity of idolatry.

—15:23 Samuel I

1
ELIZA JUNE WATERMARK

Tuesday, November 14, 2006
2nd–3rd Period

Benji Nakamook thought we should waterboard each other, me and him and Vincie Portite. We wouldn't count the seconds to see who was bravest or whose lungs were deepest—this wasn't for a contest. We'd each be held under til the moment the possibility of death became real to us, and in that moment, according to Benji, we'd have to draw one of the following conclusions: "My best friends are about to accidentally drown me!" or "My best friends are actually trying to drown me!" The point was to learn what it was we feared more: being misunderstood or being betrayed.

"That is *so* fucken stupid," Vincie Portite said. "No way I'd think you were trying to drown me."

"You don't know what you'll think," Nakamook told him. "Right now you're rational. Facing death, you won't be. That's how methods like waterboarding operate." Benji'd been reading a book about torture. "This one guy," he said, "Ali Al-Jahani, specifically stated that—"

"Ali Al-Whatever whatever," said Vincie. "I'll do it if, one, you stop talking about that book—it's getting fucken old—and two, if Gurion's down. But it's stupid."

It did seem stupid, but Benji wasn't stupid, not even remotely, and I hated disappointing him. I said I was down.

Vincie said, "Fuck."

Splashing on a kickfloat a couple feet away was Isadore Momo, a shy foreign chubnik who barely spoke English, but the rest of the class was over in the deep end. Benji reached out, tapped Momo on the ankle. "You're wanted over there," he said, pointing to the others.

"By whom?" Momo said.

"By me," said Benji.

"Sorry. I am sorry. Sorry," said Momo. He got off the kickfloat and fled.

Benji told us: "I'll thrash before my death seems real. You'll have to keep me under for a little while after that."

"How long's a little while?" Vincie Portite said.

"Decide when I'm under. If I know, this won't work."

I clutched one shoulder, palmed the crown of his skull. Vincie clutched the other shoulder and the back of his neck. Benji exhaled all the breath in his body. He let his legs buckle.

We plunged him.

"How long then?" said Vincie.

A thirty-count, I said.

"How about a twenty?"

A twenty then, I said.

Benji started to thrash.

I counted off twenty inside of my head, tried pulling him up, but he wasn't coming up. He just kept thrashing. He was tilted toward Vincie, who was staring at the water.

Vincie, I said.

"Fuck," Vincie said. He pulled Benji up.

Benji sucked air.

Vincie said, "You count fast. Did you do Mississippis? I was doing Mississippis—I only got to twelve. Gurion. Gurion."

In the deep-end, some kids had rhymed "Izzy" with "Jizzy." I'd revolved to see who: Ronrico and the Janitor. Momo told them, "*Izzy*. I am *Izzy*, for Isadore. Isadore Momo. You may call me Izzy Momo." "Jizzy!" said Ronrico. "Jizzy Homo!" said the Janitor. Momo just took it, leaning hard on his kickfloat.

Benji cough-hiccuped, hands on his waist.

So? I said to him. What was the conclusion?

"Both," Benji said.

That doesn't make sense, I said. Which one was first?

"I said, 'Both,'" Benji said.

That doesn't make sense.

"You'll see for yourself in a second," he said.

"No way," Vincie said. "I'm going fucken next. Okay? Okay? I want to be done with this."

We held Vincie under and he started to thrash. We counted fifteen and we pulled him back up.

"Both?" Benji said.

"Neither," gasped Vincie. His pupils were pinned. His flushed face trembled.

"So what then?" said Benji.

"Who—" Vincie said, but he choked on some air. He showed us his pointer, laid hands on my shoulders. "Who cares?" he said, catching up with his lungs. "I don't even know. I feel fucken stupid. Dying is fucked. I don't want to die."

Then it was my turn. I let all my breath out. My friends held me under. They had a firm hold that I couldn't have broken, and the water got colder, and my chest drew tighter, and I thought I might drink, take little sips, that a series of sips imbibed at steady intervals could gradually lessen the pressure of the strangle, but before I'd even tested this chomsky hypothesis, air stung my face and fattened my chest. They'd pulled me back up before death seemed real.

What happened? I said.

"We waited and waited. You wouldn't start thrashing."

"Vincie thought you passed out."

I didn't, I said.

Nakamook asked me, "You want to go again?"

Not really, I said. If you think it's that important, though—

"*Fuck* 'go again,'" Vincie Portite said. "I'm out. I'm done. You can drown him by yourself."

Benji said, "Vincie."

Vincie said, "Nakamook."

The whistle got blown. Free swim was over.

Benji said, "Vincie," and extended a fist.

"What?" Vincie said. "Fine. Okay." He made his own fist and banged it on Benji's.

I counted to three and we raced to the showers.

□ □ □ □ □ □ □

Were Isadore gay, I'd have probably hurt the Janitor for calling him a homo, and were he my friend, I'd have certainly avenged him—even just for "Jizzy"— but Momo was neither gay nor my friend. I'd had plans to fight the Janitor since late the night before.

I had never fought anyone without good reason, and I needed to learn what doing so felt like. I needed to see if it felt any different. I'd been fighting a lot since I got to Aptakisic, and I enjoyed it so much—maybe too much. Each fight was better, more fun than the last, and I worried I was thrilling on the damage alone, rather than the justice the damage was enacting. I worried that the people I'd been getting in fights with might as well have been anyone as far as the fun I had pummeling them went. The only way to find out was to get in a fight without justification. If the thrill was absent, or in some way different, all would be well, I'd cease to worry. If the thrill was the same, though... I didn't know what, but I'd have to change something. So I'd picked a kid at random the night before—at least *somewhat* at random; I disliked the Janitor, he disliked me, we had Gym the same period—and decided I'd fight him in the locker-room.

Benji and Vincie were still in the showers—I'd won the race—and though I wasn't finished dressing, I saw it was time. If my friends got involved it could bance up the test, and I didn't need a shirt to get in a fight. I buckled my belt and ran up on the Janitor. A couple steps short of him, I towel-snapped his neck.

He whined and revolved. He said, "You're B.D. and you smell like cigarettes, it's nasty!"

No thrill yet, but we weren't really fighting.

I snorted up a goozy and twetched it on his toes.

"Towel!" he shouted. "Gimme a towel!" The Janitor dreaded all forms of dishygiene. He hopped on one leg. He threw wild punches. One caught my shoulder.

Now it was a fight.

I towel-snapped his eyes and he fell down sideways.

Someone said, "Your towel, sir."

"No, please, a towel, really!" the Janitor pleaded. He blinked like a lizard. His breathing got labored. He stayed on his side on the floor by his basket and begged for a towel while other kids watched.

The fight was over. No thrill at all.

I returned to my locker to finish getting dressed. My shirt was all tangled but I tried to pull it on. That's when Ronrico Asparagus attacked. He came from behind and charleyed my thigh-horse. I had to lean, but I didn't get deadleg. You only get deadleg if you're willing to kneel.

"Fight!" yelled some kids.

"Pee so pungent!" yelled some other ones.

Twenty came together to form a writhing wall.

I retreated four locker-lengths, struggling with my shirt. My head was through, and my shoulders were right, but the twisted sleeves were blocking the armholes.

Asparagus charged and kicked my flank.

I coughed, saw white. I slumped on the bench.

The wall swelled and hollered, waving its fists. Kids in the back shoved up to the front. Kids in the front popped out and fell down. Asparagus posed, just outside kicking range. "See that?" he said to them. "See that?" he said. "Gurion Maccabee. Big fucken deal." The wall got more dense, inched itself closer, squeezed itself tighter, popped out more kids.

Teeth shone everywhere.

My arms in their sleeves.

"Sit back down," Asparagus said to me.

I snorted and twetched, hung gooze on his ear. It moved like a yo-yo.

Asparagus lunged.

I tagged his grill with my wrist while pivoting. The blow was glancing, but the pivot added torque; he landed on his tailbone, swiping at air.

The air was sweaty.

I limped to my locker and snatched off the padlock, jammed home the U and slid in my pointer and swear to the knuckles.

The wall of kids: silent.

Ronrico had his legs again.

I told him, Be the hero.

"Fucken," he said.

Spring so fast you blur.

He vaulted the bench.

I uppercut the sweetspot under his ribs, that charliest of horses where every nerve's bundled. He stumbled forward folded, hugging himself, the scalp in his part agleam like the padlock, inviting me to fuse the two in imagistic deathblow.

Instead I kicked his ankles, finishing his chapter. His leftward collapse on the wall of baskets clattered so loud it roused Mr. Desormie.

Desormie didn't mean anything in Italian. He taught Gym in shorts that his wang stretched the crotch of.

"What's all the noise?" said Mr. Desormie. "Who is responsible for this brand of nonsense?" The tip of his collar was curling toward the ceiling. "Why's the Janitor balanced on one of his feet instead of both of his feet?" Desormie said. "And who made Asparagus wheeze and sway like a person that's dying or fatally wounded?"

"It was Gurion!" "Gurion!" "Gurion did it!"

They ratted me out. I didn't see who; I was staring at the collar.

Desormie scratched his throat and told me, "Go nowhere."

I got on the bench to make an announcement: A kid who tells on another kid's a dead kid.

That was a line from *Over the Edge,* a childsploitation flick starring Matt Dillon.

"Hey!" Desormie said to me. He wanted to punch my nose through my face but wouldn't break rules. He crouched beside Ronrico. "Asparagus," he said. "Hey, Asparagus," he said. He hefted him onto the bench by the pits.

Someone in the distance said, "Kids who tell are dead and dead!"

Blake Acer, Shover President, ran from the bathroom, asking what happened. The Flunky whispered, "Gurion spit on the Janitor, then he whammed Asparagus deep in the solarplaces." Someone near Acer said to someone behind him, "Maccabee pissed on Flunky Bregman's little brougham. Ronrico's xiphoid process is shattered."

The Janitor continued to ask for a towel. Desormie told him to act mature.

Then the elephant sounds of lockers denting, the clicking of shock-numbed hand-bones getting shook.

Someone said, "Gurion battled two guys at once."

"Like that?" said the guy who was punching the lockers.

"Like that," said the guy who the puncher showed off for.

Back by the showers, Nakamook was shouting, "Gurion's my boy! Do not play with us!"

"Do not fucken *play* with us!" flaved Vincie, beside him.

Snarly toplip, eyebrows tensed, I mock-aggressed with my face at Ronrico. He didn't respond. Stunned? I said. He just held his chest. The gym teacher told me, "Cruisin for a bruisin."

I tried to break my fingers, to see if I could. It was something I'd try every couple of hours. I'd match up the tips of right and left and push. They wouldn't ever break. I'd think: They can't. This time was no different.

I stepped off the bench and I leaned on my locker and waited for Desormie to take us to the Office. He waited for Ronrico's wheezing to subside. The Janitor lay there, waiting for a towel. Everyone else in the locker-room verbalized.

"Your knuckles are cut." "It doesn't even hurt." "The Janitor's toe's broke."

"Gangrene set in yet?" "Do not *play* with us!" "No one fucken *plays* with us!" "Look at that latch. That's blood on that latch." "I didn't even notice the blood til you said." "Do not look at us." "…not fucken look at us!" "Bleeding's weird." "I bet I could take him." "No one here can take him. He's from Chicago." "He's only, like, ten, though—I'm twelve." "So's Asparagus." "Do not think of us. Do not talk of us. Do not try to be us." "…much *less* try fucken being us." "A sock full of flashlight batteries you're saying." "I haven't bled in a really long time." "Duracell mace." "Except for hangnails." "Blew out the ligaments with a special chi-punch." "Then the bodyslam." "Bam Slokum could take him." "Totally beside the point." "Full-nelson to suplex, closed with a sleeper-hold." "Blonde Lonnie could take him." "Blonde Lonnie *could*n't take him—he's standing right there." "Do it, Blonde Lonnie." "Blonde Lonnie fakes deafness!" "An axe-kick to the shoulder to top off the evening."

No one was speaking to any one person. All of them were speaking to every single person. Everyone was going on record. I'd performed specific actions on Ronrico and the Janitor, but the hows and the whos didn't matter to the rest of them. What mattered was something had messed up the arrangement. They wanted a part of that, so they tried to explain it, but didn't know how, so they made things up, working together, though none of them knew it, like bouncing molecules forming gases.

"Bleeding doesn't hurt." "If your *face* was bleeding, trust me it would hurt." "And the Flunky's not stepping up either, is he? And he's the Janitor's very own brother!" "A spring-loaded sap like Maholtz has." "HCl in a two-dollar squirtgun." "I've cut my lip—didn't ever hurt." "Boystar, too." "Boystar! Tch." "Co-Captain Baxter, then." "I've never seen him fight." "I'm saying your nose, getting punched in your nose." "A punch in the nose would hurt cause the bone. It's snapping the nosebone's the pain, not the bleeding." "Boystar and the Flunky and the Co-Captain together, then. Plus Bam Slokum. And Blonde Lonnie." "There isn't any nosebone." "Five guys is cheap. Especially with Slokum." "Tell it to my nosebone. He's standing right here." "A pointed fucking instrument." "Slokum's beside the point." "Nose is all cartilage." "Slokum's the *whole* point. Slokum's indestructible." "What the fuck's cartilage?" "He's fucking immortal." "He fucking jammed a screwdriver in dude's *fuck*ing earhole!"

Desormie yelled, "Quiet down!" at the ceiling.

Vincie Portite yelled, "Quiet down!" at Desormie.

Desormie yelled, "Quiet!" into the floor. To me, he said: "You've got trouble coming."

I should have said, Bring it. Instead I said, I know.

Someone said, "A dead kid." Nakamook shouted, "Ve vill crush you like zeh grape!" "Ve vucken vill crush!" Vincie Portite flaved.

Asparagus coughed, then started breathing normal. Desormie said "Good" and sat the Janitor next to him. "The office'll send for you later," he told them. "For now you go back to the Cage."

"Let's go let's move," he said to me.

After counting to seven, I hoisted my bag.

On the way to the door, I looked over my shoulder and saw the Janitor eyeing the gooze that was still on his foot, eyeing a t-shirt laying on the bench, about to decide to wipe one with the other. The t-shirt belonged to Leevon Ray. Leevon was the only black kid at school, unless you count halfie Lost Tribesmen—I don't—and he refused to speak, which is why he was Cage, but we'd sometimes trade snacks and play slapslap at lunch, so I knew we were friends, and to spread word through kids was no form of ratting, but it took me a second of sorting that out before I cued Leevon to safeguard his shirt. It took me a second because of the fight. My chemicals, after fights, often fired weird; during a fight, they were always reliable, tunneling my thinking so I could be simple, but after a fight the opposite happened and sometimes the tunnel would loop til it knotted and wouldn't untangle until I noticed.

Your shirt, I told Leevon.

The Janitor flinched.

I entered B-Hall behind Desormie. Up at the B-Hall/2-Hall junction, a red-lettered banner that hung from the ceiling read

Junior High School

Aptakisic ^ Forever

They had to jam in the "Junior High School" because of genocide and irony. Most of Aptakisic's people were gone. Aptakisic was a chief. His tribe was called the Potawatami, but the Aptakisic basketball team was called the Indians. I got called a Jew, but Jews were no longer; we were already Israelites.

I took a running start and jumped to tear the banner down. I missed the lower edge by three or four feet.

"Don't test me, Maccabee," Desormie said.

You, kinesiologist, will soon be delivered.

He said, "What did you say to me?"

I said, Into my hand, Gym teacher.

□   □   □   □   □   □   □

Admissions Record: Gurion Maccabee
DOB: 6/16/96

The Solomon Schecter School of Chicago

Admitted	Aug 20, 2001	Kindergarten
Released	May 3, 2006	Grade 4

Brief Description of Release:
  Expulsion. Physically assaulted Headmaster.

Northside Hebrew Day School

Admitted	May 8, 2006	Grade 4
Released	June 5, 2006	Grade 6

Brief Description of Release:
  Double Promotion followed by Expulsion.
  Supplied weapons to students/weapons possession/incitement to use weapons.

Martin Luther King Middle School

Admitted	Aug 21, 2006	Grade 7
Released	Aug 24, 2006	Grade 7

Brief Description of Release:
  Expulsion from Evanston Public School System.
  Assaulted student w/ brick.

Aptakisic Junior High School

Admitted	Sept 5, 2006	Grade 5 (CAGE Program)

Brief Description of Admission
  Demoted to age-appropriate grade-level. Placed probationally
  (three weeks) in CAGE Program for observation.

Update (September 26, 2006)

  Re-promoted to Grade 7.
  Observed to be appropriate for CAGE Program—
  placed indefinitely in CAGE Program.

□   □   □   □   □   □   □

The air in Main Hall was blinky that morning. Dust touched light and the particles twitched. Desormie, ahead of me, hummed out a melody with lipfart percussion and aggressively dance-walked and thought it was strutting. I was thinking how dust was mostly made of people, and that a pile of dust from a one-man home should be as easy to mojo as fingernail clippings, which was probably why Hoodoos were vigilant sweepers (self-protection), when a swollen-lipped Ashley, trailed by Bam Slokum, came out of the lunchroom, and Desormie stopped humming.

"Bammo!" he said.

I pulled on my hoodstrings.

"Hey Coach D," Bam Slokum said. Superhero-shaped and over six feet tall, Bam was Aptakisic Indians Basketball's goldenboy. I'd never even exchanged as much as a nod with him. He and Benji Nakamook were longtime arch-enemies.

Desormie said, "You got a hall-pass there, Bammenstein?"

Bam made the noise "Tch" = "I know you don't care if I've got a hall-pass," and laced his fingers in front of his chest, then pushed out his hands to pop all his knuckles. A thousand dark veins and knotty tendons raised the taut skin on his forearms.

"How about you, young lady? Got a pass?"

"Ashley's all distraught," Slokum said to Desormie. "I was helping her out. Process of helping her, we misplaced her pass."

"Oh," Desormie said. "Distraught?"

"I'm feeling much better now," the Ashley told him.

Slokum chinned the air in the direction of A-Hall. The Ashley squeezed his biceps and strode off toward A-Hall.

"Well al*right*," said Desormie. "Al*right* then," he said. "We gearing up for a righteous premiere?"

The opening game of the basketball season was scheduled for 5 p.m. on Friday.

"Sure, Coach D," Bam Slokum said.

"Main Hall Shovers get their new scarves today, boy. Just had Blake Acer in Gym—kid's *amped*. Comes up to me, tells me, 'Listen, Mr. D, our new scarves are gonna be so darn flossy, I'm scared once I see 'em, I'll just go blind.' Says, 'Bam's gonna crush and the Shovers'll *be* there. Watch it, Twin Groves. Just watch out!'"

"Yeah," said Bam. "The air's crackling with pep."

"Crackling with pep!" Desormie said. "But like what the heck's 'flossy' though? The heck does that mean, right? Heck did it come from? What happened to *killer*? Heck, what happened to *awesome*? When did the Main Hall Shovers turn to funnytalk? Maybe it's just Acer. Presidents talk weird. Good kid, though, that Acer. Don't get me wrong. Good kids the lot of them. A tribute to all of us. A boon for the team. All those Shovers. Other teams get pepsquads—pepsquads! *What?* Wussy little pepsquads waving little flags, fancy-dancing on their twinkle-toes, and, I don't know, lisping. That, Sir Bam, is what other teams get. The Indians, though? We got *Shovers.* We got us Shovers, and they don't wave flags. We got us Shovers and our Shovers *wear scarves.* Our Shovers wear scarves and they trounce any pepsquad. Right? Am I right? They trounce on the twinkletoed all the dang livelong. So what if their hand-eye's crappier than ours? So what if sometimes you want to give 'em a wedgie til the tears and the boogers go pouring down their chins? They're carrying your books. They're filling the bleachers. They're loving the Indians. Good kids all of them. A tribute and a boon. It's how you play the game. All good kids. When they almost fell apart, they could've fell apart, except they didn't fall apart because instead they came together. Overcame differences. All the stronger for it. Intestinal fortitude. Trial by fire. Awesome scarves. No limp flags. Trouncing the lispers. Pep that crackles. How you play the game. Just why the funnytalk from Acer's what I'm saying."

"Yeah," Bam said. "Shovers," he said.

Desormie made the noise "Tch" ≠ anything meaningful. Bam made the noise "Tch" back at him, and then he chinned the air at me and winked his left eye = "We just made accidental eye-contact and I am only doing what is done when that happens, but still I want you to know that we are in this together." Except for the hallway, there was nothing that Bam and I were in together. Still, I chinned back at him. His chinning made me feel brotherly. Up close to Slokum for the first time ever, acknowledged, I saw there was something I liked about him, which bothered me a lot, and not just because my best friend despised him. There were certain very few guys like Bam who something about them made me not want to harm them when I should have, or should've at least been planning how to. I thought it was probably the faces they made. Whatever it was, though, I knew those had to be the kinds of guys who Adonai used to make kings of, when He still made kings. David ben-Jesse was one of those guys, and Solomon, too; but then so was Saul, and even Jeroboam.

Hashem had to make kings because the Israelites wouldn't be led by the judges, even though the judges were tougher than the kings and knew the law better. It was actually *because* the judges were tougher and knew the law better that they couldn't lead the Israelites. That spooked me out. I didn't think it should be that way. It wasn't up to me, though.

Neither was starting a fight with Slokum. I'd given my word to Benji that I wouldn't, as long as Slokum didn't provoke me. And Slokum, there in Main Hall, wasn't provoking me. Not even a little. I thought that maybe he didn't know who I was—most Aptakisic students outside the Cage didn't—and I wanted to tell him, "I'm Gurion Maccabee, best friend of your number-one enemy, Nakamook," but before I'd said anything, he was walking away, and before he'd walked away, he'd chinned air at me a second time, and I'd chinned back, without even thinking, and felt just as brotherly and bothered as the first time.

"Baaaam Slokum," Desormie said as Slokum turned the corner.

I made the noise Tch = I am not your audience.

Desormie made the noise back = "You're lucky you're not my son."

I said, Hnh = That happens to be true, but not because you say so.

As soon as we started walking again, My Main Man Scott Mookus fell out of the Office. Aptakisic hallways always seemed picaresque.

Main Man stumbled toward us, saying, "Hello Gurion! And hello Mr. Desormie! What a shiny whistle you're wearing around your well-muscled neck. I would like to talk about it with you some time. How negligible of me not to have said so, but it is such beautiful weather that we are having today, don't you suppose? I would even go so far as to say that the snow is reminiscent of my youth in the heart of the country. Oh isn't the sky a stage, in a sense, and the snow a sort of spotlight? It is! And what of this rumor being bandied about town surrounding the subject of your tent-pitching acumen? It's truly fantastic! In all sincerity, I do wish you well. And Gurion! My captain! Captain, my captain, my great brother Gurion, the tomorrow after tomorrow's tomorrow you will lead us into battle to separate the head from the body of the heathen droves. What does that feel like? I say the silent fall of this snow won't do, that we pray for a hailstorm to dramatize the atmosphere, the thunder and pattering our background music…"

Desormie had kept us walking while Mookus stayed in the spot where we'd passed him, speaking louder and faster about weather and End Days. It was the disease. Main Man had Williams Cocktail Party Syndrome. His face looked elfy and his grammar, sometimes, sounded seriously official, but he couldn't understand himself because he was retarded. For the most part he talked because talking was social, a friendly noise, and he was nice. Almost everything he said, whatever the content = "Talk to me and I'll talk to you," and that used to get me sad, but then I figured that almost anything he heard must have also = "Talk to me and I'll talk to you," and I wasn't sad, but I was a little spooked. For a day, I was actually really spooked, and I started to wonder if I was retarded, my parents and friends all secret condescenders for my self-esteem. I even asked my mom. "Retarded?" she said. "You are the smartest and the handsomest." Exactly what I'd say to my retarded son if I wanted to hide the truth. Are you telling me the truth? I'd said to my mom, and my mom said "Yes," and I believed her, or at least I believed she didn't *think* I was retarded, and that was enough to unspook me.

Down the hall, I yelled: Mookus, you are my main man!

"Indeed I am, Gurion! I am indeed!" My Main Man Scott Mookus yelled up the hall back at me.

I wanted to know what else Scott was saying, but I couldn't hear him at all anymore. I could hear my jingling pocket and the ticking of the ball in Desormie's whistle when it swung against his pecs, the clap and squeak of our shoes on the floor, and the buzzing of the panels of light in the ceiling. Everything I could hear was not supposed to get heard. I'd been told by Call-Me-Sandy that this had to do with earlids. Earlids were figurative. They had no flesh. They closed to block out the ambient sounds. People whose A's were D'd didn't have earlids, unless they took Ritalin or Adderal or another form of speed for SpEds that stunts growth. I took no spedspeed, but still wasn't tall. Nakamook took it, but only sometimes. The ones he didn't want he'd stockpile and sell for a buck a pill to a group of sophomores with hair in their eyes who'd drive to the beach from Stevenson High School to meet him each Friday after detention.

Behind me, Scott did the Joy of Living Dance. To do the Joy of Living Dance, My Main Man would two-step and roll his shoulders like a warming-up boxer and clear all the gooze from his throat. It meant he was going to sing. His voice was beautiful and he could perfectly sing things he'd only heard once—mostly songs off the mixes Vincie burned for us weekly—and he did requests.

We took a left into the Office and I never found out what Scott sang that time. It was suck because one day soon My Main Man would never sing again. The Williams made his heart grow wrong: bubbles in his vessels and tears in his atria. These defects shrunk his chambers down. He would outgrow his pump until it would kill him, the sweetest person. He was proof of why it's flawed to call good people big-hearted. Desormie was more proof—his heart was huge from athletics, probably the biggest heart in school.

I always thought Adonai should kill him instead of Mookus.

It wasn't up to me, though. At least not the instead part.

□　□　□　□　□　□　□

In front of the desk of Miss Virginia Pinge, Desormie tried hooking his thick arm around me. The arm was hairless and tanning-bed orange. I almost hit my head on the elbow as I ducked it, but almost didn't count, so I didn't get dangerous—as a rule I'd get dangerous when my head got touched.*

Miss Pinge said to me, "What happened this time?"

Desormie told her, "Fighting."

Miss Pinge said, "You were fighting again?"

"Socking it out with Ronrico Asparagus and spitting like an animal

---

* The blossoming Gurionic oral tradition has been making far too much of this. That a touch to my head could cause me to explode is significant enough a fact to mention, but it isn't a fact that anyone should dwell on. I only dwell on it here for the benefit of a certain kind of well-intended scholar who would otherwise waste his patience and energy awaiting revelation of an origin story explaining the fact, or, even worse, fruitlessly searching *The Instructions* for evidence supporting any of those "theories" about the fact's "meaning" that the oral tradition has lately put forth. To clarify further:

1. There is no untold backstory that explains why I would become dangerous when touched on the head. No head-striking abuser haunted my past. I'd never suffered *any* kind of trauma to my head. I'd never inflicted a serious head-trauma, let alone one that I later regretted, nor had I witnessed such a trauma inflicted on anybody else, much less someone close to me. I'd never been forced to perform fellatio. I'd never seen anyone receive fellatio. No one had or would ever use my head or any other of my bodyparts against my will for any sexual purpose.

2. It is true that my head, like anyone else's, contains my brain, and that my brain, like anyone's, generates thoughts that, if unexpressed, cannot be accessed by anyone—including Adonai—but me. The idea, however, that my head-touch-triggered danger would arise because I wanted to protect my "one true sanctum" from "invaders" is patently false. I'd been exploding from head-touches since before I could remember; since the day I was born, according to my mother; since before I could make the (silly) leaps in symbology necessary to conclude that protecting my braincase = guarding my unexpressed thoughts; since before I even knew that I *had* a brain.

3. There is no genetic or biological link between my mother's "ocular neuroses" and my head-touch explosions. As my *Story of Stories* (p. 115) faithfully reports, my mother *learned* to guard her eyes zealously; she wasn't born doing it.

And so, in sum: As a rule I'd get dangerous when my head got touched, and as a rule I'd use my right hand to hold a glass of water. The former fact bears mention because it is peculiar and because it has potentiated important events and decisions I've made, whereas the latter fact doesn't bear mention (except to make this rhetorical point), for it isn't peculiar and it hasn't potentiated anything important. Both facts, however, are *simple* facts, in that they owe to chance, neurology, or the whim of Adonai, depending on the flavor of your reductive urges. Simple facts, good scholar, aren't worthy of your disquisitions, not with so many complex ones at hand.

on the Janitor," said Desormie. "Probably the Janitor said B.D. to him in a disparaging tone. That's his new thing he calls people and to me it's hilarious and ironic."

"The janitor makes fun of your behavioral disorders?" Miss Pinge said. She should have put her hand on the back of her head, where the lizard brain sits and the alarms blasts out from, but she put it on her chest instead, and kept it there.

"Not Hector with the mop, Miss Pinge, ya big loony toon. That FOB can't hardly speaky the English. You think he knows what B.D. is? I'm talking about the Flunky's little brother Mikey Bregman. The neatfreak kid. The Janitor. It's his nickname. Get it? That's why it's so ironic. Cause he's got the B.D. himself. The Janitor. Tch."

"That's not very funny," Miss Pinge said. "Where are—"

"Hey, now, it's the kid's nickname," said Desormie, "and there's a reason for that and sometimes you gotta do as the Romans and sometimes you gotta let 'em reap what they sow, cause if you're B.D. and you start saying B.D. in the disparaging tones? Then it's just like with the n-word. You're gonna get treated like you're the n-word because you're acting like someone who's the n-word. Law of the jungle. That's all I'm saying. It's the facts of life. These Cage students need to cultivate some intestinal fortitude and stop acting like they hate themselves because we know it's not very mature and it's probably why they got put in the Cage in the first place, which is also pretty ironic if you ask me, don't you think?"

"Where are Mikey and Ronrico?" Miss Pinge asked him.

Not a bad question.

Desormie chinned the air at me. He said, "Brodsky's last email said this one fights, we bring him in separate from who he fought with."

It was the first I'd heard of that policy.

Same with Miss Pinge. "Really?" she said = "That doesn't seem right."

"I do what Brodsky says," Desormie said.

Miss Pinge handed him a Complaint Against Students Sheet. Some people called it a CASS. It was the standard document for the STEP System. Cage students like me were outside the STEP system, even though everyone pretended we were in it. If I'd been in the STEP system, I'd have been expelled by then. So would at least half the rest of the Cage. You got expelled after three out-of-school suspensions. Those were OSS's. You got an OSS after three in-school suspensions in the same semester, which were ISS's. You got an ISS if you had four detentions for the same reason in one quarter. All they ever gave me was detentions and once in a while ISS's.

Desormie's auto-tinting eyeglasses were almost as big as laboratory goggles. He took them off and blew steam on the lenses. Then he wiped the lenses on his shirt and put the glasses back on to read the standard document. He'd answered the CASS questions at least five times in front of me, but still he had to mouth the words of them as he went along. I noticed a red lint-string attached to his shirt-hem by static and I wanted it removed but it wouldn't remove itself and I wouldn't ever touch him, so I scratched an itch on my head and read the pervy stories in his face: He was a notorious de-pantser in the hallways of his grade school. The first time he went to the bathroom after eating beets, he looked in the toilet and thought he was dying, so he played with himself. His wife was scared of him was why he married her. He thought *polack* was the Polish word for Polish person. That's the story of his life that his face told. It was the story of a perv in the making. The story of a perv on the make.

And the story was true. He was always caressing between his tits when he talked to women and making girls who wore spandex tights sit in front during sit-ups and leg-stretches. It was all there in the mouth. Its top lip had a pointy edge. Its word-forming movements made it look like he was chewing food that he thought was gross but wouldn't say was gross because it was impolite but he wanted you to know it was gross so he showed you—like the food was so bad he couldn't hide the ugliness of his own mouth-actions so you were supposed to admire how polite he was for not *saying* anything. I hated him. And that's not just an expression. I hated him the way the tongues of smart girls prefer bittersweet chocolate to milk. I hated him the way Jews endangered Jews and burning matter grabs oxygen. I hated him from the moment I met him, and at the moment I met him it was as if I'd always hated him. I hated him the way he hated me. Helplessly, I hated him. Without volition. And it is true that there were others as despicable as Desormie, even within the walls of Aptakisic, but I had to learn to hate those others. They had to teach me how to hate them. Desormie was the only person I ever hated a priori. Our enmity was mystical.

Miss Pinge told me Brodsky was in a meeting. She said I'd have to wait. I was already waiting, but what she meant was I didn't have to wait on my feet. To get that across, she stuck out her pointer and jabbed it back and forth. The jabbing was something Emmanuel Liebman had long ago taught me to call a blinker action. That label referred to the orange blinkers that were mounted on the tops of construction horses; the horse showed you where it was that you shouldn't go, and the blinker showed you the horse. I.e., it showed you a showing. The jabbing of the finger was a blinker action because it was a pointing at a pointing. It pointed at how the finger was pointing at the three fake-oak waiting-chairs next to the door.

I didn't like it when people blinkered for me—it seemed condescending—but I did like Miss Pinge, so I decided I'd wait just a three- (not a five-) count, before I revolved and went to the chairs. Before I'd even counted to two, though, something flat sailed over my shoulder, then landed with a clap on Miss Pinge's desk. A wooden bathroom pass the size of a textbook.

"I was nice to give you that pass," Pinge said. "It would've been nice of you not to throw it at me."

"I threw it on the blotter," said Eliza June Watermark.

□ □ □ □ □ □ □

No one called her Eliza. They all called her June. I'd seen June around, but never close up. She was flat but so pretty. She sat before I did, and not in the middle chair. I didn't know if I should sit next to her or sit so a chair was empty between us, so I tried to read her face, but I couldn't read her face because she wasn't bat-mitzvah yet—the stories wouldn't tell. They weren't available.

I did a quick eenie-meenie with my chin and the words inside my head so no one would know. I landed on *sit with the chair between us*, then knew I didn't want that, so I sat down next to her and asked why she was there. She said she was there for talking in Spanish.

I said, That's racist.

June said, "Spanish. Class." There were three slim gaps between the teeth of her top-row. She whispered, "Next stop, Frontier Motel."

"Next stop, Frontier Motel," was the first part of a rhyme people said to me on the bus, right before I'd get dropped off at the Frontier Motel. The rest of the rhyme was, "The place where Gurion's fat black dad who fell dwells." They thought I lived at the Frontier Motel, but I only got picked up and dropped off there.

I never knew what to do when I'd hear the rhyme because the guy they called my black dad was the motel owner, Flowers, a three-hundred-pound bachelor hoodooman with silvershot dreadlocks and a chrome-knobbed walking cane who'd written four novels he said cast spells. He said I shouldn't read them; not because of the spells, but because he was my teacher, and his books would interfere. So I didn't read them, because he was my teacher, and my father's old friend. He was helping me to write my third work of scripture. I.e., he was helping me out with *this* work of scripture, *The Instructions*, although, at the time, I hadn't known its title, let alone its true substance. At the time, all I'd known was that it would be different from my first two scriptures—*The Story of Stories* and *Ulpan*—which I hadn't needed help with from anyone at all, since they were exclusively concerned with my people, who I already knew how to speak to and about. My people, when I'd written those first two scriptures, were the only people I knew.

Apart from forbidding me to read his four novels, though, the only thing Flowers ever forbade was for me to portray him as a wise old black man who gave life-lessons to an Israelite boy, part lost-tribe or not, because, he said, that would signify wrong, and signifying was important to him, and since he wasn't some kind of zealous forbidder, I knew it should be important to me. And that was the reason I didn't know what to do when people called him my black dad who fell. The first thing I'd think to do was violence, because they were making fun of him, but if I did violence then they could think I was doing violence because they called a black guy my dad and that it made me ashamed. So violence would signify wrong. Plus I didn't know who they were exactly—just that they sat up front with the bandkids. They might have even been the bandkids. So I didn't do anything to them at all. Instead, I'd tell Flowers and he'd give me a book that was by someone else, or sometimes a root he'd tell me to chew. The roots all tasted like chalk.

June didn't say the black guy part of the bus-rhyme, but I was being nice to her, so it was suck of her to say any of it. I didn't even know how she knew the rhyme—she wasn't on my bus. She sneezed after she said it, though, and after she sneezed, I said God bless you. I didn't really want to be mean to her anyway.

Desormie kept trying to talk to Miss Pinge while she typed. "So," he said.

Miss Pinge shrugged = "So what?"

He said, "I guess you're recording attendance."

Miss Pinge nodded = "Yes already."

"I see you've got a system," Desormie said. "You just sorta bring up the name of an absent kid on your spreadsheet, there—Oh! Look at that. You don't even have to type the whole name in. You just sorta type the first couple letters of the last name and then there's like a box pops up you can select from... I see, sometimes it's quicker to just type the whole name in so you don't have to move your hand off the home-row of the keyboard there to use the mouse or the arrow-pad. There's a coupla systems there, huh? There's the system you're using, like in the computer, and then there's the system you're using of your own. If the kid's last name is Yamowitz—wow, you're already in the Y's and it's barely third period. As I was saying, if the kid's name is Yamowitz—and what a crappy name!—I see you just sorta type in Y A and hit enter cause there aren't any other kids with last names start with Y A in the box and you know that so you just hit enter and there's the kid's file, and then you hit shift-A. Absent! On the record. There you go. I can respect your system. I *do* respect your system. I am Luca Brasi and you are Don Vito Corleone and I am at your daughter's wedding and your daughter's wedding is the system you're using. I like it. You know what I mean?"

I thought: If history's taught us anything, it's that any man can be killed.

That's from *Part II*.

Miss Pinge stopped typing and tilted her head = "*Please* go away, Ron Desormie," but Desormie thought = "Please continue, you interesting gym teacher." He turned around and saw me watching him. Then he made his eyes wide at June and thumbed air at me = "Look at this intermittently disordered exploder who does not attend and is hyper and who thinks you want to sit next to him when what you really want is to sit in my lap." He ran the thumb up and down his cleavage. Then he winked at June and turned back to Miss Pinge.

He said, "I bet there used to be an old system where you didn't have those pop-up boxes and you had to type the entire name in. How fast our technology moves. Jeez. Look at all those absents."

Miss Pinge didn't look.

Desormie said, "What I mean is, there's a whole lot of absents you got there." Then he said, "Gotta teach gym."

He pretended to scratch his arm so he could flex it, and then he left the CASS on the desk and then he left.

I hate that perv, I said to June.

She said, "Me too."

Yeah? I said.

June made the noise "Tch" = "That was a useless thing to say, Gurion." = "What you just asked me was not a real question."

I said, Tch. It sounded inauthentic and I tried to ignore her.

It was hard for me to ignore people, especially pretty ones. It was hard to ignore noises, too. Call-Me-Sandy said the same thing as my mom said about it. They said that to be a good ignorer you had to concentrate on another thing because if you just concentrated on ignoring what you were supposed to ignore then you wouldn't really be ignoring what you were supposed to ignore because you'd be thinking about ignoring it, which was just another way of thinking about it.

So I concentrated on the face of Miss Pinge instead of June. It was not as fun as concentrating on the face of June. June was pretty and also hot. Miss Pinge was hot but she wasn't pretty. It's the faces she made that were hot. But the face that she had when she was not making a face was not pretty. It was beat-looking, her resting face. When she was my age, she got her period early and her father dragged her in front of a mirror in her pajamas. He forced her to look into it and say, "You are an ugly girl and I hate you." The face she made in the mirror acted powerfully on the bones and muscles of her resting face so that now it was a hint of the mirror-face. Certain kinds of men, on seeing the hint, would try to seduce her in hopes that once they'd gotten her naked, they could say something cruel to her and thereby elicit that original face she'd made for her father. Certain kinds of men like Ron Desormie. What a name. What a pervy name. What a perfect name for a perv like him. It could even be verbed like pasteurize. I thought: It *could* be? No. It *will* be. I thought: From now on, *desormiate* = perv the world, and *rondesormiate* will, for a while, be an acceptable, however overly formal, variant in the vein of *irregardless*, then become archaic, whereas *sorm* and *desorm,* the slang of tomorrow, will eventually dominate, rendering *desormiate* itself the over-formal variant.

At that, I was tapped, though. I'd killed about a minute, but it felt like twenty. On the June-side, my neck ached from fighting my head.

I let my head turn and said, Here's the new adjective you didn't know you asked for.

Miss Pinge said, "Shh."

I whispered, Junish: easy on the eyes, but—

June cut me off. She said, "You need to shave yourself."

A couple people had told me that, but when I looked in the mirror, I could not see where they were talking about. There were no hairs on my face. I looked very hard every day. I wanted big sideburns.

Where? I said.

June said, "Uch." Then she touched me near the area where my apple would obtrude if I grew up to have the neck of my father, and also she touched me right above that, which was the bottom of my chin, which was a part of my head, but it didn't make me dangerous to get touched there that time. It made me want to hug her in a standing position and nose her in the hair. I wanted to kiss her fingers, too. They were cool on my skin, and I thought they would have a strawberry taste. I was sure that her hair would have a strawberry smell. The hair was red, all kinds of red, and I noticed on her wrist she had a pink freckle, very light pink, shaped like a ׳. I had two like it, one on each thumb-knuck, but mine were as black as felon tattoos and under two layers of waterproof makeup my mom made me apply every morning to hide them. I was going to rub off the makeup right there to show June the freckles, but exit-laughter rumbled behind Brodsky's door. The laughter was the sound of the Boystar family, and once the door opened and Brodsky emerged I couldn't start talking without getting us in trouble, and I worried that if I just rubbed off the makeup to reveal her the letters without a word June might feel creeped. Better, I decided, to show her later.

□ □ □ □ □ □ □

Name: Gurion ben-Judah Maccabee
Grade: ⑤ 6 7 8
Homeroom: The Cage
Date of Detention: 9/22/2006
Complaint Against Student (from Complaint Against Student Sheet)
Fight in the hallway with Kyle McElroy. B-Hall. Passing period (2nd–3rd).
9/19/06. Mr. Novy.

Step 4 Assignment: Write a letter to yourself in which you explain 1) why you are at step 4 (in after-school detention); 2) what you could do in order to avoid step 4 (receiving after-school detention) in the future; 3) what you have learned from being at step 4 (in after-school detention); 4) what you have learned from writing this letter to yourself. Include a Title, an Introduction, a Body, and a Conclusion. This letter will be collected at the end of after-school detention. This letter will be stored in your permanent file.

Title

<h2 style="text-align:center">Face</h2>

Introduction

There is snat and there is face. Snat is like water, but invisible. It can become violence, depending on what kind of shape the face is in.

The face is the dam that holds the snat back.

Body
Flood

If the face is suddenly wiped out by an enemy, the snat floods, and the faceless person spends all the snat's violent possibilities in a single burst of attempted tackling, choking, or slamming the enemy's head on the floor.

While the possibilities get spent, the faceless person shakes and cries. His aim is off, and his attack, unless he gets lucky, does no serious damage to the enemy: it is usually very easy for the enemy to dodge the burst.

Once all the snat has flooded out of the faceless person, his muscles disobey him and his fists quit. The enemy can stomp him into pudding without resistance.

Trickle

If, instead of being suddenly wiped out by an enemy, the face just gets cracked a little, then the snat trickles. If the trickler tries to caulk the crack, another crack will form. If he then tries to caulk the second crack, a third crack will form. Caulking a third will form a fourth, and so on. So caulking cracks never saves the face, but not-caulking cracks eventually might.

Cannon

The best is when a brick pops out of the face. It can happen two ways.

The first way is by trickles. Trickles further corrode cracks that go uncaulked. Enough corrosion will cause the snat to pop the brick that's trickling. Snat will cannon through a brick-sized hole, and the person whose hole it is can aim the snat. He can turn the whole face in the direction of the enemy and blast that enemy faceless.

If the blast isn't perfect, the enemy might pop a brick of his own—that is the second way a brick gets popped.

Once the enemy has popped a brick, *he* can aim snat through *his* brick-hole. That's what a fight is: brick-popped enemies aiming their holes til faces wipe out.

After it's over, whoever's not faceless gets all his bricks and snat back.

Conclusion

The Judge Samson always knew what kind of shape his face was in. Because the Philistines were running Israel, his face trickled at the sight of them, even if they were sleeping. But Samson knew not to throw down while he was trickling. That is why he spent so much time getting the Philistines to start up with him. They would cheat him or attack him and these actions would pop a brick out of his face. Then Samson would aim his hole and smite everyone. He'd aim his hole as soon as his brick popped and he never waited til his face got completely wiped out. Not til the very last second of his life.

At the very last second of his life, his sense of timing was gone, and his face trickled non-stop, but it wouldn't pop a brick, so Samson got started-up-with by the trickling of the snat itself. His own snat wiped his face out all at once. Because he was Samson, his aim was amazing, even though he was blind, and his strength was astounding, even though he was shaven, and his flooding massacred every Philistine in the palace. Samson judged Israel for twenty years. In those days, there was no king in Israel and a man would do whatever seemed proper in his eyes.

□　□　□　□　□　□　□

Boystar's parents looked like monsters in disguises. The mother's eyebrows were drawn in dried-blood-colored pencil, and the hair of the father looked metal. They stood with Boystar in Brodsky's doorway, talking to Brodsky in stagey tones.

"Well this is simply wonderful, Leonard," the mother said to Brodsky.

"Yes," said Brodsky.

The father said, "We look forward to it with great excitement."

Brodsky said, "I'm glad."

"Really Leonard, it's—really looking forward to this," said the father.

Miss Pinge stopped typing so she could concentrate on what they were saying. It was exactly what the parents wanted her to do. Brodsky had opened his door because they were finished with their meeting, but the parents started talking about what they'd talked about behind the door in order to brag. The reason they kept using the words "it" and "this" instead of the words that "it" and "this" stood for was so they wouldn't seem to be bragging. They thought it would look humble to hide what they bragged about, even if the hiding drew attention to itself. I never understood why so many people thought humble = good, but I knew you weren't humble if you were trying to look humble, so the parents were liars, and even worse, they were really bad liars, and so, for three seconds, I pitied their son, who always showed off, and didn't pretend to try to not show off, which was probably because they wanted him to show off so they could pretend to not brag about it.

"So excited about it."

"I mean, really… This is… Really!"

Boystar's hand was deep in his bag, rummaging loudly. The bag was a black leather messenger bag. His shoes and belt had high-shine buckles that matched its clasp. He always wore outfits. He rarely fought anyone. Vincie Portite said it was because of his face; if something happened to his face he'd have a hard time being famous. Soon he pulled something from the bag and flashed it. It looked like a stack of baseball cards. Baseball was slow and baseball was suck. I wasn't excited. Neither was June. Boystar came over.

"So," Brodsky was saying, "I'm glad the trip to California yielded your son an enviable pop album. We're thrilled to have him back at school, and, of course, we're looking forward to this Friday's performance." The principal wasn't a stupid man. He knew they'd stick around til he said what they wouldn't.

"He and we look forward to it, too," the mother of Boystar said through a shiver.

Her son, before us now, palming the stack, told me some things that were meant for June's ears. He said, "Whuddup, skid? I guess it's like this: I'm doing a cut at the pep rally Friday. Second period, they get their first periods. That's what they're saying. That's what I hear. That's what *I'm* saying. Want a new sticker? Have a new sticker. Promote the new unit."

He gave me a sticker. The stack wasn't cards. It was stickers of him. On a background of glitter, the photographed Boystar was crouching intensely behind starry footlights. In his right hand he held a mike over his heart, and his left hand was clawed and raised in the air = "Wait, please wait, just give me a second," and his shades were low on the bridge of his nose, and his mouth half-open to tell you a secret to make you both cry. A banner at the bottom, bombstyle fonted, read: *EMOTIONALIZE. The Star's Reborn. New Album in stores this Christmas.*

June angled to see and her shoulder touched mine. I almost thanked Boystar.

June said, "Accessorize?"

Boystar had a silver Star-of-Boystar (*) earring that went with his buckles and bag-clasp. When he turned to June, the earring caught light from an overhead bulb and twinkled.

"Emotionalize," he said, and twinkled. "Ee mo shun alize."

Like June wasn't kidding. Like she needed to be corrected. *He* needed to be corrected.

You're on a sticker, I said. There's a sticker of you. You look really sensitive.

"I know," Boystar said. He said, "Girls like it when you look like a pussy, right June? And they're the ones that buy units, the girls. And girls like stickers. These stickers move units." He held a sticker out to June and said, "See? She wants my unit. She wants to give me money for it."

June said, "Nope."

"Only," said Boystar, "cause you're a dumb slut and while you're asleep your father touches you." The way he said it was really flat. Like the underdog new-kid psycho in a movie who the bad guy would shortly learn not to mess with.

I thumb-stabbed the hand that was holding the stack and slapped him on the neck. I didn't hit him hard. It was just a slap. It was just to shock him, to show him how stealth I am and how slow he is and how sudden he would end if he monkeyed with June again. Still, he became pinkish and started breathing fast to keep from crying. Whenever people did that after I'd hit them, it made me feel sad for them, as if I should help them, and then angry because I didn't want to feel sad for them since I had just hit them. I looked away.

No one but me and June and Boystar saw the stabbing or the slap, but the father saw the stickers fall and he saw the pinkishness of the face of Boystar. He stepped between us. If I was Boystar's dad? I would have known what the pinkishness meant and I would have been pissed at Gurion. I would have taken Gurion by the shirt or the front of the hair and said, "Do not make my son feel scared." It would have been a kind of justice. But the father just stood there and said to Boystar, "Come on." He said, "Don't drop the promotional stickers on the filthy floor. That will ruin them. Pick them up."

Boystar got on his knees.

June whispered, "Pick them up."

Boystar's mom huffed air through her nose; *she* wasn't embarrassed, she *refused* to be embarrassed, let *them* be embarrassed, she *wasn't* embarrassed. Brodsky bid them each good luck. Boystar picked up the stickers on his knees. Brodsky picked up the CASS from the desk of Pinge and held it close to his eyes, then at arm's distance, then in between the two points, like he needed to focus. He didn't need to focus. His eyes were fine. He was trying to look official. "Fighting again?" he said to me.

I nodded my head = Ask a real question.

"Let's go," he said.

"June's first," Miss Pinge said.

I wasn't getting up, but Brodsky told me, "Sit down." Then he said to June, "Come on."

June didn't move for an entire three-count, and when she stood, she leaned over like she would deliver a headbutt to the side of my eye, and I would have let her, but instead she kissed me very fast, just below my ear, where I wanted sideburns to be. It felt wet but was not wet and my jaw hummed and then my head got warm on the inside.

I didn't know my eyes were closed until I opened them and saw she was walking away from me, walking slowly, grinding stickers under her Chucks.

I had to do something, so I stood up and I shouted, I am in love with you!

Everyone looked at me, except for June, who stopped in Brodsky's doorway and raised fists of victory before she went inside. Even if the victory fists were sarcastic, it was the prettiest thing she could have done, and I knew it was true what I shouted.

I would no longer dream of Natalie Portman at night, and I'd quit writing broken-hearted poems for Esther Salt. I would only dream of June and all my poems would be for her. I felt like unwound rubberbands, like how I imagined Main Man felt when he'd do his dance, but I couldn't sing, plus I wasn't good at poetry—I didn't read enough of it to be any good; I didn't really like it—and even if I wrote a good love poem by accident, the best a good love poem could be was nice, and it wasn't that I didn't want to be nice to June, just that... What? Who *wouldn't* be nice to her? That was what. I wanted to do something someone else wouldn't, preferably something that someone else couldn't. No one thing seemed good enough, though.

And then I remembered the clock in the gym. How everyone said that it couldn't be smashed.

□　□　□　□　□　□　□

The window onto Main Hall in the wall behind the waiting chairs had wire outlines of diamonds inside it that suggested it was made of soundproof glass, but it turned out the glass was just sound-resistant. Half a minute after his parents took off, Boystar, from the hall-side, started knocking on the window, and I could definitely hear it. He, however, wasn't sure if I could—I was sitting in the middle chair, my back to the window—and his knocks grew more and more frantic by the second. He wanted me to turn to see him mouth a threat like "You're dead" or "I'll get you" or "I'll get my friends to get you," and when attempts to face-save were that conspicuous, it was usually because the person trying to save face was losing even more face by trying—I could think of exceptions (Tyson's assault on Holyfield's ear, Simeon and Levi's massacre of Shechemites), but Boystar's window-knocking wasn't an exception—so there wasn't any way I was turning around.

The chair I was in, though mostly wooden, was held together by metal bolts that showed at the joints of the legs and the arms. To distract myself from Boystar, I tried to pry the arm ones out with my fingers. This task proved im-possible without any tools, so I did a successful visualization that I would tell Call-Me-Sandy about in Group. Each time his knocks got harder and faster, I imagined that Boystar's head expanded. Soon it was so huge that his mouth and his eyes became thin black lines between inflated skin-folds and the only thing sticking out was his nose-tip. I flicked it with my pointer and his head popped apart, but no blood sprayed. The visualized Boystar was a rubber robot.

I timed it perfect, the flick of my visualization. Miss Pinge had been looking at Boystar through the glass while he was knocking, and then she cut her hand across the air, karate-chop style, and the knocking stopped, and it was right when she'd chopped that I'd flicked. I liked it when things went together like that. Not just timing things like the chop/flick/knock-stopping, but space things, too. Like all the man-made products that fit into other man-made products that were not made by the same men or for the same reasons. Like how the sucking wand of my parents' vacuum held seven D batteries stacked nub to divot, and my Artgum eraser, before I'd worn it down, sat flush in any slot of the ice-cube tray, and the ice-cube tray sat flush on the rack in the toaster oven, the oven itself between the wall and the sink-edge. I liked how the rubber stopper in the laundry-room washtub was good for corking certain Erlenmeyer flasks and that 5 mg. Ritalins could be stored in the screw-hollows on the handles of umbrellas. Wingnuts were the best, though. They fit over pens and many other types of cylinders with perfect snugness, and you could fasten and unfasten them without any tools. I carried many wingnuts in a small drawstring bag. They'd jingle when I walked, and often when I fought, and if I didn't want to jingle I'd tighten the drawstring.

There in the Office, I checked my pocket to make sure I had the bag on me—I did—then decided to give a wingnut to June. She could put it on a shoelace and wear it as a necklace or tie it by a lanyard to one of her belt-loops, in which case I'd tie one to the chain of my wallet, and then, sometimes, walking next to each other, our sides might collide and make a new noise, something between a clang and a click, but neither a cling nor a clink nor a clank, nothing any known onomatopoeia described.

Miss Pinge's computer beeped long and steady, and Miss Pinge growled. She clapped her hands once and held them clapped, in front of her mouth. She said, "I'm going crazy. Out of my fucking mind. I'm flipping out. I'm going bonkers." Then she remembered that I was there, and she told me: "I'm sorry. You didn't need to hear that."

I nearly said, "Don't sweat it, I won't rat you out," but Brodsky's door opened before I had the chance, and that was probably better anyway since Pinge's worried ears could have easily appended an "at least not right now" to the sentence's back end. Mine probably would've.

If Brodsky'd heard her cursing, he wasn't showing it, and she saw I wasn't ratting, at least not right then, so she went back to typing like nothing had happened.

By that point, June was already walking toward me. I didn't stand up til she got close enough that all I could see was the graying black cotton of her message-free t-shirt. She was taller than me, but only a little, and narrow top-to-center, so it didn't matter anyway. My arms could encircle her torso no problem.

"Your turn," she said. "I was told to tell you '*Your* turn.'"

Brodsky was waiting in his office, at his desk.

I stayed where I was, admiring June's face, all the many freckles in their many different forms, none of which clustered blobbily. The biggest was to the right of the curve of her right eyebrow. It was also the darkest. The lightest, beneath her lower lip, on the left, was shaped like the planet Saturn.

"What?" June said.

You okay? I said.

"Yeah. I just got a detention. It's nothing."

Are you sure you're okay?

"I'm fine."

You're sure?

I wanted her to look at my eyes and start crying so I could tell her how everything was okay.

"What's wrong with you?" she said.

Here, I said.

I removed the drawstring bag from my pocket. Thirteen wingnuts jingled inside it. I felt mean and wrong for wanting her to cry, so I instead of one, I gave her twelve.

"What's this?" she said.

I said, Wingnuts. They jingle.

I poured them in her hand. They jingled.

Brodsky coughed fakely to get my attention. It was a habit he had.

June said, "You should go in there." She pushed her thumb at Brodsky's doorway, and I saw the freckle on her wrist and remembered.

I whispered to her, I have something to show you.

She said, "Don't be sick, Gurion, I like you."

Not my wang, I said. I wouldn't show you my wang like that, June.

She said, "Show me later, then. Don't get in trouble."

I said, I'm in love with you. Be in love with me.

June said, "You're in love with me."

Yes, I said.

"Which means you'll be in love with me forever," June said.

Of course, I said. It can't help but mean that.

"Exactly," June said. "It can't help but mean that. That's just what it means."

We're in total agreement.

"Except no one can see to forever," June said. "And so no one can promise forever," June said. "So when you say you're in love with me—it can't really be true."

But it is, I said. It's true, I said.

"I'm not saying you're lying. It's just—"

I'm not lying.

"What you mean is you *believe* you'll be in love with me forever. And probably that you're glad about it—glad you believe it. That's what you're saying when you say you're in love with me."

Yes, but also—

"That's drastic," June said.

The color of her eyebrows was almost blond, and the gaps between her teeth like getting winked at so fast it might not have happened and you hope it did, plus her voice had this scratch that ran underneath it, as though last night she'd hurt her throat screaming and you were the first person she was talking to today in a tone that was louder than a whisper.

When you touch my head I don't explode, I told her.

"Mr. Maccabee," said Brodsky.

I said, I'm in love with you, and I have to show you something.

"Gurion," said Miss Pinge.

June said, "You should go. You can show me what you want to show me later, in detention. You've got detention today, right?"

I said, I always have detention.

"Good," she said. Then she chinned the air at the wingnuts in her hand. She said, "Thank you for these. And I'm sorry I said 'Frontier Motel' before. I was in a bad mood and I thought you'd be mean. You have a reputation."

June slid the wingnuts into a pocket and jingled while she walked her June Watermark walk—more than a stroll, but shy of a swagger; just a little bit swaybacked—out into Main Hall, too far away from me.

Brodsky said my name again. I looked in his office. He was pointing his pointer at the chair before his desk. "Gurion," he said. Then he blinkered with the finger. "Gurion ben-Judah Maccabee," he said.

I am, I said, that I am.

2
GUNS AND INQUISITIONS

Tuesday, November 14, 2006
3rd Period

ULPAN

1. Lay your cardboard planks down. Lay them down on the lawn. Lay them down so the short side is facing me. Lay them down so that I am facing two rows of you. It does not matter if you are in the front or the back row. From up here, I can see all of you. From down there, you can all see me. Lay the planks on the lawn so that a foot of grass-space separates you from those on all your four sides.

2. Sit down on the back half of your plank.

3. Remove the two-liter bottle of soda from your plastic grocery sack. Twist the cap off. Put the cap in your pocket. If you don't have a pocket, put the cap in your sock.

4. Empty the soda from the two-liter bottle. Empty it into the grass.

5. Remove the serrated knife from the plastic grocery sack. Hold it in your strong hand.

6. Lay the bottle sideways on the front part of your cardboard plank. Lay it down so the pouring hole is pointed in the direction of your strong hand. Hold the bottle down at its middle with your weak hand. Hold it firmly.

7. Be careful with the knife. Do not cut yourself.

8. Here is the neck, and here is the body. Here, between the neck and the body, is a nameless area that is neither as wide as the body nor as narrow as the neck. Touch the serrated edge of the knife to the place where the body becomes the nameless area.

9. Press down and saw the bottle in two.

10. Set the large piece in the grass to the left of your plank. That is garbage. After we're finished, you'll throw it in the trash. No two kids should use the same trash bin. That is an invitation to get caught. We are stealth.

11. Set down the piece that is not garbage so the pouring hole is facing the sky. Notice what you've got is a little bit tit-shaped. Laugh. Laughter is good. You are doing something important, though, and I've already made the joke, so once you are done laughing at it, don't keep saying it. It gets less funny every time you say it. Tit-shaped. It is less funny, now. The more you say it, the less funny it will be when, later on, you remember how I said it. Tit-shaped. Booblike. Mammaryish. Finish laughing and pay attention to the instructions.

12. Remove your four pennies from the plastic sack. Lay your pennies out in a safe place where you can see them. Lay them out so that you won't knock them into the grass by accident. Lay them out in a row. Any combination of Lincoln-up or Roman-looking-building-up is fine. This is not about symbols.

13. Remove the rubber balloon from the plastic sack.

14. Use the fingers of both hands to pull the lip of the rubber balloon back on itself until the lip of the rubber balloon is at the fat part of the rubber balloon.

15. With the pointer- and swear-fingers of both of your hands, stretch the rubber balloon opening wide.

16. Fit the stretched rubber balloon opening over the threaded part of the pouring hole. Fit it over the nipple. Nipple.

17. Make sure that the folded-back lip of the rubber balloon is on the threaded part. If it's not, then push it down til it is.

18. Turn the whole thing over and look inside. Make sure that the opening is clear, that it is a perfect circle, that no balloon skin is blocking the passage up.

19. Now, hold what you have in your weak hand with your thumb and pointer pressed onto the rubber-balloon-covered part of the pouring hole. Hold it so that the balloon-covered end is facing your chest. Hold it so that your weak pointer is on top and your weak thumb is on the bottom. Press hard. Make sure that no meat on your weak thumb or weak pointer is edging past the pouring-hole in the direction of your chest. Make sure that the rest of your weak hand is either above or behind the sawed-off edge.

20. With the thumb and forefinger of your strong hand, pinch the balloon.

21. Pull back on the balloon.

22. Let go.

23. Look at the pennies you lined up earlier. Understand you hold a gun.

Now you can hurt things far beyond arm's reach.

In a few more minutes you will all leave my yard. You will conceal your weapons inside your pockets. If you don't have pockets, you will use your waistbands. You'll stick the cap and other garbage inside the plastic sack, tie the sack off, and throw the whole thing in a dumpster or bin as you were instructed to earlier. You will keep your planks. You will turn them into targets. Draw bullseyes onto the faces of them, and then draw faces in the bullseyes of them. Lean them against the sides of your homes and fire on your targets with your weapons, your pennyguns. Fire first from a distance of ten feet. Once you hit three bullseyes, move back to fifteen feet. "Hit three bullseyes" does not mean get the penny to lightly graze the bullseye three different times. That will do nothing for you. "Hit three bullseyes" means get the penny to lodge itself in the bullseye portion of the plank or to cut straight through it. You have the power to do that and that is what you should do. Once you hit three bullseyes at a distance of fifteen feet, move back to a distance of twenty feet. Continue to increase the intervals by five feet after every three bullseyes until you are at a distance of thirty-five feet. Thirty-five feet is the farthest distance that you will be able to fire on someone or something from and still be able do it or him any worthwhile kind of damage.

In a couple minutes, I will tell you to leave my yard. I will tell you that I will see you Monday, if not tomorrow, when you will all be stronger than you are today. Before I tell you that though, you need to understand: Hardly anyone in the world knows what you're holding right now. They have not seen or heard of pennyguns. It is better for us that they don't know. It is better for us that they have not seen or heard of what you are holding right now. Still, some people do know and some people have heard of and seen and even fired their own versions of what you are holding, so you don't want to be a show-off. You don't want to brandish. It could make some people nervous.

Now that you have been delivered these instructions, you will receive an instruction sheet. It is a copy of the sheet I am reading from. Each one of you gets one copy. You will take your copy from beneath the paint-can at the gate. Fold it and put it in your shoe. Guard it closely. Do not guard it with your life, but guard it with your face. It is not worth getting killed over, but it is worth getting a broken face over. Tomorrow, you will make thirteen copies of your copy. You will invite thirteen Israelite boys to come to your backyard after Shabbos, like I invited you, and you will deliver these instructions from a high tree-limb, exactly the same as I have delivered them to you. If you do not have a tree with high limbs in your yard, or if the high-limbed tree you do have is unclimbable, sit on top of a swingset or fence.

Tonight, the first night on which Israelites have received these instructions, is May 27, 2006. Do as you're told and one week from tonight, 183 Israelite boys will be armed with pennyguns. Two weeks from tonight, 2,380 Israelite boys will be armed. Three weeks from tonight, 30,941 Israelite boys, and four weeks from tonight, just three days beyond the summer solstice, 402,234 Israelite boys will be armed with pennyguns. Well in advance of the start of next school year, all the Israelite boys in North America, if not the world, will be armed with pennyguns. Never again will we cower amidst the masses of the Roman and Canaanite children.

Bless Adonai, who helps us protect us.

Blessed is Elohim, Who blesses our weapons.

Chazak! Chazak! Venischazeik!

Say it.

Now leave my yard. I will see you Monday, if not tomorrow. You will be stronger tomorrow than you are today.

□ □ □ □ □ □ □

Brodsky had a megaphone on the shelf behind his desk. It was mostly white, but the mouthpiece and the trigger were red to match the jerseys of the Aptakisic Indians. It should have been Main Man's. If people tried to stop him from singing through it, he could switch on the siren and scare them away, and if they kept on coming, he could blow out their eardrums. He wouldn't get messed with so much.

"Look at me," said Brodsky.

I like your soundgun, I said.

"It's a megaphone," he said. "It's not a gun."

It's shaped like a gun, I said. It's got a trigger and it shoots sound, I said.

"That doesn't make it a gun," he said. "Guns are weapons."

Hot-glue gun, I said. I said, Nail gun. I said, Staple gun.

"It's a megaphone, Gurion."

He was trying to be nice. That's why he said my name. I didn't want him to be nice, though. It banced up the roles. So I didn't look at him. I looked at the family picture next to the megaphone. Ben was in it. I knew him before he died. He was a scholar and he was loyal to me. We had Torah Study together at the Solomon Schecter School, before I got kicked out.

Ben drowned at camp at the beginning of summer. No one knows how. He was missing for two days and his head was bruised when they found him in the lake. They thought he knocked it diving off the pier at night, but a drunken boater might have hit-and-runned him. Whatever happened, Brodsky's face changed.

I only ever saw Brodsky once before Ben died. It was at Ben's bar-mitzvah. I got invited to more bar-mitzvahs than any other Schecter fourth-grader because Rabbi Salt had promoted me to eighth-grade Torah Study and it was a custom at Schecter to invite everyone in your Torah Study class.

Before Ben got killed, Brodsky's face was either joyous or sad, and the muscles in it made the bones and the skin fit themselves to those emotions. Even though Ben's death made Brodsky bitter, his bones and skin were already finished being formed by the muscles, and it was too late for him to make convincing faces that were not joyful or sad. Like the one he was making right then: he meant to make a tough, sass-killing face, but he looked like a wifeless old cousin trying to hide his loneliness.

He said, "Tell me why you fought these boys." When he said "these boys," he poked the CASS with his finger, like Ronrico and the Janitor were right there on the page in front of him. Like it wasn't just their names, but them. I got a rush from thinking about it. My name was on the page, too. And my actions—Desormie's version of them, at least.

Brodsky said, "This is your sixth fight in the nine weeks you've been at Aptakisic."

It was my twenty-ninth fight in the nine weeks I'd been at Aptakisic, not counting exchanges like the *Emotionalize* one with Boystar. It was the sixth I got caught for. But what was important to me was that Brodsky'd poked the CASS again when he'd said the word *this*.

"Next time it's an OSS," he said.

How long til I get expelled?

"We don't want to expel you," Brodsky said. "Are you trying to get expelled?"

I said, Let's call my mother.

"Let's have a conversation first," he said. "Let's talk about why you keep fighting."

I'm not telling on anyone, I said.

"So Ronrico and Michael started up with you, then."

I'm not a rat, I said. I said, I wouldn't rat on myself if I started up with *them*.

He said, "I'm not a villain, Gurion. You can talk to me. I'm not your enemy."

I said, I never said you were a villain.

"You're implying I'm your enemy?"

I said, Talk to me like I'm a kid. Don't talk to me about implications.

He said, "Rabbi Salt has told me you're the most promising student he's ever known. He has gone on *at length* about how articulate you are. Ben, may he rest in peace, was very fond of you and—"

Can we call my mother?

"Won't you be a mensch and talk to me?"

I said, Ben didn't deserve it.

Brodsky said, "That's not what I mean, Gurion."

I said, That's the only menschy thing that I have to say to you. I said, You keep me in a cage.

Brodsky balanced his elbow on the desk and held his open hand out with all the fingers spread, like he was going to explain something important to me, but all he said was, "The Cage is not a cage."

Right, I said.

I had sarcasm in my throat. That happened sometimes when I'd get treated like a shmendrick by sincere people.

Brodsky looked hurt by it, and he wouldn't stop performing the explaining thing with his hand. It made me want to have an intermittent explosion. If he saw me explode, he would be too frightened or too pissed at me to be hurt. I didn't really care what Brodsky thought of me, but I didn't want to hurt him. There was already too much sadness in his office. It would steam off the bright pink top of his head, then condense and fall in droplets into the carpet and onto the furniture and get on you.

The second time I saw Brodsky was at Ben's shiva, where I heard him say to Rabbi Salt that he wished it was himself who got killed instead of his son.

It made me think of the part in *Genesis Rabbah* where Hashem shows Adam all the different versions of the future that could happen. I don't know what Hashem used for a screen, but I hope it was the sky, and that Adam watched it while he floated on his back in a scumless lagoon.

In one of the movies, David ben-Jesse slayed Goliath and became King of Israel. In another one, David died at birth. The version where David died is the one that Hashem said was fated to happen. But Adam told Hashem that he wanted David to live, because the Israelites, without David, would never have an empire and never build the Temple. So Hashem let Adam give seventy years of his life to David. That's why Adam lived to be 930 instead of 1000.

There in Brodsky's office, I started thinking of how almost anyone who Hashem showed David's futures to would do the same thing as Adam did, and how, if I knew a different version of the future, I might have known that if Brodsky died instead of Ben, it would have been worse for the Brodsky family and the world. I might have known, for example, that if Brodsky'd died instead, Ben would have saved the next Hitler from drowning at day camp. But that still wouldn't make it any easier to find the justice, because why did Adam have to give up seventy years of his life for David to live? Why couldn't God pull seventy years out of the serpent or a Sodomite? And so why did any Brodsky have to get killed at all? Why couldn't it be that Ben would be changing into swim-trunks in the locker-room while the next Hitler drowned? Why should there have to be a next Hitler?

None of those questions can get answered any easier than the others, but if Hashem was showing me futures, I would ask Him all the questions, and He would not be able to tell me the answers because either He doesn't know, or because understanding those things would kill a person, or make the person something less than a person. And though I would, like I said, give David my seventy, it would piss me off, and I'd cut straight to the point and ask the main question. If all of this was happening in ancient scripture, I would ask it loud. It would be a lamentation.

Gurion would lament: What is the good of trying to do justice if God will kill me and my family whether or not I do justice?

And the answer would come from God or a judge or commentary in the margins. And God or the judge or the scholar who'd comment would say, "It is good to try to do justice because God will kill you and your family whether or not you do justice."

I was thinking too much about Ben to explode, so I dug my last wingnut out of my pocket and dropped it in the palm of Brodsky's explaining-hand.

"I don't want this," he said. I was chomsky to think he'd appreciate a wingnut. He tossed the wingnut back so it would land in my lap, but before its arc ended, I knocked it sideways with a sudden backhand. It bounced off the wall and landed in a planter that held a fan-shaped tree from Asia.

"This fighting," said Brodsky. "What can I do to get you to stop fighting?"

Is my record in your cabinet?

Brodsky said, "Yes."

I said, What's in it?

He said, "Your detention assignments, the CASS's, grade reports…"

I said, Does it have my documents from Schecter?

Brodsky said, "Yes."

I want to see it.

"It's not for you to see."

I said, I want to know what Rabbi Unger wrote.

Unger was the headmaster at Schecter. I wanted to know if he wrote down that I wasn't the messiah. That's what he told me the day he kicked me out of Schechter. That I was not the messiah. He yelled it at me. He did it in his office after I destroyed his lectern. Rabbi Salt was sick that day, and Unger was substituting for him in Torah Study. Emmanuel Liebman asked Unger why carbon-dating said the Earth was billions of years old when the Torah said it was less than six thousand[*] and Unger said that time was different in the Torah, that a day wasn't just a day. He said that a day in the Torah was a day according to God, and that God was eternal, so that a God-day was "infinitely longer than a people-day." That didn't make sense as an answer because no one knows how reliable carbon-dating is, is the answer. But also it just didn't make sense because if a God-day was *infinitely* longer than a people-day, and the Torah was written according to God-time, then no amount of God-days would have passed because infinity doesn't end. That's what infinity means. I said so. Unger said, "Don't be a smart aleck with the minutiae. You know what I meant, Gurion." Unger was always calling the objects of my rigor *minutiae*. I said, Did you mean that a God-day was just a lot longer than a people-day? He said, "That's what I meant." "How much longer?" said

---

[*] Though a seventh-grader at the time, Emmanuel (along with Samuel Diamond, also a seventh-grader) had been in Rabbi Salt's eighth-grade Torah Study for nearly three years by then = they both had scholarly talent to burn, and Emmanuel almost definitely wouldn't have asked such a basic question if he didn't think the other students would benefit from hearing it addressed.

Emmanuel Liebman. "Much longer," Unger said. "A thousand times lon-ger?" Emmanuel said. "More," said Unger. "A hundred thousand times lon-ger?" said Emmanuel. "Something like that," said Unger. So a God-day lasts about a hundred thousand times as long as a people-day, I said. "Yes," said Unger. So then Adam didn't live to be nine hundred thirty, I said. I said, He lived to be ninety-three million. "No," said Unger. "You're not listening," he said. He said, "Adam was a man. When men are being written about, they are written about in people-time, not God-time." I said, Okay. I was ready to drop it, too, but then Samuel Diamond said, "Why did all the people at the beginning of Genesis get to live for hundreds of years and then after that, they didn't. Like David. Why did David only get to live to be seventy?" Unger said, "Actually, Adam *didn't* live for nine hundred thirty years. Torah says that, but what it means is nine hundred thirty *months*." So David only lived to be seventy months? I said. Even if that's solar-months, it's not even six years old, I said. "*David* is not discussed in the Torah," said Unger. "Proph-ets is not Torah," he said. "You know that, don't you?" Then Jacob, I said. I said, Torah says he lived a hundred and forty-seven years, so if a year is a solar month, then he fathered all twelve sons before he was thirteen, and if it's a lunar month, then— "Years stop meaning months at a certain point," said Rabbi Unger. It was an interruption. He interrupted me. I said, How do you know that? I said, I don't think the stuff you're telling us is accurate. Unger said, "Are you suggesting that I'm a liar, Gurion?" I *wasn't* suggesting he was a liar. I was only suggesting he was mistaken. But then, when he asked me if I was suggesting that he was a liar, I saw he'd been lying all along, intention-ally making stuff up to save face. I couldn't say that, though. If I said that, I'd be undermining the authority of the Torah Study teacher, which, at the time, seemed to = undermining Torah Study. I'd never done that before. I'd always loved Torah Study. Then again, I'd always had Rabbi Salt for Torah Study, and even though we'd argue, it was the good kind of argument—the kind where the arguers don't argue to prove they are dominant, but rather to find out what is right. And it is true that Rabbi Unger was playing the role of Torah Study teacher badly, and it is true he should not have been lying, but all the other scholars always paid so much attention to what I did and so I didn't want to demonstrate to them that it was good to undermine someone playing the role of the Torah Study teacher, because it hardly ever was. At the same time, I didn't want to tell a lie. So I decided not to answer the question Unger asked. He asked what I was suggesting, and I didn't say anything about what I was suggesting. Instead I said: I didn't call you a liar. And that was true. Slippery, but true. I didn't *call* him anything. And this is what he said: "Then you're calling the word of God a pack of lies." And when he said that—pack of lies—it was too much. He sounded like a senator in a movie, not a teacher—pack of lies. He sounded like that casuist Rabbi Bender in *The Conversion of the Jews* by Philip Roth. And his beard was scattered. It was stringy. There were holes in it where I could see his skin. And he didn't like me. He'd never liked me. He didn't even like me in kindergarten. I stood up. Unger said, "We are here to study, not to defame." I kicked my chair back into the wall. I said, You're the one calling God a flip-flopper! "Go to my office and wait there," he told me. I didn't go. I said to the students: Adam lived to be nine hundred thirty years old and David lived to be seventy. The Earth is just under six thousand. "But the carbon-dating," Ben Brodsky said. Unger banged his fist on the table. I said, It measures the decomposition of radio-isotopes. The geologists measure what's missing, and to do that they have to decide what was there to begin with based on rates and constants and constant rates of decomposition that no one can really know if those rates have always been constant, but that doesn't matter; it doesn't matter that no one's ever monitored a lump of carbon for a billion years to see if the constant holds, and it also doesn't matter that no one's even been around for that long, because all that matters is do you know what radio-isotopes are? "I don't," said Ben. "What are they?" he said. "Enough!" said Unger. I said, I have no idea what radio-isotopes are. I said, But neither does Rabbi Unger, so he's scared of what they could be. He's been studying Torah his whole life and he doesn't understand how Torah works, yet he somehow thinks that scientists who study the Earth can understand how the Earth works. "Right now!" Unger shouted. "Out!" He stood up and I leaned away fast. When I leaned, my head banged the wall and I got dangerous. I knocked his lectern off the table. It fell up-side-up, and before Unger got unshocked enough to grab me, I split the center of the lectern with a flying axe-chop. It's a trick of the wrists my mother taught me—you twist them. It adds torque. A couple students were crying by then, and Unger had me around the chest with his arm, and Emmanuel and Samuel told Unger to leave me alone, and so did Ben Brodsky, who wasn't crying at all. I yelled up into Unger's ear: You're scared of anything you don't understand so you worship it. You kiss its ass! He dragged me into the hall and through the door of his office and said he was sick of this and he would kick me out. And I told him he wouldn't. And then he said, "You're not the messiah." And I told him that all my actions had served justice, and he yelled, "You are not the messiah!" He yelled it so loud that if there was an audience, the audience would have suspected dramatic irony. They would have suspected that Unger had run out of reasons to think I *wasn't* the messiah, so all he could do was yell really loud that I wasn't. Which is even more ironic because I obviously wasn't the messiah. First of all, if I was the messiah, there'd be perfect justice throughout the world and the schmuck across from whose desk I was sitting wouldn't hold a position of authority over me. Secondly, we'd both be in Israel. Thirdly, all the dead would have begun to rise out of the peak of the Mount of Olives, the most righteous first, and I'd be studying Torah with Moses, who'd want to hear what I thought, and probably Rashi and Maimonedes and Samuel and Ruth and Rabbi Akiva too. Those are just *some* of the reasons why it should have been obvious to anyone who was scholarly that I wasn't the messiah. And I never said I was the messiah, either, and when other kids said it in front of me, I set them straight, and if they couldn't be set straight, I'd distract them off the subject, usually with pratfalls, which I had a serious talent for. What I did say, after the third time Unger yelled "You are not the messiah!" was: I might be. And that was also true. Even though my father's name was Judah Maccabee, and the original Judah Maccabee was a Cohain, we weren't Co-hains. My father's grandfather was a Judite who changed his name when he got to America—in Russia, his name was Macarevich. We were Judites, my family, and it is for sure that the messiah will be a Judite, and Unger knew the messiah would be a Judite, and he also knew that he, himself, was a Co-hain, which meant he was in the line of Moses's brother Aron, and Aron, like Moses, was a Levite, and a Levite can't be a Judite, so Unger couldn't be the messiah, and I think this made him angry. Cohains are assigned custodian-ship of the Temple, and that's an honorable thing to be assigned—but there's no Temple. It takes the messiah to build the Temple. It takes a Judite. And it's true that lots of Israelites—especially Cohains—didn't like to hear that. They didn't like to hear that the Temple needed *building*. They liked to say the Temple would descend from the sky, but I never believed that, and nei-ther did any number of other scholars, Maimonedes included. We did not believe the Temple would descend from the sky. So when I said to Unger what I was just about to say, and I used the word *you*, I did not mean *we*, and Unger knew that. What I said to him was this: You can't build the Temple. And what Unger did was laugh at me, right in my face, and he told me, "The Temple will descend from the sky. No one will build it. That is the truth. But that's well beside the point, isn't it, Gurion? Because even if I'm wrong about that—even if the vast majority of the rabbinate is wrong and the Temple will after all be built by the messiah, Gurion—and who knows, right? it's possible, I guess, that we're all wrong about that—the one thing we know for sure, the one thing no one, not even anyone *in this room* disagrees with, is that the messiah will be... what? He'll be Jewish. The messiah will be a Jew. Do you understand? Do you understand what I'm expressing? To you? To Gurion Maccabee? Do you understand what I'm telling you, Gurion? The messiah, Gurion, will be a Jew." It was the all-time snakiest thing anyone had ever said to me. He was talking about my mother. I was half lost-tribe. You couldn't see it in my skin unless you were trying, but my mother's parents were from Ethiopia, and a few Ashkenazis still thought that meant I wasn't an Israelite. Unger was the only one who'd ever said it to me, though. Right to my face. I grabbed the nearest thing on his desk and I flung it. I flung it at his head. The nearest thing was a stapler. It opened in the air and caught him on the eye-corner. He shrieked. Blood streamed down onto his shoulder. That's how I ended up at Northside Hebrew Day. And when I got kicked out of Northside for teaching my brothers to protect themselves in the one way our Israelite schools refused to, I went to public school in Evanston. And when I got banned from the Evanston School System for protecting myself in the most basic way, I went to Aptakisic in Deerbrook Park. It was all connected, all the things that kept happening with me and schools, and I wanted to read what others wrote about it, then use what was relevant to give my scripture—*this* scripture—more context. Context was the one thing I wished there was more of for Torah. That isn't to say I thought Torah less than perfect—I didn't think that at all—but if, say, archaeologists somehow dug up parchments that were authored by Pharoah or any one of the twelve spies, let alone by Aron, Zipporah, or Jethro, and especially if those parchments were commentaries on the events in Torah in which their authors played a role, I would want to read them. I would want that so much.

Brodsky said, "I'll make you a deal. If you promise to stop fighting, I'll have Miss Pinge give you a copy of your file."

Promising's against the Law, I said. If I tell you I won't fight anymore, that should be good enough.

"That *is* good enough," he said. "You agree not to fight anymore?"

I said, No.

"You're impossible!" he said. Now he was pissed at me.

I felt better and I egged him on. I said, My mom'll get my record anyway.

"That'll be up to her," said Brodsky. He picked up the telephone and

dialed. A few seconds later, he said, "I'd like to speak to Judah Maccabee...
Yes, I'll wait."

Judah Maccabee was not my mother.

PENNYGUN

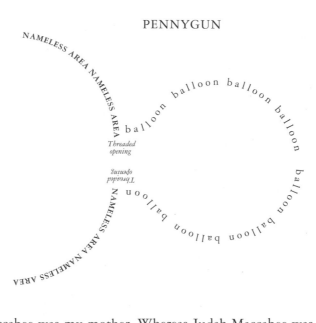

Tamar Maccabee was my mother. Whereas Judah Maccabee was my father,
whose voice was louder than anyone's. You were not supposed to bother him
at work, especially not in the middle of a trial, and he was at work, in the
middle of a trial, representing Patrick Drucker, a local White Supremacist,
in a case against the city of Wilmette, Illinois. My dad knew about my
fight at King Middle School in Evanston, but he didn't know about any of
the ones at Aptakisic. My mom thought it was better if we didn't mention
those to him, and I agreed—I wanted to protect him from disappointment.
I still remained calm though, for roughly three seconds, because I decided
Brodsky had just made a mistake, and I was going to tell him that he must
have dialed the wrong number, that he was supposed to dial the number for
Tamar Maccabee, not Judah, but right when I opened my mouth to speak,
Brodsky nodded at me, half-smiling, his eyebrows cranked up to what used
to be his hairline = "Surprise, Gurion, it's you who's made the mistake."

I saw my curved reflection in the bend of Brodsky's handset, down by
the mouthpiece. My neck was three or four times the width of my face

in there, just bulging out—begging, it seemed, for a chop—and the hairs June had touched were glossy and sharp. When at last I found my eyes, just barely pinpoints, reflected blood-red by a trick of the light, I thought: I could take you. I could wipe you out, Gurion. I could end you, easy, with just these bare hands.

Then Brodsky moved the handset, held it out before me, and I was looking at the pattern of holes in the earpiece. Brodsky said, "Gurion." So did my father. I rumbled some gooze, brought the thing to my face.

Hello, I said.

"Are you hurt?" said my father.

I said, There was a charleyhorse, but I fixed it.

He said, "I'm glad you're not hurt. I am not glad about this phone call."

I said, I'm sorry you're bothered at work.

He said, "It's not that, boychical. It's the fighting."

That's when I started crying. It happened sometimes when I'd get worked up and he'd call me something nice in Yiddish. I tried to cry quietly so he wouldn't hear.

"Why haven't you told me you've been getting in fights? And why did you fight with these boys today?" he said. "Did that Benji put you up to it?"

No, I said. And he's my best friend, I said, and you shouldn't talk about him like—

"He's a criminal," my dad said.

I sniffled back some gooze.

My dad heard it. He said, "Crying? Are you crying? What's this crying? Is it Scott?"

Whenever I cried, my dad would ask if I was crying about the last thing I'd cried about, and the last time I'd cried was a week before, right after I'd read about Williams Cocktail Party Syndrome in my mom's *Synopsis of Psychiatry* and found out Main Man would surely die young.

I said to my father, I didn't break any laws. All I did was break rules.

He said, "This is something to cry about? Rules? If you did nothing wrong and you're not hurt and your father loves you and so does your mother and these girls that call you at night on the phone who they love you too— and you know what just came in the mail? Front-row balcony for Chaplin just came in the mail. Cry? Why cry?"

Girls hadn't called me at night since I got kicked out of Northside Hebrew Day School. Front-row balcony for Chaplin, though, was good news. Once a year, around Christmas, *City Lights*, which is the single best movie ever made, gets shown at the Chicago Symphony Orchestra Hall with full orchestral accompaniment. We'd gone every year since I was four, but we'd never gotten balcony, and I always wanted balcony.

I had to sniffle again. I did it.

Then my father said, "Not that you *shouldn't* cry. It's fine, you know, if you like it. Don't get me wrong. In fact, it's good. You're a ten-year-old boy. The world is big. It's hard. I was just asking."

I said, I'm in trouble.

"Trouble?" he said. "What trouble? You're not in any trouble. You're loved. You're unhurt. Maybe you have to sit in this in-school suspension. This is trouble? This is to cry about? No. This is the world, not trouble. Trouble is for when you do wrong, for when you break laws. A suspension: this is something else. This is a punishment. This is for when you break rules, an in-school suspension. You're a good boy but you break rules. You just have to learn to not break rules. So you go to in-school suspension. There's no trouble there."

The crying was pretty much gone. I said, I don't want to be in suspension.

He said, "If you wanted to be in suspension, it wouldn't be a punishment. So you're in suspension. So what. Avoid it from now on. Don't fight. Don't fight don't fight don't fight. Now listen, genius," he said, "I have a late meeting after court today, and your mother's seeing patients til seven. We *will* have dinner together—we need to discuss this fighting—but dinner will be a little late, so I want you to nosh on something after school. Don't go hungry. And kill some time at the Frontier. I already talked to Arthur. He has a song he wants to play you."

Arthur = Flowers. Arthur was his first name.

"So what else?" my dad said.

I said, I want my record.

"What record?" he said.

My file, I said. I said, It's got all my information in it. Mr. Brodsky won't let me have it.

My dad said, "Nonsense. If it's yours, why won't he let you have it?"

I said, It's nonsense.

My dad said, "I'll get it for you. Now what do you want for dinner? Your mother's making chicken."

I said, Chicken.

He said, "Good for you, because that's what we're having. Now wipe your face and go to class. Learn what you can learn. Let me talk to this Brodsky person, yes?"

I handed the phone to Brodsky. Brodsky was holding out a tissue. I wiped my face on my sleeve and waited. I don't know what my father said to him. All I could hear was Brodsky saying, "Yes" and "I understand but" and then "Yes" again, and by the time he got off the phone, his head had lost all its pink. He set the tissue on the desk and told me I had an ISS tomorrow, which did not get me out of having to serve the detention that I was already scheduled to serve. Then he told me to go back to the Cage, that the Office would send word when my file was ready. He spun his chair around to face the soundgun.

On my way out to Miss Pinge, I took the wingnut out of the dirt in Brodsky's fan-shaped plant's pot, but I'm not an Indian-giver—and neither were the Indians; it was the settlers—so I yanked a tall green leaf off the plant and dropped the wingnut on Brodsky's blotter, where it rattled til it came to rest.

□ □ □ □ □ □ □

Sent: June 7, 2006, 6:34 PM Central-Standard Time
Subject: RE: FWD: Headmaster Mamzer
From: 13brodsky13@hotmail.com (Ben Brodsky)
To: Gurionforever@yahoo.com (me)

Rabbi,

I will do everything exactly as you've asked, no more no less. And I want you to know that we all miss you at school. True, it is not as bad for me as it is for the littler kids, since I'm graduating anyway, and I was already prepared to not see you as often, but still it is suck.

Your Student,
Ben

----Original Message Follows----
From: Gurionforever@yahoo.com
To: 13Brodsky13@hotmail.com
Subject: Re: Fwd: Headmaster Mamzer
Date: Wed, 7 June 2006 6:07 PM CST

Ben,

Thank you. You're a good friend and I wish we'd been able to hang out more when we were still in school together. I won't say a word to anyone about the hacking, but it's very important to me that you let all the Schechter scholars with pennyguns know that they should not bring their weapons to school tomorrow, or any copies they might be carrying of Ulpan. Tell them that I told you so, and no one should have any reason to suspect the hack. If they need a deeper explanation, though, tell them I heard there were desk- and locker-searches being conducted at Northside, and I fear the same thing will happen at Schechter. If they ask HOW I heard, tell them you don't know, which isn't a lie, not, at least, if you think about it hard enough. After all, I haven't yet said whether this is the first I've heard of the the searches at Northside, and I'm not saying that now, so you don't know if it is. All I'm saying now is thank you.

I will, myself, try calling as many students as I can, but a lot of them aren't allowed to talk to me because of the thing with Unger and then also what happened at the Synagogue, so please do what I've asked.

It is no surprise to me that you are a great sniper.

Your Friend,

Gurion

----Original Message Follows----
From: 13Brodsky13@hotmail.com
To: Gurionforever@yahoo.com
Subject: Fwd: Headmaster Mamzer
Date: Wed, 7 June 2006 5:01 PM CST

Rabbi Gurion,

Remember how I told you they made me a SpEd at public school because I hacked into the faculty emails and got caught? And how you said that it's no good to hack people's emails, because emails are private, but then at the same time you were glad I did it because if I hadn't done it then we wouldn't have been able to study together since my parents wouldn't have sent me to Schechter if I didn't get turned into a SpEd at public school? You were right. It is wrong to hack faculty emails, but good that we got to study together. That is why I never told you about how I've been hacking faculty emails here, at Schechter. Because I didn't want you to be disappointed, because it was only wrong, because nothing good came of it. And I am telling you about it now, not because anything GOOD has come of it, but because something I think you should know about has come of it. I was in Unger's inbox and I read an email from your Headmaster Kalisch that was headered "Important" that said you got kicked out of Northside today, but then it also said a lot of other things that I thought you should know about. I almost forwarded it to myself, but then there would have been a sent receipt in Unger's outbox, which would not be stealth at all, so instead I copied and pasted it into an email that I sent to myself, from myself, and that's what I'm forwarding to you. I've told no one about this because no one can know that I hack faculty emails, and also I figured you should read it before others—I felt very weird reading it before you. So just tell me what you want me to do and I'll do it. Also, I wanted to tell you that I was delivered your instructions Saturday night, and so was Itzy Wasserman, though in the backyards of different Israelites, and what I thought was funny is that we drew the same face on our targets—Unger's! I like to shoot his eyes. I like to shoot them so much that I've gone through three targets already. Since yesterday, I've been able to nail him from thirty feet off, but it is most satisfying at twenty feet off, because even though twenty feet off doesn't make me feel as snipery as thirty feet off, I still feel pretty snipery, and plus I can hear the cardboard tearing at twenty, if the wind doesn't blow, while at thirty I can't even hear the cardboard tearing at all, no matter what—just my breathing and the snap of the balloon—and the cardboard tearing is such a good sound.

Your Student,
Ben Brodsky

□ □ □ □ □ □ □

Miss Pinge was peeling a spotted banana. She held it close to her face to hear the hiss of the skin tearing. In the middle waiting-chair, where I fell in love with June, a thin kid wearing tzitzit and a black fedora was chewing on the ends of his peyes. I wanted to be dressed just like him, but couldn't for another two years and seven months, when I would become a man. My father didn't want me to dress like a Hasid, or even wear a keepah—he didn't say these things, but it was easy to tell—and I had to honor him. Once I was a man, I would still have to honor him, but not at the cost of breaking the Law. My father used to be Hasidic himself, and that is why I thought for a second that I knew the kid in the middle waiting chair—it was from a picture in our family room. It's a picture of my dad, at his bar-mitzvah, sitting on a stone bench in the sun outside the Kotel in Jerusalem. He's not chewing on his peyes in the picture, but wind from the Al Aqsa side is blowing the left one against his lips, so it looks like he's chewing it. I missed my father, even though I just talked to him on the phone. I wanted to have lunch with him. My old schools were much closer to my house, and sometimes he'd come by with my mom and take me out for lunch. The last time was my third—my second-to-last—day at Martin Luther King Middle School. My dad was working at home and my mom had a sudden cancellation, so they took me to Foxies in Skokie. We had cheese fries and root-beer from a glass bottle and my mom was going to let me skip the rest of the day but my dad said I couldn't and he drove me back.

I tried to snap the leaf from Brodsky's fan-tree in half and it folded. I didn't want it anymore. What I couldn't break was already broken. The thin kid was looking at it, so I set it on his knee. He said the H'Adama blessing. Then he put the leaf between his lips and bit a piece off the tip, chewed.

The kid said to me, "I am Eliyahu." He swallowed some leaf and took another bite. "So that it shouldn't turn brown," he said. It sounded like a question and he nodded to the leftover piece = "The leaf agrees." He held it just under his chin, like Miss Pinge and her banana. "You're Jewish?" he said.

I'm an Israelite, I said. I said, Does that taste good?

"You say you're an Israelite." His hat was tipped to the right, but not rakishly. Rakishly has to be on purpose. He put the leaf to his lips, then took it away. "It tastes green," he said. "I'm also an Israelite." He bit the leaf and gave it another nod. "And so it seems we're both Israelites," he said.

I wasn't crazy for the whole "I'm weird, don't you want to know why?" bit he was working with that leaf, but I hadn't ever heard of an Orthodox kid in a public junior high school, plus I liked the way he talked.

Miss Pinge drew a hole in the air with the banana. She said, "Eli's a new student here. He's originally from the Big Apple."

"It's Eliyahu, already," said Eliyahu. "Eliyahu is the name my parents gave me. And it's not the Big Apple. Even if it was, what a shmaltzy thing to call a place. Would you like I said Miss Pinge from the Windy City?" He talked like an old man. He said, "I'm Eliyahu of Brooklyn."

Miss Pinge said, "I'm sorry. I don't know how to say that."

"What does it mean you don't know how to say it? Ay Lee Yah Hoo. What's so hard?"

"I'll try to say it correctly," Miss Pinge said.

I cocked my head at her = You're being very accommodating.

But then I thought: He's right. How hard is it to say Eliyahu?

I said, I'm Gurion.

He said, "Gurion? Your parents named you for a politician or a wild animal or what?"

Gur means cub. Like the son of a lion.

Are you good at Hebrew? I asked Eliyahu.

Miss Pinge said to me, "You better head back to the Cage."

"What is this woman talking about?" Eliyahu said in Hebrew.

I answered in English. I said, It's a classroom for B.D.'s. I'm attention deficient.

"People ignore you," he said.

I told him, Ha! You're smart. I told him, My conduct is disorderly and I'm hyper. Also I explode intermittently.

Eliyahu sat back and touched the top of his hat. "That's not funny," he said.

I said, You explode, too?

He said, "I asked you nicely."

I'm sorry, I said.

I didn't know why I was apologizing, but I didn't want Eliyahu to be hurt by me. I liked how he seemed to assume we were friends. I thought it should always be that way among Israelites.

"It's okay," he said. He sucked on the leaf.

Pinge set her banana on the desk so she could write me a hall-pass. A hall-pass was one of my favorite things to have at Aptakisic. You could go almost anywhere with it. You held a hall-pass out in front of you and the guards left you alone, even if they'd seen you walk past them six times already. There were a lot of rules in the arrangement, but the guards only needed to follow one: If you have to think about a person, send him to the Office.

A hall-pass was the only thing that would prevent thinking in a guard if they saw you in the hall and it wasn't lunch or a passing-period; even if you were throwing up or bleeding out of the head, they would send you to the Office if you didn't have one. The guards were like fingers, like robots. Like the Angel of Death that spread the tenth plague in Egypt. God sent it to kill the first-born sons of Egyptians so that the Israelites would be freed from bondage, but the Israelites still had to put sheep's blood on their doors so that the angel would pass over their houses. If there was no sheep's blood on the door, the angel would kill your first-born son even if you were an Israelite because even though it was one of God's fingers, it was still just a finger, and a finger's just a robot, and all the robot knew was to kill first-borns where there isn't sheep's blood.

Miss Pinge held the pass out to me between her pointer and swear. Her fingers were trembling, and hands remind me of dinosaurs when I stare at them, so I snatched the pass and looked away. It smelled like banana. I could go anywhere in the building. No one could touch me.

I asked Miss Pinge to change a dollar. She gave me three quarters and a stack of five nickels. Eliyahu chomped up the rest of the leaf. "Shalom," he said. I said it back. It made me warm to say it. I zipped my hoodie anyway, and pulled the hood on.

Then I left to retrieve my weapon and smash the face of the gym clock for June.

▫ ▫ ▫ ▫ ▫ ▫ ▫

Floyd the Chewer was the guard of the side entrance. When Floyd was young, he played a season of football for the Chicago Bears. He got cut fast and now he wore a Bears iron-on next to the security patch on his shirt and carried a plastic cheering cone from Notre Dame, where he went to college. The cone had a loop of skinny rope laced through a bracket near its mouth-hole and was attached to Floyd's wrist at all times. Jelly Rothstein's sister Ruth had interviewed Floyd in the "Pow-Wow" section of the *Aptakisic News* that October. She asked him why he always talked to students through the cone, and Floyd told her he hoped to one day get a job in the crowd-control profession and that the cone helped him practice. "Like how you got a wiffle-bat for wiffleball to practice baseball," he said, "my cheering cone is like a wiffle-megaphone for Aptakisic, but to practice for a riot." Then Ruth asked him if he minded that people called him the Chewer, and Floyd said that the only thing he loved more than being called the Chewer was the flavor of the cubes of the tasty grape gum he always kept packed in his cheek. But Floyd was a robot and a liar. If you called him the Chewer he'd give you the finger. It was against the rules, so he'd scratch his nose with it, or his chin. And his dream of crowd-control masked another dream: spit-control. Floyd talked through the cone because he couldn't manage his saliva. He sprayed whenever he made *p* and *b* sounds. You could hear the spit buzz the cone's plastic when it slapped against the insides. You could see it drip fakegrape purple out the widehole when the cone was dangling off his wrist and you were following him to the Office after he just finished yelling at you for a while.

But I didn't need to see Floyd, anyway. I didn't need to go past the side entrance to get to my locker. I needed to go past the front entrance, and that was guarded by Jerry the Deaf Sentinel, who wasn't deaf, but never listened. He just sat on a stool in a glass booth and kept a pencil he didn't use in the space between his head and his hat-band. I disliked Jerry a fraction less than I disliked Floyd, but it wasn't so easy to figure out why.

Both of them had a condition my mom taught me to recognize as the pogromface = their faces expressed whatever emotion the most conspicuously powerful guy in the room was expressing, and this expression would remain on their faces until another conspicuously powerful guy entered the room feeling a different emotion than the first. My mother's beliefs about the pogromfaced, though, differed from mine, however slightly. Whereas she thought them cowards filled with bloodlust, and useful only for the commission of atrocities, I, while I also thought of them as cowards, believed the pogromfaced empty of lust, available to accomplish any number of objectives at which men in power might choose to aim them. Still, we both agreed you couldn't pogrom without them. But that isn't to say they'd be able to execute pogroms on their own: though often incited, they never incited. And it isn't to say they were all the same, either—at least not exactly. The distinction, for example, between even the first man to brick a shop window and the second—or the distinction between either of them and the ones who, having grown bored with bricks, make Molotov cocktails; let alone that between any of the above and the ones who impede, however briefly, their friends' ignitions of the Molotov cocktails in order to prevent the marring of the sheen of the loot not yet taken—is no doubt relevant to Adonai, for all distinctions are relevant to Adonai, minute as they may seem, even if their relevance is totally lost on me and my mother, or any other human being. And when I looked at Floyd I could see him in Ukraine, stuffing fish into the flies of a murdered fishmonger's pants, and when I looked at Jerry I could see him right beside Floyd, stuffing fish into the mouth of the same murdered fishmonger, and I didn't know which deed was worse, though one of them surely had to be worse, at least by a fraction, but I did know I disliked Jerry a fraction less than I disliked Floyd, and I was all but certain that neither of them had ever been to Ukraine. So this is what I finally decided: It's better to be able to write something down than it is to amplify your spitty voice = if you have to have a prop, better a pencil than a Notre Dame cheering cone. And Floyd had the cheering cone, and Jerry the pencil. And that is why I disliked Jerry a little bit less.

I showed him my pass and said, This is my sheep's blood.

Jerry nodded. The nod dispatched me.

When I opened my locker, I blocked it with my body and fished my pennygun from the spy-pocket of my IDF fatigue jacket, which used to be my mom's. The gun was a new design. Instead of making it with the sawed-off top of a regular-mouthed soda bottle, I sawed off a wide-mouthed soda bottle. Also, I reinforced the balloon-skin that covered the pouring hole in order to prevent any slippage or tearing the extra circumference might foment.

I was pretty sure the new gun could project quarters, but I couldn't be certain because it was still a virgin. I'd only made it that morning, and the el-train was so late the schoolbus came thirty seconds after I got to the Frontier, where I would have otherwise conducted field tests while I waited. And that is why I hadn't changed the name of it from pennygun to quartergun yet, because I didn't want to risk disappointment. I figured I'd mostly use it for pennies anyway. Quarters cost more.

To get to the gym, I had to walk past the Deaf Sentinel again.

I held out my pass and held out a quarter and I said to him in Hebrew, I'm gonna break the glass on the gym clock, Sentinel. I said, I'm gonna use this currency to bring down the time-teller.

Jerry nodded.

□   □   □   □   □   □   □

Sent: June 9, 2006, 6:09 AM Central-Standard Time
Subject: RE: Fwd: Important
From: avelsalt@hotmail.com (Avel Salt, Solomon Schechter School)
To: Gurionforever@yahoo.com (me)

So maybe, for effect, I exaggerated a little. Good Shabbos.

----Original Message Follows----
From: Gurionforever@yahoo.com
To: avelsalt@hotmail.com
Subject: Re: Fwd: Important
Date: Fri, 9 June 2006 6:05 AM CST

Well, I didn't cry THAT much, though. Good Shabbos.

----Original Message Follows----
From: avelsalt@hotmail.com
To: Gurionforever@yahoo.com
Subject: Re: Fwd: Important
Date: Fri, 9 June 2006 5:59 AM CST

I wrote only the truth.

----Original Message Follows----
From: Gurionforever@yahoo.com
To: avelsalt@hotmail.com
Subject: Re: Fwd: Important
Date: Fri, 9 June 2006 5:57 AM CST

Rabbi Salt,
    I won't change my mind, but thank you for writing so many nice
things about me. I will not forget. And I'll see you in a week.
    Your Student,
    Gurion ben-Judah Maccabee

----Original Message Follows----
From: avelsalt@hotmail.com
To: Gurionforever@yahoo.com
Subject: Re: Fwd: Important
Date: Fri, 9 June 2006 12:11 AM CST

Boychic,

Following is what I sent them. If you change your mind, I'll post it on every listserv in the world.

In other news, I'm leaving town for a conference on Sunday morning, but I'll make sure to be back for your party. 10 years old, kiddo! That's a decade. That's big.

Your Friend,

Avel

---------- Forwarded message ----------
From: Avel Salt <avelsalt@hotmail.com >
To: Alan Kalisch of Northside Hebrew Day School <akalisch@northsidehd.edu>,
Richard Feldman of Northbrook Hebrew Day School <rfeldman@northbrookhd.edu>,
Lionel Unger of Solomon Schechter School <unger@schecterschool.edu>, Benjamin
Weissman of The Goldstein School <weissman@goldstein.edu>, Harold Nieman of
Anshe Emet <hnieman@ansheemet.edu>, Michael Kleinman of North-Suburban
Solomon Schechter School <mkleinman@nshechterschool.edu>
Date: Friday, 9 June 2006 12:03 AM Central-Standard Time
Subject: RE: Fwd: Important

Headmaster Rabbi Kalisch:

It is a shameful thing for a man, among colleagues, to slander a nine-year-old boy. It is doubly shameful when the man and his colleagues are teachers, and the boy the man's student; triply shameful when the teachers are rabbis and the student a Jew. And it is infinitely shameful, Headmaster, it is infamously shameful, it is Herodianly repugnant when the result of a rabbi's slander, let alone its very aim, is to prevent a Jewish student from properly studying Torah. But for you to have slandered Gurion Maccabee, a student already ten times the teacher you'll ever be and ten-thousand times the scholar—that is unforgivable, beyond shame, beyond repugnance. It is a travesty.

I would like to see harm come to you, Rabbi, and this troubles my soul because I know you must be damaged, for only the damaged can act as you have acted, and the damaged need our mercy, not our contempt.

It is with mercy, then, however strained, that I advise you to put aside your goyische equestrianism in favor of studying dogs. If you study with any rigor, you will surely come across those, like you, who are damaged; and you'll note these damaged dogs keep their heads down whenever they're aware that you're seeing them. Will you know why that is, Alan? why it is that a damaged dog keeps its head down when you watch it? why it lowers its eyes when it passes you on the street? A damaged dog lowers its eyes when it sees you coming, Alan, because it mistakes you for a man, and a damaged dog, unlike a broken-legged horse, knows of man's capacity for mercy. A damaged dog lowers its eyes among men lest it provoke the mercy men exercise on damaged animals. Forget your horses, Kalisch. Horses can't teach you what you need to learn.

The rest of you:

There's at least one of you who isn't wondering how the email in question got leaked. Being but a lowly, however tenured, principal of Judaic Studies, I don't know how to find out which one. I do know that the email was sent to me by my friend Michael Schloss, who received it off a listserv whose manager is based in Jerusalem. As you will see below, the Fwd "originated" from FIFTEEN23FIRSTSAMUEL@hotmail.com and then passed through two other listservs before getting to Michael. Apparently, one of you possesses this FIFTEEN23FIRST-SAMUEL account and you cut-and-pasted the original to cover your tracks. I know it wasn't Kalisch, for although a mamzer, it was clearly not his intention to commit a worldwide tarnishing-by-association of the names of the other boys mentioned (an assured outcome, that tarnishing, by the way, as well as its worldwideness, for how many Fwd's must the email have been through by now? how many people on either of the listservs to which it has been posted?). As for you, Unger, you're vindictive enough, true, and I'm sure you're raucously celebrating the takedown of the nine-year-old in question, but you're at once prideful and naked of anything that even resembles savvyness and I doubt you'd have thought to hide your identity.

So FIFTEEN23FIRSTSAMUEL is one of the other four of you.

I would gleefully go after all of you to be sure I got to the one, but your victim has asked that I refrain. Of Judah Maccabee—a profoundly talented attorney, in case you don't watch the news—Gurion has commanded compliance with the same request. Though I spent all of today devising a number of highly public methods by which to avenge him, and though his father would wrap tort around your necks like phonecord where his mother would actual phonecord, the boy himself—who was on the first listserv to which

FIFTEEN23FIRSTSAMUEL posted; who has spent these past couple days in tears at the thought of no longer being allowed to study Torah among his friends; and who, as the email circulates more and more widely through our community, is being denied access to more and more of these friends by their parents, who FEAR him now—when tonight, over dinner, we presented Gurion with the thousand possible ways in which we could ruin you, he declined all of them, saying, "What has been done to me is dirty, but no Israelite, no matter how corrupt, must ever be rendered unto the law of Caesar, much less the scrutiny of Canaanites. Apart from that, I love all of you, and will not have you sully yourselves in dirt that is mine to wash away. I will wash it away. I will wash it away truly."

May he.

Sincerely,

Rabbi Avel Salt

Principal of Judaic Studies, Solomon Schechter School of Chicago

---------- Forwarded message ----------
From: Michael Schloss <schloss@yeshivauni.edu>
To: Avel Salt <avelsalt@hotmail.com>
Date: Thur, 8 June 2006 09:40 AM CST
Subject: Fwd: Important

Avel,

Is this not the same Gurion you've spoken so highly of? I hope not.

Best,

Michael

---------- Forwarded message ----------
From: TorahScholars Listserv <tzvi@torahscholars.listserv.com>
To: Michael Schloss <schloss@yeshivauni.edu>
Date: Thur, 8 June 2006 09:11 AM EST
Subject: Fwd: Important

I can't see what this has to do with the TorahScholars listserv, but if one of you wants to post something, who is Tsvi to deny him?

—Tsvi

--------- Forwarded message ----------
From: EastCoastTzadiksListserv <rabbiprime@eastcoasttzadiks.listserv.com>
To: TorahScholars Listserv <rabbiprime@torahscholars.listserv.com>
Date: Wed, 7 June 2006 10:27 PM EST
Subject: Fwd: Important

Friends,

Were the words "no little bit disturbing" for some reason unavailable this evening, I believe I would describe this Fwd as "very compelling." Though I must also say I doubt its authenticity. Feel free to post on this topic.

--------- Forwarded message ----------
From: FIFTEEN23FIRSTSAMUEL <FIFTEEN23FIRSTSAMUEL@hotmail.com>
To: EastCoastTzadiksListserv <tsvi@eastcoasttzadiks.listserv.com>
Date: Wed, 7 June 2006 8:59 PM EST
Subject: Fwd: Important

Sent: June 7, 2006, 2:01 PM Central-Standard Time
Subject: Fwd: Important
From: akalisch@northsidehd.edu (Alan Kalisch, Northside Hebrew Day School)
To: rfeldman@northbrookhd.edu (Richard Feldman, Northbrook Hebrew Day
 School), unger@schecterschool.edu (Lionel Unger, Solomon Schechter
 School), weissman@goldstein.edu (Benjamin Weissman, The Goldstein
 School), hnieman@ansheemet.edu (Harold Nieman, Anshe Emet),
 mkleinman@nshechterschool.edu (Michael Kleinman, North-Suburban
 Solomon Schechter School)

Fellow Headmaster Rabbis:

Earlier today, one of our third-graders, Moshe Levin, was on his way to morning davening when a first-grader, David Kahn, stepped out of the doorway of a bathroom at the opposite end of the hallway and shot Moshe in the eye with a slingshot-type weapon that David and, I fear, no few others, refer to as a "pennygun." It appears that the attack on Moshe was provoked yesterday afternoon, on the after-school bus, where Moshe and some other boys teased David—by all reports rather harshly—about his stutter. Moshe has suffered a bruised retina and much psychological trauma. The doctors tell us that the ocular injury should heal shortly, baruch H-shem, but it is impossible to know how long the psychic damage will linger.

After having met with David, I am entirely confident that he is repentant and will not repeat-offend. Nonetheless, the boy must be expelled from Northside. For David's sake, justice would do well to be tempered with mercy here, but our no-tolerance policy against violence need be unequivocally enforced for the good of the school. If David should attempt to enroll in one of your schools at the start of next year, I urge you to keep that in mind. It is my hope that you would admit him as a second-grader—we are only three days away from the end of the academic year, and he is a good boy, a good student. He would come to you with my highest recommendations.

Of greater concern than the attack itself are the pennyguns. There is evidence which suggests that a number of boys at Jewish day schools throughout the Chicago area may be in possession of these weapons. This evidence comes in the form of a photocopied document, titled "Ulpan," that we discovered during a search of David Kahn's desk. A copy will be faxed to each of you. As you will soon see, the document not only offers instructions for how to build weapons, but instructions for how to teach others to build them. Most troublingly of all, "Ulpan" terminates in a call to arms in the name of the Jewish religion.

I am confident that desk- and locker-searches should do away with most of the weapons and copies of "Ulpan." We are currently in the process of performing such searches at Northside. I would imagine that the students whose weapons are not discovered (and confiscated) will—upon witnessing the penalties (one-day suspensions) suffered by those students who are found to be in possession of the weapons—see the academic, if not the moral, liability in carrying pennyguns, and will proceed, of their own volition, to dispose of their weapons, as well as their copies of "Ulpan."

Of greatest concern is the document's author, Gurion Maccabee, a nine-year-old Northside sixth-grader who most of you know, if not personally, then by reputation. After his expulsion from the Solomon Schecter School, I admitted Gurion to Northside because I believe in mercy, in second chances. Our student body had, up until this point, profited by that belief. Now we suffer for it.

Students, as Headmaster Unger can attest to, follow Gurion. Many call him "Rabbi." In class, they defer to him in all matters, whether secular or Judaic, and on the playground, they stand on line to speak to him. He is as intelligent and charismatic a boy as rumors would suggest, but he is equally as disturbed. When, earlier today, in conference, I asked Gurion why he felt the need to arm his fellow students, he said that his aim was to "help the Israelite children to protect themselves from the increasingly violent population of Canaanites for whom you (I, Rabbi Kalisch) would have us lay down." He then made reference to the antisemitic violence that took place three Saturdays ago, outside of the Fairfield Street Synagogue after services, commenting that, "Sometimes a scholar must become a soldier." When I pointed out to him that the teenagers who'd thrown the stones at the congregants had, within twenty-four hours of the attack, been taken into custody by the authorities, he said, "There's no King in Israel." When I let him know that he would be expelled from Northside, he told me, "There's no King in Israel." And when I told him that I would be sending a letter about him to the heads of all the Jewish parochial schools in and around Chicago, urging them to bar his enrollment, Gurion said, "There's no King in Israel." A short time later, while waiting in my office for his father to pick him up, he became visibly upset, and called me a "snivelling Sadducee."

The boy's mother—a mental-health professional, herself—has, since his enrollment at Northside, done everything she can to limit our social worker's access to him, has taken him off his medication (if ever she administered it at all—this was being looked into), and refuses to acknowledge that he needs help. Judah Maccabee will hear nothing against his son. The situation is impossible. I sincerely hope that some institution in this world will make Gurion better, but it is my whole-hearted belief that his continued presence in any of our schools would only be detrimental to the well-being of the local Jewish community. I hope you will not grant Gurion another chance. He would surely disappoint you.

In closing, I ask you to please forgive the informality of this group e-mail. If the information it contains did not require immediate dissemination, I would have taken the time to send individualized letters by post. Please feel free to contact me with any questions you might have. I will do my best to answer them.

Sincerely,

Rabbi Alan Kalisch,

Headmaster, Northside Hebrew Day School

PS: Janice and I will be hosting a 4th of July picnic at our family farm. The foals born there this spring (2 of them!) are not only healthy, but beautiful—just to see them walking, with all their horsey pride, is a treat—and we want to share our joy with others, as well as some kosher barbecue and traditional festivity (the fireworks, though nothing compared to those you'd see at Navy Pier, do rival the suburban), so if you're willing to shlep the kids out to Galina, please do so; we have many guestrooms for those who'd like to stay overnight. RSVP to this email address.

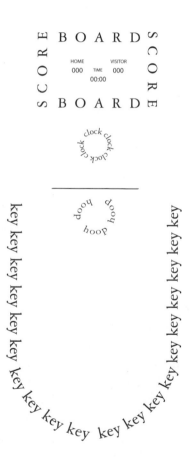

The lights were on, but the gym was empty; third-period PE had swim-unit, too. The end-of-class tone was twenty minutes away, so they'd be at the pool for at least another ten, which gave me time to piss without risk of detection, and that's what I did, though I only barely had to. I wanted no distractions when I fired on the clock.

In the language of industrial psychology researchers, the locker-room bathroom was a 2S-3U, which meant it housed a pair of stalls and three urinals. According to this study my mother once showed me—she thought it was funny—most guys entering 2S-3U's go straight for the urinal farthest from the door, unless the urinal farthest from the door is occupied, in which case most go to the one that's closest to the door so as not to stand next to a guy who is pissing, and if the only unoccupied urinal's the middle one, not only do most guys go to one of the stalls, but even though all they're doing is pissing, they stay for much longer than it takes to piss, engaging in what the authors of the study term "the phantom defecation stratagem" because they are embarrassed that they didn't choose to go to the unoccupied urinal and they feel that they need to save face.

I'd never once phantomly defecated, myself, but my choices in bathrooms, apart from that, did used to be typical. After I'd read the study, however, I quit going to the urinal farthest from the door. Whenever I'd enter an empty 2S-3U, I'd head straightaway for the one in the middle. What that did was cause most guys who came in after me to go to a stall. More than most guys, really; nearly all guys. Say eight out of ten, and call the stat reliable—I pissed a lot. Every day of the week, I beat the good sage's minimum, and usually I beat it by the end of dinner.

The Rambam (aka Maimonedes of Cordoba) said you had to piss at least ten times a day if you wanted to be a good sage. He also said you should keep your stomach in a constant state of near-diarrhea, which is not to be confused with a near-constant state of total diarrhea, which is the way of the stomachs of scoundrels worldwide. It is also important, according to the Rambam, to keep yourself clean. That is why I'd wash my hands every time. Even though doing so made people think you got some piss on your fingers. Rambam was a wiseman.

I finished up pissing and scrubbed with pink soap, dried my hands on my pants, and returned to the bright and empty gym, where my every step echoed and my breathing seemed loud. The clock was high on the western wall, ten feet over the basketball hoop, just a few inches below the scoreboard. It was masked by a box of metal rods with spaces between them too narrow for a golf ball, or even a marble, to get through. A coin, though, was thin. A coin could sneak.

Once, I got a couple pennies through the mask. All that they did was bounce off the glass, but pennies are smooth-edged, and that was the reason, apart from sheer mass, that I'd thought to try quarters. Quarters are rough-edged, and also they weigh more, and I thought that the glass might be like a man, and the edge of a penny like a bed of nails, whereas the one or two points on the edge of a quarter that would impact the glass were more like one nail that, if it was laid on, would enter the flesh.

I dropped a quarter into the balloon and stood at the top of the key. When I kneeled down to aim, it said 10:25 on the clock. I didn't know if it could happen, but I wanted the clock to stop when I smashed it, and if it stopped, I thought it would be better—a better gift to June, in case she noticed such things—if it stopped at a time that was interesting. 10:25 was not so interesting. Though $2 \times 5 = 10$, it's a cinch. And 10:26 did nothing when you played with it. So I decided to wait for 10:27, since $1+0+2+7 = 10$.

While I waited for 10:27, I could only hear my breathing and I remembered June kissing me. Not just that she kissed me, but the way the kiss felt, on my skin, in my skull. I got a shiver. When it faded, I tried to get another but couldn't. I'd worn out the memory, at least for the moment. If I thought too much about anything good, it would get less good, and everything good would begin to seem temporary. I did that the most with good songs. They'd stick in my head and go dull. And even when I'd hear one in my ears again, there were no surprises. I'd anticipate all the notes and the beats and the song would be ruined. So while it wasn't any big deal that I wore out the memory of that one kiss, I was scared that if I kept remembering the kiss I could ruin future kisses, so instead I remembered June saying, "Don't be sick, Gurion. I like you," and I got another shiver and it was 10:27 and as soon as the shiver stopped I pinched the quarter through the balloon skin and pulled back on it. I was aiming for the most middle space of the mask, the one that had the 3 and the 9 between it.

I let fly and the quarter plinked the bottom of the rod beneath the twelve, then fell straight down onto the floor. It was bad that I missed, but good to discover that my pennygun could project quarters.

It was still 10:27. I dropped another quarter in the firing pouch. This time I aimed for the space with the 5 and the 7 between it because it seemed from the first shot that I had aimed too high. There were fourteen seconds left in the twenty-eighth minute of ten o'clock. When there were thirteen seconds left, I fired. I got a direct hit, right in the middle between the 3 and the 9. It made the noise *tock*, but nothing else happened. The glass didn't fall down in pieces like I wanted. The clock didn't stop. There weren't even cracklines. Improbably, the quarter came to rest inside the mask; it lay flat on the centermost rod along the bottom.

I'd been wrong about quarters; they wouldn't do the trick. I'd smashed windows with pennies, so I was surprised. It was 10:28 and $1+0+2+8=11$, so it wasn't as good as 10:27, but it was better than nothing, and I just couldn't wait for 10:36. Though the period wouldn't end for sixteen more minutes, Desormie had to let class out extra early because the showers would bottleneck since even the dirty kids—even some of the shy ones—preferred to get warm and lather the stiff chlorine stink off their skin. If he stayed in his office while everyone showered, Desormie wouldn't hear me, but he was just as likely to stand in the gym and admire the scoreboard. He did that sometimes.

I'd have to work quick.

Since the pennygun could fire quarters, I figured it could fire small wingnuts, too. The problem was I'd given all the wingnuts I'd brought that day to June and the principal. I ran to the bleachers to see if I could find one—no. The bleachers' joints were fixed with welded-on hexnuts.

10:29, nearly 10:30.

I thought about shooting the rivet on my jeans-pocket that I used to call the grommet until my dad said it was a rivet, and then I thought about the bottom eyelet on my Chucks that *was* a grommet, but a specific shoe-kind that was better called an eyelet, but neither of those things was any heavier or pointier than a quarter, plus in order to get one I'd have to tear my jeans or cut my shoes and thus anger my mom, so both ideas were completely dental.

I opened the back door of the gym where there was an asphalt trail. Next to the trail was some mud with rocks in it. I kept my foot wedged between the door and jamb and searched for a rock that would fit in the gun. The effort got me H, but I found three in all, each irregularly shaped: one like a dog's ear bending in kindness, another like Nevada, a third like some lips with a sore in the corner. I fired Nevada first, because it was the slimmest, and also the pointiest. Nevada got wedged between the bars of the mask. It was 10:31, almost 10:32. I felt all defeated. I felt like exploding. If the slimmest and pointiest of the three couldn't penetrate... I let fly the dog's ear without really aiming; I let fly from pique; I fired from the hip. The shot was way high. Not even close. It blew out the E of the HOME on the scoreboard. The E hit the floor in three sharp pieces. The bulb remained. HOME was now HOM.

Well, that was something. Wasn't that something? I thought it was something, not much but something. As a tribute to the love that I'd fallen in with June, a broken scoreboard, so easy to engender it could be accidental, was totally worthless, but at least a broken scoreboard would upset Desormie, who if I didn't have to worry about him coming out of his office to admire the schmuckface scoreboard to begin with, I'd have had another ten minutes to find a suitable projectile to fire at the clock.

So yes, it was something, but it wasn't enough. The problem was the something wasn't on purpose. The fact that I *breathed* got Desormie upset.

It was 10:32. I was holding the lips rock. I loaded the lips rock. I had time for one shot to make it on purpose. I couldn't decide if I wanted to bust out the H so the board would read OM, or the M so instead the board would read HO. So I aimed for the V so the board would read ISITOR, because next to each other the two of them sounded like gods with the bodies of monkeys or donkeys, the kinds of gods you sacrificed virgins for, Hom and Isitor. That's right, I thought. That's *right*, I thought. You can worship *that*, you filthy uncircumsized crotch-peeping mamzer pedophile scumbomb.

I knelt, I aimed, I let the rock fly. The rock flew funny, the corner with the sore on it scraping the body of the gun on exit, bancing the vector. I missed the V. The T got blasted. The scoreboard read HOM and VISI OR. HOM and VISI OR did not sound pagan. It just sounded stupid. And now I had just under a minute to deal with all the evidence against me, to blind the world to the source of the stupidity.

I left the rocks and picked up the quarter. Then I picked up all the pieces of the broken E and T and took them to the handicapped bathroom in B-Hall, right outside the gym, and locked the door. Soon some people would see the busted scoreboard and would say that I did it, but they wouldn't have proof. That usually wouldn't matter, except since there wouldn't be any pieces on the floor, Brodsky and them would be looking for the guy who took the pieces. They would think there was a way to prove that I did it by finding the pieces. Because no one would break a scoreboard and then clean up what he broke, they would think. They would think someone would either break the scoreboard and run away fast, or break the scoreboard and take the pieces with him to show them off. Since I'd left no pieces on the floor, they would think the person didn't run away fast—they would think he took the pieces to show them off. And I was going to throw the pieces away so that if they searched my locker and my bag and my desk and my pockets and did not find the pieces, they would become confused. Because they would think there should be proof since proof was the first thing they thought of and they would think they were smart. But there would be no proof. And they were not that smart. And all my enemies who believed I did it would still believe I did it and would keep looking for proof they would never find. And all my friends who hoped that I did it would ask of my enemies, "Where is your proof?"

I wrapped the pieces of the E and the T in yards of paper towel so they wouldn't tear the bag and threw the wrapped pieces into the trashcan and covered them over with wads of goozed tissues and saw it was good. That was all the good I saw, though.

I was walking out of the bathroom when I remembered the quarter that lay inside the clockmask. I didn't think anyone would notice the quarter, especially since they'd be thinking about the scoreboard, but it wasn't impossible they'd notice the quarter. They'd see the Nevada rock wedged in the mask, and if they got on a ladder to get the rock out, they might notice the quarter. Except for Nakamook, I never showed or told anyone at Aptakisic about pennyguns, but Brodsky knew my history, at least that part of it, and if someone found my pennygun while they were searching for the pieces of the E and the T, they might think it was strange and show it to Brodsky, who might draw conclusions based on the quarter, so I took apart the pennygun and threw the balloon in one hallway garbage can and the sawed-off bottle in another one. The rubberband was thick, though, and wasn't incriminating, so I didn't ditch it. I turned it into a sideways 8 and wore it on my wrists like a set of handcuffs. I wedged the hall-pass under the left cuff. My fingers throbbed and soon I couldn't feel them. I walked toward Jerry, keeping my head down and jerking my body like the warden was shoving me along the white corridor that led to the chair, and I wanted to go as slow as I could because even though I knew that the chair couldn't kill me, the warden kept shoving and hissing, "Faster!"

I raised my hands to show Jerry the hall-pass.

They can't kill me, Jerry, but still, I said, I'll never forgive them for trying.

The Sentinel nodded.

I felt kind of childish. I felt like a dickhead. A weaponless failure playing pretend. I undid the dickhead handcuffs.

□ □ □ □ □ □ □

Sent: June 9, 2006, 12:49 AM Central-Standard Time
Subject: LAST WORD (pls fwd to any scholar not listed in the CC box)
From: Gurionforever@yahoo.com (me)
To: Gurionforever@yahoo.com
CC: SCHECHTER LIST, NORTHSIDE HEBREW DAY LIST

Scholars:

I know all your parents saw that email, "Important," that Headmaster Rabbi Kalisch wrote, and it's only to be expected that after reading that email, they'd forbid you from associating with me, and what I want you to know is that I am not angry at any of you for avoiding me, for not stopping by or writing or calling in these past couple days. There is a difference between avoiding and quitting. Sometimes you have to avoid in order not to quit. I know that. And I know you haven't quit me. And you would know if I were angry. I would tell you.

For those of you who have reached out to me against your parents' wishes: Please stop. Although the solace I get from your support is vast, it is nonetheless dwarfed by the sadness that comes over me at the thought of you breaking a commandment for my benefit.

All of you must honor your parents, and although it is true that in certain situations you must disobey them in order to honor them, no such situation has yet arisen, at least not one concerning me, and that is why, after hitting SEND, *I* will honor your parents by not contacting *you* until that time when honor demands disobedience.

Til then, remain stealth, gain strength, and protect each other.

Your Friend,
Gurion ben-Judah

3
DAMAGE

Tuesday, November 14, 2006
3rd–4th Period

C-HALL C-HALL C-HALL C-HALL C-HALL

WALL WALL WALL WALL WALL	DOORWAY	WALL WALL WALL WALL WALL
WALL WALL WALL WALL WALL	DOORWAY	WALL WALL WALL WALL WALL
WALL WALL WALL WALL WALL	DOORWAY	WALL WALL WALL WALL WALL
WALL WALL WALL WALL WALL	DOORWAY	WALL WALL WALL WALL WALL

ROOM ROOM <u>DOOR</u> ROOM ROOM
ROOM ROOM ROOM ROOM ROOM
ROOM ROOM ROOM ROOM ROOM
ROOM ROOM ROOM ROOM ROOM

Y ou were allowed to drink caffeine drinks at Aptakisic, except you couldn't buy them there if you were a student. The only Coke machine was in the teachers lounge. There was a coffee one, too, and I liked to drink coffee if it was half cream and sugar the way my mom drank it, but Coke made my stomach burn. Still, I enjoyed breaking into the teachers lounge for a Coke on occasion to practice stealth.

I didn't care about getting any practice right then, and I certainly wasn't hoping to find any joy, nor was I kidding myself that a teachers-lounge-Coke's value as a tribute was equivalent to a smashed-apart gym clock's—though no one else would have broken into the lounge, and no one else except for me ever even had, it would be, yes, my sixth or seventh time, so although it was hard, no one thought it impossible—but if I didn't do something at least a little hard for June, then…what? The dickhead, beaten feeling wouldn't go away.

Aptakisic's passing-periods lasted four minutes, which meant four min-utes, tops, to get in and out of the lounge unseen. There was always the possibility of a dawdling teacher, or a teacher who let her class out a couple minutes early and went straight to the lounge, but those things weren't worth being too concerned about, even though they ticked the clock down; with the right coinage ready, it wouldn't take more than thirty-five seconds to get the Coke and exit. Even with a balled-up dollar to flatten, I'd gotten in and out of there in under a minute. The thing to be concerned about was getting caught in the doorway.

You had to hide in the doorway so you could stop the lock from clicking when the last teacher in the lounge left. It was the kind of door that auto-matically locks when it closes, and no one had been able to steal a key yet.

So, for Coke-getting purposes, it was lucky that the teachers lounge was in C-Hall, which had doorways the size of walk-in closets. They were meant to be buffer zones between hall-noise and pedagogy. Like storm-windows that trap cold between the panes, C-Hall doorways were air chambers for trapping sounds. Soundstorm-windows.

Some of the doorways were darker than others. Benji Nakamook and I put the bulbs of most of the darker ones out for a contest we had in my third week at Aptakisic. No one had replaced them, and Nakamook told me a joke about it afterwards. Hector the Janitor goes up to Floyd the Chewer, says, "How many guards does it take to fix a light-bulb?" and the Chewer goes, "Where's your hall-pass?"

Benji won the contest 5–2. I'd have scored much higher if I'd used a pennygun, except I didn't want Benji to see that I had one; I was already considering giving him a copy of *Ulpan*, but I hadn't yet figured out the right way to doctor it, and didn't know if I'd be able to, or even if I should, so I attacked the bulbs with my bag of wingnuts, tied it up tight and underhand-chucked it. Nakamook smoked all his bulbs with his Zippo, and it was him who blanked the teachers lounge one.

The doorway was not entirely dark, though. Dim light came from the panels in the hallway, and brighter light from the other side of the door, by way of the small door-window. The window was higher up than my head, and the light it let through made a rhombus by my feet. It wasn't a rhombus I wanted to violate. To overstep its outline could mean exposure.

It turned out its outline wasn't grey like I would've assumed, but purple, and I thought that was nice, maybe poetry-worthy, whatever that meant, and it occurred to me that maybe the Coke I was getting for June, if a strong poem were taped to it, would come closer to approximating a smash-faced gym clock than would a Coke without a strong poem taped to it. Granted, I couldn't make a strong poem, but there was no doubt in my mind that a weak poem was a closer approximation to a strong poem than was no poem, and therefore a Coke with a weak poem taped to it was a closer approximation of a smash-faced gym clock than a poemless Coke, so I wrote June a weak poem in the doorway, in my head:

> I Won't Tell You I'm Not Breaching the Penumbra
> by Gurion ben-Judah Maccabee
>
> While I hide inside a doorway
> in C-Hall,
> preventing my toes from breaking
> an outline,
> I reject a fancier string of words

than this one
because when
you touched me on the head,
I didn't get dangerous,
and I don't know if you know *penumbra*.

Because the doorway was darkest by the walls, the most stealth thing to do was become a wall by getting as flat as possible against one, but I needed to get some information first. I needed to know exactly how many teachers were in the lounge so I could stop the door as soon as it started to close behind the last one. I inched to the window and stood on my toes, angling my body so no one inside would be able to see me, and I had to employ phenomenal agility so I wouldn't violate the light rhombus either. I counted the heads—seven total, two bald—and dropped back onto my heels.

Seven was a large number of people to hide from in a doorway. It got me edgy and my foot started tapping, which wasn't stealth. I crouched so it couldn't tap so easy, but that made me less flat, and then I remembered I was out of wingnuts, and I got even edgier. Usually I'd lay a wingnut on the floor in front of the door-jamb to prevent the lock from engaging. It was way too risky to stop the door with a hand. If the last teacher out lingered, which they usually did—they weren't the last out because they were rushing to teach—and you had your hand in the door, you'd be exposed in the light, and if the teacher turned around, they'd see the hand and who it was attached to. The right-sized wingnut was perfect for the job, though. It not only allowed the door to nearly close, which made it highly unlikely that a teacher would notice that anything was off, but the click of the contact between closing door and wingnut was almost identical to the click of the lock.

All I had was a pen. A chewed disposable. A very thin cylinder. I didn't know if it could do the trick. If the bottom of the door was higher off the floor than the pen laid on its side, the door would pass over the pen and lock. I was really edgy. I was so edgy that I thought it. I thought: You are really very edgy right now. And right when I thought it, the end-of-class tone came through the intercom to shock me like the punchline before the closing credits of a thousand stupid television shows.

I revolved to face the wall and got as flat as I could. Then I started telling myself a children's version of the story of the kind of holiday I wanted to one day be the hero of, the version you'd tell kids who didn't know how to read yet and couldn't understand the complexities of scripture—like the version of Chanukah where it's all about the oil, or the version of Rosh Hashanah that's all apples and honey and new year's joy. But I was not the little kid with the big imagination who half-grown nice Jewish boys star in their novels to attempt to make readers feel special and congratulated. That kid's a drip. That kid has fantasies behind his closed eyes in order to escape the facts on the ground, and somehow he doesn't know it. The facts on the ground that I had to face if I wanted to get June a Coke were these: I was highly edgy and I needed to stay pressed to the doorway wall for at least a couple minutes. In times of high edginess, I'd usually read or break things or fight, or try to break all of my fingers at once, and since I couldn't stay pressed while doing those things, but couldn't stay pressed if I remained edgy either, I had to try something else. That's the only reason I told myself a story. It was the one way I *could* face the facts on the ground. And I made it a kids' one because kids' ones lack layers and I was too preoccupied to get all in-depth, and I tried to keep it similar, at least thematically, to what I was doing, so I wouldn't lose focus on the task at hand.

So I told me one about how Gurion got out of his cell but was in such a rush that he didn't have time to get the keys to his manacles off the ring on the belt of the famously sadistic prison guard he'd clouted and left half-conscious on the third-tier catwalk drooling strings that splashed on the heads of the general population while Gurion escaped, and the ways the holiday would celebrate all of it.

The first teacher exited. Passed me. Was gone. The door squeaked three times on its hydraulics, clicked shut.

The holiday's name would be Gurion's Escape. At the holiday meal, the youngest boy present would ask his father—a second teacher passed: three squeaks and click—a set of four questions. The boy would say, "Why on this night do we wear handcuffs and leg-shackles at the dinner table?" And his dad would say, "Because our hero and his people, our people, were restricted in their movements by robots and the arrangement." And the boy would say, "Why on this night do we smash glass bottles on the pavement in the parking lots of our township?" And his dad—teacher three had a limp: two squeaks this time before the click, which meant I couldn't count on three—would say, "The glass bottles are clear like the rules of the robots, and all clear things may be broken and so all clear things should be broken and shall be broken, for the noise of their breaking is the only pleasure to be gotten from them." "Why on this night do we punch holes in the walls of popsicle-stick-models of schools after dessert?" would say the boy. "We forget," would say the dad, "that the walls of schools can be broken like bottles. We forget that we can break them. We must remind ourselves that we are stronger than the house of the arrangement." "And why on this night," the boy would say, "do we celebrate Gurion's Escape?" And the dad would say, "Gurion's Escape was the birth of perfect justice in the world." Then there would be soup and the dad would sneak off to hide a set of holiday handcuffs in a dark space between things or behind a thing. Between the meat and the dessert—the fourth and fifth teachers, I think Miss Farmer and Mr. Novy, but it wasn't worth revolving to make sure, stopped a few seconds in the doorway to flirt. She said, "I was watching you write your lesson plans and I couldn't help but admire the condition of your fingernails." He said, "I'm so flattered to hear that. You know, between lifting weights every morning at the gym and making visual art in my spare time, I always assumed that people found them cracked and nubby." She said, "Visual art! I do needlepoint! I—" but she was interrupted by the sixth teacher, whose voice I never heard before. He said, "Some kinda party here?" and they all laughed fake laughs while exiting, and I couldn't count the squeaks for the laugh-noise— Between the meat and the dessert all of the children at the table would go looking in the dark spaces of the house for the handcuffs. Whoever found them would get a prize that the father and the finder would bargain about. The father would say, "What do you want for a prize?" And the finder would answer: "Power." And the father would say, "Power can be used but it can't be had. If I had it to give, I would give it to you. You are my child." And the finder would say, "Then I want funniness." And the father would say, "Funniness is a kind of power. That is why people who try to have funniness are so rarely funny. How about some cash?" And the finder would take some cash for his prize. And there would be traditions at Schecter, Anshe Emet, and at both Hebrew Days. The students would build their popsicle-stick schools all week long. They would spend half the day of Erev Gurion's Escape in arts-and-crafts. Papier-mache handcuffs would be sculpted til noon, and they'd dry by 3:30, and the students would stay after to paint watercolor scenes of my escape on the handcuffs. They would paint me pressed against the inside of a doorway, becoming a wall. All day they'd sing a song that went "Famous in the prison/ The guard who met with Gurion/ Famous in the prison/ And Gurion bled his head/ Oh Gurion, Gurion, Gurion/ Gurion bled his head/ Gu ri on ben-Ju dah!/ Gurion Mac ca bee!" They would sing it in school and they would sing it in shul. And around the dining room table they'd dance, handcuffed to each other, their legshackles shed, singing my song and shouting *l'chaim*s, their high-kicking shins getting bruised on the chairs, their hats and their yarmulkes all flying off, fragments of popsicle sticks in their hair, the joy so huge the good silver would melt and the china for company would crack on the placemats.

Teacher #7 came out of the lounge.

I was worried the hydraulics would only squeak twice before the door shut, like with the third teacher, so I revolved after the first squeak in order to get the pen in place before the second, but the teacher paused at the outer-edge of the doorway, then turned her head to sneeze right when I was about to activate the pen-block, and I had to keep still and shut my eyes so they wouldn't betray me, flashing. The second squeak came and I opened my eyes, tossed the pen down. It landed well, right against the jamb. Another sneeze from the teacher. I closed my eyes again. There was a third squeak after all, and a third sneeze. Then the teacher's departing footsteps.

Nothing clicked.

I was in.

I plugged what remained of the change Pinge had made for me into the Coke machine, added a dime from out of my watch pocket. None of it caught funny or got rejected and, wide-mouth in hand, I was headed for the door, when I realized that the Coke would be warm by the time detention came around and so there was no way June would know, unless I told her, that I'd gotten the Coke in the teachers lounge. I didn't want to tell her because even though I knew she'd believe me if I did, I couldn't think of any words to make it sound pretty. I needed a site-specific souvenir to do the bragging for me. The bragging of a site-specific souvenir would be more elegant. Elegant could be pretty. I couldn't see anything worth taking, though. Just chairs around a long wood-colored table with a tray full of rubberbands and binderclips in the middle of it.

I pocketed the binder clips, seven in all, and saw in the gaps between the piled rubberbands a bright white something too unlikely to believe in. I picked up the rubberbands. I saw and believed. A pad of hall-passes. A thick, tall pad. I flipped through the pad. Every single one blank. A pile of freedom. I stuffed it in my bag beside the Coke. The pad wouldn't brag that I got the Coke from the teachers lounge, but gotten Coke cotton shmoke—I'd give June the pad. No one had ever gotten a pad of blank hall-passes, let alone made a gift of one. It was almost as good as smashing the gym clock.

I'd tear one pass off and write the penumbra poem on the back of it, then binderclip the poem to the lip beneath the cap of the Coke and, in detention, when June took the Coke from my hands, I'd drop the pad on the table in front of her and say, Want a coaster?

She would laugh at the coaster joke til her face hurt, and she would tell me her face hurt and I would say it was killing me, but I wouldn't mean it meanly and she'd know that.

It was time to exit.

I came to the hall-edge of the teachers lounge doorway and threw fast glances in both directions. The hall was filled with students and teachers. I ducked back and became the wall again. This time I wasn't edgy, though. I felt very good. I was stealth and loved June and broke rules.

The beginning-of-class tone came over the intercom and the footsteps stopped in the hallways and all of the teachers who would go to the lounge for fourth period—five of them—had already passed me without seeing me and I knew I was safe. I thought: As long as no one sees you, you're safe. But right when I was stepping out of the doorway, Eliyahu came around the corner, and the timing was so strange that I thought Hashem was trying to remind me that *He* saw me. Except that couldn't be it: if He could somehow tell what I was thinking well enough to answer what I was thinking, He'd know I didn't need reminding. So it had to be something else—like an argument. I didn't know if His argument was "I see you, yet still you are safe," or "I see you, *and so* you are safe," but the difference was potentially huge. Flowers might have said I was "facing a monster of ambiguity" in the hallway. It was good to face a monster of ambiguity, but sometimes what you thought to be a monster of ambiguity was just a lack of clarity, and a lack of clarity wasn't good at all. It was unclear to me if I was facing a monster of ambiguity or a lack of clarity, so that was definitely not good, but I couldn't sort it out right then. My new friend was coming toward me. From the right.

□   □   □   □   □   □   □

The top half of Eliyahu's body leaned forward like he was running but the bottom half walked and he was chewing his thumb. He had a pass in his hand.

He said, "I'm lost. I need to get to Science. I need to get to A-Hall."

I said, A-Hall's for A-holes.

Eliyahu said, "It may be so. Let me ask you, Gurion: are you a big macher? I have the sense that you're some kind of a big macher around here and I want for you to protect me. And to tell me how to get to A-Hall."

"Big macher" cracked me up.

Eliyahu said, "Already a boy yanked on my tzitzit and knocked the hat from my keppy. I'm late," he said.

For a very important date? I said.

"You'll quote cartoons to me in a singsong voice?" he said. "You're late, too."

I said, If you have a pass, it's a different kind of late.

"What kind of different late? Late is late."

I said, You won't get in trouble. Who knocked your hat off?

"I don't know his name. He was a tall boy in a basketball jersey. Taller than me, even, and also not so thin. Muscular. Two small diamonds in his ear. I was lost, trying to find this A-Hall, and then *bip*: a pulling of the tzitzit. And *bop*: there's my hat on the floor. This tall boy with the diamonds, he says, 'Nice hat, bancer'? I don't know from *bancer*, but I bend to pick my hat up, and I see there's another boy present, another tall muscular one—call him Aleph to avoid confusion—standing back by the lockers, and by the way this Aleph turns his eyes to the floor when he sees me seeing him, I know he has witnessed this whole humiliating incident, and by the rapid, unprotesting way he leaves the scene as soon as the boy with the diamonds—who has been cued by the direction of my gaze to look at him—says to him, 'What? You have a problem with this?' I see that I should be even more afraid of the one with the diamonds than I already am. And so I'm right. No sooner do I stand up than the boy with the diamonds knocks the hat from my keppy a second time, and says, 'That's a *really* nice hat, bancer,' And so what's this *bancer*? This is school-specific vernacular? Why laugh? Why laugh when I'm asking for protection? Why laugh?"

Eliyahu was hilarious. He talked like he was singing. A zadie in a movie.

I said, The kid who knocked your hat off is Co-Captain Baxter. He's in eighth grade. We can damage him easy, but I can't really protect you from anything. I'm in the Cage. They don't even let me go to lunch.

He said, "So you're saying if you weren't in this Cage, you'd be willing and able to protect me?"

I said, We're friends. I'd definitely try to protect you, but I don't know how able I'd be, even if I wasn't in the Cage. I can avenge you whenever, though. I could do that whenever. We could find Co-Captain Baxter at his locker, either right before or right after detention today, and I could put the cripple-grip on his clavicle, and then hold his arm so that his hand is partway inside the locker, and you could slam the door on his fingers as many times as you'd want, and he wouldn't be able to shoot free-throws anymore—but protection's different from vengeance.

Eliyahu showed me both his palms = "Please hold on a second." Then he turned very suddenly and took a drink from the water fountain. The water fountain made the low whistling water fountain sound and Eliyahu's curved back looked delicate, foldable like cardboard, like if I punched him between the shoulderblades, his spine would collapse. When he was done drinking, he unpressed the button and the whistling sound became a humming sound. Then Eliyahu lifted his head. Most people lift their head before unpressing the button. That way wastes water. And when Eliyahu turned back around, he did not wipe his mouth on his sleeve like most people, but skipped the water droplets from his lips and his chin with his thumb and his pointer. These were gentle things to do. They were very controlled. I noticed he was still bent forward on top. He still looked afraid of something. I thought: Maybe he always looks afraid of something.

I could not stop hearing the humming of the motor in the water fountain.

Eliyahu told me, "Not vengeance. No vengeance."

Something about how he said it made me not try to convince him, despite the singsong. It was very final how he said it. Vengeance was out of the question. But then protection was impossible.

I explained to him, Even if I wasn't in the Cage, we'd still be in different classes—I'd only be able to protect you at lunch and in the hallway.

He said, "A little bit of protection is better than none. And so what can we do to get you out of the Cage?"

Nothing, I said. I said, As long as there's a Cage, I'm in it.

"Maybe we'll get rid of this Cage," he said.

I said, Not today. I said, Do you know how to fight at all? I've never fought the Co-Captain, but he looks like the kind of kid who's never gotten hit, like if you hit him just once, he'll run away.

"I can't," said Eliyahu. "I think of hitting someone? I think of hurting him. I think of hurting someone? I become sad. My stomach aches. I cry a little. I just can't do it. So how does a boy get into the Cage?"

The Cage is locked down, I said to Eliyahu. You only get to leave for Lunch and Gym, and sometimes you can't even leave for Lunch.

"So what?" he said.

You have to sit there all day in a carrel, facing forward. The teachers don't teach. They tutor in the center, but you can't just approach them. You have to get called on, and most of the time they're not looking around to see if your hand's raised. You sit there, waiting, and you can't talk to anyone, or even *see* anyone—you're not allowed to look.

"Okay," he said. "So it's quiet in there. So no kids can bother me."

That's not exactly true, that no kids can bother you. Ways can be found.

"But you wouldn't let any kid bother me," he said. "You'd protect me from that."

That's true, I said, but the Cage is no kid. The *Cage* will bother you. And Botha, I said, who's the schmuck who's in charge—he'll bother you, too. He's a horrible man. Cartoon-level horrible. He's even got a claw instead of a hand.

"I'm bothered already by the school," he said, "and I'm certain the teachers will bother me, too. Public school teachers—they're always bothering."

You're a scholar, Eliyahu. You don't want to be there.

"And you're not a scholar?"

I'm a scholar, I said.

"So what, then?" he said. "Why should a scholar not be in the Cage? Who says it shouldn't be? Rabbi Akiva, maybe? Not Rabbi Akiva: He died in a cage. In a torture chamber! At the hands of Romans! How do I get in?"

It was true about Rabbi Akiva. It was also true that Eliyahu was determined to stay near me, where he would feel protected, no matter what it meant, and that if I didn't tell him how to get in the Cage, he'd figure out a way to get in there himself. And while it's true I didn't want him to be in the Cage because the Cage was terrible, it's also true I wanted him to be in the Cage because I was in the Cage, and to have another friend there, let alone another scholar, couldn't help but to make the place more tolerable.

"Nu?" said Eliyahu.

Break things, I said.

"Break things," he said. "And what should I break?"

I said, It's not just what you should break, but when you should break it.

"When should I break what I should break?" he said.

After you get told to do something you don't want to do, I told him.

"And what is this that I won't want to do, Gurion?"

The first thing you're told.

"And if I want to do it?"

Pretend you don't, and then break something.

"It sounds very simple," he said. He chewed his thumb some more.

I said, Don't be afraid, Eliyahu. It'll be fun if you're not afraid.

He said, "I'm not afraid of breaking things. I just don't like this school. I don't like that for protection I need to be violent. Violence causes death. I do not like death. I don't want to cause death or contribute to death. I don't want death to be. I don't want us to die. I do not like it, how everyone dies."

I said, I won't die.

"Then I will try not to fear it," he said. "I'll break a window."

I said, A window would be a perfect thing to break. It's loud and dangerous and if you broke it with your fist, they'd think you were violent, but they'd also worry that you secretly wanted to kill yourself with glass in the armveins. It would get you in the Cage for sure, for two-week observation at least. The problem is all the windows in the classrooms are highly shatter-resistant. Swung chairs can't even break them, much less fists. It's been tried. Believe me. Too bad, too. That really is suck. A window would've been—

"Science!" said Eliyahu.

Science?

"In Science, there's usually a fire-extinguisher."

That won't go through those windows, either, I said. Those are some serious windows. You can barely even open them—they're *casement* windows.

"No. Not to put it through the window. The fire-extinguisher, at least at my last school, was always in a box on the wall, a glass-doored—"

Perfect, I said. That's perfect. Break the glass door.

"I will break the glass door."

You have to be careful, though, I said, so that you don't kill yourself by accident. You can't put your fist *through* the door. And you can't wrap your hand in anything before you do it. If you wrap your hand, they'll think you were making a cry for help, and they'll only give you therapy. You have to do it barehanded, so you have to aim the punch.

"How do I aim the punch?"

It's almost the opposite of what you do when you're hitting a baseball, I said. You don't follow through.

"I don't play baseball."

Even better, I said. Baseball is suck.

"I think so, too," he said. "So much waiting. And then for what? For two seconds of action. Stop and go. Wait, wait, wait, and then wait some—"

I told him, Let me watch you throw some punches.

He dropped his bag. He jabbed the air. Whoever taught him fighting took karate in the suburbs = he held his fists at his waist. It's hard, from that position, to throw a fast elbow, and elbows are important: they're harder than hands, they tend to surprise, and when one connects with a nose or an orbit, the noise backs off potential interferers. It wasn't, however, any big deal to show him the right way to raise his arms, and other than that he wasn't bad at all. He knew to keep his thumbs outside of his fists, he knew how to stand with his feet apart so his base was wide and he wouldn't lose balance in the middle of the punch, and he knew to turn his fist a full 90 degrees between launch and target to draw extra power from the muscles of his back. If he could punch people the way he punched air, he'd win most fights at Aptakisic, I thought. I could take him easy and so could the Flunky; Benji and Slokum went without saying. The teachers, of course, could take Eliyahu, and probably Leevon Ray could too. Though no one had ever seen Leevon fight, everyone seemed pretty sure he could fight because he never talked, and not ever talking had to get him in fights because it had to make a lot of kids crazy—it made teachers crazy, which is why he was in the Cage, and teachers get paid to not get crazy—and we'd never seen Leevon bruised up or bleeding. Or maybe it was just because he was a black guy that everyone seemed to think he could fight. About Jenny Mangey I couldn't be certain: she always fought guys, and guys who fought girls were weak and sick, so even though Mangey had never lost a fight, it was hard to know if she was really any good. Vincie Portite, prior to the eye-trauma, could have defeated Eliyahu no sweat, but now the two would most likely be even. There were five or ten others at Aptakisic I'd have ranked Eliyahu even against, but the more that I watched him throw punches at air, the more certain I got he couldn't throw them at people. Eliyahu wasn't serious about damaging things. I could see it on his face. Totally calm. Not calm with concentration like a zenned-out old sensei, but more like an uncle, drunk at a wedding, in the middle of dancing to his favorite song badly. Not even that. I didn't think ill of him. His face was just… It was Eliyahuic. His violence was not sincere.

Baruch Hashem, I thought, he isn't out to hit someone; all he needs to learn to do is break glass.

You have good enough form, I said to Eliyahu. Now it's just a matter of what you pretend.

"And what should I pretend?" he said.

I said, You have to pretend that your fist is a race car with amazing brakes and that there is some power in it, and the power is like two really fat guys sitting in the front seats of your fist, and that when you're throwing a punch, your fist-car is going two hundred miles per hour, but when you hit the thing you're trying to hit, the fist-car stops the instant its knuckle-bumper impacts the thing, and because your fist-car stops so suddenly, the fat people-power inside goes flying through the windshield since the fat guys aren't wearing seatbelts, and they only stop flying after going through the surface of the thing you hit and smashing into the center of it.

"Okay," he said. "I can pretend that."

I said, We'll test it. I said, The motor in the water fountain is whistling. It is a distraction. Do you hear it?

"Yes. I think I hear it now. It's maybe more a hum than a whistle?"

I said, It's a pretty whistley kind of hum. I said, Make it stop by punching the water fountain. Punch the water fountain so the fat guys smash onto the motor. They'll splat on the motor and the motor will clog up and stop, and then there will be the sound of something dropping.

Eliyahu spun around and punched the water fountain. There was clanging noise. It was the sound of the metal shell of it getting vibrated. He shook his hand out in the air. "That hurts," he said. "And I can still hear the motor."

It's because you didn't aim the punch, I said. You tried to put your fist through the shell of it. You'll break your hands that way, and if it's a fire-extinguisher case, you'll glass up your armveins and bleed like a bibbit. What happened was you didn't put the brakes on, so the car crashed into the building and the fat guys got pressed flat between the bumpers instead of going through the windshield because the building stopped the fist-car when it should've been the brakes that stopped it.

"It's the splatting," he said. "I kept picturing them splatting, the fat men, and how it would bring them such pain as no man should ever have to know."

That's okay, I said. I said, Don't pretend they're fat guys, then. Pretend they're golems. Golems don't splat, though, so imagine they shatter.

"It could be that golems feel pain, though, no? It's possible, I think. Otherwise, the Prague golem would not have become so angry and rampaged. Without pain, there is no call for anger, much less rampaging."

I don't know about that, I said, but—forget the golems. Try boulders.

"Boulders," he said, "I like boulders. Boulders are large and without nerves, without souls. Boulders can pass through a windshield without dilemma," he said. Then he spun back around and punched the water fountain. No clanging. Then the sound of creaking and then of something dropping inside of the shell. A slow heavy sound.

Thung.

The motor stopped humming.

I said, You landed it.

Eliyahu smiled. "I want a drink," he said.

I said, Have a drink.

He pressed the button on the fountain and nothing came out of the arcing hole.

"I broke it," he said.

I said, How's your hand feel?

"My hand feels strong," he said.

I said, It's very easy to break things, and if you think the right way, you won't ever get hurt.

"This is good," he said. "Thank you," he said. "Now, how to get to A-Hall?"

I pointed in the direction of 2-Hall. I said, Go up to that opening, there. That's 2-Hall. Go left at 2-Hall, and go all the way to the end. Then take a right.

"Thank you, Gurion. I will break glass shortly."

Get told something first, I said. You don't want to look like a crazy. You want them to know you're a defiance.

"I will be a defiance," Eliyahu said.

And then he grabbed my shoulders and then he was hugging me. He wasn't pointy and cold like a skeleton, like he looked like he would be. He was softer and he smelled like oatmeal and a room of old books. He smelled like my dad's overcoat smelled, except without the cigarette part of the smell, and it made me sad because it made me wish he was my brother so that I could have known him all my life and made sure no one hurt him. I could tell that people hurt him and that he was, at least for the most part, scared of them. I could tell because he was hugging me. It was a scared thing to do. Trying to hug a person like that, a person you just met who wasn't sending any hug-me signals, might make them think that you were trying to harm them or get to their wang, and so they might try to harm you before finding out it was a hug you were going for. The only time you were supposed to do a thing like that was when you thought it was more dangerous not to do it. And even then most people didn't do it. Most people got stunned by that kind of danger. I'd never heard of anyone using the floating seat on a crashing airplane, for example. And airplanes were always crashing. And they always had floating seats you could try to save yourself with by jumping out the airlock just above the ocean. Main Man would use the floating seat, I thought, and Main Man had hugged me a few times unsignalled, but Main Man didn't really know that people hurt him and so he didn't know why he got scared, just that he *was* scared, and he'd always say so, and when he said so, I'd tell him everything was fine and he would believe me and stop feeling scared. Eliyahu was different. Telling him everything was fine wouldn't ever work. He'd know it wasn't true. It was easy to tell he knew a lot about some things. It was all those Eliyahuic faces he made. Like an old tzadik who won't squint even though his eyes are half-blind from reading so much. Soon he stopped hugging me. He picked up his bookbag and slung it over his shoulder. Then he jogged fists-up towards 2-Hall and punched the walls and lockers seven times on his way.

While he jogged, I kept thinking: Eliyahu is damaged. It got me even more sad. I didn't want to be sad, so I tried to fight it. I tried to think this: He wouldn't be the same if he wasn't damaged; you might not even like an undamaged Eliyahu.

But I knew that wasn't true. I'd have liked him either way. Maybe not as much, but then also maybe more. Eliyahu was a scholar. Everyone I liked who wasn't damaged was a scholar. Rather, everyone I liked who wasn't a scholar was damaged. Or maybe the first way. The stress kept shifting.

A door squeaked behind me, and then there were footsteps.

Swinging an empty two-gallon milk jug, the perennially dry-mouthed *Mister* Todd Frazier—*teacher* of drama, Malke*vich*ian inflector—came out of his classroom and headed for the fountain.

It's broken, I told him.

He tried the button anyway. "It's *broken*," he said. "I am *thirsty*," he said. "Let me *see* your pass."

He wasn't that bad. It was just the way he talked. I showed him my pass.

"*Do* not dawdle."

He walked me the twenty-odd steps to the Cage, watched me ring the bell, and wouldn't quit his hovering til after the monitor appeared in the doorway.

GURION

GATE GATE GATE GATE GATE

GATE   BOTHA   GATE

WALL   *DOORWAY*   WALL
DOORWAY
DOORWAY
DOOR

All schoolday long, the floor-to-ceiling gate made of chain-link fencing that blocked off the doorway of the Cage was locked. So was the door behind it. Students couldn't leave the Cage unless they were going to Gym, Nurse Clyde, their therapist, the Office, or Lunch-Recess if they had cafeteria privilege. And if you wanted to come inside between 9:10 and 3:30, there was a protocol:

1. You'd ring the doorbell on the outer wall of the doorway.
2. The monitor would unlock the door of the Cage and step into the doorway, where he'd look at you through the diamond-shaped spaces of the gate.
3. You'd hand your pass to the monitor, and if the pass was acceptable, the monitor would open the gate and let you in.

    or

   If you didn't have a pass or if your pass was unacceptable, then the monitor would write you a pass to go to the Office and get a new pass, and when you'd done that, you'd come back to the Cage and start over at 1.

There were only a few situations in which the entrance protocol didn't apply. One was if you were coming back from Gym on time: there'd be a group of you, and after one of you rang the bell, the monitor would stand behind the gate and let the group in, single-file, checking each kid off on his clipboard as they passed him. Another situation was if you were coming back from Lunch-Recess. If you came back from Lunch-Recess at the end of Lunch-Recess, it worked just like coming back from Gym on time, except the group of you would be much larger since Lunch-Recess period was the same for everyone at Aptakisic (between periods 4 and 5). If you came back from Lunch-Recess within the first ten minutes of Lunch-Recess—in which case you'd be taking advantage of what the Cage Manual called "The Hot Lunch Caveat"*—you'd usually be alone, and your tray of hot lunch would, itself, be your pass. The only other situation where the entrance protocol didn't apply was when you were coming back from your therapist's—you didn't need a pass then, either. You'd knock on the door that connected Call-Me-Sandy's and Bonnie Wilkes PsyD's office to the Cage, and Botha would unlock it, let you in, and that would be that.

Even though all but a very senior few teachers were regularly rotated into the Cage for two periods per week each, none of them had keys to get in, and, like the students, every one of them had to ring the bell and wait at the gate for the monitor to open it. There were, in all of Aptakisic, only five people who had keys to the Cage: Brodsky, Floyd, Jerry, Hector the janitor, and Victor Botha.

Victor Botha was the monitor. His righthand was just an opposable thumb, which is something certain monkeys don't have. The hand had been chopped by a crop-grinder on the island of Australia when Botha was small. It was probably a tragedy when it happened, but it was hard to tell so many years later because he became an adult who deserved a chopped hand. Botha always went beyond the entrance protocol.

That morning proved no exception. As I'd approached the gate, Mr. Frazier in tow, I'd done 1: I rang the bell and waited.

And Botha'd done 2: He came out and looked at me through the chain-link gate.

---

* "The Cage is an ever-available island of physical and emotional safety. If, for any reason, you wish to spend the Lunch-Recess period in the Cage, you may. It is your right and privilege to do so. If you would like to exercise this right, but you are in need of hot lunch, you will be permitted a ten-minute window at the start of the Lunch-Recess period (regardless of what grade you are in) in which to purchase hot lunch in the cafeteria and return with it to the Cage. Simply tell the lunch monitor that you are taking advantage of the Hot Lunch Caveat, and he or she will escort you to the front of the serving line so that you may receive your hot lunch in a timely fashion. NOTE: IF YOU REQUIRE HOT LUNCH BUT YOUR CAFETE-RIA PRIVILEGES HAVE BEEN SUSPENDED, YOU WILL BE GRANTED THE SAME TEN-MINUTE WINDOW AS DESCRIBED ABOVE IN WHICH TO GET YOUR HOT LUNCH AND RETURN WITH IT TO THE CAGE. IN SUCH CASES, YOU MUST IDENTIFY YOURSELF TO THE LUNCH MONITOR, WHO WILL HAVE BEEN INFORMED THAT YOUR CAFETERIA PRIVILEGES HAVE BEEN SUSPENDED, AND YOU WILL, AS WHEN ELECTING TO TAKE ADVANTAGE OF THE HOT LUNCH CAVEAT, BE ESCORTED TO THE FRONT OF THE CAFETERIA LINE BY HIM OR HER." From under subheading 5 ("The Hot Lunch Caveat") in "Chapter 2: Lunch" on p. 21 of *Safety and Conduct Manual for the Cage.*

Seeing Botha, Mr. Frazier took off, and that's when I'd executed my part of 3: I pushed my pass through a diamond-shaped space of the gate.

But then instead of doing his part of 3—checking to see if the pass was acceptable—Botha caulked a trickle. He didn't even take the pass out of my fingers. He said, "Show me your pass." He said the same thing every time. I had been at the gate at least a hundred times, and he knew I knew the protocol. Him saying "Show me your pass" was like a mugger holding a gun in your mouth and saying, "You better do what I say because I have a gun in your mouth." Or if a man behind the counter of a hot-dog stand who just passed you a hot dog said, "Now pay me the money you owe me for that hot dog." It makes it seem like if you do what the man says, you'll be doing it because he *says* to, when that's not true. When you do what the mugger says, you do it because he has a gun. When you pay the hot-dog guy, it's because you owe money for the hot dog. If the mugger didn't have a gun, you would not do what he said. If you didn't owe money for the hot dog, you wouldn't pay the hot-dog guy. If Botha wasn't the monitor, or if we weren't at school, I wouldn't give him my pass.

When Adonai told Moses to bring water from the rock in the Sinai by speaking to the rock, Moses not only struck the rock instead of talking to it, but he said to the Israelites who were gathered for the miracle, "Listen now, O rebels, shall we bring forth water for you from this rock?" like it was him, Moses, who would bring forth the water, when it was God who would bring it forth. Even though these were the only wrong actions Moses took in all his life, and even though Moses was understandably upset—he had just come down the mountain only to discover his brothers engaged in acts of idolatry—it was for his having taken these two wrong actions that God never let him inside of Israel.

I wanted to remind Botha of his limitations, but I was not Hashem and Botha was no Moses. There was no promised land for me to lock him in a cave outside of. So I did what is called a Harpo Progression of Defiance. The first step in the progression was that I pulled the pass back out of the diamond-shaped space and dropped it on the floor.

"Pack it up," Botha said.

Botha was the monitor and I had to do what the monitor said, so I picked the pass up.

Then I dropped it.

"Pack it up and do not drop it," he said.

I picked it up and I folded it in four. I pushed it through the gate.

"Unfold it," he said.

I unfolded it. Then I balled it up and threw it at the lockers behind me, then held up my pointer-finger = I'll be right back, and I ran toward the lockers and picked the pass up and came back to the gate and folded the pass and unfolded it and tore a notch into each corner of it.

He could not ask me to untear a notch.

So I pushed the pass through the gate. That was the end of the progression.

Harpo Progressions make me laugh because they make both the Harpo and the mark look silly. When the mark doesn't laugh at the progression, it is a sign of internal robotics, and I think that is even funnier.

Botha didn't laugh because all he could think about was how stupid he would sound if he sent me to the Office. If he sent me to the Office for doing a progression, I would get a detention, but I always had one anyway, and Botha would look like he was failing at his job as the monitor. The monitor was supposed to know how to run the Cage and the kids inside it. The monitor was not supposed to get played like a straightman.

So he didn't send me to the Office. He said, "You're late for Group."

I'd forgotten about Group. It was Tuesday. I had Group every Tuesday for half an hour before Lunch.

Let me in, then, I said.

He said, "Go around." He pushed the pass back through the gate.

It would have been faster to go through the Cage; there was a door connecting it directly to Call-Me-Sandy's office, and if I'd been allowed to enter the Cage, I could have walked a straight line to Group. Since he wouldn't let me in, I had to walk C-Hall down to 2-Hall, then walk across 2-Hall to B-Hall, and walk up B-Hall for the same amount of steps that I walked down C-Hall to get to 2-Hall. It would take at least an extra minute to get to Sandy's B-hall entrance. Botha knew it would, and he made me go around to punish me. He thought that because it was important to him that everyone got everywhere on time, it was important to me to be on time. But it was only important to him. I liked walking in the hallways. Especially by myself. And why would anyone rather go in the Cage?

But what was the most dumont about what Botha did was how he said "You're late for Group" to me, like it mattered, like it was something to be concerned about, and how then he did the only small robot thing he could to make me even later to Group. My mom would call this passive-aggressive behavior. PAB. She'd also call certain forms of laughter PAB. She'd say that

Harpo Progressions of Defiance were PAB, too, but then she'd laugh when I'd tell her about the progressions I performed at school. So would my dad. They always laughed at the same things. Except Woody Allen. On one of their first dates, they rented *Broadway Danny Rose* and nearly broke up. Even over a decade later, my dad still shivered when he recalled it. He described the experience as being "a little bit less fun, perhaps, than chain-smoking for ninety minutes while handcuffed to a dowager with asthma who used to teach Health and smells incontinent."

"What do you think is so funny about this nebach?" my mother would shout from the kitchen whenever my dad and I watched Woody Allen. We would turn down the volume, but she'd come into the living room anyway, then enumerate the qualities that made Woody Allen a nebach. He was weak and ugly, defective and ineffective and far less clever than he thought, plus cowering and phlegm-complected and proud of it. Ineffective? I would sometimes ask her. And she would tell me to just stay out of it and not smartperson at her. Woody Allen was her Desormie.

For my dad, though, Woody Allen made the top five, behind Charlie Chaplin and the Marx Brothers, ahead of Larry David and Richard Pryor. My dad's top five was the same as Nakamook's, and, in both cases, Sacha Baron Cohen was encroaching on either Pryor or David, but he had yet to prove his longevity, and neither my father nor Benji wanted to jinx him by declaiming his genius too early. I told my dad that once at dinner—about him and Benji having the same top five—but he wasn't impressed. He said, "What about the Beatles? Does he also enjoy the music of the Beatles, your Benji? Does he, like I, your mom, and Charles Manson—"

You've never even met him, I said to my dad.

"I don't need to," he said.

He's my best friend, I said.

"You'll see," he said. "You're already outgrowing him."

The thing about my father was he wasn't some kind of schmucky condescender who liked to act like he knew you better than you did; he was genuinely worried about my friendship with Benji. And the thing about Benji was that he *was* my best friend. So I was in this position, this suck position, where if I kept defending Benji my father would only worry more about our friendship, but if I quit defending Benji, then maybe that would mean that my father was right about our friendship since what kind of best friend doesn't defend his best friend against his father's assertions that their friendship is weak? I tried to break my fingers but my fingers wouldn't break.

My mom said to stop it. She *had* met Benji—a few nights earlier he'd eaten at our house, but my dad was working late at the office—and she liked him too, despite the new strike against him for liking Woody Allen. "This Benji is a loyal friend," she told my dad. "And also intelligent. Very perceptive."

She'd asked Benji what he thought of the students in the Cage, and he'd told her, "You don't have to worry, Mrs. Maccabee. Gurion's able to take care of himself, and most kids know that, and the ones who aren't sure— they know that *I'll* avenge any offense against his person." He'd said that with half a mouthful of kufta, and it had sounded less kenobi than it looks written down.

"This is not a bad kind of friend to have, Judah."

My dad kept his eyes down, sawed at his steak = "I'm dropping this subject."

So I dropped it also, even though I'd wanted to say more about Benji because they didn't just share the same top five comedians, he and my father, but both cited the same Woody Allen *scene* as their favorite (the one in *Annie Hall* where Alvie gets arrested after crashing his car). And as for Harpo Progressions—which my dad, unlike my mom, loved with no reservations—Nakamook was the champion. He had performed the only epic one that I had ever heard of. It was, in fact, by way of that progression that Benji and I became best friends. The whole thing lasted nearly two weeks and was performed on Monitor Botha, who was bald.

The baldness of Botha was the kind where the hair that remains rims the head like the seat on a public toilet. As did pretty much every other man in the world who'd balded similar while being a shmendrick, Botha grew the upper part of one side long and greased its strands flat across his sticky-looking pate. I still have a hard time understanding why men do that. Forgetting that the hairstyle doesn't fool anyone, ignoring that it highlights what it's meant to hide, the hairstyle's name—*combover*—is in the same class of words as unibrow and needlenose and muffintop and trampstamp, i.e., not only does the name mock the thing it refers to, but it's the only name there is for the thing it refers to. So any speaker of English old enough to sport a combover has to be aware of what it is called, and thereby aware that elect- ing to do what he does each morning in front of his mirror invites disdain. One time after school, I said so to Flowers, and he offered the opinion that men who sported combovers had most likely been doing so since before the word *combover* gained all its prominence; that although in the course of the preceding few years these men couldn't have avoided hearing the word and knowing the shmendiness that it connoted, a confused kind of pride kept them from changing hairstyles. Like those kids who when you tell them their foot-taps annoy you and then in response they tap faster and harder, these men kept their combovers intact to save face.

It was news to me that *combover* ever lacked prominence—it seemed so obviously to be the right word—but Flowers paid endless attention to words so I came to believe him, plus the motive he'd described for men sporting combovers seemed to be right for Monitor Botha, who was always trickling. Regardless of the motives behind Botha's overcombing, though, you'd think he'd be one of the last guys in the world to make fun of some underweight troubled kid's hair. At least that's what I'd have thought.

But Egon Marsh—his dad awaiting trial on charges of child-porn that Egon, of course, was rumored to have starred in; his older brother a tweeker, freshly kicked out of Stevenson High School for possession; his sister Mia autistic, also probably retarded, the only kid in the Cage who never once got stepped (I learned all of this a few weeks later from Benji, maybe three or four days after his epic progression ended, by which time Egon and Mia had both been removed from Aptakisic, removed from the town in which they'd grown up, removed from the custody of their suicidal mother who then committed suicide; all of the rest of Aptakisic, however, had known about Egon's family for a while)—Egon Marsh was one skinny, troubled kid, and Botha made fun of his hair three times. At least three times. The three times I saw were on my first day at Aptakisic—the Tuesday following Labor Day weekend—and for all I knew, Botha'd picked on Egon before then, too.

I didn't even know he was doing it til the third time. The first time, he sniffed at the air and he said, "Something smells rape in here!" And that was true. Something did smell ripe, and it was Egon's hair, which was matted and oily and flecked with white bits. He was sitting right next to me, and Botha, at the time he announced that something smelled ripe, was standing a few feet away from our carrels, and because I was new, and I didn't know Botha, and because I couldn't imagine a teacher could be such a dickhead to a kid so openly, I figured he was genuinely puzzled by the source of the smell, and I remember I was worried that he and everyone else might think the smell was coming from me. Short of saying that the smell was Egon's— which I wasn't willing to do—I wasn't able to figure out a way to make it clear it wasn't mine til after the moment had already passed.

Then a couple minutes later, Botha returned. He did this thing where he acted like a happy bloodhound, sniffing at the air along the trail from his desk to our carrels. This time he said, "Something smells downright bleddy *Marshy*." This got laughs from some of the students, and I got *more* worried they'd think I was the stinker—I didn't get the joke; I didn't know Egon's name; I figured that *Marshy* must have been lower-cased, and that it was either Australian or Aptakisical vernacular for *foul* or *gross*—and I still thought Botha sincerely didn't know the source of the smell, and I knew that I sincerely didn't want to start my career at Aptakisic as the kid who smells, so in order to make it clear that the stink wasn't mine, that it would stay if I left and that it wouldn't follow me, I broke off the tip of the pencil I was using and asked for permission to go to the sharpener, which was fixed to the opposite wall of the Cage. Botha told me that normally he'd give me a step for talking without raising my hand first, but since this was my first day, he'd let the whole thing slide, just this once, if I would raise my hand, wait to get called on, and then ask properly. That Botha might be actively trying to humiliate me didn't seem any more likely to me than did the possibility that he was purposely being a dickhead to Egon—I assumed the rules were really important to him, and that he was worried I didn't understand them—so I did as suggested. I raised my hand and got called on and I asked for permission.

Botha assented.

I went to the sharpener, and just as I'd started to turn the handcrank, he yelled out, "Wait! Wait, Mr. Makebee! No need to waste your affort. I think I've found a writing implement here—yes. Look. Right here in this nest!" And he made as if to pull a pen that he'd hidden inside of his sleeve from out of Egon's hair. He waved the pen around.

A lot of kids laughed. The teachers tried not to. And Botha was laughing. He was looking at me, trying to get me to laugh, and I was looking at Egon, whose lips pursed and slacked as he tried to force a smile that just wouldn't take. I didn't know what to do.

Nakamook did. He stood at his carrel. "Combover," he said.

The volume of the laughter instantly doubled.

And this was the beginning of the epic progression.

Botha stepped Benji once for not facing forward, and a second time for speaking without having been called on.

Benji said, "Combover."

The laughter got louder, and continued getting louder each of the six times the word was repeated, and the volume, I'm sure, would have gotten higher yet, but before he could name the hairstyle a seventh time, Benji got an ISS and was sent to Brodsky.

When he came back from Brodsky the following period, he wrote the word COMBOVER on three sheets of paper and taped them to the walls of his carrel. We cracked up even harder than we had before, and Botha tore the three COMBOVERs down. Again Benji got an ISS; again he got sent to Brodsky.

When he returned from Brodsky's that second time, he drew an anterior, a posterior, a sinistral, a dextral, and a bird's-eye view of Botha's head, and then he taped each to the walls of his carrel. After we fell from our chairs with laughter, and Botha tore all of the drawings down, Benji left the Cage with an OSS, and Brodsky sent him to Bonnie Wilkes, PsyD, to cool his heels for the rest of the day.

Wednesday, Benji served his second ISS.[*]

Wednesday also happened to be the last anyone at Aptakisic saw of the Marshes; that night, their suicidal mother was arrested for colluding with their father, the child pornographer, and Egon and Mia were taken into foster care nowhere nearby.

Thursday, Benji served OSS.

Thursday evening, Vincie Portite got hold of his dad's electric clippers, and Friday morning Benji returned to the Cage with an actual combover, greased-down strands and everything. This time, there wasn't just laughter. No one could take their eyes off Benji. Half the Cage got detentions for breaking the Face Forward rule, and Botha finally sent Nakamook to Brodsky, who called on Bonnie Wilkes again. They decided they couldn't step kids for haircuts, no matter how ridiculous, but they did get hold of Nakamook's mom, who left her job and picked him up.

On Monday he had a scrape on his chin, a yellow swelling along the orbit of his bloodshot right eye, and his head was shaved completely bald. I saw him in the hallway before first period.

"Newkid," he said, "I forgot my Darker—left it in yesterday's jeans." It was the first time he'd ever spoken to me.

In the bathroom, I drew, with my 12-guage RoughWriter DarkerWider Permanent, a U-shaped sequence of Charlie-Brownish black W's around Benji's scalp, then four squiggled lines across the crown. When Botha sent

---

[*] Bonnie Wilkes, PsyD, convinced Brodsky to apply the modified STEP System and consider the five periods Benji spent cooling out in her office on Tuesday his first ISS.

Benji to the Office this time, Brodsky threw his arms up, called Benji's mom, and sent him straight back to the Cage.

Tuesday morning Benji was limping. When I asked about it, he said the same thing he'd said about his damaged face the day before—that he kept wiping out on his skateboard—and then he told me his mom found all his Darkers and threw them away. He called me his "secret weapon" and "last best hope," and I remained his combover artist—his combover *re-toucher*, really; Darker ink takes multiple showers to scrub clean.

By Lunch on Tuesday, the Cage students were no longer laughing at Benji's progression so much as getting really uncomfortable about it. By Wednesday, even the discomfort had worn off. I asked Vincie Portite why Benji kept going, and I asked him if he agreed with me that Egon, wherever he was, would, by now, feel properly avenged, and want, if he were a real friend to Benji, for Benji to relent. Vincie said, "Tch. Benji's not Egon's friend. He stepped up for him, sure, but that was last week. What this is now has fuck-all to do with Egon Marsh. This is just Nakamook, Gurion." Botha, for his part, continued to trickle, stepping Benji for every minor infraction he was able to spot. Nakamook's stories about the streak of terrible skateboarding luck responsible for his body's increasing state of battery kept getting wilder.

Re-touching the combover Thursday morning, seconds after having just watched him puke a color that was way too pink to blame on bad eggs, I understood that Benji, wrong or right, saw no way to end the progression any time soon without losing face. His commitment to defiance increased in proportion to the amount of punishment he suffered; he'd keep getting stepped by Monitor Botha and claiming to streak unluckily on a skateboard he didn't possess until... what? Until some outside, benign force that had nothing to do with anyone else's authority—particulary not Botha's or Aptakisic's—ended the progression is what. The end had to come organically, or at least it had to seem to.

And the only benign force I could think of that might fit the bill was the force of his own follicles: he would quit the progression only when his hair had grown in too thick for his scalp to show ink. I thought.

I was too scared to ask him if I was right, though. Not scared *of* him, but *for* him.

This was because of something that happened on the second morning that I drew on his head. I hadn't thought twice about it at the time, but after telling me his mother took all his Darkers and I was his secret weapon,

Benji'd said, "She didn't get this, though," and he'd pulled a black crayon from his jacket pocket. I should have just taken the black crayon and used it, because you can wash black crayon from your skin with a little soap and water, so if you don't want your mom to know that you've been drawing on your head all you have to do is spend a couple minutes inside the boys bathroom before you go home. *If* what you drew on your head with was black crayon. When Nakamook had shown me the black crayon, though, I didn't think about that. All I thought was how black crayon would show duller than Darker ink, and that after showers in Gym, a crayoned combover would need to be re-applied.

It'll wash off, I'd told him, and plus it won't look as good. I'd said, I've got my Darker right here anyway.

And then I'd brandished it.

He could not admit that he'd prefer the combover to wash off; not when the less-wash-offable version of it would serve the progression better; to do so would be to openly allow that his defiance was—at least to some degree— subject to the will of someone other than himself, and he wasn't built to do that, not even when doing it would prevent him from being injured. And he was no liar, Benji—except when he lied to protect those he was loyal to—so he could not insist on using the crayon for untrue reasons, either. If I had known, on Tuesday morning, the way Benji was about snat and face, I would have understood that the crayon was a way out for him; I'd've kept my mouth shut about its washability and used it gladly. He would then have been spared at least a couple of the uglier imaginary falls off his phantom skateboard. But I hadn't considered that til Wednesday evening, after he'd called me on the telephone—a unique phenomenon (Benji hated the telephone)—and, without solicitation, taught me the principles of snat and face. And by Thursday morning I knew that asking him if he'd end the progression when his hair grew back would only make it impossible for him to allow his hair to grow back. If I asked him, then any future ink-blocking hair-growth might seem intentional, a long-term plan. And because any plan—let alone a long-term one—was not organic, he would feel obligated to keep his head shaved. So I didn't ask.

And I saw that it was almost beside the point anyway, because how long would it take for the hair to get thick enough? If after a week he was puking blood, I didn't even want to picture what kind of injuries he'd suffer after two weeks, or three. And he was my best friend by that point, one of my *only* friends at Aptakisic, and certainly the only scholar-brained kid I knew who was allowed to talk to me anymore. So after re-touching the combover that Thursday morning, I saw I needed to protect him from himself. And then I figured out how.

What I did was, during Lunch—I was still allowed out of the Cage for Lunch back then, and Nakamook (owing to all the little infractions Botha kept nailing him for) wasn't that day—I went over to the table in the cafeteria next to the one where all the Cage kids were sitting, and I got up behind Daryl Duncil, a biggish seventh-grader who I'd seen laugh at Main Man by the bus circle that morning, and chopped him sideways on the back of the neck so he leaned forward, then grabbed two fistfuls of his hair and plugged his face into the cafeteria table until he made glug-glug sounds and stopped resisting. And then, before Floyd dragged me to Brodsky's, where I received my first ISS, I grabbed Vincie Portite by the collar and told him to get the word out that if anyone in the Cage brought a Darker to school before Tuesday or mentioned to anyone—*anyone,* I stressed—the threat I was about to finish making, they'd be praying I showed them the kind of mercy I just had Daryl Duncil.

Friday morning I left my Darker at home and said so to Benji. He asked Vincie for his, but Vincie said he'd left his at home, too. So did Leevon Ray, Jelly Rothstein, and every other kid from the Cage who passed the doorway of the C-Hall bathroom. I stood behind Benji the whole time, but a little bit beside him, too. That way, anyone he solicited who hadn't gotten my message was able to see the suggestive gestures I kept making with my fist while shaking my head No.

Over the weekend, the ink on Benji's skull faded to nothing. Monday morning I hid in the teachers lounge doorway until I saw him enter the Cage.

With that, the progression was over.

□   □   □   □   □   □   □

When I got to Call-Me-Sandy's, Group was already seated in the circle of folding chairs. The arrangement was this: Call-Me-Sandy next to My Main Man Scott Mookus next to Vincie Portite next to Leevon Ray next to the Janitor next to Asparagus next to an open chair next to Jenny Mangey next to Jelly Rothstein next to an open chair next to an open chair next to Call-Me-Sandy.

I wanted to sit beside Main Man but couldn't. I either had to sit between Mangey—who often cried during Group so you felt like you should hug her, but then when you did she thought you were her boyfriend—and Asparagus—who I'd just punched the wind from an hour before—or next to Jelly Rothstein, who bit and was a girl so I couldn't hit her when she bit, or next to Call-Me-Sandy, who had a good, soft voice and looked like she probably smelled clean and sensible, like laundry detergent or talcum powder, but was also the most arranged one of all of them, which meant it was no good to sit where you had to turn your head to see her because then she could tell when you were looking.

Mookus saw me standing just inside the door. He lifted his legs off the ground and flexed his toes so they all popped at once. Then he sneezed three times and said, "Hello, Gurion. Had I known you'd be coming, I would have saved a chair for you. Do you know that?"

I know, Scott, I said.

"I'm glad you do," Scott said. "Can I take this opportunity to tell you that I am bemused? Because I am bemused. I'm filled with wonderment. I wonder have you noticed the pretty glitter makeup pattern around the eyes of our wonderful Sandy this afternoon? I think she's beautiful. And it is wonderful. Don't you think she's beautiful, Gurion? Don't you think it is wonderful? Is or is not everything very splendid today? Does or does not the beauty of our Sandy make you feel like the everything bottle is filled up to the very edge of the brim of its neck with hope for a brand new tomorrow? I, myself, am almost choking on it. It's at the top of *my* neck, too. In my throat. Inside my very throat. The joy and the beauty and the very wonderment. The very wonderment gives me a sense of the presence of a platform on which to build a better life for people like us. The common people. The people who deserve good health care and better wages. Chocolate milk. Don't you feel like a sound investment in a good retirement plan? Don't you feel as though you could love everything starting tomorrow, and everything could love you, if only you took an action to set into motion the coming of our new tomorrow and its tomorrow and that one's tomorrow? Shotgun loaded hand on the pump and no matter who you damage you're still a false prophet, but we drink chocolate milk and then we get muscles and smash down the droves with fists like hammers and then we pump the fists in the air for victory. I be the prophet of the doom that is you. You are the mess in messiah. Isn't she pretty, Gurion? Isn't she? Don't the pretty-glittered eyes of our Sandy speak of better wages and genuine possibility? No fiscal exposure?"

I said, I wish I could sit next to you, too, Main Man.

"Do you see the glitter around Sandy's eyes?" Scott said.

It's pretty, I said.

"Thank you for saying so," Scott said.

Call-Me-Sandy said, "Thank you, Gurion."

I nodded = No problem, Call-Me.

She wanted me to take a seat, but she wouldn't say so. She was good at not saying things. My mom taught me about it, that it is what you learn at schools for psychotherapy. You learn to use the invisible power in a quiet room to get other people to do what you want. But it all depends on the arrangement, so it is cheap. The power was not really Call-Me's power because it is not a person's power, even though it looks like a person's power: I wanted to sit down because it was Group and in Group you sit down. Everyone who was in there was already sitting in the circle, so if I sat down, then it would not be because Call-Me-Sandy used invisible powers, even if that's what it looked like. It would be because of the arrangement. The arrangement had the power. It was harder to stand in the Group Therapy arrangement than it was to sit down.

While I was standing there, everyone but Scott and Leevon got nervous. Mangey made dry noises by scratching under her sock where her skin was flaky, and Ronrico and the Janitor, who would not look at me, switched between looking at the ground and looking up at Sandy to try to get her to tell me to sit down. Vincie Portite kept moving his right hand to cover his eye and then putting it back in his lap. Vincie used to be one of the best fighters in the Cage, but then just after Sukkot he developed his debilitating tick. How it happened was he used to like calligraphy, so he got fountain pens with many interchangeable nibs and inks for his birthday, and there was a radiator in the Cage that Vincie dropped an ink-cartridge into the spaces of the vent of, and the ink cartridge fell into the fan of the radiator and the blades of the fan exploded the ink cartridge with a sudden cutting force. Cartridge ink shot fast from the vent into Vincie's right eye and Vincie held his hand over his eye and said, "Oh no," just like that, just once, in a crying voice, non-exclamatorily and without any cursing, and Botha said "Not brilliant, Portite" and sent Vincie to the nurse and Vincie had to wear an eyepatch for two weeks until the eye healed. He showed me what the eye looked like under the patch. It was red where it should have been white and the iris looked like someone had dripped milk in it. I felt bad making Vincie nervous, but I think it was good for him because it was like training him to be a great fighter again and lately he was doing better than before. I could tell he was doing better because while I was standing there, the hand went up at least five times, but Vincie didn't let it go all the way to the eye. It would start lifting up, but it never even got to his chin before he'd put it back on his lap. The highest the hand got was his windpipe. I was keeping my eyes on Vincie so I wouldn't look at Jelly Rothstein. Jelly was waiting for me to look at her, and if I did look at her she would tell me to sit down, and I already wanted to sit down, and if she told me to do it, it would be like Botha telling me to give him my pass. I decided I would sit down in exactly seven seconds as long as I didn't get told to.

I counted off the seconds in my head so no one would see. As soon as I got to seven, I sat down next to Jelly. When she didn't bite, it was good to sit next to Jelly. She could be very funny.

"Idiot," she said to me. When Jelly said I was an idiot during Group, there was friendliness in it because it was the beginning of a game where we alternated calling each other names. There were two ways to lose the game. The first way was if you ran out of names or repeated yourself. The second way was if Call-Me-Sandy, who would keep leaning forward to put a stop to the game but because of her therapist algorithms couldn't interrupt while someone was talking, got a word in between us. If Call-Me-Sandy got a word in, then the last one who'd said a name would win.

Dentist, I said. "Dolt," Jelly said. Leopold. "Klebold." Monorail. "Blister." Flag. "Patio." Falsified document.

"I call bullshit on *falsified document*," Jelly said. "That's like *big stupid dumbass* or something. You sound like a first-grader."

Fine, I said. Firmament.

"I call bullshit on *firmament*. There's no such thing as *firmament*."

There is, though, I said. I said, It's in Torah.

"What's it mean, then?"

I said, No one really knows what it means. In Hebrew, it's the place where Adonai resides, but it's a bad translation. It's really more like *border*— it's confusing.

"I don't think that's fair," she said. "If you don't know what it means, you can't use it."

That's your rule, I said. I said, That's not my rule.

"Whatever. That's the rule of the game."

I said, Fine, I call bullshit on *patio*, then.

"Are you kidding?" she said. "They can't pour the patio til the rain lets up. The patio is slow getting there. Mamzer."

I said, No foreign languages, Jelly.

"Whatever. That's not my rule, you schlep." You vildachaya. "Schlub." Chainik-hocker.

"What's a chainik-hocker?" Call-Me-Sandy said. She made a curious face.

"Gurion made it up," Jelly said. "It's like *hocking me in chainik* which means 'banging a tea kettle' which is what you're doing when you nag your mom and she's Jewish. But no one ever calls anyone a *chainik-hocker* but I didn't argue because I'm not a schleppy dolt mamzer like Gurion."

It was hard to tell who won. Call-Me-Sandy jumped in after I said *chainik-hocker*, which could mean that I won, but then Jelly got to say *shleppy dolt mamzer* after Call-Me-Sandy jumped in, which never happened before because it was always that once Call-Me-Sandy jumped in, we stopped calling each other names. And then, also, *schleppy dolt mamzer* was a combination of names that we already used, so in a way it was a repetition, but the combination might have made it count as a new name, and it was hard to tell if Jelly was cheating or just being very skillful when she called me a schleppy dolt mamzer. It could have been a tie.

Call-Me said, "Before we start today, has everyone heard Scott's big news?"

"What?" Scott said.

"About what you're doing on Friday?"

"It's a secret," Scott said.

"What's said in Group stays in Group," the Janitor said.

Scott stuck his lower lip out at me. He wanted to know if he should tell his secret. I didn't know his secret, so I didn't know if he should tell it, but what the Janitor said was true. As little as I liked him, especially when he recited the rules verbatim off the tear-away pad like a robot, the one thing everyone in Group—everyone in the Cage, really—was good at, was keeping their mouths shut. That a kid who tells on another kid is a dead kid went without saying among us.

To Main Man, I said: If you want to tell us, you should—no one's gonna repeat what you say.

"Okay," said Scott. "Okay. On Friday, I'm singing."

"Who cares if you're singing. You're always singing," Ronrico said.

"Shut the fuck up," Vincie said to Ronrico. "You never listen. If you listened then sometimes you might say something that didn't make you sound like such a fuckface."

"What's rule number one?" Sandy said to Vincie.

"Are you really asking me that?" Vincie said. "Because I think you know the answer."

"I'm really asking, Vincenzo."

Vincie turned around to read from the tear-away pad on the easel behind him. "'Rule number one: Always be respectful,'" he said. "But that doesn't matter, Sandy, because first of all, Asparagus wasn't being respectful, and secondly, those are rules for Group. Group didn't start yet."

"If we're all in the room," Sandy said, "Group has started."

"But you said 'before we start,' which means we didn't start."

"And we were all in the room when you said it, Sandy," said Jelly.

"We should *always* be respectful," Call-Me-Sandy said.

"That's not true," Vincie said. "You're changing the rules. Am I wrong, Gurion?"

I said, I don't know. It says 'Rules for Group' over rule number one. And Call-Me did say 'before we start,' and then she asked you what rule number one was, which sounds like she's saying you broke it, but then even if you didn't break it, maybe she's saying you should be respectful anyway, even when it's to a bancer like Asparagus who I kicked the ass of because he gave me a charleyhorse, but then I think it's useless to have Rules for Group if they're the same as rules for everywhere else. The main thing—

"A kid who tells is a dead kid," Ronrico interrupted.

Telling stuff to Sandy doesn't count, I said, because everything in Group is confidential, so don't talk out of your depth, you shmendrick.

To Vincie, I said, The main thing is that it makes Sandy uncomfortable when we're angry at each other. So she talks about rules.

"It doesn't make me—" she started saying.

"See?" Vincie said to her. "The rule doesn't matter. Even Gurion says. And I think it's unfair fighting to start in on me about the rules before Group starts. I think it's an abuse. It's abusive. You said it because you can't sit with our anger, Sandy."

"That's very disappointing to me," said Jelly to Call-Me. "I feel disappointed in you."

"I need you to be able to do that for me, Sandy. If you can't sit with my anger, who will?" Jenny Mangey said. "I feel helpless now."

Scott said, "I love you, Sandy. I'm not angry."

Ronrico clapped his hand against his knee.

Vincie's hand jumped to his eye.

Ronrico said "Flinch," and laughed in Vincie's face. He laughed so hard he started coughing. Then he chucked the Janitor on the shoulder with the fist he'd coughed on.

The Janitor wiped his shoulder with his hand and wiped his hand on the thigh of his pants and stared at the thigh of his pants, scared out of his mind.

Ronrico said "Flinch," to Vincie again.

Leevon said nothing.

I said, I made Boystar get all cry-faced.

"Did you smash him?" Jelly said. "I hate him."

"I think he's a rapist," Mangey said.

Scott said, "We're gonna sing together at the Aptakisic Pep Rally on Friday! Me and the Boystar. He's famous! I will stand in the spotlight with him and sing a duet from the new unit, *Promotionalize*. There's stickers."

No one knew what to say about that. The Janitor was still staring at his thigh. He said, "Sandy, can I have a tissue?"

"How do you feel right now?" Sandy said to the Janitor. "Do you feel threatened?"

"I feel infected," the Janitor said. He was leaning back to get as far away from the germs on his thigh as possible.

Mangey said, "Boystar is like the guy in the date-rape movie who gives girls knockout drugs without them knowing. And then he takes their clothes off when they're asleep and he date-rapes them."

"Infected. Can you be more specific, Mikey?"

Ronrico said, "Flinch," to Vincie again.

Vincie started crying, but just wet eyes and his face got red. If it was four weeks before, Vincie would have laid him out, no hesitation.

I said, No one's gonna call him 'Flinch,' Ronrico, no matter how many times you say it.

"Gurion," said Jelly, "how'd you make Boystar cry-faced? You smash him or what? You smash him in the gob?"

The gob? I said. What's a gob?

"Can you please just hand me a tissue?" said the Janitor. He started crying with his throat.

Sandy said, "Scott, how do you think Mikey feels right now?"

"I don't know," said Main Man, "but everything is very scary."

I said, We'll be fine, Scott.

"Please!" shouted the Janitor, reaching in the air for a tissue that wasn't there.

Vincie's hand jumped to his eye.

Jelly said, "You've really lost control of the room, Sandy. I mean, even more than usual."

Mangey said, "Boystar threatened to beat me up once, Gurion. He shoved into me in the hall and I said 'Excuse you' and he said he'd kick my ass."

He's all talk, I said. I said, I slapped his neck and he hid behind his dad.

"Flinch!" Ronrico said to Vincie.

Vincie's hand jumped to his eye.

I stood up fast and Ronrico fell out of his chair.

"Gurion!" Call-Me-Sandy said.

Vincie's hand jumped to his eye.

I said to Call-Me-Sandy, I'm not hurting anyone.

I stood over Ronrico. I said to him, Now who's the flinch?

Ronrico was biting his lip.

I said, You're just like Botha, but shorter and dumber.

Call-Me-Sandy said, "Please, Gurion."

I said, I'm not hurting anyone.

"I am not like Botha," Ronrico said.

I said, Why are you picking on Vincie, then? I said, You're gonna be Botha in a few years. Ronrico Botha. That's your new name. You're Ronrico Botha.

"I'm not like Botha," he said.

Not exactly, I said. You're more scared. I said, I'd have to actually hit Botha to put him down.

Call-Me-Sandy said, "Gurion, this isn't productive. Please sit."

I sat. What I want to know, I said to Call-Me-Sandy, is why the Janitor isn't helping Ronrico up. Because Ronrico is the Janitor's best friend. Ronrico got his ass kicked in the locker-room for the Janitor. I know that because I'm the one who kicked it. And it was very easy for me, but shouldn't the Janitor help him up, Sandy? Don't you think that's right?

"Mikey?" Call-Me-Sandy said to the Janitor, "Can you tell Gurion why you won't help Ronrico to stand up?"

"You strike with a fury," Main Man said to me, "and maybe you are out of control. People are afraid of you."

I said, Why do you say that, Scott? Are you afraid of me?

Main Man said, "A little bit."

It made me depressed for a second. Call-Me-Sandy saw it. I saw her lean forward. She wanted to make a moment of it. She always wanted to make a moment when Scott said something to me about feelings, but I stopped her.

I said to Scott, I protect you, though. I'll always protect you.

I said to the Janitor, Help your friend up. I'm not gonna hurt you. Just be a good guy.

The Janitor said, "What if you chop my neck? I don't want you to chop my neck."

I said, I wouldn't chop your neck like that. Why would I chop your neck for helping your friend? That's stupid.

"Do you promise?" said the Janitor.

I said, I don't promise. You know I don't promise. If you promise it means that every time you don't promise it's okay for you to be lying. I won't chop your neck. Have faith in my word.

"I need you to promise."

I said, I'll chop your neck if you don't help him up.

The Janitor pulled his sleeve down over his hand and started helping his friend up.

Ronrico said "Thigh!" to the Janitor.

Vincie's hand went to his eye. The Janitor let go of Ronrico's hand and dropped Ronrico so Ronrico fell on his own wrists. Vincie's hand went to his eye again. The Janitor held one hand in the other and squeezed. Ronrico sat up and shook his hands out like they were asleep. Sandy's hands were over her mouth. The thumbs of Main Man's hands were in his mouth. Jelly was flicking everyone off with both hands. Mangey was scratching drylegs with hers. Leevon sat on his. I didn't know what to do with mine, but I had to do something, so I dug the right one under the rubberband around the left one, twisted my wrists twice, and stretched them apart, far and fast, and the rubberband handcuffs snapped in the middle. It did not make a loud-enough sound.

I said to Scott: Mookus, you have released me from my bondage!

Scott took his thumbs out of his mouth. He said, "I have released you!"

"Bondage," Call-Me-Sandy said. She was so nervous. You could tell from how she kept pushing her fingers through the buttonholes of her cardigan. I wished she wasn't so nervous. She was actually a very kind person, Sandy. "Bondage is a curious word," she said. And you could see from her faces that she was best friends with her sisters and had proud parents who used to buy her ice cream and stickers for her sticker-book whenever she brought home an A on a test or even a quiz, which happened a lot, because she was also very smart. Call-Me-Sandy was going to the University of Chicago for graduate school like my dad and mom had, but for social work instead of law or psychology, and you had to be smart to go there. Still, she was no good at what she did. When we got loud or wild or said unkind things, she thought it meant that she was doing something wrong and it worried her and she got scared and tried to arrange us with her calm voice that shook and it made us louder and wilder and more unkind. She said, "Does everyone in the group know what *bondage* means?"

Jenny Mangey stopped scratching and sat up really straight. "It's a kind of leather," she said.

"It's a kind of *sex*," said Ronrico Asparagus. He got back in his chair.

"Fucking," said Vincie.

"Same thing," said Ronrico.

Vincie disagreed. He said, "Sex is what you do with your wife. Fucking is what you do to your mistress. You don't make your wife wear leather, and that's why bondage is a kind of fucking."

"What the fuck?" said the Janitor. "I fucking want a fucking tissue."

I said, Bondage is slavery.

"My mom doesn't fuck," Jenny Mangey said.

I said, And bondage is this school, but invisibly.

Jelly said, "No one said your mom fucks, Mange."

The Janitor said, "Fuck this fucking school."

It's the arrangement, I said. Bondage is rules you are too scared to break.

"My mom is *not* a fucker," said Jenny Mangey.

Vincie said, "No one *said* your mom's a fucker."

We were talking so fast Sandy couldn't break in because it would be disrespectful. She would have had to break the rules to break in. She was supposed to keep us under control by showing us what control looked like and it was supposed to look like control was being able to follow the rules, but all the rules did was freeze her voice and spaz her fingers around in her buttonholes. It was proof that the arrangement was a kind of bondage.

Jenny said, "My mom wears bondage leather."

"Then she *is* a fucker after all," Vincie said.

Jenny said, "That's what I said you said."

"I didn't say it til you did," Vincie said. "You're the one who said it, Mangey. If you're not ready to say something, don't say it."

"You have to accept the consequences of what you say," Ronrico said.

I said, You are a slave, Asparagus.

"A slave with pee so pungent," said Jelly.

The Janitor said, "The consequences are fucked. I fucking hate the consequences."

I said, I hate them too.

The Janitor looked at me, and he didn't look scared, and he kept on looking at me. And then I noticed that everyone was looking at me, even the ones who were crying. We were all angry at the same thing. We always had been. And I felt just like I used to feel during Torah Study at Schechter: like everyone was waiting for me to teach something. Like they weren't really looking at me, but looking *to* me. It was my second-favorite feeling. Before June kissed me in the Office, it had been my first-favorite feeling, and my second favorite, which became my third after I'd been kissed, was the one that would come when I performed the awaited teaching. My ex-third-favorite that became fourth was the feeling I'd get when someone else threw the first punch in a fight and I became undeniably justified. Fifth was the explosion that followed. The order of sixth (ex-fifth) through thirteenth (now fourteenth) favorites switched around day to day, but it included the feelings I'd get when I heard Mookus sing; when Nakamook admired how I fought; when Vincie noticed he was smart; when my dad lit a cigarette while high-speed merging onto Lower Wacker with only one finger on the steering wheel; when Flowers would tell me that my latest chapter made him want to read the next one; when my mom cursed in Arabic in the middle of laughing at a new kind of joke I'd invented; when I'd meet a tough Israelite; when Rabbi Salt wrote down what I'd say to him; and whenever a thing that was breaking made a sound I hadn't heard before.

But this time was the first time I had the second-favorite feeling at Aptakisic, and also the first time, ever, that I had trouble doing what was needed to have the third; except for Jelly, who never went to Hebrew School anyway, no one in Group was an Israelite. They might have been like Hashemites or Druzes, like Nakamook and Flowers—even the ones I thought were like Canaanites and Romans before, like Ronrico and the Janitor—but still they did not know Torah, so I could not teach them Torah, let alone Talmud, and I did not want to make things up.

The tone came out of the intercom. It sounded more like a nightmare than ever. Some teachers called it the bell, but it did not sound like a bell at all. It sounded like a malfunction alert; the sound that broken objects would make if they had souls and could complain to each other. Group was over.

No one moved.

Sandy said, "Lunchtime."

No one moved.

I said to them, We are on the same side. I said, We are all on the side of damage.

No one moved til I did.

4
FIRST SCRIPTURE

Story of Stories

Gurion ben-Judah Maccabee
Mrs. Diamond
4th Grade Reading
3/18/05

Dear Mrs. Diamond,

I love to read fiction, and I will never be able to fully express my gratitude to you for pointing me toward *Goodbye, Columbus*. I have since read
Operation Shylock, and plan to read everything by Philip Roth before the end
of the year, but I am not even remotely interested in writing a two-page
short story about made-up Jewish people eating dinner, so instead I've written scripture.

I talked to Rabbi Salt about this on the phone last night and he said he
didn't think it would be a problem for me to hand in what I'm handing in,
especially not if I wrote you a letter like this one, explaining my reasons,
and also because the part of this scripture about my father and the fires he
set, which I won't spoil by telling you any more about before you get to
read it, is a story that most people will not believe, and so you'll think it's
fiction anyway. At the same time, though, I think it would be dishonest of
me to pretend it's fiction, and therefore disrespectful to you, and I want you
to know that I've put a lot of thought and effort into making this scripture
acceptable on all grounds—to make it feel fictiony enough so you know I'm
not thumbing my nose at your assignment, but also to let it be as completely
true as it is. For example, I've written sentences which are unlike those I
have used in previous assignments, in that they have a lot of dependent
clauses as well as occasional Yiddishe inversions and inflections, so that I

sound like a narrator named Gurion ben-Judah, rather than the Gurion ben-Judah you know in real life. Also, I've arranged the contents in a fiction way that withholds certain information to the last, to keep you in suspense, and I've done so by means of frames, like how Cervantes does in *Don Quixote* (already another of my favorites of your recommendations, even though I'm not even a fifth of the way through it yet). I did other stuff too, but— Is this letter as boring to read as it is to write? If so, I apologize. What follows, I assure you, is better than this.

Anyway, I hope you like it. And I hope that Samuel has gotten over his cold and that you are proud of him. Rabbi Salt took us to the playground for Torah Study the day the cold started, and it was gloomy out there, and we were talking about whether or not the prophet Jonah intended the ending of the Book of Jonah to be as hilarious as it is, and Samuel and I said, yes, that the Book of Jonah was the most deadpan comedy ever written, and someone, Ben Brodsky I think, said how he wished the sun would come out, and right then, the sun came out, and Samuel said, "I love when the playground gets sunny," and then he looked at the sun and sneezed. It was the best-timed sneeze ever, I think. No one in Torah Study ever illustrated the complex meaning of the Book of Jonah better than your son did with that sneeze, and it made me proud of him, and I'm not even his mother. I know that that sneeze was the first announcement of his cold, but I think it was worth it, and I hope he does, too. And I hope you do, too. And I hope you enjoy this, my first act of scripture. And a blessing on your head.

Your Student,
Gurion ben-Judah

P.S. I almost forgot! Tamar of Timneh. Rabbi Salt suggested I tell you her story in case you'd forgotten it. I told him that was crazy, because how could you forget it, and he agreed that I was probably correct, but by the time he agreed, I'd already gotten nervous he might be right, and I've decided to refer you to Genesis 38, in case you did forget, and also to tell you the story myself, below, in case you don't feel like going to Genesis 38 because maybe you've gotten comfortable and your Chumash or Tanach is not within reach. If you do remember the story, though, or have a Chumash or Tanach at hand, there's no need to read the rest of this postscript...

Judah ben-Israel had three sons with the daughter of Shua: Er, Onan, and Shelah. To Er, the oldest, Judah married Tamar of Timneh, daughter of Shem, who lived in Timneh, where Judah had his sheep sheered. Tamar was not only the most righteous woman alive, but also the most gorgeous.

Er, however, was kind of a schmuck. Fearing that pregnancy would ruin

Tamar's beauty, Er took measures not to get her pregnant, and God killed him for his evilness. As was customary, Judah's next-oldest son, Onan, married her. Onan, fearing the same thing as Er, spilled seed like Er had, and God killed him, too. Now Judah had only one son left—Shelah. Judah was scared he'd lose Shelah if Shelah married Tamar, so he sent Tamar home to her father's house in Timneh to live as a widow, telling her that Shelah wasn't old enough yet to be married, but that when he came of proper age, Tamar would be sent for, and *then* she could marry him.

A long time passed—Shelah grew up, Judah's wife died—and Tamar was still living as a widow. She realized Judah wouldn't let Shelah marry her, and the next time news came to Timneh that Judah would be passing through to check on his sheep-shearers, Tamar donned the veil of a harlot and stood by the crossroads. Judah approached and, not recognizing Tamar (good, thick veil), asked her to consort. She asked what he was offering. He offered her a goat, but he had no goat on him. She said it was a deal, but she needed collateral until she got the goat. The collateral she needed, she explained, was his signet, his wrap, and his staff. Judah agreed. The two consorted.

Tamar disappeared into the night with the collateral, removed her veil, and returned to her father's house. When Judah went home, he sent his man to pay Tamar the promised goat and get back his signet, wrap, and staff. Judah's man went to Timneh, asked after "the harlot who stands by the crossroads," and was told by the people of Timneh that there was no such harlot. He went back to Judah and gave him the news. Judah decided it better to let the matter drop and let the harlot keep the collateral he'd given her, because the whole thing could become embarrassing—he didn't want be known as a guy who had consorted with a harlot.

A few months later, news came that Tamar was pregnant, and Judah said she had to die for committing harlotry. He went into Timneh to burn her to death in public, and just before she was about to be burned, she whipped out the signet, the wrap, and the staff, and explained that she was pregnant by the man who'd given her the collateral, and asked that the man be identified. Judah understood that it was he who had made her pregnant, and he admitted it publicly, there on the spot, but he never consorted with Tamar again. Six months later, twins were born, Perez and Zerah.

That the messiah will be a direct descendent of King David—a direct descendent of Judah through Perez—is not up for debate; exactly how much of that information Tamar was aware of, however... is.

STORY OF STORIES

To strap down a chicken and pluck it while it's living isn't kosher, but that's the only path to total baldness. The wispy little hairs in the feather-holes of kosher-slaughtered poultry remind my mom of eyelashes, which make her think of eyelids, and eyelids seem too thin to her to do their job.

When she was five, she saw a kosher chicken on my grandmother's chopping block and ran to her room with her hands on her eyes. This was the last day of the Six-Day War, and her dad was slaying enemies in the Golan. When he got home the next morning, my mom still hadn't taken her hands down, and when he came into her bedroom, she would not hug him until he agreed to blindfold her. He used his belt and she wore it on her face all day.

By dinner it was no longer cute, and my grandfather tossed falafels at her head. She said, "Stop it," and he said, "Who are you speaking to, Tamar? What would you like that person to stop?" She said, "Aba, stop throwing food at me," and he said, "Take off the idiot blindfold," and she said, "I need to protect my eyes." He tossed more falafel at her head. "You need to protect your head," he told her. She didn't say anything to that, and he tossed falafel until there was no more falafel and he started tossing kibbeh.

The kibbeh was heavier, and it was not as funny as the falafel, but my mother was willful, and kibbeh—no matter how much heavier or less funny than falafel; no matter how hard anyone tossed it at her head—would not convince her to remove the belt from her eyes, and my grandmother knew that, and my grandmother yelled at my grandfather, and my mom started crying, and eye-shaped tearstains seaped through the fibers of my grandfather's canvas belt.

"Your blindness is bad for us," my grandfather told my mom. "Hairy chicken is bad!" she shouted. "So stay away from hairy chicken," he said. "Buy me goggles," she said. He said, "Goggles will make you look crazy. Are you crazy? Maybe you're crazy, blindfolded and screaming about chicken." My mother swiped fried grains from her hair and her forehead. My grandfather said, "You can't protect yourself without sight." "I can't protect myself at all," said my mother. And my grandfather made her an offer: "If you stop your craziness," he said, "I will teach you how to kill with that belt."

My mother consented, and was able to avoid raw kosher chicken until she was twenty-seven. My grandmother warned her away whenever chicken was on the chopping block, and my grandfather combat-trained her so well that when she left home for the IDF his special forces team made sure that none of her two years of compulsory service were wasted off-mission, which meant no boot-camp, and so no kitchen-duty.

After she finished serving in Lebanon, she came to Chicago for school and gave up religion til I was born. All the chicken she cooked during college was traif, and all the chicken she cooked during graduate school was traif until she fell in love with my dad, who brought her to Shabbos at the house of his Lebuvitcher parents.

A couple years earlier, my dad had gone to Brooklyn to best-man the wedding of Yuval Forem. Rebbe Menachem Schneerson performed the ceremony. Traditionally, the bride and groom are the last to approach the chupa, but a lot of people believed Schneerson was the messiah, and a few still do, even though he's dead now, so he's who came out last. When the rebbe saw my father standing on the platform, he halted the ceremony and took him aside to whisper in his ear.

Although my paternal grandparents were close to Yuval Forem, they had caught the flu together before his wedding, and were unable to fly to New York. The day after the wedding, Yuval and his bride Rochel moved across the world, to a young West Bank settlement without phone service, so the first my grandparents heard of the Rebbe's weird behavior toward my father was in the postscript of a letter from Yuval that I keep in my DOCUMENTS lockbox. "P.S. The vision or dream Rebbe Schneerson had about your Yehudah must have been of the very utmost importance to merit such a taking-aside-to-whisper," wrote Yuval, "and so I didn't worry the delay. Still, I would be thrilled to know what was said between them. Yehudah left the reception before I had the chance to ask."

Within days of his return from Brooklyn, my father, who would not tell his parents or anyone else what the rebbe had said to him, dropped out of yeshiva to attend law school, and offered no one an explanation. So by the time they met my mom, my paternal grandparents had already been worried about my father's future for two years. That is what my grandfather told me, right before he died.

□ □ □

My grandfather died three days after my grandmother, when I was six and they were sixty-five. We were never close to my grandparents, even though they lived just six blocks away, and by the second evening of my grandma's shiva, my grandpa knew he was dying. How I know he knew was that he began our last conversation by saying, "It is nothing short of tragic, Gurion, that this is the only important conversation I will ever get to have with you. It is tragic that the only important conversation I will ever get to have with you will be about a rift. This rift, though, was about you, always about you, the most important person in the world, at least to me—the rift was about who you would become, and I need to know that you understand that, and I know that your father won't explain it to you properly, if at all. My son is not the explaining type, and he won't explain how important it is to his father that you continue to become the person I see you becoming, the scholar you are miraculously turning into despite your upbringing. In becoming who you are becoming, Gurion, you heal a rift by mocking it. You prove all the worries that your grandmother and I suffered to have been unnecessary. All we ever wanted was what every nice Jewish couple wants: for their children to raise Jewish children. By the time we met your mother, we had already been worried for a couple years about the path your father was embarking on. It was not we were racists," he said, "not that. But what she did with that Shabbos chicken, your mother..." He trailed off and backtracked then, explaining how they'd worried that by the time I'd be born, my dad, "who had not only traded, for that of Louis Brandeis and Benjamin Cardozo, the work of Rashi and Rambam the local rabbis all swore he was destined to elaborate, but had lately begun to obsessively clip the stragglers in his beard and—just a few days earlier—been witnessed leaning over the counter in a diner on Lawrence by our neighbor Zippy Kaplan who, yes, it's true, she had glaucoma, Zippy, yet nonetheless she swore that the substance in the glass Yehuda sipped from looked milky beside his hamburger," would become entirely secular, which would lead to secular children, and likely very few of them.

That my mother's lost-tribesmanship might mean she wasn't an Israelite, or that being dark-skinned would make her marriage to my father uncomfortable for certain Yeckies at shul, never crossed my grandparents' minds. The worry was that there would be no shul at all. My grandparents worried that, because my father was in love with a woman who wasn't observant, let alone Lebuvitcher, he would leave behind his entire religion, just as he had left behind his career as a scholar. They were a little bit right and a little bit wrong, my grandparents.

My father was moving away from religion, and would continue to do so, but it had almost nothing to do with my mother. He told me himself that he'd made the decision to leave yeshiva even before Yuval's wedding, that he'd begun longing to affect the world in a more direct way than he believed he was able to as a Torah scholar (a half-truth), and that that was why, a full six months before going to Brooklyn, he had secretly applied to law school. For a long time, that was all he told me. I learned the rest on my eighth Passover, mostly because Yuval Forem had too much wine.

Yuval's parents' house was a block west of ours, on California, and even though, like most others in the neighborhood, the elder Forems avoided us, Yuval—having brought his wife and six children from Israel for the holiday—wielded his authority and made sure we were invited. He and my father had been friends since grammar school, and roommates at yeshiva, so if Yuval hadn't moved away, or if we had moved to Israel, we'd have done Passover with his family every year. That was how he started.

"Every year, Yehudah!" he continued. Yuval's neck was so thick it could have been shoulders. His voice boomed through the mouth-hole in his wide, spongey beard, and the frayed lapels of his black robe-jacket seemed to ripple, the wales of cordurory bending and swelling. "Every year, your Gurion and my daughters would search out the afikomen together," he said. "Every day they would play together. We'd spend Shabbos together, build the suka together, have barbecues. You are a brother to me, and I love you and have missed you. And you, Tamar— you bring this brother of mine such joy. He used to be so spooky! With the studying... all the books... you can't possibly know how *weird* he was. He knew *everything*. He'd study and smoke and study and smoke, and only after ten o'clock at night would he ever relax a little...We'd go for a walk, usually for a soda over at...what was this place, Yehudah, this late-night deli where we'd go for the sodas? What was it called?"

My father, cross-hatching a half-eaten new-potato with his fork, said, "Asner's."

"Asner's!" said Yuval. "Asner's exactly! Every night, nearly—it's ten, ten-thirty, your husband says to me, 'Yuvy, I'm going blind here! Want a walk?' and of course I would agree, and Asner's we'd go to, and sometimes, if feeling particularly charitable, we'd invite Rolly Bar-Sheshet, and sometimes, if Rolly was feeling particularly less like a snivelling little shmendrick than usual, he'd come along with us— what ever happened to Rolly?"

My father made his lips fat and waved away the question with all his fingers.

I knew what happened to Rolly, though. Rolly Bar-Sheshet was the cantor at the Fairfield Street Synagogue, which is where I go because my parents won't attend shul and it's close enough to our house that I can walk there by myself. Rolly trilled a lot during the mourner's Kadish, and I did not like it so much, but his son Amit was nice. Still, I didn't want Yuval to stop telling stories, so I stayed quiet.

"Rolly-olly, Rolly-polly," said Yuval. "What I was saying is that after Asner's, we'd walk some more, usually through the cemetery, drinking our sodas, talking about everything boys will talk about. We'd talk about you, Tamar, what your name would be and what Yehudah hoped you'd be like when he met you, and you, too, Guri-on—he knew his firstborn would be a son. Sometimes the time would slip away, and it would be midnight, twelve-thirty in the morning, and you know what we'd do then? If it was midnight, twelve-thirty in the morning?"

"Litberg's!" shouted his eldest daughter. She'd heard it before.

"Litberg's, my Sara! It's true," said Yuval. "We'd walk up Devon to Litberg's bagel factory. All night long they were making bagels inside, taking them from ovens, dunking dough in vats. We'd wait near the backdoor, and this man—Morris Nussberg was his name, you see what I can remember?—Morris Nussberg would eventually come outside for a cigarette, a cardboard boat on his head to guard against the falling-out of hairs, and we'd offer him a light, and we'd chat a little about this or that, about bagels, making them, the necessity of the boiling process and so on. He'd tell us, 'Buy stock in garlic. It's the new poppyseed,' or 'Litberg's nagging again about the egg bagels are too orange for the goyim—says to lower the yolk content or Lenders will bury us by '87.' Soon enough, this Morris Nussberg finishes smoking, takes his leave, and returns with what? The freshest bagels ever. For Yehuda and I. The freshest. Ever. Delicious! And there we'd be, under the moonlight, thinking about you, and you, and you and you and you," Yuval said, gesturing with two hands at all the children around the table, knocking over an empty glass, shrugging at it, leaving it, "and you and you. Except *you*, as I recall, were going to be called Dovid," he said to me. Then, to my father: "Whatever happened to calling him Dovid?"

"You're asking the wrong person," said my father.

"This has always been your husband's second-favorite answer," Yuval said to my mom, "tied with 'It's not something I'd like to talk about, Yuvy,' both of which, as you probably know, run all too distant behind the number-one favorite answer: the half-bored/half-murderous glare on the shrugged-up shoulders which at school we'd call 'The Morton' for the way it transformed into man-size salt pillars whomsoever would dare to look directly upon it."

I didn't yet know if I liked Yuval. He was crazy and funny, but my father acted different around him. His laugh had more edges than it usually did, and when he laughed it there, at the Seder, his head went side-to-side, like to say, "Here we go again" instead of the up-and-down nod that I was used to, which always looked like, "Go on, please, go on." The laugh he laughed at the stories of Yuval seemed angry, and although my father is often angry, his usual anger is wild and unmuddled; it looks like nothing other than anger. He'll yell or slam the door, and sometimes he'll grit his teeth and go to his office. I'd never before then seen him laugh with anger, though, only with joy or sadness. So when Yuval first started describing how my father had been when they were young, what he said seemed false, except once I noticed the new way my father was laughing, it seemed not only like it had been true when my father was younger, but that it still was true—it seemed like my father had become the person you'd have expected if all you knew of him were the stories of his boyhood as told by Yuval. It seemed, in short, like he'd become a "father." And it is true that I write "father" a lot to refer to him, but I usually think of my father as "Dad" or "Aba." And that is why I didn't know if I liked Yuval, because of how he was making my dad seem like someone I should think of as "father."

But then Yuval said, "Tell us, Judah. Tell us how David becomes lioncub all of a sudden."

And my father, who had been holding my mom's hand under the table, did a very Dad thing: he raised her hand high and kissed it loudly on the wrist, on the side where the blood pulses.

"David was not an option," said my mother. "My parents had passed away before I became pregnant, and we were going to name the baby Beth, after Bathsheba, my mother; or Michael, after Malchizedek, who was my father.

"As you know," she said, "Judah had, a few years earlier, stopped practicing. No more shul and no more tefilin in the morning. Saturday became his day to read briefs. And all of this was fine with me— I had stopped practicing a few years before *him*, and my observance had never been so extensive to begin with, so it was irrelevant to me—he was a Jew either way and I loved him. What you might *not* know, however, is that my husband, in the absence of the many daily rituals he had for so long been accustomed to performing, became wildly superstitious. Constitutional Law, though it might have satisfied his Gemmaric leanings, failed to challenge him in the way that the more mystical aspects of—"

"Okay, Jung," said my father, "why not just tell the story?"

"I am telling the story," my mother said.

"This is a woman," said my father to Yuval, "who out one side of her mouth whispers hoarsely about mysticism and the meaning to be found within the shapes of birthmarks, and out the other calls herself a behaviorist."

My mother said, "Easy as a child breathes a wish at a dandelion, my love, is exactly how hard it would be for me to tear your limbs from their sockets."

"Sure," said my father. "Beat me up later, then, and be poetic about it, too. Toughguy. Sabra. Weirdo. Just get to the dream, already. You're gonna put Yuval to sleep."

"She's not—" said Yuval.

"No one asked you," said my father.

Yuval winked at me. Then my father winked at me. Then my mother. I've never been able to wink.

My mom said, "I cannot leave out the nails, Judah."

"Sure, okay," said my father. "The nails. It's better a pregnant woman doesn't step on nail clippings, yes? Because nails are the last remnants of the etcetera, etcetera… and they can cause an etcera… Yuval knows about the nails, so just let's get on with it."

"He talks," said my mother, "as if this had not all come from him."

There are arguments about the importance of nail-clippings. Some people say that they are supposed to be treated with reverence, that you are supposed to bury them. Others say they're like gooze and earwax and you can just throw them away. I don't know of anyone who actually buries their nail-clippings, though many will throw them into some fire instead of the garbage. Some people don't even throw them in the garbage, though. They stick them between couch cushions or bite them off and flick them like snots, and some even spit them on the floor. Those are the people, I think, who should be taught that a nail-clipping can still an unborn baby. Hopefully the teaching would frighten those people, because it's gross what they do, especially the spitting ones.

The belief that pregnant women will miscarry if they step barefoot on nail-clippings comes from two stories whose meanings too easily echo into noise. The first takes place on the night of the sixth day, which was the first day of Man: By the time night fell, Adam and Eve had already been expelled from Gan Eden, and were very frightened. It was Shabbos, and pitch black, except for the flames of the candles Eve had lit before the sundown. In the blackness, the only thing that could comfort Adam and Eve, the only thing that could convince them that they still had shape in the darkness, that they were still alive, was the reflection of the candleflames in their fingernails.

The facts of the second story contradict those of the first one, but I like the second one better. This second story has it that Adam and Eve were born into the world covered head-to-toe in a clear, hard, protective enamel, but that as soon as they ate from the Tree of Knowledge of Good and Bad, a pinhole in the enamel developed at the center of each of their backs. As they grew older, their enamel-holes got larger: dime- to penny- to nickel- to quarter-size, and then CDs and personal pizzas and phonograph records, and then the holes wrapped around to the front and continued to grow. It was by watching the progress of the enamel's disappearance that Adam and Eve judged how much time they had left to live. They probably believed that they would die as soon as the enamel was entirely gone—that would make sense. That is not what happened, though. They died when the enamel had receded to the middle of the top of the first joints of the fingers and the toes. I don't know if that makes Hashem more or less merciful than if he'd killed them when they were expecting it, but it's a very interesting quandary, I think, worthy of commentary and debate. It is not, however, germane to the story at hand.

What's germane is that in the first story, nails prove to be gifts given by Hashem to Adam and Eve to protect their sanity in the night, outside the Garden. In the second story, the enamel's recession lets Adam and Eve know that protection from death is fleeting. So in the first story, the gift is a consolation to Adam and Eve for being outside of the Garden; and in the second, the enamel's progressive erasure marks their growing distance from the Garden, their growing proximity to a state of no protection.

So without Eden, death approaches, which is scary; but without the approach of death, there would be no way to long for Eden. The only people who don't know this are unborn babies. Unborn babies only know the womb, which is a kind of Eden. The womb is a membrane that protects unborn babies, as Eden was a membrane that protected Adam and Eve; and nails, though membranes of a practical kind, are also, more importantly, the physical representation of the knowledge of membranes.

Before they had knowledge of good and bad—which is to say before they had knowledge of protection, knowledge of membranes— Adam and Eve, having been born adults into the womb of Eden, nonetheless knew there was such a thing as the Tree of Knowledge of Good and Bad, and they made the choice to eat from it. It is a choice every baby makes when it leaves the womb. Inside the womb, though, there is nothing like the Tree of Knowledge of Good and Bad, so the unborn baby is unaware of the presence of choice.

Unless—according to the belief currently under examination— the mother, barefooted, steps on a nail-clipping. If that happens, the knowledge that there is choice, that there is a choice to learn about membranes, as well as the knowledge of membranes itself, somehow gets learned by the unborn baby all at once, which is too much for the unborn baby to understand, and it dies before it was ever truly alive.

The problem with this belief is that it is derived from a confusion of the representational with the actual. What nails *represent* (Hashem's protection against death, the existence of choice, etc.) becomes confused with what nails actually *do* (protect the toe- and finger-tips, allow for clawing, etc). To insist that fingernails *are* choices or *actual* protection against death, would be like insisting that when the stars and stripes go up in flames, America does too.

"However," might argue a scholar, "when a man sets fire to an American flag, certain Americans get angry or 'inflamed.' Therefore, to dismiss the belief that clippings still babies on the grounds that the power of nails is *only* symbolic would be cheap of Gurion ben-Judah." And that scholar would be correct. The symbolic or representational *can* affect the actual. Obviously.

But we are still stuck with the fact that when the nail-clipping is stepped on, it doesn't enter the mother's body. I.e., if it doesn't *enter* the mother's body, how can it get into the womb for the baby to give it witness and thereby affect the baby with its symbolic power the way a burning flag will a zealous patriot? It can't. Not physically.

Yet one might argue that the clipping could get there in another, non-physical but nonetheless actual way: one might point out that to become inflamed a zealous patriot may only require knowledge that someone, somewhere, is burning his country's flag.

And one would then go on to argue that a mother feeds knowledge into her womb, as well as processed nutrients, and that the *knowledge* of a nail-clipping having come into contact with the sole of her foot is enough to still the baby. If this were the case, though, the mother would have to *be aware* that she has stepped on a clipping—but that is not part of the superstition. According to the superstition, the mother need only *step* on a clipping to still her baby.

And so the only argument left to support the superstition would be that the sole of the mother's foot has, itself, not only the capacity to acquire knowledge without the mother being aware that knowledge has been acquired, but the capacity to transmit the knowledge to the baby via non-physical means without the mother being aware that the knowledge has been transmitted.

Which is untenable.

It is untenable not because a person's body can't know things that the person herself is unaware of—the body *can* know things that the person herself is unaware of (e.g., I couldn't begin to count the number of times I've found myself scratching itches that I hadn't known were itching me til I found myself scratching them). The argument that the nerves in the sole of her foot are capable of "knowing" and thereby transmitting what they "know" about fingernails/membranes/choice into a mother's womb without the mother's awareness is an untenable argument because if we allowed for such an argument, then all bodyparts should be subject to the relevant superstition regarding nail clippings. For if foot-soles can have and transmit such knowledge, should not pregnant mothers then fear touching nail-clippings with their *hands* as well? Should they not fear *seeing* fingernails? Why should a footsole communicate more to an unborn baby than a fingertip or an eye? It couldn't, it shouldn't, and it doesn't.

And even if it could and should, it didn't. I am proof of that. Unless you go with my mother's interpretation, which we will arrive at shortly.

"...So one night," she told Yuval, "late into my third trimester, I am sitting on top of the couch in the living room, looking at the fireplace, relaxing, when Gurion starts to flop and to punch, and suddenly nature calls me, urgently, screaming. Judah is in the bathroom, clipping his nails over some newspaper that he is planning to crumple into a ball when he is finished in order to trap the clippings within the folds of the ball, and then to throw the whole package into the fire—I mean he is crazy, Yuval: it is a beautiful June evening, seventy degrees outdoors, and this crazy guy has to turn the apartment's thermostat to sixty-one because he has a fire going in the fireplace, just so that he can burn his nail clippings. Around your eyes, Yuval, I see a question forming. Is it the same question I had? I am sure it is—so ask."

"Why not just cut your nails outside, Judah?" Yuval said. "Why the fire in the summer? What's that? What were you thinking?"

"Outside," said my father, "I may have gotten distracted. It was beautiful outside, like my wife just told you. So if I sit there, on the stoop, cutting my nails, relishing the breeze, then what? I'll tell you: plip, a clipping falls onto the stoop, but I'm thinking about my childhood, and so I look at the cracks in that nice piece of sidewalk where

Yuval and I once hopscotched til the sun went down, and I look at that patch of asphalt where once we drew a four-square court, and oh that smell that comes off Devon when the wind is strong, and how I smelled that smell the day Ms. Gluckman threw the pickle jar at the mailman and came outside screaming, with no wig and no bra, and my sexual awakening had begun, and where did I hear the clipping plip again? To my left? To my right? Do I even remember hearing the clipping plip? Maybe I never heard the clipping plip on the stoop, and maybe I give up trying to find it, but maybe it's there—a nail-clipping blends so easily into concrete, the stoop is made of concrete, my wife's soles are callused like a lizard's belly from all the barefooting she did in the desert half her life and she won't wear shoes in the summer, and it's week thirty-seven with that one and she can't see past her own belly and so what? So I'm going to worry about the electric bill, Yuval? No. I'm not going to worry about the electric bill, Yuval. What I'm going to do is light a fire and set the thermostat to sixty-one. What I'm going to do is spread out some newspaper in the bathroom—clothing ads for high contrast because they're colorful and my clippings are white—and I'm going to clip and keep track of what flies, and make sure to pick it up, and make sure to set it on the clothing ads. And when I'm finished, then I'm going to *fold* the ads, very carefully—not *ball* them up like some shlub, but fold the ads up tightly, so no clipping can escape—and then I'm going to throw it in the fire, because that's the only way to prevent a woman as reckless as Tamar from miscarrying my boy. Is what I was thinking. And you can go ahead and make fun of it, Yuval, you can laugh your face off at the extremity of my caution, but I'm not the one who had his housekey turned into a tie-clip so that on Saturdays to be spent outside walled cities he could lock and unlock his front door without fear of breaking the sabbath law of carrying."

Yuval did laugh his face off, and that was when I noticed his tie-clip, and also decided I liked him. "And but why the stoop?" gasped Yuval through his laughter. "No one said anything about the stoop. What about some playground somewhere to do the clipping? Some field? The beach? I just said outside. Why not the backy—"

"Sexual awake!" said Yuval's second-youngest daughter.

"That's right, Naomi!" Yuval said, making a Harpo Marx face, "at six you will awake!"

"Six I will awake!" she agreed.

"Can you believe how smart they are?" Yuval said to us. "The rate they're picking up English—aye! Anyway, back to why your boy's not Dovid. Or Michael."

"Well you can imagine," my mom said. "I need to use the bathroom, I am banging on the door, Judah comes rushing out, this ball of newspaper in his hands, I hear him fall in the living room, he shouts to me he is okay. Okay. By the time I finish up my business, though, Judah is making all kinds of noise in the kitchen, and I go to see, and he is screaming at me, 'Get back in the bathroom! Take a bath in the bathroom! Stay out of the living room! I spilled! Where is the broom and the dustpan?'

"I do not know where the broom and the dustpan are—when do I clean the house? Do I not go to work like him? Am I not thirty-seven weeks pregnant? Do we not have a nice woman who comes on odd Wednesdays and hides the cleaning supplies? If the broom is not in the pantry or the closet, how am I to know where? I tell him that he is crazy and I go to the living room, and he chases after me. And this is silly, is what I am thinking. My husband, I am thinking, this lovely man, this powerful, beautiful man, is losing his mind over fingernail clippings. And so me, a wiseguy sometimes, I do a little show. A little dance atop the fingernails, a bump and grinding. What can he do? Tackle me? I am pregnant. And what does he say, Yuval? He says nothing, becomes white. Totally white. And yes, I feel awful. Now I feel awful.

"And then we go to sleep. And while I am sleeping, I have a dream. In this dream, I am in the backyard of the house I grew up. My father is there—he has been dead already eleven months, my father, and I am not much of a dreamer, Yuval, I am not someone who remembers what she dreams, but this was vivid. He had tzitzit on under his fatigues, not a custom he adhered to, the tzitzit, and he was wearing tefilin, facing the Old City, his back to me. I said 'Aba,' and then, in a very formal tone, not a tone I can ever say I had heard him take, he answered me, saying, 'Your indiscretion looms large over the child you carry. Only because he is especially beloved by God will this boy in your womb survive your womb and enter the world. If you wish him to live beyond his bris, you will name him Gurion, for a lion cub will he be, and as a lion will he conquer, red-eyed from wine and white-toothed from milk. And you will raise him as would befit a lion cub born of Tamar and Judah lest he depart from this world a boy, trampled beneath the feet of his brothers. And you will take that ridiculous belt off your face. Stop trifling! Now, Tamar!'

"The belt is a story for itself, I will leave it alone. As for this 'Stop trifling' that he said, it was a thing he shouted to me only one other time, years before, when I was twenty, in Beirut. My father was not at all a shouter—he was a loud, loud man, but he did not often shout, and it happened that in Beirut, we were waiting inside a building for something to happen, it is not important what, but we were waiting in this building, on an upper floor, the fifth if memory is serving me, and there was a young woman on the ground, crossing the street, holding the hand of her daughter, who was so fumbly and small she must have just learned to walk, and because of this thing we were waiting for, and how beautiful they were, amidst all the hideousness, the wreckage that Beirut had become, like a bruise on a scar was Beirut, and how gorgeous the mother and daughter, and this thing we were waiting for to happen... I fired a few rounds out the window, in the air, so that they would take cover. And my father, he shouted at me, 'Stop trifling!' and by the time the last of the three syllables was out, I'd been struck in the shoulder by sniper fire. What we'd been waiting for to happen, it happened then, and there was no more sniper fire, there were no more enemies left breathing in the vicinity, and I was evacuated, and I went back home, where I had to spend two months recovering before returning to Beirut. It is the only time I was ever shot, right after my father yelled at me 'Stop trifling!' And in the dream, as he says it for the second time, I tense suddenly, and awaken, and the sheets are soaked. My water has broken.

"Now, Judah has not yet even fallen asleep. He is up and he has me up, and we get to the hospital, and I go into labor for, what, Judah, for eight hours?"

"Ten hours," my father said.

"Ten hours of labor, and the whole time I am thinking: 'This is not because of the fingernails. This is because of some guilt I feel about the fingernails. I feel some guilt about scaring my husband white, and I have a dream about my father, and he tells me something horrifying about my son, it is nothing. Maybe my water broke because of the shock of the dream, maybe I had the dream because my water was about to break… These things can be explained, okay? Right?' That is what I think.

"And then *this* guy is born. And it is not just that he is born with a full head of hair—and I do not mean to imply the fine, silky baby kind, but the very same coarse, uncombable mess that you see before you, though much more of it than he has now: this hair he is born with, all wet, it hangs to his shoulders—all I think of the hair is: 'Strange, nu? What isn't strange? Life is strange.' And the obstetrician, he is cradling this newborn son of mine, and telling me to look at the full head of hair, it is amazing, the hair, 'Amazing, amazing,' he carries on, and then he strokes the hair, the obstetrician, and the moment he strokes the hair, this newborn son of mine *bites him on the neck*, right where it meets the shoulder, and the obstetrician lets out a little scream, but I think it is just surprise, and I think, 'Well, my baby does not like strange men to touch his head—okay, neither do I.' But then, you see, Yuval, blood starts coming through the white of this obigynie's doctor-jacket. My son has drawn blood. My son, he has a mouth full of teeth. And these teeth—these are the last nails in the coffin of naming my boy Michael, of naming him anything other than Gurion. I tell this to Judah, and what is he going to say? The whole way to the hospital, he is convinced I am miscarrying. He could care less what we call the boy. So that is why Gurion, and not Michael nor Dovid."

"This is true?" Yuval said to my father. "About the teeth and the hair?"

"He had four teeth," my father said, "not a mouthful, but they were the right four teeth—that doctor was *bleeding*. The hair, as I remember, was even longer than she said, but what do I know?"

"Amazing," Yuval said, not really believing what he'd been told.

"Tell us more stories about Judah," my mother said to him. "It is good for Gurion to hear."

My mother left a part out of the story of my birth. That Seder was a long night of leaving parts out of stories. I knew the part she left out because she'd told me the story hundreds of times. She used to put me to sleep with it when I was younger. The part she cut picks up right after I bit the man for touching me on the head, right after he started bleeding:

"...But then you see, Gurion," she'd tell me, "blood starts coming through the white of the guy's doctor-jacket, and this worries me a little, because now I am going to feed you, and what will your teeth do to me? It turns out they do nothing—you know you have teeth, you know I am your ema, you love me, you do not want to hurt me. And you are laying there against my chest, and you stretch your arms up like babies sometimes will, you stretch them so your hands are just under my chin, and my first impulse, I have a strong impulse to put your little fists inside my mouth, to see if I can fit them both, and I see that you have pressed them together, your tiny little fists, as if that is what *you* want, too, you have pressed them together for *me* I think, and as I take hold of your wrists to guide your hands inside my mouth, I see you have these birthmarks, these yud-shaped birthmarks, and this stops my heart. These birthmarks are the last nails in the coffin of naming you Michael, of naming you anything other than Gurion. And I tell this to your father, and what can he say? The whole way to the hospital, he is convinced I am miscarrying you. I knew I was not, but he was convinced. So he could not care less what I wanted to call you, just that you were alive. And that is why you are Gurion."

And this is why my mom left that part out at the Seder: because, of course, I still had the birthmarks. If she told about the birthmarks, then Yuval might have asked to see them. Then I might have had to scrub the makeup from my knuckles and shown him. And then he would maybe suspect that everything my mother had just said was not only a story to tell about your son in front of your son to make him feel like there was no one else like him in the world; Yuval might suspect it was not merely a pretty way to dress up the fact that I was born rough and ugly, like how they call retarded and handicapped people "differently abled" (and it was those things as well, surely, for she's my mom, and she's a psychologist)...My mom has always been scared that if Yuval, or anyone else, were to learn about the birthmarks, it would somehow lead, as her dreamed father warned, to my being trampled beneath the feet of my brothers.

I do not believe that is true. I never have. My brothers will never trample me, and if ever they do, I don't see how my birthmarks could cause it. But my mom—she is my mom, and the thought of me getting trampled spooks her. When I used to complain about the makeup, she'd get very worried- and scared-looking, and she's a killer, my mom. She has killed a lot of people, and she won't say that, but she will tell me that her dad did, and but what was she doing in Beirut? What was she doing getting shot in a building with her dad's special forces team? She wasn't cooking chicken for them. She was killing enemies with them, lots of enemies, and at the same time, all of those enemies were trying to kill her, but she didn't die and the enemies did, because my mom was a much better killer. If you know your mom is a great killer, and you think of your mom as a great killer, and you know she would kill for you, not just metaphorically, but really end lives for you, without hesitation, you don't want to make her sad and worried because how can you repay her for all the things she's willing to do? You can't. So the least you can do is make it so she worries less and doesn't get all sad-looking about some birthmarks. That's what I think. So I put the makeup on every day and I don't complain or make faces, and if I believed that anyone were, anytime soon, going to read this *Story of Stories* as the scripture that it is, then I wouldn't even mention the birthmarks. So it is good that you read it as fiction for now—my mom can relax. By the time you know it's scripture, I will have proven, even to her, that I am untramplable.

"So where was I before?" Yuval said.

"Litberg's!" shouted Sara.

"Yes, Litberg's," said Yuval. "Delicious bagels. We'd get our delicious bagels gratis and walk around, and talk about all of you, our futures, how we'd one day bring you to Litberg's, maybe at midnight twelve-thirty even, like how the Spanish do in Barcelona. When we were bar-mitzvahed together at the Western Wall, we fathers of yours, we had a day's layover in Barcelona on the way back, all because of these two here," Yuval nodded to his silent, smiling parents, "and *your* grandparents, too, Gurion, may they rest in peace. The four of them wanted to make us worldly, and we loved them for it and we love them for it. And on the Ramblas at midnight twelve-thirty, what you see is men pushing strollers and holding hands with their dramatic wives. The Catholic Spaniards! We'd do it like them, but without a Rambla or Gaudi facades. It would be Devon Avenue, true, but what we had was Litberg's bagel factory, and those poor Spanish ham-eaters—they didn't. Just a lot of pickpockets and a giant Lichtenstein at the end, some fantastic coffee, true, and some tomato-stained bread that seemed like maybe it was the perfect snack, a snack to end all snacks, and yet we never knew for sure since we couldn't try for its proximity to all that ham."

"Traif!" shouted a younger daughter.

"Traif like you wouldn't believe, Kreindeleh. The ham was *every-where* in Barcelona! As if striving to forbid us from joy, the ham. But we had a great time, anyway, a great time *despite* the ham. Am I making this up, buddy? Tell them—am I making it up? About the ham? About how we'd talk about them all the time, about taking them to Litberg's?"

"Oh the ham," said my father, mashing flat with his fork's curved part the cross-hatches he'd earlier sculpted from his potatoes. "He's telling the truth."

My mom said, "We went to Litberg's on our first date, and for all of this time I thought because Judah was broke."

"He doesn't like to tell anyone anything is why you thought that, Tamar. It's how he is, it's been very well established. And probably he *was* broke—broke never damaged the charm of a nightwalk to Litberg's—but what I'm telling you," said Yuval, "is that your husband beside you, smiling wryly at his old friend, at ease enough here among us to register a little embarrassment at the revelations I'm spouting, him; to violate with nervous hand-movements the physical integrity of these delicious potatoes my mother never fails to cook in just enough juice from the briscuit that they become flavorful but still maintain their firmness, your husband—they *slice* rather than *crush*, the potatoes, is what you always said, hey Pop? What *I'm* saying, Tamar, is when we were young, Judah dreamed of you without ever having met you. When he wasn't being this weirdo with his nose in arcane scripture even the rabbis couldn't teach him from, your husband, or writing these articles insisting first that Leviticus was enjambed, and then that it was *incorrectly* enjambed, he would talk about you; your husband was a romantic above all else, and he would pray to meet you, he lived to meet you, and to raise *you*, Gurion. Others might have said, 'Yehuda, he's a cold S.O.B.,' but I was his closest friend and I roomed with him, and I knew him the best, I knew it wasn't for books that he lived, but family, that he studied in order to be better at family; that when he wasn't arranging various syllables of the ten sephirot for seemingly dubious purposes that turned out would save that girl from—"

My father dropped the fork on his plate and it clanged and he said, "Yuval."

"What?" Yuval said.

"My son is here," said my father.

"Yes?" said Yuval.

My father set his hand on Yuval's and told him something, but quietly, so that I, at the other end of the table, with the other children, couldn't hear.

Yuval, in full voice, said, "Bobe-mayses what, Yehuda? I saw with my own eyes. Why the whispering?"

"My son is here," said my father.

"I see him," Yuval said. "He's beautiful. Why keep secrets from such a beautiful boy? You keep so many secrets... I still don't know," Yuval said to no one and everyone, "what Rebbe Schneerson told him on my wedding day! Imagine! It's my wedding day, the ceremony is halted by the most important rabbi in the world—the most important *man* in the world—so that he can whisper something to my closest *friend* in the world. Do I complain? I don't complain. Do I expect to hear what it was, this big secret? No. I don't expect, because this closest friend of mine is a peculiar and highly secretive individual. However... However! Do I *hope*? Do I *dare* to *hope* that this veritable brother of mine will one day tell me, or even *hint* to me what it was that was so important that my wedding was halted? Yes! I hope. And still: what? Disappointment... And now he says, now he says, 'Oh...'"

"Gurion is *my* son," said my father, "and you're in your cups, my friend, and in your cups you are expansive."

"Maybe, maybe not," said Yuval, "but this—"

"This is nothing to argue about," said my father.

Yuval said, "I agree! Why talk me in circles? All I said—"

My father said, "Please."

My father's voice is fuller than anyone's, even Yuval's, so when it goes quiet suddenly, like it did when he said "Please," it is normal to notice how shadowed and angly and completely unjolly my father's face is, how coiled it is, how ready, how unreadable its stories, and it is normal to be shaken. I shook, but I wanted to hear more. When Yuval said the thing about changing around the syllables in the ten sephirot, I knew what he was talking about. The ten sephirot are: Malchut, Yisod, Hod, Netzach, Tiferet, Gevurah, Hesed, Binah, Hochma, and Keter. Their meanings, translated respectively, are: Kingdom, Foundation, Splendor, Victory, Beauty, Power, Mercy, Understanding, Wisdom, and Crown. Sometimes they are diagrammed into something called the Tree of Life or Tree of Man. The words on the right side are believed to refer to aspects of Love, and those on the left side are believed to refer to aspects of Justice. The words in the center are thought to refer to aspects of both:

JUSTICE   LOVE

Keter
Crown

Binah   *Hochmah*
Understanding   Wisdom

Gevurah   *Hesed*
Power   Mercy

Tiferet
Beauty

Hod   *Netzach*
Splendor   Victory

Yisod
Foundation

Malchut
Kingdom

It is also believed that these aspects correspond to different parts of men's bodies in such a way as I have diagrammed on the following page.

Yet the ways in which the ten sephirot can be diagrammed are not as important as why so much time is spent on thinking about them by those who would diagram them: They are the ten words that Hashem speaks billions of billions of times per second to hold the world together. Everything that happens gets said by Hashem first, and he says everything into happening with combinations of those ten words. I think that when you combine the sounds of them in a certain order, you get His true name, Hashem's, the name the Cohain Gadol used to speak in the Temple on Yom Kippur, when there was still a Temple. It is said that if you recite the ten sephirot in certain orders, fast enough, you can affect the world—physically. You can walk on water, maybe, or heal people, or make someone's head explode. I'd often thought of recombining the syllables myself, but a No! from Adonai would exact swift paralysis on my muscles whenever I'd sit down to try, so I'd never actually tried.

While I shook in the silence after my father's "Please," my thoughts about the sephirot led me to thoughts of nice Amit Bar-Sheshet, son of Rolly the trilling cantor, to a story Amit had told me when I was six, and it was that story I meant when I said to Yuval: Were you going to tell about the fire?

And my father became pale.

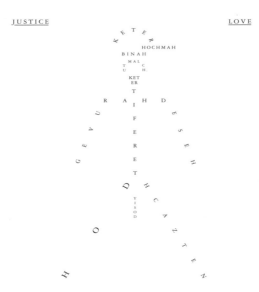

Amit had told me that when my father was still at yeshiva, he killed a mugger in the middle of the night by setting him on fire. Amit said that that's why my father became a lawyer—to defend himself in court.

When I heard the story, I asked my mom about it. She told me, "Became a lawyer to defend himself over some fire? It is nonsense." Her answer seemed like it had loopholes, like that comma that might or might not be there in *Noach*, when, after the flood,

> Hashem said in His heart: "I will not continue to curse again the ground because of man, since the imagery of man's heart is evil from his youth; nor will I again continue to smite every living being(,) as I have done."

With the comma, it might be a promise to never again destroy the world, but without it, it's only a promise to never again destroy the world *by flood*. Sometimes there's a comma and sometimes there isn't, and even though my mom's answer seemed tricky, I'd never asked my dad about the fire story; partly because he didn't like to talk to me about his days as a Torah scholar, but mostly because I wanted to believe he set fire to a man who tried to take something from him and I worried he'd tell me it wasn't true.

"The fire!" Yuval said to the table. "He already knows," he said to my father.

My father said, "We'll see what he knows, Yuval, and when it turns out he doesn't know what you think he knows, we'll allow the subject to drop."

"Agreed," said Yuval.

"I'm not asking," said my father. He turned to me. "Tell us what you think you know," he said.

His voice was quieter and harder than I'd ever heard it.

I said, You set fire to a mugger. I said, Then you became a lawyer to defend yourself.

"There," my father said to Yuval.

"It's dropped," said Yuval.

"It's not true, what you heard," my father said to me.

"Yet it has true pieces," said Yuval's Sara. That sentence was so pretty, and if I weren't so in love with Esther Salt, I think I would have fallen in love with Sara Forem, just for her nervous Israeli English, but I wanted to hear the story right, so I told her to tell me in Hebrew.

I said, Tell me in Hebrew. And my dad said, "Gurion," but my mother, who'd spent the last few minutes as quiet and content as the rest of us to watch the two giant fathers tease each other, spoke up. She said, "Know your son, Judah. He can hear this story now, in front of us, from the daughter of your oldest friend, or he will ask around the neighborhood until he will ask someone at that synagogue, and few will know the story he is hoping for, yet all of them will have something to say of you, and, unable as your son is to believe that anyone could harbor true contempt for his aba, he will be open to every twisted bobe-mayse any of these hundreds of local mamzers who would like to see you ruined will tell him. And it is not you he will ask to corroborate their whispered half-truths. He will ask *me* to do so, Judah, and I will, as I have, do my best to confuse him, and soon he will stop forgiving me for it. And soon after that, he will do exactly what you fear. Look on the face of your son and notice the smoothness around the orbits. There is not a trace of a line to be found. He sees everything, and can hear just as well, but he has not yet learned to squint. He has never squinted once."

It was a very dramatic speech to hear in the middle of the most dramatic Seder I'd ever been to. It is very dramatic to hear your mom call everyone at your shul a mamzer and then say you don't squint and that she confuses you on purpose and your dad is afraid of something, and I wanted to squint and tell everyone that my father was not afraid of anything, but before I could do that, Sara Forem was already saying, "I will tell you, but in English, because my smaller sisters don't understand well."

Her sisters understood *that*, though, and they began to cry, so Yuval told them, "Girls, go find the afikomen. Ma, Papa, Rochel—get them outta here, please." The girls' tears stopped falling, and their grandparents and their mother led them away, to further parts of the house.

Sara said, "What about us?"

"Would you rather look for matzo in an envelope, Gurion?" said Yuval.

No, I said.

"You," Yuval said to Sara, "are twelve years old." = "You've been bat-mitzvahed and the afikomen is no longer yours to find."

Sara said, "Fine." Then she said, "I forgot." Then she told the story in Hebrew because her sisters were already running around out of earshot, looking under and between things throughout the house. "Years before we were born," Sara said, "my father and your father were returning to the yeshiva from Litberg's with the shmendrick Rolly, when they came to an alley where there was a very bad struggle between two men and a girl. Our fathers and the shmendrick went to help the girl. One man, he turned to them with a pistol, while the other man, he struggled with the girl. These men should have run from our fathers, but instead there was this pistol in the hand of the one and the girl was still struggling against the other, so there was nothing else to do, so your aba said some words that no one else can pronounce, and this man with the pistol, he was covered in fire. When he fell he was dead and then he was ashes and then he was nothing, he blew away. The shmendrick and my father, they struck the other man's neck and held him against the ground, and then your father gave his coat to the girl, and he said some more impossible words, and she fell asleep against his shoulder, and he carried her home while my father and the shmendrick brought the man who struggled with her to the police, who put him in jail for the rest of his life."

I said to my father, For the rest of his life?

It was proof I could squint, but no one seemed to hear me because my father was saying to Sara, "Go look for the afikomen."

Yuval nodded to her that it was okay, and once she left the room, my father said, "All this narishkeit from you about keeping secrets, but you lied to your own daughter?"

"Not lied. Made a lesson," said Yuval.

My father dropped his head on the backs of his hands and made air-sounds with his mouth.

Yuval stood up and was wobbly. He leaned on the table. He said, "She's a child. What good is a complicated story to a child? What kind of protection does that offer?"

"Why tell it at all, then, Yuvy? Why are you like this?"

Yuval said, "Don't start with the Yuvy why are you like this. This is what I'm like and it's a good story about a good man doing good and there are very few of those, so I told it to my daughter. In a slightly simpler form."

Now my father stood up, unwobbling, and he told my mother, "We'll be back soon," and to Yuval he said, "Keep my wife company," and to me, "Let's you and I go look for Elijah."

We walked six blocks in silence, to Litberg's. My father knocked on a door in the alley, and a black man wearing a paper boat on his head and a pin on his shirt that said CARL came halfway outside. Carl said, "Who is this?"

"My boy."

"Hello his boy—two tonight?"

My father held up two fingers, and Carl ducked back inside.

My father said to me, "You knew that second man didn't go to prison."

I said, Yes.

My father said, "How did you know that?"

I said, Because you don't go to prison for life for anything less than murder or treason, and Sara said the man went to prison for life, so I thought he probably didn't go to prison at all.

Carl reappeared with two hot poppyseed bagels and my father gave him money and he went back inside. The bagels smelled delicious, and I was about to bite into the one my father handed to me when I remembered it was Passover.

I said, This is chometz.

"So don't eat it," said my father.

It's chometz, I said.

"I'm your father," he said.

I didn't know what to do. We just stood there holding bagels for a minute, then started heading toward the cemetaries on Western Ave.

My father said, "How do you know the man didn't kill her?"

What? I said.

My father said, "You knew the end of the story was false—how did you know the *way* it was false? How did you know that the lie was about the man going to prison and not about what the man did to the girl?"

I said, Yuval would never tell the story if the man had murdered the girl.

And my father said, "How do you know that?"

Because he said he told the story to make a protecting lesson for Sara, I said, and he would not have thought to make a protecting lesson of a story that ends with a girl being killed. He would only think to use the story if the lesson was there somewhere.

And then I said, The part about the fire, though—that was true, right? You did it with the ten sephirot? You rearranged the syllables? You can tell me and you don't have to worry that I'll do the same thing. I'm pretty sure I could figure out how, but I've never tried, and I won't if you say not to, and I probably wouldn't even if you didn't say not to.

"Don't," he said, "ever."

I said, I told you I won't. I said, Tell me what happened, though.

Instead of telling me what happened, my father bit into his bagel and began to chew it. I didn't want him to, but he was my father and I could not tell him what to do. He led us into the cemetary. It was not the cemetary that his parents are buried in, but the one beside it that he sometimes confuses for the one his parents are buried in when we go for walks together at night and talk about things.

The first time we did that was a week after his father died, the night he told me what Rebbe Schneerson whispered to him at Yuval's wedding.

The Rebbe had led my father to a table at the back of the shul where there were challahs and wine, and whispered: "Destiny is a Greek and muddled business, Judah. The story Avram read in the stars was, 'Avram will father no children by Sarai,' and as you know, it was true: Avram would father no children by Sarai. And so Hashem changed Avram's name to Avraham, Sarai's name to Sarah. And of Avraham and Sarah, the stars told a different story. By augmenting a name with a single syllable, Hashem rendered a ninety-nine-year-old man the patriarch of patriarchs, and by altering a vowel-sound a childless eighty-nine-year-old woman the matriarch of matriarchs. He made them the parents of Isaac.

"One wonders why, if the stars tell true stories, Avram did not, in the stars, read the story of his new name. It was surely there, the story of Avram's name being changed, but Avram on the ground did not see it. And so bearing in mind that his story was available and that he was capable of reading it, one can only conclude that he didn't find that story because he wasn't *looking* for that story. It follows: His mind was on babies, why should he look for a story about names?

"Don't speak yet, you haven't heard me out. We haven't talked about Yakov. When he wrestled the angel, and when, as daybreak came, the angel begged to be set free, Yakov demanded a blessing, and the angel gave him the name Yisrael. Of course, *Yisrael* is a combination of the words *yisra* (to overcome) and *El* (the divine), and the angel tells Yakov that he is being granted this new name because he has overcome the divine *and man*. Now, I know that you know these things, Judah, I've dreamed of you, and I know there are a *number* of things you know, probably too *many* things you know—too many, I say, not because any kind of knowledge has the capacity to be bad in *itself*, but rather because certain kinds of knowledge, particularly those kinds we often describe as *arcane*, can, by way of their very arcanity, serve to obscure the knowledge-bearer's understanding of the mundane. And we need to talk about the mundane, you and I, but you're receiving me as a particle physicist would a man who asks him for help building a bridge. The physicist, he thinks, 'Who cares about a bridge? We know all there is to know about bridges. Ask me about quarks and the pathways of neutrinos, or ask me nothing.' The difference between you and the physicist is that he *does* know how to build a bridge—he doesn't make the mistake of believing that what he once learned about building bridges somehow became false after he learned about subatomic particles—whereas you, Judah, ever since you began plumbing the arcane, you have, in increments, forgotten, if not dismissed, what you knew before. You have not lately considered the story of Yakov. And you need to. So lower your eyebrows, and let me get you in the mood; indulge me in this reconstruction, this brief blow-by-blow.

"According to Torah, Yakov and the angel wrestle all through the night, and then, as dawn is breaking, the angel perceives that he cannot overcome Yakov. What does the angel do then? He punches Yakov in the socket of the hip—hard, really mangles Yakov's hip, *dislocates* it. But Yakov holds on. Dislocated hip, dislocated blip, he's not letting go of the angel. Yet, at the same time, he doesn't *strike* the angel. One wonders why. And I submit that it's because he can't, simple as that—he has the angel in a hold, and if he lets up to punch or kick or throw the angel, the angel will get the better of him. If these were two men wrestling, we would call this situation a stalemate, a draw. No one's winning, no one's losing; they're stuck in this hold.

"It's *not* two men wrestling, though. It's a man wrestling with a divine being. It's a man wrestling with God. And before dawn breaks, God does not perceive that he has *been overcome* by Yakov; what he perceives is that *He* cannot overcome Yakov. Yet he names Yakov *Yisrael*. Thus: To overcome God is to reach a stalemate with Him. It's the best you can hope for, Judah. A stalemate. And no one ever told you it was otherwise. That you began to suspect it for yourself, to suspect that one could overcome God as one would a man—that's unfortunate, an overreaction, I'd imagine, to a long-since learned sense of helplessness, a sense that you would always be overcome as you were overcome as a boy in a world run by men, as we were all overcome as boys. And that may be my fault, the fault of all your elders, for teaching you to obey and praise and worship even as you had defiance in your heart. We were chosen because we allow and even encourage one another to question God, to do so incessantly—to be defiant—but maybe with you this wasn't expressed early enough. I don't know, because I don't really know *you*, Judah. I don't know your father, or your mother. I've only dreamt about you, and only last night. And I fear that what's happened to you is permanent. I fear that because men like me have failed to let you know how good and righteous a deed it is to wrestle God, you, having wrestled God with the intention of defeating Him, believe that you were rebelling against *us*, as well as Him, when after all you were doing exactly as you should have done. And I fear that you will walk away from us, and from Him. That you will choose to waste your life overcoming men, which will be easy for you, you who were able to reach a stalemate with God at so young an age, which is the best you could have hoped for, if only you knew—it was the best you could have hoped for, Judah, the best any of us can hope for... In the end, what I fear matters very little. You'll do what you will. I'm here as a signpost and only as a signpost—a signpost to point you to other signposts, at that. I am but a messenger sent to alert you that messages are coming, and my message is this: Destiny is a Greek and muddled business, and, lost as you are, names will be the only signposts available to you. Understand that you're neither Avram nor Yakov, and that you'll never be renamed. Know that you are Judah irrevocably, and, like Judah ben-Yisrael, you will make mistakes that the mother of your son will have to repair by means that will be unseemly to you. For your own good, though, Judah, avoid making at least *one* of the mistakes Judah ben-Yisrael made: Do not scorn your son's mother. Upon meeting her, know not only who she is, but that she is meant to be your wife. And marry her well."

"And how will I know who she is?" said my father, brimming with indignation despite the Rebbe's notoriously calming presence, despite the evidence that he was worth time out of the dreamlife of Menachem Schneerson, and despite being told what anyone else, faithful or not, would smile at having been told by any revered seer: that there was someone he was actually *meant* to be with… Just despite and despite and despite some more, my father. His soul was so bright with defiance that if he had not, with all his heart, believed there was such a woman as the Rebbe spoke of (despite *himself*, my father did believe there was such a woman, *and* with all his heart, and exactly as the Rebbe envisioned her, however the Rebbe envisioned her), he would have prayed to Adonai—Who at that time he did not love at all—to create her, for how could he ever get to experience the thrill of disobediently scorning her if she didn't exist?

He asked Rebbe Schneerson, "How will I know who she is?" and Rebbe Schneerson who, signposts pointed to and message delivered, was already making his way back to the chupa, looked over his shoulder and said, "I've told you everything already. You'll know."

So it was a great blessing that my parents fell in love at a distance. From 11:30 to 11:40 a.m. each Monday and Wednesday of the fall quarter of his first year at law school, my father's blood would jump and jump as he, on a bench across the street, pretending to prep for his 11:45 Introduction to Contracts class, watched my mom smoke cigarettes at the corner of 57th and Ellis while she waited for the university shuttle to take her to her field-placement at the hospital.

"The sight of her made me stupid," he begins, whenever I get him to tell me the story. "Twice a week for eight weeks, I'd spend ten minutes convinced I would die if she boarded the shuttle before I had a chance to speak to her, but at the same time, the idea that I could, in some complete and final way, screw up by saying the wrong thing kept me haunted in stillness on my bench. She made me so stupid, your mother, that it didn't even occur to me that I could get closer to her without saying anything—I mean, she was at a shuttle stop. Why did I not think to cross the street and wait beside her for the shuttle and let things 'take their course'? That would have been the smart thing to do. If I crossed the street and nothing took its course, *then* I could worry about what to say and how to say it, you know? But I was so stupid I didn't even think to act like I had a shuttle to wait for… And I don't mean to give you the impression that I didn't think your mother was interested in me. If I'd thought she was uninterested, I never would have worried so much—the prospect of screwing *some*thing up is much more daunting than that of screwing nothing up. I *definitely* thought there was something there, and so there was something to lose, you see. But she was such a cool character, your mother, and with the carriage of a princess, that long striking neck of hers, the perfectly straight posture that nonetheless seems relaxed, like her skeleton is made of something stronger than bones. She'd light her cigarettes in strong winds, yet it never took more than a single match. I thought about that a lot. On the third or fourth Monday—we've never been able to agree on which it was—she switched to a disposable lighter, and I thought that was such a shame."

On the ninth Monday, my mother couldn't seem to get her cigarette lit. She flicked and flicked at her lighter, and no flame arose, and she bit her lip and glared at the lighter, as if trying to scare it into working. After a minute of glaring, she flicked some more, but still no flame arose and she bit her lip and tried more glaring.

It was only after my mother's third failure to light her cigarette that my father—by now resigned almost to the point of total blindness by the "stupid" idea that he'd need to come up with the right thing to *say* before approaching her—felt a poke in his finger from the ballpoint in his pocket with which he'd stabbed himself while replacing the lighter he'd only just a few seconds earlier used on the cigarette presently stuck between his lips—a cigarette he hadn't even realized he was smoking—and saw his moment. Lighter in hand, he leapt from his bench, raced across the street, stumbled on the curb.

My mother started laughing.

My father got his footing, glowed red through his beard. "You had better luck with matches," he said to my mother. He held out his lighter.

My mother lit up—one flick—with her own.

"Understand, Gurion," my mother once explained, "that most things between people do not work out according to plan, and so when they do, it can fill you with joy. I was not laughing at your father for stumbling. I was laughing because I had been waiting for weeks for him to approach me and—"

Why didn't you approach him? I said.

"Because I did not want to. Men approach women all the time. That is how men are. If a man approaches a woman, she will only welcome him if she is interested in *him*. If a woman approaches a man, though, the man may become interested by the fact of the approach itself, and I did not want your father to ever wonder if it was *because* I approached him that he fell in love with me. I wanted for him to have no doubts. So you see, I was laughing because we had been noticing one another for eight weeks, and still he had not approached me, and it had been making me crazy since the Wednesday of the third week, at which time I saw he needed an impetus to approach, and I developed my plan. I decided to use a lighter for my cigarettes, thinking: If I use a lighter, my lighter can run out of fuel. If my lighter runs out of fuel, he can come across the street and offer to light my cigarette with *his* lighter."

I said, I don't get why you couldn't just run out of matches, though.

She said, "If you use an opaque lighter, such as the one I was using, you cannot tell how much fuel it contains, and so it says little about you if you run out of fuel. On the other hand, it is stupid to run out of matches, Gurion. It is no hard problem to look in the box before you leave the house and count your matches. If you do not have enough matches, you take more matches or you buy more matches or you suffer your stupidity. I did not want to look stupid. Now, if during those first three weeks, I had not felt, from all the way across the street, a certain thrill pass through your father whenever I lit a cigarette, then I might have dropped my matches in a puddle, rendering them useless, but I suspected—and correctly, according to him—that the source of his thrill was the vision of grace that is witnessed in any person—let alone one who you are falling in love with—who can light a cigarette on the first try with a match in the wind. It always impressed me—that is why I learned to do it. To drop my matches in a puddle, though—that would be clumsy. And clumsiness, though it can at times be endearing, as it was when your father stumbled on the curb, can at other times, especially if the person who is clumsy has previously struck you as graceful, be very disappointing. In any case, ever since switching to the lighter, I had been waiting for it to run out of fuel. I never used a lighter habitually, and I assumed, for whatever reason, that they could not possibly last longer than two or three weeks. I assumed that after two or three weeks, it would be plausible for my lighter to run out of fuel at the shuttle-stop. Five weeks later though, it was still going, and on that ninth Monday, I saw how stupid I was being, how stupid your father had made me: The lighter did not need to actually run out of fuel. It only needed to

as if the lighter had run out of fuel. Plausibility was not an issue.
In a million years, your father would not suspect that I would go to
all the lengths I had gone to in order to get him to come across the
street. If my lighter seemed to run out of fuel, he would assume that it
was a dud or an old lighter. And that is why, when he finally did come
across the street, I lit my cigarette with my lighter—not to make him
feel like a fool who had fallen for a trick, but rather because he had
said, 'You had better luck with matches,' when in fact I had not. It
was not matches that brought him across the street. It was matches
that kept him on the bench."

am Tamar," she'd said to him, extending her hand. But by
that point, even if he did hear her say it, it didn't matter. No matter
how strongly he'd been determined to defy Shneerson's advice, and no
matter how well he might have been able to harness that determination if he had heard her name the moment he first saw her, eight
weeks of longing is too much longing to defy for the sake of defiance.
It is a great blessing my parents fell in love at a distance.

Swallowing the last of his bagel, my dad sat on a stone bench for the
relatives of seven dead people called Farber. "This may be the wrong
cemetery," he said. "Why don't we take a little break." He slapped
the bench, and I sat. Wind moved clouds and the moon was suddenly
huge. Silverflake in the marble of Shua (Beloved Son, 1963–1995)
Farber's gravemarker twinkled, and so did the tips of taller grass-
blades the gravekeeper's mower had failed to chop.

"Spooked?" my dad said.

The moon doesn't spook me, I said.

"You got quiet," he said.

He was the one who got quiet, though.

The wind stopped.

I didn't say anything. It wasn't my turn yet.

My dad scraped a safety match against his side of the bench and
had a cigarette lit before the sulfer finished crackling. He let the
match burn for a few seconds, then flicked his wrist once to snuff the
flame. When the tip quit glowing, he set the dead match between us.
I picked it up and drew a line on my left palm with the black end.
Then I clasped my hands and a line appeared on the right palm as
well. I re-clasped with my thumbs switched and each of my palms

had a slanty X in the center. Before I entered kindergarten, I used to go to the library with my mom some mornings, and she taught me the X-palm action so I wouldn't get bored when I waited outside with her while she smoked. It took me almost a whole year to master. If you don't make the first line thick enough, then the second line won't be dark enough to cross the first line on the re-clasp; but if you press too hard when you draw the first line, the matchtip crumbles all at once, and you end up with no lines, let alone two X's. My dad couldn't perform the X-palm action. That is what he said. I never saw him try, though, and while I watched him smoke, I thought: Maybe he only pretends he can't.

He pointed the cherry of his cigarette at my uneaten bagel, said, "Nu?"

You want me to give it to you? I said.

"Are you going to eat it?"

It's chometz, I said.

"For you, maybe."

And for you, I said.

"And so you won't give it to me?"

I said, Do I have to?

"You don't *have* to."

I said, I'm not going to give it to you unless I have to.

"It would be a shame to waste a fresh bagel," he said.

It would be a shame to eat chometz on Passover, I said. When you say it would be a shame to waste a bagel, but that I don't have to do anything, but that you would like me to give you chometz to eat on Passover and I am trying to honor you because you're my father, but that the way to honor you might be to help you break the law on Passover, it is impossible for me to figure out the right thing to do, and that is also a shame.

And that is when my dad started laughing at me. It was the same edgy laugh he'd laughed at the table, and I saw that Yuval wasn't what made him laugh it—Yuval wasn't there anymore—but the four cups of wine. Whereas the sacrament had made Yuval jovially wobble, it had made my dad sad, wounded-animal sad. I didn't like him that way. He was weaker that way. He was wrong that way. He was not supposed to be wrong or get weaker, so I tried to correct him. I told him what I thought to be true.

I said, I think you killed both of those men.

He stopped laughing.

I said, I think that is good.

"You think it's *good?*" he said.

I said, It's what I would have done, if I could have.

My father said, "The second man had no gun, Gurion. There were three of us and one of him."

You did what you had to do to stop him, I said.

"And if I told you he caught fire only after he'd been laid out on the pavement by Rolly and Yuval?"

I said, If you set him on fire while he was near the girl, she would have caught on fire. It was smart of you to wait.

"And if I told you that I only spoke the sephirot once, when the first man held his gun on us?"

Why do you keep saying "if I told you," Aba? Why are you talking like a lawyer to your son? You're telling me what *happened*, this isn't hypothetical, and I will not be confused by your 'if I told you's, and Ema won't be able to confuse me later either. Two men were raping a girl and you killed them by speaking the sephirot once. That is what you're telling me. Good. It is good. I'm telling you it's good. And I'm telling you it's even more miraculous than if you'd spoken the sephirot twice, because it means that you didn't just make fire with words, and you didn't just do it to two men with a single utterance, but the fire you made was a strategic kind of fire that waited to burn the second man until he was away from the girl.

"By the time the second man caught fire," said my father, "he was subdued and defenseless. That is not *strategic.* There was no reason for him to die."

He'd been raping that girl, I said.

"Who said it was rape?" my father said.

I said, Please stop lawyering me! This is the Talmud, Aba. Be earnest here.

He laughed the edgy laugh. "So how did you know then? I'm asking you."

I said, Sara called it 'struggling.' She called it that because Yuval called it that when he told her the story. He would've called it 'mugging' if it was mugging and 'murdering' if it was murdering and 'beating' if it was beating, but he called it 'struggling' because he didn't want to say 'rape' to his daughter. They were raping that girl, I said, and that makes them rapists. I said, They had to die.

"They raped, and so I should murder?"

It wasn't murder, I said. It was killing.

"Enough with the eye for an eye business, Gurion. Even if that *were* a just system, rape does not end life, and so the life-taking was unjust, and so the life-taking was a murder." In Hebrew, he said, "Why are you walking away from me?"

Over my shoulder, I answered him in Hebrew, and it was Hebrew we spoke for the rest of the conversation. I said, Am I the simple son? Why do you talk to me like I'm simple, like I need protection from truth?

"You're eight years old," he said. "You need protection from a lot."

I can face down anything.

"It's not about what you're faced with," said my father. "Believe it or not, even those without soldiers for mothers can be safe from that which attacks from the front: they can run, you see, or hide. The attacks you need protection from don't come from the front. They creep up behind you."

You mean like the story of how you killed those two men? I said. I said, *That* one seems to have creeped up in *front* of me. *That* one seems to have been hiding behind another story, which was hiding behind a third story, which was hiding behind a blind spot pretending to be no story at all.

"And now that the story is before you, you misunderstand it. You try to make it simple. You never should have heard it."

You did not commit murder, I said. I said, You killed men who were better killed.

"They should have been jailed."

No, I said. They should have been raped by angels, but angels don't rape. And you couldn't rape them because that would defile you and displease Hashem. Plus it's gross. And to imprison a man is torture, and torture defiles the torturer as rape does the rapist. It would displease Hashem.

"You're telling me murder pleases Him?"

I said, I'm talking about killing, not murder, please stop saying 'murder,' and no, I do not believe that killing ever pleases Him, but killing is necessary, and so killing fails to *displease* Him. At the very least, it does not displease Him as much as the rape or torture of a rapist would, and surely it displeases him less than a rapist who goes unpunished.

"That is not justice. To take someone's life because you don't know what else to do with him is not just, is not killing, is murder," my father said. "Every tyrant throughout history has claimed—"

Don't start with the reasoning of tyrants, please. Your tyrants are straw-men and I'm not a jury and I'm not a tyrant. A tyrant wants peace. He takes lives to make peace, for in peace he's secure, and free to grow stronger without interference, free to take lives—to take lives *by murder*—without interference. So whatever brings peace, the tyrant calls justice. That doesn't make it so. Justice is not for tyrants to define.

"No," said my father, "just tyrannical gods."

Hashem is not tyrannical.

"He made a world full of tyrants, a world short on justice."

He made the only world we know.

"But how can you believe He is perfect, Gurion? How can you believe His Law is perfect? How can you call perfect an all-powerful being who makes a world where there is rape and there is murder? Will you tell me He works in mysterious ways? Have I raised a Christian child?"

Hashem is not perfect, I said, and I've never said He was perfect. I said, He is not all-powerful, either. I said, Only His Law is perfect. His Law and His intentions.

"Isn't that blasphemy? You make Him sound like a person."

I said, No person can make a universe, or destroy one; he can at best repair it, and at worst he can damage it. And when I say that Hashem is not all-powerful, I am not saying He isn't more powerful than us—He *is* more powerful than us; He is the *most* powerful. And when I say He isn't perfect, I am not saying He isn't *good*—He *is* good. He is at least as good as we are. It is because He is good, and because He is so powerful, that He has the potential to become as perfect as His Law. He *helped you*, Aba. Why can't you see that?

My dad pulled hard on his cigarette and I could not tell if smoke made him squint, or disappointment.

I said, If by speaking like Hashem you killed one man more than you meant to have killed, then why not understand that your failure was in what you *meant* to do, rather than in what you did? Why not decide that it was righteous to kill the second man? Why not that you are so righteous that even when you think you've made a mistake, you couldn't have? Why not think that you can't help but enact justice? Because that is what I think. I think you did right. I know it.

"You continue to miss the point," my father told me. "The man who threatened us with the gun—I did what I could to stop him, but I should not have known how to stop him that way. Had I not known how to stop him that way, then I would have had to have found another way, and that other way would not have cost the rapist his life."

If you didn't know how to use the sephirot, you might have been shot dead, I said.

"Or I might not have, Gurion. There were three of us there, plus the girl. Would the gunman have shot all of us? Would he have shot even one of us, knowing that he would then have to shoot all of us? It is unlikely."

You don't know that, I said. I said, The potential—

"Our neighbors don't like me, Gurion. They wish me ill. They vandalize our home because I defend the rights of those they despise. Yet they know I'm human, and a father, and so they know that the surest way to harm me would be to harm you. Potentially, one of them could go crazy, like that boy who shot Rabin in Israel. Potentially, one of them could go crazy and try to harm you. Should I kill them all to prevent it? Would you suggest I do that? Because I would not do that. It is dangerous to exist in the world. To exist is to be threatened. We must live with threats."

I said, That contradicts everything you said before about protection from sneak-attacks! And a loaded gun pointed at you by a criminal is far more threatening than a gun in a store that might get bought and loaded and walked over to your house and used on your son and you know it. I said, If the danger wasn't real, you would not have done what you did.

"How can you know so much," said my father, "and hear so much, and speak so pristinely, and meanwhile be so completely muddled, boychical? How is it that your loyalty enables you to justify everything your father does, but you go deaf when he's speaking to you? I am telling you that what I did was wrong and you have to trust that I am correct, if for no other reason than I am your father and you are to honor me, and to honor me—I'm telling you—you have to be a mensch. You do not need to prove to me that you are a good *son*. I believe it, Gurion. You are a good son. And I am glad that you are a good son, but a good son is not necessarily a good human being. A good son is just a son who is loyal to his father, and loyalty is not in itself goodness, and a good father would never teach his son otherwise. I want you to understand that. If you want to honor me, you will allow that I was wrong to take that man's life. You will call it a mistake, and after accepting it as a mistake, you will forgive me my mistake, rather than claiming it a victory. You will love me *despite* my mistake. You will cease to be my apologist and... Aye, Gurion, I'm sorry. I thought we were talking—I'm sorry, Gurion. I got a little carried away. Come on. Why are you crying on poor Michael Weinberg?"

There were a lot of reasons why I was crying: my father was angry at me; he was disappointed in me; he was worried about me; he used a Yiddish endearment; he believed he was a murderer; he kept trying to protect me from things I could protect myself from; and by calling me an apologist, he was calling me a bad scholar. Despite his perfect intentions, despite his saying everything that he was saying out of love for me, he was wrong and I was right. I was crying because he was not God and I was not Avraham. I was crying because I saw that to honor him, I would have to disobey him—that to honor him would be to disobey him—and it is sad to learn you have to disobey your favorite man.

I let him squeeze and play-punch my arms and my shoulders while he delivered a light, singsong monologue about tears and the grass atop the grave of poor Michael Weinberg; whether the water of the tears would grow the grass more than the salt of them would kill the grass or the salt would be the victor; whether the two would cancel each other out; whether the salt content of the tears was negligible, and what, if anything, that might say about the power of the tears; whether the tears themselves might be negligible and what asking that question might say about the fitness of the father asking it; whether or not the monologue was intentionally symbolic and whether or not one could be *un*intentionally symbolic while delivering a monologue; and if one could not be unintentionally symbolic, could one be intentionally but un*know*ingly symbolic; can a man have intentions he doesn't know he has?

And so on til I stopped crying.

On the walk back to the Forems', I gave my uneaten bagel to a homeless black guy on Western. The black guy was standing a couple feet away from two homeless white guys. I didn't give the bagel to the white guys because I worried they were Jews, which meant, I reasoned, that the bagel would harm them. Then I felt dumb about it because the black guy might have been a Jew like me, even though it was statistically less likely. And then I felt even dumber because statistics were irrelevant because even if the black guy *was* a Jew, he was starving, and Hashem should not have had a problem with me feeding a starving Jew chometz. He should, if anything, *prefer* that among three starving men, I would choose to feed the Jew, regardless of what I was feeding him. And if I was wrong, and that was not what He preferred, then He and I would already have had so many more other problems I didn't even know about that to spend time worrying about a bagel and whether or not some guy I gave it to was Jewish seemed pretty wasteful. In the big scheme of things. So I stopped worrying. I held my dad's hand and let myself be tired.

Although she favored a far less modest look—t-shirts and jeans or fatigue pants, if not tank-tops and shorts or cotton dresses that quit above the knee—my mother, who never paid attention to weather forecasts, had, on the day before she was to meet my father's parents, bought for the occasion an ankle-length skirt of unbreathing fabric and a blouse that buttoned up to her chin and down to her wrists. This was springtime, and Chicago, and despite it having been wintery on the day she'd purchased the clothing, the temperature climbed forty-five degrees over the ensuing twenty-four hours. My mom did own other slightly less formal, far less constricting items that she wore to the hospital, but those clothes were at her apartment in Hyde Park, whereas she was at my father's apartment on the other side of the city, in Uptown. She had Fridays off and had spent Thursday night there, as had become her habit, and by the time it occurred to her that she would suffocate in the clothing she'd bought, she and my father had only half an hour to get to my grandparents' house; even if she'd had enough money to buy a new outfit at a local thrift store—the only kind of store there was back then in Uptown that didn't sell liquor, candybars, or used saxophones—there was just no time to do it.

So she frummed up as originally planned, and over the course of the two-mile walk to his parents' house, my dad, nervous himself, attempted to lighten the situation with one-liners that failed to hit til he came upon, "At least the material's too thick to shvitz through," at which point my mother, bent at the knees with gallows laughter, turned her head and saw that she had, in fact, shvitzed through the fabric that covered her left underarm, and began to cry.

They got to my grandparents' a few minutes early, only to find my grandmother behind schedule. In order to finish the cooking before sundown, she needed help in the kitchen.

"We're going to have to use the pressure cooker because we are under pressure. Do you know how to use a pressure cooker, honey?"

"Yes," my mother said, dabbing a damp handkerchief behind her ears.

"And how are you with a chicken?" my grandma said.

"I fix a nice chick-chicken," said my mother, the stutter the only evidence of the gasp she'd otherwise stifled upon realizing, mid-sentence, that the chicken she was committing to would be a kosher one.

My grandma said, "You don't sound so sure," and my father, who did not yet know about the Six-Day War chicken trauma, and who was still in the kitchen at the time, believed his mother had said so lightheartedly.

My mother, on the other hand, was confident that "You don't sound so sure" = "Are you telling me that you expect my son to spend his life with a woman who balks at the thought of cooking a nice kosher chicken in a pressure cooker on Shabbos?" = "Do you expect me to believe that you are presenting yourself honestly in that high-collared get-up when already a rash is forming on that delicate neck of yours?" = "With your skin so dark, and my son's so light, how can you even consider bringing my grandchildren into the world?"

"I'm sure," my mom said.

She was shown the vegetables and the knives, the spicerack and the pressure cooker, and then she was shown the chicken. "Will you poke it just to double-check it's thawed?" said my grandmother.

My mom, a soldier, a killer, poked the hairy chicken with the knuckles of her clenched fists and got to work. She prepped the chicken with the spices, pressure-cooked the chicken with the vegetables, and set the chicken on the chicken-dish when the chicken was finished cooking. By the time they all sat down to eat, she had performed so many compulsive eyelid-checks that the small bit of mascara she'd applied that afternoon was smudged like warpaint.

"I looked like a harlot," she always tells me. "Tell him, Judah. I looked like a cheap harlot."

And "Of harlots I know only what I've read in books and seen through the windshield on North Avenue," responds my father. "So a harlot if she says so, boychic; but if a harlot, the most expensive harlot in the history of man, and of that I can be sure, for the one thing about which all the books agree is that the less a harlot looks a harlot, the more that harlot costs."

"You are such a sweet man," my mother says to him, "but so superstitious. He is so sweet and superstitious, Gurion, that in the cause of protecting me from the evil eye his mother was casting upon the shvitzing black harlot her son had brought to her sabbath dinner table, he actually convinced himself I looked as nice as I wished I did. I did not."

"You looked gorgeous!"

"He is crazy."

However my mother looked, and whatever my paternal grandmother thought of her, this is where the story of that Shabbos bends its knees for the leap into slapstick that it must make to remain true. It is at this point in their telling of the story that my father lights a cigarette to share with my mother, to pass back and forth with her like soldiers in a forest, the filter pinched between thumb and pointerfinger, the cherry pointed down, their cupped hands turned to shield the orange light from the eyes of snipers who hide behind anterior trees; it is at this point that my parents lean toward me and fictionalize unabashedly and I lean toward them and listen without questioning and we get so involved that I sometimes take the cigarette from one of them and put it to my own lips before any of us becomes aware of what I'm doing; this is the point at which we three conspire. We agree to act as if what's about to get said actually took place. Hardly any of it did, but the meaning of what my parents describe is truer than the meaning that would come across if they attempted to describe what actually happened—what actually happened was, I am led to believe, mostly unlistenable, if not untellable: a series of uncomfortable glances cast in near-silence, a few cutting remarks that echoed off the soup tureen, the damage of these remarks magnifying even as the decibels diminished. What actually happened, I am led to believe, was not funny at all, was painful and dull. Yet so would have been the life of the tramp in Chaplin's *City Lights*, if the tramp were not fictional; so would have been the life of the blind girl the tramp loved, if the girl were not fictional; so would have been the operation the tramp struggled to pay for and the struggle to pay for it, were the operation and the struggle not fictional. And that operation never would have worked if it weren't fictional, and even if by some miracle it had worked, the tramp would never have been able to get the money for it. But in *City Lights*, the tramp does get the money, the operation does succeed, and everything eventually works out for the lovers. And all of it *should* be true. And so in a way it *is* true. And they are worth crying for, a non-fictional tramp and the non-fictional blind girl he loves—in real-life such a doomed couple would deserve our tears. Yet had Chaplin presented them as they would have been had they not been fictional, we would turn away after five minutes instead of staying til the end and weeping as we should. I once asked my father: Why do we go to the symphony hall once a year to see *City Lights* with orchestral accompaniment at seventy-five dollars a head? "Because it is the greatest movie ever made," he said. And what makes it the greatest? "It is the truest," he told me. And why do we only weep at the end of the movie? Why do we weep once we know that everything will be alright? "We weep because the only way everything could ever be alright is in fiction. We weep because what we've seen can't be true, no matter how badly we wish it were. We weep at the truth." And so to go challenging the *facts* in this portion of the story—like some lawyer, some headshrinker—would be to act against faith, to act against truth, to dishonor my mother and father. To monkey with the slapstick would be to lie, and I will not lie.

However my mother's mascara might have made her appear at the dinner table, no one has ever argued over whether or not some dried chili peppers had been cooked into the nice kosher chicken. They had been. As for why they had been, there were two opposing claims.

My parents': My mother had cooked chili peppers into the chicken in good faith, for the sake of better flavor.

My grandparents': My mother had cooked chili peppers into the chicken in bad faith, for the sake of worse flavor.

And why would my grandparents make such a claim? Why would they believe that my mother would want to make the chicken taste bad? Opinions vary.

"Because she wasn't Lebuvitcher," my father says.

"Because they knew I was taking their son away," says my mother, "and they thought I was out to destroy them."

"If she didn't ruin the chicken on purpose," my grandmother said to my father from across the Shabbos table, "then why won't she eat any?"

"She told you, already," my father replied. "She doesn't like to eat chicken."

"What does that mean?" said my grandfather. "She's a vegetarian? Are you a vegetarian, Tamar? And if you're a vegetarian, are you the kind of vegetarian who eats fish?"

"I am not a vegetarian," my mother said. "And I do eat chicken—you misunderstood. I don't eat *kosher* chicken."

"You're sitting at our dinner table and telling us that not only do you eat traif, but you eat traif *exclusively*?" said my grandmother. "You're saying you refuse to eat that which *isn't* traif? I have a hard time understanding."

"I am not exclusive with traif," my mother said, "I—"

"She's *not* exclusive with traif!" said my father. "She's eating from every other dish on the table. Every other dish on the table is as kosher as the chicken. I'm sorry, I interrupted you, Tamar—"

"It's okay," my mom said, "I—"

"Is it because she's Ethiopian? Is it Ethiopian Jews, they don't eat kosher chicken?" said my grandfather.

"If she doesn't eat it," said my grandmother, "why would she cook it? Why would she think she would know how to cook it and now the meat is ruined?"

"I think it's delicious," my father said.

"Oh, Judah, it is not delicious," said my grandmother.

"I'm telling you I think it is," my father said.

"It is not delicious, Judah, not remotely," said my grandfather. "It is not remotely delicious and you should stop eating it, or else your stomach will tear apart."

"Chili peppers!" said my grandmother. "Where did she even find them?" said my grandfather. "Why do we even have them?" he said. "They came with the spice rack," my grandmother said, "I should throw them away? I suppose that I should now. I should throw them away. I'll throw them away. I should have before, but that shouldn't be so. That should not have been so. It never should have been so. Of all things, chili peppers! Peppers she puts! Peppers on chicken!" "On chicken!" said my grandfather. "On Shabbos!" "And for what?" "For what? For what he wonders. For what is: To hurt us!" "To hurt us!" "And why hurt us?" "Yes, why hurt *us*?" "Because we were nice enough to—" "Because we were foolish enough to—"

"Enough!" my father said. "No one is trying to hurt you, and you are being unkind."

"I am not trying take your son away from you," my mother interjected.

"Excuse me?"

"I am saying please do not worry," my mother said. "I am not trying to take Judah away from you."

"*Please do not worry? I am not trying to take Judah away from you?*" said my grandfather. "If not to take him away, then what are you trying to do with him?" said my grandfather. "And why should you tell us not to worry about a thing about which we have heretorfore expressed no worry if not precisely because we *should* worry; if not because when you say to us 'Don't worry,' you are making a threat, a veiled threat, true, but a threat nonetheless and that threat is exactly what you say it isn't, which is to say that it is nothing *other* than a threat to take Judah away from us and... and... I have lost my antecedent... I have lost my own antecedent, young lady, but I have not lost my mind, I have *not* lost my mind, not *mine*, and what it is that I mean to ask you is: Why else, when we have expressed no worry about Judah being taken away by you, would you say such a thing as you have said about not trying and don't worry, if not to suggest that we *should* in fact worry and that you *are* trying? Why say it that way when it could be much more easily expressed if you just spoke the one word over and over very quickly so it sounded like: Worry! Worry! Worry!? Why not just be forthright and honest and say to us: Worry!?"

"And why *aren't* you trying to take Judah away?" my grand-mother said. "He's not good enough to take away? You're looking for someone smarter, maybe? Someone handsomer? As if you even *could* take him away! You should be so lucky. You should be so lucky, youshouldbesolucky."

"She should be so lucky!" "Yes, she should *be* so lucky!"

"What is it you sound like?" my father said. "Robots," my father said.

"Yes, *she* should be so lucky!" "Yes, she *should* be so lucky!" "No, she should *not* be *so* lucky, or else she would be very lucky, which is not a thing I would want, given what so much of her luck would mean for us!" "We would be *un*lucky, then! You will *not* be so lucky with our son!"

"A pair of shtetl robots clucking," my father said.

"Should she be so *luck*y, we should be *un*lucky is the thrust of the matter." "Luck for she is no luck for we is the thrust." "That *is* the thrust."

"I want you to be my wife," my dad whispered to my mother.

"When?" my mother said.

"Her luck would be our tragedy is the *real* thrust." "A *tragic* thrust for us, not her!" "No: not tragic for her, but *luck*y!" "Lucky for *her*, that thrust!"

"Next Saturday night," my father said.

"The *worst* of luck is what we should be wishing her."

"You are drunk with defiance," my mother told my father.

"The worst of luck is what we *are* wishing her."

"Then a year from next Saturday, so you know I'm sincere," said my father. "In the meantime, live with me."

"...the thrust!" "...should be so lucky!"

"I will," my mother said. "And I will."

And my parents rose from their chairs.

My father bowed and my mother curtsied.

My father set his right hand on my mother's waist and my mother set her left hand on my father's shoulder.

My father clasped her right hand with his left.

With her left my mother clasped his right one back.

And the dancing began.

At first they did a mid-tempo waltz: one step for every *thrust* clucked, two for every three *lucky*s. They dipped and spun away past the table.

The musicians, insulted, launched into a furious cha-cha.

And my parents furiously cha-cha-ed.

They cha-cha-ed in the living room, and they cha-cha-ed in the foyer, but no matter how far away from the stage they went, the clucking grew louder and faster. Before it could deafen them, they cha-cha-ed out the door.

On the stoop the night was quiet.

And in the quiet on the stoop they did a box-step.

And while they box-stepped in the night, they told stories.

In fifty-three weeks and a day they would marry.

5
THE ARRANGEMENT

Tuesday, November 14, 2006
Lunch–Last Period

THE CAGE

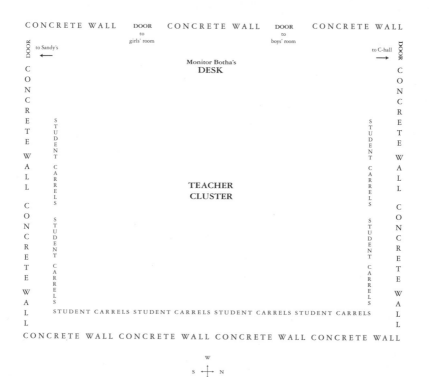

During Lunch-Recess, I sat at the teacher cluster with My Main Man
Scott Mookus, Benji Nakamook, Leevon Ray, and Jelly Rothstein.
Vincie Portite would have normally been there too, but he had a long-time
secret crush on a girl in normal classes—he wouldn't tell us who—and once
or twice a week he'd leave the Cage for Lunch-Recess in order to look at
her. No one who was there with me that day had to be except for Jelly. She
was on two weeks cafeteria- and recess-suspension for telling the hot-lunch
ladies there was a corn on her wiener and it hurt. After she said it, her milk
carton dumped out on Angie Destra's shoes and Angie cried onto the sneeze-
guard over the pudding. People started calling her "There'sNoUse Angie
Destra," but the name didn't last because it took too much time to say it,
and so it got shortened to "NoUse Angie" and "There'sNo Angie," which
became T.N.A., and that's the name that stuck because it sounds like T'n'A,
and Angie Destra didn't have any.

Sometimes milk just falls off the tray, and that kind of milk is spilled milk, not poured milk. Spilled milk's the kind that got on Angie Destra, but people believed Jelly poured milk on Angie, and Jelly wanted for them to persist in that belief since she didn't like to bite people, and wasn't getting uglier—not even a little. Jelly Rothstein was a Sephardic beauty in the loudest, sharpest, meanest kind of way. She was dark-eyed and black-haired and wholly unadorned, but light found a way to reflect off her whitely, giving the impression she wore a diamond nosestud and glittery makeup, that silvery bangles clashed and clanged on her wrists, that silvery ear-hoops bounced next to her neck. Her shape was narrow, but she wasn't skinny so much as she was taut—even in gym clothes, her body called out—and her skin was the brown of lead whitegirls in movies that take place at sleepaway camps in Wisconsin. Like her older sister Ruth, she was one of the sexiest girls at Aptakisic, and everyone knew it, though few would admit it because, unlike Ruth, most girls despised her, the Jennys and Ashleys especially. Why they despised her is hard to explain—it started with her face. It was not a cheery face. Jelly had a way of squinting at the person she was talking to, a way of sucking her teeth, of cocking her chin and twisting her lips, and whereas to me these actions of her face revealed the lithe intelligence at labor behind it, to some—to many—they looked like contempt. This isn't to say she didn't harbor contempt for most kids at school—she certainly did—but rather that even toward those she was friends with—me, for example—she made the same faces, and if I had to guess, she'd always made those faces, and by making those faces, she had, unknowingly, alienated herself, which eventually caused her to hold in real contempt the kids from whom she was alienated. After all, she must have thought, what had *she* ever done to deserve their mistreatment? whenever they spoke, she had paid attention, and she'd even thought hard about what they were saying.

What all of this meant was that guys at Aptakisic who weren't in the Cage were not supposed to like Jelly, and so those who were drawn to her—most guys were—would be cruel from a distance, shouting out "bitch" or "prude" or "slut," or, if they found themselves inside her orbit, would shove or molest her with bookrockets, ass-grabs, titfalls, or pinchings. That's why she'd bite when people got close, especially guys. She'd found that when she hit or choked or kicked, it led to more touching as often as not, but biting through skin, drawing blood with her teeth—that never failed to back off her aggressors. She'd bitten enough people that it was mostly automatic; even her friends had to approach her pretty slowly. Yet she didn't like to do it—she wasn't crazy—and, as already stated, she wasn't getting uglier; that's why she wanted people to believe that she'd poured that milk. She figured they'd try harder not to get too close to her, and then she wouldn't need to bite them as often.

But letting people believe that her spilling was a pouring was a bad idea, the oldest kind of bad idea in the world.

On the sixth day of Creation, right after Hashem made Adam from earth, He told him that if he ate from the Tree of Knowledge of Good and Bad, he would surely die. But later that day, when Hashem made Eve, He didn't teach her the law; He told Adam to teach her.

According to mishnah, Adam told her, "If you eat from the Tree of Knowledge of Good and Bad, you will surely die. Even touching the tree will kill you."

That same afternoon, Eve was standing by the Tree of Knowledge of Good and Bad, and the serpent, who was still an unscaly biped, came up to her, saying, "Why don't you eat a fruit from this healthy-looking tree?" And Eve said, "If I eat from it, I'll surely die." The serpent said, "No. You'll become like God." And Eve said, "My husband told me what God told him. He told me that even if I touch it, I'll die." The serpent knew the Law, and so knew that wasn't accurate, what Adam had told Eve about touching the tree. So the serpent plucked a fruit from the tree and held it out to her. He said, "I touched it. I'm not dead." Eve said, "The Law is different for serpents."

And the serpent shoved Eve and she fell on the tree. "See?" said the serpent. "You're still alive."

Then the serpent waved the fruit in the face of Eve.

"You'll become like God," the serpent said.

And Eve ate the fruit and she wasn't dead.

She brought the fruit to Adam and Adam ate it. Not because Eve told him it was a regular fruit, though—she loved him and so wouldn't lie to him. She told him the fruit was forbidden fruit and Adam ate the fruit anyway because he'd confused himself when he'd twisted the words of God to his wife. He'd confused himself into believing that words from God were the same as words from man. God had told Adam one thing, Adam changed it to another thing, and then Adam forgot what the original thing was; he forgot that the original thing was different from what he'd turned it into. So while Eve was pushing the bitten fruit in Adam's face, Adam thought: Eve is not dead, I'll become like God.

But just as God hadn't told Adam that it was against the Law to touch the tree, He hadn't said the fruit of the tree was fast-acting poison either. He'd said, "If you eat from the Tree of Knowledge of Good and Bad, you will surely die." "You will surely die." ≠ "You will *instantly* die." Adam, however, had concluded it did, and since Eve hadn't died instantly after eating the fruit, Adam assumed that God had either lied to him or been incorrect.

The point of the mishna is that it's even worse to twist the wording of a Law than it is to break that Law, even if you twist it to protect someone you are in love with. If you twist the wording once, it becomes hard to stop twisting it. It's because Adam twisted it that people die. And that's why it's banced to call Eve a temptress. Eve was reasonable, and when it came to Jelly calling spilling pouring, the problem was that she would not always have milk available to pour, and even if she happened to have milk to pour, she probably wouldn't have it in her to pour it; that's not the way she was. She'd never once poured milk on anyone; she'd only ever spilled it.

So even if people didn't go near Jelly for a while because they were afraid of getting milk poured on them, all it would take was one person to accidentally get close to Jelly and *not* get milk poured on them. After that happened, she would have to bite people a lot more often than she would have had to bite them before people ever thought she was a milk-pourer, and I explained that to her the day after the incident with Angie Destra. I told Jelly that letting people believe she was a milk-pourer was like saying that *touching* the tree was suicide, since even after the next time she bit somebody, people who weren't there to see the biting would think, "It was said of her that she poured milk on shoes and it was not true that she poured milk on shoes. Now it is being said that she bites those who stand close to her. Why should I believe it?" And they wouldn't believe it, even though it was true—Jelly always bit people who got too close to her—and more lies would spread. They would spread without cease. There's no killing lies. Lies uncovered change shape, but never die. When Eve got pushed onto the tree by the serpent, she didn't think, "What Adam told me about touching the tree was untrue." She thought, "What God told Adam about touching the tree was untrue." Adam's lie made God's truth look like a lie, but God never lies. Still, it was a very normal mistake for Eve to make. It is the kind of mistake that happens all the time. I'd said that to Jelly, too, and she'd said, "You're telling me I've been a bad Jew?"

Israelite, I'd said.

"I've been a bad Israelite?"

No. Of course not. Where'd you get that? *You* didn't lie. I'm just saying that—

"So what can I do, then? What should I do? 'There's no killing lies,' right? It's too late to fix it. What can I do, Gurion?"

Nothing. You're right. It's too late to fix it. Don't get upset. You're not a bad Israelite. You're good. You're great. I think you're great. So does everyone else, I said.

"Right. Sure. Everyone. Great."

Jelly had a soft thermal lunchbox with a shoulder strap. Inside it was lettuce in a tupperware cube, clingwrapped croutons, ziplocked chicken strips, oil-based dressing in a babyfood jar. Her lunch preparations were intricate as usual. She unwrapped the croutons, put some in her hand, and made a loose fist. Then she shook her fist around just above the salad and the croutons came out of the bottom fist-hole a couple at a time for a sprinkling effect. Once she was finished spreading all the croutons, she opened the chicken baggie and laid out the strips on the salad in a hexagon. Then she uncapped the babyfood jar and tipped it so a thin line of dressing came out. She guided the line over the salad so that each part of the salad got the same amount of dressing on it.

Nakamook told her, "You pay so much attention."

Jelly screwed the cap back onto the jar. She said, "I think I will be a chef." She had a real fork, a full-sized metal one, and she stabbed it into a wad of lettuce.

I never wanted to bring lunch-things to school that I would have to bring back home. That was why I didn't carry a lunchbox. Plus you couldn't pop a lunchbox. In my brown paper bag was a peanut-butter sandwich on raisin-bread toast. It was wrapped in aluminum foil instead of a baggy because toast got damp in a baggy and I liked it to crunch. I also had baby carrots and cheesepuffs and a box of BerryBerryGood–flavored FruitoDrinko.

Nakamook didn't have any lunch. I didn't ask him why because I knew he'd say his mom forgot to pack it for him again and also forgot to give him hotlunch money. I handed him half my sandwich and carrots, but it didn't make me any less sad until I got angry that I felt sad because I should have just felt angry because Nakamook's mom hadn't forgotten to do anything: she was punishing him.

Starvation was a cruel punishment to inflict on any son, but to inflict starvation on Benji Nakamook was not only cruel—it was snakey. If his mom knew him at all, she knew her cruelty would lead him to lie; that he would, out of loyalty to her, tell lies to keep her cruelty a secret. If she knew him at all, she knew Benji kept his secrets tighter than anyone. That was the Nakamookian way. It was a tragically ironic way. His secrets had made him into a person who was willing to hurt anyone and anything he was not close with that got in his path or in the path of the people he *was* close with, but he could not get too close to the people he was close with, because to get any closer would mean telling his secrets, and Benji was scared his secrets would hurt the people who he was close with, so he'd hurt himself by keeping the secrets, and that was a secret, too. That is how my mom explained it to me after we all had dinner together. Right after Benji told her he'd avenge any offense against my person, my mom said that she liked how he ate everything on his plate like he'd never been fed a hot dinner before, and Benji stopped talking and looked like he would cry.

My mom was pretty much always right about people, and yet, for some reason, I never believed her. At least not at first. What secrets? I'd said. He doesn't have secrets. You're being dramatic.

But then, a couple weeks after he'd come over for dinner (on the morning of my fourth Tuesday at Aptakisic Junior High, exactly five weeks before I fell in love with June), it came clear that Benji did have secrets. This was when he told me not to fight Bam Slokum, and I gave him my word that I wouldn't. He was Darkering SLOKUM DIES FRIDAY on a wall while I stood watch, and I asked him if all such bombs were his—I'd seen more than a handful of SLOKUM DIES FRIDAYs throughout the school—and he told me they were, and in the same breath added, "Bam's my arch-enemy. I don't want you fighting him." So I asked him why he wouldn't want me to fight his arch-enemy, and this is what he told me: "Regarding vengeance and arch-enemies, one must not only be timely but prideful, and pride exacts propriety."

Benji didn't usually talk so kenobi. Whenever he did, I'd just back off. He had read a lot of Shakespeare and Homer and Euripides, and I didn't understand those guys' justice enough to know if he'd actually mastered it or not, so getting Halakhic with Nakamook about things like vengeance was rarely fruitful. It was usually better just to listen to him—he was, after all, the one who first taught me about snat and face—and I'd found that what he said was usually right, even if it didn't seem to make sense sometimes. More important than any of that, though, was Benji was my best friend. By then I'd even given him a copy of *Ulpan*. It is true that the copy was specially doctored—I'd cut out all the Israelite and Adonai parts, changed the title to *Instructions*, and added a directive to burn the document as soon as he was through with it—but still he was the only non-Israelite kid who I'd ever given a copy to. If my best friend didn't want to tell me his own backstory—whether because parts of it caused him pain, or just because he didn't know how to tell it yet—I could understand that, and I didn't want to attempt to pull it from him. Especially not if I could hear it from someone else.

I decided to ask Vincie Portite about it.

We were dressing in the locker-room, and Nakamook was showering—we'd raced from the gym; Vincie had tripped him; Benji was the last kid to get through the door—but Vincie, nonetheless, had whispered, "Keep it fucken down. I'll call you tonight and tell you, okay?"

And he'd called me that night and told me:

Two years earlier, when Bam was in the sixth grade, Nakamook—in fifth—had been *his* best friend. Bam wasn't yet superhero-shaped back then, but his cousin Geoff Claymore, an eighth-grader and legendary shvontz, was gigantic. Claymore took steroids and sometimes kids' lunch money. He'd vow silence to shy girls at parties in darkened basements, then leave hatermarks on their necks and spread sex stories about them. He subjected Bam Slokum to noogies and bookrockets and everyone in sight had to laugh, including Bam, who, if he didn't, would find himself arm-locked or thrown.

Either despite or because of the humiliations Claymore inflicted on him, Slokum worshipped his cousin, hearing any insult to Claymore as an insult to himself. So Nakamook, who hated Claymore, no little bit on behalf of Bam, coiled his anger and kept his mouth shut about it—not because he was scared of Claymore, but because he was loyal to Slokum. A few times, Nakamook even found himself defending Claymore's name by proxy: Someone in earshot of Bam would say something about Claymore's shvontziness, Bam would start a fight, start losing the fight, and Nakamook would help him, siding against the guy who shared his hatred.

One day during the lunch-switch, though, when the fifth- and sixth-graders were going to the cafeteria from indoor recess in the gym, and the seventh- and eighth-graders were going to indoor recess from lunch in the cafeteria, Nakamook and Bam got ahead of everyone to race topspeed down B-Hall. Halfway through the race, Claymore—heading up the crowd that was coming from the opposite direction—tripped Bam, who flew through the air until he got concussed against the corner of a water fountain.

This went well beyond pink-bellies, past petty arm-bars; Bam lay prone, unconscious on the linoleum, blood in his hair oozing down along his cheek, and Benji, who knelt beside him, exploded. He rose and spun and swung on Claymore. Claymore ducked the punch and took half a step back, as if in retreat, but instead he went forward and dropped Benji hard with a kick to the stomach, then pinned him at the elbows and called his mom a wino and slapped him for a while as half the school watched.

Nakamook set fire to Claymore's house that night. The Claymores were all out to dinner, but in court they claimed that Geoff's bedroom light had been left on to scare burglars away. If what they said was true, then Benji was lucky the house burnt to the ground. Had the lightswitches withstood the fire, he might have been convicted of attempted murder as well as arson.

I thought Benji probably did try to murder Claymore, but I didn't know for sure since the story came from Vincie—which isn't to say that Vincie was a liar, just that he definitely wanted to believe that Nakamook had tried to do murder. Whatever he tried or didn't try to do, Benji got sentenced to six months in juvie.

In juvie, his arms—the first things you noticed when you met him— grew long. Comicbook-villain long. But not all thick and knuckle-draggy-looking. Apart from the arms, Nakamook had a build like Tommy Hearns, which kept any thoughts of cavemen far away. Plus, the arms seemed to be set a little bit higher and more forward on his shoulders than most people's arms. If he'd been an actual comicbook villain, he'd have definitely been called the Mantis, and if I was a Thai boxer and I saw a kid endowed with guns like Nakamook's—a kid who could reach nearly as far with an elbow as others his height only could with a fist—I'd teach him to Thai box in a second, just for the potential advancement of the art. Which might be why the guy who taught Benji to Thai box in juvie did so.

Whoever that guy was, he taught him well. Within a week of his return to Aptakisic, Nakamook was sitting wherever he wanted in the Cage. There weren't that many kids in there yet, but the kids who *were* there weren't just slow or hyper or overtalkative—in the early days of the Cage, you had to be violent to get locked in, and those were some of the earliest days. The Cage program had only been adopted a couple months after Nakamook burned Claymore's house down. It might have even got adopted *because* Nakamook burned Claymore's house down. I asked Vincie and he said he didn't know. He said that one day there was no Cage, and then the next day he was in it.

What Vincie did know was that by the time Benji came back to Aptakisic, Bam wasn't only huge, but pals with Claymore. According to Vincie, the pal part surprised Benji, but I don't think it should have. Bam and Claymore were cousins after all, and even if Nakamook hadn't tried to kill one of them, he'd burned down one of their houses. So Bam's only options were extreme: either forsake his best friend or forsake his family. That the best friend in question was Nakamook must have made the decision pretty easy. Some best friends who your people hate, you might stay friends with on the sly and they'll understand; Benji Nakamook was not one of those, and Bam, of all people, would have known that. I'd never met Claymore—he was a sophomore in high school by the time I arrived at Aptakisic—but no matter how much of a shvontz he was, he couldn't have entirely missed the fact that picking on his cousin had set events into motion that led to the burning down of his own parents' house, and so he had to have wanted to right things. Slokum's having grown too large to continue to abuse probably didn't do much in the way of impeding Claymore's decision to befriend him, either.

After Vincie told me Nakamook and Bam had been arch-enemies for two years without ever having fought each other, I still didn't doubt Nakamook's line about the importance of being timely when revenging on arch-enemies. If he were anyone else, I would have. If he were anyone else, I would have thought he was just scared of Bam.

Nakamook fought all the time, though. A lot of people would say he was a bully, but really he was just sensitive. And it is true that he might have beaten you up if you looked at him in a way that he believed was offensive but, unlike a bully, he wouldn't have ever faked being offended just to have occasion to beat you up. He didn't care to damage anyone who hadn't damaged him first. And plus he was like me: fighting was fun for him. The act of it, not just the outcome. It's not the same for a bully. They're not scared of fighting, bullies—that lie only seems true because it describes an irony—but they don't enjoy it much, either. What bullies enjoy is being recognized as dominant. They'd much rather have just won a fight than be fighting one. And though he never fought anyone as big as Bam—no one else at Aptakisic was anywhere near as big as Bam—Nakamook fought some seriously big kids. Like the Flunky. It was hard to imagine him being scared of anyone.

Even if I was wrong, though, and timeliness *was* just an excuse for Nakamook to avoid stepping up to Bam, I couldn't see how Bam would have any better an excuse for not stepping up to Nakamook. Bam didn't fight as often as Benji (or as often as me for that matter), but he had been in enough fights to be as generally feared as Benji, so I knew the excuse couldn't be that he was a pacifist. It wasn't possible that Bam didn't know he was Nakamook's arch-enemy—not with all those SLOKUM DIES FRIDAY bombs everywhere—but maybe he needed some more immediate kind of provocation to fight. Some people were like that—they possessed mellow snat and resilient facial masonry. My dad was like that. Had I been Bam, though, the bombs would have provided me more than enough reason to step up to Nakamook.

I remembered bumping into Bam in Main Hall that morning. I remembered all that brotherly chinning of air and got pissed at myself all over again. Here was Benji, loyal, lunchless Benji, my best friend Nakamook, starved by his mother and yet uncomplaining. How could I act brotherly toward his arch-enemy? How could I give my best friend half my sandwich and carrots, then stiff him on the cheesepuffs? I couldn't, unless I was a dickhead—I wasn't.

I flattened my brown paper bag to make a plate and dropped half a handful of cheesepuffs on it. When I delivered to Benji what remained in the baggie, I had snap-style energy from getting angry, and instead of just pushing it across the table, I flung it at his chest, and without even looking up, he caught it.

Botha, eating hotlunch left-handed at his desk said, "Mind the cheese doodles, Maccabee." It sounded like, "Moinda chase daddles, Makebee." He said it to remind me he was watching. The Cage was set up so we could be watched with great ease by the monitor and the teachers. Everyone in the Cage knew it, always. Except for how they locked you in, that was the main thing that made it the Cage. There was no reason to remind anyone, especially not at Lunch.

I said to Botha, The mind Maccabee, cheese doodles.

I liked that joke. I used the exact same words that Botha had used but the words meant nothing the way I put them in order, and they sounded like they meant something since I said the sentences in the same way as he'd said the originals, and with the same rhythm, and that demonstrated that English words were meaningless by themselves, that they were just lung- and mouth-sounds unless they were in the correct order, which was a paradox because the correctness of the order of a string of words depended on what the words meant, but if correct order was what gave words their meanings, then how could their meanings determine the correctness of the order? No one knew, and no one else thought the joke was funny, either.

Except for Scott Mookus, who told us all, "Ha! Haha! Ha!" That's how he laughed. It was because of the Cocktail Party Syndrome that he didn't have a real laugh. You could get him to do it forever, though, just by doing it back to him.

Nakamook said, "Scott ha ha. Ha ha ha."

Mookus said, "Ha! Haha! Ha!"

Botha said, "Quiet the nonsense." Quoydanawnsinz.

I said, Australia used to be a prison.

"Main Man haha!"

"Haha! Haha!"

Jelly said, "Georgia was a prison."

"Australia's a country," Botha said. "Australia's a contnent."

We didn't respond.

He said, "A whole contnent."

I smelled nasty hotlunch.

Main Man and Leevon had it. I didn't look at what it was. If I looked at their trays and I saw something that I usually liked, I would like whatever it was less the next time I had it because I would think of how bad the smell of the cafeteria version was. If I found out what they were eating and it was something that was one of my favorites, it would be like falling in love with the wrong person; how if you fall in love with the wrong person, then when you fall in love with the right person later on, you will remember the smelly version of being in love and it could threaten to make the good version less good.

When I was wrongly in love with Rabbi Salt's daughter, Esther, I told her I loved her and she said she loved me, too, but after I got kicked out of Schechter we hardly ever saw each other, so I wrote her a poem without a title, which at the time didn't seem half as hammy as it was. I thought it was funny.

> I got my dad
> to get Caller ID
> so I would know when you called.
> They gave us a box.
> It costs five bucks a month
> but it doesn't work—

your number and your name
disappear from the window
the second right before I check it.

On the Shabbos after I got officially kicked out of Martin Luther King Middle School, my family had dinner at the house of the Salts. I passed my poem to Esther under the table during the chicken. She read it through the glass of the tabletop. Then she told me that my poem made her sad and that since I wrote it, it was me who made her sad, and that sadness of the girl was a sure sign of a bad match. Then she broke up with me, but I didn't believe it at first. I thought she was just upset, just talking. She said, "Any bond between two people is only as strong as the desire of the one who wants it the least." We were in the Salts' backyard by then, and a rabbit was watching us. I said *tsst* to the rabbit and the rabbit took off. I repeated what Esther said to me and I noticed that it was not officially correct English because it was only two people. It should have been, "Any bond between two people is only as strong as the desire of the one who wants it *less*." I told Esther about the grammatical problem because I wanted to change the subject because I still didn't think she was serious about breaking up. And then she started crying and, for a second, I thought maybe she was serious about breaking up, but then I thought: No way. We're in love with each other, and people in love with each other might argue, but they don't break up with each other, not when they're in love. And I decided she was crying because it was Rabbi Salt who'd spoken the relationship wisdom to her, and no one likes to think their father is mistaken.

Esther sniffled in a way that I thought was cute because it wasn't gross at all, even though it meant wet snot was moving around inside of her face. The sniffling made me want to touch her sleeve, but I did not touch her sleeve. She was Hasidic, and the sleeve was too close to the hand for them.

So I said, It doesn't matter, Esther, because it sounds better with 'the least.' It's really impossible to know which is the right way to say it, because the problem might not be 'less' and 'the least' but 'any two people.' If you said, 'Any bond between three, four, or five people is only as strong as the desire of the one who wants it the least,' that would have been correct English, but correct English is not usually the strongest kind of English, anyway.

She was wearing a brown scarf that had fringes and she wiped the tears on her cheeks with the fringes mashed together. The rabbit came back and it was staring at her. I threw a woodchip at its head and it ran. I didn't like rabbits at all. They'd stare off like thinkers, but I knew they weren't thinking.

I love you, I told Esther. I said, I don't want to make you cry.

She said, "I don't feel like you love me. Why are you always correcting people? If you didn't correct people so much, we would still be in Schecter together and you never would have written the poem and made me sad with it and then we could still be together."

She wanted me to cry and I was failing. I didn't want to fail. I wanted to cry for her, but I couldn't.

I told her, I'll cry soon.

Esther said, "No you won't. I've seen you cry." She said, "You only cry about crazy things like the Intifadas, and Jonathan getting passed over for David, and Moshe getting banned from Eretz Yisroel. You don't cry about the things you are supposed to cry about." She stopped crying then. It was my turn more than ever. I thought: Esther is being mean to you so that you will cry because it is your turn to cry and you're late.

I said to her, I cry when I'm angry and my dad says something nice in Yiddish.

She said, "That's a crazy thing to cry about, Gurion. It makes no sense."

By then I knew she'd really broken up with me, or that at least she thought she had. Because it wasn't like we stopped being love with each other, I thought, and Esther wasn't even saying we stopped. And if we were still in love, that meant we'd get back together eventually, because that's what you did when you were in love, was be together.

I said, I'm sorry, Esther Salt. I said, I hope we can get back together soon.

"There is nothing to be sorry about. You can't help it," she said. "You just make me sad and it means we are a bad match. I wish we never fell in love with each other."

Rabbi Salt came out on the patio and told us it was time for honeycake. He waited at the sliding glass door for us, and Esther stared at me for an extra second to see if I would cry and I couldn't cry and she went inside ahead of me. When I passed her dad, he put his hand on the back of my neck and squeezed a couple times. It was a warm, rough hand. "My favorite student," he said. "I hear you've been expelled from King. For a fight."

I said, A seventh-grader attacked me and I beat him into submission, then his friends came, seven of them, and I picked up a brick, and right then is when the recess lady came, and everyone said I used the brick on the first kid.

Rabbi Salt said, "You didn't use the brick?"

I said, I don't need a brick for one kid.

"I know," he said. "Relax."

Let me back into Schecter, I said.

"I can't," he said. "It's not up to me."

I said, I want to study Torah with peers.

Rabbi Salt said, "Go to Hebrew School."

I said, Hebrew School is not for scholars.

He said, "Gurion, you need to be realistic. You threw a stapler at Rabbi Unger and everyone knows it. And that email from Kalisch—it's too late now for damage control... Maybe in high school, if you act like a mensch in the meantime, people will forget, but please don't waste your energy on false hope. It will warp you. You'll be lucky if I can get you into this Aptakisic."

I said, What's Aptakisic?

The Rabbi said, "I'm going to speak to your father about it after cake, but my friend Leonard Brodsky—the father of Ben, may Hashem bless his soul—is the principal there. I called him up and he's considering you. The school's in Deerbrook Park is the only problem—we'll have to figure out a way to get you there, or at least to one of the bus stops. But we'd likely have to do this for any school, so—"

I said, I want to be a scholar.

He said, "Think about the future. You act well at this Aptakisic and who knows? Maybe Ida Crown Academy lets you in for high school." He squeezed my neck again. Then he went into his dining room to eat cake and I stayed by the glass door and watched the rabbit while I cried. Its haunches kept twitching. I thought: This is not a crazy thing to cry about. And it turned out not to be. Aptakisic was twenty-five miles from our house, so I couldn't have friends outside of school, and there was no other choice except Catholic school, with all its miniature false messiahs hanging from miniature torture instruments hanging from the walls, or boarding or military school, which my mom would never allow. And then I get there and Brodsky puts me in the Cage and calls me B.D.

It was hard to find the justice.

I thumb-drummed the teacher cluster's fakewood surface, chewed cheekfuls of cheesepuffs, made a decision: I was never in love with Esther Salt to begin with. If we'd been in love, she wouldn't have told me it was crazy to cry about the stuff I cried about. I decided that the only reason it ever seemed like I was in love with her was because I said it a few times.

And when I said it, it was true, but when I stopped saying it, it stopped being true. When I stopped saying it, it made me a liar. It made it so I was lying those times when I said it. So maybe I was a liar, but I'd never been in love before June. So there was no danger of the smelly version affecting the good version: there never really was a smelly version—it was something else completely. The thought cheered me up a little, and I ate a couple bites of my sandwich, but then I thought: How do I know I'm in love with June? I thought: If all it ever was with Esther was that I kept saying I was in love, then later on, if I ever stop saying it to June, I'll just be a liar again.

So I wrote it down, because when something is written it has a better chance of being permanent. I wrote it down with a Darker on the brown paper bag.

I wrote:

I AM IN LOVE

Jelly saw. She said, "With Jenny Mangey? I knew it. You should be in love with me!"

I finished writing what I was writing:

WITH ELIZA JUNE WATERMARK.

Jelly said, "That girl June? I know that girl! I had Art with her in fourth! She painted violent things!"

I looked at what I wrote and I saw there was a problem—No one who saw it would know who loved June. So I signed it and it looked like:

I AM IN LOVE WITH ELIZA JUNE WATERMARK.
TRULY,
GURION BEN-JUDAH MACCABEE

But then the "truly" part made it sound like I doubted it. If I saw it, I would think: The person who wrote this is unsure of himself. I would think: Gurion ben-Judah Maccabee must have written "truly" because sometimes what he says isn't true, which means he is a liar. And if he is a liar, I'd be a shvontz to believe him just because he says he's telling the truth.

So I scratched out "truly" so that it looked like:

I AM IN LOVE WITH ELIZA JUNE WATERMARK.
~~TRULY,~~
GURION BEN-JUDAH MACCABEE

Except now it looked like Gurion was even more unsure of himself.

I blacked out all of what I'd written entirely.

And Jelly said, "Thank God! I knew it wasn't true."

I flipped the bag-plate over. This is what I wrote:

GURION BEN-JUDAH MACCABEE IS IN LOVE
WITH ELIZA JUNE WATERMARK

That was the most concise sentence I'd ever written, so I left it.

Jelly said, "But you can't be, Gurion! She paints so many violent things! She painted a comicstrip one time of a pink monkey telling a man about the ass of another man who was fat and then the first man goes and cuts the ass of the fat one off and brings it to the monkey and the monkey pays him money and takes the ass of the fat man and puts it on a plate. A silver one."

I said, Did the monkey chew the ass?

"It was implied," said Jelly.

How? I said.

She said, "The monkey had a bib on."

That's subtle and hilarious, I said.

"Hahalarious!" said Mookus.

Yes haha, I said.

"Yes haha!" Scott said. "The mastication of the ass is made possible by the people who brought you I-teeth. Let Us make man! And in the image! The crown and the wisdom and the understanding. The judgment and the love, the beauty and the splendor. Let us not forget the victory. Let us not forget the kingdom and the foundation. The kingdom is the mouth! In the mouth, there are teeth! The foundation is the penis of Us!"

"Scott Mookus," said Botha.

"He calls me 'Scat Mucus' and I scream to him, 'Penis!'"

"Close up your idiot mouth," Botha said. "Stop acting the moron."

Benji Nakamook mumbled, "One day I'll cut your tongue out and paste it to your shirt."

"What was that?" said Botha.

Benji said, "I'd like to spray accelerant on your mustache and toss matches at your face."

"Are you saying something to me?"

Benji half-rapped, "While you're munchin' at your luncheon, I'm plannin' your assassination. Pling." It was from "Zealots" by the Fugees.

Botha said, "You have to speak up, Nakamake."

"I don't have to do anything," said Benji. "It's lunchtime."

Jelly said, "That girl's so weird, Gurion."

Benji said, "What girl?"

"And she used to go out with Ruth's ex's little brother," Jelly said, ignoring Benji.

When? I said.

"Just last year," Jelly said.

For how long?

"Who cares how long? His brother's a dickbag, and he worships his brother, and he tried to go out with me because Ruth is my sister and he wanted to date a Rothstein like his dickbag brother, but this Rothstein wasn't having it. I would *not* go out with him, not after I saw how his brother treated Ruth. And after I said 'No, man, go away, you worship a dickbag,' he went out with June. Do you want to know his name? Ask me his name. I've been keeping you in suspense, but I'm ready to end it. Don't you want to know the name of June's ex?"

Maybe, I said. I don't think I do, I said.

"Well that's dumb cause you should, cause his name's Josh Berman."

I thought: Berman, Josh Berman. I know that name; how? At least he's an Israelite.

That latter thought looks a lot more racist than it was. The wording is accurate, but At least he's an Israelite = At least I know for sure now that June's not one of those Israelites I read about who doesn't want to date other Israelites.

And then I remembered how I knew his name: I'd read it in the *Aptakisic News*. I'd read it in an article written by Ruth about the Main Hall Shovers.

"Josh Berman," said Jelly. "Josh Berman!" said Jelly. "Not just a Main Hall Shover," said Jelly. "And not just a Jewish Shover," said Jelly. "But the alphadog king of all Jewish Shovers," said Jelly. "How's *that*?" said Jelly. "What do you think of *that*?" said Jelly.

What I thought was that I didn't want to think of that at all. I didn't know any Israelite Main Hall Shovers; I only knew *about* them—I only knew what Ruth wrote about them in the *Aptakisic News*—and I knew I didn't like them—I disliked all Main Hall Shovers on principle, and as for the Israelite ones, *hate* was probably too strong a word to describe what I... I didn't want to think about it, there at lunch. I didn't want to think about Shovers or any of it.

Did she kiss him? I said.

Jelly said, "Tch."

I wanted, least of all, to think about them kissing, but I saw that I had to.

Did she? I said.

"Probably," said Jelly. "I can't say for sure."

Then don't say probably.

"They went out for *a while*. Maybe three *weeks*. That's why I said it."

But you don't know for sure, I said.

"No," Jelly said, "but I don't know for sure that she didn't kiss him either."

I thought: If June kissed him, this person Josh Berman, it was only a kiss. Then they broke up. She broke up with him. She broke up with Josh Berman, if they kissed or they didn't kiss, and that meant she wasn't in love with him.

But then I thought: You don't know what a kiss is; you've never kissed anyone! *Only a kiss?* That's a line from the movies! A lyric from a showtune! You don't know what it is any better than you know who broke up with who, who June loves or doesn't, who June loved or didn't.

I must have looked bad, because Jelly backed off.

"All I'm saying's she's weird," Jelly said. "She's just weird."

"Who's weird?" said Benji.

Jelly said, "Pay attention."

"But I heard everything you said," Benji told Jelly. "I was just being polite because I wanted to be in the conversation, but you weren't talking to me and it sounded like your conversation was private, and I didn't want you to feel like I'd invaded your privacy, so when you said some girl was weird, I asked you which girl, so that you wouldn't think someone had been eavesdropping on you. I'm highly sensitive when it comes to other people's privacy. You should know that about me, Jelly. So I'm asking you, 'What girl?' even though I know. I'm asking it as a favor *to you*. So you won't feel invaded. So I won't feel invasive. So we won't feel awkward. So we both feel the same. And now we do feel the same—that much is true. But the same in this case is no good kind of same. We both feel uncomfortable. You criticized my gesture and made us feel uncomfortable, and now we have to work together to repair the situation. And so, to that end, I'm asking again, '*What* girl is so weird?' And you should be polite enough to tell me, Jelly."

Jelly's lips puckered to beat back a smile her flaring nostrils betrayed the strength of. "June Watermark," she said. "She draws violent things, she went out with Josh Berman, and whoever's in love with her should be in love with me instead."

"Who cares what June draws?" said Nakamook. "I don't care what she draws. I mean, say that for instance I was in love with you, Jelly, and Mangey started saying I shouldn't be because you bite people. It wouldn't matter to me, because being in love with you would make it so I didn't care that you bite people because you're really hot and you're very funny, let's say, and then maybe I'd enjoy it when you bit me because I loved you so much that I couldn't even tell you about it directly since if I did that and you said you didn't love me back I would have to kill us both or something."

Jelly said, "Are you in love with me, Benji?"

Benji wasn't even looking at her, though. He was squinting at me, like he was measuring something.

A kiss, I kept thinking. A kiss is just a kiss. What is a kiss?

"And who cares if she went out with Berman?" said Benji. "That kid is a dentist and he never laid a hand on her."

How do you know? I said.

"He couldn't kiss a baby asleep in a cradle. He couldn't kiss his grandma. He couldn't kiss a lapdog. He's never kissed anyone," Benji said.

How do you know? I said.

"I can tell," Benji said, "if someone's never been kissed."

How can you tell?

"It's a talent," said Benji.

You can't tell, I said.

"You've never been kissed. Jelly's never been kissed. Leevon's been kissed. Main Man hasn't."

"You're guessing," Jelly said.

"Am I wrong?" Benji said.

"He's just guessing," she said.

He at least wasn't wrong about me or Jelly.

Benji said, "Listen. Gurion, listen—"

Main Man interrupted: "Listen to *me*. You've fallen in love with the girl of all girls, the queen of queens, the one who will mother the most righteous sons of you! Hers is the all-American ponytail of all American ponytails. I am walking on air for you. I am singing in the rain."

"Benji," said Jelly.

"Gu Ri On," said Nakamook.

"And what does love feel like?" Scott went on. "Does it feel like the sound of cantaloupes smashing beneath fleshy hammers? It does indeed feel like melons exploding! Have you warmed her by the balustrade near ornamented parapets? Embraced her in the sandstorms of the Negev and the Sinai? Wherefore art thou, Gurion Maccabee? Will you leave us all behind for this lovely tomato? Will you be a shaved Samson in the nosebleed seats, watching from the bleachers while all of our keesters get handed to us red by basketball and pervs and robots and tall people, your ass's jawbone long-gone and unswinging? Must she dull your ferocity? Can't you be a lover and a fighter, Gurion? Can't you be righteous and also be awesome? Can't you even remember the justice love needs for protection? Please?" Mookus said.

I said, I'll still bring the justice.

"So said Jesus," said Scott Mookus.

Nakamook said, "Jesus never fell in love, Scott—but Gurion, listen, I learned a new action last night."

Jelly said, "Please don't do eyelid flips. Don't ruin... *lunch.*"

Nakamook said, "It's not eyelid flips. This kills eyelid flips. I'll never do eyelid flips again," he said. "Watch."

Then Nakamook raised his shoulder-tops up to the top of his neck and his head started shaking in this tight, twitchy way, like a wire getting boinged. A couple seconds later, the breath of his nose was hissing and his face was completely red and his eyes were wet. He said, "You see? Do you see?" and when he said it, the voice was coming out of the top of his throat, Grover-style, like it was grinding against itself.

Scott said, "Ha! Haha!"

Leevon was sitting on the other side of me. I'd forgotten he was there until he poked my elbow. Then he did the same action as Nakamook did, and he did it even better so that the water on his eyes dripped down his cheeks and his cheeks looked loose.

Then Main Man did the action.

Then Jelly did it.

Then I tried to do it but I couldn't.

Nakamook stopped after a minute, and when he stopped, breath came out of his mouth in one heavy push. He said, "It's called 'I'm Ticking.'"

I said, Why?

He said, "Because when you do it, you can hear that ticking inside your head. I think it's from drops of brain-blood that whack themselves against the backs of the eardrums. Didn't you hear the blood ticking?"

I said, Don't be a wang to me because I can't do it—you know I didn't hear any ticking of blood.

He said, "I wasn't being a wang, you spastic wang. I didn't know because I couldn't see. When you do the 'I'm Ticking' action, it's hard to see. There's a bright flying saucer shape that blots out the middle of anything you look at."

I said, Tell me how you did it.

Nakamook said, "I can't explain it. I just did it."

I said, Tell me how you discovered it.

He said, "I was in my room and I was bored and I wanted to break something, but there was nothing good to break except the window and I didn't want to break the window, so I beat on the heavy-bag, but it wasn't good enough, I didn't want to hear thuds, let alone gaspy thuds, I wanted a breaking sound, a snapping kind of crunching sound, a shattering window sound, the one sound I couldn't hear without doing something I didn't want to do, and that's when I decided to invent a new action, and I performed my first I'm Ticking."

I said, Come on! How did you do it? I said to Jelly, How do you do it?

She said, "I just did it."

Then Leevon did it again.

Main Man said, "Leevon is I'm Ticking-ing and he doesn't talk. Jelly can I'm Ticking and she is a biter. Benji I'm Tickings and he is maybe psychopathic. Even I can I'm Ticking and I am diseased in a very rare fashion. What's wrong with you?"

I don't know, I said.

Mookus said, "Watch me like a vulture watches a fat mammal that is limping across the floor of a rocky canyon with its tongue out even though I'm your friend who you would never eat."

Main Man performed the action again and I watched him closely. After a few seconds, I got scared for him because of his heart.

I said, Stop Scott.

He stopped. He was breathing very heavy. This was called hyper-ventilating. It was also called catching your breath. It did not look like Main Man was catching his breath, though. It looked like Main Man's breath was catching him. It looked like Main Man was getting breathed.

I told Benji, You shouldn't have shown that to Main Man.

Scott said to me, "Please don't worry."

I said to him, Don't I'm Ticking again.

Nakamook said, "Main Man's fine. You're just pissed you couldn't do the action, you baby."

It is true I was pissed, but I wasn't *just* pissed. I was desperately trying to not think about kissing.

Main Man said, "Ha ha."

I told him, Yeahyeah.

The end-of-lunch tone got born and died.

"Go to your carrels," Botha said. He was standing by the doorway, clipboard in claw.

□   □   □   □   □   □   □

As I was getting up from the teacher cluster, Ronrico Asparagus and Jenny Mangey entered the Cage and rushed me so fast I flinched. "We have questions," said Mangey.

The two of them came across the room with me and when I turned my head to look at Benji, he made a crumpled face = "Why is Asparagus walking beside you as though he were other than a longtime foe of ours?"

At my carrel, I sat, and Mangey handed me a piece of paper that looked like

WE DAMAGE

DAMAGE WE

WE DAMAGE WE

"Which one is right?" Mangey said.

I stared at the words, trying to understand.

Mangey leaned in close. She was bright pink along the hairline from scratching. Ronrico leaned in close, too, not smelling like pee. If his pee was as pungent as it was said to be, then he did not get any on his pants, which was a blessing. I had never peed beside him, so I didn't know the true strength of his pee's smell. The "Ronrico Asparagus has pee so pungent" saying was invented before I got to Aptakisic. Most people said Nakamook invented it, but Nakamook said it was the Janitor. I thought it was Nakamook. It was just the kind of pithy saying Benji would've invented, and he was the kind of person who would have given credit to someone else for it, if giving credit to someone else would have made it funnier, which it definitely would have since the Janitor was Ronrico's closest friend, and his being the inventor would not only be very kaufman—the only thing more kaufman than to sniff a friend's pee was to sniff a friend's pee and then speak of what you'd sniffed—but would augment the saying with a sub-plot of betrayal.

"Which one?" Mangey said to me.

Ronrico said, "It's one of the first two. I know it."

Mangey whispered, "Ronrico was bombing the lunch tables and the bleachers with the first two, and he thought he was so smart, but I told him he was not so smart and that he should write WE on *both* sides of DAMAGE."

Ronrico said, "You didn't say which side of damage we were on, Gurion, but you did say we were on *the* side of it; not the side*szzz* of it. You said *the* side."

Oh! At the end of Group you mean, I said.

"Yeah," Mangey said. "What do you *think* we mean? Jeez."

The Janitor came over, and he leaned in. That was three people leaning close to me. I thought: Now it is a huddle. I thought: Don't touch my head.

Ronrico said, "Back off a little, Mikey."

The Janitor said, "I have a question about the side of damage, though. I'm not sure exactly what it means."

Ronrico said, "None of us are, but if you don't stop breathing on me, I'll touch you on the skin."

The Janitor leaned closer to Mangey.

"I'll lick you on the cheek," Mangey said.

The Janitor stepped back and Vincie Portite came into the huddle. He said to me, "What the fuck is going on here? Why are these people standing here at your carrel? Are we friends with these people now? I thought we weren't friends with these people, except for Mangey who we were kind of friends with. Now we're all fucken friends?"

"Why don't you just go ahead and stare at June Watermark, Vincie, you stalker," said Mangey.

Wait, I said. Wait. June's the girl you have a crush on?

"Nope," said Vincie.

Why'd Mangey say that then? Why'd you say that, Mangey?

"He stares at her at Lunch!"

"I don't," Vincie said. "I stare at someone else. She sits near June a lot."

I'm in love with June, Vincie.

"Really? Does she love you back? I hope so, man. I'm not even in love, I don't think, just in very deep like, and it's really fucken lonely not to be very deeply liked back. I can't imagine how—"

Not to be very deeply liked back by who? I said.

"I'm not saying," said Vincie. "I don't want to fucken say. But you know I'd tell you if it was June because you just said you loved her. That would be a big fucken problem if she was my crush—so I'd tell you."

Mangey said, "But—."

"Mangey's a fucken troublemaker. Listen to me. I told you I've liked this girl since kindergarten, right?"

A million times, I said.

"And June didn't go to school with me in kindergarten. Did she, Mangey? You went to school with me in kindergarten, so you would know—was June in fucken kindergarten with us?"

"No," Mangey said. "It's true. She wasn't."

"See?" said Vincie. "All is well, except for how the girl I like deeply does not like me deeply back."

I banged fists with Vincie, all kinds of relieved.

Sorry, I said.

"No problem, man. But what I was saying is," he said, chinning air at Ronrico and the Janitor, who were making kiss-faces at him, "are we friends with these two knuckleheads now, or what?"

We're all on the side of damage, I said.

"So we're all friends or what though?" Vincie said.

"I told you we were friends now," Ronrico said to Vincie. He said to me, "Vincie tried to say at recess that you didn't mean we were friends and I told him he was wrong, just like how I told Mangey she was wrong about the bombs on the tables and the bleachers."

"I said to Ronrico that he was a fuckface," said Mangey, "because when you said we were on the side of damage, you didn't mean that we were *to* the side of damage: you meant that damage is on one side, which is the side we are *for*, and then something else is on the other side, which is the side we're *against*."

"And then," said Ronrico, "I told her that it was not me who was the fuckface since it was her mom who was the fuckface, because of how we already decided in Group that it was her mom who was the one who fucks like a fucker and that Gurion would not have said 'We are all on the side of damage' and left it that way if there was this whole other something else that we are against like Mangey is saying—I told Mangey it was maybe her that was the fuckface because of genetics and that you would have told us what the something else was, and I told her that it is true that I don't know if we are on the right or the left side of damage, but I do know that it is one or the other. And that's why I switched off the sides with the bombs. I did thirteen, starting with the WE on the left. So now there are seven WE DAMAGEs and six DAMAGE WEs."

"Who's right?" Mangey said.

Botha said, "In your seats."

Those huddling around me pretended not to hear him.

I spoke fast. I said, We are all against the arrangement, always. I said, Sometimes we are on the left side of damage and other times on the right. Often we are on both sides, so both of you are correct.

"So I don't have to fix the bombs?" Ronrico said.

I said, The bombs are good.

"Thank you," Ronrico said. "Tomorrow I'll scrape a huge WE DAMAGE WE into the four-square court with a rock. I would've done a four-square one today, but we had indoor recess, so I did the bleachers with a Darker instead—Oh we forgot!"

"Hey!" said Botha.

"Hey back at you!" said Vincie Portite, hand over eye. "I didn't hear a tone yet!"

"The scoreboard," Ronrico said.

Mangey said, "It's smashed."

Vincie said, "He knows already. God! You don't listen to Vincie."

"Did you really know already?" said the Janitor.

The beginning-of-class tone sounded and Botha scattered the huddlers to their carrels by shouting, "Mind the loin there!" What he meant was my tape-line.

```
L  WALL WALL W
I         DESK  A
    chair  DESK
N         DESK  L
E  WALL WALL L
L  WALL WALL W
I         DESK  A
    chair  DESK
N         DESK  L
E  WALL WALL L
```

Forty carrels were bolted to the walls of the Cage; sixteen to the east wall, and twelve to each the north and south. Stuck to the floor behind every student's chair was a line of masking tape the width of his carrel. The rule was that you were supposed to keep the back legs of your chair in front of your line at all times. As long as your back chair-legs were in front of your line, your head would be between the walls of your carrel, which rose five feet higher than the surface of your desk and extended two feet beyond the desk's edge. Because only the thinnest, most flaccid carpet covered the Cage's concrete floor, and because all the feet of the chair-legs were metal, the noise of the feet rubbing the floor when you'd scoot your chair was a squeaky kind of groan that was wholly distinct from other Cage sounds, so breaking the Tape Rule was a risky move, since Botha—at his desk between the bathroom doors, in the middle of the west wall, facing east—or a teacher at the cluster in the center of the room, was likely to look in your groan's direction. If you were over your tape-line, you'd get step 1. Step 1 was a warning. Three warnings in the same half-day = step 4: detention.

While following the Tape Rule, the only direction you could look that wasn't walled off and didn't end in floor or ceiling was behind you = you weren't able look at anyone else without conspicuously revolving your head. And so there was also the rule of Face Forward, which was exactly what it sounds like. The rules of Quiet At All Times and Always Be Sitting—those were exactly what they sound like, too—combined with those aforementioned to make it near-impossible for students to initiate communication with other students without getting noticed, then stepped, by the robots.

On top of the rules, the stain-colored carrel walls were insulated thickly so that whispers below the robots' audial threshold couldn't break through them, and if you wanted to send a written message to someone, not only did you first have to ball the paper (folded notes' trajectories just weren't reliable), which got too noisy if you didn't crumple slowly, but you basically had to be sharing a wall with the intended recipient, for it was near-impossible to arc even a balled note much greater a distance than the next carrel over with any kind of accuracy, which meant that if Benji Nakamook, say, was more than one carrel away from you, a note you wrote him, in order to get to him, would have to be tossed to every student between you, and since each between-student would need to unball it to see if it was intended for him or another, and because no student could see what any other was doing inside of his carrel anyway, every between-student could and would read the note without any fear of getting beaten up, so even if every kid between the two of you was willing to risk steps for tossing your note, and even if the note did eventually get to Nakamook without being detected by Botha or the teachers (the likelihood of which decreased with each potentially noisy de- and re-crumpling), you wouldn't have written anything important in the note, and thus probably wouldn't have bothered writing to begin with.

And for those of you scholars who, at this point, wish to accuse me of blithe exaggeration or of lying for effect; for those of you assuming I'm engaging with metaphor or trucking with expressionism, thinking to yourselves, "This place about which Rabbi Gurion tells us *seemed* so overbearingly stifling and hellish that it *felt like* he wasn't ever allowed to speak to his friends, and at times it even *felt like* he wasn't allowed to look at them; it *was as if* they had to stare at flat, unadorned surfaces six hours a day in total silence, and *as though* to do otherwise would garner them punishment"; for all of you scholars who'd like to insist that a classroom like the Cage, given all the violent uprisings its very existence would daily incite, couldn't possibly abide for any longer than a week: believe me, I understand your objections. I was prepared no better by Schechter and Northside to experience the Cage's smothering reality than you've been prepared by your Israelite schools to accept that smothering reality's description.

As for *why* the Cage wasn't plagued by daily (or weekly, or at least semi-annual) savage insurrections, the short answer's this: Apart from me—the new kid still studying the others in the Cage to learn how it worked and how it got worked—its population was not comprised of scholars who'd spent their lives studying Torah and Talmud, but rather of kids for whom junior high had always = Aptakisic, if not the Cage itself.

The long answer's harder, a lot more complicated. The long one will take a little while to get across, and I haven't even finished describing the rules. I haven't even gotten to the rule against me.

If you were me, you could rarely even toss notes to a kid sitting next to you. Unless there was no one absent that day, enough empty carrels would be available for Botha to enforce the Gurion Has to Sit Next to No One Whenever It Is Possible rule.

For a while, that rule had been unconditional—Gurion Has to Sit Next to No One, Ever—because, back in my third week at Aptakisic, when Botha originally made up the rule (after catching me toss eleven notes in one hour), it was *always* possible for me to sit next to no one since the number of carrels in the Cage was forty and, until the end of my seventh week—the week before the week before I fell in love with June—the number of students who were sentenced to the Cage, though it had increased fairly steadily from its initial thirty-five,[*] never surpassed thirty-eight. Then came Ben-Wa Wolf, #39, a white-haired sixth-grader who cried all the time, which is why people called him The Boy Who Cried Wa-Wa. Other than how easy and often he cried, nobody really knew anything about him, let alone the reason he'd been removed from normal classes—he never broke rules or spoke to anyone at Lunch—but as soon as Ben-Wa got sentenced to the Cage, there was hope that I'd sometimes get to sit next to someone. For that to happen, there would have to be no absences at all, and although that circumstance rarely arose—just twice in all of my nine Caged weeks—having something to hope for, no matter how unlikely, was better than nothing (at least that's how it seemed), and from the moment Botha banned me from sitting next to others til the day Ben-Wa thirty-nined our roster, nothing's what I'd had in the way of hope.

I've learned forthright descriptions of hopelessness are boring, though. I learned that from Flowers on the same day that Botha issued the edict described above, which was also the first day I tried to write scripture concerned with the Cage, i.e., the first day I tried to start *The Instructions* (even though I didn't know what it would be called yet, or what it was about, or who I wanted to read it). Right there at my carrel I wrote a whole chapter, and I saw it wasn't good, but then I thought I might not be qualified to judge: the chapter wasn't, after all—at least not directly—about Israelites, Torah, or Adonai. So that afternoon, at the Frontier Motel, I showed the chapter to Flowers to see what he could tell me.

"This boring," he told me.

He was sitting on the couch in the Welcome Office waiting-space, chin on his hands, hands piled on the knob at the top of his walking cane, staring

---

[*] I.e., I was #35, then Egon and Mia Marsh disappeared; Renee Feldbons, Jerry Throop, and Ansul Entsry arrived a week later, all the same day, bringing the tally to thirty-six; #37, Remus "Chunkstyle" Heany, came a couple weeks after that; and Forrest Kennilworth, who arrived in mid October, was #38.

at a wall-mounted statue of Legba. I was on the couch next to him, waiting for more, but he wasn't saying more; it was my turn to talk.

I said, the Cage is boring.

He said, "Don't matter—pathetic fallacy."

I didn't hear it right, though. I heard, "Don't matter, pathetic phallus," like he was calling me a littlewang, or saying I had one.

I said, What do you know about the size of my wang?

He'd never seen my wang.

"The what?" he said. He took his chin off his hands and turned to me. "I'm telling you about the pathetic fallacy, and you're talking to me about wang? Learn."

I was embarrassed for hearing him wrong. I used to hear Flowers wrong a lot. He had an accent from Robert Taylor Homes combined with an accent from University of Chicago Law School, and his grammar, at times—especially when he was teaching you something—would become Hoodoo grammar, the kind he'd cast spells with. Before starting Aptakisic, I only met Flowers once—it was at a fundraising dinner for the United Civil Liberties Advocates of America, which was the organization my father worked for and the one for which Flowers used to work until he quit lawyering to be a writer when his brother died young and left him the Frontier—and for the first few weeks after starting Aptakisic, I'd get embarrassed to hear him wrong because he hardly knew me, and so when I'd hear him wrong, I'd think it seemed like I wasn't paying attention, and I'd think that if I explained to him that I *was* paying attention then it would seem like I meant that the way he talked was banced, which is not what I'd have meant, so instead I'd say nothing and just be embarrassed. The pathetic fallacy day, though, was especially embarrassing because it wasn't just that I heard him wrong, but that I heard him talking about my wang when he wasn't talking about my wang, which made it seem like I was always thinking about my wang.

So I said to Flowers: Sorry. I said, Pathetic fallacy.

Flowers said, "Forget the pathetic fallacy. There's what you write and there's what you write *about*. Even if what you write *about* is boring, you can't be *writing* boring. Seem to me like you want to write about you wang, anyhow. Now you wang—that's a good example cause it's boring to me. You wang is boring to most people. Half the world's got wangs and half all writers already written bout em. Only thing *ain't* boring to me about you wang is how you're callin it *wang*. You're a creative little boy, know some Yiddish slang like *shvontz* or *schmuck* or *pizzle*, could call it anything you want, and you call it you wang. Wang outlandish. I mean: wang. Wang nuts. As it were. Still, it ain't much to write about. Say it enough, word sound lose it charm fast as anything. For fact, it already has."

I don't want to write about my wang, I said. I never even think about it.

"Never even think about he wang, he tells me. Now you're lying. Don't matter anyway. Point is, you want to write about some boring things, fine, just don't make me feel you boredom. I don't read because I want to get bored. Take this root," he said. He pulled a root from the bag around his neck and put it in my hand. I put it in my mouth. It tasted like chalk and mushroom.

Flowers banged my rolled-up chapter on his knee. "That was harsh of me," he said. "Ain't all boring, actually. It was harsh of me, but you just gotta see what's not worth keeping and wipe it out."

I said, I can't tell what's not worth keeping.

"Cause you too obsessed with being methodical," Flowers said. "Systematical. I wish you'd quit it. 'Cept I guess that like asking a bumblebee to leave some pollen alone. Click click click," he said. It was one of my favorite things that Flowers would say. It was supposed to be the sound of thoughts gathering, and when he made it, it meant he'd forgotten what he wanted to say next but he wanted you to give him a second to think of what it was before you interrupted him... like spoken elipses... like he was trailing off, but would return in a moment with something important. Usually when he'd return, the subject of what he was talking about before would be changed a little...

"Click click click," Flowers said, and then: "Main thing is it sound like you gotta find the chink in the system, Gurion." He said, "Find that chink and exploit it."

I said, Exploit a chink and my scripture gets better?

"Secondarily, yes," he said. "What I'm talking about is you *life*'ll get better, though. This Cage sound like prison."

Flowers was right. I re-read the chapter and the whole thing was swollen; full of abstract words like "desperate" and "hopeless" and "anguish" and "mental." The whole thing was static. The whole thing was suck. I'd never skip a paragraph in a book I was reading—I was too afraid to miss something important—but I sometimes wished I was the kind of person who would skip a paragraph because then all I'd do is read the dialogue and the action. Those were the only parts of books I ever really enjoyed. The conflict parts. The parts where people act on things and words and other people. All the other parts seemed there to be gotten through: too many nouns and adjectives, too few verbs. This chapter was the kind that made me wish I was a skipper. I threw it away. I wiped it out.

And then, the next schoolday, I searched for a chink. For a little while, I even thought I found one. Late in the afternoon, I witnessed my first Hyperscoot: three kids scooted their chairs in rapid succession, each one loudly groaning the floor, and then a couple other kids groaned the floor with their chairs, and then another one, making six kids who groaned the floor in less than ten seconds. No one went over their tape-line, so no one got in trouble. What was even more interesting to me than that, though, was how the second three scooters never even got *seen* by Botha or the teachers, who were too occupied with checking to see if the first three were in violation of the Tape rule. And not only that, but a lot of us revolved to watch the action after the first three groans, and none of us got steps for breaking the Face Forward rule since we were done breaking it before the robots were done failing at trying to figure out who the second three scooters were.

As soon as school let out, I asked Nakamook about it. We were sitting in prop thrones on the stage in the cafeteria, waiting for the detention monitor to arrive. Nakamook said, "I've been in the Cage two years and seen maybe nine or ten Hyperscoots."

So they happen once or twice a quarter? I said.

"Nine or ten divided by eight is somewhere between one and two," said Nakamook = "Yes, once or twice a quarter on average, but I am not very interested in this subject." He was using a house-key to scrape the gold paint off the dog-head on the arm of his throne.

I said, Why don't people Hyperscoot more often? It's so simple.

Nakamook said, "It's not like anyone does it on purpose."

But why not? I said.

"What do you mean?" he said. "It's an accidental thing. A few spazzes groan their chairs at the same time by accident—that's why it's called Hyperscoot. Because it's hyper. Hyper's never on purpose. If it was on purpose it would be called Superscoot or something. Riotscoot." He blew his pile of scraped paint off the dog-head and walked away from me.

I disagreed with Nakamook about being H—I believed you *could be* H on purpose, or at least use your H *with* purpose—but I figured that the potential purposefulness of H was beside the point. I figured that Nakamook had simplified a good explanation; that he knew some complicated set of reasons why Hyperscoot couldn't happen more often but didn't want to talk about them because, for some reason, they made him touchy. Even though we'd blanked hallway bulbs together a few days earlier, and even though I'd drawn on his head and he'd gone to my house for dinner once, I hadn't yet given him that copy of *Ulpan* with all the Israelite parts cut out, so I thought it was fair for him not to want to talk about touchy stuff, and I didn't want him to get upset, so I dropped the conversation and gave up on Hyperscoot.

That afternoon, when I got to the Frontier, I told Flowers I couldn't find the chink. He said I shouldn't be a quitter and told me I should look where I didn't usually look.

The next day, I revolved my head a conspicuous number of degrees to look behind me. This broke the Face Forward rule, but Botha was spaced out and didn't see, and neither did the teachers at the cluster, who were busy grading papers.

Across the room, directly behind me, was Nakamook. Jelly's and Mookus's carrels were along the same wall. The problem was that all their backs were to me. Everyone's back was to everyone else because of how the carrels were arranged to face the walls. Still, I stared at Nakamook's back for no less than two minutes and none of the robots noticed. I thought of throwing something at Nakamook's neck so that he'd turn around, but whatever it could have been would have had to be heavy enough to travel the length of the Cage while also being light enough not to hurt Nakamook, which didn't leave me any options other than a very compressed ball of paper bound with Scotch tape, which would be inaccurate to throw, noisy to crumple, and also, since it would have to pass the teacher cluster in flight, too large and white to sneak under the robots' radar. Plus then there'd be this ball of paper on the floor.

Having thought, for the second time in two days, that I'd found a chink, and then, for the second time in two days, finding that I hadn't, I started getting angry that I'd ever looked, and angrier still that I'd ever had to look. My friends were sitting just yards away, but I couldn't communicate with any of them openly... Rather, I *could* communicate with any of them openly—all I'd have to do was use my voice—but I would get in trouble if I did so. And that I was expected to accept that was... what? An insult. One of a thousand that went with being in the Cage. And I *did* accept it. All of us did. That was the thing. That was the thing that started to eat at me, even though I didn't yet understand it. This is the thing that was starting to eat at me, even though I didn't understand it yet: In trying to find a chink with which to game the Cage, I, like the rest of them, was playing along with the Cage, accepting the insult, accepting—in action (or lack thereof), if not in thought—that the Cage possessed the authority to lay down rules = Even when the actions that would get us in trouble were good, human actions—e.g., talking to friends, making eye-contact, searching out something other than solitude and blankness—we did our best to stay out of trouble. And why? For what? They didn't teach. They didn't even *teach*. If someone were teaching, it might have been different; if you had to be quiet so as not to interfere with a teacher's lessons, that, although stifling and totally unlike the way I'd been schooled at Schechter and Northside, would at least have made a little sense, but quiet *at all times*? Quiet at all times, though no one was speaking, let alone about anything you'd be better off knowing, plus always facing forward, *away* from the teachers? The Cage Manual said that students in the Cage were there to learn through "self-direction," but all that meant was that since we were all in different grades, with different abilities, there was no way for the teachers to give us group lessons. What they did was give us "individually tailored" writing assignments and readings, and then "tutored" us on an "as-needed basis" at the teacher cluster. If you had a question, you could raise your hand and wait to get called on, but since the teacher cluster was in the center of the room and your back was to the cluster while you faced forward, you couldn't tell if the teachers had seen your raised hand; until they looked up and called on you to join them, you just had to wait, arm held high. Newer students often tried to groan the floor inside their tape-line to get the teachers to look in their direction and see their raised hands, but this drove people crazy, teachers and students both, and Botha called it Aggressive Squeaking, and Aggressive Squeaking broke the Quiet At All Times rule. Those words: Aggressive Squeaking! They got me explosive, and just before third period on that second day of my search for a chink, I couldn't stop hearing them inside my head, Aggressive Squeaking Aggressive Squeaking, and I probably would have exploded by fourth, but my nose beat me to it; my nose had to sneeze.

I didn't like anyone to see me sneezing, so I revolved to face forward and sneezed into my carrel, and Botha said, "Gehbless you," and I thought: God damn you! and within half a second, I'd discovered the chink and how to exploit it, for as soon as Botha had said "Gehbless you," I'd revolved in my chair, breaking the Face Forward rule once again, and I found that he was just as spaced out as before. Despite my sneeze and his automatic blessing, he wasn't even looking in my direction. Neither were the teachers.

Sneezing drew no real attention.

It took me less than five minutes to work out a sound-code. At lunchtime, I handed it out to those concerned. I would cough when I wanted Benji's attention, fake-sneeze when I wanted Vincie's attention, clear my throat to signal Mookus, pop my spine-nodes for Jelly, sniffle for Leevon, and wheeze for Mangey.

Without knowing sign language, there wasn't much we could say once we were facing each other, so we resorted to gestures that didn't mean what they seemed to—we shook our fists, thumbed our front teeth, dragged fingers across our throats like knives—yet performing these gestures, at least for a while, felt like a victory over the arrangement.

Within a few days of the sound-code's inception, though, all of the Cage had caught on to its rudiments, and everyone likes to see rules get broken, so whenever I made a body noise, half the room would break the Face Forward rule to see what I'd do next, and Botha would notice and then he would yell and hand out some steps. Soon enough he figured out what I was doing—or at least he figured out that when I made a body noise, people got disarranged—and after that, I couldn't even tongue-click or sigh in awe of a Philip Roth paragraph without getting shut down in booming Australian.

The most important thing, though—at least to me, at least at the time—was the new way that I learned to think about chinks: since they were spaces between rules, the more rules there were in an arrangement, the more chinks. Once the robots found out that a chink was being exploited, they'd create a new rule to fill the space between the two rules containing the chink, but the new rule never filled the space completely—there is always space between rules—and so what happened was that every time a new rule got shoved between two old ones, two new spaces would arise, two new chinks, one on either side of the new rule, so that

$$\overset{\text{chink}}{\text{R}\text{ULE } 1} \quad ^\wedge \quad \text{R}\text{ULE } 2$$

would become

$$\overset{\text{chink}}{\text{R}\text{ULE } 1a} \,^\wedge\, \overset{\text{chink}}{\text{R}\text{ULE } 1b} \,^\wedge\, \text{R}\text{ULE } 2$$

The two new chinks would be much narrower than the one they'd replaced, but still they would be chinks. So the more that exploited chinks got filled with rules, the more chinks there were.

It was hard, however, to keep finding the chinks, and it was even harder than that to exploit them in a way that was fun.

Once the sound-code failed, we tried a time-code, i.e., we agreed that at certain times we'd revolve to face each other. Benji and I, for example, agreed that we would revolve at every eleventh, seventeenth, thirty-first, and fifty-third minute of the hour, whereas Vincie and I would revolve at the second, twenty-seventh, and forty-fifth minute, and Benji and Vincie at the fifth, thirty-ninth, and fifty-eighth minute. We arranged revolve-minutes with Main Man and Jelly and Leevon and Mangey also, but after a week the time-code died. This was partly because people would get confused and re-volve at the wrong minute or face the wrong person, which caused a mutual and reflexive loss of faith (as Main Man put it: "Because when I revolted you did not revolt with me, I became revolted, and I revolted less, which got you revolted, so you revolted less"), but it was mostly because of how using the time-code felt too much like obeying the rules. With the sound-code, I'd been able to give the revolve signal whenever I felt like it, while with the time-code, it was all arranged in advance, like recess. Recess could be good because, unless you were banned from it like I was, you got to go outside. But at the same time, you only got to go outside when the arrangement let you go outside—at recess. It is true we picked the minutes for the time-code ourselves, but because they had to be decided on in advance, it was never as fun as it should have been. It was just another arrangement. Like recess.

A day or two after the time-code disappeared, we replaced it with a random three-code. Whenever three events of a certain type occurred, two of us would be signalled to act. Mine and Vincie's event, for example, was rising = every third time anyone rose from their chair, like to go to the bathroom or the nurse or the teacher cluster, Vincie and I would revolve and gesticulate. Because the frequency of the three-part signals varied un-predictably, using the random three-code was a little bit more fun than using the time-code, but our revolving still depended on decisions we'd made in advance (we chose which events would elicit our responses), so there was no spontaneity (as there'd been with the sound-code). As well, and as with every other way we'd exploited the chinks, all we could man-age in the way of communication was a gesture that, regardless of the movements of the hands comprising it, always meant the same thing:

"Look, I exist, and you exist, too; but for the fact that you are seeing me make it, this gesture is totally meaningless."

Nonetheless, the random three-code stuck. We'd been using it for a month; the robots couldn't crack it. Even while I stared down at the WE DAMAGE WE piece of paper Jenny Mangey had given me, I was waiting on a third floor-groan to signal that I should revolve and show Benji my swear, or maybe pump a pointer inside of my fist at him, but it was so boring, so desperately boring. If asked beforehand, I probably would have guessed that having fallen in love a couple hours earlier would've made this boredom a lot more tolerable, but the opposite was true, for now I was imagining how weak June would think me if she were to know how I sat there perpetually, hopelessly suffering.

On Flowers's sound advice, dear scholars, to write in the cause of averting *your* boredom, I've avoided directly describing our hopelessness in favor of describing how we tried to fight it, but make no mistake: our methods all failed. Even those that seemed to succeed were failures—especially those. The sound-code, the time-code, the random three-code; what did they get us? How many times could you give your best friend the finger before it just quit being any fun at all? And how dumont was it to believe that doing so accomplished anything meaningful, let alone useful? Wasn't to believe that but a way to be arranged? Maybe even the worst kind of arranged? The kind where you think you're overcoming the arrangement, when, in fact, you're serving it perfectly? Flipping a covert bird instead of screaming a curse instead of throwing a punch instead of throwing a rock? Revolving in a chair you might have otherwise swung? Cheering for underdogs and calling it action? Smirking at the powerful and calling it subversive? Embracing your meekness instead of getting strong? All day long we *coped* with the insults, with being insulted; we did what we could to avoid further insults. But that original insult—the one I mentioned earlier, the one that took a while to really understand: that we were expected to accept all the insults the Cage dealt out, all of its rules; to accept that the Cage was allowed to deal them out, was the maker of rules, the *only* maker of rules, and rules, no less, that were only there to dominate us; only there to show us that the Cage made the rules—that one loomed, grew ever more evident, and even more powerful. And worst of all, we let its power grow; we *helped* its power grow. You can render unto Caesar that which is Caesar's, but if you don't keep from Caesar that which is yours, Caesar will take some, and then take some more, and if you don't put a stop to it, though you won't lose everything—you *can't* lose everything; there's things he *can't* take, at least one or two—a time will soon come when you'll *think* you've lost everything, when you'll think *all* is Caesar's, and by then you'll be too weak to take what's yours back, too tired to remember what was yours to begin with, and you'll end up, perversely, scheming for his leavings and, even more perversely, grateful when you get them.

The Cage was no Rome, nor Botha a Caesar, and if I had been a Yeshua I wouldn't know to be ashamed, but the sound-code, the time-code, and the random three-code, all of our meaningless gesticulations—these were our schemes to get Botha's leavings, and we were verging on grateful, at least I was. Ashamed is just grateful waiting to happen. You only taste your own dignity right before you puke it up.

My tongue was all sticky and dignified.

Fuck, I said.

A bunch of kids laughed.

"Who said that?" said Botha.

No one told.

I kept my head low, stared down at the WE DAMAGE WE slip of paper. I felt a little better.

Then I felt a lot stupid. Why should I take pleasure in getting away with something that I should have been entitled to do to begin with?

Fuck it, I said. I said, I'm the one who said it. I could've fucken gotten away with it, too.

"Stap four for three curses," Botha said. "That's one detantion for Garrion Makebee. Two staps for speaking twice; that's two thirds to a second. Have anything more to add, Mister Makebee? Would you like another stap, a second detantion?"

I wanted to say something because fuck him, but what? I wanted to say a thing that didn't mean anything, to say a thing to show him that I was breaking a rule for no other reason than to break the rule... It was written before me.

We damage we, I said.

"What was that, Makebee? Whadjeh say? Now that you've earned yourself a second detantion in ander a minute, you've got three more whole staps to burn before your third. Say more. Please."

I wanted to say another meaningless thing, and Botha wanted me to say another any old thing. No matter what I said, he'd give me a step.

And so I kept my mouth shut, choosing not to do what I wanted to do over doing what it was that he wanted me to do because what, scholars, really—what was the point? To take pleasure in getting away with something you should have been entitled to do to begin with was dumont enough; to take pleasure in pretending to take pleasure in *not* getting away with it, though... that was about as useful as trickling. In fact, it *was* trickling. And what ever did we do in the Cage but trickle, except for submit? We trickled in submission, or we just submitted.

I kept facing forward, and stared at my walls, and I swallowed til Botha quit trying to bait me.

□ □ □ □ □ □ □

Right when the end-of-class tone sounded, the doorbell gonged. It was such an unlikely timing of sounds that no one gesticulated or rose to stretch legs and bang fists like they usually did during passing-periods.

Botha let the teachers out of the Cage, and when he came back inside, Eliyahu was behind him, and was no longer leaning; not as much, at least, as he had been before. He looked more like a determined professor than a late white rabbit. It made me glad.

Monitor Botha said, "Lasten up."

Everyone revolved.

"This here is a new student named Ay lie... Ay lie... Ay lie..." Botha looked to Eliyahu for help.

Eliyahu said, "I am—"

Mookus said, "He's wearing a hat!"

The Flunky said, "A kid who tells on another kid is a dead kid."

"Enough," Botha said. "This is Aye lie—"

Main Man said, "But I wasn't telling, the Flunky. I was only just saying."

"I don't see the difference," the Flunky said.

"That's because you're a foog," said Nakamook.

"I am not a fool," said the Flunky.

"Students!" Botha said.

"Botha!" said students. It wasn't as tough a thing to shout as it seemed; since we were between tones, Botha couldn't really do anything unless we cursed or hit each other.

Eliyahu loudly de-pocketsed his hands and placed them on his hips. His upper row of teeth shone from under the hat-shadow.

"No one said you were a fool," Nakamook told the Flunky. "I would never call you a fool. I like fools. Fools know that they're fools. It's a kind of wisdom. What I said was that you are a *foog* and a foog—"

"*I'm* a fool," said Main Man. "A fool for you. I'm a fool to do your dirty work," he said. "I'm a fool for love and an ice-cold pop on a sunny day when the ground splits open under America and the sky falls down and so forth."

"But what's a foog?" the Flunky said.

"It's almost exactly the same thing as a fool, except I don't like you," Benji told him.

"At least I'm not a fool," the Flunky said.

"But why does that boy get to wear a hat, though?" said Mookus.

Eliyahu said, "I am—"

The Flunky said, "Why do you get to wear a hat?" to Eliyahu.

Eliyahu very suddenly removed his fedora and held it out for all the Cage to look at, but no one looked at it because they were all looking at his face. Eliyahu's eyes were doing something I hadn't ever seen eyes do before, something I knew at once was called "burning." "Burning eyes" is a confusing thing to call eyes like that, though. Eyes like that have lids so narrowed that the only reason you can even see the sliver of white at the outside corners is the contrast against the irises which have gone completely black with pupil. They are called burning eyes not because they look like they are on fire, but because they make you feel like *you* are in danger of catching fire, like they could set you on fire from the inside if you do the wrong thing while they're seeing you.

Eliyahu said, "I am Eliyahu of Brooklyn and I am a defiance. Will you try to take my hat from me?"

No one answered him.

Eliyahu put his hat back on. Then he pointed to the empty carrel to my right. He said to Botha, "There is where I will sit."

Botha started to say "No," but then he saw he couldn't argue. Except for the one on my left, the one on my right was the only carrel that was open. To reduce his loss of snat, Botha turned to welcome the teachers who'd entered, then went to the doorway and locked it down early.

I pulled Eliyahu's chair out for him, and Nakamook flashed me almost the same crumpled face as when Ronrico'd walked next to me, except it was a little more crumpled than that first time.

I whispered to Eliyahu, "*You* got tough sudden."

"It was a blessing to break that case," he said.

I thought: You are the blessing.

Eliyahu said, "The glass didn't cut me at all, and I thought to myself: Nothing can cut me. True, it is not a thought I haven't had before, but this time it felt good to think it."

I squeezed him on the neck, like how my father will sometimes squeeze me on the neck, and then Eliyahu did what I usually do when that happens. He looked down at his own chest and nodded his head a few times = "Yes, okay, yes okay" = "This is nice, but if you don't stop, I will become embarrassed for reasons I don't understand."

Like my father usually does, I stopped squeezing the neck before his embarrassment started.

Botha was back. He said to me, "Don't get so appy, Makebee—it's only tempory."

He meant getting sat next to. Eliyahu had brought the Cage population to maximum capacity, though. More than one absence from the Cage was as rare as none, so Eliyahu was effectively the end of the Gurion Has to Sit Next to No One Whenever It Is Possible rule.

Botha dropped a Cage handbook on the desk of my newest friend's carrel.

"That's for you, Aye Lie."

"And I've got something for you, Mr. Bertha," said Eliyahu. "From Principal Trotsky."

Main Man said, "Ha ha."

Eliyahu handed Botha two notes on office stationary.

Botha looked at the first one and said to me, "Go to the owfice before detantion."

I said, My record's ready?

He said, "Can't say I know what your talking about."

I said, What does the note say, Mr. Botha?

"Says to go to the owfice before detantion, Makebee."

Botha went to his desk, reading the second note. Then he called Ronrico and the Janitor over and wrote them one pass. Brodsky had summoned them for our fight in the locker-room—that had to be it. It seemed so long ago.

Standing in the doorway behind the grumbling, key-clanging monitor—Botha hated that he had to unlock the gate just after having locked it—Ronrico shouted back to me, "Don't worry. I won't tell on you—and neither will he."

"I won't," said the Janitor.

Soon the the beginning-of-class tone sounded and all of the Cage went quiet again. I touched my neck on the hairs. June had said, "Show me later, then. Don't get in trouble." I shivered big. It was almost later. Coke, poem, and passpad. I yearned for detention.

□ □ □ □ □ □ □

Before Eliyahu had the chance to get us steps, I sent a note over the wall that told him to send a note over the wall when he wanted to communicate. His response took so long, I worried he fell asleep. A lot of Cage students would sleep in the afternoon. Since the robots couldn't see your face, it was easy to get away with if you didn't put your head down onto the desk.

While I waited for Eliyahu to write me back, I returned to the problem of the random three-code—of why I couldn't come up with something better. I started to think about how Flowers had said I was too methodical, too systematic; how I'd thought he was probably right ever since he'd said it, and for weeks had kept trying to be different than he'd said. Like when I towel-snapped the neck of the Janitor that morning. That was the most successful I'd been; I didn't have any reason to towel-snap his neck. Rather, I had a reason to attack *someone* who didn't deserve it (I had to find out if I was a sadist), and a reason to attack that person in the locker-room (teachers were scarce there; most fights went unpunished), but my target could have been any one of at least ten kids who I had Gym with and didn't like. From that list of ten, I'd chosen the Janitor at random the night before. But then, because it was him I chose, his best friend Ronrico started fighting with me, and that fight was noisy enough to rouse Desormie, who brought me to the Office where I got to flirt with June, then meet Eliyahu. And now I was in love and getting sat next to. So it was definitely *good* that I towel-snapped the neck of the Janitor—I didn't doubt that—but now that I thought about it, "because there was no reason to pick a fight with the Janitor" seemed like a reason to pick a fight with the Janitor, and if that was the case, there was reason in everything. Or maybe it was more like reason was inescapable. At least for me. And if reason was in everything, it would seem to make sense for me to continue to be methodical and systematic.

And if reason was inescapable, then I couldn't help but continue being methodical and systematic. Except... except...

I felt snared in a word-trap and cowardly for it. Like a guy on a gallows worrying about rope-burn. The Cage was the trap. The Cage was a cage.

A kid groaned his chair. I revolved to face Benji. He pointed at Eliyahu and shrugged his shoulders while curling his lips in around his teeth = "I don't understand who this person is."

I nodded once and showed Benji a power-fist = He is a friend.

Then Benji made two fists, held one on top of the other the tall way, and did circles with them at chest level. I didn't know what that meant, but he followed it with the lips-curl and the shrug. Next he waved a sideways goodbye under his nostrils, which at first I thought = "It stinks in here," but then he followed it with the shrugging and the lip thing again, which seemed to = "I don't understand why it stinks in here," but because I couldn't smell any bad smells, and because it didn't make any sense to tell me that he didn't understand why the Cage was so awful, I was confused.

I heard the tap of a note landing on my desk and I revolved to face forward. Instead of balling up the note, Eliyahu had folded it into a box. That took longer than crumpling, but it didn't make noise, and a thrown one's trajectory was at least as reliable as that of a balled one's. I'd never even thought of boxing a note.

I opened the note. It said: *This Cage Manual is long and full of topys.*

I wrote: *I don't know "topys." Is it Yiddish or Hebrew? You are smart to box this piece of paper. I always crumple.*

I boxed the note, tossed it.

A kid groaned his chair. Two more and I'd revolve again, gesture at Benji.

The note came back: *To crumple is noisy. Topys is a spelling joke in English.*

I wrote: *You are a very quiet kind of funny, Aye lie Aye lie Aye lie.*

Boxed it, tossed it. I heard a fly buzz. A kid groaned his chair.

Tap. The note said: *Better this than a very funny kind of quiet. It is a very funny kind of quiet in here. It's no picnic. You weren't kidding before. How much longer til the day ends?*

I checked the clock, wrote: *1.5 periods + 1 passing-period = 60 min + 5 = 65 min.*

I have no work to do, Eliyahu wrote back. *I will doze. Please enjoy a disc of butterscotch—my favorite.*

A disc of butterscotch came over the wall. It shattered in its wrapper when it hit the desk.

Chair-groan, chair-groan, chair-groan, chair-groan—aggressive squeaking. I revolved to face Benji. He revolved, too, but not to face me. He looked, instead, at Ben-Wa Wolf, the source of the chair-groans—which hadn't yet ceased—and so did most of the rest of the Cage, including the teachers and Botha.

"Aggrassive squeaking," Botha said.

Ben-Wa stopped. He said, "I've had my hand up for—"

Botha interrupted him. "Stap one, Mr. Wolf. That's what you get for agrrassive squeaking, isn't it? Stap one and tan minutes til you're called on, plus—"

"I—"

"*Tan minutes til you're called on,* Mr. Wolf, plus another two mannits edded for each word you speak. 'I' is a word, so that's twailve mannits."

Ben-Wa chewed his lips, shut his eyes to the wrinkling, crossed his legs at the knees like a lady being interviewed. A bunch of kids giggled. Someone said, "Ben Gay." I didn't see who.

"Face ford, all you," Botha commanded.

I counted to seven and did it.

To Eliyahu, I wrote, *Thank you for the butterscotch.* I folded the note, but then I unfolded it and wrote, *Don't write "You're Welcome" back to me. It is not worth risking a step to toss a note that says "You're Welcome." Or even "Thank you." I'm only writing "Thank you" this once so you'll know I'm not thoughtless. From now on, though, if you give me something in the Cage, assume that I am thankful. I will do the same with you. Dream of victory.*

Over the wall.

I untwirled the wrapper of the butterscotch and put the two biggest pieces in my mouth. I fought off my teeth. My teeth wanted to chew.

A fly buzzed into my carrel, then left. Then came back.

And then the note came back. It said: *You're welcome—I will write that just once, too. But I mean it. I carry many discs of butterscotch in my pockets. It is something I learned in Brooklyn—I would give butterscotch to Bathsheba Wasserman, who is the love of my life. When I give away discs of butterscotch, it helps me remember Bathsheba, who I hope to dream about instead of victory, or maybe as a kind of victory, the best kind, loving her. Either way, I should thank you for helping me to remember. Bathsheba is so very beautiful, with black eyes and ringlets, and dresses so long she hovers when she walks away from you. Even as I fail to describe her well,*

*and even amidst these humiliating conditions (what is that teacher's PROBLEM
with the tiny white-haired boy?! he looks like a nice boy, no?), I have joy. And now
a snooze.*

I tucked the note in my pocket. I would save it in my Documents lockbox and, on the twentieth anniversary of their wedding day, I would give it
to Bathsheba, along with a drawing I would ask June to make of Eliyahu as
a boy. Bathsheba would weep tears of happiness and all of our sons would
practice stealth in the yard together, speaking Hebrew to each other. This
would be in Jerusalem, behind the limestone house where my mother was
a girl. We had pictures. One was in a frame on the living room wall. My
mother is sitting under some blossoms in it, eating a Jaffa orange that her
father is peeling apart the segments of and handing to her. It was the first
picture I ever saw of my grandfather, who was a very dark-skinned person
who died the same year I was born. I'd seen it a million times in the frame
on the wall, but one time, when I was three, I saw my mom stare at it, and
I looked at it more closely and I asked her, Who is the man?

It is the earliest conversation I can remember.

My mom said, "He is my aba."

I said, No he is not.

She said, "Why do you say that?"

I said, He is not Jewish.

She said, "He is."

I said, No.

She said, "I do not lie to my son." But I didn't believe her and she knew
it, so she showed me his medals. The letters engraved in them were Hebrew.
I couldn't read it yet.

"You see?" she said to me. "He was a soldier in the Six-Day War, in the
Yom Kippur War, and in Lebanon. He was a hero. Do you see how young
I was! Just older than you."

I said, Why was he a hero?

"What?" she said.

What made him a hero?

"He kept the people he loved from being killed by others."

How? I said.

She said, "Speak in sentences to your mother."

I said, How did he stop the others from killing?

My mother said, "He killed them first."

I can never remember when my father came in the room, or where he was sitting or standing, but he was there by then and they had a fight. I do not remember what they said to each other, either, just that it was loud, and that while I cried the tears magnified everything, and my mother looked browner than me, and my father pinker. After they finished fighting, we all got ice cream on Devon, and then we went to Rosenblum's Books, where they bought me a Chumash with a leather-colored cover. I read half of *Bereishis* in English before I went to bed, and in 14, at the part where Avram arms his 318 servants and takes war to the five armies under Chedorlaomer, who had captured Lot, I could see Avram put his fist to the ground and the desert cracking open to swallow his enemies and I could see his face. It was the face of my grandfather and I saw that it was good.

The fly whacked himself against the inner walls of my carrel. The buzzing and the ticking D'd my A like crazy, so I turned the wrapper inside-out and rubbed a streak of butterscotch dust across the desk. The fly put his hose down and fed on the thinnest part. I moved my hand and he flew to the wall, clung on a fiber. I remained still until he returned to the streak.

A minute before the end of the period, a girl on the other side of the Cage said, "No!"

Then someone else said, "Aww!"

"Quoydanawnsinz!" Botha said. "Sit down!"

I revolved. There was a half-circle of students standing around Ben-Wa Wolf. I could see his white hair through the gaps between the hips.

The whole Cage had revolved.

Botha told the standers to get back in their seats. They shifted. That is when I and everyone saw that Ben-Wa Wolf was wet. He was crying without tears and without any throat-sounds—only with his breath—and his hand was raised. His hand is raised, I thought, and he wet himself, I thought. His right hand is raised and his piss is dripping into the carpet, I thought, staining the carpet, I thought, his hand in the air.

The end-of-class tone sounded as Botha approached Ben-Wa with a pass. "Go to the nurse and clane up," he said.

Ben-Wa ignored him, revolved his chair slowly til he faced the center of the Cage. He said to us, "This isn't normal. I am eleven years old. This is not normal at all. Can you believe this? I can't believe this. Can you believe this?"

No one answered him.

It was the worst thing.

"Ben-Wa," said Botha.

"It was past twelve minutes. Why couldn't you call on me?" Ben-Wa said. You could hardly hear it, but you couldn't help but hear it.

Botha shook the pass until Ben-Wa finally lowered his hand and took it.

I thought of a song, a terrible, cloying, cute little meansong:

Hey Ben-Wa Wolf/ Why's your hand in the air?/ You're crying and soaking/ Piss streams from your chair/ I wonder and wonder/ And wonder and wonder/ I wonder and wonder/ What makes you so scared?

I had to press my tongue to my mouth-roof with my eyes rolled up while I dug a thumbnail into my neck to make the song go away. There were always songs and they always rhymed and everyone laughed when they sang them. No one sang any songs this time. The day's last teachers came in and sat at the cluster. It was English. Mr. Meineke, Ms. Kost, Miss Beepee, and Mrs. Anoko. Ms. Kost assigned me a Kurt Vonnegut story called "Harrison Bergeron." Flowers had me read it two weeks before and I loved it. I read it again there, in the Cage, and loved it less. The ending was cheap. It happened too fast.

When Ronrico and the Janitor returned from the Office, we all revolved at the gong of the doorbell.

Benji pointed to Ronrico and then to the Janitor and then he did the shrug/lip-curling very frantically at me = "That's who I was making confusing gestures about before."

I showed him the power-fist. = They're friends now.

He waved me off with two hands and looked sad doing it.

Ronrico took a look around the Cage. "Who died?" he said.

"Wolf," said Main Man.

"The Boy Who Cried Wa-Wa?" the Janitor said.

"The Boy Who Went Wee-Wee," said Forrest Kennilworth.

I was across the room before I knew I'd left my chair, across it so quick Botha hadn't finished chuckling yet. Nakamook already had Kennilworth's wrist bent. Kids crowded fast and thickly behind us, shoving close together to get a better vista, their jammed-together bodies blocking all Botha's sightlines.

"Entertain the monitor," Benji said to Forrest. "Make him laugh again."

Kids were saying, "Hurt him." Kids were saying, "Break it." By "kids," I mean all of them but Jelly, Eliyahu, Main Man, and me.

Botha was shouting, trying to clear his way, shouting for the teachers to help him clear the way.

"He should get more than a wrist-twist," Vincie told Benji.

"Please," Forrest said. "I'm sorry," he said. "It's just fucked up. I was making a joke. It's just fucked up."

Main Man said, "Nakamook, Forrest is sorry. He was making a joke and it's just effed up."

"He's crying," said Jelly. "He means it. He's sorry."

Benji let Forrest go as Botha got through, and we all dispersed. The teachers stood dumbly by their chairs at the cluster. Even though Vincie, retreating to his carrel, thumb-stabbed him stealth on the side of the neck, Forrest didn't rat anyone.

Botha handed out steps for the following offenses: noise, talking, swears, standing.

The fly was on my desk, his hose in the candy dust. I cupped my hand and covered him, then brushed him past the edge to see where he'd go. He returned to the dust, as if I hadn't just demonstrated that I could kill him, as if I hadn't just shown him right there in the dust.

I snuck the hall-passes out of my bag and wrote the penumbra poem on the back of one. I held the bottle of Coke between my knees, under the desk, and binder-clipped the poem to the lip beneath the cap.

The fly sucked dust. The end-of-class tone sounded. Eliyahu went straight to the bathroom.

I secured June's gift inside of my backpack and charged the locked door with everyone else.

6
DARK ENOUGH

Tuesday, November 14, 2006
Interim—Detention

Principal Leonard Brodsky
Aptakisic Junior High School
9978 Rand Rd.
Deerbrook Park, IL 60090

Rabbi Avel Salt
Principal, Judaic Studies
The Solomon Schechter School
2911 W. Albion Ave.
Chicago, IL 60645

September 1, 2006

Dear Leonard,

I want, first of all, to thank you for admitting Gurion Maccabee to Aptakisic, and secondly, to apologize for having had to cut short our conversation after services last week. I'm not sure if you saw her there or not, but my daughter Esther was sitting on the stair beneath the one on which we stood, and, being yet another great admirer of the boy in question (not to mention a habitual eavesdropper!—though this is no thing to complain about: after all, what better indication of a child's love for you than her belief that what you have to say to others is actually *interesting*, baruch H-shem?), she became very sad at Gurion's mention (she misses him at school), and she'd been tugging at the hem of my pant-leg and whispering, as if in prayer, "Please let's go, please can we," for all but the entire duration of our overly brief dialogue. So while I'm already at it here, with the gratitude and the apologies, I'll use the occasion to address as best I can the concerns you expressed. I'll begin with the issue of the weapons, as it seems to be—very understandably—your greatest source of unease.

I can't remember if I've mentioned it, but over the summer months, the afternoons Gurion didn't spend gallivanting in our backyard with Esther and her sisters, he spent in my study, reading Chumash and Talmud, so I've had a number of opportunities to discuss with him what he was thinking when he wrote and delivered those instructions of his last spring. Before we go into that, though, you must first understand that when I initially contacted you about Gurion, I was in no way exaggerating his peculiar intelligence, nor the promise it entails. It is my belief that, if given the proper chance, Gurion will become the foremost Jewish scholar of his generation, if not his epoch. I recognize that the magnitude of such a claim might seem, to someone who doesn't know the boy, cartoonish—even reckless—but...an anecdote in its defense:

On Gurion's first day at Solomon Schechter—he was a kindergartner, five years old, and without any capacity to read Hebrew—he approached me in the hallway and said, "Because you are the principal of Judaic Studies, I would like to ask you about the importance of truth." He spoke that way when he was small, like a boy with maybe a governess, surely a summer villa somewhere coastal in western Europe. Now he speaks differently—with character.

In any case, "Truth is very important," I told him.

He said, "I know. Except sometimes it is less important than it is at other times and this is what I want to ask you about. The matter, however, is a private one."

"The matter!" I thought. "So that's how it is!" Queen's English or not, I was confident he would tell me about having stolen something, or hurt somebody, only to ask if he should be honest about it, and then I'd tell him yes, be honest.

That is not what happened.

In my office, he sat cross-legged in the chair on the other side of my desk and said, "My mother has a colleague with a baby named Isaac. We went there yesterday, to Isaac's house, for a barbecue. We ate steak because I like steak and the steak that afternoon was delicious. After the steak, while our fathers smoked cigarettes, our mothers cleared the table and brought out bowls of ice cream. Isaac was laying on a blanket in the grass next to the table and, in the middle of my first bite of ice cream, a glinting in my eye came from his direction and I turned and saw that he held a steak knife. It must have fallen off the table when our moms cleared the dishes. It might have been my steak knife, it might have been anyone's—I don't think it matters. But I saw this baby, Isaac, holding this very sharp knife, playing with it. He was making the sun reflect itself onto his chest and his belly—he was wearing only a diaper—and it was very beautiful to Isaac, how the sun was being reflected, the way he could bend his wrist to push the sun around his body or turn it off or change the size of it and how it would multiply in number when he caught it on more than one tooth of the serration at once. And probably the knife felt to him differently than anything he'd ever held before because I know Isaac's parents would never let him play with dangerous metal things, and so it was very sad to me that it was a knife since he could accidentally stab himself in the eye or cut himself on the hand or the belly or stab himself in any of those places with it, or cut his forehead, or even if he just pricked himself a little bit and then dropped the knife, or dropped the knife *on* himself, pricking himself, it would be harmful… I jumped off my bench and snatched the knife away. I did it very quickly. All those thoughts I said I was thinking about the reflections on his belly and how he could hurt himself, I remember thinking them, but it seems impossible because they take so much time to say, and it was really as soon as I saw the knife in his hands that I took it from him. Isaac has big eyes, even for a baby, and they became even bigger when I took the knife. And then he started crying. And I said to his dad—because it happened so fast that no one could make out what exactly the situation was and maybe it looked like I made him cry on purpose—I said, 'He had a knife and I saved him,' and then my father, who was sitting next to me, picked up his ice-cream teaspoon, reached around me, and handed it down to Isaac, who grabbed it and stopped crying immediately. Which is what I should have done—the teaspoon. My father is smart. He tricked the baby. The baby thought the spoon was the knife. The spoon was smooth and metal and it could reflect the sun onto his belly. And I know that was the right thing to do, to trick the baby.

"And it is not that what I did was bad. What I did was very good. It is very good in a left-handed way to take a knife from a baby, because babies can be harmed by knives they're playing with, so it is a very clear kind of justice to take a knife away from a baby, only: there is very little love in taking the knife away. And I *do* love Isaac—he's a very funny baby…but even if I didn't love him, even if he were someone else's baby who I didn't know and didn't love, I would've taken the knife away. So it really had nothing to do with love, what I did. The spoon, though, giving him it, that *is* out of love, unless it's just to make him stop crying because the crying annoys you, but like I said, in the best circumstances I would've given him the spoon myself, before he even noticed the knife was missing from his hand, and he would never have started crying or even felt like crying. So here is where the question of the importance of truth comes up. The right thing to do is to balance justice and love, and giving Isaac the spoon after taking the knife away is one of the most balanced actions that I can imagine—but you end up tricking the baby when you do that. The spoon is not the knife. And you can say that the baby didn't know the knife was a knife to begin with and so there's no trick, but that's cheap—because it *was* a knife to begin with and tricks are *always* about what the mark doesn't know. So you're tricking the baby, and if you say you're not tricking the baby you're tricking yourself. There's no way to get around it. And tricks are dishonest and there's no way to get around that. And tricking the baby is the right thing to do, and there's no way to get around *that*. So truth is, and therefore must be, less important than some other things. And there are the obvious ones, like life, like if someone I don't like very much puts a gun to my head and says, 'I will kill you if you don't say that you love me,' I have to say I love them, but that is easy to figure out. It is worth lying to save a life. But why is it worth lying to Isaac about a knife that's already been taken from him? Maybe you say to save him pain or injury, but so then how much pain and how much injury? Because what if it's an adult? Is it different for adults? They can take a little more pain than a baby, maybe? What if it's an older kid? I'm an older kid, and if I found out you lied to me to save me some pain, I would trust you less and things would fall apart between us. At least I think that's how it is. I'm five and I am sure there are things that I don't know about: exceptions. But either way, since yesterday, whenever I think about Isaac the baby, I start thinking about Isaac, the father of Jacob. How when Isaac is blind and dying, Jacob glues the goat fur to his chest and pretends he's Esau, who's hairy, so Isaac will give him the blessing that is Esau's birthright. Jacob tricks his own father! But it is definitely the right thing to do. It has to be. Esau was mean. He secretly sold his birthright to Isaac for a bowl of soup years earlier, and then, when the time came, he tried to get the blessing anyway. And if Jacob didn't trick Isaac, we probably wouldn't even be here, there'd be no Israelites! And then on top of it, I read a commentary that said that Isaac *knew* he was being tricked. It said that he *wanted* to give

Jacob the blessing and that he was only pre*tending* to be tricked. But if Isaac was only pretending, then who was he pretending *for*? Because it seems to me like if he was pretending, he was pretending for H-shem. Like he was tricking H-shem! And that H-shem let Himself be tricked! It's very confusing to me and what I'm asking you is what other things, specifically, are more important than truth? And also why? And is it possible to trick G-d? And if it's *possible* to trick G-d, does that mean it is *okay* to trick G-d?"

Stuttering, I asked Gurion to come back later, to let me think about his questions, the answers to the simpler of which, to my mind at least, have to do with the tension between the abstract nature of truth and the fact that truth actually functions, physically, and in variable ways no less, such that one of the truths about the knife is that it was a vehicle of the sun's reflection, as was the spoon, and that what the baby became upset about, when Gurion took his knife, was the loss of his sun-reflecting vehicle. And so what soothed the baby was the acquisition of a new sun-reflecting vehicle: the knife was not, for the baby, ever functioning as a piercing or sawing instrument (thank G-d!), and the spoon was not, for the baby, ever functioning as a scooping instrument (or as a knife), and so there is no good reason to believe that the baby was tricked. There is no good reason to believe, as Gurion believed, that the baby believed the spoon was the knife. Knifeness or spoonness (to us distinguished, respectively, by the properties "ability to pierce/saw" and "ability to scoop"), if even the baby was aware of knifeness and spoonness, were likely irrelevant to the baby. So where's the trick? Nowhere. Imagine if it were a pet. My Esther had a pet mouse and the mouse died of a rare cancer and Esther moped until I replaced the dead mouse with a hamster. She did not believe the new rodent was the same rodent as the old rodent, but the new rodent did function similarly enough to the old rodent that she was able to forget, for the most part, the pain brought on by the old rodent's loss. She wasn't tricked out of being sad, but soothed.

The story of Jacob and Esau, however, is more complicated. (And you'll please forgive me for going on like this, Leonard; I realize I must sound more like a blowhard proud father than a concerned teacher, here, but it is so important to me that when you put down this letter, you understand the kind of talent of which Gurion is in possession, and I feel that the best way to help you understand is to detail what he has done for *me*. I.e., if even I, an adult, a lifelong Torah scholar, can be inspired by this boy—the *kindergartner* version—to re-examine fundamental notions about Torah, just imagine what he, five years later, can do for other *children*. I tell you he makes them *better*. Not merely *smarter*—though he certainly does that—but more *decent*. Kinder. More reflective. Of our children, he makes mensches. This is not a boy you lock away in a room. This is a boy to whom you introduce *everyone*.)

On one hand, Esau's birthright was voluntarily forfeited by Esau for the bowl of soup our star student mentioned, indicating that it was not *his*, was never his (What kind of son trades his birthright for a bowl of soup? Not the kind who is deserving of a patriarch's birthright, I can tell you!), and so one might say that Isaac, rather than being tricked by Jacob into giving Jacob Esau's blessing, had actually been tricked earlier, by his sons' birth-order, into thinking the birthright *ever belonged* to Esau: Jacob's trick could then be understood as a correction. Even so, Jacob deliberately misleads Isaac, via the goat-fur, into believing he's Esau. And although a number of scholars suggest that Isaac knew Jacob was pretending, that Isaac was colluding in his own trickery, that Isaac was thereby *not* tricked, the fact of some kind of truth being undermined cannot be dispelled: Even though we can all agree that the trick of the goat-fur served a higher truth (i.e., the birthright rightly belonged to Jacob), and even though (rather, even *if*—for we don't all agree on this part) we can agree that Isaac was not actually tricked by the trick, we cannot deny that *a* trick is being played. But if not a trick played on Isaac, then on whom? For whose benefit or detriment this trick? The reader's? Of course not. Though possibly an unreliable narrator (more on that in a moment), Torah's is not an unreliable author—He's G-d. And there's no need to trick Esau, who sold the birthright and isn't present anyway. As for Rebecca: we know for sure by the scripture that she has colluded with Jacob, orchestrated the whole goat-fur bit. So whom does that leave to trick? Rather: So Whom does that leave? H-shem? Yes. At least: Maybe. And this is not to say that G-d, for even a second, would have believed that Jacob was Esau, but that maybe G-d believed that *Isaac believed* Jacob was Esau, when that was not necessarily the case. And if G-d believed such a thing, despite its being untrue (which it may or not be), it would suggest—as many other portions of scripture do—that G-d has only limited access to the minds of men, if any at all. We know He cares greatly about what is "in our hearts"—that is plainly stated throughout scripture—but we do not know how it is that he learns what is in our hearts. Though we surely cannot hide what we do from Him, it may be the case that we can hide what we *think* from Him, and even what we think *of* Him. This may be why we are commanded to engage in so many rituals, why we are taught to pray aloud, never silently. It may be that H-shem, because he cannot access thoughts that we don't express in words or deeds, cannot completely understand Torah—a book about men that He, Himself, wrote—without our interpretation, without scholars or sagacious little boys to talk about it within His omnipresent earshot, to write about it so that He may read about it. It may be that Jacob and Isaac colluded to trick G-d, who loved them both, and that because He loved them He wrote of them so that we may read of them, because it is only by our reading of them and writing of them and speaking of them that He may come to understand them. And Gurion's capacity, as a five-year-old boy, to be haunted by certain of these possibilities, was shocking to me. And his ability to think scripturally in his assessment of everyday events was shocking to me, and that he could describe the sun on the belly of a baby at a barbecue as gorgeously as he had. And when, after I dismissed him, he said to me, "I'm sorry if I'm being very complicated. I'd ask my father these questions, but he doesn't like to talk to me about Judaism. He'll do it, but I can tell he doesn't like to. He quit it before I was born. He was supposed to be a great rabbi and kabbalist"—when he said that, I was shocked, too, for I knew his father to be Judah Maccabee, Esq., and all I'd known of the man was exactly what everyone else knows: that he defends the rights of Nazis to hold parades in the streets of Jewish suburbs. A complicated person, Judah Maccabee.

And so when Gurion left my office, I rushed to write down everything he said to me, as best as I could remember. You see, Leonard, he is a born tzadik, this boy, such a quick one, and it was apparent even then.

This letter is running long, and still I've not addressed your signal concern, so I won't, as much as I'm tempted to, go into detail about my ensuing series of awestruck and often—unfortunately—*fumbling* scholarly endeavors with Gurion, other than to say that, until the very end of his fourth-grade year, the only thing he seemed to like as much as learning was teaching. And in all of Schechter, there was not a boy or girl who did not profit by or enjoy being taught by him. And yes, this led to some talk among the children at our school of Gurion's being more than a genius (*genius* an epithet that no few of our students—some, like Gurion, deservingly; and others, of course, not—have had hurled at them by their loved ones); some talk of his being Moshiach. And yes, there were a few teachers here who were made uncomfortable by this kind of talk, and yes, there was one in particular who maybe did not like Gurion so much to begin with, and true, that one happened to have quite a high professional standing (the highest), and maybe that person acted unprofessionally one day, and surely he provoked an outburst of a violent nature from the quick tzadik in question, and possibly that outburst was not appropriate, and but then likely it was.

What I know for sure is that Gurion had not once acted violently toward others in our school until the day he was forced to leave; had not once in the five years he spent in my classroom offered any encouragement to those who, if you'll excuse the pun, lionized him; and had *but once* (in his third-grade year) lost his temper in my presence, which was apparently the result of his remarkably sensitive cranium coming into sudden contact with the underside of an oak table while he retrieved a pencil that he'd accidentally, it seemed, swept to the floor with his fiercely animated hands, hands he'd been using, with perfect pedagogical intent, to punctuate his learned commentary on the flawed nature of angels (one-legged, soulless) and the origin of the lisp of Moses (a hot coal the infant brought to his own lips in Pharaoh's court, if you don't know the Midrash). (Later, I asked Gurion why he even bothered to pick the pencil up in the middle of his lecture—it had been going so strongly when he dropped it—and he told me that Simon Rothschild, a new boy at school who was sitting at the far end of the study table, was wearing on his face a look of envy and annoyance, and Gurion knew that if he wanted Simon to pay attention, a gesture of endearing clumsiness would be required to win him over. "So I knocked the pencil under the table," Gurion said, "but Simon didn't see. So I got under the table to get the pencil, to show him that I knocked it down there. But then when I banged my head getting it, that was an accident, and I got very angry because I don't like it when my head is touched, and so when I came up from under the table, I was thinking: Simon made me bang my head. That is why I spun and knocked the chalk-trough off the blackboard—because I wanted to jump across the table and knock Simon's face off his head, but at the same time I didn't want to. And it was good that I didn't go after Simon, but still, I'm sorry I wrecked your blackboard.")

And furthermore, as you might or might not have noticed by way of his permanent record, Gurion did not, after leaving Schechter, engage in any violence at Northside Hebrew Day School. He is not some loose canon. He wrote those instructions after having witnessed an act of antisemitic violence outside of the Fairfield Street Synagogue, where he used to attend services (without his parents, by the way—their home is secular). If you followed the newspapers last Spring, then what you read was that a group of local Muslim teenagers, claiming to have been inspired by the current Intifada, threw stones at a group of Hasidic congregants on a Saturday and that no one was critically injured. What you did not read was that those congregants who did not duck back inside the synagogue for cover froze where they stood, and that the rabbi, a good man (I know him a little), came forward, apparently in an effort to reason with the stone-throwers, and managed to utter one word, "Please," before receiving for his trouble a block of jagged concrete in his mouth.

Gurion was one of those who had frozen, and he told me that by the time it occurred to him to chase the fleeing boys, they were already too far ahead of him; that he ran after them fruitlessly, catching sight of them through gaps in backyard fences, turning numerous corners, and ducking into various alleys and gangways, until he became sick from exertion, and that it was not until he stopped running that he realized that no one was behind him, that he was the only one who had tried to catch them. This upset Gurion greatly, and when he returned to the synagogue, he was reprimanded by the rebbetsen for having endangered himself. He told me that, as he received his reprimand, a group of boys gathered behind the rebbetsen and that what he saw on their faces was not the remnant of fear and shock that he would have expected, but rather regret, and that he knew that what they regretted was that they had not helped him chase down the stone-throwers. And he also told me that the rebbetsen was right—that he *had* endangered himself—and that he should not have endangered himself. He told me that what he should have done was picked up a brick of his own, "or something with better range," he said, and convinced the others to do the same, and to follow him. Unreasonable? Maybe. Maybe not. Not so very unreasonable, in any case. As Gurion put it: "We're taught not to bow down before idols or men. *You* teach us that. *Torah* teaches that. We're taught that it's better to *die* than to bow, but isn't it better yet to do neither? When someone comes at you and says, 'Bow or die,' isn't it better to lay him out? And I know what you'll say, Rabbi Salt, I know: You'll say there's a difference between ducking a blow and bowing down, that there's no sin at all in ducking a blow. But that's only true to a certain extent. To duck a direct blow is only to duck—I'll give you that—but to duck a blow that has yet to be launched, let alone a blow that only might be coming, which is to say nothing of ducking in hopes of averting a blow's being launched to begin with—that, Rabbi Salt, is to bow, is it not? It is. Of course. That's exactly what it is. And I say this: It's better to shoot. It's better to shoot til you no longer have to, to shoot til those people who'd have you bow down duck to avert the launch of *your* blows."

Once the rebbetsen had finished admonishing Gurion, the boys who had gathered behind her walked him home and, at his front stoop, he told them that if they were to return the following Saturday evening, after shul, he would teach them how to avoid losing face, how to live without bowing to idols or men. And he invented that weapon and wrote those instructions and he sent to those he'd invited an e-mail containing a list of supplies they should bring to his home, and the boys came to his home as originally planned, and the rest you know about. You can see, if you read *Ulpan*, that Gurion never instructed, or even suggested, that the weapons be used to attack other students, much less fellow Jewish students.

Now, if you put a weapon in the hands of a child, of course an accident is bound to happen. And of course Gurion knew this as well as any adult. Nonetheless, he is a boy. Despite his talents, a boy. And a boy is more idealistic than a man, and high ideals in the hands of children can be as dangerous as weapons. He thought he was in the right, and because he thought he was in the right, he thought there would be an exception. That's that.

As for what happened at the Martin Luther King Middle School, it seems, now, to have been inevitable. Gurion, owing to that highly alienating and pejorative e-mail from Rabbi Kalisch, was made to see a social worker, who promptly diagnosed him with all sorts of nonsense disorders and then placed him in a lock-down program for disturbed children not dissimilar to this CAGE program you described to me outside the shul on Saturday. On his fourth day there, being both new and the youngest, Gurion was attacked at recess by one of the boys from this program. He fist-fought the boy, apparently injured him badly, and then a number of the boy's friends crept forth, ready to avenge the boy, and what did Gurion do? He did what you would have done and what I would have done, if we were not the types to run away—he took hold of a cinderblock. The friends stood their ground, but stayed their attack, and soon a recess supervisor had arrived on the scene, and saw Gurion holding the cinderblock, and saw the bleeding child at his feet. The friends claimed that Gurion had used the cinderblock to beat the boy, the boy confirmed the lie, and, owing to Rabbi Kalisch's e-mail (which I really do believe should be expunged from Gurion's record), this claim seemed more than plausible to the principal, and Gurion was expelled.

These days he's not so fond of school. That is true. But it's on you to fix that, Leonard. It's your turn. I would remind you, sympathetically, that your very own sons came to Solomon Schechter because you felt—and correctly so—that the mental health people at their public school had wrongly damned them to what you yourself called "the ever-growing ghettos of special education." I would remind you that your son, Ben, may he rest in peace, was a school-friend of Gurion's, despite the gap in their ages, and that Gurion attended his shiva, and that Gurion wept at his burial. Please forgive my tone if it is too strong. I only hope, in reminding you of these things, that you will reconsider your stance, and see your way to *not* placing Gurion in your CAGE program; that you will do everything in your power to be good to him, to understand that he is coming to you damaged but that the damage is not irreparable, that our prophets are always treated like criminals, and that if you treat Gurion like a mensch, he will act like one. And if it is, for some reason, impossible for you to keep my student out of your cage, maybe there's a compromise—maybe a trial period, a couple of weeks to observe him. But I must say that I have a bad feeling about even that. For a ten-year-old, especially one who is so readily fascinated with the world as Gurion, a day is as rich and significant as a history of everything. A day can change everything.

A blessing on you and your family.

Your Friend,
Avel

P.S. Gurion's new legal residence—on Lincoln Road between Holmes Parkway and Skinner Drive—is a motel (The Boarder, I think it's called, or maybe The Border) with a rather large driveway. Gurion has been instructed to wait on the corner of Lincoln and Holmes for the bus, but his mother would prefer the bus to pick him up in this large driveway, which one can see from inside the motel office, where it is warm and dry, and where, for that very reason, the motel owner has given Gurion advance permission to wait. I told her I was certain you could speak to the driver or dispatcher and get them to accommodate her preference. If I was being presumptuous, please let me know, and please accept my apology in advance. If I was not being presumptuous, I thank you in advance, and if I was maybe being a little presumptuous, but you'll nonetheless accommodate Mrs. Maccabee's request, I thank you in advance, apologize in advance, and then thank you again for working with me here, despite my presumptuousness. In advance.

□   □   □   □   □   □   □

Nakamook shoved through half the exit bottleneck to bookrocket Ronrico. I caught up as he lowered his fist.

I said, Benji.

Nakamook launched it.

The books popped from Ronrico's grip and scattered.

"Jesus!" Ronrico said.

"Just shut the fuck up," said Nakamook.

Botha, at the door, twenty kids plus two teachers–deep, shouted out "Hey!" except he didn't know to who. He couldn't see.

Ronrico was trying to back away from Benji, but Botha got the door open and the crowd was pushing forward, up to the gate, so Ronrico bounced off us. He said to Nakamook, "We're all on the side—"

Nakamook plugged his hand in, beneath Ronrico's chin, and lifted. He lifted swiftly til his mantis-arm was straight, and then, in smaller increments, at less rapid intervals, he lifted higher and higher from the shoulder. This action was called the Impossible because no one else at school could perform it. Also that's how it looked: impossible. Nakamook often performed the action on people who, unlike Ronrico, were taller than him, and to keep his balance he had to stand bowlegged, which, to the eyes of observers, always made him look shorter. I'd never been Impossibled before, but I didn't think it would be that hard to disengage. You'd just have to kick him a good one in the torso, or dig your thumbs deep into the soft part of his wrist til the tendons gave. It must have been that the suddenness of the action erased your sense of options though: no one had ever gotten out of a Nakamookian Impossible before Nakamook had let him, and many even seemed to cooperate with the action, bending their knees in midair the way a baby does when you lift it by the armpits.

The Janitor stepped out of the bottleneck as soon as Ronrico's feet left the ground. Benji hammered down on his skull with his free hand and the Janitor said, "Ow. Ow. Ow." He half-sat against the crowd, rubbing a sleeved forearm briskly through his hair, his dazed face slack.

Thirteen inches above Benji's head, the bugged-out eyeballs of Asparagus revolved at me. He wrinkled between his pulsing temples = "Why?"

Nakamook didn't miss it. "Don't act ignorant," he said to Ronrico, shaking him a little.

I set my hand on Benji's elbow and waited for him to feel it. When he felt it, he one-shoulder-shrugged at me = "Fine." To Ronrico, he said, "Do not try to be us," then lowered him slow and let go of his throat.

Ronrico crouched down to gather his books. The Janitor helped him. Botha unlocked the gate. The crush of the bottleneck got heavy, then ended.

I picked a rocketed book up and gave it to Ronrico. I said, This won't happen again.

Ronrico looked at his feet.

"The fuck!?" Nakamook said to the air next to my face. Then the Flunky walked past us. "Foog," Benji told him.

The Flunky stalled for a second, walked on.

Benji followed him past Botha, into C-Hall. I followed Benji. C-Hall, lockerless, was always empty after school except for Cage students, who always got out of class last because of the gate.

I told Benji to hold on.

He slowed his pace. "You're friends with the Flunky now, too?" he said.

He's not my enemy.

Nakamook stopped walking. He said, "None of these guys are your friends. They're just scared of you."

So what? I said.

"Whenever I'm scared? I wait for a chance to damage who's scaring me, and then I do that. Isn't that what you do?"

I don't get scared of people.

Nakamook said, "Well that's what everyone else does."

I said to him, Even if you're right, I still don't lose anything, having them on my side.

He said, "Listen. When someone's scared of me, I know they'll try to damage me the second they have the chance, and that makes me scared of them. And so I think: I better damage them first, while I have the chance— You should be scared of these people *because* they fear you, Gurion. You should damage them first. You should damage them again and again. You should damage them until they stop being scared of you. Until your dangerousness is undeniable and you're like highway traffic or the edge of a cliff— something they wouldn't even *consider* crossing. *Then* you make friends. It's the only way."

I said, You and I never damaged each other.

He said, "We weren't ever scared of each other, but look, forget it—my mood just switched. So did yours."

I touched my face. My face was smiling. We stood at the C-Hall/Main Hall junction. People shouting and shoving and flirting with each other. At the other end, the front doors opened and shut and the hallway had wind. I could look in any direction I wanted.

Benji said, "I feel like a millionaire on the back of an armored jet-ski my samurai girlfriend who loves me is charging at a cartel speedboat to win a game of chicken. Isn't this the day's best part? You don't even have to remember to enjoy it. It enjoys you into itself."

I could not imagine June as a samurai on a jet-ski, but a ninja—she could be a ninja, hang-gliding. And she could be my wife.

I said to Benji, Walk me to the Office.

"Office shmoffice!" Benji said. "You're killing the momentum. What's in the Office, anyway? We've only got fifteen minutes before detention—twelve minutes, just—don't you wanna go outside by the buses?"

I said, I got called.

He said, "That note the new kid brought? That was so long ago—say you forgot."

I said, You know I did the scoreboard, right?

He said, "I know *I* didn't do it, and Vincie and Leevon were in the Cage all day, so…"

I said, Brodsky's expecting me to come to the Office and get my record. I made this really big deal out of getting my record this morning, and if I don't go and get it now, then he'll think I'm avoiding him. It should only take a minute, anyway—then I'll come out by the buses.

Benji said, "I'll walk you."

Eliyahu came up beside us, raving, "…and this Cage should fall—that boy who wet…"

I said to him, This is Benji Nakamook. I said, Don't fear him.

"And why should I fear him?" said Eliyahu.

I said, You shouldn't.

He said, "But I don't. Still, this wet boy, I think it was the second-worst thing I've ever seen—with his hand in the air. Did you see his hand in the air?"

It was too hard to think about Ben-Wa right then. Right then, I was thinking about gliders and June and getting my record.

I said, Eliyahu, did your mood just change?

He said, "Why should my mood change?"

I said, Look at Main Hall.

He said, "It's filled with people who are desperate to get out of it. This I should celebrate? They will get out shortly and I will go to detention. *This* I should celebrate?"

Benji said, "You drain my buzz, new kid."

The three of us headed through the Main Hall rush together, Benji in the middle and two steps in front of us, squinting his eyes, cutting a tunnel from the crowd with his elbows.

Halfway to the Office, I saw June putting books in her locker, talking to some shaved-headed girl I didn't know, and my throat went dry and chokey. I had the poem to give her, and the Coke and the pass-pad I'd risked getting steps for, but I couldn't give them to her in front of some girl I didn't know, and even if I could, there was no table there to throw the pass-pad onto while I made the "I thought you might need a coaster" joke. If I threw the pad on the Main Hall floor, the joke would lose conceptual integrity and the pad would get stomped on by the traffic.

What I did then was chomsky. If, after Hashem replaced Isaac with the goat, Avraham, instead of slaying the goat, had thought to himself, "But I was prepared to kill my own son!" and then turned from the goat and slain Isaac, it would have been just a little bit more chomsky than me, once I saw June in my path, thinking, "It's not time yet," and then ducking between Nakamook and Eliyahu before she could spot me. But that's what I did. I mistook a blessing for an inconvenience.

Nakamook said, "She's right there, klebold. The girl of your dreams."

I said, Keep walking.

We kept walking.

"Which girl is this?" said Eliyahu.

Nakamook said, "The redhead."

Eliyahu looked over his shoulder. He said to me, "You love a Gentile?"

I said, She's not a Gentile.

"She looks a Gentile," said Eliyahu.

"Who cares?" said Nakamook.

I said, Hashem wouldn't fall me in love with a Gentile.

Nakamook asked Eliyahu: "You think I look pretty Gentile?"

I didn't hear what Eliyahu said, though. I'd already turned into the Office by the time he'd responded—either that, or he spoke too softly.

▫ ▫ ▫ ▫ ▫ ▫ ▫

Jelly Rothstein's sister Ruth was leaning against Pinge's desk, tapping a mint against her teeth so it clicked. Across from her, crowding the waiting chairs, were four Main Hall Shovers who seemed short of breath. June's ex, Josh Berman, was one of the four, but I wasn't yet aware of that; Blake Acer's face was the only one I knew. (What's more is despite the fact that Berman's existence loomed sudden and huge over all of my thoughts, I didn't even consider the possibility that he, himself, might be standing before me. In the few hours since Lunch, when I'd banished the thought of him, Berman had become, by way of said banishment, a mythic figure of such towering stature that to just bump into him would've seemed about as likely to me as just bumping into an American President, or Natalie Portman. Philip Roth, even.) In Acer's right hand was a bright orange boxcutter, on the far chair a cardboard carton. He knelt on the chair that I fell in love with June in, sliced through the tape, reached into the carton, and came out with a handful of 2006 scarves. The scarves were, as Ruth had reported they'd be in "Nada y Pues Nada"—the last installment of "State of School Spirit," her three-part series for the *Aptakisic News*—entirely absent of disputed embroidery. I stepped a little closer to get a better look, partly because June had dated a Shover—but only partly. I'd been following the controversy surrounding the scarves ever since I'd started attending Aptakisic. For the Main Hall Shovers, this moment was colossal.

*Ten weeks earlier, in the first week of school, Blake Acer got elected Shover president. The margin was narrow, 31 to 30, and the platform he ran on was scarf redesign, though by Rothstein's analysis, his win was dynastic.

Acer's brother Wayne had founded the Shovers. This had happened back in 2002. Rothstein couldn't get an interview with Wayne, but according to a sidebar titled "Dawn of the Shovers" (also by Rothstein), Shoverlore had it that, after seeing Scorsese's *Gangs of New York*, Wayne read fifty pages of the book in one day. Pausing only for dinner in front of the TV, he saw footage of a riot in England on a newsbreak: soccer fans storming the field of a stadium, stomping on rivals, trampling each other, uprooting seating, full story at ten. Wayne glugged down some milk and went back upstairs, googled the search terms "soccer" and "violence," and came across an excerpt from a book about hooligans—no one remembers the title. He biked to the bookstore and purchased the book, took it back home and read fifteen pages, then broke for the news and an ice cream. The hooligans profiled protected each other. The clubs they belonged to had tough-sounding names, and they were always together, sharing a cause, making up cheers, and probably— even the fat ones, Wayne bet, even the pimpled—getting girls. They wore

---

* Because both of my faithful translators have convinced me that there are scholars out there who will be made confused by my decision to include a "somewhat intricate" ten-page history of the Main Hall Shovers at this point in the scripture, and because there is, unfortunately or not, no better point in the scripture to include said history, I've elected to provide this cumbersome footnote (all eighteen footnotes to the scripture proper, are, I should mention—as long as I'm embracing cumbersome explaininess—after-market parts that owe their inclusion to similar advice from my translators, to whom I owe much, and to whom you owe much, and to whom, above all, we'll owe even more just as soon as I'm finished here, for they'll be the ones to field your questions in my stead) in which I will, following the colon, state something I'd have hoped would be obvious to everyone, but apparently isn't: Without knowing the history of the Main Hall Shovers and their scarves, scholars of today (ca. 2013) will not be able to fully comprehend the mechanics of the Damage Proper, nor will scholars of tomorrow (e.g., ca. 4013) be able to understand the Gurionic War's larger context. Furthermore, I want to assure you that if you feel a little lost, it's not because you missed something, but rather because I haven't gotten to it yet. So now I'll start getting to it, and finish later when I'm finished. You *will* understand.

matching scarves sewn with intricate crests that despite being scarves were totally masculine, and all because of soccer, the girliest sport you could play without a shuttlecock.

The next day at Recess, Wayne told his story. No one wrote the speech down, but its opening was famous: "I've read sixty-five pages and we need to get scarves because basketball is better than soccer."

By the end of the week, the paperwork was finished. Wayne filed a petition with twenty-five names and Miss Kimble signed on as the faculty sponsor. Like the Sci-Fi and Fantasy and Pastry-Lovers clubs—unlike Squaw Squad, Debate Team, or Band—the Shovers got semi-private status. They could meet twice a month after school in the gym, under Miss Kimble's supervision, but the school would provide no bus-space for away-games, no section in the bleachers, no official uniforms. Shovers ordered and paid for their scarves themselves.

Twenty-one guys formed the club that first year, about 7 percent of Aptakisic's male students. Anyone who wasn't a bandkid could join. Band-kids were the enemies of the Main Hall Shovers: partly because their purpose rivaled the Shovers' (though they did give an annual concert in Spring, the primary function of the Braves Brass Band was to "support" the Indians during pregames and rallies and homegame halftimes); partly because they got the best seats on the bleachers; mostly because the Shovers needed kids to harrass to buttress their identity and keep up morale, and whereas the few counterparts they had in the conference (i.e., the Knifelike Fangs at Heinrich Junior High, the Uberdunk Slammies at Twin Groves Middle, and the Kinderpop Pep Squad at Sandburg Middle) were encountered but twice per season at most, the bandkids were everywhere, always.

From "Red Zeppelin, Led Inddian," part one of Ruth Rothstein's "State of School Spirit":

> ...and only two years after having founded the Shovers, Wayne Acer, as a freshman at Stevenson High School, fell in with a crowd not known for loving sports, not known for the pride they took in their school, their family, or even themselves—a crowd that is known to everyone at Stevenson.
>
> A crowd everyone at Stevenson knows as "the skids."
>
> Wayne bought a chrome-zippered black leather jacket, cut holes in the knees of his jeans, and smoked. According to Blake, Wayne changed for a girl.
>
> "You just shouldn't ever change for a girl like that," the new

Shover President told me over lunch. "If you change for a girl, who are you, really? You don't know who you are. And I'll say so right to Wayne's face cause it's true. I HAVE said it right to Wayne's face, last May. 'Who are you, now? Who are you, Wayne? What about basketball? You FOUNDED THE SHOVERS. You lived for the Indians. You knew all the stats.' And he did, Ruth, he did. And not the stats for only just Aptakisic, either. He knew all the stats IN THE CONFERENCE. Where do you think I learned all that stuff from? Wayne wasn't just some average older brother. Wayne was my mentor. Everything I know, I know because of Wayne.

"But I asked him who he was now, or who, you know, HE THOUGHT HE WAS, and he looked at his feet and giggled this really uncomfortable giggle, and what that giggle meant, Ruth, was: 'I don't know who I am, Blake. I really need your help. I'm lost.'

"Lucky for us, the Bulls were playing the Sixers, and Wayne was fighting with this girlfriend who will so-called BE A FAMOUS DRUMMER ONE DAY, and I convinced him to watch the game with me. He wouldn't do any of the cheers we used to, and he kept going outside to smoke stinking disgusting death-causing cigarettes, but he only did it during timeouts I kept noticing. See, in the end, he hadn't shaken basketball. He never will, either, cause no one can. Once you catch that bug. And so on.

"That was last May, and since then things have gotten a little better. Wayne still says he doesn't care about the Shovers, or the Indians, let alone The Stevenson Patriots, but once in a while, Ruth—three times now, to be exact—he'll throw on a Bulls game on the TV in his room, and invite me upstairs to watch with him. And the silver lining—gold lining, really, even platinum if you think about it—is that during timeouts and half-times, we listen to all this music Wayne's into, and even though the guys who sing it seem fruity, it's okay because they're joking about the fruitiness. What they're really doing is making fun of dudes who think it ISN'T fruity to look all fruity. Wayne and the other skids don't get that at all because they're always so serious, but all you really have to do is have a sense of humor to see that even the bands who might actually be a little fruity have earned the right to be fruity like that because of how they're geniuses. Mostly they're joking on skids, though—it's subtle. It's great music Wayne listens to, though, is my point, and plain and simple? Wasn't for Wayne, I'd have never even heard OF Led Zeppelin. And if I'd never heard of Led Zeppelin, I'd have never HEARD Led Zeppelin, you see what I'm saying? I'd have never known "Stairway to Heaven," hands down, was the best song ever, on what is, bottom line, the best album ever, in all the history of music. If Wayne, to sum it up, never became a skid and started, in a nutshell, listening to their music, then no doubt I couldn't've, long story short, had my creative revelation, and so, the 2006 scarf, to put it plainly, wouldn't be as sharp as you'll see in November when the order comes in and you'll see what I mean."

Apart from not being a bandkid, all it took to be a Shover was the annual scarf. It was made of red wool with white fringes and embroidery, and all of the Shovers wore it the same: tied around the neck in an overhand knot with the right leg two times the length of the left so that none of the signifiers went unexposed. On the right, by the shoulder, was Chief Aptakisic, feather-headressed and -earringed, a sillhouette in warpaint, the year of the season in thin roman numerals that looked like whiskers along his square jawline; beneath that the numbers assigned to the players, JV and varsity, varsity on top; and on the left above the fringe that hung just beneath the heart, the names of the varsity A-team starters, captains at the bottom (so they wouldn't get covered if the knot slipped low), then up to the neck reverse-alphabetically.

This design had been constant for five years running, but its left leg had always been a problem. Since players improved at various rates, line-ups were always subject to adjustment, and by the start of every season since the Shovers had been founded, at least one Indian off the bench or the B-team took an A-team position from another player whose name had already been embroidered on the scarf. The cause of the problem was variously diagnosed. Some blamed the scarf's maker for the six weeks its factory took to fill orders, which required Desormie to give to the Shovers his rosters that far in advance of the season. Some blamed Shover presidents for failing to find a maker of scarves who required less lead-time. A few—mostly presidents— blamed Desormie himself for being fickle with his lineups, or the victim of brain disease. Many of the Shovers didn't care either way; the important thing to them was for the scarves to identify Shovers as Shovers. Among the proponents of scarf-reform, though, 2004 was invoked almost daily. That year a captain got bumped from the lineup: within three weeks of the scarf being ordered, Bam Slokum, til then but a middling sixth-grade player, had grown four inches taller and ten times as dominant. He came off the bench of the JV B-team to play A-team on varsity as a starting point-guard, and went on to break, in the eight weeks following, three Aptakisic and two conference scoring-records. The captain Bam replaced was called Gregory Gumm, and to *get Gummed* became slang that for Shovers was fighting words, harsher even than any phrase it might have euphemized.

Not that Shovers ever actually fought. The events they called fights were chest-bump engagements where one guy said "What?" and the other "So do something," and sometimes a third and a fourth said "Yeah, do something." A few of the Shovers were stooges for Indians—carrying their textbooks, doing their homework, hearing hints of affection in their verbal abuse—but most of them only aspired to be stooges. They met twice a month, shoved around Main Hall, and as of only very recently had seemed poised to schism over trouble that stemmed from their scarf's new design.

By the end of the 2005–2006 school year, the scarf-reform issue was so starkly polarized that the Shovers had forgotten its mechanics. You either wanted reform (whatever that meant) or you didn't want reform (regardless of what it meant). Most of the Shovers' debates went like this:

"They may not be perfect but our scarves are the best, so don't rock the boat, homes, it's dangerous."

"All I'm saying is 2004, dude. Two-gumming-thousand-and-four."

Thus, when during his pre-election speech, Blake Acer spoke of his scarf-redesign plan, a plan that would alter the scarf's left leg's looks but didn't address the real problem at all—the problem of immanent roster-change/scarfmaking-leadtime/embroidery-permanence itself (taboo)—the majority by which he would soon acquire victory was simple in more than one sense of the word. The really dumb Shovers fixed on *redesign* which sounded a lot like *reform*, and those among them who wanted reform thought Blake backed their cause and voted for him; those among them who didn't want reform thought Blake opposed their cause and voted against him. The less dumb Shovers—both those who wanted reform and didn't—saw that Blake Acer, intentionally or not, had undermined reform with redesign, and they voted the opposite of those really dumb Shovers who shared their position on reform. The split between the two kinds of dumb was pretty even, but the few undecideds knew Blake to be the brother of the Shovers' founder, and they figured the blood was good, so Blake won.

The morning after the election, during announcements, Blake reiterated, for all of Aptakisic, the details of the scarf-redesign plan. "Over the summer, I had a creative revelation, and the creative revelation that I had was this: However smartly colored and intelligently organized and totally perfect on the right leg our scarves are, they'd be even better without English on the left. This creative revelation was what got me elected, so that's why we're getting rid of all the English and replacing the names of our starters with symbols: symbols the starters will choose for themselves; symbols that really mean something to them, like the symbols the guys in Led Zeppelin chose to represent their souls on the cover of *IV*; really deep symbols that mean more than words, that mean more than names; symbols that capture the spirit of each starter as a person as well as a player. Thank you!"

Co-Captain Baxter, at lunch that day, stood on a table and shouted for attention, then raising his can of protein drink, said, "Bam and I were sitting here, talking to the Indians, and we all agree that this moment's historic, and we all agree this year's Indians are historic, and this school is historic, and, on behalf of all the school and especially basketball, Bam and I want to thank the Shovers for voting for Acer, who's really got a vision here that's also historic. Even though it can only happen for five of us, none of us can wait to see our symbols on the scarves, but especially not Bam and I, who are both looking forward to this chance to be creative, and know that the opportunity to be creative will motivate our teammates to seize the opportunity: it's just one more reason to work hard to make starter, and bring home the victory and the glory and so on, so thumbs up to Acer and his Main Hall Shovers. We value all of you, and not just as the army of goodguys you are, but each and every one of all sixty-however-many of you, on a first-name-type individual basis. We don't listen to Led Zeppelin, me and Bam and the Indians, but you can bet we're gonna start to this very afternoon. Right after practice, y'all, right after practice. Three cheers for Acer and his Main Hall Shovers. Three cheers for Acer. Three cheers for the Shovers."

Acknowledged and praised, their three cheers resounding and rifts all healed, the Shovers bore Blake like a casket or champ on their shoulders to recess, feeling like brothers and knocking down bandkids, smashing the fast ones against walls and lockers.

The rosters were posted twenty days later, and the varsity starters gave Acer their glyphs. Blonde Lonnie Boyd chose the cap of a jester, Co-Captain Baxter a tomahawk. Bam Slokum, for reasons no one could or would say, chose peace symbols flanking a bigtop tent, and the starter whose name no one ever got straight—the one whose replacement was himself replaced twice in the weeks leading up to the opening game—chose a bow and arrow surrounded by a garland. The last of the starters to turn in his glyph was Gary "The Quiet Indian" Frungeon, who Main Man attended weekly Pentecostal mass with, a kind-eyed niceguy who liked to shake hands, who no one at school—not even Benji Nakamook—had ever even wished to bring any damage.

Frungeon gave Acer a red-on-white ichthys.

Shovers who were Israelites remembered they were Israelites.

An emergency meeting by the dumpsters was held.

The Israelites stated that wearing an ichthys was against their religion, like wearing a cross.

Yet, argued Acer with all due respect, the ichthys was the symbol Frungeon chose to express the depths of his soul creatively with, and who were they to suggest that the Shovers had the right to stifle the creative expression of a soul, let alone that of the soul of an Indian?

Jews, they said. They were Jews, they said. They were Jews who couldn't wear an ichthys.

So then they couldn't wear an ichthys, Acer told them, so what? Maybe they could get themselves a different kind of scarf, or cover the ichthys on their scarf with marker, though on second thought marker would be disrespectful, and on third thought another kind of scarf would be, also—anyone would see they were singling out Frungeon, then—but what about another item of apparel? A smaller item that didn't feature starters, an item on which five symbols couldn't fit? Something like a hat, but not exactly a hat because you couldn't wear a hat in the classroom; maybe a wristband or headband or handkerchief? Maybe a patch they could sew on their outerwear?

No, said the Israelites, that didn't make sense: without the scarf you were other than a Shover.

But weren't they saying they were other than Shovers? If no Jewish Shovers could wear the ichthys, but all of the non-Jewish Shovers could, then didn't that make them different from the others?

If being a Shover meant wearing Christian symbols, then yes, said the Israelites, but that's not what it meant, so no.

The Shovers don't wear Christian symbols, Blake explained: the Shovers wear symbols of the starters' souls, one of which only happens to be Christian.

The atheist Shover, Trent Vander, weighed in then: One thousand pounds of this, said Vander, and half a ton of that. Vander told them Jesus was used to make war and do evil and kill the environment, so Vander wasn't crazy for the ichthys either, but Vander knew God wouldn't punish the Jews for wearing a symbol that meant nothing to them, not if God was full of total love, which didn't matter anyway because there was no God, so why not decide the ichthys wasn't a Jesusfish? Call it two meaningless arcs intersecting because that's what it was, and that's what he was doing, was being open-minded, and so should they.

The Israelite Shovers demanded a plebiscite.

Acer scheduled the vote for the next official meeting.

Then some of the Israelites, led by Josh Berman, went to see Brodsky. If I was among them, I'd have told them not to, but I didn't tell them anything: I wasn't among them. I'd only read of them, and after the fact. Before I fell in love with June and met Eliyahu, my only Israelite friend at Aptakisic was Jelly, who told me they teased her for being in the Cage—not just the ones who were Shovers either, but all of the Israelites, or nearly all of them, none of whom I knew. I'd decided when I started at Aptakisic that I wouldn't talk to Israelites who didn't approach me. They were secular there, and they likely hadn't heard of me, but still they might have, which meant that their parents might have barred them from being my friends, and their being secular didn't make it okay for me to risk leading them toward break-ing the fifth commandment. Still, of course, I'd hoped *they'd* approach *me* and tell me their parents didn't know who I was, but then after Jelly told me they teased her, I began to hope that they *wouldn't* approach me. After I'd read about the nonsense with the scarves, the latter hope only got stronger and stronger.

They were right about one thing: Adonai would get pissed if they wore the ichthys. But that was whole miles beside the point. The majority of Shovers clearly wanted the ichthys, regardless of how the Israelites felt. And Adonai doesn't care if Gentiles wear ichthii any more than He cares if they eat pork or have foreskins. And no one, let alone Adonai, ever told anyone he had to be a Shover. And so, if the Shovers didn't care about the Israelites, or just didn't care enough to honor Israelite laws—and why should they care? the laws weren't theirs, and, Vander aside, the ichthys was—why would an Israelite even want to be a Shover? If I'd been a Shover... but I'd never be a Shover, maybe that was the difference... If, though, I *had* been, I'd've just walked out.

In any case, I'd never have ratted to the principal about the ichthys, especially not after demanding the plebiscite. Apart from being wrong, to rat was self-defeating. If the other Shovers found out (which they did), then the passive disregard they already had for the cause of the Israelites would, by many, be replaced with active contempt (which it was), and worse than that, it would give *them* a cause, make *them*—the Gentile Shovers—the underdogs, and Brodsky their oppressor, a figure to defy.

And that happened, too.

As soon as he learned of the dispute from the finks, Brodsky announced that nothing religious could appear on any item of school apparel, and thereby banned the ichthys from the scarf.

But Acer said the scarf was not school apparel. He said that the Shovers, being a semi-private club, paid for and ordered and designed it themselves, and now it was they whose creative souls were at stake, so it wasn't Brodsky who'd make the decision, but the "majority of Shovers who would hold a democrat [*sic*] vote."

Yet a club at school with semi-private status was nonetheless a school-sponsored club, Brodsky told them, and the principal of the school had total jurisdiction, so plebiscite narishkeit, referendum dumb pudendum.

Despite Brodsky's assurance it would be illegitimate, the vote was taken at the next official meeting. The pro-ichthys faction won 48–13.

No one can know what would have happened had Acer and the Shovers followed through on the results. Nor can it be known if, by the time the vote was taken, they'd had any intention of following through. Ruth Rothstein opines, in "Nada y Pues Nada," that all of the Shovers, including Blake Acer, had been long-since resigned to Brodsky's decision, their votes meek gestures they'd back with no action, hollow as bird-bones, forty-eight balloted chest-bumps. (Ruth's heart, Jelly'd told me when I'd first read the article, was once broken by a Shover—this was Berman's older brother, although, at that time, she hadn't named names.) If it's true that the Shovers had been only caulking trickles, then indeed Frungeon saved them many facefulls of snat. If it isn't true, it's hard to guess what he saved them—Brodsky talked tough, but what could he do if the Shovers, as Acer suggested in whispers, did order scarves embroidered with ichthii and had them delivered somewhere other than school? Expel them? Who'd stand for it? What about the kids who wore crosses and chais? We weren't in France or Saudi Arabia. Maybe Brodsky could sue for trademark infringement? the use of the mascot up near the shoulder? Maybe take away the Shovers' semi-private-club status? But then they'd meet at recess, wholly private, with impunity. Ban scarves in the classroom? What about cold kids? Apart from maybe holding a grudge—and maybe, for a Shover, the threat of that was enough—Brodsky really couldn't do much to punish them. Whatever might have happened in either case, though, it was Frungeon, to everyone's surprise, who prevented it.

He appeared, according to Rothstein's account, at the meeting just after the vote-counts' announcement. His scrimmage jersey soaked in the sweat of earnest basketball, he came straight from practice, nearly breathless from the rush, and proclaimed to the Shovers, without bile or guile: "I never wanted to cause you guys trouble. The Lord Jesus, my savior, cares not about scarves, and He'd never want anyone to fight about scarves, and I've prayed for the past two nights for His guidance, and this morning as I woke, the Lord Jesus provided: I fell to the floor—no worries, my brothers, my parents have carpet—and shook like the dickens, for the Lord Jesus Christ had come to me. He told me, Bring peace to your school, Aptakisic, and let the Jews be, son, for I was a Jew, and My Father, My son, is their Father too, and Our Father, My son, shines His holy light upon them, for it's they who will bring Me, they who'll announce Me, they who will bring Me to you, My son, in body then and there, as in spirit here and now. Do not cause them strife. Help Me save them."

"So you don't want the fish on the scarf?" Vander asked.

"No," said Frungeon.

"It's the creative expression of your soul," Acer said.

"It's a symbol for who I am," said Frungeon, "but there's no good reason that should be on your scarf."

"So what do you want for a symbol then, Gary?"

"Nothing," he said.

"Nothing?" they said.

"There's nothing could stand for me better than the ichthys, so let there be nothing to stand for me."

"Nothing at all?"

"Nothing at all."

"Not even a white stripe where the ichthys would have been?"

"A white stripe?" said Frungeon.

"Cause white's like nothing. A white stripe of nothing: a blankspot."

"A blankspot," said Frungeon, "I'll gladly take you up on."

"A blankspot!" cheered Acer.

And they all cheered a blankspot, a blankspot that stood for "If not Christ, then nothing."

Ruth was the first one in the Office to notice me. She chinned air in my direction, and that was surprising. One time, for three minutes, I had a hot crush on her. I bet every guy at Aptakisic had had a three-minute crush on her.

With mine, I'd just read "Nada y Pues Nada" and decided she was smart, or at least a good writer, and she was waiting for Jelly by the buses after school. She had Jelly's shiny eyes and fast-moving face, but was brighter-haired and even more compact—not petite, and not skinny either; more like sharp, or maybe economical, the same way June's body was economical, really, but more narrowly shouldered, and with a lot less ass, which sounds kind of bad, and usually would be, but was nice on Ruth, or not on Ruth, depending on what you expect an ass to be like. Jelly'd told her, "This is Gurion. He hates the Shovers, too." And I said, I don't hate them; I just want to hit them. Your newest article's the best one yet, though. Blankspots for Jesus. Those guys are so chomsky. "I think you missed the point," Ruth Rothstein said. I said, What point? "Blankspots for Jesus? Tch," Ruth said, and my crush died faster than a magazined spider. I said to her, No, I think *you* missed the point. I thought you were being subtle not saying it, but you weren't. Those blankspots mean *If not Christ, then nothing.* "You're wrong," said Ruth. "They just mean *nothing.* I mean: they don't mean anything. They're meaningless." I said, Only nothing is meaningless, and a blankspot is something; nothing would have to be no spot at all. "Gurion's smarter than you," Jelly told her, "ha ha." And Ruth bit her lip and said "Tch" and walked off.

But now, in the Office, she chinned air = "C'mere," and I went without a three-count since it meant she didn't hate me. "Excited?" she whispered. "You're about to be anonymous."

I don't know what that means.

She told me, "Watch this," then swallowed her mint and went over to the Shovers.

Acer saw her coming and held out the scarf. "My statement," he said, "is officially this: 'This year's scarves are flossy flossy, which is two times flossier than even I predicted, and as you well know, Ruth, I was, from the beginning, very optimistical.' If you want, you can take out the part where I say your name, but I do want you to emphasize—"

"The question on everyone's mind, Blake," said Ruth, "is how do the Shovers respond to accusations that the scarf's white stripe is a blankspot for Jesus?"

"I—"

"Who made *that* accusation?" said one of the others. He was tall and his arms had machined definition—not so much strong as muscular, not so much conditioned as cut. If something unguarded and heavy were in front of him, and it had parts to grip, and it wasn't animate, and its weight was symmetrically distributed, he could lift it no sweat.

"Just calm down, dog," Acer told the Shover. "The question was directed to me."

"Josh is more than welcome to comment," said Ruth.

Josh? I thought. No, I thought. No way, I thought. Not this vain swallower of multivitamin supplements. Not this morning drinker of protein milkshakes. This wasn't the guy. A million kids were named Josh. This was some other guy.

"I want to know who's asking," he said to Ruth.

"*I'm* asking, Josh. Ruth Rothstein, ace reporter."

"Cut the slippery shit."

"Wow that's gross."

"You know what I'm asking you. Who said the blankspot was Christian?" Josh said.

"I can't give up my sources."

His shirt got tight against the force of his pec-flex. "Don't talk to me like I'm stupid, Ruth. Sources give *information*, not opinions."

"This was an accusation."

"That's a *kind* of opinion. Whose opinion is it? Is it *your* opinion?"

"I wouldn't say it's my opinion," Ruth said.

"What would you say?"

"I'd say it's an accusation that, while I'm by no means certain of its accuracy, I did find somewhat compelling til just a second ago, when you started getting whiny, and then it became *very* compelling."

"Nyah nyah nyah nyah nyah nyah. My brother says you're titless, even flatter than you look."

"But he's hung like an insect," Ruth said, entertained.

"It's not true. He's my brother. Our men are hung."

"Matt's hung like a cicada, and I know you must know that. What I don't know is how you trust what a person—even your brother—says about size, if what he's got is a wa but he calls it a wang."

Wait. No. But yes. But no. That happened too fast. So no. But yes. Actually, yes. Jelly'd told me her sister had dated Josh Berman's brother; Ruth was Jelly's sister; Ruth had dated this guy's brother; this guy's name was Josh, but... Okay: so maybe June was...maybe this Berman...so she'd been his girlfriend, for whatever weird reason, but...Nakamook was right; he had to be right. They'd never kiss. She wouldn't have kissed him. She would not have kissed *this* guy. I was certain. I was. Pretty certain. I'd been pretty certain, though... I'd been pretty certain she wouldn't have been his girlfriend either, though... I'd been... And... His wang? Really? This is what I had to think about, there in the Office? June's ex-boyfriend's wang and his brother's wang too? Standing there shaking their wangs, the two of them? One with a face, and the other with no face but the first one's body, both shaking their identical wangs at June and Ruth and Jelly, too, for some reason? Shaking their wangs while flexing their pecs and high-fiving each other and kissing their biceps? That's what I had to do in the Office was picture that?

"You catch that?" said Acer to the fuming Josh Berman. "She just admitted, in so many words, that she's seen your brother's dick."

Enough with the dick, I said. Enough with the dick.

"What up, dog," Blake said to me. "I didn't even see you there."

Enough with the dick.

"You the man," Acer said.

Get bent, I told him.

Ruth reached her hand out and put it on my shoulder. It was nice of her to do that. It calmed me a little, though I felt even worse for having pictured her getting dick-shook at. She said to Acer, "Josh has seen his brother's unit too, Blake, is I guess what I was getting at, and since size is relative, and oneself what one relates to, and since Josh seems to genuinely believe that his brother's other than tiny, it doesn't take much of a leap to conclude that, well, you know..."

Good, I thought. Yes. Berman's got the tinywang. Way too tiny to shake at a girl. He wouldn't even whip it out. If she saw it he'd be... I felt like a bancer. I knew what it was you did with your wang when you had a girlfriend and she would let you; I wasn't two years old; I read a lot of books. I knew that you didn't just shake it at girls, but if what you did with it was what Berman did with it with June... As bad as it was to picture him shaking it at her, that wasn't as bad as what he really would have done, if he'd done anything that she would've let him, so I pictured him shaking it and felt like a bancer. Everything seemed gross. I wanted to hide. I was hiding.

"Just keep talking," Berman said to Ruth. "Keep on talking. No one here's listening. You're not even in the room."

"You heard the question about the blankspot for Jesus, though, right?"

"That's not what it is at all!" said Berman.

"Who are you getting angry at? I'm not even here."

"It. Means. Nothing. A blankspot is blank. Blank means nothing."

"But if I'm not here, then who're you trying to convince?"

"Aren't you supposed to be objective? Aren't you supposed to be a reporter? Is it my fault you're flatter than a wall? Is it my fault Matt met another girl at Stevenson? Yes and yes and no and no, so listen to me: It's meaningless. The blankspot is meaningless."

"Well, not totally meaningless—it's Frungeon's," said Acer. "The white stripe of Frungeon, Frungeon's own nothing, the innermost symbol of his soul."

"Exactly," said Berman. "It's got nothing to do with Jesus at all."

"But it's the innermost symbol of Frungeon's Christian soul?"

"Fuck. You. Ruth. Rothstein," said Berman, and grabbed his scarf and rushed out into Main Hall. One of the others grabbed his own scarf and turned.

"Cory," Acer said to him.

"What?" the Shover called Cory said.

Acer hesitated.

Cory walked off to follow Josh Berman.

"Goldman!" Acer shouted. "Berman!" he shouted. "Don't sweat it, you guys!"

And the other Shover added, "She's just one of those kids who hates on the Shovers."

Ruth said, "Drop the preposition and you're onto something, fatso."

That's when Blake Acer tried to make friends with me. "That was sweet how you beat down those SpEds," he told me.

You're a cheesedick, I said.

"No, I didn't mean… I meant in the locker-room…This morning's what I meant… That Janitor SpEd and his friend with the smelly piss or whatever? Like the way you messed them up like that? I saw it with my own eyes and it was badass, man, those guys had it com—"

You're a cheesedick, I told him.

"Oh, a cheesedick," he said. Then he turned to the kid who Ruth had called a fatso. "Cheesedick," he said. "Cheesedick, right?"

And each of them said "Cheesedick" and "Cheesedick, Tch." = "We know how CageSpEds show affection with insults, we've heard them do it on the buses, and we can be down with it: cheesedick is a shibboleth we can all pronounce."

I'm calling you a cheesedick, I said. You're the both of you cheesedicks, and all of your friends. You're smegmatic foreskins. Stinking, fungal, sebaceous fleshfolds.

"Smegma!" said Acer. "Fungal!" said the other one. "That's funny!" they said, and they laughed it up loud, stealing glances to see if I was joining them yet. A couple seconds later, the laughter'd grown louder, like all laughter does when the laugher starts to force it. They no longer believed we'd soon laugh together, but they pretended they did to save face. It was the same move they'd pull when B-team bully Bryan "Bry Guy" Maholtz would grundy or push down a Shover in the hallway, the same laugh they incited the bandkids to laugh when they'd trip or wallslam or bookrocket a bandkid. It was textbook caulking, this laugh-along laugh, an offering of peace that = "We don't want to fight you" while managing to ≠ "We don't want to hurt you."

In the middle of the laughter, Brodsky's door opened, and then out came Miss Pinge, and Acer said her name. He showed her the scarf.

"Dashing," she said, and sat down at her desk.

"Says it's dashing," said Acer to Fatso.

To me, Pinge said, "Your ears must be burning." = "Brodsky's been talking about you." = "Brodsky's got you made for the scoreboard."

It took me a second to figure that out, though. My A was a little bit D'd.

Are the lobes very red? I said to Miss Pinge.

I disliked Berman, but that wasn't it. Or that was partly it, but not all of it; the wangtalk and meanness to Jelly's sister, the being June's ex, the maybe having kissed her and the dickshaking imagery—it got me pissed, but none of that was what D'd my A. It was Cory, Berman's friend. I'd disliked him on sight, as I had all the others, and that didn't bother me—because he was a Shover, it didn't bother me—but when Acer said his name and I found out it was Goldman, I liked him even less. That was what bothered me. I never liked, to start with, when I didn't like an Israelite. Whenever I met one I didn't like, instead of trying to find reasons why I might come to like him, I'd try to find reasons for why it was okay not to like him. I'd try to find a way to like not liking him, and I didn't like that about me—it seemed weak.

"The lobes?" said Miss Pinge.

And suddenly I understood what she'd meant about burning ears, but Brodsky's door was open and he might have been listening, so I kept up like I didn't know what she'd meant. I approached her desk, asking, You got my record?

"I do," she said, leaning forward a little.

Behind me, in his office, Brodsky coughed—fakely?

Can I have it? I said.

"I don't know," Miss Pinge said.

The Shovers packed up, went out to to the bus circle, Ruth taking down their statements on a stenopad.

You don't know? I said.

"Maybe," Miss Pinge said.

Brodsky coughed again, a string of—yes—of fakes, and a ball of muscle heated up between my shoulders, right where he aimed the beams of anger that shot from his eyes. He was definitely coughing to get my attention. It was not a good sign. I'd assumed that if he was going to question me about the scoreboard that day, then the note Eliyahu'd brought would've said for me to come down to the Office immediately, not when school let out. Except Brodsky probably knew I'd think that, and that's probably why he did it the way he did it. It was a solid tactic and it was stupid of me to expect that showing up for my record would game him out.

Is this a can I/may I thing? I said to Miss Pinge. Or a magic word thing? I said.

"Yes," she said.

May I please have my record?

"Yes," she said. She reached under her desk and came up with two thick manila envelopes, the kind with the bobbin and the red twine fastener. The red twine fastener gets wound around the bobbin.

I said, Two copies?

"Just one," she said.

I said, How many envelopes does Nakamook have?

She said, "That would be confidential."

I said, I bet mine are thicker.

Miss Pinge said, "I bet so, too."

I said, Lots of people have written about me.

"That's a very positive way to see it," she said. "I think Mr. Brodsky wants to talk to you, kiddo."

□   □   □   □   □   □

In his doorway, I told Brodsky: Miss Pinge said you want to talk.

And then I stepped over his threshold and saw that the wingnut I'd given him was gone from his blotter. It wasn't anywhere on his desk.

He said, "I've been doing some math."

I unwound the twine from the bobbin of the top envelope and started pulling out the contents—vaccinations, prescriptions for drugs I wouldn't take, copies of birth certificate, Social Security card, admissions records—

Brodsky stood up fast behind his desk. He said, "The average number of students in Tuesday detention is twenty. Do you know how many students are in detention today?"

I shoved the contents back down in the envelope.

He said, "There are forty-one students in detention today. That's over one fifteenth of the school. There are so many students in detention today, Gurion, that we had to assign a second detention monitor."

The top item in the second envelope was my first Step 4 CASS from Botha. The offenses listed were "Destruction of School Property" and "Incitement to Destroy School Property" = I'd bent paper-clips into grasshoppers and taught Main Man and this slow boy, Winthrop, how to sculpt and trigger them.

Brodsky slammed his fist down onto the desk, wishing it was my nose. He said, "You, Ronrico and Mikey Bregman account for three of the students in detention. And Eliyahu, who, this morning, was every bit the tragic posterboy for sweetness and piety, put his *fist* through some *glass* some sixty minutes after meeting you. He's a fourth."

I said to Brodsky, I like Eliyahu. I said, He's a scholar.

Brodsky said, "That's just what he said when I asked him about you. No few people have said that about you, Gurion, but I am beginning to believe that the praise is hollow. You are failing to live up to expectations— Don't smile!" he said.

I couldn't help it—I'd found a copy of this letter from the social worker at Northside Hebrew Day that asked my parents for permission to meet with me regularly. I'd seen the letter before, right when my mom received it in the mail, but I hadn't seen my mom's response, which was stapled to the copy. The response was in her usual all-caps handwriting, in marker, sideways, on top of the text of the social worker's original letter: "YOU WERE ALREADY TOLD 'NO, THANK YOU' ON THE TELEPHONE. THIS TIME IT IS 'NO.' I WOULD RATHER NOT HEAR MYSELF SAY WHAT I WILL SAY IF THERE IS A THIRD POLITE REQUEST. SINCERELY, TAMAR MACCABEE." I covered my mouth with my hand.

Brodsky said, "Listen to me!" = "Look at me!"

But first I looked to see what the next document was—something by Sandy called "Assessment of a Client: Gurion Maccabee," and the one under that was a letter to Brodsky from Rabbi Salt; I put both on top—and then, when I looked up, I saw the clock on Brodsky's desk. It said 3:41. Four minutes til June.

I shoved all the contents back in the envelope.

Brodsky said, "After Eliyahu was sent here? Six other students in the lab advanced from step 1 to step 4 in under thirty minutes."

Maybe it was because Brodsky's "I've been doing some math" bit, which was about a thousand beats too long to be intimidating, was actually starting to intimidate me a little anyway; maybe it was how Sabra my mom was; maybe it was because I was thinking I'd see June in less time than it takes a beginning-of-class tone to follow an end-of-class tone; maybe it was because that made me nervous; maybe it made me nervous just because I was in love with her or maybe because I was in love with her and had seen her ex-boyfriend who she might have kissed; or maybe I was just nervous... whatever it was, I laughed a little. Something made me laugh a little.

Brodsky hit the desk again and leaned forward and his head was pinker than ever. He said, "Leevon Ray and Vincent Portite are in detention for taking wingnuts off the vents in A-Hall yesterday. They said they were having a contest." He said, "Don't interrupt me."

I hadn't interrupted him.

He said, "Not including you, eleven of the forty students in today's detention are there as a result of your influence, whether directly or indirectly. What do you have to say about that?"

I said, I'm not only responsible for the actions of my friends, but for the actions of people who see my friends act—that's what you're saying to me.

"And now you choose to speak like an adult," he said. "You only act like a mensch when your ass is on the line?" He pounded the desk rapidly, five times, once for each syllable in "ass is on the line."

I said to him, I don't know what speaking like an adult has to do with being a mensch, and I don't know how it is that you expect a person to defend himself to you when you don't even have a handle on free will.

"Free will!" Brodsky said.

I said, If those kids you listed aren't responsible for their own actions, then why would I be for mine, let alone theirs? If I said there was a bomb in the cafeteria and people got trampled, that would be one thing, but I haven't done anything like that.

His hands were shaking in the air. He stilled them, then knocked his pencil cup sideways off the blotter. It hit the wall and spilled and I got a little startled.

He said, "Who wrecked the scoreboard?"

I said, I don't tell on people.

He said, "So you know who it was, then."

I said, I don't tell on people.

He said, "Was it Nakamook?"

I said nothing.

He said, "Was it Portite? Leevon Ray? Angelica Rothstein?"

I said nothing.

"Did you wreck the scoreboard?" he said.

I said nothing.

"I asked you if you wrecked the scoreboard," he said.

I said, I heard you.

His whole face twitched then, like the muscles he was forcing to scowl were losing a rebellion, or starting one. "I will keep you here until I get a sufficient answer to my question," he said.

It was a completely dumont condition. I'd never heard anything so babylike from Brodsky before, and that is when I understood—he was desperate.

It wasn't just that he had no proof that I'd wrecked the scoreboard—I'd known he had no proof: I'd gotten rid of the pieces and was the only one who saw me do it = I had total control over all the evidence against me—it was that he actually *needed* proof.

Wrecking the scoreboard was big. I could get arrested for wrecking the scoreboard, taken to court, expelled. Wrecking the scoreboard was so big that suspicion, no matter how strong or who it belonged to, was not enough to nail me, and it never would be. I'd had the upper hand the whole time and I hadn't known it.

"Answer me," Brodsky said.

The clock said 3:45 and I was safe, but being safe was not getting me any closer to June. I knew Brodsky couldn't keep me there forever, but he could definitely keep me there til the end of detention if he wanted.

"*Did* you wreck the scoreboard?" Brodsky said. "Did you?"

The first "did" was too loud and his voice faltered on the second, like he heard the first one and didn't like what he'd heard.

I thought: He doesn't like treating me the way he is treating me. He's treating me differently than usual because he wants me to act differently than usual.

Click click click.

I thought: There are a million kinds of different-than-usual.

I decided to try the first one I could think of.

In between deciding and actually trying, though, I got completely paralyzed. The paralysis lasted twice as long as a decision to blink takes to become the action of my eyes blinking. That is less time, even, than it takes to say the word No. The first time I ever got paralyzed like that was in a shopping cart when I was four. My mom took me to the Jewel for fruit to make fruit salad for a barbecue at her colleague's house. The lemons were shiny and I wanted one, but I didn't want to ask my mom to buy it for me because I was playing a game that day where I would not ask my parents for anything, so I just grabbed one of the lemons and looked at it and waited for my mom, who was looking at whipped toppings, to see the lemon in my hand and *offer* to buy it for me. She didn't see. She put some whipped topping in the cart and pushed us past the melon stand, where this kid in a baseball uniform was pulling on his little sister's hair while she cried and their mother sniffed cantoloupes. We got some apples and walnuts and went to the checkout line. We were right behind the mean kid's family. The mother got her change and took the mean kid's hand and told him to hold his sister's hand while she pushed the cart, which was very full. I still had the lemon. I had put it in the pocket of my hoodie by then. The mean kid's family started walking off, and I saw by the way that the sister was moving side-to-side in these little circles that the mean kid was either crushing her fingers together or twisting her arm, and I reached my hand into my pocket to take the lemon out and set it on the runway so my mother, who was looking in her wallet for her credit card, would offer to buy it, but then I thought: I will steal this lemon, and right when I was about to remove my hand from the lemon to leave it in my pocket, the paralysis passed through me and I knew it was my muscles reacting to the sound of Adonai telling them No! so I kept hold of the lemon and took it from my pocket after all. Then I threw it hard at the mean kid's neck. His head jerked forward and he let go of his sister's hand and spun around to see who did it. I pointed at him and he started crying. He didn't revolve again til I dropped my finger, and then he was pulling on his mother's shirt, but she shooed him off and I didn't get in trouble. I still can't say for sure how it is that Adonai knew I was about to steal the lemon, or how He ever knows when to shout No!

at the muscles, but I do know He can't hear your thoughts, and so I believe that He must be a highly talented reader of faces, and that there must be something very startling to Adonai that a human face does right before the human it belongs to is about to do wrong. In Brodsky's office, it was different than the time with the lemon because I did not understand how what I was about to do was wrong, and the paralyzing No! of Adonai lasted only as long as it always does, which, if you're not expecting it, is little enough time to deny it just happened. So I denied it, quick as a blink, and did what I'd decided to do to get out of there:

I pretended to have a pretend itch in my eye, to pretend-rub that pretend itch with my wristbone, and in as trembling a voice as I could fake, I said to Leonard Brodsky:

I think you're really bullying me.

It was like I'd suddenly died. It was like I'd pulled my own head off and tossed it in his lap. I said "bullying," and the wrinkles around his mouth disappeared and he sat down in his chair and he sat back in his chair and, on the shelf behind where his head had been, three things glinted at me: the bell of his soundgun, the glass in the frame of his family portrait, and—this last one between the first two, and duller, barely visible—the wingnut I'd given him that morning.

With his hands on his knees, rubbing them, Brodsky said to me, "I didn't... I got carried away, Gurion. Please accept my apology." His eyes were suddenly very wet.

Another No! passed through me, and I did not deny it happened this time, but I kept up the fake-out, anyway: I ducked my head a little, like I was hesitating, and then I nodded many small nods = I reluctantly accept your apology.

While I did that, my own eyes got wet, not fakely, and I blinked the wetness away because it was not my privilege to be sad. Leonard Brodsky was the one who was hurt, and I was the one who'd hurt him, and it didn't matter that I hadn't wanted to hurt him or that I didn't know how I'd hurt him. It didn't matter that I knew not what I did to him. It didn't need a name to be wrong. It didn't need reasons I could understand. Verbosity is like the iniquity of idolatry.

Adonai had twice shouted No! at me and I had twice ignored it.

I was dismissed.

In the outer-office, Miss Pinge wrote me a hall-pass, my favorite thing to have at school. I went straight to detention.

It was 3:48 and I was safe, a miserable sinner. Then things got ironic.

□ □ □ □ □ □ □

I wasn't allowed in detention: I had entered through the southern doorway of the cafeteria, but before I'd even gotten past the first bathroom, Miss Gleem rushed over, saying, "Go to the library."

Why? I said.

Miss Gleem pressed a finger against her glossed lips and shooed me back into Main Hall. I spotted June at the table by the stage on the eastern side. She had her back to me. My sadness over having hurt Brodsky made me slow, so instead of shouting June's name across the room, I only thought about shouting June's name across the room, and by the time I decided I should actually do it, Miss Gleem had gently pushed me through the doorway.

"I'm so sorry," Miss Gleem said. She meant about the push, but Miss Gleem was always exaggerating her emotions. Even if she was sorry, there's no way she was *so* sorry. The push was fine with me, anyway. Miss Gleem was a big-time toucher, but it wasn't perved. It was affectionate. In her head, I'm sure she called the push "encouragement." She was the art teacher. She monitored detention on Tuesdays and Wednesdays against her will. She told me that once. I liked her. She wore fake tortoiseshell combs in her fuzzy hair, like the sweeter, less pretty sister of a bony princess whose combs are made of gold. It wasn't just me who liked her, either. She was mostly pinged-out and everyone liked her, and if I'd met Miss Gleem first I'd have probably called Miss Pinge gleemed-out.

She bent her knees and leaned toward me and I could see the tops of her tits in her shirt. Her tits were really white and pushed together. I thought about how if I put a watercolor brush on her tits sideways, then while the brush rolled forward it would trail a fleeting, tubular dent in the skin be-hind it. By the time the brush fell on the ground there'd be goosebumps on her tits and maybe even her throat because the rolling watercolor brush would feel like how it feels when you run a hangnail along the paler side of your arm. I don't know why I thought of that. What her tits mostly did was make me want to press the side of my face against their top parts while I was kneeling in between her legs and she was sitting in a rocking chair. I would reach up with my hands to put them on her ears and in her hair and then go to sleep on my knees, just like that. But then I thought about how I would rather put the side of my face on June's tits and reach up with my hands and fall asleep. But June didn't really have tits, so then I thought it would be better to put the side of my face on June's stomach while we were laying down in the shape of the letter T, and my arms would be long like Nakamook's, and only one of my hands would be in her hair and the other hand would be holding her ankle, and I would fall asleep hearing the sounds inside her stomach, and the sounds would be humming sounds, and she would have one of her hands on my head, too, but none of that could happen, not any time soon, not with me in the hall and her in the cafeteria, a sound-killing wall of cinderblocks between us.

"You're so upset," Miss Gleem said. "Why are you so upset?"

I said to her, I have to go in. I have detention.

She said, "We have too many students in here. We tried to seat everyone, but the chatter was too much for Mr. Klapper to handle, so he took ten of you folks to the library, and I'm sorry, but that's where you've gotta go now."

Again with the sorry.

Mr. Klapper taught Social Studies. I'd heard that he was very old. He was one of the only teachers at Aptakisic who didn't have to teach in the Cage once a week. I never met him.

I said, But I'm here already.

She said, "I'd love to have you in detention with me, Gurion, except I don't have your assignment form—Mr. Klapper took it."

I said, I know the assignment by heart. I said, I'll just write it out on looseleaf.

She said, "They make a big deal out of the forms. Looseleaf won't cut it."

I said, Miss Gleem! I said, No one even reads those things.

She said, "Who told you that?"

I said, It's just I know some people fill the page up with swear words and no one gets in trouble for it.

She said, "I don't think that's true. *I've* never seen an assignment like that. And I read them all when I'm the monitor. It's part of the STEP System. After we read them, we pass them on to Bonnie Wilkes and Sandy Billings and they read them. Sometimes Mr. Brodsky does, too. So a lot of people read them. And I've always liked yours, actually—they're so angry, but in a very literary and deep way, and though it's clear to me that you think verbally rather than visually, that's nothing to be ashamed of, Gurion."

I said, I'm not ashamed.

She said, "But why should you be?"

I said, I shouldn't.

She said, "I was just trying to compliment your writing."

Thank you, I said.

She said, "Now go get a hall-pass from the Office before you go to the library—Mr. Klapper's a stickler."

I already had a hall pass. I had one from Miss Pinge, and one with a poem on it, and then a whole pad of them with no table to throw it on and make my coaster joke.

I headed slowly toward the Office, but once Gleem was back inside, I spun and ducked into the cafeteria's northern doorway. That doorway was deep, but doorless. I leaned back against its sidewall and slid down onto the floor. I could see the back of June. She was sitting on her knees on the bench of the table, writing her detention assignment, crouched over the page with her shoulders up to her ears like she was cold.

I tried to move heat around. I thought of blankets, a pile of them. She didn't look any less cold. I thought of the blankets catching fire, and a high-powered fan built into my chest. It didn't work. I failed. No. I didn't *fail*. I never had a chance. I didn't fail at anything. A high-powered fan? Blankets catching fire? A high-powered fan in my chest and burning blankets? What the fuck was wrong with me? I was thinking like a whiny escapist special-kid, a nice little Jewish boy who'd tell Mr. Brodsky, "I think you're really bullying me," and actually mean it. Gee aw gee. Such heartbreaking heartbreak. So scared inside, so lonely and helpless, just wants to be accepted. Aw gee aw gee aw *fuck* you, Gurion. Kill the limp magic thinking, and act like a mensch. Figure out how you hurt him, see the sin for what it was. And repent. And atone.

I reviewed the encounter, beat by beat:

1. Brodsky starts flipping out, talking about math.
2. I don't back down.
3. He tells me I won't be able to see June until I tell him who broke the scoreboard.
4. I see that he doesn't want to be flipping out.
5. I get an idea.
6. Adonai shouts No! at me about my idea.
7. I pretend I'm very scared by pretending to wipe pretend tears from my eyes that I'm pretending inside my pretend-game are actually

an itch that I'm pretending inside my pretend-game to scratch with my wrist and then I say to Brodsky, I think you're really bullying me.

8. He acts like someone died, then apologizes and lets me leave.

I thought: But his son died and that's the worst person who can die and someone saying he thinks you're a bully…it's nothing compared to your son dying, especially when it's just some boy who's saying it, some boy who, when you look at him there, in front of you, the first thing you do is you wish it was him who'd been killed instead of Ben.

Then I thought: Oh no, because—

I thought: Another way to say that Brodsky wished the boy in front of him had been killed instead of his son was: Brodsky wished the boy in front of him were his son.

And I had been the boy in front of him.

And he would not have treated his son the way he'd been treating me. Ben, though a hacker of email accounts, was no stonewaller of principals. He did not drive his father crazy.

I'd pretended, to a good father, that I, the person he wished was his kind, dead son, was as afraid of him as his kind, dead son would have been if that son had just seen his father act the way Brodsky had acted.

And Brodsky became ashamed, and there was nothing pretend about it.

And now I wasn't even looking at June's face from across a table, but at her back through a doorway = I had shamed Brodsky needlessly.

I did math:

Of the forty-one students in detention, eleven of them, not including me, were there as a result of my influence, whether direct or indirect. And then eleven students, including me, were not allowed in the cafeteria. Why two elevens? Why not eleven of forty-one and then eight or nine of forty-one? I was the last one to arrive, so if Hashem merely wanted to keep me from June, it wouldn't even matter if it had been one of forty-one and Klapper had left the cafeteria with no kids and one blank detention form—I'd have still been the one of the forty-one, the one who'd have gotten sent to the library to fill that one assignment out: I'd have still been barred from the cafeteria, still would have been sitting in that doorway, Juneless, punished, and that would have been suitably ironic and terrible. Being barred from the cafeteria would have caused me to suffer, regardless of how many others were barred.

But it was not one of forty-one, or eight or nine. It was eleven influenced and so eleven removed, and you only find Justice that symmetrical in scripture, and only when there is a message attached.

The elevens were a message.

And because Hashem knew I didn't need reminders that He ran things, Him saying to me, "I run things," could not have been the message. The message of the elevens was that He didn't just want me to suffer, and He didn't just want me to know that I had made Him make me suffer: Hashem wanted me to suffer from the knowledge that when I had made Him make me suffer—that when I had disobeyed his No! and made Brodsky suffer— I had made Him suffer, too, Hashem. I had made Hashem suffer.

So I dropped my head between my knees and suffered all of it.

□ □ □ □ □ □ □

Soon, setbuilders sent sawings and bangs through the fake-velvet stage-curtain, which hung slanted in the middle where whoever shut it caught the tassels at the bottom in a footlight, and I lifted my head. Every few seconds, a few hammers struck their targets at the same time and the noise boomed. When that happened, June's back tensed and she'd cringe her neck.

After the fifth or sixth boom, she revolved her head, annoyed, and I saw her face. I didn't think she saw me. I would not have let her see me right then—a sufferer, a sinner, unable to warm her—and I thought the combination of doorway-shadow and jamb blotted me out of her line of sight, but a couple booms later, she revolved a second time and was smiling. I didn't smile back. I couldn't. I was trying to suffer and she was such a good smiler and it stunned me.

Then she was raising her hand. Miss Gleem walked over.

June said to her, quietly, "I need to get out of here for a minute."

Miss Gleem said, "What do you mean, Juney?"

June said, "It's important."

Miss Gleem whispered a question to her.

June made a single laughing noise: *Tss.* She said, "It's not that."

"Well..." Miss Gleem said. You could tell she wanted to let June leave.

June said, "It's fine, Miss Gleem, I promise—and did I tell you about the idea I had for the sculpture competition?"

Miss Gleem lit up. "I thought you wouldn't enter."

June said, "I wasn't going to, but then yesterday, I found this website with paintings by Jean Dubuffet, and also some Alberto Giacometti sculptures, and I had this idea about shadows and a flattened animal made of clay, glazed ultra-brightly—not like a cartoon roadkill or anything, but a very shiny and complicated mammal that won't look right in two dimensions. Like say it's a rhinocerous, but smashed down flat like a stingray, so how could she walk? is what you'll ask yourself. How can the many chambers of her stomach perform the exertions required to digest exotic grasses? is the feeling I hope to evoke. And then an outline. A thick black one bordering the entire rhinoceros on both sides. Do you see what I mean about the outline? Because an outline is what you do before you learn shadows, right? And I'll set the sculpture on its side, thin-way-down, on a set of casters, the super-cheap kind that won't go in carpet, and then, attached to the back part of the back caster wheel will be a rigid length of wire that'll be bent so that I can hang a sun-colored styrofoam lightbulb from the end of it, like the midmorning sun, and bracketed to the front part of the front caster wheel will be a large pane of smoked plexiglass that'll lay flat, in what do you call it? perpendicular respect to the rhinoncerous plane—I have to learn to cut and stain plexiglass, first—but this plexiglass will be cut into the shape of what the shadow of the three-dimensional version of the rhino would be at midmorning, which will basically be the same shape as the 2-D rhino, but foreshortened to account for the rhino's position relative to the lightbulb, which, like I said, will be at the angle of the midmorning sun, in summer I'm thinking, on the summer solstice, in Illinois. Don't you think that would be a funny sculpture, though? A 2-D rhino with a fixed shadow in a 3-D world? Or is it pretentious? I think it's funny, but my mom said it was pretentious, but I think that maybe when I told her about it, I did a bad job explaining."

June looked at me when she said "Jean Dubuffet" and again when she said "rhinocerous" and "midmorning-height," but didn't make a face or anything. It was stealth.

"It does sound funny," Miss Gleem said, "and also completely wonderful!" She said, "I take it you liked the Dubuffets?"

"I loved them," June said.

Miss Gleem said, "There was an exhibit in Amsterdam a few summers back—I went right when I finished grad school, and they were so amazing." She fiddled with her combs, remembering. "Did you have any favorites?"

June said, "Of course, and I'd tell you, but I don't like titles, so I never checked them."

Miss Gleem said, "That's because you think visually, June, and you should be proud of it. Can you describe the paintings you liked? How about the cow ones?"

While June described cows by Jean Dubuffet, the Janitor farted twice with his armpit. I couldn't see, but I knew it was him.

Miss Gleem turned from June and said, "Mikey Bregman! We know it's you."

"Sorry, Miss Gleem," said the Janitor.

"Sorry, Miss Gleem," said Vincie Portite, in a sissy voice. I couldn't see him either, the liar—Vincie was the one who told me no one read the detention assignments.

Miss Gleem said, "Vincie."

Vincie said, "Miss Gleem."

"Okay," she said.

"Okay then," said Vincie.

Miss Gleem clicked her tongue and turned back to June.

June said, "I've really gotta get out of here for a minute, Miss Gleem."

Miss Gleem said, "Only a minute."

"Maybe five or six," June said.

"Five or six."

June came toward me, not looking at me.

I heard Ronrico say, "Oh but I've got feminine problems, too, Miss Gleem!"

June laughed.

Miss Gleem said, "Just stop, Ronrico."

Ronrico said, "Sorry, Miss Gleem," and June flicked her eyes at me = "Get out of the doorway"/"Come into the hall," and then turned into the doorway and continued past me.

As soon as I started getting up, I remembered how I was supposed to be suffering and, instead of standing, I crouch-walked along the doorway's sidewall, and when I made the turn into Main Hall I pressed my spine on the corner as hard as I could.

□ □ □ □ □ □ □

We sat next to each other, leaning back against the lockers with our knees up.

"What happened?" June said.

I said, I'm sorry. I said, I got stuck in the Office and—

June said, "That's fine. What happened to *you* is what I mean? You look like something happened to you. Or at least you did a minute ago—now you look happy."

I told her, I said a terrible thing to Brodsky. I said, I hurt him in his own office.

"Why?" she said.

I was trying to speed things up, I said, so I could sit by you in detention.

"It worked out, then."

How's that? I said.

She said, "You hurt someone to get something you wanted, and then you didn't get what you wanted and that hurt you. It's fair."

I said, But you're here, now. I said, I'm not really hurting anymore.

"Probably Brodsky isn't either," she said.

I'd wanted her to look in my eyes and see me suffering, then tell me everything was fine. And, in a way, she did tell me that, but we were next to each other and she was facing forward, and I wasn't suffering anymore. Still, I wished she would hug me, so I tried to think of something that might evince her sympathies which might become a hug. It was hard to think of anything like that, though. What did I have to complain about, really? If I had failed at something that might undermine my self-image or whatever, that might work, but—boom.

I said, And plus, the thing is, I couldn't do this action.

June said, "What action?"

I said, Nakamook discovered this action that everyone at lunch could do except for me. I said, Your whole body shakes and your face gets red and tears fill up your eyes. It looks like a seizure.

June was already doing it. She I'm Tickinged for about half a minute. Her face became darker than her freckles and her irises shook inside the whites. I didn't like to see it, but it was good to see it, because while she was doing it, I thought: If June had a disorder that made her I'm Ticking for minutes at a time out of every hour of every day, would you, Gurion, still want to sleep beside her on the beach of the Dead Sea, even though she would shake you awake every night and probably drool on you while she did it? and I thought: Yes, it would be hard to do, and sometimes very gross, but I believe I would still want to sleep next to her.

And then I got happy because June didn't have any disorder like that.

When she was finished with the action, she said, "That's called the Electric Chair."

Benji calls it I'm Ticking, I said.

"It's been the Electric Chair for years now," she said. "Since 2003. That's when I invented it."

How'd you do it? I said.

She said, "I used to want to be a modern dancer, and one time, in the third, while I was home from school with strep, I was watching this amazing video of a solo dance by a choreographer from Philadelphia named Kathryn TeBordo who all she did was sit down in a folding chair and then get up from it, but it took her twenty minutes because the dance was so slow that you could hardly see her moving, and it hurt to watch it, in my sternum. My sternum vibrated and I started thinking how completely in control of all of her muscles Kathryn TeBordo was that she could move that slow, and how I wished I could do that with my body and I would never be able to, but that maybe I could do the opposite. I thought maybe I could be totally out of control of all of my muscles at the same time. But I couldn't figure out how that would work because if I just started flopping around, it might *look* like I was totally out of control of my muscles, but really I'd be controlling them—I'd be making them flop around. And so then I thought—and it was only because I had this really sweaty fever that I was able to think it, I think—I thought that in order for a person to truly be out of control of all of their muscles, they first have to be trying to control all of their muscles, and their muscles have to disobey them, because you can't actually *try* to be out of control, right? That doesn't make sense. That was the problem. You can only try to be *in* control, and then *fail* to control—that's what out of control is, a kind of failure. So I decided I would try to make my muscles do something impossible. I decided I would try to make my muscles tear themselves and maybe even crush my own bones while they tore. And I tried, and then I tried harder, and then I was doing the Electric Chair, which at first I called the anti-Kathryn TeBordo, but I changed that fast because I loved TeBordo's dancing and 'anti' made it sound like I was some kind of hater."

I said, You're the smartest girl I've ever met.

June looked at her knees and shivered.

You're my favorite person, I said.

She brought her knees up to her chest.

I remembered how I'd failed to warm her with specialkid visions and took off my hoodie to spread it over her shoulders.

She said, "I'm not cold. Take it back."

I took it back.

You're my favorite person, I said again.

But she wouldn't look at me, so I tried to do the Electric Chair, and I thought I was maybe getting it.

I touched her left elbow and got a friction shock. When I pulled my hand back, I saw the corner of her mouth lift and fall and lift and fall. She was trying not to laugh.

I said, June.

She said, "You're just nodding your head and flopping around. It's the opposite of what you want to do."

I stopped nodding and flopping.

She said, "Make a fist."

I made a fist.

She said, "Close it as hard as you can... See, your whole arm's shaking." She said, "Just do that with your neck now, and then the rest of you."

I did what she said and the brain-blood started whacking itself against my eardrums. A silver dot appeared in the center of June's forehead and bloomed into a bright white flying saucer shape. I was doing the Electric Chair.

June said, "Stop now. You look gross." It echoed when she said it.

I stopped.

"In a second," she said, "I have to go back into detention, and there are still things we have to talk about."

I said, I love you.

She said, "That's what I mean. I've been thinking about you all day and I believe you, and I like believing you, but it's too soon to believe you. You don't really know me."

Tell me what you think I need to know, I said.

She said, "I knew you'd say that, and I think that even if I told you, you'd love me anyway, if you really do love me, but the thing is that I don't really want to tell you, so..."

I said, So then I *don't* need to know. And so you don't have to tell me. I love you anyway.

"But—"

All I need to know is there's things you don't want to tell me, and that those things are things that I don't need to know. So now I know that. I know all I need to.

"That's—well—that's a pretty good answer, actually, but—"

I said, Good.

She said, "But still, let me finish what I was saying—I was talking to Starla Flangent during lunch, and she thinks you're not dark enough for me and I think she's right."

I said, I'm half-Ethiopian.

She said, "Really? You don't look Ethiopian."

I said, Half.

She said, "That's not what I mean, anyway." She said, "You have all this joy. There's nothing wrong with you."

I said, I get sad all the time lately.

She said, "It's nice to be sad. You have to have joy to be sad, and if you're dark you don't get to have joy, so you don't get to be sad. You only get to be anguished if you're dark."

I said, I'm angry, though. I said, I get in fights all the time.

She said, "Anger's not anguish and I've seen you fight. I saw you fight Kyle McElroy at the beginning of the year. I saw you dance on his back after you finished choking him—you did a kind of pirhouette. It was fun for you. And this morning, with Boystar—"

I said, I fell in love with you this morning.

She said, "That's not dark at all."

I said, But I've got all these disorders. I've got ADHD and Conduct D. and Intermittent Explosive D. and Antisocial P. D., and you can't even have the last two ones unless you're an adult, but I have them.

She said, "You don't really have any of them, though, and you know it."

I said, But people think I do have them, so that's how I'm explained. I said, I'm very dark. I said, I've been kicked out of three schools. You should have seen how cruel I just was to Brodsky. I said, It was awful. It was a dark way to treat a person—I'm a tyrant.

She said, "If you were cruel, you wouldn't think it was awful."

I said, I'm not cruel—I *acted* cruel. I said, And that is what makes me dark.

I didn't even know what we were talking about anymore, only that I had to prove to June that I was dark.

June said, "Listen. There's this thing I just saw that's carved into the lunch table. It says 'We Damage,' right? And I was thinking how that's not dark, it's just violent. But right next to it, there's another carving that says 'Damage We.' That's also violent, but it's dark too."

I said, Fine. I said, Why's 'Damage We' dark?

She said, "Because dark people might do damage, but they're only dark if damage comes first—if they've *been* damaged. You're not damaged."

That much was true—if dark meant damaged, then I wasn't dark.

I said, Fine. So so what? So Josh Berman's dark?

"Josh Berman?" June said. "Where did that—"

Did you kiss him?

"Bluck!" June said.

Bluck? I said.

"Bluh-luh, bluh-luh, bluh-luh-luck. Did he tell you I kissed him?"

I don't even know him.

"Did someone else say I kissed him?"

Wasn't he your boyfriend?

"Yeah," June said. "Last year. So what? All of a sudden that means that I kissed him?"

Well—

"I guess that's not crazy. But no. I didn't kiss him. And no he wasn't dark. That's why I went out with him."

Now I'm confused.

"I thought if I was his girlfriend, I'd get less dark."

But so—

"I didn't though. I stayed just as dark. I probably even got darker because of how I stayed just as dark and thought I should have gotten less dark—and I bet he told people I kissed him, that bancer."

No, I said. I mean, at least that's not what I heard, but look: Why'd you break up with him?

"Do you know that kid at all? He's a total dentist."

But you were his girlfriend!

"Now you're being mean."

I'm not, I said. I just don't understand why you'd let someone be your boyfriend who you thought was a dentist.

"I thought maybe he wasn't really a dentist," June said. "I mean, I thought: Okay, he seems like a dentist, but sometimes people who seem like dentists are only acting dental because they think you'll be mean to them, so maybe if I'm nice to him, he'll stop acting dental."

You went out with him just because he might not have been dental?

"Well not just that, Gurion. It's complicated. Also, like I said, I thought I'd get less dark—it's just... You've gotta understand: girls really hate me for some reason. I don't know why. This therapist said it was because I'm pretty and I have red hair, but first of all that doesn't make a lot of sense. Those aren't good reasons to hate somebody. And secondly that's exactly the kind of thing you say to someone who you're trying to make feel good, who you're *paid* to make feel better—"

You had a therapist? I said.

"The thing is—"

You don't know that your gorgeousness is objectively factual? I said.

June bit her lip and squeezed her lids shut. = "I'm frustrated," "I'm flattered," or "I'm ready to cry." I couldn't tell which.

I didn't mean to interrupt, I said. I'm sorry.

"It's okay," she said. "The thing is, though," she said, unsqueezing her lids, "what I was trying to say was that most girls hate me, so most boys hate me so those girls will like them, so most boys don't ask me out, and Josh asked me out, which meant he was different, at least in that one way, and since most boys are dentists, and Josh wasn't like most boys, at least in that one way, I thought maybe he wasn't really a dentist either, and maybe I should give him a shot."

And then? I said.

"And then what? I broke up with him."

But why'd you do that? What'd he do? What made you break up with him? Was it something I should hurt him for? I could hurt him, I said. I could break—

"No. Stop. He didn't do anything."

But so why'd you break up with him?

"Gurion, wow. You're just drilling it in. Fine. You're right. I was acting stupid. It was a stupid way to act, to be his girlfriend. Those reasons I told you were the reasons I was, and those reasons weren't good reasons, okay? I barely believed he might stop acting dental. Even at the beginning when I first said yes. It seemed stupid even then. It was just what I told myself because I thought it would be nice if that's how things were. It would be a nice story, a nice hopeful story. But I wasn't in love with him. I didn't even really like him. So there wasn't any reason to be his girlfriend. There wasn't any good reason to try to be hopeful. And so I broke up with him. You don't have to laugh at me."

I'm not, June, I said. You didn't kiss Berman. This all makes me happy. Because I'm in love with you.

"And again," she said. "That isn't dark at all."

I said, What does it matter if I'm dark or not, though? If that dentist wasn't dark and you gave him a chance, then unless you think I'm dental, or secretly dental—

"Everyone gets damaged eventually," she said, "so everyone eventually gets dark," she said, "and that's always a tragedy."

I said, Well, I'll be dark soon enough then, and so—

She said, "But I like you *not* dark, and if I love you, I *love* you not dark."

I said, I really don't understand the problem, June.

She said, "I'm dark and I might end up being what damages you, and then you'd be dark and the tragedy would be my fault."

I said, How would you damage me?

She said, "Maybe I'll break your heart."

I said, You'd break my heart?

She said, "Well, not your heart-heart that beats, but your heart of hearts: the place in your brain where your love's at. The frontal lobe? Yes. Maybe I'll break your lobe."

I said, You want to break my lobe?

She said, "I'd rather tear my eyes out—why don't you pay attention? If I broke your lobe, then you'd be dark, and it would be a tragedy. And my fault."

I said, If you don't love me, it'll break my lobe.

She said, "But if I love you for a while, then break your lobe later, it'll be even more broken."

I said, If you break my lobe, you break my lobe. Broken is broken and I break things all the time, so I know. I'd rather have you break my lobe later, I said.

June was hugging herself.

I reached out and put the hoodie on her shoulders again.

She said, "You'll be cold."

I said, I don't get cold. You want a poem I wrote you?

"You wrote me a poem?"

I set it down on the floor between us and finally she stopped looking away from me. She wasn't looking *at* me, but if she looked up, she would have been. I decided to skip the coaster joke. I touched the part in her hair. It seemed the right thing to do, though I didn't know why.

She said, "Your poem's attached to a Coke. I don't like Coke so much. I like coffee."

I said, Same here, but I wasn't sure if you liked Coke or not, so I—

Miss Gleem came into the hall. She said, "Five or six minutes, June? And you," she said to me, "you haven't even gone to Mr. Klapper yet, have you? And what is that? There's no drinks allowed in detention."

June was standing already. She said, "Tell me the Coke story tomorrow."

Miss Gleem said, "People, please."

I said, I'll call you tonight and tell you.

June said, "I hate the phone."

Miss Gleem said, "People! If you don't move along right now, I'll have to give you detentions."

I said, I'll tell you by the buses, then—rush out to the circle when detention ends. It'll only take a minute. And I still have something to show you.

I'd completely forgotten about the birthmarks.

June said, "I don't want you showing or telling me anything else today. I need to think."

I said, But how will I see you tomorrow?

Miss Gleem said, "Fine. You've got detentions."

"That's how," June said. She was so tough.

I said, I want you to tell *me* something, then.

June said, "I'm stealing your hoodie."

I said, It's yours. I'm giving it to you.

She said, "Let me steal it, okay?"

I said, Give me back my hoodie.

"No," she said, "I'm stealing your hoodie."

I said, You're stealing my hoodie.

"Yes I am," June said.

Then she went in the cafeteria and I put the Coke in my bag. The Coke was poemless. The poem was gone. June stole it.

⬜ ⬜ ⬜ ⬜ ⬜ ⬜ ⬜

Mr. Klapper checked e-mail at a computer-carrel and touched his mustache at both ends. The mustache was white like his suit, and I thought: He is Missouri-looking. The thought surprised me because I didn't know what I meant yet—I'd never been to Missouri.

I waited beside his chair for him to notice me. After a minute of nothing, I dropped my pass on his keyboard. His shoulders jumped like I'd startled him and he revolved. It was a fun thing to watch—him seeing me. His tri-focals were smeared heavily with finger-grease, and on top of that, I was standing in an unfocused middle-ground he'd have had quadrafocals for if they made them. His eyes wobbled in their sockets and he moved his head down-and-toward and then up-and-away from me like a strolling pigeon.

"I know," he said, pulling on his string-tie. "I know. If Mark Twain were a pigeon and etcetera."

I said, You're my favorite teacher.

"But you never come to class, you little firebrand!"

I said, I'm not in your class!

"How come?"

I'm in the Cage, I said.

"Hell with the Cage!" he said. He checked his roster. "Gurion Maccabee?"

Would you like a warm Coke? I said.

"No thank you," he said. "Burns my guts, that stuff. Check your email?"

I said, I'll wait til I get home.

"Well," he said, "that's discipline! I have to check mine every hour, or I get nervous, know what I mean. Now, I want you to take a seat, but before you do that, I want you to take this asinine assignment off my hands and, once you're sitting, I want you to fill it with assininities multitudinous."

I said, Where should I sit?

"Wherever," he said. "Just don't yell or kill anyone."

He handed me the detention assignment and I headed to a table at the back of the library to sit with Nakamook.

Nakamook said, "That Klapper? He pretended to be all fuddy-duddily angry about how noisy the lunchroom was, and then as soon as we got out of there, he told us, 'Not to worry, students, I'm no fascist—just wanna check my e-mail.' And then he let *us* check our e-mail if we wanted. I got one from my cousin Phil in New Hampshire. His dad just bought him a rifle. He's lucky. I want a gun. Not to shoot anybody with or anything, but to clean it and know the parts of. The barrel and the trigger and the stock and the sight—that's all I know. But there's all these other parts, the parts that make it work. And plus you could shoot people with it."

Where's Eliyahu? I said.

"Probably trying to decide if someone's a Jew."

I said, He's a good person.

"He's a weird person," Benji said. "He lives with his aunt and uncle.

Why's he live with his aunt and uncle? He mentioned something about it in a way like he wanted me to ask him, and so I didn't ask him cause I don't like being hinted at."

I said, I don't know why he lives with his aunt and uncle, but he's friends.

Benji said, "He said you shouldn't be in love with the girl you love—that's not friendly."

I said, He didn't say that. He just said she didn't look like an Israelite. And she doesn't really. Not particularly.

"It's what he meant, though," Benji said. "It's like a kind of racism."

I said, I can't marry a girl who isn't an Israelite—Eliyahu was looking out for me.

Benji said, "Of course you can marry a girl who isn't an Israelite."

I said, But my sons wouldn't be Israelites.

Benji said, "What if she converted?"

I said, Conversion's complicated—you don't so much convert, it's this other thing. It's called converting, but if you do it, it means you've been an Israelite all along, so it's not really converting and—

He said, "But either way, she could do something?"

I guess so, I said.

He said, "And if she wouldn't, then you'd—"

I said, My lobe would break.

"Your what?"

I said, It doesn't matter. I said, She's an Israelite.

He said, "Calm down. How hard is it to convert, anyway?"

I said, I told you it doesn't fucken matter.

He said, "I'm just asking."

Why? I said. I said, *You* wanna marry me?

All of a sudden, Benji acted real interested in the grain of the library table's fakewood. So I wrote my detention assignment because I wasn't going to apologize to him.

□ □ □ □ □ □ □

Name: Gurion ben-Judah Maccabee
Grade: 5 6⑦8
Homeroom: The Cage
Date: 11/14/2006

Complaint Against Student (from Complaint Against Student Sheet)
Speaking out of turn, inappropriate tones, speaking out of turn, turning in seat.
The Cage. 1st Period. 11/07/06. Mr. Botha.

~~Step 4 Assignment: Write a letter to yourself in which you explain 1) why you are~~
~~at step 4 (in after-school detention); 2) what you could do in order to avoid step 4~~
~~(receiving after-school detention) in the future; 3) what you~~ have learned ~~from being~~
~~at step 4 (in after-school detention); 4) what you have learned from writing~~ this letter
~~to yourself. Include a Title, an Introduction, a Body, and a Conclusion. This letter~~
~~will be collected at the end of after-school detention. This letter will be stored in your~~
~~permanent file.~~

Title

Actual, Potential, and Potentially Potential Messiahs

Introduction

A potential messiah is born once every generation.

No one ever knows who he is, since there are so few restrictions on who he could be. If you look into the face of any male Judite, you may be looking into the face of the potential messiah. You probably aren't, but you may be. And because the diaspora has left so many of the records of our paternal lineages mangled, you may find yourself looking into the face of a Judite while believing he's a Levite, which means that you are potentially looking into the face of your generation's potential messiah whenever you are looking into the face of any Israelite male. And so if you are an Israelite male yourself, and you are looking in the mirror, you might be a lot more important than you look. You probably aren't, but you might be.

It is surely true that the prophets were aware of this problem and wanted to address it—there are many prophecies about who the messiah could be. But it is just as true that when facts can't get bent to fit prophecies, prophecies can bend to fit facts. Either kind of bending could be an exercise in sacrilege. Some might call that statement an exercise in sacrilege, which means some might call me sacrilegious for making it. That does not mean they would be right. They could be sacrilegious themselves. Yet even if they were pious they might not be right. If I am right, it might make me a prophet, and a prophet is a bright thing, and while those who can't see a bright thing are blind, those who do see a bright thing can get blind doing so.

Either way, it is surely true that when facts can't get bent to fit prophecies, prophecies can bend to fit facts.

Body

Persons

For example: Yeshua.

Yeshua came to Jerusalem from Nazareth, and the priests believed prophecies which stated that the messiah would come from Bethlehem. The Christian gospels say that Yeshua, though he was raised in Nazareth, was born in Bethlehem. Maybe he was, maybe he wasn't. Either way, who can really say where Bethlehem is? If the actual messiah turns out to have been born in Big Fork, Montana, a wiseman at a later date will manage to determine that Big Fork, Montana is, in some relevant and probably figurative way, Bethlehem. Either that, or that the meaning of Bethlehem is something entirely different than what we've suspected for thousands of years. In that sense, Bethlehem could be anywhere, and so the Bethlehem prophecy is useless.

In fact, nearly all the prophecies regarding the person of the messiah are useless; if not because they were penned by humans, then because humans can edit and interpret them to suit their needs. That is what humans do—edit and interpret. That is 50 percent of what makes them human. It is an outcome of having a human soul.

More importantly, it doesn't matter all that much who the potential messiahs of the past generations were. A tree might grow from a seed, but that does not make the seed a tree. Yeshua might have been the potential messiah of his generation. So might have been Sabbatai Tsivi. Or Shimon bar-Kokbah. Or Menachem Schneerson. But not one of them was the messiah. The messiah doesn't die. And Yeshua and those others—all those guys are dead.

What matters is who the *actual* messiah is, and the only way we will know the actual messiah is by his effect. He will bring perfect justice to the world. He will build the third Temple. The dead will rise from the Mount of Olives. No one will doubt Whose kingdom is the universe. The messiah may be a soldier, a king, a rabbi, or all three. His methods may be military, scriptural, miraculous, or all of these. No one will know until the messiah has succeeded. And the messiah cannot fail. That is what will distinguish the messiah from all the potential messiahs before him, whoever they were or are: victory undeniable.

Environments

For a generation's potential messiah to become the messiah, the environment must be right; the world must be in the right condition. There are prophecies about that, too, prophecies about what conditions = the right conditions. There is a prophecy that states the potential messiah will become the actual messiah if all the Israelites celebrate a single Passover together in the land of Israel. Another one says it will happen if all the Israelites in the world, wherever they are, observe the same two consecutive sabbaths.

Probably the most talked-about condition, most likely because it is the most interpretable one, is the Brink of Destruction condition, which is exactly what it sounds like: the entire (human) world's very existence just being a moment or two away from assured erasure. This prophecy, however, is subject to the same difficulties as the prophecies mentioned under the heading Persons, and it is subject to those difficulties to an even greater extent because who could possibly know if the world is on the brink of destruction or not? At any given moment, some madman genius in a basement with a few plane tickets could complete his fast-acting doomsday virus and go around the world contaminating all the water and who would know? And say someone did know—like the Mossad. Say the Mossad knew all about it, and so, at any given moment, the Mossad could be at the basement in question, destroying the virus or the man: if the Mossad were to know about this and were able to prevent it, would it be right to say the world was ever on the brink of destruction? I don't think it would be right. I don't think you can know what the brink of destruction is until the destruction has well begun—and even then... Maybe the madman will have invented the virus because a girl he thought he loved as a boy did not love him—maybe the brink was the moment just before she called him a bancer, or laughed at his engagement proposal, or kissed some other boy in front of him. You can't know, so the prophecy is useless.

Apart from all of that, the Kabbalists tell us that Hashem holds the world together by speaking the ten sephirot at a rate of uncountable billions of times per second and, were He to stop, the world would stop existing. So, from where we stand, as humans, the world is always on the brink of destruction, and so the world is never on the brink of destruction.

And so the Brink of Destruction condition is a useless condition to consider, not because it isn't truly a condition under which the messiah might come—it *is* a condition under which the messiah might come—but because it is impossible to determine when the world is on the brink of destruction.

Adonai

No few scholars claim that the actual messiah will hear the voice of Adonai and that the voice of Adonai will *tell* him—in advance of his undeniable victory—that he'll become the messiah. Rabbi Avel Salt himself once made this claim, and, for a moment, it seemed reasonable.

But then the scholar Emmanuel Liebman, in what might have been his finest moment in all of eighth-grade Torah Study, opposed the claim with oratory of such high caliber that when he was finished we applauded for minutes. Emmanuel stated that Adonai would most certainly *not* tell the messiah that he was the messiah—ever; that not only would "having heard Adonai tell you in your ears that you were the messiah" be insufficient reason to conclude that you were the messiah (this insufficiency a qualification that Rabbi Salt *had*, to his credit, stipulated), but hearing Adonai's voice in your ears would necessitate that you were *not* the messiah.

"First of all," Emmanuel said to us, "it's been millenia since He spoke to anyone in their ears. He didn't speak like that to Chaim Weitzman nor Theodor Herzl, nor Maimonedes, nor Nachmanedes. He didn't speak in Rashi's ears either, and He didn't speak into the Bal Shem Tov's. No king, but for Saul and David—and even then only mediated by judges and prophets—ever heard Adonai in his ears. When the time of Judges was over, He stopped speaking into ears.

"And granted: to argue that examining what Adonai has *not* done can predict, with any kind of certainty, what He *will* or *might* do— that would be blinkered, and I would never even dream of attempting to put such sophistry into *your* ears and call it wisdom. I say, 'The time of Judges is past,' and Rabbi Gurion, who breathes deep, hands animating, he wants to say, 'While no longer in the time of Judges, Emmanuel, we are no longer in the time of Kings, either, and this, the time of the disapora, is certainly on its way out.' He wants to say, 'Times change, earnest student, and times are always changing. It is impossible to define clearly the characteristics of our own era, let alone those of eras to come.' And with Gurion ben-Judah—by whose suddenly relaxed posture I can see is satisfied with the words I have put in his mouth—I would, as always, agree. The argument from eras may be compelling, but it is well shy of convincing. I only note the history as an introduction to the following explanation, which, among other things, may help account for the history. And while you consider the following explanation, I ask *you* to note that you're being asked to do nothing other than consider, however more explicitly, that which you already consider every waking moment of your lives.

"We have the written Torah. We have the one document that contains the universe, and therefore all the truth in the universe; all the truth that is, was, and will be. As well, we have this world; a world that Adonai is constantly acting on. And finally, we have scholars who study both—the Torah and the world. We *are* scholars who study both, and we are scholars who study the methods by which we study and the methods by which others who were like us have studied.

"In other words, all the truth is before us, arranged perfectly. And so I submit that it would be *inelegant* of Adonai to speak into ears with words. And Adonai is elegant. I submit that it would be sloppy, and He is not sloppy. For Adonai to speak into ears with words would furthermore be shmaltzy in the slickest, schlockiest Hollywood tradition, and He is no more a Spielberg than was Moses a homesick alien or Ruth a tragic cutie pie in a little red dress.

"It is through studying Torah, the world, and the way others have studied them that the messiah will know how to bring about the events which will characterize the messianic era. It is through studying those same things that *we* will know how to recognize the messiah when he arrives; for though he will be a scholar like the rest of us, he will be better than us; he will teach us how to be like him and we will be ready to learn. In the end, that is why we seek truth, why we study Torah: Our scholarship speeds the coming of the messiah. If we did not believe that, we would not be scholars. In sum: The messiah will not *need* to hear the voice of Adonai in his ears, and so the messiah will *not* hear the voice of Adonai in his ears.

"And now Samuel Diamond, my wise, forward-leaning friend, leans forward, wisely, wondering to himself, 'How does all of this fit itself into Rabbi Gurion's teachings about potential messiahs and proper environmental conditions?'"

"It fits perfect," said Samuel Diamond, elbows on the table, chair balanced on two legs.

"*Perfect* you're saying?" said Emmanuel, averting his eyes. "You're saying *perfect*? Does that mean I should be flattered or anxious? Because I am beginning to feel anxious. Have I mistaken an enumeration of the obvious for a strong argument? What must you guys think of me? 'Loquacious Liebman'? 'Mamzer, stop asking questions you and we already know the answer to'? 'Button up, you windbag shmendrick'?"

"No," the scholars protested. "Tell us," they said. "Finish," they said. "Tell us how it all fits together."

With shaky hands, Emmanuel touched his yarmulke. It was still there, held fast by black bobbypin. "If not the *sole*," he said, "then we are, at the very least, *the most central* environmental condition that needs to get proper. We are the ones who will make actual the potential messiah. And as I have already said in so many words: that is why we are scholars."

And that is when the applause started. It was me who started it.

In*Conclusion*s

It seems to me that even though the messiah can't know he is the messiah until he has had the undeniable victory of the messiah, it would not be unreasonable to assume that he would, prior to the victory, *suspect* he was his generation's *potential* messiah.

Therefore: A person who suspects he is his generation's potential messiah is not necessarily false, or crazy.

But what would such a person do with this suspicion? What, if anything, *should* he do with this suspicion? There is no doubt that he should keep the suspicion to himself, no doubt that he should not speak about it to anyone, at least not directly, that's a no-brainer: Were he to mention the suspicion, those who already shared it—assuming there were any—could overreact and annoint him too early, spoiling his potential. Those who did not share the suspicion could spoil the potential in other ways. They could—as is done with so many of those who claim they *are* the messiah—lock the person up.

But what should he *do*? In the world. How should he act?

What if, for example, a part of the world is persecuting him? What if he's already locked up?

What is the righteous thing for this person to do?

Is it righteous for him to throw his hands up and say to himself, "Right now I am, at best, only this generation's *potential* messiah, and I suffer persecution because the proper environmental conditions that would allow me to become the actual messiah and bring perfect justice to the world have clearly not been met"? = Is it righteous for this potential messiah to be humble about his potential? To allow that messianic actuality is solely in the hands of the world at large?

Or is it righteous for him to say to himself, "In persecuting me, a potentially potential messiah, my persecutors may be haunting the world's future, and I will therefore rise up and smite them?" = Because the potential messiah might one day become the actual messiah, might not smiting his enemies be righteous? Might not this smiting, in itself, help to render him the actual messiah?

Clearly, if the person who suspects he is the potential messiah is being persecuted because he is an Israelite, he must try to rise up and smite his persecutors—not necessarily because they are *his* enemies, but because they are the enemies of the Israelites, and therefore the enemies of the world, who all Israelites must face down. But if that's not the case, or if—even more confusingly—some of his persecutors are, themselves, Israelites, then what is righteous becomes much harder to figure out.

It is what I am trying to figure out.

□   □   □   □   □   □   □

It wasn't easy to stay pissed at Benji, the way his chin would drop. After I finished my detention assignment and Nakamook still hadn't said anything, I saw I'd really hurt his feelings. I was trying to figure out how to make it up to him when I noticed the top half of his assignment was sticking out from under his nearer arm. I saw the title of it was *Villainy*, and I started to read the intro:

> The world may be villainous, the world may be virtuous, but to believe the world wholly villainous is no less blinkered than to believe it wholly virtuous, for a virtuous world is one in which the virtuous overcome the villains, and a villainous world one in which the villains overcome the virtuous. Thus: without virtue, there can be no villainy; without villainy, no virtue. So if we value our belief in the tendency of the world to be virtuous, we must be grateful for the villainous aspects of the world which test the instances exemplifying that tendency. Yet that is a macro-level assertion, and such assertions are easy. What of true love? What of mine? Or yours? We can agree that true love is the sweetest of all things, yet love untested cannot be known to be true. And who tests true love if not villains? And so if we value our true love, must we not, in turn, be grateful for the existence of the villains who would thwart it? Must we not be grateful for their attempts to thwart us? And how do we reconcile this gratitude with our insistence that they are villainous? How can anything that is necessary be considered villainous? If, for example———————————

But then Nakamook's arm was suddenly blocking the rest.

"Why are you making that face at my paper?" he said.

I said, It's weird—it doesn't sound like you.

"What do you mean?"

The way the sentences move—and the words you're using.

"The diction and the rhetoric?" he said.

The syntax, too, I said. Doesn't sound like you.

"You always write the way you talk?" he said.

Half the time I don't even talk the way I talk, I said.

"Me neither," said Benji. "Let alone talk the way I think." He didn't want to be pissed at me anymore.

I pulled the Coke out of my bag and set it on the table.

I said, Want a warm Coke I got from the teachers lounge?

"Thank you," he said. He sipped the Coke and set it down. Benji loved Coke.

I said, You're leaving rings on the table. What kinda slob are you—the Coke's not even sweating. It's room temperature.

"Shut up," he said.

I said, No. I said, You shut up. Look at those rings.

He said, "There's no rings."

I said, You must be crazy, because look at those rings. I said, Look at the rings, Benji. I said, I think you need a coaster. Look at the rings! Don't you think you need a coaster? Say you need a coaster.

"You're a spaz," he said.

I said, Say it. Say you need a coaster.

"Wow," he said, "I need a coaster."

I said, Luckily, I've got a coaster for you.

Then I dropped the hall-pass-pad on the table, and even though my sucky timing ruined the joke, Nakamook laughed his face off because he was my best friend.

I said, You can have half of those, but if you sell them—

He said, "They're my favorite things to have at school. You can go any-where with them. No way I'd sell them. Thank you," he said.

He liked me again. I said, You're welcome. I said, Know what else? I said, Before I came in here? June snuck out of detention to meet me in the hallway.

He said, "Nice. Is she your girlfriend now?"

I said, She said she never kissed Berman.

"I told you," he said. "Is she your girlfriend now?"

I said, I don't know. I said, I should've asked her.

"No way," he said.

Benji was single, but girls went nuts for him. He'd had six different girlfriends in the first five weeks of school and broke up with all of them because he wasn't in love. Even though he'd have told you fighting, girls was Nakamook's favorite subject to talk about. I don't even think fighting was his second favorite—I think it was manners.

He said, "Any time I've ever asked a girl if she was my girlfriend, she got angry at me, like I should know already, and anytime I've ever asked a girl if she'd *be* my girlfriend, she got freaked out, like I should know that if I had to ask, there was no way."

I said, That's crazy.

He said, "It's only sorta crazy, actually. I think I figured it out a little. I think it's like this: If you're asking a girl if she's your girlfriend, it's probably because you kissed her, and if you kissed her already, then she already thinks she's your girlfriend, which makes sense, and so by asking her if she's your girlfriend, it sounds like, 'Did you kiss me because you're my girlfriend, or just because you're easy?' which means you think it's possible that she's easy, which is a mean thing to think about a girl who was nice enough to kiss you. And then if you ask a girl to *be* your girlfriend, you probably haven't kissed her, and so it's more like you're asking for permission to kiss her, which is not a cool thing to do because why would you ask that?"

I said, Why wouldn't you ask that?

Benji said, "Girls decide who gets to kiss them, right? So if you haven't kissed a girl, it's because she hasn't decided to kiss you. And if she hasn't decided to kiss you, and you ask her to be your girlfriend, which is the same as asking her to kiss you, then it's like you're telling her to go faster, which is like telling her she's prude—it's either that or she just doesn't want to kiss you. And that's the part that's the most suck, because after you ask her to be your girlfriend and she gets freaked out and stops talking to you, you can't even just be glad it's over and that you got it out in the open so that the healing process can begin; you'll always have to wonder if you might have had a chance that you ruined by asking, and maybe, instead of feeling relieved about having put everything out on the table, what you should do is run very quickly at a picnic table so you trip on the bench of it and your head smacks the boards and gets splintered."

I shouldn't say 'girlfriend' to June, I said.

"Right," he said. "You just have to wait and see if she decides to kiss you."

But I shouldn't *try* to kiss her, I said.

Benji said, "Of course you should try—if she decides."

I said, And she'll tell me if she decides?

He said, "Don't look worried, Gurion. You're smart. You'll be able to tell if she decides to kiss you."

I said, How will I tell?

He said, "Wait and see. There's signals. You'll know."

And then I thought of something that made no sense if what Benji said before was true.

I said, Esther Salt was my girlfriend and I knew it and I never kissed her.

He said, "How'd you find out she was your girlfriend?"

I said, She told me I was her boyfriend.

"There you go," he said. "She decided."

I said, But you said the girl decides about the kiss, and the kiss decides the girlfriend part.

"I said the kiss decides the girlfriend part, but that doesn't mean the girl can't decide the girlfriend part, too, without the kiss," Benji said. "There's really not much that a girl can't decide about. They don't have rules."

I said, I don't understand.

He said, "I don't really, either. I'm kinda just making it up."

I said, Maybe June decided she was my girlfriend but didn't tell me.

Benji said, "It's possible."

She stole my hoodie, I said.

He said, "Well I guess if she—"

I said, This is making me explosive. I said, I really want to kiss June.

He said, "Who wouldn't?"

I said, I will break your skull.

He said, "I didn't mean *I* wanted to. I meant who, if they were you, wouldn't want to? You're in love with her, you said. You wrote it down. Of course you want to kiss her."

I won't really break your skull, I said.

Nakamook said, "You can't get to my skull." Then he touched my earlobe to be a show-off, and I put mock-strangulation to his throat.

Mr. Klapper let us out of detention a couple minutes early. When he collected the assignments, he handed out dum-dum lollipops with weird, texty wrappers. "Not because you're a bunch of dum-dums," he said, "but because my son is a dentist."

Eliyahu caught up to us at my locker.

Where were you? I said.

"Afternoon davening," he said. "In the reference section. My aunt and uncle become verklempt when I daven in the house."

I said, They're not orthodox?

He said, "They're not."

There was a note in my locker from My Main Man Scott Mookus.

H LLO!
Soon th nd.
—Mookus

Main Man dropped all his E's. He'd pronounce them when he spoke, but couldn't see them written, so he'd leave blanks for them when he wrote. It is fin sinc you can assum th sound of th m. And ink is saved.

Nakamook yanked a string of Eliyahu's tzitzit and said, "What's your intramural bus?"

"I was told Bus One," Eliyahu told him.

"Mine too," Benji said.

I said to Benji, Co-Captain Baxter's on your bus.

There were nine regular buses, but only three intramural ones.

"That bancer," said Benji.

I said, He knocked Eliyahu's hat off.

"Want me to avenge you?" Benji said.

"Thank you, but no," said Eliyahu. "If need be, Gurion has taught me how to send forth metaphoric boulders from my hands, but I hope need won't be. Such a need fulfilled would pain my stomach."

Benji said, "If you don't wreck him, he'll come for you again."

"Boulders in his brains when he comes for me then, but boulders no sooner," said Eliyahu. "However, if he does come for me, and when he comes his friends accompany him—"

"Sure," Benji said. "I'll cripple his friends."

"I was thinking restrain," said Eliyahu.

Nakamook said, "A wheelchair restrains."

"True," said Eliyahu, "but just short of a wheelchair is a cane, and what is a cane if not but a bludgeon waiting to happen? Surely it would be better if those we once restrained were not, the next time we encountered them, carrying bludgeons, let alone bludgeons whose contact with our bodies would be made somewhat ironic by the origin of their carriage's necessity."

Nakamook said, "Actually, to be a bludgeon, in the purest sense of the word, a cane would have to be extra stout and weigh more at one end than it does at the other. Still, even if they were just canes, we'd be—"

"We'd be in a very cocked-up situation with a bunch of needless chazerai that who would want to bother with it?" said Eliyahu.

"Killing would make more sense than crippling," Nakamook said.

"There's no need to talk that way," Eliyahu said. "It's uncalled for, really."

Benji said, "Just pattering, man."

"My apologies for misunderstanding," said Eliyahu. "I have a hard time with the deadpan esthetic. I love Charlie Chaplin and Harpo Marx, and can enjoy Groucho, but Buster Keaton and Andy Kaufman, who—though I occasionally find them delightful—they trouble me the rest of the time. While we're on the subject, I might mention my belief that girls who like Woody Allen movies are nicer girls than girls who don't, and I have little use for Jerry Seinfeld. That is not to say *no* use, but rather—"

"You have to like Kramer, though," Nakamook said. "You have to love George Costanza."

Eliyahu said, "Those two are wonderful, sure, but Seinfeld himself?"

"Well, he's no Larry David, I'll give you that, except—"

"I share that opinion," Eliyahu said.

The cafeteria detention let out. Vincie exited through the southern doorway with Asparagus and the Janitor, who nodded at me = We'd come to your locker, but Nakamook is dangerous. I didn't wave them over. I knew Nakamook wouldn't attack them, but he would not be happy to stand next to them, either, and he was getting joy from talking comedy with Eliyahu— they'd moved on to Sacha Baron Cohen and Sarah Silverman; Nakamook claimed Cohen might be as good as Larry David, and Eliyahu, like my father, agreed with Nakamook, allowing that it was possible the two were equals, yet holding that Cohen had yet to prove his longevity, that only time would tell, and the same went for Silverman as for Cohen, but she was so gorgeous that her future seemed sadly to be a lost cause; she'd most likely drop serious comedy for animatronix and family pap like Robin Williams and Billy Crystal and Eddie Murphy and Steve Martin and Bill Cosby and almost every other truly funny performer of the previous half-century who hadn't died by forty and wasn't Gilbert Gottfried or Richard Pryor—and I saw that it was good: Benji seemed either to have accepted my defense of Eliyahu's concerns about June's Israeliteness, or, at least, forgiven him those concerns in favor of being friendly. It was warm, there in Main Hall, in the day's last minutes, and now here was June, making it warmer—her locker was just down the hall from mine, and she was smiling while she twisted her combination. Right when I noticed, she pulled my hood on to hide her profile, and it seemed like she did so *because* I noticed: like it was my noticing itself that pulled my hood on, and plus it was my hood, in her freckled hands, and this time it didn't feel chomsky at all for me to be in her proximity and not approach her. It felt like flirting. She'd told me not to talk to her til the next day's detention, and I would do as she told me, and she would know I was willing to do as she told me, and maybe she would wish—maybe she was *wishing*, right there at her locker, behind my blue hood—that I wasn't forbidden from what she'd forbade, and that, good scholars—that would be even better. Vincie banged fists with Ronrico, came over.

I said, Eliyahu, this is a liar called Vincie Portite.

Vincie said, "I'm no liar."

I said, You told me you fill the detention assignments with curse words and never get in trouble.

He said, "I said no one reads them. I never said anything about curse words."

I said, They do read them and I can't believe you're still lying to me. I remember exactly what you said. It was my first detention and you said, 'Don't worry, no one even reads these.' And then I said to you, 'Well why do you even write on them?' And you said, 'I get bored, so I just write fuck and bullshit.'

"Fucking bullshit," Vincie said. He said, "I said 'fuck*ing* bullshit.' Fuck-*ing*. Get a hearing aid." Both times he stressed *ing*, his hand jumped to his eye, so I let him keep last dis. Then I gave him my dum-dum. It was cherry.

"Everyone's favorite," Vincie said. He stuck it in his mouth and made a face at the wrapper. "Who's Dr. Harmon Klapper, DDS?" he said. "Why should I call him at (847) 459-0638? Why should I visit him in Wheeling? I hate fucken Wheeling. Wheeling is suck. And what about Ben-Wa? We haven't even talked about that. That was *really* suck! Except for after that ink shot into my eye, and Botha told me, "Not brilliant, Portite," and my eye blocked pieces of things I looked at and made the unblocked pieces look shadowed and when I got sent to the nurse because of it and I stopped in the bathroom to piss and when I took out my wang to piss and my wang looked like a disappearing trombone, that was the worst thing I've ever seen, that kid pissing on himself. That's weird, huh? How the two worst things involved piss? I think it's weird."

And that's when I got the idea to give Ben-Wa some blank hall-passes. I thought I'd drop a couple through the venting of his locker, and then he'd find them in the morning and would feel like his luck had changed.

I asked Vincie: Do you know where Ben-Wa's locker is?

"I don't think you should be mean to him, Gurion," Vincie said. "I don't think you should write things on his locker or leave him some rhyming poem about how he pissed himself because that is one kid who has suffered enough. And I'm not the only one who thinks so either. You saw how the whole Cage almost killed Forrest for Boy Who Went Wee-Wee. You were one of the first ones, yourself. I saw. He's suffered enough, that kid."

I said, I'm not gonna do anything mean, Vincie.

Then I explained to him.

He said, "You've got blank hall-passes and you're not gonna share?"

"Easy, Spastic," Nakamook piped in. "I've got some, too, and *I'm* gonna share. But I don't know about Ben-Wa, Gurion—he doesn't seem like the type of kid to get excited by blank hall-passes. He doesn't seem like he'd use them. I mean, instead of getting up to piss without permission, he pissed himself *waiting* for permission. You see a person like that forging a robot's signature and roaming the hallways?"

I don't know, I said. I said, Why's he in the Cage with us if he's not that kind of person?

"No one knows," Vincie said. "It's probably a mistake."

Eliyahu said, "Mistake mishmake, it's always better to give tzedaka than withhold it."

"I hate that guy's voice and I don't know what he has to do with anything we're talking about, Eliyahu," Vincie said.

"What guy?" said Eliyahu.

"That singing fuckface asshole Sedaka who my fuckface old smelly asshole stepdad loves, what do you mean what guy?"

"I'm talking about tzedaka, and you're talking about a singer?"

"Who do you *think* I'm talking about, man? Are you trying to make me crazy? He's that fuckface asshole who sings that fuckface asshole song about breaking up is hard to do and commacomma down doobydoo downdown and now it's stuck in my head and I'm going crazy and there's an even more annoying one than that, and what's really fucken sick is that for some reason I'm trying to remember it anyway and, when I do, that's the one that's gonna be stuck in my head. Any second now. Any fucken second now."

Tzedaka is charity, Vincie, I said.

"Sedaka is a fucking asshole fuckface, Gurion!" shouted Vincie, hand on his eye throughout.

Do any of you know where Ben-Wa's locker is? I said.

Nakamook said, "Nope."

"If I knew, I would say so," said Eliyahu.

"'Run Samson Run,'" said Vincie.

"And why would Samson run?" said Eliyahu. "The strongest man in Israel? He should run? He shouldn't run, unless—"

"He should run because Sedaka would sooner trust a hungry lion than a gal with a cheating heart because he. Is. A. Fucking. Asshole. Fuckface. Shithead. Fuckface. Asshole. Fuck. Face. Shit. Fuck. Wang..."

"Well," Eliyahu said, "Sedaka may in fact be right in that case—if, that is, Delilah is the gal to whom he's referring. I don't usually think of her as a *gal*, for although a *gal's* looks may fall on the attractive side, they surely wouldn't do so in a spectacular way, whereas Delilah's beauty is believed to have exceeded that of all other women during the era in which Samson reigned—and I'd believe it, too. He was a judge of Israel, and Delilah a Philistine. Would a judge marry a Gentile, let alone a Philistine, were that Philistine not a stunner? I would tend to doubt it. However, given the context in which *gal* appears, Delilah would seem to be the one your Sedaka is advising Samson about. Samson surely would have been better off avoiding her, though who is to say whether Israel would have been better off? At the end there, Samson killed a lot of important Philistines, Vincie. Any one of them might have been a plague on Israel, and who's to say Samson would have ever gotten to kill that one—assuming such a one did, in fact, exist—if he hadn't run *toward* Delilah? It's a rhetorical question, so you don't have to respond."

Vincie was punching the sides of his own head.

Nakamook said, "Why did Samson kill so many people?"

"You want the short or the long answer?" said Eliyahu.

"I don't trust long answers," Nakamook said.

"The short answer is Samson was a holy man, devoted to God, and God wanted some people killed because they were trying to hurt the Israelites, who God was loyal to, so Samson did it. For God. And the Israelites."

"Out of loyalty," Nakamook said.

"For justice," said Eliyahu. "Loyalty's the short answer. Justice—takes a while to explain."

I said, Does anyone ride Ben-Wa's bus in the morning?

"Nope," said Nakamook, who was leaning back on a locker now, his eyes closed and squinty at the edges.

"I do," Vincie said.

I tore off three hall-passes and handed them over, told him to give them to Ben-Wa in the morning.

"What about for me?" Vincie said.

Nakamook said, "I told you I'd give you some." He gave him some.

"Instead of breaking up, I wish that we were making up again," said Vincie.

"And this is how you thank a friend for a gift? With nonsense?" said Nakamook.

"You would make fun of the way I speak?" said Eliyahu.

And Benji said, "So what good is an homage without a little fun?"

7
SIGNIFY

Tuesday, November 14, 2006
4:45 p.m–6:15 p.m.

AN ASSESSMENT OF A CLIENT:
Gurion Maccabee

(Week Three Assignment)

Sandra Billings
9/25/06
Psychodynamic Methods I, SSA 545
Professor Lakey

Introduction

Over the past three weeks, I have had five forty-minute individual sessions with the client, Gurion Maccabee, who has also participated in three thirty-minute group sessions.*

A ten-year-old Jewish-American boy of mixed racial background, Gurion lives in the West Rogers Park neighborhood of Chicago, from where he commutes to Aptakisic Junior High School (my first-year field placement) in Deerbrook Park by means of Metra, el-train, and school-bus. For most of his life, he has flourished at school, both socially and academically. Historically, his grade-reports are glowing, particularly those authored by his Reading and Bible Study teachers. It was not until May of last year that Gurion began to violently act out. The incidents of violence, which are duly represented in the accompanying documents, led to his expulsion from three separate Chicagoland-area middle schools: the Solomon Schecter School of

---

* As per the assignment, all five sessions were recorded on mini-cassette and are available at your request.

Chicago, Northside Hebrew Day School, and Martin Luther King Middle School. Owing to the nature of his expulsions (see *Admissions Record*, attached), Gurion was placed in the Aptakisic Cage program for a three-week probational-observational period and, based on the assumption that he would enter into the regular student population at the termination of this period, he was demoted from the seventh to the fifth grade, the rationale behind this decision being based the assumption of myself and my supervisor (Bonnie Wilkes, PsyD*) that Gurion's difficulties had their roots, at least partially, in his being surrounded by classmates two years his senior. Since meeting with Gurion, I have revised my opinion about the origin of the dif- ficulties' roots. Beyond that, I am going to recommend that Gurion remain indefinitely in the Cage and, because grade-level is socially irrelevant in the Cage anyway, I will also recommend that he be re-promoted to Grade 7, the schoolwork of which would at least be a bit more suitable to his intellectual gifts than that of Grade 5. I do not anticipate any resistance from my supervisor or from the principal in either of these regards.

Psychosocial History

MEDICAL

The client is of average height and weight for his age. His medical records and self-reports offer no indication of his having suffered head trauma or any other physical ailment that might provide an organic account of his behavior.

---

* Is it so weird to see your actions and motives discussed in an academic paper, Bonnie? It was definitely weird for me to write about you, knowing that you'd be reading what I wrote—not to say that I take issue with your (from what I've been told) highly uncommon policy of reading everything your interns write about their clients, not at all. That is to say that if the paper at hand does shed any light on Gurion that may prove useful to you, I'll be proud. Either way, I hope we'll have time to process all of the weirdnesses in our next supervision session. (Btw, for obvious reasons [like formality and relevance to the assignment at hand], this footnote does not appear in the ver- sion of the paper that I handed in to Professor Lakey—It may be the case, as you sometimes seem to be telling me in veiled ways during supervision, that I'm a little too permissive or forgiving sometimes and that I have a convoluted and tangent-ridden explanation-style, but I'm definitely not some kind of flake or weirdo who'd include a footnote addressed to you in a paper being read by one of my professors. Anyway, jIH muSHa' Daj tlhej Hoch wIj tIq [that's, "Have a good weekend," in Klingon. (JK!—not JK that it's Klingon, but JK that I'd think Klingon was appropriate.}])

PARENTAL

Gurion is the only child of Judah, a civil rights lawyer, and Tamar, a clinical psychologist.

Since he was added to my caseload three weeks ago, I have been in sporadic telephone contact with the client's mother. Mrs. Maccabee has refused to allow my supervisor (Bonnie Wilkes, PsyD), to administer any standardized Psych. or IQ tests to her son (the trial-by-fire-type challenge that this lack of cooperation on the part of a client's primary caregiver provides a new caseworker being, I believe, a feature reason for why Ms. Wilkes, PsyD, added Gurion to my caseload*), and has displayed some measured hostility toward the probational-observational process. On one occasion, the mother stated, "I know about Cage programs, Ms. Billings. I know that there is no such thing as an appropriate candidate for a Cage program. Furthermore, I know what a behavioral disorder is, and I can assure you that Gurion does not have one." On another occasion: "You lack the capacity to fathom my son."

I have only once spoken to Gurion's father, Judah, who "defer[s] to Tamar in all matters pertaining to Gurion's psychological well-being in the scholastic environment and so would appreciate it if [I] just went to [his] wife with [my] nonsense, which is not to say that [my] nonsense is objectively nonsense, as in 'a verbal phenomenon that fails to convey anything even fractionally meaningful, let alone compelling,' but rather that to [him], personally, that's how [my] nonsense comes off, and so why not just always call Tamar and never [him] with [my] nonsense is what [he's] hoping to get across to [me]."

PRECURSORS AND WARNING SIGNALS

The physical assault against the headmaster of the Solomon Schecter school, which resulted in Gurion's expulsion from that learning institution, was the first atypically violent behavior to appear on Gurion's scholastic record. Gurion denies that any major change in his home-life had occurred prior to the assault, and his parents (I hesitate to say "corroborate his denial," as "corroborate his denial" seems so darned criminal justicey and no one's on *trial*, here) affirm his denial's accuracy. Furthermore, the teachers at Schecter who I've interviewed over

---

* Am I right, Bonnie?... supervision on Monday.

the telephone have all remarked on the utter dearth of warning signs preliminary to the assault, as have those at Northside Hebrew Day and MLKJH in regard to the acts that earned Gurion expulsion from their respective schools.

Gurion, himself, justifies the three "actions" that led to his expulsions in the following ways.

1. The Solomon Schechter School of Chicago
   Unger [headmaster of Schechter –S.B.] basically called me and my mom and her whole side of the family a worthless lot of Godless n*ggers. So I exploded.

2. Northside Hebrew Day School
   I taught those Israelites [a group of students at Northside Hebrew Day-S.B.] how to make weapons that are legal to carry, legal to fire at non-living things that don't belong to anybody, and can't accidentally go off. I was trying to help them protect themselves from people like the ones who attacked my synagogue. It's not my fault they turned on each other— You wouldn't blame an arsonist's parents for teaching him to light a match any more than you'd blame the proverbial fisherman for teaching— Is there any way you'd turn your fan off?... Not cold, bothered by that rubbing sound, though, thank you. What I was saying is that I'm not anyone's father, not yet, and even if I was their father, if I was the father of *all* those kids, the crime still wouldn't be teaching them to build pennyguns; it would be raising them to be the kinds of people who'd use pennyguns on members of their own tribe. All that I, who is their not-father in the first place, did was teach them to build pennyguns. They came to my backyard because they thought they needed protection and I agreed they needed protection, so I did what I thought was right, and I would do it again... Because I still think it was right... With all the scholars who had pennyguns—not to mention all the ones who've made pennyguns since Northside kicked me out—there's been only that one shooting incident. Why doesn't anyone remark on that?

3. Martin Luther King Middle School
   First of all, I didn't use the brick [a brick Gurion was discovered

holding when the MLK recess supervisor broke up the fight –S.B.]
—I only picked it up to defend myself against the bleeding kid's
seven friends who were coming after me. Secondly, the only reason that kid, who, by the way, had about twenty pounds on me,
was bleeding was because he called me a "motard" which, if you
don't know, is a combination of "homo" and "retard," which is bad
enough already, and then, after calling me motard, he slapped my
head, which leads us to thirdly: if I was someone else, someone
who'd have needed a brick to end that kid's chapter, I'd have been
totally justified in using one, anyway.

Although the client's explanations, however suspiciously elo-
quent (Gurion's eloquence will be further explored below, under the
rubrics Codeswitching and Diagnosis), have the ring of being sound,
the behavior he has engaged in since coming to Aptakisic (again, to
be explored below) throws a shadow over them: a shadow of a doubt.

RACIO-ETHNIC BACKGROUND

Gurion identifies himself as "Israelite," a term he prefers to "Jewish," and all but ignores the fact of his African lineage. He provided
me with an explanation re: his rejection of "African-American" as an
appropriate descriptor of his background and, although I would typically summarize such an explanation rather than set it down word-
for-word (you can hear it on side 2 of tape A, from indiv session 2 of
3), I believe that it is important, in this particular case, to remain
faithful to the audio-recording,* as it will serve to further illustrate
the precocious linguistic abilities that will be discussed later in this
assessment, under the rubric of Codeswitching.

> GURION: African-American is a misnomer, and an irrelevant one
> when it comes to me... A misnomer because it refers to very
> general geographical origins that have little if anything to do
> with the identity of the people who claim the misnomer—their

---

* That said, I am determined, despite the length of the quotation, to stay within Assignment 3's
15–18 page-limit, since, judging from certain comments you've penned onto Assignments 1 and 2,
it seems you'd rather have us, or at least me (lol! Professor Lakey, lol!), err on the side of saying too
little, rather than saying too much, which is, I think, totally understandable, and so, to that end, I
have cut out my own contributions to the discussion (again, if you want, you can listen to the audio
tape), and replaced them with ellipses.

identity is not based in having *African* ancestors any more than a Polish-American's is based in having *European* ancestors... I *guess* maybe *Rwandan-American* or *Nigerian-American* could potentially be more worthwhile descriptors of someone's ethnicity, though not much more worthwhile, come to think of it—those countries haven't been around that long and weren't established as nations by anyone all too indigenous. A tribal identification would make the most sense... Like if people called themselves *Tutsi-Americans* or *Hutu-Americans*. Anything less is just... I don't think you're hearing me, Sandy. What I'm saying is that you wouldn't imagine Tutsis doing too much identifying with Hutus, even though they're all from the same continent, which is Africa, which makes them all *African*... Because they genocide on each other for kicks is why not... I guess that's a pretty way to think about it, but even if you're right, *African-American*'s mostly just a fancy way to say dark-skinned, and who cares what color anyone is? I mean a lot of people care, but those people won't usually admit it—that's why they like to say *African-American*... I agree we should set it aside, but not for later; we should just set it aside... Irrelevant when it comes to me because even though my mother's parents were born in Ethiopia, they were taken to Israel on this special program in 1955 when my grandfather was eighteen and my grandmother twenty and... Of course voluntarily! The idea was that the Israelites of Ethiopia—the Beta Israel—whose status as their brothers some lighter-skinned Israelites denied (and a few still deny), were behind the times religiously—they'd been isolated from most of the scripture and commentary that was written after the Torah—and the idea of the 1955 program was to take a small group of the most intelligent younger Beta Israel to the land of Israel in order to educate them in the relatively newer ways of our people, and that these Beta Israel would then return to Ethiopia and teach their Beta Israel countrymen the new ways they'd learned. So my grandfather and grandmother, who had never met prior to the journey, fell in love on the airplane over, and, once they arrived in Israel, they married and decided to stay there... Because the reason they decided to stay there was that, first of all, it was Israel, which was promised to them by God, and secondly, they knew that in Israel they wouldn't be subject to the rapes and lynchings and hut-burnings they'd been suffering at the hands of the Canaanite Ethiopians, whose skin was the same color as theirs and whose country went by the same name... So here's another way to put it, then: That my grandparents came from the continent of Africa and had dark skin is only relevant to me insofar as certain unenlightened Ashkenazis make a big deal out of it, which is a great reason to get explosive—the big deal that gets made out of their skin color—but it is not nearly a good enough reason to call myself *African-American*... I am an Israelite because all my people are in the line of Israel, who was Jacob, who wrestled an angel and won, and I am a foreigner among all others, nearly all of whose ancestors tried to wipe mine out... Yes, I believe literally wrestled an angel... Sure there's metaphorical value—very rich metaphorical value—but why would that deplete its literal value?... Listen, I was born to be who I am and I know who that is better than you do, which... Just check whatever box you want to check and record my name without the patrinomic, then... ben-Judah... It's not my middle name... I said it's fine... I said don't worry about the ben-Judah... Maybe a little frustrated, yes... Forget it... Stop... Forget it... It doesn't matter...I said whatever you want to put is fine... I'll never know your dumont language as well as you do, anyway, social worker... Flat and imperceptive like Margaret Dumont... The greatest straightman in the history of the world... Yes. She was a woman... Because straightwoman or straightperson would mean heterosexual... No, in fact it has nothing to do with my thoughts about the term *African-American*.

PRESENTATIONAL

During individual sessions, Gurion's conversational style is highly animated—filled with much movement of the hands and face (I'm tempted to describe this animation, particularly that of the face, as being "caricatured," but "caricatured" seems to imply a level of theatricality or falsity, when, in fact, I don't believe that's the case at all—rather, by using "caricatured," if, that is, I were to settle on using "caricatured," I would only mean to get across the "intensity" or "poignancy" of the facial expressions) that appears to seem almost caricaturey—and typically contains a number of humorous gambits, many of which I must admit I do not follow, although, I must also admit, I tend to laugh along with, as Gurion's emotional state, whatever it may be at a given moment, is highly infectuous/contagious.

The infectuousness/contagiousness of Gurion's emotional states is not only evidenced by my reaction to him, but by the reactions of his peers. The parallel in Group Session to Gurion's animation in Indiv. Session is an extremely labile affect. I have twice seen him, in a single instant, affectively leap from an almost-trance-looking state that could indicate anything from sleepiness to hostile disinterest, into a state of total emotional intensity, and then back again. These affective leaps have, both times, included postural, facial, vocal, and manual activity. On the first occasion, owing to what must have been a visual cue on the part of M.B., the boy Gurion would momentarily address (I was engaging another group member in eye-contact at the time, which prevented me from being able to see what the rest of the group was doing, and, added to that, I did not hear anything out of the ordinary, so I must assume it was a visual cue), Gurion stood up with such suddenness that his chair was forced into a backwards double-tumble, and, in a boxer's crouch, one fist on guard, the other overhead with an extended index finger, he shouted, "Do not!" at M.B., who wept openly in response.

The second affective leap occurred during a session which had, I must admit, reached a chaotic peak that I could not for the life of me control, wherein all of the group members, except for Gurion and a mentally retarded boy (Williams Syndrome) who I'll call S.M., traded swear-peppered insults and cross-talked without cease. S.M. appeared sad throughout the chaotic period, and often looked to Gurion, who, when he wasn't engaging eye-contact back at S.M. in what appeared to be a gesture of comforting solidarity, stared fixedly at the ground. After about twenty minutes of the aforementioned group chaos, S.M. began to pray aloud, though too quietly for anyone to make out the words he was pronouncing, and it was at this point that Gurion ceased staring fixedly at the ground and leaned forward. I don't believe I can describe the intensity of this leaning forward—I don't believe I can describe what aspect of it communicated what it communicated, but what it communicated was a capacity, and even a willingness, to paste the walls of my office with the bones and organs of anyone other than S.M. who dared continue making noise. (And I should note, here, that I am not attempting to sensationalize or to startle you, Professor

Lakcy, with that kind of imagery, but to produce a reproduction of actual events: at that moment [whatever it may say about me as a person or a therapist], I actually thought to myself, "Sandy! Pay attention to S.M., or Gurion will make a paste of your bones and your organs with which he will cover the walls of your office.") Within moments, the other group members had ceased riotously acting out in their various ways and given their total attention to S.M. At the conclusion of his prayer (which, once it had been rendered audible by our silence, proved itself to be melodically familiar, however in another, completely unfamiliar language), S.M. sang "She Said, She Said" by the Beatles (S.M.'s singing voice is angelic), and at the conclusion of the song, Gurion applauded S.M., as did the other, formerly chaos-making group members, and then fell back into staring fixedly at the ground, as did the other, formerly chaos-making group members. They would not speak, not any of them, for the session's remaining ten minutes.

PEERS, FRIENDS

Though he is not, at the time of this assessment's writing, generally well-liked by other students in the Cage program, Gurion is offered a wide social berth by his peers (I have never seen him sanctioned for any of his behavior), and, more often than not, it is the case that, as the saying goes, "all eyes are on this kid."

Other than all of them being Cage students at least two years his senior, the few friends at Aptakisic who Gurion has acquired do not share any notable similarities; their personality traits vary greatly, as do the forms taken by their acting-out behaviors. Nonetheless, the few who Gurion considers to be his friends share a group identity. It is unclear whether they are aware of this group identity, but other students respond to it, as do teachers. In fact, the Cage Monitor, Victor Botha, even has a name for the group, a name, albeit, that he only uses in the teachers lounge, but a name nonetheless, and one that has caught on among some of the other teachers (though they, as well, only use it in the teachers lounge). Victor Botha calls the group Spooky and The Spastics. For obvious reasons, I find this name offensive, and prefer to the think of the group as the Maccabeean Collective. The Collective's roster is outlined below:

1. The aforementioned S.M.

2. L.R., a selectively mute African-American boy (I only mention his racio-ethnicity because, apart from Gurion—who, as we've seen, denies the affiliation—L.R. is the sole African-American student at Aptakisic).

3. V.P., a short-tempered and often violent boy who has been, unlike Gurion (see below, under Diagnoses) *correctly* diagnosed with Conduct Disorder.

4. J.R., a girl who, apart from a tendency to become overexcited when she is interested in the subject matter at hand, along with a kind of verbal ferocity when placed in competitive situations or situations wherein an authority figure seems vulnerable, as well as a tendency to bite people who stand "too close" to her, is a quiet, attentive, and, if I may be permitted to say so in an academic essay such as this one, *very sweet* girl.

5. J.M., a girl who has been diagnosed with Pica, OCD, and ADHD (again, accurately), who often engages in physical confrontations with other students—mostly boys—and who, curiously enough, all but refuses to participate in one-on-one conversations, but becomes quite loud and communicative when faced with a peer-group of 2+. (J.M., like Gurion and all the others listed, with the exception of B.N. [description forthcoming], is in the open therapy group I lead, and I have noticed that she only enters conversations that are in progress.)

6. Sixthly, finally, B.N., a very—for lack of better terms— *troubled* and *angry* boy; the son of an alcoholic single mother who neglects and (we suspect [he refuses to speak against her]) physically abuses him, and who has already been (B.N, I mean) through the juvenile justice system for having committed arson on a local residence at the age of ten; fights incessantly (is recognized by many of his peers as the "toughest" boy at Aptakisic); has been diagnosed with ADHD (once more, accurately, I believe); who would, were it not for the efforts of

Bonnie Wilkes, PsyD (who meets in Indiv. session with him {B.N.} regularly), have long since been permanently expelled from Aptakisic; and who Gurion sees as his only intellectual and masculine equal, and even (in certain senses that Gurion will go to great lengths to qualify) as his superior—Gurion looks up to B.N.

Prior to Gurion's arrival at Aptakisic, certain members of the Macabeean Collective were already socially involved—specifically S.M. with B.N., V.P. with B.N., L.R. with V.P., J.R. with J.M., and B.N. with L.R.—but otherwise they held themselves aloof from one another. Since Gurion's arrival, however, it is hard to find any one of them without another at his or her elbow or, at the very least, within arm's reach.

Unfortunately for Gurion, the close relationships he has formed at school do not have extracurricular counterparts. Because he lives in Chicago, it is hard for him to spend time with his Aptakisic friends (all of whom live in Deerbrook Park) when not in school. I only know of one occurrence of Gurion's engaging socially with an Aptakisic friend outside of school—About a week ago, B.N. had dinner at Gurion's house. (By all indications, it went well.)

Furthermore, the client claims to have no social interaction with others in his age group—not even his *relative* age group—outside of school. According to Gurion, as well as to his parents and his teachers, he was quite popular at Schechter and Northside, many of whose students live walking-distance from Gurion. However, the parents of his old friends, owing to gossip about Gurion's recent scholasto-behavioral history and the wide dissemination of a mysteriously leaked e-mail (see *FWD: IMPORTANT*, attached) from Northside's Headmaster Rabbi Kalisch, have forbidden these friends from spending any time with Gurion and have, furthermore, shunned his parents, who (again, according to Gurion), owing to his father's secularity and his occupation as a civil rights lawyer known to handle (and win) court-appeals for racist political groups on the political fringe, as well as their interracial marriage (Gurion's parents'), were already (Gurion's parents were already) closer to the bottom of the community's social hierarchy than desirable.

When asked how he felt about his mostly asocial extracurricular lifestyle, Gurion said, "It gives me time to write. And plus I have Flowers." *Writing*, from what I can gather, refers to Gurion's diary. How I've gathered that is deductively: Gurion refuses to explain to me the subject matter of his writing, often calling it, comically (I think), "[his] autobiography" or (just once) "[his] scripture" when pressed. And what kind of writing is private, I ask myself, if not the kind that goes in a diary? None that I know of. As for Flowers, Gurion won't talk about him either, other than to say that "he is a badass Hoodooman who teaches [Gurion] at the Frontier [the motel near the bus-stop at which the schoolbus picks Gurion up and drops him off –S.B.]," which, by means of deduction similar to those applied to *writing*, I have concluded to mean an imaginary friend—Flowers, that is. I have concluded that Flowers is Gurion's imaginary friend.

RECENT ACTS OF VIOLENCE AND UNDERMINING BEHAVIOR

From his first day at Aptakisic, Gurion has been placed in after-school detention nearly every day, and in-school suspension twice. For the most part, his offenses against the STEP System (Aptakisic's disciplinary rubric) have been non-violent (e.g. standing on his chair and shouting [e.g., "What we have here is a failure to communicate!"; "My mouth is open wide against my antagonists!"] at the top [tops?] of his lungs; removing the wingnuts that affix the whiteboard to the wall of the Cage and refusing to return them [Gurion told Monitor Botha that he was willing to "pay 1.5 times the fair-market price for the wingnuts, and re-bracket the carrel walls to the desk with hexnuts {he} would bring to school along with {his} father's 5-in-1 ratchet if {we} would just let {him}" but that "the wingnuts {were} no less {his [Gurion's]} than the power to open wide {his [Gurion's]} mouth against {his} antagonists," at which point, presumably for the purpose of demonstration, he shouted, "You are a robot!" and Monitor Botha gave Gurion a detention]), but he has also engaged in at least two physical confrontations (i.e. in the cafeteria, during his second week at school, he mashed and pounded the face of a rather large seventh-grader against a lunch-table for reasons he has since refused to elaborate other than to say they were "good"; more recently, in the hallway, just after school and just prior to detention, after an eighth-grade boy I'll call K.M. made a derogotory comment to S.M., Gurion, who was standing nearby, took hold of the hanging-loop at the top of K.M.'s backpack, kicked the back of K.M.'s knees so that K.M.'s feet were swept from under him, and, still holding K.M. up by the backpack loop, used his own (Gurion's own) knees to repeatedly strike K.M. in the lower back until K.M. fainted, at which point Gurion dropped him, stood atop his chest and, before being taken to the office by one of the school security guards, stated to the crowd of students who had gathered around him: "This boy underfoot trifled with my main man S.M. My main man is not to be trifled with.").

Diagnoses

Over the past six months, Gurion has been diagnosed by four separate mental health professionals with the following disorders, in various combinations: Conduct Disorder, Oppositional Defiant Disorder, Attention Deficit Hyperactivity Disorder, Antisocial Personality Disorder, and Intermittent Explosive Disorder. It is my opinion that all but one of these diagnoses—Oppositional Defiant Disorder—are, to varying degrees, inappropriate. My reasons appear below.

CONDUCT DISORDER

Although Gurion does meet the criteria required for this diagnosis, he meets more of the criteria for Oppositional Defiant Disorder and, because the two cannot be applied to the same individual, I gravitate away from the former and toward the latter.

INTERMITTENT EXPLOSIVE DISORDER

Regardless of how much he would like to (despite my protests to the contrary, Gurion, who thoroughly enjoys using the word "explosion" to describe the internal phenomenon which occurs prior to and during his violent outbursts, insists he has IED), Gurion does not meet the criteria for Intermittent Explosive Disorder. Though he has been in a few exceptionally violent fistfights and destroyed some public property, he does not report having had the sense of being overtaken by violent/destructive impulses prior to or during these instances, nor has he ever expressed regret for the pain and destruction that any of his actions have brought about. I.e., no matter how inappropriate his reasons, Gurion always *has* reasons; he is always able to explain why, in a given situation, he has acted violently/destructively, and, furthermore, after the fact, he consistently feels that his actions were justified and proportionate. Thus, when he says, "I exploded," he does not mean, "I lost control," but rather, "I joyfully and violently *took* control." When he says, "I got explosive," he does not mean, "I was overtaken by violent impulses," but rather, "I realized (gratefully) that I was willing and able to bring the violence/destruction I believed— and still believe—the situation at hand called for."

ANTISOCIAL PERSONALITY DISORDER

It is spiteful, if not just shy of criminal, to diagnose Gurion with Antisocial Personality Disorder. In any case, it is ignorant. *DSM IV* makes it abundantly clear that one must be at least eighteen years old to be diagnosed with any personality disorder.

ATTENTION DEFICIT HYPERACTIVITY DISORDER

I take cautious exception to the ADHD diagnosis. Like Conduct Disorder, ADHD is another disorder for which Gurion meets the criteria (as well as one which, like IED, he would, owing to the verbal idiosyncrasies it permits him [e.g., "My A got D'd by {Monitor} Botha's mouth-breathing."], prefer to keep). However, as with Conduct Disorder, I do not believe it is an appropriate diagnosis. Gurion's claims of easy distractability, his visible motor agitation (e.g., tapping feet, manual flux in the form of wild expressive gesturing and the drumming of tabletops and thighs while sitting, the pocketing and un-pocketing and re-pocketing of hands in sweatshirt pockets [accompanied by balling and un-balling of fists] while standing, constant pulling on the drawstrings of his hood, occasional chest-drumming and self-embraces that rapidly alternate with the dropping of hands to the sides), and his near-constant attempts to communicate with other students in the Cage (where total silence is the first rule) seem to be (all of these symptoms do) functional outside of the Cage.

To put it inversely: these behaviors are only dysfunctional insomuch as they are causes for disciplinary action *inside* the Cage, where the authority–subject dynamic is far different than that of a regular classroom, let alone a "real world" situation. Gurion's high level of motor activity, for example, does not disturb or distract me in session, nor does it seem to disturb or distract the group in Group session.

When I interviewed Gurion's former Jewish-American School teachers (before enrolling at MLKJH, Gurion had never been in a Cage program), not one of them even mentioned his high level of motor activity, much less complained about its effect on their students. When I probed further, drawing examples (such as those mentioned above, parenthetically), one of the teachers commented, "He *did* bring a lot of passion to the bimah," and another stated, "His excitement about his studies was surely palpable: his contributions to classroom discussion were unmatched and very inspiring to the other children."

Because of the nature of the situations in which the aforementioned behaviors cause him trouble (again: situations in the Cage, where an atypically high level of authority is ever-present and exercised regularly [and, I sometimes think, *excessively*]), I believe that the symptoms of ADHD that the client manifests can be accounted for by his Oppositional Defiant Disorder. Finally, as demonstrated by his uses and misuses of clinical terminology (as shown under the present sub-rubric, as well as under the sub-rubric Intermittent Explosive Disorder), Gurion takes his diagnoses to heart, and, I believe, he does so to his detriment—affectionately embracing one's symptoms is unlikely to aid in the cause of overcoming one's disorder(s)—such that, although diagnosing him with ADHD would be "safe" from the C.Y.A. P.O.V., it would not be all too therapeutic.

Codeswitching

The "voice" in which this paper is written is not the voice I would use at dinner at my ma's in Bridgeport. Nor is the "voice" you use when lecturing the class the same as the one you use in individual conferences. If you and I were to "get together over a beverage" some time, Professor Lakey, we would be unlikely to use any of the aforementioned "voices" while doing so. And if the beverage we decided to "get together over" were coffee, the "voices" we'd use would be different from those that we'd use were we to decide instead on beer. And if, *while* "having coffee," we decided to "make it a girls' night out" and "get beers," the decision would likely have to do with the kinds of "voices" we found ourselves using while "having coffee." These are all examples of codeswitching, and anyone can understand what

I'm getting at when I use these examples, even if they're unfamiliar with the term "codeswitching." The reason anyone can understand codeswitching (which, btw, is usually explained by linguists as an outcome of assimilation, and by evolutionary psychologists as a sort of speakerly camouflage) is that everyone *engages* in codeswitching.* It is normally a very powerful way to signify a group affiliation.

When Gurion codeswitches, however, it is harder, and maybe impossible, to understand because a) he switches codes at unlikely and unpredictable times (e.g., in the middle of a diadic conversation without tertiary witnesses), and b) the codes he engages are his own, i.e., though each code contains recognizable influences, not one of them, on the whole, signifies any single group affiliation, much less any affiliation with a group whose members are present at the time of the code's engagement.

I have noted three distinct codes between which Gurion alternates when speaking and writing (for written examples, see attached "Detention Assignments"), each of which is exemplified by the quotations that appear earlier in this essay (under the rubrics Precursors and Warning Signals and Racio-Ethnic Background):

1. A highly refined, organized, and even scholarly English rife with dialectic that is vocalized at breakneck pace, as if Gurion is highly irritated.

2. A syntactically complicated, analytical style that makes use of both clinical and idiolectic vocabulary, is often peppered with

---

* I do not mean to imply, by describing it, that you, Professor Lakey, are unfamiliar with the term codeswitching. Quite the contrary—it's that, seeing as you have a B.A. in Linguistics from the University of California at Santa Cruz ('93), I'm sure you're more than familiar with the term, and, being that you're my favorite professor (and believe me: I'm not grade-grubbing when I say so— I'm not a grade-grubber), who I respect in so many ways, I become fairly nervous when writing papers for your class and only hope to convince you that I know what codeswitching is. And what's worse is that I realize how overcompensatory I'm coming off right now, like I'm even maybe trying to hide something, and probably I am, but I don't know what it is, if not the aforementioned nervousness, which, on one hand, seems reasonable (to be nervous seems reasonable), but on the other hand seems dubious (that this feeling I have which arises from the copious amount of respect I have for you is merely nervousness seems dubious), and so maybe you, who are as well-renowned (as you know) as a clinician as an academic could provide me with some insight into what the root of this nervousness might be some time outside of class. I wouldn't dream of asking you to do so— help me with my dubious nervousness re: you—during your office hours, which I respect as your time to meet with students in an academic way, but maybe at some other time, outside of school. If you can spare the time.

biblical references, and is vocalized either a) slowly, explanatorily/revelatorily, as if Gurion were soliloquizing by the footlights; or b) at the aforementioned breakneck pace.

3. A clipped manner of speaking that mixes the dialectical speech and vocabulary of #1 with the vocabulary of #2, while also incorporating the slang and imperative tonality of a street-thug. This code is vocalized in any number of ways, often in as many as three or four within the span of a single utterance.

The peculiarity of the above-described styles and the times when Gurion chooses to engage them allow us three possible explanations for Gurion's codeswitching: 1) Gurion is completely unaware that he codeswitches, which would indicate that his codeswitching is symptomatic of an undiagnosed cognitive disorder; 2) his codeswitching is highly purposeful and totally conscious, indicating that Gurion either a) knows the reasons for his codeswitching are inscrutable to listeners, which, if this is the case, would indicate that Gurion aspires to inscrutability; or b) is attempting to appear unaware (as in 1)) of what he's doing (codeswitching); or 3) is experimenting with a variety of codes in order to inspire in his audience the alternating impressions of both 2a and 2b so that he may, while indicating, via his verbal behavior, a capacity to understand wildly complicated ideas, simultaneously maintain enough of a childlike persona to "charm" his audience so that he might more easily "get away with" a larger portion of his more "childlike" or "mischievous" (read: antisocial) behavior (verbal and non-).

Regardless of what Gurion's codeswitching might indicate at any given moment, what's most notable is that whichever code he happens to be using is nearly as infectious/contagious as his emotional state. I.e., when Gurion codeswitches, those members of Group who belong to the Maccabeean Collective do so with him (and so, I find, do I). In light of his dominant personality (alternately: his *charisma*), it is not surprising to discover that changes in his behavior (verbal or otherwise) would elicit (at least to some degree) similar changes in the behavior of those around him, nor is it surprising that when Gurion speaks thuggishly, those around him speak thuggishly (cursing often begats cursing), but what *is* surprising, is that members of the Maccabbean Collective not only engage a more scholarly code when Gurion does, but they engage it *convincingly*, i.e. they don't just adopt Gurion's lexicon (which adoption could certainly be "faked," i.e., just because someone pronounces a word doesn't mean they understand what it signifies), but his syntax (unfakably analytic).

In sum, Gurion's codeswitching behavior merits further, closer attention, and I hope that you, Professor Lakey, given your expertise in linguistics, will help guide me more closely through the process of further attending it.

Recommendations

1. Gurion should remain in the Cage program indefinitely, and be permitted leave of the Cage only when attending state-mandated Physical Education, Lunch/Recess (at the discretion of Monitor Botha), weekly group therapy, and Assembly (again, at the discretion of Monitor Botha). Although it seems, as I've noted throughout this paper, that many, if not most, of Gurion's disruptive behaviors are exacerbated by the Cage program dynamic, his *violent* behaviors (e.g., the hallway incident with K.M.) may or may not be. That is to say that there is no telling whether or not Gurion would cease assaulting other students if he were a member of the regular student body. It may be the case, as many of his former teachers claim, that Gurion is by nature an ideal student who, at one time, rarely, if ever, acted out; and it may be the case that his troubling record, which appears to describe a dangerous and even doomed young boy, only reflects a combination of a) unlikely circumstances of which Gurion has been a victim and b) mistakes made by administrators in response to these unlikely circumstances. On the other hand, it may be that Gurion, once an ideal student, has *become*—via the aforementioned combination of unlikely circumstances and mistakes made in response—the dangerous and even doomed boy indicated by his record. It may be that, were he admitted into regular classrooms, he would exert bodily harm on other children at a similar, if not—Cage restraints lifted—higher, rate. CYA POV aside, that is not a risk which a conscientious social worker can take.

2. Owing to Recommendation 1, Gurion should be re-promoted to Grade 7, the work of which is better suited to his intellectual abilities than that of Grade 5. Whether or not Gurion's disruptive and violent behaviors have historically resulted from the social awkwardness of being surrounded by students two-to-three years his senior is irrelevant as long as Gurion is in the Cage program, where 5th-, 6th-, 7th-, and 8th-graders are mixed together willy-nilly, anyway.

3. In addition to twice-weekly Group Therapy, Gurion should attend once-weekly individual Therapy with me, Sandra Billings, Student Social Work Intern. His treatment plan should focus primarily on anger-management and the prevention of the onset of Antisocial Personality Disorder via psychodynamic methods we've been studying in your (Professor Lakey's!) class.

4. Like so many other students in the Cage, Gurion should henceforth be disciplined according to what is unofficially termed the "modified" STEP System. If this exception is not made and Gurion continues to behave as he has over the course of the probational/observational period, he will be expelled from Aptakisic within two days. If he is expelled, we cannot help him.

5. Regarding the attached detention assignments (about which, in obedience to this essay's page limit, hardly anything has been said): Gurion should be permitted to continue using them as he has in the attached examples—as an aid to fantasy and a tool for venting.

□   □   □   □   □   □   □

Detention ended at 4:35, but the buses wouldn't leave until 4:50, in case band and the teams got out of practice late. Usually we'd wait on the curb of the bus circle playing slapslap even if the buses were there already, which they were that day, but it started raining right after we came outside, and all my friends raced. I didn't like to get rained on either, especially not without a hood in November, but I'd known some girls who didn't mind getting rained on, and even liked it, and I always enjoyed how those girls would stroll in the rain like it was the cleanest, nicest blessing, and how they'd sometimes stop and face the sky, winking. I had never seen June in the rain, but I thought she would be that kind of girl, and that kind of girl made fun of you when you ran from the rain, so I walked slow to Bus 3, and even paused a couple times to look at the clouds. I didn't know if June was watching me, just that revolving my head to check would be a mistake if she was, but Vincie, who was sitting on the blocky stairway in the bus and breathing heavy from how he'd sprinted to get there, was staring straight at my face and saying, "You sexy nature boy! You're such a dreamy—" when cherry dum-dum juice got swallowed down his wrong passage and he choked a little and raised his hands and coughed. Marnie the heavy bus-driver slapped his back. Her cheeks and neck-meat shook and flapped and I looked away.

The value of the wheel-well seats on the bus was different from school to school. At Schechter and Northside Hebrew Day, getting a wheel-well seat was prized, but at Martin Luther King Middle no one cared, and at Aptakisic it was as generally dreaded as sitting bitch in a compact between a pair of bickering people who spit. The argument against the wheel-well seat was that the hump prevented you from stretching your legs, but—maybe because I went to Schechter first—the hump, to me, meant less a lack of leg-room than a bonus of floor, so I always preferred a wheel-well seat. It is true that you had to sit with your knees at the height of your neck, but at the same time, if you leaned back, you could push your knees against the seat in front of you while resting your feet atop the hump's peak, which gave you a warm, protected feeling that you could not get in a regular schoolbus seat, unless maybe you were very tall. To have just been rained on at the end of a schoolday pleasantly boosted this fortified feeling, and that afternoon, I got sleepy fast.

Vincie sat across the aisle from me, spreading a hole in his seatback's vinyl with his thumbs. He pulled a piece of foam out. He said, "You ever set this stuff on fire? It smells."

I said, When you were coughing just now—

"Stop being so fucken quiet. I can't hear you."

I said, When Marnie was slapping you, your hand didn't jump to your eye.

He said, "So what?"

I said, Don't act sensitive—can you fight Thai-style?

He said, "Nakamook showed me a little."

I said, Get in the stance.

Vincie shoved the foam back in the hole, then stood bent in the aisle and held his fists fingers-forward at forehead-level.

I slapped my thigh loudly. Then I slapped the seat loudly. Then I yelled Flinch! at him.

He said, "That's not cool, Gurion."

I said, When it's above your eye, your hand doesn't jump to your eye.

He said, "Really?"

I said, Flinch!

It didn't jump.

Vincie said, "I'm cured!"

I said, Wait. I said, Stand American-style.

He dropped his fists to chin-level.

I waited a couple seconds, then I said, Flinch!

His right fist opened, revolved, and covered his eye.

"Fuck!" Vincie shouted, and his hand repeated itself.

"Vincie!" said Marnie.

"Marnie!" said Vincie.

"Okay!" Marnie said.

"Okay, Marnie!" said Vincie.

The hand had repeated itself four more times. Then the sky got white outside the window and thunder struck and the hand repeated itself.

I said, You're not cured, but you can fight Thai-style no problem.

Vincie slumped when he sat. He said, "I'm suck at Thai-style. Benji throws his elbow at my chin and lands it every time. I can't see to side-step. Also when he does the knee-to-kidney thing, too—and it hurts."

I said, But that's Benji, so it doesn't matter.

Some bandkids got on the bus and I waved hello to them. They sat down fast, clanking instrument cases.

"Why do you wave to them?" said Vincie. "They never wave back. They're scared of you."

I said, But they shouldn't be scared of me, and I've always waved to them, since before I knew they were scared of me. If I stop waving to them now, they'll get even more scared of me because they'll wonder, "Why doesn't Gurion wave anymore?"

Vincie said, "Maybe I should wave to them, then."

I said, But they're scared of you, too, and you never wave to them. I said, If you wave to them now, it'll be like if I stopped waving to them.

He said, "That's what I'm saying. You stop waving and I'll start—it'll be funny."

We aren't Shovers, I said.

"You don't have to be a Shover to enjoy a scared bandkid." He held his hands above his head and told me, "Watch this." Then he yelled to the bandkids, "Hello! Hello!"

They ducked their heads.

"Sorry!" said one of them.

"We're sorry!" said another one.

Vincie said to me, "I think that's pretty funny."

It was pretty funny, but laughing felt cruel. We weren't Shovers.

We aren't Shovers, I said to Vincie.

Don't worry about Vincie! I said to the bandkids. He isn't a Shover! Neither am I!

"We're really really sorry!" they said, all of them still ducking.

"Really!" they said.

"Sorry!" they said.

And I stopped feeling cruel because why did they keep apologizing? Maybe they did something to me that I didn't know about and they were scared that I found out about it, but probably they did nothing to me and so their apology was a kind of lie. And I'd told them not to worry—but it was like they couldn't hear the words I said, just my voice that scared them.

Why are you apologizing? I said.

"We're sorry!" they said. "Please."

Please what? I said.

"We didn't mean to offend you."

I said, How did you offend me?

"We don't know."

So what good's apologizing? I said.

"We're sorry."

Soon more bandkids got on the bus, and then some Indians in their school-colored windbreakers: Maholtz, Shlomo Cohen, and Bam Slokum himself. They went to the seats in back. Marnie drove us out of there and I cracked my window to smell the storm. The plastic latches you shove into the frame were tight and my thumb-flesh got dented. I shook out my hands like thermometers, like the flesh-dents were mercury.

Vincie said, "That makes you look gay. Why's Slokum on our bus? He's not supposed to be on our bus."

I said, Why don't you ask him?

Vincie made the noise "Tch" = You trickle my snat, friend.

I let it go. It was mean to challenge Vincie about Slokum, but I didn't like it when people used *gay* like a swear. There was a gay kid who used to go to Schechter with me who I won't name because it's a secret. He was in eighth grade when he told me, and I was seven. I was the first one he told. We were close and stayed that way until after I delivered *Ulpan* and his parents banned me from talking to him. I wished he wasn't gay because it made him sad to be gay, and it would've made his parents sad if they knew, so he had to hide it, and Adonai didn't like it either, there was really no getting around that—I tried hard to find a way the day this friend of mine told me, because that's what he'd wanted, that's why he'd told me; he wanted me to tell him that it was okay. But it's clear Adonai doesn't want Israelite guys to be gay. It's exactly as clear as His not wanting us to use condoms, get blowjobs, play with ourselves, tell lies, speak ill of others, mix linen with wool, mix dairy with flesh, eat pork, eat shellfish, or shave, I'd explained, and so my friend was cheered after all—but when someone said *gay* like an insult, or *fag*, or *homo*, it was like they were saying something bad about my friend, which is like saying something bad about me for being a friend to my friend. And plus my friend was an Israelite, and Vincie wasn't. Since it was Vincie saying *gay*, I knew he didn't mean anything bad about me or my people, since if he did he'd also be saying something bad about himself since he was friends with me too, but still I didn't like him saying *gay* that way because what *he* meant didn't matter that much—he was saying something bad about us whether he wanted to or not.

The bus stopped at a red and Shlomo Cohen started walking up from the back. Shlomo played second-string point-guard for the Indians and I'd never spoken to him before. Marnie shouted at him to sit, so he ran. He ran to the seat behind me, put his head in the aisle, and said, "Which one of you is Gurion?"

I said, I'm Gurion.

He said, "They want you to come back there and talk."

"Who?" Vincie said.

"Bam and Maholtz."

"What for?" Vincie said.

Shlomo shrugged.

All three of us got up. "They don't want to talk to you," Shlomo said to Vincie.

"I don't want to talk to *you*," Vincie said.

I set my hand on Vincie's shoulder = It's fine.

Eighth-graders talked way more than they fought. And plus, if they tried to attack me, I knew I could handle them for at least as long as it would take Vincie to get there. I was good at bus-fighting. I knew how to use inertia and I could always tell when the driver would hit the brakes. That was the best time to throw a guy.

Marnie shouted some more and Shlomo shrugged some more and Vincie sat down a couple seats closer to the back. I decided I didn't like Shlomo. He wasn't friendly to me and I believed in his shrugging. I believed it was true that he didn't know why Bam and Maholtz wanted to talk to me, but he came to get me anyway, and that was not very Israelite of him. Israelites who didn't act like Israelites disappointed me the most.

Shlomo sat in the second-to-lastseat on the right and Bam stared out the window from the 2/3-size lastseat behind him. Maholtz was standing in the aisle, gesturing to the other lastseat with his right hand, which was his weak hand. He had his left hand in the pocket of his windbreaker, where he kept his weapon. It was a sap with a lead-ball head that was spring-loaded for more than the sake of concealment. Cocked, it was about five inches long. Sprung and straight, it was nine. You sprung it with your thumb— there was a button on the grip. The grip was black steel and the button was silver like a stilleto's button. When it was cocked, the sap did not look like a weapon. It looked like the missing piece of something useful and electric, like a drill or motorcycle. The rod the lead-ball head was attached to was rubber, a very heavy kind of rubber, but because it was rubber, it was bendy, and that was good because of torque. If you flicked your wrist at the pinnacle of your swipe's arc, the rod's bendy action would create an extra swipe for the lead-ball head, and the impact would be exponentially greater than what it would have been if the rod wasn't bendy, and the lead-ball head would, on contact, turn your enemy's bones into a powder so fine it would appear to be mist if the flesh and blood weren't there to block you from seeing it.

Maholtz said, "Step ingto my office, Gooreeing."

Bryan "Bry Guy" Maholtz was a high-stepping, button-nosed, prettyboy bully from Pittsburgh, Pennsylvania. He suffered from a combination of a stupid accent and cloggy adenoids that added *ng* and *nd* sounds to the backs of certain vowels and gunged up some of his consonants, too. His smile was the kind that said, "Wait'll this kid seends what I've got up my sleengve." On top of the creepy speech d., Maholtz always kept his eyes slitted, like he was waiting to violate something quietly. And his jutting chin, his pushed-out lips—it was like he was rondesormiating the whole bus. He was not very good at basketball, either, but he sold steroids to the varsity starters so they'd be friends with him, which worked. Maholtz didn't scare me, but I was not going to sit between him and the window.

"Have the window. Pleandse," he said.

I said, I like the aisle.

He said, "Your pleandsure is my pleandsure."

We sat.

He said to me, "Thing about Boystar: no one reandlly likes him much. I don't reandlly like him. Bam over there doesn't reandlly like him." I looked at Bam Slokum. He leaned on the opposite window, his forehead on his arm. "You like him, Shlomo Coned?" said Maholtz.

"Not really," said Shlomo Cohen, in a bored voice.

"See?" said Maholtz. "Not. Reandlly. Still though, the ladies like him. They like his musinc. It gets them horngy. *He* gets them pretty horngy, the girls, just by doing his little dances in the hallngway. It's a very curious thing. But the poind is, there's only one of him. And then therend's us, his friends. Do the mangth—I will: Many girls mindus one *for* him > many of his friends mindus one *of* him = many more girls for his friends than friends for the girls and therefore don't mess with our play, Goo-ree-ing. Right?"

As long as Boystar didn't bother June again, I had no reason to go after him, but if I agreed with Maholtz, it would be like saying that I wouldn't go after Boystar because Maholtz told me not to, and plus he was a disgusting person.

So I said to him, I'll think about it.

Maholtz said, "Think abound what?"

I said, Your question.

He said, "You misunderstood. I didn't *ang*sk you a question. I told you that you will, from now on, leave Boystar aloned."

Do people ever call you 'Bry Guy' to your face, Bry Guy? I said.

His pocket-hand flexed around the handle of his sap and the knuckles stretched windbreaker nylon, but I knew he wouldn't pull the weapon. How I knew he wouldn't pull the weapon was that I was watching his face, and all his face did was fold up into little sickly colored pouches of totally normal rage. If sapping Gurion was truly his plan, the face would've signalled Adonai to yell No! at Maholtz's muscles and I was sure I would've seen it. But even if I was wrong about the existence of a pre-sin face signal, or about my ability to see one, I knew for sure that his weapon was useless in the face of my stealth. I'd have made claws of my fingers and palmstruck his windpipe into stickman dimensions before he had the chance to find the silver button with his gangly thumb, let alone to bring his arm back for the swipe. The second he pulled his weapon, I'd have made it mine. I liked his weapon. I wished he'd pull it.

All he did, though, was remove his empty hand from his pocket and cut it across the air slowly, left-to-right = "Luncky for you, Goo-ree-ing," and when I didn't do whatever it was that Maholtz was used to people doing when he offered them a very clear example of trying to save face, he did the same hand-cutting thing again while shaking his head left-to-right-to-left-to-right = "You don't even know enough to know you're luncky, much less how luncky, dumbass," and when I still didn't do whatever he wanted, he said "Tch" to me, and I said to him, Bry Guy, and he said, "You hearnd this kid, Bam? You hearnd this kid?"

Bam Slokum continued staring out the window and leaning on it with his forehead and one elbow. The hollow between his neck muscles where the top of the spine is housed was wide enough and deep enough to secure a superball, and he could actually do it, too—he could flex the back of his neck and hold things with it. I saw him do it in the hall once, to the thumb of a girl called Kylie Watson. He had to get on his knees so Kylie could reach, and then once she got the thumb in, Bam tightened his neck, bowed down like a Muslim on a prayer mat, and Kylie, following the pull on her thumb, fell on Bam's back, giggling.

When Bam spoke, in the direction of the window, he moved his thick hand around above his head to emphasize certain words. His voice was yawny and quiet and weirdly punctuated. It surprised me, the way he talked. I'd only ever heard him speak in very short sentences. The waving hand was the only thing that showed his impatience, flicking at the wrist on words like "pick" and "most" and "sit" and "mewling." He said, "Maholtz you're a scumbomb, no one likes you, why you always gonna pick on people? Gurion I want you to leave Boystar alone. He told me all about what happened, and probably it was lies, I'm not saying you were wrong, you were probably right, and this isn't about who did what to who but who'll do what to who in the future, tomorrow, day after, whenever, first who being you, and the second one Boystar. You came out ahead, I hope you'll leave it at that, I anticipate no objections on your end, you seem like a solid no-bullshit-type person, you don't vibe me funny, I can tell that you listen and you want to understand, so I'm asking you to hear me, to listen, understand: Lana Mary Wilder is endlessly beautiful, the most gorgeous sophomore at Stevenson High, and for two years of Fridays she sat for the kid—pro-grade sitter, Lana, sat for me once, too, actually, we made these weird cookies, a whole nother story, it was years ago anyway—but she stays in touch with him, Boystar I mean, and she gets all upset if he calls her up crying, and he calls her a lot. Mewling and whining like a fraidycat crybaby famous little brat. He calls her up, worries her, and then she feels troubled, she gets all upset. I'm about to go see her is why I'm on your bus, I'm going to her house, and he'll have already called, probably called her at lunch, so understand I want to tell her that it's all taken care of. So she won't be upset. You understand."

"If Wilder's all upsendt," Maholtz explained, "she won't be giving up the tints and sweet pussy."

Bam reached across the aisle and the width of my body, and held Bryan Maholtz by the front of the hair. His arm was so long that he was able to do this without rising even a little from his seat. He said, "I'm really just super tired of hearing you, Bryan."

Once his face was exposed, I could see that Bam's jaw hardly moved when he spoke. His voice stayed yawny and even and, watching him close-up like that, I saw that I'd been right in the hallway that morning when I'd guessed his kingliness came from the faces he made—the face, actually: there was just one. It was as unchanging as his voice, the face, and describing it as a half-smile doesn't explain much except for what it would look like on someone else in a photograph. A half-smile can mean almost anything, I think. It can fit almost any situation—it can mean whatever the person watching the half-smiler thinks is most appropriate at the time. Bam's face was more intentional. It was set in a *pre*-smile. It was the face of someone who has just leaned in your direction to hear something important that you are about to say—maybe the punchline of a joke he is expecting to be entertained by, or the conclusion to an argument he thinks you'll convince him with. When someone pre-smiles like that, it is impossible to read the stories in the person's face—at least for me. It is also impossible to want to hurt the person. You want to perform for a person like that. You don't want to disappoint him. Bam was impressive.

Vincie ran down to us. He must have seen a blurred version of the hair-pulling action and thought I was in trouble. I showed him my palm = Not yet, and he stopped short beside the seat of Shlomo Cohen.

Shlomo made the noise "Tch."

"So I'm asking you to leave Boystar alone," Slokum said to me.

Vincie said to Slokum: "Nakamook'll fucken—"

Bam said, "I don't stress Benji Nakamook and I wasn't even talking to you Portite with your fists in the air like that like maybe you want to do something we all know you won't do anyway so you might as well relax. I'm just asking your friend to leave someone else alone so my life can be a little easier, what do you say?"

I said, I'll think about it.

Bam said, "Good," to me. He said to Vincie, "You can tell Nakamook a lot of Fridays have passed and I don't feel too dead."

"I'm not your fucken messenger," Vincie said.

"My messenger or Nakamook's asskissy lackey, whatever you call yourself," Bam said, "you'll deliver my message."

By the time Bam said "whatever," Vincie had already spun and started back down the aisle, slapping his fingers along the tops of the seats on the way to his own. Right when Vincie spun, Bam's pre-smile twitched away, like the stories in his face were fighting to get told, and if the twitch had lasted another billionth of a second, I could have read the stories, but it didn't last another billionth, and Bam finished speaking his sentence. Then he started talking to me again. He said, "The thing about Nakamook—"

"Would you pleandse let go of me?" Maholtz said.

Bam said, "Only if you promise to quit talking about girls in front of me because when you talk about girls Maholtz it makes me want to hide every girl in the world in a castle you can't get to and I don't have a castle much less one you can't get to and even if I did have a castle you couldn't get to it wouldn't be big enough for all those girls so promise?"

"Yes," said Maholtz.

Bam twisted the forelock. "Promise," he said.

"I promise!" said Maholtz. Bam let go and Maholtz hid his face.

Some kids I couldn't see were singing, "Next stop, Frontier Motel/ the place where Gurion's fat black dad who fell dwells." Was it the bandkids? Is that why they'd apologized? The song was definitely coming from toward the front of the bus.

I stood up to check, but then, in this whisper that seemed to project like a shout—even as it managed, because of its whisperiness, to sound like the voice of total reason, like he was explaining something neutral and scholarly—Bam, leaning further into the aisle, said to me, "I don't like Benji Nakamook, but I do respect him."

I should have left right then. If Bam wasn't starting up with me, I couldn't fight him—even if I'd wanted to, Benji had my word—and if I couldn't fight him, I had no good moves. With every beat that passed, although I didn't quite know it yet (I rarely ever trickled; the feeling was foreign), I was losing snat. Yet instead of leaving, I sat back down. I sat back down and tried to caulk. That like-and-respect line was just too tempting; I'd heard it in movies and never thought it meant much—all its abstraction, its gangster profundity. I thought I'd caught Slokum speaking out of his depth.

And so I played dumb, to get him to talk more.

I said, I've never really understood what that means—you like a person, but you don't respect him. Sounds like nonsense.

Bam said, "It means I want to empty your best friend's face but I wouldn't want to do that if I didn't know how much snat was behind it."

I thought: So much for caulking.

And yet I caulked more.

I said, Why should I care what you think about Benji, anyway?

Bam whispered, "Should? Who said should? I'm not the one who told you you should. That said, it's pretty normal you care what I think of him—you're his friend. But the thing is, you want to be my friend, too—why wouldn't you, right? We're sitting here, talking, totally peace. The thing is, you want to be my friend too, but you don't believe you can be a friend to both of us. Why is that, Gurion? Did I say you couldn't? I'm not really asking that. I know I didn't say it. So who was it said you can't be my friend? Actually, I guess I'm not asking that either. We know who said it. What I guess I'm asking is why you would listen. That's a question for real. You don't have to answer out loud you don't want to, you think it'll somehow betray him or whatever. I understand. Believe."

I don't need your—

"Permission. Right. I know. You don't need my permission to speak or withhold. I didn't even kind of mean it that way, kid—colloquial trappings, my mistake. And I know you think you're trickling, here, but you're the only one who thinks that. All you're really doing is hearing me out, and listening never compromised anyone."

The bus stopped in front of the Frontier Motel, balding brakes squealing; Bam paused til they quit.

"You want me to put out my hand?" he said. "I'm gonna do the friendly thing and put out my hand. I'm gonna put out my hand just so you can refuse it, and when you refuse it, you'll see what I do. You'll see I'll do nothing. So here goes," he said. "Get ready for victory."

He put out his hand. I walked past his hand. I went to the wheel-well seat for my bag. I banged fists with Vincie and crept off the bus.

□ □ □ □ □ □ □

Flowers kneeled on a striped blanket, arranging pebbles and sticks in the mud under an evergreen shrub along the outer wall of the Frontier's Welcome Office. He sang his spells quietly, almost mumbling them, so no one could make out the words. A generator next to the shrub gave the songs extra cover with its fan-noise. On the shrub's other side, where Flowers had laid the blanket, was a concrete walkway that led from the motel's drop-off circle to the front door of the Welcome Office. A whole hedge of evergreen shrubs grew on the opposite side of the walkway, but Flowers only ever hoodooed the one shrub. He'd been doing it for a couple weeks by then, since autumn had kicked in.

It was already November, but the hoodooed shrub had berries, and bugs and insects got confused into hatching. In the mornings, when I went there to wait for the schoolbus, the walkway would be speckled with the dew-covered bodies of newborn ants and beetles who'd died trying to get across to the shrubs that weren't hoodooed. I'd ring the bell and Flowers would come out the door with broomy paintbrushes we'd use to sweep the bodies into square, sand-colored envelopes. It always chilled me up to do it because I couldn't help thinking how the bugs died freezing. I'd seen flies invade air-conditioned houses and get slow til they fell, but air-conditioned houses aren't as cold as Illinois at night, in the autumn, where it gets below 32 degrees sometimes, and I'd wonder if the liquids in the bugs I'd swept started turning to ice before or after they'd died. When I'd imagine before I'd get chilled up the most.

All the winged insects, though—lived. Flowers called them sentries. The sentries nested in the hoodoo shrub, never flying farther than the drop-off circle, and they always returned to the shrub after a minute or two. Somehow they didn't freeze to death. They never tried to get inside the Welcome Office either. Mostly the sentries were lightning bugs, but also there were earwigs and at least ten cocoons between the branches, so there would be butterflies soon, or moths. I didn't know how long the insects would survive, and Flowers only gave me a funny look when I'd ask him, but I hoped they'd make it through winter—I wanted to see the glow of lightning bugs during a snowstorm.

Aside from that, I didn't really know what to think of the hoodoo Flowers did on the shrub. He said hoodoo wasn't magic but a science derived from arcane knowledge, except what was magic if not a science derived from arcane knowledge? Even that question seemed to piss him off, though, so I called hoodoo science when I didn't call it hoodoo.

Being magic wouldn't make it bad anyway. Not necessarily at least. Adonai disliked magic that looked like miracles since that kind of magic threatened to screw up the arrangement, but not all kinds of magic were wrong, I didn't think, even though former Kabbalists (not the moviestar kind with the red bracelets and bottled water, but the real kind), like my dad, would have disagreed. Avraham himself not only knew magic, but taught it to the sons that he had with Keturah, and the way that moment's described in Torah, it says that Avraham, on his deathbed, "gave all that he had to Isaac. But to the concubine-children who were Avraham's, Avraham gave gifts." The gifts were the magic, and gifts are good things.

I think Flowers got touchy when I called hoodoo magic because he wanted to teach me to be a hoodooman and he assumed that I thought magic was bad (even though I'd told him I didn't), and that that's why I didn't want to learn to be a hoodooman. That's not how it was, though. Good or bad, arcane science or magic, I didn't care to practice hoodoo any more than I cared to practice Kabbalah. I didn't care to make golems or help fireflies live through autumn and winter. Golems always backfired and fireflies were bugs. What I wanted was to learn to write better scripture and to be a better scholar, and since I could learn those things from Flowers—an experienced writer with a scholarly brain—and since those things were infinitely learnable, those were the only things I wanted him to teach me.

I walked across the drop-off circle from the bus and stopped when I saw him atop his blanket. He had his back to me, and I knew that between my stealth and the fan-noise of the generator there was no way he could hear me if I didn't want him to. And I didn't want him to. I didn't want to interrupt his spell-casting. After about ten seconds of watching him, though, one of the roving insects—an earwig—landed on my pointer, and even though I stayed still and kept silent Flowers revolved to face me as soon as the thing touched down.

"Why you all pissy?"

Pissy? I said.

"You face all pissy. Don't bring the pissy here."

Don't bring the pissy.

"You like that one."

I did. It was funny. I was no longer pissy. Don't bring the pissy'd knocked the pissy right out of me. Fun words to say. I said them once more, and wanted to again, but then I got afraid that I'd wear them out, so I tentatively offered up another one to Flowers: Quit hauling that pissy?

"Not so much," Flowers said.

Keep the pissy in the commode?

"I don't even—"

Don't drive Miss Pissy?

"That's actually alright, but don't put I said that in you scripture. People take the joke wrong cause you're lousy at funny, and by the time you get done with it, I'm the angry black man, no sense of irony, hates all the white people *and* Morgan Freeman til one day a whiteboy melts his hard heart. I do not hate white people, or Morgan Freeman, nor are you white. But you're gonna put it in, I can tell the way you're grinning. So fine. You put any of this in, though, you put all of it in. Right?"

Right, I said.

"And I'm no kind of fucken Queequeg, either. I'm a lawyer wrote three novels, old friend of your dad's—a white man, Judah, I hasten to add."

I said alright, I said.

"This doubly important because soon I'm gonna talk about a rap song."

Really? I said. You listen to rap now?

"*You* listen to rap, and you put this one on that mix you made me."

The mix was actually a mix that Vincie'd made me. I liked it so I burned it for Flowers.

'Zealots'? I said.

"Yeah, that's the one," said Flowers. He was folding up his blanket. The earwig flexed its pincers and flew back to the hoodoo shrub. "So what's your favorite rhyme? Take a minute to decide." He opened the door and his deformed cat, Edison, bounded out to the lawn in the center of the drop-off circle. Edison's front legs were half the length of his back ones and he looked jacked-up like a hotrod. Whenever he leapt too high or ran too fast, he'd fall on his throat.

I followed Flowers inside, saying, My favorite's when Pras goes, 'And for you bitin' zealots, your rap styles are relics. No matter who you damage, you're still a false prophet.'

"Yeah," said Flowers. "See, that's the wrong one."

It's my favorite, though, I said.

"Well it shouldn't—something ain't right. Click click click." Flowers set the blanket under the altar in the corner. "I left 37 outside," he said.

37 was Flowers's cane. When I went out to get it, I saw this squirrel hiding behind an oak in the drop-off circle. The squirrel was hiding from Edison, who was chewing the end of a fallen branch. The cane was in the grass by the hoodoo shrub. It came up to my elbows and weighed eleven pounds. Its shaft was cut from a petrified redwood, and the silvery knob screwed into the top of it was a chromed ball of lead, about twenty times the size of the one at the end of the sap of Maholtz. The cane was functional, but not because Flowers had a limp—he didn't. The Frontier Motel was thirty miles from Chicago, which meant it wasn't close to anything good, unless your family was good and they lived in Deerbrook Park or Glenfield, and even then, since Deerbrook Park and Glenfield families mostly lived in houses, there was usually enough room for relatives to stay over. Especially with all the finished basements. Flowers lamented the basements and so had his brother Aaron, who'd had a fatal heart-attack a few years earlier, and left Flowers the Frontier. Aaron had had the cane made and he'd itemized it in the will as item 37, right below the motel, which was item 36, which is why Flowers sometimes called the Frontier 36 and the cane 37. He loved his brother and it reminded him. The cane was functional because guests at the Frontier often weren't. A week before, I'd seen Flowers kick one out. There was a poisony smell coming from Room 12, which was right next to the Welcome Office, and Flowers told me to stay in the office while he took care of it, but I came out front and stood in Room 12's doorway to watch, which was easy, because the Room 12 bathroom was opposite the doorway, and all the action was happening in the bathroom. This guy was making drugs in Room 12's tub, and when Flowers came in, the guy spun around with eyes like tomatoes and he cursed Flowers and Flowers cursed back and told him he was ruining the bathtub and told him he had to leave. Then the guy stopped cursing and said to give him a couple hours and Flowers told him to leave again, and the guy went for this arm-length lucite rod that he'd been using to stir the mixture in the bathtub, and as soon as he got ahold of it, Flowers plugged the ball-end of his cane in between the guy's shoulder and chest, right

in the rotator cuff, which made the guy's hand drop the rod and stumble backwards. Flowers followed through, using 37 to pin the guy against the wall, and told him, again, to leave. Then the guy swung at Flowers's head with the hand of his free arm, and Flowers dodged it Tyson-style—not ducking or blocking, just tilting his head out of the path of the punch, the skin of the guy's knuckles grazing the point of the ivory horn Flowers wore in his earlobe—and then Flowers lifted the cane and brought it down on top of the guy's shoulder, which became like gravel. I heard the shattering. The guy dropped to the tiles, screamed, and passed out. A lightning bug landed on my neck and Flowers spun around and told me to call the cops while he kept an eye on the guy. I didn't want to call the cops, because it was a kind of ratting, but then I didn't want the guy to come back at night and hurt Flowers in his sleep, so I called them. That was the first time I'd ever seen grown men fight who weren't on a screen. I didn't like it so much. It seemed like it shouldn't have been happening. As stealth as Flowers was with the cane and his Tyson-style, the thing on the whole was very clumsy and ugly, especially the part when they were cursing each other and then when the guy swung his lame punch and the way he began to shudder, broken-shouldered and unconscious, while Flowers stood watch on him. I kept thinking that they were too big to be fighting each other— not too old, really, but too big. While they were fighting each other, they didn't look like people, or even animals. They looked like giant marionettes constructed from meat who the puppeteer was frustrated with. My mom cooked steak for dinner that night and I made myself eat it because I always ate my steak and I knew that if I didn't eat it my parents would be worried that I was psychologically harmed from seeing the fight, and then they would decide I shouldn't go to the Frontier anymore after school which they were already considering since Flowers told my dad about the fight over the phone that evening. If I couldn't go to the Frontier, then there'd have to be other arrangements made for where I'd get picked up and dropped off by the schoolbus, and that would be an extra hassle on top of all the hassle I'd already caused by getting kicked out of everywhere, and plus I really liked Flowers. So I ate all my steak and then I went to the bathroom and threw up quietly.

The squirrel behind the oak saw his moment and shot across the drop-off circle, startling Edison, who ran up the sidewalk til he fell on his throat, then made a hurt-cat noise and followed me back inside.

Flowers waited on the couch, seeking through "Zealots" with a remote.

A chapter (#43, p. 199–205) of what I thought would be this scripture, *The Instructions* (though back then I was calling it *The Autobiography of Gurion ben-Judah Maccabee* or *Another Guide for the Perplexed* or *Israelite Scholarship among Gentile Friends in a School Run by Romans*—I kept changing my mind), was leaned on a music-stand next to the ottoman. The margins on the front page were totally empty, and there weren't any red marks anywhere. I wondered if Flowers thought the page was perfect, but I knew it was more likely that he just hadn't read it yet.

I handed him his cane and sat down beside him, and Edison jumped up into his lap. "You ain't paid enough attention to the girl," he said. He paused the disc. He said, "Pay attention." Then he hit play and Lauryn Hill of the Fugees rhymed, "Even after all my logic and my theory, I add a motherfucka so you ign'ant niggas hear me."

Flowers stopped the song and thumb-flicked his swearfinger at the center of my chapter with so much force the music stand tilted and almost fell. Edison jumped over my legs and hid his face like an ostrich in the gap between two cushions. Flowers said, "Now listen to this." Leaning forward on his cane, he read a sentence with a royal accent:

"'When one wishes to render oneself undetectable in the doorway of a scholastic facility wherein authority figures bent to disciplinary action who long to beset one lurk vigilantly in the many vestibules and passageways, one must not only find shadows within which to bestill all of one's own twitchings and other visible muscular activities, but these shadows must be engaged by one in only their darkest parts, for to even momentarily breach such shadows' penumbras will surely invite one's detection by said parties of the other.'" Flowers said, "Now why you gonna write like you Sir Alec Guinness?"

Who's that? I said.

"Obi-Wan Kenobi, man. Why you writing Obi-Wan style? You didn't used to write Obi-Wan style at all. Every chapter you give me's more kenobi than the last, though. Been gradual. This one here—it's just too much. And I'm trying to understand. You writing for the learned order of the Jedi or what?"

I said, I'm writing for rabbis.

Flowers said, "Why rabbis?"

I said, Because it's scripture.

"Damn," Flowers said, "you mean like capital-S scripture, don't you? All this time I thought you speaking figuratively. That's lofty," he said. "Lofty and loftier. Not that lofty's a bad thing. I admire the lofty impulse. What don't make sense to me, though, is how come if it's supposed to be scripture for rabbis, you ain't writin in Hebrew?"

I said, Cause then you couldn't read it, or Nakamook, or June.

"I don't know who June is," he said, "but I know you boy Nakamook ain't but a fraction more a rabbi than Edison over there, who's a fraidy fraidy fraidy, ain't you kitty cat?"

Edison was walking in place, or maybe climbing in place. He was trying to get his whole body into the cushion-gap, but there was no room. He couldn't push through.

I said, I'm in love with June.

He said, "I thought you loved that Esther what's-her-name—you other teacher's little girl."

I said, I was lying to myself. I didn't know til today. I was eating cheesepuffs.

"You're a funny little boy," Flowers said. "At least you're trying to be honest. You daddy the same way. Maybe you been lying to yourself about who you want for an audience, though, too. Anyone else you want beside the forementioned?"

I said, All the Israelites and anyone who's on the side of damage.

"What's the side of damage?"

I don't know yet, I said, but the people on the side of damage don't know it either, so it's okay I don't know.

"Even better," he said. "Click click click." He took Edison by the scruff and held him over his face. Edison liked it. He kept trying to mark the wrist of Flowers, who said in a kitty-cat voice, "How a bunch of autobiography gonna be scripture?"

I said, If I interpret or demonstrate law, or if I become an important leader, like the messiah, or—

Flowers dropped Edison then, on the floor, and burst out laughing. When Flowers bursts out laughing, it is so booming that after you see it, it is hard to describe anyone else's sudden laughter as bursting out without feeling like a liar.

Once he caught his breath, he said, "That's amazing, man. You just out-loftied 'I wanna write scripture.' For fact, you just out-loftied anything anyone's ever said to me straightfaced. The messiah!"

I said *if*, I said. And that's only one of the—

"*Hell* no on 'if' and 'one the ways'," Flowers said. "I say chuck the 'if' and pick the loftiest way. I hope you the messiah. Same time, I think you best not harp on about being the messiah too—"

I wouldn't, I said.

"Let me finish. You don't want to harp on about it too early in this scripture you gonna write, cause that could discredit you, being that it's so lofty, but same time, unless you gonna hold onto you book until *after* you're famous for saving the world, it's not the kinda thing you should avoid mentioning altogether. It's something you're gonna have to explain at some point. You know, like, leak it in slowly while you're hooking everyone, and then blast! That's first of all.

"Second, you should re-examine you people's scriptures. They all got plots. They got dramatic arcs. Thus far, you don't. And they don't read Obi-Wan style, neither. That's the most important thing for you to learn right now—nothing good reads Obi-Wan style. I thought you knew that—that *Story of Stories*, Obi-Wan couldn't hack that, that piece was *on*—but maybe you got lucky, or maybe you forgot. Anyway, that's why I played you the rhyme from the song. So as to give you the context needed to understand what I'm asking you when I ask you what's you motherfucker."

My motherfucker, I repeated dumbly.

He said, "So far we got rabbis, me, June, Nakamook, and Israelites for you niggas. And then the ign'ant niggas the ones on the side of damage don't know what it mean. You got more than enough logic and theory, we both know that, but what is you motherfucker? Like you motherfucking vernacular? You goin' get heard, you gotta signify, right?"

Flowers was always right.

I said, Bancer.

He said, "Bancer's good. What else?"

I said, Pennygun? Chomsky? Snat? Dumont? Hyperscoot, blinker action, bookrocket?

He said, "Good. Use those."

I said, What about firmament?

"Why firmament?"

I said, Not firmament, but the word in Hebrew that gets translated into firmament.

"A word that means firmament?"

I said, It doesn't mean firmament.

"What's it mean?" Flowers said.

I said, No one knows. I said, In Torah the translation says, 'God split the firmament into land and sea,' but rabbis argue about what that means, so I'm thinking firmament is motherfucker for rabbis. Unless—wait—do the rabbis need a motherfucker, you're saying, or just the people on the side of damage?

"Need it or don't, no way a motherfucker for rabbis could hurt," Flowers said.

I said, But if I signify Scholar and I signify I Am In Love and I signify The Side of Damage—if I signify all those things, it'll be too confusing.

"*Could* be," Flowers said. "But you can explain a little, and then the plot should make sense of the rest. That's what all the best plots do, man—they bring together disparate elements, linguistic and otherwise. You web-search 'brings together disparate elements,' you gonna land a thousand pages of gushy book reviews."

I said, My life has no plot.

He said, "Sure you life got plot. Especially if you're the messiah, right? Being the messiah's you conceit. As it were."

I said, I'm not the messiah, though.

Flowers said, "But you say you might become the messiah, right?"

I said, Yes.

He said, "So pretend you know you'll become the messiah—If you become the messiah, then you'll always have been the messiah, right?"

I don't know, I said.

"What you mean you don't know?"

I explained about potential messiahs. Flowers got bored and spaced out. When I finished, he said, "Do better you write it out and show me. Know, though, that a boy who might or might not be the messiah—that's no less interesting to me than a boy who's the for-sure messiah. Maybe it's even better. I know that because I like you a hell of a lot, and I ain't sure you the messiah. Now I'm gonna have at this Jedi scripture of yours with my red pen, see what's there to salvage. You want an ice-cream pop or something? I picked some up—they in the freezer if you want them." He took my pages off the music stand and rolled them into a cylinder. Then he headed toward his desk, tapping the cylinder on his thigh.

I tried to break my fingers with the forces of diametrical opposition. The knuckles popped but nothing broke.

I said to Flowers, I'm starting over.

He said, "Starting over what?"

The scripture, I said.

Flowers said, "You given me, like, two hundred pages last couple months."

Doesn't matter, I said.

Flowers said, "If you *can* scrap that many pages, then I suppose you *must* scrap that many pages."

I'm starting over tonight, I said. You want an ice cream? I'm getting one.

Flowers said, "Nah, man. I had one already."

I'd been taught to never eat ice cream alone. I'd lived by that rule, and it had served me well, or at least it hadn't harmed me; I'd never eaten ice cream without enjoying it. I buttoned back up and left for the Metra.

I searched my school record when I got on the train. No document by Headmaster Unger was in there. His signature appeared on a few official forms—e.g., an enrollment one one which he'd entered "ben-Judah" as my middle name; an expulsion one wherein a box beside the phrase FOR REASONS OTHER THAN THOSE LISTED ABOVE was checked, and beneath the box, on the two lines provided, were scrawled the words "unacceptable violence: student assaulted his headmaster (myself, the signatory, Headmaster Rabbi Lional Unger, M.Ed.) with a stapling implement"—but there was nothing that he'd authored all by himself, let alone an account of what preceded my flying stapler attack. Apart from what I'd already found in the Office while Principal Brodsky talked about math, there wasn't much in my record I could use in my scripture. Rather, there was, but all of it was stuff that I'd written myself—detention assignments, a copy of *Ulpan*, an essay for English called "9-1-1 Is a Joke"—and as with everything else I'd ever written or read, I had all those writings memorized anyway.

I tried to decide whether to read Rabbi Salt's letter to Brodsky or Call-Me's *Assessment*, but then I remembered I had in-school suspension the next day, and if I saved them to read in ISS, then ISS almost became worth looking forward to. Plus I was tired.

I leaned on the window and fell asleep for a minute. I woke up more tired, and hungry, too.

☐   ☐   ☐   ☐   ☐   ☐   ☐

In Evanston, I got a large coffee and a slice at this place called Pizza by

the Davis Street station. I bolted the slice and brought the coffee to the
el stop.

On the platform, I saw Emmanuel Liebman. He was staring at the sky
and rocking heel to toe. A wobbly plank beneath him kept squeaking. The
noise made the people under the heatlamp act nervous. One guy smoothed
his mustache three times in a row. Another worked his eyebrows, and a third
his pants-wrinkles. A woman with nostrils the size of dimes chomped on
gum the way kids stomp bugs that keep not dying.

I sat in a patch of rock salt by the mapstand, holding my cigarette like a
French guy to hide it. I couldn't decide if I should say hello.

I knew that I wanted to. Along with Esther and Rabbi Salt, Emmanuel
had been my favorite person at Schechter, and I hadn't seen him since the
day I got kicked out of Northside. He was taller and had some whiskers,
very thin ones, but was easy to recognize from far away since his head was
shaped like a mallet.

If you were a Cohain, having a mallet-shaped head would automatically
bar you from becoming the Cohain Gadol, which translates to "the Big
Cohain," which means the high priest of the Temple, the one who'd get to
speak Hashem's true name once a year on Yom Kippur when we still had
a temple. Some scholars think that Judah Maccabee—not my father, but
the hero of Chanukah who led the rebellion against the Greeks to briefly
take back the second Temple in the second century B.C.E.—was mallet-
headed, and that that is why he was called Maccabee, because maccabee
means hammer, or mallet. I don't know why a mallet-head barred you from
high-priesthood. Emmanuel was hugely smart and kind, despite his mallet-
head, and I think that Judah Maccabee probably was, too, but maybe only
because he had the same name as my father and the same-shaped head as my
loyal friend, Emmanuel.

When the woman with the nostrils leapt from the bench, the smoothing
guys leaned forward. She put her foot down on the wobbly plank, and the
squeak got zeroed and they stopped their smoothing.

Emmanuel did a slow revolution, blinking his eyes like he'd just left a
trance. He double-taked on seeing me, then chinned the air in the direction
of the stairwell. I followed him there at a ten-pace distance.

"I'm sorry, Rabbi," he said. "I thought I saw my mom's friend Susanah
on the other side of the tracks, and I didn't want her to see me talking
to—I'm probably just jumpy. My grandfather—Schechter's closed today—
service day for the teachers—I came up to visit him. We watched an awful

documentary. Sabra and Shatila and Ariel Sharon. Not very cheering. Not very easy to come away from undistracted, unjumpy. But then look who's here." He clapped both my shoulders. "I was almost starting to think you were imprisoned in a juvenile hall," he said. "Of all the rumors I've heard about you since the schoolyear started—death, flight to Israel, employment by the Mossad—the imprisonment one's been the most popular. I've pooh-poohed it from the get-go, but then, last week, I looked at the last email you sent, the one called "Last Word." I looked at the sent-date, and did some arithmetic, and realized it had been five months since we'd heard from you. I thought how five months is a lot longer than we were counting on, and when you consider all the strife in the Land of Israel in the last five months... I began to wonder if the rumors might be true. I began to think to myself, 'Many of our tzadiks do end up imprisoned,' but even then I would think, 'not often while in middle school.' So what are you doing in Evanston? And what are you doing with my collar?"

Even if it is said kiddingly, it is such a nice thing to be called a tzadik that I never knew how to act when someone called me it, so I'd started straightening Emmanuel's collar with my free hand because that way I could make a face like I was concentrating and not look at his eyes.

He touched my cup and said, "Did you just eat at that pizza place Pizza? With the swastika guy?"

Emmanuel was referring to a guy called Mongo who sometimes worked behind the counter at Pizza. Mongo had a swastika on each of his wrists, but it wasn't how it seemed. Mongo was Indian—you could tell by his accent. He wasn't a Nazi. The tattoos were religious.

Mongo's Indian, I said.

Emmanuel said, "That's what I used to think: he's Indian, the swastika means something else. But even if it does mean something else, he's cruel about it. My grandfather took me there over the summer," he said, "to Pizza. We were thirsty and we knew they had soda in cans. And my grandfather asked the guy, 'What are these tattoos for? What do they mean?'—he was trying to understand. And the guy said, 'I owe you no explanation.' So we left without getting any cans of soda because even though it was true he didn't have to explain anything he didn't want to explain, so what? If he was nice, he *would* explain. If he was nice, he'd understand he was mak-ing an old man uncomfortable, that the old man was only trying to get comfortable, and that all it would take is a couple words to make the old man comfortable. Because what? It's my grandfather's fault the Nazis stole this guy's religious symbol? What if some old guy from Mississippi came into Pizza in a Confederate flag bandanna and said to Mongo, 'You coloreds are wonderful'? Do you think Mongo would say to himself, 'It's okay he says *coloreds* because he's saying he likes me and *coloreds* used to mean something different when this guy was young, and all his bandanna stands for is Southern pride?' Do you think Mongo would be thrilled about serving this guy pizza? I think Mongo would pore Borax into the cheese of such a guy's pizza, but then you have my grandfather, who all he wants is Mongo to say, 'Swastikas used to mean something different,' and he'll be happy to talk to Mongo, and Mongo won't *explain*? What kind of name is Mongo, anyway? You sure it's Indian?"

Loose slats on the tracks clunked and the whine of metal rubbing metal bounced between the stairwell walls. "You getting on this train with me or what?" said Emmanuel.

We ran up the stairs and got on. I was going to ask him if maybe his grandfather didn't ask Mongo about the swastika as nicely as it seemed like he had; if it was possible that, with his voice, Emmanuel's grandfather made the question sound like an accusation, like when someone says, "Are you a Jew?" but then there was this homeless guy with no thumbs. Not even nubs where the thumbs would have been. Two smoothnesses. He stuck out his hands and said, "I was born this way."

I gave him a dollar and he took it with his pointer and swearfinger, then turned to Emmanuel, who gave him another dollar.

The guy blessed us and walked off.

Emmanuel said to me, "Why'd you have us give away our fathers' dollars?" He said it in Hebrew, and that is the language the conversation continued in.

I said, That man was cursed with thumblessness.

Emmanuel said, "By Whom, though?" = "His thumblessness is the will of Hashem."

I said, So maybe the thumblessness was a blessing. Maybe that man's homelessness was not caused by his thumblessness—maybe he's homeless for some reason we don't know, and Hashem granted him thumblessness so more people like us would give him dollars.

Emmanuel said, "Is that different than saying the Shoah may have been a blessing for us because, without it, the West might not have backed Israel in 1948?"

The train stopped. I was in the seat to the left of Emmanuel and two men in yarmulkes got onto our car through the door to his right, then went to the right so we didn't see their faces and couldn't tell if they knew us.

Emmanuel tried to make himself invisible with slouching and it didn't work, so I switched to the seat to Emmanuel's right and became as wide and tall as I could. Emmanuel nodded = "Thank you," and once he'd relaxed a little, I said to him, It is not much different to say those two things. But I think you answered your original question with your new one. I said, Should not the West have helped Israel in 1948 regardless of the Shoah? Is the Land of Israel not rightfully ours? Should we, when we see a man without a home, not help him survive as best as we're able, regardless of whether or not he is somehow crippled? Is life not rightfully his?

The men in yarmulkes leaned at the sound of my academic Hebrew. I didn't see it happen, but I felt it on my back, their attention, and Emmanuel ducked his head even lower than it had already been ducked.

"Fair enough," he whispered, "but then there's the how of it. There's giving fish away, and teaching the skill of fishing, and we have all heard it said that not only is it better to teach the skill of fishing to the hungry so that they may perpetually eat, but that it may actually *harm* them to give them fish. Being given fish, we have heard it said, may prevent them from learning to fish, for they may think, 'Why should I learn to, when I get my fish for free?'"

I said, Who do you know that thinks that way? Who would rather rely on someone else's help? Would that not be a kind of sickness in itself? And even if *everyone* was sick that way, I said, does that mean that if we can't teach them to fish, whether because we don't know how to fish ourselves or because we don't have time, we should let them starve? I do not know how to give a homeless, thumbless man a home or thumbs, let alone how to teach him to get a home or thumbs, so if he believes a dollar can help him, and I don't believe a dollar will hurt him, should I not give a dollar?

Said Emmanuel, "I see your point, Rabbi, but I have walked with you many times—I think of these times often, and miss them, and wish, even now, as I sit beside you on this train, they were not so impossible to reclaim with regularity—so many times, Rabbi, I have walked with you past homeless people to whom we did not give away our fathers' dollars. And so I can't help but to wonder: Why did we walk past them? Because they had thumbs? Might they not have been crippled in ways we couldn't see or understand? And were they not, either way, homeless?"

I chugged my coffee, leaving only one sip. I liked to drink the last sip while I stepped off the train, then victory-spike it into the garbage barrel at the station = I am finished with this part of the day!

I said, I don't know why we walked past them.

Emmanuel said, "Maybe because there are so many homeless, and so few dollars, we save the dollars to give to those who need them the most?"

I said, I don't know that we save.

Emmanuel said, "Maybe we save the dollars to give to those who will use them best?"

I said, I don't know why we save them, if we save them.

"And how do we know who needs them most or will use them the best?" said Emmanuel. "There is no law about it. There is no law that says it is worse to be thumbless than alcoholic, or, for that matter, better to be sober and homeless than drunken and homeless. How do we know what to do?"

I said, We do whatever seems proper in our eyes.

Emmanuel said, "That's a terrible answer."

I said, That does not make it false.

"But it should make it false, though, Rabbi. Don't you think it should?"

I said, No. I said, We would be angels if it was otherwise, if the laws for everything were always clear and absolute and we always knew what to do. We would never doubt or question. We would be robots.

Emmanuel said, "The suffering of others is the price we pay for our humanity, then."

I said, And suffering is a price others pay for our humanity.

Emmanuel said, "That shouldn't be so."

I said, If you were an angel, you would not be able to imagine that it shouldn't be so. If you were an angel, you would love the suffering as you would love everything else, because all of it is the creation of God. If you were to love the suffering, you would not be able to love the world *despite* the suffering. And then you could never hope to repair the world, and so you could never hope to repair God, and God's love for you would be no greater than his love for the angels, which is no greater than your love for your thumb.

Emmanuel said, "I love my thumb."

I said, I love my thumb, too, but I would chop it off in a second if doing so was needed to save your life; it's only a thumb, after all, not a human.

Emmanuel said, "I would chop off my entire hand to save your life."

I said, Only if you could cauterize it immediately, though, since you'd be unable to tie a tourniquet singlehandedly and the blood-loss would certainly kill you.

I was trying to lighten the conversation a little—I hadn't seen Emmanuel in too long, and I wanted to joke with him—but he wouldn't have it.

"Even if I could not cauterize it," said Emmanuel, "I would give my life to save yours, Rabbi."

Risk your life, maybe, but not *give* it, I said.

"Give it," said Emmanuel.

I said, That's dumb.

"How can you say that?"

I said, I would never do the same for you. Your life is worth no more than mine.

"*Your* life is worth more than *mine*," said Emmanuel. "And that is why I would give mine for yours."

I said, It would be a sin.

"A lesser one than letting you die," he said. "I mean, if you can die."

I said, If I can die, then who so special am I to be saved at the cost of another boy's life?

The train slowed and we swayed.

Emmanuel said, "You know who you are." He looked really disappointed in me. He kept squeezing the knees of his pants. "Is it just you want me to say it?" he said. "Did all those fakes have the right idea after all? You find someone else to annoint you, and then, what, you're not accountable? *You* never claimed to be anything more than just a person, a son of man, we have no business expecting anything from *you*. Is that all you've been waiting for, these five months? Because I'll say it if that's what you want, if that's all it takes to make it so. It's been said thousands of times about you, but what? Not in the proper way? Not at the right venue? Not by the right scholar? If all you need is annointment, just tell me how and I'll annoint you. But you must know by now that what you're called is beside the point. With or without annointment, we expect a lot from you. We expect everything. And I apologize for my tone. I should not raise my voice like this, we have been having such a pleasant conversation, Rabbi, but all of us have waited for five months now, and not out of obedience to our parents, who we believe to be misled in regard to you, but out of obedience to *you*, the one they tell us not to listen to, the one who tells us to listen to them. I am tired of waiting. We are all tired of waiting."

I said, Emmanuel, I'm ten years old.

He said, "And you're the only one who thinks that makes a difference, Gurion."

The only one? I said. I said, There's millions of Israelites who don't even know who I am, let alone—

"There are millions of Israelites who call Torah "the Old Testament" and think that means the Ten Commandments. Millions who think Moses was an orator and Adam a Jew. Rashi an Indian God with a giant shvontz and lots of arms. My father's own cousin Bernie in Highland Park, Gurion—my family got stuck for the night at his house last January, during that blizzard. In the morning, before davening, I ask Bernie if he has any phylacteries I can use, and after winking slyly, he takes me to the master bathroom and pulls from the cabinet an assortment of condoms. Latex ones, intestines ones, reservoir-tipped, no-tipped, with spermicide or without, anesthetically lubricated purple ones with built-in pleasure-giving rivets. Bernie says I can have as many prophylactics as I want, just as long as I'm safe. Says he won't tell my parents, I don't have to worry, it is natural to want to have sex with girls, 'It *is* for with girls, right, Emmanuel? Not that if it's not there's anything wrong with that,' he says, chuckling, play-punching my arm, this ability to appreciate a reference to *Seinfeld* the deepest thing we have in common, two Israelites. So yes. I misspoke. You're the only one *of any relevance*—the only scholar with a pennygun—who thinks it matters that you're ten years old. And before you start talking about your father, or Rabbi Salt, about what they believe, about how *that* matters, let me do the most obnoxious thing a person can do to his friend. Let me quote you at you. Let me tell you what you told me when I described to you how the implications of Chapter 15 in First Samuel gave me headaches. You said, 'A prophet is a bright thing, and those who can't see a bright thing are blind, and those who do see a bright thing can get blind doing so.' I would suggest to you that your father and Rabbi Salt, wise as they certainly are—they see you and get blind. And let me tell you something else, please, before I lose steam, and this is maybe the most important thing: You're the only one who thinks you need to be the messiah in order to lead us. It is true that none of us is certain you are the messiah, and it is true that a number of us aren't even certain you'll *become* the messiah—and I have no problem telling you that's the camp I'm in (though were *you* to tell me you will become him, I would believe it)—but every single one of us agrees that if you are not already the messiah, you *might* become him. And not merely because you are a Judite, but because you are Gurion Maccabee. You are the person we want to lead us. We believe you were born to do that. And if following you, as we suspect, turns out to be the environmental condition that makes actual your potential, that would be ideal; but even if following you doesn't do that, Gurion, we are certain it will still bring about an improvement. We are certain that following you will help bring the messiah, whoever he might be, whether in this generation or the next."

I really didn't know what to say. Whenever the subject of my possibly being the messiah got brought up this explicitly at Schechter or Northside, it was always by one of the lesser-abled scholars—most often a first- or second-grader, occasionally a sweet, lower-IQ-type or new kid— and if after I then gave them my thumbnail lecture on potential and actual messiahs, they still failed to take the lesson, I would fix a collar or do some kind of pratfall, and the conversation would end. None of the truly talented scholars had ever brought it up to me directly, let alone Emmanuel, who was the most talented of them all. And after what he'd said, I knew that any of the arguments I came up with would sound like a coy invitation to get annointed. And annointment really wasn't what I wanted. Like everyone else I knew, I did want to be the messiah, and certainly, at times, I suspected I would be, but at the same time, there was almost nothing I could think of that I wanted less than to be a *false* messiah. To lose June, to see my parents get hurt—what else besides variations on those two themes? That was it. To be a false messiah would be the third worst thing in the world.

"Rabbi," said Emmanuel, "You look frustrated. Are you silently pooh-poohing me?"

I said, I just don't know what to say to you.

"Say that you'll lead us."

Lead you how? I said.

"I don't know," he said. "*Some*how, though. Something needs to be done soon. There is too much strife in the Land of Israel. Everyone agrees."

I said, There has always been strife in the Land of Israel.

"Exactly," he said. "And always too much, and everyone has always agreed on that. It's wisdom as old as history. Something needs to be done already."

The train slowed and we swayed.

"Aren't you getting off here?" Emmanuel said.

It was our stop, but Emmanuel could not be seen entering our neighborhood with me, so I told him to go ahead, that I would stay on til Loyola and walk from there.

"It makes me angry, Rabbi—at myself. I'm your student. Why should I have to worry I'll be seen with you?"

Because you're a good son, I told him.

"It feels like I'm a coward," he said. "Either way, I'm the one who should walk the extra blocks—not you. And there's no time to argue."

Emmanuel was right.

When the doors slid open, I snatched the yarmulke from his head and flung it onto the platform.

He leapt out to get it, grabbed it and kissed it, and it was only after the train pulled away that I saw we'd created needless drama, that things had actually been *simpler* than they'd seemed. We could have both disembarked at our stop no problem if one of us had just hung back an extra minute while the other one entered the neighborhood.

I stepped off the train at the next stop, Loyola, and gulped down my last sip of coffee. The nearest garbage barrel was twenty feet away. By the time I got to it, the victory spike felt forced, like a knock on wood, and nothing seemed finished at all.

8
VANDAL

Tuesday, November 14, 2006
6:30–Bedtime

Maccabees aren't

```
MATMATMATMATMATMATMATMATMAT
MATMATMATMATMATMATMATMATMAT
MATMATMATMATMATMATMATMATMAT
MATMATMATMATMATMATMATMATMAT
MATMAT         MATMAT
MATMAT WELCOME MATMAT
MATMATMATMATMATMATMATMAT
MATMATMATMATMATMATMATMAT
MATMATMATMATMATMATMATMAT
MATMATMATMATMATMATMATMAT
```

Patrick Drucker wanted to stand on the sidewalk in the Wilmette shopping district and speak through a megaphone while handing out pamphlets about conspiracies. The City of Wilmette didn't want him to speak or hand out pamphlets, and after he refused a request to desist, the Wilmette police put him under arrest, and Drucker contacted the United Civil Liberties Advocates of America, at which point my father became his lawyer. Patrick Drucker vs the City of Wilmette had been getting publicity for weeks. Closing arguments had begun that morning. My dad was convinced he'd defeat Wilmette, and so was most of the rest of the Chicagoland area—my father always won—but the Israelites of West Rogers Park weren't happy about that, they never were, and one of them, in protest, had spraypainted "Maccabees aren't" above the welcome mat on the front stoop of our house. I couldn't be sure how long the new bomb had been on the stoop—I hadn't seen the stoop that morning (Tuesday) because I'd left out the back door like my parents, like usual—but I knew it hadn't been there the afternoon before (Monday), and I had a hard time imagining someone vandalizing a stoop before midnight or after 5 AM, so I figured the vandal had come in the night.

Drucker's pamphlets had titles like *Aspects of Zionist Power in the United States* and *Zionists and the "Antisemitism" Cry.* Those were the two that always got mentioned on the news, but there were five or six others, and one of them was called *NBC, ABC, CBS, AIPAC.* Whenever interviewed on television, Drucker would ask why it was that although the titles of his other pamphlets were regularly cited during newscasts, *NBC, ABC, CBS, AIPAC* was never mentioned. And then he would answer his first question with a second one; he would ask if the absence of the title's mention might not be "very ironic proof" that "a small group of Zionists" was controlling all the major media outlets and "doing everything in their power to obscure the truth from the eyes of the viewing public."

Drucker was always very careful to say "Zionists" and was not a stupid guy. When one of his interviewers responded to the media cover-up accusation by stating, "But Mr. Drucker, we're an ABC affiliate. If this controlling group of alleged Zionists are doing what you claim they're doing, how can you account for this broadcast?" Zucker responded like this: "You guys are out to make me look crazy, and since your so-called 'producers' and 'editors' are at the controls, you succeed to a degree. This is all pre-recorded and you do studio-tricks to my image. Anything from lowering the number of pixels per square inch in the area of my eyes so even the pupils look like an outdated video game, to simply shooting me from a slightly oblique angle which makes it appear that I am not, as they say, a 'straightforward' individual, not to mention sitting me on the right side of the table so I'm always leaning in what's known as the 'sinister' direction to answer questions, and the way you raise the volume on my voice, and speed it up ever so slightly, and the way you 'edit' me, or should I say 'censor' me, the way you cut out portions of what I'm saying while I'm in mid-sentence... I come off like I'm disturbed, and if a disturbed man mentions my pamphlet *NBC, ABC, CBS, AIPAC*, the pamphlet is sure to be associated with a disturbed man, and such a man might as well be talking about a UFO sighting—you completely undercut my credibility. If one of your starry-eyed talking heads so much as even gave a list of the surnames of the men and women who run the networks, let alone the types of—if I may be permitted to scare-quote aloud—'philanthropic' Zionist organizations to which these men and women tithe, the implications would be examined at dinner tables all throughout Chicago, if not on a national level; but when a slightly diagonal Pat Drucker bends sinister to discuss these same executives, to alert the viewing public to the money-hungry, war-mongering Zionist cabal that's controlling this very interview, well, it's obvious he's nuts, right? Cause just look at him, yeah? He's a pixel-face!"

Drucker's accusations about how the media undercut him were crazy in themselves, but at the same time, if you considered them for a second, you couldn't avoid wondering if they could be true; and if it was *possible* that the only reason the accusations sounded crazy was because the TV networks were doing to his image what Drucker claimed they were doing, then it was also possible that all the other things Drucker had said weren't as crazy as they might seem. His tactic made me think of that Lauryn Hill line that Flowers loved, "Even after all my logic and my theory, I add a 'motherfucker' so you ig'nant niggas hear me." Lauryn's not only telling you about what she does, but in telling you what she does, she's *doing* what she tells you she does. She makes truth by saying it. Drucker wasn't making truth when he talked about the studio-tricks, but he *was* making tricks. It was pretty smart of him.

That does not mean that I liked Drucker. I didn't like Drucker, and I didn't like that he and others like him existed. I understood why someone had to defend Drucker's right to speak against my people, and I even understood why it was a good thing that Drucker *had* the right to speak against my people, but I didn't understand why the person who rose to his defense couldn't be one of *his* people. I didn't understand why it had to be one of my people. I didn't understand why it had to be my father. And neither did the Israelites of West Rogers Park. And so I understood why some of them vandalized our house. If I had not been Gurion, I might have vandalized our house myself.

But understanding is not the same as approval. I could have very easily understood how someone would fall in love with June, for example. And I could understand why someone in love with June would try to kiss June, but still I would not have hesitated to wreck anyone who tried to kiss June. And because he would love her, this boy who would try to kiss June, he would understand why Gurion would wreck him, and he would try to wreck Gurion for trying to kiss June. And that would have been fine with me, because that boy would not have been Gurion, and so he would've been unable to wreck me. And no matter what justification whoever spraypainted our stoop thought he had for spraypainting our stoop, it was the stoop of the Maccabees, and even though the meaning of the "Maccabees Aren't" graffito was made as limp by its over-clever use of the WELCOME mat as any WAR ever tagged beneath the STOP of a stopsign, the vandal had been bold enough to climb our seven steps and crouch before our front door to convey his limp insult, and for that trespass he would have to suffer.

In the past, no vandal had ever breached our sidewalkline. They would bomb our fence or the city-owned curb, fling boxes of eggs at our greystone façade, and brick our windshields and sugar our gastanks before we built the garage off the alley, and once, when I was six, someone slung a rock through our living room window and my mother ran outside with a fireplace poker as the vandal's squealing tires smudged lines on the street—but this was different. This time the vandal had been only a crobar and a wish away from overstepping our very threshold, and it isn't hard at all to get hold of a crobar, and to make a wish is even easier than that, so I decided I'd stay awake at my window that night with my weapon at the ready. If I crumpled his lenses with U.S. currency, the vandal would never return.

I would first have to hide the graffito, though, so my dad wouldn't see it and call the cops. If he called the cops, they would send a squadcar like they had in the past, and the squadcar would scare the vandal off before he got close enough for me to target properly. After a few days, the squadcar would stop coming around, and the vandal would return. It's what always happened. And it made sense that the vandals kept returning. When a particular threat has been keeping you from doing something dangerous, and then that threat suddenly disappears, you feel twice as safe doing the dangerous thing as you felt before you ever encountered the threat, like how all the enemies of Jelly Rothstein who believed the untrue version of the Angie Destra milk-spilling/pouring incident would—once the truth revealed itself—flood into Jelly's biting-range at a higher rate than they had before they believed the spilling was pouring. And the squadcar was a weak threat, anyway: for the squadcar to be effective, a vandal not only had to imagine what would happen to him if he got caught, but he had to imagine it was likely that he *would* get caught. That was too hypothetical. Even though the squadcar threat had kept the vandals at bay in the past, I knew it was too hypothetical because it wouldn't have kept me at bay if I was one of the vandals; if I was one of the vandals, I would know that the likelihood of me getting caught would be very low, and I would do what I came to do. That the vandals of the past were cowards without stealth, or maybe just cowards with no faith in their stealth, was only a matter of chance. And who knew what kind of person the vandal who bombed my stoop with "Maccabees Aren't" was? Was he like me, or was he like those who'd vandalized us in the past? He was probably not so much like the ones from the past, I thought, because the ones from the past never breached the sidewalkline. But even if he was like those other vandals, he would, like those other vandals, come back once the squadcar was gone. So I knew the new vandal would eventually return, and I knew that other vandals would follow, unless, maybe, the new vandal was marked with something that required little imagination, like blindness. If while bombing the Maccabeean stoop you were made unable to see, you would be unable to bomb the stoop again, and those who'd learn what you'd been up to when you were blinded wouldn't have to use their imaginations so terribly much, because there you'd be, before them; falling all over the place while learning to walk with a stick and a dog, your shirt scabby with foodsmears you didn't even know about. You would be marked by Gurion ben-Judah as a penalty for vandalizing his family's property, and all the vandals would give witness.

And inflicting blindness on the vandal would *not* be an extreme reaction like my father told me it would during Shmidt vs Skokie, when a vandal wrote "jewhater" on our garage door and the squadcar got called against my protests, for how much simpler would it be to take the King-Middle Brick of My False Accusation from my Relics Lockbox and just drop it on the head of the vandal? My bedroom window overlooked our front stoop, and it was surely easier to drop a brick accurately on a head than to get a pair of pennies into a pair of eyes from the same distance as you'd drop the brick. And a dropped brick would kill the vandal, or at least leave him retarded, and that was far harsher a punishment than blindness, and to exercise a gentler option when a harsher one was more readily available was to exercise restraint, and that was the opposite of being extreme.

Before going inside, I pushed the WELCOME mat on top of the graffito, then went back down the steps and placed five pairs of pebbles at twelve-inch intervals along the walk-up.

When I got to my room, I took a pennygun and some pennies from my Armaments Lockbox and set my deskchair at the open window. Kneeling on the chair, I nailed the first seven pebbles in consecutive projections, missed the eighth, hit the last two, and then tried for the one I missed and missed it again. It was weird to miss the same pebble twice. I got it the third time. The whole thing took fifty-three seconds.

□   □   □   □   □   □   □

After retrieving the pennies and the eighth pebble from the walk-up, I returned to my room and turned my computer on. While the OS loaded, I pulled all my lockboxes from under my bed. I dropped the eighth pebble into the Relics Lockbox. Into the Documents Lockbox, I filed the paper-bag plate with my love declaration in the Aptakisic manila, and then I unfolded and filed the note I'd tossed with Eliyahu of Brooklyn right next to the manila, but when I got my School Record out of my bag, I could see that there wasn't enough room for even one of the two folders.

I had known that this problem would eventually come up—my lockboxes were only half the size of banker's boxes and I kept on making and finding documents—and I'd decided weeks before that when the time came I'd consolidate my Armaments Lockbox with my Relics Lockbox and put some of the documents from the Documents Lockbox into the former Armaments

Lockbox, except I'd thought I had at least another few months before I'd have to come up with an organizing principle that determined which documents went into which box, and now I had to come up with one immediately.

I sat there and tried and I couldn't come up with one. I kept getting distracted, thinking about the vandal, and Emmanuel on the el talking strife in Israel and rumors about me, and poor Ben-Wa Wolf, and Israelite Shovers, how to start my new scripture, and Slokum on the bus, and how I had trickled and how I had caulked. Plus I was starving. It was like I never even ate that slice of pizza. The sound of my thoughts was whiny, too, like "Plus I was meowmeow. It was like I meowmoew even meow that slice of meowmeow."

I punched my desk on the fake copper mailslot—my desktop used to be our front door—and it dented in the middle, but I didn't feel better, I felt even worse, that desk was important, a gift from my father, I felt like a jerk, I meow like a meow, and then the chime chimed, the hopeful new-mail chime, I opened my inbox, found stuff off listservs, got disappointed, but what was I expecting? something from June? vandal fucken vandal, vandal at the threshold, consolidate the lockbox you'll get the vandal later, it was time to stop whining, to get something done, something simple that functioned, something that worked. I wrote Rabbi Salt:

Sent: November 14, 2006, 6:49 PM Central-Standard Time
Subject: Updated List Please?
From: Gurionforever@yahoo.com (me)
To: avelsalt@hotmail.com (Avel Salt, Solomon Schechter School)

Rabbi Salt,
I was hoping you could send me an updated list of email addresses of Schechter students, both former and current—mine's from last year.
Your Student,
Gurion ben-Judah

I thought I heard the back door open, but decided to ignore it. Something about typing the words "Your student, Gurion ben-Judah," cleared my head a little, so I typed the words another ten times. Then I deleted all of them but one and sent the email. I still didn't have an organizing principle for my documents, but I saw I might as well consolidate the relics and armaments. The consolidation was a cinch. (Except for the bells of a couple pennyguns, the Armaments Lockbox didn't contain anything that could get crushed too easily—there were washers, some coins, a bunch of wingnuts, and a very primitive, however effective mace that I'd made by wrapping a fist-sized ball of penny-laden duct tape around a doubled-over bootlace—and apart from the eighth pebble, the Relics Lockbox only held my passport, my broken water-resistant watch, an envelope with a cut-off dreadlock that had formed in the middle of my head after I'd refused to let my mom brush my hair for a week one time when I was four, the King-Middle Brick of My False Accusation, and some teeth I'd lost.) All I had to do was remove the pennyguns, dump the Armaments Lockbox into the Relics Lockbox, then put the pennyguns on top, lock the box down and call it my Relics & Armaments Lockbox.

Performing the consolidation completely un-D'd my A, and I came up with an organizing principle that was so easy and simple it embarrassed me to think how the problem had gotten me explosive enough to dent my mailslot:

The original Documents Lockbox would become my Documents By Or About Gurion Lockbox, and it would contain all my emails and letters, my school record (minus, for the moment, Call-Me-Sandy's *Assessment* and Rabbi Salt's letter to Brodsky, which I set aside to read in ISS the next day), the original copy of *Ulpan*, the scripture that Flowers had been redpenning, the scripture that I told Flowers I'd start that evening (once I started it), and *The Story of Stories*.

The former Armaments Lockbox became my Other Documents Lockbox, and that is where I put the hand-to-hand combat manual my Grandfather Malchizedek wrote for the IDF; an upublished manuscript my father wrote at yeshiva called *Justice in Samuel I*; my mom's doctoral dissertation, *The Creation and Utilization of "Accidental" Contingencies in Diadic Behavioral Modication Therapy*; and her galley-proofs of *New Directions in Functional Analytic Psychotherapy*, which was about to be published by University of Chicago Press.

I'd just gotten all the documents into their boxes when I heard my mom yelling up the stairway.

"Gurion, *bavakasha boy*." (Please come here!)

A "please" from my mother, especially a Hebrew "please," is its own exclamation point. Probably she'd been calling me for a while and I hadn't heard her.

Five minutes! I shouted.

I wanted to fix my desk's mailslot before going downstairs. My dad built the desk when I was five, after my parents got an addition on the house. He told me he'd had a frontdoor desk at yeshiva just like it, and I thought it was the nicest present, and that it was important that he wanted me to have the same kind of desk that he used to have, and now I'd damaged it with my fist like a real schmuck. I could pound the dent out later, but if I didn't start the fix—if I didn't at least find my screwdriver and take the lid off its brackets—I'd have too much sadness to eat dinner across the table from him.

"Now!" my mom shouted.

Is Aba home? I shouted.

"He's coming now from the garage!" she shouted.

Three minutes!

"Now!"

There was no way that dinner would be on the table in less than ten minutes, though, and I found my screwdriver on the windowsill.

Twenty-five minutes! I shouted.

"Gurion: *boy!*" *Boy* without a "please" is for puppies and three-year-olds who are readying to stumble into highway traffic.

Seventeen hours and twenty-three minutes! I shouted.

I heard her walk back to the kitchen.

My screwdriver was too thick for the bracket-screws' X's. I threw it like a dagger and it stuck in the wall, then fell a second later. I was about to punch the mailslot again when I saw my envelope-slasher in the pencilcup. I tried its corner on a screw and got movement.

"I'm home!" my father shouted.

"Tell your son to get down here," my mother said.

"Soup's on, boychic!"

I didn't want him to come get me in my room and see me removing the mailslot lid; he'd ask me why was I monkeying, and I'd have tell him, and then he'd be disappointed. He wouldn't be disappointed because I showed disrespect to a thing that he built for me, but because I'd exploded, and that was not the right reason to be disappointed, which would disappoint me, so after finishing the screw I was working on, I laid the envelope-slasher on the mailslot for later and came down the stairs shouting, Forty days and forty nights! at the two of them.

My father let go of my mother's hand and headed to his room to change from his suit into jeans and a t-shirt. When he passed me, he poked me and pinched at my shoulder and then, like a rowing viking, he sang,

Detention, detention,
And in-school suspension!
What shall
Become of
My son?

=

I killed in court!
Oh, how I killed!
My Nazi
Shall be
Free!

I walked to the kitchen with my mom, who kissed me. "So are you hungry for a nice chicken from Selig's?" she said.

I snatched a glass from the clean-rack and filled it with tapwater. I glugged it down.

No, I told her.

"It is what we are having," she said. "So what? You were in trouble today?"

Not trouble, I said.

"What do you think? That you can beat me up suddenly? I can beat up all of you. I have carried up hills in one arm a carbine that weighs two Gurions. Do not lie to me."

A carbine, I said, is smaller than a rifle.

She said, "Why was the crazyman singing on the stairs?"

I broke rules and got an ISS, I said. I said, That's not trouble, that's punishment. And no carbine weighs two Gurions.

"You will make fun of my language?" she said. "I am fluent in four and hold a Ph.D. and people pay me to speak, it is how I heal them. You, in junior high school, know three languages, one of which is dead, you spend the money that people pay me to speak to them, and you will make fun of me? It is not nice. I do not find it to be very charming."

Aramaic isn't dead, I said. Not exactly.

"And if I say a carbine when I cannot possibly mean a carbine, then you should know that I meant a cannon, smartperson. It was a cannon for making helicopters drop. Do you think no cannon could weigh two Gurions?"

You blew up helicopters with a cannon? I said.

She wasn't paying attention anymore. She was pouring matzoball soup from a styrofoam cylinder into three bowls. She said, "I must carve the chicken. Kiss my cheek and bring the long knife."

She'd never told me she used to blow up helicopters.

□ □ □ □ □ □ □

If chicken is a certain level of wet, it squeaks between my teeth and my tongue gets heavy. I swallow that kind of chicken as fast as I can, trying not to picture the chewed-looking meat that dangles near the throats of roosters like earlobe. Sometimes I swallow too fast, but not usually, and when I coughed at the beginning of dinner, it was not because chicken choked me. Apple juice had entered the wrong pipe.

"You are inhaling your chicken," my mom said.

It was juice in the airpipe, I told her.

"Yet you are inhaling your chicken," my mom said.

It's wet.

"Don't talk that way at dinner," said my father.

She asked, I said. And plus if I was actually *inhaling* the chicken—

"She didn't ask," my mother said. "She observed. And 'inhaling' was meant figuratively and you know this, you are being a wiseass today."

I said, Your observation was wiseass—it was a question, disguised. It was, 'Why are you inhaling your chicken?' That's a question.

She said, "Not a question, Gurion, a request: Stop inhaling chicken."

That's a command, I said.

"When the request was not met, it became a command, but never was it a question," she said. "There is never good reason to inhale chicken, and so there is no purpose in asking you why you have inhaled chicken."

Whenever my mom was upset with me at dinner, we'd have a conversation about our conversation. I thought it was because she'd spend all day practicing FAP, which is a kind of psychotherapy where talking is called *verbal behavior*. If you were my mom's client and you told her, "I want to kill myself," she would not tell you, "You should not kill yourself," or "If you kill yourself, you will never be able to decide to kill yourself again," and she'd never ask, "When do you plan to kill yourself?" or "How do you plan to kill yourself?" or even "Why do you want to kill yourself?" This is what she'd ask: "Why are you telling me that you want to kill yourself? What do you get out of it? What is it that you are trying to elicit from me by telling me you want to kill yourself?" Since I'd been old enough to remember conversations at dinner, no fewer than thirty people had told my mom they wanted to kill themselves, and this is how many of those people killed themselves: zero.

I said to her, Eyelids.

It was a little bit cheap of me, but I didn't feel like having a conversation about a conversation.

My dad said, "That is *very* impolite." He cracked a chickenwing in half.

I rubbed my eyes with my thumbknuckles and my eyes made squishing sounds.

My mother told me, "It does not affect me, Gurion. And it would be cruel of you if it did." She said that flatly, but her upperlip kept trying to smile itself because she liked it when I teased her. She didn't want to have a conversation about a conversation, either. "Did you hear what I said to you?" she said.

I did simultaneous eyelid flips and she spit chicken into her napkin and pushed her plate away, laughing.

"You are so *mean*," she said. "How can you be so mean? Your father, he is not mean."

My father, his mouth full of chicken, jabbed air with his pointer in the direction of my mother.

"*I* am mean?" she said. "I am *not* mean!" she said. "Gurion, do you think I am mean? Is that why you told your principal to call your father instead of me?"

Yes, I said.

"Because you thought I would be mean to you? I am not mean to you. I am your mother and I love you."

My father touched a sideburn and lifted one eyebrow = "How ironic that my wife is upset with my son over this tiny aspect of a larger phenomenon about which I am upset with her," and said, "Your son's winding you up for kicks, so relax a little. This Brodsky called of his own volition. When he called I told him that he was to call *you*, that *you* were the one who handled such calls, and Brodsky said he knew of the arrangement, but that he was hoping for a different approach, which, as you would likely expect, led me to wonder aloud: 'Different from what?' He then explained that by different, he meant different from the approach my wife takes when he calls to tell her that our son has been in a fight. And then I wondered: What fights has my son been in? Of course, that latter wondering was performed silently."

"If you are angry at me," my mother said to my father, "please do not be coy about it."

He slid his knife beneath the skin of a breast and sawed and pried til the skin came off in one piece, and then he set it on my plate. I liked the skin when it crackled. This skin flapped. I poked it. My dad said, "That was not coyness, Tamar. That was a question: Why is it I'm not told my own son is getting into fights at his new school?"

My mom pulled her plate back onto the placemat to fork meat, but dropped the fork and said "Uch," and touched her eyes to make sure they were still there, and put her hands in her lap to stop checking on her eyes. Then she said, "If there was something for you to be concerned about, I would have told you. The fighting is normal."

"It is not normal," my father said to her. "Do not tell him it is normal. It is not normal to fight," he said to me. "You are surrounded by delinquents and idiots. *They're* the ones for whom it's normal, and what's normal for delinquents and idiots is what? Is delinquent. Idiotic."

"They start up with him, Judah," my mother said. "He should be picked on?"

"Are you picked on?" my father said.

I said, Not exactly. I said, People start up with me, though.

"They started up with you today?" he said.

I said, Kind of. I said, I towel-snapped the neck of this one boy the Janitor and he called me a name.

"Why did you *towel-snap his neck?*"

There wasn't exactly a reason, I said, but he wasn't a nice kid. Him and his brother used to make fun of Scott Mookus. I don't think he'll do that anymore, though. We're friends now. But after I towel-snapped his neck, he said I smelled and was a B.D., so I towel-snapped his eyes and spit on his foot. That's when his friend Ronrico charleyhorsed me from behind and kicked me in the ribs.

"You see?" my mother said. "It was just some snaps of towel, and then the second boy came."

"The second boy," said my father, "came to protect his friend from our son."

I said, That's not true. I said, He came to *avenge* his friend. It wasn't protection. I wasn't fighting the Janitor anymore—he wasn't getting up.

"The second boy came from *behind*, Judah," said my mother.

Yes he did, I said.

My mom said, "And what did you do?"

I loved my mom. She was always so interested.

I said, "I landed a glancing blow on his face."

"This ended it?" she said.

My father exhaled loudly, made a fist around his chin = "I will wait this out, and you will both be aware that I am waiting."

The blow pushed him back, I said, but he wasn't out, and this crowd that was watching kept growing, so I grabbed the padlock off my locker.

"You did not," said my mom.

I did, I said. I said, And I hooked the ring around a knuckle and blasted that kid's lungs out with a blow to the solarplexus just before he would've knocked me over.

"Gurion!" my mother said.

He bent like he was praying, and I swept his legs, I said. When he went down, he hit all these metal baskets and it was so noisy everyone backed off, Ema. They were gonna crowd me up more, I knew it, but they backed off because of the noise and how the padlock gleamed.

"You are very smart," she said.

"What the *fuck* are you telling him?" my father said.

In almost all of the books I have ever read, and many of the movies I've seen, when a husband curses at a wife, or a wife at a husband, it signals that they are fighting. That was not true about my parents, though. My parents were often a little bit explosive, always very loud, and when they'd curse it was usually with joy. When it seemed like they were fighting, they were usually playing. The loudness was fun for them. The back-and-forth way they'd become outraged with each other was a contest like the name-calling game that I'd play with Jelly during Group; neither one cared to win, they only tried to make the contest last. It is true, though, that when the subject of the outrage contest was Gurion, it would *become* a fight as often as not.

You could tell a fight from a contest by what they'd do with their bodies. During contests, they would touch each other, usually with pinches and gentle thumb-stabs, and they'd always look at each other's faces when they were talking, like to say, "What then! What!" When they'd fight, though, they didn't look at each other much, and instead of touching, they'd use a prop—usually a cigarette, sometimes an eating utensil—to occupy their hands, and their voices would become quieter. The problem was that most of their fights would start out as outrage contests, and even though the body-indicators made it pretty easy to tell the difference between a fight and an outrage contest, I had never been able to figure out what caused an outrage contest to *become* a fight. I knew it wasn't cursing, though, so I didn't get upset when my father said, "What the *fuck* are you telling him?" and then my mom said, "And why the *fuck* do you yell?"

"He hits a boy with a padlock and you call it smart!" said my father.

"That boy hurt our son, and there is no boy who saw it happen that will ever *fuck* with our son again, Foulmouth."

"Unless our son *fucks* with another boy, himself, Toughguy, in which case *that* boy will have long since known to carry a weapon to defend himself against Gurion Maccabee because Gurion Maccabee is a crazed lunatic." He said to me, "You're not a crazed lunatic, but you are acting like one, and eventually you'll be treated like one, and even if you were one, I would love you because you're my son, and I would never want you to get beat up either, but this is not the way to act, the way you have acted, you are smarter than this, and you will act like a mensch, not a Philistine, you will use your gifts to avoid fights, not to start them—there are other ways to win."

I said, That's why I do Harpo Progressions. I said, I did one just today. To Mr. Botha.

That was excellent timing, for me to mention the progression right then. My father made his bottom lip fat and leaned at me. "Nu?" he said, faking impatience.

I said, Remember I told you about the protocol for getting in the Cage? With the passes and the clipboard?

"The gate, and the locks, yes yes go on."

I was coming back from Brodsky's office, I said, and Botha told me to hand him my pass like I didn't know that I was supposed to hand it to him, like I hadn't done that a hundred times already, and so I folded it before I handed it to him.

"He gave it back?" said my father.

He wouldn't even take it, I said. I said, He told me to unfold it.

My father slapped the table and said, "Ha! Bureaucratic robot mamzer. So what? So you unfolded it, you refolded it…"

Yes, I said, and then I dropped it and he told me pick it up, and I picked it up and crumpled it, and—

"Get to the point," my mother said. "This story does not entertain me."

You think it's hilarious, I said. I said, You're looking down at the placemat's dandelions to hide your face, but the corners of your mouth are crosshatching the rays off the corners of your eyes is how big you're smiling.

My dad jabbed his pointer at my mom.

I said, I had to do something to the pass that couldn't be undone because that was the only way to win, was to do something permanent. So I tore it in four places, and that's how I won.

"Now *that* is smart," my father said. "You used your head."

"To what end was his head used?" my mother said. "What do you think you encourage?"

"His teachers are idiots, we can't hide that from him, and there is little to do about it as long as he's enrolled at that school," said my father. "So what? Do I tell my son: 'Obey these idiots'? Do I tell him: 'Be docile in the mitts of fools, amid subnormals'? No. And no. I encourage him to subvert these idiots whenever possible, but without violence."

"And how do you think he subverted the idiot, Judah? By tearing some paper? All he did was incur idiot wrath. This method is worse than ineffective—such a method undermines whoever is enacting it."

My father grabbed her leg, and her knee hit the table-bottom. She said, "I am being very serious."

"We can't flirt when you're serious?"

"You can flirt to me all that you want, but if I am being very serious, you cannot expect me to flirt back to you," she said. And then, as if the over-immigranted English weren't enough (my mother knew as well as anyone that people flirt *with* each other, not *to* each other; knew that the more she sounded like the earnest academic Sabra, the more endeared my father became), she flicked a blush-colored spot onto my father's neck with her pointer.

"Are you paying attention to this, Gurion?" said my dad. "This is a useful lesson, here: when a female talks about flirting, the talk itself is flirting."

"That is only partly correct," my mom said. "For the smartest and the handsomest male in the world, a mention of flirting is almost sure to be a flirtation in itself, but when the male is not the smartest and handsomest, the rule fails to predict. Therefore, if a woman talks to this man about flirting, she may well not be flirting with him, for how can he be the smartest and the handsomest while also being the father of the smartest and the handsomest? He cannot."

I said, Pssh = Stop looking at me that way.

My father said, "Your mother's mostly right, Gurion, but she fails to tell you that when a female who you are flirting with is some kind of toughguy, and that female pulls your earlobe or flicks you on the neck rather than smashing your nose or belting you where it counts, both of which she, being such a hardnosed brawler, is capable, the neck-flicking or lobe-pulling is a sure sign that she is flirting with you, regardless of how smart or handsome you may be."

My mom pretended to punch my dad in the nose and he kissed her on the knuckles.

Again I said, Pssh = Stop being such characters.

I didn't mean it, though. I said it because I was supposed to. It was what you were supposed to say when your parents acted deeply in love. It made them feel young to hear it said.

"Seriously, Judah," my mom said. "Stop kissing my hand and be serious."

"Seriously," said my father, "if we're going to be serious, I think we should talk about Northwestern again."

"That is not serious."

"Maybe if he takes the class, he'll see the kinds of things that he has to look forward to when he finishes—"

"Northwestern is moot," said my mother.

My dad said, "Why don't you go to your room, Gurion."

I pretended to be confused and stayed where I was.

"He does not want to take any class at Northwestern," my mother said, not waiting for me to go to my room, "and I do not want him to, either."

"*He* isn't old enough to know what he wants, and I'm sure Professor Schinkl's invitation's still open."

"Always with this antisemite."

"Schinkl is a Jew."

"He hates himself," my mom said.

"In fact, he does not hate himself. He just disagrees with your politics." My dad picked up his fork, then set it down.

When I was eight, this man Schinkl, an Israelite who taught at Northwestern University, read a copy of *Story of Stories* that his friend Mrs. Diamond, my Reading teacher at Schechter, had given him. He wanted to meet me and probably to become my teacher—he taught Literature and Jewish Studies—but my parents wanted to meet him first, and when they met, they started talking about Israel, and while they were talking about Israel, he called a suicide-bomber a "freedom fighter" and my mom called him a twerp and a nebach. She tore my scripture from his hands and told him she'd never let me study with him or anyone else at any school that would employ him.

"Why are you still here?" my father said to me.

I said, You're talking about me.

"Fair enough," he said.

"Fair enough?" said my mom. "He is not old enough to know what he wants, but he is old enough to listen to this? He is old enough to take classes at college? He is old enough to become an abnormal? He should be made the mascot, if not the object of derision, of eighteen-year-olds? Of twenty-year-olds? He should suffer daily heartbreak at the sight of pretty girls who are one and two feet taller than him, who want nothing more than to pinch his cheeks and make him blush and get some extra help with their homework? He should befriend boys who smoke drugs and wear the keffiyeh on their necks to impress these girls? He is old enough for that, do you think? Do you think we should let him move out and find himself? Do you think—"

"Stop yelling!" my father yelled.

"I am not yelling, you only wish I were yelling, and you will not tell me what to do," said my mother, "you who would cancel not one, but two summer trips to Jerusalem, where your son has never been, so that you may defend Nazis in American courtrooms. You who—"

"Criticism from a mother who teaches her boy the quickest ways to kill men with his bare—"

"Please do not exercise sophistry on your wife," my mother said.

"Sophistry!"

"To speak of your son as if he were a typical boy is sophistry, and you are not in court, you are at my dinner table. If you do not see the need for Gurion to know how to protect himself, you are blind."

"So send him to karate," said my father, "not backyard assassin camp, you who would teach him to use bootlaces for handcuffs and salt shakers for cudgels." He waved a salt-shaker.

"Do not youwho me, Judah, with your 'backyard assassin camp.' For how long have you been waiting to deploy this clever phrase, anyway? Where did you write it down? Is it on the back of your clever hand, you clever man? Do not giggle like a girl, Sir."

"And which end of this cudgel," said my father, wagging the salt-shaker at me, "*would* you hold, Gurion, if you wanted to win a fight with it?"

I knew he didn't actually want an answer to the question, but I couldn't tell what he wanted, so I looked at my mother.

She said, "I do not know what he is trying to prove, either, but he is your father." = "Answer him."

So I answered. I said, I wouldn't use it as a cudgel. My knuckles are harder, pointier too. That salt-shaker's brittle and the couple inches I would gain in range by swinging it aren't worth the force the blow would lose to the shatter at impact. If I wanted to use that salt-shaker, I would pour salt in my hand and fling it in the eyes of my enemy—salt is an eye-irritant of the second-highest order.

"The *second*-highest order," said my father. He was curious even if he didn't want to be.

I said, It stings, and plus it's grainy, and the enemy's first reaction would be to get the graininess out of his eyes, which means he'd rub them, and make the sting worse.

"And what," said my father, "would be a first-order eye-irritant?"

I said, Pulverized glass is one, which though it wouldn't sting too bad after the impact, would actually corrode and soon lodge itself within the surface of the eyeball when it was rubbed; or a high- or low-Ph chemical in liquid or powder form that can burn holes in the eyes' jellies, even something like Borax, or—

"To protect himself he needs to know these things?" my father said.

"I did not teach him to throw salt in eyes," my mother said.

"Just the first-order ones you taught him? The Borax and pulverized glass?"

"No, Judah. He has figured it out for himself."

"Based on principles you've taught him, Tamar!" To me he said, "What is it she tells you? 'The world of objects should be divided into two categories. The good weapons and the better weapons'?"

Again, I didn't know how he wanted me to answer that question. I didn't know if he was misquoting my grandfather's 'Relevant Tenets of Ninjitsu' chapter on purpose or by accident, so I corrected him.

I said, 'If an object is not, on its own, a weapon, then it is a part of a weapon.'

My mom laughed.

"So you think it's entertaining," my father said to her.

"Lighten up, Judah. You react as if this isn't your son telling you how he would defeat an enemy, but the enemy revealing how he will defeat your son; as if your son were his own enemy."

Neither of them were holding a utensil or looking away from each other, but their voices had lowered and I didn't know if they were fighting or still having a contest, and I didn't know if they knew, either, but I really wanted to change whatever was happening. I couldn't think of how, though.

"Enemies," said my father. "How can you talk of children having enemies? They compete. They have rivalries. Children do not have enemies."

"Children are the only ones who recognize their enemies," my mother said. "Men fail at that. Enemies are too simple for men. Enemies are too forthright. Some men so needfully require complication, they find themselves defending their enemies."

That was a cruel thing for my mother to say to him, even if it was true. He lit a cigarette and I knew they were fighting for sure.

I tried to imagine what it would be like to fight with June, and I couldn't, I just couldn't imagine it, but thinking of June right then was lucky.

I said, I fell in love today, Aba.

"What?" he said. He heard me, though. The "What?" was to maintain form. If it were a fistfight that I was breaking up, and I had just gotten my arms around some guy to keep him from punching some other guy who I knew the guy in my arms didn't really want to punch, then my father's "What?" was like the half-strength lunge forward that the guy in my arms would make before finally giving in to my hold and agreeing to back out of the fight. As long as the "What?" was taken seriously—as long as we all pretended it was more than just form, as long as we all pretended the content mattered, that the "What?" was actually a question, "What did you say?" or "What did you mean by what you said?"—everyone would get to save face.

So I said, I fell in love with a beautiful girl today, and she is an artist.

"And what happened to Esther Salt?" said my mother. To my father, she said, "You get him this caller ID he begs you for, he gets a new girlfriend."

"Casanova," said my father. "Is she in the Cage with you?"

I said, She's in normal school, in seventh grade.

His relief lit him up. He really thought the Cage was bad. "An older woman," he said. "An older woman!" He winked at me, clicked his tongue.

"What is her name?" my mom said.

Eliza June Watermark, I said. She's red-haired.

"That is a very interesting name," my mother said.

"Who cares, Tamar?" said my father. "He says he's in love with her. That's all that matters. It's all that matters, Gurion."

"It is not all that matters, Gurion."

"He's ten years old," my father said.

"Ten years old so what? Ask him what he plans to do with her. What do you plan to do, Gurion?"

I'll marry her, I said.

I didn't understand what they were arguing about yet.

My mom slapped my dad's shoulder.

My dad slapped her shoulder back. He said, "We'll see how he feels about Eliza June Watermark when he's old enough to get married, Conniptionthroat." My mom's carotid throbs when she's worried.

"Eliza. June. Watermark," said my mother. "It puts George William Saunders to shame. Ryan Todd Jones cowers. Ashley Elizabeth Johnson quietly swallows every Tylenol in the house. I think, Gurion, that Eliza June Watermark may be the single most goyische name I have ever heard in my life."

I said, Oh! I didn't know what you meant before. She's definitely an Israelite.

"Her mother is Jewish?" said my mom.

I guess, I said.

"You guess?"

I said, Maybe her father is, too. I said, I don't know for sure, but Hashem would never fall me in love with a girl who wasn't an Israelite, Ema.

Both my parents laughed, then, and both at the same thing, but for different reasons; my mother because what I said signified the exact way she wanted Gurion to approach the world—like it was all arranged for him, the smartest and the handsomest; and my father because of how foolish he thought it was for Gurion to approach the world that way. And even though they were laughing at me with condescension, I started laughing like I thought they were laughing *with* me. But I was only pretending to think they were laughing with me. I pretended because their laughing was keeping them from fighting, and that is what I was laughing at.

And then soon enough we were all laughing at the same thing, for the same reason, in the same way: first at how we kept laughing, and then at the sounds of the laughing and the way it warped our faces and made our jaws ache. Finally we were laughing at laughing, the nonsense of it, how when you first start laughing it seems like you're laughing because something is funny, but later, as you continue to laugh, you see that the funny thing is funny *because* you're laughing at it.

After that, we were quiet and my father went to the pantry. He removed an oily block of halvah from its butcher-paper package and halved it. He cut the first half into three slabs, and re-wrapped the second one. "For tomor-row," he said, "for lunch."

My mother crumbled her slab and spread it on white bread. My father broke pieces off with his fingers and I used a fork. We ate halvah and sucked at our teeth.

I said, What is halvah made of?

"Have you ever failed to ask that question when we have eaten halvah together?" my father said.

I said, What is halvah made of?

"How many times can you ask the same question?" my father said.

I keep forgetting, I said.

He said, "It's mostly sesame seeds. Got it? Halvah: what's it made of?"

I forget, I said.

"Do you see what he's trying to get at, Baby?"

"You," said my mom.

"It doesn't work!" he shouted, faking an angry face, dealing out the next day's halvah.

□   □   □   □   □   □   □

After I smoothed its dent flat with the round side of a hammerclaw wrapped in t-shirt to prevent scratching of the finish, I refastened the mailslot-lid with the envelope slasher. I grabbed my grey hoodie from my closet then, and attempted scripture. I typed

> There

and the phone rang. I didn't recognize the number in the ID box.

Hello? I said

"Did you shave your chinhairs yet?" It was June. She was whispering.

I said, June!

"Did you?" she said.

I told her I didn't.

June said, "Good. I was being mean when I said you should. And not because you have a reputation. I'm not scared of you. And maybe I like your reputation. I was mean because it was styley at the time. Sometimes I'm mean because it's styley. That was not an apology. There's no reason I should feel sad for being mean to you. I am glad I originally told you to shave, even though I'm taking it back now. Anyway, your chinhairs are very ugly, and that throws the rest of your face into relief. That was a styley compliment. Don't return it. And don't call back, I hate the phone, goodbye." She hung up.

I couldn't tell whether I was really not supposed to call her back, or if it was like shaving the chinhairs—if I was supposed to disobey her.

She *had* said "yet" about the chinhairs. She'd said, "Did you shave your chinhairs *yet?*" which meant she thought that if I hadn't shaved them, then I was going to shave them = she'd thought I was going to do what she'd told me to do unless she stopped me = she was expecting that I would do whatever she told me to = she wouldn't tell me not to call back if she thought it would make me call back = she didn't want me to call back.

And I hadn't corrected her "yet." I hadn't said that I'd never considered shaving my chinhairs, even though that was true. All I'd said was that I *didn't* shave my chinhairs. The "yet" could have been implied by me, or not, from where June stood.

At the same time, though, maybe I had June's "yet" wrong. Maybe the "yet" was to pre-empt the need for trickle-caulking. Maybe she knew all along that I wasn't going to shave the chinhairs, and she only called to tell me not to shave them so that it would seem like I was obeying her because that way she could avoid having to save face the next time she saw me, when I would still have my chinhairs despite her original wish. And if she knew that I would have disobeyed her to begin with, that meant that she expected me to disobey her, and so then telling me not to call back = telling me to call back.

If calling back was like shaving the chinhairs.

The biggest problem of all was that the chinhairs might have had nothing in common with the potential callback. What I knew for sure was that I wanted to call her back—I didn't even get to wish her goodnight or sweet dreams—and because I wanted to call her back, maybe I was just looking for a reason to call her back despite how she told me not to.

I was confused. I had to write scripture.

I typed the word *is* and the screen looked like:

> There is

And the phone rang again. I picked it up before the first ring terminated. June! I said.

"Who?" said Esther Salt.

I said, Esther Salt.

Esther Salt said, "Why don't you ever call me anymore? You haven't called me in weeks. I even got Caller ID to make sure I'd know if you called, like in case you didn't leave a message, and so I know *for sure* you haven't, so don't try to lie."

You broke up with me, I told her.

"I know," said Esther, "but I didn't know that meant we couldn't talk anymore."

What did you think it meant? I said.

I said that way too fast and it sounded cold. I didn't mean it to be cold, though, so I said, All we ever did was talk, Esther, and if all you ever do is talk, then when you break up it means you stop talking.

"We didn't only talk," she said. "We'd see each other."

I said, We still see each other every Wednesday.

She said, "No, that's not true. You and my dad see each other every Wednesday; you and I just *look* at each other. Why don't you say what you really mean?"

There was no way I could think of that Esther could have known about June, and even if she somehow did know about June, I'd fallen in love with June only that day, so there was no way Esther could think I hadn't called her in weeks because of June, plus it wasn't why I hadn't called her in weeks.

What do you mean what I *really* mean? I said.

"Maybe that I'm too *modest*. Maybe that I'm not *easy* enough," said Esther.

That's not what I mean at all! I said. I said, I never even tried to hold your hand!

"Exactly," she said, "because you think I'm too prude for you."

"Esther," I said.

"Esther!" said Rabbi Salt in the background.

"What?" she said.

I don't think you're prude, I said.

She wasn't paying attention, though. She didn't answer me. She was talking to her dad.

Then she said, "Did you get my dad's email? He sent it twenty minutes ago."

I said, I don't know—I haven't checked.

"He says he sent it and he wants to know if you're coming over tomorrow to study."

Tomorrow's Wednesday.

"What's that?" she said.

Of course, I said.

"Of course *what?*" she said.

Of course I'm coming over to study tomorrow.

"He'll be happy to hear that," said Esther Salt. She said, "I am going to sleep." She hung up.

I knew Esther's feelings were hurt, but I couldn't see how I could be the one who'd hurt them. She hurt them. She hurt them herself. And she was the one who broke up with me. And I thought that if I called her back out of niceness and June found out, then June would get upset, and even though I knew June wouldn't find out, I wouldn't want June calling someone who I wouldn't want her calling even if I didn't find out. But then what if it was Berman? Would I mind so much? I couldn't tell. She said he was a dentist and she'd never kissed him, so if she called him back, it would just be out of niceness. Except if she called him back out of niceness, then wouldn't I worry it was something other than niceness? Because why would she be nice to someone she thought was a dentist? I wouldn't want to think about that, I didn't want to think about it, and I wanted even less to not be able to think about it because I didn't know about it. I wouldn't call Esther. I didn't even *want* to. I didn't want to talk to her. I wanted to talk to June, and it wouldn't be nice of me to call Esther and spend the whole conversation wishing she was June. But I wouldn't call June, either, I decided. Because of Esther. Because Esther decided I was implying a bunch of things that I wasn't implying and I didn't like it, so I didn't want to do it to June. I didn't want to do something she wouldn't like. She'd said not to call back. If what she meant was the opposite of what she said, it wasn't for me to know.

I went online and got Rabbi Salt's email. It had all the updated Schechter addresses in the body. After cutting Esther's out, I pasted the addresses into a new list I cc'd, along with my list of Northside Hebrew Day addresses, and then I wrote this:

Draft Saved: November 14, 2006, 9:49 PM Central-Standard Time
Subject: THE TRUTH ABOUT GURION BEN-JUDAH MACCABEE
From: Gurionforever@yahoo.com (me)
To: Gurionforever@yahoo.com
CC: NEW SCHECHTER LIST, NORTHSIDE HEBREW DAY LIST

Scholars:

I am no more angry at you for avoiding me, for not stopping by or writing or calling, than I was when last I wrote you five months ago. I see no less a difference between avoiding and quitting than I did then, and I have no shallower a well of conviction that you and I must both honor our parents. However, I am troubled by some conclusions that some of you have lately drawn about my recent silence and seeming invisibility. I am troubled by the thought that you have failed to grasp fully the lesson of the weapons you have built.

Your weapons, when not projecting, are silent. Your weapons, when concealed, are seemingly invisible. Most of the time, your weapons aren't projecting. Most of the time, your weapons are concealed. Do these conditions (unprojecting, concealed) render your weapons ineffective? Would it be correct to say that your weapons, in their silent concealment, are somehow *defeated*?

No. And no. Your weapons are stealth.

And I am neither dead, nor in prison. I am in love with a red-haired seventh-grader and I attend Aptakisic Junior High School in Deerbrook Park, 60090. There are other Israelites at Aptakisic, but I am unknown to nearly all of them because they aren't scholars and I spend my days in a cage. These Israelites think themselves Jews, for the arrangement at this school, though operated in part by Israelites, is nonetheless constructed by Canaanites and Romans in whose best interests it is that Israelites fear themselves. Rejoice that you still get to go to Schechter and Northside. I wish we could still be studying together.

And yet I see it is good to be in love, and were I still attending school with you, I could not have fallen in love. I hope to tell you the story one day. I hope that day will be soon.

Soon,

Gurion ben-Judah

I moved the cursor over the SEND button, daring myself to click it, knowing I wouldn't. I'd known I wouldn't since halfway through the first paragraph, but had kept writing anyway, hoping the message, completed, would reveal a justification for its own sending. The stated one was legless. Emmanuel Liebman would tell the scholars he'd spoken with me, and they would believe him because he was Emmanuel Liebman. They would know

I wasn't dead or in prison. And simply missing them wasn't a good enough reason to contact them. If I contacted them, no few would conclude it meant that it was okay for us to be back in contact—it wasn't. And they would contact me, and I would tell them it was not okay, that it was not yet time for them to disobey their parents, and some of them would listen, but most of them would argue, pointing to the wording I'd used in my "Last Word" email (p. 71), and though I'd eventually convince them, they would, in the meantime—while getting convinced—be breaking a commandment, and I'd be abetting the breakage.

I closed my browser and started writing scripture.

> There is love. There was always love, and there will be more
> love, forever. Were there ever to be less love, we would all be at
> war, and Your angels would learn suffering.

I stared at these lines for a couple of minutes, then noticed the clock read 10:07—eight minutes til bedtime—and saved the document, shut down my computer, washed up and brushed, and got into bed. I lay there fake-reading Dostoevsky's *Adolescent*, which Flowers had given me a couple weeks before.

My parents came in at 10:21. My dad thumbed my bookspine and told me he liked *Notes From Underground* better. My mother said Dostoevsky was an antisemite, and they each kissed my forehead, then went to their bedroom.

Ten minutes later I retrieved ammo and a pennygun from my Relics & Armaments Lockbox. Then I cut the lights and pulled my hood on. I set my chair before the open window and waited on my knees to blind the vandal.

9
SOPHISTRY

Wednesday, November 15, 2006
6:00 a.m.–Interim

A nd there was night, and there was morning, Wednesday.
Wednesday didn't take as long as Tuesday.

My mom came into my room at 6:00 and pressed her chin to my forehead to wake me. "I have already turned your alarm off," she said. "Sleep late today, but not in this chair. Why are you in this chair? Why is this chair set in front of the window? Get in your bed." She was holding my pennygun.

My neck pinched when I turned and I remembered the vandal, saw that I'd failed to be vigilant.

I've got ISS, I said.

"Do not snap at your mother, who will drive you to school. Get under the blanket and bless your aba when he comes." She dangled my pennygun by the firing pouch. "I will hide it," she said, "but where?"

My schoolbag.

She put it in my schoolbag. "Sleep now," she said.

I shut my eyes and pushed my face in a pillow. Soon I heard metal scraping flint by the doorway, then an exhalation.

Into the pillow I said, Judges love your voice. Wilmette will cower.

My father said, "You're a good son." He stepped into the room to ash in the wastebasket. "No more fistfights."

I said, I can't sleep when you're watching. Intimidate Wilmette. I love you.

"I love you, too."

I slept four hours and woke up angrier than the last time.

My mom wasn't in the kitchen or the office, so I ran down to the basement. I found her in desert fatigues, in the punchingbag circle. She'd set it up when I was still a baby. There were seven bags, all heavies, and the circle's diameter was ten feet. The bags, five feet tall, hung by eighteen-inch chains from a nine-foot ceiling.

You forget about me? I said.

"That is a stupid question," she said. "Would you like to exercise?"

I'm late, I said.

She set the heavies in motion and started weaving and jumping and throwing blows while I tried to stay angry, watching her. The object of the exercise was to land as many blows as possible without being struck by the bags as they swung. It was a much easier exercise for me than for her because I fought from a squatty, wrestley stance, and was closer to the ground to begin with—I could duck any or all of the bags at even the lowest points of their arcs without dropping to my knees, which meant I could pop back up and deliver a worthy blow without having to regain my feet. My mom was tall, though, and her stance was the gawkiest, most uncomfortable-looking fighting stance anyone has ever seen. That was because of her neck. It was long and vulnerable-looking and had no wrinkles or horizontal lines on it at all. If she turned her head, even a little bit, tendons appeared and the hollowed area within the clavicle got deeper. My father called her neck *striking* whenever he'd kiss it, and that was a little bit poetic of him: if you were her enemy, the likelihood was high that you would strike first at her neck.

My mom's fighting style was built to increase that likelihood, to make her neck even more difficult to resist. She'd accentuate the illusion of her neck's vulnerability in every possible way, not only by using the gawky fighting stance—tiptoed and stiff, her shoulders back so the blades were almost touching, she'd bend slightly forward at the waist and keep her hands open at her sides the way Christian saints do in paintings—but by tipping her chin a few degrees higher than normal and swallowing as often as possible. If she knew in advance that she'd come across an enemy, she'd pin her braids up in a pile to cut down on the thickening and foreshortening effects the ropy shadows would otherwise create. She wore lots of V-necks, too.

If the enemy didn't know my mom, he couldn't possibly suspect the vulnerability was a fakeout; encountering the long, seemingly unprotected neck, he was as close to dead as an insect giving witness to the bright white promise of warmth in a bug-zapper's coil. He would attack my mom's neck, and because she was expecting exactly that, she could and would lay into him with a kind of suddenness that, even if he remained conscious afterward, would leave him too stunned to get up. And then she would kill him. Unless he was me. I'd only ever gone at her neck once—she put me on my back so fast I thought the ceiling was the floor. And that was when I was six, when she'd still handicap for my height by sparring on her knees. She put me on my back that fast, and she couldn't even use her legs.

She landed nine blows—one to each of five bags, and two to the remaining two—before one of the bags caught her, in mid-roundhouse, on the outer right thigh. If that bag were an actual enemy, the hit to the thigh might have sealed her doom, but at the same time, if that bag were an actual enemy, he would not have kept swinging back and forth while my mother slayed his buddies. He would have been lying dead at her feet from the toe to the windpipe she'd delivered thirty seconds earlier.

"I will make you breakfast," she said, bobbing and weaving as the bags swung dumbly toward exhaustion—it would be minutes before they were still.

I'm late, I said.

She ducked and bobbed.

Mom! I said. I grabbed a bag and pulled it back.

"'Ma-ahm,'" she said. She never liked the word *mom*. She thought it sounded like the name of a puppet. Mom the puppet. She slipped through the gap I'd made and tugged at my hair. "I did not know you were in a rush to sit in ISS," she said.

I said, If I show up too late, I'll have to serve it tomorrow. Don't you have clients to see?

"It is Wednesday. I had class this morning, so I cancelled class. I had one client, and I rescheduled with him. I did this so you would not have to sit in ISS all day—I know you do not like ISS. And I will not allow your principal to put you in ISS tomorrow. You will wash up and I will make you breakfast and then I will drive you to school for the second half of the day. Why did you fall asleep on a chair by the window holding a projectile weapon?"

I said, How will you stop Brodsky from giving me another ISS?

She said, "Uch" = Tch = "That is such a stupid question that I am going to walk up the stairs without saying anything else and cook an omelette."

She walked upstairs and cooked an omelette.

On the way to my room, I opened the front door and checked the stoop. The stoop was clear, so I went outside and did a perimeter-check. Nothing. I hadn't missed my chance to blind him, whoever he was, and the omelette was perfect, not a foldover, and not the kind they make at diners where the ingredients go on top either, but a fully integrated cheddar and tomato one like chefs cook at brunches in hotel lobbies. It was a delicious omelette, and eleven o'clock, and a forty-minute drive—just a half day's wait til detention, June.

In the car, we listened to National Public Radio. There was a long, sad story about a family whose house got bulldozed by the IDF in Gaza in 2003, and then a shorter one on Drucker vs Wilmette. In the second story, my father's name got mentioned more than anyone's, even Drucker's. NPR loved my father. At least three times a year, he'd participate in on-air panels as their Constitutional law expert.

My mother did not love NPR. She said, "These mamzers. One story about the violent Jews of Israel, and then another about the ethical Jewish defender of Constitutional rights." She drew fire into the end of her cigarette. "This seems like balanced press for the Jews, yes, Gurion? The balance is an illusion. In the first story, it is the bad Jew, they are telling us, who harms those who would destroy him. And in the second story, it is the good Jew who protects those who would destroy him. It is the same argument both times: the Jews should let themselves be destroyed. I could kill them for how they use your father."

No one uses Aba, I said.

"You are right," she said. "I spoke with too much force."

She kissed her hand three times—loudly, rapidly—and touched the crown of my head with it, and then we were quiet.

I kept trying to fix my eyes on a single tree along the highway so it wouldn't blur when we passed it, but all of them blurred.

□ □ □ □ □ □ □

My mom had lit a cigarette just before we pulled into the Aptakisic parking lot and was still smoking it on the way to the front entrance when she tried handing me a paperback. I was spaced out, looking at the school's outer wall. A WE DAMAGE WE bomb spanned six bricks above the bushes. I still didn't know what exactly it meant, but it had to mean *something*, and I liked that. I could see my mom's hand insisting with the book in my left periphery, but my eyes were doing a nice soft-focus on the bomb and I didn't want to break the trance.

My mom wagged the book and the pages flapped, sharpening everything. "To read in ISS," she told me.

Thank you, I said.

I took it from her hand. It was Philip Roth's *My Life as a Man*, one of his only three books that I hadn't read yet, unless you counted the autobiographies, which I didn't; I was determined never to read those. I didn't want to know what was true and what wasn't when it came to Roth, or any other writer of fiction I liked for that matter, but him especially. As long as the information I'd learned about him and what he believed did not come directly from him, I could ignore or embrace it at will, and it couldn't then interfere with the fictions he made—at least not that much—nor with what others made of those fictions, which was also important. Sometimes at least.

I said to my mom, I thought you said Roth was an antisemite.

"I have never said that," she said.

We stopped before the doors of the front entrance so she could finish her cigarette.

I remember, though, I said. I said, You argued with Aba about it once. You said, 'Roth is bad for the Jews.'

"He is," she said, "bad for the Jews. But that does not make him an antisemite. He loves the Jews."

But you argued—

"Ask Aba what I argued. You misunderstood. That can happen when you hear conversations you were not meant to hear. In the meantime, I just gave you a book by Philip Roth that I liked when I was younger, a book I rushed to the bookstore to buy for you this morning while you were asleep so that you would have something to read in ISS, so—"

So thank you, I said.

"You are welcome," she said.

That is when Jerry the Deaf Sentinel came outside. He said, "Ma'am, I have to let you know that there is no smoking permitted on school grounds."

"Good morning," my mother said, flashing teeth. She flicked ashes and took a drag.

Jerry waited til she took another drag to say, "I'm going to have to ask you to extinguish your cigarette."

"Very shortly," she said. "First I must finish it."

"Then I'm going to have to ask you to leave the school grounds, Ma'am."

"And now you have done so," said my mother.

"Ma'am—"

"Sir," my mother said, "I do not know who you are, or what authority that beaten felt crest on your pocket is meant to represent, but I am confident—I am *certain*—that I am not within the, the, the—what is the word, Gurion?"

Reach, I said.

"Not *reach*," she said. "There are more syllables."

Jurisdiction is too fancy, I said. I said, You want to say *jurisdiction* but *reach* has more force. *Reach* sounds like *punch*.

"Pow!" she shout-whispered, mock-swinging a fist at my chin.

"Ma'am—" said Jerry.

"I am certain, sir," said my mother, "that I am not within the *reach* of whatever authority it is that you represent. Stop bothering us."

And Jerry said, "I really don't know how to respond to that, ma'am." His whole face was twitching, but especially this one jumpy muscle under his left eye. He didn't seem angry, though, just confused.

"Maybe you should let it go," my mom said. She said it in her concerned voice, the same voice in which she must have said the same thing a thousand times before to clients.

"I'd like to let it go," Jerry said, "but I've gotta do *some*thing." He kicked his left heel with the toe of his right boot, concentrated on the pavement.

My mom exhaled some smoke. "How would you usually respond?" she said.

"There's no precedent," Jerry said. He raised his head, and I saw his eyes twinkled a little. The muscle under his left eye had gone still, as if the twinkling were an outcome the earlier jumping had manufactured. It was not entirely surprising to me, the way Jerry was acting. My mom is seriously pretty, and not the way everyone else thinks his mom is pretty because she is his mom and he gets confused because she is nice to him, but truly pretty, and in an uncommon way, at least in America; to be addressed by her at all, let alone in the concerned voice, makes people weak, even me sometimes, and I see her every day. "I'm Jerry," Jerry said.

"No precedent at all?" my mother soothed, ignoring the introduction. "Would you have me believe," she said, "that your superiors have failed to establish a protocol for dealing with those who illicitly smoke cigarettes on school grounds?" The cherry was almost down to the letters. Probably three more drags.

"There's a protocol," Jerry said, grinding his kicking-toe into the pavement. Then he spoke the largest string of words I'd ever heard from him: "I've followed the protocol, but when it comes to what to do about someone who, after you've followed the protocol, continues to smoke, there's just nothing in the manual. If you were a student, I suppose I'd go inside and write you up."

"That is what you should do, then," said my mom.

"But that's just silly," said Jerry.

"Maybe it is you who are silly, Jerry," said my mom.

"May*be*!" Jerry said, eyes gone wide and hopeful at the sound of his name on her lips. He choked on something that would have bloomed into laughter if he wasn't a robot.

"Look at this contraband," said my mom. Jerry leaned forward. "The fire," she said to him, "is burning the letters. There is more tar under the letters than I am willing to inhale." She dropped the cigarette and stepped on it.

Then she stepped past Jerry and held the door open for me. Carved into the door's pneumatic pushplate was another WE DAMAGE WE. I ran a finger over it, barely touching it, and the dry topskin of my fingertip perforated whitely from the roughness of the engraving. I wondered what Ronrico had used to make the words so mean—a nail? a key? If you held a guy by the hair on the crown of his skull, I was thinking, and pressed his forehead hard enough against the bar, the words would make the forehead bleed, and the guy would be marked by them. In a mirror, his scab would read WE DAMAGE WE.

"Let's go," my mom told me.

Right when we stepped into the Office—I had just got my hand up to wave hello to Miss Pinge—my mom asked, "Where is Leonard Brodsky?"

Brodsky's door was open, and he was pacing. Hearing his name, he revolved to face us and I pointed at him. My mom entered before Brodsky had a chance to invite her. I wished she had waited, and thought to wait myself—after my Tuesday snakiness, I wanted to at least be polite to him—but followed anyway because she was my mom and he was only my principal.

"Leonard," my mother said, "I am Tamar Maccabee and I would like you to excuse Gurion's tardiness. It is my fault that he is late."

"Fair enough," Brodsky said, no hesitation or anything. He said, "Go on ahead to the Cage, Gurion."

I have ISS, I told him.

"You can serve your ISS tomorrow," Brodsky said.

My mom said, "I told him he would not have to serve ISS tomorrow, Leonard."

"Well, I don't—"

"Leonard, he spent all of yesterday and this morning mentally preparing himself to be in ISS today. We must take into account his mental preparation."

The wingnut I'd given Brodsky glinted up from the palm of his half-open fist when he shrugged = "I don't know what you're talking about."

My mom could not have known what she was talking about, herself. As a rule, she avoided using the word *mental*—she did not believe the word described anything real. In the introduction to her doctoral dissertation, she wrote, "*Mind* is to the study of human psychology what *the ether* once was to that of pre-Einsteinian physics—a convenient and groundless homuncular hypothesis that obscures exactly that which its proponents insist it describes; an illusion to be dispelled." At best, she had *mental preparation*ed at Brodsky the way I'd sometimes *Jew* at Israelites who didn't know they were *Israelites*. At worst, she was being a sophist. She was about to respond to Brodsky's shrug when the beginning-of-lunch tone came through the intercom.

As soon as it ended, she said, "The mental preparation is arguably the largest part of the ISS punishment." Sophist. "Beyond that, Leonard," she continued, "I told him he would not have to serve ISS tomorrow. Will you make a liar of me before my son?"

Brodsky tried to gesture with his shoulders in a way that would have = flabbergasted, but midway through the gesture, the wingnut popped from his hand and bounced off the back of my mother's. Brodsky bent to retrieve the wingnut, which interrupted the gesture and made it so the gesture, not only *despite* but also *because of* its failure to signify *flabbergasted*, actually heightened Brodsky's signification of *flabbergasted* = Brodsky was so flabbergasted, he couldn't even express *flabbergasted*. It was perfect, and I got a rush because I knew it was perfect, perfect in the exact way that I knew the entire universe would be perfect if I, or someone else, became the messiah. I knew of many outcomes in the universe that were affected either despite *or* because of a given reason—like for instance hatred of the Israelites and the contributions of Israelites: You can say that we are hated *despite* the good things that we have done for the world = the haters don't care about the good things we've done; or you can say that we are hated *because of* the good things we've done for the world = the haters are sick of us being the ones who do so many of the good things; but for any given hater, it has to be one *or* the other in order to make sense; either the hater says, "There are no good Israelites, and the ones who seem good are but tricksters," *or* he says, "The good ones are the exceptions that prove the rule that Israelites are bad"—but Brodsky's expression of *flabbergasted* was one of the very first outcomes I knew of that came about both because of *and* despite the same reason. What spooked me out was that the last time I considered that kind of perfect relationship between an outcome and a reason—early on Tuesday, on page 41, when I thought about how it was good to do justice because God will kill you and your family whether or not you do justice—I was also in Brodsky's office. Brodsky hadn't intended for me to consider what I considered either of those times, but I felt gratitude toward him anyway, for cueing me in to something perfect, only I could not come up with a way to thank him without sounding like I was making fun of him for accidentally hitting my mom's hand with a wingnut, so I just smiled at him. He didn't look at me, though. He didn't see it.

Standing again, wingnut retrieved, Brodsky said to my mother, "I'd like to speak to you alone."

"I would prefer if we could settle about Gurion's ISS first," she said.

"He can serve the rest of today and go back to the Cage tomorrow," Brodsky said. "Go ahead," he said to me.

He shut the door as I cleared the threshold.

□ □ □ □ □ □ □ □

Name: Gurion ben-Judah Maccabee
Grade: ⑤6⑦8
Homeroom: The Cage
Date: 9/26/2006

Complaint Against Student (from Complaint Against Student Sheet)
Impersonating the following: Mr. Gerald's walk, my step 1 warning for the impersonation, Mr. Gerald's laughter, my step 3 warning for the impersonation. 5th period. 9/21/06. Mr. Botha.

~~Step 4 Assignment: Write a letter to yourself in which you explain 1) why you are at step 4 (in after-school detention); 2) what you could do in order to avoid step 4 (receiving after-school detention) in the future; 3) what you have learned from being at step 4 (in after-school detention); 4) what you have learned from writing this letter to yourself. Include a Title, an Introduction, a Body, and a Conclusion. This letter will be collected at the end of after-school detention. This letter will be stored in your permanent file.~~

Title
Underdog

Introduction

The underdog is a story. This is the story: Someone is trying to

overcome unlikelihood and therefore that someone is the hero.
Unlikelihood describes size or numbers relative to power.

Body

The underdog in one-on-one combat

When two individuals engage in combat with one another, the underdog is rendered by the storyteller as either a) large but weak, or b) small yet powerful. The larger the underdog, the lesser his strength; the smaller the underdog, the greater his strength:

SUPERPOWERFUL

vs./=

POWERFUL

vs./=

WEAK

The underdog army at war

When armies war, the underdog army is rendered by the storyteller as either a) consisting of few soldiers, all or most of whom are powerful, or b) many soldiers, all or most of whom are weak. The greater the underdog army's numbers, the weaker its soldiers; the lesser the underdog army's numbers, the stronger its soldiers:

Some examples of the large one or the many who fight the small one or the few

Unionized Workers vs. Factory Owners. Any sweetheart-fatboy vs. any prettyboy-bully. Fijian Natives vs. Indian Colonists. Russian Peasantry vs. Tzarists. Russian Army vs. Nazi Army. Big Chief vs. Nurse Ratchett. The U.S. vs. the American Indians. Europeans vs. Israelites.

To win their battles, these kinds of underdog rely on their own and one another's ability to absorb violence. They find their might in their nature. They believe victory is assured by their nature, and that as long as they act in accordance with their nature, they will claim it.

Because they are able to fight, they must fight.

Some examples of the small one or the few who fight the large one or the many

Corleone Family vs. The Five Families. Moses vs. The Egyptians. Israel vs. The Arab Nations. Samson vs. The Philistines. Yeshua vs. Rome. The Nazi Party vs. The World. McMurphy vs. Hospital Security. The Palestinians vs. The Israelis. Warsaw Ghetto Soldiers vs. The Nazis. Mosada Soldiers vs. Roman Centurions. Al Quaeda vs. The West.

These kinds of underdog rely on stealth, craftiness, or technology to win their battles. They have faith that their might comes from outside of them. They believe their fight is meant to be; that their might, whether it is in the form of stealth or craftiness or technology, is a gift from God that they must use if they wish to claim victory.

Because they must fight, they are made able to fight.

Conclusion

Had their birth not been thwarted by the decimation of their ancestors, a billion Philistines would today be crying out against David for having cheated in the contest that ended their giant.

Underdog stories are easy to tell. It is best to be suspicious of underdog stories.

□ □ □ □ □ □ □

The ISS desk faced the back of the Office to prevent conversation with kids in the waiting chairs. No one was waiting when I came out of Brodsky's, except for Miss Pinge, who wanted to leave. She handed me my ISS assignment and pardoned herself to the bathroom. Then she went out to her car to smoke.

I reversed my chair to watch Main Hall through the window. It was already a minute into Lunch/Recess-rush, and my eyes went straight to the the Main Hall Shovers.

The blankspot for Jesus on their scarves was loud, way more prominent than it had seemed the day before, when I'd only seen the scarf get brandished for a second. Not only was it centermost on the scarf's left leg (beneath it were the symbols that stood for the co-captains; above it, the ones for Lonnie Boyd and the fifth guy, A-teamer X, whose unknown last name, it could now be deduced, began with a letter between B and F), but whereas the other starters' symbols were thinly embroidered—just scant white thread-shapes on deep red fabric, the fuzz of which seemed to be trying to suffocate them—Frungeon's white stripe was dyed bright in the wool.

The Shovers kept touching their scarves on the knots, triple- and qua-druple-checking their integrity, but otherwise nothing they were doing was new to me. Their actions in Main Hall, though usually conspicuous and often offensive, were always predictable. If a bandkid was around, they'd call him a bancer and shoulder him sideways at the wall or trip him. If a girl who wasn't an Ashley or a Jenny was pretty and standing or walking alone, then one or two Shovers would push another into her, the pushed one would sly-grope a tit or some ass, explain real loud how he had to catch his balance, then apologize softly and ask if she was hurt. When an Indian came by, they'd show him their thumbs and say, "Gumm 'em!" or "Yope!" or "Gumm it up! Yope!" and try to shake his hand, unless he was a starter, or Bryan Maholtz, in which case they'd step to the side so he could pass. Most of the time, though, the Indians ignored them, and the bandkids and pretty non-Jennys and -Ashleys kept enough distance to dodge molestation; most of the time the Shovers only had each other, and their Shover-to-Shover routine went like this: One would toe the heel of the one in front of him, the heel-toed one would shove the one in front of *him*, and the one who'd been shoved would stop short and go rigid so the heel-toed one would walk into his elbows. Sometimes, too, they'd make a Shover sandwich, i.e., the heel-toer would walk into the elbows of the one who had just walked into the shoved one's elbows. And occasionally the heel-toer's own heel would get toed by a fourth Main Hall Shover, then the fourth by a fifth, then the fifth by a sixth, and etc. and so on. The only thing that might vary was the size of the sandwich.

None of the Shovers ever wrecked school property, or ever got in trouble, let alone damaged, yet from the way they'd chin air and slap backs post-routine, you could tell that they thought they got away with being dangerous. Mischief wasn't danger, though, and they'd only been mischievous, and you didn't have to get away with that during Lunch—mischievous was what you were supposed to be. The whole purpose of Lunch outside of the classroom was to provide time and space for students to engage in benign little fits of halfhearted assault that would dull their urges to damage the arrangement. So while the Main Hall Shovers thought themselves defiant, like some paddling gang of finns on the foamy rapids, they were just a bunch of sawyers in school-colored scarves eating candy in a barn before supper. They'd have brought more damage singing Aptakisic's fightsong while marching down Main Hall in a singlefile line—at least then their behavior might have seemed ironic.

After their first routine (a three-man sandwich), I looked past them to the action on the farther side of Main Hall. The seventh-grade Jennys—Jennys April, Khouri, and Flagg—knelt under the fire alarm to retie their shoes. The shoes were brand-new white with a steel toe on the outside and a bright-colored tongue: a red tongue for April, a green one for Khouri, and an orange for Flagg. No one in the hallway seemed to notice the Jennys, so they pulled the knots loose and tied them again, and then again, and again once more, when finally two Ashleys—Dunkel wearing an EMOTIONALIZE head-band, and Doer a wrist one embossed with a Star of Boystar—stopped to admire the shoes. Dunkel slapped her forehead, and Doer used her wrist to touch each Jenny on the shoulder. They kissed each other's halos and giggled loud giggles.

Then an Israelite Shover thumped the window chin-first, and my line of sight got blocked, and he fell. A second kid tripped on the fallen one's body, and the tripped one got grundied by Maholtz. Maholtz then blindly collided with Slokum, who one-arm bounced him off the window hard and continued forward without breaking stride.

Maholtz saw me see him, stuck his hand in his pocket, and pulled out his sap and snicked it. I stood up fast and he backpedaled. I reached in my hoodie and pulled out my swearfinger, mouthed the word "Bryguy," and there might have been a stare-down, and Maholtz might have won it, but I looked at the ground, overcome with confusion, and so I didn't know if there'd been any staredown.

What confused me was how it was that I'd known that the Shover who'd slammed against the window was an Israelite. To read a face takes too much effort to do it without noticing, so I knew I hadn't, inadvertently or otherwise, read an Israelite story in the slammed Shover's face. I could barely remember the shape of the face. What I did remember was blonde hair and light eyes, and though no few Israelites had such features, the features themselves far from signified Israelite. His nose I couldn't picture, but big-nosedness would have indicated little, anyway. To really get across that Nazi propaganda look, you had to reveal your profile to the viewer, and the glance that I'd gotten was totally frontal. By the time I started picturing the area under his scarf-knot to see if he wore a hamsa or chai or mogen David, the image was already becoming unreliable—it flickered and the chest expanded and contracted, cycling through various breadths and shirt-colors, none of which seemed to be accurate. Was it possible I made a mistake? What kind of mistake was that to make, though? Why would I see an Israelite where there was no Israelite? Because I *wished* he were an Israelite? *Did* I wish that? What I really wished was that *no* Israelites were Shovers. However, being that some were, did I wish them more harm than I did the other Shovers? Did I wish hard enough that the wish banced my eyesight, banced it enough to Israelitelate a window-slammed Gentile? I didn't think so. I didn't believe people's brains worked like that, or at least not mine, and I still don't. But that stopped mattering, anyway. What came to matter was that, yes, when I thought about it, I did wish the Israelite Shovers more harm than the others. I wished them all harm, all of the Shovers, but there was a sharper kind of satisfaction in my stomach when I thought of the Israelite ones getting damaged. They seemed, somehow, to deserve it more. Or maybe it was just that I would never hurt them myself, at least not for being Shovers. All Shovers were chomsky for being Shovers, but the Israelite ones, in addition to being chomsky, got me disappointed. Despite that disappointment, I wouldn't bring them damage, because they were my brothers, chomsky or not. And because I wouldn't bring them damage despite the disappointment, because they were my brothers, chomsky or not, it made me feel frustrated and wish them extra damage.

To have even thought these explanations *could be* correct, seems now, in itself, to mean that they were. Right then, though, I didn't have time to sort it out. Eliyahu, having spotted me through the sound-resistant window, charged into the Office with a hand atop his hat and shouted my name. Then he was hugging me. I hugged him back one-armed, looking over his shoulder. Maholtz was gone, having maybe won a staredown.

We sat in the waiting chairs.

"Baruch Hashem," Eliyahu said. "I thought you'd died."

I told you, I said, I'm not gonna die. And I asked him, Where's Nakamook?

"Nakamook," he said. "Nakamook, exactly. Nakamook, he's in the Cage eating lunch with your friend Jelly Rothstein. And I know you told me that you wouldn't die, yet still I worry. You were not in the Cage this morning, and when I asked Nakamook did he know where you were, he said you were here in this office. But the word of Nakamook…" His mouth half-open, Eliyahu used both hands to wave the rest of the sentence away from his body.

What? I said.

"Maybe it's not so important," said Eliyahu. "And a blessing on Benji's head. What I am trying to explain is that I thought it better to see with my own eyes that what he said of you this morning was true. So, to see with my own eyes, I raised high my textbooks, one by one, and dropped them the flat way. Such a boom they made upon meeting the floor! For each boom, Monitor Botha gave me a step. And so boom and boom-boom and a fourth boom: detention. Then bip: he wrote a CASS. Bop: he sent me to Mr. Brodsky, who revoked the detention when I explained my concerns. That was two hours ago and you were not here, and so what else could I think? I thought maybe you were dead. What else was there to think?"

That I'd stayed home with a cold? I said.

"Maybe," said Eliyahu, "and I did consider the possibility, but then I began to think of how you'd told me that you wouldn't die. I thought: If I'm to believe that Gurion won't die, it's the same as believing that Gurion *can't* die, and if Gurion can't die, then is it so likely he can catch cold? It didn't seem so likely. It didn't seem likely at all. It seems to me that if you can catch cold, you can die. So I thought: Maybe he was mistaken when he said he wouldn't die— maybe he would, in which case he could, which is to say he *can*, so he probably has a cold. So probably a cold, I thought, and thank God it is probably just a cold. And this was comforting for a moment, until the stress shifted, at which point I thought: If Gurion can have a cold, he can die, so it is not so outlandish to worry that he is dead. So I worried you were dead."

I don't have a cold, I whispered. I slept in. And Nakamook can be trusted—he's loyal.

"I am glad you don't have a cold, and it is not really a question of is Benji loyal, or even does he lie," Eliyahu said. "It's maybe he's a little crazy. Maybe he gets a little carried away sometimes. For instance, yesterday: On the bus-ride home, we sat next to each other, and this Co-Captain person did not come near me—I could see in his eyes that he wanted to bother me, but he did not bother me—and yes, it made me grateful for Nakamook's protection. But then Nakamook became crazy, or maybe just carried away. Is there a difference? I don't know. Who am I to know the difference? It seems as though to act *carried away* is to respond excessively to something actual, and that to act *crazy* is to respond improbably to something that may or may not be actual. It seems like the *carried away* person, if he slips like a clown on a banana peel, assaults those who laugh at him, whereas *crazy*, it seems, would be a person who, when people are laughing at a clown who has slipped on a banana peel, believes the people are laughing at him—laughing at the crazy person, I mean, not the clown—and then he, this crazy person, assaults the people. The ones who are laughing. Or maybe the crazy person is the one who, even when people aren't laughing at all, and there is no banana peel, he attacks people because he believes they *would* laugh at him *if* he slipped on a banana peel. Whether Benji is crazy or just gets carried away, when this morning he told me you were serving ISS there was no reason for me to think he would lie, but there was also no reason for me to believe him—he could have seen you, true, but also he could have thought he'd seen you and seen someone else, or he could have seen no one else but believed he'd seen you."

What did he do on the bus? I said.

"Aye! The legs! I got ahead of myself. I forgot to explain. I left out the important part. It happens sometimes, you should know it about me—I get ahead of myself. I get carried away and leave out the important part. The important part is what Benji did with his legs. True, it began harmlessly, it was a little funny even: He stretched his legs onto the seat across the aisle from the one on which we sat, and he kept them there, the legs. At bus-stops, when a girl needed to pass him, he would clear the path, but when it was a boy who needed to get by, Benji would keep the legs stretched until the boy did something for his entertainment. It was, at first, playful, like a game. Some of the fifth-graders seemed to like it. On reflection, I suppose they enjoyed how the fearsome Nakamook was talking to them without any threat of smashing up their bones, or maybe just that he wanted something from them that they could deliver. He would have them tell a joke or sing the chorus of a song, and he would applaud when they did so, even when the joke wasn't funny or the song was off-key. He was nice to them.

"But then Aleph comes along—that tall, muscular boy I told you about yesterday, the one who looked away when the Co-Captain knocked my hat off—he's also on the bus—and the nonsense with the legs stops being playful. Nakamook tells him, 'Sing me a song,' and Aleph, he doesn't want to sing, so he offers Nakamook a dollar.

"'What is this?' says Nakamook.

"'A toll,' Aleph tells him.

"'A *toll?*' says Nakamook.

"'For so I can pass by you—I'm offering to pay you a toll,' explains Aleph.

"And Nakamook, here, gets all verklempt. He gives Aleph this speech, this carried-away, if not crazy, speech, and then he says to me—"

Wait, I said. What speech? I said. You're getting ahead of yourself.

"You want the speech?" said Eliyahu.

Do you remember the speech?

"Who could forget such a speech!" said Eliyahu.

So nu? I said. I'm stuck here all day. Give me something to think about.

"Okay, so okay, so Aleph proffers the dollar, Benji says what is it, Aleph tells him it's a toll for so he can pass, and then, and then…" Eliyahu cleared his throat, made his eyes squinty, and held his hands before him in half-open fists, fingernails up, and made the fists rotate in little circles. "'*Toll?*' Benji says. '*Toll?*' he says." Having gotten into character, Eliyahu stilled his wrists. "'*Toll* is not what you mean. *Toll* sounds like a lie. *Toll* you pay a builder to cross a bridge he built. *Toll* you owe the builder because he built the bridge. When *you* say *toll,* kid, it sounds like something else. When you say *toll,* it sounds like the price of safe passage, and *the price of safe passage* like a fee being extorted from you, an unjust price; a price you pay to prevent the advances of unjust forces against your physical integrity. But to pay a price like that, to pay a price in advance, to the *unjust,* a price *to prevent advances against your physical integrity*—that is to compromise your dignity.'"

Eliyahu stopped squinting. "Just to be clear," he said, "you know I'm doing Nakamook—this isn't me saying this."

Right, I said. It's good. It's a good impression.

"Really? Thank you. Okay, so, okay, so where…"

'To pay a price in advance to—'

"Right. Exactly." He fell back into character, and this time spoke louder: "'To pay a price in advance, to the *unjust*, a price *to prevent advances against your physical integrity*—that is to compromise your dignity. And dignity compromised is no longer dignity. Whoever says otherwise is selling you a bridge, kid. And I am no extortionist. I'm only a person with his legs across an aisle. Why not just ask me, *Benji please move your legs*? Years we go to school together, never speaking… Years go by, you never introduce yourself to me, you never nod hello to me in the hallway or even so much as drink a Coke at my lunch table—and all this time I give you the benefit of the doubt. I tell myself, *He's shy. He is not avoiding you. He is not snubbing you.* But now, when you would have me do something for you, some nothing so small as moving my legs, a gesture I never said I wouldn't perform… It is only after I've requested, in a spirit of good will, that you sing me a song… Only now do you reveal that you *were* avoiding me. All a*long* avoiding me. Snubbing me. I *request* of you a little entertainment, and you respond as you would to a petty extortionist. A common bully. I *request* and you hear a *demand*. Behind the demand you hear a *threat*. Such is the nature of demands. I ask you for a song and you offer up your dignity instead. You treat me like a common bully.'

"So, and this is the part where he stops the speech for a second," Eliyahu said. "He stops the speech and cracks a handful of knuckles against the side of his own neck. He's not facing me, Gurion, so he can't see me, but he says to me, 'Fear is contempt, whether the fearful know it or don't. Look on me with fear, Eliyahu, and it will be the last open glance you cast.'"

What did you do? I said.

"*Do?*" said Eliyahu. "I looked out the window, telling myself Aleph did nothing for me earlier that day. That when the Co-Captain knocked my hat off, Aleph only watched. That the obligation I felt to step in between Nakamook and Aleph and prevent any further humiliation from happening was misguided. In truth, I even began to long for Aleph's further humiliation. As if that were justice. It was awful. At the time, though, it maybe didn't seem so awful… Anyway. Aleph, he says to Benji, 'I didn't mean to treat you like a bully.' And Nakamook, he says, 'You didn't *mean to* treat me like a bully? Meaning you couldn't help it? You couldn't help but treat me like a bully? Is that supposed to *lessen* the insult?… I asked for entertainment, and you could have refused and held your head up. I never asked for your dignity. That is what bullies do. I am not a bully. A bully has no dignity. You treat me like I have no dignity. How can I possibly lower my legs for you now?

How the eff do you expect me to lower my legs and hold onto my dignity? Why have you done this to us? Answer me.'

"So Aleph apologizes. 'I didn't know what I was doing,' he says. And when that apology fails to soften Nakamook, Aleph tries a second one: 'I didn't mean to do what I was doing.' Nothing. He tries a third: 'I thought I was doing something else.'

"'Put your dollar away,' Nakamook tells him, 'and pray you never again mistake dignity for a toll, nor safety for peace, let alone justice.' High-minded stuff, right? Or crazy stuff. Carried-away stuff, maybe. Who can really tell? Not Aleph—not him. Aleph, he's frozen. What's Nakamook saying? He forgive him or what? It isn't so clear. Benji's made it sound like he's forgiven Aleph, but his legs, Gurion, are still stretched across the aisle, and Aleph doesn't understand, and neither do I. The silence: it grows. It grows and grows more, Aleph just standing there, and Nakamook's legs.

"Finally, Nakamook, he says to Aleph: 'I told you to put your dollar in your pocket. Put your filthy effing dollar in your filthy effing pocket with your filthy trembling effing hand.' Aleph swallows hard. Does it. Puts the dollar in his pocket. Benji's legs haven't moved. They're still across the aisle. He says, 'Now get past me. Do so with the understanding that I will be unable to bear any further insult. Understand that I will be unable to bear the insult of contact. Get past without touching me, or to preserve my own dignity, I will show you your blood, and I will be just.'

Here, Eliyahu took a fast breath, then blew out slow.

"Am I to trust a boy who would get this carried away, Gurion?"

I said, But what happened?

"It was shameful what happened!" Eliyahu said. "Aleph, first he removes his scarf and folds it and tucks it inside of his coat. Then he reaches over Nakamook's legs and drops his backpack onto the floor of the bus. And then he makes the decision—and, look, it's the only decision he can possibly make, for Nakamook's legs are bent at the knees and so too high to jump, and Aleph, he's too tall to get under them in a crouch—he makes the decision to crawl under Nakamook's legs. He crawls along the floor on his belly. Am I to trust a boy who would act so crazy as to make another crawl on his belly? Gurion?"

That wasn't the only decision he could have made, I said. I said, He could have fought.

"He would have lost," Eliyahu said.

I said, He would have lost, but it would not have been shameful.

"It might not have been *as* shameful," said Eliyahu, "but it would have been at least a little bit shameful, *and* he would be damaged."

I said, I'm sure Benji had his reasons for doing what he did. What was Aleph's real name?

"If I knew, I wouldn't call him Aleph."

I said, He must have done something wrong to Benji.

"When?" said Eliyahu. "In daycare? Benji himself said they hadn't spoken in all the years they'd gone to school together... Say he *had* wronged Benji in daycare—it was a long time ago. Why not let it go?"

I said, Maybe Aleph *did* wrong him in daycare, and Benji was unable to do anything about it at the time. The million different answers to 'Why not let it go?' have just as many good ones among them as the million you can get from 'Why *should* I let it go?' And look, Eliyahu, I know this place is weird, and the people in it—this school is not a member of the Associated Talmud Torahs Network. But you should trust Benji, and the reason you should trust Benji is that he is loyal to everyone who has ever shown him loyalty. He can't help it. He is loyal to me, and so he's loyal to you, so he wouldn't mislead you about something like whether or not I'm in the Office for ISS.

"But he *did* mislead me, Gurion. You weren't here before."

He told you I was here because he knew I had ISS today, I said. I said, He told you what he thought was true, and not because he was crazy or carried away, but because it *should* have been true, what he told you. I said, There was no reason for him to believe it wasn't true.

"He threatened me," said Eliyahu. "He told me to stop looking at him in fear, or else—"

That was not a threat, I said. It was a warning.

"I hear this phrase in gangster movies," said Eliyahu, "cowboy movies, television reruns about oil barons and men who own vineyards—I have never understood its meaning."

I said, A boy makes a threat when he wants to damage you. The threat itself is a minor form of damage—it makes your snat trickle. When a boy gives you a warning, though, it's because he doesn't want to damage you.

"What is snat?" said Eliyahu. "It sounds like something sticky and unpleasant."

Brodsky's door opened.

I said, I'll give you something I wrote about it.

"Eliyahu," said Brodsky, "you cannot talk to students who are in ISS."

Eliyahu didn't even look at Brodsky, though. He started speaking Hebrew to my mother. "You are Gurion's mother," he said, "I can tell."

This is Eliyahu, I said to my mom.

She touched his cheek with the bottom of her hand and said, "Eliyahu? I am glad to meet you, Eliyahu."

"Thank you," he said. Then he looked at his feet. Then he went to lunch.

My mother bent as if to kiss me, and she whispered in my ear, "Eliyahu is an orphan. You—"

How do you know that? I whispered back.

Into my other ear she whispered, "Do not be thick. I know the face of an orphan when I see one. Protect him. He loves you. So do I. Now act like I have told you that we must have a long talk when you come home from school." Then she stood up straight.

A long talk about what? I said.

She made her voice weary and said, "We will discuss it at home, Gurion," and, with her back still to Brodsky, she winked.

I thought: My mother is not carried away or crazy, but some third thing—she is something else.

□ □ □ □ □ □ □

It's true that Philip Roth wasn't good for the Jews, but it bothered me that other Jews ever said so. It bothered me not only because he was as good for the Jews as any Jew of his generation could have hoped to have been, but because *they*—Roth's accusers—were also bad for the Jews, and for the most part worse than Roth, who was always trying to protect them from themselves, which is what they believed themselves to be doing by accusing Roth of being bad for the Jews. I knew it wasn't really their fault, though—not most of them, anyway—nor his for that matter: Jews couldn't help trying to protect themselves from themselves any moreso than they could have helped being bad for the Jews. That is a lot of what made them Jews. And that is why it wasn't good to be Jews. And that is why I've been good for the Jews: because I've been the end of the Jews (except, of course, for the fictional Jews: Zuckerman and Glick, Stern and Kravitz and Golk, Shylock, Gimpel, Tevye, and Flesh, each Paley-made granny and sister and aunt, Kosinski's boy and all his Ruthenians—Jews forever the lot, and baruch Hashem: fiction needs Jews). All Israelites know this now. Even Philip Roth. Especially him.

But he didn't used to. Not when he wrote *My Life as a Man*; not til after the so-called "11/17 Miracle." In that he was no different than most of the rest of you.

I, on the other hand, had known all my life—or at least since age three, when I'd first read Torah—that I was never a Jew, but always an Israelite, and that all of us were. Therefore I knew, whether there in the Office on 11/15 or anywhere else on any day prior, that I could not have been so very much like Roth, no matter what my mother might have thought; no matter what she might have thought that *I* thought.

My mom thought I thought I was like Philip Roth, and because she thought I thought myself like Philip Roth, she assumed I'd be willing to take a lesson from Roth. That's why she gave me *My Life as a Man*.

(Briefly, for scholars unfamiliar with the book: *My Life as a Man* contains three distinct parts. The first two are short stories about a fictional Jewish writer called Zuckerman[*] who marries a crazy, lying shiksa who ruins his life and then kills herself. The Zuckerman stories are written by another fictional Jewish writer called Tarnopol, and the third part of the book is the novel-length autobiography of Tarnopol, who marries a crazy, lying shiksa. After ruining his life, she kills herself.)

The lesson I was supposed to take was this: I shouldn't marry a shiksa.

But that wasn't the lesson of the book at all—there was no lesson; books with lessons are not good books; *My Life as a Man* was a good book (a *great* book)—nor was June a shiksa, let alone a crazy, lying shiksa; and Tarnopol marries the crazy, lying shiksa in the book not because he loves her as I loved June, but because she lies to him about being pregnant.

To be clear, scholars, my mother was as lucid and concise a thinker as just about anyone I'd ever heard of. Among radical behaviorists, her renown as an innovator was spreading before she'd even finished grad school. Whenever she started to think about her son, though, her thoughts, like so many moms', got seriously disorganized.

Thus, while she knew Roth's book contained no lesson concerning shiksas (she *had to* have known; she was too smart not to), she wished it did, and she gave it to me thinking something along the lines of, "Gurion

---

[*] Despite their having the same name, the fictional Jewish writer Zuckerman of *My Life as a Man* is not the same Zuckerman as the fictional Jewish writer Zuckerman of Roth's "Zuckerman Novels" (e.g. *The Ghost Writer, American Pastoral, The Human Stain*).

will see the lesson that I *wish* Roth was teaching him, and Gurion will come away from that wished-for lesson no longer wanting to marry June." And that didn't make sense. It wouldn't have even made sense if *My Life as a Man did* contain her wished-for lesson. = While she took me seriously enough to believe that I loved and would marry June because I'd said so, she not only didn't believe it when I'd said June was Israelite, but she believed that a book by Philip Roth would have the power to fall me out of love with June. How could you believe your son was in love with a girl and at the same time believe a novel could make him stop loving her? Muddledly is how, and only muddledly.

This isn't to say that the great degree to which her thoughts were muddled was *solely* an outcome of my love declaration. There was also my father—he enhanced the muddle, muddled it further. Had my dad reacted the same way as my mom when I told them about June at the night before's dinner, I doubt she'd have thought to give me the book. Instead, he got all calm and laissez-faire. This wasn't because he took my declaration more seriously than my mom had, though—at least not necessarily. His thinking most likely went something like this: "Gurion is just a boy and so is probably not actually in love with June, but just excited about her; if he *is* in love with June, though, really and truly in love, there is no way to stop it; so either he isn't in love and there's nothing to worry about, or he is in love and there's no *use* in worrying."

In any case, that was their usual pattern: my father believing I'd warp if taken too seriously, and my mother that I'd warp if not taken seriously enough; the one going one way, and the other the other, pressing against each other, further and further, til they overlapped deep into one another's spaces like the fingers of a cage you might make with your hands to surround a ladybug or firefly. It was how they loved me and, on the whole, it was nothing to complain about.

I wasn't thinking too much about any of that, though. I hadn't even read *My Life as a Man* yet. After my mother had left the Office, I read the summary on the back of the cover and from that I got a basic handle on her motives, and, deciding that knowing them would interfere too greatly with my enjoyment of the novel—I wasn't in the mood to feel condescended to—I put the book away and instead I read Rabbi Salt's letter to Brodsky.

At first the letter cheered me—thrilled me even. He testified to nearly everything I wanted to believe about myself. But at the end of the letter, where he claimed that the Cage would be the end of me—that got to me a little, then more than a little. I tried to tell myself he was just hamming things up in order to persuade Brodsky not to put me in the Cage, but I knew Rabbi Salt, I knew him well, so I knew that he wouldn't have brought out the big guns—Brodsky's dead son, my old friend Ben, "Gurion attended his shiva… wept at his burial"—if he didn't desperately believe in his argument. Rabbi Salt was not a heartless man. To use another's emotions about a dead son to strengthen an argument he didn't fiercely believe in; that was beyond him. That was beneath him. At the time he wrote that letter he had to have believed that the Cage would destroy me.

Or maybe I was wrong about him. I might have been wrong about him. I was wrong about something, because if he wasn't the kind of person who'd use a dead son on that son's loving father (in the same nasty way, no less, as I had the day before; same father, same son—I'm not trying to be coy), he'd either lost faith in me and since pretended—every time I'd seen him since the letter was written—to still have faith in me, or he'd lost faith in me at the time he wrote the letter but gotten it back before the next time I saw him.

Since it neither entailed his being cruel or condescending, the last of the three options seemed to be the most generous to Rabbi Salt, so that's the one I chose, but it wasn't like that option got me feeling all joyful—it still meant he'd thought less of me than I wanted him to think of me, even if just for a day or two. The Cage couldn't break me. Nothing could break me. I wanted him to know that; I wanted him to have *always* known that.

I put the letter away to write my ISS assignment, but I couldn't get my mind off Rabbi Salt, and to ignore a thing you have to concentrate on another thing, so I read Call-Me-Sandy's "Assessment of a Client: Gurion Maccabee." When I got to the end, my reaction was the opposite of the one I'd just had to the letter. I wanted to feel *more* upset at its writer. I wanted to hate her. I thought: You should hate her. If it wasn't for her, you would be in normal classes; you might even be in class with June right now.

But that whole Klingon bit, and how she'd concluded that Flowers was imaginary, and the codeswitching part where she thinks she's being slick, asking her professor on a date in a footnote—I couldn't see her doing *anything* with malice, let alone to a student she seemed to like. To hate Call-Me-Sandy for dooming me to the Cage would be like hating a dog for farting. And so I gave up, and then gave up some more: on attempting to be happy about Rabbi Salt's faith-loss, my mother's muddled thinking, my father's skepticism.

At least Philip Roth was good for the Israelites.

□   □   □   □   □   □   □

I put "Assessment" away and was about to ask Pinge for a pass to the bathroom when Desormie burst into the Office, frothing.

He said, "You think you're funny, Maccabee? You think *I'm* funny?" Some of the froth had built up and hardened into paste in his lipcorners and I didn't know what he was talking about. I could barely think is how bad I wanted his paste to disintegrate.

I looked away, saying, The Gym teacher is talking to me during ISS, Miss Pinge.

Desormie leaned at me.

"Ron—" said Miss Pinge.

"And now you're tattling like a tattle-tale telling tales outside school? Isn't that ironic!"

"Lower your voice," Miss Pinge said.

"Lower my voice?" Desormie mock-whispered. "I'll lower my voice," he mock-whispered.

He was leaning with his hands on my desk and he wanted to break my nose. He was leaning so close, and he wanted to break my nose so bad, that his eyes were crossing to keep my nose in focus. I scratched it on the septum. I should have used my swearfinger, but instead I used my ring one. The one good thing about him being that close was I could look right at his eyes like a killer and not see the paste in the periphery.

"The Indians," Desormie said, "have worked their butts off to get good enough to bring you glory on Friday. They've slaved to develop the skills it takes to bring decisive victory that will reflect for the better on all of us. It! Is! Un! Grateful! To! Damage! Their!—"

"Stop yelling, Ron," Miss Pinge said.

"Stop yelling?" Desormie said, standing up straight. "Don't you want to know *why* I'm yelling, Ginnie? Don't you wanna know? Because I wanna tell you why I'm yelling."

"What's the yelling about?" Miss Pinge said.

"I'm gonna tell you," said Desormie.

Tell it, I said.

"You don't tell me what to tell."

I said, Stepitup, man. Tell 'em where it's at.

"Oh, I will, and—"

Break it down righteous. Take 'em to the bridge.

Miss Pinge said, "Are you making James Brown jokes, Gurion?"

"Who knows what kinda jokes he's making? They're inappropriate jokes is what I know. And what else I know is whatever kinda jokes it is, ever, not only don't I think his jokes are funny, ever," said Desormie, before revolving to look at my nose again. "Not only don't I think your jokes are funny, ever," he said to me, "but I don't even *get* your jokes. And I don't think *any*one does. And even if they do, I don't think *they* think your jokes are funny either, because you're not mature. Maturity, Maccabee, is control of yourself, and I don't think you've got control of yourself. You make jokes because you can't help it is what I think. If you had some intestinal fortitude, you *could* help it, but you don't have any intestinal fortitude because that's a part of maturity, too. For example, I don't think you've got the intestinal fortitude to fess up to what you or those so-called friends of yours did today is an example of what I mean by maturity. Maybe you think what you did took a whole lot of intestinal fortitude, but it didn't. Maybe you think the silence you're keeping about the crimes you and your friends have committed is the same kind of silence Frank Pentangeli kept to protect Michael Corleone, but it isn't. The silence of Frankie Five Angels was the silence of *omerta*, which is honorable, and Frankie Five Angels became a suicide in a bathtub to keep that silence so he wouldn't dishonor himself and shame his family, which believe me he was tempted. *That* is the kind of silence that requires intestinal fortitude. And I don't see you in a bathtub. And I definitely don't see you *bleeding from the wrists* in a bathtub. What I see is you sitting beside an administrative assistant, reading a book, trying to save your own hide and thinking, 'I'll never rat on my friends and I'll always keep my mouth shut,' like that's omerta, but it isn't. It's not omerta. It's what Henry Hill thought is what it is, and guess what. Eventually he *did* rat on his friends. He *didn't* keep his mouth shut. And look at him. Look at where his path has led him. To witness protection, probably in Arizona—no one's for sure about it, of course—but what is for sure is the marinara there is ketchup and he's a shnook. I don't think you want to be a shnook, Maccabee. I don't think you want to be on that path, but the way you're mistaking the saving of your own hide for omerta, and the way you're mistaking jokes for control, not to mention how you're mistaking gutless silence for intestinal fortitude, well let me tell you: You're worse than on that path. You're taking the *shortcut*. The shortcut to shnooksville."

When he was finished giving his speech, Desormie chinned the air at Miss Pinge = "My interrogation method, though unconventional—some might even call it 'controversial'—is pretty impressive, if I don't chin so myself."

Miss Pinge looked at her lap.

You're tall, I said to Desormie. How tall are you?

"Tall enough," Desormie said. "Don't try to change the subject with non-sectarians."

But how tall are you exactly? I said.

"Quid pro quo," Desormie said. "Quid. Pro. Quo... Means you answer my question, and only then I answer yours."

You didn't ask a question, I said.

"You know what I mean by a question, Maccabee."

A question? I said.

"Stop playing the fool."

Maybe I'm playing the foog, I said.

"What the heck is a foog?" he said.

I said, Quid pro quo, Clarice.

"You said I'm a Cla*rice*?" he shouted.

"Stop shouting," Miss Pinge said.

"Yes, Ron," said Mr. Brodsky from his doorway. "Please stop shouting."

"The scoreboard is destroyed!" he shouted.

Brodsky said, "I've already discussed the matter with Gurion, and further-more, the scoreboard is not destroyed. Two letters are missing from the—"

"I'm trying to tell you it's destroyed, Mr. Brodsky. It's no two letters. The whole reason I came in here is to deliver the information that at nine this morning it was two letters, which is the last I checked was nine this morning—the last I checked until ten minutes ago, that is—and some time between nine this morning and ten minutes ago, while I was at the pool or in my office, him or his so-called 'friends-of-him' went into the gym and threw so many rocks at the scoreboard that almost all the letters are broken and almost all the bulbs, and those bulbs that are left won't even light up anymore because those thrown rocks those kids threw blew the fuses or something. Scoreboard. Is. Destroyed!"

I wondered about the clock—if Nakamook or Vincie or whoever hit the scoreboard also got the clock. I was so excited I even started asking before I caught myself. I said, What about the—

"What about the *what*?" Desormie said.

I recovered, saying, Does smoke purl from the sockets when you give the thing juice?

"Look at him smiling about it!" Desormie said. Forgetting again to use my swear-finger, I touched my mouth-corners with my thumb and pointer, and this triggered Desormie to touch his own mouth-corners, which smeared the paste onto his cheek a little.

"Let's talk about this in my office," Brodsky said to him.

"Good," said Desormie. "Let's go," he said to me.

I have to use the bathroom, I said.

I really did have to.

"Go ahead, Ginnie," said Brodsky, "give him the pass."

"But we have to discuss the—" Desormie protested.

"Gurion was with his mother this morning, and he's been in the Office since noon," said Brodsky.

"That wasn't the case yesterday," Desormie said. "It wasn't the case when the E and the V got busted out. He's unaccounted for for yesterday."

"You think that he damaged the scoreboard yesterday, but someone *else* did it today?" Brodsky said. He said it like it was the dumbest thing anyone could possibly suggest.

And I thought: Why *not* think that?

And then I thought: Brodsky wants for you to be innocent. He wants to keep you from being bullied.

I thought: Count your blessings, you're off the hook.

"But why *not* think that?" Desormie said. "They're all copycats. And/or they're organized."

Brodsky set his hand on the back of Desormie's elbow and pushed on it, just barely. He pushed Desormie's elbow gently in the direction of his office, and took a step toward the Office, and said, "Who's they?"

And Desormie, who only a split second earlier was dying to break my nose and yell about me, followed Brodsky's cue—took a step in the direction of Brodsky's office without hesitation—and when he said, "I don't know who they are, but I know there's a group of them, Mr. Brodsky," his voice was all but entirely drained of anger.

Miss Pinge handed me the bathroom pass, and I didn't have to piss as bad.

I wanted to do something nice for Brodsky.

I said, "Gym teacher."

And Desormie revolved. He said, "My name is Mr. Desormie to you."

And I said, You are suggestible, Mr. Desormie.

And Desormie said, "What the heck are you talking about?"

And I dragged the back of my hand back and forth across my mouth twice.

And Desormie dragged the back of his hand back and forth across his mouth twice. And Brodsky coughed fakely to mask his laughter. And there was no more paste in the mouth-corners of Desormie. And Brodsky would not have to stare at paste while they talked in his office. That was nice of me.

I went to the gym.

The clock was intact. Floyd the Chewer knelt beneath it, examining the shards of plastic letters and scoreboard bulbs the gym floor was strewn with. Hector the Janitor, on standby beside him, gripped a pushbroom with one hand and a dustpan with the other. I watched them from the doorway. The Chewer held a shard up to the light, made a face like he was deciding something important, then dropped the shard and buzzed a go-ahead through his cheering cone. Seizing his pushbroom just above the brush and using only the bristles along the edge of its short side to avoid accidental contact with shards Floyd hadn't yet approved for disposal, Hector crouched to sweep the rejected one into his dustpan, then stepped back into position. Floyd picked up another shard and the whole thing began again: examine, reject, command, sweep. After the fourth or fifth cycle, I remembered I had to piss.

And then I remembered I had the bathroom pass.

I headed for the locker-room.

"Evidence?" the Chewer was complaining to Hector. "More like garbage for the garbage dump. Sweep! —Oh well, oh hey, just look at who it is." Who it was was me. "Halt it," Floyd said. So I halted at center-court, my heels on the gnarled and overwrought nose of the floor's red, murder-eyed Chief Aptakisic. Floyd came out of his crouch and approached, stumbling on his way on a pile of rocks that was stacked at the top of the key—the rocks scattered—and, once he'd recovered his footing, said to Hector, "Re-organize the admissable evidence and secure it somewheres safe, preferably outside the scene here so no one has to break his neck on the way to apprehend suspects is a lesson we'd do better to learn fast rather than later, Hec."

Hector hopped to action without a word. He was as quiet as Leevon. I'd never heard him speak, but usually he smiled. And he always walked on his toes. He wasn't smiling when he pushed the rock-pile to the corner with the pushbroom, but he did walk on his toes, and I looked away feeling like a shmuck for noticing because "Does Floyd the Chewer really believe the Deerbrook Park Police Force, who probably doesn't even have a crimelab, will run fingerprints on all of those rocks?" is what Hector must have been wondering. It is what anyone but Floyd—who not only seemed to believe the scoreboard's damager might have touched the shards as well as the rocks, but that he could see, with his naked eye, whether the damager had done so—would have been wondering, but no one so much as Hector, who, if he didn't wonder about the fingerprints, would have surely had to wonder why he was taking orders from a man like Floyd.

"They always return to the scene of the crime, Hec," Floyd said. "You hear what I just said, Gurion?"

I didn't, I said.

"Didn't what? I didn't ask you about doing anything. You hear that, Hec? I ask him if he heard what I said to you and he starts in about how he's innocent. Innocent of *what* is my question. Far's I can tell, we've got a guilty conscience on our hands. What didn't you do, Gurion?"

I didn't hear what you said to Hector, I said.

"Just now, you mean? Or originally?"

I said, Originally.

"Right, right. You didn't hear. Says he didn't hear, Hec. Well, I'll tell you what, then, Gurion: I was just telling Hector over there about how they always return to the scene. Of the crime. Now, let's talk, you and I, man to man. Off the record. You won't see me taking notes. I don't even have a pencil to take notes *with*. You want a pencil, you see Jerry over by the front entrance. He's got a pencil. Keeps it in his cap. I'm the one's got the cone. So where were you this morning at such-and-such a time?"

With my mom, I said. I said, I really have to pee.

The bladder is a mystery. I'd had to piss bad in the Office, and then I didn't, and then it was stabbing me again.

"Tie it in a knot there, kid, because my next question's a zinger," said Floyd. "My next question is how come when I ask you about where were you at such-and-such a time this morning, you're so quick with an alibi that's your mom when I didn't even specificate the exact time? Are you trying to tell me that you, who we were put on alert for by Brodsky himself because he was ditching the ISS, were with your mom *all* morning?"

All morning, I said, and I've been in the Office since noon and I have a pass, and I need to piss.

"Let's have a look-see," Floyd said. "Let's. Have. A look. See."

I flashed the pass, and Floyd looked dizzy. The two conflicting protocols—ALLOW STUDENTS WITH PASSES TO PASS vs. OBEY ALL ORDERS GIVEN BY BRODSKY UNTIL OTHERWISE ADVISED—were melting his circuits. He was mumbling to himself. "Looksy. Look *see*? Look see. Looksy?"

My wang ached hotly and my thigh-muscles were jumping. I thought: Ten times a day. The bladder is a mystery and Maimonedes was smart.

I said, Floyd, you can take me to the Office after I go to the bathroom, or you can take me to the Office after I piss on your shoes. I said, In ten seconds, I will pull out my wang and piss on your shoes.

Floyd tilted his head and made a mock-curious face he scratched the cheek of with his swearfinger and said, "Fine then. But only because maybe I have to use the facilities myself, and so I'm going with you so don't even think about escape."

I walked fast into the locker-room with Floyd at my heels. I would have run, but I thought running would cause piss to leak. Floyd overtook me by the window of Desormie's office. I saw purple spit-droplets jumping out from the bell of his cheering cone, which flailed at the end of its wrist-string, and I had to slow up so I wouldn't get spattered.

Floyd went to the urinal farthest from the door, and six seconds later, while I planted myself before the middle one, I heard the sound of his zipping. By the time I was unzipped, he was already headed for a stall, grumbling into his cone about what a creep I was.

I pissed so hard the soap flipped twice, and when I was done I said, Floyd, back in the nineties, did anyone ever call you a Two-Point-Five?

And Floyd said, "What?"

I said, I saw this movie once called *Boyz in Da Hood*, which was about gangsters in Compton in the nineties, and all the gangsters in the movie called the cops 'Five-Oh' and I asked Benji Nakamook why they called them that and he asked his cousin, and his cousin told him it was because cops in LA drove Mustang 5.0s, which were really fast.

"So what?" Floyd said, not pissing anymore, not flushing, just waiting behind the stall door, trying to save face.

So they were called 'Five-Oh,' I said.

"So you're asking did anyone call me 'Five-Oh' in the nineties?"

No, I said, they called real cops 'Five-Oh' in the nineties. I'm asking if anyone ever called you 'Two-Point-Five.'

"I don't think so," he said. "I can't remember anyone ever calling me that."

I washed my hands. Floyd fake-moved his bowels for another minute. The metal rectangle on the door between the bathroom and the locker-room read WE DAMAGE in drippy Wite-Out.

□ □ □ □ □ □ □

Benji Nakamook, Leevon Ray, and Vincie Portite were waiting in the waiting chairs when we got to the Office. Just past the threshold, Floyd went hipshot like an R&B diva on a magazine cover or an infantry general getting sculpted by a master. Hands on his waist, he raised his chin high.

Vincie sat in the chair that was closest to the door, and as I passed him on the way to the ISS desk, he put up his hand and I punched his palm. The punch was automatic—we'd quit high-fiving a couple weeks earlier in favor of pounding fists.

Vincie grabbed my fist with the hand I'd punched, and slapped the side of it with his other hand. Then he did a kind of grinding of the slapping hand's palm against my fist-side, which was also unusual and confused me.

A folded square of paper fell to the floor when I retracted my fist.

I thought: A note from June.

Vincie stepped on the note so Miss Pinge wouldn't see.

Miss Pinge was distracted by Floyd the Chewer. She had failed to congratulate him for having brought Gurion in, and during the few seconds it took me to klutz Vincie's note-passing plan, Floyd had begun nodding slowly, knowingly, and making the noise, "Eh? Eh?"

I sat at the ISS desk, hoping the note said June loved me.

"Eh?" Floyd said.

Miss Pinge said, "Can I help you, Floyd?"

Vincie pulled his foot toward his body, but the friction of the carpet fuzz gripped the paper more powerfully than Vincie's sole, and the note got exposed, and again he had to step on it.

Breaking his victory pose to point at me with one hand and hold cone to mouth with the other, Floyd said, "That one over there returned to the scene of the crime that was perpetuated on the scoreboard in the gym." Then he put his pointing hand back on his waist and added, "Just like Ronny D and myself predicted."

Vincie tried dragging his foot really slowly but the carpet wouldn't let the note go.

"So where is Ronny D, anyway?" said Floyd. "He said he'd be in here if he wasn't in his office, and he wasn't in his office, so…"

Leevon elbowed Vincie and Vincie took his foot off the note.

"Ron's talking to Mr. Brodsky," Miss Pinge said to Floyd.

Leevon is stealth, but even when you're stealth, you can blur a periphery. Leevon made a blur when he bent to grab the note.

"What's *that?*" Miss Pinge said.

Leevon shrugged.

"Leevon," she said.

Leevon chewed thumbskin.

Benji ran distraction. "So," he said, "did you kiss June Watermark?"

"No talking to students in ISS," said Miss Pinge. "You know that, Benji."

Leevon flipped the note into Vincie's lap.

"You know you want to know the answer," said Benji. "Just let him say yes or no."

"I want to know," Pinge said, "what Leevon just did."

"But not as much as you want to know about Gurion and June."

"You've got the dimples of a con-man." Benji was her favorite.

"When's the chief gonna be done with Ronny D?" said Floyd.

"So?" Benji said.

I haven't kissed her, I said.

"Better hurry," Benji told me, "or she might start to hate you. I was thinking about that all last night—how I forgot to tell you about the way she might hate you if you wait too long to kiss her. It's almost always better to jump the gun than latestart off the line." He twitched his head sideways = "Pay attention to Vincie and Leevon." (I waited, so Miss Pinge wouldn't follow my eyes.) "Do you know why we're here?" Benji asked.

Miss Pinge said, "Benji, what did I just tell you?"

How long is too long? I said.

Benji never used sports metaphors, so I thought at first that he wasn't serious about jumping the gun's superiority to a latestart off the line— I thought it was just banter to throw Pinge off of Leevon. But then I thought how it was sound advice for a fight: It is surely better to strike before you're sure you're in a fight than to not strike til after the fight is on its way. Maybe kissing was like fighting. Lots of things were like fighting. Benji didn't answer me.

"I wasn't asking Gurion," Benji said to Pinge. He jerked his head sideways again for my benefit. "I was asking you, Miss Pinge: Do you know why we're here? Because those CASS's say one thing, but why we're here is another thing."

I looked at Leevon, who showed me his palm ≠ "Stop," but seemed to.

I squinted.

Leevon showed me his pointer ≠ "One," but seemed to.

Stop one? I mouthed.

Leevon shook his head = "No." He cut his hands through the air and showed me both palms and closed his eyes = "I'm starting over now."

"The CASS's say we're here because we started wrestling each other on top of the teacher cluster," Benji said to Pinge, "but that's not really true."

Vincie leaned forward and made his eyes poppy, faking big interest in Benji and Pinge while he formed the note tighter between his clasped hands. I wanted him to throw it. I wanted that note.

Once again, Leevon showed me his palm ≠ "Stop," but seemed to.

Five? I mouthed.

Leevon lip-bit, nostril-flared, shrugged = "Kinda, but wait. Let me finish the message."

"Botha wrote 'wrestling,' on those CASS's," said Benji, "like we'd just started wrestling, which would be a pretty hyper thing to do, but it was the exact opposite of that—we were totally in control. And plus we were only play-wrestling. And we were only play-wrestling because we heard Gurion had finally gotten to ISS and we wanted to come see him."

Leevon made a fist and showed me his palm again, but this time with the thumb down = "Four." Or "Kinda four."

Floyd cleared his throat. "Any working estimation of the length of this meeting of the minds between Chief Brodsky and my man Ronny D?"

Pinge didn't reply. She was listening to Benji.

Leevon made a fist, then he showed me three fingers = "Three."

Five (kinda), four (kinda), three (kinda)... Countdown? A countdown? Scoreboard? I mouthed.

Leevon nodded and smiled and stopped counting down.

But I knew about the scoreboard. Who cared about the scoreboard? I wanted that note.

At Leevon, I mouthed: I know. It is broken.

He shook his head and mouthed silent words ≠ "You know," but seemed to.

I know, I mouthed. I know, I know!

Leevon mouthed, "You don't know," and I saw that what I thought had = "You know" had actually = "You don't."

What didn't I know? I wanted to know.

He mouthed silent words that ≠ "Bet what didn't," but seemed to. I squinted.

"Bet what didn't!" Leevon didn't really mouth again, but seemed to.

I wanted to punch him a little. I wanted to punch us all a little. More than that, though, I wanted to understand the message. And even more than that, I wanted the note.

Vincie wouldn't look at me.

"Really, Miss Pinge. How long for the chief and Ronny D?" said Floyd. "Are they having a serious pow-wow? I don't want to stand around here giving the impression I'm just standing around here is why I ask. Because I love this job."

"I'm not sure how long, Floyd."

Leevon seemed to mouth, "Bet what *would* didn't," but that could not have been what he was mouthing, and I knew that—it was nonsense.

I waved Leevon off because I didn't want to want to hit him, and then I waved my legs around for Vincie's attention. He pretended not to notice; Pinge was still facing him.

"See, before we started wrestling," Benji was saying, "we told Botha to send us to the Office, and he wouldn't, and so we told him we would have to force him to send us, and still he wouldn't send us, so we play-wrestled each other on the teacher cluster. The teachers at the cluster scattered because it's not their job to break up fights, even fake ones, and Botha—he tried to break it up, but we put each other in these diametrically opposed holds that stalemated us and made it hurt when he tried to separate us, and I told him that. I yelled it so everyone could hear. I said, 'Mr. Botha, we are only

playing, and if you keep pulling on my knee my ankle will dislocate between Vincie Portite's forearms, and Leevon Ray's throat will fall on my heel
and he'll flatten his trachea and go limp on impact. Vincie Portite will then
drop nose-first onto the surface of the cluster and his septum will deviate.'
Finally someone yelled, 'Lawsuit!' and Botha backed off."

"Sure," Floyd said, "I mean being the guard of the Aptakisic side entrance ain't exactly crowd control, but I see it as a kind of apprenticeship and
I take pride in it, and the last thing I'd want to do is give you the impression
I'm just standing around like a lazy guy who's looking for any excuse in the
book to not do his job."

"Stand around all you want," Miss Pinge said to Floyd.

"Are you even paying attention to me, Miss Pinge?" said Nakamook.

"I'm paying attention! Jeez," she said.

"It seems like you're paying attention to Floyd."

"I'm paying attention to far too many people at once, Benji, but you're
one of them, okay?" she said.

I know what you mean, I said to Miss Pinge.

"Oh meow meow meow, Miss Pinge, my friends got in trouble just to
come see me and now I'm complaining," Benji said.

Baby, I said.

"You. Must. Not. Talk. During. I. S. S.," Pinge said.

"I'm not the one who's your baby, baby," said Benji. "June Watermark's
your baby and you should kiss her before she starts hating you and you
should be quiet because you're in ISS and I'm talking to Miss Pinge."

I haven't even seen her since yesterday, I said.

"Then she probably won't hold it against you," said Pinge. "Benji is
yanking your chain."

Are you just saying that to be nice? I said. I said, Because it's something
I would say just to be nice, if I thought Gurion's cause was lost.

"You're sweet," she said.

So you are just saying it to be nice, I said.

"No more talking, Gurion," Miss Pinge said. She said, "Finish your
story, Benji."

"Something blah blah Ronny D," said Floyd.

"Bet what would didn't," Leevon didn't but seemed to.

Vincie wouldn't look at me.

"We were in the stalemate hold, the three of us," said Benji, "and I told
Botha to write up the CASS's and the passes and put them in my mouth to

ensure that he didn't destroy them while we were busy getting out of the stalemate, and he did exactly what I told him, and I clamped them between my teeth, and then the three of us let go of each other, and Botha unlocked the Cage and sent us down here, but the CASS's don't say anything about that is what I'm trying to tell you. They don't say, 'I, Monitor Botha, am sending these students to the Office for wrestling because I refused to send them to the Office for *not wrestling*,' and they don't say, 'I, Monitor Botha, when given the choice between seeing students under my watch do mock violence, and seeing students under my watch do no violence, chose the first option.' All those CASS's say is 'wrestling.'"

"So Mr. Botha is a liar because the CASS's say 'wrestling,'" Miss Pinge said.

"Exactly," said Benji. "That's all I'm trying to say."

Leevon seemed to "Bet what would didn't!" at me.

I tried to break my fingers with diametrically oppositional force and they wouldn't break.

"So what about any updates on Ronny D and the chief, there?" said Floyd. "You got a potentially predictional ballpark figure regarding the time for their pow-wow's overage, maybe?"

"No I don't, Floyd," Miss Pinge said.

"You keep saying *Ronny D*. Is Ronny D *Desormie?*" Nakamook said to Floyd.

"You bet," Floyd said. He was so excited, he forgot to use the cheering cone, and Nakamook had to duck the spray off the "bet."

"The two of you go back, don't you?" said Nakamook. "That's why you've got such a great nickname for him, huh?"

"Came up with it myself," Floyd said.

"Maybe you should be a writer, Floyd, because that's really something," Nakamook said. "Don't you think that's something, Virginia Pinge?"

Miss Pinge blushed and looked away. She always blushed when Nakamook called her by her full name. He told me the first time he ever did it was the day he came back from juvie. He said he did it to be disrespectful, but that when she blushed he liked it, and after that he was never disrespectful to her again, even though he teased her the exact same way someone else would've if they were being disrespectful.

"I guess she really *does* think it's something," said Floyd, confused by the blushing, taking a couple steps toward Miss Pinge's desk. "And if Miss Pinge thinks something's something, well...a little something-something we might have indeed."

The spray of the P left purple dots of spit on Pinge's beige blotter, and her mouth went pinched and I wondered if she was wondering what I was wondering: whether or not it would be better for her to tell Floyd to call her by her first name. If Floyd started calling her Ginnie or Virginia instead of Miss Pinge, he'd have fewer opportunities to pronounce labial plosives, which meant less projectile saliva, but then also Ginnie and Virginia were more familiar than Miss Pinge, and it would probably encourage Floyd to further pursue the investigation of his something-something hypothesis.

I was weighing the pros and cons when Vincie finally flipped me the note. It landed in my lap and I made a very unstealth startled movement that caused Miss Pinge to look at me, so I left the note be and waited.

Nakamook picked up the slack. He said, "I think that nickname is a work of genius, Floyd. I commend you. If I had a thousand years, I don't think I could have ever come up with a pervier name than Ron Desormie. And if you'd have asked me to? I'd have told you *no one* could do it."

"Benji—" Miss Pinge said.

I grabbed the note, held it on the desk in my fist while Nakamook continued:

"You, Floyd—you did it. You *out*did it, Floyd. *Ron nee Dee*," said Naka-mook. "If I had a sister?" said Nakamook. "If I had a sister, and she was talk-ing to some guy in our backyard? And if my sister, she said to me, 'Benji, this is Ron Desormie'? I would kick him in the lower back, and when he fell, I'd drop a knee on his face and drag him out into the street unconscious so a car would run him over, and then he'd be dead and that would be that, but if I had a sister and I came into our backyard, and my sister said, 'Benji, this is *Ronny D*'? I would slap him on the neck and slap him across the chops and slap him on the neck again, then across the chops again, and I think it would be the end of me, Floyd. I think that *I* would die. I'd be like those lab rats from the filmstrip where they hook them to cocaine drips and the rats can step on the lever so the cocaine spikes into them and they always kill themselves fast because they can't stop stepping on the lever. If I were a rat in a lab, the slapping of Ronnie D would be my cocaine, Floyd. I mean, I could really slap the Jesus outta some Ronny D. Even dead—I'd just keep slapping him; even after he was dead, Floyd. I'd slap him to death, and then a few days later, in the middle of slapping his corpse, it would be me who was dead. I'd lose all interest in hydration and nutrients and I'd just die slap-ping him. You really nailed it, Floyd. You call it like it is. You tell the truth.

His parents might have named him Ron Desormie, but you came to know him, and you saw that he was really *Ronny D*. I mean, you're a robot just like Botha, Floyd, you're a real machine, a total gizmo, but at the same time, you're also the opposite of Botha, because you tell the truth. You should be a writer. Good job."

"Good job, Floyd," Vincie said.

Leevon shot Floyd with his pointer.

Floyd said, "Thanks to all you guys, but especially you, Benji. Sometimes I really don't know what you're talking about because you get all abstract like that movie *The Matrix Trilogy* and I think maybe you're being condescending to me like how a wiseass does. Same time, though, *The Matrix Trilogy* does have some pretty great moments in there where they're doing swords and kung fu and like that. And I like that. I like to think of those parts as 'the other side' of *The Matrix Trilogy*. And I can see that there's something like that in you. Like the other side of Benji. The other side of *Benji N*, if you get my drift."

Nakamook said, "Will you start calling me Benji N, Virginia Pinge?"

I was hoping Miss Pinge would face Benji so I could unfold and read the note in my fist, but "Whatever you say, Benji," she said, looking at me.

"Benji *N*," Vincie said to Miss Pinge. "*Ben ji Ennnn.*"

"Don't talk to Miss Pinge that way, Vincie," said Benji.

"Sorry," said Vincie.

"Okay, boys," Miss Pinge said.

"Okay, Miss Pinge," said Vincie.

Benji punched Vincie's arm.

"Benji!" Miss Pinge said.

"Sorry," said Benji.

"I was just saying *okay*," said Vincie.

"You weren't being nice to her," Nakamook said. Then he said to Miss Pinge, "I've got these lighters. These jetflame ones. I know a girl who knows a guy who has a cousin who works at a BP station where they sell 'em, except for the ones that go missing, if you know what I mean."

"I don't know what you mean," Miss Pinge said.

"Well but *who* do you know? That's what I mean. Who do you know, Virginia Pinge? You know me, don't you, Ginnie-Gin Pinge?"

"Nice one!" said Floyd. "Especially for a beginner."

"You know *me* is what I'm getting at," Nakamook said, "and I happen to have some jetflame lighters that went missing, like ten of them, and

I'm trying to tell you that the fire comes out of the firehole like fire from a blowtorch, or the butt of a fighter-jet. On ignition there's a hissing noise that ramps up the excitement. I want you to have one. I want to give you one. You'll find new joy when you light your cigarettes."

That got her to finally look at Benji. I unfolded the note.

"I'm not a smoker," Miss Pinge said. "And what's more, I sincerely hope you're not telling me you have these lighters here at school."

"G-Gin-P's right," said Floyd, "because lighters belonging to students are grounds for actionable displination when we're talking about having them on school grounds, be they inside lockers, desks, or even pockets, which are searchable with due cause of suspicion."

"Would I bring lighters on school grounds?" Benji said to Miss Pinge. "Do you think I'd do that, Floyd?"

"That totally depends on you and only you," said Floyd.

"Either way, Benji, I'm not a smoker," Miss Pinge said.

"Of course not," said Benji. "*Smoker* is a label. There's no need to label things. We all know that. And we all know you smoke cigarettes, too, and all I'm saying is I'd like to give you one of these crack-lighters that I have because I'm fond of you, and I hope you'll accept my offer."

"If you take that lighter from him, Miss Pinge, you can't use it to smoke on school grounds," Floyd said, "because it's against the rules and you'll get in trouble, unless of course someone who has the power to look the other way when you use it to smoke cigarettes looks the other way when that happens."

The note said:

> Dear Gurion,
>
> I am an Enemy of Botha and an Enemy of the Indians and of the Cage and Aptakisic. I am an enemy of the whole Arrangement and I want to join the Side of Damage. They said they'd tell you what I did with your gift. If what I did was not enough then tell me what to do and I will do it. I am sick of fuct rules and fuct tears and fuct tapelines. Let me be a soldier.
>
> WE DAMAGE WE

I thought: This note is not a love letter from June.

And then I thought: *Your gift?*

"Give me the note, Gurion," Miss Pinge said.

I ripped the writing from the note and handed her the blank part.

Fuct tears? I thought. What was torn? And who did I give a gift to?

"The whole note, Gurion," Miss Pinge said.

"Bet what would didn't," Leevon didn't mouth but seemed to, while doing the countdown with his hand.

I crumpled the note's remnant.

Maybe the "ea" was hard and the *fuct tears* the wet kind? Did *gift* mean "talent"?

"Gurion," Miss Pinge said.

I thought: The countdown = "The scoreboard."

I tossed the remnant to Leevon.

"Leevon," Miss Pinge said.

Bet what would didn't—the scoreboard. Wet tears and talent.

Leevon popped the remnant in his mouth.

"Leee eee von," Miss Pinge said.

I saw I was right the first time: *Gift* meant "present," not "talent." Whatever the note's writer had done, he could not have done it with any talent of *mine.*

Bet what would didn't—the scoreboard.

So wet tears and a present. Or ripped tears and a present. What present had I given?

Brodsky's door opened.

"Don't be sad, Miss Pinge," said Benji. "We like you."

"Well just speak of the ding-dang devil!" Desormie said from Brodsky's doorway. Then he made the noise "Tch" at us = "You are immature non-basketballers without intestinal fortitude."

What I thought had been a "You know" from Leevon had actually been a "You don't."

"Bet what would did*n't?*" Or "Bet what would did *it?*"

They said they'd tell you what I did with your gift.

"Ronny D," said Benji.

"Ronny D," said Floyd, "I caught that one at the scene, just like our prediction forecasted we would."

"Wasn't him, Floydinator—it was them. Or one of them. Or two of them."

Bet what would *did it.* And the scoreboard.

"Who's up first?" said Brodsky, flipping through CASS's.

"Benji," Miss Pinge said.

"*What's* on first," said Benji. "Who's the one on second."

Bet what would did it—the scoreboard.

"Floydinator is a suck nickname," said Vincie.

"I'm not the one came up with it," said Floyd.

"Heck is wrong with you?" said Desormie.

Wet tears from eyes, the Boy Who Cried Wa-Wa.

I'd had Vincie give the kid three blank passes.

Ben-Wa Wolf did it. The scoreboard.

□　□　□　□　□　□　□

Some minutes later, the pencil-cup jumped as Benji, returning from Brodsky's office, smacked Miss Pinge's desk. The jetflame lighter was under her hand before the cup's contents finished rattling. Pinge was stealth.

Brodsky had startled at the sound of the smack, but instead of looking at the desk, he took a fast breath and said, "Inappropriate, Benji. That's what we mean by *acting out*. I asked you if you could live with the way our conversation concluded, and you told me you could and I believed you. Do we need to go back inside and talk some more?"

"No," said Benji, chewing a half-born smile to death. "I'm content with our mutual decision that I continue serving detention indefinitely. I was just feeling a little hyperactive for a second. It happens. I was acting out, like you said."

"Get a pass and go back to the Cage," said Brodsky.

As soon as Brodsky had closed his door for his meeting with Leevon, Miss Pinge pushed the lighter in Benji's face and told him, "That wasn't a very smart thing to do."

"It worked out fine," Benji said.

"Take it," she said, waving the lighter, blinkering it.

"It's yours," said Benji. "It always has been."

"And how did you know I'd cover it up when you put it on my desk like that? How do you know I won't tell Mr. Brodsky that you've been carrying a lighter around?"

"You would never do that, Miss Pinge, because then Benji would get in trouble," said Vincie.

"I'm throwing it away," she said.

"Whatever you want to do with it, it's yours," said Benji. "Just try it out once before you junk it so you can see how cool it is."

She put the lighter in her purse, saying, "I'm throwing it away as soon as I get home." She scribbled on a hall-pass and handed it over.

"See you after school," Benji said to me. "Bus circle, yeah?"

I said, I'm not going there today. I'm meeting June in the cafeteria.

"Nice!" he said. "I'll walk you."

Miss Pinge threw her arms up and shook her head side to side = "It will be more aggravating to enforce the no-talking-to-students-in-ISS rule than to just let them say goodbye."

"I'll come too," Vincie said.

No, I said. I said, It's gonna take too long for you guys to get out of the Cage. By the time we get there, I'll only have twelve minutes before detention. I want fifteen. I can have fifteen if I go straight there and June also goes straight there.

"You don't know if she's going straight there?" said Vincie.

She said she'd meet me in detention today, but we weren't clear on the time, I said.

"It's better if she gets there first," Benji said. "You don't want to be the one waiting."

"You don't want to sit there and get all worked up and nervous and then screw up the big first kiss," said Vincie.

"That's got nothing to do with anything," said Nakamook. "Vincie doesn't know anything," he said. "If you're waiting for her, you'll look anxious. You don't want to look anxious."

I am anxious, I said.

"You don't want to *look* anxious," said Benji. "You want to kiss her, and if you want to kiss her, it's better you don't look anxious, right Miss Pinge?"

"I don't know about any of it," Miss Pinge said, "but anxious isn't usually an attractive quality."

"That's what I was saying," Vincie said.

"No it's not," Nakamook said, "and you know it's not, so you should watch out for that. What are you gonna tell Brodsky when he starts asking you things? Because when I was in there, he started asking me things, Vincie, not just about the wrestling but about the scoreboard which of course I have no idea about and I'm sure you have no idea about it either, but the way you're pretending to know things that you don't—worries me a little. What're you gonna tell him?"

"Nothing!" Vincie said.

"You sure?" said Nakamook. "Because it seems like you can't stop talking today."

"Whatever, Nakamook," said Vincie. "I hardly said anything that whole
time the Chewer was in here and it was cause I was practicing for silent-
mode, which you're screwing up right now by accusing me of things and
I have to defend myself. And don't say that's exactly what Brodsky is gonna
do is accuse me and so then I'll think I'll have to defend myself by talking because I know that's why you're making that fucking face at me you
fuckface I'm not stupid. Maybe it's you who's stupid for saying everything
you're saying in front of Mr. Brodsky's secretary, because maybe she doesn't
like you as much as you think she likes you. For all you know, she thinks
you're doing that thing you're always quoting about in weird old English
about exclaiming too loud of a doth protest or whatever and how it makes
you look suspicious and maybe she'll say so to Brodsky. I at least know the
difference between my friends and the Arrangement so don't start up with
me, just don't start up with me."

"Wait for us," Nakamook said to me.

Vincie ripped a sleeve off his T-shirt. He could get very explosive when
anyone ignored him, but especially Nakamook.

I said, It's like a lie to pretend I'm not anxious when I'm anxious.

Benji said, "No one's saying you should pretend anything. I'm just saying you should wait for us, and we'll walk you. If you agree to wait for us,
it's true you'll be a little late to your meeting with June and that'll make you
look less anxious than if you were early or on time, but that doesn't mean
you're lying. All it means is you told us you'd wait for us and you didn't
want to break your word to your friends."

But if I agree to do it now, I said, after you just said all of that, it's fakey
even if it isn't a lie.

"Fakey shmakey," Nakamook said. "If she asks you if you're anxious,
you'll tell her the truth. There's no reason to telegraph that you're anxious if
she doesn't ask, though."

I said, But if I *hide* it in advance—

"Gurion, say that detention comes around and you're in the bathroom
and it makes you late for your meeting with June, okay? When you finally
get there, to detention, are you gonna say, 'Hey June, the reason I'm late
is I was playing Victor Dumpenstein to this brown monster I was sadly
compelled to bring into the world?'"

Miss Pinge, who'd leaned in about nine times with the intention of telling Vincie to stop cursing and Benji to stop talking to me, made a gros-sout face and sat back in her chair.

I said, Of course I wouldn't tell her that.

"Right," said Benji. "Of course," said Benji. "You wouldn't tell her," he said, "but wouldn't not telling be fakey? I mean, if you were, in fact, a young Dumpenstein?"

No, I said.

"So why would it be fakey to not let her know that you're anxious?"

I don't know, I said.

I really couldn't think of why right then.

"So I win the argument. Agree to wait for us," he said.

I agreed to wait.

The whole rest of the schoolday, no one said anything to me except for Vincie, who mouthed "Ben-Wa Wolf" as he came out of Brodsky's while shrugging his shoulders = "Can Ben-Wa Wolf be on the Side of Damage or not?"

I shrugged back with squinted eyes = Ask me later.

I still wasn't sure what the Side of Damage was exactly, let alone how to make decisions about who was a part of it; I didn't even know if I was the one who should make those decisions. I was too distracted by my anxious thoughts about June and my anxiousness itself and how to make it stop to consider the possibilities with any rigor.

Plus I still had to write my ISS assignment, or else I'd have to be in ISS again the next day. And so what I did was, I wrote about distraction, and once I was finished, I was no longer distracted, I was no longer anxious, I was ready to think about Ben-Wa Wolf or the Side of Damage or anything else I might've wanted to think about, but no sooner had I handed the assign-ment to Pinge than Boystar's mom came in for an appointment, ushering a skinny, raccoon-eyed blond guy, a guy she bragged was "the best acoustics man in the business," and this guy was wearing a company trucker cap embroidered with the words *Sound by Highway 61* and a t-shirt for a metal band I'd never heard of—But the Angel Was Tardy—on which, in cartoon, Avraham opened up Isaac's carotid while a drunken-looking seraph who'd tripped on a vine lay on his back just inches away beneath a big speech bubble reading "Oh shit!"

Which of course got me anxious about June again.

□ □ □ □ □ □ □

Name: Gurion ben-Judah Maccabee
Grade: 5 6⑦8
Homeroom: The Cage
Date: 11/15/2006

Complaint Against Student (from Complaint Against Student Sheet)
Fistfight with Ronrico Asparagus and on on top of that assaulting Michael Bregman by spitting on the guy. Gym locker-room. 2nd Period. 11/14/06. Mr. Desormie.

~~Step 5 Assignment: Write a letter to yourself in which you explain 1) why you are at step 5 (in-school suspension); 2) what you could do in order to avoid step 5 (receiving in-school suspension) in the future; 3) what you have learned from being at step 5 (in in-school suspension); 4) what you have learned from writing this letter to yourself. Include a Title, an Introduction, a Body, and a Conclusion. This letter will be collected at the end of in-school supension. This letter will be stored in your permanent file.~~

Title
Kinetic Principles of Your A and H

Introduction

1. Attention (A) must fix itself on something. Once a thing is fixed on, that thing demands concentration.
2. If we measure A in units, and we assert that 100 units of A = the amount of A it takes to concentrate on one typical task (one fullthing), then most people in the world have exactly 100 units.
3. Some people, like me and Benji Nakamook, have more units of A than are needed to concentrate on a fullthing. People like us have 175 units of A. These people will henceforth be known as You.

Body

Hardly anything in the world demands exactly 75 A-units for concentration, let alone 175.

Normal Places

In normal places, ones that are filled with brief actions and randomness, there are, in addition to some fullthings, thousands of things for A to fix on that are not full. Therefore, if You are in one of these normal places, it is not unlikely that Your A will fix on a set of things that, together, demand exactly 175 units = It is likely, in a normal place, that You will be able to concentrate on whatever things You're doing = Your A probably won't get D'd.

Abnormal Places

In abnormally still and quiet places like classrooms, although there are many available fullthings for A to fix on—many available things that demand exactly 100 units of A—there are hardly any that demand less than 100 units. Fidgeting, for example, demands just 10–20 units, depending on the intricacy of the fidget. Another 20–30 units, depending on the quality of the sound, may be demanded by the task of listening to the background noise that gets past where Your earlids would be if You had any. But even if while concentrating on one fullthing, You fidget *and* listen to noise, 25–45 more units remain, and all of them must fix on something.

The Remainder

What the remainder fixes on will be the nearest thing, which—as You are in a place containing few brief actions and little randomness—is almost always going to be a fullthing.

Because a fullthing demands 100 units of A for concentration, the 25–45 unit remainder is insufficient.

But even if You don't fidget or listen to noise—even if Your 175 units of A are divided between only two fullthings—You are still 25 units shy of the A required to concentrate on both: While 200 units are being demanded by a pair of fullthings, only 175 are available, and that is why the fullthings enter into a cycle of thievery.

An Ultimately Doomed, However Momentarily Useful, Analogy

To understand the thievery cycle, it is a little bit useful to think of A-units as electrons—to think of A as being stolen back and forth between fullthings to fill their concentration-demands the way electrons get traded between bonded atoms to complete their outer-rings.

With atoms, the trading of the electrons happens at the speed of light—so fast that it is as if at any given time, each atom has a full outer ring, which is why it is only a *little* bit useful to think of A like electrons: A does not move nearly as fast as light, and so A is never as if in more than one place at a time. When demanded A arrives at one fullthing, that fullthing holds onto it for a second or two while the other fullthing demands it back; not only that, but the A takes time to travel from one fullthing to the other.

So then, with two fullthings demanding Your A, the following four arrangements cycle over a period of seconds:

1. Fullthing1 has 100 units and Fullthing2 has 75 units

2. Fullthing1 has 75 units, Fullthing2 has 75 units, and 25 units are traveling from Fullthing1 to Fullthing2

3. Fullthing1 has 75 units and Fullthing2 has 100 units

4. Fullthing1 has 75 units, Fullthing2 has 75 units, and 25 units are traveling from Fullthing2 to Fullthing1

In a vacuum, this cycle would repeat forever, but You are never in a vacuum. This cycle is only the beginning of a larger one.

The Larger One

Within a few passes, something, usually a fullthing, will get in the path of the traveling A-units (i.e., during arrangement 2 or 4) and the units will fix on that something so that now there are three fullthings demanding concentration = three fullthings demanding 100 units each. This not only decreases the frequency at which each fullthing within the cycle possesses 100 units, but increases the overall number of units being demanded at any given time. Worse than that, the amount of time that the A is in transit increases, which creates more opportunities for things—again, usually fullthings—to get in the path of your traveling A. The process thereby continues to degrade at an exponential rate. Nonetheless, it is not an entropic process. If it were entropic, it would eventually stabilize—single units of your A would come to free-float around the universe, fixing on and being stolen from so many random things, both fullthings and non-, that you could never concentrate again. That very sad kind of math, baruch Hashem, is entirely avoided by means of hyper (H).

A Blessing

H is a blessing. Here is how it arises:

After a certain number of things—usually between 9 and 11,

depending on how many are fullthings—have entered the cycle, the paths of the traveling A criss-cross and the A begins to act like a thing, itself = the traveling A itself demands A = You get distracted by the fact of Your distraction = You find Yourself paying attention to Your attention.

And paying attention to Your attention, You find Yourself.

Before, You operated as if the A *was* You, as if it was You being divided and shuffled between fullthings. But now that the A has begun to demand A, You—the most basic You, the part of You that never changes, the part that is always there, that has always been there, watching—You think: If I can *pay* attention *to* my attention, then I must be something other than my attention. You don't actually think that so much as You watch it get thought, yet it's at this point that You come to know, however briefly, that You are neither Your A, nor what Your A fixes on, but a soul. This is where You find out, for the billionth time, that You are partly God. If You were not partly God, how could something like A, something that emanates from You, demand anything of You? If there were no God in You, how could something like A, something that is completely subject to Your will, be capable of willing things on its own, much less things that go against Your will? It couldn't. And it is here that You become hyper = here You watch, in softer focus than is normally comfortable, every insufficiently concentrated-upon thing that Your A has fixed on at once, and You respond to all of it, at once. You do not necessarily respond in ways that are best for You, and You do not necessarily respond in ways that are best for the world around You, but You respond to everything. You respond to everything in some way or another because that is the nature of the most basic You, the nature of your God. The nature of God is hyper.

Conclusion

Unlike God, You are not all God (although God is not all *of* God, all of God *is* God: where much of You is made of something else like blood and bones and muscle, He has nothing but Him; He is only God minus the pieces of Himself that are inside of us) so You cannot remain hyper for all too long.

After a few minutes of H, the A units spasm like an overworked muscle. They lose their fix on the things they have fixed on, and the things they had been fixed on no longer demand them. Now only You demand them and so your A returns to You, a few units at a time. How long it all takes to amass depends on how far the units that were fixed on the farthest thing have to travel. Once it's all gathered in You, the A quits spazzing and the cycle starts over.

For Further Consideration

The question arises as to whether or not Your A can be aggregated with the A of other Yous in such a way as to satisfy the concentration-demands of fullthings.

I.e. Suppose there are 4 Yous. With 175 A-units per You, the aggregate number of A-units is 700, which is exactly as many A-units as it takes to concentrate on 7 fullthings.

So, if A can be aggregated, then 4 Yous should be able to concentrate on 7 fullthings at once= 4 Yous should be able to perform the tasks of 7 normal people within the same amount of time and space as it would take 4 normal people to perform 4 tasks. In concentrating on 7 fullthings, then—if 4 Yous can in fact aggregate their A to do so—4 Yous would not become hyper; the kind of A-unit slippage that leads to the thievery cycle that occurs when 1 You attempts concentration on 2 fullthings would never begin, for there would be no remainder of A-units in the case of 4 Yous and 7 fullthings.

And just because 4 Yous who are concentrated on 7 fullthings would almost definitely *look* very H to an outsider, that does not make it so. Looking H to the eyes of outsiders may, in fact, be to the advantage of 4 Yous.

E.g. If 4 Yous were soldiers, the 4 Yous could conceivably prepare for and maybe even launch a war's decisive battle right in front of their enemy without their enemy knowing it = The appearance of the 4 Yous' H-ness could provide a kind of cover similar to that of David ben-Jesse's youth or the Yiddish accent of that Palmach operative's telephone voice when he gave fair warning to the British. For what did Goliath see from across the battlefield? He didn't see a killer taking aim with a deadly weapon. He saw a boy inexplicably swinging a leather strap over his head. A moment later, Goliath was gone. And what did the British colonists hear when the operative phoned in the

Palmach's warning to vacate the King David Hotel? They didn't hear the voice of a stealth guerilla group that was about to explode British headquarters. They heard a nut with a Yiddish accent making a prank call. A couple hours later, there was one less place for the Brits to sleep, and quite a few less Brits.

The capacity to aggregate A would be a very useful capacity. Whether or not such a capacity exists, and how one (or 4 or 8 or 12 or 40) might engage it if it does exist, is surely worth further consideration.

10
ARTFUL

Wednesday, November 15, 2006
Interim–Intramural Bus

The tale of Avraham's tenth test is not about faith, no matter how bad any Israelite or Danish scholar wants it to be. If you're enough a wiseman to patriarch all Israelites, and you know you're being spoken to by Adonai—the same Adonai Who made your disobedient in-law a salt-pillar, your barren wife fertile at the age of eighty-nine—you do what He says because you know that if you don't, He'll do it Himself, then punish you and the world for your disobedience.

The tale of the tenth test is a testament to Adonai's mastery of language.

To Avraham, He said, "Please take your son, your only one, whom you love—Isaac—and go to the land of Moriah; bring him up there as an offering upon one of the mountains which I shall tell you" which ≠ "Sacrifice Isaac on the mountain," even though it seemed to, to Avraham.

And it would have seemed that way to me if I was Avraham, instead of Gurion reading about Avraham. If I was Avraham instead of Gurion, I would not have suspected God of artfulness. I would not have suspected Him of having built a sentence around loopholes. And I would have done exactly as I was told—exactly as I thought I was told. I would have brought my son up the mountain, prepared to kill him. I would have thought: "Better by my hand than an angel's, for Isaac is my son, not Theirs, and I will kill him better than would They."

But despite my sympathies with Avraham, it would be chomsky to insist that Adonai ever explicitly told him to sacrifice Isaac. He only told him that he should bring Isaac up the mountain "*as* an offering," which is a very slippery phrase, since it could mean at least a couple of things that ≠ "Sacrifice Isaac on the mountain" (e.g., "*bring* Isaac as you would *bring* an offering" or "*place him on a mountain* as you would *place* an offering"), so although Adonai didn't *lie* to Avraham, or even reneg, He did mislead Avraham, and He knew He was misleading Avraham, and that has always seemed shady to me. Avraham loved Adonai, and Adonai Avraham. And both of them knew of the other's love, but only one of them acted like he did.

To hide my anxiousness from June, then, was not to lie to June, and to show up second to detention was not to reneg on her, yet to do these things was shady. Whether she would consider my level of anxiousness or even notice I'd arrived second was beside the point—I hoped she would notice and consider (I knew that I would), and I knew she'd be misled if she noticed and considered, but I would show up second anyway. It is true I had a justification: I'd told my friend I'd wait for him. It is true the explicit trumps the implicit and that the spoken is a contract, the unspoken at best an understanding, and June and I hadn't spoken about the exact time at which we'd meet (I'd asked her in Main Hall the day before, leaning back on the lockers, sitting beside her, But how will I see you tomorrow? at which point Miss Gleem said we both had detention, and June answered, "That's how"), so the most we had was an understanding. But it is also true that I'd arranged my justification (or at the very least allowed for the arrangement of my justification by Nakamook) with no less lawyerliness than Adonai had placed His "as" in that shady commandment.

By the time Benji returned to the Office with Vincie and Leevon, I'd spent an hour hoping to be undermined. If only June could arrive second, I thought, despite my artfulness...

But that's not what happened.

We arrived at the southern doorway of the lunchroom thirteen minutes before detention started, and June was already inside, at the northern end— Benji'd rushed the last few steps ahead of us and checked.

He told me, "She's waiting for you. I'll shut this door and guard it. When the monitor comes up Main Hall, I'll give you a warning. Get to the other doorway," he said to Leevon and Vincie, "and if you let anyone in, or start spying on our boy, I'll pull your guts out through your mouths and feed them to Botha with a shovel. I'll cut your arms off and roll you down a hill like logs."

Vincie and Leevon went to the northern doorway. The northern doorway was doorless. They stretched their arms like tortured Yeshuas across the space between its sidewalls.

"Don't look so worried," Nakamook told me. "It's fine you're jumpy. It's a serious thing to be in love with a girl, but worrying is stupid. If she loves you back, it's because she can't help it, and if she doesn't love you back, then you can't help it. All you're about to do is find something out. You have no control over this. It's not a fight and it's not an argument. Don't strategize. And forget what I said about anything having to do with girls and how to kiss them. It was just talk. I was just talking to talk because it's fun to talk. Especially about girls. You look like you're about to cry. Don't cry. Don't cry and don't strategize. This is exciting. That's why you're jumpy. No one knows how to first-kiss anyone, Gurion. That's why it's so good. That's why you're so nervous. It's probably why you look like you're gonna cry."

If I was about to cry, it was because Nakamook had spoken over a hundred consecutive words without cracking a single joke, and he wasn't talking about killing someone—he wasn't even angry at all. He was supposed to act Nakamookian, not concerned; not like someone I could disappoint. And it wasn't only how he was talking, but what he was saying. I'd been worrying so hard about my shadiness that everything else had gotten blotted out. Over the previous hour, I hadn't once thought about kissing June, or what I would say to her, and now that Nakamook brought it up, I couldn't stop thinking: You are not only shady, but unprepared.

My throat was closing. I swallowed to fight the choke and a noise came from my neck like stepping in tar.

I'm not gonna, I said, cry.

"You'll cry if I tell you to cry, crybaby," said Nakamook.

It was the right thing to say.

I thumb-stabbed at his chest and he blocked it, flicked my ear with his swearfinger.

I thought: If she breaks your lobe, she breaks your lobe.

Benji stepped aside, kicking the stopper out as I passed him. The door closed slow and quiet behind me.

The curtains of the cafeteria stage were open. All that banging and sawing during Tuesday detention had been the noise of props being built and affixed to the stage for *Ponies and Rainbows*, a play I'd never heard of. Four rainbow-skinned rocking horses, rings in their noses, stood in the foreground. Ten wooden, 2-D, sitting-up teddybears smiled behind them. The bears were all day-glo, and larger than men, and their arms were stretched forward to hug.

June was at the lunch table nearest the stage, farthest from the door through which I'd entered. She sat the bench the same way lone cowboys sit horses, and stared at her lap, or something in her lap. She looked so much prettier than I remembered, it was impossible. How could I act shady to a girl that pretty? All I wanted was to kiss her lips. I didn't know how to start. I didn't know how to know if she wanted to kiss.

I thought: If she breaks your lobe, your lobe will stay broke, you'll be damaged forever, you'll never recover.

I tried to remember characters in books, how characters start kissing in books the first time. That was easy to remember. Characters firstkissed in many books. But I couldn't remember any books where characters actually moved from not-kissing to kissing, let alone to firstkissing. One sentence they weren't kissing and the next sentence they were. But what about the space between them? Before they kissed, there had to be space between them, between each mouth, and they had to close the space in order to kiss, but how did they close it? Did they just suddenly close it? Maybe they just suddenly closed it, I thought. It was possible they just suddenly closed it, I thought, but how did they know *when* to suddenly close it? How did they know if it was okay with the other character to close it?

I remembered that in movies there was sometimes some touching of hair. Almost always, actually. There was almost always hair-touching in movies, before the kiss. Or the ear. Was it the ear or the hair? It was the hair. The ear was something else. The ear was how you pick a fight in Fiji. My mother told me and I told Nakamook. A Fijian UN soldier once taught my mother you start a fight in Fiji by touching a guy's ear. If you touch his ear and he doesn't fight you, his snat trickles for the rest of his life because how could you let some guy touch your ear like that, like you were his to be touched on the ear by? You have to save face if your ear is touched by some guy. I told Nakamook once and he thought it was funny is why he'd sometimes go for my ear when we'd fakefight. And that was one way I knew we were best friends. Because my ear was a part of my head and I didn't explode when he'd touch it.

So I thought the way to start would be to touch June's hair. If I touched her hair and she let me, then I could bend my head sideways. If she bent her head sideways, then I could lean forward. And if she leaned forward, then I could press my lips against her lips, and then we would be kissing. The only way I'd lose face would be if she did everything but kiss me at the last step; if I pressed my lips against her lips and she didn't press back. She could say, "You tried to kiss me," and it would be obvious that it was true to any third person who might be looking, and there I'd be, a very trickling bancer.

If she didn't let me touch her hair, though, or if she didn't bend her head, or didn't lean forward, then I could stop touching or trying to touch her hair and sit back like normal, and my face would be safe because a third person could think that maybe I wasn't trying to kiss her, that maybe I was only touching her hair and bending my head and leaning forward. I thought: That is why this is a good plan.

But then I saw it was also a real dickhead way for me to scheme about someone I was in love with, and for a second I thought I was going to stand on top of a table and dive into the floor to flatten my neck discs because my plan was like Desormie making the girls sit in front for stretches. If a girl told someone, "Desormie makes me sit in front during stretches so that he can look at the contours of my vagina through the spandex," it would be impossible to prove. Desormie could say that the girl was a lazy stretcher and that he put her in front so that he could make sure she stretched the right way. He could say that she talked to her best friend too much during class and that he put her in front to separate them. Whatever he said, he would make the girl sound crazy, and she would look like a wolf-cryer, and people would want to know what was wrong with her and was her father touching her, and so her father would look bad, her whole family would, and her people. All of them would look bad because Desormie desormiated and the girl tried to stop him. Everything in the lunchroom looked like a weapon or a piece of a weapon.

The acids of my stomach stabbed me in the lining. The props on the stage would have been good to look at if one of them had a screwdriver in its forehead or the claw-part of a hammer. The claw-part of a Maccabee, I thought. Gurion Maccabee, I thought. Lioncub Hammer. Like the name of a secret war. Operation Lioncub Hammer. Like the end of the world. Gurion ben-Judah Maccabee. Lioncub, son of Judah the Hammer, I thought, but it didn't really help.

There was a fire-extinguisher mounted on the wall.

A weapon, I thought. There are so many weapons. Few people know it; you're one of the few.

That didn't help either.

I thought how if I tried to kiss June, I might find out that I was like Desormie.

I thought I could take the fire extinguisher off the wall and throw it high in the air and stand under where it was going to land so my skull would get bent and my brains would get softened.

If I touched June's hair and she let me and I bent my head and she bent her head and I leaned in and she leaned back and so then I leaned back, we would both know that I tried to kiss her, but if she said, "You tried to kiss me," I would say, "You're crazy." And that was a wrong thing to do. And what's worse is she would never say it. She wouldn't say, "You tried to kiss me," because she would know that Gurion would say, "You're crazy." It was cheap of me.

There were ovens in the kitchen behind the cafeteria counter. I could turn them on and put my hand in. I could burn my hand so bad that it would always look bloody and June would never let me touch her hair with it, even if she liked the rest of me.

There were thousands of millions of ways to be a coward, I decided, billions and trillions of googols of ways, and no less than half of the ways were ways to save face or ways to act so you could save face later.

My stomach hurt so bad, though. If I didn't try to kiss her I could get ulcers and become a tyrant. If I did try to kiss her, I could end up desormiating. I had my left fist up in front of my face to see which side of it would do the most damage to my nose if I punched my face and I was turning the fist when I saw the makeup flaking on the thumb-knuckle and I remembered the marks: that I was going to show my two ʾs to June. The ʾs reminded me of the Law. And there are no Laws about thinking. Not one out of 613. There are only laws about doing. And then I thought about Maimonedes again, who said that there is a right order that all things you can do should get done in. Maimonedes said it's just as important to do things in the right order as it is to do the right things. You don't build a house to live with your wife in until you're married. You don't make cribs for babies who aren't born yet. I decided that I could try to kiss June in the exact way I thought to try to kiss her, with the hair-touch and the head-bend and the forwardness first. I decided that it was the only right way to try to firstkiss someone. It was the best order because at each step she would have the chance to stop me, and I decided that was why I thought of it originally. It would be a cinch to stop me. She wouldn't even have to say anything to stop me is why it was the best order. All I had to do was pay attention. And then if she didn't want to kiss me, I would stop and I would not pretend I hadn't tried. Pretending was the only thing that would make it like desormiating, the saving face. Trying to kiss June was nothing like Desormie staring at vagina contours unless after failing I acted like I'd never tried.

Walking toward her, I felt clumsy, like the only thing bracing my bones at the joints was some old, shot elastic. If I didn't concentrate, my forearms would fall off my elbows. If I didn't lay my weight down in just the right way, then when I took my next step I'd leave a foot on the floor, and then the other foot so I'd be walking on my ankles, and then my shins would get left behind and I'd be on my knees, and next my thighs and I'd be on my waist, and then I would be bouncing, destroying my sack, and I wouldn't even notice any of what happened until my shoulder-socket dropped my last piece of arm and I couldn't put my body back together again. All I would have to defend myself would be the teeth in my head.

June touched her hair to push it behind her ears and it changed in darkness. Her hair had at least seventeen shades of red in it. The coat she was wearing to detention showed many of them off. She wore it over my hoodie. It was a long red overcoat made of wool. It had a hood of its own and five wooden pegs on leather strings that shoved through the buttonholes to close it for protection. The red of the wool was the same red as rich blonde women's lipstick in old movies. There was nothing on June's head that was the same color as the coat.

I sat down on the bench on the other side of the table from her. I sat forward like I would eat, instead of like a cowboy. It was hard to figure out where to put my hands and my arms; if I should put them in my lap or on the table. If I put them in my lap, they would be under the table, and if they were under the table, it would take a lot of movement to touch her hair, and also it would look pervy in the meantime. If I kept them on the table, though, then they would be between us, doing the movements my hands do when I talk, which is distracting to some people because I point a lot with my pointer finger and sometimes raise the thumb to make a harmless gun-of-flesh that I jab in the air or swing around in a fast way with snaps from the wrist when I am saying something important. I didn't want to scare her with wild hand movements and I didn't want to look pervy, so I balanced it out by keeping my right arm on the table and my left arm in my lap. But maybe I looked perved out and scary at the same time.

"A penumbra is a part of a shadow?" June said to me.

The lighter part, I said. On the border.

"It's a pretty word."

I took the half-pad of hall-passes from my pocket and set it on the table. I said, I got you these yesterday, so you can go anywhere.

June said, "I'm worried about you."

I said, I won't get in trouble. I'm stealth.

She said, "I know you're stealth. I'm not worried about you getting in trouble."

I told her, I missed you.

"And maybe you're crazy."

I said, I like your coat because it shows off how many different reds you are.

Her face blushed and she turned away from me, pulled her hair into a ponytail. When she turned back, she was wearing two hoods.

I said, The color of your blushing is exactly the same as the color of the freckles on your face. I was thinking that the freckles were red until I saw you in your coat. Now I know the color of your freckles and your blushing is actually a very light pink color. What's amazing is when you blush your freckles disappear. I've never seen that happen before. It's beautiful.

"No one else thinks it's beautiful," she said.

I told her, Everyone thinks it's beautiful. Everyone thinks you're beautiful.

She said, "No one ever tells me."

No one? I said. Really?

"No one I trust," she said.

I said, I'm telling you. I said, I think that what happened is that when you were a baby, when you knew some words but you couldn't talk yet, you were just as gorgeous then, and everyone who saw you would say how gorgeous you were and you knew what it meant, but you couldn't say anything because you didn't know how to speak, and so you blushed because you knew how to do that, and you knew it meant thank you, even though you've forgotten now. And so one day—

June said, "Gurion," = "Stop/Go on," and then she smiled like she was getting tickled and she liked getting tickled but she didn't want to like getting tickled.

I said, One day your mom took you out somewhere, like to the beach, to Oak Street Beach, and you were on a striped blanket the size of a bath-towel and it was such a hot day that half of Chicago was there and so people kept walking by you non-stop, thousands of them, and they all saw you and said how gorgeous you were and you kept blushing to say thank you, and that is how you got your freckles, because you blushed so much that the freckles got left behind permanently, like the wrinkles my father has at the sides of his eyes from squinting while he reads. It looks like he is always reading and it looks like you are always saying thank you.

"Shh."

I said, The reason people don't tell you how gorgeous you are without cease is that they think you can read their minds because of the way your freckles make you look like you're always saying thank you, which is lucky for you, since I'd imagine that conversation would get old fast.

I took a breath.

"So you don't think I can read your mind?" June said.

I said, No one can read my mind, June. Not even God. Maybe you can read my face, though, like Him. But even if I knew you could read my face, I would still tell you you're gorgeous. Because you make me into a kind of sissy is why I tell it to you. Because I am scared not to tell you because I am scared that if I don't tell you, it will cripple me from the inside not to tell you and I'll become a tyrant because I am in love with you.

She said, "Stop."

I said, And plus your hair is no less than seventeen separate shades of red.

She said, "Stop it, Gurion." Then she took the barrel of the gun of my hand and closed it and then she closed the thumb so I had a fist and she pushed the fist down onto the table between us and turned it over so the fingernails-side was up. She undid the fingers and pressed both of her hands on top of my open one.

It was quiet and it would have been the perfect time to start trying to kiss her by touching her hair with my hand that was under the table, but I was way too nervous to reach it up. We stared at each other very hard in the eyes, but not like a staring contest, and mine got heavy in the sockets and then numb and then I was about to start crying, but June started crying first, so I didn't. But it was not like a crying contest.

I said, Why are you crying?

She said, "I am sad and worried."

I said, Why are you sad and worried?

She said, "Because what if you die?"

What was wrong with everybody?

I told her, I won't.

And then it made *me* sad and worried because what if *she* died? People died all the time, and what if June died? What would happen then? I was sitting there, across from her, and it was so much better than before when I wasn't, when I was only thinking of her. And before, at least, I knew I'd soon sit across from her. If I couldn't even walk around knowing that, though... If I knew that I could never see her again, I would have to go crazy. Time would pass and June would become like Hashem's revelation at Sinai, like manna, like the parting of the sea, and I'd have to suspect that maybe there never really was a June I knew, let alone a June I loved, that she was only a person I once longed to believe and failed to fully believe had ever existed. I'd tell myself lies and believe my own lies, or else I'd have to go an even worse kind of crazy.

"I was sketching," she said. She let go of my hand and took a sketchbook out of her lap. Then she stopped sitting cowboy-style so she could face me with her whole body. I looked at the picture in the sketchbook. It was a picture of a boy in the center of a large room kneeling on the chest of another boy in a way that made it look like he was trying to pull the second boy's face off, but neither boy had a face.

I said, The boys have no faces.

She said, "It's a sketch. I don't know who they are yet."

June wasn't crying anymore and she touched her face with her arm to get the tears off. The tears got trapped in the overcoat fibers. They didn't smear. They shivered like raindrops on a windshield on a highway when she set her arm down on the table. She said to me, "So do you like the drawing?"

I said, I don't know.

June said, "Good."

I said, Good?

"If you don't know," she said, "it is bad to pretend like you do."

I didn't say anything

She said, "Everyone is a liar."

I didn't say anything.

She said, "You are a liar."

I didn't say anything.

She said, "I'm a liar, too, but it doesn't matter if we're liars, as long as we lie about the same things." She said, "What do you have to show me?"

I couldn't remember which wrist had the י on it, so I pushed both her sleeves back and turned her hands over so the soft sides of her wrists were facing the ceiling. They both had a י.

That's amazing, I said.

"What?" June said.

I pushed her wrists right next to each other so they were touching.

I rubbed the backs of my thumbs on my jeans til my skin burned. The makeup came off and I put my fists on the table, pinky-sides down. She saw my יs.

She looked a little freaked out.

I said, Are you freaked out?

"It's weird," she said.

Do you know what it says? I said.

"What what says?" she said.

The letters.

"They're letters?"

They're an abbreviation of Adonai's best written name. It's such a good name, most people can't even pronounce it.

"Whose name?" she said.

God's name, I said.

"He has another name?"

He has a lot of names, I said. I said, Don't you go to Hebrew school?

She said, "I'm Unitarian."

I said, What's that?

"I don't know," she said. "We don't go to Hebrew school."

But you're an Israelite, I said.

"No," she said.

Come on, I said, you know what I mean—a Jew. You're a Jew, right?

"I'm not," she said.

I started to get up to get on the stage, to swing a rocking horse at a teddybear-head and snap the head off at the neck and then smash the rocking horse against the floor of the stage and chew on the head of the bear. It was all very clear in my mind what I would do.

Then June was standing up. She was hugging herself while I climbed over the table to go up the stage-steps to smash the prop monsters. I was walking up the steps and she said, "You don't like me anymore."

I was on the stage and I had a rocking horse by the nose ring. I held the nose ring in both hands and I dropkicked the horse in the front of the chest and its nose broke off. I hit the floor on my back while the rocking horse's body flew back to the back of the stage and crashed into a teddybear. The teddybear fell. I was laying there, holding the nose ring. June came up the steps of the stage.

I said, I'm in love with you. It's everything else—these fucked-up props.

June dragged a teddybear to the back of the stage and laid it on a slant against the rocking horse I'd dropkicked. She jumped on the teddybear and it snapped in two. The jump jarred her hoods. The outer one was off completely, and mine hung onto her ponytail's cinched part. She pulled it back on and I hid my eyes, pressing my forehead into the stagefloor.

Then June was standing next to my body.

I said, I want to marry you. Do you want to marry me?

June said, "I do."

I rolled onto my back. I said, But you're not an Israelite. It's impossible. She laid down next to me.

"You're so dark," she said. "You don't have to be so dark. I'll convert."

I said, But what about the Unit god? I mean the Unity god? I mean what about your parents? Won't you be scared of the wrath of the Unit or the Unity or Unitary god that will come down on your head for betraying your parents?

She said, "My parents don't care and their god has no wrath."

What kind of God has no wrath? I said.

"Tell me," she said.

Your parents' god is nothing, I said. There's only one.

June said, "Okay."

What does that mean? I said.

She said, "I'm an Israelite."

You still have to convert, I said.

"So convert me," she said.

Could I convert her? There was a ceremony that couldn't be performed there, on the stage—that is true. You needed a mikvah to perform the ceremony; there wasn't any mikvah anywhere in sight. Even if we had a mikvah on the stage, though, I wouldn't be allowed to perform the ceremony, but the ceremony, in the end, was mundane. In the end, when it came to Israelites, converts or otherwise, you'd either been one all along or you hadn't. The conversion ceremony was more for the benefit of the Israelite community than it was for the convert; it announced to other Israelites that, all along, this person who was being ceremonied, despite not having an Israelite mother, was born with the soul of an Israelite, and no one worth listening to disagreed about that. That's why calling it "conversion" was bad English. Because to convert something means to change it, and to convert an Israelite does *not* change that Israelite. To convert an Israelite means only that you recognize that all along, regardless of who their mother is or how she raised them, the Israelite has been an Israelite, and that they will continue forever to be one.

I thought: June is an Israelite.

Then I counted off silently to seven, waiting for the No! of Adonai, the paralysis. He did not say No!, and I was not paralyzed, but then I worried that maybe He couldn't read my face, so I said it out loud in Hebrew.

I said, June is an Israelite, Adonai. I said, I will recognize that she is an Israelite.

I gave Him another seven-count, and again, there was no No! or paralysis.

I said to June, You're an Israelite.

And it was true.

I got up on my knees.

June got up on her knees.

I said, We will stand under a chupa my father will build out of trees from our backyard.

I touched her hair.

She let me.

I said, I will smash a glass beneath my right foot in remembrance of our suffering and we will drink from one cup before thousands.

I bent my head.

June bent her head.

I said, We'll raise sons who'll lead armies and rule righteous city-states, and we will never die.

I leaned forward.

She didn't lean forward.

I leaned back.

She laughed at me.

I was a bancer.

I pulled my hood on.

I said, I just tried to kiss you.

And then she leaned forward and I kissed her.

☐ ☐ ☐ ☐ ☐ ☐ ☐

At first it was all tick-tock. I kept switching which side of June's nose my nose was on and landed puckered ones rapidly. She did the same back to me. Our faces made smacking sounds and I couldn't understand why kissing was important. It wasn't that I was unhappy to be kissing her— I *was* happy—but I would have been at least as happy to thumb-wrestle, and even happier to play slapslap, if slapslap or thumb-wrestling signified what kissing signified.

For a second it seemed like maybe I was homosexual.

I thought: Are you homosexual? Maybe you're a homosexual.

I didn't want to be a homosexual. To be homosexual, I'd've had to like wangs, and wangs looked dumb to me: blind, fumbly animals needing sonar and lacking it. And also I'd probably have to like nuts, which looked even dumber—how they bulged out the sack, the way they'd flop and sway and that scarry line in the middle when it was cold. They were like brawn to the brain that was the wang atop them, and barely even that, for even when thinking of it as a personified animal, it was hard to grant the wang much beyond a basic invertbrate nervous system, let alone a brain capable of leadership, so the nuts thugged for wangs that were but stooges themselves; minions to lackeys were the nuts. It would've been too hard to be a homosexual. And plus I was in love with June, a girl.

Still, kissing her wasn't great. And if it wasn't great for me, then it could not have been so great for her, and it was obviously my fault. When she'd kissed me where my sideburns would be, that was perfect, but now that I was responsible for half the kissing, it was only a little bit nice. Something needed to be done.

She'd said she wanted us to lie about the same things, so I thought about asking her to lie with me about the meaning of slapslap—to agree with me that *slapslap* meant the same thing as *kissing*, and maybe even call the game of slapslap "kissing," so that if she said to me, "Gurion, let's kiss," I would put my hands out, palms-down and parallel, and she would put her hands under mine, palms-up, and we'd start to play slapslap. I would always give her the first turn, unless she'd made me angry before. If she'd made me angry and she wanted to make up with me, then when she said, "Gurion, let's kiss and make up," she'd put *her* hands out palms down, offering me first turn, and when I put my hands under hers it would mean she was forgiven. Soon enough, no one would even have to say anything about kissing or forgiveness—we'd just put our hands out to play slapslap and know what we meant. So slapslap would make a lot more sense than kissing, because slapslap wouldn't just signify love—it would also be fun to do.

I stopped switching nose-sides to make the slapslap proposition, but when I opened my eyes and saw her, the way her freckle-sprays were triangular and the colors of her eyelashes not black but one of the browner reds of her hair, I didn't want to play slapslap, I wanted to kiss her, which didn't make much sense, but we kissed some more, and it was more of the same tick-tocking, and I stopped again to look at her. The gaps in her top row winked, and we tick-tocked, and I stopped to look, and the lighter color of the hair above her ears that wasn't long enough to be ponytailed, and tick-tock and stop, the one-stitch scar that notched her cheek beside the left mouthcorner, a permanent dimple...

It was impossible to not want to kiss her while I looked at her, but no matter how bad I wanted that, once I was kissing her the kissing wasn't satisfying and I'd start thinking: slapslap. Slapslap's no fun with your eyes closed, though, and looking at her made slapslap impossible to concentrate on because of how badly it made me want to kiss her. Looking at her, I couldn't concentrate enough to even talk about slapslap. I was getting H.

There were freckles on her eyelids so I kissed the freckles on her eyelids, and while kissing on her eyelids I pushed her hood back and smelled her hair. It did smell sweet, though not as brightly as strawberries, not as red-and-greenly. It was a better, lazier kind of sweet than strawberries and it seemed to be made of smoke. If a hammock swaying in slomo between telephone poles in the poppyfield from *The Wizard of Oz* was a smell, that would be the smell of June's hair.

With my thumbs and pointers I worked her hair-tie back until the ponytail was gone. Her hair curtained down and I slipped my fingers into it, deep, the topjoints touching her scalp. Her hair was as thick as its smell, and I was glad to have my hands in it. I became *more* satisfied than when I was only looking, but still not really satisfied. I didn't know what to do.

"Keep your hands there," June whispered. Her eyes were still closed. She told me, "Close your eyes again." I did. She pushed my hood back and her palms on the sides of my neck felt fresh and this time our mouths weren't puckered when we kissed. And we didn't tick-tock. There weren't smacking sounds. June's lips parted to surround my bottom one, to press down on it a little, warm and slippery here, cool and steady there; she did these small pullings on my bottom lip and soon I did the same to her top one at the same time and something splashed bluely across my lobe, left-to-right, and I saw it on my eyelids like a waveform with tracers and these muscles in my temples slackened. I thought: Who knew the muscles in my temples had always been flexed? Who knew I even had muscles in my temples?

I thought: This is exactly what we should be doing right now. This is exactly what needs to be done.

June turned her head then, like she was arguing with my thoughts, saying, "No not that, but *this*," and her tongue brushed mine, and it was such a good thing, my hands fell from her hair. She squeezed my neck and our tongues brushed again and that is when the kiss became perfect. I couldn't tell my face from her face. I couldn't tell the difference between the movements of her mouth and the movements of mine. I couldn't separate June from Gurion. It was like being in the first and third person at the same time, the kiss not just something we were doing, but something that was happening to us.

I thought: This is not us kissing; this kiss is ussing.

Ussing? I thought.

Like hyperventilators getting breathed, I thought.

And then I heard this violent *chucketa-cracketa* noise like a helicopter crashing.

And Nakamook was shouting, "Goddamn!"

That was the end of the kiss.

The monitor, I said.

Across the cafeteria, pennygun in hand, Nakamook was racing to the bathroom. Right next to me rocked the rockinghorse he'd shot. It was not the same one that I'd dropkicked. Half this one's face was gone, and inside its hollow, busted head lay a black wingnut I reached in and snatched.

"That was a serious," June gasped, "kiss."

Pink ghost-shapes spreading all over her neck.

I pulled her into the doorway at the side of the stage.

Become the wall, I told her.

"Our stuff," she said. She kissed my chin and pulled me back out.

Miss Gleem entered the cafeteria, came fast in our direction when she noticed the props.

"Can you believe this?" June said to her. She smacked the wingnut-shot rocking horse on the back of his head. He bounced. Then rocked. June laughed. Nakamook sprinted from the bathroom to Main Hall.

"Who would do this?" Miss Gleem said.

"Some genius," said June.

"Junie!" Miss Gleem said. "Someone destroyed art."

"It wasn't art," June said, "until it was destroyed. It was a very badly executed set for a play, and someone made an installation piece out of it. I was just about to draw it. You see where my sketchbook is?" She pointed at the table by the stage where her sketchbook lay—covering, I noticed, the half-pad of hall-passes, baruch Hashem. She said, "I think that's the perfect angle to draw it from. But I want to draw it with this rocking horse rocking—that way it'll look like it's just been struck by whatever genius struck it with whatever it was he used to take its face off. That's good, right?"

"It's not good at all, Junie," Miss Gleem said.

I was thinking: Here we are, redhanded, and instead of being stealth about it, instead of hiding, June has shoved our redhands so close to the face of the art teacher that they don't look red anymore because they don't look like anything anymore, because they are covering the art teacher's eyes.

"You're right," June said, "it's not good. I can get it to rock the way I want it to by smacking its head, but the rocking will stop before I can get back to my sketchbook. That's why I'm showing Gurion how to smack the head. That way I can sit by my sketchbook, and Gurion can smack it, and I can get a sense of how the rocking horse's motion relates to its surroundings, which is, I'd think, one of the keys to understanding the installation artist's intentions. So give it a shot, Gurion. Let's see what you can do for me. Smack the horse."

"I don't think this is very nice," said Miss Gleem.

I was thinking: June is doing something new. She is doing a new kind of blinker action.

"Who cares if it's nice?" said June. "It's art."

I thought: GURION AND JUNE DESTROYED THE PROPS = the construction; GURION AND JUNE ARE STANDING RIGHT NEXT TO THE DESTROYED PROPS = the construction horse that draws attention to the construction; and JUNE HAS OPEN CONTEMPT FOR THE PROPS = the blinker on the construction horse that draws attention to the construction horse that draws attention to the construction...

I thought: The new thing is how THE WAY JUNE KEEPS GOING ON AND ON ABOUT HER OPEN CONTEMPT = a surge of electricity so huge that the blinker pops its bulb, and the flash of the pop is temporarily blinding, temporarily disorienting, and by the time Gleem's eyes adjust, she will be more concerned about the surge and the blinker than the presence of the construction; the more she worries about the surge and the blinker, the less the construction horse will seem to her to signify the presence of the construction.

"Smack the horse," June said to me.

I love you, I said.

"Smack the horse," she said. "Smack it on the head."

I smacked the horse on the head. The horse hopped, then rocked.

"Why'd you smack it like a sister?" June said. "Smack it harder, like this." June smacked the horse on the head. The horse hopped, then rocked.

"Junie, please," Miss Gleem said.

"Smack it!" June said.

I smacked it. The horse hopped, then rocked.

Other detentioners had come to the cafeteria. They filled up the tables in back by the bathrooms and they laughed. Miss Gleem revolved to face them and shook her head left-to-right = "Not funny."

"Just last night," June said to Miss Gleem, "Gurion's friend called me up to tell me how Gurion was all tough, and I believed him, but now— don't you think he hits like a little sister?"

Who called you? I said.

"Benji. Don't worry—he said nice things. Anyway," she said to Miss Gleem, "I need the horse to be smacked the way I smacked it, not the way Gurion smacked it—you saw the difference, right?"

"I think so," Miss Gleem said.

"Of course you saw the difference," June said, "but Gurion didn't."

"Some people aren't visual thinkers," Miss Gleem said. The voice of Miss Gleem sounded flat like a zombie's—she was so surprised by what June had been saying and by how happy the sight of the busted-up stage made the detentioners, who were shouting new words out like, "Knocking-horse!" and "Deady-bear!" that she was distracted from what she, herself, was saying. The surge had worked.

June kept it working.

"It's true," she said. "A lot of people aren't visual thinkers—especially the ones who designed this ugly set—but do you think, Miss Gleem, that since you can see how I want it to rock, that you could maybe smack it for me while I watch from the table?"

"I want you to get off that stage and sit down and I want you to think about what it would be like if some vandal destroyed your art," Miss Gleem said.

"You mean if my art wasn't actually art but set-design and my set-design was *suck*?" June said. "Because I don't think I can imagine what it would feel like if someone destroyed my set-design that was *suck* and I called *art*, because set-design is not *art* and *my* art is not *suck*."

Miss Gleem said, "Well, you try to imagine it, June. You try until you figure out how." She wasn't distracted from herself anymore, just really angry. "Get off that stage," she said.

While I followed June down the steps to the table where our stuff was, Nakamook was trailing Vincie and Leevon into the cafeteria. All of them showed us victory fists, and I showed them mine back. June kept her head down, her hands in her pockets.

Once we were sitting, she went at her sketchbook like I wasn't even there, and I thought: It's important to let her draw, don't bother her. But then, when Miss Gleem handed us our detention assignments, June started working on hers without saying anything to me, or even signalling anything, and I whispered to her, You are the mother of the hyper blinker action.

She still didn't say anything, or give any sign that she'd heard me, and I thought she was being stealth: I thought she didn't want Miss Gleem to hear us talking. But we had just kissed perfectly and I felt less alive not talking to her. Plus, the worst that could happen would be if we got another detention, and that didn't seem so bad at all. Still, I waited awhile to say anything else. I waited til Miss Gleem went to the opposite side of the cafeteria to quiet down some kid who'd started whistling.

You really tricked Miss Gleem, I whispered to June.

Again: nothing. Like she hadn't heard me.

I whispered a little louder: You really tricked Miss Gleem.

"I know that," June said. "You don't have to tell me that," she said. Then she kicked my shin, hard, and my knee banged the table-bottom.

From the other side of the cafeteria, Miss Gleem said "Hey!" but she didn't know to who.

"Did that hurt?" June said to me.

I said, Hurt?

I thought she was flirting.

"Hurt," she said, full-voiced.

She didn't sound like she was flirting.

"*Hurt*," she said.

"June!" Miss Gleem snapped.

June was showing me her teeth, but it wasn't a smile. Her jaw was shut and her lower eyelids were trembling. "Did it *hurt?*" she said, kicking at my shin again.

I grabbed her ankle before the impact. I was totally confused.

June kicked my grabbing hand with her free foot. I dropped the first foot.

It hurt, I said, it hurt.

June made the noise "Tch" ≠ "I love you."

"June and Gurion," Miss Gleem said.

"Sitting in a tree!" sang someone I didn't spin to look at.

"K-I-L-L—" sang Vincie, who then yelled, "Fuck!" because Nakamook had punched him.

I said, Why are you mad at me?

June said, "Stop talking to me."

I said, But why?

Miss Gleem said, "You've both got detention tomorrow."

"Tell me what I did," I said to June.

"Eliza June Watermark," said Miss Gleem, "you pick your things up and get over here. Now."

June got away from me so fast, she forgot her sketchbook.

□ □ □ □ □ □ □

Nakamook disagreed. He said, "She left it for you."

We were gathered on the curb of the bus circle by then—me, Benji, Vincie, and Leevon. June had cut out of the cafeteria as soon as Miss Gleem dismissed detention. I had run into Main Hall with the sketchbook but wasn't able to find her, so I went to the front entrance and looked out the window. Just buses in the circle.

I asked the Deaf Sentinel if he'd seen her.

"Show me your pass," he said.

Detention's over, I told him. I said, No one needs a pass anymore.

He said, "I guess I'm off-duty, then."

Robot, I told him.

He chewed his pencil.

I ran outside to the circle to look in the windows of the buses. No one was in the buses.

I dropped my backpack and tore my coat off. I swung the coat over my head and let go, but it only made me angrier, and cold. Puddles were slushy. Molecules were slow. I slammed my fist into the flank of bus 2. Blood went to my knuckles and my fingers got warm. I switched which hand held the sketchbook and hit the bus with the second fist.

The driver, who I'd assumed was gossiping like usual with the other drivers on the grassy island in the middle of the bus circle, came down the chunky steps saying "Hey." I'd never seen him before.

Hey? I said.

"Stop doing that," he said. "Don't hit my bus."

I said, You're not Marnie.

"Marnie's got the flu. Don't hit her bus."

I said, As long as you don't tell me not to hit it again, I'll only hit it once more.

I hit the bus. This time with my head.

"Jeez," said the driver. He got back inside.

My friends showed up.

"Your head's all red," said Vincie.

Leevon banged his head on Vincie's backpack, which was huge with textbooks. Vincie met the pavement on his knees and Leevon stumbled backward til he sat on the curb. When they got their bearings they wrestled.

Did you see June? I asked Benji.

"No," he said, "but calm down."

I said, I kissed her and I thought she loved it, but then she kicked me and forgot her sketchbook.

"She left it for you," he said, "so you could bring it to her."

I said, How would you know that? And why did you call her? She said you called her last night.

"I know because I called her, and I called her because, I don't know, man—you're in love with her and you're my friend and being in love with her's making you act a little, I don't know... out of character? Uncharacteristically insecure?"

Insecure how? What do you mean insecure?

"*That's* what I mean. And how you just *had* to be early, *had* to arrive first to detention. And the way you got about Berman. And the super-knit brow thing you're doing right now, like you're trying to make your eyeballs explode. *This* is what I mean. And I wanted to make sure she knew you weren't a dork, that you're dorked out only in this one specific area because you're in love and that is new for you, and also I don't know her that well, and I wanted to make sure she wasn't gonna somehow accidentally dissapoint...that she wouldn't...doesn't matter. That part was groundless. But look. You've got her notebook because she left it for you, but it's good here to hesitate. It's good here to wait awhile. Stop bouncing around like a spaz, okay? Joke around with your friend Nakamook and don't bring her that notebook. Just laugh like I'm saying a bunch of really funny stuff and make her come and get—look out."

A pebble struck me sharply on the back of my neck. I spun and saw June. She ducked behind a hedgerow halfway to the entrance.

"Don't go there," Benji said.

I went.

"At least slow down!" he shouted after me.

June was bundled in her coat, laying down behind the bushes.

I said, Why—

And she swept my legs out at the ankles. I fell next to her, still holding the sketchbook.

"Still love me?" she said. "Even though I'm mean to you? Even though I kicked you twice and hit your neck with a pebble and made you bring me my sketchbook and then tripped you?" she said. She said, "I wouldn't love you if you did that to me. If you did that to me, I'd think you were a dentist. I would think you were crazy, too, and I wouldn't trust you and every morning I'd bake a clay doll that was shaped like you, and every night before I slept I would smash it on the floor beside my bed and kneel on its shards with no pants so my legs would bleed and I could hate you even easier the next time. But don't worry about it, I disappointed my teacher and she hates me now, too, so at least you're not alone." I was too glad she was talking to me to be angry at her.

Miss Gleem doesn't hate you, I said.

June said, "I don't care."

I said, It's a little bit like what happened to me in Brodsky's office yesterday afternoon, and you told me—

"I don't care!" June said.

I said, If you didn't perform the hyperblinker action, Miss Gleem would have known you helped destroy the props yourself, and she'd feel even worse—so even though your hyperblinkering was artful, it was kind. You saved her some pain.

June said, "Go away, Gurion."

I said, Why?

She said, "I don't want you near me."

I said, Then you go away.

She didn't go away. She got up on her elbows like she was going to, but she didn't.

You just want me to think you're crazy, I said.

"Get bent," June said.

You want me to think you're crazy since I can't convince you Miss Gleem's not disappointed, I said. Because if I think you're crazy, I'll tell you you're crazy, and then you might believe it. If you believe you're crazy, you get to doubt everything that you know to be true but wish were untrue.

That's why you kicked me—because it was the kind of thing a crazy person would do. And that's why you're telling me to go away now—because it would be a crazy thing to tell me if you really meant it. And that's your secret plan, but it doesn't make sense.

"Why doesn't it?" she said. Her voice had less nails in it.

It's yossarian, I said. If I tell you you're crazy and you believe it, then you have to doubt that you should trust my opinion to begin with because how can a crazy person judge whose opinion to trust? They can't. They're crazy. So then you have to doubt that you're even crazy because the person who told you you're crazy—me—might not be trustworthy. And you come out with nothing that way. And so I come out with nothing. So I'm not going to tell you that you didn't disappoint Miss Gleem. And I won't tell you anything that would mean that you're crazy. You did disappoint her—not tons, but a little. And you aren't crazy.

"I hate that," June said.

Me too, I said.

I didn't know what I meant, just that I should agree with her.

"I hate worrying about disappointing people who want me to be a way that I'm not," she said. "Because I *did* think the stage looked better after we were through with it, you know? It looked fake before. It looked lifeless, but then when we destroyed it, it looked dead—once we destroyed it, it looked, at least, like it *used to* have life, you know?"

That was exactly how it looked.

We laid there, sighing. The sun was an ugly winter sun. You had to squint, but it didn't warm you. June rolled on top of me and pinned me at the wrists.

That's not how you pin someone, I told her. I said, Look at all this leverage I've got.

I shoved my chest up and bumped June's. Not hard, but just to show her.

"I know how to pin someone," she said. She pinned me at the elbows. "Keep your arms strong," she said, "so I can balance." Then she did a handstand on my biceps. Her hoods and hair fell down on my face.

Your hair is my favorite smell, I said.

"Mine too," she said. "It's not the smell of my hair, though." Her voice was croaky, ground-down—the muscles of her neck were flexed, pressing on her voicebox, her air-passage. She said, "It's amber resin. I put it in my hair."

How are you doing this? I said.

She came out of the handstand before answering and laid on me. Her stomach pressed on mine and then didn't, pressed on mine and then didn't. Her eyelashes were on my ear. She was blinking.

"I used to think I wanted to be a gymnast," she said, "so I became a master of the handstand." Her breath made my neck tingle.

I thought you used to want to be a modern dancer, I said.

"I used to want to be a lot of things," she said.

Me too, I said.

"Like what?" she said.

I said, I don't know... I keep spacing out on your body.

"I'm flat," June said.

I like your body, I said. I said, I like how you're pressing it on me.

"I can tell," she said = "Your wang is chung."

My wang *was* chung. It was supposed to be, because I was heterosexual.

"You said you wanted to be a lot of things," she said.

I said, I used to think I wanted to be a scholar, then a soldier—but now, whenever I'm near you, I start to think I've been confusing means with ends. I think I wanted to be the messiah all along and I didn't know it. I mean, I knew I wished the messiah would come, and a lot of times I wished I was the messiah, but the wishing—it wasn't *wanting*; there's a difference, I think. Like how everyone wishes they could fly, or walk through walls, or be invisible... There's no pain, you know? To wishing like that, I mean. Because there's no possibility. With wanting, though—there's some pain, I think... This is hard to explain... What I'm saying is I *want* to be the messiah, now. Or at least I want to *bring* him. Whenever I'm near you, I do. And I think that all along I thought that being a scholar or a soldier would help me become the messiah, or bring him, but—

June said, "How can you want something and not know it? I don't think you can. I got sent to a social worker for a while and he kept telling me I wanted something and I didn't know it, but what he said wasn't true and I stopped going."

What did he say you wanted? I said.

"I don't want to talk about it."

Why did you get sent to him?

"Stop asking questions," she said. "You're always asking questions when you're supposed to be answering them."

I said, Since yesterday—since right after you kissed me on where my sideburns will be—I've been thinking that all my life I wanted us to be in love, but I didn't know it, because I didn't know you.

"Oh," June said. Her left eye-socket was cupping my left cheekbone and she squeezed it.

But, I said, that doesn't make it so. Because you're right, I think. It is true that all my life I wanted to be in love—I have always known what *in love* is—but how could I have wanted to be in love with you, if I didn't know who *you* were? I couldn't have. You're definitely right that I couldn't have. But still, it has seemed that way to me since yesterday—that I've wanted to be in love with *you*, with *June*, all along—and that has to mean something. Now that I'm saying it, though, I think that *want* is the confusing part. It is *need* I mean by *want*, I think. Because you can need something without knowing it. I know that is true. Sometimes when I'm at my desk, I forget to eat and don't know I've forgotten, and my A gets D'd and I get angry and explosive and I don't think to myself, 'Gurion, you have forgotten to eat,' and I don't think to myself, 'You are hungry.' All I think is, 'You are fucking up. You are going too slow. In the time it took you to word the previous sentence, which isn't even a perfect sentence, Israelites have died.' Eventually my mom will call me downstairs for dinner and I'll go have dinner, and my A won't be D'd anymore and my anger and explosiveness subside a little. It is only after eating the dinner that I tell myself, 'You needed to eat and you didn't know it.' So I'm thinking the truth must be that all along, though I've *wanted* to be *in love*, what I *needed* was to be *in love with you* and didn't know it; and now, because on top of needing it I want it so bad, because I want it to keep happening, because I want to keep being in love with you, the wanting hides the needing and seems to replace it, even though the wanting actually has nothing to do with it. I'm glad I'm in love with you, I love that I'm in love with you, but it doesn't matter. Whether or not I want to be in love with you, I need to be in love with you. And yesterday, after you kissed me on where my sideburns will be, I started thinking that all my life I hadn't *wished*, but *wanted* to be the messiah, or to bring the messiah, and didn't know it, but it can't be true for the same reason that it can't be true that all along I've wanted you. I cannot have wanted something I didn't know I wanted, even if I wished for it sometimes. So it may be that all my life I've *needed* to become the messiah, or bring the messiah, regardless of what I thought I wanted, or knew I wished for. It may be that all the things I've done that I thought I'd done to become a better scholar or a better soldier were things I was doing to become the messiah, or to bring the messiah. It's like I've been a crying just-born baby who doesn't know he's hungry, let alone that he's hungry for his mother's milk. The newborn doesn't know who his mother is, or even what *mother* is. He doesn't even know what crying is, right? I don't think he knows he *is* crying, June. He's just doing what he's doing and it is only after his mother has begun to feed him that he begins to understand what he was doing, why he was doing it. It is only after he's been fed that he can know what hunger is. And so it is only then that he can choose to cry when he is hungry. Before he can go after what he wants, he needs to know what he wants, but before he can know what he wants, he needs to get what he needs. The world must come to him first. I've been as dumb as a just-born baby. Do you understand me, June? When I'm near you, I need to become the messiah no matter what I might want. Or at least I need to *bring him* no matter what I might want. But I want to become the messiah—or bring him—because I need you to always be near me. I need you to never die. Do you understand what I'm saying or not? Because I want you to understand. This isn't just me wishing.

She squeezed my body with all of hers until the buses gave off one-minute-warning honks for stragglers. Then we ran at the circle, June yelling a song that went:

> I am sorry I was mean to you,
> Gurion Maccabee!
> I kicked and I tripped you
> And said go away!
> I am sorry I was mean to you,
> Gurion Maccabee!
> I am so sorry!
> I was mean!

Kids piled up at the buswindows and stuck their heads out and looked at us. The ones who were shmendricks made faces, smooched air. Still running, I looked into the eyes of three of them, none of whom I recognized. Each of the three fell back from his window and ducked below the frame.

At the door of June's bus, she said, "I'm forgiven."

I said, Yes.

"I wasn't asking," she said, then gave me a fast but painful tittytwist. "I'm sorry," she said. "I'm forgiven."

I didn't say anything.

June said, "Good." She pulled her hoods on and climbed the steps.

I watched her make her way down the aisle til she got to the wheel-well seat and sat.

When I spun, I almost broke my nose on Bam Slokum's elbow, but he moved it just in time.

"June Watermark," he said to me, "is crazy."

Take it back, I said.

Bam said, "There's no such thing, kid. And no one's listening but you and I and I'm not even fucking with you, just giving you a friendly warning because she's crazy and crazy girls—they're dangerous, especially when they're beautiful. So lighten up."

I said, You're not my friend.

"I'm no one's friend," he said, "but that doesn't mean I don't *have* friends, nor does it mean I can't act friendly, and it doesn't change the fact that you need a friendly warning." He said it in the same yawny whisper he'd used on the bus the day before. He said, "You're ten years old and I've got at least ninety pounds on you and the way you're talking to me—it's like a Pomeranian or a Shih Tzu or some long-haired fucken Chihuahua in a blonde girl's purse baring his teeth at a Chow. You know what a Chow is? He's the most loyal guard-dog in the world, but only to one master. Pretty, too. A mane like a lion's. Comes from China. We got a Chow at my mom's house. He's hers. You want to pet him when you see him, his melting black eyes, the mane—he looks almost fake, like a stuffed animal, something to cuddle, but what he wants most is to tear the face off your head. And no warning, either. Chow's boundaries—not clearly defined. Maybe he lets you pet his mane, maybe his nose even, but then all of a sudden you touch him on the haunch, the knee, someplace you wouldn't expect was so personal— Chow bites all your fingers off, goes at your vitals when you hit the ground if he's in the mood, and if you're reckless enough to backtalk me, you're reckless enough to think you understand girls like June Watermark, and you don't understand her because she's crazy and crazy people—they're misunderstood. It's why they're called crazy. And you probably think you're in love with her—it's what Boystar told me you said in the Office, and that's a fine thing to *say* to a girl, even a crazy girl, but if you think you mean it, it's a different story. Because what's love without understanding, Gurion? A fucken lie it is."

June isn't crazy, I said.

"Just warning you," said Bam.

Busdrivers honked and I turned a little, saw Nakamook looking at me through his buswindow. I thought: You have failed your friend, listening willfully to this kingly basketballer's monologue.

"Bus can't leave without you," Bam said. "Not as long as you're standing here."

I said, I know.

He said, "Ah, right. Nakamook. I see him. He sees me seeing him. He saw you seeing him. Everyone's seeing everyone see everyone and it's twisting you up in the face because you think you've gotta do something to slight me to show him you're loyal. It's always loyalty with that kid, right? Loyalty this and loyalty that. Thing is though, Gurion, your buddy Nakamook knows me, studies me, is on the edge of his seat in terms of when he's gonna try to end me, and it's because he thinks I'm his enemy, and maybe I am, but why should you be worried about what he's thinking right now? Why is it your loyalty getting tested and not his? He hates me so much? He thinks I'm so dangerous, so untrustworthy and dangerous—why isn't he rushing out here to protect you from me, understand? There's two possible answers. One, is that he *is* testing your loyalty—and that ain't a very loyal thing to do to a friend, ain't a very friendly thing to do to someone to whom you claim loyalty; and the other possibility is he's scared. But if he's so scared then what does he expect of you here? Bravery? These questions are rhetorical. What I'm getting at is that's no dumb guy, Nakamook. He's sharp, right? Knows himself. Knows it's either he's testing you or he's scared, knows the implications of each, so how can he fault you for having a conversation with me? He can't. Not if he's your friend. And so how can you fault yourself? You can't help it that you like me. People like me. Even people I've hurt. Not *while* I've hurt them, but after, see. And I'm not hurting you right now. So what are you supposed to do?"

Someone honked a car-horn then. It felt like a rimshot. I revolved. The car was a Jeep. A Cherokee in Aptakisic's parking lot. Another rimshot. Behind the wheel: a high-school blonde guy, snowboarder sunglasses. He reached a bulgey arm out the window and smacked the fender. "Bam!" he shouted.

"That's Claymore," said Slokum.

Geoff Claymore? I said.

"Bam Slokum!" shouted Claymore from his Jeep.

"You want to meet him? We'll give you a ride. Tell you some stories about your pyro friend over there." He pointed at Nakamook. Nakamook looked puzzled and off-guard. His eyes looked glassy, but it might have been the bus window. "Look!" Bam shouted to Claymore. "It's Benji Nakamook."

"I thought that smell I smelled was pussy, not gasoline!" Claymore shouted back.

"Turned out it was both!" Slokum yelled. "Don't look at me like that," he said as he walked away from me. "Don't look at me all stunned. I'm exactly what's called for, kid, at all times, and wide open as your mouth may be, you're not calling for anything. You're just standing there, a little boy. Have fun on the bus."

11
TEACHERS

Wednesday, November 15, 2006
Intramural Bus–Bedtime

ANSWER THE FOLLOWING QUESTION IN 1–2 PAGES. BE
SURE TO HAVE A CLEAR THESIS STATEMENT, CLEAR TOPIC
SENTENCES THAT SUPPORT THE THESIS STATEMENT, AND
SUPPORTING EVIDENCE FROM THE TEXTBOOK TO SUPPORT
YOUR TOPIC SENTENCES.

THIS ESSAY IS DUE ON OCTOBER 31.

QUESTION

HOW DID THE EVENTS OF 9/11 CHANGE
WHAT IT MEANS TO BE AMERICAN?

9-1-1 Is a Joke
or
How We Did It at the
Solomon Schechter School of Chicago

Gurion Maccabee
10/31/06

Ancient/Prehistoric

Slapslap is older than giving the swearfinger. It is probably the oldest game human beings still play. The slappee holds his hands out,
knuckles-up, above the held-out, knuckles-down hands of the slapper; the slapper tries to slap the tops of the hands of the slappee, and
the slappee tries not to get slapped. Some slapslappers play a flirty,
unscored form of which the object is only to play the game, but most

play to win. You win when you score a previously agreed-on number of points—usually 13 or 21.

Scoring

It is always the case in scored slapslap that if the slapper attempts to slap one of the slappee's hands and connects, the slapper gets a point. Apart from that, however, the way the game is scored can vary. Whether the slapper gets one or two points if he slaps both hands, or no points if he only slaps one while trying to slap both; whether when he serves but fails to slap he loses a point, the slappee gains a point, or the failed serve is point-neutral (though never turn-neutral); whether flinching at a fake loses the slappee a point or gains the slapper a point, or balking on a serve loses the slapper a point or gains the slappee a point—all of these rules depend on what has been negotiated by the players prior to the game. And the same goes for when the players switch roles. It is most common for the slapper to become the slappee as soon as he misses. In some games, though, players switch roles after every point scored regardless of who scored it, and in other games a player plays his role for a fixed number of turns (usually 3 or 5), as in ping-pong.

Agreement and Disagreement

It is not uncommon for a slapper to slap so fast that a slappee doesn't see the slapper's hand make contact with his own, but the slap will always leave a tactile trace—usually the kind that stings. Therefore, when the honorable slapper correctly declares that he has scored, the honorable slappee won't doubt or deny it, for even if he failed to see it, he'll have felt it. Yet even between two honorable slapslappers who have agreed beforehand on a given set of rules, disagreements are bound to come up. The disagreements will not be concerned with slapping itself, but with flinching vs. twitching, and balking vs. faking, which, because they involve no physical contact, can only be perceived (or mispercieved) visually. Though never quite *resolved*, these disagreements are dealt with practically via one of two means: do-overs or rotating gimmes. Both options are problematic for the same reason: it is in the slappee's best scoring interests to claim that all flinches are twitches and all fakes balks; it is in the slapper's best scoring interests to claim the opposite (that balks are fakes, and

twitches flinches). And even among the honorable, who, by definition, do not make claims they believe to be false, self-doubt arises.
How couldn't it? How couldn't an honorable slapslapper allow for
the possibility that he saw what he wanted to see rather than what
he should have seen (i.e. what truly happened)? And how could an
honorable slapslapper with any bent toward rigor whatsoever fail to
question whether his opponent's ability to see what truly happened
isn't complicated by motives similar to those of which he suspects
himself?

One Solution

Most great and honorable slapslappers eventually end up playing a
form of slapslap in which the only way to score is by slapping, and
the only time a turn is counted is when a serve has been attempted.
In other words: balking and flinching are considered both turn- and
point-neutral actions, thereby making it irrelevant to distinguish a
flinch from a twitch or a balk from a fake.

This newer form of slapslap, which everyone initially referred to
as *simple slapslap*, has become so dominant in the past few years that
a great number of its adherents have seen fit to forsake the modifier;
these days they refer to the form, simply, as *slapslap*. And the name
they give to the original slapslap is *olden slapslap*.

On the other hand, adherents of the original form (of whom I
am most certainly one) have continued to call the newer form *simple
slapslap*, and to call the original form *slapslap*, even while—in order to
avoid ambiguity when speaking in mixed company or writing mid-
term papers—they will occasionally deploy the term *real slapslap* to
describe the one they love.

Robotness vs. Roboticness

Though I can understand the motivation to play it, simple slapslap
gets me worried and mournful. You cannot simplify what is complicated without subtracting subtlety, and thereby richness; and the willful subtraction of subtlety, no matter how practical it may be (or seem
to be), strikes me as a non-scholarly—even *anti*-scholarly—endeavor.
It is not true that a person's urge to erase or prevent controversy via
simplification necessarily indicates that he aspires to become a robot;
that urge existed before anyone even dreamed of robots. Nonetheless,

by giving in to the urge to render simple what could defensibly remain complicated, a person becomes more robotic.

Furthermore, real slapslap is just more fun than simple slapslap. The scholar Emmanuel Liebman once told me that the latter was checkers to the former's chess. I think that's an understatement.

Imagine the rules of boxing were such that boxers weren't allowed any footwork, were forced to stand in one spot in the middle of the ring and trade blows, one for one, the block their only legal defensive move. The champions would always be the soundest-bodied heavy-hitters. Muhammed Ali would never have lasted a round with Joe Frazier, let alone ever rope-a-doped Foreman. Eventually, as scientific techniques of measurement grew more advanced, boxers wouldn't even need to enter the ring, much less hit each other, to determine the winner of a given match; the same kind of violence-allergic people on the state boxing commissions who invented the TKO and made it illegal to fight for more than twelve rounds would employ hack physicists to measure the PSI of the boxers' punches, the rigidity and pressure-aborption capacities of their upper bodies, their pain-tolerance levels, and the physical integrity of their blocks, then plug all these variables into an algorithm and declare the winner. To box, at that point, *would* be as barbaric as the haters say: two men clobbering each other to prove nothing that isn't already known.

Just as the stronger will always win in such a contest of strength, so will the win always go to the faster in a contest of speed. And simple slapslap is but a contest of speed. Strategy is nearly impossible. Thinking is all but useless. The game allows for no details in which a devil, let alone a human being, might reside. It's like a novel about people who use common sense to arrive at comforting, commonsense conclusions.

When, however, the distinctions between balks and fakes and between twitches and flinches *are* of consequence, a great variety of slapslapping strategies can't help but develop; strategies based on faking and faux-faking, on drawing balks with skillful twitches, on toying with opponents' expectations by establishing and then departing from rhythms, etc. Yes, gimmes and do-overs are frustrating, born of and then bearing only more epistemological discomfort, but for every instance of controversy over a balk/fake or flinch/twitch, there are, between honorable slapslappers, at least ten instances free of controversy; ten in which the slapslapper scores by his wits, by his capacity to be unpredictable, and is properly recognized.

Simple slapslap only *wishes* it were checkers to real slapslap's chess. Simple slapslap is tic-tac-toe.

The Way It Was Done at Schechter

When I started kindergarten at the Solomon Schechter School of Chicago, Emmanuel Liebman and Samuel Diamond were the only great and honorable slapslappers there who hadn't quit real for simple. That is one reason why, despite our differences in age—they were both in the third grade—I became such close friends with them so fast.

On the first day of school, I arrived twenty minutes early and went to the fenced-in playground, where scores of early students sat shiva for summer break. Some older boys were playing tournament-style slapslap-to-13 by the bigtoy. They needed a sixteenth, so I volunteered, and they told me I looked like a kindergartner. I said I *was* a kindergartner, but that I'd been slapslapping for approximately three-fourths of my life, which was true—my mom taught me slapslap before I'd learned to walk (I'm told that from the crib I aborted a round of pattycakes—I don't remember ever playing pattycakes, but I do get a shake of disgust through my shoulders at the sound of its cloying melody—with a thumb-stab to her wrist, and she, as she explains it, figured, "And so why not?")—and the older boys let me play, thinking they were humoring me.

I won the first three rounds 13–nothing, but Simon Katz, the sixth-grader I was to face in the championship round, was much better than my first three opponents. I'd watched the last two points of his semi-final. He wasn't as fast as me, but he was really fast, so I decided I'd mess with him out of the gate.

I won the roshambo for serve (scissors to his paper), and opened with a fake. Simon Katz flinched. I called 1–0 Gurion. "You didn't slap me, kid," said Katz. I told him he flinched. "What do you think this is, a nursing home?" he said. I asked him what that was supposed to mean. Simon Katz just said "Tch," and I figured that he was trying to tell me that he hadn't flinched, but dodged, the implication being that I'd balked and so it was not 1–0, but either a gimme or a do-over. I figured that when he asked me if I thought we were in a nursing home, he was saying that people in a nursing home often had weak vision, but that he didn't have weak vision like someone in a nursing home, so if he saw a balk, then a balk there had been.

I knew I hadn't balked—my fake was all chin—but I also knew there was no way to settle the argument. So I said to Simon: Are we playing do-overs or rotating gimmes?

Simon said, "The score's 0–0."

I took that to mean do-overs.

Then I did another chin-fake, and Simon flinched again.

I called 1–0, Gurion.

"What is wrong with this kid?" Simon said to the crowd—this crowd had gathered to watch the finals.

I said, Look, I know I won't convince you by insisting, but that was not a balk. I didn't even move my hands. Why don't you pay attention to my hands instead of my face. And stop calling me kid, because I'm Gurion ben-Judah Maccabee, and unless you're really small for your age, you're not thirteen yet, so you're a kid too, and I don't keep calling you kid, so don't call me kid.

It was not a very elegant speech—I didn't know how they talked on the playground yet, and I had yet to learn concision.

Simon Katz was not a dickhead at all, and he immediately ceased to call me kid, but when he said, "Look, Gurion ben-Judah, we play slapslap here, not olden slapslap," I thought I sensed contempt in the unfamiliar phrase *olden slapslap*, and the presence of this contempt was then corroborated by some other kid behind me who said, "Olden slapslap is Lame Lamey von Lamey McLamensteinowitz." The popular X Xey von Xey McXensteinowitz joke-form was unfamiliar to me at that time, and I thought this kid behind me, on top of the contempt for whatever any of them meant by *olden slapslap*, was expressing contempt for the many syllables of my name.

And I said, You are all a bunch of fuckers.

There was a collective gasp, a giggle or two, and then someone said, "You can't swear."

I can't what? What can't I do? I said.

The concept of swears was, at that time, also foreign to me.

"You can't say the eff-word."

What's the eff-word?

"The word you just said." "You called us effers."

I didn't call you effers. I called you fuckers. You're all fuckers,

I said. You're fuckers because you're not honorable slapslappers and you're fuckers because of how you make fun of my name, which is a good, strong name my parents gave me, you fuckers.

"That's a bad word!" they said, and half of them went to the other side of the playground.

The fuck are they scared of? I said.

That is when I first noticed Emmanuel Liebman and Samuel Diamond. They were laughing, and even though I wasn't laughing, it seemed like they were laughing with me somehow, and that gave me a good, brotherly feeling, so I decided I liked them.

"The eff-word, Gurion ben-Judah," said Simon Katz, "is the word in the question you just asked that begins with the letter f. It's a *swear*."

No it's not, I said.

Even though I didn't know what exactly a swear was, I could of course tell by the context that a swear was bad, and so I knew the word fuck could not be a swear because it was a word my mom used to say a lot. To an Israeli, who has grown up cursing in Arabic, "fuck" seems like *fiddlesticks*, "fucker" like *meanie*. How could it be otherwise? When you curse in Arabic at the rock that has stubbed your toe, what you say to the rock is *Coos em ach*. Coos em ach = Your mother's cunt. If someone pisses you off a little, and you don't want to say something too vile, you tell them they're the offspring of ten thousand donkeys and a whore. I didn't understand all of that at the time, nor would I til that afternoon, when after Headmaster Unger heard about my saying the word, he yelled and called my parents, and we had a talk, and my mom decided to stop saying *fuck* so much and so did I. All I knew right then, on the playground, was that my mom said *fuck* and *fucker* when she was mad or annoyed, and so it wasn't, at least to me, a bad word any more than the word *bad* was a bad word.

It's not a swear, I said.

"It is," said Simon.

So what the fuck is a swear then?

"It's a word bad people say."

I said, Take it back.

"I can't take back facts, Gurion ben-Judah."

I said, Take it back now, you pussing leprosy from between the scabrous vaginal lips of a discount vestigially-tailed prostitute for whom any one of your sixty-seven possible syphilitic fathers were either stupid or crazy enough to pay nearly twice her value for at eighteen cents, fuck.

"Whoa."

Woe unto you, you filthy crevice-sniffing—

But Simon Katz—a nice boy—was already walking away.

I started choking up because of how everyone I'd met hated me for doing nothing other—at least as far as I could tell—than playing unimpeachable slapslap and defending my family. I had not had much contact with other kids my age, but I'd always assumed that people who I wanted to be friends with would like me. I sat down in pebbles and took deep breaths, and the sting behind my eyes softened before any tears fell.

Soon, Emmanuel and Samuel sat down beside me and said their names. Samuel told me about simple slapslap, and how it made the two of them angry. Emmanuel seemed more disappointed than angry, and he told me that Simon Katz, though nice, was not very bright; that he believed swears were words that bad people said because his mother, knowing that Simon was so nice and therefore wouldn't want to be a bad person, had told him so. Then he told me what swears were. "They are words that a large group of people agree are forbidden, and so they are good, for if Adonai's true name were the only forbidden word, then, other than lying, the only way to rebel by speaking would be to break the Law handed down to us by Adonai, either by saying his true name or taking his lesser ones in vain, and since people must rebel by speaking—it is part of being a person, yes? I know you know that—it is better if they have something other than Adonai's Law to rebel against. It is better for them to have the option to rebel against the rules of man, which are all, ultimately, imperfect."

Since they'd sat down with me, Samuel had been whipping pebbles at the bigtoy, Emmanuel absently hoisting fistfuls to shoulder-level and spilling them one- and two-at-a-time into a small pile in the middle of us. When Emmanuel was through speaking, I back-handed one of the spilling pebbles so that it struck one of the whipped ones in mid-air and the ricochet was audible. CLACKSH.

I liked for things to ricochet, but as soon as I'd backhanded that pebble, I worried Emmanuel and Samuel would think I was a show-off. I'd never worried about being a show-off before. I didn't even know the word "show-off," but I knew the idea from Torah: Moses wasn't allowed into Israel because he'd acted like a show-off in the Sinai, during the second water-from-the-rock miracle. The stakes were not that high here, and I had performed no miracle, just an impressive feat of timing and aim, but I had, at least partly, performed the feat to *impress* them with my timing and aim, when I could have just as easily done it for better reasons: to let them hear a new sound or witness the rare and pretty physics of a missile striking a missile.

They didn't treat me like a show-off, though. They kept doing what they'd been doing with the pebbles, totally straight-faced. I thought maybe they hadn't seen, but after Samuel had whipped a couple or three more, he said, "Can you do it again?"

I said, Maybe.

"Try."

So I did it again. CLACKSH.

They stopped monkeying with the pebbles and slapped me on the back.

Can we be best friends? I said. I really liked them. I said, I think we should be best friends. We all prefer to play slapslap correctly and judging by what I've seen this morning, here on the playground, I believe a love of real slapslap is a deeply meaningful affinity to share; the kind of affinity from which friendships of great longevity have the opportunity, if not the impetus, to grow.

Samuel said the beginning of a "Yes," but Emmanuel cut him off. "Are you a scholar?" he said.

Are you? I said.

"Yes," they said.

"But that doesn't make you one," said Emmanuel. He said, "You have to worry about what things mean. Especially things in Torah."

I do, I said.

"Like what?" said Emmanuel. He wasn't acting mistrustful, just cautious.

You know when Jacob tricks Isaac on his deathbed? I said.

"What about it?"

First of all, I don't think he really tricks him.

Emmanuel said, "A number of great rabbis would agree with you" = "You are not impressing me with originality."

I said, But I think maybe Adonai gets tricked. By Isaac, though, not Jacob.

"That is a very compelling statement. What would make you say such a thing?"

"He'll have to explain some other time," Samuel said. "First bell's about to ring."

I'll explain at recess, I said. I said, But what you asked me was to tell you what I am worried about, which I can do very quickly: I am worried that if Isaac did trick Adonai, then not only would it seem to indicate that Adonai *can* be tricked, but that maybe He *should* be tricked sometimes, and I am worried because I don't know how to trick Him.

"Listen," said Emmanuel. "You explain this to us after school. At recess, I want you to find Rabbi Salt, the principal of Judaic Studies. He is a very smart man. He teaches second-, fourth-, sixth-, and eighth-grade Torah Study. We're in fourth-grade Torah Study, Samuel and I, instead of third-, because Rabbi Salt was our teacher last year and he double-promoted us. You need to go see him at recess and get promoted out of kindergarten Torah Study because it's Rabbi Unger, the headmaster, who is a fool, who teaches kindergarten Torah Study, and you will learn nothing from him but foolishness. I am certain that if you search him out, Rabbi Salt will promote you, at least to second-grade Torah Study, and in the meantime, Samuel and I have Torah Study right after lunch, and we'll try to convince him to promote you twice again so you can study with us."

"You know, you're really socially stunted sometimes," Samuel told him.

"You're always saying that, and I never know why."

"Right. Exactly. Tell him you're his best friend, already."

"Why don't you tell him?"

"He already knows I am, Stunted Stuntedy."

"I am, too, Gurion," Emmanuel said.

And I saw that it was good.

We went to Assembly in the multipurpose room together, to line up behind our teachers and pray and be counted.

Territory

No Chicagoland junglegym could beat Schechter's bigtoy. The bigtoy's creator, except for (years later) Philip Roth, is the only person I ever wrote a fan letter. Unlike Philip Roth, who thought I was a prankster,* the bigtoy's creator was dead. I didn't find that out til I'd written the letter, though.

How I found out was I approached Headmaster Unger to acquire the creator's name and address, and Unger told me he couldn't remember the man's name, but he knew he was dead, that he'd died on Schechter's campus on a summer's day in '97 or '98 while overseeing the bigtoy's construction, but that if I wanted, he (Unger) could look through some receipts to find the name of the man's company, and from there I could look the name up in the yellow pages and find the company's address. I asked Unger why he thought I would be interested in something like that, and he told me that although he hadn't seen the letter I'd written, he knew I must have put effort into writing the letter, and he thought I would prefer not to waste the effort. I still didn't understand, and I said so. Unger said he was thinking I could send the letter to the creator's construction company. But the letter, I told him, wasn't written to the creator's construction company; it was

---

* Roth's response to my letter, in its entirety:

Dear Lioncub, Son of Judah the Mallet,

Whereas the praise you've showered on my work is deeply flattering, your reading of *Operation Shylock* eerily incisive, and the section of your letter in which you mimic recent so-called Jewish wunderkind authors both terrifically cruel and on point, your insistence that you are a grade-schooler—despite being mildly entertaining at first—quickly grew as tiresome as your pseudonym. Normally, I wouldn't mention it—normally, I don't respond to fan letters at all—but because you strike me as a serious writer of slapstick (I did a Kosmo Kramer–worthy spit-take while reading the part of the letter in which the junior rabbis on the playground debate whether hanging the Natalie Portman poster would violate the second commandment; specifically the section of that dialogue in which Rabbi Samuel claims the poster would be kosher if only the mole on Portman's cheek—"This mole a dark half-centimeter of flesh which, in failing to be dissonant with the rest of her face, commands the viewer's acknowledgment that Natalie Portman is perfect"—weren't showing, and Rabbi Emmanuel responds tangentially, however talmudically, that the mole is not a mole but a birthmark, "for a mole is a squinty animal in the light of day, and one cannot both squint and wink at once; surely you will not insist, Samuel, that Ms. Portman's birthmark fails to wink at us in the light of day."), and because you seemed, as well, to be soliciting my advice, I thought I would offer you some: You don't need this conceit that you're a nine-year-old. Nor the pseudonym. Your jokes and insights the both would come across better if instead of writing from the unconvincing POV of a boy-genius whose name suggests a messianic fate, you wrote from your current POV: that of someone who remembers, or at least chooses to remember, his childhood as a time when he, like so many of us, suspected that he was the messiah, knew his friends to be kind and loyal, and was convinced that most everyone, to some degree, seemed preoccupied with questions as to what it meant to be good.

Best of luck to you. If ever I write you again, it will be after I've read your first book. Of course I won't know its author is you because I don't know your real name, but I am certain that once you publish a book, someone will get it into my hands. Til then, I have my own novels to complete, and thus no time for pen-palliness. I trust you understand.

Nearly Yours,
Philip Roth

written to the creator, and I didn't get why anyone would deliberately send a letter to someone to whom that letter wasn't written. "So as not to waste effort," Unger snapped at me. But the effort was already wasted, I told him. Since the letter wasn't written to the company, to send the letter to the company would just waste more effort: the effort of looking up the address in the yellow pages, the effort of writing it on the envelope, of printing the letter out, of affixing the stamp, and not least of all the effort of whoever in the company would read this letter which didn't concern him or anyone else at the company still living.

Unger, though able to muffle the contemptous *hrumph* that his nose made, seemed unable to silence it entirely, and I got the sense that we'd been having a metaphorical kind of conversation without my knowing it, and that I'd insulted him somehow, but at the same time I didn't feel bad about insulting him, if that's what I'd done, because that nose-noise—especially because he seemed to have purposely failed at silencing it (how hard is it to hold back a *hrumph*?) as if to indicate that the place from which he just realized he had to condescend to me was so many miles high that he couldn't, despite all his efforts, even *pretend* to get fully down to my level—indicated, if nothing else, that his was an M.O. of total penility. If he hadn't made that noise, I probably would have eventually taken the name of the company from him, and even sent the letter, all the while trusting that Unger's being an elder of mine granted him access to an understanding of the world that I did not yet have. Instead, I thanked him and returned to lunch.

It might be better that the bigtoy's creator never read that letter anyway. Having recently reread it myself, I see now how it would've been possible, even likely, for the creator to misconstrue my sincere praise as backhanded. It would've all depended on what kind of guy he was. The attribute the letter claimed to be most important—the one that made the bigtoy great—was not, I don't think, an attribute the creator even knew about, much less one he intentionally designed.

Although it's true a slide descended from each corner of the bigtoy's platform, and true that all four of these slides were fast, it wasn't the number of slides or their speed that rendered the bigtoy superlative. And while the 7' x 8' wackywall intersecting the eastern side of the platform had footholds and grips spaced perfect for climbertag, it wasn't the wackywall either. Neither was it the monkeybar dome that rose ten feet above the platform's safety railing. Nor the seemingly dangerous wood-and-wire bridge off the platform's south side, which led to the old castle-themed junglegym (the smalltoy) and creaked loud in the cold and would bounce like a waveform if just two big kids jumped hard and no one else was on it. And certainly the yellow ropenet that sagged between the platform's north side and four ground-anchors seven feet away was a remarkable achievement in itself—twice as remarkable when you noticed the skewed grey grid of shadow it left on the pebbles, and three times so if you ever saw that shadow go bendy during storms—but remarkable as the ropenet was, even it paled beside the true source of the bigtoy's superlativeness. All of these aspects combined did. It was not the sum of the bigtoy's parts that made the bigtoy superlative, but the difference between that sum and the portion of the universe containing it. It was what the bigtoy surrounded.

With the *possible* exception of certain eighth-grade girls (their preference for the swingset had always seemed fake), everyone's favorite part of the playground was the territory ceilinged by the bigtoy's platform. Five steel poles that were set in cement held the platform level seven feet above the earth. The platform's gapless planks, rubberized for traction, kept the territory dry in the rain and the snow, and the shade it provided was thorough enough to make everything it covered look blue. This shade, in the morning, was perfectly square-shaped. To slapslap within it—especially when other kids were gathered outside it—made you feel like a performer in a reverse-lit arena. And it wasn't just the best spot at Schechter to slapslap. It was the best spot at Schechter to do nearly anything. Gossip you heard there always seemed urgent, and secrets you told completely secure. The baseball-card kids would go there to trade. The handheld kids would crouch there and game. If you cried with your back pressed to one of the poles, your sobs would leave your throat so heavy and loud that by the time you slid down to sit in the pebbles, your palms on your cheeks, your fingers all gooey, you'd know you'd never cry about the same thing again. After every school-dance, some couple firstkissed there. It was where you would meet to share cigarettes on weekends. At night, it was said, teens went there to drink, to lay in the pebbles and go to third base. So if you wanted a spot there before the first bell, you had to rise early, rain or shine. No more than nine kids could fit uncrammed within the boundaries. No more than six if you wanted to slapslap.

Everyone wanted to slapslap.

Overthrow

It was from under the bigtoy that we'd end the reign of simple, me and Emmanuel and Samuel Diamond. On my second Monday at Schechter—August 27, 2001—our plan got formed during lunch:

First we made a pact that we wouldn't simple slapslap, not with each other or anyone else. Second, we'd take the territory every morning. The schoolday began at 8:30, so at 7:25 I'd meet Emmanuel and Samuel at Rosemont and Artesian, and if the weather was nice we'd walk the twelve blocks, and if it was lousy we'd ride the bus. Either way we'd get to school by five to eight, beating the earliest early-morning regulars by at least ten minutes, and we'd get under the bigtoy and slapslap. There'd be room enough for three more kids. If not the best simple slapslappers at school, we knew they'd be some of the most die-hard; they'd have had to rise extra early to get their spots, too.

Six slapslappers under the bigtoy = enough slapslappers to keep three slapslaps going at once. Owing to our pact, though, no more than one of these slapslaps would ever be simple. Either two of the three would be real and one simple, or only two slapslaps—one real and one simple—at a time would be played, while the third member of each group spectated.

In the latter case, the crowd who gathered to watch—the crowd was always thick by a quarter after eight—would protest that the space taken up by the third players was wasteful = a lot of pressure on those players to get a third slapslap going. Since the other three wouldn't have a pact, their third would be less able to withstand that pressure than ours. Thus, the former case would obtain, if not by the first or second day then certainly by the third = Two reals, one simple. That is how we would get others to start playing real slapslap with us.

There were four main reasons why they'd *keep* playing real slapslap. As previously noted, to master real slapslap entailed mastery of all the skills of simple slapslap, plus more, and therefore the more the simple slapslappers played real, the more dominant they'd become at simple. Second, once they got used to playing real, simple would seem a lot less fun. Third, crowds liked controversy. They liked to argue with umps and refs. Being that real slapslap entailed scoring controversy where simple didn't, the crowd around the bigtoy would pay more attention to the real slapslaps than the simple ones. And then finally, there was me. I was unbeatable. Simple, real, it didn't matter. Few could even score on me. And who was I? Who was Gurion ben-Judah if not the new kid who swore and insisted real slapslap was the ultimate?* They would want, if not to be like me, then to beat me. In order to do either, they'd have to real.

That was the softpower part of our plan to end the reign of simple at Schechter.

The hardpower part was to be put in effect exactly two weeks from the day the softpower part started: I would challenge all comers to whichever form of slapslap they wanted to play. If anyone beat me, then Samuel and Emmanuel and I would permanently relinquish the territory under the bigtoy. If no one beat me, the bigtoy would be declared a real-only zone.

This hardpower part we thought of as a contingency plan. We assumed the softpower part would end simple on its own.

It almost did. By recess of the thirteenth day since the softpower part's enactment—September 10—we anticipated only two challengers: Shmooly Gooses and Joshua Pritikin. Whereas Gooses was a slow boy who couldn't grasp the rules of real, let alone the psychology of faux-faking, Pritikin was not just a champion of simple, but a completely uncompromising loyalist. He was the one simple slapslapper in all of Schechter who'd refused beneath the bigtoy to cave to the crowd. He'd point to us and tell them, "Blame it on these three." But no one would blame it on us. Instead they'd boo Pritikin, call him a mamzer, demand that he real with our third.

Though I admired Pritikin for being such a hardhead, I didn't doubt for a second I'd rout him. Shmooly Gooses only scored when someone let him, and we'd already decided that for his sake we'd make an exception. To ban Shmooly from playing simple under the bigtoy

---

* Actually, by the end of my second week at Schechter, my reputation as a scholar was beginning to spread, and a lot of kids had started making friends with me; at the time we devised the plan, however, only the kids in my Torah Study liked me.

= banning Shmooly for being slow. He really couldn't understand the rules of real, so he'd still be allowed to simple in the territory, as would anyone else—just as long as they were doing it with Shmooly.

In short, we saw the hardpower part of the plan as a formality. Pritikin was honorable, so we knew he'd take the challenge, we knew I'd shut him down, and that he'd accept the consequences. Shmooly I'd go through the motions of almost losing to, and I'd then, for his benefit, explain to him and the crowd that his near-defeat of me granted him the privilege described above.

Victory Undeniable

We were halfway to Schechter when the first plane hit the Trade Center. I was warming up with Samuel when the second one struck. We didn't know about any of it. Neither did the first twenty or thirty kids who showed up at the playground, and none but us three knew of the challenge we'd make. The plan was to announce it as soon as fifty kids had gotten to the bigtoy, but last minute I changed it a little.

At 8:06, Pritikin rolled up on his GT Compe. He performed a triple bunnyhop at 0 MPH, then dismounted into a kind of handstand with his legs like an L; its horizontal bar propped the bike from falling sideways. It made me admire Pritikin more and wish I was good at bike-tricks. He clamped the Compe to the rack and came over. He walked like he always walked, and didn't make any extra eye-contact. To me this proved Pritikin wasn't a show-off. He'd done the bike-trick for the beauty of the bike-trick, not so kids would admire him. The thought of that led to my seeing the single problem with our plan. To surprise Pritikin with my challenge in front of fifty people, while it wasn't just unnecessary to secure his defeat, might later provide him with an excuse for having been defeated. For the longevity of real slapslap's imminent reign, it was important he and everyone else knew I beat him fair and square. So I took him aside and let him know I'd challenge him publicly, as soon as fifty kids got there. He said he'd accept the challenge, then paced by the wacky wall, waiting.

By the time fifty kids showed, it was twenty after eight. Though usually there were fifty by 8:15, none of us thought twice about it. We didn't think twice about Sheldon Markowitz, either. At twelve after eight, he got out of his mom's car. He took a few steps toward us, then his mom yelled his name. He got back in the car, and they drove away. We just figured he'd forgotten something at his house. Maybe his lunch, maybe his gymshorts. (Sheldon was heavy and hated Gym, which was probably why his mom always drove him to school even though they lived only a few blocks away.) It wasn't til nearly a half hour later, when everyone was gathered inside the multipurpose room, that Emmanuel offered a stronger hypothesis: between the time Sheldon opened the passenger-side door and the time his mother called his name out, NPR, to which Mrs. Markowitz—if she was anything like the rest of our mothers—was listening, received word on the second plane and announced it.

At 8:20, I explained the challenge to the crowd. I told them Pritikin had already accepted it, but it was open to the rest of them as well. Shmooly, as predicted, was the only one who stepped up.

Gurion 21, Pritikin 3.

Gurion 21, Shmooly 19.

Everyone agreed the territory was a real-only zone. Everyone agreed on the exception for Shmooly. Then the first bell rang. We went to Assembly.

Surrounded by Underdogs

During Announcements, moms appeared in the doorway. Not one or two, but ten or eleven. They took away their children, and news started spreading. From radios in cars and TVs at breakfast, some kids had learned some things about a plane and a building. Or planes and buildings. The center of the world. It wasn't very clear. At first everyone had thought whatever'd happened was an accident, but why were all these moms showing? Take a look around. Teachers chewed hangnails, pulled tieknots, were quiet.

After Attendance, before morning prayer, Rabbi Unger said everything was fine. Most of us knew then for sure: not everything.

We started to daven. More kids' moms came. Most were in and out in under thirty seconds, but one started crying, another arguing with a teacher. The arguer wanted to take her daughter's best friend home with them, claimed the girl's mother had asked her to. The teacher wouldn't budge without written permission; but if written permission were gettable, explained the arguer, the best friend's mom would have shown up herself.

"But yet nonetheless—"

"But yet nonetheless nothing! Today of all days is no day to play the bureaucrat."

Rabbi Salt went over and whispered to the teacher. The mom left the school with both girls.

The news, spreading fast, became rumors faster. A plane had hit the Sears Tower, it was said. Later that day, I'd wonder which schmuck had spread that, but it was probably no schmuck, just some kid who mis-heard the message he'd been passed. If between mouth and ear the World Trade Center could so quickly become the center of the world, it only followed that the tallest building in the country would get confused for the one that used to be.

A couple syllables into the Shemoneh Esreh, everyone but Solomon Schenk had stopped praying. Schenk's bar-mitzvah had happened the previous Saturday. At Schechter that meant he'd lead prayers all week. Schenk was the boy whose mother was crying. His eyes were on scripture and he'd failed to see her. She was slouched on the opposite side of the multipurpose room, waiting politely for Solomon to finish. When finally he noticed that no one else was praying, he lifted his head, and there she was. Through the mike on the podium, he said, "Where's Aba? What happened to Aba? Where is my aba?"

"Your aba is fine," she yelled back to her son, then from the same kind concern for decorum that had caused her to wait in the corner, crying, she incited a panic she'd intended to cull. "Everyone's parents are fine," she said.

And we knew what that meant. We thought we did.

"Sears Tower's destroyed!" "And the center of the world." "Planes are missing." "Planes are missiles." "Where's our parents?" "We want our parents."

Rabbi Salt took the podium and told us what he knew. Two planes had hit a building in New York. The building was called the World Trade Center. Nothing bad had happened in Chicago. It was alright to weep, even he felt like weeping, weeping made sense, but we should know, he told us, what exactly it was that we wept for. It wasn't our parents, it wasn't our parents. "Please sit back down and we'll continue to daven."

"How do you know?" "How does he know what's happening?"

"Keep down your voices," we were told by Rabbi Unger. "Sit down in your seats and we'll continue the service."

No one sat down in his seat. Kids with cellies* called home, checked in, then passed the cellies on to kids without them.

Rabbi Salt, wise, buzzed the media-tech. A few minutes later, CNN was on the wall-screen. We sat on the floor in front of it. Towers were burning, people were falling, no few planes were still in the sky. Most of us began to enjoy ourselves. That might sound cold, even arch, to a moron. Our parents were fine, though, and plus we had enemies.

Just minutes earlier, when the possibility that our parents were dead had seemed, for the first time ever, real, we'd discovered we were not as bad as we'd suspected. Who among us hadn't, at one point or many, entertained reluctant fantasies of being orphaned—all those guys you'd know more than, all those girls who'd notice, all those good reasons to cry and lash out, the allowances granted you for all of it, the admiration you'd get for having overcome? And who of us hadn't wondered what was wrong with himself for having entertained such fantasies? Who hadn't worried that in his heart of hearts he was selfish and guilty, a wishful parricide? And now we knew we weren't, that we hadn't ever been. During those couple minutes in which we feared our parents' deaths, we learned their deaths were the last things we wanted; that those fantasies, like nightmares, said nothing true about us. We were good after all, we'd been good all along, our dreams of orphanage the outcome of frustrated longings we hadn't known we'd had, longings for actual, unadulterated enmity = It turned out we'd just always wanted enemies. Worthy enemies. Materially demonstrable injustice to (after some struggle) beat. Explicit threats to rise above. Good reasons to dominate, a righteous path of conquest, the chance to exhibit strength without being a show-off. Ways to do violence while remaining a mensch. The need to do violence to remain a mensch.

I'm not saying all of us. What I'm saying is most of us. (Emmanuel, for instance, showed no signs of power-surging. He just stood

---

* *Real* cellies, these, of which there weren't so many at Schechter. (Cellies were still expensive, the technology was as yet mostly frowned upon for kids, and controlling-parent-friendly call-plans didn't exist. This was still two whole years before New Traditions in Safety Industries—maker of the kid-hostile Nojack phone—had even been venture-capitalized.)

there, worried, quietly saying, "This is not good, people are dying," while keeping his tears welled, not wanting attention.) And I'm not claiming all of us knew why we were thrilled. I'm not claiming any of us knew why we were relieved. I'm saying we were thrilled. I'm saying we were relieved. I'm saying that for the first time in most of our lives, these two previously contradictory feelings served to complement each other. We were good and we had enemies. We had enemies, were good. We had enemies because we were good. I'm attempting to account for the secret reasons why this all seemed true to us, why it all made sense to us. I'm attempting to explain that it wasn't just the on-the-spot cancelation of classes, or the feeling of productivity you get watching news in a group, or even the oft-reported rush that comes of surviving intact a force others like you have not. We had this feeling of importance, of total purpose, that most of us had never experienced before.

We suspected we had become the underdog.

By the time the South Tower collapsed, we were sure. And then some new questions arose, or tried to. When, exactly, had we become the underdog? Was it possible we'd been the underdog all along? Without knowing? And was it right to speak of a group as an underdog; i.e. was an underdog group not comprised of many individual underdogs? And if comprised of many, was it not likely that some were more underdoggy than others? Which ones?

"I've *been* to Manhattan." "I was born in Manhattan, so I know what you mean." "You're right, you're right: my father was just there on business last week." "I have cousins in Brooklyn, just over the bridge." "Here, take my phone, Yoni. Call your cousins."

"They might go for downtown." "My dad works downtown." "Mine's in the Hancock." "Mine's at One Mag Mile." "Board of Trade." "Prudential." "Lake Point Tower." "Daley Center." "Birthday Cake."

"I've got cousins who live in actual Manhattan." "You know what, Yoni? Give the phone to Shayna first." "But it's busy, Saul, I haven't gotten through to—" "But her cousins live in actual Manhattan."

"My dad's in Sears Tower, and that's the tallest so they'll hit it." "If they hit it, Ran." "What're you trying to say?" "Who cares what he's trying, cause you're all of you wrong. The Aon buiding's what's getting hit if something's getting hit." "I don't even know what that is." "You'd know it if you saw it, that's why they'd hit it. Listen to Blitzer. It's all about symbols."

"Where in Manhattan?" "I don't know exactly where." "She says she doesn't know where, but it's actual Manhattan." "But just cause mine are in Brooklyn doesn't mean hers are closer." "Brooklyn's a totally different city, though." "So what? Pizza is in Evanston. It's in a totally different city from Chicago, but still Pizza's closer to us than Comiskey Park, right? Or even Wrigley Field. Admit it, Shayna." "No. It's not like you're saying. They're islands."

"Who's that guy with the big brown eyes?"

"My father always said this would happen."

"Sears Tower you'd know if you saw it, plus its name." "Aon building's white. Monolithic." "Lake Point Towers is shaped almost like a clover. It's right next to Navy Pier and it's black. It's where the real action happens, where my dad works." "The real action happens in the Hancock, which you'd not only know if you saw it, and it's name, but it's way more important architecture. Sears Tower's ugly." "Aon's not ugly." "No one knows it's name, though, the Aon." "Lakepoint's close to Navy Pier." "The Empire State's what they'd have hit if they cared about names." "Statue of Liberty's what they'd have hit if they cared about tourist attractions." "The White House and the Pentagon is what I'd've tried to hit." "Don't act like a seer; they already announced the Pentagon was hit." "They announced they heard something about the Pentagon. They didn't announce if it was true yet." "The point is anything is vulnerable."

"That's true? They're islands?" "They've got these big bridges because of how they're islands." "They're boroughs." "What's a borough?" "They're islands. Evanston and Chicago aren't islands." "They're *not* islands. They're boroughs." "Is a borough a kind of island?" "Only New York is islands [tears]." "Now she's gonna cry so she can use the phone first." "She's crying because she's upset." "She's upset about the phone if she's upset about anything." "She's upset about her family. They live on the same island as the Trade Center." "It's busy, anyway, so here." "Good man, Yoni." "I didn't hear a thank you." "She's too upset to thank you. Plus if anyone should be thanked, it should be me, don't you think?" "No, I don't think." "But it's my phone she's using." "But I was the one who was using it." "You didn't thank me either, come to think." "Times like these, it's pretty much your duty to lend out your phone." "Why my duty? I'm not the only one with a phone." "You're the one with a phone sitting closest to us."

"Look, I'm not complaining. I'm glad to lend my phone. And maybe even it's my duty, but if it's mine it's everyone else's too." "You're the closest." "We're talking distances measured in feet here, Yoni." "Whatever, I'm upset, I've got family in Brooklyn." "Except maybe I've got family in Brooklyn, too. Maybe even in Manhattan." "Maybe? What does that mean?" "My uncle in Connecticut does a lot of work in Manhattan." "Then why didn't you use the phone to call him?" "Maybe I was being selfless."

"Nine-one-one." "What?" "Today is September 11." "So?"

"If anything is vulnerable, everything is vulnerable." "All of us are vulnerable." "We've always been vulnerable." "It's true, we have." "How didn't we notice this?" "Because of what Mrs. Diamond said about Lancelot and boobytraps." "What did she say?" "About how come he always fell in the same kind of boobytraps even though he was a great knight." "How come?" "Because he never used deceptions since he was such a goodguy, and so he never suspected badguys would use deceptions. He'd go to the fort of a goblin to save Guinevere and the goblin would say, 'Okay, she's yours, just cross that discolored area of tile and I'll bring her,' and Lancelot would try to cross and the goblin would pull a lever, then *blau*, trap door, and he'd fall into a pit. And the pit would have a beast. And the beast would try to eat him. And Lancelot would have to kill the beast." "Like Skywalker."

"Eleventh day of the ninth month. 9-1-1, emergency." "Emmanuel Liebman thinks he's a kabbalist." "Sounds more like he's saying that Brown Eyes is the kabbalist." "Don't call that mastermind 'Brown Eyes'—it's irreverent." "Little Sammy Diamond's got a short fu—Ow!" "Samuel." "Let go." "Say my name." "Samuel." "Say it again." "Samuel. I said it! Let go!" "You let Emmanuel reason out loud. Off the cuff he'll say things you couldn't think in a decade." "Okay." "You don't distract him." "I told you I told you I said it: okay!" Do Amalekites dial 9-1-1 in emergencies? "I see what you mean. Who'd know?" Rabbi Salt?

"Maybe you forgot about him, your Connecticut uncle." "That's not a kind thing to say to someone, Yoni, especially someone who just lent you his phone." "Indian-gave his phone, and it wasn't unkind. I was saying that maybe, since you only seemed to think of your uncle in Connecticut just now…maybe you're not that close with him.

Maybe you're not as close as I am with my people in Brooklyn is all I'm saying, so it was right to let me call mine before you called yours." "Or maybe I did think of my uncle, but knew I could take it, the wait for others with relatives to use my phone first, I mean. Maybe I just knew I was strong enough to take it." "Maybe so, maybe so, but that doesn't really contradict my hypothesis, does it? I mean maybe you were strong enough cause you're not that close." "Or maybe I didn't realize how close til the implications of this tragedy we're suffering began to come clear. They're coming clearer and clearer, wouldn't you say?" "We are definitely getting clearer and clearer." "We are. It's true." "It's true." "I agree."

"Exactly like Skywalker, but Lancelot fell for it every time. It happens, like, nine times with a bunch of different goblins, and he never learns to expect it." "Cause he's so pure and good, he trusts everyone and gives them the benefit of the doubt." "Exactly." "We *are* like Lancelot." "I didn't have Mrs. Diamond, but Lancelot sounds pretty doofy to me." "That's what we said to Mrs. Diamond! But then she explained about his pureness and we believed her. She's smart." "We should probably stop being like Lancelot so much, though." "Lancelot, Shmancelot. We're now, at this point, more like Guinevere." "I think you're right." "Yeah, it's safe to say the goblin's got us." "But Lancelot's on the way." "We've got a lot of Lancelots." "That's the benefit, in the end, of being like Lancelot; you make a lot of friends along the way." "Or if you're pretty like Guinevere." "Pretty like Guinevere?" "Pretty like Guinevere, because the goblin's got us, which means we're like Guinevere, not Lancelot. We're like Guinevere with Lancelots on the way, like you said." "I was speaking figuratively. I was saying we're like Guinevere cause the goblin's got us and we've got Lancelots on the way, but we're actually Lancelot in the end, ourselves." "Um."

"I don't know what they dial, Gurion." Do you know what they dial in Israel? "I never had an emergency in Israel. Don't you think more important questions are afoot, boychic?" Not ones you could answer, no offense. "I don't see the relevance—" "Because why on 9-1-1? It hardly seems arbitrary." "On that I agree, Emmanuel, but—" "Who's the message for, is the question we're getting at." If 9-1-1 means nothing to Amalekites, this mastermind's talking to— "I see, I see."

"Can I get my phone back, Shayna?" "My family's line's busy." "All the more reason to give it back." "Three more times." "One more time." "Three more times, so I know I'll have tried ten. That's how desperate I am to contact them." "Seven's enough, Shayna." "Three's enough, but I'm so desperate to get in contact I have to try seven more, I'm compelled to do so, even at the cost of alienating those who'd help me is how desperate, so just bear with me." "I have already." "Just wait your turn." "It's my phone." "It's my family." "It's my family, too. My uncle." "My cousins." "Connecticut." "Manhattan." "Brooklyn."

"We're like Lancelot if Lancelot was like Guinevere." "I don't think that makes sense." "Think harder." "Don't get confrontational in times like these." "Who ever thought we'd live in times like these?" "No kidding. And that's not the craziest part, because we've always lived in times like these, it turns out." "That's what being Lancelot gets you, blindness to the times you live in like these." "Goblins inside every shadow, laughing at you." "But you hold your own. You don't change for goblins." "When you change for goblins, that's when you're defeated." "If they've been there all along, the goblins, then we know we can survive them intact as Lancelots." "But still you have to wonder, if we've always lived in times like these and didn't know they were times like these, then how were these times like these affecting us?" "Probably they were really doing some job on us." "Probably these times have been doing bad stuff to us we thought was just from bad luck or ourselves." "It's true. How much of our woes owe to times like these because we didn't know about them!" "That makes it sound like it's our fault for not knowing." "Maybe it *is* our fault for not knowing, after all." "How can you ignore your times, especially in times like these with hiding goblins?" "It's our fault for being so good despite the goblins." "That's all I'm saying. We're good and pure. We've been taken advantage of for being good and pure."

And then the fall of the North Tower, and Flight 93. Air Force One missing, celebrations in Gaza, firemen dying, bin-Laden, bin-Laden. Taliban, Taliban, Osama, etc.

Pritikin's Complaint

At eleven, Pritikin asked for a re-match. I told him no re-match, the territory was ours. He told me he'd been distracted; that he'd seen

Sheldon Markowitz get back in his mom's car and known something bad had happened. I told him that I'd seen Sheldon, too, that all of us had. He asked if I'd known something bad had happened, though. I told him of course I hadn't known, but neither had he, he'd only convinced himself after the fact. He told me it wasn't right to exploit 9/11. I couldn't tell if he was casuistic or simply confused. Maybe both. Maybe the latter had engendered the former. I did know he was wrong, though.

He walked away from me angry.

By noon he'd gotten Gooses to tell the same story. They marched around lobbying, and a lot of kids backed them—not everyone, but roughly 30 percent. Even though just a few were still simple adherents, Pritikin's complaint harmonized easy with their underdog sense of entitlement.

For the sake of the definitude consensus would foment, I chewed my tongue raw and agreed to a re-match.

Fuck Yourself

You will get no conclusion beyond that, Mr. Beagle. The truth is I don't understand why you would ask me or anyone else at Aptakisic to write about how 9/11 changed what it means to be American. The textbook enlightens nothing. It says the fall of the towers confirmed the same things here that it refuted there, that what 9/11 means or meant varies according to who you ask. You teach from the textbook, so you're no help either. And me, I was five years old when it happened. Five years later, I know the world much better, but it's still almost always impossible for me to distinguish change from revelation. I'd imagine it's the same for any scholar. I'd hope so.

This is what I know for sure: Neither on 9/11, 9/12, or anytime thereafter did anyone who was in the multipurpose room at Schechter think, "This is how it is now." We thought, "This is how it is." Whether we were correct or incorrect, it's impossible to tell, but the distinction between what a person becomes and what he finds out he's been—let alone what a people becomes and what it finds out it's been—is too important to ignore, so I won't. Not for some chomsky Social Studies essay.

Go ahead and flunk me for begging the question, then go ahead and fuck yourself for asking it.

Coda

On September 12, Schechter was closed. On September 13, I re-matched with Pritikin and Shmooly Gooses. Emmanuel and I had come up with new terms of the contest the night before, and I explained the new terms to the crowd around the bigtoy.

I said, Since I didn't see the way 9/11 gave me an unfair advantage last time—and since I still don't see it—I'd be foolish to trust my vision this time. So what I'll do is simple with Pritikin and Shmooly until either one of them beats me, or both are satisfied I beat them fair.

We began.

Gurion 21, Pritikin 3.

Pritikin said unfair—he'd had a series of itches.

Gurion 21, Pritikin 3.

Pritikin said unfair—someone kept sneezing.

Gurion 21, Pritikin 2.

Pritikin said unfair—I'd yawned in front of him and he had to keep fighting the yawns my yawn had suggested.

Gurion 21, Pritikin 0.

Some kids told Pritikin to give it up already. Pritikin said the way they were scowling had screwed him up. Kids walked away.

Gurion 21, Pritikin 0.

Pritikin said the kids who were walking away had done so too noisily for him to concentrate. It was almost as if they were deliberately kicking the pebbles around.

Gurion 21, Pritikin 0.

Pritikin started saying something, and I told him not to worry, fair was fair, and unfair un-so, he didn't have to explain. The crowd around the bigtoy had dwindled to half its peak size.

Gurion 21, Pritikin 0.

Unfair.

Gurion 21, Pritikin 0.

Unfair.

Gurion 21, Pritikin 0.

The crowd shouted that I'd beat him fair. I told them only Pritikin could say for sure what was fair. I asked Pritikin if I had beat him fair.

Almost, but no. There'd only been a few turns this last time during which he was distracted, and although the points he'd lost on those turns wouldn't have made the difference in themselves, having lost them distracted him from gaining other points.

Gurion 21, Pritikin 0.

Almoster, but still no.

Gurion 21, Pritikin 0.

The crowd told Pritikin that simple was boring. They told him it didn't matter if he won because they'd never simple with him again anyway. Pritikin said there was no point in continuing then. I told him the point was fairness. I told him he was obligated, by honor, to make sure he'd been beaten fair. After all, if he couldn't be sure, how could he expect the rest of us to be? And where would we be—where would slapslap be—without absolute definitude?

Gurion 21, Pritikin 0.

It seemed fair.

Seemed wasn't enough. You need to be certain.

Gurion 21, Pritikin 0.

Now he was sure.

But was he sure he was sure?

He was sure he was sure. I'd beaten him fair.

Shmooly's turn. Shmooly said he didn't need a turn, just as long as he was still allowed to simple under the bigtoy with people. I told him he wasn't. He asked what if he scored on me? What if he scored as much as he scored the last time? Could he simple with people under the bigtoy, then?

Sure, I told him.

He couldn't remember the score from last time, though. What did he have to score?

I told him last time shmast time. If he scored 3 on me, he could simple under the bigtoy. This lit him up. He said that was fair.

Gurion 21, Shmooly 2.

Unfair—some itches.

Gurion 21, Shmooly 2.

Unfair—cold hands.

Gurion 21, Shmooly 2.

Unfair—wind in his eyes. Plus 3 seemed high, didn't 3 seem high?

I told him score 2 and he could simple under the bigtoy.

He agreed that was fair and wiped the tears from his eyes.

Gurion 21, Shmooly 1.

Maybe 1 was more fair, he suggested.

Sure thing.

Gurion 21, Shmooly 0.

Maybe he was just too tired. His mom had a cold. He'd only had a hard-boiled egg for breakfast.

Emmanuel gave him a granola bar and he ate it.

Gurion 21, Shmooly 0.

It was unfair, explained Shmooly, it was just unfair. I was Gurion and he was Shmooly. It was unfair that Gurion was faster than Shmooly. How could that be fair? He was born Shmooly and I was born Gurion and that was unfair, it was always unfair and would always be unfair. He didn't have a chance. He never had a chance. I asked if he wanted me to let him score. He said that he did. I told him to go fuck himself, I wouldn't let him score; I would simple with him til he was satisfied, but I wouldn't let him score. He told me to go fuck myself. I told him he couldn't score on me even if I was fucking myself while he tried to score on me. I told him anyone at Schechter could shut him out while they fucked themselves because he was Shmooly and they weren't. He told me again to go fuck myself, and that I was a crybaby. He knew everything I was telling him already, he said. He didn't care anymore what was fair. Fair could go fuck itself, he said. It wasn't fair that what was fair got to be fair and what wasn't fair didn't. Fair was unfair. Everything could go fuck itself. Everything should fuck itself. Everything should fuck itself but not everything fucked itself plus fair was unfair was why I should let him score. That's why other people let him score, and that's why I used to let him score, so I should go fuck myself now because it wasn't fair to change like that and I knew it, he knew I knew it because of how I was crying like a fucking kindergarten fucking crybaby, he told me. I wasn't the one who was Shmooly, he told me. I wasn't the one who suffered for fair's unfairness, he said. He was the one who was Shmooly, he told me, and Shmooly was the one that suffered for fair's unfairness, and it was unfair for me to make Shmooly feel bad by being a fucking kindergarten crybaby because it was Shmooly who deserved mercy, not me. It was Shmooly, not me from Shmooly. Go fuck myself, he wouldn't show me mercy, go fuck myself, go fuck myself. Go fuck myself or let him score.

By then I couldn't distinguish the one choice from the other.

I held my hands out to Shmooly, palms down. Shmooly held his under mine, palms up. And then he scored. Probably I let him.

There was finger-writing across the fog of the bus-door's windows. It looked like this:

$$
\begin{array}{ccc}
 & \text{D} & \\
 & \text{A} & \\
\text{W E} & \text{M} & \text{W E} \\
 & \text{A} & \\
 & \text{G} & \\
 & \text{E} & \\
\end{array}
$$

I wiped it out with my sleeve and went to the wheel-well seat, where Vincie had put my coat and backpack.

"Why'd you wipe what I wrote?" he said.

It signified wrong, I told him.

"It fucken *whated* wrong?" he said.

I said, You wrote it in the shape of a torture instrument.

"I was saying we're like crucified," said Vincie. "The like crucification of the Side of Damage," he said.

We're not crucified, I said.

"I didn't *say* we were fucking crucified. I said *like* crucified. Like we're crucified*ish*. By the Arrangement. Like you said. Why do I have to play the dumb one all the time?" He stabbed the cushion of his seat with a Bic.

You're not dumb, I said. You're smart.

"I'm *not* smart, Gurion, but I'm not dumb either, and I didn't say that I was. I asked why do I have to *play* the dumb one if I'm not dumb, which I'm not?"

I said, You don't have to play the dumb one, no one said you have to play the dumb one, and we're not crucifiedish, I never said that. Even if we were, it still doesn't make sense to write WE DAMAGE WE that way because WE isn't crucified on ARRANGEMENT the way you wrote it. WE isn't even crucified on DAMAGE the way you wrote it—the way you wrote it, the WEs are the arms of DAMAGE.

He said, "People can see it better if it's shaped like a cross. At least I can. But what do I know, since I play the dumb one, which I'm not asking you if I have to play the dumb one or not—I'm telling you: I play the dumb one. Like, I've had a crush on the same girl since kindergarten, and I have a million things to say to her, and I don't think they're dumb, but I play the dumb one when I see her. She sees me seeing her, and I know what to say, but instead I play the dumb one. I pretend I wasn't looking. I squint at fucken nothing. I don't say fuck-all. I play the fucken dumb one. But I don't know why I do that and what I'm asking you is why I do that. Why the fuck do I do that?"

What's the girl's name? I said.

"I'm *not* fucken telling you. But see? That's exactly my fucken point, what just happened—you thought you could catch me off-guard, like if you asked me fast enough, I'd tell you her name, like a tricked fucken dumbass, and you think that because of how I always play the dumb one. And so I'm asking you why I always play the dumb one."

I said, How should I know why you do what you do?

He said, "You're the leader of the Side of Damage. If anyone should know—"

Who says I'm the leader? I said.

"*Everyone* says you're the leader. Even Asparagus. We were tagging the foursquare court at recess and Main Man saw us, and Asparagus was nervous Main Man was gonna narc him out because of how Main Man's retarded, so Asparagus told him, 'Remember we're all on the same side.' And Main Man said, 'Gurion said that.' And Asparagus was like, 'That's what I'm saying. Gurion's the leader of the Side of Damage.' And then all afternoon, Mookus kept writing the same note over and over and tossing it to everyone. Look." Vincie unfolded a square of paper and showed me:

H LLO!
GURION IS TH L AD R OF TH SID OF DAMAG !
—MOOKUS

"And Mookus is only first of all, because then *Ben-Wa* said you were the leader—he didn't actually say it, but he asked us to give you that note we gave you. The note asked *you* if he could join the Side of Damage—it asked you and not us. So we thought: Gurion must be the leader. And thirdly it made sense for other reasons, too, because you lead us. And because who can beat you up? No one can beat you up. Maybe Nakamook could, but he wouldn't, so no one. So you're the leader."

I said, What if I don't want to be the leader?

"Why wouldn't you want to be the leader? I'd kill to be the leader."

Exactly, I said.

"I wouldn't kill *you*, Gurion. You're my friend."

I'm not everyone's friend, I said.

He said, "You could be if you wanted. At least in the Cage. Everyone in there wants to be on the Side of Damage now. Nakamook tell you about the carrels yet? I bet he didn't, cause it fucken tweaked him, but you should see the carrels. All of them are tagged with WE DAMAGE or DAMAGE WE or WE DAMAGE WE. I bet Benji didn't tell you cause it got him so pissed cause he thought we'd get in trouble even though I told him we wouldn't get in trouble because you can't get in trouble for being suspected of vandalism—you have to get caught in the act of vandalism. If you could get in trouble for just being *suspected* then me and Leevon and him would've all gotten in trouble with Brodsky for the scoreboard today, because one thing we were, man, was fucken *suspected*. By Brodsky *himself*. And where's the trouble? Where's the fucken trouble? There isn't any trouble. We're in no fucken trouble. And then Botha himself proved me fucken right cause right before the end of the day he saw one of the tags on scabby-ass Mark Dingle's desk and he started to yell at Dingle, and Dingle said he didn't do it, that the tag was there when he arrived that morning. And Botha didn't believe him, and he tried to make a rat of him because he remembered that Dingle's boy Salvador had sat at the desk the day before, and he told Salvador he'd be suspended for the vandalism on Dingle's carrel because he thought it would get Dingle to confess, which is so fucken stupid because Salvador's weird but he's no kinda dumbfuck and so he said he didn't do it, but that he'd noticed the tag was there when he came back from lunch yesterday. Real smart is how he said it: 'I *noticed* it for the first time when I got back from lunch,' he said, meaning, like, 'It could've been there for weeks, for all that I know.' And everyone was watching, Gurion, because Botha was having such a fucken fit, and since everyone was watching, they all learned the fucken blueprint for how to lie about the tags without ratting anyone out, so when Botha gave up on Dingle and Salvador, and he saw the other tags all over the carrels, he went for Jesse Ritter, who told the same story as Dingle'd told, and when Botha went for Forrest Kenilworth who'd sat in Jesse's chair the day before, Forrest told the same story as Salvador'd told, and then Botha—Gurion, he fucken *gave up*. Just sat at his desk and acted all busy til the tone. Anyway, I was right: Benji shouldn't have been worried that we'd get in trouble, and I told him that, too, but he told me he wasn't worried we'd get in trouble, and he said I missed the point, that's not why he was pissed, and when I said, 'What the fuck's the point, then? Why the fuck you pissed?' he was just, like, 'Tch,' and I threw him at a locker and he swept me at the knees, and then he picked me back up and we came and got you in Brodsky's to take you to June. But what I'm saying is this: none of those tags on the carrels were there before lunch, and that means they weren't there til after everyone heard the scoreboard got totalled—which seriously upped Ben-Wa's snat by the way—and what I'm getting at is no one told anyone to tag the carrels—at least not me or Benji—we didn't say anything to anyone, so everyone did it on their own, not from any fucken peer pressure or threat or any kind of fucken bullshit like that, so what I'm saying is I don't think those kids want to kill you. And even if they did— could they? No way they could. Not with how stealth you are, and then me and Nakamook and Leevon and Asparagus on your side. We could bury all those fuckers, but we wouldn't even have to is all I'm saying. And probably they're not fuckers is all I'm saying. Probably they're our friends if we want them to be, I'm saying. Probably they're on the Side of Damage and would never even think of trying to kill you."

I said, No one can kill me, anyway, Vincie.

"That's all I'm saying," said Vincie. "So why don't you want to be the leader?"

I said, I just asked *what if* I didn't.

"Why even ask that?" said Vincie. "Why make simple things complicated?"

Why play the dumb one? I said.

He said, "I don't *know*—but it's what I fucking do. Do you wanna go to the back of the bus and wreck Maholtz and that Shlomo kid now, or what?"

I kneeled on my seat and looked at the back of the bus. There they were, Maholtz and Shlomo Cohen, staring out opposite windows.

That's really strange, I said.

"What's really strange?" said Vincie.

They haven't said anything to us, I said. I said, Did they say anything to you before I got here?

Vincie said, "They didn't say fuck-all to me and it isn't even a *little* strange—Slokum isn't here. They're not so bold by themselves, those two. Let's bust the grins off their mugs."

I said, They're not grinning.

Vincie said, "They want to be grinning, but they're scared of us." He kneeled on his seat and looked back at them. He raised his fists over his head. "You dentists!" he shouted. "You bancers!"

The muscles in their faces tightened, but they kept looking out their windows, like Vincie wasn't talking to them.

"Vincie!" yelled the busdriver.

"Yeah, yeah, yeah," said Vincie. He sat down. "So?" he said to me. "We gonna go back there and fight?"

I did want to fight Maholtz. I wanted him to pull his sap so I could take it justly. But I didn't want to fight Shlomo Cohen. And I definitely didn't want Vincie to fight Shlomo Cohen. Shlomo Cohen was still an Israelite.

I said, We're not fighting them.

"How come?" he said.

I said, Bad timing.

Since *bad timing* could mean almost anything, it was a certain kind of truth. A low kind.

"What do you mean 'bad timing'?" said Vincie.

Just trust me, I told him.

And that was even lower.

I said, Let's play slapslap to thirteen.

Vincie Portite trusted me, and about the time I was up seven-nothing, I was feeling awful. Then I had an idea that I thought could fix everything.

I thought: Make Vincie an Israelite.

But I was immediately struck with the paralysis of God's No! and I couldn't fix anything. And on second thought, that move wouldn't have solved much anyway; an Israelite Vincie fighting Shlomo Cohen would be a little better than a Gentile Vincie fighting Shlomo Cohen, but it wouldn't by any means be *good*. Here we'd have my brother hurting my brother, there we'd have an outsider hurting my brother. Either way, a brother would end up hurting, and though brother hurting brother was better than the other way, I was supposed to protect my brother in both cases, even when my brother was a bancer like Shlomo. The problem, ultimately, was that my brother was a bancer. To make Vincie an Israelite wouldn't solve that problem—it didn't even *address* that problem.

So on top of feeling low, I also felt stupid, and the paralysis inflicted by Adonai lasted just long enough to lose me a point.

And I noticed Vincie's hand, which had gone to his eye each time I'd scored those first seven points, stayed in the air of the aisle when I lost that eighth one. I thought it better not to tell Vincie about it, at least not yet. Then I let him have the next point on purpose, and again the hand failed to rebel against him.

I started switching off—giving him this point, taking that one—til we got to twelve-twelve. Vincie's hands stayed in the aisle every time he scored.

I thought: If he defeats you, his hand will never rebel again.

I thought: Let him defeat you.

And again, I was paralyzed by a No! from Adonai.

Vincie won the point, and the point the game. It was not the will of God, but it owed to the force of God. The force of God acted in accordance with the will of Gurion, against the will of God, and I saw that it was good. I had not sinned. I had not disobeyed. I'd only been as paralyzed as God forced me to be.

"I won!" Vincie shouted, clapping my shoulders with both hands, leaving them there. "I beat you," he said. "I'm stealth!"

I said, Flinch!

"Don't ruin my victory," he said, shaking me.

I said, Flinch right now!

"No!" said Vincie.

"Oh," said Vincie.

"Fuck," he said. "Thank you." He put his hands out, palms up.

We played slapslap to thirteen til the kids in front sang the rhyme of my bus stop.

□ □ □ □ □ □ □

A firefly touched down on my ear and Flowers shouted, "Come quick!" from the other side of the Welcome Office door. He was watching the Local 5 News in back. Edison, asleep on Flowers's outstretched legs, startled when I came inside—he fell, struck the floor nose-first.

"Gift for timing," Flowers said to one of us about the other.

The cat bolted at me, tripped on lint, laid there.

I set the previous night's scripture on the music stand.

"You daddy," said Flowers, pointing at the television.

"...v. the City of Wilmette is nearing its conclusion," said an offscreen anchor. Onscreen was footage from outside the Drucker trial. The anchor said, "Here we see protesters gathered on the courthouse steps for the tenth consecutive day." A mob of Israelites stabbed at the clouds with picket signs. Some of the signs said NEVER AGAIN and others showed a photo of Patrick Drucker sieg-heiling that didn't look doctored. The majority of the signs were protests against my father, though. One kind featured his photo with a large-lettered legend that read ROY COHN FOR DISTRICT ATTORNEY OF COOK COUNTY on one side, and HAMAS, AL QUAEDA, HEZBOLLAH, MACCABEE on the other. Others inverted the arrangement—a photo of Roy Cohn and the legend JUDAH MACCABEE FOR DISTRICT ATTORNEY OF COOK COUNTY; ear-to-ear headshots of bin Laden, Nasrallah, the dead wheelchair guy from Hamas and a black circle with PASTE JUDAH MACCABEE HERE in white letters in its center. Another sign had no photo at all and just said PASTE JUDAH MACCABEE. I'd seen similar signs a few months earlier during Shmidt v. Skokie, but there were more of them for this trial, fifty easy.

The other side's signs were more varied; unlike the protesting Israelites, who had all come to the courthouse on the same chartered bus, the other side, though smaller, comprised a number of separate factions. The Neo-Nazis' signs read HEIL DRUCKER! over an American flag with fifty tiny swastikas where the stars should have been. The head Nazi waved an actual flag of that description in the air above his helmet. Another group, much larger, who stood nearly as far from the circle of Nazis as they did from the Israelites, carried signs that read ZIONISM = NAZISM and ADVANCED INSTITUTE FOR THE PUPPETEERING OF AMERICAN CORRUPTION. The graphic on those was an outdated caricature of Ariel Sharon (no longer the prime minister of Israel, he'd been in a coma for ten months by then), with an extra-hooked nose and blood-dripping fangs, his claw-tipped fingers in the loops of strings connected to the limbs of an Uncle Sam marionette who wept while stepping on the neck of a baby in a turban. A third group's signs were maps of the Middle East, all beige, except for Israel, which was black—one legend read THE UNHOLY LAND and another LAND OF BILK AND MONEY. A lone, clueless man who wore a keffiyeh over his ski-mask carried a sign with a target on it, and WTO was written in the bullseye. There were at least five other small groups, all of them forming different circles and carrying different signs, but the camera didn't linger long enough for me to make them out.

The anchor said, "Inside the courthouse, however, things weren't so calm," and three drawings appeared onscreen for a few seconds each—the first of a group of white-haired audience members on their feet, their mouths open wide, their fists in the air, while my father, in the corner of the drawing, leans on the jurybox, hanging his head ("Here we see an artist's rendition of Judah Maccabee being shouted down during closing arguments by a group of several elderly Jewish protesters," narrated the anchor); the second drawing was of the frowning judge banging his gavel ("…our artist's rendition of the Honorable Michael Hall calling for order"); and the third was of the shouters being led out of the courtroom in zip-tie handcuffs ("…officers arresting the protesters on contempt-of-court charges…").

The screen switched. It showed a pair of vans, cops holding the doors open.

Flowers said, "Whoah. This not exactly common."

The anchor was saying, "…live broadcast of the jurors boarding—are we allowed to show this? Well… What you're seeing is a rare, live broadcast of the jurors boarding the vehicles that will return them to their motel, where they'll deliberate the fate of Patrick Drucker and his pamphlets." Approaching the van, the jurors hunched their shoulders and turned their faces from the camera like red-handed felons. "Good luck to them," said the anchor. "We'll return with the weather."

Flowers hit the POWER button just as a used car commercial started jingling.

"You dad gonna win," he said, "and quickfast."

I said, Those jurors didn't look happy.

"You wouldn't look happy neither, you had to hand down a verdict favor Drucker."

So why do *you* look happy? I said. It came out of me like an accusation. I wasn't pissed at Flowers, but the way I asked the question, it seemed like I was. Who I was pissed at was Adonai for making men who hated Israelites, and at the Israelites for hating my father, and at my father for defending men who hated Israelites. Why was the world always uniting against the Israelites? Why were the Israelites always uniting against Israelites? Why was each question the only answer I could ever come up with for the other?

So why do *you* look happy? I said to Flowers. I said, I don't think Drucker loves black people much, either.

"I'm happy cause you dad an old friend about to win something he been fighting for. And I'm *sure* Drucker don't love black people, but that don't mean he should be outlawed from *saying* so in Wilmette… click click click… Now, how you said that—that's bothering me. Drucker don't love black people *either*—what's that? What's that *either*? You ain't black youself the sudden?"

It was the start of a conversation that I didn't want to have, but it was important to Flowers that we have it every couple weeks.

Only bancers care if I'm black, I said.

"I guess you calling me a bancer then, ever the hell that means."

I said, You don't really care about the color of my skin, Flowers. I said, You just think you're supposed to. I said, I'm your friend Judah's son who writes and that's what matters to you. That's why you're my friend.

"That don't change that you black."

I said, I'm an Israelite.

"You a black Israelite."

And I'm an Israelite with detached earlobes and I'm an Israelite born in Chicago and I'm an Israelite who usually wears a hoodie and an Israelite who ate chicken last night. An Israelite is an Israelite, I said.

"Black is black," said Flowers.

I said, Only because you say so.

"A lot of people would say so," Flowers said. "And from what you tell me, ain't no shortage of Israelites who'd reduce you to *only* black."

You and them—you're all just people, though, I said.

That cracked him up. "Oh, I guess I misunderstood—you're like a hippie, now," he said. "That girl from yesterday must be doing some job on you, man. Good for her. Good for you. It's a healthier way for you to be."

Good teachers are so busy listening for a sign that you've learned what they've tried to teach that they almost can't help but eventually hear it, even when it isn't there, even when it's the opposite of what you're really saying. Flowers heard *we* where I'd said *you*. He heard "We're all just people," as in, "If we could only get over our superficial differences, we'd all love each other," when that wasn't what I meant at all. What I meant was that I was the Israelite Gurion ben-Judah, so I didn't have to answer to people. What I meant was Adonai doesn't care what color my skin is, but He does care that I have the soul of an Israelite—He treats me differently because of it.

"So how *is* that girl?" said Flowers. "June, right?"

I kissed her, I said.

Saying that, my mouth remembered the push of June's tongue, and I shivered. I knew the memory would wear out with use, and I saw I had to be careful not only about how many times I used it, but when I used it, too. If I hadn't remembered June's tongue, I would have stayed pissed about Adonai and my father and the Israelites, and I should have stayed pissed—it was important to stay pissed about those kinds of things, to hold onto the pissedness until it thickened and became useful—but the shiver thinned the pissedness, made the pissedness seem less important. I felt warm, but less dangerous.

"Kissed her!" Flowers said.

We banged fists.

"You figure out what's the Side of Damage?" he said.

A thing I lead, I said.

"You're talkin' like a koan. Got something to show me?"

It's on the music stand, I said, but it's only three lines long.

"Don't say *only*," said Flowers. He said, "Right three lines—specially they the openers—that's big. They the right ones?"

I think so, I said.

But I was mistaken. I hadn't even swapped love for damage yet, let alone made forever not always.

The right ones follow the table of contents, 496 pages ago.

□   □   □   □   □   □   □

Esther Salt sat alone on her stoop without a jacket. From a block away, I could make our her shape, but her face was blurry—I couldn't tell whether or not she looked pretty. Nor could I decide if I wanted her to. It seemed to be an important thing to decide in advance, so even though I was running a few minutes late for my meeting with her dad, I slowed my pace by 50% and kept my eyes on the sidewalk. The problem was I didn't know which kind of love was truer: the kind where some girls would look pretty to me but I wouldn't try to be with them because I loved June, or the kind where no one but June would look pretty.

The last I'd seen Esther was seven days earlier and she'd been pretty in the way Natalie Portman would be pretty if I took a time machine to the set of *The Professional* in 1994, when Portman was young enough to be my girlfriend, yet I somehow failed to realize Portman wasn't Mathilda, budding schoolgirl assassin, but rather the actress playing Mathilda. I.e., the last I'd seen Esther, I'd believed she was meant to mother my sons. I had just finished studying in the study with the Rabbi and there were still a few minutes to kill before dinner. Esther was playing backgammon with a couple of her sisters, Kinneret and Ayelet, at the dining room table. I pulled up a chair and, quick as a slap, I felt like a shmendrick who'd screwed up his life—Esther wouldn't look at me, or even say hi.

It is true that I'd quit having conversations with her ever since she'd broken up with me, but it wasn't because I hadn't wanted to have conversations with her—I had only quit on my mom's advice. She'd told me Esther would feel how gone from her I was and then decide to get back together with me. I didn't understand how that plan could work if Esther didn't try to talk to me first—if she didn't even try, how could she know for sure that I refused to have a conversation with her?—but I trusted my mom and I'd stuck to the plan.

Kinneret said, "Gurion, do you know how to play sheishbeish?" *Sheishbeish* is backgammon, and Kinneret was the kindest and eldest of the Rabbi's seven daughters. She had purple eyes and always bit her lip while squinting at me nicely from across the table at dinner whenever I asked Esther to pass me food and got ignored.

A little, I told her. I've played a couple times.

"Have you played with the cube?"

What cube? I said.

"What cube?" mumbled Esther, eyes on the board. "The doubling cube," she mumbled. "It's only half the game." She was talking to herself as if she didn't really want to say anything, as if not knowing about the doubling cube was so stupid to her that no matter how hard she tried, she couldn't hold the contempt back—like the contempt was so fierce that it was able to force its way out of her mouth against her will.

"I know the cube!" Ayelet said. She didn't say it mean, though—she said it excited and, right after she said it, she touched her right cheek to her right shoulder and made a pop-eyed crazyface and a hissing sound. Ayelet was seven, and very shy, and that was what she'd do when her voice came out louder than she'd planned. Esther used to do the crazyface hissing, too, but not because she'd been loud—Esther was never loud. She'd do it whenever we were alone, staring at each other and saying nothing, wondering what we were supposed to do next, which would have been kiss if she wasn't Hasidic.

"When you play with the doubling cube," said Kinneret, "you can form strategies of intimidation. Do you want to learn?"

"It's fun," said Ayelet.

"There's no time to teach about the doubling cube," said Esther. *Teach about*—she wouldn't even put the *him* between the words. "Ema said five minutes til dinner."

"Ema said ten minutes," said Ayelet.

"Yes," said Esther. "She said *ten* five minutes ago."

"Ten means twenty when it's dinner, anyway," said Kinneret, and then she taught me about the doubling cube, and I saw that Esther was right—it was half the game. At the beginning, the cube didn't belong to anyone, and either of the players could pick it up and use it. You used it to double the stakes. The best time was when you were at a slight advantage. If your opponent accepted the double you offered, the cube belonged to her, unless she decided to re-double. If she decided to redouble and you accepted, the cube became yours again. If at any point a double was offered and the player it was offered to didn't take it, that player had to forfeit the game. I liked the cube.

We had dinner.

"She said *ten* five minutes ago," was the last thing Esther had said that evening, one week earlier, six days before I fell in love with June.

I arrived at the stoop before I could decide which kind of love was truer. I arrived at the stoop and saw Esther looked pretty—Portman-pretty, not Mathilda-pretty—and I saw that the truer love was the kind where you don't want to be with any other girls even when they're pretty like Natalie Portman.

Because Esther had already called me the night before and I didn't care anymore whether she wanted to get back together, I started a conversation with her. I said, You're shivering.

"I'm cold," she said.

I said, Why aren't you wearing a jacket?

She said, "Can I wear yours?"

What's wrong with yours? I said, taking mine off.

"It's inside," she said.

I said, Why don't you just get it? I said, I'll get it for you. I said, Wear this while I get it.

I held my jacket out to her.

"Why are you so mean to me?" she said.

Mean what? I said. I just offered to get your jacket for you, I said. And I offered to let you wear my jacket while I got yours. I said, Why don't you just wear my jacket?

I blinkered my jacket.

"I can get my own jacket," she said, leaving me holding my jacket out for no one.

I waited a minute for Esther to return before giving up and going inside. I hung my jacket on the coat tree.

Rabbi Salt sat at his table in the study, poring over Zohar. "You too, Gurion?" he said. I thought of the loss of faith in me he'd revealed in his letter to Brodsky, but then he rose and squeezed my shoulders and by the time he'd let go, the thought had disappeared. And that's how I preferred it, for everything between us to be as it seemed. "I'm asking you," he said. "Have you been conspiring with my wife? Are you being used? It only takes two, you know—a conspiracy—and she's already got my doctor in her pocket. She wants to make a conspiracy, she doesn't need *you*, boychic. So what? Is she trying to make a patsy of you? Does she think she can make of Gurion Maccabee a patsy? How dare she even."

I didn't know what he was talking about, but he wanted a straightman, so I played one.

I said, I'm no patsy!

"And the coffee?" he said.

Usually I brought a carafe to the study with me, but on the way to the study I'd heard Esther in the kitchen and skipped it.

I don't know from nothing about no coffee, I said.

"Exactly," said the Rabbi.

That was the end of the routine.

The Rabbi said, "Seriously—do you not want any coffee? I tell my wife I drink coffee with you so late in the day because it would be rude to leave you drinking it by yourself, and that used to be true—that used to be why I drank coffee so late, but now, come Wednesday at six-thirty, I find that I hanker for coffee. It's like the story of the Shabbos Non-Smoker, but in reverse... You know that story?"

Yes, I said.

"Yes you want coffee or yes you know the story?"

Both, I said.

"Let me hear you tell it," he said. "In the kitchen."

We went to the kitchen for coffee, and Esther was at the counter eating grapes. Her father said, "What a nice-looking bunch of grapes."

"Try one," she said. She plucked a single grape from the bunch, handed it to him, then went to the living room with the rest.

"Do you want it?" said Rabbi Salt.

No, I said. Then we fixed coffee and I told him the story he'd asked for:
The Shabbos Non-Smoker was a Hasidic tzadik who smoked two packs

a day, except on Shabbos, when he smoked no packs a day, because lighting fires is a kind of work and working breaks the Sabbath. Because the man never smoked on Shabbos, he never craved nicotine on Shabbos. One day he was arrested in Eastern Europe. He was held alone in a basement cell for years, awaiting execution. Every so often, a guard would bring him his meals, but none of the guards would tell him what time it was, let alone what day. The guards wouldn't speak to him at all. To stay sane while awaiting his execution, he needed faith, but to maintain faith he needed to observe the Sabbath. To observe the Sabbath, he needed to first know when it was, and because he didn't crave cigarettes on Shabbos, he knew when it was, so he stayed sane til they hung him.

The story was a bobe-mayse, but it got told a lot. There were two different, conflicting, points the storyteller could use the story to make. The first point was that the Sabbath is one of the greatest gifts Adonai gives us, and we should never forget it—that even while you await execution, the Sabbath, if you honor it, will provide you with a level of peace and dignity that you couldn't otherwise experience.

The second point the story could be used to make is that it's foolish, possibly even sinful, to place the Sabbath, or any religious practice, ahead of your life—the storyteller who wants to make this point stresses that the Shabbos Non-Smoker was executed *despite* keeping the Sabbath; that had the man not been so faithful to the Sabbath, peace would not have come upon him; that had peace not come upon him, he might have taken a guard out and tried to escape, which would have, even if the escape were unsuccesful, at least depleted the number of enemies of Israel. The implications of this second point are that it is not sane to strive for the kind of sanity that will allow you to await your own execution peacefully; that if faith brings you peace and comfort, you're a sucker—that you must struggle to make sense of faith; that Adonai would prefer killing you Himself to having you die at the hands of men, and that he wants you to fight for the privilege to be killed by Him; that to risk likely death at the hands of men in order to save yourself from assured death at the hands of men is to act the way Adonai wants you to act—that He will like you better if you risk your life to save your life, and He will therefore be more likely to help you if you do so.

And so it is always better to force the issue. It is always better to place your faith in your ability to save yourself from men than to have faith that Adonai will save you from men. To be favored by Adonai, you must first truly love Him, yet to truly love Adonai you must love your life more than Him.

In the kitchen with Rabbi Salt, I drove the story toward the second point.

He said, "You've made it your own."

Not good? I said.

He said, "It's a bobe-mayse—it's not scripture." = "Do what you want with the Shabbos Non-Smoker."

Back in the study we drank coffee, read Rashi.

Eventually the Rebbetsen knocked and said we had twenty minutes til dinner, but the Rabbi closed his Chumash anyway. "What was this business with the grape before?" he said. "My daughter's upset with you?"

He and I never talked about Esther and I, but I knew the two of them did, so I decided it wouldn't be ratting to talk about us.

She's upset, I said, but she won't be for long. I said, We weren't speaking for a while because we broke up and I didn't want to break up, but now I understand it's much better that we broke up, so we agree now and should soon be able to speak again.

"I see," he said. "And what made you change your mind?"

I said, I haven't told Esther yet, and I don't know if I should, but I'm in love with another girl. Eliza June Watermark.

Rabbi Salt said, "She goes to Aptakisic, this Eliza?" = "Is she as much a shiksa as her name would seem to indicate?"

I said, She's an Israelite. Her parents aren't, but she has an Israelite soul. "She has a Jewish soul?"

You say that like it's a weird thing to say. Her soul was at Mount Sinai when Torah was delivered. If that's weird, then fine, but that's what it means, and everyone agrees that that's what it means. Her soul was there at Sinai when Torah was delivered, and therefore she has an Israelite soul.

"But how do you know she has a Jewish soul if she doesn't have a Jewish mother?" said Rabbi Salt. "How do you know that her soul was at Mount Sinai?"

I said, I converted her.

The Rabbi grabbed his lapels and laughed.

It's true, I said.

"For the sake of argument, let's say you, Gurion Maccabee, *did* have the power to perform a conversion on someone," he said. "This person you say you've converted is still a child, meaning she still lives with her Gentile parents, and therefore no one in the community would consider the conversion legitimate."

I said, Well, *my* parents aren't observant—their household isn't kosher, we don't keep Shabbos. Still, you'd never deny that I'm an Israelite.

"You've been provided with a strong Jewish education," he said.

And I am happy for my education, but if having a Jewish education is what makes a person an Israelite, the vast majority of Israelites would be Gentiles.

"You're right," said the Rabbi, "the family and the education are beside the point in this matter. A Jew born a Jew is always a Jew. It's simply not the same for Gentiles."

I agree, I said. I said, But June's an Israelite, not a Gentile.

"If her mother is a Gentile, then June is a Gentile. It's very simple."

I said, But her soul—

"She can have as much Jewish soul as Barbara Streisand, yet she's been born into a Gentile family, so she's not a Jew until she's been converted and the conversion is recognized by the community. That's how it is."

I said, I don't know that that's true.

"Then why did you attempt to convert her, Gurion? If you believe she's Jewish regardless of what your community thinks, why even bother?"

Are you angry at me? I said. I said, Your voice just got—

"I'm not angry," he said. "Frankly, I'm a little worried."

I said, We're having a conversation—don't be worried. I'll convince you I'm right.

"You won't convince me, Gurion. It's you who needs convincing—that's why I'm worried."

I remembered his letter, the end of his letter, the part where he wrote that I needed repairing, that Brodsky could *fix* me... I was talking to a man who'd believed I'd been broken, who'd believed I'd stay broken were I kept in the Cage for over two weeks, and now, ten weeks later, I was still in the Cage. What now did he believe? What now did he imagine he was he doing here with me? Charity work? No, I thought. Not charity work. Remember who this man is, I thought. This is Rabbi Avel Salt. Your favorite teacher ever. He has always had your back, never been condescending; he's not act-ing condescendingly now, so calm down. Were he condescending now, he wouldn't voice his doubts to you. He'd let you live in what he thinks is a fantasy, rather than trying to end that fantasy. He'd say, "Fine, June's an Israelite, if that's what you think." And that's not what he's doing. Instead he's voicing doubts. But doubts aren't certainties; they're not assertions of wrongness, just questions of rightness. Doubts you can deal with. Doubts you can remove. That's something you're good at.

I was sure I would convince him.

Zipporah, I said. I said, What about Zipporah? She was raised by Gentiles, and it doesn't say anywhere that Moses converted her, let alone in front of any community, yet no scholar has ever said that she wasn't an Israelite, not even *before* Torah was delivered—and he *married her* before the Torah was delivered, had *kids* with her before—

"Different times," said the Rabbi.

That's never the right answer, I said, and you know it. I said, Anyway, times weren't so different. There was no king in Israel then, and there's no king in Israel now.

"Then how about this: You're not Moses."

You're angry at me, I said.

"Because I say you're not Moses, you think I'm angry?"

I said, It's the way you said it. I said, You said it like: 'Who do you think you are, Gurion? You're not Moses.' You said I'm not Moses like I don't know I'm not Moses. You said it like I think I'm Moses. I *don't* think I'm Moses. And I don't think Moses thought he was any kind of Moses— not when he married Zipporah. And he *wasn't* really Moses when he married Zipporah, not the Moses we know. He hadn't led us from bondage. He hadn't transcribed Torah. And he didn't even know that he would. Adonai hadn't told him anything about that stuff. Moses was just an outlaw and a fugitive from Egypt. He was hiding in a desert. His greatness was only potential.

"But who is to say, Gurion, that Zipporah would have been accepted as a Jew if Moses had not eventually made actual his potential greatness?"

Fine, I said.

"Fine?" he said. "You're telling me *fine*?"

Yes, I said.

"You're saying 'fine' and 'yes,' but at the same time you're giving me the Bob Dylan routine." He meant about how I'd pulled my hood on.

I said, I have to think.

"What do you have to think?" said Rabbi Salt. "What do you need her to be Jewish right now? If you marry her, it won't be for years yet. Be friends for now—there is nothing wrong with that. And if, years from now, when she's no longer living with her parents, she still wants to convert? Baruch Hashem."

I told her she was an Israelite, I said, and Adonai did not object. He would've objected if her soul had not been there when Torah was delivered. And He would not fall me in love with someone who is not an Israelite.

"This is not the kind of thing you can expect anyone to take your word for."

I pulled on my hood-strings.

"Gurion," said the Rabbi. "Gurion?" he said.

I said, It *is* the kind of thing I'd expect *you* to take my word for.

"Gurion," he said, "I—"

Or would've expected.

"But—"

No, I said, you're right. When you're right you're right. I said, But just because you're right doesn't mean you know the truth.

"Stop for a second. Listen, okay? Even if I did believe you… Even if I did accept your girlfriend was Jewish, I'm saying no one else in the community would. And that is a *good* thing, isn't it? We practice Judaism, yes? Not Gurionism. This is a good thing."

I know, I said.

"You don't seem to like it, though."

I have to go home, I said, and write scripture.

"No commentary, no matter how thoughtful," he said, "will be powerful enough to persuade the Jewish community that you have the authority to convert this girl, Gurion. Not when your motives are so clearly personal."

And I thought: You hear "Jew" when I say Israelite, and "commentary" when I say "scripture." You see Esther's husband while looking at June's.

My personal motives? I said to the Rabbi.

"Where are you going? Please sit back down. Stay for dinner."

I said, I'll write scripture and you'll know the truth.

"You're unhappy with me, Gurion. You're in distress. Don't run out of here. Stick around for dinner. There's no need to run. We're talking," he said. "We've got more to say. We've got more to study."

You've been a good teacher, I said.

I went home.

MATMATMATMATMATMATMATMAT
MATMATMATMATMATMATMATMAT
MATMATMATMATMATMATMATMAT
MATMATMATMATMATMATMATMAT
MATMAT **WELCOME** MATMAT
MATMAT MATMAT
MATMATMATMATMATMATMATMAT
MATMATMATMATMATMATMATMAT
MATMATMATMATMATMATMATMAT
MATMATMATMATMATMATMATMAT

to Canrovsky's

There was a new, semi-literate bomb in front of the WELCOME mat on our stoop. It was supposed to say "Welcome to Carnovsky's" but the vandal switched around the r and n.

I knew it was supposed to be Carnovsky because Carnovsky is a fictional character made up by the fictional character Nathan Zuckerman, who is the protagonist in many books by Philip Roth. A lot of Jews in Roth's first few books about Zuckerman think that Carnovsky is a self-hating Jew and that because Carnovsky is a self-hating Jew, Zuckerman is a self-hating Jew.

But any smart Israelite who ever read Roth's books knows that Carnovsky is *not* a self-hating Jew, which negates the assertion that Zuckerman (for creating Carnovsky) and Roth (for creating Zuckerman who creates Carnovsky) are self-hating Jews.

So to say that my father was a Carnovsky was to say that my father was falsely accused of being a self-hating Jew, and that was a nice thing to say—it was what I said.

But no one would vandalize the stoop of a man he wanted to be nice to.

So it was easy to conclude that the vandal misunderstood what a Carnovsky was—that the vandal, like so many of Roth's fictional Jews, was *not* that smart, and missed Roth's point, and thought Carnovsky *was* a self-hating Jew, and thus thought my father was a self-hating Jew.

And that's what I concluded at first, and for a second I almost felt a little good, thinking, The enemies of my family are such stupid bancers, they not only mistake Carnovsky for a self-hating Jew, but they can't even spell his name.

Except then I started wondering if the transposition of the r and n wasn't an accident. I.e., wasn't it possible that the vandal knew Carnovsky wasn't a self-hating Jew and had switched around the letters on purpose—like Eliyahu did the o and y of *typos* in his joke about the Cage manual—in order to ironize the bomb? Maybe the message was: "Look, the only kind of guy who'd claim that Judah Maccabee is, like Carnovsky, falsely accused of being a self-hating Jew can't even spell *Carnovsky*."

It was possible. And not only that, but it made the bomb a lot more effective: The enemies of my family who were stupid enough to believe Carnovsky was a self-hating Jew would forgive the misspelling out of admiration toward the vandal for his having bombed the Maccabeean stoop; the enemies of my family who didn't know who Carnovsky was wouldn't know the name was misspelled and would admire the vandal without need of forgiving the misspelling; the enemies of my family who were smart enough to know that Carnovsky wasn't a self-hating Jew would not only admire the vandal for bombing the stoop, but admire the cleverness behind his misspelling; and my family itself... we'd stand there staring at our enemy's message, thinking about it, trying not to admire its cleverness and failing. I would, that is. No. I wouldn't. I thought: I won't.

I pulled the mat down to cover *to Canrovsky's* and the stoop looked like:

Maccabees aren't

MATMATMATMATMATMATMATMAT
MATMATMATMATMATMATMATMAT
MATMATMATMATMATMATMATMAT
MATMATMATMATMATMATMATMAT
MATMAT **WELCOME** MATMAT
MATMAT MATMAT
MATMATMATMATMATMATMATMAT
MATMATMATMATMATMATMATMAT
MATMATMATMATMATMATMATMAT
MATMATMATMATMATMATMATMAT

I tried adjusting the mat so that it covered both lines of grafitti, but the mat wasn't large enough, so I took out my Darker and got on my knees.

When I finished editing, the stoop looked like:

Maccabees aren't

MATMATMATMATMATMATMATMAT
MATMATMATMATMATMATMATMAT
MATMATMATMATMATMATMATMAT
MATMATMATMATMATMATMATMAT
MAT **unWELCOME** MATMAT
MAT MATMAT
MATMATMATMATMATMATMATMAT
MATMATMATMATMATMATMATMAT
MATMATMATMATMATMATMATMAT
MATMATMATMATMATMATMATMAT

It was the best I could do. As long as the vandal kept coming around while I was at Aptakisic—and why shouldn't he? he kept getting away with it—I wouldn't be able to blind him. Not unless I ditched school. I wasn't going to ditch school. School was where June was.

I thought: Is she thinking of you right now, too?

And I thought: She might be.

I thought: You need to go inside and write scripture.

I thought: Your scripture will outlast the bombs of the vandals.

I pulled my frontdoor keys from my spypocket and found rolled-up commentary wedged in the ring. The paper was pink and printed double-sided in Lucida Calligraphy, the favorite font of Esther Salt and soon-to-be brides everywhere:

> *Dear Gurion,*
>
> *I beg you be sensible and sensitive like you used to. Do you really think I would spend thirty minutes waiting for you in the cold of the mid-to-late autumn chill on my stoop without a coat if I didn't want you to do a kind thing for me by giving me your jacket so you could prove that you are still the sweetest boy to me who will always be my first and only true love no matter what?*
>
>
> *Oh Dear Gurion,*
>
> *Don't you understand that I was angry for all these many and varying weeks we have spent away from each other in our respective lonely and cold solitudes since that sad and fateful Shabbos on which you delivered me your heartbreaking poem? How could you not see that when I broke up with you it was not to break up with you but to let you know that I wanted you to come see me more and at least try to kiss me at least once because we were together for so long and you never even tried to hug me or even ever hold my hand and I was scared that you only said you loved me because you are my father's student and you wanted to be a good student because that is the only thing that is important to you?*
>
>
> *Oh Dear, My Gurion,*
>
> *That last question was the question I was asking myself from*

the time we broke up until one week ago today, when you came over and learned the doubling cube, and I thought: Some people, even very smart people, play sheishbesh without the cube, and they don't even know they're playing without the cube because they don't even know there is a cube...they don't know what the cube means, these people, and if you were to offer them the cube in the middle of a game you were playing with them, they wouldn't even know that an offer had been made—they would think you were just pushing dice at them, and maybe not even that because maybe they'd only think you were doing something nervous with your hand to the dice. And I thought: Gurion is one of these people.

And Oh My Dear, My Gurion,

I thought how if you didn't even know what the doubling cube was, then it was likely that you didn't know that when I was breaking up with you it wasn't because I wanted to break up with you but because I wanted you to kiss me, the exact opposite of breaking up. And I have been getting less and less angry at you because it is not your fault that you don't know how to double, and I've just kept remembering that all week long. But then today I waited in the cold on the stoop, and you weren't acting happy to have the opportunity to give me your jacket, and you definitely weren't offering it to me nicely. You were acting like I was being dumb and you didn't even think about it. You didn't even think: Esther isn't dumb, Esther must be telling me something. You just didn't think! And it made me angry and lonely all over again, so I didn't offer you a grape. But now I'm here at my desk in my room and I am thinking: Gurion isn't dumb. Gurion is the smartest (and the handsomest) boy there ever was, and so he knew what he was doing on the stoop today! He was doubling you! He wanted you to apologize for doubling him on that fateful Shabbos when he didn't know he was being doubled, and he would have gladly given you his jacket, held it open for you to put your arms in it, and even maybe hugged you once you got your arms in, and when you hugged him back maybe even kissed you if only you'd thought to apologize.

And so I am sorry, Gurion Maccabee. I am sorry and filled with regret for misunderstanding and treating you badly and I want you to know that I'll accept your double if you offer it to me again.

I love you,
Esther Salt

Esther's letter was too flowery to think about, and not just because of the *Oh*s and *Dear*s. I took it upstairs and rewrote it til it made sense:

Gurion, please be nice to me even though I have tortured you with shadiness for eight weeks.

I know I told you that I broke up with you because you caused me pain, but the real reason I broke up with you was to manipulate you in such a way as to get you to stop respecting the traditions of my family. Even though you wrote me poems and were always kind to me, I didn't believe you when you said you loved me. I thought you were only saying it and writing those poems because you were a highly dedicated sycophant of my father's and you knew that showing love for me would please him. When I broke up with you, I believed that you knew I was doing it to manipulate you. I thought that you were only pretending to think I was being forthright so you could get out of our relationship without having to break up with me yourself.

But then, when you came over to play backgammon last week, I realized you were a dumb shmendrick who never even suspected anyone might try to manipulate him, and that made me happy. It made me happy because it meant that you'd been straightforward all along, which meant that you actually had loved me and still did love me, even though I kept being so shady to you.

And now I'm thinking that if you were a dumb shmendrick then, you might still be a dumb shmendrick. In fact, I'm all but certain that you remain a dumb shmendrick, and this letter is evidence. After all, if I weren't counting on your continuing to be a dumb shmendrick, how could I—unless, I, myself, am a dumb shmendrick—think that a letter such as this would bring you back to me? For who, besides a dumb shmendrick, would ever return to a girl who tortured him with deliberate shadiness for eight weeks and then sneakily called him a dumb shmendrick with flowery words rendered in my favorite font, Lucida Calligraphy? I am sorry for not realizing you were a dumb shmendrick sooner.

Please continue to be a dumb shmendrick.

Esther Salt

I reread the rewrite and thought: Gurion ben-Judah let himself be tricked by love's smelly version into saying he was in love with Esther Salt, which was a lie. Esther knew it was a lie even though Gurion believed it, and because she knew it was a lie, and because she wanted it to be true, she told lies to Gurion that he thought were true. And only now that Gurion knows his love was a lie does Esther think his love was true. And only now that Esther thinks his love was true does she stop lying, and reveal that she thinks Gurion is a shmendrick, a shmendrick who she believes she loves. But Gurion is not a shmendrick, so Esther can't possibly love him. Esther cannot be in love with a shmendrick who is Gurion ben-Judah Maccabee because there is no such person. So she has also let herself be tricked by the smelly version of love.

We lied about the same thing, but the lies we told were different.

I saved and closed the document and was about to attempt scripture when a plate of cut-up apple appeared beside my keyboard.

"I hear you have had no dinner," my mother said.

I blanked my screen.

He called you? I said.

"I am told you have learned to make Jews of Junes."

My notifier chimed.

I've got email, I said.

"I am told you have learned to make Jews of Junes," my mother said again.

That's not nearly as funny as you think, I said.

"You are laughing," she said.

Because you think alliteration is funny, I said. I said, I'm laughing *at* you.

She kissed my cheek. "One day," she said, "you will look back and be amazed at how much of a little shit you were to your mother who loves you, and you will come to me, and you will say, 'Ema, I was such a little shit to you. I was such a little shit! I said cruel things to you so casually. So often I spoke to you like you were a stupid immigrant, or someone with mental illness. I spoke to you like people speak to stinking, drunken beggars who approach them in the rain. I had so much contempt.' And I will say to you, 'Gurion, you remember through the eyes of a boy. I saw your small cruelties for what they were. You were only trying to be charming. You read *Portnoy's Complaint* and believed it was charming to have contempt for your mother, to be cruel to her, and you acted as charming as you were able.' Have some apple I cut for you."

I'm sorry, I said.

"I do not want you to apologize. I want you to be kind to me. I want you to speak kindly to me."

I handed her a piece of apple. She had a bite, then set it on the plate and took my thumbs in her hands. "What happened to the makeup?"

I showed June, I said. I said, She has the same freckles on her wrists.

She kissed my thumbs and let go of them. "The same ones?"

They're pink, I said, but they're the same size, and they're definitely yuds.

"I wish you would have covered them after you showed her. You will cover them again tomorrow, yes?"

Yes, I said. Are you upset with me?

"Why should I be upset? Eat that apple."

I had a bite of apple. I said, It doesn't make you angry that I showed June the freckles?

"Were you trying to make me angry?" my mom said.

I said, I was trying to show June how we were the same.

"If I had strange birthmarks, and I met someone who had the same kind, and I liked that person, I would also show that person. I would think it meant something."

So you think it means something? I said.

"If it does not mean something," said my mother, "then you risked nothing by showing her, and my worries about others seeing the marks are senseless. In either case, there is no room for me to be angry. I am not a policewoman. I would not have you obey me only for the sake of obeying me. I just want you to be careful. It is careless that you did not cover them again before going to your teacher's house, but it does not seem that he saw, and if he did see, he did not think enough of the marks to even mention them to me in passing. So no harm has been done. Just cover them tomorrow before you leave the house. Do not become careless."

And the conversion doesn't make you angry? I said. I said, Rabbi Salt was upset—he said it didn't count.

"That is not so important to me, what Rabbi Salt thinks," said my mom. "What is important to me is that you believe it counts. It is important to me that it is important to you to have children who are like us. Whether or not June is actually like us—we can worry about that later, if you decide to marry her. And if it turns out that she is not like us, that is fine, too, as long as she becomes like us—as long as I know you'll make sure of that."

Really? I said.

"What is this new habit you have that when I tell you something you want to hear, you doubt my sincerity? I do not lie to you. Eat the apple I brought you. Make sure the girl you marry is Jewish when the time comes to marry her. Cover the marks tomorrow."

Do you believe the conversion counts, though? I said.

She said, "I have no opinion. I am not a Torah scholar. If you are asking me if I believe it *should* count, the answer is yes. I believe the world should be as you wish. You are my son, and who is better than you? No one. What do you have against the apple?" She took another bite of the apple. "I suppose it is a little soft. Check your email, then come downstairs. We will see what we have here for dinner. Your father has been delayed."

The email was from Jelly.

Sent: November 15, 2006, 7:09 PM Central-Standard Time
Subject: THE PLOT THICKENS
From: jellyjellyjellyjellyjellyjellyjelly@gmail.com (Jelly Rothstein)
To: Gurionforever@yahoo.com (me)

Dear Gurion,

How was ISS? The Cage was crazy today. Every carrel's got a WE DAMAGE WE bomb now, and someone put one on Botha's blotter when he went to the bathroom during a passing period. You ever think about Botha going to the bathroom? I never did til I just wrote it. It is a very sad thought, actually, but not because of why I'd think it was sad if someone told me it was sad which is because of how he probably has a hard time with his fly, which I think is actually funny since he's such a bancer and I hope everything in his life is hard. The sad part is how after the fly's open, and he's using his hand to aim because it would be too cold to use his claw, what does he do with the claw? In the movies, the unholding hand either hangs straight at the guy's side or they put it on their hip or on the wall the urinal's attached to, except I picture Botha like I'm standing a few feet behind him and holding a length of pianowire, and he's peeing into the urinal, aiming with his real hand, and there's his claw, and he can't decide where to put it, so he lets it dangle, then puts it on his hip, then lets it dangle, then puts it on the wall, but then no, the hip, the wall, dangle, and so on until he's done peeing and it gets me sad and I can't get myself to garrote him after all. Isn't that stupid?

Anyway, the reason I'm writing is because I know how you've been following my sister's stories on the Main Hall Shovers, and there's new news she just told me I thought you should know. When they came to school today, they all got their new scarves, and during lunch, three of them drew thick Jewish stars on their blankspots with Darkers because Berman, who Ruth told me you saw her fight with in the Office, told them they should draw the stars because the blankspots meant Christian even though they weren't Jesusfishes. So then after school, the Shovers all had an emergency meeting by the dumpsters and Ruth was there to do a report, and the Shovers voted to kick out Berman and the other two whose blankspots were starred because Acer said they defaced official Shover apparel, and then he told them to give back their scarves, and Berman said no way they were giving their scarves that they paid for to Acer to burn in an oven like his mom's grandma's cousins who were burned in ovens and had to wear stars, and Ruth said Acer never said anything about an oven, but that after Berman said oven all the rest of the Shovers who were Israelites took out Darkers and starred their blankspots, and they all walked away with their scarves still on. It really pissed off the other fifty-however-many Shovers, who voted to kick out ALL those kids who starred their blankspots, who there were thirteen of, and who before they walked away said that they were Main Hall Shovers no matter what anyone else had to say about it.

Ruth says the whole thing is very stupid. She says the Israelite Shovers are the stupidest part of it, and that Berman is the stupidest part of them because of the ovens. I think she's right about the ovens being very uncool because that's not even what Acer said, and even if he said it that's probably not what he would have meant, and I think Ruth's right that it's stupid to put Jewish stars on the scarves, but then I also think it's stupid to kick people out for starring their scarves because the scarves are theirs, but Ruth doesn't agree that that part's stupid because of how they all went through all that trouble with the Jesusfish and the blankspot, and the Israelites got their way and agreed to it. But I told Ruth they didn't really get their way because it was Frungeon who finally decided no Jesusfish, not the Shovers, and that meant the Shovers didn't care about their friends as much as their friends wanted them to, and that was the important thing, not the Jesusfish, and that would really piss me off if I was one of those friends, so whatever the blankspot meant, I wouldn't have been happy about it. I would have quit because you can't let people push you around like that and if they do you have to ditch them, I think. But then I imagine what if Mangey did something like that, or you, or, like, Benji, and how hard it would be to decide we weren't friends anymore because a lot of the way that I think of myself is that I'm Benji's friend, and if I stop being Benji's friend, then I am not who I was, and who wants to stop being who they are? I don't. And then I also think that maybe I just don't understand something those Shovers who starred their scarves do understand because of how I'm less Israelite than any of them, and so is Ruth, and so maybe she doesn't understand either because we never went to Hebrew School, but I know that you're the most Israelite person who I ever met, so what do you think?

I really want to know what I should think so that I don't have to think about it anymore. All of it makes me uncomfortable and I don't think that's really fair. Who cares about the stupid Shovers, right? They're stupid. But still. I feel bothered.

XOXO

Angelica Rothstein

PS Benji told me you were really in love with June Watermark and I wanted to tell you that what I said about her painting violent things and being weird I didn't mean. She does paint violent things and was always weird since a couple years ago, but that's not bad, and I was teasing you. I like her a lot, actually, and of course she didn't really kiss Josh Berman, that was just me teasing too hard because I like to wind you up because it's exciting for some reason, and if one day you don't have to go to Chicago right after school and you want to hang out, like you and June and me and maybe Benji or Jenny or Leevon, but probably not Jenny since her mom's always grounding her, and probably not Leevon because Leevon rides his bike to school and probably wouldn't want to leave it and it would be weird if he had it while the rest of us walked, we should go to eat pizza or something else and a movie or maybe just not get on the buses and walk to the lake instead if someone has cigarettes, the four of us, or maybe but probably not the five or six of us, since come to think of it, it should probably just be me and June and you and Benji because we probably shouldn't invite Leevon or Jenny since they probably couldn't go anyway for the reasons I just explained and so the invitation would only make them wish they could, and that would be suck.

PPS Ruth is standing here, looking over my shoulder, and she just told me that it is dumb to use a PS because the PS was invented before computers which means before you could cut and paste and delete stuff and that people used it because they had to write or type their letters, and once they got them perfect, they didn't want to have to retype or rewrite them to make room for anything they real-ized they should have said before they signed their name, so they put what they realized they should have said in the PS, but now there's no need to do that, so it's dumb to do it, Ruth says, and I should just cut and paste the PS content (Ruth keeps calling it "the PS content") into the space above the XOXO Ruth says, which is why I won't do it, and also why I will type PPS after I finish saying what I'm saying here, which is what I am calling the PPS content, and then cut and paste it into the space right before the first "Ruth" of this paragraph (even though you can already see the "PPS" before the paragraph's first "Ruth" right now, while I'm writing this, I mean, since there's only just one skipped line that divides the Ruth from the "suck" that ends the PS) because if you could see how much it is bothering her right now, the way she is biting off the nails of one hand and holding that hand's elbow with the other hand and getting sweaty because I know how to use and will use cut and paste but still won't use cut and paste the way she wants me to and how she can't do anything about what I want to do because I can beat her up so easy even though she's older than me, you would laugh at Ruth as much as I am laughing at Ruth and you would want to make that last as long as you possibly could.

I wrote her back:

Sent: November 15, 2006, 7:27 PM Central-Standard Time
Subject: RE: THE PLOT THICKENS
From: Gurionforever@yahoo.com (me)
To: jellyjellyjellyjellyjellyjellyjelly@gmail.com (Jelly Rothstein)

Hey Jelly,

You should write to me more often. I love long emails that aren't in leetspeak, and this one especially because it helped me figure something out. While I was in ISS, I saw this Shover through the window for a second, and I instantly knew he was an Israelite, but I didn't know how I knew he was an Israelite, and now I'm pretty sure I knew because he was one of those first three to star their scarves = I must have seen the star for a split second and registered what it meant without really registering that it was there

More importantly: There are no degrees of Israelite. You either are one or you're not. That is how it has always been. You, Jelly Rothstein, ARE one, so nobody in the world is more Israelite than you, and no one ever, in all of history, has been more Israelite than you.

Second: Israelites or not, the Shovers are dickheads because they are Shovers. On top of being dickheads, the Israelite ones are rats because they finked to Brodsky about the Jesusfish back in September. At the same time, the scarves, like you said, are theirs, and no one should be able to stop them from drawing whatever they want on the scarves, so I agree with you on that, but no one HAS stopped them, and no one CAN stop them, just like no one ever forced them to become Shovers. Should the Shovers have kicked them out for drawing the stars on the scarves? Maybe. I'd even say probably. I can't say for sure because I'm not a Shover, and it's not up to me to decide what it means to be a Shover (though it clearly means to be a dickhead). If the democratically elected president of the Shovers, shmendrick or not, says that drawing on the blankspot is an offense punishable by de-Shoverment—and especially if the vast majority of the Shovers agree with him—then it seems to me that drawing on the blankspot is an offense punishable by de-Shoverment, even if the de-Shoverment is hiddenly motivated by antisemitism (which I really don't think it is, not unless it's also antisemitic to say that Jews can't be mullahs or cardinals), or insensitivity, which it might be (but even that's complicated because the Gentile Shovers could just as easily say—and for all we know actually BELIEVE—that the Israelite Shovers had been insensitive to THEM; that instead of taking into account the Gentile Shovers' feelings about Frungeon or the Indians or whatever other feelings they feel that led them to think a Jesusfish or blankspot needs to be on their scarves, The Israelites ignored those feelings, insulted those feelings, etc).

The thing is, it isn't wrong to wear a Jesusfish on a scarf. It's wrong for ISRAELITES to wear a Jesusfish on a scarf. And furthermore, it's neither right nor wrong for Israelites to wear a scarf with a blankspot on it. And Adonai (God) couldn't care less either way if an Israelite wearing a scarf with a blankspot covers the blankspot with an Israelite religious symbol. He just doesn't care. So there's nothing good or noble about those Israelite Shovers starring their scarves, nor is there anything bad or cowardly about them breaking Shover rules—Adonai doesn't care about Shover rules either.

I'm with you when you say that the Israelite Shovers should have walked out on the rest of them the second it became clear that the rest of them wanted the Jesusfish regardless of what it meant to The Israelites. And I'm also with you on how hard it would be to stop being the friend of someone who betrayed you, and I would say that when a friend betrays you, it is normal, and understandable, and probably even good if your first impulse is to figure out a way to forgive the betrayal.

And probably some Israelite Shovers DID have friends among the Gentile ones, and those who did probably felt betrayed when their friends supported the Jesusfish, but obviously they chose to forgive those friends. And probably those same friends felt betrayed when the Israelites finked to Brodsky, but obviously those friends chose to forgive the Israelites. Except then they each betrayed each other again: the Israelites when they starred their scarves; the Gentiles when they kicked out the Israelites for starring their scarves. Whether or not they should forgive each other again isn't for anyone to say—there's no laws about it—but since they are all dickheads, it's a safe bet that whether they forgive or don't, it'll be for dickheaded reasons.

Another safe bet: tomorrow we will see some Jesusfished scarves.

Your friend,

Gurion

PS The PS may have been invented and used for the reasons Ruth said, but either way the content of a PS is an afterthought, so I don't see any reason why it shouldn't—as it does—look like one. Unless it's only pretending to be an afterthought, which would make the writer shady, except in certain situations like, for example, at the beginning of Part One, how everyone goes to Don Corleone's office during his daughter's wedding bearing gifts and giving blessings, but even Don Corleone knows they're there to ask a favor, even though the favor gets asked after the gifts and blessings are delivered = If every party knows that every party knows a given pretense is a pretense, then the pretense, even if it's unnecessary, isn't offensive.

PPS I think the best idea is to go to the beach and smoke, since I could walk to the train after that if it's not too cold. We should see how the weather is next Wednesday because I just quit the thing that I usually do on Wednesdays after school, so I'll have time to kill.

PPPS Sorry if there're a lot of grammar or spelling errors in this email. My mom's been yelling for me to come downstairs to eat dinner for the past five minutes, which is distracting.

□ □ □ □ □ □ □

Having eaten a little too much too fast, my mom and I leaned in opposite directions, against either arm of the three-cushion sofa, one leg apiece stretched over the ottoman, on which plates crusting with hummous and baba specks abutted a napkined basket of pita crumbs. Somebody'd slashed my father's tires. He'd caught a ride home from his office with a clerk. He entered the family room holding a pastry box ribboned with twine, and my mom and I waved. He set the box down atop the TV. *Seinfeld* was playing, disc 2, season 4. Kramer made noises, Elaine's mouth twisted, George's voice tightened, and Jerry rolled his eyes. My mother and father caught up on their day in voices whose volumes matched the TV's. Everything was fine, or seemed to be fine, the laughtrack mixing with my parents' conversation, and I started spacing out, started falling asleep, maybe even fell fully for a second or a minute—and then I snapped to with a hiccup.

"...on the stoop?" my Dad was saying.

"No," said my mother. "I came through the back."

I hated the hiccups. They made me feel hopeless. I hardly ever got them; when I did they'd last hours.

"'Maccabees not unwelcome,' it says. This guy doesn't understand the effect of double-negatives—either that or he likes me," my dad told my mom. "I don't know what's more spooky."

I could heal the hiccups instantly, but not when they were mine. When a friend had the hiccups, I'd take out my wallet, then take all the money out of my wallet, then count the money slowly, out loud.

"Both ways are spooky," my mother said. "I'll call the police."

I'd have eleven dollars, or maybe just three—it didn't matter, but call it eleven.

"I called them already—after the tires. They're sending a car. It'll be here at nine. They'll send it every night til the trial blows over."

I'd slap the money, or I'd slap a table *with* the money, and I'd tell my friend: This right here is eleven dollars cash. If you can hiccup one more time, I will give you all of it.

The cure never failed. No one ever hiccuped after I'd say that. Even the people who I'd done it to already. None of them would ever perform the cure on me, though. I think they thought that since I'd invented it, it wouldn't work, and then they'd have to give me the money.

"Not unwelcome," my father said. "Why not skip the *not* and the *un*? Why not just write—

"Boo!" my dad shouted.

I startled. I hiccupped.

He laughed with my mom and the fake studio audience.

Then I explained to him about the *un*, and only the fake studio audience laughed.

"You're telling me," he said, "that someone comes along, vandalizes our property, and your solution to this is to *further* vandalize our property? How is that something my son thinks to do? How is that bright?"

I hiccuped.

"I'm asking you, Gurion."

I was planning to blind him, I said, from my window, but he only comes around while I'm at Aptakisic.

"Why not call the police?" said my father.

I said, Because—

And he cut me off—he hadn't been asking. "Even if being stricken with blindness," he said, "were an appropriate punishment for committing an act of vandalism—and it isn't, by the way, it's *tyrannical*—why let your life be controlled by your ill-wishers? Why lose the sleep that they want you to lose? I don't understand you."

The police eventually leave, I said, and the vandals—

I hiccupped, this time cutting myself off.

"What?" said my father. "The vandals *what*?"

They always come back.

"It is true," my mother said.

"Don't encourage him, Tamar. He's not joking, and neither should we joke. If you blind someone, Gurion, you think no one will ever bother us again? Because that would be a fantasy. They will always bother us. You will always be bothered by others. And if you act violently toward those who bother you today, then tomorrow, they will return the favor."

I'm—*hiccup*—stronger than them, I said.

"You know what?" he said. "Let's accept your baseless premise, for the sake of argument, and see where it takes us. So fine, you're the strongest person in the world, no one can harm you, you can kick everyone's ass, you're safe… I'm not, though. Not me. Not safe. I can't kick everyone's ass. And your mom can't either, believe it or not; not everyone's. So imagine one day the father of someone you blinded, vengeance-hungry, gathers his friends together and, knowing you're an immortal asskicker, he rationally—notice I'm not even bothering to quibble over whether someone acting on vengeful impulses can properly be called *rational*—this vengeful father, he rationally decides to come after me, or your mother—both of us, say, for an eye for an eye is not good enough for this fellow and his buddies, he wants a two-for-one—and you're at school, busy fighting janitors and vegetables with padlocks when they come—what then? We're both blind is what then, your mother and I. And that's only if the man and his friends settle on the two-for-one exchange, and I don't see why they should; if two-for-one is acceptable, if an-eye-for-an-eye goes out the window, why not an eye for a life, two lives even? Especially when the woman keeps getting up, cursing in Arabic, breaking noses—any vengeful shmo with half a brain would certainly worry how your mother might avenge *her*self later, no? And even if they didn't have half a brain, the damage she brings to these attackers before they get to her eyes—this is damage for which they would seek even more vengeance. And so what? What happens? We're dead is so what. You've effectively killed your parents is what happens. How's that for a fantasy? You blind a vandal and get to be an orphan. Gurion ben-No One," he said. "Is that what you want? No one around to stop you from burning down houses with your delinquent friends and going to jail? To sink like a fucking ball of lead, no one to obstruct you?"

I wouldn't, I said and hiccupped. I said, I wouldn't let anyone kill you.

My mother said, "We know. No one will kill us, Gurion. You won't be an orphan. Your father has had a hard day."

"Please keep feeding the fire!" said my father. "Please undo everything I say to him!"

"You are yelling, Judah."

"And you, Tamar, are not paying attention! You spoke to Avel Salt earlier, did you not? Your son is delusional. This is *our* fault."

"Our son is imaginitive. You, on the other hand, are as *touchy* as you always become whenever you have just made closing arguments, and this is making *you* delusional."

My father chewed a lip, turned away from my mother. My mother changed her posture. Good, I thought. Pinch him. Pinch him on the neck. Pinch him or reach out and thumb-stab his thigh. Instead she lit a cigarette and studied the cherry.

My parents were fighting.

"So tell me," said my father. "You converted someone today?"

Yes, I said.

"And how is that possible?"

I explained. Or I tried to. The more I talked, the worse the hiccups got. The worse the hiccups got, the more H I got. And I had to look at *Seinfeld*, which looked like disrespect—I could look at *Seinfeld* or I could look at my father, who my hiccups were annoying, who I didn't want to look at, whose lips got twistier, whose nostrils got wider, whose eyes got squintier with each word I spoke.

"Wow," he said, once I'd finished explaining. "Wow!" he said. "I had no idea! Sabbatai Zevi and Shimon bar-Kokhba, Yeshua of Nazareth himself—how violently their bones must be quaking with jealousy. Your power to deceive yourself, Gurion—it's unmatched. And that's to say nothing of your ability to articulate your self-deceptions. Truly amazing. You keep it up, sonnyboy, you might actually be the end of us. And by 'us' I mean the Jews, of whom your girlfriend is one. Of course she is. Of course she's Jewish. Your girlfriend is Jewish because she has a couple birthmarks and you've got a gift for casuistry."

And you'll have the cops watch over your house because *you've* got a gift for *bravery*, I said.

He pulled me from the couch and held me in the air, under the arms so we were eye-to-eye. He was giving me The Look of The End.

"This is the gaze of someone you would do better to hide from," he said, in a whisper so calm Bam Slokum would envy it. "Someone looks at you like this, no matter who it is, it always means the same thing. It is how I've been looking at you for the past ten minutes. Memorize this gaze, and the next time you encounter it, you'll know to run in the opposite direction *before* you lose the use of your legs."

He set me down on the couch, onto my feet. Outside of daydreams, I had never seen him so dangerous, and I just stood there, slouching, on cushions, staring. How can I explain it? My father could have exploded and turned all of Chicago to dust at that moment, and though I, if he did explode, would have been ground zero, he was my father, and the thrill that filled me was not just the thrill of being afraid—it wasn't even mostly that. I kept on thinking: Look what he can do. I am his son.

"Did you not hear me?" he said.

My mother stepped between us. She lifted me off the couch and set me down on the floor beside the nearer arm. "Go to your room," she said.

I went to my room. My hiccups were gone.

◻ ◻ ◻ ◻ ◻ ◻ ◻

If the point of fighting with people you love is to kill your desire to fight them; if it is best, in the course of this killing, to inflict as little lasting damage as possible; and if that means fights fought smartest by loved ones can't but scream topspeed toward stalemate, then let no scholar confuse the following for overstatement: My parents fought like geniuses that night.

Though their words got incoherent by the time they reached my bedroom—the shapes of their vowels lost between the floorboards, their consonants made mush by the rugs and insulation—there was no mistaking that those words were being shouted. I didn't enjoy that, but I saw it was good. Charged with enough decibals, any verbal attack, no matter how ugly, could later be blamed with little effort on the heat of the moment. As long as they stayed loud, I knew we'd be fine. By bedtime, the fight would seem as much a thing that happened to them as it would a thing they made happen. By morning it would seem like a place, static and passable; not "That time I fought you" or even "That time we were fighting," but "That time we got *into* a fight."

Knowing everything would eventually be fine was not the same as everything actually being fine, though. If it were, then scholars wouldn't try to bring the messiah, my parents wouldn't have fought, and I'd have had the concentration to write immortal scripture. Instead I checked email, where nothing was personal—two weekly digests from scholarly listservs and a spam from a pornsite: "I'm Suzy CUM fly me."

I tried calling Nakamook, but his mother picked up. "What?" she said.

Can I please speak to Benji?

"No," she said, and then she hung up.

I tried calling Vincie, but the phone was off the hook.

Eliyahu wasn't listed in the Aptakisic directory, and I didn't know his uncle's last name for 411. He'd never told me his own last name either. All I knew was it wasn't Of Brooklyn.

Main Man's dad said, "Scott's in bed," but Mookus picked up on a different extension, saying "Gurion is the leader of the Side of Damage, and that which he brings will be once and for all yet all for one. Our plastic muskets, though powderless, will frontload, and our coup will not be bloodless, nor will the blood be lambly. It will stain the lion's den whose bars though invisible are verily there as we roll along, doo-da doo-da and a thousand lonely dirges. Time alone oh time will tell, and peanuts to you there, pally. When first he is king we'll be first against the wall, then it's pop goes the weasel in your opinion, but that's hardly of consequence goodnight."

Scott sounded tired.

Ha-ha, I said.

"Ha-ha!" said Main Man. "Ha-ha! Ha-ha!"

"Goodnight, Gurion," said Mr. Mookus. "Goodnight, Scott," he said. The phone clicked.

"Ha-"

The phone clicked again and they were both gone. The noise from downstairs had ebbed and cut out.

Soon my father came in with the pastry box, twineless. He opened the lid and showed me stacks of flour-dappled poppyseed cookies. These cookies were a longtime family favorite he got from a bakery whose name and locale he refused to divulge. He sat on my bed and tried to look at my face. I didn't let him. We ate a couple cookies without saying anything. They were better than I remembered. They were hard and they crumbled and the crumbs were buttery.

"We should never again speak to each other the way we spoke to each other downstairs," said my dad. He lit a cigarette. "Do you agree with that?" he said.

I did not disagree.

"I am not used to being scared for you," he said. "I have always believed you, and I have always believed *in* you. When you were kicked out of Schechter, I thought: My son reacted to a provocation that would have caused me to react as well. He *over*reacted, I thought, but he is a boy, and a boy is a child, and a child overreacts. I wasn't scared."

He ashed his cigarette into the cup of his hand.

He said, "When you were kicked out of Northside, again I thought you'd overreacted, but you were overreacting to a provocation that would have also caused me to react, albeit not by telling people to take up arms, let alone teaching them how to do so, but still... Your intentions were good. I believed that, and I still do. And when I read that email from the Northside headmaster, Gurion, I was going to destroy his life as thoroughly as I could without doing the same to ours. He was trying to harm you, and I am not willing to let anyone harm you. You told me that if I sued him, it would make the whole episode worse for you. I didn't sue him."

He half-stood and leaned across me. He flipped my desk's mailslot open, turned his cupped palm over it, and then he flicked his cigarette against its lip. The ashes hit the floor beneath my desk and flattened. I stepped on them, caught them up in my sock fibers.

"And I will not pretend," he said, "that the idea of your being prevented from studying Torah with those people didn't strike me as a blessing in disguise. I didn't think that studying with them was doing much in the way of helping you live a good life. I still don't think so. That said, I knew that my experiences as a scholar—as one of *them*—were peculiar and misled, and that surely it was impossible for me to consider what studying with them was doing to you without that consideration being haunted by what I knew it had done to me. And so when you resolved to continue working with Rabbi Salt, I did not raise any objections."

Again he leaned over me and ashed into the mailslot. And again I stepped on the ashes and caught them in my sock fibers.

What are you doing? I said.

"Did I just ash in your mailslot?"

Twice, I said.

"I'm sorry—I'm tired. It's what I used to do at yeshiva. I had the same kind of desk, you know—I lined the mailslot with tinfoil, though. I thought I was very clever. A desk with a secret built-in ashtray. We weren't supposed to smoke in the dorm. Why don't you pass me the wastebasket."

I passed it to him.

"Where was I?" he said.

You didn't object to me studying with Rabbi Salt.

"No. I did object. Just not wholeheartedly—I didn't object enough to *raise* objections. And in August, when they kicked you out of the King School, I believed what you said, I believed you were innocent of hurting anyone with that brick. I worried about what your mother had been teaching you—it worried me that the thought to even heft that brick occurred to you—but also I was glad you picked up the brick. I was glad because, in the end, doing so prevented you from being hurt by those other boys. None of it scared me, Gurion. I worried like a father worries, but I did not experience *fear*.

"But then yesterday, when I heard that you'd been fighting all this time, it got me a little scared. Not because you were fighting, which is worrisome, and not even because you and your mother have hidden it from me, which is *very* worrisome, but rather because all the time you were hiding this from me, I never suspected it. I never suspected it for a moment. And so I have to wonder what other hidden business I am failing to suspect. And that is not a nice thing to wonder about. That is a fearsome thing to wonder about. And then, just now, downstairs, you say to me—"

I said, I didn't mean what I said, Aba.

He said, "I know you didn't. You wanted to hurt me because I had hurt you. That is natural—to want to hurt what has hurt you is natural—but what hurt you, Gurion, is not that *I* said what I said. It is that what I said was accurate, and a large part of you knows it. A large part of you knows you are not the messiah."

All of me knows I'm not the messiah, I said. I said, And all of me knows I might be. I *am* a Judite.

"If that's the only criteria, then so might I be the messiah, and millions of others, but I don't act as if I am just because I *might* be. Nor do the vast majority of them."

Maybe you should, I said. I said, Maybe if you act like the messiah, you'll become the messiah. Maybe that's what the messiah needs to do.

"I don't want to be the messiah, Gurion. I don't even think I believe in the messiah. This is an absurd line of inquiry. We're talking about *you*."

I said, Well I didn't do anything messianic, anyway. I don't have to be the messiah to convert somebody. Moses wasn't the messiah.

"You're not Moses either, Gurion."

I said, I know I'm not Moses. I just had this conversation with Rabbi Salt. You are in total agreement with the Blackhats, Aba. You have returned to the fold to unite with those you abandoned in an orgy of total dismissal of your son's heartfelt words.

"Don't be so dramatic," said my father. "I'm not uniting with—"

I wasn't being dramatic, I said. I said, I was being arch. Bitingly ironic.

My dad laughed = "I want everything to be right with us."

I don't have to be Moses, I said. I said, Israelites will read the scripture I'll write—I'll have authority like Moses.

"Are you still being bitingly ironic?"

I said, I'm being completely sincere.

"That's a hard sentence to pull off without sounding a little ironic. If someone were listening, they might think you were making fun of your father."

I'm not making fun of you, I said.

"Even that one—hard to take at face value after the ones just preceding it, no?"

He lit a new cigarette off the old one, set the old one on its filter, cherry-side-up on my desk so it could go out.

"Moses didn't have authority just because he wrote Torah," he said. "He also led the Jews out of bondage. God chose him to do both of those things, and writing the Torah was the *second* one, which is pretty significant, I'd think. And even if I'm wrong about that; even if his taking us from bondage was causally unrelated to his being chosen to write the Torah—even if God would have given the Torah to Moses regardless of what Moses did for us in Egypt and the Sinai—I think it's pretty safe to assume no Jew would have listened to Moses if he hadn't ended our slavery. I mean, would you? If he hadn't led you from bondage? Would you have listened to him? I wouldn't have. Why should I believe some dandy prince with a stutter should be the one to receive the word of God?"

I said, Torah is what tells you the story of the stuttering prince. And it's the stuttering prince who wrote it down.

"The Torah's important," said my father. "It's the most important thing the Jews have—I'm not saying it isn't. I'm just saying that its author... Uch! This is all beside the point. It's not even that you're delusional—you *are*, but it's not that; it's the nature of your delusions. If you wanted to believe your girlfriend was a Jew and so you merely insisted that she was a Jew, that wouldn't be so bad. But why you want those who have hurt you to think that she is a Jew—"

An Israelite, I said.

"Fine. An Israelite... what you call it doesn't change anything. That it is important to you that she be known to *them* as an Israelite... that you feel the need to prove it, or anything else, to the same people who have expelled you from their schools, the same mamzers who have kept you from your friends, who have vandalized our home and threatened our family, who have rejected you at every opportunity... It doesn't follow for you to want their approval. You were just telling me you wanted to blind one of them. Why do you want to blind someone who you want to accept you? Why do you want acceptance from someone who you wish blindness on? What does it matter if they think your girlfriend is an Israelite?"

I said, I am loyal to June, and—

"If you're so loyal to June, what do you care if she converts or not? Why can't you just love her regardless? When I married your mother, there were still a lot of Jews who did not consider her Jewish, and I—"

Those Jews were wrong, I said. They didn't know the truth and you did and you married Ema without any hesitation because you loved her and you knew the truth. And I know you were defiant. I know all about you. You were defiant, and because you were defiant you married her without regard for what your community endorsed. But we aren't talking about you, anyway, right? That is what you said a minute ago. We are talking about me. That is what you said. And I am not defiant, not like you were. I am loyal.

I said, I am loyal to the Israelites as well as to June and to Adonai and to you, Aba. I don't care if June converts. Whether or not she converts, she is an Israelite and that is the truth. I said, I know it and June knows it and

Adonai knows it. The Israelites don't know it, though, and neither do you. So it would be disloyal of me not to convince you and them of the truth. I am obligated by loyalty to do so.

"You're not going to convince anyone, though, ever. And what will happen when you realize that? I worry, Gurion. You're not so good at disappointment. You get disappointed, you do rash things."

I said, You say I won't convince anyone because you believe it is true and you are loyal to your son, Aba. I said, You say it because I am your son, and you feel obligated to convince me of the truth. And you *are* obligated. And so you will *always* try to convince me of the truth. And you're my father, and I'm loyal to you, and so I will always do the same for you. I know you understand that.

"So much fancytalk only to come to let's agree to disagree?"

You're making light of what I'm saying, I said.

"I'm trying to end this conversation on a nice note," he said. "I'm trying to be the soft Yiddishe dad you admired in that *Story of Stories*. I'm trying not to be the angry father who killed rapists and made threats in the family room. I want you to be softer and more Yiddishe. I want you to be less angry."

He'd said "killed" and not "murdered," so I hugged him and kept my mouth shut. In time, I knew, he would come around.

□   □   □   □   □   □   □

There is love. There was always love, and there will be more love, forever. Were there ever to be less love, we would all be at war, and Your angels would learn suffering.

Alone in my room, I awakened my computer, then looked at what I'd written the day before, and I saw it wasn't good. I liked the rhythm of the words, but that didn't make them true. Though more war didn't strike me as a particularly unlikely outcome of less love in the world, there was at least as good a case to be made for an outcome of less war. And to say that angels would learn suffering, ever—it was hard to figure out how that could be. Angels delighted in every aspect of Adonai's creation of the world. That is what He'd made them to do. How could beings who delighted in everything suffer? It didn't seem possible.

And these were the least of the paragraph's problems.

The biggest one was that the whole third sentence read threatening—and in the lowest, least effective kind of way. It was a four-year old stomping grocery-store linoleum and telling his mom he'll hold his breath til he dies if she doesn't right this minute buy him brightly colored, mock-food, toy-bearing cereal. "You better not decrease the amount of love in the world, Hashem, or we're gonna start killing each other, and You'll really regret it then."

Whatever consequences might come if there were less love in the world was beside the point, anyway. The point—rather, what *should* have been the point; what is *always* the point of scripture, even as it speaks about what has been and what will or might be—was to get across, directly or not, what *is*. So I deleted everything but the first seven words, and went from there:

> There is love. There was always love, and it has always been righteous. Were love not righteous, then nothing would be righteous, and we would not serve justice, let alone study Law, but allow the peace of tyrants to fall upon us like a blanket, and all things dangerous to scare us away.
>
> Bless Adonai for making Law of love's corrolaries, and bless Him for making love's protection Law's objective. Blessed is Adonai, King of the Universe, for granting us our potential to be just.

I read the scripture over four or five times, eating two of three cookies my father had left me, and I thought it was good enough to deliver. I knew that to only *think* it was good enough was not a good enough reason to deliver it—I had to know for sure. But I saw that I couldn't know for sure if it was good enough until it had actually been delivered. I decided I'd deliver it and find out for sure. How I'd do that—it unfolded as I wrote, as if the plan itself were being revealed.

Sent: November 15, 2006, 9:07 PM Central-Standard Time
Subject: NEW SCRIPTURE
From: Gurionforever@yahoo.com (me)
To: Gurionforever@yahoo.com
CC: NEW SCHECHTER LIST, NORTHSIDE HEBREW DAY LIST

Scholars:
When last I contacted you, I said I wouldn't do so again until

such a time when to disobey your parents, in regards to me, would be to honor them. But I might have been wrong about that. It is hard to tell. It is true that I am contacting you, yet I am not certain that a situation indicating an equivalence between disobedience and filial honor has arisen. I'm not certain it's okay for you to contact me yet.

Nor am I certain, when I really get to thinking about it, what exactly *contact* means.

I am certain, though, of some of the things *contact* does not mean. For instance: If you went to shul last Saturday, and you davened with the congregation and then left, you did not—even though you knew he would be there, leading the service—you did not contact the rabbi. And if you were a Cohain, and the rabbi called out for Cohains to approach the bimah and bless the congregation, and you went up and stood near him and spread your fingers and blessed the congregation— even then, though it could reasonably be argued that the rabbi con- tacted you, it could not be said that you contacted the rabbi.

I am also certain of other things. I am certain that yesterday I fell in love with a red-haired girl, today I wrote scripture, and tomorrow, at 11:00 a.m., with the red-haired girl beside me, I will deliver this scrip- ture atop the higher of the two hills across the street from Aptakisic Junior High School, directions to which are attached to this email. I am certain that were you to stand in the valley between the two hills and hear my recitation, it could not be said that in doing so you contacted me. And, finally, I am certain that if after the recitation—if, maybe, *as a consequence of the recitation*—we find that we have entered a time when to disobey our parents is to honor them, then we will *all* be certain of it, every last one of us.

Your friend,
Gurion

———————————

AptakisicDirections.doc
24K View Download

I ate the third cookie as I read the email over. I had one bite left when the phone rang.

"Gurion," whispered June.

June! I said, I've been eating the best poppyseed cookies in all of Chi- cago and—

"My mom said I could be Jewish if I wanted to be Jewish, but that I can't just say I am and then be it," said June. "I told her I didn't just say I am. I told her *you* said I am, and so I was, and she said that was impossible and I yelled at her and got grounded."

What did your dad say?

"I haven't seen him in three years. Am I Jewish or not?"

I said, There are no more Jews. There are only Israelites. You are one of them.

"That's what I said," June said.

Three years? I said.

"I can't wait to see you again," she said. "I don't want to wait til detention."

Good, I said, because tomorrow I need you to get out of class at eleven and meet me in the doorway of the boys' locker-room.

"You think cause I'm an Israelite you can just tell me when and where we're gonna make out next?" she said.

It's—

"Just kidding," she said. "Of course I want to make out with you at 11 a.m."

I said, I'm not talking about making out.

"Well so what's so special about 11:00, then?" she said. "It's third period. I've got Social Studies."

I said, A bunch of my friends are gonna meet us in the two-hill field.

"Tell them to come after school," she said.

They can't, I said. They'll be coming from Chicago, and by the time they'd get here, the intramural buses will be gone, and so you wouldn't have a way to get home. Plus, where would we wait between the end of detention and what, like, seven-thirty? It's gonna be cold tomorrow. And then now you're saying you got grounded. So what my friends have to do is, they have to ditch school. To do that, though, they're gonna have to act like they're going to school, but instead come to Aptakisic.

"Can't they come during recess?"

They'll be walking from the Metra station in Deerbrook Park, so it'll take them forty-five to sixty minutes more to get to Aptakisic than it takes me to get there, which means if they leave at 8:00, which is the time that most of them leave for school, they'll get to the two-hill field by 11:00 at latest, right? And they're gonna want to do that—they're gonna want to be on their way here, and way the hell out of the neighborhood as early as possible, because once the principals of their schools realize they're all ditching, calls will be made and parents will be set in motion. If they're still in the vicinity of where they live, they might get busted. If they're on their way here, though, they won't get busted, at least not before we all get to hang out, and no one in a million years is gonna guess that hundreds of scholars all ditched school to go to Deerbrook Park.

"Hundreds?"

I'm guessing about two to three hundred, I said. And so if they get here at 10:45, and we make them wait til recess—

"You have hundreds of friends?"

That's what I'm told, I said.

"Well then, no," June said.

June, it's really important, I said.

"No, I didn't mean 'No' like 'No, I won't do it'—I'll meet you. I meant 'No' like 'You're right, we can't make them wait in the cold like that if they come all that way just to visit us.'"

"Good," I said. I clicked SEND and the email was disseminated.

And then we both talked at the same time. June said, "I can't wait to see you," and I said, Three years?

Then she said, "Bring me a cookie, okay? I miss you so bad I hate the sound of your voice." And then she hung up.

Goodnight, I said to no one.

I finished my cookie and there was night.

12
DEFACE

Thursday, November 16, 2006
6:00 a.m.–3rd Period

A nd there was morning, Thursday.

I woke to the smell of piping-hot fat, which meant my dad was restless. When I got to the kitchen, he was scrambling brie cheese and green peppers in a pan of frying eggs.

"You want a chub?" he said. A chub is a smoked whitefish with a head without eyeballs. "There's chubs in the fridge," he said, "also some sable. You want sable?"

I don't like that stuff, I said.

"When're you gonna learn?"

It smells fishy, I said.

"Fishy."

I like lox, I said.

"Bully for you," he said. "You know who likes lox? William F. Buckley likes lox. He calls it smoked salmon. He likes bagels, too. All those goy bluebloods like lox and bagels. Salmon and rolls. You know who William F. Buckley is?"

A goy? I said.

"A goy in a blazer with gold buttons," said my father. "Men like him put lox-bagels in wicker baskets and eat them for lunch on their catamarans. You know what a catamaran is?"

No, I said.

"It's some kind of boat," he said.

Catamaran, I said.

I liked to say it.

"Or else a schooner," he said. "If you've got a gold-buttoned blazer for the weekend and it's blue, you might have a catamaran, but also you might have a schooner, which is what?"

Some kind of boat? I said.

"You got it. Do you have a schooner or a catamaran?"

I started laughing.

"Are you some kind of yachtsman in a special sports-jacket?"

No! I said.

"So learn to love fish that smells like fish," he said, "or drop a syllable, become Greg, and add a prominent middle intial. An F, probably." He turned the pan of cheese-eggs over a plate, but they wouldn't come out. He tapped the pan with the spatula, once, twice, three times. The eggs flopped from the pan, landed on the plate as a single, crisp-edged glob. "Gregory F. McCabe," said my dad, "of the textile and petroleum McCabes of West Texas. Not to be confused," he said, sawing the egg-mass in half, shoving one of the portions onto a second plate, "with the shipping and armaments McCabes of East Texas." He said, "I didn't get you any lox, Clark Kent." He set the plates on the table in front of me and went to the oven. "Christopher Peterson," he said. He wrapped his hand in a towel, pulled a dish from the oven, said, "Bryce Matthew Pemberton-Exley." He set the towel on the table and the dish on the towel, sat down next to me, then immediately got back up and took a chub from the fridge. "Lox you want a bagel for," he said, "and I knew I was making cornbread. You can't have bagels and cornbread in one meal. You'll be snoozing by second period." He cut me a piece of cornbread. He said, "Have some cornbread, Jimmy."

We ate our cheese-eggs and cornbread.

You'll win, I told him. I said, You probably won already.

"I know," he said.

If you knew, I said, you wouldn't have been up at five, mixing cornbread batter, waiting for the deli to open.

"I got up at four," he said. "This is the second meal I've prepared today. Your mother—I went to the Jewel for the cornbread mix and got some plain yogurt and fresh fruit for her. I chopped the fruit, and she still wasn't up, so I started peeling almonds. Not that she cares if they're peeled, but it was something to do. Then I mixed it all into the yogurt. You know that when we yell, it's not really fighting, right? Even when it sounds like it. We're just yellers."

I know, I said.

He said, "You come from a loud family, kiddo." He slit the whitefish at the tail, pulled away its gold-scaled skin with his fingers, then flipped the fish over and repeated the process. "She left for work after the yogurt, and that's when I went to the deli," he said. "I went out twice for food already. This is the second meal I've prepared this morning. I said that already. But it's not I don't think I've won," he said. "Probably I did—I usually do. But I don't know for sure, and so I have to wait. I have to wait around til they call. For all I know they won't call til next week. What do I do in the meantime? If I start working on the next thing, and it turns out I have to appeal this one, then…I don't know."

I said, Rambam.

"Rambam what?" he said.

I said, You don't want to start the next thing before the first one's finished. You're trying to do things in the right order, like the Rambam said.

"I'm trying to do things in a certain order because I'm superstitious. You shouldn't be like that. It's foolish. And for future reference," he said, "this is how you get the meat off the fish. You don't want bones in it, okay? So you turn the guy upside-down, press lightly with the fork, right here, under his spine, and push, away from the spine. If he's right-side up, you end up pulling—pulling, you get more bones. You probably get a couple bones, anyway, so you have to be careful. You have to push gentle."

He ate a forkful of fish. "It's delicious," he said. "Salty. Try some." He wedged a piece between knife and fork, held it up.

It looked mushy. And it wasn't white, but beige with shots of bruisey purple.

No, I said.

"Well I don't want it either," he said. "I wasn't even hungry the first time I ate today. It's a shame to waste a nice chub like this. I'll leave it for you while I take a shower. Then I'll drive you to school because I have nothing else to do. Sound good?"

You got your car back? I said.

He said, "Ema took the train."

Can we listen to the Fugees? I said.

"We can listen to anything you want as long as it's on NPR," he said. "Your mom put your lunch on the foyer table. I'll be down in six minutes. Be ready."

I went to the foyer, got my lunch off the table. Stapled to the fold of the bag was a note:

> I SAVED YOU FOUR POPPYSEED COOKIES FOR LUNCH. DO NOT GIVE THEM ALL AWAY TO JUNE. IF YOU GIVE HER ALL YOUR COOKIES, THEN SHE WILL NOT BELIEVE THAT THEY ARE AS VALUABLE A GIFT AS WE KNOW THEY ARE. RATHER,

SHE WILL WONDER, "IF THESE COOKIES ARE SO ENJOYABLE AND DELICIOUS, WHY DOES GURION NOT TAKE AT LEAST ONE FOR HIMSELF?" AND WHEN SHE EATS THE COOKIES, SHE WILL NOT ENJOY THEM AS MUCH AS SHE OTHERWISE WOULD HAVE.

SO KEEP NO FEWER THAN TWO FOR YOURSELF. MAKE SURE TO EAT AT LEAST ONE IN FRONT OF JUNE. IF YOU CHOOSE NOT TO EAT A SECOND ONE IN FRONT OF HER, SHE SHOULD BE MADE AWARE THAT THERE IS A SECOND ONE, SO SHE WILL KNOW THAT YOU DID NOT EAT THE FIRST ONE OUT OF MERE POLITENESS. SHE NEEDS TO KNOW THAT ALTHOUGH YOU ARE GLAD AT THE IDEA OF GIVING HER DELICIOUS COOKIES, PARTING WITH THE COOKIES IS NOT IN ITSELF ANY KIND OF SPRING PICNIC.

AND ALWAYS REMEMBER THAT ALL OF THOSE COOKIES HAVE ALWAYS BEEN YOURS, AND THEY ALWAYS WILL BE.

LOVE, MOM THE PUPPET

□ · □ □ □ □ □ □

When his celly chimed, my father was merging onto the highway at 50 while lighting a cigarette and lowering the driver-side window. He dropped his lighter in the center console, kept the lit cigarette in his mouth, reached for the phone in his pocket, set his window-button hand on the steering wheel, and then thrust us off the ramp, into the slow lane, which was going fast.

"Radio," he said.

I turned the volume knob all the way left.

"What time?" he said into the mouthpiece. Then: "Good."

He handed me the phone while pressing the end button.

What am I supposed to do with this? I said.

"Doesn't matter," he said. "They've got a verdict. Came in last night. I have to wait til 3:00 to hear it. We have to listen to music now, loudly."

Fugees? I said.

"*Fugees?*" he said. He said it like I was crazy. He said, "Find the Mix."

The Mix was a CD of anthems, mostly punk rock ones he missed out on as a yeshiva boy. My dad made the Mix when I was two and he got his first burner. It was all he would listen to on days that a verdict was going to be delivered, and he would never listen to any of the songs it contained on other days. He made about twenty copies of the Mix and stashed them all over the place like a gangster does with his money. There were two copies in the car. I pulled out the one that was under the seat.

"Get the other one—that one's scratched," he said.

I got the other one from the glovebox.

It was also scratched. The only songs that worked were the first two: "Gotta Gettaway" by Stiff Little Fingers and "Guns of Brixton" by the Clash. As soon as "Guns" would end, the player would skip back to track 1 and "Gotta Gettaway" would start again.

"Gotta Gettaway" wasn't fun to sing along with, but we traded off screaming verses at each other during the third round of "Guns" and came together on the choruses.

> (*Judah*)
> When they kick at your front door
> How you gonna come?
> (*Gurion*)
> With your hands on your head
> Or the trigger of your gun?
>
> (*Judah*)
> When the law break in
> How you gonna go?
> (*Gurion*)
> Shot down on the pavement
> Or waiting on death row?
>
> (*Judah and Gurion*)
> You can crush us
> You can bruise us
> But you'll have to answer to
> Oh, oh, the guns of Brixton

We were two-thirds through a fourth round of "Gotta Gettaway" when we pulled into the Aptakisic parking lot. I waited in the car for the song to finish. I didn't want it to be stuck in my head all day and get ruined. Songs I knew always stuck when I'd quit them before they were over—they'd get stuck from the point where the song left off and repeat. It would have been especially bad if "Gotta Gettaway" got stuck right then because the last third of that song was, itself, a bunch of repetition: "Gotta. Gotta. Get away. Gotta. Gotta. Get away," and then, "Gotta gotta gotta gotta gotta gotta gotta get away" over and over with another singer going, "Oh oh," in the background.

Unfinished songs stuck to my father the same way, so I didn't have to explain why I wasn't getting out of the car. The two of us just sat there for a minute, watching students walk from the bus circle to the front entrance. The Main Hall Shovers poked each other and did secret handshakes, and I saw that some had, yes, drawn icthii on their blankspots. The Jennys and the Ashleys made exasperated faces and hugged basketballers. The basketballers acted bored and copped feels. Bandkids leaned left or right, depending on which hand held their instrument case. The jolt of every step taken by a tiny girl I'd never seen before pushed a looseleaf binder closer to ejection from her half-unzipped backpack. Then I saw Ben-Wa Wolf and three other Cage kids—Casper Lunt, Fulton Market, and Derrick Winnetka—doing this thing that looked like some kind of game. Ben-Wa would pratfall, and the others would surround him to help him up, but they didn't help him immediately—they faced away from him for a few seconds first, as if they were worried others might see them. After the third pratfall, I gave up trying to deduce the game's rules and decided I'd ask them about it later, but in the meantime "Gotta Gettaway" had ended and "Guns of Brixton" had started. I looked at my Dad and he waved a short wave with one hand = "So wait out 'Guns of Brixton.' I don't have to be downtown til three."

Soon, a yellow pickup truck driven by a girl with high bangs and blue eye-makeup pulled into the lot a couple spaces to our right and Bam Slokum got out of the passenger side. He chinned the air at me as he passed our car, and I chinned it back and felt dumb.

"What the hell does that guy teach?" my dad shouted over the music.

I said, Ha!

"Ha *what*? He's wearing ripped jeans. That's not a good examp— Who's this?" he said, suddenly looking over my shoulder.

My shoulder got cold.

June had opened my door.

"Who are you?" my dad shouted at June.

She pinched my shoulder. "June!" she shouted back.

My father halved the volume of the Clash. "I'm Judah," he said.

He's my dad, I said.

"He's not dark at all," she said. "What's this music?"

The Clash, I said.

"You're not so dark either," said my dad to one of us.

He's not the Ethiopian one, I said to June.

"The Clash is good," June said.

I said, June and I are getting married.

June squeezed my hand.

My dad said, "The same taste in hooded sweatshirts *is* a solid foundation on which to build—"

She stole it from me, I said.

"I stole it," June confirmed.

"That strikes me as sweet for reasons I don't quite understand. Why don't you get in the car. You look cold."

"You're a stranger," June said.

"So are you," said my father.

"I'm the girl Gurion loves."

"Gurion lives at my house."

"Fine," June said, and I moved over and she sat on my seat with me.

"Gotta Gettaway" had started up again.

"Now what?" June said.

"Now we all listen to this song by Stiff Little Fingers, and then the two of you go to class."

We listened to the song, then got out of the car, but I was way too happy to go to class so I didn't.

□   □   □   □   □   □   □

The spots where Ben-Wa pratfell all said WE DAMAGE WE. The words were jagged-looking, and some of the letters were barely there—he'd used a rock to scrape them into the pavement. I knelt and touched one, and June knelt next to me.

She said, "These things are everywhere now. I like it the best when they're scraped like this."

Me too, I said, but I don't know why.

"It looks like the words have always been here, waiting to get uncovered," she said. "They look revealed. Like old marble sculptures—like the art was hidden inside the stone and all the sculptor did was chisel away the stuff covering it."

I said, If I hugged you right now, then your ribs would snap and cut your heart.

"I had this dream the other night I made a cage for a piglet by tying spareribs together with tendons," she said. "When I woke up, decoding it, my thigh had this cramp, and I was sure I'd torn my hamstring, but I hadn't—I was fine."

We entered the school a couple minutes after the first-period tone, and Jerry sent us to the Office for a pass. We walked toward the Office until he stopped watching us, then ducked into B-Hall where I wrote one with my left hand, and on the way I saw that June was right: the bombs were everywhere—I counted thirteen without even turning my head to look for them—and all the scraped ones were better because of subtractiveness.

Deface, I thought. *De*face. To deface is to damage; to scrape DAMAGE to deface. The words were enacting what they described, and I got a rush from thinking about it.

Even the guard-booth was bombed. I showed Jerry the forged pass and he waved us on to our lockers, but then June wouldn't ditch with me because she had Art.

I offered her a pass to give to Miss Gleem.

"I don't want to lie to her again," she said. She was hanging her coat and pretend-accidentally bumping me with her left shoulder and hip. "I want to hand her a ruler," she said, "and hold out my knuckles so she can bash them like nuns do in books by angry Catholics. I want to look in her face so she'll see my eyes blur when I wince."

Is a forged pass really a lie? I said. I said, Because even if it is, you didn't have any problem with me flashing one at the Deaf Sentinel.

"I don't care about The Deaf Sentinel," June said. "Did you bring me a cookie?"

I said, Are you dying to have one?

"You said they were the best," she said.

I gave her all of them.

She took two from the baggie, handed one of them to me.

"These have a lot of butter in them," she said, looking at the shine her cookie left on her fingertips. "Do you ever press really buttery cookies against the roof of your mouth til the butter starts falling down the sides of your tongue and the rest of the cookie becomes a dense ball that you store in your cheek and pull apart slowly by sucking it through the gaps of your teeth?"

It's good to do it that way, I said. I said, But my mouth always wants to chew, so I chew.

"Me too," she said. "I think what we should do is chew one cookie, and do the pressing thing with a second one."

Which first? I said.

"It would be easier to do the pressing to the second one because the chewing desire will have already been fed by having chewed the first one," she said, "but if we do the pressing first instead, then our teeth will be teased before they get satisfied by chewing the second one, and the teasing will make the chewing full of relief and that much better."

So we should chew the second one, I said.

She said, "The only problem with that is that it might be impossible. If we try to do the pressing to the first cookie, but the cookie is so good that we can't control ourselves and so we start chewing it, then what?"

What? I said.

"Well then we can't justify having the second cookie on the heels of the first."

Why do we need to justify a second cookie? I said.

She said, "You told me these are the best poppyseed cookies in Chicago, and we only have four, which means we can't waste any, which means they need to be savored. To savor the second one immediately after we've already savored the first, we need to eat it differently from the way we ate the first—we need to eat it in a way that our mouths can't remember. If we press and chew the first one, then what can we possibly do to the second one that our mouths won't be able to remember?"

What? I said.

"Nothing, Gurion."

So we should chew the first one, satisfy the chewing desire, and then press the second, I said.

"But that's playing it safe," she said. "And we're in love, which means it's safe for us to be dangerous. If we act safe while it's safe for us to be dangerous, we're not taking advantage of being in love, and we could ruin it that way."

I didn't understand exactly what June was saying, but I decided to believe her because it is dangerous to believe in what you don't understand,
and I thought she was saying she wanted me to be dangerous, and I wanted
to be what she wanted me to be.

I said, So then let's try to press the first cookie and chew the second, and
if we end up chewing the first, we'll wait til later, when our mouths forget,
to have the second.

June agreed to the plan.

And we tried to press and ended up chewing the first cookie.

She started putting the cookies away, and I said, Wait. Eating the second
cookie now would be a waste, and being wasteful is dangerous.

"Yes!" she said.

So we each ate a second cookie. I put the whole thing in my mouth and
chewed it into a paste without swallowing and then stuck my paste-covered
tongue out at June

She yanked down on my hood-strings and pretended to chop me on the
throat. I staggered and came back to land a drunk-looking haymaker on the
locker next to her and dented it. Then I collapsed against the dented locker,
swallowed the cookie-paste, and put my pointer in my mouth. I flexed my
swearfinger and dropped the thumb, made a shooting noise and shuddered.
I was feeling very good.

"Is that how you'd do it?" June said. "With a gun in your mouth?"

I wouldn't do it at all, I said.

"Me neither," June said. "If I did do it, though, I'd want to do it with
a gun in my mouth, except I'd have to be a cartoon first, so I could pull the
trigger nine times."

Nine? I said.

"Maybe," she said, "Bangbang. Bangbangbang. Bang." She extended a
finger every time she said bang. "Six times," she said, "not nine. And if I did
it with my back to a sheet of clangy steel, I could pull it just three times
because every gun report would get followed by the bang from the back of
my jerking head smacking the clangy steel."

I said, It wouldn't be the same, though. It wouldn't be the same rhythm
as the one you just said. You said, 'Bangbang. Bangbangbang. Bang.' With
three shots and a sheet of clangy steel, you'd get six bangs, but it would
sound like: Bangbang. Bangbang. Bangbang.

"You're right," she said. "It would either have to be six shots, and
no sheet of clangy steel, or there would have to be two sheets of clangy

steel—the second one just behind the one behind me—attached to pulleys, and someone operating the pulleys, so that only the first sheet was lowered for the first gunshot (bangbang), then both for the second gunshot (bangbangbang), and none for the third (bang)." She kissed me on the left eye-corner. "You pay so much attention to what I say," she said. She said, "So how would you do it?"

I said, I'd kill as many hard-to-kill enemies as possible. I said, I'd go straight to the center of the Arrangement and explode.

"Like with a bomb?" she said. "Like a suicide bomber?"

Like Samson, I said. I said, And probably with a bomb, but I wouldn't be a suicide bomber. I'd only make power-kills, generals and political figures.

"If while bombing you commit suicide, you're a suicide bomber—doesn't matter who the target is."

A forged pass is no more a lie if you use it on Miss Gleem than if you use it on Jerry, then, I said.

"That's true," June said. She said, "Showing a forged pass to Jerry is a lie. I never said it wasn't. You're the one who tried to say it wasn't. What I was saying is everyone's a liar, and I don't care about the Deaf Sentinel, so lying to him isn't any kind of betrayal. Miss Gleem, though—she's my friend and I don't want to betray her. I'm not a betrayer."

I really wanted June to ditch with me.

I said, The pass doesn't have to be your lie, anyway. It could be my lie. I told you I forged it, but maybe you didn't see me forge it—maybe you thought you did when really you didn't; maybe I was only faking the forgery—so for all you know I've been lying about it being a forgery; for all you know, it was given to me by Miss Pinge to give to you for being late to Art, and I'm just trying to impress you with forgery skills I don't really have.

"But that's cheap," June said, "because I do know it's forged. Plausible deniability is cheap."

I said, So you might as well just ditch with me and then get punished.

"I like Art," she said, "and if I ditch, Miss Gleem will feel bad—I know her. I'll see you at 11:00." She sandwiched my right hand between both of her hands, lifted it high, dropped it, and ran to class, twelve wingnuts jingling in the pockets of her stolen hoodie.

I had wingnuts too—I had thirteen in a drawstring bag. I had a lot of things. I had an Israelite girlfriend who I loved and I had nearly half a pad of hall-passes and an IDF fatigue jacket with a wide-mouthed pennygun in the secret pocket. And I had the Side of Damage. I thought: What is the Side of Damage? And I thought: The Side of Damage is the thing you lead. I thought: The Side of Damage is dangerous.

I was still too happy to just go to the Cage. I wanted to do something—I wasn't sure what. I flipbooked the passpad, made it a cylinder, flattened the cylinder, pocketed the passpad. I tried to break my fingers and my fingers wouldn't break. I poured the bag of wingnuts in my hand and they jingled. The paint on the wings of the black one was nicked; this was the one with which Nakamook had blown off the rockinghorse's face while June and I kissed on the stage in the lunchroom. CHUCKETA-CRACKETA. That was the noise it made. I pinched it between my thumb and pointer. It was small enough to sneak, if I wasn't mistaken, between the metal rods of the gym clock's mask.

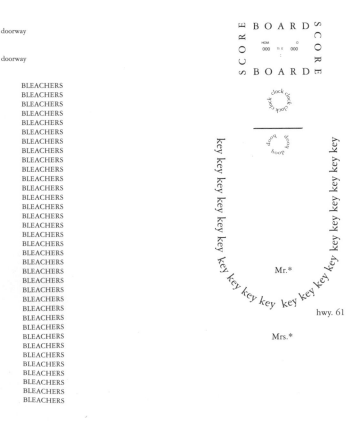

The gym wasn't empty like it should have been. Boystar was throwing a tantrum under the hoop beneath the clock. The heap of scoreboard wreckage had been removed, and he stomped on the spot it used to occupy, yelling "Jesus! Jesus Christ!" At "Jesus!" he raised his arms. At "Jesus Christ!" he slapped his hips. The person he was yelling at was his father, who stood slump-shouldered at the free-throw line, his pomade bending light into a halo. He shook his head = "No, this behavior is nothing I can brag about," and the halo got dull and tilted.

I was in the midcourt doorway, trying to be a wall. It wasn't easy. B-Hall doorways were smaller than C-Hall ones. They barely buffered sound and their shadows were thin.

"Listen to me!" Boystar was yelling. "Please! I'm telling you!" He kept raising his arms up and slapping his hips.

There were other people there, too, but none of them watched the tantrum.

At the top of the key, Boystar's mother was crouching beside the Highway 61 acoustics man I'd seen the day before. He knocked his fist twice on the floor in front of him, then revolved and did it again. The mother leaned in.

Another man was on his knees on the bleacher-side sideline at half-court. He was outlining three sides of an air-rectangle like actors playing directors do in art movies about old Hollywood. He squinted through the rectangle and tsked his tongue in concentration.

My chemicals were ticking. How could I smash the clock with all these people in my way? Why was this guy framing shots on the sidelines? I dropped the black wingnut into my pennygun.

If I shot the clock and the shattered glass fell like I imagined, shards would slice off Boystar's nosetip and knife deep into his shoulders, his feet. The problem was the bleachers—they blocked my vector of attack and there was nothing I could do about it. Even if I risked moving to the center of the doorway and edging into the gym proper, where anyone in there could see me if they turned their head, the post the hoop hung from would deflect the projection.

Could I run at the acoustics man, shove him out of the way, then shoot the clock from the top of the key?

A guy in a suit as metal-looking as the hair of Boystar's dad came out of the door of the boys' locker-room. "Our star the Boystar!" the guy said to Boystar, adjusting his belt.

"I'm not happy about this, Chaz. I'm not happy about this at all," said Boystar. "I'm really fucking unhappy."

The guy in the glitzy suit—Chaz—put his arm around Boystar's shoulder and whispered something in his ear.

Boystar said, "You're a real sweetheart, too, Chaz Black, but that's got nothing to do with anything. *Emotionalize* is about being sexy."

Explosive as I was getting, I probably *could* move the acoustics man and hit the clock. Or I could even just race across the gym and hit the clock running—my chemicals were making me simple; my aim would be true—but I would get seen, caught.

Chaz said, "Sexy is as sexy does, my friend."

Boystar's dad clutched his own neck and looked at his feet.

As if he knew what I'd been considering, the acoustics man moved to the southeast corner of the gym. He struck a tuning fork and said, "Nice."

It was too soon to get caught. Would it always be too soon? I didn't think so, but I knew it was too soon right then. I turned my pennygun upside-down above my palm and shook it til the wingnut fell out.

Boystar's mom touched the elbow of the acoustics man. "Is that a tuning fork you're using?" she asked him.

"Sexy people aren't diseased," Boystar said. "And you said I'd get a blue faux-hawk and we'd shoot in LA and you'd CGI me doing fly aerial shit in halfpipes. You tricked me and it's stupid and I'm thinking hard about hiring a lawyer."

There was an X of masking-tape on the sideline where the shot-framer had stood. He was working his rectangle at halfcourt now.

Chaz was saying to Boystar, "No one tricked you, buddy. Circumstances have changed. And for the better, I might add. Frankly, we got lucky. This video's gonna nice up your image and it ain't gonna cost much."

"I don't care what it's gonna cost. I'm gonna be rich. I'm gonna be so rich. The only reason I even agreed to sing with that retard was so Brodsky would let me go on tour. Like that ever even mattered. Tch. If he had any faith in me," said Boystar, pointing at his father, "he'd know how big I'm gonna be, and he'd just withdraw me from this shithole and hire a tutor. Now the whole world's gonna see me chumming some Jerry's kid? *Emotionalize* is not about dances with retards, Chaz. It's about being sexy."

I pulled pennies from my pocket.

Chaz said, "Listen. You treat this Mookus with affection—smile at him, put your arm around his shoulders, make wowie-zowie kindsa faces if he breaks out the fancy footwork like they do in that sensitivity-training video we watched together—and all this advance negbuzz we're getting about *Emotionalize* being too explicit for the tween set is gonna disappear forever. Churchmoms around the world are gonna be humming 'Infantalize Me' over the pot-roast like it was the Cats! soundtrack or something. And 'The Way You Mmm'? Forget about it. Platinum."

"I'm a star," Boystar said. "I'm a star and I'm sexy and retards do not move units."

I dropped a penny in the balloon and I aimed.

"I want to get a punky haircut and dress like a skateboarder. I want—"

I shot him in the knee and he dropped to all fours, yelling, "Help me! Something happened! Help me!"

"Stand up and stop acting like an idiot," his mother said.

"Something happened!" Boystar wailed.

"Get off the filthy floor," said Boystar's dad. "You are ruining your slacks."

"My *slacks*?!" yelled Boystar. "I'll ruin *my slacks*?! How about this, Dad? Emancifuckingpation! I want emancipation! I'm gonna fucking *sue* you for emancifuckingpation! You can fuck these fucking slacks in the face with a big fucking stupid fucking… cock! For all I care. But I'm gonna be *rich*, and you won't get my money! You won't get fucking shit! Ruin *your* fucking slacks! How do you like *that*, you fucking fucker stupid ass?"

I didn't get to hear what his father's response was. I'd been heading west slowly since the first "emancipation," doing the walk of the oblivious innocent, and after "fucker stupid ass" I was too far away.

□ □ □ □ □ □ □

I cradled a ball of gooze in the curl of my tongue and rang the Cage doorbell. As soon as Botha came to the gate, I fake-sneezed the ball into the middle of my hall-pass, and tried to hand it over.

"Kape it," Botha said.

Coming through the door, I slapped the pass on the wall over the light-switch and it stuck.

I heard Vincie whisper, "I told you he was alive," and I revolved to wave at Eliyahu, who blushed.

"Gurion. Yo!" Mark Dingle said.

"Yo, Gurion," said Dingle's friend, Salvador Curtis, who was sitting at the carrel to Dingle's right.

"Quoydanawnsinz!" snapped Botha. "Face ford!"

Both Dingle and Salvador showed me a power-fist.

Dingle'd been in the Cage since the very beginning, and we rode the same bus but didn't speak. He was one of those guys who was always reading *Fight Club*. I'd never heard of him fighting anyone, though. He'd probably never had to. He was the scariest-looking kid at Aptakisic. He might have been the scariest-looking kid in America. It's true he was taller than most other eighth-graders, and nearly as wide and muscley as the Flunky, but his height and build weren't what made him scariest. His homemade tattoos—lopsided black aces on three of his knuckles and a stick-figure hangman on the light side of his forearm—weren't it either. In the fang-shaped shadow of his super-lubed pompadour, behind his masking-taped, shop-teacher glasses, Dingle's face—every centimeter of it that wasn't teeth or eyeballs—was gruesomely deformed. The first and only time I'd gazed directly at the face, I bit my cheeks raw and gave away my lunch. You'd guess Dingle's leprosy'd contracted the mange before infecting him through lesions in his acne vulgaris, but according to Vincie no disease was the cause. All those swollen cross-hatches and discolored volcano-shapes, every gouge and slash and shiny pouch: they'd all been self-inflicted with razor-blades and cigarettes, pushpins and paperclips, at least twice a pencil-lead dipped in hydrochloric. Each of his scars had won a small-stakes bet for him. "If you don't believe me," Vincie'd said, "go up to him at lunchtime and tell him you got three dollars says he won't rip a new hole in its bottom part's ass-thing." That's a chin-cleft, I'd said. "Whatever keeps your nightmares at bay, young man."

The other guy who'd yo'd and powerfisted at me, Salvador Curtis, was the only kid who ever talked to Dingle, and he was known in the Cage for his uncommon talent: he could suck whole limes with no facial puckering. Every day he brought a baggieful to school. Once, on a bet, inspired by Dingle, he squeezed a lime dry on a freshly bleeding knee-wound he'd gotten at recess and didn't wince once. Three guys paid him a dollar apiece. The next morning, on the bus, he squeezed limes in Dingle's eyes. That time it was Dingle who paid him a dollar.

I chinned air at both of them.

Benji said, "Tch."

The Cage, that day, was at full capacity, a beautiful thing; I'd have kids on both sides of me. The carrel that was open was between Scott Mookus and a sixth-grade guy called Chunkstyle Heany, who was regular-sized but smelled of canned tuna. Chunkstyle's real first name was Remus. He got sent to the Cage after the third time he gently cupped the cheeks of his Social Studies teacher, Mrs. Mingle.

Cheek-cupping a teacher—especially with gentleness—is surely pervy, but Remus Heany hadn't meant it that way. Third period on Mondays and alternate Thursdays, Mrs. Mingle was assigned to the Cage, and every single Monday and every other Thursday, at some point near the end of third period, Chunkstyle would push his glasses up his nosebridge and stand to recite a lengthy apology that Anna Boshka—who was put in the Cage because she'd only address her teachers in Russian—helped him write in the perfect, formal English of an eager new immigrant. The apology always began the same: "Barbara Mingle, my love for you is a powerful thing that drove me to behave in a manner I do not quite understand and so cannot honestly account for. However—" We never got to hear the rest of it, though. Botha'd always shut him down before he could finish.

I barely knew Remus, but I assumed he was a good person because he never made fun of My Main Man Scott Mookus. Plus, the t-shirts and folders of Anna Boshka all had dolphins on them, and if she loved dolphins even half as much as it seemed, she had to have been very impressed with Remus's kindness to befriend him despite all the Starkist he ate.

He pitched a note over the wall we shared. It said:

We the undersigned want to join the Side of Damage.
Tell us how. We will do anything. We are:

1. Ben-Wa Wolf 2) Mark Dingle 3. Chris Perrot 4. Cody von Braker 5. Stevie Loop 6) Exar Tea 7. Flunky Bregman 8 Casey Sabado 9. Jackie Friday 10 Summer Weekint And) Winthrop! 12. Miles Minton 13. Clive Spearmint 14 Renee Feldbons (15) Paulina Mulvina 16; Jerry Throop 17: Fulton Market 18 Casper Lunt 19 Ansul Entsry 20. Janie Glencoe 21, Forrest Kennilworth 22. Derrick Winnetka 23) Rick Deerfield 24! Jesse Ritter 25: Glen Murphy 26) Aarron Worley 27) Anna Boshka 28. Christian Yagoda 29 Salvador Curtis 30. Remus Heany

I thought: Me + Benji + Mookus + the Janitor + Ronrico + Vincie + Mangey + Jelly + Leevon + Eliyahu = 10.

And: 10 + 30 = 40.

Vincie'd been right. Every student in the Cage—we were all on the Side of Damage. And that wasn't the only thing Vincie'd been right about: on the desk of my carrel, near the Remus-side wall, someone had planted a WE DAMAGE WE. It was thin-lined enough that I'd missed it at first. It was bombed with a ballpoint in the hand of a girl, the hand of a Cage girl who must not have had a Darker, a girl who was neither Jelly nor Mangey. I looked around the carrel, found another on the facing wall, and another one yet right under my elbow. Same ink, same size, same feminine hand. I'd forgotten to check the other carrels when I'd entered, but if a girl who didn't even have a Darker was willing to bomb, then the rest of the kids...

The chair of Scott Mookus groaned the floor.

"Gurion," he whispered. He was leaning into my carrel and no one was stopping him, so after a two-count, I broke the face-forward rule. The teachers at the cluster were working with students. Botha shuffled papers at the monitor's desk.

I leaned toward Mookus = Go.

"Plans to lay well-laid plans are best laid to rest," he whispered, "for their very scripting would tire the fingers that need grip steady so many disguised bodkins we shall launch into the thrumming parts of tomorrow's bancing, fleshy targets. Lord, get we simple enough to be earnest, and stealth enough to be harrowing in our damage-making. Let our laces outlast the soles of our Chucks and Sambas. We would never order hamburger buns without something between them. It's not nutritious and it might feel like slavery. We want to find props on our feet that help us pretend to be superheros but we can't have new kicks til we need them. We can't just put some butter on salt-crackers and call that dinner, either. We can't stuff up on bread, skip the meat, and expect dessert. How can you have any pudding if you don't eat your meat? We're not gonna take it. The words of the prophet were written on the studious crowd noise. All the world's indeed a page and we must loudly tear it. May our disarrangement be a joyous and brutal project. May The End come once and pretty, Gurion, and once and for all. Your sons' mother's love shines blinding off your skin like the light of God off Adam's at Creation's apex, and I pray you do not lock us up but give us tomorrow our daily guns, and today bind us safe inside your danger. Never forget to protect me."

I squeezed his shoulder.

"I believe you," he said, and ducked back into his carrel.

It felt good and strong having people on both sides of me. It had been over two months.

I turned over the petition and wrote:

> Remus,
>
> To be on the Side of Damage is to be a defiance. So be a defiance. Spread the word by mouth during the passing-period. Return this note to me for safekeeping as soon as you're done reading it—we are stealth here.
>
> —Gurion ben-Judah Maccabee

I tossed it over the wall and then broke the face-forward rule again.

On the side of the Cage perpendicular to mine, Ronrico tossed a note to Eliyahu who passed it on to Vincie while Jelly tossed a second note to Mangey, who got it to Nakamook. Botha was still shuffling papers, but the teachers at the cluster—Mr. Powell and Ms. O'Connor—weren't occupied, and Mr. Powell was looking right at my friends, and Ms. O'Connor was looking right at me, and neither of them were doing anything about the rules that were getting broken. Peculiar, I thought.

But then I thought: Is it?

I tried to remember the last time someone in the Cage got a step from one of the teachers at the cluster. Mine always came from Botha.

The note came back to me:

> You can call me Chunkstyle if you want, Gurion. I mean it. It is good to have a nickname when your parents named you Remus. Before the Cage, I was Rabbit because of Uncle Remus, but that was always too obvious and I hadn't discovered tuna yet. I hear you are in love with Eliza June Watermark. I know how it feels because it's the same with me and Barbara Mingle, only she won't even talk to me because I didn't act like a gentleman. I don't know what to do.

I wrote:

> Your love for Barbara Mingle is only a ~~smelly~~ weak version. Anna Boshka is where it's at. Open your eyes. She's ten times prettier than Mingle and already fluent in two languages, plus not married. If you fall in love with her, she'll let you cup her cheeks, I bet, and probably she'll cup yours, too, if you want that. Find a ceramic dolphin that opens up to reveal another

ceramic dolphin which opens up to reveal a third that contains a fourth and so on. Then buy the dolphin, give it to Boshka, and tell her you'll quit eating tuna before she has to ask you, and make sure you do it before you kiss her. And get this note back to me.

I tossed it over the wall. I tried again to remember a time when a teacher at the cluster had handed out a step, and I couldn't. Even if there was such a time, though—even if there were two or three or even ten such times—they were obviously exceptions; if they weren't exceptions, I'd have had a much easier time remembering them.

But so why didn't the teachers ever—or hardly ever—give us steps, then? According to the Cage Handbook, they were allowed to.

I got half a rush, thinking the teachers were on the Side of Damage, too, and they just didn't know it.

But then I saw it couldn't be true.

To be on the Side of Damage meant nothing if not to be against the Arrangement. You could not be against the Arrangement without being against the STEP System, and in classrooms outside of the Cage, where the teachers at the cluster spent most of their time, they all handed out steps left and right. I'd never been in a normal classroom at Aptakisic, but everyone else in the Cage had been, and for the most part it was the teachers at the cluster who'd sent them here.

But then why would the teachers act different inside the Cage?

I thought of a few possible reasons. It could have been they were scared of us—that they knew we were more dangerous than the students in their regular classrooms, and so thought it was too risky to make us angry; that maybe the reason they got so many of us sent to the Cage in the first place was so they wouldn't have to be scared of us in their regular classrooms.

It could have been they thought we were hopeless—that even though they were pro–STEP System, they didn't think Cage kids were good enough to benefit from the STEP System, and so we weren't worth the time it would take to discipline us and fill out the paperwork.

Or maybe the paperwork part was right, but it had nothing to do with hopelessness; maybe they were just lazy and uncaring and knew that Botha would do their dirty work.

A benefit-of-the-doubt way to think of them was that they didn't like the STEP System at all, that they only gave steps when in their classrooms because the Arrangement demanded that they do so, while inside the Cage the Arrangement allowed them to give steps but didn't demand that they give steps and so they didn't give steps. Maybe in their hearts, they *were* on our side. Maybe they weren't so much fingers and robots of the Arrangement; maybe they were the Arrangement's fiefs and draftees.

But then maybe they had nothing in their hearts. Or maybe their hearts were confused. I couldn't see into their hearts with any more clarity than I could Slokum's face.

Chunkstyle sent the note back over the wall.

> Anna Boshka is ten times prettier, maybe even twelve times prettier, and I will try to fall in love with her eventually, but before I can move on I need Barbara Mingle to forgive me for my uncomely and inexplicable behavior that was untoward at her. I can't wait to tell everyone to be a defiance. Thank you for the privilege. Down with the Arrangement!

I decided it didn't matter what was in the teachers' hearts. At least not yet. Whatever was in their hearts, they never once protected us from Botha. And they could have. Or at least they could have tried to. Even if they were fiefs and draftees, their toil and their soldiering was good for the Arrangement. That was what mattered.

Soon the end-of-class tone complained and Miss Pinge's voice came through the speaker to introduce the announcement-maker. To be an announcement-maker, you had to have stayed below step 4 and gotten nothing lower than a C for the entire quarter prior to the one during which you'd do the announcement. Also, you had to write your own introduction.

Miss Pinge said, "Performing today's announcements will be Tanya Taylor." Then she read the introduction: "'Tanya is in the eighth grade, and has made honor roll every quarter since she's been at Aptakisic. Last year she won bronze at the State Science Fair, and this year she aims to bring home the gold. And don't worry, Girls' Varsity Volleyball—Tanya isn't talking just about science. As team captain, she's going to apply herself on the court, too. She wants to give a shout-out to the team, and as for the rest of you Indians, she wants you to know that this year will be a great year for Aptakisic. And in case any of the rest of the junior highs in the conference are listening, she wants to tell them that they're gonna get served, and when Tanya says served, she means on the court. So bring your A-games, Rand Middle and Twin Groves and Longfellow

Middle, bring your A-games Sandberg and Frost—bring your A-games all you want, but understand the curve's getting blown by Ms. Taylor and company. Understand how even though it's your A-game you're bringing, you're a C-student anyway because you're coming into the house of Tanya, and even a ten-ton semi looks small when it's parked in front of the Sears Tower, unless it's packed with explosives, and it's not! Go Indians!' And here she is: Tanya Taylor."

"Um, thank you, Miss Pinge," said Tanya.

I had no idea who she was, but she didn't sound like the person who had written her introduction. She sounded scared, and she kept mumbling and screwing up the punctuation of the announcements.

"Today's big news. Is that tomorrow, at the pep-rally for the opening. Game of the basketball season Boystar and a special guest will. Perform a song off the new Boystar album *Emotional Eyes* and the performance will be filmed for use in the first Boystar video we'll be dancing in our seats and—"

"The special guest is me!" shouted Mookus.

"Lies," said the Flunky.

"Foog," said Nakamook.

"Quoydanawnsinz!" snapped Botha.

"Is it true, Scott?" said Eliyahu.

"Yes!" said Mookus.

"Quoydanawnsinz during nouncemints!" said Botha.

"Congratulations," said Eliyahu.

I nearly said congratulations, too, but then I didn't. Neither did Naka-mook or anyone else. It was complicated. It was like my dad and the Drucker case. If the Side of Damage had been more like Flowers, we would have all said congratulations because Main Man was our friend and something good was going to happen for him. We weren't more like Flowers, though. We were more like me.

"...less happy note if anyone has any information on who has been de-stroying the school's property which is a criminal offense then please let us know it will be confident... confidench—" said Tanya, who was interrupted by a scuffling noise, and then the sound of Brodsky clearing his throat and then the distant voice of Miss Pinge saying, "Sorry, Leonard, I must have spaced out when I was typing it up and put your part under—"

"Thank you, Tanya," Mr. Brodsky said into the microphone. "You have all seen the graffiti," he said. "You have all seen the scoreboard. These are acts of vandalism. Vandalism is a criminal offense, and it will not be tolerated.

It is our first priority to find out who has been vandalizing our school, and we *will* find out.

"If anyone has any information regarding the identities of the vandals and would like to share that information, you will have my deepest respect, as well as my pledge to keep your name in the strictest confidence. And if any of those responsible come to my office and admit what they've done, provided they share me with the names of those with whom they share responsibility, they will be shown leniency."

The mike clicked off.

"What's leniency?" someone said.

"Nothing worth dying for," said Nakamook.

During five-minute free-swim at the end of Gym, Isadore Momo got a nose-bleed in the pool. He was doing the deadman's float with his eyes closed.

I one-hand hung beneath the springboard and shivered, watching the blood change shape. Gravity pulled threads from the black-red swirl under Momo's face, and the chlorine thinned out and broke the threads to kill between the cellwalls. Ripples spread and stretched the mess wider.

The first two times Momo turned his face for air, he kept his eyes closed, then put his head back onto the cloud he'd made and bled in it some more.

The third time, he opened his eyes and said, "No!"

His terror and his foreign accent made it sound like "Heneh!"and he swam away from the blood, fast, like he thought it was the blood of someone else. He kicked the water loudly and people turned to see, but the blood kept following him and he was too afraid to understand why.

Someone said, "Hermaphrodite."

I saw it was Blonde Lonnie Boyd.

Momo got out of the pool and Blonde Lonnie laughed and repeated it. "Hermaphrodite."

It was funny that Momo tried to escape his own blood and it was funny that Blonde Lonnie Boyd thought hermaphrodite meant bleeder, but Blonde Lonnie wasn't laughing at either of those things, and I didn't want to laugh with him, especially not against a chubby kid who could barely speak English and never showered til the locker-room was empty, so I didn't laugh at all.

Other kids did, though, many of them Shovers. Blonde Lonnie was the third highest scorer on the basketball team, right behind Bam and Co-Captain Baxter,* and those who believed good basketballing was a tour de force would try to please Lonnie Boyd by laughing with him. It made him even less funny than how he started. He'd used to just be an unfunny guy who made mean, unfunny jokes sometimes, but after a lot of people had laughed along with him, he began to think he was hilarious and, on top of the mean, unfunny jokes, he started making this one same joke over and over again, a tagline-joke stolen from the comedian Damon Wayans, who used it on an old TV show called *In Living Color.*

Lonnie's favorite way to deliver the joke was to use it as an answer to a question Desormie would ask the class when he wanted to make someone feel worthless. A lot of times in Gym, when someone defied the Arrangement, Desormie would blow his whistle for attention and say something to the class, like, "People! When he misses the shuttlecock, Ronrico Asparagus whacks his racket against his knee in anger, like it's the racket's fault, or maybe even the shuttlecock's fault, when really what it is is that it's his fault for not having the skills that would prevent him from missing the perfectly good shuttlecock with the perfectly good racket that he's ruining little by little, and one of you guys—or ladies—whoever it is of you who next time gets assigned that racket he's damaging… When that racket breaks in your hands, it's gonna be who's holding that racket who's gonna pay the fiddler for the cost of that racket, and not just the money fiddler who is our athletic supplies supplier, but the fiddler of point and serve, which is to say the rules of badminton, and possibly—as a result of the impending loss of the match that is the thing that would result from a racket that breaks in the middle

---

* For most intents and purposes, Blonde Lonnie might as well have been Co-Captain Baxter—both were blonde and both were tall, both were bullies and A-team starters, both of their mouths seemed to sneer in repose—which accounts for why Reuters would so often miscaption those stills from the videos of the Damage Proper in which both would shortly appear, but Blonde Lonnie hadn't picked on Eliyahu of Brooklyn whereas Co-Captain Baxter had knocked off his hat, and so, for Eliyahu, to whom that meant a lot at the time, and thus for those scholars of coming generations whose commentaries' focus will be Eliyhau, distinctions between the two blondes need be made.

of a point in what could very well turn out to be a tie-breaking situation—a third fiddler who is the fiddler of grades who is me the teacher who does not give A's for effort but only victory and who's the fiddler who's gonna get paid by whoever next time gets assigned that racket when it breaks, even though it's Ronrico's fault for getting it in the kinda shape that makes you break it by accident. Is gonna get paid by you. In grades. So what do we think about the way Ronrico's whacking his racket? Is the question. Except let me better yet put that important question another way that doesn't individuate, since what I don't mean to do is make it seem like Ronrico is bad because he is Ronrico, but instead that he's bad because of how he keeps *behaving* like Ronrico. So the newer, better version of the question I'd like to ask you guys and ladies today is: What do we think about whacking rackets? In general." And as soon as Desormie was finished talking, he would make the noise "Tch" = "The response is obvious," and that is when Blonde Lonnie would answer Desormie's question with the stolen joke:

"Lonnie don't play that."

And all his mooks and stooges would laugh. Sometimes, Lonnie thought it was even more hilarious to be around Lonnie than usual and, instead of saying, "Lonnie don't play that," he would say, "*Funny* Lonnie don't play that," or even "Funny Lonnie don't play that, *friend*." And that is why the people who would laugh began to call him Funny Lonnie and Funny Lonniefriend.

None of them were willing to call a nipple a nipple, though, let alone Lonnie, who, if he were truly funny, would have made lots of jokes that had to do with nipples. He had an extra on the left he was always pinching, but he called it a mole and no one ever argued.

"Hermaphrodite," Lonnie said a third time, pointing at Momo, pinching the extra.

The laughers laughed louder. Their laughter echoed and Desormie came.

"Everyone outta the pool," he said. "We got blood. Class dismissed."

"Come on, girls," Miss Kimble said. Miss Kimble was stacking kick-floats in the kick-float cage. She was one of the few robots in school who was dumber than Ron Desormie. She'd do whatever he wanted and wink at him while nodding her fluffy head, like there was a very deep understanding you could have of what Desormie meant when he said stuff like "Gather up the bats and the bases," and she was the only one in sight who had that understanding. She led a bunch of the girls back to the locker-room.

Desormie said, "I said outta the pool, Maccabee."

I stared at the blood while I counted to seven and got a little hypnotized thinking how the way the chlorine made the blood harmless to animals and useless to hemophiliacs was by over-cleansing it. Cleaning it to death.

The water near the blood looked shinier than the other water, and by five-one-thousand my eyes were putting auras on the halogens and my forehead felt empty, but at seven-one-thousand, I snapped myself out of the trance. I reached overhead with my dangling hand and pull-upped into a backflip onto the springboard. Then I dove deep and swam across the bottom to the ladder.

A crowd of laughers—mostly guys, but also some of the seventh-grade Jennys—stood together in the shape of an eyebrow over the pupil that was Isadore Momo. The laughers all pointed at him while he knelt on the tiles with his head back, pinching his nose. They wanted to see if they could get him to cry or change face-color. They wanted to make him embarrassed. Blonde Lonnie Boyd was the eyebrow's apex. He had the longest finger of all the ones that pointed.

Momo didn't seem to care about any of them. Even though he'd let his own blood chase him in the water, he held his nose calmly now, and didn't cry, and I wished he was on the Side of Damage.

One of the laughers said, "Hermaphrodite." Then another one. And then all of them.

Desormie stood beside Momo and said, "That's right, pinch that sucker good. Pinch it. Just like that. Right on the bridge, there. Pinch it." But you could tell he thought the hermaphrodite joke was really hilarious because he kept looking over at Lonnie and the Jennys and rolling his eyes = "Can you believe how this kid keeps bleeding!"

Then he touched Momo on the elbow for a second and said, "Okay? You're okay. Good guy. Okay. Okay guys, nothing to see here," and walked off to check the lock on the kickfloat cage.

Benji and Leevon and Vincie were in the shadows of the doorway to the locker-room. Ronrico and the Janitor were just outside of it. I thought: They're all waiting for me. I thought: I am the leader of the Side of Damage. And I decided: If Isadore Momo is not on the Side of Damage, he is at least on the same side as the Side of Damage.

And I saw that it was good.

I walked at the left wing of the eyebrow the long way, hoping to bump a couple laughers, but the laughers moved when they saw me coming and the eyebrow lost its curve. When I got to Lonnie Boyd, he was still pointing at Momo and saying, "Hermaphrodite."

So I pointed at Lonnie, and even though I thought I'd say something about his nipple, or Momo being on the Side of Damage, I changed my mind and said, Basketball.

I said it loud. Then I said it again.

Basketball, I said.

The laughers stopped laughing and waited for someone to drown me. They were always waiting for someone to do something. I kept my finger pointed at Lonnie and said it again:

Basketball.

Then I stepped forward until the nail of my finger was close enough to Lonnie's extra nipple for Lonnie to reach out and break my finger off and I said, Basketball.

"Psycho," Lonnie said.

I pressed my finger on the nipple. Not hard or anything, but it was my finger and it was his nipple. Extra or not, he should have hit me. I would've hit me. He didn't hit me.

Basketball, I said.

Desormie said, "Class dismissed, guys."

No one moved. The snat dripped down Lonnie's chin and I took my finger off his nipple because I didn't like touching it, but I continued pointing to it.

That's when Nakamook said, "Basketball." By then, him and the others had already come over and started a second eyebrow over the pupil that was Lonnie and I.

The original eyebrow fell back into the new one.

And Ronrico said, "Basketball."

And the Janitor said, "Basketball."

Vincie said, "Fucken basketball."

"Hey!" said Desormie.

And Leevon pulled his cheek down to show Lonnie the red part of his eyeball.

Isadore Momo, still holding his nose, came up next to me, and to Lonnie Boyd, Momo said, "Nipple." It sounded like "Neepo."

Someone said, "The chubby bleederkid says that Lonnie's a nipple!"

"A nipple!" said someone.

Lonnie said, "It's a mole!"

"*What's* a mole, Lonnie?"

"My mole," said Lonnie, "is a mole."

"Nipple!" said someone.

"Enough!" said Desormie.

"Nipple!"

"Nipple!"

"Nipple!"

"Hey Lonnie?" said a Jenny.

"What?" said Lonnie.

"Your mole?" said another Jenny.

"What about my mole?"

"Oh my God is it a nipple!"

Lonnie's body jerked, but instead of attacking anyone, he revolved and went to the locker-room. He had to walk around to the end of the new eyebrow to get there since who would step aside for a trickling wonder like that?

"You're really cruisin' for a bruisin'," Desormie said to me.

"You make the rhyme," Momo said to Desormie.

Laughter boomed from the eyebrow.

Momo bowed.

"That's it!" Desormie said, looking around.

"That's what?" said Ronrico.

"Did you just look at Jenny's nipples?" said Nakamook.

"Hey!" Desormie said.

"Jenny, did Mr. Desormie just look at your nipples?" said Vincie.

"Probably," said the seventh-grade Jennys. Then they all giggled.

"I thought I was just imagining it?" said Jenny April.

"Sometimes he looks at my cha-cha," said Jenny Khouri.

"Always the nipples during swimming, though," Jenny Flagg said.

"Why you always lookin' at the Jennys on the chest?" said Ronrico.

"I wanna know that, too," said the Janitor. "Isn't it illegal? What do *you* guys think?"

"It's definitely ickish," April said. "I agree with Jenny that it's gross," said Flagg. Khouri said, "I don't like the faces he makes at me."

"Ladies," said Desormie.

"And he calls us 'ladies' which is creepy." "We're girls." "Will you stop looking at us the way Ronrico said?"

"Now, I don't know what you're all talking about," said Desormie. "But," he said, "all you gotta do if something bothers you? Is tell me. Tell me *while* it's bothering you. If you tell me *while* it's bothering you, then maybe I'll know what you mean, cause right now? I just don't know what you mean."

"Stop looking at us like that."

"Like what?" said Desormie.

"Like that," said Jenny April.

"You ladies are crazy and I'd go back to the locker-rooms if I was you because I for one am not writing hall-passes for this nonsense so if you're late, tough luck, it's your fault."

While I was getting dressed, kids I never spoke to chinned air at me and showed me power-fists. President Blake Acer wasn't among those kids, but he wasn't showing Lonnie any mooky solidarity, either. Nor were his two or three Shover underlings; they all just kept their eyes at ichthi-level.

Then, out in B-hall, by the locker-room entrance, Ronrico and the Janitor were waiting for me beside Nakamook and Leevon and Vincie Portite, all together, like it was the most normal thing to do in the world.

And we all walked back to the Cage together.

At the gate, instead of ringing the doorbell, I pulled the hall-pass pad from my pocket.

I asked them: You guys got Darkers?

□   □   □   □   □   □   □

"WE DAMAGE WE is tired," whispered Nakamook.

It was ten minutes after the beginning-of-class tone, and Benji and I were on opposite sides of the teachers lounge doorway's light rhombus. The Chewer was checking his image in the glass of the C-Hall firehose case. He'd locked up the side entrance in order to rove. According to Ronrico, the roving had started at lunch on Wednesday.

"You might think it was because of the scoreboard getting killed," Ronrico'd explained when we first noticed Floyd wasn't at his post, "but don't blame it on Ben-Wa. Floyd was roving even before that—because of how I tagged up Main Hall. It's my fault and I'm sorry."

"Shut up about it already," Nakamook had said.

"Sorry, Benji."

"Stop saying sorry. If you want to brag about tagging up Main Hall, brag about it, but don't pretend you're reluctantly confessing for the good of Ben-Wa."

We'd decided to work in pairs so one guy could always be on lookout for Floyd. It would have been more economical in terms of passes and defacement-per-minute rates if we worked as a single group with one guy on lookout and five bombing, but we decided on pairs because two's the most guys that could hope to hide safely in a doorway. I wrote out one pass for each pair and designated different times to return to the Cage since if we trickled in separate it would look less suspicious.

Tired how? I whispered across the rhombus.

"Everyone's writing it," Nakamook said.

I said, Some people are still writing DAMAGE WE and WE DAMAGE—I've seen probably ten of those.

"Yeah," said Benji, "but those just seem like screw-ups. The one kind looks like the tagger was dyslexic, and the other like he got caught before he could finish. That's not the point, anyway, how many people do one or the other. I don't like writing what *any*one else writes. It's team-spirity."

I said, If the tags all say the same thing, they'll be more powerful. They'll look more like a message.

"What's the message?" said Benji.

It's what it says, I said. WE DAMAGE WE. It is that it is.

"What does that mean, though?"

I said, Every time someone reads or writes *Damage* now, the Arrangement gets damaged and the Side of Damage gets stronger.

"Maybe that's what the message does," Benji said. "Maybe. But what I'm asking you is what it *means*."

It means what it does, I said. Beyond that, it doesn't matter. At least not yet. What matters is the Side of Damage has the power to send messages—that we can send messages the Arrangement doesn't want sent.

Benji said, "Even if that *does* make sense, someone's gonna get—"

Here he comes, I said, and became the wall.

Benji did, too.

Floyd paced past the doorway.

When he was out of range, I whispered, Maybe someone'll get caught, but that's not so bad. If they rat—and I don't think they will, but even if they do—we'll continue. Everyone'll know we're unstoppable.

"Not if they kick us out."

They can't kick us all out, I said.

"Why not?" he said.

So fine, I said, so say they kick us out—maybe we're still victorious.

"How's that?" Benji said, then became his wall.

I became my wall, waited.

Floyd passed by again, hands crossed at the wrists at the small of his back, cheering cone bopping the backs of his thighs. I snuck to the edge of the doorway. The way I cocked my head, I could see C-Hall to 2-Hall before my line of sight got obscured. If Floyd took a right into 2-Hall, we'd wait because there wasn't much 2-Hall to the right of C-Hall—the side entrance was just three classrooms from the junction, and it wouldn't give us enough time to deface anything well. If he took a left, though...

I said, If we get kicked out, we'll get sent to other schools and maybe we'll do the same thing there with other kids. The Side of Damage could spread out from Aptakisic like—

"First of all, that's crazy—the only reason all those kids even joined the Side of Damage is because it means that we'll protect them. If they go to a new school, we won't be there to do that. Secondly, what do I care anyway? They're not my friends. Any loyalty they have to me comes out of fear. And any loyalty I have to them is only by proxy; it's only cause I know they're on *your* side."

I said, That's good enough, Benji.

"Loyalty without friendship creates hypocrisy."

That's just a whiny word, I said.

Benji said, "There's only so much loyalty to go around, Gurion. And there's even less friendship. If you're loyal to someone who isn't your friend, and they come into conflict with someone who is, then what are you supposed to do?"

I said, Be loyal to the friend.

He said, "But you still end up being disloyal to someone who you were supposed to be loyal to, and that's hypocritical."

I said, It's not hypocritical—it's just how it is. Friendship creates— Floyd's gone, I said.

We stealthed into C-Hall. It was my turn to play lookout. Benji led me to the water fountain.

Friendship creates loyalty, I told him, but loyalty doesn't necessarily lead to friendship. So friendship and loyalty are separate, and it's better to have both than just one, but it's better to have one than neither.

"Whatever," Benji said, gesturing at the water fountain.

He'd written I EXPLODE in the basin, just above the drain.

"You got a problem with that?" he said.

I said, The marker's gonna wash away if someone takes a drink before it sets.

"No one's gonna take a drink," said Benji. He pressed the button and nothing came out of the arcing hole, and I remembered: it was the water fountain Eliyahu had punched. "I was asking about *what* I wrote—you got a problem with it?"

I said, You're Benji Nakamook.

"What's that mean?" he said.

I said, You're my best friend.

He said, "You sure about that?" = "I saw you talking to Bam by the bus circle yesterday."

I said, Don't get subtle on me, Nakamook. You asked me not to fight him.

"That doesn't mean you've gotta be his buddy," Benji said.

I'm not his buddy, I said.

"You looked pretty friendly."

We're not, I said. I said, He thinks we are, but we're not.

"But you do like him," said Benji. "Everyone does."

That's what he keeps saying, I said, but that doesn't make it so.

"Let's drop it. Pride and propriety."

You're the one who started talking about him, I said.

"I didn't start shit. You think I should do more I EXPLODEs or what?"

I said, Write what you want. I said, It's probably better to change it up, anyway—it'll confuse the robots.

And when I said that I got an idea.

I said, I just got an idea.

On the wall across from the Cage, I wrote *EMOTIONALIZE*, hugely, using an entire cinderblock for each letter.

"That is just smart as hell, man," said Benji. He liked it so much.

We admired what I did for a few seconds, then heard human noise and ducked back into a doorway. It turned out to be Ronrico and The Janitor, returning to the Cage, right at the time I'd told them to.

The Janitor rang the doorbell and Ronrico noticed the *EMOTION-ALIZE*.

"'Boystar Emotionalize Boystar'?" said Ronrico. "He's biting my fucken steez, Mikey."

"Gurion's steez," said the Janitor.

"Whoever's steez it is, that kid's biting it. Hard."

Nakamook bit into his fist and barely stifled nose-noise.

"Come lunch, I will blot that bullshit out," Ronrico said.

"Don't get so emotional," said the Janitor, "because then you're just doing what he tells you to do."

Botha came to the gate then, but Ronrico was still staring at the wall.

"That kid can't tell me to do anything," Ronrico said. "I bet he didn't write it anyway. It was probably one of those Jennys."

"A Jinny wrote what?" said Botha.

"Leave me alone," said Ronrico.

"A kid who tells on another kid is a dead kid," the Janitor said.

"Tails about what?"

"We're not rats," Ronrico said.

Botha said, "Rets about what? Jinnies?" He saw the wall then. He rushed Ronrico and the Janitor into the Cage, but didn't lock the gate behind him. Half a minute later, he came back out. He was heading toward Main Hall, the Office.

▫ ▫ ▫ ▫ ▫ ▫ ▫

It was ten to eleven when I finished the twelfth *EMOTIONALIZE*, a block-lettered one that spanned three floor-tiles. Benji's last bomb was a SLOKUM DIES FRIDAY, the words stacked vertically on the face of the 2-Hall juice machine. He used his cracktorch to burn the characters into the plastic. They looked like they'd been scooped with an action figure's snow-shovel. We briefly deliberated the fate of the residue that had gathered in some of the letters' corners. I argued for wiping it since its blackness testified to burntness, and Miss Pinge knew Benji had a cracktorch. Benji said owning a cracktorch was circumstantial evidence and the residue looked badass. I allowed that badassness was manifest in the residue, and that, in itself, was a good thing, but noted that circumstantial evidence was usually enough for Brodsky to nail you. Benji stated that clearly wasn't the case when it came to expellable offenses such as vandalism—that if it were, the whole Cage would by now have been expelled—and added that Pinge would never fink him anyway, and it was Benji's risk, so the residue remained. I handed him a pass and he asked where I was going.

I'm meeting June, I said.

He tilted his chin up and grasped it. In a low, slow, Jedi-council voice, he told me, "Always respect her in the Vaunted Hutch of Hector."

The Vaunted Hutch of Hector was the janitor's closet in 2-Hall. It was said kids snuck in there to sex down, but I don't think that was true. I'd never met anyone who'd actually done it. It was just something fun to say.

"Be certain to protect her in the Vaunted Hutch of Hector."

We're not going there.

"If by chance you reject her, or even just neglect her, never again shall you enter the Vaunted Hutch of Hector. Not if she can prevent her—"

We're not going there, I said.

"To play the gentleman is correcter, so I won't play inspector, or pressure you to conjecture like some kiss-and-tell...uh..."

Yeah? I said.

"Director? Director of something something love's sweet nectar in the Vaunted?—no, that's suck, I'm tapped. You're really not going there? Where you going?"

Two-hill field, I said. We're meeting some people.

"Some people," he said.

Old friends, I said. Guys I used to go to school with.

"Like in Chicago?" he said.

Yeah.

"They happen to be passing through Deerbrook Park this morning or...?"

No, I said. I said, I wanted them to meet June, because—it's a long story.

He said, "From Jewish school, these guys."

Right.

Benji didn't say "Aha!" or anything, but the way his eyebrows jumped—

"You know," he said, "I still have a bunch of those passes you gave me, so if I dumped this one, it wouldn't be a major loss or anything."

That's not, I said, necessary.

"So June's not, after all... You're gonna do that thing you told me about the other day, right? The thing that's like conversion, but isn't conversion? I kinda want to see that," he said. "I mean, I'm really kinda interested in that. Since you mentioned it the other day."

I said, It's probably better if it's just June and—

"Oh. Okay. No. That's fine."

Why would you even want—I mean, the other day you said... What did you say?

"No, I know. Seriously. No. It was just curiosity. I was curious how it works. I understand if you can't have, you know, *guests* or whatever. But good luck, though. To June, I mean. Or you. Good luck to whoever needs it. Mazel tov, right? All the nachos in the world."

We didn't bang fists so much as press knuckles.

◻ ◻ ◻ ◻ ◻ ◻ ◻

While I waited for June in the locker-room doorway, I pictured us outside. The way the scholars in the valley would murmur and then quiet when we appeared atop the high hill. From the pocket of my hoodie, I'd produce the scripture. I knew it by heart, like everything I'd written, but failing to show the page would be as chomsky as pretending to read it—it might make it seem like I was speaking off the cuff. So I'd hold out the scripture like the head of a prized enemy, the side with the words on it facing the scholars as would that enemy's lightless eyes, and with my own eyes on theirs, I'd speak.

I was trying to imagine the booming "Amen" when the door behind me half-opened. Though surprised, I wasn't startled—June snuck with finesse. She whispered, "All clear," and led me back through the locker-room.

Crossing the gym, we didn't squeak the floor once. To jam the backdoor's autolock, I slid *My Life as a Man* between the bolt and the strikeplate while June waited outside to test it—all of this without either of us speaking. I wanted to tell her I was thrilled by her stealth, but I thought my surprise might come through my voice, and she'd hear it and be disappointed.

June tried the door and it worked. I caught the book before it landed, then performed the re-jam from the outside.

All along the asphalt trail, we swung our arms like bancers in musicals. When we got to the sidewalk, June said I was a dentist, so I pratfell on a hydrant, and she mock-stomped my head.

"By a blow to the brain dies Jellybean," she said. "I am the one who killed Jellybean."

Who?

"Jellybean," she said. "It doesn't fit you at all, and I didn't think it would, but during second I decided it might fit me, and I was hoping you'd take the hint. Since you haven't, I've resorted to an explicit request, which is suck because now you'll have to wait awhile."

I'll have to wait to call you Jellybean.

"Yes. Til such a time when it'll sound inspired."

What if I never get inspired?

"You only have to *sound* inspired."

So force it, you're saying.

"Wait awhile first, then force it if you need to, but don't sound like you're forcing it."

Practice the art of artlessness.

"Whatever, Zenpoetface, it's cold out here."

We crossed Rand Road and climbed the western slope of the high hill. I kept my eyes on the ground as we climbed. I didn't want to see the scholars til my scripture was in hand. I didn't want to smile before the recitation. I heard the expected murmur as we ascended, but it wasn't theirs—just the throb and swish of my brainblood.

At the crest, I took the page from my pocket and saw that the valley was empty. I looked up the road and no one was coming. All the joy in my chest zoomed out like ghosts.

"Your friends are late."

They're not, I said.

There was no way they were late. Not all of them.

I pulled my hood on and sat. The valley stayed empty. June swiped the scripture from my hand and read it.

"Adonai is God?"

Yeah, I said.

CAGE CHAIR

italics = thin carpet over concrete
bold = metal

Though my pennygun was in my pocket, and the gym as empty as we'd left it, it didn't occur to me to smash the clock. I wrote June a pass, then snuck to the library. The computer room was empty.

So was my Yahoo inbox. Not one scholar had emailed to tell me he wasn't coming. And after all that Emmanuel had said on the el on Tuesday... It was hard enough to believe he could have been so mistaken about where they stood—*Say that you'll lead us; I'd give my life to save yours, Rabbi*—but for *him* not to email: it stunk like a plot.

What else could explain their inaction's uniformity? Simple apathy was not sufficient. Even if all two-hundred-plus kids I'd invited didn't care enough to show, a few of them—or at least one of them—would have cared enough to RSVP. I knew them that well at least. They may have, every one of them, fallen away from me on their own, but they would not have done so identically.

My chemicals fired at this thought, dutifully catalyzed the simplifying process. They had to have been *kept* away or *led* away. From me, away. And as for Emmanuel... Whether he was keeping or kept, led or leading... That he'd manipulated me—using praise and flattery and false beholdenness, every single Roman trick he was able to muster, to fuel what now seemed the basest, dumbest kind of hubris, the Gurionic hubris—appeared undeniable.

And that Emmanuel would be able to manipulate me was no revelation—he'd always been the brightest of my fellow scholars—but that he *would* manipulate me... That is the thought that boggled me. Had I ever wronged him? No. Had I wronged my Israelite brothers? Never.

And so maybe my father had the right idea. Maybe all the scholars, despite their scholarship, were as blind and simple and reactionary as he claimed their parents were. Maybe they hated those they thought better than them, and maybe they thought I was better than them. That notion in itself was hubristic, true, yet it seemed so obvious—that they thought me better than them had *always* seemed obvious, and that was why I'd always rejected the suggestion. But what was it to deny the obvious if not to act from hubris? And yet and yet and meow and meow. What thought could I think that wasn't hubristic? What concern that lacked hubris could be called responsible? I couldn't imagine one. And since when did I care about hubris, anyway? The voice I was thinking in wasn't mine—it was Nakamook's. By the measure of Shakespeare and Euripides and any number of Benji's other favorite wisemen, every Israelite scholar in the world was hubristic;

to believe you are chosen by Adonai to bring justice, the messiah—what is that if not hubristic? And I never cared if I was hubristic before, so why should this—this betrayal, this *harm* done to me—why should *this* cause me to care? I was not the one who ditched his friend; I was the friend who got ditched. Yet I did care. Obviously.

Unless maybe not. Maybe it was the other thing, the thing that haunted my house. That type of needless complication of which my mom accused men and claimed boys innocent. Maybe I kept seeing hubris so as not to have to see my enemies. Maybe I was protecting my enemies. Fighting with myself to avoid fighting *them*. What, scholars (and this is not a real question), could be more Yiddishe?

It would not be true to say that while sitting in the library, before my Yahoo inbox, I decided the scholars of Schechter and Northside were my enemies. That was too much. Their offense, if it could be called that, was passive. They had not attacked me—not to my knowledge, at least—they had simply failed to help me.

After sneaking back out of the library, however, while making my way past hallway walls now dense as scripture with WE DAMAGE WE bombs, I *did* decide that the aforementioned scholars *were not my friends*. And what was peculiar, or rather not so peculiar—for I wasn't obliged to suffer any longer, to expend half my energy awaiting permission, convincing myself that simple acts of malevolence on the part of my elders were complicated acts of misdirected loyalty, piously and reverently abiding the malice of their cowardly parents for the sake of their souls, their Israelite souls, the Israelite souls of my Israelite friends (we were no longer friends!), so they wouldn't transgress the fifth commandment, *just in case* I'd been wrong*, just in case* I'd been bad for them in ways I couldn't see, and because I felt beholden, all because I was their friend (we were no longer friends!)—but what *struck* me as peculiar at the time was this: I felt relieved. And relieved, I remembered all the kids in the Cage. I thought: I'm the leader of the Side of Damage; at least I'm the leader of the Side of Damage. And at last I'm the leader of no one else.

And I felt *more* relieved. Relieved, in neither case, in the sense of *unencumbered*, though; it wasn't as if "a burden had been lifted." It was more like I, with my burden yet shouldered, no longer had to worry how to lay it down properly; more like when you slouch on sore-arched feet, shivering and exhausted, beside your warm bed, a thick towel wrapped capelike around your clean body. How you can, if you want to—and you have for a while, it turns out you have; you've wanted to forever even though you didn't know—just go ahead and fall. Finally, finally, and finally, the end.

I handed my pass to Mrs. Plotkin—Botha was in the bathroom—and dodged Benji's glances on the way to my carrel. I didn't want to talk about the two-hill field with him, let alone in hand-signs. I wanted to hold to that feeling of relief.

Already it was leaving me. The Cage was too—what? There wasn't enough—what?

The Cage was still the Cage.

No cursing or throwing things, no yelling or breaking things, no defiant group action to greet my return. No defiance at all. If Chunkstyle, as instructed, had whispered my message, it certainly wasn't apparent. I didn't know what I'd expected, but it wasn't this. Kids wrote, kids slept, kids read, faced forward. A few of them even had their hands in the air. *Ben-Wa Wolf* had his hand in the air.

I set my chin on my fist and attempted to doze, but those hands, raised hands—how you had to ask the question "May I ask a question?" before you asked a question, and how a raised hand *was* that question, how you had to raise your hand to *ask* that question, how handraising blinkered your own domination—those raised hands jacked up my pulse like a potion. Sleep was impossible. I couldn't escape me.

My disappointment in the scholars came back on me amplified, enhanced now by disappointment in myself, my weak-kneed, cowardly, glass-jawed self. It wasn't just that I'd been ditched by two-hundred-plus friends I'd been fool enough to count on; it wasn't just that those friends had, it seemed, gone out of their way to maximize the pain they would cause by ditching me, but that, once ditched, once suffering that pain, I'd let myself trick myself into seeing a brighter side. I'd behaved like an angel, convinced myself that damage, plain-as-day damage, was actually a blessing—the consolation I'd taken was no consolation. That relief that I'd felt was a loser's relief. A meek-shall-inherit/karma-will-balance/love-the-one-you're-with scorned sucker's relief. I was the leader of the Side of Damage? At least I was the leader of the Side of Damage?

You get socked in the mouth and wait a couple heartbeats, whoever you are—Nathan Zuckerman or Huckleberry Finn, Peter Tarnopol or Peter Pan, Tom Sawyer, Holden Caulfield, or Akaky Akakievich, Seymour or Zooey or Franny Glass—the sting will numb out, you'll feel some relief.

You wait a couple heartbeats, your chemicals will warm you, armor your nerves. Not just so you can abide the pain you've been dealt, though, let alone so you can stand there taking more of it, but rather so you can return the pain two-fold, ten-fold, twenty-fold, fifty-. So you can stop its inflicters from finishing you. So you can have a chance to save yourself. That's why Muay Thai geeks kicked trees and punched rocks and used hurt extremities to strike the enemies who'd hurt them. That's why you didn't crumple when socked in the mouth, that's why you didn't lay there, why you came back swinging: to use what you were given—that advantageous, brief burst of numbness—to harness and use it, not wallow in the fleeting relief it provided.

Yet here I was, wallowing, or trying to wallow; and there that relief, not fleeting but fled now. At least I was the leader of the Side of Damage? At *most* I was the leader of the the Side of Damage. At *best* I was the leader of the Side of Damage. And what the fuck was the Side of Damage? Forty kids inside a cage who were staring into boxes, asleep sitting up, waiting to get called on. At last I was only the leader of *them*. At best that meant nothing. My father'd been right, and Rabbi Salt too: Moses I wasn't. I'd not have used my staff to strike the rock a second time. I'd have stove my brother's head with it, then all the golden-calfers', then laid in the sand to die of thirst with the rest of them.

My eyes were closed, but I still couldn't sleep.

And then there was Botha, butchering my name. "Makebee!" he said. "I said Makebee!" he said. He was next to my chair. He dropped a pass on my desk—the one I'd handed Mrs. Plotkin. I'd forgotten the signature.

"Who wrote this?" he said.

Leave me alone.

"Whatsametteh, Makebee? Not feeling good? Sneppy answers eluding you?"

Just step me and leave me alone, I said.

"You're the one brought this, though," Botha said. "Mrs. Platkin?" said Botha to Mrs. Plotkin. "He's the one what brought the pass, yes?"

"He gave me a pass and I put it on your desk," Mrs. Plotkin said. "That's all I know."

"Well, sance this was the only pass on my dask," Botha started to say, but his sentence's predicate, whatever it was, got zeroed by a noise that came from behind us.

This noise was being furnished by Ben-Wa Wolf and, like so many other famous instances of defiance, it came on so suddenly that, at first, it didn't seem like defiance; it seemed a mistake. It was, after all, just the groan of a chair being scooted on the thinly carpeted floor. The noise sounded no less accidental than it had on any of those thousand occasions we'd heard it in the past, those thousand times when it *had* been accidental. As the seconds passed, though, and the groaning failed to relent, no one in the Cage failed to break the Face-Forward rule, and all of us saw that Ben-Wa's hand was in the air. We began to suspect the mistake was on purpose.

And then, so to speak, the second plane hit the building.

"I've been raising my hand for thirty-four minutes and all you care about is passes!" Ben-Wa shouted, his chair still scooting. "I have questions!"

"Stap one for you," Botha said. "Aggrassive squeaking."

Ben-Wa continued scooting. Back and forth and side-to-side. He was way beyond his tapeline.

"Questions!" he shouted, his neck showing muscles as he strained to look over his shoulder at the cluster.

The teachers did nothing.

Ben-Wa kept scooting.

Botha moved toward him, forgetting the forged pass—I tore it up.

"The Boston Tea Party!" Ben-Wa shouted.

"Stap two," said Botha, closing in.

"It was terrorism! Why does this book call it a party?!" Ben-Wa dropped his raised hand to knock the history book from his desk. "Why won't anyone answer my questions?!" he shouted at the teachers.

Then Botha stopped the scooting himself. He took Ben-Wa's seatback in hand and claw and stilled him.

"Let go of my chair!" Ben-Wa yelled at Botha. "I've got questions about terrorism!" he yelled at the teachers.

"Why not answer his questions?" said Eliyahu.

"Stap one for you, Aye lie!"

Let his chair go, I said.

"And stap one for you, Make—"

"Let go of my chair!" Ben-Wa yelled at Botha. "Let go of my chair! Just—!" His voice cracked then, all pleading-sounding and defeated, and silence came over the Cage. Mrs. Plotkin took a breath, as if she was about to say something, and then didn't. Mrs. Mingle did and then didn't do the same things as Mrs. Plotkin. Botha kept his eyes down and held the seatback. He was the only one who believed he knew what should happen next.

The rest of us studied Ben-Wa.

He rocked his torso like he was crying, or praying. And there *were* tears on his cheeks, but they weren't the weepy kind. He was squeezing the sides of his seat, struggling to scoot out of Botha's grip and failing, the veins in his hands throbbing, those muscles in his neck, and the Cage seemed to dim, and he to smolder, his bright white hair drawing light from the periphery, channeling it down to his face. It became red and aglow, a speeding firetruck face, yet his chair remained still as a photo of a chair.

It hurt, to look at him trying so hard. It hurt the way it hurts to watch a baby stumble across a room—how your left side tenses when the baby's about to fall to his right, your right when the baby's about to fall to his left. And it hurt like watching great boxing does—that twelfth-round tightness gripping your chest and how your hands wince like Vincie's to block telegraphed punches—the gasp and shiver when a knockout blow lands and then all the startled blinking. It hurt like visceral descriptions of hurt hurt, and it hurt all of us, and all at the same time, and we all knew at the same time that that was how it was for all of us at the same time.

And it is true that you cannot box a man who you are watching on television. And it's true you can't balance a stumbling baby who's out of reach. You can never bleed from another's wounds, and no one, no matter Whose son he says he is, can bleed from yours. But your body can describe the condition of another's. Your body can describe the condition *to you*, and that kind of description is also an action. The action is sympathy. Sometimes you can push it. Sometimes it pushes.

Our vicarious suffering at the sight of Ben-Wa's struggle couldn't get his muscles strong enough to free his chair from Botha's grasp, but the line between description and action in our own muscles was thin, erasable: we had our own chairs.

We acted on them. We forced them to describe us.

It happened all at once.

It was the most noise we had ever heard indoors. It was the noisiest noise we had ever heard anywhere. There wasn't a rhythm, just constant inconstancy. No mappable peak or valley to the volume. No predictable ebb and flow of squeak and groan. No arc. It was hyper. It was everything at once.

After two minutes of everything at once, it was over.

If Cecil B. DeMille had directed the scene, the hair on all our heads would have been the color of Ben-Wa's.

Instead, our battered eardrums vibrated to a tone no longer sounding.

Our arms ached. The teachers' faces were slack. Only Botha was un-changed.

Let Ben-Wa go, I said.

"Let go of his fucken chair!" shouted Vincie.

"He's got questions!" shouted Eliyahu.

"Barbara Mingle!" shouted Chunkstyle.

Eliza June Watermark! I shouted.

"He's got questions about terrorism!" shouted Nakamook.

"We've got questions about terrorism!" shouted Asparagus.

"Tea Party!" shouted Winthrop.

"And the hilly highways a-roll with the heads of infidels whose eye-holes—!" shouted Mookus.

"Barbara!" shouted Chunkstyle.

"Mingle!" shouted Chunkstyle.

June! I shouted. Maccabee!

"Let go of him!" "Terrorism!" "Emotionalize!" "Let his chair go!" "Ques-tions!" "Fucken let go of him!" "I have questions!" "My love for you is a pow-erful thing that drove me to—!" "The chair!" "Get off me!" "Homotionalize! "My pee isn't pungent!" "And the cities smashed against the mountains by tsunamis like flies breathed on by boy-Gods eating wantons—!" "Get off him!" "Foog!" "We have some fucken questions!" "I do not understand and so cannot honestly account for—!" "—Terrorism!" "The party!" "Let him go!" "Homo's lotion in your eyes!" "I'm no foog!" "However I hold one belief forever true—!" Gurion ben-Judah Maccabee loves Eliza June Water-mark! "My mother's no fucker!" "Slokum dies Friday!" "All my desires and motivations—!" "Bleeding at our feet, begging for mercy on their families, vengeance on their enemies, and cinnamon their toasts!" "*You're* the foog!" "Let go of my chair!" "Let go of his chair!" "Let go of our chair!" "Get off me!" "Get off us!" "Let us go!" "We damage we!" "The Side of Damage!" "Gurion!" "Gurion!" "Gurion Maccabee!" "Came out of love, truest love, the kind of love that never dies!" "Let go of him!" "We can be together like—!" "The Side of Damage!" "And love like—!" "The Side of Damage!" "And the world will be great for us like—!" "The Side of Damage!" "And the world will be smiling at us like—!" "The Side of Damage!" "For, in a certain way, the world will belong to—!" "The Side of Damage!" "—a terrorism party!"

Suddenly Ben-Wa stood, and just as suddenly the shouting stopped.

The teachers uncovered their ears.

"Sit down," said Botha to Ben-Wa Wolf.

The Side of Damage stood, awaited his next mis-step.

"Detantion for all of you for that first nawnsinz," said Botha. "And lunch in the Cage for all of you for this nawnsinz."

The end-of-class tone harmonized with our acute tinnitus.

Botha returned to the monitor's desk.

"We are a defiance," Ben-Wa said to us.

"But we've all got detention." "And lunch in the Cage." "And no one answered your questions." "And Botha didn't let your chair go til the tone sounded."

"That's right!" snapped Botha from the monitor's desk. "You've done nathin' but catch a banch of trouble for yourselves. Kape it up and I'll kape giving you all the trouble I ken."

"Botha says," Benji said, "that he'll keep giving us all of the trouble he can."

"All of it?" said Vincie.

"He's been giving us all the trouble he can?" said Eliyahu.

What the monitor's given us, I said to my army, is all the trouble he can.

The Gurionic War

Emmanuel Liebman: Diaspora Judaism is what? I missed the last part.

Terry Gross: "Diaspora Judaism is masturbation."

Emmanuel Liebman: And who'd you say you were quoting?

Terry Gross: A.B. Yehoshua.

Emmanuel Liebman: Who's that?

Terry Gross: A novelist.

Emmanuel Liebman: He sounds Israeli.

Terry Gross: He is Israeli.

Emmanuel Liebman: An Israeli *novelist*?

—*Fresh Air with Terry Gross,* 11/17/12

TRANSLATOR'S NOTE

Except for where otherwise noted, Rabbi Gurion ben-Judah Maccabee wrote all of what you have read so far, the first twelve books of *The Instructions*—our most important work of scripture but for Torah itself—in English between the ages of ten and twelve years (between late 2006 and early 2009), and the latter ten books in Hebrew between the ages of thirteen and sixteen years (between mid-2009 and mid-2013). Upon completing the first twelve books (which the Rabbi had yet to title "The Side of Damage"), Rabbi Gurion asked Emmanuel Liebman—who has, of late, gone completely underground and thus could not, regrettably, help me write this introduction—to translate them into Hebrew. The rabbi gave Emmanuel eight weeks to do so. Considering that Books One through Twelve comprise approximately 230,000 words, this was no small task. Nonetheless, Emmanuel met his deadline, the rabbi approved the translation, and a couple days later (on March 14, 2009), asked me to translate Emmanuel's translation back into English by June 18, 2009, which was three days before the Rabbi would become bar-mitzvah, at which point he would cease to speak English, write English, and—inasmuch as it would be possible—hear or (with the exception of studying the canons of Philip Roth and Don DeLillo, whose *End Zone* he has lately, for hobby purposes, been translating into Hebrew) read English.

Of course I protested: Why so Borgesian an assignment? Weren't there more important things for me to do than translate a translation back into its original language?

"No," said the Rabbi. Nor would he let me see the original. Just Emmanuel's translation.

Long made short, my task was surprisingly easy. I brought the re-translation to Gurion on June 18, 2009, and I told him so. He informed me that Emmanuel had reported similarly. He took out his original English version and compared paragraphs for a few minutes, a quarter-hour tops, then told me, "It's good. Thank you, Eliyahu."

To have three months of work, however easy, merely browsed by the friend for whom you did that work, and even if he tells you it's good—not to mention that it seemed insincere, he wasn't smiling, scholars, I'll tell you that—it was infuriating.

I said so.

The Rabbi pushed the two versions across the table. "See for yourself," he said.

And so I saw: My re-translation was, word for word and jot for jot, identical to the original.

"I thought it might be this way," the rabbi said. "I guess I probably knew it would. I guess this means I have to finish."

My re-translation's having turned out identical to the rabbi's original meant—to him—that his scripture was translingual, and therefore definitive. That is what he told me. Had it turned out otherwise, i.e., *not* definitive, he would have, he explained, ceased to write scripture and stayed silent forever, never allowing what he'd written to be read by anyone other than myself and Emmanuel, never completing what he'd spent nearly three years starting. As scholars can imagine, the thought of that shook me, still shakes me today (had I somehow managed to screw up the re-translation, "The Gurionic War" would not have been written; *The Instructions would not exist*), though not half as much as did the look on Gurion's face when he uttered the words, "I guess this means I have to finish." That look, scholars, the grimness of which I'd not seen in evidence since the so-called "11/17 Miracle" itself... That look would have wilted young David ben-Jesse astride Gath's giant in the Valley of Elah; the head would have dropped from his capable hands.

Even so, while I do agree without hesitation that the scripture you hold in your hands is definitive, I cannot share—try as I might—in Gurion's certainty that it is "translingual" (though for reasons I trust by now to be obvious, I did not argue when he first claimed it was). However remarkable, the identicality of my re-translation and Gurion's original—along with the identicality of the original and re-translation of the latter ten books, which you're about to read, and to which Emmanuel and I applied the same methodology as we had to the first ten (Hebrew-to-English-to-Hebrew this time)—might be otherwise explained by what's lately known in social-science communities as "The Gurion Effect," and "Gurionic Solomony" among non-pseudoscientists. Both Sandra Billings, in her "Assessment of a Client" (p. 291), and Rabbi Avel Salt, in his letter to Leonard Brodsky (p. 217), glancingly refer to certain outcomes of Gurionic Solomony, but neither really describes it, not even briefly. And so, to describe it, however briefly:

Anyone who reads or listens to Gurion ben-Judah without enmity becomes more like him; demonstrably more like him. E.g., before I, at the age of twelve, met Gurion, I was no doubt booksmart, even exceptionally so, but I was not on a path toward finishing college at the age of nineteen. Now, at the age of nineteen, I'm in law school. I will not detail it here for security reasons, but Emmanuel

Liebman's experience has been highly similar to mine. Suffice it to say that among those who have encountered the Rabbi and/or his work, instances of grade-skipping and a generally increased talent for verbal articulation are not only manifold, but well documented. You can even witness these changes happening (to Vincie Portite, for example) over the course of the four days on which the vast majority of *The Instructions* focuses. And lest I be accused of coyness, let it not go without saying: If you are with us, you will certainly witness such changes in yourself as you proceed through the scripture. I would not be too surprised were I to learn that you have already.

But the point I'm trying to make is this: Given the effect of Gurionic Solomony, Emmanuel and I, two of the five people with whom Gurion has maintained the closest contact over the last few years, might be two of the *only* five people with the ability to translate/re-translate *The Instructions* in the way that Gurion himself would have. And so the fact that we have done so does not—not necessarily, at least—indicate that *The Instructions* is translingual, at least not in the general sense. It only indicates the *potential* of *The Instructions* to be translingual. It might, of course, further indicate that if you're a scholar without enmity toward Gurion, and you were to come to know him as well as we do—it is his hope, and ours, that reading *The Instructions* will itself engender such knowing, or at least a sufficient approximation thereof—*The Instructions* would in turn *become* translingual. For you. The scholar. It might. We hope. And so maybe I'm merely splitting hairs.

Yet maybe, though splitting hairs, I'm not *merely* splitting hairs. In either case, who am I to split hairs? To you. Who, to you, am I to split hairs? You don't know me from Adam. Not really. Not yet.

Come heavy next year in Jerusalem.

—Eliyahu of Brooklyn, December 2013

13
THE FIVE

Thursday, November 16, 2006
4th Period–5th Period

Fourth period, I had individual therapy. Call-Me-Sandy had a bag of wrapped caramels. She held it out across her desk. A one-pound bag, an inch above the blotter, her elbow at rest between the lips of a tissuebox.

"So?" she said. "How are things?" she said.

Her bony wrist, her medium-length nails, raggedy cuticles, the bag slightly trembling, its stiff plastic rattling. The overhead light panel flickered twelve times.

"I'm worried about you."

Thirty more flickers, and she set the bag of caramels to rest on the blotter, put her hand in her lap, took a sip from her coffee.

Ninety-six flickers. Three sips from her coffee. Uncountable flickers. She chinned the air at the bag of caramels.

Twenty-seven flickers.

She lifted the bag, held it over the blotter. Again the bag rattled.

"I'm worried about you."

You said that already.

"You didn't respond."

You're not worried about me. You're worried because you're nervous.

"I worry that I'm nervous?"

Maybe that too, I said. What I meant is you're a nervous person and nervous people worry. The nervousness comes first with nervous people. The vector proceeds from nervousness. Like how you're worrying that bag of candy. As it were. Your hand's not shaking because the bag's rattling—the bag's rattling because your hand is shaking. And maybe you don't notice the bag rattling and it stops there, or maybe you do notice the bag rattling and you realize your hand is shaking, and so maybe you stop your hand from shaking, or maybe seeing that your hand shakes makes your hand shake worse, which makes the bag shake worse. Either way, though, your worries are a rattling bag of caramels in the hand of your nervousness. Some people, though: their nervousness is a rattling bag of caramels in the hand of their worries. Those people look calmly on the world until they come across something worrisome, and only then do they worry, and only when they worry do they get nervous. They act upon themselves prior to being acted upon *by* themselves. They're the healthier kind of people.

"That's an almost gestalt kind of observation."

No it's not, I said. I said, It's homuncular. It's nonsense. Games with prepositions to impress and intimidate.

"Was your mother a gestalt practitioner at any point?"

Mama always said life was like a box of chocolates.

"Are you upset with me, Gurion?"

Why should I be upset?

"I'm asking."

Why are you asking?

"You don't usually make fun of me."

Was I *making* fun? I said. I knew I was *having* fun, but—

"It sounded like you were making fun of me," she said.

How long have you known you were a lesbian? I said.

She choked and coughed—wrongpiped coffeespit—and dropped the caramels. "Excuse me?" she said.

You heard me, I said.

"I don't…"

How long have you known you wanted sex from women?

"This isn't appropriate."

If someone with a vagina likes vaginas but tells herself she doesn't like vaginas, or tells herself she likes penises but just hasn't found the right one, or admits to herself that she does like vaginas and doesn't like penises but consistently refuses to act on her desires for vaginas, is she a lesbian, Sandy? What do you think?

"This is not appropriate."

How about this one: If someone with a vagina, at age, say, twenty, realizes she likes vaginas and has never liked penises—i.e., realizes she's a lesbian—has she been a lesbian all along, or has she only been a lesbian since the moment she realized she liked vaginas? And if it turns out to be one of the latter two cases, is 'realize' the correct verb? That is: Do lesbians become lesbians, or are they born lesbians?

"I can see that you're angry, Gurion. That's why—"

Are you getting any? Sex from women, I mean. Have you gotten any sex from your professor? Did you switch voices over coffee and decide to get beers?

"Please, Gurion. You're worrying me."

But did you say it like Obama or Daley, Call-Me? That is, if you said anything, how did you suggest it? 'Join me for a beer, Professor Lakey?' Or 'What say we blow dis popstand and get some beerce?' Which code did you use? Was the moment all postmodern and meta and intertextual and post-ironic because both of you knew that Professor Lakey had read "Assessment of a Client: Gurion Maccabee"? Or was the moment, after all, just nice and straightforward and full of tension and potential romance because even though she'd read the paper, you couldn't be sure she'd read it *right*—you couldn't tell if your encoded, footnoted professions of love for her had even come across—and your professor herself was worried that maybe she'd only seen in the footnotes what she wanted to see, a student with a desirable vagina who wanted to see *her* vagina where there was but a desirably vaginaed student who wanted to talk about linguistics? Did you end up going home together? Did Professor Lakey take you home, Call-Me, or did you end up alone that night, using her, in fantasy, as a tool for venting?

"You were never supposed to have read that paper."

That's the response you're settling on? Blame the victim? That's the response?

"The victim?" she said.

The victim being me. The victim being sentenced to the Cage indefinitely.

"Gurion, you hurt people."

I hurt people.

"You hurt people, Gurion. You have a history of hurting people. You cause physical harm to people, and you show no remorse. That's why you're in the Cage. I will admit that a lot of what I said about you was inaccurate. This owed partly to my not having known you so well at the time I wrote the paper, but—"

University of Chicago dialect, now. Nearly stentorian. And from such a small head. You are one bold lesbian. You are—

"Make fun of me all you want, Gurion, but I'm coming clean here. I will even admit that many of the inaccuracies in the paper weren't mistakes, per se, as much as they were—how should I say this? In gradschool—well—"

Sometimes you have to go analytically overboard to prove to your teachers that you're worth their time.

"Yes. That's about—"

You constructed me in such a way as to allow yourself room to riff. You needed room to riff on all the valuable knowledge you absorbed in your beloved professor's writings and lectures. That would get you the A. Or the date.

"Yes."

Did I mention that I think professor Lakey is imaginary? I think she's your imaginary friend.

Sandy pushed me the tissuebox. I pushed it back. I wasn't crying. Not even close.

"You were never supposed to have read the paper. I don't know why Bonnie filed it with your records. I didn't know she would when I wrote it. She's—"

It's your supervisor's fault.

"Yes."

The buck stops there.

"Stop it now. Please. If you know half as much as you seem to, you know that despite my mistakes, I care about you, Gurion. I am fond of you. I worry about you. You should not have read that paper. You should never have seen it. I am very worried about you right now."

You're nervous.

"That too."

And I'm in the Cage because I'm remorselessly violent.

"Yes."

If you had the chance to do it all over again, you'd still have me placed in the Cage indefinitely.

"When you put it like that—"

From the CYA POV—

"It's not just to cover my ass, Gurion, no. It's because you hurt people. You cause disruptions and you hurt people. You cannot be in regular classrooms. You are Cage-appropriate."

No one is Cage-appropriate.

"That's a separate issue. You hurt people, Gurion. That's what we're talking about."

I hurt people.

"Yes. You commit acts of violence. You endanger other students. You're someone from whom other students need protection."

She pushed me the tissuebox. She *wanted* me to cry. To share a tender moment. She was trying to create one. I was not feeling tender. I pushed the box back.

Funny sentence, I said.

"Excuse me?"

'You're someone from whom other students need protection.'

"I don't see how it's funny."

It's all stress and context. Repeat it three times. 'You're someone from whom other students need protection.' It'll sound like the opposite of what you meant.

"You're someone from whom other students need protection. You're someone from whom other students need protection. You're someone from whom other students need protection... Okay. I see. More wordgames with prepositions. So what?"

Try to kiss her.

"What?"

You're too passive.

"What?"

Touch her hair first. If she lets you, lean in. If she leans in too, then kiss her. That's the right order.

"We're done talking about this. This isn't appropriate."

Don't say 'I love her' in Klingon, I said, then pretend it means 'Have a good weekend.'

Sandy's eyes welled. She blew her nose. Through her tissue, she said, "'With all of my heart.'"

Pardon?

"*jIH muSHa' Daj tlhej Hoch wIj tIq* means 'I love her *with all of my heart*.'"

In Klingon.

"Yes."

In a footnote.

"Yes." She tossed her crumpled tissue.

You proclaim your love in Klingon in a footnote addressed to your supervisor. A footnote you claim—within the footnote—that you will not include in the copy that goes to your professor.

"I *did* include it."

You included the footnote in the copy to your professor, hoping she'd get the message. You hoped she'd read the footnote and conclude that you had forgotten to remove it, or that you were 'unconsciously motivated' to 'forget' to remove it. You hoped that your declaration of love for 'her' would come across, in Klingon, and would—because it was buried in a footnote that she wasn't supposed to see and was thereby a 'secret'—not only enhance the thrill of her discovery that you love her, but put the ball in her court, yeah? Because you figured: 'She'll see the footnote, and she'll realize that I, Call-Me-Sandy, can't bring myself to approach her romantically, and so she'll have to approach me if she's interested.'

"Yes."

Does your professor speak Klingon?

"I don't know."

You don't know?

"She used to want to be a linguist. She majored in linguistics. Even if she doesn't know Klingon, you'd think she'd look it up."

No. I wouldn't. I wouldn't think she'd look it up. You wrote that the phrase meant 'Have a good weekend.'

"You looked it up."

I *didn't* look it up.

"You know Klingon?"

I knew a kid who used to say 'jIH DIchDaq chargh Canaanite' all the time.

"'I will conquer the Cannanite?'"

Yeah. So *jIH*, I knew, meant 'I.' There's no 'I' in 'Have a good weekend.'

"But how did you know it meant 'I love her'?"

Context, I said. I guessed. It was either that or 'I hate you,' as in 'I hate you, Bonnie Wilkes, PsyD for making me hand in a copy of this paper.'

"But—"

Touch her hair and lean in. If she leans in, kiss her.

"This is so inappropriate!" Sandy said.

No, I said. This is termination. This is Good Will Huntingstein and Thursdays with Gurion. The saccharine and cinematic moment when the tables turn. The helper getting helped by the one she came to help. I'm done with you now. You aren't my therapist.

"That's not up to you."

If you want me to come on Thursdays still, fine. And you can write whatever you want to write about me for whatever papers you need to turn in, and I won't even call you out, because I like you. I think you're a kind person. But I'm not saying anything to you anymore. I'll sit here writing scripture or reading Philip Roth. And don't look so down. Just don't. Just don't. This could've been worse. I could've been worse. I hurt people, right? That's what you said. I could've thrown a stapler, but I didn't, did I? I could've been worse but I wasn't. Remember that.

She pushed me the tissuebox.

It's not gonna happen, Call-Me, I said.

Sandy said, "Tch." Then she said it twice more. "Tch," she said. "Tch."

I plucked her a tissue.

The argument started five minutes after the beginning-of-lunch tone. Half the Side of Damage had left the Cage to get to-go beef stroganov in the cafeteria. Benji, Jelly, Mookus, Vincie, Leevon, Mangey, and Eliyahu sat with me at the teacher cluster. The other twelve or so brownbaggers and lunchboxers formed a circle on the floor surrounding us. To speak to us from the circle, you had to make your voice louder than conversational. You had to make it public. Ben-Wa Wolf was the first to do it. He said to us, "What do we call that action we did with our chairs?"

And Benji said, "Riotscoot."

And I said, Hyperscoot.

"Hyperscoot already means something else," said Benji. "A couple or three spazzes groan their chairs at the same time by accident—that's hyperscoot."

I said, Any time two or more people groan their chairs at once, it's hyperscoot. It doesn't matter if they do it by accident or on purpose. Intention's invisible.

"Lots of things are invisible," Benji said, "but they still count. They still get their own names. Spare a cheesepuff?"

I pushed my baggie into the lunchless space before him.

"This point of Benji's is not a weak one," said Eliyahu. "I ask you: What is the meaning of this face?"

He let all the muscles in his face rest.

It's a blank face, I said.

"A scared face," said Benji.

"It's a fucken bored face," said Vincie.

"A sad face," announced Cody von Braker, from the circle. "It's a doubtful face," said Miles Minton to Cody. "A face like it's very hard to push the poop out the ane," Jesse Ritter said to everyone. "We're eating here," said Exar Tea. "We're not eating chocolate brownies or brown gravy or anything," retorted Jesse. "It's a face like your brother's dog died but she bit you once and you were always scared of her," said Jerry Throop. "It's not always brown," claimed Exar. "Exar shits snot-colored." "You feel sorry for your brother because he's your brother, but also happy the scary dog's dead, and maybe even a little sick of your brother because of how he keeps whining to your mom. You want to punch him a little." "Not snot-colored. Maybe sometimes beige like peanut butter." "Half the room's eating peanut butter, Exar. That's banced of you." "Jesse started it." "I'm not the one who said beige." "It used to be that whenever you wanted to punch him a little, you didn't do it, except for that first time, when the dog bit you. Which is why you didn't do it after that. But now the dog can't bite you because that dog is dead, you're thinking." "I think it's a face of Protestant determination," said Forrest Kenilworth. "That fucken dog is fucken dead, you're thinking. And now? Now you're gonna punch your brother a lot, even though you only want to punch him a little. You're gonna punch him for all those other times you wanted to punch him a little and couldn't because of the dog. And when he says, 'What are you doing, Jerry? What're you doing?' You'll be like: 'It adds up.' Just that. 'It adds up.' All cold and minimal and shit. Maybe you even drop the 'It.' You just say, 'Adds up.' All dirty and real."

It's a blank face, I said again.

"Or a pensive face," said Eliyahu.

So which one is it? I said.

"You see?" said Eliyahu. "It matters. The feeling behind the face is invisible, but it matters. Even to you."

"Exactly!" said Benji. "It matters. Even to you."

I'm not saying the feeling doesn't matter, I said. All I'm saying, I said, is that the feeling is invisible. The face *is* visible, though; it is visibly *blank*. If I say, 'Eliyahu wore a blank face,' people can try to figure out why it's blank, and maybe some of them'll even be right about why it's blank, but none of them will imagine that it *isn't* blank. If I say, 'Eliyahu wore a pensive face,' though, then even though some people might picture a blank face, others might picture a face with a crinkled forehead or jutted-out lip or squinted eyes. That's why if you were pensive when you made that blank face, Eliyahu, it's better I say, 'Eliyahu was pensive. He wore a blank face,' than if I just say, 'Eliyahu wore a pensive face.' My way's more accurate.

"So you're right," said Eliyahu.

"Traitor," said Benji.

"I'm loyal to the truth," said Eliyahu.

"I was kidding around," Benji said. "I don't think you're a traitor. You think I'd call you a traitor over that?"

"There's no need to make it federal," said Eliyahu.

"Federal?" said Vincie.

"Like a federal case," Jelly said. "Like there's no need to make a federal case out of it, he's saying. "

"It's hard for me tell when you're kidding," Eliyahu said to Benji.

Invisible intentions, I said.

"No way!" said Benji. "That doesn't prove your point at all. That's the opposite of proving your point. The reason he didn't know I was kidding was because he didn't *pay attention* to my intentions. He only heard the word 'traitor.' He didn't hear how I said it. I said it real deadpan."

"Nakamook is scary," the circle around the cluster was saying. "Gurion's scarier." "Not scarier, but better at fighting." "Not better at fighting, but faster at fighting." "Maybe a little faster at fighting, but also a little slower to fight." "And Nakamook's stronger." "Thai boxing." "Short fuse." "Those crazy arms." "It's weird he's not a basketballer." "He's not like a basketballer, so don't say that." "Looks like someone who bites people might have a crush on a rumored pyro everyone's scared of." "She can hear you. They can all hear us, you know. They're sitting right there. We're right next to the inner circle, which is shaped like a rectangle." "A square." "They can hear us, but only if they're listening." "A square's a kind of rectangle." "Even if they listen, it doesn't mean they can hear us." "Wrong. A rectangle's a kind of square." "You got it backward: The girls listen to the lyrics, the women hear the voice. The voice is more important than the words, so hearing's deeper than listening."

I said to Benji, Deadpan's funny when it's funny because it's hard to tell when the person who's deadpanning is making a joke. It's hard to tell his intention. And that's his intention—to make it hard.

"What are we even talking about, here? I don't even know what we're talking about anymore," Benji said. "I'm trying to tell you that if we call that action we did 'hyperscoot,' then it sounds much more pussy than it actually is because it sounds like it's by accident. 'Hyper' means out of control. The things you do when you're out of control are necessarily accidental."

I said, What about riots? If we have a riot, it means we get all out of control, but if we have a riot it's because we decide to have a riot, and if we decide to have a riot then it's on purpose.

"A riot's not out of the control of the rioters! A riot's only out of the control of the people the rioters are rioting against!"

"It's okay, Benji. It's okay," Jelly said.

"You're getting a little outta control there yourself," Vincie told him.

Benji reached across the cluster, sweeping Vincie's daily lunch-apple sideways.

Ansul Entsry caught the apple in his lap and smiled.

Vincie leaned over the cluster, holding a fresh-opened pudding cup. He tried to turn it over onto Nakamook's head, but Benji grabbed his wrist and thumbed deep to disable Vincie's finger control. When the pudding dropped, Nakamook caught it face-up in the palm of his free hand, and Vincie backhanded the pudding with *his* free hand, and the pudding landed sideways on the cluster in front of Jelly, who righted it just as the surface tension broke. Only a dime-sized puddle of pudding spilled.

"Now the pudding's Jelly's, Vincie," said Benji. "That's what happens."

"Hyperscoot," Vincie said. "Hyperscoot, hyperscoot."

The doorbell rang and Botha rose from the Monitor's desk to answer it. Nakamook, still holding Vincie's wrist, pinned it to the cluster so that Vincie had to bend low and Botha wouldn't be able see the grappling unless he came close. The circle around the cluster closed in. I sensed something good about this closing-in of the circle, something improved. On Tuesday, when Forrest Kenilworth had called Ben-Wa Wolf "The Boy Who Went Wee-Wee" and the whole Cage rushed him, they'd done so to see what Benji would do to him, which only happened to shield Benji from Botha's witness; this time, though, there was little they could see by way of getting in closer that they couldn't have seen from where they'd been sitting; this time they'd closed in *in order* to shield Benji—it wasn't just a circle getting closed, but ranks; they were *closing ranks*.

And something else was good, too—maybe even as good as the show of esprit de corps. Up until the moment the doorbell had rung, I'd almost forgotten that Botha was in the Cage. He'd been so quiet. Silent, even. How many *fuck*s and *shit*s had he let go unanswered? On countless occasions, he'd

stepped kids for *bastard*s and *damn*s and *wang*s, for *hell*s and *jerkoff*s, *dickhead*s
and *pussy*s; twice I'd witnessed him stepping for *suck*. And he had to have
heard them—those *fuck*s and *shit*s of our Thursday lunch. It's true he may
have failed to identify who'd spoken them, but in the past, swears whose
speakers he couldn't identify had garnered a "Quoydanawnsinz" at the least.
But not anymore. Or at least not right then, at Thursday lunch. Then again,
this *was* lunch, and at lunch the rules slackened—but no, not this much;
they hadn't ever slackened quite this much. The hyperscoot had scared him
into choosing his battles. At least that's how it seemed. At least for the
moment. Even if just at least, though, I saw it was good.

"Hyperscoot, hyperscoot, motherfucken hyperscoot," Vincie, writhing
in wrist-grip, told Benji. "No one listens to you, anyway," Nakamook said.
"No one listens to *me*," said Main Man. "I don't want any pudding," said
Jelly. "I'll have your pudding," Mangey said. I said, I listen, Scott.

"You listen but you don't hear," said Main Man. "Tomorrow I'm gonna
sing. Listen to them!" he said. He pointed at the doorway of the Cage. All
the kids from the cafeteria were coming in with their hotlunch, Ronrico and
the Janitor in front.

"Slokum told me to tell you a bunch of Fridays have passed and he
doesn't feel too dead," Vincie said to Nakamook.

"And what did you do, Vincie? You just listened to him, didn't you?
You just nodded and smiled and listened," said Benji, "like a whiny basketballing messengerboy wannabe Shover who's had a crush on the same girl
since kindergarten and never spoken to her."

"Cold," said Vincie. "Fucken cold."

"Don't kill the messenger," Main Man said. "Just hear what he had to
listen to."

"You gonna let go of my wrist?" said Vincie. "Not yet," said Benji.

I smelled Chunkstyle.

"You would hurt a friend over a message?" said Eliyahu. "He's not hurt,"
said Benji. "No I'm not!" yelled Vincie.

"Quoydanawnsinz," Botha said from the doorway, but no one seemed to
hear him, and he seemed to be content with that; he stared at his clipboard,
looking busy.

Benji doesn't hurt friends, I told Eliyahu.

"What do you call a cow that's...?" said Ronrico, laughing. "What?"
said the Janitor. Ronrico kept laughing.

"There's props on the stage for a play we never heard of—smashed!" said

Chunkstyle. "Smashed to pieces," said Anna Boshka. "The set-designers: they glue them."

"He would humiliate a friend, though?" said Eliyahu. "He would make a friend powerless at his whim and then expect us to trust him?" "They're playing," said Jelly. "Vincie ain't powerless," said Benji. "It's just his right hand. He's got another hand." "I've got another one on the left, Eliyahu! And I'm about to use it! As soon as I figure out how!" "Use it, Vincie," said Benji. "I got no leverage!" "You can't reach anything vital on me anyway." "What do you call a cow that's playing with himself?"

"Quoydanawnsinz!" shouted Botha.

"The rules change at lunchtime, Australian!" yelled Vincie. "Australian!" yelled many. "Australian!" yelled more.

Botha went to his desk, but we all got quieter—a ceasefire feeling, grudging but practical.

"What already?" said the Janitor. Ronrico kept laughing. "It pains me to see others experience pain," said Eliyahu. I'm telling you they're just playing, Eliyahu. It's okay. It's how they play, I said. "And suddenly there's these new tags everywhere of 'Boystar Emotionalize Boystar,'" said Chunkstyle. "I asked Chunkstyle, 'What is it, a Boystar?'" said Boshka. "This is no way to play," said Eliyahu. "And Chunkstyle, he told me, 'The Boystar is a brownstar.' Very clever."

"Beef strokin' off," punchlined Ronrico to the Janitor.

The Janitor instantly dropped his foam lunchtray. Carrots spilled on his khakis, and Stroganov his Sambas. He did a panicked little dance and it flung the debris.

With his left hand, Vincie finally grabbed the wrist of the hand with which Nakamook held Vincie's right hand. Vincie dug his thumb in. Nakamook let go of him.

"I got it?" Vincie said.

"Yeah," said Benji, "but you gotta get it quicker next time. A hell of a lot quicker. You wasted your flood on knocking that pudding out of my hand, and then you were still in my hold, all stunned and smack-talky, trying to figure out what to do next. You can't miss when you flood, Vincie, you know that. I could've pulled the teeth from your head one by one in all the time it took you to get your snat back up. If you have no leverage and you can't get to your enemy's vitals, you have to dig in to anything you can reach. That's the rule. Ill-targeted flooding is the way of the dead, flinchy Vincie, okay?"

"Okay," said Vincie, hanging his head.

"Don't act all defeated, it's weak," Benji said. "You have a gift for flooding. You're the only person I know like that. You're the only flooder I've ever taught to fight who I haven't taught not to flood, and that's because you're able to harness sick-high volumes of snat, way higher volumes than me or Gurion, for example. It's good that your first instinct is to hit, man—it's a good instinct, unless there's nothing you can get to worth hitting. Then, like I said, you gotta dig. So you just have to get a better sense of what's possible. It'll come with practice. You're really tough, Vincie. If I was anyone but me, I'd think twice before fucking with you."

"Thanks," Vincie said.

They banged fists. Leevon grabbed each of their wrists as the fists touched, and did the thumbing action and the fists opened involuntarily.

"You're a scary kid," said Nakamook.

Leevon did a pantomime of Nakamook telling Leevon he was a scary kid.

Then he did a pantomime of himself pantomiming Nakamook telling Leevon he was a scary kid.

Then he snatched a cheesepuff off my brown paper bag-plate and got it in his mouth before I even knew he'd snatched it.

Leevon was a scary kid.

"Can I have my pudding back?" said Vincie.

Mangey coughed on Vincie's pudding.

The Janitor limped away from the germs rapidly, dragging his sullied foot as far behind him as possible.

Ansul Entsry handed Vincie his apple, and when Vincie thanked him, Ansul blushed and seemed to bow.

"Now where were we?" Benji said to me. "Right. I remember. *Riot*'s a tougher word than *hyper*."

But the action's already called hyperscoot, I said. I said, The action already has a name. I said, You can't just change the name of something because—

"I'm not changing the name of anything. Riotscoot isn't the same phenomenon as hyperscoot. The intention makes it different, no matter what you say. Anyway, even if I *was* changing the name of something—aren't you the guy who calls Jews 'Israelites'?"

I said, We were Israelites first, Benji. I said, And what about explosions? If a gas main accidentally blows up and kills twenty people, it's called an explosion. If I blow up a bomb that kills twenty people, that's also called an explosion.

Eliyahu was tugging on my sleeve.

"But it's also called terrorism," Ben-Wa piped in. "Because you did it on purpose."

Not if it's on a battlefield, I said. I said, If I use a bomb to blow up twenty enemy soldiers on a battlefield, it's called heroism, not terrorism. In all three instances, though, it's an explosion.

"Please stop," said Eliyahu.

"Yeah, quit it already," said Vincie. "You're both right, or both wrong, and it's totally fucken boring, so why don't you just slapslap for it?"

"No way I'm gonna slapslap with Gurion," said Nakamook.

Why not? I said.

"Why don't we arm wrestle?"

No way, I said.

"Why not?" said Nakamook.

I said, How about the Electric Chair?

"What's the Electric Chair?"

It's what you called I'm Ticking the other day, I said.

"You can't change the name," said Benji.

It was the Electric Chair first, I said. I said, Actually it was the anti–Kathryn TeBordo, then the Electric Chair, but the girl who invented it changed the name of it, so we should honor that.

"You just call me a girl, man? Like as an insult? That's sexist. And also kinda pussy."

You didn't invent it, I said.

"I invented it Monday night," Benji said.

I said, June invented it years ago. She had a fever. You're just a Tesla.

"I fucken hate Tesla," said Vincie. "What was that song? 'Love Song'? 'So you thi-ink that it's o-vah-ah.' Why can't he pronounce his fucken r's, that guy? I hate when they don't pronounce their r's. It's only the singers with hairstyles that don't pronounce their r's. Hairstyles are fucked." "Is that true about the r's?" said Chunkstyle. "Vincie likes sweeping statements," said Mangey. "This is a rhetorical trick characteristic of many tyrannical world leaders," said Anna Boshka. "Rhetorical trick? You're so smart, Boshka." "You are a nice boy, Remus," said Boshka, "and if you were to ask me to go walking with you, I would not refuse the request."

You're that Indian calculus kid, I said to Benji.

"Now Gurion speaks of Srinivasa Ramanujan." "Sriniwhatta Whosajon? You're so smart!" "Soon your surprise at my wit will begin to sound like contempt, sweet Chunkstyle. Tell me about my eyes." "You've got the most beautiful hazel eyes."

"You couldn't even I'm Ticking for a second on Tuesday. I'll have a contest with you. Winner names both actions."

Bring it, Ramanujan.

"You want to count us down, Vincie?"

"Don't you even worry pretty darling. I know you'll find love again," Vincie half-sang. Then he said, "Three."

And Benji and I faced off.

Then Vincie said, "Two."

And the Cage got quiet.

Vincie said, "One."

And we inhaled deep.

And Vincie said, "Go."

We started to tremble.

Ten seconds into the contest, a bright white flying-saucer shape bloomed from a silver dot in the center of Nakamook's forehead. I was sure I had one on my own forehead, and I wished there was a mirror. I tried Nakamook's pupils, but they didn't reflect me; they were aimed at the ceiling. The ticking of my brainblood wasn't very loud yet at all, and although they were muted as if they had to pierce fuzz first, voices from the Cage filled those spaces of the soundscape that the ticking didn't occupy. "Look at how red they're getting!" "This is not a thing I like." "It's just a contest, Eliyahu of Brooklyn." "...a grand-mal—" "The nasty way their jaws are bulging." "...don't pop a filling." "I hope their tongues are safe."

At the thirty second-mark, Benji's eyes began to wobble in their sockets, and the saucer started throbbing. With every throb, the saucer expanded a little, covering more and more of Nakamook's face. The ticking's rhythm stayed steady, matched the throbbing's beat for beat, and each drop of brainblood whacked the backs of my eardrums louder than the last.

I thought: The decibals are mounting at an incremental ratio equivalent to the one by which the saucer expands, and language is turning weird on me.

The fuzz between the ticks thickened, and the voices of the Cage began to blot out. "Looks bad like____or a seizure." "My uncle____and got comatose." "___long?" "___til today." "Youth_____merciful thing." "_____orkian."

By sixty seconds, I wouldn't have been able to see myself even if I was nose-to-glass with a mirror—Benji's face was obscured to the neck and the hairline by bright white throbbing light. I couldn't even see the corners of the saucer anymore. I felt good, though. Warm.

I thought: You need to breathe.

I breathed.

The saucer kept throbbing, growing. The brainblood whacked harder, the fuzz between the ticks became impenetrable. I lost count of the seconds at ninety, gave up tracking time. Breathe, I thought.

I breathed.

There was no more Nakamook. Only bright white light. Not even the saucer's outline remained within my field of vision. There was throbbing, ticking, breathing, and me. Breathe, I thought.

I breathed.

A silver dot appeared in the center of the whiteness. It bloomed into a brighter, whiter flying-saucer shape that began to throb in time with a new ticking of blood against a less taut part of my eardrum. This ticking was basser than the first one.

I thought: I am making this happen. I don't know how, though.

And then I thought: How do you make anything happen, like—?

Breathe, I thought.

I breathed.

How did you make yourself breathe? I thought.

You *didn't* make yourself breathe, I thought. You *let* yourself breathe, I thought, and barely even that. You can *slow* your breathing—you can halt the in- and exhalations of your lungs temporarily—but you cannot halt them indefinitely. Eventually your lungs will inhale and exhale, whether or not you want them to. Eventually you will be breathing.

Breathe, I thought.

I lifted the halt on my lungs. My lungs breathed for me. Out, then in.

I thought: They are only your lungs in the way that June is your girl-friend, Nakamook your best friend, Judah your father, the Israelites your people: they are only your lungs inasmuch as you are their Gurion. To be yours does not mean you control them. To be theirs does not mean they control you. It only means there is mutual influence. And the more one element influences the other, the more the other influences the one. What you animate animates you back.

Exhale—no don't, I thought.

And despite the hot pain in my chest, I did not lift the halt on my lungs. My lungs strained. Strained against what, though? Strained against the halt? Against me? *My* lungs strained against *me*? Against my *will*? The idea of me, an integrated being with a singular will, much less a will that could be exerted with predictable results—let alone *desirable* results—grew less comprehensible as my oxygen shortaged and the heat of my chestpain increased.

I thought: That control is an illusion is no new idea. But what produces the illusion? What is the thing the word *control* fails to describe? And if there is no such thing, then from where does the urge to describe it arise?

There was a sideways feeling.

There was a falling feeling.

There was a coarse feeling in my elbow and an upside-down feeling all over.

Then I leapt out of my chest, a silver dot centered on a throbbing field of white. The shape I'd thought was a flying saucer had been, I now understood, the outline of either of my eyes, of one stacked on the other, paralaxical. Free now from their boundaries, the throbbing white was limitless. I hovered silver in the center of it, a few feet above Gurion Maccabee.

Gurion had fallen sideways off his chair, rolled onto his back, and was now thrashing, spastically scraping his carpet-burned left elbow back and forth over the floor like some malfunctioning robot. His torso arched and then flattened, arched and then flattened. He was halting his lungs, clenching every muscle in his body, and this was the response of his lungs and muscles: to throw him down, to hurt him back. Parts in conflict take it out on the whole. The only way Gurion could end his own conflict would be to die. But Gurion was a death-proof Israelite. He was not remotely a cross-legged Buddhist.

And an angel came, from my right. One-legged and faceless, skin humming a thousand psalms. He knelt beside Gurion and placed his index finger in Gurion's mouth, then his hand. Then his arm up to the elbow. I tried to stop him, but I had no mass. I was just this silver dot.

The angel continued climbing into Gurion. It was cheap. A low blow. Gurion gagged, coughed him out. All the air he'd held in his lungs left in a single burst. The angel shot past me, back into the white, and the lungs gathered new air, and again I was Gurion.

The ticking in my ears became the sound of my name and the throbbing white resolved into a face.

"Gurion! Gurion! Gurion!" shouted Eliyahu. He was crying.

Heavy, I said.

I did not mean it like hippies do on sitcoms.

"He's not dead!" said Eliyahu. "It's just he feels heavy!"

That's almost how I meant it.

"Hyperscoot then," said Nakamook. "And The Electric Chair."

Botha pushed him aside. He said, "You're blading. Go to the nurse."

Leevon and Vincie lifted me to my feet. I'd carpet-burned my elbow raw. Little dots of blood in the bunchy part.

"You were dying from a seizure," said Jelly Rothstein, "but you aren't dying anymore."

"What was it like to be dying?" asked Ben-Wa Wolf.

"And do you feel any lighter yet?" asked Eliyahu.

The Side of Damage was not a group of scholars, so I did not say: If ever you are asked whether Adonai can create a boulder too heavy for Him to lift, you will answer the fool who asked you: 'Fool, we are two of seven billion such boulders, you and I.' And when the fool insists that Adonai cannot then properly be called almighty, you will not argue, for the fool will be correct. Instead you will answer: 'He is Adonai nonetheless.'

And the Side of Damage was not a group of Israelites, so I did not say: We are superior to the angels not because we control ourselves, but because Adonai does not control us.

What I said was this: We are better than the robots not because we control ourselves. We are better because the Arrangement can't control us.

And whether the inspiration for that statement had been a holy vision— which I doubted (my ability to doubt it the best evidence that it wasn't; i.e. shouldn't a visitation from Adonai strike the person visited as being *undeniably* a visitation from Adonai?)—or a hallucination brought on by an oxygen-starved brain, I saw that what I'd said was good. That is: I saw that what I'd said was true, and so did the Side of Damage.

Botha handed me a pass to the nurse.

□   □   □   □   □   □   □

Nine of the twelve *EMOTIONALIZE* tags in C-Hall had already been monkeyed with. Seven of the nine were entirely blacked out. On the other two, the first Star of Boystar and the six letters following it were slashed through by the crossbar of an A.

EMOTIONALIZE

I figured Ronrico had only sodomized two of the tags he'd monkeyed with because he didn't think to do so to the first seven, but I wondered why he'd left the other three alone. It was probably because he'd seen someone coming and didn't want to get in trouble, except his reason might have been better than that. It might have been that he wanted people to see what the blotted out and sodomized tags had originally said; if no one could see what the ostensibly Boystar-fanatical writers of the *EMOTIONALIZE* tags had ostensibly intended the tags to say, no one would know that the ostensible writers and what they ostensibly stood for were under inostensible attack. The thought of a real attack on non-existent beings filled me with the feeling I'd get from watching Mookus do the Joy of Living Dance, so I looked around for something to damage, and that's when I noticed I wasn't the only one in C-Hall.

Floyd the Chewer stood puzzled before the water fountain. He pressed the button and nothing came out. Then he pressed the button and nothing came out. He grasped the edges of the sink and shook it. Again he pressed the button and nothing came out. He punched the fountain in the grill and cursed. He pressed the button and nothing came out. He slapped the sink on the graffito and cursed. He pressed the button and nothing came out. He banged on the button and nothing came out.

To the spigot, he said, "*I'll* explode. How do you like that? *I'll* friggin explode! How do you like that?" He kicked the fountain in the guts and it dented.

I said, You're gonna break the water fountain.

He revolved, raised his cone. "You know who wrote this?" His circuits were frying. He was so angry he didn't even ask for a pass.

Who? I said.

"I'm asking you."

Why do you care so much? I said.

"I'm the guard," he said.

I said, But you're not really the guard. I said, You're just the guard because you're paid to be the guard.

"I choose to be the guard," Floyd said.

Because it pays you, I said. I said, If you could choose, you'd do crowd control, right? That's what you said to Ruth Rothstein in that interview.

"If I could choose," Floyd said, "I'd play starting linebacker for the Bears. Doesn't mean you gotta be disrespectful, telling me why I do what I do is because of pay. I am the boss of me. Everyone is the boss of himself. I do what I want to do."

Except play linebacker for the Bears, I said, or crowd control.

Floyd slurped his saliva thunderously and his knuckles got as white as his cheering cone. He looked over both shoulders, and on seeing no one else was in C-Hall, he said to me, "Hey, fuck you, Gurion. Eat shit. How's that?"

A little bit funny, I said.

"Right. Funny. You think you're all clever and cute? 2.5 and like that? I asked my wife and she told me what you meant. You think I think you're cute? It's not cute to make fun of a man's job he's gotta do so he can eat. It's not decent. It's not what decent people do. It's what shitty people do. You're not decent. You're shitty. You should eat shit to see what you're like."

He checked over both shoulders again, and while he did that, I started getting scared. Not scared of Floyd, but scared that he was right; that I was wrong. It *wasn't* decent to put someone down for their lousy job—it was snakey, low. It is true that Floyd had the pogromface, that it took no effort to picture him standing in some cobblestone town square, shoulder-to-shoulder with scores of other dummkopfs like Jerry, their eyes and the tines of their pitchforks flashing orange in the flickering light of their torches while they wait for Desormie to pick the right storefront, the worst usurer, the most defenseless wife... However, even if by looking at him I *did* know the crimes Floyd was capable of committing, the crimes he *would commit* if given the opportunity, that didn't mean it was right, in advance of his committing those crimes, to treat him like a criminal. Not necessarily, at least. Adonai Himself did not deal with men according to their *potential* deeds; it's what men did that mattered to Him, not what they would do or might.

I was about to apologize, but Floyd, satisfied C-Hall was still empty, picked up where he'd left off. "If I went to school here?" he said. "I'd *make* you eat shit, huh? Me and *all* my friends would. We would find some shit and make you eat it. In front of everyone. We'd take you out to the playground and feed you shit and when you passed out from humiliation, we'd piss in your eyes. For the rest of your life, you'd be the little bitch who ate shit and got pissed on. It'd help to solve the problems of the world. All you little smartasses who look at us like you know something we don't. All you little know-it-all parasites with your comments and your sportscasts trying to make us feel bad about who we are, trying to make us feel bad for doing what we gotta do to make our way through this world that's only fucked up because of guys like you, behind the scenes, whispering your poison into the air and meanwhile without us you'd be nothing? Without us you'd have nothing to feed on? If we made you eat shit and pissed on you, you wouldn't have nothing to say to us. You wouldn't have nothing to *think* about us except, 'I am an abnormal piece of shit who clogs up the plumbing that's the society these good men who pissed on me and made me eat shit are trying to make the world a good place with.' Your mouth's wide open, now, huh? You got something to say me?"

I did have something to say to him, or at least I should have had—it felt like something needed to be said by Gurion—but I didn't know what. I just kept thinking: Why *don't* You punish men for the wrongs they would do?

Floyd lowered his cone, leaned at me.

I thought: Because You don't *know* what they'll do. Not for sure. You don't know what they'll do for sure, and You believe their thoughts can change their course in the world—the course You've set them on, the future You know—yet You can't read their thoughts any better than You can read mine. Our thoughts to You are what You are to us. Noisy, but hidden. Endless, but unseen. Even if You can read our faces, You can only do so in the way we read Your scripture. Our faces may potentially tell You every-thing that we think, but often You misread them, often enough that, out of fairness—because You are good—You will not act according only to what You've read.

I closed my gaping mouth and lowered my eyes, saw globs of saliva dripping from the bell of Floyd's cone, pooling between the toes of our shoes. In case he'd start talking again, I took two steps back to get out of spraying range. Floyd understood it as a retreat, understood retreat as a show of weakness—maybe it was; I was rarely speechless—and liked it. It puffed him up, cued him to continue. The cone stayed down.

"I'll tell you what," he said. "If I was in the junior-high school again, I'd do it better. All we ever did to guys like you was beat your asses til you hid in the corners, reading, jerking off, whatever you did. And you had years to tell yourselves that all it was was you were weaker, smaller, one against many. You made a hero-story out of it. You thought you were like Jesus. So many little Christs, suffering because you were the only good one in the world—thousands of you thinking that across the country. And my friends and me, while you were hiding in those corners, we had no idea—we thought you'd learned your lesson. Once in a while you'd come out and show yourself, and we'd beat your ass again, to teach you again, but we were decent, not like you, and innocent, not like you, and as soon as you hid again, we let you be. Every single time, we were sure we'd finally taught you. But you always came out of the corner eventually. You never learned your lesson, never learned to keep your head down or your mouth shut. We thought that while you hid you were getting decent, but all that time, all's you were doing was rubbing your grimy palms together and plotting revenge. And eventually you grew up, all of us grew up, and you were out of our reach. You were safe. Protected. We were working, being productive Americans, we didn't think about you, and if we did we still thought we'd crushed the evil right out of you, but then suddenly you'd pop up, you'd make even more wisecracks, you'd look at us even squintier than before. You would fuck with us, out of vengeance. Instead of learning the lesson we taught you and being grateful, you'd do vengeance from behind your desks, from behind your fucken glasses, behind your fucken telephones. And it's our fault, partly. It's our fault for being decent human beings, for believing in the good of man, believing a beating was all it would take to teach you humility. What we shoulda done is force-fed you shit. Pissed in your squinty little fucken eyes. God knows we wanted to. God knows the only thing kept us from it was respect for the idea of humanity and decency. Too much respect. We shoulda made you eat shit and pissed all over you. Dragged you out to the playground and did it, in the middle of recess, so everyone would see, so everyone would remember, so everyone would remind you what you are even when you forgot. You mighta learned something then. If I was in junior high school again, I swear to God, I'd save the world. And if I was in *this* junior high school? I'd start with you."

Midway through Floyd's monologue, the switch had come, and he'd lowered his voice accordingly. Seventh- and eighth-graders were shoving past us now, on their way from recess to the cafeteria while fifth- and sixth-graders headed in the opposite direction.

I was thinking: You *can't* punish men for their potential wrongdoings, or else You would. You cannot fix Your own damage.

I thought: It is good I am not You.

"I'd start with you," Floyd repeated, louder than the first time, in case I hadn't heard him over the crowd noise. "You hear that, fuck?" he said. "I'd start with you."

I said, You're the one who's like Jesus, Floyd.

"You don't know anything about Jesus," Floyd said.

I said, I know that by the time he'd gotten himself all covered in spit, he wasn't able to do much more than talk.

Floyd shook like the Electric Chair, aching to hit me. Aching.

I held out my pass, said, This is my sheep's blood.

I passed.

□ □ □ □ □ □ □

Stealth in a crowded hallway works the opposite of stealth in an empty one. You have to walk forward with your shoulders high and stare at the heads of the people you're walking toward. They will sense you coming, even if their backs are turned to you, and they'll move out of your way without ever looking at your face to see who you are. All you have to do is see them first. People feel when they're being seen and it moves them.

I was not being stealth on the way to Nurse Clyde's, and got bumped a few times. I was looking all around me, trying to spot June. The looking strained my neck and I got vertigo watching the faces turn.

At the junction with Main Hall, I stopped to close my eyes and breathe out the dizzy. When I opened them again, I saw Josh Berman's sidekick— the kid from the Office, what was his name? Goldman, Cory Goldman— getting monkey-in-the-middled by a pair of icthiied Shovers. Bare-necked between them, turning 180s in rapid succession, Cory Goldman shouted, "Give it! Hey hey! Give it back!" as they arced his balled scarf back and forth above his head. I considered stepping in—I *really* didn't like him, but yes, he was an Israelite, but—but before I could decide one way or the other, Berman himself emerged from somewhere behind me and barreled at the Shover who had Cory's scarf. That Shover saw him coming, and before he got floored, tossed the scarf to the other one, who caught it and ran in the direction of B-Hall, Cory on his tail now, and Berman on Cory's. Shovers they ran past joined in the chase—some of them Israelites, others of them not—and they grabbed at each other, attempting to capture each other's scarves, and the Shover Berman'd floored got back on his feet, revolved to face B-Hall, as if to join the chase himself, but encountered a bandkid and stripped him of his flute. He twetched on the flute, told the bandkid, "Get gummed," then touched the flute's goozed part to the bandkid's cheek, and the bandkid cried.

That was when someone yanked my hood and I spun. I grabbed his face by the chin. It was Isadore Momo.

"Aye-yay ah-yah!" he shouted. "I am Momo I am Momo!"

I said, Sorry, Momo, you surprised me.

Beside Momo, an even squattier kid, a kid so chubby his forehead had dimples, seemed to be floating above his own shoes.

"He is my friend Beauregard Pate," Momo explained. "Beauregard Pate is a man of ideas, and when I tell to him the story of our Gym class and the nipple, he is wanting for to tell you something. Tell to Gurion what you tell to me, Beauregard."

"You are nice!" shouted Beauregard Pate, nearly breathless. "That is first of all!" The Shover who'd performed the goozeflute on the bandkid popped out of the C-Hall crowd-stream then to accidentally-on-purpose elbow Beauregard sideways. I ankl>swept him hard, he hit the floor one-kneed, crawled a couple yards fast, then got up and ran. Beauregard seemed to have noticed none of it. "You were nice to Isadore!" Beauregard continued. "And you have all my best wishes! So secondly, I would like to say, God bless you, Gurion Maccabee! All my best wishes are with you!"

Momo slapped Beauregard on the shoulder and Beauregard high-fived him. They tilted their heads in opposite directions and made meaningful-looking eye-contact, as if cuing one another to patter for the benefit of their Broadway audience, like, "Are you thinking what I'm thinking, Isadore?" "I'm thinking we should turn up the music, Beauregard." "You mean turn up the music and do a little dancing, Isadore?" "I mean turn up the music and do *a lot of dancing*, Beauregard!"

The sight of the joy of the chubby always puzzled me. When the chubby had joy, I knew in my heart they were forgetting their chubbiness, but to my eyes it always looked like a celebration of their chubbiness, and I'd feel like an invader and have to go away.

I tried to go away, but Beauregard said, "Wait! I didn't say what I wanted to say! Please wait?"

I waited. Where was June? The crowd kept pushing by. Beauregard swallowed hard. He said, "We want to ask you if you like gangs commited to social reform. We want to start a gang called Big Ending to end our oppression. We believe that girls would like us more and teachers would stop making faces."

Why do you believe that? I said.

"Because we believe that girls do not find oppression to be a sexy phenomenon, and we also believe that teachers don't know they're making faces when they're making faces, but that the faces they make encourage our oppressors to oppress us, and therefore we must raise teacher awareness. Will you be the leader of Big Ending?"

I said, Some girls think oppressors are sexy, and some other girls think the oppressed are sexy. I'd never say you shouldn't start a gang, but you can find a nice girl without starting a gang. And teachers know exactly what they're doing when they're making faces at you. Because they're tall and you're nice, you think they're all like your mom who loves you and tries to understand, and some of them are like your mom that way, but most of them aren't. Most of them think of you the way everyone else thinks of you, because the way everyone else thinks of you is always the easiest way to think of you, so if you want them to stop making faces, you have to stop being oppressed. If you stop being oppressed, then everyone else will think of you different, and so will the teachers who make faces. And they'll stop making faces.

"So it's our fault?" said Beauregard. "It's our fault the teachers make faces?"

No, I said. It's your enemies' fault. Stop beating yourself up. It's your fault that you beat yourself up instead of treating the teachers who make faces like enemies, when that's what they are. Those teachers are your enemies.

"Will you to lead the Big Ending then?" said Isadore. "If we say the teachers are the enemies?"

I said, No way. I said, Not if you guys are in it.

"But you were so nice to Isadore, Gurion. I thought you were on our side," Beauregard said.

I am on your side, I said. I said, That's why I'd never lead Big Ending. The two of you were born to lead it—I'd only get in the way.

They blushed, the red climbing their faces like a juice-spill up mop-strands, and again I tried to go, and again Beauregard said, "Wait!"

And Isadore said, "Will you join us in the Big Ending?"

No, I said. I said, Sometimes I lead things, but I never join them. You have my blessing, though, and if you want Big Ending can be a special arm of the Side of Damage.

"What's that?"

The thing I lead, I said.

"What is it, though?"

An army.

"What can Big Ending to do for your army?"

I don't know yet, I said.

"We will do what you want us to do when the time comes."

To my right, a single cracking sound rose above the crowd-noise in Main Hall. As the three of us revolved, there was another. Maholtz was demonstrating the power of his sap to some seventh-grade girls. He was striking the cinderblock corner of the northern entrance to the cafeteria. "Look out, Jenndy. Stand bank," he said. "Bank. Come on. Bank. Angshley," he said, "get Jenndy outta the way, put her over by Jenndy, there. Good," he said, "now I'm gonnda show you." Another crack. "Seend?" he said. Another crack. "Seend that?" he said. "It's just paint," said an Ashley. "No, it's wallnd. Don't you dount me, now." Crack. "Seend?" said Maholtz. "That's wallnd. Try and tell me thant's not wallnd." "It's paint." "I think it's wall, Ashley." "It's not wall, Jenny. If it was wall, it would be a different color than the paint." "Okay okay," said Maholtz, "here." Crack. Crack. Crack. Crack. "And?" he said. "Fine," said the Ashley, "that's wall. But before it was paint." "I can bring down wallngs, girlies, is the poind. You want Maholntz to bring downd the wallnds for you? Maholntz is bringing downd the wallnds for you."

"I am dreaming very badly of a time to see the Bryguy Maholtz writhing with frantic in the throes of pain and anguish," said Momo.

"Making that dream come true," said Beauregard Pate, "will be one of Big Ending's primary objectives."

I like that, I said.

And again they blushed.

▫ ▫ ▫ ▫ ▫ ▫ ▫

Four sleepy-looking fifth-graders were sitting in the corner of Nurse Clyde's office, leaning on each other and whispering. I'd never seen them before. They were short, narrow guys and they all had cartoonface: eyes and lips as large as men's, jaws and noses and chins that were boy-size. You'd expect them to turn blue when cold, green when sick. If you frightened them and their teeth chattered, it would not be surprising. Or if puffs of steam whistled from their earholes when you slapped them.

And I did want to slap them a little, mostly for that reason, but also because each one of them wore a Chicago Cubs batting glove on his right hand, and baseball was suck, and so was cuteness, and here was a combination. Except then I thought how one of their dads probably took them to a baseball game and bought them the gloves so they would always remember, and I felt bad for wanting to slap them at all. They were probably just nice.

When I came through the door, they stopped talking but pretended not to see me.

Hello, I said.

They huddled closer and whispered quieter. Then one of them asked, "Who are you? Are you Ben-Wa Wolf? Are you from the Cage?"

I couldn't tell which one said it. It could have been any of them.

I said, "Where's Nurse Clyde?"

Two of them said, "With Shpritzy," a third one pointed at the Quiet Room door, and the fourth said, "Nurse Clyde said anyone who comes in should knock." Their voices were identical. The office smelled like mouthwash.

I didn't know who Shpritzy was, but the four guys, on closer inspection, seemed to be more sad than sleepy, so instead of knocking on the Quiet Room door, I sat down next to them, but with a chair between us, and instead of asking who Shpritzy was, I made a joke.

What's shpritzy? I said.

"'What's Shpritzy'!" one of them said. "This boy just said, 'What's Shpritzy'!"

Two of the other ones slapped their knees. One of them clapped his hands together.

"Shpritzy's not a what! He's our best buddy," one of them said. "He's the best guy in the world besides these other guys here, who are also the best," said another one of them. Then they all gave each other affirmative nods.

That was not a good enough reason to slap them.

I said, Is Shpritzy sick?

"He's in pain." "He got choked." "And he got headlocked." "He got thrown on the floor a lot."

What about you guys? I said.

"We got full-nelsoned." "And tackled." "And held by the waist." "Some of us were half-nelsoned for a little while." "Some of us got our shoulders banged against the sinks during the half-nelsons." "And some of us got knocked on the wall between the urinals while attempting to lunge at Shpritzy's attacker."

It's good you tried to protect your friend, I said.

"We're losers." "We're not losers, but we don't know how to fight so we suck." "We don't suck, but we suck at fighting, so we're sissies." "We're not sissies, but we're small guys right now, and when we try to act brave we get held back and Shpritzy gets hurt." "Ah, Shpritzy!" "Shpritzy's such a good guy." "We're all good guys." "We are. There's nothing wrong with us." "It's the messed-up people who always want to fight that make us feel like there's something wrong with us when really we're fine and it's these violent people that aren't fine." "Even they're fine. It's just that they don't have great buddies like we do. Because they're messed up." "And their parents are alcoholics and divorced and very abusive. They're messed up because they *got* messed up." "It's true. Those other guys are really okay, except that they think violence is okay, which isn't okay because violence is wrong. But they only think it's okay and not wrong because they got messed up."

I said, You're wrong. I said, Are you messed up?

"No way." "We're good." "We're nice to people." "We don't do violence."

I said, But violence did you. I said, Violence did you just now, so you should be messed up.

"We're different." "It doesn't work like that." "We got messed up, but we're not all messed up by it." "Not like those other guys."

How come, though? I said.

"I see what you mean. Do you guys see what this boy means?" "I think I do see what he means. He means that we just got messed up, but still we're not all messed up." "I think what he means is the guys who messed us up didn't mess us up just because they were messed up by someone else, but because of some other reason." "I think what he's saying is that even though the people who mess up other people were probably messed up by different other people, it doesn't mean they have to mess up the first other people since look at how we just got messed up but we're not messing anyone else up." "We're just sitting here being sad about Shpritzy." "So if we can get messed up and not be all messed up, then why can't those other guys who messed us up not be all messed up?" "He means it's their fault that they messed us up." "He means we shouldn't be so easy on them." "We should mess them up ourselves." "They messed up Shpritzy." "We should mess them up back, but we can't." "But that's why we were looking for Gurion Maccabee to begin with." "No, we were looking for Gurion Maccabee to begin with because we wanted protection from getting messed up, not so he would mess up the guys who messed us up." "We said to each other that it was protection we wanted, but we wanted him to mess up those other guys a little bit." "We only wanted him to mess them up a little bit?" "No. We wanted, a little bit, for Gurion to mess them up a lot." "But we called it protection." "Right. We called it protection, when really it was mess-up." "Are you Ronrico Asparagus?"

You're looking for Asparagus, too? I said.

"Well we know he's in the Cage." "And so he knows Gurion." "Are you from the Cage?" "Do you know Gurion?"

I said, Sure, but what makes you think he'll mess these guys up for you?

"Gurion is the Lion Hammer!" "He brings justice." "And he likes to mess people up." "And we're Jews." "Our God is Adonai." "Our homeland is Israel." "Saturday's our day off." "We're men at thirteen." "And Gurion protects the Jews from the Canaanites and the Romans." "And from the Jews who act against the Jews." "And the righteous from the tyrants." "And the kind from the wrongus." "Except he doesn't say 'Jews.'" "He talks about Israelites cause of Hitler." "Cause Hitler killed Jews." "And Nebuchadnezzar did too." "And Abdul Nasser." "And Yasser Arafat." "Haman." "Saddam Hussein." "Ismail Haniyeh." "Stalin the Russian, in Russia and Poland." "And lots of peasants everywhere." "The Israelites became Jews and people kept killing them." "Like in *Night*." "And *The Painted Bird*." "And the Olympics." "And Tel Aviv and Gilo." "There's this Jewish school called Solomon Schecter and Gurion went there til he got kicked out because the principal thought he was the messiah. Then he went to Hebrew Day and got kicked out of there for teaching the Jews they were Israelites. Nathan Feingold told us." "What he didn't tell us, though, was that Gurion goes here." "We only found that out yesterday!" "We think we found it out yesterday, at least." "Well, we sort of found it out a couple months ago." "If we found it out yesterday, then we'd already found it out a couple months ago when we heard this rhyme that you probably heard that goes, 'Next stop Frontier motel, the place where Gurion's fat black dad who fell dwells.'" "It was this kid Brad Snad who was singing the rhyme." "And Gurion's a really uncommon name." "So we told Nathan Feingold about it." "That a boy named Gurion went to our school." "And we told him the rhyme." "And Nathan Feingold, he told us, 'Gurion's dad's not the black one. It's his mom who's black. And no way Gurion lives at a motel.'" "And that seemed very true." "Because this Gurion's dad is a famous lawyer." "What lawyer lives in a motel?" "Except then about a week later, there was Brad Snad again, talking about Gurion." "He told us about this kid Kyle McElroy getting stomped by Gurion for messing with some retarded kid called Lucas." "But this time, when Snad told us about Gurion, he also said Gurion's last name." "Or at least he tried to." "We thought he tried to." "What Snad said was, 'That Gurion MacIntyre is something.'" "And that made us think about how once he called Jerry Seinfeld *Gary Steinfield.*" "Snad did." "This Snad is a kid who says *lie-berry* for library." "And William Jeffenface *Clim*-ton and Gustav *Clint.*" "A boy who calls animals *am*-inals." "Vice President Lon Cheney." "Last Feb-*you*-ary, he told me that suntanes he gets real lonely on Valen-*time*'s day." "Stevedore Milosovic." "So we knew he was a dummkopf who was bad at remembering the sounds of words and names." "Which is probably a serious blessing if your name is Brad Snad!" "You're so funny, man! Seriously." "I'm so glad we're best buddies." "Me too." "And me three." "Me four." "Do you hear this, guys? 'Me four,' he says!" "I'm really cheering up here!"

I said, Nathan Fein—

But they had only stopped to take a breath.

"And so we thought that, in the language of Snad, MacIntyre had to be Maccabee." "And Maccabee is almost as uncommon of a name as Gurion." "And so the combination of the two already uncommon names Gurion and Maccabee…" "Because that was the Schechter Gurion's last name, Maccabee." "Gurion Maccabee was his name." "So we told Nathan Feingold." "And Nathan told us to give it up." "He said, 'Give it up. Gurion Maccabee does not go to your school. He is either in prison or dead, or working for the Mossad who are disinforming people that he's in prison or dead so he can go deep cover.'" "And that sounded a little crazy." "About the Mossad doing that." "And Nathan is our friend, so we believed that he believed it, but that didn't mean that we had to believe it." "So we asked around." "We asked other Israelites at school." "We know almost all of them." "And they all know about Gurion." "The Gurion who Nathan told us about, that is." "We asked around to see if any of them had ever seen a boy named Gurion at Aptakisic." "And some of them had, and the ones who hadn't—some of those ones had done the same thing as us." "They'd asked around." "And we found out a bunch of stuff from asking around." "And what we found out made it seem like Nathan might be right, after all." "Because first of all, we found out that Gurion was in the Cage." "And the Gurion we were looking for was a scholar and why would Mr. Brodsky put a scholar in the Cage?" "The Cage is for retarded people who don't act right and future killers and con-men." "No offense, if you're from the Cage." "But that's who it's for." "Not scholars." "And then, from those Aptakisic Israelites who had seen Gurion on the bus or in the halls, we found out that he hung out with Benji Nakamook and Vincie Portite and did not look half-black." "And the Gurion we were looking for was supposed to be half-black, and Nakamook and Portite are not the kinds of guys Gurion would hang out with." "Those are mean, scary guys who are not scholars, but please don't tell them we told you that if you know them." "The meanest and the scariest." "They're not even friends with Bam Slokum is how mean and scary." "And then plus, the main point is there's all these Israelites at Aptakisic." "There's, like, forty or fifty." "And that's just the guys." "And we know all of them, or almost all of them, and none of them had ever even spoken to this Aptakisic Gurion." "And so we figured that even if Brodsky or whoever *would* put our Gurion in the Cage, and even if, for some reason, our Gurion *would* be friends with guys like Nakamook and Portite, there's no way Gurion would go to school with all of us Israelites and not, like, lead us." "Let alone not even talk to any of us." "And much less allow kids to sing that rhyme about him living at a motel that they're always singing. I'm sure you've heard it." "And plus it would be too lucky." "For us to go to school with Gurion." "That was really the main thing." "We're good guys, all of us, but we're not that lucky of guys when it comes to certain things like being strong." "And basketball." "And girls." "We're only lucky because of how we've got such great best buddies." "That's pretty much the only way." "And cause our parents aren't alcoholic abuser people." "That too." "But the kind of lucky we'd be if we went to school with Gurion is the exact opposite kind of lucky of the lucky we usually are." "We've never been lucky that way." "So we decided Nathan Feingold must've been right after all." "But then yesterday afternoon, we get this email from who else but Nathan Feingold himself." "And Nathan Feingold tells us that on Tuesday night, some kid saw Gurion on a train and Gurion talked to the kid and even did something with the kid's hat, so he wasn't dead or in prison after all." "And if he was in the Mossad, he wasn't deep cover." "And Nathan told us that if we heard anything more about this Aptakisic Gurion, we should alert him at once." "And now, after what just happened to Shpritzy, the timing seems fateful." "Especially because it was on our way to the computer room that we all stopped to pee." "We were with Shpritzy, at his locker, right?" "Good old Shpritzy." "This was just right before lunch started." "This was barely half an hour ago." "We were with Shpritzy at his locker and Brad Snad came over to us and told us that this Aptakisic Gurion just saved that chubnik Isadore Momo from that yutzy Blonde Lonnie who's always saying how he's funny." "But he isn't funny." "He isn't funny at all." "And he's got three testicles, but no one ever said so, until Isadore Momo did, which got Lonnie pissed." "Lonnie was gonna tear Momo to pieces, but Gurion was there and he cooled Lonnie's jets with a punch to the chest." "And, clutching his nipples, Lonnie fell in the pool!" "But he didn't drown, but he almost did, except Desormie gave him the kiss of life, which saved him." "But only barely." "And so as soon as Snad finished telling us all of that, we decided to go to the computer room in the library." "To email Nathan, who goes to Hebrew Day." "We didn't know for sure, but we thought they probably let you check your email at Lunch at Hebrew Day." "And we didn't know when Lunch was over there, but we thought it might be the same time as here, so we wanted to get that team-email out to Nathan Feingold as soon as possible." "Post-haste." "But we all stopped to pee on the way to the computer room so we wouldn't be distracted by the need to pee if we ended up needing to pee." "And that's when that jerk attacked Shpritzy." "While we peed!" "He said Shpritzy bumped into him, but it wasn't true so Shpritzy wouldn't apologize." "And then the jerk attacked." "And then we attacked." "And then we got messed up." "And the jerk told us, 'Make sure to say hi to Josh Berman for me. Make sure he knows I think his scarf's *real* sharp.' And his jerks friends laughed." "And I was all, like, 'What's Berman's scarf have to do with us? That's Shover stuff and it's not like we're Shovers. And we're friends with Berman, yeah, but it's not like we're buddies.'" "I was all like that, too." "We were all all like that." "But it wasn't like we said it." "We couldn't have said it." "It was too hard to talk." "I was choking on spit." "I was holding my guts." "I was holding my shoulder." "I was choking on something." "And now we're here." "And Shpritzy's a mess." "And the email to Nathan has been back-burnered." "Why do you keep leaning forward with your fists balled up?" "Why does he look so tense?"

They huddled to discuss me, and I saw my moment. I asked the question as fast as I could.

I said, You keep saying Feingold, but you really mean Weinblatt, right? Nathan Weinblatt?

I said that because I thought I knew everyone's name at Northside Hebrew Day and, though I remembered a Nathan Weinblatt, this was the first time I'd ever heard of a Nathan Feingold. It is true I only went to Northside for a month, but it wasn't that big of a school.

"Weinblatt?" "What's a Weinblatt?" "You think we're some kind of Snad?" "Nathan. Feingold."

Are you sure? I said.

"Of course he's sure," said a different one than the one I asked. He said, "And so am I. Nathan's my friend, too." "We're all friends with Nathan." "He's not our best buddy, but he's definitely our buddy." "A very good buddy." "Nathan is a great buddy." "We go to movies with him on weekends. "But not Cubs games." "We usually go to Cubs games on Saturdays, and Nathan's Orthodox." "Most of the kids at Hebrew Day are Orthodox." "That's why none of them can go to Saturday Cubs games." "And that's why none of them talk to Gurion anymore." "Because their parents are scared of him." "Because they think he's a bad influence." "Because they're the ones who Gurion told them they were Israelites." "No, not just that. They're scared because of the other thing he did when he told them they were Israelites." "That's true." "It was that other thing." "See, when Gurion told them they were Israelites, he also gave them—"

"Wait!" yelled the three who hadn't just been speaking. Then they asked me if I was an Israelite. I wanted to hear the rest of their story, so I kept playing along like the truth wasn't mine and I wasn't me. I told them I was an Israelite, and they told me to prove it and I spoke to them in Hebrew, saying: Listen to me, now. Would an American Gentile who's my age know Hebrew?

But *they* didn't know Hebrew, for they weren't scholars, just non-observant Israelites, looking at me blankly.

"That's supposed to be Hebrew? How do we know it's not nonsense?" one of them said. "Or Farsi or Arabic?" said another.

I said, Do you even go to Hebrew School?

"Yeah." "But they don't teach us Hebrew." "They teach us stories." "And prayers, too." "That's the only Hebrew we know is the prayers." "Well we don't really know it." "We don't know what it means." "We just know what it sounds like." "We can sound out its letters." "We know how to say it."

Okay, I said, do you know what the Sh'ma Yisroel sounds like?

"Who do you think we are?" "Who does this kid think we are?" "What's wrong with this guy?" "They teach you the Sh'ma first thing." "We've known the Sh'ma since the days of juice and animal crackers." "Of course we know the Sh'ma." "And we know what it means, too." "Well not exactly." "It's very mystical, what it means, but we know how it translates."

I said, Hear O Israel, The Lord our God, The Lord is one.

"Yeah, but do it in Hebrew," they said.

I recited the Sh'ma in Hebrew and they believed me.

You were explaining why Israelites stopped talking to Gurion, I said.

"Right. Exactly," said one. "Because of their parents," said another. "A little bit because their parents got scared of him for telling them they were Israelites," a third said. "But mostly," said the fourth, "because of this."

He pulled a beat-looking sheet of paper from his pocket, and shook out its folds. I saw it was my second scripture.

The kid said, "This is how it goes: First Gurion makes jokes about boobies and nips and they are funny jokes, but they are not as funny the second time, and you are not supposed to repeat them, so I won't. But then he tells you how to make the gun in twenty-three steps and then, listen to this: he says, 'Now you can hurt things from a distance.' Here." He handed me his copy of *Ulpan*.

I looked it over and gave it back.

I said, So where'd you get that?

"From Nathan. He had a party in his backyard and gave these out."

I said, Where'd Nathan get it?

"From this boy Saul Benjamin he goes to school with, who we're kinda very good friends with, but not buddies, just very good friends."

I'd never heard of Saul Benjamin, either. I said, You're *sure* these guys go to Hebrew Day?

"Definitely." "For sure." "We know where our friends go to school." "Yes."

I said, Northside Hebrew Day?

"The one that's in Northbrook." "North Hebrew Day." "North-*Suburban* Hebrew Day, it's called." "There's another Hebrew Day?"

I said, Gurion went to Northside Hebrew Day. That's twenty miles from the Hebrew Day of your friends, I said.

"This boy knows an awful lot about Hebrew Days all of a sudden." "And Gurion, too." "An awful lot." "A suspicious awful lot."

I thought: Twenty miles!

"I think maybe he's Gurion." "I was thinking that, too." "I can't say the thought isn't one I wasn't thinking."

I thought: The scholars spread my scripture far and wide, but fail to help me when I need them? What is that?

Twenty miles! I thought.

I wasn't really bitter, though. I even got the Joy of Living Dance feeling a little. So these four here weren't scholars—so what? Neither was my mom. Maybe this was just as well. Maybe even better. It wasn't two-hundred-plus *secular* Israelites who'd just ditched me. It wasn't two-hundred-plus *non-observant* ones.

These four here, in the meantime, said nothing. The three who'd last spoken were looking to the fourth because something was off—consensus was lacking. The fourth had yet to fourth his suspicion of my being Gurion. Instead he kept squinting at me, bancing up their rhythm, breathing heavy through his nose. "Pinker?" one of them finally said to him. "Pinker." "Hey, Pinker!" And this loud-breathing fourth, the one they called Pinker, stopped his loud breathing, and turned to his friends. He said, "Okay, fine, *maybe*; but except then again…"

"Well exactly."

"Right! Right? Right."

"*Exactly* then again, I agree because you're right since…"

"Since because of how he…" "Right! Since because of how he doesn't…" "Since because of how he doesn't even *look like a lion*!" "Since because of how he doesn't even look anything like a lion *at all*!" "Or a hammer." "Exactly!" "And he doesn't look black." "He's not supposed to look *that* black, though." "But he's part Ethiopian." "*Part* Ethiopian and they're not that black." "Right! Wait. So what you're saying is…" "No, not… They're at least very very tan, though, the Ethiopians, and he's not what I'd call very very tan, this guy." "Maybe not very very, but he's more than just plain tan, for sure—very tan, I'd say." "Wait, what are we saying, here?" "And actually he *does* have hair like a black guy." "But he doesn't have any hair on his face." "He doesn't!" "Yes, well, no, that's not true; he does have some there, on the bottom of his chin." "That's the top of his neck. That's not his chin." "What's the difference?" "Buddies! Best buddies!" "I don't know what's the difference." "My great best buddies! Where do we stand on this, buddies?" "Where?" "Exactly!" "It's a really big deal!"

Philip Roth was no scholar. Or Stanley Elkin. Or Andy Kaufman. Or Barney Ross or Lenny Bruce or Larry David. Kafka was no scholar, and neither was Elaine May. Nor my zadie Malchizedek, nor Arnold Rothstein, nor Meyer Lansky. Forget about Isaac Babel and forget about the Stern Gang. Forget about 90 percent of the IDF. And be he Chico, Harpo, Zeppo, Gummo, or Groucho, among the Marx Brothers there was not a one.

Where are your pennyguns? I said to the four of them.

None of them heard me. Either that or they ignored me. They kept talking faster, leaning in closer, trying to believe that I wasn't Gurion, or trying to believe that I was Gurion, believing either way that whatever they believed about who I was mattered.

"Okay, look, let's go one thing at a time: Gurion's only a seventh-grader. Why'd we think he'd have hair on his face?" "Not only that. He's supposed to be a fifth-grader, so he's our age, and we don't have hair on our faces." "Plus he's got the chin ones, or neck ones, whatever." "So that gets us nowhere." "So next up, okay: this guy's small and he does not look that tough." "Good point, except David was small and he looked like a young version of the rich man from that movie *Pretty Woman*." "But he had a slingshot." "True, he had a slingshot, except this boy has a hood, though. Didn't you picture Gurion having a hood?" "Yes." "And his wallet has a chain. I always thought he'd have a chain, but he's bleeding on the elbow, and I didn't think he'd bleed." "Did he jingle when he came in? I heard he jingles when he walks." "I might have heard him jingling." "Are you Gurion or not?"

I said, Who do you want me to mess up?

"Right, see? Of course. So now he's saying he's Gurion, but that somehow makes it seem—" "Maybe he's lying." "Exactly. Lying." "I'd want people to think I was Gurion." "So would I." "Who wouldn't?" "What did we expect? You don't just ask him 'You Gurion?' and expect the kind of answer that'll set things straight." "We have to test him." "How do we test him?" "What would such a test measure?" "Any number of things, but mainly: Can he fight?" "Can he fight four guys, like?" "Just like that." "Yeah. Let's attack him." "Attack him?" "Attack him." "If he's Gurion, we'll get messed up for the second time in one day!" "I don't want to get messed up twice in one day." "It wasn't that bad the first time, though. We're alive, remember." "It's true, we're alive." "You're right. We're not dead." "We're not dead at all." "We are not dead at all."

Just as the fifth-graders rose from their chairs, flexing their fists, their batting gloves squeaking, eyes nothing like sleepy, Nakamook entered the Nurse's Office.

"Gurion," he said.

And the attack was called off.

"Oh God!" "Oh man!" "Oh gee!" "We didn't mean to—" "We're sorry!" "Please don't—" "We're sorry!"

Benji held up his right hand, which was bleeding from the center—it looked like something wooden was in it.

"Jesus!" said one of the fifth-graders

"Not at all," said Nakamook. He brought his hand closer, a step at a time, and they backed away smoothly, like same-charged magnets, and once they were sitting, huddled as before, he thrust the hand between their heads, deeper and deeper, til they all leaned away from each other with their eyes winked and squinted. Nakamook's hand was a mess.

Soon he got bored and put it away.

The fifth-graders re-huddled.

Benji turned to me and said, "I wanted to hang with you, but Botha wouldn't unlock the gate, so I took a pencil, right? And I stabbed my hand and broke off the tip, right? And this is what it looks like. This is my stabbed hand!" he yelled. He shoved his hand back into the fifth-graders' head-space and shook it around. The huddle split again and some blood-drops dripped on some laps.

"Jelly told me I was crazy," Benji said. He stopped shaking the hand and sat next to me to whisper. He said, "Botha was so pissed, he mumbled curses in Australian. He said 'shate' and 'crep' and he said 'basted.' I said the curses back to him, too. I said, 'El crep en yer ed, yeh shate-ater, yeh saley basted!' Then Main Man starting belting out ha-has and Leevon was standing behind Botha and doing impersonations of Botha's pass-writing movements. Leevon's perfect at impersonations. Perfect. Did you see that grip he laid on me and Vincie? It was the exact same grip I'd just demonstrated. Got me thinking we should show him Bruce Lee movies—he'd become a one-man special-ops force fast, I think. And I think that's what we need. I've been thinking maybe the Side of Damage is a good thing. If we can run the Cage like we did during— Hey." He pointed his finger at the huddle of fifth-graders. "Hey, Gurion," he said, "is that what I think it is?"

What? I said. I was really stunned out.

"That," he said, blinkering the finger.

The boy who'd shown me the copy of *Ulpan* had it under his thigh, folded in thirds. Step 23—*Look at the pennies you lined up earlier. Understand you hold a gun.*—showed just above the crease.

"What the fuck is that?" said Nakamook.

Identical to the *Ulpan* I'd delivered in April, the fifth-graders' ended as follows:

Now that you have been delivered these instructions, you will receive an instruction sheet. It is a copy of the sheet I am reading from. Each one of you gets one copy. You will take your copy from beneath the paint-can at the gate. Fold it and put it in your shoe. Guard it closely. Do not guard it with your life, but guard it with your face. It is not worth getting killed over, but it is worth getting a broken face over. Tomorrow, you will make thirteen copies of your copy. You will invite thirteen Israelite boys to come to your backyard after Shabbos, like I invited you, and you will deliver these instructions from a high tree-limb, exactly the same as I have delivered them to you. If you do not have a tree with high limbs in your yard, or if the high-limbed tree you do have is unclimbable, sit on top of a swingset or fence.

Tonight, the first night on which Israelites have received these instructions, is May 27, 2006. Do as you're told and one week from tonight 183 Israelite boys will be armed with pennyguns. Two weeks from tonight, 2,380 Israelite boys will be armed. Three weeks from tonight, 30,941 Israelite boys, and four weeks from tonight, just three days beyond the summer solstice, 402,234 Israelite boys will be armed with pennyguns. Well in advance of the start of next schoolyear, every Israelite boy in North America, if not the world, will be armed with pennyguns. Never again will we cower amid the masses of the Roman and Canaanite children.

Bless Adonai, who helps us protect us.

Blessed is Elohim, Who blesses our weapons.

Chazak! Chazak! Venischazeik!

Say it.

Now leave my yard. I will see you tomorrow. You will be stronger tomorrow than you are today.

Whereas, apart from all the other doctoring done to it (e.g., any statement conspicuously addressed to a plurality had been individualized, any line that read speakerly made writerly, all references to backyards and Israelites omitted, the title changed from *Ulpan* to *Instructions*), the document I'd delivered to Nakamook had ended like this:

Now that you have been delivered these instructions, make of them ashes. Burn and never speak of them lest we enter into enmity.

And so, on seeing *Ulpan* (or, more accurately: on seeing what he thought was *Instructions*) in the possession of an unfamiliar fifth-grader, Benji assumed betrayal was afoot, and even if I *had* known what to say to stop him, I would not have had time to.

Nakamook flew.

With the nasty hand, he grabbed the kid's shirt's alligator and pulled him to his feet. He took hold of the kid's nose. "Where'd you get *Instructions?*" he said, "I'll twist your cute fucking nose off I swear to God I'll dot your i I'll fucking kill you."

I told him to stop, but he couldn't hear me. The others were saying, "Unhand our buddy," and "Hurt him and you're dead," and "You're dead."

Now came the beginning-of-fifth tone and, as if it were a go-signal, one of the fifth-graders punched Nakamook in the back. I had to jump up and hug the kid away because Benji had let go of the nose kid and turned.

I spun us and my hood whipped sideways. Benji's fist caught in the peak and tore an inch off at the seam, but he missed the kid, baruch Hashem. He said, "Let me cross his t, Gurion. Let me double-space him."

I said, He was protecting his friend.

Benji said, "He punched me."

But he didn't hurt you, I said. I said, You're not hurt, right?

"He *wants* to hurt me," Benji said. "Look at him."

The kid's jaws were crab-appled with teeth-clenching. I said, "This is Benji Nakamook. This is Nakamook, okay?"

The strain against my arms faded and the kid said, "He attacked Mr. Goldblum!"

"Who the *fuck* is Mr. Goldblum?" Nakamook said. He started laughing a special pirate-laugh he'd only laugh when he was murderous. The first time I'd heard it, I thought to call him Captain Kidd, but the moniker died on my tongue because I killed it. No nickname could ever rightly stick to Nakamook.

The kid half-tried to force himself out of my grip again. He made a sound like *nyah*, like he really meant it, but he'd realized who he'd punched and he was already shivering. I put a hand on his head to calm him. He pushed his face into my armpit and cried.

Benji turned to the one whose nose he'd just held. "Are you Mr. Goldblum?"

"You're dead," the nose kid said.

He was Mr. Goldblum.

Benji said, "I'm not anything even *like* dead. And I think you're Mr. Goldblum. Do you like being called Mr. Goldblum?"

"I don't care if you're Nakamook," said Mr. Goldblum. He said, "My friends will kill you anyway."

"We'll kill you in your sleep." "You can't fight while you're unconscious." "We'll burn *your* house down." "Nyah!" "You can't fight when you're tied up." "And suffocating on fumes." "And dying of fright." "You'll be shocked to the very marrow." "The very *very* marrow." "Nyah!"

Then two new events took place at the same time. Nurse Clyde rushed out of the Quiet Room to investigate the noise we were making, and a tiny sick-looking girl in a dress made of t-shirt came in from the hallway. The sick girl sat where I'd been sitting before I'd had to hug the kid I was hugging.

Nurse Clyde said, "What's happening here?"

Mr. Goldblum said, "The Levinson tripped on his shoelace. Gurion picked him up."

"I tripped," said the kid in my arms, who was called The Levinson.

"Why didn't anyone knock?"

Nakamook said, "I just got here, Clyde. Check the partial stigmata." He waved the hand and blooddrops dripped on the carpeting.

Nurse Clyde ignored Benji. He said to The Levinson, "Your shoelaces are tied, little man."

"It's a miracle." "He's very clumsy." "I tripped on my heel." "Spontaneous knotting."

"Unfortunately, 'e doyed of spawntineous comboostion," Nakamook said. *Spinal Tap.*

Here the sick-looking girl threw up on her legs. Just one heave. Then she apologized.

"Oh, honey," Nurse Clyde said. He carried the girl into the examining room, which was right next to the Quiet Room.

Benji said to Mr. Goldblum and The Levinson and the other two, "Good move not ratting."

"Nakamook dies at dawn." "Darkness forever." "Choked." "Strangulation."

Benji said, "Who *are* these little guys?"

Israelites, I said. They tried to protect their friend Shpritzy from getting beaten up by a Shover and—

"You mean like Bernard Shpritz? That violin whiz?" said Benji.

"That's him." "That's Shpritzy." "And he's not just our friend." "He's our best buddy." "He's the best violinist ever." "He's the best guy in the whole world, next to these guys, who are also the best guys." "And it wasn't Shovers who messed us up." "And it wasn't a Shover who messed Shpritzy up." "What do we have to do with any Shovers?" "What does Shpritzy have to do with any Shovers?"

You said you were friends with Berman, I said.

"Friends, sure, but not buddies!" "And barely even friends!" "There's a distinction! A huge distinction!" "Huge." "That's why it was weird that the kid who hurt Shpritzy said 'say hi to Josh Berman' and 'tell him sharp scarf,' cause what do we have to do with Berman? We're not Shovers and we don't have anything to do with any scarves." "Let alone Shpritzy!" "Poor Shpritzy! Man!" "Stupid scarves!" "Shpritzy had nothing to do with Berman!" "Shpritzy had nothing to do with those scarves!" "Shpritzy!" "Aw, Shpritzy!" "Poor Shpritzy!" "Aw, Shpritzy!"

Nakamook said, "That Shpritzy kid really *is* a good kid. He plays *The Godfather* theme-song for me on the bus whenever I ask him to. I don't even have to ask him anymore. I just make a twetching noise, like I'm twetching on the floor in anger, and I say to him, 'I'm a Cor Lee O Nay,' and he plays it. Who beat him up? Give me a name. I'll beat *that* guy up. And steal his bike."

I said, These guys are gonna do it.

"We'll do it." "Don't say who it is." "It's ours to do." "We'll get that guy." "Don't say his name." "Don't even hint." "He's ours." "We'll damage him from a distance." "He's ours, Nakamook."

Nakamook said to them, "He's yours."

"He's not ours because you say so." "He's ours because we say so." "And because Gurion says that what we say is so." "And you didn't even say sorry."

"If you apologized to me, it would mean nothing," said Nakamook, "and nothingness commands nothing if not reciprocity. If I apologized to you, nothing I said would ever be worth anything again and so *I* would be worth nothing. And what happened, anyway? Mr. Golbfarb's nose got held? The Levinstein cried into someone's armpit? In the end, no one really got hurt, and that's lucky for you. So spit twice and toss a pinch of salt. Count your blessings. Are we friends?"

They huddled for a second. Whispered, nodded. Then they un-huddled. "Friends, but not best buddies." "Not buddies at all." "Or even great friends or good friends." "We're just friends."

"I don't keep buddies, anyway," Nakamook said, "and if you wanna take care of the guy who hurt our friend Shpritzy, that's cool, but if you get your clauses spliced while you're trying, I'll gladly indent your enemies. Count on it."

"What does *that* mean?" "What's he *talking* about, indent?" "Spliced clauses?"

Don't act ignorant, I told them.

I let go of The Levinson, but The Levinson didn't let go of me. I said, How many Israelites at Aptakisic have pennyguns?

The Levinson said, "All of us, Gurion." "We delivered your instructions to all of us," Pinker added. "*Almost* all of us," Mr. Goldblum corrected, in a low, conspiratorial tone.

I said, What do you mean *almost*? What's the tone?

Mr. Goldblum popped his eyes out at Pinker and The Levinson.

The Levinson and Pinker winked at Mr. Goldblum. "Well there's a... there's a new one we're not friends with," said The Levinson, "and we don't know about him. He might be an Israelite, but he also might just be a Jew." "He only started school this week," said Mr. Goldblum. "He's orthodox." "Co-Captain Baxter knocked his hat off."

That's Eliyahu of Brooklyn, I said, and there are no more Jews, only Israelites. So don't get toney just cause someone who dresses sharper than you knows more—

"It's not cause he's Orthodox." "Nathan Feingold's Orthodox." "And he's a really good buddy." "It's just we didn't know him, right guys?" "Right." "Yeah." "He's new." "We didn't know him."

I know him, I said. And he's your brother, and if you saw him get his hat knocked off and didn't do anything about it, you should be ashamed and repentent. Not toney.

"We didn't see him get his hat knocked off." "We just heard about it." "And if you say he's our brother, then he's our brother." "And if you know him, then maybe he has a pennygun." "We can't say for sure." "We can't say for sure, but we're not being toney about him, Gurion. Really."

And it was true. At least it seemed to have become true: the tone was gone.

Do you have them on you? I said. Your weapons?

"We keep them at home," The Levinson said. "We're waiting."

For what? I said.

"More instructions."

There aren't any more, I said.

"You're instructing us to stop waiting?"

Sure, I said.

Then Shpritzy came out of the Quiet Room. He had a fat lip and a temple-bruise. His shirt was torn on the sleeve-seam. Besides that, he looked just like the rest of them.

"So who messed you up?" said Nakamook.

"Don't say!" said the four. Shpritzy didn't say.

I'm Gurion, I said to him.

"Finally," he said.

He sat down in the middle of his friends. They were, the five of them: Shpritzy, The Levinson, Mr. Goldblum, GlassMan, and Pinker. They leaned into each other, back-slapping.

Nakamook said to me, "Why's it okay for them to betray your *Instructions?*"

I said, They didn't.

"How's that?" he said.

Their document's different.

"Different," said Nakamook.

From yours, I said.

"Why different?" he said.

They're, I said, Israelites.

"Okay," he said. "So what, though?" he said.

You're not, I said.

"But so *what*, though?" he said.

So I didn't want you spreading my instructions.

"Spreading them to who?"

Others.

"Other goys."

Goyim.

"Goyim, whatever. Other goyim like who? Like Vincie? Main Man? Goyim like Leevon?"

Hey—

"Or no, you mean goyim like Botha and Slokum, right? Like Floyd and

Desormie? Acer and Berman? Pinge and Brodsky?—no, not Brodsky; not a goy, Brodsky. Not Berman, either."

Listen—

"Right—I know. It's okay. I know. I'm making it too complicated. Just goyim, right? All of the goyim. Any of the goyim. Vincie and Slokum, Main Man and Botha, Leevon and Floyd and Sandy. Same difference."

Benji.

"What?"

I—

"Why would I spread your instructions, anyway?" he said.

I didn't say you would—it's just theirs say to spread them.

"These five little Cubs-fan knuckleheads here."

Yes, I said, but—

"These little guys you don't know—theirs say to spread them."

Yes, I said.

"And mine not only doesn't say spread them. Mine says burn this document or we're enemies," said Benji.

I know what yours says. I wrote it, I said. I wrote both of them, I said.

"Mine says if I don't burn it we're enemies," he said. "Theirs say, 'Strangers, please spread this to other strangers.'"

Other Israelites, I said.

"Other Israelite strangers."

Yes, already. So what? I said. I said, Why don't you just take it as a compliment, Benji?

"A compliment?" he said.

A compliment, I said. I said, You're the only non-Israelite I ever gave it to.

"You didn't, though," he said. "You didn't give it to me."

I—

"You changed it," he said.

But—

"You didn't?"

I did. That's established. We've long since established that. I did it for you though. Because you're you.

"Nakamook the goy. Gentile me."

Nakamook the friend. My best friend Benji.

"A mensch among the goyim, but a goy nonetheless."

The only non-Israelite to whom I'd give *Ulpan*.

"*Ulpan?*"

That's what it's called. I changed the title of yours.

"Whose is better?" he said.

That's, I said. That's a weird question. I don't think it makes... It depends on who—

"To *you*," he said. "To Gurion. Whose is better? The one you gave strangers to spread to strangers, or the one you gave the goy containing the threat?"

In answer, I shrugged = I don't want to lie to you.

"He shrugs. He's speechless. He stammers and shrugs."

Back off now, I said.

"'Back off now,' he says."

What do you want from me? I said.

"What do you *think* I fucken want, man."

You're not an Israelite. I can't do anything about that, Benji.

"Jesus fucking Christ."

You want contrition? You want me to *apologize*? Cause you're not an Israelite? Because I *am*?

A tube above us flickered and made him look dead.

Benji said, "Tch." He said, "Nevermind." He pulled the pencil-stub out of his hand with his teeth. "Flesh wound," he said, and forced a laugh. He folded it up in a "Say No" brochure from the D.A.R.E. shelf by the door, said, "Relic in an envelope." Another forced laugh and he left into Main Hall.

I had done, from the beginning, the best I could. Why couldn't he see that? Why can't he see that? Why can't he see my side of things? I thought. But he did, I knew—he did see my side. And so I attempted to see his side and saw it, and saw that I'd seen it—I'd always seen it; I hadn't missed anything—I just wasn't *on* it. Benji'd get over it. He'd have to get over it. It wasn't a thing I had to get over.

I pressed all my fingers against all my fingers while cracking sounds echoed all across Main Hall; Benji was flying at ceiling-hung EXIT plaques, overhead-punching them off their cheap mounts.

My fingers wouldn't break.

The cracking sounds stopped.

For three or four seconds, Main Hall was quiet.

Then Benji set off the fire alarm.

The sky was always prettiest when I hadn't known I'd see it. It seemed less round, more like a blanket. The clouds all looked sewn in and deliberate.

As soon as we got outside, I felt watched.

For mid-November, it wasn't cold. The air didn't make steam of our breath or crust our gooze, but still I was coatless and I shivered a little.

Nurse Clyde, who was holding the puker in a fireman's carry, led me and the Five across Rand Road to the two-hill field and told us to find our fifth-period teachers and let them know we were safe. Then the nurse set the girl in the grass and she puked more.

Most students and teachers were still exiting the school. The Five followed me past the ones who'd already exited—none of whom were June—and I took us up the high hill for a better view. I started a circle by leaning on a stump. The Five finished the circle and we sat facing west.

A paramedic and a cop were consulting with each other outside the front entrance, from which students and teachers continually emerged to cross the street in single-file lines. Each teacher, once her class arrived in the field, ordered her students to stay where they were, then headed to an area just east of the sidewalk where a growing group of teachers huddled and gossiped. No one else climbed the high hill, but many of the students, once their teachers had gone, abandoned their classes to find their friends, and they all faced the school, some hugging themselves and some rubbing others' shoulders and others playing slapslap for warmth. As their numbers grew and their density thickened, more and more of them stood, and more cop cars and fire engines came up Rand Road.

The Levinson said, "This is the best. Look at that crowd!" "That crowd doesn't see us!" said GlassMan. "But we see them!" Shpritzy said. "And look at those clouds!" said Pinker. He pointed his Cubs-gloved finger at the blankety sky. "It's a cluster of commas," said Mr. Goldblum. "It's a bunch of apostrophes," said GlassMan. Shpritzy said, "It's a gang of yuds." "We're a gang of Yids." "We're a gang of kids." "We're a gang of Yid kids under clouds of yud, and despite the chill, we're not catching pneumonia!" "Where's that one kid?" "Let's find that kid." "Let's kill that kid." The Five looked around for the kid who hurt Shpritzy and I looked around to try to spot June, but got spotted first by Eliyahu of Brooklyn. I felt a tap on my elbow and looked to my right. He was blowing into his hands.

He said, "Are you okay?"

I said, Where did you come from?

He said, "I came from Israel, I came from Brooklyn, I came from the other side of this tree stump. I came to my uncle's house to live and they sent me to this Aptakisic where I broke a window. I came to the Cage, and you kept disappearing. I went to my new gym class and waited to change— I'm shy—and no sooner had the last boy gone to the pool than this alarm goes off and I'm all alone. I rebuckled my belt and I ran. I'm troubled." He got inside the circle and sat close, facing me. He said, "This kind of thing doesn't thrill me at all." He was shivering, too, and not looking me in the face. With his teeth, he kneaded the corners of his lips.

I said, I didn't disappear, I just went to the Nurse. Here, I said, meet the Five.

The Five revolved, waved, then got back to the task of finding their guy.

Eliyahu wasn't paying attention anyway. He said, "This kind of thing happens? I think about my family. How I was washing my face. Have you heard about my family? If you heard, it doesn't matter," he said. His eyes were darting around and he rocked back and forth as he spoke. "If you heard, you heard wrong." he said, "because no one knows about my face. We had mango ice cream at a café on Ben Yehuda street. Do you know Jerusalem? My sisters and I and my mother, we had mango ice cream at a café on

Ben Yehuda street in Jerusalem, and my father drank coffee with ice in it. It was hot outside and the Jerusalem-stone was blinding. It was too bright outside. There were no shadows. You would squint just to look at a building. I finished my ice cream before anyone else, and my father he says for me to lean close to him? He was on the other side of the table and, when I leaned, I leaned over the whole table, and my father licked his thumbs, saying, 'You've got shmutz,' and he started to rub the thumbs on my cheek. I didn't like it because I was eleven already and it was embarrassing. I pushed his hands off and he smiled. He said, 'I'm sorry.' He said, 'You're a grown boy.' And when he said it, I knew he didn't mean it. It's not the kind of thing you can say and mean it. You can't tell someone he's a grown boy and mean it, even if you think you mean it. And my father didn't even think he meant it, and it made me angry because if you say that someone is a grown boy, then you're saying they're not a man yet, but what's a grown boy if not a man? I was thinking of this so much, then, because we were in Israel for my sister Miriam's bat mitzvah, and I kept thinking she was a woman now and what was I? It was a very important question. I leaned away from my father and he said to me, 'So go wash your face.' And it made me even angrier because now he was telling me to wash my face, and a grown boy, or a man, *would* go wash his face. A grown boy would not leave his face shmutzy just because his father said to clean it, but that's what I was going to do. I was going to leave my face shmutzy because he said I should clean it. And I knew I should clean it, but I wasn't going to, because I was not a grown boy. I said nothing to my father and I didn't move. He said, 'Look, there's a napkin, there's a glass of water. You can dip it.' I told him, 'No.' I said to him that it was not something that I was going to do. And then I decided to go to the bathroom in the café to wash, because now that he was telling me I should dip the napkin in the water, it gave me the chance to wash my face like a grown boy, like I wanted to do, without doing it how he told me, like I also wanted. So I got up and went to wash my face in the café, in the bathroom in the back of it, and my father, as I stood up, he reached over the table and touched his hand on the top part of my arm, right here, almost on the shoulder. He wanted to get me to look at him, because now he was sorry and he wanted me to look at him so he could say it, and what I thought was how tall of a man he was that his arms could be so long, that he could sit on the other side of the table and reach over to me while I'm standing and get his hand on my shoulder. And I thought how before he could have just reached over with the spitty thumbs if he'd wanted to. He didn't have to ask me to lean closer to get the shmutz; he could have just reached, you know? I thought it was strange he said for me to lean close to him when he could have reached. He was six and a half feet tall, my father, and I did not want to look at him because I thought I would cry. It was something I did a lot at that time was to cry when he was sorry for something he said to me. So I shook off his hand from my arm and went inside the café, to the bathroom, without looking at him, and in the bathroom I looked in the mirror and I saw there was nothing on my face. There wasn't any ice cream on my cheek at all. Not anything, and I would've seen it. The ice cream was a very bright orange color, it was mango-flavored, and I've always been a very pale person, even after a week of sun on my face in Israel, I was pale because I wore sunblock. I washed my face anyway. I bent forward into the sink and splished some water here, some water there. I thought to myself, why would my father kid me about having shmutz and, when I thought it, the door of the bathroom, it got bent a little, curved. The door curved in and I heard this blast. It was louder than anything, and my ears must have been ringing from it and the door was curved, but I didn't think to myself about an explosion yet—I wouldn't think about an explosion for a long time. I kept thinking about why my father would kid me like that and I thought maybe he just wanted to touch my face, you know? I'm in this bathroom thinking maybe he wanted to touch my face because I'm a grown boy or not a grown boy and now Miriam has become a woman and then I stop thinking about it because there was that blast. The door was curved. My face was clean and I had to leave. I had to force my way out by laying down on the tile and kicking the door since it was curved and as I walked through the café, out to Ben Yehuda Street, there were people on stools with their heads down on the counter and there were people by the tables in front and these people were torn. I never thought about living things being torn. Blankets I think of are torn. Paper. Shirts and sheets. Living things are not the things you think about when you think about things that can be torn, but these people were torn and I knew not to look at it, but I thought I saw Leah, my other sister. I didn't want to see her, but I was out in front of the café, on the sidewalk, and I was trying to get between the fires and I did not want to trip on the torn people on the ground, so I looked down, to see where to put my feet to walk and like I said I think I see my sister Leah. She has a nail in her face. And she has no legs? My sister has a nail in her face? She should take the nail out of her face, I think. She has hands. She can take the nail out of her face. My sister Leah is a quiet person and she does not make many jokes.

She is not a very funny person yet. She won't be very funny for a long time. All the things that are very funny about her are accidental. She falls down and she says, 'Oops, I must have fallen down,' and that is very funny. The cat comes into the room while my mother gives her Hebrew lessons and Leah points at the cat and says, '*Chatul, chatul.*' It's not her. She wouldn't put a nail in her face for a joke because she does not make jokes yet. Her jokes are accidents. I thought: This is a joke my father is making on me because I didn't want him to touch my face. This is his kind of joke. He tells jokes when he becomes angry. They are not funny, but it is how he stops being angry, telling these jokes. And I knew they weren't my family because none of them looked like they were supposed to look. My father had gotten the faces right, but the bodies were not right. The bodies were in pieces. He didn't get the pieces right, you could see they didn't fit together. I knelt on the ground and I waited a few seconds because I was not tricked by my father and I wanted him to see it was not funny. Sometimes I would laugh at his jokes just to make him stop making his jokes. It's the laughing we'd do that would make him less angry, I was wrong before when I said it was the joke-telling, it was not the joke-telling that made him less angry, it was the joke-telling that made *us* less angry, it was the joke-telling he did to *make* us less angry—*at him*, less angry—and I would laugh sometimes when it was not funny because it was the only way to make him stop making the joke and I don't like to hear jokes when I'm trying to be angry, but I did not want to laugh on Ben Yehuda because I was still angry and still trying to be angry but I wanted the joke to stop so in the end I decided I should laugh and I laughed in a fake way. I said, 'Ha ha.' I said, 'Ha ha ha,' and still he didn't stop making this joke on me, since he could tell that my laugh was not a real laugh, but a laugh to make him stop, and he wanted a real laugh, but that was impossible because his joke wasn't funny at all and that is why I started looking at everything closely because none of them looked like who they were supposed to be, do you understand? I looked at all of them. I crawled around on my knees and moved the people around because I did not believe that I had seen my family and I wanted the proof that I hadn't seen them and that it was only a joke my father was making on me that he wouldn't stop making because I couldn't laugh. I wanted to find them, my family, underneath the joke-bodies, because it would be proof. I thought I could prove that they weren't torn, that these were dummies, made of cloth, burned closed at the edges, paint splashed upon them, and I—it doesn't make any sense, but that is what I was thinking and how it ended up I saw everything very close, on my knees, touching all of them, pushing on them with my hands to move them, and how heavy they were, I could only tilt them, and the sirens began and a soldier lifting me up and this sort of thing, here, it does not thrill me at all, Gurion. I am not a good defiance and I don't like it here. It doesn't feel safe. Everything becomes unsafe. "

I was crying pretty hard. I kept imagining my father telling me to wash my clean face. I needed to say something to Eliyahu, and I didn't know what to say, so I said the first thing I thought of:

You knew I was in the nurse's office.

But when I said it, I was wiping my nose off, and the words went into my sleeve. When I said it, Eliyahu didn't respond, and I thought he hadn't heard me, that I had a second chance, and I said what I should have said:

I said, I wasn't joking on you.

And he said, "Someone is."

And that was when GlassMan whispered, "Kill." He'd spotted their guy.

14
DEATH TO THE JEW

Thursday, November 16, 2006
5th–6th Period

And GlassMan jumped up, shouting, "There!" The guy was way up at the front of the crowd, looking around for who he should sit with. The guy was Shlomo Cohen.

There was something very wrong with that. Something didn't make sense, or at least didn't seem to, but struggling as I was to keep my gooze in my face, while trying, with my hands, squeezing his shoulders, to help Eliyahu keep his gooze in his, it took me longer than normal to figure out what. Shlomo, I thought. Cohen, I thought.

Shlomo Cohen, Shlomo Cohen.

Why should Shlomo Cohen care about Berman and his scarf, let alone care enough to harm Bernard "Shpritzy" Shpritz? Shlomo Cohen was an Indian, a B-team Indian; what concern of it was his? What was the angle? Neither side of the Shover schism had beef with the Indians; and not just no beef; it went well beyond beeflessness = they were, the Shovers, schisming over who had the right to be the Indians' semi-official humps and lackeys = both sides of the schism were on the Indians' side = there wasn't any reason for an Indian to choose sides. If anything, you'd've thought that Shlomo Cohen, the one Israelite Indian, would've sided *with* Berman and the Israelite Shovers, unless—but no… but then again I remembered when he brought me to Bam and Maholtz, on Tuesday's intramural bus, recalled my disappointment in him for taking me back there without his even knowing why he was taking me back there, how it wasn't very Israelite a thing for him to do, but that didn't mean… at least not necessarily it didn't…Was he—was it even possible?—could Shlomo Cohen be a *self-hating Jew*? Was there really such a thing outside of fiction? Maybe, I thought. Maybe, maybe. My mom believed there was, and had, on occasion, convinced me there were self-hating Jews in universities—Noam Chomsky, say, or that Finkelstein guy—except that was universities…

But even if there was such a thing as a self-hating Jew who was not a professor, and even if Shlomo was one of those—even if, say, he didn't want to be thought of as an Israelite by others (which, fat chance, *Shlomo Cohen*); even if he felt some need to distinguish himself from the Israelite Shovers, or maybe just the Israelites (the Israelite Shovers as proxies for the Israelites?); even if Shlomo, when the scarves got starred, believed it necessary to demonstrate that he wasn't on the side of those who had starred them, that he wasn't one of them, or anything like them—why should he attack Shpritzy? Why not go after Berman? Because Berman was big? Sure, Berman was big—and there he was in the field, on the fringe of the crowd, among ten or so other Israelite Shovers—Berman *was* big. He was *really* big, actually, June's ex was, huge, June's huge ex-boyfriend who *didn't kiss her* so there was no reason to picture it, to picture her tilting her head with her eyes closed, under the moon, in front of a door on a concrete stoop, not a stoop but a porch, stoops were for cities, a front-door porch in Deerbrook Park, no reason to think of her up on her tiptoes to meet him halfway as he leaned down and—

Shlomo Cohen found a spot in the center of the crowd, revolved to face the school, and sat where he'd stood, and Berman was huge was the point to keep focused on, while squeezing Eliyahu's shoulders continually—squeezing them *hard*, squeezing them *firmly*, a *steady* squeeze, and not one you pulsed like *I'm comforting you*, not like *Here is an armless hug for you, a boy who needs to be hugged*, but firm and steady like *My hands are strong, and my hands, like yours, are capable of smiting, I have strong, smiting hands, and I'm on your side, and we will smite, with ferocity, will face down our enemies*—Josh Berman was huge. Not Bam-huge or Flunky-huge, not overactive-glandular-huge, but reasonably huge, Co-Captain Baxter-size, really big for a kid who was in junior high, and so maybe Shlomo Cohen, who was maybe, it seemed, a self-hating Jew, attacked Shpritzy because—but no, because Shlomo wasn't small. He wasn't hardly small. Even if it made sense for a self-hating Shlomo to go after someone other than Berman, someone smaller than Berman, a proxy for Berman the Israelite Shover, there were no few potential proxies who fit that bill—*all* the Israelite Shovers were smaller than Berman, for example—and Shlomo could have attacked any one of those guys, any one of these smaller-than-June's...

If he didn't have the snat to pick a fight with Berman, Shlomo could've attacked any of these smaller-than-Berman-size Israelite Shovers to make his point. None were so small as Shpritzy, true, but the kind of coward you'd have to be to go after a kid *so* much smaller than you when there were bigger ones available, ones your size or even just four-fifths your size—because Shpritzy was what? two-thirds Shlomo's size? maybe even just four-sevenths his size?—that kind of cowardliness was—what? Akin to the cowardliness of hating your own people? Of being so ashamed of where you came from that you'd attack your own people in order to show others that you had overcome your origins? Well, actually...

"There!" the Five said. They passed the word around their circle like a stolen cigarette. "There!" said Mr. Goldblum, blinkering with his finger. "There!" said Pinker, who jumped in place. The Levinson said, "There!" and bounced fists on his thighs, and Shpritzy cracked his knuckles on his temples, saying, "There!"

And then the Five were streaking down the hill's western slope, each one's bare hand open in front of him, each one's gloved hand balled at his side.

They had to slow their advance when they came to the crowd, and as they made their way through, high-stepping laps and legs and heads, June came across the street, into the field. She held her hand above her eyes as if to block the sun, but there wasn't any sun, the sun was in clouds, and I thought to wave, but I didn't want my girlfriend to see my face tear-streaked, and my hands were still busy with squeezing Brooklyn's shoulders.

As the Five closed in on him, Shlomo revolved. It was hard to imagine how he couldn't have spotted them, but the way his head was tilted, like the head of a squirrel, a squirrel being fed in the park by a stranger—he could not have known the Five were after him. And how could he not have known that they were after him? For the same reason he'd thought to attack Shpritzy in the first place: he couldn't believe—refused to believe?—*failed* to believe who he actually was.

I kept my eyes on Shlomo, my hands on Eliyahu.

The Levinson yelled something. Then all the Five yelled something: "Death to the Jew!"

I knew what they meant. Still, it signified wrong.

Eliyahu took off first; shook my grip and bolted. I followed him, shouting, Don't hurt them, Brooklyn!

We were ten yards away when they fell upon Shlomo—Pinker, Shpritzy, and The Levinson. Shpritzy pulled the head back by the hair both-handed, The Levinson pinned the wrists, and Pinker stood the hips, crouching, jumping, landing where he'd started. Shlomo screamed. And then Mr. Goldblum and GlassMan arrived. GlassMan dropped all his weight on the crotch, elbow-first. Mr. Goldblum reared back and kicked Shlomo's jaw in.

His leg was cocked for a second face-shot when I got there and threw him aside. Eliyahu dragged GlassMan away by the ankles.

Mr. Goldblum said to me: "But you said!"

About then is when Brodsky began to catch on. At the edge of the crowd, with most of the teachers, he was too far away to see more than blurred movement, but the movement blurred fast, fast meant violent, and Shlomo kept screaming. The principal yelled, "Break it up!" through his soundgun, and the sitters in the field all leapt to their feet. The standers were already thickening around us.

Mr. Goldblum attempted to make his way past me, faking to the left, slipping to the right. I side-stepped to block him, left-right-left, til he caught me off-footed with a sideways shoulder-thrust. I landed on my ass and he helped me back up, saying, "Sorry, I'm sorry. Sorry, sorry."

We were standing nose-to-nose, Mr. Goldblum and I, and I thought: We're nose-to-nose, Mr. Goldblum and I, and I'd think we'd be nose-to-clavicle, us, or at least nose-to-thrapple.

Was I also cartoon-looking? I touched my nose.

I noticed his copy of *Ulpan* on the ground. I knelt to pick it up, still a little bit stunned, and he shot right past me, returned to the fight. I jammed the paper in my pocket, tried to follow him in, but before I'd even landed a second footfall, I got yanked back, then up in the air. Two arms wrapped tight around the crooks of my own, and my elbows pressed into my gut so hard some lunch got displaced and I puked in my mouth.

I spit it out.

I thought: Desormie.

I kicked my legs around, trying to get free. The stun was entirely gone now.

I saw Eliyahu wrap The Levinson's torso and wrestle him off of Shlomo Cohen's wrists.

The Levinson's face was soaked with tears and he was screaming at Shlomo: "Where's your friends now? It's *my* friends who saved you! *My* friends! Mine! You—" Then he was knocked away by the Chewer, and Eliyahu got arm-barred by Maholtz.

Eliyahu's fedora fell in the grass.

Finally my heel made contact with something soft on my holder and my holder said, "Fuck," but he didn't drop me. He swung around, and I could no longer see Eliyahu and the Five, and then I made contact again with my heel, and my holder swung us back to the first position. If I was him and he was Gurion, I would have leaned forward and fell on Gurion, stuck my knee in one of Gurion's kidneys and sideways-chopped on Gurion's neck, but he was not me and I was not him. He just kept holding me in the air while I kicked, and walking us backward, away from the fight, further into the crowd, and laughing, he was laughing, a peculiar laughter. It was forced, but not loud enough for anyone to hear—not anyone but me. He was laughing for my benefit.

I heard Brodsky screaming for Jerry and Floyd. He was still far away, trapped back by the crowd.

My holder kept swinging me left and right. Kids opened a path so they wouldn't get kicked.

Boystar, now travelling beside us, was thrilled. He got in my face and talked news like it was his: "Maccabee's a dead man! Maccabee's dying!"

I wanted to say something back but I was gasping. Every time I exhaled, the pressure on my center got tighter. My holder adjusted his grip a little, and for a few seconds, I could see over everyone's heads. I saw Co-Captain Baxter. He crushed the crown of the fallen fedora, then stepped to the Maholtz-grappled Eliyahu and took his yarmulke. He threw it behind him, frisbee-style, into the crowd. Maholtz reached his leg around the front of Eliyahu, released the arm-bar, and shoved forward so Eliyahu tripped. He fell bad. He caught his own knee in his beauty, and his wind got blasted. I needed to get loose to help him and I couldn't. Co-Captain Baxter flipped him over and pinned him, slapped him, twetched in his eye. Everything in sight spun for a second.

I put all my strength in my shoulders to spread them, inhaled as hard as I could. This got a little air inside my cramped lungs, but blinking sparks were already falling, scraping their way down my visual field.

All the Five were cleared away by teachers except for Shpritzy, who was nearly horizontal, stretched in mid-air, his arms locked tight around Shlomo's head, Desormie pulling him west by the ankles while the Chewer pulled Shlomo east by the waist. Floyd dropped his cheering cone and Main Man grabbed it. He shouted through the bell: "Nakamook? Nakamook? Where is Benji Nakamook? Is Benji Nakamook in the two-hill field?"

I wanted to know where Nakamook was, too. And Vincie. Leevon. Where was the Side of Damage? If the cheering cone was a soundgun, then Main Man could—but no. There was no need for a soundgun. There was the

Side of Damage! All of them but Benji—no! There was Benji. They were standing right there. Not helping me.

Watching.

"Nakamook!" shouted Mookus. "If you are Benji Nakamook please report to the center of the penultimate crowd scene! Please step back to allow Benji Nakamook access—"

Shpritzy and Shlomo had suddenly separated. Floyd's elbow struck Main Man. The cheering cone dropped. All the Side of Damage glanced between me and Benji.

Again my holder re-adjusted his grip, turning us a little. I caught sight of some Shovers shoving each other, yanking scarves off each other, lofting scarves in the air, then my eye-level sunk to the crowd's neck-and-back-plane. Any breath I had left in my body was stale. I heard ticking in my ears, and the sparks ceased to blink, and they grew tails like comets and were falling so quickly I was seeing bright lines, phosphorescent white.

And I wanted to know how Desormie could possibly hold onto Shpritzy way over there while he crushed all the air from me right over here.

The white lines thickened.

Desormie couldn't be in two places at once.

I tried some more kicking. My legs were floppy. My holder said, quietly, "Don't make me hurt you." The calm of his voice was unmistakable.

I thought: But he's only just another boy, though. I'm being defeated by another boy.

"I'm saying calm down, kid," Slokum said.

I turned my head as hard as I could and used my last halfbreath to twetch in his face, but it only drooled out of me.

Kids were staring.

"Okay now," said Bam, and he set me down. "You're okay now. Good guy. Okay."

I sucked air, gulped air, wiped my face on my hood. Slokum was leaving.

Wait! I shouted.

He stopped. He waited.

I caught my breath and jumped straight at him. He turned away, and I bounced off his arm. "Smacked-up Maccabee," Boystar said. He thought it was hilarious. "I'm gonna write a song."

"Just disappear now," Slokum said to one of us. "Don't make it all knotty. Don't complicate things."

When I got back on my feet, he was gone, in the crowd. The crowd had gone calm, lining up to be counted.

I walked around the hillside and sat in the valley, cold and faceless in a puddle of snat.

GURION

I lay back on the stiff grass and stared at the yud-shaped clouds. They drifted together into pairs while I daydreamed an audience that filled the risers in the gym. I paced inside the tip-off circle, denouncing Slokum's tactics through a megaphone. I explained how I'd have wrecked him if he'd faced me honorably: if he'd attacked head-on instead of creeping up from behind. And if I'd have wrecked Bam Slokum, I explained, he'd be the one in front of an imaginary audience, protesting the unfair tactics of Gurion ben-Judah, explaining how he'd have wrecked Gurion if Gurion had faced him honorably and how in that case it would be Gurion in front of an imaginary meow meow, explaining meow meow meow meow meow meow meow.

Fucker! I yelled at the clouds of yud.

And the clouds said nothing. They were only clouds, mute symbols at best.

I was a snatless wonder.

I didn't want to fight Bam. I liked him. Even as I'd regained my feet and jumped to attack him, I'd liked him. Even as I hated to like him. Why did I have to like him? And why did he just hold me in the air like that? Was it mercy? Some scholars would argue it was mercy. They would argue that because he could've done any number of other things—any number of things that would have seriously damaged Gurion's body—it was merciful of Bam Slokum to do nothing more than hold Gurion in the air, and that Gurion should therefore be grateful.

Other scholars would see it differently. Maybe Bam held Gurion in the air, they would suggest, because he thought that was the only way to keep his advantage. Maybe he thought that if he fell forward and broke Gurion's back or damaged Gurion's kidneys or lifted Gurion higher and dropped him on his head—maybe Slokum thought actions of that kind would incite Gurion's friends to step in. Maybe he thought Nakamook, or Vincie, or the Side of Damage, though presently kept at bay by their fear of him, would be incited to rally against him if he actually damaged Gurion.

Or, would argue a third group of scholars, maybe Slokum just thought he'd get in trouble if he damaged Gurion. It could be Slokum knew that what he seemed to be doing, to the eyes of Brodsky and the teachers—if they were even watching—was stopping a fight = restraining Gurion = restoring order = separating the undesired prefix from the disArrangement. It is true that Gurion had been stopping that same fight himself, but Bam might not have known that; and even if he had known it, he could plausibly deny the knowledge as long as all he did was restrain Gurion, who few at Aptakisic would ever suspect of attempting to break up a fight.

But then again, maybe Bam knew that being held back helpless while otherwise able to function at full capacity was, ultimately, more humiliating than having that capacity beaten out of you with blows that broke bones and bruised organs. Maybe Bam, like the Cage, was just another fractal of the Arrangement, operating perfectly, in concentrated miniature, according to the central principles on which all its rules were based: The less violent the measures of restraint, the more humiliation those measures inflict on the restrained; the more humiliated the restrained, the less violent need be the measures to restrain them.

What would seem an act of mercy to some scholars would, to

others, surely seem a quiet, snakey assertion of dominance, a prelude to enslavement.

But even if those latter scholars would be wrong and it *was* an act of mercy, who was Bam Slokum to show me mercy? And why should *I* consider the possibility that it was mercy? Wasn't that a kind of weakness in itself? Giving him the benefit of the doubt? Why did I have to like him? Ever? But especially now? Why did I have to *still* like him? Why was I compelled to posit scholars who would come to his defense? Why did I have to play his apologist? Why couldn't the story be that I used to like him, and then, after he'd humiliated me, I gave up on him and didn't like him anymore? Why couldn't I just feel disappointed and then betrayed and then get on with the vengeance or whatever it is you're supposed to get on with when you've been disappointed and betrayed? I could never get disappointed at the appropriate time. I was always so late. It took me nine weeks to see Esther Salt's shadiness, and it would have surely taken longer if I hadn't fallen in love with June. And those scholars who had ditched me third period—why *not* call them enemies? Why resist? What was wrong with me? I wanted to damage someone, but I was the only one in the two-hill field's valley and I wasn't getting up.

I thought: You've been laid low. Pray.

But I didn't think: You've been laid low by an enemy. Fight.

I thought: Stop thinking. Thinking only makes it worse.

But I didn't think: Stop praying. Self-pity only makes it worse.

I should have been thinking those things I didn't think, but instead I just laid there, tight-chested and pitiful, trying to make hearty the hollow Hebrew praise I found myself whispering in the direction of the same yud-shaped clouds I had cursed only moments earlier.

And then I heard jingling, and grass-blades getting crushed. And then there were knees, next to my face. Girl's knees. June's knees. Under the denim they were naked, freckled. I'd never seen them.

"Who are you talking to?" she said. "Get up. They're about to take attendance."

June, I said, don't look at me. I just got defeated.

She said, "I know."

You saw? I said.

"No," she said. "I saw Benji Nakamook crying and I—nyee-yah!" She got a chill from the cold that rolled her shoulders. "Eee!" she said. "I saw Benji crying and I asked him why."

Why didn't he help me? I said.

"I think that's why he was crying," she said. "But get up, okay? If you don't show for attendance, you'll be in trouble."

I said, I don't care if I get in trouble.

"That's fine for you," she said, "but I care. If you get an OSS or expelled, then it'll be hard for me to see you."

I said, You're gonna stop seeing me if I get in trouble?

"With my eyes," she said. "If you're not in school, it'll be hard for me to see you *with my eyes*. What's wrong with you? I told you I'd marry you. We're engaged. Why would I break our engagement because you got in trouble? And why would you care, anyway? If I was the kind of person who would stop being engaged to you because you got in trouble, then I'd be a suck kind of person and you'd be better off without me, and we both know you wouldn't be better off without me, so that means I'm not that kind of person. What I want is to make out with you a lot and crack jokes. I want to make out with you a lot *after school today* and crack jokes. If you get kicked out, how will we be able to do that?"

I followed her halfway up the high hill, where she spun around to face me, like she had something new and sudden to say.

The Side of Damage was just over the crest. Botha told them to quiet the nonsense and line up. I didn't hear any nonsense that needed quieting. I heard Nakamook clicking his Zippo open and snapping it shut inside of his pocket, an action he'd sometimes perform to calm himself. A brittle elm bough was creaking behind us, adjusting in the wind. Someone played spastic percussion with a zipper. A fought yawn forced crackling from someone else's jaw-joints. The sound forced me to yawn, then June to yawn, and me one more time, but otherwise I didn't care about any of it. June was staring at me and she was letting me stare at her. She didn't turn her head away when she yawned. She hid her mouth behind her wrist and her eyes got even wetter-looking.

She said, "You always look really alive. I want to draw you. Line up now, okay? Get counted." She touched my hand, dashed over the hill.

As soon as she was out of sight, I remembered my defeat; limpness washed through my muscles. I got on my stomach and army-crawled to the crest.

Chin on the ground, my field of vision sliced into portions by hard, dead blades of grass, I looked down on the field full of lining-up students. Eliyahu and the Five were nowhere. Probably the same nowhere as Brodsky and Floyd. I couldn't spot Maholtz, Co-Captain Baxter, or Shlomo either. Blonde Lonnie and Slokum stood in parallel attendance lines, low-voicing jokes. Boystar, ten yards away from them, kept shouting their names. When they'd revolve to see what he wanted, he'd turn his thumbs up.

Looking at Boystar, at his little celebration, I finally had a thought that was smart. I thought: It's not that you like Bam Slokum despite the fact that he humiliated you, Gurion. I thought: You like Bam Slokum *because* he humiliated you. Like some cowardly Pascal wagering, you suspected all along that Bam could hurt you, so you decided to like him. As long as you told yourself you liked him, and for as long as you continue to tell yourself you like him, you have had and will continue to have an excuse not to fight him, an excuse to make excuses for him and his actions, actions you wouldn't hesitate to condemn if anyone else had performed them.

I may have helped to wreck the pagan scoreboard, but I had made of Bam a Christian deity, and these days were not like the days of Avram. To smash idols was not enough. It only infuriated the idolaters. We must smash what the idols stand for, I thought. We must smash their gods, bone by bone, starting with the fingers and ending with the skulls, and that is only the beginning, for we must also bring down the shelves and the altars on which new idols could be mounted; we must bring down the walls to which new shelves could be attached and bury all the flooring on which new altars could be balanced, then smash apart the wreckage so that none of it may be salvaged.

I had been operating too symbolically. I had been too verbose. Verbosity was like the iniquity of idolatry. I had been iniquitous, a sinner, and there in the two-hill field I was repenting.

Repentance is easy when you've been defeated—I knew that. I needed to figure out how to atone.

Itching to flash his upturned thumbs some more, Boystar shouted Slokum's name again. Slokum ignored him, and I enjoyed it too much, enjoyed it the wrong way. To enjoy the revelation that the bonds between two of my enemies were weak would have been fine, but what I enjoyed was so instantaneous that it could not have been that. What I enjoyed was that Bam showed Boystar disfavor, which meant being in Bam's favor was still valuable to me.

You were humiliated by him, I thought, well before he laid hands on you, and yet even now, after he has held you helpless in the air, you can hear it echoing, the angelic robotvoice in your head that assures you might makes right even while might is wronging you, that it is good to accept the dominance of those who dominate you, that your enemies are friends as long as you cheer for them.

I thought: The more violent the measures of restraint, the less humiliation those measures inflict on the restrained; the less humiliated the restrained, the more violent need be the measures to restrain them.

I thought: Being humiliated only makes it easier to restrain you. And being restrained makes it possible to torture you, for the unrestrained cannot be tortured; the unrestrained can only be fought. So to be restrained is to be unable to fight, and to be humiliated is to be readied for torture. To know you have been readied for torture is to await torture. And to await torture is, itself, torture.

I thought: There is nothing more glaringly unmerciful than torture. Those who would restrain you will be subject to your atonement.

Botha started taking attendance.

"Haspaygus!" he said.

My eyes opened at the sound of it. I hadn't known they'd been closed.

"Yeah," said Ronrico Asparagus.

Looking on the Side of Damage, now, I thought of Nakamook's judgment in the teachers lounge doorway: that they were only loyal because they wanted protection.

"What's the proper response, Mister Haspaygus?"

The moment I was unable to protect them, they cowered, abandoned me.

"'Here' or 'prasent' is the proper response, Mister Haspaygus."

Except so had I. I had cowered, was cowering.

"Yeah," said Ronrico.

"That's a detantion, Haspaygus. Bashker!"

They had cowered before the same false god that had humbled me, their protector.

"Tut," said Anna Boshka.

And to see your protector being humbled—what can you do? Can you step in to protect him? Yes, you can. But do you think to? Do you ever think to protect your protector? You should, but you probably don't. You probably take for granted that what overpowers him will overpower you. And you cower.

"Moykil Braigmin?"

So was that the end of their loyalty, then?

"Yeah," said the Janitor.

Is loyalty measured by the ends to which you'd go to protect the object of your loyalty, or is it measured by the ends to which *you'd hope* you'd go to protect him?

"What's that?" said Botha. "What's that?"

Maybe, I thought, there is *actual* loyalty, and that is measured by the ends to which you'd go; and maybe then there is also *potential* loyalty— measured by the ends to which you'd hope you'd go. Surely the second kind is not as important as the first, but that wouldn't make it *un*important; all things potential can be made actual—that is what it means to be potential. And apart from Adonai, what in all the universe was actual that wasn't once potential?

"I said, 'Yeah,'" said the Janitor.

"That's so romantic," said Botha, "to side with your baddy Hespaygus." Then he fake-coughed. "Lotsa jairms out here," he said. He fake-coughed again, said, "All that blad from Aye-lie and that Shy-lomo boy on the ground that you're stendin' on."

The Janitor knew he was yards away from where Shlomo and Eliyahu had bled into the grass, but still you could almost see the germs he imagined floating up from near his shoes, their cellwalls slimily marbled hot pink and piss-colored, little barbs protruding from their goozy-shaped bodies, trying to cling to his skin, to crawl into his openings. Though he hesitated, the Janitor was only able to hold his ground for a three-count before succumbing to Botha's power of suggestion and moving a couple steps back.

Botha, still trickling—doomed, as all caulkers, to trickle forever—said, "It's in the air by now I'd think, the jairms. Enexcapable, I'd suppose."

"Leave my brother alone," said the Flunky.

The Janitor tightened his lips, hoisted the collar of his t-shirt over his nose.

"Your dumb behavior is the dumb behavior of a foog who's like a fool except I don't like him," the Flunky said to Botha.

The sound of more than four consecutive words from the Flunky—let alone words acknowledging his genetic ties to the Janitor—startled all of us, but no one as much as Botha, whose claw, with a click, pinched so hard and suddenly on the drizzle-slick wood of his clipboard that the clipboard shot from his grasp. Reflexively, as if a champion of that shvontzy sport hackeysack, Botha extended a leg and kicked the clipboard, which bounced once then twice off his inner-arch before it hit the ground. He was bent over to retrieve it when he said, "I guess that mains Rachid Braigmin's present," but by the time he said, "and I guess Rachid Braigmin wants to serve a detantion with his little brother and his little brother's little frand Haspaygus—I'll oblige you that, Rachid Braigmin, I'll oblige you that," he was standing up even straighter than before, shoulders thrust back proudly. "Cattis!" he said.

"What did you just say to the Flunky, Mr. Botha? I couldn't understand," said Salvador Curtis.

"Jest mind yourself, Cattis, and kape your nose to the tesk at hand. Deerfailed!"

I thought: Maybe it's the duty of loyalty's object to transform the potential into the actual. Maybe it's my fault they didn't protect me. Maybe when they saw me being humiliated, they didn't believe what they were seeing.

"Present," said Rick Deerfield.

"Dangow," said Botha.

"Present," said Mark Dingle.

Maybe they didn't believe I *could* be humiliated.

"Hentsary!" said Botha.

"Present," said Ansul Entsry.

"Failedburns," said Botha.

"Here," said Renee Feldbons.

Maybe they thought, moment to moment, that I would break free of Slokum in the next moment. That was definitely what *I* thought when it started happening, and by the time I knew otherwise, I didn't have enough air in my lungs to call for help—but they didn't know that. My lungs were not their lungs.

"Freudy!"

"Present," said Jackie Friday.

My lungs were not their lungs, and my humiliation wasn't their humiliation. It didn't have to be, at least.

"Glanncow!"

"Here," said Janie Glencoe.

They didn't *have to* be humiliated by my defeat.

"Hyeney!"

"I'm here," said Chunkstyle.

And they didn't *have to* be ashamed for letting me be defeated.

"Kannilwath!"

"Present," said Forrest Kenilworth.

Yet they were humiliated. And ashamed. I could see it in their faces.

"Layp!" said Botha.

Stevie Loop said, "Here."

Their faces were blank; I saw shame in their faces, shame in their blankness. And maybe I just wanted to. Maybe I *needed* to—maybe I wanted, that much, to forgive them; maybe to forgive them I had to see shame that wasn't really there—but shame's what I saw.

"Lant!" said Botha.

They wished they'd done more for me, regretted they hadn't.

"Right here," said Casper Lunt.

They wanted to do more.

"Make-bee!" said Botha.

They wanted to atone.

"Make-bee!" said Botha.

They wanted to be loyal.

"Make-bee?" said Botha. "Where's Make-bee?" said Botha.

Someone cleared his throat—Leevon Ray. "Here," Leevon said.

"Nice to finely hear from you, Layven," Botha said, "but don't eff around with me. Where's Garrion Make-bee?"

"Here!" the Side shouted.

And Leevon Ray spoke: "Word is bond, you prison-colony trick. Outback gimp-ass vegemitebrain. Coyotebugger. Stingraybait. Wallabee-eating marsupialsack. Crocodile ugly walkabout cripple. Bent Australian clawfisted lame inbred Foster's-pounding bowie knife…"

I came down the hill, damaged and relieved and forgiving as the rest of them.

□   □   □   □   □   □   □

Mounted behind glass in a wallcase outside the art room was Miss Gleem's Quarterly Student Themeshow. The theme for the quarter was "Exploring Black & White." In the center of the display, amid would-be photoreal ink-drawings (moons, penguins, busts of tuxedoed Bruce Wayne types) and construction-paper cameos (all 19th-century-looking except Leevon's: a spear-cleft Centurion's helmet), hung the only unsigned piece. According to the little card Miss Gleem had pasted above the upper margin, it was made by June, and titled "Visual Thinker."

This is exactly what it looked like:

```
GRAYGRAYGRAYGRAYGRAYGRAYGRAYGRAYGRAYGRAY
GRAYGRAYGRAYGRAYGRAYGRAYGRAYGRAYGRAYGRAY
GRAYGRAYGRAYGRAYGRAYGRAYGRAYGRAYGRAYGRAY
GRAYGRAYGRAYGRAYGRAYGRAYGRAYGRAYGRAYGRAY
GRAYGRAYGRAYGRAYGRAYGRAYGRAYGRAYGRAYGRAY
GRAYGRAYGRAYGRAYGRAYGRAYGRAYGRAYGRAYGRAY
GRAYGRAYGRAYGRAYGRAYGRAYGRAYGRAYGRAYGRAY
GRAYGRAYGRAYGRAYGRAYGRAYGRAYGRAYGRAYGRAY
GRAYGRAYGRAYGRAYGRAYGRAYGRAYGRAYGRAYGRAY
GRAYGRAYGRAYGRAYGRAYGRAYGRAYGRAYGRAYGRAY
GRAYGRAYGRAYGRAYGRAYGRAYGRAYGRAYGRAYGRAY
GRAYGRAYGRAYGRAYGRAYGRAYGRAYGRAYGRAYGRAY
GRAYGRAYGRAYGRAYGRAYGRAYGRAYGRAYGRAYGRAY
GRAYGRAYGRAYGRAYGRAYGRAYGRAYGRAYGRAYGRAY
GRAYGRAYGRAYGRAYGRAYGRAYGRAYGRAYGRAYGRAY
```

Though the themeshow went up in mid-October, I didn't get the whole joke til early November, when, returning to ISS after going to the bathroom, I happened to see the piece from thirty paces off.

I pointed as we approached it on our way to the Cage. The Side of Damage looked, and I told them to go closer. All of them did so—and fast—except Benji.

He'd stayed out of speaking range since I'd come down the hill. I'd been telling myself he was waiting for privacy, but now that I was alone—the others half a hallway off, either puzzled or giggling in front of June's artwork—I saw how stupid that thought had been. If Benji'd wanted to speak to me alone, he would have scattered the lot of them and spoken. And had he done that, even if all he'd said was, "Hey" I think I would have forgiven him on the spot. I think I would have assumed I'd missed something obvious; that there'd been a solid reason for him not to help me in the field; that despite, if not because of, my efforts to forgive the others, this reason eluded me like a deer a duckhunter. Indeed, the very fact he couldn't be forgiven on the same grounds as the rest of them—while always his friend, I'd never been his protector—might not have occurred to me at all. Had he only said "Hey."

But he hadn't. He didn't. He kept on not. He wouldn't even look at me. What I decided was he'd write me a note.

And after we'd been in the Cage for ten minutes, I decided the note he was writing was long, more like a letter than a note, and I decided the letter would right everything between us.

The anticipation got me H with vigilance. It was the last letter in the world I'd want Botha to intercept. In the meantime, though, just about everyone except Benji was tossing me notes—"We Revenge We" "The Side of Damage is the End of Basketball" "You got snuck up on!" "Slokum dies Friday!" "I am a defiance!" "Death to the Arrangement!" "*EMOTIONAL-IZE*" "Robots will melt!" "Tomorrow I'm singing at th p p rally with

Boystar! Can you wait? I can't wait! Lov , My Main Man Scott Mookus"—
and because Benji was on the opposite side of the Cage, his hypothetical
letter would have to pass through the hands of at least three intermediaries
before it could get to me, and I didn't know who would toss it, or which
direction it would come from, and soon I did a very unstealth thing: reaching for a ricochet, I scooted my chair.

The Side of Damage believed I wanted a hyperscoot.

And so there was a hyperscoot.

Botha beat his fist on his desk and we couldn't hear it over our noise.
But the teachers, Miss Lang and Mr. Wadrow, though they covered their
ears, looked on in simple amazement, even smiling a little: it was the first
hyperscoot they'd witnessed, and they didn't know to be terrorized—they
thought it was just random weirdness. Clearly they hadn't spoken to Miss
Mingle or Miss Plotkin since before fourth period, and Botha must not have
told them about hyperscoot, either. That surprised me for a second, but it
shouldn't have: it was, above all, his authority that hyperscoot damaged,
and a trickler like him would want that information to remain hidden for
as long as possible.

Though I was glad the Side of Damage was so battle-ready, the teachers
needed to understand hyperscoot was a tactical weapon, and because the current hyperscoot wasn't in response to any obvious offense the Arrangement
had provided us, they couldn't have understood, so I stopped it. I waited til
all robot eyes were directed elsewhere—there was nothing to be gained by
letting them know there was a leader, let alone who that leader was—and
then I showed the Side of Damage my palm. They stilled their chairs.

"Tomorra you're eating lunch in here," Botha said.

It was a show of weakness and he knew it. We would have all stayed
in the Cage for lunch on Friday anyway: I was banned from the cafeteria,
and the rest of them would have wanted to eat with me. So then what was
the point of his sentencing us to lunch in the Cage? This was the point:
He knew we would think of the punishment as our having gotten away
with something—and we did think of it that way; half the hands in the
room were hiding sly smiles—and that therefore we wouldn't respond with
another hyperscoot.

And if we didn't respond with another hyperscoot, Lang and Wadrow,
who Botha was so concerned with impressing, and who had no clue that we'd
want to eat lunch in the Cage, would believe that Botha's power was intact.

So we should have hyperscooted in response to the sentencing. If we had,

Botha still would have known that he'd shown us weakness, but he'd also have looked weak in front of the teachers. It took me a minute to think of that, though—for those first sixty seconds after the sentencing, I was, like the others, too busy being impressed with our small victory to imagine a larger one—and after that it was too late. A delayed response would not look like a response. Just more randomness.

As the minutes after the hyperscoot quietly passed, I became less and less convinced that Benji was writing me a letter, more and more convinced that he'd been too afraid of Bam to help me, that he'd been just as afraid as the rest of them and was ashamed. That kenobi line of his about timeliness and vengeance and pride and propriety—maybe it *was*, after all, just impressive-sounding babbling, a clever-phrased reason to explain away the fact that after two years of arch-enmity he'd never once stepped to Slokum; to make it sound to others, maybe also to himself, like he wasn't plain scared. If there is such a thing as a disloyal thought—and I'm not sure there is—that would be an exemplary one. But my options were narrow. Either I could (disloyally?) believe that Benji was ashamed for having been afraid to fight the one guy he swore up and down was his enemy—and in the perfect storybook situation no less, a situation in which the fight would rescue his best friend—or I could believe that Benji wasn't loyal to me.

But why would he be disloyal? Because despite all his naysaying about the Side of Damage, he actually wanted to lead it and he thought my defeat would put him in that position? Or maybe his naysaying was understatement; maybe he *hated* the Side of Damage, and he thought my defeat would break it apart? Maybe he wanted the Side of Damage to break apart because he thought that would mean that we'd go back to how it used to be, just me and him and Vincie and Mookus and Leevon and Jelly and sometimes Mangey against everyone? When he seemed to come around to the idea of being friends with the Janitor and Ronrico and Eliyahu and Ben-Wa, could he have just been faking it? Was it the earlier two-hill field thing? that I hadn't invited him to meet the scholars, who didn't, in the end, show anyway? Was he jealous of June for being invited? All of these things, though possible, didn't ring even slightly true, and, more to the point, they were too abstract: They didn't supply motive enough for anyone capable of preventing it to stand by and watch his closest friend get humiliated. So either he'd been too afraid to fight Slokum or... what? Or he had quit our friendship.

And what reason could he have had for quitting our friendship? The only one I could think of didn't seem good enough at all. Maybe finding out that you've been given an inferior version of *Ulpan* justifies smashing exit plaques and pulling alarms—*I* was certainly pissed enough to do something like that by the time Nakamook had exited the Nurse's—but it doesn't justify abandoning your best friend. Benji wasn't an Israelite, and I would not act as if he were. To do so would be to pretend. To do so would be unfaithful of me and condescending to him. To do so would be chomsky. And Benji was the most anti-pretend person I'd ever met. He wouldn't have wanted me to merely *act* like he was an Israelite; he'd have wanted me to believe he *was* an Israelite, or that Israelites *weren't* Israelites. And I didn't believe those things. And I couldn't believe those things. And it is no easier to change what you believe than it is to change what you want, and my beliefs were far older than Benji's desire—if my changing my beliefs even was Benji's desire—so if either of us needed to bend, it was him.

And when did it ever really come up, anyway? When was the fact that he wasn't an Israelite ever a practical consideration? Only with *Ulpan*. Only in that one instance. And he could so easily make of that the opposite of what he'd made of it in Nurse Clyde's office. It was the easiest thing in the world to flip: Nakamook could just as easily decide to believe that my giving him a doctored copy of *Ulpan*—a copy I'd made specifically for him—signified my loyalty to him, my friendship, my trust. And it did. And, in so many words, I'd explained that. I had taught him to build a weapon intended for Israelites. I had trusted him enough to share with him the means of protection I'd given my first brothers. I had, in all but name, made of him a brother. Could the name really be that important to him?

He'd either been afraid, or he was no longer my friend. Both options were suck, but I definitely preferred the former. If he had been too afraid to fight Bam, I would have a sad and ashamed best friend who wasn't as brave as he or I had imagined. If he had quit being my friend, though, I would have no best friend at all.

I looked over my shoulder and saw, by the way Benji was bent, that he was writing.

Good, I thought.

For a while I wrote potential responses to the forthcoming letter to see which one might be the most comforting:

> I probably would have been too frozen with fear to help you,
> too, Benji.

Because I've never seen you helpless, I bet I wouldn't think it possible that you ever could be, even if your feet were alternately kicking at and dangling in the air while some giant's arms were wrapped crushingly around your chest right before my eyes, so don't sweat it; I understand.

Bam's too big for any one kid, and although the Side of Damage would have surely helped you take him down if only you'd led them in his direction, if I was you I probably wouldn't have realized I had an army either, so stunned would I be at the sight of my best friend's humiliation.

Botha's voice suddenly gloated from the opposite side of the Cage. "Something to share with the cless, Miss Rotstain?" he said.

I revolved. So did everyone else.

Jelly threw a folded note into Mangey's lap and Mangey tried to swallow the note, but Botha snapped it from between her teeth with his claw before she could get it all the way in her mouth.

"Let's see," Botha said to the class, once he'd wiped the note's saliva on the wall of Mangey's carrel and read it through to himself. He said, "Says here, in the handwriting of Mister Nackamake, 'Bibey, will you be my bibey?' And then, beneath it, in the handwriting of Miss Rotstain, 'Mate with me after school boy the bus circle? Yours, Jaily.' Seems there's a badding rowmentz happening in this clessroom of ours. Well, whuddya think Nackamake? You gonna mate with Jaily boy the bus circle?"

"Wherever she wants," Nakamook said to Botha. "I'm in love with her. Anyone in here have a problem with that?" he said to the Cage. He was standing. "Anyone in here wanna make a pun about it?"

"Stap two," said Botha.

No one made a pun.

I was thinking: I get humiliated, and Nakamook courts a girl? Courts—wait—courts *Jelly?*

"C'mon," Benji said to us, "pun's right there for the taking. Right before your very ears. Jelly asks to meet me and the Monitor tells you about it in order to embarrass me, only he can't pronounce the word 'meet,' so he says 'mate,' which is a verb as well as a noun."

"Enough, Nackamake. You're at stap three as of now."

Benji said, "I asked you all a question. If someone who knows how to speak English says to you 'Benji went to the bus circle to mate with Jelly,' what would that person be saying? What's 'mate' mean when it's a verb?"

"You've got a detantion now. Anyone answers him's gonna get a detantion, too."

"If anyone answers my question," Benji said to us, "I promise I won't punish you for it."

There was silence. No one was going to say anything. Least of all me, thinking: Benji wasn't scared. Benji was done with you. Benji's *been* done with you. Out in the field, he was already done with you, there's no other explanation; if he'd not been done with you, then here in the Cage he'd be feeling ashamed, apologetic and ashamed, not in the mood to court Jelly Rothstein, flirt with Jelly Rothstein, whatever they've been doing. Nakamook was done with you. And now you're done with him.

Then Jelly said, "Sex."

And Botha said, "Detantion for the star-crest lovers, both."

And that's when I thought: Jelly's an Israelite.

And I knew Nakamook knew I was thinking it. And I knew Nakamook had thought I was thinking it before I'd actually thought it.

And I saw that was the practical consideration that mattered to him— not the doctored copy of *Ulpan*. What mattered was that I didn't think Israelites should—or really even could—marry Gentiles. What mattered to him was that I wouldn't believe in their marriage if they ever got married. I'd basically told him as much during Tuesday's detention in the library, when he kept trying to talk to me about June converting. He'd been thinking about Jelly. About him and Jelly. I could see that now. But what? How long had they been together, anyway? They flirted, I remembered, on Tuesday at lunch—"Say that for instance I was in love with you, Jelly," he'd said, "and Mangey started saying I shouldn't be because you bite people..." he'd said. "Are you in love with me?" she'd said—but both of them were flirts, and I'd thought it was just banter, but nothing was just banter, nothing was ever just banter, and no, it wasn't true that both of them were flirts, Jelly wasn't a flirt, and yet the two of them were flirting on Tuesday at Lunch, and I'd somehow missed it, or maybe not so much *missed* it (I couldn't have missed it if I was now recalling it) as failed to consider what their flirting might mean—and I remembered Jelly's email from Wednesday night, where after giving me her news about the Shovers and their scarves, she kept going on about what now essentially seemed like a proposal that we all double-date after school at the lake—"it should probably just be me and June and you and Benji"—which made it seem, by the tone, at least *now* it seemed this way, *if* I was remembering right... made it seem by the tone that they hadn't hooked up yet; it seemed like Jelly was trying to get into a situation where the two of them could hang out with June and I, who she probably figured would go off to make out, leaving her alone with Nakamook, so... unless maybe I was wrong about the tone. Maybe they'd been hooked up for a while in secret and Jelly's tone was toney in that email because she and Benji had been keeping their couplehood hidden and wanted to... what? To *premiere* it to me and June? But why would they keep that kind of secret? If they were in love with each other, why would they care what anyone else thought? Why hide it? Had they thought I'd disapprove or... If they'd disapproved of me and June, I wouldn't care, or rather I'd care, I guess I would care, but I wouldn't hide that I loved her; I'd tell them to get over it... But if they did keep that kind of secret from me, for *whatever* reason, then why would they choose to premiere it when... unless maybe they thought all along, before I'd ever said anything about it, that I didn't think Israelites and Gentiles should be together, and then, once I told everyone I was in love with June, they thought that maybe they'd been wrong about *me*, or that I'd *changed my mind* about Israelites and Gentiles, because they knew—*thought* they knew—that June was a Gentile, and so now they could tell me that they were together... But... And Benji'd called her Tuesday night, after that conversation in detention. June. He'd called June. Had he called her to tell her she—had he told her I thought she was an Israelite? Had he told her I needed her to be an Israelite? What if he had?...Because she hadn't hesitated, there on the stage; she hadn't hesitated for a second to say to me, "I'll convert"—she'd said, "You don't have to be so dark. I'll convert" and—and that lack of hesitation, it had meant a lot to me but—if Benji'd explained to her... no... It didn't matter. It didn't matter anyway: I'd said she was an Israelite and Adonai had failed to object, He'd sent no No! through my bones, through my muscles, my skin, no No! He hadn't. Why June hadn't hesitated was totally beside the point, and even considering it—questioning her motives, the authenticity of her Israeliteness... It was like my dad had explained the night before in my bedroom, about being scared about me; how finding out he hadn't known that I'd been getting in fights made him scared that there were other things he didn't know that he was supposed to know, and so now he was scared about things which I knew for a fact that he shouldn't be scared about. But no, no way, it wasn't like that. It wasn't like that at all. It was less called for than that, even. I'd found out nothing.

This was all hypothetical. Why was I getting so hypothetical? I was getting worked up about one thing in order to avoid facing another. Yes. That's what I was doing. I was thinking about June instead of thinking about Benji, who I should have been thinking about. About him and Jelly. Either they'd been together for a while in secret, or they'd only recently hooked up—or maybe they hadn't even hooked up yet; maybe they'd only been talking, flirting; maybe they'd only liked each other, loved each other—"Wherever she wants," he'd said, "I'm in love with her"—loved each other for the past couple days, which, how serious could that really be? Well but actually, well, so... Yes so maybe very serious, but that wasn't the point... It wasn't what mattered. It didn't matter. What mattered was Benji'd gotten pissed off and silent in detention on Tuesday when I cut off our conversation about conversion—He'd said, "I'm just asking," and I'd answered him, Why? *You* wanna marry me?—and then, when I gave him the stolen Coke and the passes, he'd gotten unpissed, which meant he must have decided, at that time, to believe I didn't mean it; he must have decided to believe that I didn't mean it when I'd told him that I didn't believe Gentiles could or should marry Israelites, plus all that implied, and all that seemed to imply—to imply *to him*; *seemed to imply to him*—and whether he'd been with Jelly for a while, or just a couple days, or even just a couple hours—however long it had been—he, ever since I'd given him the Coke and the passes, must have been telling himself that I didn't really mean it, that when push came to shove or worse came to worse (worse came to *worst?*) or whatever stock phrase he'd imagined best suited the occasion, I would change my beliefs—*overcome* my beliefs, is how he'd think of it—he'd thought that I would change my beliefs for practical reasons—because it isn't practical to believe that Israelites and Gentiles shouldn't be together if your best friend was a Gentile and his girlfriend an Israelite—or that I'd change my beliefs for reasons of loyalty—because it's disloyal to believe that Israelites and Gentiles shouldn't be together when your best friend's a Gentile and his girlfriend an Israelite. He'd thought. He'd thought that once I learned that he and Jelly were together, I'd be okay with it, that I'd "come around" or "see the light" or realize that what "really mattered" to me wasn't what I'd thought "really mattered" to me but what he'd thought I *should* think "really mattered" to me = Until he found out I'd doctored *Ulpan*, Benji'd thought I was just talking, all along *just talking*.

A lot of people think that about me, I thought. A lot of people believe I'm just talking. These people aren't my friends, I thought, but Benji Nakamook had been. At least he was supposed to have been.

Benji'd quit our friendship and watched me get humiliated, I thought; he had quit because I didn't believe a Gentile should marry an Israelite. Or because of what he thought that implied. And what *did* it imply? I didn't necessarily know what it implied, but that didn't matter. That was beside the point, or at least beside *my* point, so I didn't have to think about it, at least not right then. At least I thought I didn't have to think about it right then.

He quit being my friend because of what I believed. That was the point.

And I believed what I believed because I was an Israelite. That was the point.

Benji quit being my friend because I was an Israelite was the point. He wasn't scared of Slokum *at all.* He was an anti—all along, a *crypto*-anti—but except no because he loved Jelly—so a *closet* fucken crypto-anti... Whatever he was it didn't matter anymore. He wasn't my friend, had quit our friendship for no good reason, so I wasn't his. I wasn't his friend.

We were no longer friends.

And for you scholars who protest, who say, "Wait now, wait a minute. *This* was your conclusion? *Closet-crypto-anti dot-dot-dot? No longer friends?* This seems a little crazy, Rabbi, no? It seems kind of easy, kind of—how should we say it? Not Gurionic. What about what June told you, in the two-hill field? She'd said Benji was crying. Why would Nakamook have cried in the two-hill field after you'd been humiliated if he wasn't your friend? Shouldn't that, to say the least, complicate matters? Why would you not take his tears into account?"

And I tell you, good scholars, I did. I took Benji Nakamook's tears into account. I took his tears into account and rapidly dismissed them. I'd spent the six months since I'd been booted from Schechter taking all sorts of things into account that it turned out I shouldn't have. I'd spent six months positing empathetic rationales for people who'd disappointed me, six months telling myself not to be disappointed, not to feel hurt, but to be understanding. That the scholars of Schechter and Northside who'd abandoned me had done so to be good sons and daughters—I'd convinced myself of that. That their parents had to fear me to be good parents—I'd made myself understand that as well. I'd told myself I wasn't in any real trouble, nothing end-of-the-world, that the stakes were lower than they seemed to me to be, and that if ever I did face any real trouble, if push came to shove, if I was backed into a corner, caught in a pinch, if worse came to worse (worse came to *worst?*), all those who'd disappointed me would step up and... help me. Fight for me, even. They'd remember, all at once, that we were on the same side. They'd see I'd never cursed them, blamed them, mistreated them; they'd see I never thought of them the way they'd thought of me, and we would all reunite as if never divided. Except then I'd needed help. And none of them had helped me. None of them were helping me. Even the two who I'd believed were most separate from their like. First Rabbi Salt, then Emmanuel Liebmann. In rapid succession. In less than a day. And all at once it seemed I'd been offered a lesson from Adonai himself: quit counting blessings, start tallying offenses; quit providing excuses, start recognizing enmity; quit your forgiving, start bringing your vengeance. Nakamook had cried in the two-hill field? I was supposed to accept that as evidence of something good inside him? His tears were supposed to mitigate something? No. Not so. I'd been accepting too much, letting too much mitigate. I'd been acting like a Jew instead of an Israelite. When the twelve spies were sent out to scope the land of Israel, Caleb and Joshua said it was a go, and the other ten protested, saying to everyone, "Giants! Giants! There's giants down there, Amalakites and Canaanites and Jebusites and giants! We'll never be able to conquer them! They'll smite us! We're grasshoppers next to them! Grasshoppers, brothers!" and so God never let them, or anyone who believed them, into the land of Israel, and why? Because *fuck* those ten spies. Those spies were faithless. Those spies were crazy, as were all those who believed them. God took them from slavery and still they were faithless. Is that not crazy? To see God here, and not see Him there? They were crazy and they didn't deserve to live in Israel. And even crazier than that? What's even crazier, scholars, is on hearing God's curse, a curse from a God in whom they lacked faith—on hearing the curse from a God they doubted, I tell you good scholars: all those spies cried, as did all of those who'd believed them. Crazy, all of them. And so was Nakamook. Nakamook, after all, was crazy. A psycho. A bully. After all, just a crazy psycho bully. And all crazies cried, all bullies and psychos. Who knew what they cried for? Really, who knew? Not me. I wasn't one of them. I wasn't *like* one of them. And not you, scholars— you're not crazy either. So no. Just no. It just didn't matter why Nakamook cried, and so it didn't matter *that* Nakamook cried. All that really mattered was that Nakamook abandoned me. You don't abandon friends. We were no longer friends. And just as I had earlier, just a couple hours earlier, on returning from the first of Thursday's two two-hill-field abandonments, I felt relief. Things felt a lot simpler. Things felt like this: Fuck him, fuck them, fuck it all, it's done.

And I pressed all my fingers against all my fingers and none of my fingers would break.

Benji was still grandstanding next to his chair. "No one else?" he said to all the Cage. "All this whispering about the side of this and the side of that and none of the rest of you wants to step up against the Monitor in solidarity? Not one of the rest of you has anything to say?"

The Side of Damage was more loyal to me than even I was—they'd been through with Benji since the moment they realized he wasn't helping me on the high hill. And now they were all looking to me. It was just like the end of Group on Tuesday, except there were more of them. They were waiting for me to teach them something. They were waiting for me to show them what to do.

I revolved my chair and faced forward in my carrel.

All of us did.

Not a minute later, I heard a chair scoot, followed by Jelly yelling, "Don't!"

Everyone turned again.

"Now give me a pass to the nurse lest this piddling wound grow fatal with infection," said Benji to Botha. A black bic pen pinned his t-shirt to the flesh beneath his bottom right rib. The shirt was a light blue. When Jelly pulled the pen out, the stain the blood made was lavender. She fainted for a second, falling forward onto Benji, who caught her with a wince, and for a second, yes, I did wish I could hang out with them, but only for a second. Or maybe ten seconds.

Botha wrote passes and sent them to the nurse.

15
TACTICAL

Thursday, November 16, 2006
6th Period—End of Schoolday

J ust before the end of sixth, Eliyahu returned to the Cage with a note. Small cuts were swelling below both his eyes, and some cotton plugged a nostril, but he'd quit the lean of the determined professor and acquired a menacing slouch. Head tipped to the left, he gave the note to Botha, then started toward my carrel, arms straight at his sides like holstered police batons, barely shifting and stiff.

"Sit down, Aye-lie," Botha said, as he read the note.

Eliyahu got taller and taller.

"Note says you're wanted in the owfice, Make-bee—I said sit down, Aye-lie."

"I need to talk to you," Eliyahu said to me. Up close I saw that his tzitzit were mud-caked, his fedora in tatters. Its felt was all matted and the crown bore a pattern of tiny dents that matched the tread on the Co-Captain's Jordans. The hatband was gone. "Forgive me," he whispered, "for yelling."

"What dad I jes' say," said Botha.

Eliyahu shot a glance at Ben-Wa Wolf, who scooted his chair.

And half the Side of Damage began to hyperscoot.

Eliyahu urged the other half on. He raised an arm overhead and beckoned nonchalantly, almost lazily, as if this were the ten-thousandth hyperscoot he'd captained that week. A black ribbon tied around his elbow—the one that used to band his hat—flapped pennant-like.

Botha went to the nearest chair—Stevie Loop's—and stilled it. The rest of the hyperscoot continued.

"I want you to know!" Eliyahu shouted into my ear, "that I was given an in-school suspension, but I told Brodsky nothing of your part in the fight!"

You would never do that! I shouted back.

Botha moved on to still Renne Feldbons's chair, and Stevie Loop started scooting again. Lang and Wadrow were covering their ears. They were not amused this time.

"I am nonetheless verklempt!" Eliyahu shouted. "What I do not understand! Is why you protected those five boys who yelled 'Death to the Jew'! Why you said to me 'Don't hurt them!' It makes me very uncomfortable!"

The Five are Israelites! I shouted.

"Now I am especially verklempt!" shouted Eliyahu.

The teachers hated the noise so much, their eyes were closed.

I pulled Mr. Goldblum's copy of *Ulpan* from my pocket and pressed it into Eliyahu's hand.

Read it! I told him. I'll explain more later!

He spun to face the Side of Damage and the hyperscoot stopped.

"None of you's—" said Botha. The end-of-class tone sounded. "None of you's going to the pap relly tomarra."

"That's a good one," said Ronrico. "If by good you mean great," said Ben-Wa Wolf, "and great means an ingenius way to punish us without all the paperwork."

Making their way to the gate, Lang and Wadrow shook their heads at Botha = "You are a fuckup." He let them out, keeping his eyes on the pass he was writing for me, pretending to ignore all of us. There was little else he could do. It was a passing-period and no one was hitting anyone. No one was even cursing.

"Forty'd be a lot of CASS's to write," said the Janitor. "A lotta testimony against us." "A lotta hard evidence that you've lost control of your students and Brodsky should replace you." "So let it be unwritten that it may remain undone." "All that pep will be wasted on the already peppy while we sit in the Cage, lamenting our lack of pep." "We need that pep." "We need a rally to inspire it."

"Make-bee," said Botha, waving the pass at me. "Go. To. The. Owfice."

Why? I said.

"I already told you."

So tell me again.

"Note your frand brought," Botha said to me, "says you're wanted in the owfice."

What's a frand? I said.

Botha chewed his face.

"We don't get to see enough serious high-fiving between basketballers, Mr. Botha." "We don't get to see enough Jennys stacked in pyramids." "Or hear enough words get spelled out with clapping." "The special way the words sometimes sound like swears but aren't, even though they really are." "Double-entendres." "Homonyms." "Spelled-out homonyms cleverly masking double-entendres." "With clapping."

"Make-bee!" said Botha. "Go to the owfice!"

"We don't get to see enough Desormie in a tight suit, either." "His love of cheerleading." "His gameday tent of finest gabardine." "And don't forget about the music!" "You're gonna make us miss the Boystar."

The air vibrated on my right: Mookus was crying.

I flashed my palm at the Side of Damage.

Some of them didn't see.

"We won't get to be in his video now!" "Shucks! Aw shucks!" "And he'll probably win a Grammy." "Word on the street's he's next year's favorite for best female vocal—"

Hey! I said.

The Cage went quiet.

To Main Man I said, You'll be fine.

"Okay," he said. He kept crying.

"Go to the Owfice, Make-bee."

"You'll be fine, Main Man," said Vincie.

"Go to the—" said Botha, cut off by the beginning-of-class tone.

I decided to give him a chance to be decent. I got up from my carrel and went to the gate—I didn't even do a three-count—and when I stepped into C-Hall, I said, Tell Main Man he can go to the pep rally.

I said it quiet so that no one could hear, so Botha wouldn't lose any face for acting decent, so being decent wouldn't feel like a defeat.

"No," he said.

□   □   □   □   □   □   □

As I approached the mouth of 2-Hall, spacing out on dead-end thoughts about who'd ratted me to Brodsky, Call-Me-Sandy turned the corner into C. She had to pull her fingers from her cardigan's buttonholes to wave hello.

"I'm sorry, Gurion," she said.

Why? I said.

"You must have been waving at me forever."

You waved at me first, I said.

"Oh, I'm sorry."

Don't be, I said.

"I'm—I guess I'm just feeling a little jumpy," she said. "Distracted. That false alarm. Rattled my bag of caramels, right? Or so you might say... because of how you put it when last we—"

Sure, I said.

"Right," she said. "And now I tell myself I'm going for a drink of water, but in fact the destination's arbitrary. I'm on a disguised amble. I tell myself, 'Sandy, you're taking a walk to get a drink of water,' but the truth is I'm not even thirsty. It's just the water fountain's the first destination that came to mind."

Why can't you just take a walk? I said.

"Because that would be a blatant, undisguised amble and it would defeat it's own purpose: I'd know I was taking a walk because I was jumpy, and so I'd be thinking about my jumpiness, which would only make me jumpier."

But you *do* know you're taking a walk because you're jumpy, I said. You just told me that.

Her fingers slid back into her buttonholes. "It's not kind, what you're doing. Undermining my healing strategy."

I wasn't trying to undermine your healing strategy, I said.

"Well, that's what you were doing."

There was nothing worth saying in response, so I made her high-five me, and then I made her high-five me again, and she laughed a syllable and I got away fast, thinking: Rat. Thinking: Deadkid. If Brodsky had seen me in the fight himself, I'd've been brought to the Office with the others.

I took a left at Main Hall, which was mostly empty—just a couple or three late kids speedwalking. Jerry in his booth to pass-flash at. WE DAMAGE WE bombs were everywhere: scraped, Darkered, pencilled, lipsticked. Too many of them to count accurately while walking at a leisurely pace, too many for the Side of Damage to have written all of them. I wasn't sure what to think of that. At first it seemed completely good. The bombs weren't just enacting damage—which, dayenu—they were actually inciting it.

But then I had to wonder what the taggers who weren't on the Side of Damage believed their WE DAMAGE WEs signified. I had to wonder how many of them, if any, had even heard of the Side of Damage, and whether that mattered.

If the taggers hadn't heard of the Side of Damage, and enough of them got in the habit of bombing WE DAMAGE WE, then soon—in the way of the Indian swastika, say—the bomb could stop signifying the Side of Damage. It could end up signifying whatever those who planted it decided it signified.

If the taggers *had* heard of the Side of Damage, and *thought* they knew what it was, and *intended* the tags to signify the Side of Damage, then that meant the taggers considered themselves members—or at the very least allies—of the Side of Damage. Which might or might not be good: it depended who the taggers were. If, for example, they were part of Momo and Beauregard's Big Ending, that would be fine, but if they were Main Hall Shovers or basketballers or singers of the rhyme of my bus-stop, that might not be fine. It was hard to decide.

Yes, a WE DAMAGE WE tagged by a Main Hall Shover would, for now at least, damage the Arrangement exactly as well as a WE DAMAGE WE tagged by anyone who was actually on the Side of Damage, but if Main Hall Shovers went around signifying the Side of Damage, others would come to think the Side of Damage was made up partially of Main Hall Shovers, which it wasn't. No Main Hall Shover was one of us, and no Main Hall Shover would ever be one of us. If I let Main Hall Shovers join the Side of Damage, it wouldn't be the Side of Damage anymore. We'd just be another part of the Arrangement.

Then again, maybe it wasn't so bad if people who weren't on our side—even, and maybe especially, our enemies—thought they were. At the rate the bombs were spreading, I'd have to decide soon.

I passed a pink nail-polished *EMOTIONALIZE* under the instructions on the glass of a firehose case, and though I knew I didn't write it, I wasn't sure Benji hadn't. He could have done it on his way from the Cage to see me in Nurse Clyde's, just before we stopped being friends. Though the color of the nail-polish made the *EMOTIONALIZE* seem devotional, it could have been a Nakamookian joke for my benefit. He could have been feeling arch. Maybe he'd planned to tell me he'd written it only after I told him I'd seen it; or maybe he'd planned to never admit to it, like with his authorship of the "pee so pungent" saying. Then again, it might not have been a joke at all. Maybe he'd wanted to inspire Jennys to vandalism and figured it would seem more heartfelt if he spoke to them in glossy pink.

Although this pink *EMOTIONALIZE* would have marked a kind of victory for the Side of Damage if it had been written by a Jenny—and it probably had been—the thought of Nakamook being clever enough to urge Jennys on with pink nail polish was far more thrilling. But why should I have been thrilled at all about Nakamook's cleverness if he was no longer my friend? I shouldn't have been. And I definitely shouldn't have been *more* thrilled about it than about a Jenny's transformation into a vandal, yet still I *was* more thrilled, out of habit—the habit of admiring Nakamook. It was poison to think of him, and thinking it was poison didn't make it any less poison.

Rat, I thought. Deadkid. Think about *that*. Someone got Brodsky to call you to the Office. Someone was a rat. Someone was dead.

Through the sound-resistant glass, I saw Brodsky was standing in front of Pinge's desk. I entered the Office.

"Gurion," Miss Pinge said.

"Gurion indeed." Brodsky revolved and set his hand on my shoulder. "Gurion Maccabee," he said. He was smiling.

Then we were sitting across his desk from each other, the wingnut I'd given him centered on his blotter. It didn't seem like I was in trouble, but I hadn't forgotten Tuesday afternoon—the way he'd outgamed me—and so I stayed cautious.

"Why do you like wingnuts?" Brodsky said.

I said, They hold as well as hexnuts, but you don't need a tool to fasten them; just your fingers.

"Fasten them?" he said. "Or unfasten them?" he said. He winked for some reason. He said, "Either way." Then he rested his pointers on the wingnut's wings, pressed, spun it. "I believe that you are partially responsible for this sudden rash of vandalism," he said. Just like that. "However, I know you aren't entirely responsible—you couldn't be. There are hundreds of instances by now, and a large portion of them occurred while you were in ISS yesterday. I'm not going to ask you who else was responsible because I know you won't answer me."

You're just expelling me, I said.

"No," he said. He said, "I don't believe that'll solve anything. Why must everything be so extreme with you, Gurion? You're not in any trouble and I am not threatening you with any trouble. I want to have a conversation with you. Can we have a conversation?"

I won't tell on anybody, I said.

"I won't ask you to."

We can try to have a conversation then, I said.

"You have a very powerful influence over some of your fellow students," he said, "particularly the ones who are vandalizing our school, pulling fire alarms, getting into fights. Deny it to me all you want, I believe you know it's true."

I didn't say anything.

"I want all this trouble to stop. I suspect that you want that as well. At least some of it."

I didn't say anything.

"Those five boys who fought with Eliyahu and Shlomo told me that you tried to break up the fight. I am proud of you for doing that."

Be proud of Eliyahu, too, then, I said. I said, Revoke his ISS.

"Eliyahu," said Brodsky, "was not trying to break up that fight. He was trying to harm those five boys. They said something he objected to, something he wouldn't repeat, and he tried to harm them—he told me that himself. The other two—Bryan Maholtz and Billy Baxter—they were the only ones who claimed to have been doing anything noble, but looking at the bruises on Eliyahu's face, anyone could have seen they were lying. All eight of them will be in ISS tomorrow, and Shlomo Cohen as well, if he recovers enough to return to school."

I said, If you were Eliyahu, and you'd believed what he believed, you would have done the same thing he did. You would have had to.

"I am glad you are a friend to Eliyahu," said Brodsky. "He is in a very sensitive place right now. He will be for quite a while. And I urge you to continue to be a friend to him. I also urge you to consider the influence you have on him, to take into account that his mistakes, as those of so many others in the past few days, are at least partially being made to impress you. You have sway, Gurion. You have power that teachers and principals don't have, power that teachers and principals *can't* have. I want you to use that power to better ends. I believe you broke up that fight because you want the same thing. That's why you're not in trouble right now. I want to give you a clean slate. I want to offer you the opportunity to be good."

I am good, I said.

"I want to offer you the opportunity to *act* like you are good."

You want me to make your job easier, I said.

"When you put it that way, you make it sound conniving. If you do what I'm asking, my job will become easier, but that's not why I'm asking you to do it. I want you to improve yourself and I want you to see that improving yourself will improve those around you. You will find it satisfying, Gurion. You have my word. And yes, I will find it satisfying too, but not because it makes my job easier. I took this job because I care about the world and I believe that the better children are educated, the better the world becomes. Children cannot be well-educated in an unsafe environment. I want you to help me make Aptakisic safer because I want the world to be better. Don't you want a better world?"

Get rid of the Cage, I said. I said, If you get rid of the Cage, a lot less kids will act like they spend their days in a cage.

"That's Jerusalem you're asking for. The district requires we have a lock-down program."

So have a lockdown program, but don't put anyone in it, I said.

"That wouldn't fly."

Fire Botha, I said. I said, Hire a monitor who isn't a schmuck.

"Mr. Botha can be a hard man to deal with, I know, but we've had worse in the past. I'll tell you the truth: his job's not a terribly desirable one. Those who want it... It takes a certain kind of personality."

I said, So you won't do anything. I said, You want me to act different, but you won't do anything different.

"I am reaching out to you, Gurion. I'm not bargaining."

I said, Botha banned us from the pep rally, the whole Side—the whole Cage.

Brodsky said, "Why?"

It wasn't to make the school safer for the benefit of better education, I said.

"I can't undermine his authority, Gurion. If he's suspended your pep rally privileges... that's within his power."

What about Scott Mookus?

"What about him?"

I said, He's supposed to sing with Boystar at the pep rally.

"And he will."

Won't that undermine Botha's authority?

"Mr. Botha said *Scott Mookus* couldn't go to the pep rally?" said Brodsky.

Everyone, I said.

He spun the wingnut a couple times. He wanted to let Main Man sing, but something was making him hesitate, and I realized it was exactly what he'd claimed. He really *didn't* want to undermine Botha's authority. He believed in Botha's authority. Believed it was good that Botha had author-ity. As wrong and arranged as he was, Brodsky was trying to be ethical. The choice to override Botha and let Main Man sing was actually the *easier* choice, here; Brodsky was Botha's boss and Botha was as much Brodsky's sycophant as any of the other robots. Whatever Brodsky would do, Botha would not complain. The Boystar people, though—the parents and the Chaz and the shotframer; all of them but for Boystar himself… If Mookus wasn't allowed to be in the video after all the preparations *those* sleazebombs had made, after all the money they'd already invested ("the best acoustics man in the business," etc.), they *would* complain. Loudly. Yet Brodsky was willing to suffer them, if that was the ethical choice…

Not that it impressed me so very much. It is not impressive when people try to do what they believe is right. It is only right. Yet I was a little surprised.

Still, what Brodsky suspected was right *wasn't* right. Main Man did *not* deserve the brunt of Botha's collective punishment. He didn't deserve anyone's punishment. Anyone who punished him deserved punishment. The severest.

One time I asked my father what he looked for in potential jurors during the selection process. He told me, "Ethics," a much simpler answer than I had expected. I'd thought that he would've laid out a matrix: X-type juror for Y-type client in Z-type dispute, B-type juror for C-type client in D-type dispute. And so on. But he said, "Ethics," and for a second I thought he was making a reference to that movie *Miller's Crossing* that he loves, and I chuckled, and he told me, "Ethical people—even those whose systems of ethics may appear hideous—can, by their very nature, be reasoned with. And I, boychical, am a very, very reasonable man." And then *he* chuckled. I still don't know what that chuckle was about. Maybe he'd just caught himself being cocky, or maybe he hadn't meant what he'd said at all and thought it was funny that I seemed to believe him. Maybe he really did want me to believe the world was a place where there were enough ethical men to fill juryboxes, but knew I doubted it. It was a back-of-the-throat, possibly arch, likely uncomfortable, nearly atypical Father-type chuckle, but whatever it indicated, the idea that ethical people were inherently reasonable seemed like it made sense.

And so to Brodsky I said, I bet Maholtz and the Co-Captain and Shlomo get to go to the pep rally, even though they've got ISS.

"Everyone in ISS tomorrow will go to the pep rally," said Brodsky, "but that decision belongs to me, not Mr. Botha—I'm the one who gave them their ISS's."

He was certainly using reason.

Fair enough, I said, but where are Maholtz and the Co-Captain gonna sit? Are they gonna sit with Eliyahu and the other five?

"I hadn't thought about it. I suppose, though, that they'll sit with their teammates."

They'll get special treatment, I said.

"Well—"

Not because they deserve it, though, I said, but because the school deserves it, right? The school deserves to have a look at every one of their basketballers at the pep rally. The school deserves to have a proper pep rally. Especially after all the panic from that false alarm. The school needs to heal.

"Something like that," he said, leaning over his desk a little = "Go on."

I said, Even though the special treatment might be unfair to the others in ISS, it would be unfair to everyone else at Aptakisic if that special treatment weren't granted. So it's *unfair to the few* vs. *unfair to the many*. You do the math and the choice becomes obvious.

And this time he said it: "Go on," he said.

The plan is for Scott to sing with Boystar, I said. I said, This morning, that Tanya Volleyball person announced there'd be a special guest. Most people don't know it's gonna be Scott. They're expecting someone famous. Instead they're gonna get a retarded kid. You knew all of that, and you planned it that way; to keep the special guest a secret. You must have figured it was good for the school. Maybe it's a little manipulative—get their hopes up, sink them suddenly, and then they're thrilled beyond they're wildest imaginings because it turns out the elfy-looking boy is a great singer... And after about six notes, they're gonna decide to be nice to this boy, and respect him for having talent, and maybe think twice about being cruel to other retarded people, of which the world has a great many. Yet none of that happens if, to be fair to Botha, you don't let Scott sing. So it's *unfair to Botha* vs. *unfair to the whole world.*

Brodsky spun the wingnut.

"I'll let him sing. We'll have to work out another punishment for him, though."

I said, That's very reasonable of you, Mr. Brodsky.

"I'm glad you think so. You see how far you get with me when you talk like a mensch? Now consider what I've asked of you, okay?"

I let the mensch thing slide.

I said, I'll consider it.

"And that's reasonable of *you*," he said.

Reasonable of you, John. Reasonable of *you*, Dick. No two Israelites had ever pattered so goyischely.

By the time Miss Pinge started writing my pass, I'd finished considering. And this is what I decided: Brodsky had only been flattering me. If he really believed I had as much sway as he said—and I did, regardless of what he thought—he would have been willing to bargain.

□ □ □ □ □ □ □

Call-Me-Sandy hadn't returned to the C-Hall water fountain.

"I never left," she cried.

She cried like a television beauty. Her breathing wasn't sniffly, just deep and sudden, and she didn't make any choked sounds. Her bright blue eyes were much brighter wet, and when she wiped at them with the hand that wasn't on the button, her sleeve, rather than sopping up the tears, spread them all over her face.

I thought about hugging her, but then I thought it would just make her cry more and I didn't want her to cry more.

She chinned the air at the I EXPLODE Benji'd Darkered in the basin, and said, "I think this water fountain might explode if I take my finger off the button. Don't smile about it."

It's not a bomb, I said.

"I was calling out for help, and no one would help me," she said. "At first I was just waiting for Floyd to come by, but—"

He's roving, I said, and the water fountain's not a bomb.

"He didn't come by, and after a while I gave up and started calling out, but no one would help me. I started having crazy thoughts. I started thinking that maybe I was so lost in my own thoughts that the schoolday had actually ended without my noticing, and no one was around anymore."

I said, It's just C-Hall. The doorways are sound-buffers. No one heard you. And it's just past three, which means school hasn't ended.

It meant something else, too—what did it mean, though, just past three?

"I know that," she said. "I know what *time* it is. But I started having the thought that the day had ended, and it was crazy. It was a crazy thought to have, and I recognized that, and I thought, 'This water fountain's not a bomb—that's just another crazy thought you're having, Sandy,' but that didn't comfort me at all—"

Because for a little while you believed the crazy thought about the schoolday ending, I said, and if you weren't able to distinguish the crazy thoughts from the normal thoughts at one point in time, who's to say you could do so at any other? Not you. It wouldn't be rigorous. So maybe the thought of the water fountain being a bomb isn't crazy at all. Maybe it only seems crazy. And plus even if it is a crazy thought—in fact, *especially* if it's crazy, and you're not normally crazy—then might not your craziness attest to the water fountain bomb being real?

"Right," she said. "Because my—"

Because why, if you aren't usually crazy, would you get suddenly crazy? There would probably be a reason.

"Intuition," she said.

I said, Maybe you're highly attuned right now. I said, Maybe your intuition is telling you something. It's never told you much before, and you never really even believed in intuition, but that could be all the more reason to believe in it right now. This moment could be exceptional because it could be a life-and-death one, and maybe, right before a person dies, they acquire—by unknown means—the knowledge that they're about to die. Maybe right before someone dies, they intuit their death—maybe that's how it is for everyone. And maybe some of them scoff at the intuition because they don't believe in intuition, but then maybe others don't—it's not a thing that we can know. But maybe the intuition is God telling you something loud and clear—telling you you're about to die—maybe He's telling you as a sort of courtesy, so you can think pretty last thoughts, say goodbye to the world in your heart of hearts, send a message telepathically to your loved ones which, at the moment of your death, will cause a change in the air surrounding them, and they'll either think something of it because they believe in intuition or think nothing of it because they don't believe in intuition—maybe God is loudly and clearly telling you you're about to die, but you don't necessarily believe what He's telling you because His language isn't concise, or maybe His language is so concise that it doesn't even seem like language, and that's why you doubt it came from outside of you. Maybe the only reason you'd even *think* to doubt that you're about to die by exploding water fountain is that God speaks so concisely that when you hear Him, it's as if He simply planted an idea in your head, a feeling in your chest—maybe His language is so concise, so perfectly convincing, that it doesn't even seem to *communicate* the messages it communicates—so concise and convincing that the thoughts and feelings His messages stir are incited *instantaneously*, making it seem as though the messages have come from *within* you. Or you might be crazy. But I'm telling you you're not about to die.

"This *school* has gone crazy. All these kids throwing scarves. All these tags on the walls, that false alarm. The way you spoke to me in session today—what's predictable around here anymore?"

I suddenly remembered what just past three meant. The verdict on Drucker v. Wilmette had been read, or at least it was about to be. A victory for hatred; no, for civil rights. A victory for both. Whatever it meant, my father had won—he had to have won; he always won—and now he knew he won, or at least he was about to know, and now he could relax, for a couple days at least, so I let myself be happy for a second, and it showed.

"You think I'm being *funny*?" Call-Me-Sandy said. "I thought we were—"

No, I said. No, I said. Look: I'll stand here with you while you take your thumb off the button.

"So what?"

That's how sure I am the water fountain's not a bomb, I said.

"That's how sure *you* are, Gurion? You don't believe you can die. You think you're the messiah."

I don't think I'm the messiah, I said.

"I read your Step 4 and 5 assignments," she said.

I said, All those say is I think I might become the messiah.

"Do you hear yourself? Please just go to the Office and have Mr. Brodsky call the police."

I said, I know who wrote the I EXPLODE on the water fountain. I saw him do it and he didn't plant any bomb.

"And it just so happens that the water fountain doesn't work," she said.

I said, I saw the water fountain get broken, too.

"You saw a whole lot of things."

You think I'm lying? I said.

"Why wouldn't you have told me those things to begin with?"

I didn't think about it, I said.

"Or maybe you're still angry at me about the paper and you want me to die. Or maybe you're just so confident you're right that you're willing to pretend you saw things you didn't see. Just please just go to the Office."

I said, If Brodsky catches you like this, he won't let you work here any-more. And then what'll happen at the University of Chicago? I can't help you get kicked out of here.

"You're such a friend all of a sudden."

I'm kind of a friend, I said.

"A friend would comfort me in my distress, Gurion, even a 'kind of' friend. And whichever one he was, he wouldn't argue with me about why I shouldn't be distressed."

I thought about hugging you, I said. I said, It was the first thought I had, but then I thought it would just make you cry more.

"So what?" she said. "What if I do cry more? Sometimes people have to cry. That doesn't mean you have to be cold."

So I hugged Call-Me-Sandy.

She hugged me back one-armed, my right temple against her left breast, bigger and softer than I'd have thought. And she smelled sparkly, Sandy, not like baby powder or laundry detergent—she smelled like expensive hairspray.

My hands were under her cardigan, pressing on her damp cotton blouse, the strap of her bra poking my wrists. My hands weren't underneath out of perviness—it was accidental, and when I noticed I removed them. I set my right one on her back, outside the cardigan, and with my left, I took hold of her right wrist and pulled. Her thumb came off the water fountain button and she shoved me in the chest.

Hey, I said.

"You should have convinced me first," she said.

I said, I tried.

⬜ ⬜ ⬜ ⬜ ⬜ ⬜ ⬜

The schoolday proper was almost over. Nakamook and Jelly weren't in the Cage, and I doubted they'd be back before the last tone. Benji had a lot of hall-passes left, so no one would catch them out at ditching, at least not for the rest of the afternoon, and even if they got in trouble the next day—if Botha spoke to Nurse Clyde once school let out, say, and discovered Clyde had sent the two back to the Cage—who wouldn't be willing to serve detention, or even ISS, to hide out with someone he loves, kissing? Especially when the alternative was to sit in a room full of people who'd disappointed him. No,

I thought, they wouldn't return, and that was fine with me. It was. It was fine. I might've wanted him to suffer, but I didn't particularly want to see it.

When I got to my carrel, I said Main Man's name, and Monitor Botha tried to shout me down. "Make—!" was all he could manage before the hyperscoot thundered.

At the cluster, Mr. Voltz and Mrs. Sepper clutched their heads like boxers doing crunches.

I allowed the noise to rage for thirty seconds, during which time the monitor stilled no chair—he didn't even try—and then, at waist-level, I flashed my palm, and all at once the Side of Damage was quiet.

I said, My Main Man Scott—

Botha said, "Sit—!"

And I hid my hand in the pocket of my hoodie—I'd thought first to show a fist, but then figured I'd have to keep showing it til I wanted the Side to stop, which wouldn't be stealth, and plus it was hammy; *ham-fisted*, I thought—and a hyperscoot erupted.

At first, Mr. Voltz and Mrs. Sepper just clutched their heads as they had the last time, but soon they were mouthing the word "Please" at me = "Despite your efforts to be stealth, we know it's you who's in charge, Gurion."

So when I showed my palm after a minute of hiding it, I held it high and didn't drop it.

As soon as it was quiet, Botha said, "Make-bee—"

This time it was Voltz who shut him down. "Let him talk, Victor. Please. They can do this all day."

"It's a mutation!" said the Flunky.

No one corrected him.

"We're going deaf," Mrs. Sepper said.

"I mean a mutilation!" said the Flunky.

"Allow him to speak, Mr. Botha," said Voltz.

Botha didn't know if he should shrug at the teachers to signify the reluctance of his obeidance, or wave them off to prove he could defy them. So he shrugged, and then he waved them off. And then he shrugged while waving them off.

I said, My Main Scott Mookus will sing at the pep rally tomorrow.

"Is it true, Gurion?" said Scott.

"No," said Botha. "In fect, it's nothing like—"

I dropped my hand.

Hyperscoot. A solid two minutes. The duration of this one was arbitrary, though. I would have let it last for however long it took the teachers to snap.

I thought Sepper would be the first, but it was Voltz who rose from the cluster. He stalked over to Botha and pointed a finger. As he opened his mouth, I showed my palm.

"—is wrong with you?" Voltz accused at the tops of his lungs. Then, more quietly: "They've been doing this all period. Every time, it's in response to you. Can't you see that?"

"Can't you see that!" Mrs. Sepper said. She slapped the cluster hard, both hands, then shook out the skin-sting. She was actually crying. "Please stop," she said to me.

It's deafening for us, too, I told her. Still, I said, if I don't get the last word, all our ears will ring til kingdom come.

"Fine," said Mrs. Sepper.

I know it's fine with you, I said.

"It's fine with me and Mr. Botha, too," said Mr. Voltz.

That's when Botha started to giggle.

I did a silent three-count, then stood on my chair.

He wants us to look at him, I said to the Cage. Monitor Botha. He wants us to look at him and see that he's smiling. He wants us to hear him—to hear that he's giggling. We should, we should look at him. Look at him giggling. Look at him now. We know what that's like, to giggle like the monitor. We've done it ourselves. All of us have done it. We get stepped for this, we get stepped for that, we giggle—why? We just got caught. Getting caught isn't funny, getting stepped isn't pleasant, why do we giggle? Embarrassment? Shame? No. We're not embarrassed. We're not slightly ashamed. We're angry. Angry. We took measures in order not to get caught, and now we've been caught, and it makes us angry, but now that we're caught, and now that we're angry, what can we do? What can we do that we'd want to do? What is there to do that we want to do that won't get us in deeper trouble? Nothing. And now that we're caught, we're being watched; watched more than before. Watched ever closer. And so we giggle. We might as well dance, though. We might as well waltz with invisible partners. We might as well cha-cha. We might as well sneeze. What we do, though, is giggle. We giggle and hope it looks dangerous, tough. We giggle to say, 'You can't fire me because I quit. You may have won the battle but the war isn't over.' We giggle to suggest that getting caught doesn't matter. We giggle and hope that the one for whom we giggle begins to suspect that we *planned* for him to catch us. 'Curses! Foiled again!' we hope he thinks. We hope he thinks, 'No, oh no, oh no; it seems I've just played right into their hands. Oh dear, what's up their sleeve? What exactly is up this giggling person's sleeve that allows them to giggle even though I just caught them?' But listen, let's be honest: when we're giggling, caught, our sleeves are empty, we don't have bubkes, we know we've been fired, and even though it's true that all we lost was a battle, we also lost the last one, soon we'll lose the next, and what's more is the war won't ever end. We know that. Don't we? We do. We know. All we're doing by giggling is trying to save face, and all we do when we try to save face so blatantly is lose more face. And all of us know this, but we keep on doing it. Giggling when caught. Leaking precious snat. Caulking the cracks. We know it, but we hope that others might not. I'm telling you they do, though. I do. You do. Above all: he does, Monitor Botha. Look at him now. Have a long look. Have a good listen. Look at him smiling and listen to him giggling. I'm not saying 'Curses! Foiled again!' Nor am I thinking it. Neither are you. I'm not getting worried what he's got up his sleeve. I'm certain that none of this is part of his plan. Look at the beaten monitor, soldiers. Smiling, giggling. He looks to us just like we have to him on all those occasions where he caught us and we giggled. For *that* be ashamed. For *that* be embarrassed. No more of this giggling for us, I said. No more.

"No more."

No more getting caught.

They said, "No more."

Good, I said. And no more of this giggling or getting caught means no more trying to get away with things. You can only get caught if you're trying to get away, so from this moment on, we don't try to get away—we get and we get and then we get more.

"Get," they said.

We get, I said. We've already gotten. We've gotten with hyperscoot, and we'll get more with hyperscoot. Hyperscoot alone's not enough, though. And too much hyperscoot will make hyperscoot useless. They'll figure out a way soon enough to prevent it—thicker carpeting, sound-eating walls, friction-reducing caps on the chair-feet... They'll figure out a way, and the more we use hyperscoot, the faster they'll figure it. So we'll use it sparingly. We only need it sparingly. We know we are on the same side, now, I said, and so does the monitor. We don't have to keep proving it. Hyperscoot, soldiers, is just the beginning. The beginning ends now, and now it's time for the middle. The middle is quiet, *always* quiet. The middle is where we decide what to do with the strength we've gathered. The middle—

His claw flailing weirdly, almost epileptically, Botha, who still hadn't ceased to giggle, interruptively slapped his khakied thigh—*slap!*—with his five-fingered hand and, at twice the volume of his spectacle thusfar, expelled a long series of cough-gasped syllables intended to resemble howling laughter. Soldiers gripped their seats, dug their heels in the carpet. Voltz and Sepper stuck their pointers in their ears. I showed the Side my palm, not wanting them to miss this—I didn't want to miss this. I wanted us to witness his face going snatless.

Pay attention to the monitor, I said to the Side. He's bleeding out. He's got a big punchline. He wants us to cue his big punchline, I said.

They un-dug their heels, loosened their grips. Sepper and Voltz dropped their hands to their sides. All looked to Botha, who said to the teachers: "Thinks he's Morc—thinks—boy thinks he's Morc Antney!"

Sepper bit her lip. Voltz sucked his cheeks. No one on the Side had ever read Shakespeare.

"That's not his last name," said Salvador Curtis.

"He doesn't even *got* one," Mark Dingle agreed. "Why would he have one? He doesn't even *need* one. Dude's *from Ork.*"

Most of the Side had never seen *Mork and Mindy*, but "Ork" sounded funny, so some of them smiled.

Botha's howling crashed on a "Tch" and ebbed. His grin went sneer and the sneer went purse-lipped, became another grin—saggy at the corners but a grin nonetheless—and the giggles that pushed through his husk of a face were made only of air now, purest breath, quick swishy sniffs and staccato exhalations; even his vocal cords refused to cooperate.

Pay attention to the monitor, I said to the Side. Always remember the monitor, I said. Always remember that you used to be like him. Understand that you could be like him again. All it takes is a giggle. *Listen* to that giggle. How hollow it is. Just so much quick breathing. He is caulking a face behind which is *nothing*. He doesn't have a drop of snat left to trickle, and yet even as I speak of the Side of Damage, of the gathering of strength and the need for decisions, the giggle keeps shaking him, the grin keeps twisting him. Does he not believe the Side of Damage exists? He acts like he thinks he's humoring us, no? Maybe he does. Maybe he thinks that. I speak as if I know he's pretending, but maybe he's even more desperate than I thought. Maybe he isn't pretending at all. I've been talking in very certain terms about him, but the truth is, I don't know what he's thinking. At least not exactly. None of us do. At least not exactly. He might really believe that he's humoring us, soldiers. It's not within my power or yours to know. It's not within anyone's power but his. Some things are like that. Secrets forever. Look at baby smile. Baby smiles baby happy? Or baby just gassy? Maybe baby happy *because* baby gassy, right?

Leevon Ray burped.

Half the Side of Damage burped.

The other half tried, but didn't know how.

Botha's giggling had stopped, but the grin stayed in place.

Whether Botha, I said, is pretending or not, full of happy gas or just full of gas, convinced that he's humoring us or faking his conviction, I say we're better off assuming that he isn't pretending. We are better off believing he *does* think I speak now at his discretion, that he *is* confusing fleeting stalemate for victory, and middle for end, and our threat for submission. We are better off believing he thinks he's letting *us* save face. So let us let the monitor be with his thoughts, whatever they are. Let us let him believe whatever he believes. If he knows our strength, he knows we own him; if he doesn't, we're underestimated, and that works too. Main Man will sing at tomorrow's pep rally, and tomorrow we'll be stronger than we are today. We'll see tomorrow if Botha's still grinning. As for today: Today's almost over, and a few minutes back I made a contract with the robots. I told them their ears would ring til kingdom come if they didn't allow me to have the last word. When I made that contract, was I speaking for you?

"Yes!" the Side shouted.

Do I speak for you still?

"Yes!" it shouted.

Will you make us a liar?

No! we shouted.

There are fifteen minutes left in the schoolday, I said. That's fifteen minutes before the no-hyperscoot contract ends. As long as the robots keep to the terms, the contract is ours to keep or to break. I say let us keep it. Let us honor the contract because our word is good. And so that no one may be mistaken, so that no one may think that we honor it out of fear of what the monitor might be hiding inside of his head, so that everyone will know that we honor it because we choose to, because our word is good, let us honor the contract *beyond* its demands. Let us be like the sweetest dream of the Arrangement. Let us be as the Cage has never been able to make us. Let us now all at once face forward in our boxes, still and silent as nightmares.

We did.

16
NAMES

Thursday, November 16, 2006
Interim–Intramural Bus

"What they meant was death to *the idea* of the Jew is what you're telling me," said Eliyahu of Brooklyn.

Pretty much, I said.

We were speaking Hebrew. At the end-of-class tone, the Side of Damage had lined up single-file and silent, gone out the gate one at a time, not one of them running or shouting til they'd stepped over the threshhold. I'd been last in line, Eliyahu just in front of me. Now we were weaving our way through Main Hall. I wanted to go find June at her locker.

"So the Jew of their rallying cry," said Eliyahu, "wasn't this Shlomo person, but some kind of abstract Jew for whom the Shlomo person stood."

Could've been, I said. It was ambiguous. It might not have referred to Shlomo at all—they might have been talking about themselves.

"I don't understand," said Eliyahu.

Just then, a Shover coming toward us decided not to make way. I could see by his eyes. They'd flicked at my chest, then over my shoulder.

I checked him into a locker and we didn't lose a step. A couple seconds later, the sound of the impact repeated. Vincie was behind us. He'd locker-slammed the Shover on the rebound.

A little out of breath, he said, "I need to talk to you."

It can wait, I said.

"English," he said.

Can it wait? I said in English.

"I guess," said Vincie, continuing to follow us.

Back to Hebrew: Are you a Jew or an Israelite?

"An Israelite," said Eliyahu.

When did you become an Israelite? I said.

"If I understand what you mean by Israelite, then I have always been an Israelite," he said. "However, if I understand what you mean by Jew, then I have, admittedly, sometimes behaved like a Jew."

I said, You understand. You're a scholar, though—the Five aren't.

"And so?"

So when they shouted 'Death to the Jew,' they might not have understood they were Israelites who had been acting like Jews, I said. I said, I think they might have believed they were Jews who *had to become* Israelites. And to become a new kind of person, you have to kill the person you already are— I think the Five might have believed they had to kill the Jews they were.

"Even though they were never Jews, but always Israelites."

To our left, Ben-Wa Wolf played the pratfalling game on linoleum with Chunkstyle, Boshka, Derrick Winnetka, and a rock.

Even though, I said.

Eliyahu was frowning.

Look, I said, the Five *aren't scholars*, and in one way that's unfortunate, but in another it's not.

"How can you say that? How is it not?"

A lot of scholars did me wrong today, I said, and—

"How?" said Eliyahu.

I'll explain some other time. For now, just trust me. What I'm trying to say is think of it like this: No one on the Side's a scholar except for us, and the Side is good, right?

"We're not talking about the Side. No one on the Side yelled, 'Death to the Jew.'"

That's true, Eliyahu, and I'm not saying… You're right. It was a foolish thing to yell, I said. Let's leave it at that, though. They made a mistake. They yelled something foolish.

"And so maybe they're fools."

I said, Maybe even foogs.

"You'll makes jokes now?" he said.

Yes, I said. And so should you. These fools are with us, that's all there is to it, and everything else is working out okay.

"It's working out I have an in-school suspension."

In a room less prisonlike than the Cage, I said, and with five new friends.

"Maybe so, but those others will be there, too," he said. "I should have to sit all day in a room with a boy who bruised my face and crushed my hat?"

Two, I said. And if Shlomo's back, then a third who'd like to do the same.

"That does not sound like something that I will enjoy. In the Office, that Co-Captain Baxter kept showing me his fist, his middle finger—"

Only because he knew it was safe, I said. I said, He knew you wouldn't attack him in the Office.

"And why should he have been so sure?"

He shouldn't have, I said.

"People look at me and think I'm weak," Eliyahu said. "They push me around. I can't hide it."

Hide what? I said.

"That I'm an orphan—who are these chubniks saluting you?"

Isadore Momo and Beauregard Pate stood shoulder-to-shoulder with three other short, husky guys by the southern doorway of the cafeteria. Each one had a line of thick writing across his chest in Darker:

Beauregard
FIRED A BULLET THROUGH HIS RIGHT TEMPLE.

Chubnik X
LIKE AN OVERGROWN HALO.

Chubnik Y
VANISHED COMPLETELY INTO THE DARKNESS OF NIGHT.

Chubnik Z
ONLY HATE AND HATE, SOLID AS STONE.

Momo
I PUSH THROUGH.

They were showing me victory fists.

That's Big Ending, I said to Eliyahu. I said, They're with us, too.

"What's with the shirts?"

I don't know, I said.

Like an overgrown halo and *I push through* were familiar phrases, but I couldn't place them. *Vanished completely into the darkness of night* also seemed familiar, except how couldn't it?

"I was saying—"

You don't need to hide that you're an orphan, I said. I said, Anyone who knows you're an orphan—and I don't think that many people do—could just as easily be scared of you for being an orphan as think you're weak for being an orphan. So the ones who do think you're weak—don't let them push you around.

"I know I shouldn't let them, but I do."

I said, Not always. I said, You led that hyperscoot. And before that you fought back hard in the two-hill field—I saw some of it.

"I was very verklempt then. I told you that. I didn't know up from down. If I knew up from down, I never would have done those things. So what am I supposed to do? Be verklempt all the time? I think it would be worse than getting pushed around."

I spotted June. She wasn't at her locker. She was about a quarter of the hallway away, talking to a big-eyed girl with an almost-shaved head and clown-pants.

I said, Anything you do, Bathsheba Wasserman might hear about it.

"Sure," said Eliyahu. "And probably from me."

I said, So imagine she hears you're getting pushed around.

"I should worry Bathsheba will think I'm a coward? Don't manipulate me."

That's not what I'm saying at all, I said. If Bathsheba hears that you get pushed around, it'll cause her pain. Protect her from that, I said. There's June. Would you like to meet her?

"When can I talk to you?" Vincie said to me.

I'd forgotten he was there.

Just let me talk to June first, I said to Vincie.

"Oh God," he said.

Oh God what? I said.

Before he could answer, we were saying hello. I kissed June's cheek and she pinched my neck. "This is Starla," she said to us, chinning air at the clown-pantsed girl. Then to Starla: "You know Vincie Portite. *Do* you know Vincie? Anyway—this is Vincie. And that's Gurion, and I don't know who you are."

"I am Eliyahu of Brooklyn," Eliyahu said.

Vincie's face was all red.

To Starla I said: I hear you don't think I'm dark enough.

June punched me in the shoulder.

"Gurion's dark as fuck," Vincie told Starla. "And bracelets for causes are not punkrock." He pointed at a yellow plastic bracelet on her left wrist. It looked like one of those Cancer Foundation bracelets that said LIVESTRONG.

Starla made the noise "Tch," and turned the bracelet so we could see it said LIVESTOCK.

"That's subtle," said Vincie. "And your name is really fucken pretty, too. I've been wanting to tell you that since kindergarten."

"Is that why you're always staring at me at lunch?" said Starla.

"Yeah," said Vincie. "That's the reason. Cat's outta the bag now."

Wait, I said. Since kindergarten?

"Yeah," he said. "Yeah. Just like I said. Cat's outta the bag."

"What cat?" June said.

"Don't worry about the cat," Vincie said. "The cat's no concern of yours."

"Gurion," June said.

Vincie's cat, Vincie's bag, I said.

"Anyway," Vincie said to Starla, "that's a pretty fucken name you've got, that's all I'm saying."

"It's the name of a song," said Starla.

"I know," said Vincie.

"Liar."

"When you can't decide what's on your mind, it's clear. I'm here. Starla dear. Please take me home."

"You know it!" said Starla.

"Yeah, and it's fucken hammy, don't you think?"

"Vincie," June said.

"What?" said Vincie. "Starla knows the lyrics are hammy. It's got nothing to do with her. It's her fucked-up grunger parents I'm laughing at. Who names their daughter after a Smashing Pumpkins song, right Starla?"

"I know!" said Starla.

"It's still a pretty name, though. And a pretty song, too, if you don't pay attention to the words too close."

"Weird, right?" said Starla.

"Not that weird," said Vincie. "My favorite kind of pretty's always mixed in with a little fucked-up. You got a bike, right?"

"Yeah," Starla said.

"You should ride your bike to my house around midnight and we'll go to the railroad tracks and smash some bottles. I got all these bottles in the recycling in my garage."

"Why don't we just meet at the tracks?" said Starla.

"I can't carry all those bottles by myself," Vincie said.

"What if we just skipped the bottles?" said Starla.

"How the fuck are we gonna skip bottles if we don't have any bottles?"

"What? No. Wait... Not skip them like throw them, skip them like forget about them."

"Why the fuck would we go to the tracks if we didn't want to break some bottles?"

"I—I don't—"

"If we're not gonna break anything, we might as well just hang out in my room."

"What about your parents, though?"

"After midnight? Why do you think I got so many bottles? We could smash bottles on *them* and they wouldn't wake up."

"Okay," said Starla. She was breathless.

"*Okay?*" Vincie said. "What's wrong with you?" Vincie said. "I was *exaggerating*. I'm not gonna let you hit my mom with a fucken bottle."

I kicked Vincie's shoe and when he tried to kick mine back, June stomped his foot away. Eliyahu was chewing the insides of his cheeks.

"No, I—your room," Starla was saying. "We could just hang out in your room."

"Sure," said Vincie, "if you say so. Whatever. But there's not much to do in my room, so if it's boring, then tomorrow night I'm smashing bottles, with or without you."

Vincie wrote his address down while June and I agreed to ditch detention, and Eliyahu, eyes burning, told me, "Don't help."

Help what? I said.

He'd already gotten past me.

"I've attained verklemptness!" he answered as he ran.

A familiar cracking noise resounded and I spun.

BryGuy Maholtz was doing wallnd tricks. He and Blonde Lonnie had Big Ending backed up inside the south doorway of the cafeteria, and Brooklyn and the Co-Captain were rushing toward them from opposite directions.

I dropped my bag and gave June my jacket.

"Steal these and meet me in the field," I told her.

Vincie showed teeth, said, "Maholtz or Lonnie?"

Maholtz, I said.

□ □ □ □ □ □ □

Big Ending, in the doorway, bit lips and twitched. Every time Maholtz sapped a flake of wall off, Blonde Lonnie said, "What! Play *that*, you hermaphrodites!" Vincie muttered curses. I muttered commands: Walk slow, be stealth, we'll get there any second. As soon as he noticed Eliyahu was rushing him, Co-Captain Baxter used basketball skills. First he went from topspeed to floor-squeaking deadstop in just two steps. Then he tried to pivot. He should have faked left.

Eliyahu caught his backpack by the loop with one hand and rabbit-punched him twice with the other. Squinching his neck up, the Co-Captain yelped, spun them in circles til he wiggled from his straps, and then from the thin boy whose hat he had stomped, this thin pale boy who he'd thrown in the mud, the Co-Captain, pop-eyed and whinnying, sprinted—just tucked in and bolted the long way down Main Hall, stunned and cowering, swift and southerly. The freed-up inertia of the captured backpack sent Eliyahu a couple yards north. When he regained his balance, he got a running start, hoisted the bag, deployed it like a natural. The bag's arc ended at Baxter's knee-backs. He didn't fall, but his stride got limped. Eliyahu chased him into C-Hall.

Vincie, in the meantime, kept trying to run at the scuffle in the doorway, but running would bring on the robots too soon—Brooklyn'd just spent the day's luck for the stealthless—so I held Vincie's elbow and kept our pace steady. I wanted that sap.

Out of nowhere I placed *like an overgrown halo*: the last four words of Roth's "Conversion of the Jews."

That chubnik had excellent taste in big endings. What was his name? I didn't know his name.

Blonde Lonnie knocked him hard into Isadore Momo and slugged him in the gut. Then Blonde Lonnie slugged Momo in the gut.

Beauregard Pate and the other two chubniks threw shoulder-blocks while Momo hugged himself and puked. Lonnie sidestepped the blocks and slapped the chubniks. Beauregard flooded. It looked like Sumo dog-paddling. His swearfinger caught inside of Lonnie's shirt. The shirt popped a button.

Kids in the hall started pointing at the doorway.

Other kids looked.

Maholtz kicked Beuregard square in the ass, which turned him around.

The first chubnik puked on Momo's puke.

Maholtz sapped the wall and Beauregard backstepped, foot in the mixture.

Beauregard slipped. Beauregard puked.

"Hermaphradite Homo," Lonnie said to Momo. He pushed the slapped chubniks into the lunchroom.

Vincie had just shaken free of my grasp. He ran six steps before jumping at Lonnie's face. His chest smashed Lonnie's nose; Lonnie's skull struck the wall. They both hit the floor. Vincie got up first, onto his knees. He head-locked Lonnie, pulled him blindly toward the lunchroom. Lonnie crawled like a baby, but fast to save his spinal cord.

Just outside my striking-range now, Maholtz was poised to kick Vincie in the ribs.

BryGuy! I said.

He took a step back and sapped the jamb.

Vincie straightened up. Arm still locked around Blonde Lonnie's skull, he palmstruck his mouth with his free hand. The squishy clicking noise the blow made was loud. Lonnie drooled in color.

Momo puked more. Beauregard Pate and the remaining chubnik dragged him inside of the cafeteria.

Vincie dragged Lonnie after them.

In the seconds since those kids started pointing, a crowd had developed around the doorway, drawing attention. It wouldn't be long before robots showed up. I was currently doing nothing against the rules, but I wanted to do something against the rules. I wanted to be in possession of a deadly weapon, and I didn't want to get it taken away.

Open my skull, I said to Maholtz.

"In front of all these peenple? I may be crazy, you stupid angshole, but—"

They've been waiting to see you use that thing forever, I said. I said, All you do is brandish.

Some kid in the crowd behind me said, "Brandisher."

You're just the mantel, I said.

"Mantel!" another kid in the crowd said.

Stuck in Act One, I said.

"Mangtel?" said Maholtz to those gathered behind me. "This guy's a psycho." He gave forth a giggle.

I twetched in his eye and he closed it.

Then I closed some space between us.

Now you're winking at me, I said.

Someone said, "BryGuy."

Someone said, "Floyd's coming."

I closed more space.

And then I took his weapon. I took it one-handed. I grabbed hold of the lead ball, exerted no more downward force than I would on a pen if I were to write scripture with a pen instead of a computer, and the deadly weapon was mine.

No hurrahs arose from the crowd. A couple people said "Winker" and "BryGuy," but they sounded—even to Maholtz, I was sure—like embarrassed afterthoughts, not provocations. The rest of the crowd booed. Not so much at Maholtz as the implications of the anticlimax he and I had just provided them. To see an oppressor felled without a hint of violent struggle can't help but tarnish the shine on your victim badge. To see Maholtz made to cower so easily had to make those who would have otherwise cheered wonder how they, for so long, could have cowered so readily before him. They were booing themselves.

As I entered the cafeteria, Blonde Lonnie limped past me into Main Hall, bleeding.

I heard Floyd command him to "Halt it, fella!" and I raced to the northern doorway. Vincie and Big Ending were ducking into the bathroom. I pulled on my hood and walked into Main Hall.

On my way to the front entrance, Ben-Wa and Leevon, playing slapslap by the lockers, paused their contest to show me victory fists. Just as I mirrored the gesture, Co-Captain Baxter whipped past me so fast I didn't think to trip him.

Eliyahu, at his heels, shouted "Mamzer!" and long-jumped. He axe-chopped the Co-Captain's shoulder on landing. Baxter said "Ah!" but lost little momentum.

Jerry exited his booth while, a few feet south of it, Eliyahu picked up speed going north. "Stop!" shouted Jerry.

Eliyahu didn't stop.

Fakefight loud, I said to Leevon. Now, I said.

Locker-metal clanged. Ben-Wa shouted, "Fight!"

Jerry revolved at the sound of the word. Fighting trumped running. Ben-Wa and Leevon kept it up til he got there.

Eliyahu was safe.

As long as enough of us acted dangerous enough, most of us would be safe.

Through the glass of the front doors I saw Slokum heading away from the school.

A bright white tickle shot across my heart.

▫ ▫ ▫ ▫ ▫ ▫ ▫

My pennygun was in my jacket, my jacket with June.

I stalked Slokum with the sap in my fist, cocked. He stopped walking at the far end of the parking lot, just past where it curved around the building. It made no sense for him to wait for his ride so far from the driveway. He was hiding something.

I ducked behind a dumpster five yards back.

He checked over both shoulders, and then his hands disappeared in front of him. His jacket's Chief Aptakisic iron-on drew taut across his back. His neck muscles did a rolling thing.

With a running start, a well-timed leap, and the extra few inches by which the sap, when snicked, would extend from my hand, I could tag the base of his skull. Level him. Then stomp.

I got a running start.

When he revolved at the sound of my footfalls, a lit cigarette between his lips, I looked away from his eyes, saw his throat, and sprung. He stepped to the left and I hit the ground ugly. Elbow in the beauty. Windless. Choked sounds. I curled up and gripped the sap's handle tight, trying to catch my breath, coiled to crush his ankle when he tried to kick me.

He didn't try to kick me. He smoked.

I got my breath back.

I've got a weapon here, I said.

"Get up," Bam said. "You want some help I'll help you up."

I popped up.

I said, Try and take my weapon.

"No one's watching us kid so quit playing pretend with me and calm down," he said.

I didn't get H like I usually did when somebody'd tell me to calm down. I even calmed down a little. I told myself to keep my eyes on his throat and have contempt. His throat was a massive target, too large to miss if you could reach to swing on it, but then the chin compensated. Squarish, bristly, and nearly as wide as his neck, it looked bulletproof. He could tuck it. It was made to be tucked during fights, a shield of bone.

I heard kids heading to the buses, but couldn't see them. The part of my field of vision not blocked by the corner of the schoolbuilding was filled with Bam.

"Swing it or pocket it kid I don't want to take your prize, you like to smoke cigarettes?"

I should have said nothing and swung. Instead I said, Sometimes.

There was no reason to avoid looking at his face anymore. I didn't have the snat to attack him head-on.

"Sometimes is smart," Bam said. "All the time gets you killed."

Why are you talking to me?

"I like you," he said. "A lot of kids at Aptakisic are starting to like you, and if I wasn't talking to you, I suspect you'd do something injudicious and then I'd be getting your blood all over my clothing, and what would I gain by that, I'd gain nothing, certainly not a conversation. So I'm glad, not anywhere inside, but on the surface—it makes me *act glad*—that you've decided to quit behaving injudiciously. I enjoy our conversations, Gurion, which is to say that during our conversations I find myself acting as if I am experiencing joy, you're a rare good audience, someone who listens, and the way you handle yourself publicly is occasionally admirable. Like for instance just a few minutes ago, how you got that sap. I was there, you know. At the back of the crowd. You didn't know that, did you, but now you know. Anyway that was elegant, how you took what you came to take, spent hardly any energy doing it. Admirable. But beyond that, and maybe more to the point, everyone likes to see the little guy win, and I don't want to bear them the bad news about how he doesn't, which is a warning and not a threat so lower the hackles there. Like most small toughguys, you think it's weak, I know, to cheer for someone just because he's smaller, and you think it's backward to base your actions on what people are gonna cheer for, but the fact is smaller's what they cheer for and, barring few exceptions, what they cheer for's what I act on, so that's why it's a warning and not a threat, and that's why I'm talking to you instead of wrecking you—I'm somewhat invested in your well-being. Believe."

He held out his cigarette.

"Not a peacepipe, but a cigarette," he said. "Let us not engage in acts of symbolism, let alone expect others to behave symbolically. I don't like to interpret things. And it's not that I don't understand your dilemma, it's just it's got nothing to do with this cigarette."

I took the proffered cigarette and dragged at it.

I was more curious than I wanted to be.

"You won't ask, so I'll just tell you. You like me as much as any of them do but you fear me, too, and anyone you fear you figure you've gotta damage. But then anyone you like you figure you've gotta protect. I understand all

the machinations of that dilemma, and that's how come I avoid it by playing to the crowd, so long as necessity doesn't dictate otherwise, see. Like for
instance if you swing that sap, which I can see still ain't in your pocket you
know, necessity would dictate I separate the two of you. After that, it's a safe
bet you'd be in some pain. Apart from that, though, it's a safe bet I act like
a friend, an older brother even."

And if I had no sap, but the crowd wanted you to hurt me? I said.

"Then I'd hurt you."

I told him, You'd be a hypocrite.

He said, "That's juvenile, Gurion, hypocrisy's a juvenile idea, an accusation slaves throw around to gain a false sense of empowerment, it's beneath
you."

But I'm right, I said. I said, If you liked me, but you hurt me just to
please a crowd, you'd be a hypocrite.

He beckoned with a sideways peace sign. I hit the cigarette again,
handed it back.

"When you say stuff like that, like '*just* to please a crowd,' you indicate
your failure to understand the Way of Barnum because what I'm telling
you is—"

The way of what? I said.

"I just *said* the Way of Barnum, didn't I? That's a little dorky of me,
though I hope endearingly so. Sometimes I think of myself in the third
person, which is actually a by-product of practicing the Way of Barnum,
believe it or not. I can sort of watch myself, from the outside, and it monkeys with my use of language on occasion."

Your name's *Barnum*? I said.

"I wouldn't put too fine a point on it I were you. Follow the bloody trail
to that bureaucrat Mohan's left ear you want to see what happens," he said.

"Mohan" was Martin Mohan, a yearbook kid with arty hair. He was
always snapping photos of Jennys in the hallways, saying stuff like "Fantastic tableau! Don't move a muscle!" and extending his bottom lip to loudly
blow the pricey bangs off his over-knit brow while reading his light-meter
for far longer than it takes to read a light-meter.

"Last year," Bam said, "I was seeing this girl on yearbook staff and she
tells me Mohan, who's like, some kind of underling editor at that point, she
tells me he's got a photo of me titled 'Barnum Slokum Dunks.' Tells me
Mohan won't call it 'Bam Slokum Dunks' because Barnum's the name on
the copy of Desormie's roster Mohan's gonna print on the facing page and

something about 'verbal consistency' or 'verbal integrity' or some nonsense. But you ever seen Desormie's writing? It's like a palsied monkey's if you made it use its left hand. And he can't spell either. He misspells the word 'coach.' And not just occasionally. He regularly spells it C-A-U-T-C-H, like how Mike Ditka would say it. Anyway no one was gonna be able to read the roster anyway. So I found Mohan and I said so, and I told him it was my name, not his and he should respect my wishes. I was nice about it. I cited relevant precedents. Earvin 'Magic' Johnson did not go by Earvin all too often and hardly anyone knows the great bambino was *George* Ruth. But Mohan, he kept saying the word 'officially' to me. He said, 'Bam's not *officially* your name. *Officially*, your name is Barnum.' And that's true. My name is definitely Barnum. And it's a family name and I'm fond of it. It's a strong name. Barnum. But a person's name loses power on the lips of others. And so the person whose name it is loses power. That's a long-established fact. 'That's my name, don't wear it out.' The third commandment. Etcetera. So I don't like other people saying my name. To say 'Barnum' while not simultaneously *being* Barnum is to take my name in vain. And I explained to Mohan that to write my name would urge others to take it in vain, but he couldn't hear me at first, so I explained some more, until I was all he could hear, and then some more, until he couldn't hear much of anything for a while."

Bam dragged deeply at the cigarette and squinted at the cherry, exhaling slowly as he spoke.

"Anyway," he said, "what I was saying before we so fascinatingly digressed together was that when you say stuff like '*just* to please a crowd,' you're missing the point of what I'm trying to tell you, which is this: Except for self-preservation there's no higher motive than crowd-pleasing, and my situation here at Aptakisic and in the world at large greatly minimizes the chances that acts which are needed to please crowds would ever come into conflict with acts needed to preserve myself. It's an elegant system. I'm very elegant. There's no room *for* hypocrisy in an elegant system such as the Way of Barnum because the point is I *wouldn't* like you if they wanted me to hurt you, and so I'd hurt you, no qualms.

"Today, you know, it looked like you and those other little guys were attacking that B-team Shlomo kid who because he plays basketball everyone expects me to protect him from outsized beatdowns. Truly I couldn't care less about that kid, but if I stood by and let seven guys hurt him, see, I would be failing to live up to expectations. Same time, there was no call to damage you—just to protect B-team. So there was nothing to be gained by damaging you. So I pulled you out of the fight and let you be. Even after you jumped at me I let you be. And I'm letting you be right now. I'm a simple animal. Consistent, elegant. The proof's in the pudding. Yet you're still confounded by my inaction just now when you were making Maholtz your bitch, let's have another."

He lit a second cigarette off the first, which he then dropped between us. I stepped on it.

"You're confounded because, once again, you're not paying attention to what I'm saying. Everyone hates Maholtz, and so I hate Maholtz. The only reason I don't fuck him up is because he supplies me with a couple things that no one else in this school can get their hands on, and what he supplies is good for the cause of my self-preservation. The fact that he's on the basketball team excuses me from having to fuck him up—in the eyes of the crowd, see. See, if I did fuck him up, they would be happy about it, but that I don't fuck him up is readily excusable because of how we're teammates and teammates aren't expected to harm each other. Nonetheless, I am in no way obligated to step in to *protect* him from you—or anyone else, except maybe Nakamook—in any kinda one-on-one deal. Or, in any case, the crowd didn't want that. What they *wanted* was for you to make Maholtz your bitch. At least until you did so—and with great aplomb, I commend you—at which time they felt like pussies but that's a spooky train of thought we don't need to pursue because the only thing I'm getting at is if I'd stepped in against you, they would have been displeased with me. And in the end, it turns out you did me a solid. Listen to them tommorrow and hear it yourself. Listen to what they'll say. See, since I let Maholtz take his lumps within such close temporal proximity to the incident with B-team, the crowd assumes that I'm a righteous human being. They assume I'm not blindly loyal to basketball players just because they're basketball players but that I'm filled with some clumsy complicated system of archaic scruples that their parents taught them was good and that these scruples I'm filled with dictate that I protect the B-team kid and let Maholtz suffer a little."

And really you're just filled with shit, I said.

It came out of my throat halfhearted, less an accusation than a challenge. "And why halfhearted?" scholars ask. Half-hearted partly because I said it with the future scrutiny of scholars in mind—if I didn't call bullshit, what would you think of me? Mostly, though, because I was trying to caulk back the snat that trickled from my face at the idea of being dominated by a monologue while I held a deadly weapon in my hand. I wanted to hear more of what Bam had to say, and I didn't want to want that, so I pretended I didn't want it.

He said, "Now see, I got no real issue with us having a conversation wherein you make ineffective—not to mention irrelevant—attempts to save face by telling me I'm full of shit, but for future reference if you say stuff like that to me when people can hear? I'm gonna have to hurt you pretty bad, cause it's no good for the cause of my self-preservation to get spoken to that way in public. It happens that no one's close enough to have heard, so good for you, you've made your meaningless little gesture and you continue to survive. In the meantime I'm gonna contest what you said because I'm not full of shit, because what I'm full of is nothing. Behind this face that you keep staring at so weirdly, like it's gonna speak to you on its own without me knowing, like it's gonna let you in on some secret, I've got but zen and zen and endless zen. I'm a colorless canvas flag atop a mile-high pole and I don't move a single fucken fiber but for when the wind flaps me see."

I put out my hand. He gave me the cigarette. I was done caulking. I'd resigned myself to trickling, to acquiescing in the form of open curiosity, telling myself this was no different an approach than most any kid standing before a freakshow cage would take. What, if not a freak, was a superhero-shaped eighth-grader who wanted to flatter and generally act friendly toward a kid who'd just tried to kill him? Even if I wasn't blameless, I was the next best thing—I was empathetic. Though someone in my place could have conceivably taken action—could have swung the sap at Bam, told him to get bent and meant it, or even just walked away—it was hard to imagine who.

I said, The other day you said you didn't like Nakamook, though. You said *you* didn't like him, and that you respected him.

"The respect line was a flourish I picked up from the movies—there was an audience see, a bus full of everykid no-ones," Bam said. "An occasional flourish is pleasing to an audience. You know that as well as anyone. As for liking or not liking Nakamook, I *don't* like him. And I don't like him because no one likes him. He's a fucken bully. You and Portite and Leevon Ray and then Scott Mookus—you're the only ones around who like him, and one of you is mentally retarded, another fakes muteness, the third one's a less effective bully himself, and then there's you with all your weird notions about snat and face and hypocrisy, and you're standing here, a deadly weapon in your hand, having a relatively civilized conversation with your best friend's—what's his favorite term now?"

Now I was laughing. Something about Bam's rhythm. I hated that I was laughing, and how I wanted to get him to laugh in return. And though Nakamook wasn't my friend anymore, I hated even worse that I was laughing at his expense.

Arch-enemy, I said.

"Like Lex Luthor," said Bam. "The Joker. Fucken Magneto. It used to be 'nemesis.' So dramatic, that guy."

And after that bit of collusion I could no longer think of myself as a kid at a freakshow. I was pathetic without any prefix, feeding Bam cues to punchlines like a pagan offering tribute, a Phoenecian peasant before a dog-headed oracle.

I said, Still, though, you're wrong about who likes him. I said, Girls go crazy for Benji.

Bam heard in my voice what I couldn't quite hide with my words, despite how oblique to the request I'd arranged them: I was asking to be set straight.

He said, "Girls go crazy for what's dangerous, kid, at least most of them do, so girls are irrelevant here because as long as I'm more dangerous they prefer me, the girls. And apart from them, no one likes him. And why they don't like him ain't just cause he's a bully, but cause he's a psychopath. He comes to school and just fucks with anyone who's near him. You've seen it happen. Everyone's seen it happen. You heard the stories about my cousin Geoff and his house burning down, I'm sure— Geoff was also a bully. The difference between Geoff and Nakamook is Geoff was never a psychopath. He's always been predictable. You knew what you had to do to stay on his good side. You just had to treat him like he was the dominant force in the room. If you didn't treat him that way, then he'd hurt you. But otherwise you'd be just fine. I'm not saying everyone liked him either—a lot of people didn't, but enough did. Nakamook alienates himself more than Geoff ever did because ever since he came back from juvie, being acknowledged as dominant and reaping the benefits of that acknowledgment—that ain't been enough for him. He wants to *actually* dominate. Like in the moment. And at all moments. You can't like a guy like that. You *can* like a guy like me, though. I've never acted like either of those two. People fear me, but I just keep the peace, so they like me, too. I don't ask anyone to kiss my ass—just so long as they don't fuck with me, see. So Bam walks quiet with his big stick, they think. He only fights kids we don't like, they think. Anyone he fights must be unlikable, they think. And so to remain on Nakamook's bad side makes me likable. He does me a favor, writing that SLOKUM DIES FRIDAY shit everywhere. Everyone knows it's him, and it throws us into mutual relief. Look how likable is Bam when contrasted with that bully. Look how decent. That's what they think. An elegant system, mine. I do what I want, everyone thinks I'm right, and I'm ascribed the best of intentions, the most noble motivations. You should adopt this system. You're a very sharp kid and you're rapidly becoming beloved. That damage nonsense everyone's writing now. The bitch-making of my less amicable teammates. I've been hearing about you all day. You and Boystar. You should take a lesson from him. Primpy little poodle that he is, he knows what he's got and who he's got and where he stands, and he uses it all to maximum effect. And you're smarter than that kid. It's a shame to waste a brain like yours on scruples. I hope you'll stop. It's only confusing for you. I ask you to ask yourself: 'Why like Bam *despite* my screwball loyalties when I can so easily ditch my screwball loyalties and just plain like Bam?'"

Geoff Claymore's Cherokee entered the lot and parked in a spot, honked. Without revolving to face the Jeep, Slokum signalled to his cousin with his palm = "When I'm ready."

"Now I have to get going," he said to me. "There's a girl, you know, who I really like to kiss on the neck. I won't tell you who because that's unseemly, but she makes these pretty sounds, this girl, and that's what I need to hear right now, some pretty girlsounds to preserve me for the game tomorrow. It's Desormie's mistake not having practice the day before a game. The energy he thinks it saves us just gets spent on girls. Not that I'm complaining. So now I'm gonna walk away from you without offering my hand because you still have to think about some things before you can make peace with the fact that you and I have no quarrel. I'll give you a little help, too, a little elder-brotherly push in the right direction. Here it is: It's not your face that holds your snat back, but your snat that holds your face *together*. And your snat's not what you think it is, either—it's got nothing to do with truth and it's got nothing to do with loyalty and it's got nothing to do with love or toughness or any kind of interior nonsense. It's just public opinion. You're only what they say you are, and if you're only what they say you are the only thing you gotta do is make sure they're saying what you want them to. Look at Holden Caulfield—you don't wanna wind up like him, do you? I don't want you to. I like you. It preserves me. At least for now. So as-salamu alaykum, shalom, and om," Bam said. And then he was walking away.

I almost shouted after him: Wait! You're right! We have no quarrel! We *can* shake hands.

But guys like Bam—guys of the kind Adonai once made kings—they rule with their presence. With each step Bam took toward the yellow pickup, the spell he'd cast weakened. My urge to shout about alliances got flatter and flatter under the weight of something shakey and hideous I couldn't name yet.

I stayed quiet.

With Bam out of the way, I could see the crowd gathering by the bus circle. So many of them wanted to be my friend now. Whatever it meant to them, they believed they were on the Side of Damage. Claymore, sunglasses on his forehead, shot me with his index finger and winked. And June, who was in love with me, slid through the crowd, bearing our books. In a couple minutes, I'd be making out with her. But even that was little consolation.

It was only after they'd driven away, after Bam had reached over Claymore's gearbox to beep the horn friendly—two times, then four—and after the pickup's engine had gunned and its tires had screeched their long, cheesy peel-out—only after they were gone was I able to name it, the hideous thing that was making me shake: I had been arranged. Not with any Cage or Step System, though. Not by any sadistic and claw-handed monitor, nor by any pervy, tight-crotched gym teacher. Not by any closet racist headmaster, pogromfaced lowlife, or well-read vandal, let alone some well-meaning, sad sack principal. I'd been arranged, scholars, by Barnum "Bam" Slokum, whose face was unreadable; a pre-smiling king who pandered peace to the weak to keep them from bringing any manner of damage that might get them stronger, that might get them *strong*; a practical king who dealt power to the strong to keep them from breaching his peace; Barnum "Bam" Slokum, who claimed we were similar, and then convinced me—if only for a minute, still a minute too long—that I was actually glad about that.

They rule with their presence, these king-types, I thought. They dissolve, with their immediacy, all of your enmity. The Law, like the rest, like everything else, gets blotted out white by their glowing charm. You want, when they're near, to follow their rules, to please them, be like them; you want to be like them in order to please them. That's how you get arranged. It's how you go robot.

I don't know what it was that got me more explosive: that I failed to be exceptional when faced with such charm, or that I didn't possess that charm myself.

One thing I did know, a thing I should have already known, a thing that I had, in fact, already known, until I had somehow let myself forget: To damage kings true, you had to strike from out of arm's reach.

I stepped out from behind the corner of the building, pulling my hood-strings, and someone said, "Gurion."

The voice came out of Blake Acer, Shover president, who stood over by the dumpsters, ichthys near his heart, his face telling stories of proudly attended semi-annual dental appointments, baggie-gloved strolls beside a golden retriever, dipped cones of soft-serve after Little League victories.

"Gurion," he said. It was the first time he'd ever spoken my name to me. It was the first time any Main Hall Shover had spoken my name to me. "Check this out," he said.

He was scratching WE DAMAGE WE on a dumpster with a rock. I was beside him by the time he finished. He ta-da'd at the bomb with one hand and bright teeth. The rock in his other hand was fist-sized.

Do not try to be us, I told him.

"What?"

I said, I'd hold onto that rock if I were you.

He dropped it.

I kicked him in the stomach. He showed me the top of his head and I turned him, pushed his face against the dumpster, raked it back and forth across the jagged letters until I felt human.

Tell your friends, I said.

□ □ □ □ □ □ □

The field was all empty. June should have been there. I knelt in the valley between the two hills and scraped my hands clean against stiff blades of grass, watched red globs of Acer dry brown on the tips. She said that she'd be there. Why did she test me? Along with perfect justice and the end of death, being near her was the simplest thing I'd ever wanted. Why did she have to act so complicated? Or maybe she'd only acted impatient. Maybe she'd shown, and then taken off. Maybe I'd taken too long to arrive. But that was the difference between us, I thought. That was the difference between me and everyone. It's not that I wasn't impatient—I was. I had as little patience as anyone else. I'd tap my foot at the slightest inconvenience. I'd claw at my clothes, suck air and flare nostrils, attack all manner of inanimate objects, but one thing I'd never do was ditch you. That was the difference. I'd show up and wait for however long it took you. If I told you I'd meet you, I'd meet you; I'd wait. I'd wait til I saw that I'd waited too long, and then I'd wait more; I'd wait for as long as it had taken me to see that I'd waited too long, I'd double it up, telling myself it was best to be patient, that if I wasn't patient, I'd worry later on that you'd shown once I'd gone, that you'd think that I'd ditched you, and I'd think about patience and think about waiting, and how it always seemed like I was always waiting, and how it always seemed like other people weren't, and how it probably seemed the same way to those others, that they were always waiting and other people weren't, and I'd see it was true, that it seemed the same to everyone, and because it was true, a universal human truth, that everyone always thinks himself impatient and everyone thus tries to act more patient while telling themselves they're always waiting for others who never seem to have to wait, I'd think that the thought should provide me some comfort, but the thought would never provide me comfort, and the failure of the thought to provide me any comfort would make my lack of comfort that much more salient, and I'd end up wishing I wasn't so much like everyone, wishing that I wasn't so much like anyone, particularly you, the person I was waiting for, which meant I didn't like you, for how could I really be said to like you if my foremost wish, at least right then, was to be less like you, and why should I wait for someone I didn't like? Why should I wait for you? I shouldn't. I'd leave. I didn't even really like you, and so I would leave. But I didn't leave. I stayed where I was. I knelt in the valley of the two-hill field, a few yards away from where last I'd been left—by the Side, by Benji, by Benji, by Benji—in a spot where the scholars who'd ditched me that morning would've stood had they shown, and I waited for June because she was June and what was the point if June didn't come through? What was the point of caring about anything? What was anything's point if you cared about nothing? Was that even possible, to care about nothing? And why so dramatic? I thought. Why so desperate? Why so whiney? Why so all-or-nothing? Why so meow-or-meowmeow? Why be such a baby? Because you're in love? That's exactly the reason you *shouldn't* weak out, you whiney, meowing baby, get angry or something, get any way other than—

All at once I was getting tackled sideways, kissing, wrestling a little. June did things to my neck with her mouth that felt so different from any feeling I'd ever had in my neck I panicked my deepest nerves were exposed, that she'd opened my flesh so gently I hadn't noticed and now the wind was going into my throat, and pints of blood, warm as summer, were flowing out of me and Adonai was merciful—not just kind enough to numb my pain as I expired, but to mask it with the most gushing rushes of pleasure, as if, in the last seconds of my life, the thing He most wanted was to secure my high opinion of Him—and I thrust my whole torso away from her and saw no blood. How could I have been upset? How could I be upset about what either of them put me through if it lead to this?

"You taste like cig—" June said, and I did to her what she'd been doing to me, and soon it made her make sounds like I was killing her, which panicked me again, and I stopped for a second to look, and I saw she wasn't bleeding any more than I'd been.

The way I understood it, now: she wanted me to withhold a little. That's why she kept doing it to me, making me wait, making me chase her, calling the gift of my hoodie a theft. So I decided I wouldn't kiss her neck again until she opened her eyes. But then when she opened her eyes, she saw something.

"Hello, deadly weapon," she whispered.

That June, having seen what at first I thought to be my pennygun—fallen, I imagined, from the spy pocket of my IDF jacket, which she had layered between my stolen hoodie and her coat—would know, by sight, that it was a weapon... surprised me. But something else was off, too.

You've seen one before? I said.

"I invented it."

I invented it, I told her.

"Then how did *I* get it?"

You got it from inside my jacket, I said.

She reached into my spy-pocket and took out another pennygun: mine. I knew it was mine because the firing pouch was a black balloon. Rather, I realized the one on the ground beside us *wasn't* mine, because its firing pouch was an orange balloon.

"You ripped me off," she said.

You ripped *me* off, I said.

She said, "When did you invent it?"

Last spring, I said.

"So did I," June said. "Why did you invent it?"

To protect Israelites, I said.

"I invented mine for extra credit," she said. "I had Mr. Klapper for Social

Studies and I wasn't doing that well because all his tests were fill-in-the-blanks that you had to memorize all these dates and locations for, and I'm much better at essays. Everyone thinks Klapper's crazy because he makes uncomfortable-looking neck movements and says 'damn' and 'hell' a lot, but he also looks like Mark Twain and I told him so, and he took it like a compliment, so I always liked him, and near the end of the semester I told him his tests were too hard, and that he should give us essay tests, and he said he thought essay tests in junior high school were overrated and that they undermined something—what was it? He said that, 'Owing to their emphasis on rhetorical skills, essay tests undermine the importance of scholarly exactitude in the arena of historical facthood, and thereby serve to strengthen the reliance of our youth on their ability to sell hopeful-sounding horsepucky like "the pen is mightier than the sword," an assertion that will keep down and dumb the lot of you as you age,' and I said, 'But the pen *is* mightier than the sword, Mr. Klapper,' and he told me that he'd forget all my grades so far and give me an A for the class if I could show him evidence that the pen was mightier than the sword. So I invented the pengun and got an A."

The pennygun, I said.

"The *pen*gun," said June. If you don't believe me, ask Vincie Portite. I used Vincie's pens to demonstrate—not the whole pens, but the nibs. He has all those fountain pens."

I use pennies, I said. They're cheaper, I said.

"You can't kill with a penny," June said.

I said, You can debilitate with a penny, and then kill the enemy you debilitated with your hands.

"But a penny isn't mightier than a sword if you can't kill anyone with it," June said. "A pen is mightier, though, if it's a fountain pen, or the nib of one, and you project it into that neck artery, the one you were just kissing on—the carotid artery. If you project a nib into the carotid, you can kill a swordsman who can't reach you because you fired from a distance greater than his arm plus his sword. And don't try to argue with me by saying that the swordsman can use his sword as a projectile because even if he can, its accuracy and range don't match the pengun's. Not to mention its speed. Which is why Mr. Klapper gave me an A."

I—, I said.

"And I'll bet if you're close enough," June said, "you can shoot the nib into his eyeball—the swordsman's eyeball—and it might go deep enough to enter his frontal lobe and kill him that way, or at least cause braindeath. It would be hard to get that close, though, and take aim, I think, if the man still had his sword. So in that situation, maybe the pen is only *as* mighty as the sword. I got an A, though. You can ask Mr. Klapper."

I love you so much, I said.

"Good," June said. "If you didn't still love me, I would feel really tricked. I want you to kiss my neck again in the same exact spot. You kissed it right on the carotid artery and I tingled in so many places I almost had a grand mal seizure. It made me so warm, Gurion, and then cool and then warm again and then cool and it started switching so fast, warmandcool and warmandcool, that I couldn't tell the difference and my jaw was grinding and then yawning, and my eyebrow muscles were very concerned and then very surprised, all of it switch-switching and your tongue doesn't gross me out. I was worried that your tongue would gross me out. Right before I kissed you yesterday, I thought your tongue would be thick inside of my mouth, that it would taste like cardboard and be dry like other tongues, and then your tongue wasn't like that at all, but it was strange inside of my mouth and I couldn't make a decision about it and I worried til now that it was because it was just about to gross me out, that you stopped only a second before my grossout would've started, and that the next time you put your tongue in my mouth it *would* gross me out, but this was the next time and it wasn't gross at all. I like it so much that when you were kissing my neck, I almost made you stop just so I could suck on your tongue, but I didn't do it because I wanted to have a grand mal seizure first, and I was almost there until you started talking about penguins." She grabbed my hands and said, "Will you do it again til my hemispheres crossfire? You're blushing. Good. I like when you blush. It's because you want me to do it to you again, don't you? I will. I'll do it to you until you seize, but you have to do it to me again, after."

A hot red face does not always = blushing. A hot red face only means blood has risen. I said, What tongue was thick in your mouth?

She said, "What?"

I said, You said that other tongues were thick in your mouth. Whose?

"I said other tongues are thick and like cardboard," she said. "And dry."

But how do you know that?

June said, "Come on."

Come on? I said.

She said, "I kissed this other boy, once, but it was nothing."

How could that be *nothing?*

"How? Because it was. It was at a party at the beginning of the school-year that it happened. We were playing this stupid game that was like a combination of Truth or Dare and Spin the Bottle."

A game, I said.

She said, "We went in this closet together and I had to tell him a secret, and I didn't. I told him something that was a lie, and he told me something that was true. But it was about me. He told me something true about me that I'd never told anyone and it freaked me out that he knew it, and I said, 'How did you know it?' and he said, 'I know you. I've always known you and I love you.' And that is when we kissed. But it was gross, Gurion, because he was a liar and he didn't love me and I didn't love him and I never said I did."

I said, Was it Berman?

"Of course it wasn't Berman. I never kissed Berman. I told you that already."

Tell me who it was then, I said.

"That's dumb."

I said, Right now I'm imagining you kissing every kid I know, and I'm going to keep imagining that. Every time I see someone, I'm going to picture you kissing him.

"So stop imagining things," she said.

I can't, I said.

"Come on," she said.

I know you're trying to protect me, I said, but it isn't working. I said, Your protection is a form of torture. If you tell me who it was, I can figure out a way to make it alright. If you don't tell me, I can't make anything alright, and now that you know that you're torturing me, you need to stop. If you don't stop, then it's like you're doing it on purpose.

"I don't like the way your voice sounds."

Neither do I.

She mumbled something.

What?

"Boystar," she said, pulling on grassblades.

I felt like the center of me was a vacuum and the vacuum sucked all of my bones and muscles into my chest cavity and the density of my chest cavity was so high that the center of me was being pulled into the center of the earth, into this tiny hole that had formed in the ground underneath me, and all the rest of me was attached to the center and was trying to follow it down into the hole but it couldn't follow because the hole was too small and that is why I started breaking. And it wasn't so much the kiss, either. That there had been a kiss—I didn't like that at all, but that wasn't really it.

June said, "Gurion."

I said, He knew a secret about you? Do I know it?

She said, "I don't know. Do I have to tell you that too? I didn't want to tell you. I told you I didn't want to tell you before and you said I didn't have to, but you look like you are going to die. You were all red and now you're all beige and I'll tell you if it'll make you red again. Will it make you red again?"

I don't know, June, I said.

She said, "You have to become red again. It's so pretty when you're red, with your black hair and eyes. You're the end of death."

And then she told me the secret of her darkness.

I forgot about Boystar and grew red and cried and I asked her why she didn't use her pengun and she said because she hadn't invented it yet and that even if she had she probably wouldn't have been able to use it and then she was crying too and she kissed me on the carotid and it was just like she described it and I forgot everything and so I kissed her on the carotid and she forgot everything, but while she was forgetting I couldn't stop remembering.

□ □ □ □ □ □ □

When the one-minute warning honks sounded, we were still at each other's throats. We raced over the crest of the high hill, shouting til the drivers saw us, then crossed the field and Rand Road slow, trying and failing to say goodbye right.

What can I do? I said.

"About what?" June said. She held my hand between us by the wrist and stared at it.

About what you just told me, I said. About—

She bent my fingers back so hard and sudden I knelt. "You can go ahead and fuck off if you ever bring it up again, Gurion. Especially in that whiney, desperate voice," she said. "We cried and now it's done so forget about it, or at least act like you have. I didn't fall in love with you because you were cute. I didn't fall in love with you because you were sensitive."

My fingers, I said.

"You think I can break them?"

I said, I don't know, Jellybean.

"Well so worry about that."

□ □ □ □ □ □ □

At the front of my bus was too much heat. The bandkids were flushed and sleepy-eyed.

"We Damage We," said a chunky trombonist behind the driver.

I told him, Next stop Frontier Motel.

He lowered his eyes.

Vincie was waiting in my wheel-well seat. He wanted to whisper.

"You look dead," he said. "Are you worried about tomorrow?"

I said, What's tomorrow?

"That's exactly what I said to Eliyahu, which is the point of this whole story I want to tell you," said Vincie.

Then he told me the story.

"I was in the cafeteria with everyone else, and I saw Co-Captain Baxter run down Main Hall, toward the front entrance, and then Eliyahu. There was about ten minutes to go before the end of detention, which meant Eliyahu was chasing him for, like, fifty minutes. You chase a kid for fifty minutes, it's more like you're hunting than chasing. It's gonna end in some kind of fantastic fucken asskicking, and of a basketballer too, so I didn't want to miss it. I was sitting right by the doorway, and there were so many kids in detention, I thought I had a chance of sneaking out and getting away with it. Ben-Wa said he'd hand in my detention assignment for me, so we'll find out tomorrow.

"Anyway, I get out to the bus circle, and there's a bunch of bandkids on the sidewalk part, watching Eliyahu. He's kicking the shit out of this backpack that's on the asphalt. Bodyslamming it. Swinging it over his head and banging it on the curb. The backpack's Co-Captain Baxter's, who's barracaded himself on the bus. The drivers have no idea what's going on. They're on that grassy island thing in the middle of the circle, talking shit about busdriving or whatever they talk about. They've got no idea.

"Soon Eliyahu starts swinging the backpack against the side of the bus, and Co-Captain Baxter sticks his head out the window over the rear wheel.

He goes to Eliyahu: 'Tonight I'm gonna rape your mom *and* your sister. Over and over,' he says. 'Until they start liking it,' he says. 'And then I'll tie them to a rock,' he says, 'and cut off their clits so they bleed to death.'

"Some of the bandkids start laughing because dude said 'clit.' I twetch a goozy on one of their shirts and he hides behind the other ones. Eliyahu doesn't notice any of it. He just keeps thumping The Co-Captain's back-pack like he's gonna chop a hole in the flank of the bus, and the bus does *dent* a little and its paint gets scratched—there's textbooks in the bag, all these zippers—but Eliyahu's not looking satisfied. And then the main zip-per opens, and the bag dumps its contents. Now Eliyahu drops the bag, plucks this little bottle out of the mess, unscrews the cap and starts flinging steroids through the air, right?

"So now the Co-Captain's trickling all over the place. He goes, 'You think I can't get more of those? Not that I've ever seen 'em before or know what they are, but I'll fucken chop those retarded fucken sideburn things off your mongoloid head because you *think* they're mine.' But all he's doing is shouting through a window, you know? And I'm thinking: Eliyahu has *beat* this fucken kid, and that is truly fucken wonderful, but these drivers are gonna be done talking to each other soon, and he bet-ter calm down, right? And get away. But instead of calming down, he's just getting madder and madder, Gurion. Like a fucken crazy madman. He's walking in this tight little circle between the bus and the curb now, kicking all the junk he spilled out of the bag and staring at his feet and muttering to himself: 'I want to kill him and it is wrong... I am Eliyahu of Brooklyn... that earring... to sever him from his jewelry...' And the Co-Captain, he says to the bandkids: 'Psycho's mumbling prayers.' And the bandkids laugh, and I twetch another one on the nose of the one I twetched one on the shirt of a minute ago, and he hides behind his friends again, and they laugh at that too.

"And Eliyahu's still, like, muttering. And he's throwing Yiddish into the mix, now. Stuff I never heard you say before, like *cappy* and—

Keppy, I said—it means head.

"And what else? This really great sounding one that goes, like, *a-fat-stink-on-her* or *fuckatitioner*."

Farshtinkener.

"Definitely! Yes. What's it mean?"

Pretty much what it sounds like, I said, but what happened already?

"Oh, so Eliyahu's muttering all this stuff, like, '...knock the hat from my keppy?... the uncircumcised dog... to push his filthy Canaanite teeth back so his farshtinkiner mouth may accommodate this... I will... I will force this thermos down his throat with my fists,' and he pulls The Co-Captain's thermos from the pile of bagjunk, and it's right about then that I see through the gaps between the buses how the drivers in the circle are shaking hands and banging fists or whatever, and I figure I've gotta get Eliyahu outta there, so I touch his elbow, and he swings on me, man!"

Did you—

"No no, it's okay—I ducked it, and he saw I was me, and I told him, 'We gotta go now, the drivers are coming.' And Eliyahu says, 'Tell me I will damage him tomorrow, Vincie, or I will never be able to stop pacing this facocta circle.' I love *facocta* by the way, it's my favorite of all of them I think, but I know Eliyahu's got ISS tomorrow, and so I tell him, 'If not tomorrow, then Monday.' And then he goes, 'Am I a child? You would talk to me about Monday? There will be no Monday.' And then the Co-Captain, through the window, *he* says, 'Am I-uh the child? You woulda to talka to me about on Monday?' like trying to mimic Eliyahu, but it sounds way more like Chico Marx than like Larry David's dad—not his dad-dad, but his show-dad— what's his name?"

Shelley Berman, I said.

"That's it. The impression sounded nothing like Shelley Berman, which is pretty much what you'd go for if you wanted to make fun of how Eliyahu sounds, right? But Eliyahu whipped the thermos at his face anyway, and the Co-Captain pulled his head inside the bus and the thermos tonked off the windowframe and I caught it, which was really smooth of Vincie, I think.

Stealth, I said.

"Thank you. Because Eliyahu didn't fucken appreciate it at all. He just tried to grab it from me, the thermos, and I didn't let him because we had to get outta there because like I said: those facocta drivers.

"But so Eliyahu goes, 'Give me the thermos and don't give me nazarite about Monday, Vincie.'

Narishkeit, I said.

"That's the one. And I said, 'I don't know what you mean about Monday, but please don't be upset like this—we fucken have to fucken go.'

"And Eliyahu says some Hebrew stuff I can't even begin to imitate, but The Co-Captain could. And he did. He did it pretty good, like, 'Chuh chuchaluh shicha hucha lachama.' And then Eliyahu swiped the thermos out of my hand and let fly at the Co-Captain's grill again. This time he got chin: *cronk!* And the Co-Captain yelped, ducked under the windowframe. And I said to Eliyahu, 'Feel better?' and he goes, 'Only a little. I want his earring,' but he lets me kinda lead him away from the buses, and what's funny is this: The Co-Captain's on Eliyahu's intramural bus, which is Bus One, but the one he's barracaded himself on is Two, and there's no way he's gonna ride on the same bus as Eliyahu now, so he's stuck on the wrong bus! And not only that, but he was supposed to go home on the regular bus like those other fuckers because he's got his big game tomorrow. And plus, even though we got away from the bus circle a little so the drivers wouldn't bust Eliyahu, Eliyahu made us stay in seeing distance so the Co-Captain was too scared to even get off Bus Two to gather up all the junk that fell out of his bag, which was strewn everywhere! I had no idea Eliyahu was like that, man. That he was the kinda guy to think of that—sticking around like that. He's so fucken angry. Who knew? I mean, yeah, when he came into the Cage he did that thing where he held out his hat and said he was from Brooklyn, but then—I mean he asks me if you're dead, like, five, six fucken times a day, and, every time, he looks ready to cry. The whole point of me telling you this is this, though: While we're standing there watching over the bus circle, I'm going over it in my head, everything that just happened, and I ask Eliyahu, I say: 'What was that shit you were saying before about no Monday?' Because remember, he said, 'There will be no Monday.' So I ask what he meant, and he goes, 'Are you kidding with me?' Real snotty, he said it, like he was offended or something. So I was like, 'What the fuck?' and he goes, 'Tomorrow we destroy the Arrangement.' He said it like I was a dumbass not to know that, and I thought: Maybe I am. But what's weird is, it didn't feel like I was a dumbass. It felt more like what I was saying yesterday on this very bus; it felt like I was just *playing* the dumbass. It felt like that because when Eliyahu said we'd destroy the Arrangement tomorrow, it sounded true, like we'd all agreed on it, but I couldn't remember doing that. I couldn't remember agreeing on it, and it seems like the kind of thing I would have remembered, right? So I said, 'There's a plan to destroy the Arrangement?' And Eliyahu said, 'A plan I don't know—an understanding, though? Surely there's an understanding.' 'Well who says?' I said. And Eliyahu said, 'Everyone says.' And I said, 'Like who, though?' And he said, 'Like your friend the Main Man Scott Mookus.' And I said, 'Main Man says a lot of crazy stuff.' And Eliyahu said, 'Our friend Gurion says.' And I said, 'No way. I'd remember if Gurion said that.' And Eliyahu said, 'If hyperscoot was the beginning, and hyperscoot began third period, and by seventh period we're already in the middle, what can be tomorrow if not the end, Vincie? And what can be the end for the Side of Damage, who is against the Arrangement, if not the end of the Arrangement? And what will bring about the end of the Arrangement, if not the destruction of the Arrangement? And who will bring about the destruction of the Arrangement, if not the side that is against the Arrangement?'

"So is it true, Gurion?"

I didn't know if it was true. It was just like Vincie said.

I said, It's just like you said—it *sounds* true, but I hadn't thought of it til you said it. I mean...

"Well, I just play the dumb one, man, but I'll tell you: This morning, right after that first hyperscoot? I would've said fuck yeah for sure we're doing it and we fucken well should do it: destroy. But today was long and full of weird fucken shit. Like what happened with Nakamook? That's the thing I wanted to talk to you about before. That was fucked up, right? And it was the same kind of fucked up as this kind of fucked up that we're already talking about. We should have all rushed Slokum in the two-hill field—we were all there, and I don't care who he is, he can't take thirty-odd kids out, especially not while holding onto you—but at the same time, we were waiting for Nakamook to do something first. Actually, first we were waiting for you to kick Slokum's ass, we figured you'd get it under control. But then there was like a solid half a minute where we all knew you *weren't* gonna get it under control and what we did was look to Nakamook, and he wasn't doing anything, and by the time we gave up on him—at least by the time *I* did—Bam had already set you down. That was some weird shit. No one ever said Nakamook would be the leader of us if you were in trouble, but we all acted like he was—there was an *understanding.* And that first hyperscoot, too—no one decided to do it, right? Not out loud. And then suddenly we were doing it. And it was great. But that other shit with Slokum? I feel really bad about that other shit. And I'm sorry about that fucken shit. And I feel like I gotta prove myself to you now. Or get Leevon and Ronrico and Ben-Wa and probably a fifth guy together and try to kick Benji's ass or something, which is really the most fucken upsetting part, because he's been my fucken friend for two years, which is more than one-sixth of my life, and since I can't really remember shit from before kindergarten, it's like more than that—it's like one third of my life. Or two-fifths even, I don't fucken know. But you're the only guy besides Mookus and Leevon who never once made fun of me during that horrible flinching phase

I was going through, and not only that but you healed it, and so what am I supposed to do?"

The idea of anyone, let alone my friends, kicking Benji's ass just made me sad. I thought it should make me happy, though, so I didn't say anything. Instead, I hugged Vincie, like how Eliyahu had hugged me in the hallway on Tuesday. And Vincie was happy I hugged him, and he hugged me back, but then you could tell by the nature of the ensuing non-sequiter that he got weirded out a little by the hug.

"Starla Flangent is so hot," he said. "And I'm pretty sure she's into Vincie. We'll see if she comes over."

She's into Vincie, I said.

"But that's the other thing about tomorrow, too," Vincie said. "What happens if Starla comes over tonight and we fall in love like you and June or Benji and Jelly or Chunkstyle and Boshka or—if it doesn't sick you out too much to think about—Ronrico and Mangey, who I saw holding hands? I mean, it seems like we're gonna fucken fall in love, right? It's in the air or whatever, and so what if that happens?"

What do you mean? I said.

"If we destroy the Arrangement—say we *can* do it—but then afterward, when they put us in a new school—do you think it'll be the same school for all of us? Because if not, then... I don't know, man. I don't know if I've fully fallen in love yet. It seems iffy, though. I mean, it's supposed to be a big deal to fall in love. It's supposed to be the biggest deal, and even though I probably haven't fully done it yet, it's pretty fucken hard for me to imagine a good reason to do something that I thought would stop me from being able to see Starla. At the same time, though, when I think about her, I get all filled up with this feeling like I'm great because she's great and maybe she loves me and so I shouldn't have to take any shit off anyone, ever, and it makes me want to destroy everything around us that's suck. Actually, no—I already wanted to destroy everything around us that's suck. What it makes me feel like is that I *can* destroy everything around us that's suck. And that if I *can*, I *should*. And if I *should*, but I *don't*, then I'm gonna get fucked for it. If I should, but I don't—and at the first chance I get—then something will happen so that I *can't*. And even if I'm kidding myself—even if I never *could* destroy everything around us that's suck, maybe because Starla *doesn't* love me or maybe because being in love with her *isn't* the biggest deal—then I might as well destroy as much suck shit around me as possible anyway, because what's the fucken use of any of it. What's the fucken use, you know, in taking shit off anyone? What's the use? What's the fucken use? I mean, what the fuck's the use? And now I feel like a fucken dumbass again, though, because now I'm all the sudden full-on 'fuck-yeah let's destroy the Arrangement tomorrow,' which I wasn't a second ago, but like I said, I don't think I'm even fully in love yet, and so what the fuck do I know about tomorrow?"

You're in love, I said. I said, You just described it perfectly.

"I don't even understand what I described, Gurion. I just know that I said 'fuck' way too much. Who talks like me? No one."

You're Vincie Portite, I said. I said, Vincie Portite says 'fuck' a lot.

"Call-Me-Sandy says that when I say 'fuck' it's because 'fuck' is a really angry word, and when I say it, I trick myself into getting angry and saying it more, and that gets me more angry, and I start believing that I'm completely right about everything, which is what I do when I'm angry is start believing I'm right about everything, which Sandy says is why I like to get angry to begin with, and I think Sandy's right because I just said 'fuck' a whole lot and I believe I'm completely right about everything I just said, even though I have no idea what the fuck I just said. What the fuck did I say?"

I said, You said you were in love with Starla and that being in love with Starla makes it seem like it's safe to act dangerous, and that if it's safe to act dangerous, then maybe it's dangerous to act safe; maybe if you act safe when it's safe to act dangerous, you said, then you endanger the thing that made it safe to act dangerous. You said that not to be dangerous while you're in love is to endanger your being in love.

"So how are we gonna destroy the Arrangement?"

We'll act dangerous, I said.

"But how?"

It's less dangerous if we plan it out, I said.

No one sang anything when we got to the Frontier.

17
SCUFFLES

Thursday, November 16, 2006
5:05 p.m.–Bedtime

Outside the Welcome Office, I bobbed and weaved to stealth past three sentries. I slammed the door behind me, but Flowers wasn't there to surprise. Just Edison. He fell off the coucharm, landing on a haunch.

I called my dad so he could tell me how he'd won in court—he liked that—but I got sent to voicemail, and so I tried my mom, in case they were together. While it rang, I noticed a note was taped to the television:

> G,
> Amateur plumbing for screaming primadonnas. Fiercely clogged pot, engineer out with flu. Rm 16. Come get me.
> —F

Without saying hello first—she must have recognized Flowers's number and known it was me—my mother told me everything was fine, though they'd be at the hospital for a while. I asked her why she was at the hospital. She was surprised Arthur hadn't said anything. I asked her again why she was at the hospital and she told me not to raise my voice. Then she told me there was a shuffle. And I didn't know what she meant and she raised her voice and told me a scuffle, and not to pick on her, right now was not the time to pick on her. "There was a scuffle outside of the courthouse and your aba fell down." What does that mean he fell? "In the scuffle. Do. Not. Yell at me." Who was he in a scuffle with? "Who? Who? *He* was in a scuffle with no one. He was peripheral to the scuffle. This was an accident that he fell. They were after the Nazi." They who? "No one tried to hurt your aba. And he is fine. He is in no danger. He has some bruises, and he may have torn a ligament, and this hurts, but it is not the end of the world, Gurion. And there is no concussion, just a little swelling on the outside. He is in no danger." She'd said "no danger" twice and I told her so and she told me not to have crazy ideas, that she was my mother and she had never lied to me and

I said, He's fine? And she said, "I promise," and I told her I didn't ask her to promise and she made the kind of frustrated pleading sound that you do not need to clench your teeth to make but you always clench your teeth anyway, then took an audible breath, and said, "Please, Gurion. I am not happy that he has been hurt either, and I wish I could be with you right now, but Aba cannot be alone in a hospital, it upsets him. Arthur said he will drive you home, and if we are not back yet, he will see to your dinner. I am very angry at him for not being there when the bus dropped you from school." I told her a toilet was overflowing and the janitor was sick. She told me it didn't matter now anyway, that he would drive me home and wait with me til they got there. And then I asked her why Flowers had to wait with me and she told me it was because I was upset and I told her that *she* was upset and she agreed and told me I wasn't helping and I told her I wanted to come to the hospital and she said she didn't know how long they'd be there, that my father might talk to the reporters or might not and had yet to talk to policemen and that if certain tests showed certain results certain other tests would have to be administered and that could take hours or who knew how long and I was not welcome at the hospital but they would wake me if I was sleeping when they got back to the house and go get Arthur now and please do not, for God's sake, watch the news, and I told her God didn't care if I watched the news, and who did she think she was telling me I wasn't welcome at the hospital when my father got in a scuffle and she told me she was my mother and my father's wife and she could beat me up even if I had forgotten and that if I watched the news to spite her she would remind me and I told her I would not watch the news to spite her, and it was true that I would not watch the news to spite her, and it was true that I would watch the news, though I didn't say that. She loved me and now the doctor had to talk to her so she hung up and I took the remote off the coffee table and hit POWER.

I found my dad on CNN, shielding his eyes from the sun and descending the courthouse stairway beside a smiling Patrick Drucker, then stopping halfway down before a handful of reporters holding microphones.

"Mr. Drucker," says one of the reporters, "is your—" and the rest of the question gets lost beneath a studio-imposed bleeping sound: someone offscreen has cursed.

The camera turns a 180 to reveal scores of protesters. Except for their consignment to the parking lot—six cops in sunglasses are holding a line at the bottom of the stairway—the scene looks no different than it did the day before. The same picket-signs stab the sky. The same swastikas-and-stripes flag flaps overhead. That guy in the skimask and keffiyeh—he's waving his fist.

A second camera feed is cued and the time signature in the corner jumps from 3:44:21 p.m. to 3:47:36 p.m. The new visual field contains the whole scene as witnessed from just above and behind the protestors.

"...feel great," Drucker is saying. "I feel like this victory is—" and there's another bleeping sound, this one lasting five or six seconds.

Just before the bleeping stops, Drucker sieg-heils.

My father grabs the back of his own neck.

A stitch of blackness blinks on the screen and the time signature jumps again. 3:47:36 becomes 3:48:20. Same feed.

The entire parking lot has begun to roil. Shoulders press shoulders. The swastikas-and-stripes is tipping, draping a picket for a second, now sucking under, now disappeared. "See, it's these kinda people," Drucker says, hand still aloft, "who control the media. Who control the money. Who don't believe in the first ammend—" *Bleeeep.* Sieg heil. "...damage the—" *Bleep.* Sieg heil.

Protesters push onto the sidewalk, cops pull batons from their holsters.

My father backs up a step. *Bleeeeeeeeeeeeep.* Two cops walk into the fray, exit the fray.

"...parasites..." *Bleep.*

Sieg heil.

"...and Spielberg..." *Bleep.*

Double sieg heil.

Another stitch of blackness. The time-stamp reads 3:50:45. The angle is the same as it was before the stitch, but it has to be a different feed with an unsynched time-stamp because it makes no sense for my father, Drucker, or any of the reporters to have continued standing there for two more minutes on the courthouse steps—they must have seen by then how the lot was roiling, and they must by now see what is starting to happen there: the pickets parallel to the ground, the pickets swinging.

The keffiah guy takes an elbow to the gut, stumbles out of frame.

All six cops ascend a step backward.

Drucker keeps talking, the bleeping keeps bleeping.

Drucker: Sieg heil.

A cop falls down.

Drucker: Sieg heil. A picket flies like a spear.

Sieg heil. Bleeping. Nazis chased out of frame.

A flown picket hits a reporter in the ass. The reporters spray out in six directions.

The cops stutter-step, retreat. Drucker revolves, starts climbing stairs.

My father's holding his ground, showing his palms, yelling something. A protester knocks him sideways. He falls. The crowd rolls over him slow, then fast. The backs of heads and torsos (vague pain in my hand) fill the screen where he'd stood.

More flown pickets. One of them, its sign torn off, strikes Drucker on the back of the neck as he reaches for the courthouse doorknob. He's down. Protestors get there, stomp. Then more. And more.

(More pain in my hand.)

The last of the mob having ascended the stairway, the center of the screen opens up. My father is laying across three steps, a lipstick-red disposable lighter peeking out of a tear in his nearer slash pocket. He's blinking rapidly—the one eye I can see is. Then he's rising, holding his head, turning toward the camera, looking beyond it, tieknot askew, blinking, squinting, sensing the lighter slipping through the tear, attempting to get the lighter back where it belongs, both hands off his head, using two hands, missing the mark, widening the tear, reaching to catch the lighter as it drops. His keychain follows, bounces off his wrist, lands on the lighter on the stair below. And then my father takes a step toward the camera. His brow goes high. His jaw muscles bulge. He stands up straight, straighter than straight, hard intake of breath. His eyes roll. His lids drop. He buckles and plunges.

I don't know if the CNN producer intentionally froze the frame at that point, or if it was the outcome of technical difficulties, but my father, collapsing, arms limp at his sides, chin inches from concrete—the image lingered on the screen for seconds. The time signature in the corner read 3:51:18 p.m.

The pain in my hand throbbed sharp.

Cut to newsdesk.

A blue-eyed anchor with a wet-combed widow's peak was saying that Patrick Drucker was in critical, then Flowers was standing there, blocking the screen, doing something to my wrist, saying, "Open up."

He meant my hand. I opened it up. Shards and dusty particles of the shattered remote fell into my lap. Two slim Duracells. A splash of blood. I shook off what stuck.

Flowers reached back and offed the power just as the anchor started bungling a sentence. "The protestors, mostly comprised of Jews—Jewish people—"

"Gurion," Flowers said.

It was not an uncommon syllable for a Roman to stammer, but when the Roman was a newsman it always chilled me up. I could remember three such newscasted "Jews" off the top of my head.

"You dad's fine," Flowers said.

But the thing was I could remember three such newscasted "Jews" off the top of my head, and since I could, I did. I heard the first one after the Ishmaelites attacked the Fairfield Street Synagogue: "The youths assaulted the Jews-the Jewish congregants with stones," said an NBC 5 Local News reporter. A week later, on the ABC 7 Nightly News: "The Jews-the Jewish-the Israeli soldiers entered Gaza at seven this morning." A month after that, in a round-table discussion on CSPAN, the Reuters Middle East Bureau Chief was asked by the moderator: "To the best of your knowledge, what percentage of Jew-Zionist-Israeli citizens would support the release of imprisoned Hamas freedom fighters in exchange for a cessation of hostilities against the militant settlers?" Those were just the ones I remembered verbatim. There were others, too, each of them uttered in a discussion occasioned by violent activity. Sometimes the Israelites had done the violence; other times they had suffered it. Sometimes the stammer seemed to unmask something and other times it just seemed like a stammer.

"Shit," Flowers said, staring at my hand.

A plastic sliver was jammed in the muscle of my thumb. I pulled it with my teeth. The hole was triangular.

Flowers shuddered, wadded leaves of Kleenex the color of lemon ice cream, pressed the wad to the wound.

"You dad's fine," he said.

I spit the sliver into my cupped left hand, dropped it into a pocket, watched the tissue get wet and orange.

"Say something," said Flowers.

I said, Now I'll say 'a Jew' and just the word 'Jew' sounds like a dirty word and people don't know whether to laugh or not.

"Lenny Bruce?" Flowers said.

Yeah, I said.

"Funny man," said Flowers. "You—"

Sometimes, I said.

"You dad's *fine*," Flowers said.

       □ □ □ □ □ □ □

Scholars recognize three significant aspects of the conversation Avraham has with Hashem on the eve of Sodom's destruction. First, the conversation is an argument: the patriarch of patriarchs, the original model of exemplary Israelite behavior, tells Hashem that He is about to make a mistake. Second, Hashem, rather than smiting Avraham for arguing—He does not punish Avraham at all—listens to what Avraham has to say. Third, there is the substance of what Avraham says: that when faced with the choice, it is not only more important to save a righteous person than it is to destroy a wicked one, but more important to save a righteous person than to destroy *numerous* wicked ones.

Even though, if not because, these three aspects of the conversation are so significant, others of no less significance tend to get overlooked. One is *how* Avraham says what he says, another *when* he says it. He enters the conversation like an accuser—raging, scornful, indignant above all—and he does so at a moment when a scholar would expect indignation to be the last thing he would feel. It was only three days earlier that Hashem told Avraham he would have the thing he wanted most in the world—a son with Sarah—and, for that reason, a scholar might expect Avraham to feel joyous; or, if not joyous, then maybe weak, for immediately after learning that Isaac would be born, Avraham circumsized himself, and the third post-operative day is known to be the most painful, more painful even than the bris itself. That Avraham would feel exhausted is another possibility. If neither weak with pain nor joyous with news of a son-to-be, then maybe, a scholar might think, Avraham would be exhausted by the tasks of dutiful hosting: only *seconds* before Hashem told him of His plans for Sodom, Avraham bade farewell to the angels Hashem sent to his tent to test his hospitality, a test he passed without complaint, despite the pain of the third day.

Then again, it is *within the very same utterance* of His plans for Sodom that Hashem reiterates His pledge to give Avraham a son with Sarah—more than a son, in fact. "Shall I conceal from Avraham what I do," Hashem begins, "now that Avraham is surely to become a great and mighty nation, and all the nations of the earth shall bless themselves by him?" At which a scholar would expect Avraham to feel—if not in addition to joyous or weak or exhausted, then in place of those feelings—safe, protected; certainly not indignant.

Yet Avraham, once Hashem is through speaking, once the plans for Sodom have been laid out before him ("Because the outcry of Sodom and Gomorrah has become great, and because their sin has been very grave," Hashem has just finished saying, "I will descend and see: If they act in accordance with its outcry which has come to Me—then destruction! And if not, I will know."), Avraham does the most dangerous thing imaginable. He lashes out at the guarantor of his safety, raises his voice to challenge his protector. He yells at God.

"What if there should be fifty righteous people in the midst of Sodom?" says Avraham. "Would You still stamp it out rather than spare the place for the sake of the fifty righteous people within it? It would be sacrilege to You to do such a thing, to bring death upon the righteous along with the wicked. It would be sacrilege to You! Shall the judge of all the earth not do justice?"

And Hashem not only listens to Avraham—this brown old man shouting accusations in the desert, this defiant creation waving his fist—but attempts to *appease* him. And this makes a scholar wonder—or at least it *should* make a scholar wonder—if coming to Hashem full of rage is not sometimes (on those occasions when the scholar faces injustice, for example) a better idea than coming to Him full of praise. "If I find fifty righteous people in Sodom," says Hashem, "I will spare the city on their account."

And Avraham, though no longer as indignant, is nonetheless unappeased. "What if there are five fewer?" he says. "What if there are forty-five righteous people in Sodom?"

And Hashem says that for forty-five, he'll spare the city. And Avraham continues to bargain. From forty-five to forty, forty to thirty, thirty to twenty, and then, says Avraham, "Let not my Lord be annoyed and I will speak but this once: What if ten should be found there?"

And Hashem says, "I will not destroy on account of the ten."

The next line closes the chapter: "Hashem departed when He had finished speaking to Avraham, and Avraham returned to his place."

When *He* had finished speaking: not when *Avraham* had finished speaking to Him; not when *they* had finished speaking to one another. "When He had finished speaking to Avraham" = "Avraham was not finished speaking."

So what would Avraham have said, had Hashem not departed just then? It should be as obvious to scholars as it was to Hashem.

He would have said, "Five righteous men?" And if Hashem tried to appease him, he would have said, "Three righteous men?" And if Hashem agreed to three, he would have said, "And one?"

There are some scholars who will disagree with these assertions. Some scholars will argue that there is no way of knowing if I am right or wrong, no way to know if Avraham was as settled on the number ten as was Hashem. Some may even argue that the phrase prefacing Avraham's last spoken sally of the argument, a phrase which, to me, reads as nothing more than an act of formal self-effacement that one who has just finished yelling indignantly at the Creator of the Universe would, on calming down a little bit, think wise to employ—some scholars might argue that "Let my Lord not be annoyed and *I will speak but this once*" indicates that Avraham had no intention of continuing to bargain. And those scholars would have a point, just not a very significant one.

Whether or not Avraham was finished speaking, whether or not he ultimately did come to terms with Hashem, the last line of Genesis 18 contains the most significant aspect of the conversation that gets overlooked by scholars: the revelation of Hashem's (if not also Avraham's) final stance on collateral damage. Namely: that some collateral damage is acceptable.

And how much is some? How much collateral damage? At first, it seems easy to calculate: 9 parts per the population of Sodom. And scholars do have a rough idea of that population—between 600 and 1200. But then, on second thought, neither Avraham nor Hashem would speak of children as being righteous or wicked (until one comes of age, one's behavior is attributed to one's parents), so scholars must subtract the number of Sodomite males under the age of thirteen and Sodomite females under the age of twelve from the denominator. Scholars don't know this number, but can assume, conservatively (in terms of allowable collateral damage), that the percentage of children in Sodom was equivalent to the percentage of children in Jordan today ≈ 40%, which is relatively low for that region.

So the denominator (the estimated population of Sodom minus 40% of itself) is somewhere between 360 and 720. The acceptable proportion of collateral damage, then, is somewhere between 9 parts per 360 and 9 parts per 720. Reduced to their greatest common denominators, these proportions become, respectively, 1 part per 40 and 1 part per 80.

In other words: If a scholar were to approach the issue of collateral damage as conservatively as possible, that scholar would conclude that to kill 1 righteous person in the course of killing 79 or more wicked ones is acceptable to Hashem. If, on the other hand, a scholar were to approach the issue of collateral damage as liberally as possible, that scholar would conclude that to kill 1 righteous person in the course of killing *39 or more* wicked ones is acceptable to Hashem.

In either case, to say "Hashem treats the righteous with mercy" is omissive.

Hashem treats the righteous with mercy when it is cost-efficient.

His standards of cost-efficiency are the ones by which Israelites must strive to live. Therefore even those who play the numbers as loosely as possible cannot justify bringing a proportion of collateral damage that is greater than 2.5% of the total damage brought. When death is the unit by which damage is measured (as seen above), these calculations are simple enough. When injury is the unit of measurement, however, it is a bit more complicated. How many righteous noses, for example, may be collaterally broken in the course of smashing 39 wicked femurs? Certainly more than one—a broken nose is little more than a flesh wound compared to a broken leg—but how many? And what is the acceptable ratio of crushed and righteous strong-side wrists to crushed and wicked weak-side ones? It is true that without the use of his left hand, David could not have sawn past the neckbone of Goliath of Gath, and so could not have hoisted high the massive head, but without the use of his right, he would never have even felled the giant.

Patrick Drucker was in critical. A coma, the radio was saying. A broken back. Six ribs snapped. One punctured lung.

My father had some bruises. Maybe some torn ligaments. Was his damage ≤ 2.5% of the total damage brought? I think it was—even if his ligaments *were* torn and Drucker *didn't* die.

And so, assuming Drucker was wicked, my father's damage was acceptable in the eyes of Hashem.

And so I found myself at odds with Hashem.

And not just Him.

Flowers turned off NPR and said, "Talk to me, man. You gotta talk."

We were heading south on Sheridan in his old Volvo wagon. According to my dad, Sheridan was known as the second most beautiful road anywhere. It wound a lot, often sharply, and that kept you from driving too fast and missing it. For miles you could see Lake Michigan between the gaps of the tree-shaded mansions. The white one with the Spanish-tiled roof was supposedly built by Capone. A few miles farther, the road widened to four lanes and the B'hai temple appeared in the distance. In all the world, there were only seven B'hai temples. The one in Haifa was known for its garden.

"You need to talk, Gurion."

I don't feel like talking.

The first most beautiful road anywhere was said to be in Monte Carlo. I could never remember what it was called, but my mom had driven it, and she said Sheridan was prettier.

Flowers said, "You spooking me out."

Heebie-jeebies, I told him.

"Oh, I see. We jokin' around. You break my remote, quote some Lenny Bruce, stare out the window twenty minutes so salty you jaw muscles bout to tear through you cheeks, then make some silly wordplay with some racial slurs and now it's all better. That something, man. Least it might be. I don't think I believe you, though. I think you bottlin up. I think you gettin heavy."

We passed Capone's, then the B'Hai—a dome set atop a pair of stacked hexagons, all stone and white.

Flowers blew air through his lips, pulled a folded paper square from his jacket, dropped it in my lap. "Not a single redmark," he said. "And it ain't cause I didn't read it."

I unfolded it. "There is love," it said. "There was always love, and there will be more love, always. Were there ever to be less love, we would all be at war and Your angels would learn suffering."

I tore it seven ways.

Flowers said, "Why you do that?"

It's nonsense, I said.

"You the one called it scripture."

That was a mistake, I said. It's just fiction.

He didn't like that.

"*Just* fiction. You believed it well enough yesterday. Maybe what you sayin right now is *just* fiction. Maybe you actin a little fictional."

Fiction is lies, I said. I said, I have no use for lies.

He liked that even less.

"So why you tell me you don't feel like talkin?" he said.

I don't, I said.

"No," he said. "You don't feel like talkin *to me*. That different than you don't feel like talkin. And what you said was, 'I don't feel like talkin.'"

I was being polite.

"Feedin me some maggoty-ass apple and callin it protein-enriched what you doin—polite's evasive, man."

I just saw my dad get trampled on television. I don't feel like talking to you about it.

"It ain't cause you saw you dad get trampled you ain't feel like talkin."

Why are you picking on me?

"Pickin on you—shit. What am I, some sadsack principal? I don't like the *reason* you ain't feel like talkin to me. You someone else, it be different. Might say to myself, 'He into some stoic, Hemingway yang.' That ain't you, though—you nothing like stoic. You a little boy don't shut the fuck up less he hidin something. And that what you doin. You leavin some vital information by the wayside. I pay attention to what you say. I pay attention to you *scriptures*, be they disavowed or not. I pay more attention than anyone else who reads them, if there even is anyone else, but that don't matter to you cause who the fuck am I, right? A Gentile. You friend, sure, but just some goy. No kinda person to talk to about the people you want to read you work most—people who couldn't care less what you have to say. And they the ones put you dad in the hospital. And they the ones—"

Stop treating my paradox like it's irony, I said. It's not that simple.

"Retreat to the abstract—that's good. Paradox versus irony: discuss."

I know who hurt my dad, I said, and I'm not *retreating* from that, I'm trying to figure out how to approach—

"Go on," said Flowers. "Whizkid youself into *total* fucken anguish and confusion."

Let me out of the car, I said.

"You cry all you want. I'm takin you to you folks." He dropped his handkerchief in my lap.

I threw it back at him.

"Too common a mistake in this world," he said. "Thinkin' ingratitude a form of pride. What it get you but some crusty sleeves?"

We're not friends anymore, I said. Let me out of the car.

He said, "The one ain't up to you any more than the other, Gurion."

Again he dropped the handkerchief in my lap. This time I used it. But let that not confuse any scholars. My tears, as usual, were well beside the point.

```
                    FRONT DOOR
                    FRONT DOOR
                    FRONT DOOR
                    FRONT DOOR
                    FRONT DOOR
                    FRONT DOOR
                    FRONT DOOR
                    FRONT DOOR
                    FRONT DOOR
                    FRONT DOOR
                    FRONT DOOR
                    FRONT DOOR
        STOOPSTOOPSTOOPSTOOPSTOOPSTOOPSTOOPSTOOP
        STOOPSTOOPSTOOPSTOOPSTOOPSTOOPSTOOPSTOOP
        STOOPSTOOPSTOOPSTOOPSTOOPSTOOPSTOOPSTOOP
        STOOPSTOOPSTOOPSTOOPSTOOPSTOOPSTOOPSTOOP
        STOOPSTOOPSTOOPSTOOPSTOOPSTOOPSTOOPSTOOP
        STOOPSTOOPSTOOPSTOOPSTOOPSTOOPSTOOPSTOOP
        STOOPSTOOPSTOOPSTOOPSTOOPSTOOPSTOOPSTOOP
        STOOPSTOOPSTOOPSTOOPSTOOPSTOOPSTOOPSTOOP
        STOOPSTOOPSTOOPSTOOPSTOOPSTOOPSTOOPSTOOP
        STOOPSTOOPSTOOPSTOOPSTOOPSTOOPSTOOPSTOOP
        STOOPSTOOPSTOOPSTOOPSTOOPSTOOPSTOOPSTOOP
        STOOPSTOOPSTOOPSTOOPSTOOPSTOOPSTOOPSTOOP

R  STEPSTEPSTEPSTEPSTEPSTEPSTEPSTEPSTEPSTEP  R
A  STEPSTEPSTEPSTEPSTEPSTEPSTEPSTEPSTEPSTEP  A
I  STEPSTEPSTEPSTEPSTEPSTEPSTEPSTEPSTEPSTEP  I
L                                            L
I                                            I
N  STEPSTEPSTEPSTEPSTEPSTEPSTEPSTEPSTEPSTEP  N
G  STEPSTEPSTEPSTEPSTEPSTEPSTEPSTEPSTEPSTEP  G
R  STEPSTEPSTEPSTEPSTEPSTEPSTEPSTEPSTEPSTEP  R
A                                            A
I                                            I
L                                            L
I  STEPSTEPSTEPSTEPSTEPSTEPSTEPSTEPSTEPSTEP  I
N  STEPSTEPSTEPSTEPSTEPSTEPSTEPSTEPSTEPSTEP  N
G  STEPSTEPSTEPSTEPSTEPSTEPSTEPSTEPSTEPSTEP  G
```

As we approached my stoop, the scrape of jostled pebbles sounded from the shadows beside the steps and there were whispers. We ascendend the stairway and I unlocked the door. Flowers went inside.

"You comin?" he said.

I'd already jumped the railing. A boy was crumpling beneath me.

Flowers said my name.

The boy hit the ground on his stomach, me atop him, and I dug my knuckles between his shoulderblades and then knee-hopped on his kidneys and he was still. I began to turn him over—I would deliver him his blindness with my bare hands—but I heard another vandal behind me.

I donkeykicked.

Though one of my heels connected, nothing buckled or squished = I'd missed both his knees and sack. I leapt off the still kid to finish the kicked one. That was when Flowers flipped the stooplight on and someone said, "Please." It was the second kid who said it.

The second kid was Emmanuel Liebman. He was sitting in the pebbles, leaning on my house, clutching his thigh. The still one was Shai Bar-Sholem, another boy who I'd been in Torah Study with at Schechter. Two more—Samuel Diamond and a Satmar I didn't recognize—were helping Shai to his feet.

"Why—?" said Emmanuel.

Why? I said.

I grabbed his face. I would dig my thumbs into the corners of his orbits and pull. *Why are you bombing my house?* I would pop his sockets. *Why did you lie to me?* And while his eyes swung from gory strands near his peyes—"Rabbi," he was saying, "Rabbi!"—I would carve matching tunnels in his mallet-shaped brain.

I thought.

But all I was doing was pressing the heels of my palms against his jaws. And not even that hard.

When Flowers pulled me into his bearhug, I barely struggled. "Hell you doing?" he said.

"Unhand him, sir," said Samuel, before us now.

"*Pardon* me?" Flowers said.

Samuel lifted 37 from the spot on the ground where Flowers had dropped it. He gripped it like a bat and stepped behind us.

"Please let go of the Rabbi, sir," said Emmanuel, the reflection of the stooplight's bulb a white square in the bell of his drawn pennygun. "We don't want to hurt you."

And of Shai Bar-Sholem, the Satmar asked, "This is the tzadik?"

"That's him," said Shai.

And now the Satmar drew his weapon and, training it on Flowers, said, "Am I holding it right, Rabbi Gurion?"

□   □   □   □   □   □   □

"Had we known about your vandals," said Emmanuel Liebman, once I'd finished apologizing and given him an icepack, "we would have hidden *behind* your house." He sat on the floor in front of me, leaning against my dresser, the Satmar and Samuel Diamond flanking him. On the other side of the room, Shai Bar-Sholem stood stooped at my window and held his kidneys.

Flowers had left. Having spent no small amount of energy squinting to reconcile the bruised scholars' testimonies of our friendship with the very battery that had bruised them—"He's our teacher, sir," had said Shai; "We trust this bit of violence, if anything other than an unfortunate mishap, must certainly be some kind of valuable lesson," Emmanuel had added—he eventually became placated enough (or maybe just weirded out enough) to suggest we all eat some dinner, then ordered us Pizza Pnina, which, though glat kosher, and therefore suitable for the scholars to ingest, wouldn't deliver south of Devon. And then he left us there on the stoop, gladly it seemed—chuckling as soon as he flipped his phone closed, and continuing all the way to his car—to go pick it up, along with some paper plates.

"At the very least," said Emmanuel, pressing down on the icepack, "we should have thought to come out from the shadows in a more timely fashion—after these horrible things that happened to your father, we should have guessed you'd be jumpy."

"I can't even imagine," said the Satmar. "A broken neck is bad enough. To have it broken by trampling protesters, though—much less Jewish—"

"Don't remind him," said Samuel Diamond.

The Satmar covered his mouth in shame.

"What's *wrong* with you, Weiss?" snapped Shai Bar-Sholem. He winced, clutched his kidneys.

I chinned the air from him to the heating pad I'd set on my bed = Lay down already.

He said, "Your sheets, Rabbi—I'm all muddy."

I said, I made you all muddy.

"That's true," he said, and laid down.

The Satmar's mouth was still covered. He reminded me of Eliyahu a little.

I said to him, What is your first name, Weiss?

"Solly," said Solly Weiss the Satmar, from behind his hand.

It's okay, Solly Weiss, I said. My father's neck's not broken. You must have heard an early report—they inflate those for drama. He might have torn some ligaments in his knee is all.

Is all? I thought. Maybe, I thought.

"Baruch Hashem," said the scholars.

But I wasn't willing to join them. It was certainly good that my father hadn't suffered greater damage, but that didn't mean it was a blessing, or that I should thank Hashem. If anything that fails to be worse than it is is a blessing, then no one would say anything *but* baruch Hashem, for everything could be worse, and so everything would be a blessing. We would all be angels, one-legged and faceless, seething with endless, hopeless praise. Desormie desormiated all the girls in spandex, but he never raped them; I should say baruch Hashem? Eliyahu's family was murdered, but, baruch

Hashem, they weren't tortured first? The Shoah—as many Israelites had remained as were destroyed—baruch Hashem?

That they—the three who I knew—had ever been my friends at all, though, let alone that they'd remained my friends after I'd attacked two of them: that was certainly a blessing, and for *that* blessing I might have thought to echo their baruch Hashem, but I was distracted by Solly, who continued to suffer from Shai's unnecessary, however well-intended, shaming; he was sniffling, and I saw his eyes had begun to well, golden swirls in the blue iris of the nearer one magnifying.

I removed the sap from my pocket and held it out to him, said, Look what I got today.

He took it with the hand that covered his mouth and soon the weapon cheered him. He thumbed the button and the rod snicked out, and while he tested the bendy action, his tears sucked back into his ducts.

I gave him a few seconds, then asked, Why haven't I met you before?

"We just moved here a couple weeks ago," he said, reaching over Emmanuel to give the sap to Samuel Diamond—Samuel had been making grabbing movements from the moment I'd brandished the thing. "We came from New York," said Solly. "Upstate. The Teitelbaum brothers are feuding with each other over who's in charge."

I heard about that, I said.

"It's very ugly," Solly said. "People throwing punches in shul. Breaking windows. My father didn't want to take sides, so we moved here. We're not really Satmars anymore. Still, I like to wear the flathat. It's a very nice hat. And not cheap." He took the hat off and held the brim between his pointers, then did circles with his wrists that spun it. He set it on my head. "Very handsome," he said. "Please accept it as a token of peace. I am sorry for what I said before. I want us to be friends."

I gave the hat back. I said, It *is* a nice hat, but for now I like my hood.

Solly seemed unconvinced.

If we weren't friends already, I said, I'd never have shown you that weapon.

"We thought you would need friends to talk to is why we didn't end up waiting for your response," said Emmanuel, exhibiting no interest in the sap which Samuel now proferred.

Mallet-headed or not, Emmanuel Liebman was one of my favorite people.

My response? I said to him.

"Yes, to my— Oh, of course!" said Emmanuel. "Of course. *That's* how come you still thought I might be the vandal, even after you saw my face. You didn't read our email, did you? Of course you didn't. You hadn't even gotten home yet. Here's what happened: That email you sent—Solly didn't show it to us til just a couple hours ago and…"

Email? I thought. Oh, the email I sent them! "New Scripture"! I thought. The two-hill field! I hadn't thought once about any of that stuff since they'd stepped up to Flowers. I was far more surprised to remember than angry. I tried to get angry. I thought I should be angry and found I wasn't angry. I seemed to have forgiven them without really trying—no, I didn't *seem to*, I *had* forgiven them—another surprise, though it shouldn't have been. Just twenty minutes earlier, in under ninety seconds, I'd gone from suddenly wanting to murder a former best friend to suddenly discovering I didn't have it in me to do so to suddenly seeing that this former best friend was not only not the enemy I'd thought he'd been, but a friend so good that, despite my having just attacked and injured him, he was willing to threaten a scary-sized man in order to protect me. To be surprised by anything at that point seemed dumb. So I made my voice angry, interrupting Emmanuel, who, while I'd spaced out on the above-described thoughts, had apparently not stopped speaking.

"…but the ambiguous nature of—" Emmanuel was saying.

And I said to him: Wait. Why didn't you come to Aptakisic today?

"Gurion, I just said… I just finished explaining…"

I didn't hear it.

"You didn't… What? Okay," said Emmanuel. "So okay," he said. "So Solly didn't show us the email you sent til just a couple hours ago, so—"

Solly? I said. What Solly? I said. What does he have to do with it? I sent it to all of you, every single scholar whose address I had.

"Yes," said Emmanuel. "We saw the CC box. And that's why as soon as Solly showed us the email, we forwarded it to every scholar therein, but that wasn't til just a couple hours ago."

"I would have myself forwarded it last night if I knew who you were," said Solly, "but I didn't know who you were til after school today, when I stopped by Emmanuel's to borrow his graphing calculator and happened to mention the strange email I received. He gave me your *Ulpan* then, and explained—"

Back up, I said. I don't understand. I sent that email to *all* of you. I sent it to everyone at Northside and Schechter—and the Schechter list, at least, was totally updated from Rabbi Salt.

"Yes, Rabbi," said Shai, "but email from your Gurionforever address is blocked by our parents, ever since the meeting."

The meeting? I said.

"You don't know about the meeting?" said Shai.

"I told you he didn't know about the meeting," Samuel said. "If he knew about the meeting, why would he have sent the email from Gurionforever?" To me, he said, "They had this meeting. At the J. Back in June. It wasn't *about* blocking your email address, Rabbi—it was a planning session to do a fundraiser for Sudanese refugees. But. The meeting was right after everyone saw that email from the Northside Headmaster."

"And right after you sent that 'don't call me I'll call you' one," said Shai.

My parents never told me, I said.

"With all due respect, Rabbi, our parents don't speak to yours, so…"

I know, I said, but Rabbi Salt speaks to *them* sometimes. And what's more, he speaks to *me*, and *he* never told me either, I said. And Esther, I said. I said, Esther didn't tell me, either.

"They probably wanted to save you some pain," said Shai.

"They were probably trying to protect you," Emmanuel said. "And if your parents knew, I'm sure they were, too. It wasn't such a nice meeting."

Samuel said, "Once they were finished talking about African genocide, they started talking about you and your dangerous influence and, long made short: in the course of the discussion, Sidney Beber's tech-savvy mom, who my mom said is the one who originally told her and every other scholar's mom north of the Mason-Dixon about these stupid Nojacks*—Beber said

---

* A Nojack was a walkie-talkie-type celly without a numberpad—just a dial and a CALL/END button—that came packaged with a plan which allowed parents to program the Nojack in such a way that it could call and be called by as few as one and no greater than twenty-five phone numbers. Some parents programmed the Nojacks to permit calls to and from their kids' closest friends, but for the most part they were programmed only to communicate with family members and emergency services. I don't know if Sidney Beber's was the only, the first, or even the loudest mom to push Nojacks—though neither Samuel nor Mrs. Diamond were liars, they each, like so many good storytellers, did have the tendency to exaggerate the truth whenever the effect of doing so might serve to entertain or to ironize or to amp up tension—but by the eighth day of Chanukah of 2005, nearly everyone at Schechter who had asked for a cellphone wound up with a Nojack, Samuel being one of them; and because at Schechter (and at Northside, too, I later found out), the existence of Nojacks allowed a new justification for the headmaster to ban regular cellphones (he had tried before, in 2003, and been shot down by parents of cellphone-having kids—at that time, such parents tended more than not to be near-psychotically overprotective—on grounds that they needed to have immediate access to their child in case of emergency, and vice-versa, and that it wasn't his right, or anyone else's, to take such access away), he did so, he banned them, Headmaster Unger, made all non-Nojack celly's illegal to possess at school, and these same parents (gladly, in most cases), cancelled their kids' old call-plans and bought them Nojacks. I, that year, received a set of CD ROMs of Talmud, which Ben Brodsky (iPod Nano) cracked so I could burn them for Emmanuel, who in turn had Ben crack his Zohar CD ROMs and burn them for me.

how easy it would be to block your email address, and everyone at the meeting thought that was a good idea."

"A lot of them had seen the 'don't call me I'll call you' one, too, and got scared," said Shai, "because the implication was you'd eventually get back in contact."

"So then instructions got emailed to everyone for how to block email through all the different email clients, and these emailed instructions all listed Gurionforever specifically," said Samuel.

"This egghead mump named Malinowitz even wrote some code called BanGurion.exe," said Shai, "which was this small program for Windows users that you download and click it and it blocks Gurionforever just like that."

Samuel said, "People forwarded the instructions with the code attached and posted them to listservs and so on—you know how word spreads. It's pretty surprising, actually, that Solly's parents didn't get those emails."

"I'm sure they did," Solly said. "We were still in New York, though, in the middle of that feud, and my parents were probably receiving too much email about the alleged demagoguery of various New York–area Teitelbaums to be concerned with a supposedly false messiah from Chicago. Anyway, it turns out it was a blessing. If your address had been blocked by my parents, the email wouldn't have ever gotten to me, and so it wouldn't have gotten to anyone."

I said, Why didn't any scholars tell me my address was blocked, though?

Emmanuel said, "Please don't be upset with us, Rabbi. I know *I* would have told you, but I thought you'd know, and I think everyone else thought the same, and that it didn't really matter because how hard would it be for you to get a new address to send emails from? A new address—it's free to get one. I have four, myself."

"And plus you told us not to contact you in that 'don't call me I'll call you' one," said Shai.

"Stop calling it that," Samuel said. "It's disrespectful. Call it by the title Gurion gave it."

"I can't remember the title."

"'Last Word.' How hard is that to remember?"

"But my kidneys hurt, Samuel."

I felt like I was in *Romeo and Juliet*, or maybe the Book of Esther. Happenstance and simple misunderstandings—piling up, convoluting, resolving. I felt like I was in a sitcom. Had I known that my email address was blocked, I'd have sent them 'New Scripture' from a different address, and had 'New

Scripture' gotten to them at the time I'd sent it, they'd have all shown up at Aptakisic. Had they all shown up at Aptakisic, I wouldn't've gotten back to the Cage for third, let alone been distracted enough to forget to sign my pass, in which case Botha would not have yelled at me, in which case Ben-Wa might not have snapped, in which case there wouldn't have been a hyperscoot, and if there hadn't been a hyperscoot, I wouldn't know the Side of Damage was my army, and if Ben-Wa'd snapped anyway and there *had* been a hyperscoot and someone—say, Benji—told me about it but I hadn't felt betrayed by the Israelite scholars, I might not have cared that the Side was my army, and either way I, not having seen the hyperscoot, wouldn't have argued at lunch about what to call it, and there'd've been no contest about what to call it, and I'd've not scraped my elbow during the Electric Chair and then gotten sent to Nurse Clyde's and met the Five, and I'd've not offended Benji, and he'd've not pulled the alarm, and I wouldn't know the source of Eliyahu's damage, and there'd've been no attack on Shlomo Cohen, no 'Death to the Jew,' no humiliation at the hands of Bam Slokum, no failure of Nakamook to step in and help me, none of the post-alarm hyperscoots either, no self-stabbed Benji, no call down to Brodsky's, no giggling Botha, no transformed Eliyahu, and as for my father—actually, no. What had happened to my father would've happened the same, and my sorrow and my anger at what happened would have been the same, though maybe, had I known that the scholars were still on my side, I'd've been able to address it all differently somehow, been able to do better than smash a remote and alienate Flowers: I'd've felt less helpless, at least a little. And I felt less helpless, at least a little, though still more helpless than I wanted to feel.

To Emmanuel, I said: I don't understand. How many listservs was this email-blocking email posted to?

"A lot," Emmanuel said.

How could I have missed it? I said.

"You subscribe to a lot of community listservs?"

None, I said, but I subscribe to every scholarly listserv I know about.

"Those are different, though," Emmanuel said. "Why would a post about blocking your address be on a scholarly listserv?"

Why wouldn't it?

"It was not a very scholarly kind of post. I mean, yes, it had to do with you, our greatest scholar, but it didn't actually say much about you, other than your email address. I mean, it didn't say anything about your teachings or anything."

They posted the one Kalisch wrote about me, I said.

"Someone *sent* that to those listservs, though," Emmanuel said. He said, "I'm not saying a scholarly listserv wouldn't have posted the email about blocking your address if someone had *sent it in*, but who'd send it in? I mean it's pretty strange anyone sent that Kalisch one to those scholarly listservs—pretty inelegant, no? If whoever was out to damage you had half a brain, he'd have posted it straight to the community ones. The scholarly listservs are there to discuss scripture. You getting kicked out of a school—to anyone who doesn't know who you are, at least—it's not exactly a talmudic type concern, right?"

Well if they don't know who I am, I said, then exactly.

"Exactly what?" said Emmanuel.

I mean: you're right, I said.

By then I was at my desk, waiting for my inbox to open. It was taking longer than usual.

"In any case, Rabbi," said Emmanuel. "We still haven't addressed the ambiguity about which I wrote you."

The loading icon in the corner of my monitor—a tiny pair of animated thumbs—kept pausing mid-twiddle.

"About whether your offer was a one-time offer," said Samuel.

My offer?

"The offer to receive your scripture," said Shai.

"On one hand, you invite us to your school to receive your scripture," said Emmanuel, "and you say that once it's delivered, things might somehow change in such a way as to make disobeying our parents a form of honoring them—a big *might* to be sure, but a might nonetheless—and that after the scripture gets delivered, we'll know if we can be in contact with you again."

"But then," said Samuel, "we didn't get the invitation til after the time you wanted us to come meet you."

"And so," said Emmanuel, "it seemed to us that we might have blown our chance."

"And not just us as in the us who are talking to you right now," said Shai, "but a lot of the scholars you meant to CC, who, from five minutes after Emmanuel forwarded your email to them, were jamming his phonelines and inbox, offering very clear opinions on the ambiguity."

The thumbs had grown still and become 2-D. I minimized the window, mazimized the window.

"Most of them don't see an ambiguity is what Shai means."

"That could have gone without saying, Samuel. Gurion knew exactly what I meant."

"Enough out of you."

"Most of the scholars think it's one way or the other," said Emmanuel. "Some say, 'By having not gotten the invitation til it was too late, we blew our chance to be led by Gurion.' And then the others say, 'We did not blow our chance. We'll visit him at his house on Saturday, after Havdallah, just like with his *Ulpan*, and he'll deliver the new scripture as he delivered his *Ulpan*.'

"So while it seems to us, us here in this room that is, that there is certainly an ambiguity," Emmanuel continued, "we are in the minority. And the ones who are ready to come over after Havdallah; they've already gotten carried away. "

I clicked STOP, then RELOAD. My inbox flashed—just the frame—then disappeared, but now at least the thumbs twiddled rhythmically.

Carried away like how? I said.

"Like they're already into the bobe-mayses," said Emmanuel. "This girl you mentioned, for example—all you told us is she's got red hair and you love her—but these scholars who are talking about visiting after Havdallah, they're all convinced there's some big story behind it, how you fell in love with her, and that it has to do with the new scripture. And granted, you mentioned her in the email, suggesting she's got something to do with the scripture and with your contacting us, so it's not unreasonable to assume there's some kind of story, but the kind of stories these scholars are predicting—they're not just stories, but parables or allegories about the diaspora and persecution or the diaspora and salvation or a coded set of further instructions, like a second *Ulpan*, wherein this girl you love is the Land of Israel or Torah or maybe Adonai Himself, and this Aptakisic the world or the United States or the whole of the Middle East, and this Cage the Canaanites or the Romans or the law of the land. And that's not even the half of it.

"Silly, Rabbi, in our opinion—they were all silly, these assumptions being made; ungrounded speculations the lot of them, Samuel and Shai and I felt," said Emmanuel. "And then: potentially dangerous, too. For despite all the excitement, despite how grateful we would all be to receive this scripture from you, let alone to be in contact again, despite how thrilling it would be to let ourselves get carried away like these other nutsos, it still wasn't clear to us—the three of us, I mean—whether or not we would even get to receive this scripture, now that we'd missed the invitation. And if we aren't to receive the scripture, if that invitation was a one-time offer, and if, as the invitation seemed to be stating, the righteousness of being in contact with you again had been contingent on our having received the scripture, then all these scholars who are certain we *are* to receive it anyway... If they were to come over here on Saturday evening, they would not only be transgressing against their parents, but against you as well. And so the three of us, plus Solly, we gathered by my computer and took it upon ourselves to ask you to clarify the ambiguity via email. Although asking for such a clarification was no doubt a form of contact, which might count as a transgression against you (and if so, then certainly a transgression against our parents), we figured it would be a much smaller transgression than contacting you via telephone, let alone in person, and we figured that if, in your response to our email, you stated that it was *not* okay to resume contact with you, that the invitation *had* been a one-time offer, we would tell all the other scholars what you said, thus preventing hundreds of transgressions this Saturday, by way of our four today. And so we sent an email to all the CC'd scholars that told them of our plan, and we wrote you our email, and were ready to wait for however long was necessary for you to respond. But no sooner had I hit the send button than, as I mentioned earlier, we saw the news about your father on television, at which point we decided, 'You know what? Enough of this. Whatever else he may be, Gurion is an Israelite and a friend of ours, and if it is a transgression to comfort our Israelite friend in the wake of a personal tragedy, if to do so is to dishonor our parents, then so be it. Let us transgress. Let us bring them shame and wrath and endless shame.' And then we were here, waiting in the shadows so as not to be detected by any passersby who might fink to our parents, and then you were pummeling Shai's internal organs, and then you were kicking me in the legs, and now we're in your bedroom, asking: Was the invitation a one-time offer? Will you deliver us the new scripture despite our failure to appear at the appointed time? Do you sanction this visit we've made to your house? If so, does that mean you will lead us? And lastly, who is she, this girl you love?"

Suddenly, my screen became a field of backlit blackness, and then it blipped and I was in. I had 248 new messages, every one of them titled "RE: FWD: NEW SCRIPTURE."

The thumbs in the corner continued to twiddle.

Her name's Eliza June Watermark, I said to the scholars.

And all of them leaned in, and none of them looked at me funny.

□ □ □ □ □ □ □

Flowers came back with the pizza in the middle of the story, so I told the rest of it in the kitchen, the rapt scholars pointing at slices and nodding at liter bottles, flicking their eyes in the direction of napkins and chinning at packets of parmesan and pepper flakes. They didn't squint once—not when I told them I never loved Esther, or even when I described the conversion on the stage. With the exception of a couple whispered mazel tovs, no voice but my own was audible til I finished.

Then Emmanuel suggested a metaphorical kinship between June's Gurion-independent invention of the pennygun and the desert monotheism Zipporah had practiced before she met Moses which was, itself, Emmanuel insisted, certainly akin to the righteousness of the matriarchs in the days before they met and wed the patriarchs.

Samuel wanted to know when they'd receive the new scripture.

Solly wondered whether June had friends, or maybe sisters.

Shai asked what they should tell the other scholars about visiting me after Havdallah, and then Samuel asked Shai how he could fail to notice I'd risen from my chair and shown them my back.

Samuel had me wrong, though. Their reaction to the story had been perfect, the reaction I'd've wanted most from anyone, and it made me feel artful—in describing the moments leading up to the conversion, I'd skipped all mention of mine and June's birthmarks. So the reason I'd risen was to go to the sink, to scrub the makeup from my thumbs and reveal the yuds, not doubting for a second that my mom would understand. These were the last four brothers in the world who'd trample me.

Yet as they rose from their own chairs, apologizing for outstaying their welcome, expressing their gratitude for my "patience and hospitality in the midst of upsetting events" (Emmanuel), assuring me and each other that I'd answered enough of their questions for one day, "the longest day I've ever heard of outside Irish literature" (Samuel), I saw they were right—not right that I felt stretched or put out by their visit, but right that I'd already said enough.

One time, at the Frontier, Flowers and I watched this show about pets where a dog did the moonwalk when its owner held its elbows. It was so weird and funny it got all over the web. Within a couple days, someone CGI'd the owner out and gave the dog a hat it doffed with a diamond-studded paw. We agreed the doctored video wasn't as funny as the original—it wasn't really funny at all—except I didn't get why til Flowers explained it. He said, "Gild the lily, the stem collapse."

It was the right explanation. And if faith and trust worked anything like comedy, which I suspected they did—I suspected most good things did—then the reason I wanted to show the scholars the yuds could just as easily be a reason not to show them the yuds. That is: They already believed June was an Israelite, and they believed it because I told them she was. So while the revelation of my birthmarks, which aspired to hard evidence, might strengthen that belief, it might also insult their intelligence, damage their faith, and thereby endanger (structurally and otherwise) the integrity of the stem from which their trust blossomed.

I followed them out of the kitchen without a word or a gesture. It is true they were mistaken about outstaying their welcome—their visit made me feel much better, kept me from staring into my head at my falling father's image, or at least from *ceaselessly* doing so—but it was, nonetheless, still time for them to go, time now to stare at that image excessively, to work myself up to interrogate my dad. I was angry at him, but not angry enough, and it was already 8:00, he'd have to come home soon. Plus, the later the scholars stayed, the more likely it got that *they'd* be interrogated. I knew they'd never fink on me or each other, but silence could get them grounded too, yet if I told them that, they'd only say grounding was a small price to pay, then attempt to stick around to prove that they meant it. Better if they thought they'd overstayed their welcome.

I have to make some decisions, I told them, but I'll send word before Shabbos on what's to come. Tell everyone we know to lay low til then.

All of them but Emmanuel were bundled. He'd gotten everything on except for his boots, then sat on the floor to attempt doomed contortions. Unable to reach past his knees, he rose and shed his entire wooly bulk—overcoat, pullover, hat, scarf, and gloves—then sat back down and pulled on the boots, the laces of which kept slipping from his fingers. The others, in the meantime, overheated. Shifting their weight from foot to foot, they tucked their toplips and extended their bottom ones to aim huffy air at their darkening foreheads.

"Go ahead," Emmanuel told them.

"We're fine," said Samuel. "Just hurry."

"No, really," said Emmanuel, "I have to stop at the pharmacy anyway."

"For what?" Shai said.

"You don't ask for what when it's the pharmacy," said Samuel.

"Why not?" said Shai.

"Because maybe he's got a fungus or the runs," offered Solly.

"Do you have a fungus or the runs?" said Shai to Emmanuel.

"You don't ask that, Shai," said Samuel.

"I bet Solly's right, though. Look how silent Emmanuel's being suddenly. He's almost as silent as Solly," said Shai. "We've come to expect that from Solly, silence, but silence we don't readily associate with Emmanuel. It might be he's been suffering all along. Suffering in silence. An uncharacteristic silence indicative of a medical unpleasantness. We're all among friends, though, and what's a fungus among friends? Who hasn't had the runs? I've had the runs, we've all had the runs. You know what it is that my dad calls the runs? It's the trots, what he calls them. My dad calls the runs the trots."

"My dad calls you 'that shvontz with the gums,' so let's go already," said Samuel.

"What's wrong with my gums?"

"Nothing, you shvontz."

"Then why's your dad specify the gums if it's nothing?"

"*Specify*. He doesn't even know who you are."

"But I see him all the time."

"You're not memorable, Shai."

"What's wrong with my gums?"

"I'm telling you I made it up."

"Why, though? Why'd you say 'with the gums'?"

"It was the first thing that came to mind."

"But *why* was it the first thing that came to mind?"

"Probably I was looking at your gums."

"What's wrong with my gums, you look at them?"

"You're crazy."

"Maybe *you're* crazy, Samuel. Did you ever think of that? Maybe you can't stop looking at my gums."

"Now that you mention it, my eyes *are* drawn to them," said Samuel. "What is it about them, I wonder, that draws my eyes?"

"Stop messing with me."

"No," said Samuel. "Before, I was messing with you. Now I'm thinking: you got a lot of gums. They're…"

"What? No. You're messing with me. No. What? They're what?"

"Meaty."

"Meaty?"

"You got a lot of gums, Shai."

Shai looked to Solly. Solly looked away.

"What?" Shai said. "They're meaty?"

I missed you guys, I said.

"We missed you, too," said Shai.

"You know, you're thick sometimes," said Samuel. "The Rabbi already knows you missed him. That was his polite way of saying, 'Go home.'"

"Well, I did miss him, though," said Shai.

Emmanuel had yet to tie his second boot, and I saw that he was trying to linger. Samuel now saw too and, saying goodbye, he shouldered the others outside.

I pressed my spine against the doorframe, bracing to hear June's conversion get questioned. Emmanuel put his hat on, took it off, stared at it. Maybe I'd overestimated my effect—my lily a sunflower, or even just a dandelion. He put the hat on again. Then he took it off again.

Nu? I said to him.

"This hiding," he said. "That we're supposed to 'lay low.' How you told us to tell the other scholars to 'lay low'—it troubles me."

I dropped to the floor beside him, pretended to give him a deadarm.

"What?" he said.

I thought you were gonna say something else, I said.

"Something having to do with June and your being in love with her and her so-called conversion, you thought."

Yeah, I said.

"I might have. I might have unpacked the logics of love and Israelite conversion and then discussed your theory of potential messiahs as it relates to those logics. I might have said something like, 'Gurion, if love is forever, and therefore what it means to be in love is that you stay in love forever, then one can never truly know if he is in love until the moment he dies. And yet you say you are in love with June.' That might have been premise one. If I wanted to introduce premise two, I might have gone on to say, 'Since all it means to be an Israelite is you have the soul of an Israelite, and the soul is eternal, and the soul from its creation is immutably Israelite or non-, then no one can truly convert; they have or haven't been an Israelite all along, and therefore conversion ceremonies are only ceremonious. At best such ceremonies acknowledge a truth that requires no acknowledgment to be true—*This Israelite is an Israelite*—and at worst these ceremonies are but lying declarations—*This non-Israelite is an Israelite*. So if June is an Israelite, she has always been an Israelite, whether you or I or she believed it to be so, whether you or I or she *currently* believe it. And no matter what we say about it, either. Yet about it, you say, "June is an Israelite." And in response, we say, "Amen." And all of it is heartfelt.'

"Then," he said, "if after presenting these premises, I felt you were still listening to me, I might have offered some preparatory commentary before arriving at the heart of the matter, like: 'To fall in love, two people must meet somehow—fatefully, accidentally, or on purpose; doesn't matter here—they must meet by way of their eyes, their ears, their scent, whatever. Maybe they have to do other things to fall in love, too—speak endearments, write letters, kiss, who knows?—but we are certain that before they fall in love, some type of observable phenomenon that qualifies as 'meeting' *must take place*. We know for a fact that no two people have ever fallen in love with each other without having met. To fall in love is to *become* in love. We all believe that is true. It is not controversial. Yet that there's nothing anyone can do to become an Israelite—that's not controversial either. As I already said, you are or you aren't one, and we all believe *that* is true.'

"And after saying all that," said Emmanuel, "I might have attempted to bring it all home like this: 'So despite both truths, by nature, being immutable—once in love, forever in love; once an Israelite, always an Israelite—one truth is set in motion, at least partly, by human beings, and the other is set in motion solely by Adonai. And that is complicated enough. But now we move on to your theory of potential messiahs, which concerns itself with both types of immutable truth at once: Adonai creates a potential messiah, one per generation, and then that potential messiah becomes the actual messiah when human beings do or fail to do something or some set of things—who knows what exactly?—to set his potential in motion. So while the potential of a potential messiah is set in motion solely by Adonai, the actualization of that potential will be set in motion, at least partly, by human beings. Agreed?'—"

Agreed, I said.

"I was only asking the hypothetical Gurion, to whom I might have said all of this, but I'm glad you agree. The hypothetical one would have agreed as well. He would have agreed exactly as you have, and I would have gone on to say, 'According to you, Gurion, we should not say that anyone is the messiah until he has had "victory undeniable"; until perfect justice is visited upon the world; until calling the messiah "messiah" is, for all intents and purposes, redundant. And that seems cautious, safe. And that is the appeal of your approach, for false messiahs haunt our history. We have followed them, and suffered greatly for it. But there are a pair of potential pitfalls to this safe approach, and these are major. The first one is this: faith becomes irrelevant. If we cannot call the messiah "messiah" til doing so is no more risky than calling a lemon sour, a goat smelly, or Natalie Portman a world-class knock-out, what is the point of ever looking for the messiah? When he comes, we'll know it, so why bother looking? What is the incentive for waiting or hoping? Why bother trying to bring him at all? He will be self-evident, and so the end of faith. And maybe you'd say, "That is the point, Emmanuel. We should not have faith *because* the messiah will come. We should have faith because faith is good, and part of faith is to believe *that* the messiah will come." And maybe you'd be right. Maybe those scholars whose faith is bolstered by its own promise—the promise that faith's objects, despite their current state of unfalsifiability, will one day become evident to everyone and in turn reward the scholars for their faith—maybe those scholars are lousy scholars. Selfish, self-centered would-be know-it-alls, driven by the desire to one day say to the faithless "I told you so" or the fear of having ever to hear that statement addressed to them. Maybe their faith is not a noble faith in what *should be true*, but a lower kind of faith in what they *fear is so*. And maybe that latter kind's not faith at all. And so maybe most of us are faith-less, impurely motivated, heartened only by our so-called faith's promise of coming worldly empowerment. And yet surely some of us aren't...

"'But is it *faith*, Gurion, anyway, that will bring the messiah? It doesn't seem like it to me. *Acts* of faith, maybe. But faith itself? When has faith itself ever served us? And how often has faith been used against people? For just as there are acts of faith, there are non-acts of faith, no? Most tyrants don't get assassinated, let alone trampled to death by mobs to whom they've been unjust. Why not? Often because crooked or misled clerics urge faith and its non-acts on the faithful is why not. And that is what makes us dif-ferent, no? That is why our religion is good. We are not taught to abide injustice through our faith; we are not taught to wait for Adonai to reach a hand down and save us. We are taught to faithfully destroy injustice; we are taught that to do so will force His hand. Taught that, at least, by you.

"'And so in the end, what's in a scholar's heart should only matter to us inasmuch as how it leads him to act. In other words: what's in a scholar's heart doesn't matter as long as he *acts as if* it's faith. That said, if you teach us faith is irrelevant, Gurion, how can we know how to act? And why should we listen to you? Maybe you say, "I will tell you how to act, Emmanuel, and you should listen to me because I'm the strongest and wisest of all of us." And that works if you become the messiah, Rabbi. Of course it does. And in that case, and only in that case, is the first potential pitfall successfully dodged.'

"And then I'd have gone on to discuss the second pitfall, which would take fewer words since, having gotten worked up, I'd probably abandon all subtlety and just form a string of rhetorical questions, like, 'What if the thing we must do to set the messiah's potential in motion is call him 'messiah'? What if the words need to come first? What if it must be written before it can be done? What if he must be said to be before he can become? Is that not how the universe became, Gurion? Is it so crazy to think that the final chapter might end as began the first? So crazy to think we'll create truth by speaking it? Why should that seem crazy? Because it would be perfect?'

"In any case, I decided that all went without saying," said Emmanuel, "and had you not leaned forward at so acute an angle when first I began to say it, it would have remained unsaid, but you leaned forward, and I got going, so now that it's said, what do you say?"

I'd become so engrossed in listening to him—somewhere in the middle of his remarks on the first pitfall, I got this highly familiar rush I couldn't place just then—that when he asked that last question, it took me a second to realize it wasn't the hypothetical Gurion who was supposed to answer, but me.

"Rabbi?" he said.

I think you're the most talented scholar I know, I said.

"That's good to hear. I think maybe when you spoke of this Eliyahu of Brooklyn, I became a little jealous, and I thought that was shallow of me, and wanted to prove—I don't know. Let's not get tender, shall we? What I *was* going to say, originally I mean, was that I'm troubled by this instruction to 'lay low' because I assume that 'laying low' means, at least for the most part, not telling our parents we were here."

Yeah, I said, that's what it means.

"But if telling them we've been here is not the right thing to do, then how can we be honoring them? That is: if we have, through our disobedience of them, honored them, then why should we be dishonest about it?"

Would it be dishonest if they didn't ask where you were, and you didn't tell them?

"No."

Would it be dishonest, if they did ask, to tell them you've been with Samuel discussing Judaism?

"In a certain light: no. That *is* one of the things I've been doing, discussing Judaism with Samuel. However, that account would not exactly be forthcoming."

Who says you always have to be forthcoming? I said.

Emmanuel squinted = "This sounds demagogic."

I said, 'Always' as in 'at all times.' You weren't originally gonna tell me you were jealous about Eliyahu, right?

"That's true, but then I did tell you."

Because the time was right, I said.

"Okay," he said. "But when will the time be right to tell my parents we're friends again?"

Not before I deliver my scripture, I said.

"So you'll still deliver it."

Yes.

"When?"

After I write it, I said.

"I thought you already wrote it."

So did I, I said. But listen—are you still troubled?

"Not about laying low," he said.

I said, Good enough. I said, Go home.

A genius of bundling, a worried mother's wildest dream, Emmanuel covered his face to the eyes with his scarf like a ninja. Then he jumped from the top of our five-step back stoop, exploding a half-frozen puddle.

⬜ ⬜ ⬜ ⬜ ⬜ ⬜ ⬜

Up in my room, I read ten of the scholars' emails, each equally and sufficiently representative of the rest (I've since examined all 365). Some of the emails mentioned Emmanuel's email—the one where he told them that he and the other three would contact me in order to find out for everyone if contacting me was transgressive. The authors of these emails explained that despite their initial willingness to do nothing til after Emmanuel reported on my ruling, they'd since reasoned that *contact*, at least as it seemed to be defined by my "New Scripture" email, was a two-way street, and that therefore to write to me was not, in itself, a form of *contact*—not unless I chose to read what they'd written—and that if contacting me *did* turn out to be transgressive, they reasoned, then I *wouldn't* read what they'd written, for I was the last teacher in the world who'd ever lead them to transgression, and so there was no danger in writing to me. Other emails didn't mention Emmanuel's. Apart from that, any variance among them was little more than grammatical. They were all signed "your student," they all wished a speedy recovery for my father, they all contained blessings on "this red-haired girl you love," and every single one requested further instructions.

I was in the middle of the tenth when my parents came home. I didn't click any more envelope icons, but I didn't rush to the door either. I didn't want the conversation I'd have with my father to be compromised by his good manners—Flowers was still reading in our living room, waiting to give them the babysitting report.

I shut off my light and looked out the window, and a couple minutes later the Volvo tweeted. Flowers got in and I headed for the stairway.

Distracted by Emmanuel's close reading of my teachings, then tempted by my overloading inbox, I hadn't, as I'd planned to, bolstered myself with focused recollections of the courthouse-steps imagery, but it turned out that would've been unnecessary anyway.

Halfway down the stairs, I could hear them in the kitchen; my father saying I was probably asleep, my mother that she'd promised to wake me if I was. The scrape of metal against flint. I stealthed to where the wall became banister, leaned long and downward and watched them through the bars.

My father's damaged leg lay across two chairs, swollen and braced in elastic. My mother reached over the table, stole the cigarette from his lips.

He reached for the pack in his jacket.

"Do not have conniptions," she told him. "I only wanted one puff."

"No, have it," he said. He shook out a fresh one.

"You say this like you are being generous, but in fact—"

"Not now, baby," he said.

"'Not. Now. Baby,'" she said. "Should I feel offended or charmed? It is hard to say, no?" She dragged and the cigarette crackled, but she kept it there in her mouthcorner. "On the first hand, it is a kind of brush-off: he does not want to hear the affectionate small jab I was about to make regarding his mood. On the second hand, he calls me 'baby' which is sweet, but on the third hand, it is precisely because 'baby' is sweet and he is using it to brush me off that saying to me 'baby' is a little condescending. Do I decide that he is sweet for painting with honey the brushoff, or cruel for pretending to me that a brush-off is honey?"

Here, a chunk of ash fell off the end of her cigarette, exploding on impact with the placemat. She might have paused because she noticed or she might have noticed because she paused. It was impossible to tell, but now she addressed herself to the ashes, and my father didn't notice—he just kept looking at his lap.

"Let us assume that I truly love him, this Judah Maccabee, and that I call it honey on a brush-off. Say that I can even empathize with his need to exercise a brush-off, that I understand he has had a trying day and needs to enjoy an uninterrupted cigarette in its entirety before he can feel human again. The question then becomes: How do I get across to him that despite all of that, he is not the only one who has had a trying day, that I have also had a trying day, and that if I empathize it is at least partly because I need someone to do the same for me? How do I get it across?"

She blew the ashes into the cup of her hand.

"Do I drop the lit cigarette down the back of his shirt and then become alarmed? Do I just thank him for the cigarette and continue to smoke it while I fetch him an icepack from the freezer?" She was at the freezer now, the icepack in her hand; noticing its softness, she gave it dirty looks. "Do I attempt to return the lit cigarette to his lips? Maybe continue to soliloquize until he reacts, until he tells me how sexy my accent still is to him, or until he tells me in a prideful, almost fatherly way how little my accent inflects my speech anymore? Maybe he will pay me the compliment I want to hear but he will mean the opposite and I will know it. Maybe it is only a sentimental kind of love we have now, a warm thing, but not fiery. Maybe he knows I want him to tell me how sexy my accent still is and he tells me, or maybe he knows and so he tells me the opposite, to tease me, for teasing is more youthful, less porch-swinging, a more convincing denial. Teasing is fierier." She set the icepack on his knee, said, "Is this a word? Fierier? It should be. That is not the point. What is the point? Maybe it is all a put-on, is the point. This teasing. Maybe this teasing is all a put-on, a clever double-feign arranged, however lovingly, to confirm that he—"

"This icepack isn't very cold," said my father. I couldn't see his face.

"He broods!" she said, "and she continues to speak. What does this make her? What else but a twit? Is not a twit one who twitters? And what is it called in the American language when a foreign wife ceaselessly banters into the ear of a husband who is brooding cross-armed with a burning cigarette in his fingers? What is it called, Judah? What, if not twittering?"

"Baby, come—"

She kissed him on the cheek and he dropped his cigarette and grabbed her wrist and she giggled a syllable.

They started making out.

All the other times I'd come across them making out in the kitchen, I'd snuck away quietly. This time I smacked the wall, because who were they trying to kid?

My mom, still kissing, opened her eyes.

"A spy," she said.

Again I smacked the wall. A couple of the scabs from the remote control opened on impact and the blood left dots.

"Boychic—" my dad said.

Why didn't you set those people on fire?

"Not even a hug first?" he said.

I came down the stairs. I could see his crutches leaning on the fridge.

Why didn't you? I said.

"Even if I could still—"

Did you try? I said.

"Gurion!" my mother snapped.

My dad set his hand on her arm. He said to me, "I hurt my knee a little, Gurion. I bumped my head. Men should die for that? I fell and they left me alone."

Before they left you alone, they were coming for you and you didn't—

"They were coming for Patrick Drucker."

You were in their way, and you didn't know what they would do. You could not have known.

"And?"

And *what*? You should have stopped them.

"I should have killed them, you're saying."

They might have done the same to you.

"I fell and they left me alone."

You didn't know they *would*, though.

"And I didn't know they wouldn't. To pre-emptively—"

They didn't leave your client alone, I said.

"My *client*?" he said. "You would expect me to— What can you possibly think of me, Gurion? Do you think we're that different?"

Who?

"You and I."

I don't understand you.

"Nor I you. Patrick Drucker is a Nazi in a cheap suit. You would expect me to kill Jews—*murder* Jews—to protect a Nazi?"

I sat where I'd stood. I sat on the floor, not knowing how to answer. Because that was, actually, what I'd have expected of him. It hadn't *been* what I'd have expected—not for the last ten years it hadn't; not until the previous few hours. Not until the expectation was useful. When I saw him get hurt I was angry at him for getting hurt, at least as angry at him as I was at those who'd hurt him, and at Adonai. I was angry because it is right to be angry at people who are guilty. People who are guilty should have—which means that they *could* have—done something different from what they did. To be guilty, you have to have had some control over the thing you did, and if he had had some control, my father... if he had *deserved* the enmity of those Israelites... if he had brought it on himself... if he had *gotten himself attacked*, then it only followed that in the future he could *avoid* getting himself attacked. In the future, he could keep himself safe. And I wanted to believe he could keep himself safe. That was why I had decided he was just as his attackers claimed he was; it would have been easier to love him despite his being an enemy of the Israelites than to have to worry about him getting killed for being righteous; less world-shattering to lose my trust in him than my faith in Adonai; more tolerable to be angry at him than to fear for him. And if these reflections seem too complicated for me to have had in the middle of an argument with my parents, while my mother, who was rising by then, puffing up warriorstyle to deliver me a rhetorical slap that would not, as it would turn out, bring me pain, but relief—if this all seems too complicated a stream of thoughts for me to think in the moment my entire understanding of the previous six months of my life was getting re-arranged, that's because it was. Too complicated. I didn't think these things then, not all of them, not nearly, and certainly not in this order. All I thought was: You are good, Aba, and they trampled you anyway. And struck as I was by the implications, I only managed to speak a bastardized version of the predicate.

I said, They trampled you anyway ≠ "But those Israelites you wouldn't kill to save a Nazi trampled you and so you should have killed them." I wasn't arguing at all, only lamenting, but judging by my mother's response, it must have sounded like arguing.

She said, "Yes they did, Gurion. And Jews every one of them. They ran right over him. They did not give a fuck about your father, or you, or your mother." Who was leaning at me now, my mother, yelling these words.

"Baby," said my dad.

"No." my mother said. "He is in the wrong, Judah, and it is not cute. It is not smart. Now is not the time to speak softly. You are terribly wrong to say such things to your father, Gurion. You are being heartless and reckless and abominably stupid. I do not know who you ate dinner with tonight. I do not know with whom you ate dinner while your aba and I were at the hospital because Flowers did not seem to catch their names, but all of their heads, he said, were covered, and so I assume these were boys you went to Schechter with. Yes? Boys you call your friends? Are they still your friends, Gurion?"

They're my friends, I said, but—

"But *nothing*. Who do you think it was at the courthouse? Whose blood, Gurion? Whose cousins and uncles? Whose older brothers? Whose Jewish fucking parents?"

I know, I said.

"You know, yet you are friends with them? After what their parents did to your father—and never mind what has been done to you—after what their parents did to your father, you call them your friends?"

They can't be held—

"They cannot be held to account for the crimes of their parents?" she said. "Is that what the fuck you were going to say?"

Yes, I said.

"Are you sure you want to say that? Are you sure it is true? Are you sure they cannot be held to account? Because if they cannot be held to account, Gurion, I do not understand why you would have them suffer. I do not understand, if they cannot be held to account, why you would have your father turn your friends into orphans."

I wouldn't, I said.

"No?"

No, I said.

"No but what?" she said.

No but nothing, I said. I said, I was wrong. You're right. I was saying stupid things, Ema. I was doing everything you said I was doing.

"Are you lying to me?"

No.

"Are you still angry?"

Not at Aba, I said.

"Are you still angry at me?"

No, I said.

"So enough yelling," she said.

I'd never watched myself cry, so I didn't know, but I thought I must be one of those people who smiles before he cries, because my mom sat next to me on the floor and did stuff to my hair while my dad kept reassuring me that everything would be alright, and I wasn't crying at all. I was smiling so hard my face hurt.

☐ ☐ ☐ ☐ ☐ ☐ ☐

An entire night and then some would pass before I'd learn about the Gurionic War, weeks on top of that before I'd start writing *The Instructions*. By the time I left the kitchen, though, I already knew the first of the blessings of both of them, and it was the first thing I wrote when I got to my room.

> There is damage. There was always damage and there will be more damage, but not always. Were there always to be more damage, damage would be an aspect of perfection. We would all be angels, one-legged and faceless, seething with endless, hopeless praise.
>
> Bless Adonai for making us better than angels. Blessed is Adonai for making us human.

I saved the file, hit PRINT, and was about to get a fresh address from which to send email to the scholars when I noticed how late it was, and that June hadn't called. I worried she wouldn't, so I called her.

"Are you still in love with me?" she said.

More than ever, I said.

"Because of what I told you?"

No.

"In spite of it?"

Regardless of it.

"You always say the right thing," she said. "You should write me a book."

I said, Tomorrow I want you to bring your gun to school.

She said, "I always bring my gun to school. I love you." Then she hung up.

Two minutes later I had my new address, and ten after that I'd written the "Sudden Holiday" email. Still, I spent an hour hesitating before I sent it. Not because of what I'd written—I liked what I had written. If it was possible, as Emmanuel had argued, that the messiah needed to be proclaimed the messiah before he could do those things the messiah was supposed to do; and if it was good to declare you were in love prior to the moment just before you died (and I was beginning to think it was more than good; I was beginning to think it was necessary, beginning to suspect it could not be true *without* the declaration = starting to believe that before you could actually *be* in love, you needed to *say* you were in love); if Adonai's hand could be forced with words, then there was no reason why a holiday, let alone a potential holiday that was acknowledged as such, couldn't or shouldn't be announced in advance of the events it might commemorate.

What made me hesitate was the new address. Whether or not I should use it. I already had an address the scholars' parents hadn't blocked, and Ben Brodsky was well beyond need of my protection. If anyone did end up figuring out how I originally got hold of that Kalisch email (it wouldn't be that hard; Ben's penchant for password-cracking had been notorious), what difference would it make? Yes, a kid who tells on another kid is a dead kid, but not when the kid being told on is, himself, dead. Ben's death had done to Ben what death always did to dead kids: Ben's death had all but sainted him. The revelation that he'd hacked Unger's mailbox—whether Brodsky's, Emmanuel's, Rabbi Salt's, or anyone else's—wouldn't sully his memory, but enliven it, fondly reminding the rememberers of the extra-bright sparkle in Ben Brodsky's eyes they might or might not have actually witnessed, let alone appreciated, while he was alive.

And I wasn't ashamed that I'd forwarded Kalisch's email to those list-servs, either, much less incapable of describing why I'd done so. In fact, I did describe it. At one point during the course of my hour-long hesitation, I became convinced enough that I should come clean that I wrote half an alternate version of "Sudden Holiday" in which I explained what I'd hoped to gain:

...I forwarded Kalisch's email because I wanted the elders of Israelite communities outside Chicago to learn of the persecution I was suffering at the hands of our headmasters. I believed that if the elders knew of it, they would stop it. I believed, scholars, that they would stand up for me and convince your parents to embrace our friendship. I believed we would again be allowed to study Torah together.

It was my mistake to expect such help: an honest mistake, but mine nonetheless. The Israelites of Chicago, especially those other headmasters to whom Kalisch originally addressed the email—they were the ones who should have stepped in to help us. To go outside of our community for help, even if only into the wider Israelite community; that is always a mistake. I know that now more than ever.

I stopped writing there, unsure of how to begin the next paragraph. Certainly the scholars would want to know why I took so long to tell them what I'd done, and that would have to be the next thing I addressed. And maybe they would accept what I told them. Maybe they would accept that I had to protect Ben. And maybe they would allow that, although Ben had been dead since July—that although it had been four months since last he'd required my protection—no opportunity or need to let them know I was FIFTEEN23FIRSTSAMUEL@hotmail.com had arisen in the last four months, and maybe they wouldn't hold against me my silence during those months. Maybe they wouldn't question any of it. Maybe they would just assume that I had done what was right at the time. Or that I hadn't done what was wrong. Maybe they would believe that I had done what seemed proper in my eyes, and maybe that what was proper in my eyes, despite its failure, was proper nonetheless. Or maybe not.

But even if they didn't feel the slightest bit betrayed, and even if they saw that my reasons for forwarding Kalisch's email were good, they would see that my doing so had been a mistake. How could they avoid seeing that? I said so outright, and there was no way to avoid saying so outright, not without lying. Not without blaming people who weren't deserving of blame. It really *wasn't* the fault of those elders outside the community that they'd failed to step in to help me. People don't step in to help you, not from outside. That's just not the way the world works. And overall, that's probably a good thing. They didn't know me, those elders. They didn't know

Kalisch or Unger. All they knew was that Kalisch and Unger were headmasters of Israelite schools, were pedigreed, authorized by the Israelites of Chicago to exert certain powers. And maybe they'd heard of my dad, probably they'd heard of my dad, and certainly whatever they'd heard wouldn't have been good. Why would wise Israelites step in to help a stranger, the son of a reputed self-hating Jew whose own schoolmasters had called him dangerous, had called him detrimental to the Israelites? They wouldn't. And they shouldn't be expected to. To insist otherwise might have been convenient for me, but it would have been a lie, and I wasn't going to start lying to the scholars. So what, then? So I made a mistake back in June. It was a forgivable mistake, and taking as long as I'd taken to admit to it—that was forgivable too. But if I could make one mistake here, I could make another there. And it was easy to understand how they might see it that way, the scholars. They might think, "Gurion made a mistake in June. How do we know he's not making a mistake in November?" And then they might not do what I wanted them to do.

And I saw it was better they be misled by me than not led by me. Nothing was worth the risk of failing to protect my father.

I could send them an email from FIFTEEN23FIRSTSAMUEL some other time.

□　□　□　□　□　□　□

Sent: November 16, 2006, 11:51 PM Central-Standard Time
Subject: SUDDEN HOLIDAY
To: 49_17ISAIAH@gmail.com
CC: NEW SCHECHTER LIST, NORTHSIDE HEBREW DAY LIST

Scholars,

If we are just, then tomorrow a new holiday will arise. I believe we are just, and so I am canceling school for all of those Israelites who wish to observe. Services will be held in the field across the street from Aptakisic Junior High School, in the valley between the two hills. Directions to get there from Schechter are attached.

This news comes late, I know. Most of you are in bed already. Most of those in bed won't check email before school tomorrow. But for those of you who Hashem has chosen to receive this email, I suggest He chose you for a reason. And though I have cancelled school, there is no reason for you to think that showing up early at Hebrew Day or Schechter to wait covertly near the entrance and spread the news to our brothers would be a bad idea. In fact, if we are just, then to do so would be a mitzvah.

Lastly: There may be a toll to pay. As this potential holiday creeps closer, I am less and less certain about what exactly it will celebrate, and I see it would be irresponsible, even criminal, to leave out mention of a toll's possibility. What's curious, scholars, or maybe not so curious at all, is that despite not knowing if there will be a toll to pay, I do know what that toll will be, should we have to pay it: a dollar per scholar, delivered in parts. From a distance.

I pray that we are just.

If we are just, then tomorrow a new holiday will arise.

Rabbi Gurion

AptakisicDirections.doc
24K View Download

18
COMMENTARY ON COMMENTARIES

So far, Tanach aside, *The Instructions* has predominately been concerned with things that general readers, and even most scholars, were not aware of prior to reading *The Instructions*. The majority of the exceptions haven't required any correction: the previously published texts* have appeared as they were written; the differing opinions of editorialists—those of academia and mass-media both—have been enough at odds as to mutually nullify one another's authority; the facts of the War and my earlier childhood have, for the most part, been reported accurately by the press.

In cases where facts have been made up, misinterpreted, or warped by proximity to the agendas of those presenting them,** the lies and warpage and misunderstandings have been easy enough for me to correct in passing by simply telling the story of the Side of Damage and the Gurionic War as I experienced them, free of nearly all reference to what was to come.

At this point in the story, however, owing to the motives that I've since been erroneously ascribed for having written "Sudden Holiday"—motives *universally* ascribed to me, by my supporters as well as my detractors—I have

---

* E.g., the many reprints of *Ulpan* and the "Important" email by Kalisch, which—apart from having been disseminated by Israelites both electronically and via backyard-handoff since the summer of 2006—appeared in most Reuters- and AP-sourced newspapers after 11/17/06.

** E.g., (most conspicuously) in the Pulitzer-winning "profile" of me in *The New Yorker*, with its blame-the-mother retro-pop psychology; the ostensibly regretful yet subtley self-congratulatory "Critic at Large" one (also in *The New Yorker*) by Malcolm Gladwell, who claimed I'd "maliciously used [my] innate understanding of tipping points in order to ignite the current nationwide epidemic of radically defiant tween-group behavior"; the "Person of the Year" article in *Time*, with its sidebars on my mom, dad, Nakamook, June, and Eliyahu, which said I was a Karaite, a vegan, and fan of Ayn Rand; the interview with my former and would-be "teachers" on that episode of *Nightline* where Kalisch referred to me as a "Jewish-Supremacist," Unger described me as an "antisemite," and Schinkl (either making fun of them or attempting to create accord between them or maybe even sincerely calling it as he post-post-colonially saw it) said I was "the living dawn of the antisemitic Jewish-Supremacist movement"; and the peerlessly demagogic feature in *Harper's*, which compared me in one windy, weirdly punctuated breath to Moshe Dayan, Benjamin Netanyahu, Osama bin Laden, Yasser Arafat, Jonathan Pollard, the Rosenbergs, Ari Fleisher, Ariel Sharon, and Sabbatai Tsvi, then repeatedly used the word "Zionist" the way Marxists and neocons use "liberal," and ended by forming—accidentally or not—an acrostic of the word "kike" with the first letters of its last four sentences.

to look forward, however briefly, in order to correct you all directly, friends and enemies alike.

In case the reader is scratching his head, unaware of the misconstrued motives to which I am referring—whether because he has been living in the wilderness between the end of 2006 and the present, or, more likely, because the present in which he is reading this is far enough ahead of the present in which I am writing it that *The Instructions* has become hegemonic, and the miscontruances thereby forgotten—he'll just have to take my word that I am justified in temporarily (as temporarily as possible) breaking the mostly old-timey flow of the narrative here, in Book 18 in C.E. 2013, and push on like a good soldier, a good scholar.

The rest of you are certainly aware that "Sudden Holiday" has been regularly cited as material evidence that I, Gurion ben-Judah Maccabee, had been plotting since at least the night prior to that YouTube-crashing geologic razzle-dazzle which far too many people (*one* would be too many) have taken to calling "The 11/17 Miracle," to execute what is currently known by my supporters as "The Damage Proper" and by my detractors as "The Gurionic War."

Once and for all, friends, and once and for all, enemies: While I do accept full responsibility for bringing the Damage Proper, I did not plan the Damage Proper until *minutes* prior to the Damage Proper. Furthermore, I had no idea that there would *be* a Damage Proper. No one did. Not even Eliyahu. Not until I planned it. How could we have?

Yes, it is true that the recurring themes of Main Man's ramblings contained what might now be construed as the stuff of prophecy; that had we understood his words to be prophetic, we might have better predicted what would happen on Friday. But—with the exception of Eliyahu—we did not understand his words that way, I least of all. Or no moreso, I should say, than I understood my vision during the Electric Chair wager or my dream of the Tower of Restraint (to be described shortly) to be prophetic. I will not deny that these three phenomena seemed to me to be possessed of insight, nor that I trusted and eventually acted upon those perceived insights to a certain degree. However, because they could all, as well, be mundanely explained—i.e., "Williams Cocktail Party Syndrome leads its sufferers to engage in a novel kind of verbal behavior characterized, for the most part, by 'mash-ups' of previously overheard statements"* to

---

* p. 147, *Linguistics Is for the (Language of) the Birds* by Tamar Maccabee, Hebrew University Press (forthcoming, pending change of title)

explain the utterances of Main Man, who split his time outside the Cage between Pentecostal Mass and marathon sessions of network television, and fell asleep at night listening to mixes Vincie'd burned him; an oxygen-deprived brain to account for the Electric Chair vision; a combination of latently understood evidence and my not-so-latent desire to salvage my friendship with Nakamook to account for the Tower of Restraint dream—I did not take it for granted that Adonai was trying to tell me anything.

Seven skinny cows cannibalizing seven fat ones as dreamed by a man who'd never dealt with cattle: that, with its crystal-clear one-to-one relationship between the symbols and what they corresponded to—and without anything extra, without spilling a single drop—*that* is what I believed a prophecy was supposed to look like.

Though wholly beloved, Main Man was retarded, and, as with no few other famously compelling lies—e.g., beautiful girls can't get dates, powerful men father weak sons, terrorists are the new freedom fighters, enmity breeds respect, no one hates the Jews more than the Jews, etc.—the lie that being retarded inherently makes a person closer to Adonai only seems true because it describes an irony. So even though, on reflection, Main Man's weird utterances seem to have been obliquely prophetic—and maybe they were—there was no good reason to believe they were prophetic at the time.

"But what about Vincie Portite?" ask both the haters and scholars alike. "What about what he said to you on Thursday's intramural bus?"

What Vincie Portite said to me on Thursday's intramural bus was that he, Eliyahu, and the rest of the Side believed, to varying degrees and for nebulous reasons, that something big was to happen soon; whether as soon as Friday or not, no one but Eliyahu seemed to be certain at all, and even he, as he has himself since testified, "was somewhat less than reliable due to [his] overwhelming state of verklemptness" when he told Vincie, "There will be no Monday." Furthermore, the "something big" that Vincie and the rest of them believed was soon to happen, was described to me as "the destruction of the Arrangement."

Now, it is true that *when* Vincie described it, I quickly came to believe he was correct. I quickly came to believe that "the destruction of the Arrangement" was imminent. I knew it to be true the way I knew Adonai was real and I was in love with June, and I will not deny that. However, what this phrase meant to me—"the destruction of the Arrangement"—was hardly comparable to what ended up happening on Friday. I imagined we might arrive at a means of action that would cause Botha to quit his job, or Floyd to be humiliated, or Desormie to never desormiate again. I thought certain deserving basketballers might receive some come-uppance, and that maybe, if I was lucky, I might find justification to cause our local up-and-coming young popstar to bleed a little, or even get deformed. In sum: I thought of Vincie's and Eliyahu's use of "the destruction of the Arrangement" as a kind of overstated euphemism for such events. Kind of like how when a tough-guy in a movie threatens his enemy with an "I'll break every bone in your body," and everyone watching, as well as the toughguy and the guy he has threatened, knows full well that if there is a physical confrontation in which the toughguy is victorious, there will nonetheless be enemy bones—many, if not all of them—which will remain unbroken; and furthermore that none, let alone all, of the enemy's bones *need be* broken for the toughguy's threat to come true. The every-bone-threatening toughguy who acquires victory by way of any act of violence—a single blow to his enemy's windpipe, for example—is not considered a liar, let alone called one.

But "Sudden Holiday": If I hadn't already planned the Damage Proper, then why, in the email, did I tell the scholars to bring their weapons to Aptakisic? Why did I tell them to come to Aptakisic at all? Could I not have met with them in my backyard after Havdallah on Saturday, as so many of them had already been planning?

I had them bring their weapons for the reason I stated in the email. If there was to be a holiday, I didn't know what the holiday would celebrate. I didn't even know if "celebrate" was the right verb. Some holidays, like Yom Ha-Shoah, only *commemorate*. Some, like Simcha Torah, do both. Yom Kippur does neither—it's a day of *atonement*. What I knew was I would deliver my scripture to the scholars. Maybe the holiday would celebrate the deliverance; maybe, if I was somehow wrong to deliver scripture, the holiday would mournfully commemorate the folly of my having done so. Maybe the deliverance would lead to something else that the holiday would celebrate or commemorate. Maybe what it led to would be military, for no calendar, let alone the Israelite calendar, is short on military holidays. And again, maybe there would be no holiday. *If* there were going to be a holiday, though, and *if* that holiday were going to be military, I wanted to do all I could to make sure it was more like Chanukah or Yom Yerushalayim than the Fasts of Tammuz or Tevet. I wanted to be sure that victory for the scholars was at least possible. So I told them to come heavy.

And as for why Aptakisic instead of my backyard: I was finished with stealth. It was time to get caught, witnessed. I wanted to incite as boldfaced a brand of defiance as I could. For a scholar to leave his home after Havdallah was not uncommon, so it was possible, even likely, that if the scholars came to my house after Havdallah, many of their parents would not find out—let alone all at the same time—where the scholars had gone. The absence of two-hundred-plus scholars from a few Israelite schools, however, could not help but get noticed. Calls would be made. Panic would ensue. Furthermore, for the scholars to compound the forbidden act of contacting me with that of ditching school—which they would have to do to get to Aptakisic on time—would attest to my being in possession of a much larger influence over them than would their merely coming over to my house.

The greater the demonstration of my influence, the more the scholars' parents would fear me, and I wanted as many of them to fear me as possible, and I wanted them to fear me as deeply as possible. I wanted them to dread evermore what I might, if crossed, do with their sons. Since they had not thought once, let alone twice, then let them think a thousand times, I thought, of what I might be capable if again harm came to my father.

I expect that many scholars, even those with the best of intentions, will, at first, attempt to resist this commentary on commentaries. Since the Damage Proper, well-meaning factions have been culting up my personality, and although I'm flattered by the intent behind this culting, efforts to render me and my actions perennially good and cohesive lead—at least in some cases— not only to Orwellian doubletalk ("the people's prince," "peacemaking warrior," etc.), but also bad scholarship, a kind that permits and even sometimes encourages lazy, unrigorous interpretations of the as-yet-quite-young Gurionic oral tradition, wherein I'm put forth as everything to everyone, and all at the same time. Which is bad enough. And it will be even worse if this lack of rigor establishes itself as a habit, for such a habit will certainly have undermined—will certainly *be undermining*—the study and interpretation of this, *The Instructions.*

Nothing, scholars, nothing in all the world is good because I say it is good. Nothing is right because I say it is right. What I say is good is good for the reasons I cite. What I say is right is right for those reasons. If you don't understand the reasons, you will one day—if you study—but you can't just take my word on what is right and good and expect that to suffice. If you could do that, I would never have mentioned my reasons.

And when I say something is bad or when I say that something I did was *wrong* or *foolish,* or when I say that something excellent that you want to ascribe to me is not something I am responsible for, or that something you call a miracle was the opposite of a miracle, then, as inconvenient as it may seem at first to believe it, the proper response is not "Gurion is too humble to admit that he was good all along, too humble to admit he was right all along," or "He is too humble to admit that he made a miracle happen, too humble to call it a miracle." I am not humble, much less am I what the well-meaning doubletalkers among you have taken to calling "a humble egotist." There is no such thing as a humble egotist. And for that matter, I'm not a "peacemaking warrior," either; I'm a scholar and a soldier. There is no paradox there, no euphemism, no contradiction. I'm both. And so should you be.

If you want to resist this commentary on commentaries, scholars, it's because the notion I'm attacking—the notion that I'd had the Damage Proper elaborately planned well in advance of the opening sally—strikes you as appealing. Maybe it strikes you as appealing because it suggests that I am a gifted general, or a talented forseer, maybe because it's the easiest explanation to imagine. I don't know exactly why the notion appeals to you. However, I do know why it appeals to the Arrangement. It is in their best interests that you resist this commentary on commentaries; it is in their best interests to spread the claim that I planned the Damage Proper well in advance of when I actually did. The implications of the truth are bad for the Arrangement because the implications of the truth are good for us. In denying the truth, in spreading lies, the Arrangement protects the Arrangement.

The fact that I only planned the Damage Proper minutes before we executed it means that you are each a much greater threat than you know. It means that despite all the early-detection procedures and other "safeguards" that have, since the Damage Proper, been put in place by various houses of the Arrangement—and manifold they are, these "safeguards," well designed to foil days and weeks of planning, as well—future war campaigns could be just as successful as the first one. They can be just as successful as long as they are undertaken as suddenly and spontaneously as the first one.

Damage, damage, and damage, the end.

19
WE

Friday, November 17, 2006
12:13 a.m.–10:41 a.m.

A nd there was night, and all through the night I kept waking from the same dream.

In the valley of the two-hill field stood a tower of restraint. Slokum held Nakamook in the air like Slokum had held me during the false alarm, except Nakamook's arms weren't pinned to his chest. Instead, they held a second Slokum, and the second Slokum held me, and I a second Nakamook, and that second Nakamook a second me:

The tower swayed. To keep from falling, we had to continually redistribute our weight. It took a lot of concentration at first, but soon I got the hang of it and noticed there was clapping. There'd been clapping all along, but my earlids had been blocking it, pushing it into the background. I looked around to see where the sound came from and saw it was Patrick Drucker. He stood before the tower, applauding.

There were two things wrong with him. The first was his pants. It was windy in the field, but the pants lay perfect on his legs, unmoving. The second was his hair. The wind didn't blow that either.

Soon clouds parted and the sun shone and both his nose and the apex of his left knee's pant-crease glinted. The glint was identical and I knew both were plastic: the face and the pants. Then I saw his eyes did not look like eyes, but television snow. I saw that he was not Patrick Drucker. He was an angel in a Patrick Drucker mask, standing behind a legs-shaped podium, applauding.

It got me edgy.

The Slokums both said, "Thank you," to the angel. "Really, you're too kind," they said. "We'd bow if we could, but as you can see…"

That got me even more edgy.

What should we do? said the Gurions.

"Which 'we'?" said everyone.

I don't know, said the Gurions.

"Is that right?" said the Nakamooks.

The effect of both Benji-voices saying the same thing at once was that it flattened the question's intonations so that I couldn't tell if "Is that right?" = "Is it really true that you don't know to which 'we' you are referring?" or if it was a sarcastic, accusatory question that = "No shit, Gurion. You *obviously* don't know to which 'we' you're referring," or if I was being asked about the moral implications of not knowing to which "we" I had referred = "Do you believe it is right to not know to which 'we' you're referring when you ask the question 'What should we do?'?"

This is when the dream would start to seem familiar, and I'd remember I was supposed to be pissed at Benji.

Meanwhile, the angel continued applauding, and the Bams kept talking about how they'd love to bow to show their appreciation for the applause, but they couldn't bow, not responsibly at least. Everyone would fall if the Bams bowed, even if just one of the Bams bowed, mused the Bams, and the angel didn't think it was worth everyone's falling down just so a Bam could bow, did he?

The angel kept applauding.

The tower of restraint kept swaying. It was exhausting.

I kept wondering what we should do.

Nakamook kept asking me which "we" I meant.

I kept forgetting and then remembering I was pissed at him.

On waking, I'd decide I wasn't pissed at him, but when I fell back asleep, the dream would start again and I'd forget what I had decided, then remember I was pissed at him, then forget I was pissed and then remember it again.

When finally there was morning, and I woke for the last time, I was no longer pissed at him.

□ □ □ □ □ □ □

While upstairs, painkillered, my father slept deep, I prepared a forkless breakfast with my mom in the kitchen. On a breadboard on the counter, I smashed walnuts with a rolling pin. She, at the table, opened soft-boiled eggs. I liked eggs soft-boiled, but in the morning couldn't prep them, not if I wanted to put them in my stomach. Those insect-like screams emitted by the shell when you pried its fragments from that film they clung to—the mastication of wet chicken sounded musical by comparison.

Walnuts in pieces, I dumped the sip of cloudy topwater from a tub of Greek yogurt. I globbed honey from a jar across the yogurt's flat surface. I folded and stirred til the color was even, then folded some more til my mom's task was finished. When she signalled it was, I came to the table, the tub in one hand, breadboard in the other; we liked to add the walnuts as we went.

The yogurt of our forkless breakfasts was for the most part treated like dessert. Though we'd always cool our mouths before we ate our eggs, we'd only use a spoonful, never even two. While the roof-blisters you'd get from a scalding one stung, nothing eggy was as nasty as a gluey tepid yolk. Plus our egg-cups, glass, were shaped like half an ostrich, and the closer the temperature of what you drew from them matched yours, the less cute the images your brain coughed up. Half-formed wings and beaks of high plasticity. Goo that would be claws and bone. A pulsing spaghetti of veins and tendons. Ligaments and cartilage not quite yet chewy. Throbbing, webbed red membranes.

Our attack on the eggs was double-fisted. We spooned them up rapidly and salted with abandon. Ninety seconds later it was over.

You inhaled your egg, I said.

My mom pinched my shoulder and I passed her the walnuts. We ate yogurt without speaking til I saw she wore fatigue pants and said so. She explained she was staying home with my father. I told her she could have slept in with him. She said not to talk nonsense because who would make me breakfast. I told her I would've made breakfast and she sneered at cold cereal and microwaved starches, praising flame-heat and animal protein by implication. I thanked her for making eggs. Then she told me what she'd heard on morning radio. She told me Patrick Drucker had died in the night.

Good, I said.

"That is not nice to say."

I have to say nice things about him now?

"You should not dance on anyone's grave. It could have been your father."

It could not have been my father.

"We are lucky it was not your father."

If hypothetical death is on the table, I thought, we are at least as unlucky Drucker hadn't died younger, before my father ever met him. But she wasn't really talking about luck. It was just an expression, and though I didn't agree with what she said, I did with what she meant.

I said, I'm glad it wasn't Aba.

She kissed me on the cheek and handed me my lunch. I looked inside the bag. A sandwich in foil, a box of peach-apple fruit drink, and baggies of carrots and pretzel sticks.

"Do not give away your carrots," she told me.

◻ ◻ ◻ ◻ · ◻ ◻ ◻

Tracks were being rehabbed and the el moved slow. Near the front of my car, which was barely half-full, two women in headscarves I'd seen around my neighborhood threw me the Look of The End and whispered. They often walked along Devon, each with a grocery bag, a mother and daughter chattering. Whenever one saw me, she'd bite down on her lip, tug the sleeve of the other, and they'd lower their voices. I'd always taken them for typical haters of Maccabees—nothing I wasn't used to near home—and decided, on the el, that that's all they were; that the reason they appeared less harmless than usual was I wasn't accustomed to getting hated on the train. I turned my eyes to my lap, read *My Life as a Man*.

By the time we'd gotten to Davis, our car—the last—was empty except for some high-schoolers. The women got off first, the others, then me. By the exit, the women stepped aside for the rest of them, but I didn't see that til I came down the stairs, and by then the last high-schooler was out on the sidewalk. I went to the turnstile the younger woman blocked.

Excuse me, I said.

"You are Gurion," she said. "Do you know who I am?"

I pointed to the mother, said: You're this woman's daughter. I need to get to school.

"Do you know who my son is?"

I had no idea who her son was, and I didn't like her questions. She could have just told me the answers. I read the stories in her face.

I said, Moshe Levin.

"That's right," she said, "I'm Michal Levin," and though Moshe's grandma grasped her hamsa between thumb and pointer, the mother was not impressed at all. Neither was I. Only a schmuck would pick on David Kahn for his stutter, and retinal detachment via pennygun or no, Moshe had finked to Headmaster Kalisch. He'd told on David, on me, on all of the Israelites. I knew he didn't mean to rat on anyone but David, but his ratting on David got me booted from Northside, and a rat was a rat was a rat was a rat. Moshe Levin was a rat-fink schmuck.

"Do you know what I think of you?" said the mother. "Do you want to know what I think of your injured father?"

Even before the No! rushed through me, I knew I would disobey it. I knew that if I didn't disobey it—if instead I who's-there'd her frenzied maternal knock-knock—she would spit some version of the following punchline: "I think your father is suffering for your sins, and you, in turn, are suffering for his." And maybe that was true, but even if it was, I didn't think I was obliged to hear it from her, so I sinned just as hard as I needed to sin in order to shame her into silence.

In superformal Hebrew, I said to this mother: Maybe ocular damage is not always so much the outcome of projectiles as of cruel words that invite projectiles, Michal Levin. And maybe such ocular damage is not merely the cause of psychological trauma, but its effect as well. Maybe Moshe wouldn't be so quick to pick on younger boys with speech impediments if your husband wasn't always bullying him. Maybe he wouldn't pick on anyone if the one person who could protect him from your husband ever did so. Probably you should forget about my father and concern yourself with Moshe's.

At which point Moshe's grandmother struck me across the jaw.

Though I showed her my other cheek, it was not because I loved her.

You should have taught her that before she had a son, I said.

And the daughter struck me, and my sense of righteousness multiplied, hardening my bones, swelling my lungs.

Your Moshe may redeem you yet, I said. When I call, he'll follow. Get out of my way now. We're all shored up, you mothers and I.

I barely made the Metra. By the time I got on, the upper level was full, and I had to share a seat on the bottom. The woman I shared with smelled like a cantaloupe and she made it impossible to read. For the duration of the ride, she chewed granola from a bag and, though graciously muffled, her crunching was audible, and oat particles gathered on her lap unswiped.

In Deerbrook Park it was drizzling coldly. Coming up the sidewalk, I saw Flowers by the hoodoo shrub, sweeping dead bugs off the walkway into envelopes. I was half across the drop-off circle when the bus pulled up and honked. Flowers must have heard it, but he kept his eyes on concrete.

The bus wouldn't leave as long as the driver saw me, so I waved and he shrugged and I continued toward Flowers, saying what I had to say.

I said, I'm sorry I said fiction was lies—I didn't mean it.

"*That's* what you're sorry about?"

And when I said we weren't friends anymore, I said. I take that back.

"And?"

And nothing, I said.

I revolved and went to the bus.

"I'm still pissed at you," Flowers said to my back.

That wasn't up to me, though. Maybe getting slapped had made my voice a little wooden, and the apology'd come out less sincere than it could have, but I'd apologized for exactly as much as I'd felt apologetic, and Flowers gave me nothing, wooden or otherwise. I boarded the bus still pissed at him, too.

Three people called my name. The first two were Dingle and Salvador Curtis. I didn't know the third guy, but Dingle and Salvador were near the back of the bus and this third guy was closer, so I took the seat behind him.

"I'm Ally Kravitz," he said. He put out his hand and I left it hanging. A blue pelican was embroidered on the tit of his shirt and when he saw I wouldn't shake he touched it. "Pinker called me last night," he said, "and so did The Levinson. Pinker called to tell me that you were *the* Gurion, and then The Levinson called to say the same thing, just in case I'd thought Pinker was yanking my banana." He unzipped his bag and showed me a pennygun. "Show him," he said to a boy across the aisle. "That's Googy Segal," Ally Kravitz said to me. Googy Segal's face was a tiny, pointy face beneath a big blonde bubble of coarse-looking curls. I'd noticed him before; he was hard not to notice. Pop-eyed and ruddy-cheeked, even in repose, he always looked startled. In greeting me, he hissed out a quiet, lilting sibilant— the high, lipless whistle little kids playing war use to imitate incoming missiles. "Googy's shy," Ally said. "He doesn't like to speak much. Words cause him trouble if gets too excited—Go on, Goog, show him. Show him the you-know." Googy pulled a pennygun from the spy-pocket of his jacket, then put it back in and zipped up fast.

Seeing Israelites with weapons did make my lungs tingle, but for Ally Kravitz I would show no joy.

Your voice sounds familiar, I said to him. The sound of my name on your lips, I said.

Googy sucked loud spit from his mouth-corners.

Ally said, "I'm not gonna lie to you, Rabbi. I made up that rhyme and I'm sorry. I really wasn't doing it to be mean. People made it mean, but I was just trying to be funny and that's why it rhymed. I bet I would've made it up even if I did know who you were, and we'd have been friends then, and you'd have liked the rhyme, I think. You'd have known it was good-natured, all in fun. See, me and Googy—he's my cousin—we're always putting bits together. I do the monologues, or just play the straightman assistant or whatever. Googy's the star. It's all about the Googy. He's a genius of pantomime and clowning, my cousin. Right, Goog? Right? Come on. Admit it."

Googy looked behind himself, like a parakeet napping, and Ally pulled a ski-cap from the pocket of his parka. "We'll show you," said Ally. And when Googy turned back, his eyes were crossed, and his cheeks were roundly inflated. Ally said, "We've been massaging this bit for a month. The title's the working kind: 'Googy and the Hunger.'" Ally set the ski-cap atop Googy's curls. Googy lowered the cap so his forehead disappeared. He rolled his crossed eyes up as though his brow puzzled him.

Ally, leaning toward me, said in a stage-whisper, "What do you think? Googy looks like he's hungry. Do you think he wants a herring and some onions for a sandwich?"

Googy nodded with vigor and twisted in his seat.

Ally raised his voice: "If Googy wants a herring and some onions for a sandwich, we can manage a herring and some onions for a sandwich—my herring and onions guy's just up the block. But what about the bread, though? Herein lay the problem. My bread guy was murdered. My bread girl, she left me. But wait. Aha! There's a charming young filly, a friend of a friend's, lives just around the corner. I've heard tell that she has a line on baguettes, that she plays her baguettes very close to the chest, but she'll give up that bread if you bring her some beer. So we'll bring her some beer, get us some bread! Just grab me my coat while I reach in the icebox and grab her a—no. Oh no. Here's a problem. Herein lay the problem. We're all out of beer. Our drunk uncle drank it, that rowdy, that lout. A bigger problem yet? My beer guy's in prison. My beer girl's got mumps, she's quarantined, deadly. Aw Googy, poor Googy, poor young master Googy, no sandwich of herring and onions for Googy…"

Googy and Ally both swayed right and left, and Googy grabbed Ally's hand, as if to offer comfort. When he started to pet it, Ally jerked it away, stuck it in his coat.

"If only Googy," Ally said, "wanted anything else, any food not a sandwich of herring and onions, or any kind of sandwich, or beer— What's this?" He removed from his coat an unwrapped fortune cookie.

Googy horse-clopped his hands on his thighs eight times.

"Look what we have here! Just have yourself a gander at this elegant contraption, this perfect endeavor on which to embark after gobbling down a plate of hot chop suey, and that's to say nothing of a bowl of lo-mein! Too bad we don't have any hot chop suey. Too bad my lo-mein guy winters in Poughkeepsie—"

"Nnnnng!" yelled Googy, reaching for the cookie.

Ally dropped it on the floor and stomped it to crumbs. "Don't act like an animal," Ally told Googy. "You gotta ask polite. What happened to your manners? Remember where you come from! Remember your glory! A champion you were! A champion of hopscotch at the school for the maimed! A bronze medalist—twice! not once, but twice!—in their semi-annual boxing round-robin! What happened to you, Googy?"

Googy waved Ally off and reached in his own coat, pulled out five cookies, and started to juggle. After nine or ten passes he juggled one-handed, using his free hand to take off his ski-cap.

"No way!" Ally said. "It's never been tried."

Googy closed his eyes and positioned the cap upside-down near his heart, and after he'd caught all the cookies in the cap, he opened his eyes, looked deep into the cap, filled his cheeks up with air and, shuddering violently, turned the cap over, dumping all the cookies, and stomped them to crumbs while performing a sequence of face-slapping raspberries. Only after that did the cousins take a bow.

So?" Ally said. "What do you think?"

Wow, I said. That was pretty good, man. I wasn't expecting—

"No no," said Ally, "it's still rough, we know, but what I'm asking is do you believe me now that we never meant it mean, the rhyme about your bus stop?"

Yeah, I said.

It was true.

"Good," he said. "So what do we do now?"

What do you mean?

"What do you want us to do with the weapons?"

Protect each other.

"Of course," said Ally, "but what's the plan?"

The plan? I said.

"It's okay," Ally whispered, "no one can hear us but Goog."

Googy pinched his lips so they flared.

No one can hear us what? I said.

"Discussing the plan."

I don't know what you mean.

"Rabbi, come on. We showed you our weapons. I explained the song. I thought you forgave us."

I did, I said.

"Then don't cut us out."

Ally, I said, I don't know what you're talking about.

"The plan," he whispered, "to deal with the Shovers."

The Shovers?

"Are we pattering?"

What?

"Are you trying to start a routine with me, Rabbi?"

What? No.

"I'm asking you about the plan for the Shovers. I'm really asking. I'm not joking with you."

I didn't say you were, I said. I said, I don't know what the Shovers have to do with anything.

"The stars and the fish? Isn't that why you revealed yourself yesterday? Isn't that why you ripped Acer's face up with the dumpster? Isn't that why you instructed the Five to tell everyone to bring their weapons to school?"

I told the Five the pennyguns were meant to be carried, but all the rest of that stuff—who told you all that stuff? Where'd you get all those reasons from?

"No one told me," Ally said. "I mean, no one in particular. Everyone I talked to told me," he said, "but no one had to tell me, or anyone else.

779

There's an understanding. With the timing and everything—there's an understanding. We all figured, you know, 'Why would he reveal himself, now? If not because of—'"

Who's we?

"The Israelites, Rabbi, of Aptakisic."

Well, I have no plan for the Shovers, I said. That's a misunderstanding.

"But they're enemies of the Israelites!"

No, I said. No they're not. They're enemies of *some* Israelites, I said.

"*Because* they're Israelites," said Ally. "Which means they're enemies of all Israelites." He was standing up by then. So was Googy.

Sit, I said.

They sat.

The Shovers, I said, are the enemies of those Israelite Shovers who defaced their scarves with stars of David. They're the enemies of those Israelite Shovers because those Israelite Shovers—who are dickheads, by the way, bigger dickheads even than the Gentile ones—broke Shover rules.

"I always thought they were dickheads, too, Gurion, and so did Googy—they're all the enemies of comedy, and that's not up for argument—and the Israelite ones, we thought, were especially big dickheads—not everyone thought that, but some of us did, and me and Goog especially, because they embarrassed us—so you have no disagreement from us that the Israelite Shovers have been dickheads. But then, like you said, they broke Shover rules, and the reason they broke Shover rules was because they wanted to be good Israelites. Or at least because they didn't want to be bad Israelites."

They should have just quit.

"They did, though. They quit."

They didn't, I said. They got kicked out.

"I'm telling you they quit—you must not have read the email. They got kicked out on Wednesday, but yesterday afternoon they held an emergency meeting and they quit, and Berman sent this, like, press release to everyone announcing it last night."

I said, Tch.

"Tch what?" said Ally.

I said, They'd already been kicked out by then.

"I see your point," Ally said. "And I'm with you," he said, "and I know it looks weak. It probably even is weak—quitting after you're fired, it looks like caulk, but still, they're no longer Shovers, and they *are* Israelites, and since they're Israelites, it seems like they should be given the benefit of the doubt. At least it seems that way to me. That *I* should give them the benefit of the doubt. Am I wrong, Rabbi? Isn't that the right thing to do?"

He wasn't wrong. It was the right thing to do.

I told him so. Then Googy nodded vigorously, pointed at me, peek-a-booed, shrugged, choked himself, and shrugged again.

Ally said, "What Googy wants to know is why did you reveal yourself yesterday if it wasn't to bring us together to attack the Shovers over the scarves?"

The Five were looking for me, I said to Googy.

Googy waved me off like a beggar.

"Googy finds that hard to believe," Ally said. "So do I. They just happened to be looking for you yesterday? The timing's too perfect. There has to be some connection between—"

There is, I said, but it's not through me. Shpritzy got attacked by Shlomo Cohen yesterday—

"It looked more, to us, like he attacked Shlomo. Him and the other four."

Shlomo attacked Shpritzy first, I said. During Lunch-Recess. He beat Shpritzy up and some other guys restrained the other four so they couldn't interfere, and when he was finished beating on Shpritzy, he made it clear it was because of the scarves. He said, 'Say hi to Berman for me. Tell him, 'Sharp scarf,' and—'

"Tell *Acer* sharp scarf, you mean," Ally said. "Acer's the one who started the fishes."

No, I said, *Berman*, who started the stars.

"I don't like that," said Ally. "That's lousy. I don't like it. You know, when the Five brought *Ulpan* to Aptakisic, Shlomo was the only Israelite who didn't get it. I was there. So was Googy. In Pinker's backyard—Pinker was the one who invited him, Shlomo, but Shlomo didn't show. There were only twelve of us at Pinker's. Everyone else was divided up between the rest of the Five's backyards. Everyone else but Shlomo, like I said. And anyway, we waited for an hour for him to show, and he didn't show, and he didn't even call. And since the way Pinker invited everyone to receive your *Ulpan* was by going up to them in the hall and handing them a list of supplies with his address on it, and saying, 'Tonight, my place. Secret meeting for Israelites,' lots of people, that night, said Shlomo was a self-hating Jew. That he didn't come because he hated Israelites. But I told them no. I defended Shlomo. I thought that was too much, them calling him that name. That's a bad thing to call someone. It's one of the worst things to be. And, really, I thought Shlomo probably just didn't want to hang out with us, but now you tell me what you're telling me, and I'm thinking you're saying maybe Shlomo Cohen is, after all, a self-hating Jew. Like, you know, like Noam Chomsky, or Philip Roth or whoever, so, I mean, is that what you're saying?"

I said, Philip Roth's not a self-hating Jew. I said, No one with half a brain even considers that a possibility anymore. It's not even a conversation. Shlomo Cohen, though—yeah, he must be. I guess I'm saying he must be. It's the only explanation, right? Shlomo Cohen is a self-hating Jew, so when all of a sudden the Israelite Shovers start making a big deal out of being Israelites, he wants to distinguish himself from them, I'm saying. He wants everyone to know that even though his name's Shlomo Cohen, he is not on the same side as you'd think—he is not on the side of starred scarves, loud Israeliteness, and—

"Except but then he'd attack Berman. Berman's the one who started the scarf-starring."

You'd think so, right? But Berman's a big kid, I said, and Shlomo, as we all saw yesterday in the two-hill field, is a serious bleeder, and if all you thought you needed to do to get your message across was beat up a conspicuously Israelite kid at Aptakisic, a conspicuously Israelite kid who's a known associate of all the other Aptakisic Israelites, and so a known associate of the Israelite Shovers, you wouldn't pick Berman. Not if you didn't know how to fight. And not if you were a giant coward. If you didn't know how to fight, and were a giant coward, you'd pick the smallest kid you could to inflict your message, the kid who'd put up the least resistance.

"Shpritzy," said Ally.

The violin whiz himself.

"Okay. I'm sold. You've sold me on that. Shlomo's a self-hating Jew and Berman starred the scarves, so Shlomo attacked Shpritzy, told him say hi to Berman, and that's why the Five came looking for you. Okay. We're sold. Me and Googy the both. But we're still not sold on not attacking the Shovers, and—"

Googy grabbed hair from the back of his own head and smashed his face into the seatback in front of him.

"Exactly," Ally said. "Why did you mess up Blake Acer so bad?"

Acer was writing WE DAMAGE WE bombs.

"You're *against* the Side of Damage?"

I lead the Side of Damage.

"That's what we heard, but—"

Acer's not on it.

"But he's not the only one not on it who writes WE DAMAGE WE."

You?

"Well… yes."

Don't worry, I said. I said, Write it all you want.

"I'm on the Side of Damage?"

You're an Israelite, I said.

"Israelites are on the Side of Damage?"

Some are, I said, but that doesn't matter.

"You're really confusing me. If I can write WE DAMAGE WE whether or not I'm on the Side of Damage, why can't Acer?"

Israelites are my brothers.

"Acer's not."

Acer's a Shover.

"So tell me again why we shouldn't attack the Shovers."

Who said you shouldn't?

"You said you didn't have a plan."

I don't have a plan.

"And then you said they weren't antisemites, the Shovers."

They're not, I said.

"But they're dickheads, you're saying."

Total dickheads. Arrangement gizmos.

"So we should attack them for that?"

You'd have my blessing.

"But no further instructions."

I said, I taught you how to build weapons and use them. I told you to protect each other. I'm telling you you're Israelites. What better instruction do you need? Damage dickheads and gizmos whenever you get the chance, and protect each other while you do it. Adonai will take care of the rest.

"That's all?"

What more do you want, Ally?

"Will you help us?"

I *have* helped you. I *am* helping you.

"But will you lead us?"

Am I leading you right now?

"I don't know."

Then neither do I.

"Riddles."

I don't speak in riddles, Ally. Riddles are for pagans. If you're following me, I'm leading you.

"I'm following you."

Good, I said.

And I saw that it was.

The rest of the ride I sat by Dingle and Salvador. Dingle said, "Bro," and banged fists with me. Salvador offered me a lime-wedge. I sucked it and tried not to wince, but did. "Almost," said Salvador.

"You almost had it," said Dingle. "For real. You want to see me bleed? I won't even charge you."

That's okay, I said.

"What's your favorite Palahniuk?"

I've never read him.

"Bro," said Dingle.

What? I said.

"Dude," he said.

□   □   □   □   □   □   □

The parking lot was thick with unfamiliar vehicles and non-scholastic personnel. Long-haired guys wearing leather eased a giant spotlight down an eighteen-wheeler's trailer-ramp. Men chokered with chunky headphones erected broadcast dishes in the beds of tricked-out pickups. It wasn't that cold outside, just a touch below freezing, but the air was damp from the morning drizzle, and the first breath I took after stepping off the bus gave me a one-shake chill and came out white.

Main Man and Vincie played slapslap on the curb. Scott kept saying "Smack." I didn't see June anywhere.

"Smack," Scott said, and Vincie pulled his hands away.

I came up beside them. None of us wore gloves.

"Smackattack," said Main Man, and he scored again.

Vincie cocked his chin at me and winked ≠ "I am letting Main Man win," though I thought it did, and I didn't believe him—his flinching seemed authentically defensive. He said to Mookus, "Four–one you, but that's the last time I fall for it."

He fell for it once more, or seemed to, and then it was his turn to slap.
Main Man said, "Smack." Vincie balked, lost the point.

"That's cheap," he said.

Haha, I said.

Main Man looked past me, saying nothing.

It would take him another minute to rout Vincie 13–5. Between the
clouds, strips of sky shone green. Wind blew low and hard and sudden
enough to tousle the loops of our shoelace-knots. A shallow puddle on the
pavement spread.

"Smack-ack," said Main Man, and the game was over.

Vincie cocked his chin and winked.

He beat you sound, I said.

"Fuck does that have to do with anything?" Vincie said. He cocked his
chin once more and I saw that his winking wasn't conspiratorial. It was a
blinker-action for the chin-cocking, which had, itself, been a brandishment:
there was a mouth-shaped welt near his collarbone. That's what I was supposed to look at.

Nice hatermark, I said.

"It's called a hickey when you're in love."

Wouldn't that be when it's called a lovebite? I said.

"If you're some kinda gothy fucken sap, maybe," said Vincie. "You ever
get one, though? You should really get one from June, man. Starla Flangent,
I'll tell you *what*. When Vincie held her hand she felt e lec tric ity."

Benji, I said.

"Fuck does Benji have to do with anything?"

When *Benji* held her hand.

"I don't think you're right."

I'm right.

"We're talking about the same song?"

'The Love You Save,' I said. I said, Jackson 5.

"Whatever, Gurion. All I'm saying is getting a hickey like this one—
I want to play drums for a Motown outfit. I want to rob banks. Listen—"

"No you *fucken* listen!" Scott said.

"Okay," said Vincie.

Okay, I said.

We'd never heard Main Man curse before, and his eyeballs were trembling like Mr. Klapper's, as if straining to take in a sight too large for Main
Man's field of vision to accommodate. He lifted his left foot a couple inches

off the pavement, said, "I'm singing today? I'm singing today," then lost his balance and set the foot back down.

What's wrong? I asked him.

"I forgot," he said. Then he did the foot thing again.

"He's nervous," Vincie said, "cause his parents aren't coming."

That true, Scott? I said.

Main Man wouldn't look at me.

"His little brother Jimmy called me last night to tell me," said Vincie. "I never even knew there was a little brother Jimmy. What a nice little brother. You got a nice little brother, Scott. Jimmy called and told me their parents had to go to some long-weekend Christian retreat thing in Wisconsin today, and Scott forgot all about it til they reminded him last night during dinner when he told them he was psyched for them to see him perform. But I say: So what? I say: So fucken what? I say: Better no parents, especially real Christian ones, since how many girls are gonna be in that audience, and girls are the ones that give hickies, not parents. So no parents isn't something to be nervous about, right? So he shouldn't be nervous about that, Gurion, should he?"

No, I said. You shouldn't, Scott.

"If he's gonna be nervous, he should be nervous cause he's about to get famous, right?"

Right, I said.

"Why he should be nervous is cause, starting second period, every Jenny and Ashley at Aptakisic's gonna chase him through the hallways *Hard Day's Night*–style for the rest of his life just to touch his fucken shirt, right?"

Exactly, I said.

"'Scott Mookus! Oh my God! It's Scott fucken Mookus! I want to touch his shirt! That's a shirt he once sweated in! I want to touch his shirt and then suck on my hand and make him a part of me!'"

Vincie put his fist out, but Main Man wouldn't bang it.

Main Man, I said, Vincie's telling you—

"Am I still singing today?" he said. "Do I still get to sing?"

Yeah, I said. Of course, I said. I said, Don't worry. What're you worried about?

He handed me a letter in an unmarked envelope. I didn't need to open it to know from who.

11/16&17/06

Gurion,

For the past few hours, I've been thinking I'd call you as soon as I figured out what to say, but I haven't been able to figure that out, and it's almost ten, and I hate the phone anyway, so instead I've decided to write you this letter. I still can't figure out what to say, though. I can't figure out the right way to start. I know THIS isn't it, but I'm thinking: Well, at least it's honest so far. At least you can be honest. Try and stay honest.

We've had about forty imaginary conversations since sundown, and none of them have gone the way I wanted them to. You call me one name then I call you the same name and then we start yelling, or I deliver some high-flown speech that explains pretty much everything but for what it's supposed to. One's about the meaning of love. Another's about the trappings of loyalty. A third's about friendship, a fourth about enmity. You get the idea. Anyway, after each speech, you call me out. You say, "That's all just great, Benji. You're a really smart guy, what a talent for discourse, what a way you have with words, but why the fuck did you stand there in the two-hill field, crying like a fucken baby instead of helping me?" And I tell you, "I thought I just explained that, man." And you tell me I didn't, and I see that you're right, and then I launch into some other irrelevant soliloquy.

I'd like to tell you, "I froze," but that sounds like I'm saying I didn't have a choice. I did have a choice, I know I had a choice, and what's more is I knew I had a choice at the time. I chose at the time to stand there and watch. And I could say, "I wish I hadn't made that choice," but that doesn't really hit the mark either. It's more like I wish that I hadn't been me, a person who'd have made that same choice every time. I might as well be wishing we lived on the sun.

So. What.

You ever know a kid who says he's in love, and then a little time passes, maybe even a lot of time, and he tells you he's fallen out of love? Instead of just saying, "Look, I thought I was in love, but it turns out I was wrong," this kid twists the whole thing around. Because you can't fall out of love, right? You fall in love forever. Any kid who says otherwise—he's either a fool or a snake. He's misunderstanding the meaning of the word, or twisting the meaning deliberately. I think usually the latter, he's usually a snake. Either way, his word is worthless. And I don't want to be that kid. I don't want to be anything like that kid. You don't either. I know you that well, at least. We're alike in that way.

With loyalty, it's different, though. You and I, I mean. We're different on that. Loyalty's as permanent as being in love for me. Not so for you, which is probably one reason why none of my imaginary speeches to imaginary Gurions were able to get across what needed getting across.

This morning, in C-hall, I asked you what would happen if a friend of yours got into a fight with someone you had given your loyalty but not your friendship. Your answer came fast and easy. You said you'd side with your friend.

I don't get that, though. For me, if you give your loyalty to someone once, you've given it forever. For me, in order to be truly loyal, you have to be loyal despite preference and hardship—even despite betrayal by the person you've given your loyalty to. Which means you can't let your heart govern your loyalties, right? Your heart's the first thing you have to lock down. Because your heart's what bucks the hardest against the loyalties that are hardest to maintain; and those loyalties—the ones that are the hardest to maintain—their maintenance is the only real measure of your loyalty.

So then how do I decide, right? How do I decide, if a friend of mine gets into a fight with someone who has my loyalty but not my friendship—how do I decide who to side with? I can answer just as quickly and easily as you. I decide by duration—by the loyalties' ages. That's the only way. It's a heartless way, but that's why it's reliable; that's why it's consistent. I solved the whole problem when I was nine years old and I had to choose who to live with. I liked my father better. He was a sober marine who taught me to curse and to swim, but I chose my mom, who was always screaming and falling down. I didn't want to choose, because to choose was to betray one of them, but I had to choose so I chose her because she'd carried me, and that's what I told the both of them. I'd been with her longer and that was that. This solution's a good one, because it's so simple. You can't really fuck with it. You side with the one you've been loyal to longer because time is an absolute. Time isn't subject to the whims of your heart. It can't be interpreted, and therefore it can't be misinterpreted, willfully or un-. Can you see where this is going yet? Probably you can, so before I get there, I need to go somewhere else.

What happened in Nurse Clyde's during Lunch today had no part in the choice I made once we were in the two-hill field, but I know you've got your hypotheses, Gurion, you always have your hypotheses, and I don't want you to think I was in possession of motives unknown to me, so here:

Yes, Slokum and I were best friends until he betrayed me for a blood loyalty—everyone knows that. And yes, lately you've been my best friend, and—in Nurse Clyde's office—I found out you'd betrayed me for a tribal loyalty. And yes, despite your betrayal being far smaller than Slokum's, it gave me flashes of Slokum's, and I thought of Jelly, and I thought of what you'd said to me in the library on Tuesday about conversion and Israelites, and I worried you and I would soon become enemies. But no, that was not a lasting worry at all. I pulled the fire alarm, the moments proceeded slowly, as my most anguished moments always do, and by the time everyone got outside, I was over it. "Gurion's not Slokum," I thought. I thought: "His Israelites aren't Geoff Claymore... He isn't ditching me... He just has to get his loyalties straight..." Etcetera. I saw I didn't have to get fucked up just because you were. I'm not the one in love with a girl his own people won't accept—you are. I'm not the one whose own people fear and shun him. That guy is you. And I don't see why anyone—let alone anyone you've never actually met—should have your loyalty just because they share some distant ancestry with you. Maybe that's because I don't really have people, just a couple friends and a mom, but either way, when it comes to Jelly: I love her, and I don't care so much what you or anyone else think about that, as long as you don't try to interfere. And you hadn't and haven't tried to interfere, and you haven't given any sign that you would. And by the time we were out in the field, I was all sorted out.

By the time we were out in the field, I was ready to laugh with you about pulling the alarm, how I knew I'd get away with it (I went straight to Miss Pinge and said "Is this a drill?" and Pinge said it wasn't, and I said, "Miss Pinge. I don't wanna die. I don't *wanna*!"). But then you were in the air, in the hands of my arch-enemy. And I did nothing to help you. And in a certain light—certainly a *very* certain light (I'm not trying to get off the hook on a technicality)— I betrayed you.

I need to explain about Bam now, my original best friend Bam, my first friend ever, the one who claims, though never out loud, my third-oldest loyalty (apart from my parents, I can't remember anyone before kindergarten, which is when Bam and I became friends), the one who held you helpless in the air.

I am loyal to Bam Slokum because at the age of five I claimed to be, and if I were to now side against him with anyone other than my own parents, it seems to me that all other loyalties I have ever claimed would become dubious. Dubious in FACT, even if not in my heart. I would be no better than that kid who says he's fallen out of love. And I would be the snake variety of that kid, because I would know what I was doing. To side with anyone other than my parents against Bam Slokum would make me a worthless snake, Gurion.

And let me be clear on this: I'm not scared of Bam. He knows it, too. SLOKUM DIES FRIDAY—on his locker, on the walls, the floor, desks. I write it and everyone sees it, and they know it's me who wrote it because Bam tells them. But THEY don't matter to me. What matters to me is that BAM sees it, SLOKUM DIES FRIDAY, and when he sees it, he knows how I despise him, but he also knows that I'm loyal despite his betrayal, that his betrayal lost him the friendship of a truly loyal human being; a guy whose loyalty is able to tolerate his own hatred of its very object. Or maybe not. Maybe he doesn't see that. I don't know. That all seems a little crazy when I see it written down, but that's what I hope, or at least what I've hoped.

In either case, SLOKUM DIES FRIDAY is both a provocation to fight and an expression of loyalty. If I weren't loyal to him, I would write something other than SLOKUM DIES FRIDAY. And he knows exactly what I would write—how easy it would be for me to just add the one word—and he doesn't want it written, and that is the provocation, that is the threat: that I could write that word if I wanted to. But still I *don't* write that word. I don't write it for the same reason I don't disclose it here and for the same reason I don't swing on him when we pass in the hall: because as long as I am not being assaulted by him, I have to protect him—loyalty demands it. I think he knows that, too, although, again, writing it down makes it seem a little crazy————

But that's not as important, whether he knows I'm loyal. What's important is I know. What's important is you know.

And he's not scared of fighting me, either, Gurion. He should be. I'd tear him down if he attacked me, but he's not scared of fighting me, I'm not saying he is. And whether or not he's aware of my loyalty's resilience, it's definitely not regret for having betrayed me, much less any feeling of guilt, that keeps him from attacking me. The reason he doesn't attack me is the same reason he tells everyone it's me who writes SLOKUM DIES FRIDAY: my public displays of enmity *serve* him.

He knows I'm a villain in the eyes of all those kids he wants to worship him (there is no denying it; neither of us can deny how little I'm liked, how many kids would love to see me ended), and he knows that if their villain is Bam's enemy, and Bam's enemy appears afraid to fight Bam, that makes Bam their hero. Crazy as THAT might look written down, I'm positive I'm right. And he's right, too—I make him their hero. Or at least I help to. And a hero under threat, Gurion, always appears more heroic than a hero victorious. If he were to beat my ass—and he *does* believe that would be the outcome (another thing I'm sure of—I *know* this kid)—they would worship him less, because what enemy of Slokum could take my place? Who do they fear more than Benji Nakamook? Who do they hate more than me? No one. So my hatred of him—no matter its forthright nature, its snow-white purity—it doesn't hurt his standing; it's all to his benefit. And so I get to have my cake and eat it too. I get to hate him out loud and protect him all at once. I go forth without compromise, integrity intact, the unbetraying villain.

At least until this afternoon, when I betrayed you, letting him hold you in the air like that. Out of loyalty to my own code of loyalties, I maintained the older of two loyalties. I preserved my own integrity. But it wasn't pleasant. I didn't enjoy it. My heart was bucking.

And now you say, "Who cares? Who cares, though?" right? This is the part where you say, "Who cares what your heart did? How about your legs? How about what they DIDN'T? How about your fists?

You sound like a bancer, talking fancy betrayal and loyalty bullshit, principled bullshit, self-dramatizing bullshit. You sound like a trailer for an action movie. You should have HIT that kid. You should have HELPED me."

And you're right. But so was I, Gurion. And what I'm trying to tell you is I did the harder thing. I didn't do what I wanted—that would've been the easy thing. I hated just standing there, but thought I had to just stand there and so I just stood there. I did what I thought I had to do, and I hated what I thought I had to do, and because I hated it, I knew I was right... or thought I knew I was right. I don't know anymore. I don't know what to do.

If what I've always believed is true—that without our loyalties we're nothing—then our worth is determined by nothing other than the strength of our loyalties. And if I conclude that what I've always believed is false—that our worth is determined by something other or more than the strength of our loyalties—I would, according to my current code of loyalty, be doing so out of worthlessness, or snakiness. So what should I trust? The code I've always trusted that now rings false, or the urge to abandon that code, which is an urge I've always defied with contempt, but which screamed true in the two-hill field, and has continued its screaming ever since? I have to decide. I'm not saying I don't. If I don't, I'm a pussy. And I'm not going to get all purple and sobby about it, but except for in those moments prior to choosing between my parents, I have not felt worse than this. I want you to know that. Juvie was cake compared to this, and Slokum's betrayal an ice-cream sandwich. I'm all backward, Gurion. Most people, they get fucked up the worst when someone else fucks them up. Not me. The only thing that really fucks me up is when I fuck up. I don't understand any of us.

And I don't expect you to understand why I betrayed you, but I'm hoping you won't MISunderstand. I'm telling you I'm your friend, and if you want to hate me for what I failed to do, okay, I get that. I accept it, even. If you hate me, though, Gurion, you'll be hating a friend—a lousy friend who betrayed you, that is true, but not an enemy, not by a longshot. I don't want your hatred. An enemy would. An enemy would court it. What I want is your forgiveness. And I guess that's how I should have started. That would have been the most honest way, to ask you to forgive me for the way that I am—if not for the way I've made myself, then for the way I was made. Whichever way you see it. Any way you can forgive me. I've been trying to give you one without telling lies.

I know, at least, that I've told you no lies.

Your loyal blowhard friend who betrayed you,

Benji Nakamook

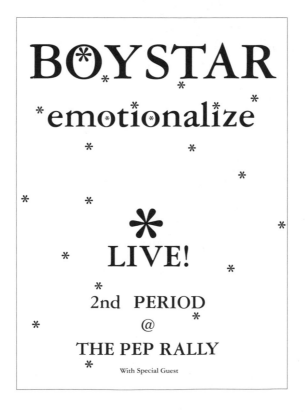

The tower of my Tower of Restraint dream explicated, I returned the letter to its envelope. Then I climbed off the hood of the car I'd been sitting on—a maroon Ford Escort I was pretty sure was Botha's—and made my way out of the parking lot.

Ten steps along, a limo crept past me, a stretched SUV with a jacked rear axel. Its wheels were chrome-spinnered, and its plates read NEWTHING, its custom-made hood-ornament a gold-plated microphone. The men in the back hung cigar smoke out the windows, and when it parked beside the dumpster Blake Acer had bombed—his blood clung like rust to the second WE—I saw they were Boystar's dad and Chaz.

Chaz waved a hand to beckon to a woman who was chanting, "Unaccept-able," into her celly. She stepped out of her heels and ran tiptoed to the limo. She leaned through the smoke and kissed Chaz on the cheek, and it was boring so I looked away.

The lot had gotten busier. More roadies hauled more implements down the semi's tongue-like ramp: speakers, footlights, a soundboard. Techs inside newsvans keyed at rugged-looking laptops; dish antennas rotated and bowed. A curious bandkid leaked gooze out both nostrils while a high-haired Ashley did a curtsy at a cameraman. Some Highway 61 guys fought about a chapstick and three talking heads traded sugar-free chiclets, smiling like it hurt when smitten Jennys turned to gape. Two of these Jennys manned a table at the curb. Across their foreheads, in lipstick, was INDIANS. In front of their table, girls stood ten-deep, waiting in line to get their own foreheads INDIANS'd.

As I approached the front entrance, June leapt from the shrubs. She bit my shoulder, and I called her Jellybean and pinched her hip til she wiggled. The smell of her hair got me warm and relaxed, and we bumped each other sideways as we staggered at the building like our legs were manacled.

I think I'm friends with Benji again, I told her.

"You never weren't," she said.

I said, How long do pep rallies last here?

"A period."

Good, I said. Can you get sent to Nurse Clyde a few minutes after third starts? I'll do the same thing and we'll meet up like yesterday.

June said she'd do it and we entered the school. The Sentinel halted us just past his booth. No surprise there—we'd both ditched detention. "Two of you: Office," the Sentinal said.

June said, "You office."

Jerry didn't hear. He asked me, "How's your mom?"

I flashed him the Look of The End.

He pretended confusion, and we followed him through Main Hall.

Boystar flyers were all over the place, taped to anything flat and stationary. Support pillars were plastered with red and white construction paper. Matching streamers hung in clusters from the ceiling like curtains. Jerry before us, we tore as we went. Helium balloons nodded and swayed, the taut lengths of ribbon that anchored them to locker-vents angling sharp in our wake. June freed a balloon and pulled out its plug. She aimed at my face, let fly, and I ducked it. It spiraled six feet and fizzled on an Ashley. She glowered at June, and June flicked the plug at her. The Ashley's INDIANS went crumply.

Just outside the Office, sitting on a dolly, was the spotlight I'd seen in the parking lot. Inside, Brodsky's door was closed. Empty ISS desks crowded the floor, and Pinge was smiling at a notepad. She wrote something down for a big, blushing roadie, who was leaning one-handed on the border of her blotter.

We sat in the waiting chairs we'd fallen in love in. June put my hand on the weapon in her pocket. She narrowed her eyes and bit on her lip, digging her nails in my wrist.

Miss Pinge slid the notepad across her desk.

The roadie pushed his bangs back and asked of her softly, "This your home or your celly, ladyfriend?"

"Shh," she said, seeing us.

The roadie said, "What?"

Pinge chinned air in her own direction and the roadie leaned way over the desk. This blocked Pinge's sightline, I saw my moment, and I kissed June's neck and the kiss made her gasp.

I'd started by her ear and was going toward her shoulder, about to, with my free hand, squeeze her thigh so she'd gasp more, but a guy with a soul-patch was standing in the doorway.

He lifted one lip-corner and gave me the cockeye = "I can see what you're doing, there, but I won't tell."

I liked him.

"The hell, Raymond," he said to the one who loved Pinge called Raymond. "We're chewed we don't get a move on already."

"Just a minute," said Raymond.

"Are you the lighting guys?" June asked the soulpatch.

"We're the lighting *grunts*, cutiepie."

"Installation experts," said Raymond.

"We push the lights on dollies, hoist the lights on guywires, secure the lights to their end-locales, and finally we plug them in. After that we go smoke in the truck."

"We also gotta calibrate—"

"We don't gotta calibrate nothing. The only other thing we do is what I already told you, but backward to the truck. That's why you stay in school there, cutie. So's when you meet someone you want to date with, you don't feel pressured to prevaricate about calibrating when in fact there's no calibrating you do."

"Jeez, Tony," said Raymond.

"Hey," said the soulpatched Tony, chinning the air at Miss Pinge. "She cares about you don't calibrate? Then pretty or no, she's the wrong girl for you. Let me tell you, Miss: Raymond here is a progressive rock and roll musician of the temporarily defunct funk-metal genre. His talent is genius-par. World was fair, he'd be rich and famous already. We both would cause he's my cousin and we got a band together, Blaine the Minority, and I'm not so bad at bass he'd ditch me once he made it, but even if I was that bad at bass, he wouldn't ditch me, because he's a good friend, and if you think that's common in this world, you live a truly blessed life, but also you got another think coming, and you should think that think twice or even three times first."

"Excuse me, sir," said someone behind him. Tony moved and I saw it was Shpritzy.

Miss Pinge sent Raymond away with a hand-pat. Tony followed at his heels and made wet kissing sounds.

The Five had entered the Office with Berman.

The Levinson told me, "A friend of ours: Berman."

Berman chinned air at June and gave her a wink. June chinned air back and did not give a wink, and that might have reassured me, but for all I knew June couldn't wink—I knew *I* couldn't wink—so for all I knew, she'd have winked were she able. It happened, however, that she was holding my hand, and she certainly could've given it a reassuring squeeze, but no squeeze came, and I wasn't reassured. Reassured of what, though? That she didn't still like him? Well… yes. Except why should I want reassurance of that? They'd broken up. They'd never kissed. They didn't speak. Above all, June and I were in love. I wanted reassurance because she'd gotten winked at, but it wasn't her fault that she'd gotten winked at. It was Berman's fault. He shouldn't have winked. He shouldn't have gotten me wanting reassurance. Especially because there could be no reassurance. That's what was chomsky. To think that a hand-squeeze would reassure was chomsky. Had June squeezed my hand, I wouldn't feel reassured; I'd only wonder why she thought I wanted reassurance. I'd worry that she thought I wanted reassurance because Berman's wink was, in fact, worth worrying about. = If June had squeezed my hand, I'd want *more* reassurance. And I saw it was good that she hadn't squeezed my hand. Which isn't to say I stopped wanting reassurance, but that all at once I saw what needed doing, not to me or for me, but by me: I had to tell Berman not to wink at my girlfriend. Had he not been an Israelite, I'd've thought of that sooner, gone straight to confrontation. Instead of burning sweaty seconds lamely sorting useless feelings, I'd have risen to my feet and said, Don't you fucken wink at her.

And that is exactly what I was just about to do. I'd let go of June's hand and planted mine on my chair-arms, but no sooner had I started leaning forward to rise than Josh Berman chinned air and winked *at me*, undermining my resolve, my whole sense of what was called for.

I leaned back, puzzled.

Berman opened his coat like a stranger-danger flasher to show me the pennygun riding at his flank—it was held to his fleece by a strip of velcro.

The unspoken subject at hand shifted quickly.

I shrugged and made my lips fat = Glad you have a weapon, but why not hide it in your pocket?

He clicked his tongue against his teeth = "Clever, my holster, I know."

Then he closed up the coat and said, "Finally we meet." He was acting as if we'd never laid eyes on each other. It didn't seem possible that he wouldn't remember—we were in the same place where we'd met the first time—but maybe he hadn't noticed me there. Or maybe he was embarrassed for how he'd acted toward Ruth. He deserved to be embarrassed, and that was punishment itself, so I didn't say anything; I channeled Ally Kravitz, attempted to give Berman the benefit of the doubt. My face must have, despite that, betrayed what I remembered.

"Wait a second!" said Berman. "I think I saw you right here on Tuesday. Crazy. Wow. No idea. I had no idea."

That's something, I said.

I didn't like being so casual about it. Benefit of the doubt, I thought, benefit of the doubt... But he should have either said something, or he should have said nothing. He shouldn't have said nothing *and then* said something, much less with fake surprise... Or maybe he should have? Maybe he was being just as human as anyone? Maybe I wanted to think he did something he shouldn't have done because that would make it easier for me to believe I disliked him for being, in some objective way, a dickhead, rather than because he used to date June and I was petty and jealous? What worried me more? Not liking an Israelite for my own petty reasons, or liking a dislikable Israelite because he was an Israelite? I couldn't tell. Meow meow, meow

meow. I squeezed my own hand.

That's something, I said.

He said, "*Something* is right. I got set *straight*. You saw it yourself."

Yeah? I said.

"About the blankspot, I mean. That really got to me."

Right, I said. I said, Ruth's smart.

"Yeah," he said. "She's pretty smart."

No, I said. Ruth's *really* smart.

"I guess, you know, I don't know. I guess I must not have come off so—you know, she and my brother had a really ugly break-up." Was he being sincere? Was he truly apologetic? What did that even mean, *truly apologetic*? He was saying all the right things, things I didn't want to hear. "I'm real tight with my brother and—"

I said, None of my business.

"I'm just saying," Berman said.

Yeah, it's none of anyone's business, really, right? Not even your friends'.

"I totally agree. Believe you me. I got seriously burned for bringing it up, didn't I?"

Scorched, I said. I said, I wouldn't mess with Ruth.

"Believe you me," he said.

Berman had been shaking my hand since "No idea." Here he finally let go. Then he clicked, and flashed the gun again. "So wuddup, June Dub?" he said. "Long time no—"

"Joshua Berman, get to class," Miss Pinge interrupted. "The rest of you. ISS starts in about ninety seconds. I suggest you choose a desk."

They all did as they were told, Berman chopping air near his temple as he left.

"What a dentist," June said.

Yeah? I said. Yeah, I said.

June squeezed my hand.

You guys know June? I said to the Five.

"Nice to meet you, June!" said The Levinson. "I'm Mr. Goldblum," said Mr. Goldblum. "You can call me Shpritzy," said Shpritzy. "This boy right here is Glassman," said Pinker. "And this young soul who so kindly just introduced me is a fellow known affectionately as Pinker," said Glassman.

By the time they got to Shpritzy, June was laughing her face off, and I loved her so much. Everything was fine.

They're best buddies, I told her.

She balled fists around her hair and pulled toward her shoulders, her freckles all fading in the flush of her face as she began to squeak and hyperventilate.

"June's laughing." "At us or with us?" "Who cares? She's pretty." "Still, I hope it's with us." "Ask her." "She can't talk right now." "Is it with us, Gurion?"

She likes you guys, I said.

"Who is she, anyway?" they said.

We're getting married, I said.

"Mazel tov!" they shouted in unison. Then they started to clap. The sound was slightly muted by their batting-gloves, but their celebration brought me joy nonetheless.

Soon the clapping gave way to high-fives, and a roll of pennies fell from Pinker's pants pocket. Mr. Goldblum kicked it to Shpritzy. Shpritzy rolled it with his hand to The Levinson, and The Levinson swooped the roll up and over, onto the lap of Glassman. Glassman stuck it in the pocket of Pinker's that was opposite the one it had fallen from.

Miss Pinge cleared her throat, looking dizzy.

She said, "You're cute, but the clowning stops after the tone, understood?"

"You're really nice, Miss Pinge. Isn't Miss Pinge really nice?" "She's so nice." "She's so nice, she should be the spokeswoman for an important charity because she'd raise millions." "Probably even billions." "She should go on Oprah."

Brodsky's door opened.

Maholtz, the Co-Captain, and a mangled Shlomo Cohen exited. Eyes on their shoes, they adjusted their ties, but none took a seat at the open ISS desk.

I said, Tattle and asskiss your way outta trouble?

"I can't waint til Bam seends what you did," said Maholtz.

And what's that? I said.

I really didn't know.

Maholtz said, "Tch." Shlomo Cohen and the Co-Captain echoed it.

Then Pinker honked his dickhorn at them, and soon the other four honked their dickhorns at them, too. I thought honking my dickhorn might ick June, but I wanted to back the Five, so I just said, Honk, and kept both my hands far away from my wang.

Out came the gym teacher, stiff in his suit. As soon as he saw me, he glared.

"Don't vibe at boo," said June.

"Don't *what* at *who*?"

Don't rhyme with wifey, I told him.

"You don't even speak correct English," said Desormie, "and that is a testament."

"A testament?" said The Levinson. "Testament's like testicles," said Mr. Goldblum. "Patriarchs grab the ones on their sons when they're making a promise," said Pinker. "Patriarchs grab thighs," submitted Shpritzy. "Thigh's a euphemism," retorted Glassman. "How do you know?" "Cause it's called a testimony, not a thighamony." "Their dads touch their shvontzes?" "Their bollocks." "Their yarbles." "Still, that's pervasive." "*Pervy.*" "Right. Pervy." "Except it didn't used to be in the old days." "These days, though, to touch your son on the nutbag—" "These days it's total pervasion." "Perversion."

Desormiation, I said.

"What?" said Desormie.

I showed him my palm and pointed at it.

Delivered, I said.

That was the last word that I would ever say to him.

"Come on," he told his basketballers.

They followed him into Main Hall, away from ISS.

The Five got up in arms.

"They just get to leave? Where's the justice?" said Pinker. "This is a testament." "Balls!" "Why do they get to leave, Miss Pinge?"

Miss Pinge said, "Look around. Do you see any room in here for three more desks?"

"But yesterday Mr. Brodsky said—"

"I miscalculated," said Brodsky, emerging from his office. "They'll serve ISS on Monday, though."

"So they get to go to the pep rally." "I smell a rat." "The rat smells like Desormie." "A testimonious sack is what it smells like."

"You'll go to the pep rally, too," Brodsky said. Then he left to go to the bathroom.

"What about the Orthodox kid?" "Where's he at?" "There's still an empty desk." "It's saved for that Elijah, right?"

Hey, I said.

"What?" "What's wrong?" "What'd we do?"

I said, When Eliyahu comes in here, you make him your best buddy.

"You can't just make someone a best buddy like that, Gurion." "It takes time." "There's a whole set of things that goes into it." "We've never even seen a movie with him on Sunday." "Let alone on seven consecutive Sundays." "And batting gloves?" "Forget it—we've never even watched a game on TV with him." "He might be a Sox fan." "Best buddies, at this juncture, even if we wanted to… it's impossible." "We can do friend, maybe even pal."

Pal shmal, I said.

"Good pal."

Sounds pally to me, I said to June.

"It does," June said.

"Now she's weighing in?" "Fine." "She says good pal sounds pally, maybe it's pally." "Straight-up buddy's the final offer." "Can we really do that, Mr. Goldblum?" "Franklin Gurstein. Three weeks ago. Precedent's been set." "That's different." "How's it different?" "Franklin Gurstein told us what frottage was, and the Brumpy." "And the Dirty Sanchez and the Angry Dragon." "He told us all about the Ray Charleston Chew." "Point taken. But maybe this Eliyahu can tell us what something dirty is?"

He can teach you words for penis in Yiddish, I said.

"We know all those words." "Shvontz." "Putz." "Schmuck." "Shlong." "Pizzle."

There's more.

"How many?"

At least ten more.

"If he can teach us ten more, we'll call him Buddy."

Five more and good buddy, I said.

"Good buddy's too much." "Just a half-step below best." "Straight-up buddy, Gurion." "And only if he asks." "And he has to teach us seven words for penis in Yiddish."

"That's enough with the penis," said Miss Pinge.

"Miss Pinge said penis."

Miss Pinge bit a smile back.

Pretty good buddy, seven words for penis, and he doesn't have to ask, I said.

"There's no such thing as pretty good buddy." "Who ever heard of pretty good buddy?" "Pretty good buddy's a unicorn." "A winged unicorn." "A horned Pegasus from Atlantis with rainbows in its eyes." "Work with us here."

Pretty good buddy, three words for penis, and he doesn't have to ask.

"That's not how you do it!" "We go lower and you go higher." "We meet somewhere in the middle."

Pretty good buddy, one word for penis, and he doesn't have to ask. Anything less I walk away unhappy.

"Do you see what he's doing?" "Look at what he's doing!" "It's an affront to the process." "He's undermining the process." "It's now or never." "Gurstein's gonna call it a ripoff." "Everyone's gonna call it a ripoff!" "Pretty good buddy!" "Is it even real?" "It's definitely *not* real, but can we make it real, if we really try? That, best buddies, is the question." "Let's say we could, let's say we can make pretty good buddy work. If Gurstein hears of it—" "Why would Gurstein hear of it?" "If Gurstein hears of it, we'll make him a pretty good buddy, too." "We'll have to." "No way around it." "Can we do that?" "If we can make pretty good buddy real, how hard could it be to make of Gurstein a pretty good buddy?" "It's settled then." "It's settled then?"

It's settled then, I said.

Brodsky returned. "Who wants to go first?" he said.

June poked my knee.

□   □   □   □   □   □   □

Next to Brodsky's phone was a box of donut-holes shaped like a house. He pushed it my way and opened the roof. He wasn't just offering me donut-holes, though.

I'm not talking about my father, I told him.

He showed me his palms, chuckled *hurt hurt hurt*. Then he tapped on the box and said, "Please. I'll be diabetic by noon."

All the chocolates were gone. I wrapped three cinnamons in a napkin, and Brodsky handed me a spreadsheet. Thursday's detention roster jammed in a grid. Since June and I had gotten collared together, I already knew we were in the Office for ditching detention, but what surprised me was that next to Eliyahu's last name (Weitzman, it turned out—a small surprise in itself, to learn he was a Yeckie), instead of a blank space or check-mark, were the letters EXC. A couple slots above Eliyahu's name was June's, and next to hers another EXC. I scanned the whole STATUS column and failed to find a blankspot, let alone an INEXC or ABS.

"EXC means excused," said Brodsky. "You won't receive an ISS for ditching detention."

I snapped a curled, stray thread off the cuff of my hoodiesleeve.

"Neither will June. No one will."

This nub of elastic poked out from the cuff where the thread had been. I pinched it between my nails and pulled, but the nub just got longer, which I should have expected. How many out-sticking elastic nubs had I made elastic string of, pulling them?

"Do you know there were nearly eighty students on yesterday's detention roster?" said Brodsky. "Forty were from the Cage, but the average number of students in Thursday detention is sixteen, so even without the students from the Cage, who account for an average of thirty-nine percent of detentions on any given day, roughly seven percent of the school was in detention. Unheard of. And nine students skipped, also unheard of. Now: all of you will serve a detention to make up for the skipped one. None of you, however, will be disciplined for *having skipped*, nor for any other offense for which you haven't yet been stepped this week."

The move my dad had showed me was you grasp the fabric on either side of the nub and massage it; it took a few seconds sometimes to get the action right, but the nub never failed to suck back inside the garment. I rarely thought to massage til after I'd pulled the nub, though. I usually made string of the nub, and you couldn't massage string away. You could wind string around your swear-tip and yank suddenly, but half the time that made more string. The only guaranteed method was sawing side-to-side at the base with your teeth. This got spit on your garment, but was always effective, so that's what I did. I brought my wrist to my mouth and started to chew.

Brodsky hadn't stopped talking. "...Then yesterday you told me the students in the Cage act like they're in a cage *because* they are in the Cage. Now, as I'm sure you're well aware, that's not a new idea. However, it's not an entirely insupportable one either. In fact, were you to allow it to soften a little—were you to qualify it... were you to say, instead of *the* students, *some* students, or even '*Many* students in the Cage act like they're in a cage because they are in the Cage,' then you'd find yourself saying something I might entirely agree with. Whether or not I'd agree it was problematic, however—that's a different story."

The trouble was lining your teeth up right.

"Here's another idea that I'm sure you're familiar with: The world at large is like a cage. The world is bounded and governed, and those who violate its boundaries or defy its governance meet with negative consequences.

And yes, even those who stay within their cage's boundaries and allow them-selves to be governed meet with negative consequences, and indeed that happens far more often than should be the case, you'll hear no argument from me on that—I do not deny the world contains its share of injustice, but… *Most* people, Gurion—*most* people do not violate boundaries, do not defy governance, and most of them come out intact, whereas *very few* of those who act lawlessly do. And that is why school is so much about following rules. You are here, above all else, to learn to live lawfully for the rest of your life. You are here to learn how to exist in cages without acting as if they are cages, to live like mensches despite being locked in cages. You are here to learn to survive in the world. That is the most basic purpose of our educa-tional system, and it is a high purpose. It is good. I stand behind it. I want you and your fellow students to leave Aptakisic more capable of survival than you were when you entered."

You didn't just have to get your teeth down to the very base of the string. You had to get one of the two big middle ones in the top row to press the string base directly against two of the three small middle ones in the bottom row, and once you started sawing you had to go perfectly side-to-side so that you wouldn't pull the string longer, and you had to be mindful of the width of the top tooth so you wouldn't over-saw and lose the string and have to start over, and plus with your inner-lips and gums flush with the fabric, your saliva gets triggered if you don't remind yourself every half-second that your cuff isn't food, so there was that to concentrate on too, and finally I just twirled the string around my swear and wound it til it ended and my cuff was that much looser.

"In any case, when you say all the students in the Cage act like they are in a cage because they are in the Cage, it's too extreme a position. I can dismiss it with great ease. The rest of the world is in a cage as well, and the vast majority of us *don't* endanger others. The vast majority of us act quite decently. However—"

You're arguing semantics with me? I said.

"Excuse me?"

You're saying, 'For one to act like one is in a cage is for one to act decently. To endanger others is not to act decently. The students in the Cage endanger others. Therefore the students in the Cage do *not* act like they are in a cage,' I said.

"I appreciate your intelligence," he said, "but this isn't one of your detention assignments. I'm being serious here."

I said, So am I. If the world's in a cage, and most of the world acts decently, then to act decently is to act like you're in a cage.

"Fair enough, but it's beside the point. Let's forget the phrase 'act like one is in a cage.' Let's focus instead on 'endangering others.' Can we do that?"

I chinned the air at my shoes = It's your office.

"Thank you. Now. Were you to qualify your statement—were you, as I suggested earlier, to say, '*Some* students in the Cage *endanger others, at least in part,* because they are in the Cage,' I could not dismiss that, not responsibly. Were you to say 'some' instead of 'all,' and add the 'at least in part'—after all, everyone in the Cage was originally put in the Cage for having, in some way, endangered others while outside the Cage—it would be my responsibility to ask, 'How many?' And yesterday, on my drive home, I imagined a dialogue with you in which you did say 'some,' and added the 'in part.' You said 'some,' and 'in part,' and I asked you 'How many?' And you said, 'Five or six.' You said, 'Five or six students endanger others, at least in part, because they—the five or six—are in the Cage.' And I said, 'That's eight to ten percent of the Cage who endanger others, at least in part, because they are in the Cage; that's one percent or less of Aptakisic. That is not troubling. That is something to celebrate. That is a system that works for ninety-nine percent of the student population.' You see, it's about math, Gurion, it always is. Yet I thought maybe I wasn't being fair. Maybe, in our imaginary conversation, I had formed your argument of straw. So I rewound. I rewound the conversation so that when I asked how many, you doubled the number. And still your argument was weak. So I rewound again and had you triple the number. Yet again, your argument was weak. I had you increase the number by increments of eight, then ten. I had you increase it until you were back to 'All the students in the Cage endanger others, at least in part, because they are in the Cage'; until you were up to forty students. Forty students is roughly seven-point-five percent of the school, I reasoned, which would mean the system worked for over ninety percent of the school. And though a ninety-two-point-five percent success rate is not as admirable as a ninety-nine percent success rate, it is nothing to scoff at. But this is where the revelation happened.

"You, the imaginary you, said two very intelligent things to me in succession. First you said, 'Mr. Brodsky, you are rationalizing the abandonment of seven-point-five percent of your students.' And I saw that you were right. And it stung me, Gurion, it did—even in fantasy the idea stung. I am an idealist, a do-gooder, I have always been. I am not ashamed of it. I am, in fact, proud of it. Do-gooders who disregard practicality, however, are a dime a dozen. It seemed impossible to reconcile the sting with the ninety-two-point-five percent success rate. So I wasn't perfect, I thought, but no one was, I thought, and it's nothing short of hubris to strive for perfection as if it were attainable. It is hubristic to fail to leave well enough alone. Who is to say that if I changed the system, I would make it better? Who is to say I wouldn't make it worse? Could it be anything other than selfish, I wondered, to take such a risk? But then you said, 'Last month, only five or six of the students in the Cage endangered the school, at least in part, because they were in the Cage. This month it's forty. The danger has spread and the danger will continue to spread.' And that, Gurion: That was a strong argument for change, an argument based in math, however imaginary. And this is what I decided, in my car, with an imaginary you as my audience: I decided that the danger needed to stop spreading, and I saw that it was not the Cage itself that caused most students in the Cage to endanger our school, but those original five or six—that original one percent. That one percent truly wishes harm on the school. 'Damage' as the graffiti would have it. The Cage doesn't fail them so much as they fail the Cage. The rest of you—and I *am* counting you among the rest (though exceptional among the rest, which I'll get to momentarily)—the rest lack true malice. You all have good intentions, you want to be good, but the one percent has filthied up your environment, has not only made school *feel* unsafe, but has *made it* dangerous, and you can't help but respond with dangerous behavior, for dangerous behavior begats more of the same. It does so by means of undermining trust in authority. You look around at all the dangerous behavior... You look around and feel unsafe, and you think, 'The school is failing to protect me. I must protect myself. I must blend in with my dangerous surroundings.' And when you get in trouble for it, for blending in, when you get in trouble for engaging in what seem to you to be acts of self-protection, you think, 'Not only is the school failing to protect me, but it is attacking me. It is as hostile toward me as those who initially made me feel unsafe.'

"And this is the kind of thinking I want to put a stop to. I *must* put a stop to it before the damage becomes permanent. So I've decided that, along with a few other measures, a goodwill gesture on my part is in order. A gesture to show all of you that the school *is* on your side, *is* here to protect you. That we are not here to punish you for acting in ways that you feel you must act in order to remain safe. Thus: amnesty. Amnesty to show all of you that

I know—that *Aptakisic* knows—that you are in a compromised position, that you are not acting out of malice, but rather attempting, however misguidedly, to survive. A goodwill gesture to show you that we understand you: that is the beginning. That will grant us all a fresh start. And I believe this schoolwide rash of misbehavior, the fistfights and detention-skipping as well as the graffiti, and this nonsense with the scarves—because they have *not* for the most part been committed by the malicious few, but the endangered many... I believe this misbehavior will cease. By the end of next week, the graffiti will have been cleaned up, and by the end of the month we'll have security cameras installed throughout school. Those few malicious students who are causing all these problems will be neutralized, if not expelled. The good ones will feel safe again."

Here, Brodsky popped a toasted-coconut donut hole. He chewed it vividly behind an all-lips smile, nodding his head with each clench of his jaw, his chomping and swallowing way louder than necessary. I knew it wasn't possible to like donut-holes that much, but what I wasn't sure of was whether he was he trying, with his dumbshow, to infect me with enthusiasm, or if he meant to cue approval from me that he believed already imminent. Either way, he was taking too much for granted.

I said, Why'd you just tell me all that stuff?

He showed me his pointer and his Adam's apple bobbed. He sucked a flake of stuck coconut off the front of his teeth. "I thought you'd be happy to hear it," he said.

Why would I be happy to hear it? I said.

His big pink head deluminesced a little, but except for that loss of candle-power, the question didn't seem to deflate him like I wanted it to. "To begin with, as I began before, you played a big role in my decision-making process, and credit is due to you. If I failed to express that—"

I didn't ask you for amnesty, I said. I said, I definitely didn't ask you for cameras.

"Not by name," said Brodsky, "but in spirit, I think. I'm not certain, here, why you want to deny that. I heard how you helped out in the Cage yesterday, and your actions speak volumes."

What exactly do you think my actions say?

"They tell me you want us to be on good terms, that you want—as we discussed at our meeting yesterday—you want to help me. That you want to make Aptakisic safer."

I think my actions might've bumbled their lines a little, I said. What

I did yesterday was demonstrate that I *could* help you—that if you get rid of the Cage, I *will* help you.

"Did you not believe me when I said I wasn't bargaining, Gurion?"

He seemed more entertained by this than he should have.

That was before you knew I could do what you pretended to believe I could do, I said.

"No, Gurion. I pretended nothing yesterday. I reached out to you, and I did so in good faith. I was honest with you."

Reach out by getting rid of the Cage.

"It can't happen."

Fire Botha, I said.

"Your biggest backer?" he said. And laughed. "Mr. Botha admires you, Gurion."

Tch, I said.

"After school, yesterday, after I'd discussed with him what you and I had talked about regarding Scott Mookus, he described what you'd done in the Cage. He said he'd never before seen the students behave so well."

He acted more like he'd never seen them behave so badly, I said.

"He said that, too. He even admitted some culpability for the chair-scooting, but claimed that you, Gurion, and I am quoting directly, 'have shown him the error of his ways.' I was, I think, even more surprised than you look right now. Mr. Voltz and Mrs. Sepper were also impressed. But where they left off, Mr. Botha did not. He suggested that you might be ready to move on. He thinks you no longer require what the Cage has to offer."

I nearly jumped from my chest, but I swallowed me down. My voice stayed level.

He just wants to be done with me, I said. I said, He's trying to railroad me.

"Railroading usually leads *toward* locked rooms, Gurion."

Are you in on it? I said.

"What a way to speak. Back up a second. I understand you believe yourself and Mr. Botha exist in some irrevocable state of enmity, but I'm certain you've got it wrong. After we discussed Scott Mookus, and after Mr. Botha finished praising your behavior, he, without prompting, explained that he understood the reasons behind this scooting thing you were all doing."

You guys understand a whole lot, I said. There's so much understanding going on—

"He said that yesterday morning, during announcements, Scott had told everyone that he would be singing with Boystar, and Mr. Botha had not believed it—he thought Scott was confused. And he had assumed that the rest of you had thought so too. But. He said that now he realized that all along, the lot of you had known that Scott would sing, and that that was why you had reacted with the scooting behavior when he took away your pep rally privileges. And *then*, Gurion, *then* Mr. Botha told me that he thought hearing Scott sing at the pep rally could only be good for the morale of the rest of the Cage students, and so he would allow all of you to go to the pep rally. And I did not prompt him to say any of these things. He said it all out of the goodness of his heart. What do you think now?"

I think he warped everything that happened yesterday, I said, including the basic sequence of events. I think he just wants me out of the Cage. I said, He's trying to wash his hands of me.

"And I'm sure you're incorrect, but let's say you're right. That you're right about his motives. What if I remove you from the Cage, anyway?"

Now you're threatening me? I said. I said, I thought you were reaching out.

"And I thought I'd just offered you a bargain. What quarrel could you possible have?"

It's no bargain to keep me from my friends, I said.

"Maybe it is," he said. "From some of them. Maybe some of your friends hinder your education, put you at risk. Your father seems to think so—that's what he told me over the phone the other day. I think separation from them will be good for you. You'll make new friends."

I can make new friends whenever I want, I said.

"Be sensible," he said. "Who're those pastries in the napkin for?"

They're donut holes, I said.

"They're for your girlfriend. She's very talented, by the way, June Water-mark, a very intelligent girl. And more to the point: she's not in the Cage. She's in all of the gifted classes we offer for seventh-graders, classes you would certainly be placed in, were *you* not in the Cage."

I said, You can't use June against me.

"*Against* you, Gurion? If anything, I'd think she'd play carrot to the Cage's stick."

Don't give away your carrots, I thought.

I said, Stop trying to arrange me.

"I'm offering you an incentive to be good," he said. "Yes," he said, slapping the desk, "I wasn't certain before, but talking through this with you—now I see I was right. You need an incentive, not a deterrent. Deterrents backfire with you. They make you resent us. This is the right incentive. It's all over your face. You should see yourself. I'll file the papers this afternoon. You'll be out of the Cage on Monday. You won't be going back in, either. And we'll put you on the regular STEP system. We will no longer damn you with our low expectations."

I said, I'll get expelled by the end of the week.

But the words sounded obligatory, even to me.

"I hope that's not true," he told me. "I believe that after the weekend, after some time to think, you'll see this is a good decision and you'll be a mensch about it. That said, I will not tolerate you holding yourself hostage. If you try to get back in the Cage by misbehaving, you *will* be expelled. I'll explain that to your father, and he'll be fine with it, I'm certain."

I stared speechlessly at the wingnut on his desk. It shined bright without meaning, and my thoughts spun, tractionless. Hold myself hostage? Was that even possible?

Brodsky opened the door for me. "Ms. Watermark," he said.

June rose from her chair. We brushed wrists as we passed, and she whispered in my ear: "The Israelites live!" Then she looked at Eliyahu and he turned up his thumbs, and only then did I realize June had spoken in Hebrew.

Smiling, Eliyahu said: "Nice girl, this redhead, who tells you you're smart and handsome in the language of the patriarchs." He was sitting at the desk nearest Pinge's. While Pinge wrote my hallpass, he took off his hat and flipped it upside down. Two rolls of pennies were hidden in the sweatband. Affixed to the crown by tape was his weapon.

"He's a pretty good buddy, this guy," said Pinker. "He's no shmeckel."

```
SCAFFOLDING SCAFFOLDING SCAFFOLDING SCAFFOLDING SCAFFOLDING
SCAFFOLDING SCAFFOLDING SCAFFOLDING SCAFFOLDING SCAFFOLDING
     P                                              P
     I                                              I
     P                                              P
     E                                              E
     P                                              P
     I                                              I
     P                                              P
     E                                              E
  SPEAKER                                        SPEAKER
  SPEAKER                                        SPEAKER
  SPEAKER                                        SPEAKER
   F F F                                          F F F
   O O O                                          O O O
   T  T  T                                        T  T  T
```

I was glad. There was no way around it. There'd be no more tapelines. No more Face Forward rule. No more blindsiding wings extending from the walls of carrels. No more carrels. I could make out with June at recess. We could trade notes in classrooms where only one robot presided. Steal kisses. Make faces at each other across aisles between desks.

Wasn't I glad? Was there no way around it? Why was I looking for some way around it?

Why *should* I care what Botha intended? Why should I care if he got to save face? If he behaved in a way that was to my benefit, what did it matter if it was also to his? Wasn't that the ideal, anyway? Wasn't it better to make allies of your enemies than it was to defeat them? Maybe *allies* was overstating the case, but even still: wasn't it better to achieve a steady détente with your enemies than it was for the two of you to suffer? And maybe *détente* was overstating it, too, steady or no—but a ceasefire? Not so much a de-escalation of hostility, but an end to *hostilities*? No more hostile acts? That was *under*stating it, actually, *ceasefire*. This was better than a ceasefire. At least a little. It was more secure. The lines we'd have to cross to bring new hostilities weren't abstract—they were walls. The same walls inside of which we'd been trapped with one another for ten weeks. Now they'd be between us, physical blockages. I'd rarely see him, if ever. The Cage, after all, was a cage.

It is true that my exile would leave the Side of Damage leaderless, at least til someone else stepped up; and true that Botha would almost certainly regain the ground he lost on Thursday, ground now occupied by my friends. That was the suck of it, but this was the thing: what could I do about it? That was the thing. What could I do about it? Brodsky wasn't bluffing. I would not be allowed back into the Cage. It wasn't up to me. It was either expulsion or June, and expulsion would be good for none of us.

So why did I want to resist it, this gladness? Why, in Main Hall, was I dragging my feet as if beaten? Was I faking it? For whose benefit? For my own benefit? Was I playing a role, like Brodsky'd implied? Can you fake yourself out? I *did* feel fakey, but I did not believe you could fake yourself out. I'd never believed anyone could fake himself out. You could be misinformed, you could fail to see the truth, but I didn't see how it was possible, logically, to fake yourself out, especially not while suspecting yourself of doing so...

My thoughts kept spinning, and I wasn't solving anything, only getting H. I needed to do something, or maybe to prove something—something concrete and simple, something effective. I needed something to focus on, something to focus me; I needed to take aim at something and nail it. The clock in the gym.

I turned into B-hall, tearing down streamers, shredding pep rally posters and Boystar flyers, uncovering WE DAMAGE WEs. I hid in the central doorway and looked. Behind centercourt, fifteen chairs were shaped roughly like a half-flattened V, like the body of a crow in a stickman universe. A line of five chairs formed its east wing; its west was two such lines set parallel. In this west one sat Blonde Lonnie, smashed-nosed, plus all of the B-team minus Maholtz. Dominating the whole tableau was a scaffolding rig strung with light-cans and -panels and a pair of spotlights. The rig appeared to hold the laws of physics in contempt: Twenty feet high and thirty across, it stood on two legs of thin steel piping with speakers for ankles and telescoping feet—four for each leg—which should have locked into something heavy below them, something stable to stay them, a pillar of concrete or lead, but didn't. They didn't lock into anything at all.

The bleachers, extended, blocked my forward periphery. I stealthed under the eastern ones to scope more.

Maholtz and Slokum stood behind the west hoop. Eight chairs formed a row between the northern sideline and the lowest bench of the western bleachers: a special gallery in which a cheerleader now sat, stealing glances at Bam and chewing her nails. Slokum cracked his knuckles and wrote in a notebook. He looked smaller to me than the last time I saw him. His face was turned away, and maybe that's why, but his back seemed slouchy and a lot less wide. I remembered how I'd helped him to make fun of Nakamook, and I didn't want to think of that, and looked away.

I crossed the doorway's-width gap between the two sets of bleachers. Ducked beneath the western set to see what lay east.

Arrows made of cardboard were taped to the floor to form a path. They led from the locker-room to centercourt. In the tipoff circle, just a couple yards north of the chair-row, two cardboard squares were taped to the floor on either side of the halfcourt line. The locker-room-side one had a star of Boystar on it. The side-exit-side one said MOKUS. I didn't see Scott anywhere and I thought that was suck. He could memorize a song after hearing it once, and I was pretty sure that they wouldn't have him dance, so they probably didn't need him to rehearse, but still: if the basketballers got to skip first period, they were bancers for not letting Scott skip too. And they should have got his name right, the dentists. It was probably Boystar who gave them the spelling.

And there he was. He kept bursting from the locker-room to pose before the bleachers. Each time, he stopped at a different arrow on the path. Cameramen milled, coordinating angles. Chaz Black clapped and Boystar's parents made suggestions about his posture. I thought about shooting him, decided against it. Decided against it because now I could do it later, better, more repeatedly. I would not be short of chances now. Kiss *my* girlfriend? Murmur in her ear? Even stepped regular and busted every time, I could give him six beatings before getting expelled. Every day we'd have Lunch together, Recess too.

Lunch-Recess, I thought. That was another thing. I'd no longer be in the same room as my friends for class, but there was always Lunch-Recess. Rather, there *wasn't* always Lunch-Recess. *Now* there was Lunch-Recess; now I would have irrevocable cafeteria privilege. Now, whenever my friends in the Cage were also granted cafeteria privilege, we could eat together, speak outdoors in the schoolyard together, plot without whispering, no Botha down our necks. Maybe I *could* lead from exile. To do so would be hard, but to believe it was impossible was way too dramatic.

And I saw it wasn't yet time to smash the gym clock, either. It was not yet time to get caught. I had often told myself there would be a time to get caught, and I had always been certain that the time wasn't yet, but then last night I'd decided the time for stealth was over; if the time for stealth was over, though, why shouldn't I get caught? Because the end of the time for stealth was only over when it came to the scholars? Why should that be? Why should it be different with me and them than with me and the rest of the world? Why shouldn't I just rush in there and smash the clock and smash the Boystar, smash everything I could til the Arrangement put a stop to me?

Because, I thought, they'd put a stop to you, dramaface; they'd put a stop to you before you could finish.

That was one potentially good answer—good if a time was to come when the Arrangement *wouldn't* put a stop to me.

But what made me so sure that time would come? What made me so sure Adonai was ultimately with me? Why was it that when something horrible happened, I read it as encouragement from Adonai to do more of whatever I'd been doing before the horrible thing happened? Why was it that instead of thinking I was being punished for what I'd done, I thought I was being punished for what I hadn't done? for where I'd fallen short? When I got kicked out of Schechter and Northside and MLK and when those Canaanites stoned the rabbi at the Fairfield Street Synagogue and when I got banned from the homes of all the scholars and when Slokum humiliated me and when I saw my father get trampled, why was my first thought *You need to bring the messiah faster*? Why wasn't it *You need to stop trying to bring the messiah so fast*? or even *You need to stop trying to bring the messiah*? let alone *This has nothing to do with Adonai, for there is no Adonai*?

And was I even truly wondering about this stuff, there in the doorway? I was asking myself the questions, yes, and I had asked them before, thousands of times, and supplied the arguments against the beliefs toward which I tended as best as I could, but before, as now, the questions seemed merely ponderous, the arguments no better or worse than the ones opposing them, the ones I held.

Can arguments against tenets of faith do anything other than exalt faith among the faithful? Did the faithful ever say anything to the purveyors of such arguments other than, "Yes, maybe what you say makes sense, but I disagree nonetheless. That is how strong my faith is. Thank you for testing it. Now I know better where I stand"? If they ever said different, I'd never heard it. It wasn't so much different from when Jelly told me I shouldn't love June because she made violent drawings, or Slokum said it was impossible to love her. I loved her. I just did. Despite, regardless, or otherwise.

Your defiances showed you where you truly stood, but they didn't tell you if you *should* stand there. Yet they seemed to. They seemed to tell you you should stand there. Why else would you be standing there, despite?

My head was spinning so hard. My chemicals didn't know what to do with me.

I ducked back into B-Hall and headed for the Cage, still glad, still attempting to resist it, and my thoughts spun back to where they'd left off before I'd decided it was time to finally smash the gym clock:

Even if it *was* logically possible to fake yourself out while suspecting you were doing it, and even if I was doing exactly that, could I be sure about which part I might be faking? Could I be sure I was faking my resistance to the gladness? Maybe the fake part was the gladness itself. Maybe neither were fake, and I was as torn as I felt, and a scar would form, and the scar, though unpretty, would do what scars do in weak stories of coming of age: protect the torn part from getting torn again so easy. I never liked those stories, the coming-of-age ones with scars. I liked to read them fine, but they were tricks. They were tricks to make adults feel like their sellouts were wise compromises, or at least unavoidable. As if you *would* go to Hell for helping Nigger Jims. As if Goliaths *weren't* slayable.

But again, though, I really had no choice. Rather, I only had two. Get expelled or be in class with June. In either case, this was my last day in the Cage. There was nothing I could do about it. It wasn't up to me.

And I started to feel relieved. I started to feel like I'd felt just the morning before, when the scholars failed to show and I thought they'd betrayed me. It was a relief to decide you didn't have to decide. It was a relief to have faith in immutability, a relief to lose faith in your ability to change something, even when it was something you'd wished you could change. It was a relief to be imposed on intractably. Acceptance, if not brave, was at least a relief. That was the trick of it. This was the trick of it: If Brodsky had *offered* me the chance to get out of the Cage, I would have refused. I would not have abandoned my friends, yet despite and because of that I was glad he hadn't offered. And despite and because of that I wasn't glad that I was glad. In the end, though, I was more glad than I wasn't, and that wasn't up to me either.

I'd deliver a farewell speech to the Side during lunch. I'd tell them I was being removed from the Cage because Botha feared me. I'd tell them that Botha was mistaken to believe my removal a solution to the problems of the Arrangement; that soon, just as long as the Side stayed the Side, he and they would both understand that. I'd tell them I was with them all the way, but all the way for me was not good enough for them, because what they needed was a leader in the Cage. And then I would have to put someone in charge. The Side would forgive Benji for the two-hill field—I'd make sure of that—but forgiving wasn't the same thing as trusting, which was suck because he'd otherwise have been the best one to take over. So

Vincie or Brooklyn. Brooklyn would shortly get out of the Cage—he had less business being there than anyone else and, once I was gone, he'd stay quiet til the end of his two-week observation period, and Brodsky would gladly put him back in normal classes—so the leader'd be Vincie. Vincie'd be the new leader, and Vincie'd be good, and if Vincie got booted before Botha got crushed, Ben-Wa would take over—Leevon was definitely more charismatic, and Jelly was smarter, but Leevon wouldn't speak and Jelly probably wouldn't risk being cleaved from Benji—and Ben-Wa would be good, he would, he'd be good, they all looked at him different now, they'd seen him reborn. If Ben-Wa got booted, though... Then I didn't know. Hopefully by that time, the choice would be obvious, at least to the Side (I imagined other kids would step up by then), so I'd make it clear that if Vincie got booted, Ben-Wa's first task would be to choose two successors. And I'd finish by telling them... telling them what? I didn't want to lie, but I didn't want to tell them that it might not work. I didn't want to tell them that I had my doubts about where they'd be without me—that Vincie might prove too explosive and reactionary, and Ben-Wa, despite having demonstrated all kinds of strength still seemed pretty likely to break down and cry at crucial junctures, and if those two were the best I could leave in charge, then... No. Who was to say where the Side would be without me? For all I knew, they'd be better off without me. For all I knew, they'd do better with a leader who was quicker to explode or break down, right? That is what I told myself, and I'd tell them none of it. I'd just tell them I'd miss them. *That's* how I'd close. If nothing else, it was true. It was true I would miss them. Even if a loud part of me was looking forward to missing them, that didn't make it untrue; that didn't diminish what it would mean for me to miss them, did it? Maybe, actually... But it was still first period. Lunch wasn't for hours. I had hours to determine the right way to close this lunch-time farewell speech, and after lunch I'd still be in the Cage—I'd be there until the end of the schoolday. So if my close at lunch was suck, I'd figure out another one, deliver it in C-hall, before detention started, and plus I was forgetting: there were good things to come between now and lunch. Before it came time to give that speech, we'd all hear Main Man sing. Who knows what that might do for us? And after that? After hearing Main Man sing? After hearing Main Man sing, I'd fake sick to Botha and get a pass to the Nurse. I'd take June to the two-hill field and meet the scholars. I'd deliver scripture, my father would be safe, everything would be fine. Everything was fine. Fine and fine and safe and fine.

Someone behind me said my name and I spun. Isadore Momo. Across his forehead in Darker was DAMAGE.

"For to payback," he said, pointing at the word. "For your protection and Vincie's. We wear it so the Big Ending has blame for your bombings. To protect you. We vow we wear it until we have destroyed the Blonde Lonnie and made of the BryGuy a puddle."

He pronounced the second "b" in bombings. I embraced him and went to the Cage.

On the way, I saw the thing Maholtz must have been referring to—"I can't waint til Bam seends what you did," he'd said—burned into the face of the 2-Hall juice machine. It made me even gladder, even less glad to be so.

BARNUM
SLOKUM
DIES
FRIDAY

◻ ◻ ◻ ◻ ◻ ◻ ◻

Art was the one decent class in the Cage. No one had to sit at a carrel and, except for Botha, Miss Gleem was the only robot present. She'd lay tarps down before school started and bring a huge metal wheelycart with boxes of supplies. She'd let us make whatever we wanted, and since the Tape rule and the Face Forward rule couldn't be enforced on students who weren't confined to carrels, Botha had less to monitor, which got him disarranged. Half the time he didn't even step us for talking. He'd mostly just sit with his feet up on his desk, polishing his claw with breath-steam and a shirttail. He'd even let Miss Gleem answer the doorbell.

I handed her my pass and followed her to the cart. She said, "What kind of supplies would you like?" She was pissed at me.

Nails and screws and wire, I told her.

She'd have usually joked around with me after I said something like that, but she was pissed at me so she didn't. I hadn't even seen her since Wednesday detention. She'd probably decided I was a bad influence on June. I hoped so—a thought like that would mean June was out of her doghouse.

Whatever she was thinking, though, it didn't make her smile. She handed me charcoal sticks and cream-colored construction paper.

I told her, Gold haircombs look tacky on women under forty.

She snapped, "My combs aren't gold, Gurion."

I know, I said. I said, They're fake tortoiseshell, which is better than real tortoiseshell because no tortoise had to die to complement your natural coloring, which is exactly what your combs do.

"I'm so sorry," she said. "I wasn't expecting you to—"

You don't need to be *that* sorry, I said.

"Sorry," she said. She handed me a box of crayons. I had spoken like a visual thinker, and all was forgiven. "Now go draw something amazing," she said.

I shook the crayon-box like a spaz, like I was excited by our prospects, me and all those colors and what we could accomplish together. I was suck at drawing, though. I was nearly the suckest in the Cage, and Miss Gleem knew it. She knew as well as I did that I couldn't draw anything amazing, but she pretended to believe I could because she thought that having the ability to draw well was as important to her students as it was to her, and she wanted to protect me from the knowledge of my suckness. I pretended so I could protect her from the knowledge that she couldn't protect me. The goodness of our intentions was in direct correlation to the heights from which we condescended to each other.

I looked around for where to sit. Ben-Wa Wolf was shooting rubberbands at a line of origami swans on the radiator. Chunkstyle and Boshka bent pipecleaners into dolphins near the girls' room. Next to the door to Call-Me-Sandy's, the Janitor flashed homemade flashcards at the Flunky. GUM, read one of them. "Gun," said the Flunky. RUN read another. "Gun," said the Flunky.

Nakamook was under a carrel with Jelly by the northeast corner. I went there.

Kids stole glances and whispered to each other.

Benji was dotting tastebuds on the tongue of a bull. The bull was eating a dying lamb. Off to the side, a ram scraped his hoof in the dirt, about to charge the bull.

Benji was almost as good at drawing as Leevon, who was the best in the Cage.

I tapped his shoulder, and when he held out his fist I banged it = Nakamook is my boy, do not talk of us.

The Side of Damage stopped whispering.

I said to Benji: Bulls are vegetarians.

"So what?" said Jelly.

I said, No bull would eat a lamb.

"No real bull would," Nakamook said.

That's what I'm saying.

"Real bulls don't wear watchcaps either, though," he said.

Watchcaps? I said.

He drew the bull a watchcap.

"Look at Botha," said Jelly. "Pretending he doesn't care we're talking."

I looked. Botha winked at me, showed me his thumb.

Let's not get carried away here, I thought.

"What's he doing?" Benji said. "Why'd he do that?"

He's railroading me, I said, and he thinks I don't know it. He thinks I think he likes me.

"What do you mean *railroading* you?"

I remembered he and Jelly hadn't returned to the Cage after leaving for the nurse on Thursday, so I caught them up on what happened, then told them what Brodsky had said.

So this is my last day in the Cage, I said.

"What's the rub, then?" said Benji. "Back to fifth grade?"

The rub? I said. Fifth grade?

"You said the Monitor was railroading you."

He's kicking me out of the Cage, I said.

"That's not kicked out, what you just told me, Gurion. That's getting freed."

"Congratulations," said Jelly.

We won't be in class together anymore, I said.

"We're not in class together now," said Benji. "We're in the Cage together. And there's always lunch, and Botha can't keep you outta the cafeteria anymore."

I said, The Side of Damage—

"If they're worth your friendship, they'll be happy for you. Stop making that crazy face and listen: don't smart yourself out of joy. Whatever Botha's trying to do, it doesn't matter. This is great for you. I was thinking just yesterday morning how suck it is that you only got to see June after school. I was on the bus, hating that I had to come here, and then I remembered I'd get to see Jelly, and that didn't just make it okay, you know? I got *psyched* to come here.

And I thought how I would tell you that, and then I decided not to, because of how it might sound like I was rubbing it in your face, that I got to see my girlfriend all day long, and you barely got to see yours. But now I can tell you, cause you'll have the same thing. Think about how great that is."

Jelly touched his hand then, and I left them alone.

Leevon Ray sat under the teacher cluster, colorworking a flipbook about him and a ninja taking a bike ride together. Balanced on the back pegs of Leevon's BMX, the ninja threw Chinese stars at oncoming pedestrians. The starred pedestrians all fell backward, clutching their starred parts and filling dialogue bubbles with exclamation points and wingdings til Leevon bunny-hopped them. Each pedestrian was fatter than the last, and the bellies of the fallen bodies grew progressively higher and harder to jump. Finally there came a man so fat his herniated navel touched the upper border of the page when he fell. The ninja leapt from the pegs in the direction of the viewer and Leevon's eyes popped out of his face and the flipbook ended.

Next to the 3-D Leevon lay Vincie. He was the one kid in the Cage more suck at drawing than me. Neither of our circles were ever very round-looking, but mine, at least, didn't have tails. Vincie's resembled 6s or 9s and sometimes 6s on top of 9s. He was using a ruler-corner to carve STARLA from a sheet of brown clay. Beside him, Ronrico dumped sparkles from a jar on Mangey's rubber-cement-slathered jeans. Mangey discreetly sucked glue off her fingertips. I got on the floor and asked them where Main Man was. Leevon snatched the second A off Vincie's STARLA and started rolling it in his palms.

"The fuck!?" shout-whispered Vincie.

"Scott's been in the bathroom since before the tone," said Ronrico.

Leevon held out a log-shape.

I looked at the clock. 9:32. Art had started twenty-seven minutes before that. I thought of Main Man's shrunken chambers. He'd been so nervous by the bus circle, maybe his pump couldn't take it. If he'd had a heart attack in the bathroom, no one would know.

I knocked on the boys' room door. Nothing. I tried the knob—it was unlocked.

Main Man knelt beside the toilet, spitting. He said, "I think I'll be okay, Gurion. I have to sing."

I said, You don't sound like yourself.

"All the guns are ripe for the plucking," he said. "Twice smitten, one dies but once, yet still we burn the ashes and annihilate all wreckage. Wherever we go we bring the monkey with us."

Okay, I said.

He wretched and I kneeled next to him. "I need to do this for a little while," he said. "These webs everywhere, green and then purple, but then they go away. The spiders aren't real because I am real but I wish they were real so I could squash them. Once I get the second one down, I can sing til everything disappears, so just please don't look at me while I do this."

I'll stay til you feel better, I said.

"It gets me all ambulance, spiders out the eyeballs."

You're gonna sing great, I said. I said, You're the best singer in school and you have the best voice.

Mookus puked, said, "Boystar." His puke didn't smell normal. It smelled like a bakery on Christmas.

Your voice *kills* Boystar's, I said.

"Soon," he said. "Please go," he said. "Spiders dance meanly and there's no place like home."

I lingered by the sink, washing my hands so I could watch over him, but he asked me to leave again, so I left.

"You need to shave yourself," said Mangey when I sat down next to her.

"You do got some hairs there," Ronrico said. "I think they're good, though. Maybe a little long. You probably shouldn't grow 'em out til you have some more of them."

"Like a thousand more of them," said Mangey.

"Okay everyone," Miss Gleem said. "Roll up." She meant the tarps.

The first time we had Art, me and Benji held the rolled-up tarps in our pits and jousted. Shouting "Charge!" and running across a room to knock someone down with a lance made of canvas looked like so much fun that, even after Botha stepped us for it, other kids picked up other tarps and did it. Vincie and Leevon. Mangey and Jesse Ritter. Even Ronrico and the Janitor, who'd been our enemies at the time. And so I'd thought we'd all joust every time we had Art, but stuff that fun rarely happens more than once.

The Side of Damage returned art supplies to the wheely-cart and rolled the tarps without incident.

While that was happening, the doorbell rang. Botha, forgetting Miss Gleem had his keyring, went to answer it. At the door, he patted himself down until Miss Gleem said his name, his first name. "Victor," she said. And then he performed this stream of completely unBothalike actions. He spun on his heel, smiled, pointed at the keyring, and beckoned with his pointer-finger = "Toss the keyring, sexy." Then, when Miss Gleem tossed the keys underhanded, Botha used his claw to hook the ring overhanded and finished with a bow, flourishing an invisible feathered cap.

He was flirting.

Main Man was hallucinating. He had come out of the bathroom and was standing beside me, eyes shut tight, pressing a powdery orange ball against his lips. The ball was no larger than a shooter marble, but Scott's mouth wouldn't open to let it in.

Benji walked over, saying, "What is that?"

"It's the second one," Scott said.

The second one what? I said.

"The second medicine to make me sing perfectly."

"You look like shit, Scott," said Vincie, approaching us.

"What's the medicine called?" Benji said.

"I can't remember," Scott said. "Boystar eats four before every performance. I'll eat this one when the ghosts stop stapling my lips."

"Boystar gave you that?" Benji said.

"Yes. And it was nice of him. It's the secret of all his success at singing good and he let me have the secret. It's the whole key to the castle of girls peeing on themselves because that is the purpose of singing. You have to eat four of them if you're the Boystar because he's not as good as me at singing, he said, and also because he's taller. All I need to eat is three for the girls to bathroom because I'm already as good as if I just ate one, just by being me, not just because I'm short. I'm trying."

I swiped the ball from his hand.

"He said it was for me," Scott said, reaching for it.

I sniffed it. It smelled Christmasy like his puke had. I touched it with my tongue-tip. Bitter. It was nutmeg. And then it was powder, falling out the hole at the bottom of my fist.

This is amateur poison, I said. It's what's making you sick.

Nakamook bit a thumb-knuckle til it bled.

"That fuck," said Vincie.

Scott knelt before the powder at our feet.

"Fucken fuck!" said Vincie.

"It was mine," Scott whispered down at the powder.

I tapped his shoulder. When he looked up, I placed a ball of nothing in his palm. He popped the ball of nothing in his mouth, smiling, and swallowed.

He gave me the third one and I put it in my pocket, replaced it in his palm with another ball of nothing. Again he popped nothing in his mouth and swallowed.

"All done," he said. "You fix everything."

I heard gratitude, Nakamook an imperative.

"We will," he told Main Man.

"That too," Main Man said, but a tear bubbled over the scoop of his lashes. "Will I get to sing first?" he asked me.

You'll get to sing last, I told him, and wiped the tear with my sleeve.

The woman who'd rung the doorbell was a Boystar staffer with a headset. She led Scott out the door by the hand. "Alert makeup," she said into her celly. "The talent's a little bit monochrome. Over." Miss Gleem followed them, pushing her wheely-cart. Botha locked the Cage down behind her. I know the announcements had started by then, but I don't know what they said. I couldn't hear a word of them. I couldn't hear anything.

Then I heard the end-of-class tone.

I went to the door to wait for Botha to open it. Vincie and Nakamook and Jelly followed me. Botha had returned to his desk. He was sitting on it. I looked his way and, again, he winked at me.

"Why are we standing here?" Vincie said.

What do you mean? I said.

"We're going to the pep rally," Benji said.

"Since when?"

"I don't know—Brodsky told Gurion this morning, though."

Wait, I said. I said, Botha didn't tell you guys?

"No," they said.

Come on, I said to the Side of Damage. Line up, I said.

They got behind us.

"Where we going?" someone said.

We're going to hear Main Man sing, I said.

To Botha, I said: We're gonna be late.

"No one's going innywhere," he said. He stood up to say it, winked at me for the third time. "You had your chence," he said. "But you spant all first period talking. Talking's against the rules."

What? Wait. We always talk during Art, I said. I said, There's a tacit understanding that—

Then he winked again, and I saw he was joking.

"Every one of you talked," he said.

It isn't usually against the rules to talk during Art, I said, playing along with his unfunny deadpan. I said, Not during Art.

"You and Nakamake more than anyone, Make-bee."

Stop joking now, Mr. Botha, come on. We're gonna be late.

He shrugged his shoulders = "Jaking? What do you mean, jaking?"

And he really wasn't.

I said, It would be different if you'd said you were changing the understanding, but you didn't.

"Told your friend Scat," he said.

You told Main Man? I said.

I was beginning to understand.

"Told him you'd all see him sing, long's you stayed quoyt. Thought he'd want to tale you himself."

Well he didn't, I said. I said, He didn't tell us.

"I don't belave that for a sackond, Make-bee. Scat was so excited. His smile—bright as the vary sun that warms our planet. He was looking forward to it so vary much, to all his frands seeing him do what he loves to do. He wanted that more than even you, I'd bat. Yeah. I just don't belave you—course he told you! It meant everything to him."

You fuck, Vincie said.

"Stap four for Vancent Pawtight," said Botha.

The beginning-of-class tone sounded.

"Everyone sit down now," said Botha.

Brodsky's gonna fire you for this, I said. I said, We will rat you out and you'll get fired. Think about that.

Botha said, "Don't be rideckulous, Make-bee. Mister Brodsky knows I got your bast interests in mind. 'Specially yours. After all, you're the one showed me the error of my ways. Now all you: sit down," he said. And he extended his arm and panned it, as if to show us where our seats were. "Sit down and help your frand Make-bee cellbrate his very last day in the Cage."

No one moved.

Unlock that fucking door, I said.

□   □   □   □   □   □   □

"Sit down," said Botha.

We're going to the gym.

Botha started giggling. "Jest sit," he said.

I said, Where are we going?

"We're going to the gym," said the Side of Damage—they'd encircled us by then.

We're going to the gym to see Main Man sing, I said to the Monitor. Give us your keys.

Attached to him, at his beltline, by a single, flimsy loop of fabric, the chunky keyring swayed and gleamed. We were moving forward, toward each other. We'd *been* moving forward, toward each other. I think I started it, but I can't say for sure—it might have been Botha. Once the movement began, though, it felt as much like I was letting my legs carry me as it felt like I was making them carry me. How it felt was *right*. At the same time, the circle the Side had formed was growing tighter, and this banced my perspective. I wasn't rushing at Botha, but the gap between us kept closing more rapidly than I was expecting, each step we took appearing to achieve a much greater distance than the previous one.

Whether I acted too early or from too far away—that there even *could* be a difference only ever occured to me in the stealthest slo-mo moments—when I lunged for the keys I miscalculated. My fingers tapped metal, but I didn't get a grip, and Botha had time and space to pivot.

In the middle of the pivot, he hooked my hood, maybe inadvertantly, maybe only half so. The hood was a good one, stitched tight to the collar. My spine jerked straight, then my body jerked backwards.

The back of my head struck the keyring, hard.

My ass hit the floor, I popped up, angled sharp, and I palm-struck the Monitor's nearer kidney.

It would not be correct to say—as I fear well-intending scholars may wish to—that this marked a point of no return for me, let alone for the Side of Damage. Apart from death and the moment of Elohim's pronouncement that man be made in His image, I suspect there has never been any such thing for human beings as a point of no return. But even if I'm wrong about that, I was born an Israelite, I became a Torah scholar, I armed my brothers, I was put in a cage, I fell in love with June, the Side of Damage arose, I fell out with my teachers, was humbled by Slokum, my father was trampled, mothers slapped me, an innocent was poisoned, and the Arrangement double-dealt me. There is no good reason why my delivery of an excellent bodyblow to the Cage monitor should be ajudged the start of the Gurionic War. I will not deny that planting that shot in Botha's kidney severely narrowed whatever set of Aptakistico-scholastic options I might have wanted to explore if I were someone other than myself, nor will I deny it roughly coincided with my *knowing* the Gurionic War had started, but that, scholars, is not the same as calling the moment a point of no return. Narrowed options are options nonetheless, even when your chemicals are parching your mouth and swelling your muscles. I had always been at war, whether I'd known it or not.

As for the Side of Damage, why I'd just hit Botha didn't matter a billionth as much as *that* I'd hit Botha, and whatever it meant or didn't, they knew I was their leader.

I wouldn't guess my reasons for hitting him were any more important to the Monitor himself. Holding his kidney, he made an Australian noise and twisted. He shouted about expellable offenses—"axpailable erfences"—and pulled much harder on my hood than the first time. I lost my balance and jerked back into him.

He got me around the chest and arms. Lifted. The feeling, by then, was not unfamiliar.

I started to kick and he swung me left. I kept on kicking and he swung me right.

The circle of soldiers receded toward the carrels. I might have thought: Not again—but I didn't. What I thought was: Hurry up! And I continued to kick, and the Monitor to swing me, harder at each pass, backer and further, the claw's round side gouging deep in my ribs. The faster he swung me, the more my ear fluids swirled. The room lost depth fast and my kicks were barely glancing him. No one said anything. Motion looked blurred, the Cage flat and queasy.

At some point after the seventh swing—after the seventh, I was too dizzy to count—I landed a lucky heel in Botha's knee's sweetspot and, as he dipped to regain balance, a small, smudgy Benji moved in the periphery, did something fuzzy with a chair.

I bonked Botha's cheek with the back of my head, and when I bonked it a second time, we three-sixtied clockwise. I saw Vincie and Ben-Wa flip chairs at the teacher cluster, and Benji, now medium-sized, held his by one leg. He approached us like a liontamer, oriented sideways, left shoulder-first, but the chair was where the whip should have been, its seatback dragging the floor behind him.

"Let him go," Ben-Wa said.

"Let him go," said the Side of Damage.

Leevon flipped a chair near the doorway.

Another bonk from my head got Botha on the chin. It stung my scalp, and Botha stumbled us forward.

Benji got in our way.

Botha hoisted me shieldlike.

Benji stepped left fast, then I heard a thick *thump* with low, boinging echoes as the chair connected with the Monitor's shoulder.

Botha, shrieking like a car accident, dropped me. I landed all-fours.

The Flunky pulled me up onto my feet, and I leaned against him while the dizziness passed. "You're okay," said the Flunky, "deep breaths, deep breaths."

Monitor Botha was heading for the door now, clutching his shoulder. The shoulder looked low.

Benji, following, crushed the hand that clutched it. Botha's knee met the ground, but he stood back up. Stood there, gasping and surrounded. The gasping had rust in it. His pipes were wrecked. Little cuts in his throat that had trailed that first shriek's soundwaves bled.

"Axpail—" he hissed.

Ben-Wa and Vincie took turns attacking. A chair to the back put Botha on his knees. A chair to the chest kept him off his hands. They swung once more each before Nakamook finally chopped him down: an air-abrading swing ("*Ffffffih!*" the air screamed) to the broken shoulder. Botha fell on the other one.

Dropping his chair before he arrived, Leevon punted into Botha's stomach. Botha curled fetal and Leevon stepped over him, kicked him in the tailbone, straightened him out.

We stood there, watching the monitor writhe. He rolled onto his back and onto his stomach then onto his back and onto his stomach, crossing his legs and twisting his hips to guard his nuts against phantom wallops. His claw, draped over his face, didn't hide much. Involuntary muscular actions—overwrought blinking, jumping neck tendon, his forehead wrinkling, his forehead smoothing, his mustache twitching above his pursing then slackening then pursing lips—were manifest.

"Not brilliant, Botha," Vincie told him.

I tore the keyring off Botha's belt loop and righted the nearest chair. I'd thought I'd stand on it, but once I got it righted, I didn't feel so worked up. I was glad for what had happened, but it had been so easy. The Monitor had been delivered into our hands. Standing on a chair to shout about it seemed chomsky.

I sat, cleared my throat.

Who did this? I said to the Side of Damage.

About half of them looked at their feet.

Who did this? I said again.

"No one," they said.

But who did this? I said.

"Everyone," they said.

They wanted to give me the right answer and they didn't know what it was. They were scared to ask me.

I did this, I said.

"I did this," they said.

I did this, I said.

"You did this," they said.

Good, I said. Who's got a knife?

No one said anything.

I said, What's for lunch today, Jelly?

"Medallions of venison."

Get your knife, I told her, and cut the straps off some backpacks.

Boshka, Chunkstyle, and Nakamook volunteered theirs.

Pick some guys and drag the Monitor into the bathroom, I told the Flunky. I said, Hog-tie him when Jelly brings the straps.

"How we gonna hog-tie him?" the Flunky said.

"Like a hog, foog," said Nakamook.

"The claw," said the Flunky.

"My bad," said Benji.

I said, Take his claw off first, and three-quarter hog-tie him. When you're done with that, tie him to the radiator.

The Flunky deputized his brother and Dingle. Ronrico got in on it, too.

Botha kept mumbling. I pulled his cellphone—a flip—from its holster, put it in my pocket.

Give us your claw, Ronrico told him.

Lowering his eyes, Botha said, "Demmeged," ≠ "I can't detach my prosthesis with these broken phalanges," but might as well have.

Benji did a zippo trick I'd never seen before. He held the lighter side-ways in his lefthand and snapped the fingers of his right hand, which opened the lid and sent the lighter falling end-over-end. The wheel scraped Botha's forehead, which sparked the flint so the flame arose as the lighter slid down Botha's temple. It landed right-side-up, an inch from his face, flickering. "Once you're hog-tied," Benji said, "I'm gonna set you on fire." He grabbed and closed the zippo with a single swipe of his hand, arm so long he barely bent to do it. Then he placed his foot on Botha's shattered shoulder, but didn't lay his weight down. Botha stuttered moans and twitched more.

"He thinks I'm gonna set him on fire," Benji said to us.

Botha stammered, "I'm... demmeged."

"The monitor says he wants to join the Side of Damage," Vincie announced.

Nearly everyone laughed at that—some from the belly and most from somewhere else. Leevon, who wasn't one of the laughers, knelt beside Botha and whispered something I couldn't make out. Botha mumbled more.

"I said stop *talkin*," Leevon said. He rose to his feet, as if to walk away. Instead he kicked Botha's teeth in.

Kids sucked air. Leevon did a hop, holding his toes. Botha's crotch was wet.

"You see that?" Vincie said to Ben-Wa.

Ben-Wa, crying, knelt where Leevon had, measured out the shot and hammered Botha's nose flat.

The blood shot out, puddling on his chin. Spit blew off his lips and, with eyes shut tight, he turned his head flinchingly, over and over, left-right-left, dodging big punches that no one was throwing as sticky-looking strings, like rope fed through portholes, wormed from his nostrils and swung.

Renne Feldbons puked. Ansul Entsry crossed himself. Forrest Kenilworth puked and hail-Maryed twice. Most of the laughter transformed into weeping, and as it did I started laughing. I wasn't laughing at their fear or remorse or anything else they felt. I wasn't laughing at anyone's pain, but their timing. We had broken the man's one good hand and we had broken the shoulder of the arm opposite that hand and, except for Ben-Wa Wolf, who cried about everything, no one had shed any tears. Compared to being maimed, a bro-ken nose and missing teeth were mere cosmetic difficulties, yet the formerly laughing weepers didn't weep til the nose got broken and the teeth went missing. They didn't weep until the gore bubbled up. Even soldiers on the

Side of Damage required actual, bright red blood to spill before they could see things for what they were, and if that wasn't funny then I didn't want to know what it was.

"We're fucked," someone said. "We're so fucked now."

"*Yeah* we're fucked," said Vincie Portite, "and that's why we're so fucken *dangerous*."

Brandishing the keyring, I leaned at the Monitor. Which lock what? I said.

"We're going to prison!" somebody shouted. "We're getting expelled!"

Botha stopped twitching and started to enumerate, key by key. White-capped key, Cage door; orange cap, gate...

"We're so fucken dead!" "What'll we do? Look what we did!"

"'What'll we *do*?'" Benji Nakamook said. "We'll go to the *gym*. 'Look what we *did*?' We haven't done *fuck*-all. We've barely even started."

"We're not asking you, Benji!"

Blue was the copy room, purple the teachers lounge...

"We gotta settle scores," said Ronrico Asparagus.

"No one's asking you, either!"

"We're the Side of fucken Damage."

Red was the C-Hall faculty bathroom, green the front doors. The rest were all personal.

2-Hall gates? I said.

Botha shook his head.

Side entrance? I said.

He shut his eyes hard and shook his head faster.

I saw that I believed him. I sat up straight.

"We have to get it done," Jelly Rothstein was saying, "before we get nailed, and before they're all gone."

And Ben-Wa Wolf kept saying, "Now or never."

And "Fucked!" kids were saying. And "Gurion!" they said. "What can we do?" they said. "Look what we did!"

I said, *You* didn't do this. I'm the one who did this, and if you want to go before I do more than this, a blessing on your head, but we can't say goodbye before you get armed. I'm not leaving anyone who's in here unarmed.

And as soon as we tied and locked down the prisoner, I brought the Side of Damage to the teachers lounge. On our way, we stripped C-Hall of all of its pep. Some crumpled streamers, others tore posters, others yet made confetti of flyers. Every last one of us grabbed a balloon.

□ □ □ □ □ □ □

April 11, 2007

Dear Mr. Maccabee,

Enclosed, on one DVD encoded in MPEG format, is the second draft of the Video-Sync (VS). I believe this draft will more accurately match your vision than did the first, though I recognize the likelihood that at least one more draft will be in order. Thus, in hopes of getting it right sooner rather than later, I've created an annotated transcript of the VS, 390 pages in length. I believe this annotated transcript will allow us to discuss any changes you might like to make with greater economy than we've formerly been able. The way I understand it, a large part of the problem we faced last time—though, admittedly, not the largest (see below)—was that we didn't have an easy-reference guide to the available alternate footage. Now we do: The transcript not only notes—on a shot-to-shot basis—which of the 9 cameras' footage is being used in the current draft of the VS, but what other footage is available for use in the next draft (i.e. which of the 9 cameras were shooting simultaneously), as well as the general nature of this alternate footage. (A guide to the notation used in the transcript appears at the end of this letter.)

I would like you to know, Mr. Maccabee, that I'm honored to have been given this project, and I hope you'll accept my apology for the tone of our last conversation: I really *do* understand the importance of keeping the narrative linear and not using the kinds of splicing techniques which you referred to as "Goebbelsian." It's just that the technology at my disposal is so much fun to play with, and I guess sometimes I get carried away. In any case, as you'll see in this draft, I've not overlayed any sound onto any imagery that wasn't occurring simultaneously with that sound (in fact, I've avoided all sound-over-lays as much as possible, only using them on audience reaction-shots whose accompanying soundtracks don't, in their original form, pick up the the event or speaker the audience is reacting to), and every moment from the start of the VS til the end is arranged in completely forward-moving temporal order.

Please contact me with any questions, knowing I will do my absolute best to meet your editing needs, whatever they may be.

Sincerely,

Sid Feldman

PS Just to be clear, Mr. Maccabee: I'm sending you this copy of the transcript because you seem to be someone who wants to be aware of as many of his options as possible—a noble desire, to be sure. If you find the code we use confusing, though, or just don't want to bother reading the transcript, that's more than fine; please feel free to just watch the VS, and if you have a problem with any of the footage, just please go ahead and feel free to call me up or email, and I'LL check the transcript and let you know what other shots are available. I am at your service.

A BRIEF GUIDE TO THE NOTATION USED
IN THE ANNOTATED TRANSCRIPT

The appearance of a timestamp-line indicates that the corresponding footage on the Video-Sync comes from a different camera than the one that was being used the last time a timestamp-line appeared.

After every timestamp on the timestamp-line, one of the 9 camera codes (listed below) appears: this first camera code corresponds to the camera that shot the footage currently in use in the VS. Following the first code, in parentheses, is a list of other camera codes corresponding to cameras that were shooting different footage simultaneous to that currently in use in the VS. The nature of that footage is indicated by the typeface in which the camera code appears (the meanings to which each of the typefaces correspond are listed below).

CAMERA CODEKEY	TYPEFACE CODEKEY
C1: ABC LOCAL NEWS CAMERA	1. PLAINFACED: SAME SUBJECT AS PRIMARY
C2: NBC LOCAL NEWS CAMERA	CAMERA, DIFFERENT ANGLE
C3: CBS LOCAL NEWS CAMERA	
C4: FOX LOCAL NEWS CAMERA	
C5: BOYSTAR INC. CAMERA A	2. *ITALICIZED: DIFFERENT SUBJECT THAN*
C6: BOYSTAR INC. CAMERA B	*PRIMARY CAMERA, NONVIOLENT TYPE*
C7: BOYSTAR INC. CAMERA C	
C8: BOYSTAR INC. CAMERA D	
C9: BOYSTAR INC. CAMERA E	3. **BOLDFACED: DIFFERENT SUBJECT THAN**
	PRIMARY CAMERA, VIOLENT TYPE

▢ ▢ ▢ ▢ ▢ ▢ ▢

10:01 AM: C1 (C4; *C3*; *C6*; C9)

PRINCIPAL LEONARD BRODSKY
(SPEAKING INTO HALFCOURT MICROPHONE)

Welcome. Welcome students and teachers, welcome members of The Boystar Incorporated and New Thing Records, welcome news crews.

10:01 AM: C3 (*C1; C4*; *C6; C9*)

BLEACHERS
(STUDENTS AND TEACHERS APPLAUDING)

10:01 AM: C6 (*C1; C4*; *C3; C9*)

SPECIAL GALLERY (PANNING)
(MEMBERS OF THE BOYSTAR INCORPORATED AND
NEWTHING RECORDS APPLAUDING)

FOX CAMERAMAN, CBS CAMERAMAN
(LOOKING INTO THEIR CAMERAS)

10:02 AM: C1 (C4; *C3; C6;* C9)

PRINCIPAL LEONARD BRODSKY
(SPEAKING INTO HALFCOURT MICROPHONE)

We have quite an exciting pep rally to get through, but before I introduce the first part of the program, I'd like to talk for just a minute about some of the difficulties our school has been facing in the last few days. Graffiti on our walls, our lockers, our floors. The destruction of our brand new scoreboard. An increase in disruptive classroom behavior. An increase in fistfights. You're all well aware of these difficulties, and most of you are aware that these aren't normal difficulties; that these difficulties are new to Aptakisic. What many of you might *not* be aware of, however, is that these difficulties are being caused by very few students. Most of you spend your time in class peacefully and quietly. You spend your Lunch-Recess and class-interims being friendly and having fun. Most of you are wonderful students, and I want to emphasize that. I want to emphasize that because, with all these new difficulties cropping up around you, my worry is that you'll start to think of *yourselves* as the abnormal ones. I worry that if you start to think of yourselves as the abnormal ones, then *you'll* start causing difficulties, in which case I will have to punish you—with detentions, suspensions, maybe even expulsions... I don't want to have to do that. I don't like to punish. Nor do I believe that most of you want to cause difficulties. I believe that most of you realize how difficulties hurt our community, that when someone acts up in class, the teacher is made less able to teach, and the students are then less able to learn. That a broken scoreboard will detract from the fun of home games. That graffiti on the walls makes us feel unprotected, like we go to a lawless school. That fistfights not only hurt those directly involved, but the rest of us—they make us fearful, and fear makes it harder for us to learn, harder for us to trust each other, harder for us to form new friendships. I believe most of you care about your friends, your fellow students, your teachers, and I hope that this pep rally, this coming together to support our team and our school, will give you a greater sense of being a part of something larger than yourselves. A part of something larger than yourselves that cares about you. You are a part of the Aptakisic community, and the Aptakisic community appreciates it. I appreciate it. And it is in the spirit of healing and community and appreciation that I have hired crews to come in next week and clear the school of all graffiti, and it is in that same spirit that, by the end of the month, we will have a camera system up and running throughout the school. Our school will feel safer. Our school will *be* safer. But I want us to feel safe before all of that happens, despite the graffiti, and without the benefit of security cameras taping everything we do at all times. I want us to feel like a community of people who look out for one another. I want us to feel like that right now. And that is why I have decided to grant amnesty for all offenses committed up until this very moment. That means that everyone gets a clean slate, and no one will be stepped for offenses they have not yet been stepped for. I trust that this will greatly reduce the number of offenses that would otherwise be committed from this moment forward. I trust that in the future you will look out for one another and your school. And I thank you for that. We all thank you. Now, without further ado, it is my pleasure to introduce... Mr. Mussel and The Aptakisic Braves Brass Band!

10:05 AM: C6 (*C4*; C3; *C1*; C9)

BAND LEADER MARVIN MUSSEL
(RISES FROM BAND SECTION OF BLEACHERS, TURNS TO FACE THE APTAKISIC BRAVES BRASS BAND)
Braves!

THE APTAKISIC BRAVES BRASS BAND
(STANDS)

BAND LEADER MARVIN MUSSEL

Let's roll!

THE APTAKISIC BRAVES BRASS BAND
(STRIKES UP APTAKISIC FIGHT SONG)

□ □ □ □ □ □ □

Getting the widemouths out was easy. We threw our bodies at the front of the Coke machine and soon its plastic shell was pieces. We reached inside and took.

Bottles in their hands, the crying kids cried quieter.

I told everyone to set their spare change on the table. The pile they made was sixty coins tops, at least one fifth of which were dimes. While quarters were the best, and nickels were good—better than pennies if you ignored cost-efficiency—dimes were the least effective small currency. They weighed so little they'd tumble end over end when met by the smallest air-disturbance, and even when the tumbling didn't bance your dime's trajectory, your target got hit flat and round half the time, so unless that target was an open eye, there would be no damage, the shot would be wasted.

We needed to get a lot more ammo.

I pulled the Flunky and Nakamook aside, instructed the rest to unplug their balloons and empty their sodas in the sink. They got in line and started to verbalize.

"Pissbombs," said the Janitor.

"Bullshit on pissbombs," said Jesse Ritter. "We're making truncheons. That's what the coins are for—to add weight."

Benji and the Flunky tipped the Coke machine north—the coinbox held.

"There's barely enough coins there to weight even one of these things," Mark Dingle said.

"We'll use pebbles, too," said Jesse. "And marbles. Coins, pebbles, and marbles."

Benji and the Flunky tipped the Coke machine west, got it almost horizontal—again it yielded bubkes. Nakamook thought he could pick the coinbox lock. We gave up on tipping. He twisted a paperclip.

The Janitor said, "I'm sticking with piss. Uric acid. Cleanses. Stinks. Stings." "Pissbombs or truncheons or macarena cocktails," said Cody von Braker, "it's gonna be all like, 'Hey there, kiddies, hi there, Boystar: time to bleedalize! Time to fucken *bleed*alize!'" Christian Yagoda said, "Bleedalize— shit. 'Hey there, Aptakisic, it's time to explodalize!'" "We're gonna fill these balloons," Mark Dingle announced, "with hostile components. You put the soap in the red ones, the orange juice in the white ones, tie em off. You stick one of each in your bottle so they're resting on top of each other. You drop a coin in there. Then you stick a pencil in your bottle, point down. Now you've got a grenade. Time comes, you pierce both balloons with the pencil, metallic properties of your coin catalyze the reaction, and you got three seconds to toss that badboy, and after that…" He slapped himself in the face. "KABLAM! KABLAM! KABLAM! KABLAM!" Fingershapes darkened his pitted, mottled cheeks.

The paperclip snapped and jammed the keyhole. Nakamook punched a hole in the wall. My A was going D. We needed projectiles. The pep rally would end in thirty-five minutes. I nearly yelled for everyone to quiet down so I could think, but I saw that all the talk of make-believe weapons and targets of vengeance was good for morale. The louder the fight-ready among us planned and speculated, the more distracted the crying kids were getting from their lingering regrets about Monitor Botha—most of them weren't even crying anymore—so I didn't yell at anyone. I just tried to think. A lever, I thought. A lever, a lever. I looked for a lever.

Salvador Curtis chucked a spent limewedge. "We're acting symbolically," he said to everyone. "We're here to dump the favored beverages of our oppressors on the floor of the tyrannical gymnasium of their palace."

Dingle slapped himself more.

"Why you slapping yourself?"

"Gets my blood up quick. Why you always suck limes?"

"Builds tongue-strength," said Salvador.

"Well maybe you should save those limes," Dingle said.

I found a metal yardstick on a shelf in a cabinet.

"'We'll rightcrossalize, and you… and you… and you fat*lip*alize!'" shouted Forrest Kenilworth, smacking the table. "We will crippleize all of you demonizing kaisers!" squealed Anna Boshka. "Why I'm saying you should save those limes is cause we could probably use those limes for the citric acid in case we don't have enough orange juice," said Dingle, "cause it's the citric acid that—" "Shut up about it already," Jenny Mangey chimed in. "That movie's bullshit." "Total bullshit," said Ronrico. "Brad Pitt's a limp sister." "And explosives are beside the point," Salvador said, "because we're doing Sag Harbor all over again, but on land, in this very building." "*Boston* harbor, numbtongue, and we're spilling our Cokes in the sink. Not in the gym. Not even on the carpeting," said Jelly Rothstein. "We're not doing *anything* symbolic," Ben-Wa said. "That's right," said Vincie. "We're gonna *hurt* some people." "*Hurt* some people," Ronrico said, "and I'm calling dibs on funny Blonde Lonnie friend."

The yardstick bent in the coinbox doorgap. I chucked it aside.

In the Flunky's back pocket was Botha's prosthesis. I snatched it out, wedged the tip of the claw where the yardstick had been, pushed it hard, then pushed it harder; I got a little give but the lock wouldn't bust.

"Call dibs on Blonde Lonnie all you want," said Vincie, "but that guy's Big Ending's." "When I flying-roundhousealate,'" Chunkstyle offered, "'you guys blackeyealize." "What's Big Ending?" Ronrico said. "Five nice chubbos with auto-dibs on Lonnie." "Why," said Mangey, "do chubbos got auto-dibs?" "Isadore Momo," Vincie told her. "Isadore Momo?" Ronrico said.

Benji and the Flunky turned the machine onto its side while I dragged the table a couple feet closer.

"Isadore Momo. Remember? In gym? *You* were there. Hermaphrodite? Nippo? Big Ending's Momo's gang." "Oh! Fair enough! Didn't know he had a gang. But then I got Co-Captain Baxter then." "You gotta be kidding me. Baxter's Eliyahu's. Don't get in his way." "Vincie's right. Baxter messed up dude's hat." "So then how about this: BryGuy Maholtz." "Maholtz is mine!" "Get over it, Throop," Jenny Mangey said, "cause Ronrico just called dibs on Maholtz for both of us." "And I called dibs on Maholtz two minutes ago." "No one heard you, Fulton. Plus I called Maholtz *three* minutes ago." "No one heard you either, Stevie." "That's what I'm saying. If your quiet dibs count, you *don't* got dibs because *I* got dibs." "Painalize!" "Best of luck to all of you on BryGuy Maholtz." "Why you being sarcastic?" "Cause half the country's after Maholtz." "That's why I called dibs!" "Half the country's not here, man. They can't hear your dibs." "So dibs then on Slokum." "You're kidding me, Ronrico." "I call dibs on Boyst—" "Really? *Really?* You think Gurion gives a fuck about your dibs on that guy? You think *I* give a fuck about your dibs on that guy? Not to mention Benji?" "But Benji's got Slokum dibs." "I don't think he'll feel the need to limit his dibs." "Beatassalize!"

"Maimalize!" "Maim works fine, I think."

Benji jammed the claw in the coinbox doorgap, wiggled and angled it until it caught stiff. "Flunky," Benji said. The Flunky got on the table. He jumped up high, came down heavy on Botha's claw's arm-part.

Something groaned but it wasn't quite enough.

"Shlomo Cohen dibs!" "Shlomo Cohen's the Five's." "And what is the Five?" "Those kids from the field." "They're on our side?" "I think so-yeah." "I want a piece of basketball." "Try to think bigger." "'Bigger,' she says. Think bigger like *how*?" "Like how we got *the whole Arrangement* in one single place." "I should call dibs on teachers? Is that what you're telling me? We're gonna get teachers?" "Teachers, whoever. Whoever whoever. We just beat Botha's ass and tied him to a radiator." "Right! You're right." "I know I'm right. So like how about, say then, Jerry, for instance?" "Jerry's a wang, but I'd rather get Floyd." "Too late to get Floyd. I'm getting Floyd." "I just called dibs, though." "Put your dibs in your hat and then shit in that hat. Floyd's for me." "Jesus, Vincie!" "Jesus Vincie fucken what? I said Floyd's mine. I'll *show* him my pass. I'll show him *his* pass. His pass to the hospital! Like, 'Here's your fucken pass, Floyd! Come get your fucken pass, Floyd.'" "Whatever, Floyd's yours then. I'm saying Desormie." "Desormie. Sure. Desormie. Go ahead." "Scare-ize!" "Really? Desormie? Desormie's all mine?" "*Scare*-ize?" "Scare-alize! I mean." "How about *scare*, dog?" "Sure, Desormie's yours. And why the fuck not? Gurion probably isn't interested at all in fucking up Desormie, himself. Great pick. Deep cut. One from the vault. You're the only one here who ever hated the guy. The only one in all the school—" "You shoot down everything! What the fuck? I mean what's the point of even calling dibs if you shoot down everything?" "No one said there was a point. You just kept calling dibs." "Well that's not—" "Don't be a baby. You'll get to get someone. We'll all get at least someone." "Yeah, don't be a baby. The quiet middle's over. We're in the fucken *end*, man." "So who, then, who? Who'll we get?" "We'll get whoever Gurion tells us to get."

The Flunky and I climbed onto the table. He bent his knees and scooped me up. He counted to three. On three he jumped. We came down hard.

"Horror-alize!" "Crushalate!" "But who else is there to get? Like specifically, I mean."

The coinbox popped and change gushed forth.

"Quarters and nickels like mad here," said Benji.

Baruch Hashem.

"Horror-alize? No. Horror-*orize*...? No." "'Who else *specifically*?' How about the basketballers who no one knows the names of?" "And how about a million jerkstore Shovers?" "Horrorize! Yes! Horrorize! Horrorize!" "All the teachers who sent us to the Cage in the first place!" "Smackalate!" "Jackilize" "Ripalate!" "Tear-… Tear-o—no. Tear-alate? Tearalate? Tearalate!" "How about *the whole motherfucking Arrangement*!"

I was splayed on the floor, next to the Flunky. The claw had come down right next to my head. Its shape had held—a well-made claw. Maybe stainless. Maybe even titanium. I stood up and banged it like a gavel on the table.

I said, Everyone get in line for coins. Ten apiece. Forsake the dimes.

It was twenty after ten = thirty minutes til the end of the pep rally. While the Side got their coins, I called 911 on Botha's celly to report an explowsion et Deh Franteah Maytelle. The operator asked if I was safe, and I told her I was; I was in my car at Kilroy and Rand. She asked my name and I told her it was Victor Bo—then pretended to lose the signal and turned the phone off.

"They'll call your friend at the motel before they go there," Benji told me.

That's fine, I said.

"You think they'll send people anyway?"

Maybe, I said. It doesn't matter.

"Oh," said Benji. "Oh!" he said. "We're crying wolf?"

For now, I said. Is your mom at work?

"Yeah."

Call from Jelly's phone and tell them there's a fire in the basement—your mom locked you in there and went to work and now there's a fire in the basement.

"We don't have a basement."

Even better, I said.

□ □ □ □ □ □ □

COACH RONALD DESORMIE
(AT HALF-COURT MICROPHONE, USING OWN
MEGAPHONE)
Thank you. I'm glad to have your guys' ears because we need to talk, you and I, cautch to student-body. We need to talk about the elephant in the room. Can anyone tell me what that elephant is?

10:10 AM: C3 (*C1*; C4; C6; *C9*)

BLEACHERS
(STUDENTS FIDGETING, TEACHERS SHUSHING
STUDENTS)

10:11 AM: C1 (C4; *C3*; *C6*; C9)

COACH RONALD DESORMIE
(AT HALF-COURT MICROPHONE, USING OWN
MEGAPHONE)

I know it's hard to talk about, so I'll just say it. That elephant is
the scoreboard in this very gymnasium. The scoreboard and what's
been done to it. The world-class Aptakisic Indians scoreboard which
was just Monday in perfect working order only to have the H and
the V knocked out of it on Tuesday and how that was disrespectful
enough to everything we stand for and was going to be embarrassing
already this afternoon, when the Twin Groves Eagles are coming for
the *opening game* versus our Indians, without how on Wednesday it got
totally destroyed so it's not in any kind of working order and there's
unsightly dings in the floor that came from some of the pointier rocks
as an outcome of those rocks making contact with the floor after they
got thrown at the scoreboard, too. I'm here to tell you disrespect and
embarrassment will not stop the Indians, who have worked hard for
me, ladies and gentlemen. Hard for *us,* our fighting Indians, hard for
this *school*, people. In practice is what I'm talking about, hours and
hours of practice over the last nine weeks to really come together as a
team who will dominate so as to bring this school and all of us that
kind of glory known as opening-game-of-the-season glory, which is a
kind of glory you only get a chance at once per academic year because
there's only one opening game per year isn't there? Yes there is just
one, and how often does that opening game take place at *home*? And
I'll tell you how often because how often is *every other year*, meaning last year it was away, and though last year, yes, we dominated
that opening game, it was not as effective a brand of domination in
terms of the glory I spoke of as it was gonna be this year in terms
of the glory I spoke of. And then next year it'll be away again, and
though I have to believe we will dominate next year, it will, again,

be that same kind of less-effective domination that we had last year that I just described. And since this year our world-class scoreboard's been destroyed for the opening game, which is the kind of thing that diminishes the kind of domination I'm talking about here, can we go three years in a row without that kind of domination and still hold our heads up? is what I was asking myself yesterday. The way in which I was answering was: no, I don't think we can, I really don't think we can because I think we'll be lucky to *survive* after three years without that kind of domination, let alone survive with our heads up. That kind of domination at an opening game at home is unmatched in its potential to boost spirits and bolster our feelings of general confidence, not just at school I'm talking, but also at home and in our personal relationships to people who we spend time with and so on. And maybe some of you are thinking that when I was asking that question and answering how I was answering it, I was being too, how should I put it? Overdramatical. Maybe some of you are thinking: "Jeez, Cautch, a couple years ago we didn't even have a world-class scoreboard, and a couple years ago we survived just fine with our heads up." But you see this isn't like a couple years ago, people, because now we not only don't have a world-class scoreboard, but we *do* have a world-class scoreboard that has been vandalized and doesn't even work, which is worse than no world-class scoreboard at all is what I'm telling you. In fact it's worse than having no *any*-class scoreboard at all because of how a gym with no scoreboard at all could at least possibly indicate that that gym is part of a school with so little funding it can't afford even a low-class or no-class scoreboard, and that would set the stage for the kind of underdog story where the poor kids from the poor school and their poor cautch who should be coaching pros but can't because he's too passionate a man to coach pros who do it for money that isn't pure instead of the glory that these poor kids do it for, and who was booted permanently from the NCAA for losing his cool on a player who wasn't toeing the line and maybe even got a little violent with that player, and publicly, and that player whined and sued like the spoiled-rotten player for money who doesn't care about glory that he was, much less teamwork, and the public knew it and stood behind the coach who was, of course, a foot shorter and about a buck lighter than the player who whined and sued, but rules were rules said the bigshots who ran the NCAA and that coach got banned and did he suffer? No. He didn't suffer because he had long arms that coach, like my father used to say, meaning he could pull himself up by the bootstraps, which is what he did, with a fire in his eyes and also in his belly and with a ticker that wouldn't quit either, and he came to that junior high school and coached those poor kids who didn't even have a scoreboard but cared about glory and teamwork and the other values, and then they won against the kids who did have a scoreboard, but we the Indians *do* have a scoreboard. A world-class one. And it's broken. And even though I would've, if I ever coached in the NCAA and had a money player who didn't toe the line or care about glory, I never slapped a player in the NCAA, which I never coached in, it's true, and so the Indians are suffering for no reason that has to do with me. They're suffering for a reason that has to do with vandalism and ill will and no intestinal fortitude or honor of any kind on the part of others so now we have to find volunteers to keep score with flipcards, and I'm not trying to be negative. I see the long faces, but you gotta let me finish first. I was only just telling you about the way I *was* answering that question about surviving with our heads up, which was: No. Today I answer it different. Looking at my players, *our* players, I got hope and my answer now is: Yes. Maybe we're not too poor to afford a scoreboard, but two of our starters and one of our benchmen got injured in assaults yesterday, and unless lightning strikes twice in similar locales, which we all know it can't, Twin Groves' players have *not* been assaulted by schoolmates this week, meaning we've got a need to show some heart. To climb out from under what's trying to keep us under it. We got difficulties to overcome, and since the scoreboard's been destroyed, those difficulties are blessings, and once we overcome them, do you know what it is, because I'm tellin you it's glory freakin road. FLIP-PIN! GLORY! FREAKIN! ROAD!

□ □ □ □ □ □ □

We had one knife and ten of Benji's stolen crack-lighters. He handed them out once the coins were rationed, and I showed the Side of Damage where to sever their bottles. The jetflames were as precise as Benji'd told Pinge—they left all the rims at the severances smooth.

As the lighters went around, Benji called in the fire in his basement on Jelly's celly, I called in a gunman at a mall on Jerry Throop's, and Vincie on his own phone reported a beardo who left a fat suitcase on the Metra tracks. When he hung up, he shook his ammo-packed fist. It jingled and he said, "I don't get this coin-op bullshit."

I'll explain soon, I said. Why you whispering?

"It seems like you're trying to keep everyone in suspense, so I don't want to blow the suspense."

How would you blow the suspense? I said.

"Because I know what we're making," he whispered. "June invented—"

I forgot, I said.

"Well so I don't know what this fucken coin-op bullshit's all about. Why don't I get some nibs from my locker?"

How many do you have?

"I don't know—forty? I lost count. My grandparents keep sending them to me. No one ever told them my eye got inked, and their hearts would fucken break if they knew I quit calligraphy."

Go, I said, but do it fast—the pep rally ends in twenty-five minutes.

"What if Floyd's out there?"

I said, Take Ronrico to scout for you. He can run distraction if—

"Distraction's good," Vincie said, "but, you know what's a lot fucken better..."

I handed him the sap. He wanted to bang fists.

We banged fists.

"Ronrico," said Vincie, "let's go."

"I want to finish making the weapon," Ronrico said.

Give me your tit-shaped piece, I said.

"Tit-shaped! Ha!" Ronrico said. He traded me for the pennygun in my pocket.

"How do I use it?" he said.

"I'll show you on the way," Vincie told him.

They grabbed some change and split.

I called in a hit-and-run. Benji called in a dine-and-ditch.

As soon as all the widemouths were severed, I demonstrated how to affix the balloons and told the Side of Damage what to understand.

Understand you hold a gun, I said.

Then I projected a nickel into a desklamp and the bulb shattered.

The Side of Damage cheered.

I projected another one at a coffee carafe, and the carafe shattered.

They cheered some more.

Understand you hold a gun, I said, but understand you're not the only ones. Others in the gym will have them, too. I don't know how many, and I don't know most of their names. And since they don't know all of us and we don't know all of them, the only way we'll all be able to identify each other is by our weapons, so be sure to brandish and be sure to *watch* for brandishers, too: we're all on the same side. Ask your questions.

"What makes them on our side?" "What if we don't like them?" "What if they're enemies?"

I said, Even if some of them have been your enemies in the past, the past is over. They're all loyal to me, and all of us are against the Arrangement.

That was good enough for most of them, but a few—some of the smartest—were still concerned.

"Please forgive my interjection, Gurion, but how is it that you know these others are loyal to you if you do not even know their names?" asked Anna Boshka.

"Gurion knows stuff," said the Flunky. "He's the leader."

"It's true," said the Janitor.

I said, I was their leader since before I even met any of you, and they're my brothers, so they're loyal. Faith in me is the same as faith in them.

Anna said, "But what if we do not have faith, Gurion?"

"Jeez, Boshka, don't be such a downer," Chunkstyle said.

I said, No, it's an important question. If you have doubts, then you can't attack the pep rally with me. And I'm not challenging any of you when I say that. You're all feeling stronger now, weapons in your hands, and that's good, that's why I had you build them, but back in the Cage a lot of you were dying to leave, and any of you who want to leave, any of you who have any doubts—and I don't mean about will we have victory or won't we—those doubts are fine, better than fine, they are smart, faithful—I mean about *should* we have victory or *shouldn't* we, *are* we righteous or *aren't* we— you will leave with my blessing. I *want* you to leave if you have those doubts. And if you leave, you will leave with all your snat, and under my protection. No one will call you a coward or a traitor. You'll always be, as you have been, on the Side of Damage.

"What if something happens and we want to leave later?" said Ansul Entsry. "Like after we attack?"

I said, If you follow me to the gym, you have to follow me til I tell you not to follow me anymore.

"What about freedom of choice?"

Nakamook said, "If you get to leave whenever you want, no one'll know who to rely on."

I said, You make your choice here. Walk away now or stay til it's over.

"But what if we think we want to attack with you, but then, after we start, it turns out we were wrong and we didn't really have faith?" Ansul said.

"You mean like you're worried you don't have faith in your ability to know if you have faith right now?" Benji said.

"Yeah," said Ansul.

"Then you're a fucken pussy and we're better off without you," said Benji.

"But what if—"

"If you come with, then try to run away in the middle of it, I'll catch you," Benji said.

"Gurion?"

I said, You probably shouldn't come with us, Ansul.

"But I want to."

Everyone here wants to, I said, and soon, if things go well for us, almost everyone everywhere will want to, or at least wish they had—even some of our enemies. It's not good enough to just want to, right now. If you can walk away, you should walk away.

Just then Vincie and Ronrico returned to the lounge.

Take a minute to decide, I told the Side of Damage. If you're not coming with, turn your coins back in—we'll need them.

"We didn't fucken see Floyd," Vincie told me.

"Not that we didn't go looking," said Ronrico.

"Shut the fuck up, Asparagus. You wanted to get him as bad as me." Vincie handed me the sap. I stuck it in my belt. "I'm sorry," he said, "but I just love that thing. Makes me wanna fucken *use* it, you know?"

"I know!" said Ansul Entsry. "Exactly!" he said.

"Huh?" said Vincie.

Ansul batted his eyelids = either "I think you're very sexy and want to kiss you, Vincie Portite," or, "I think you're very sexy and want to be like you, Vincie Portite."

"Anyway, I was thinking about it, and I'll bet you anything Floyd's in the gym," Vincie said.

Why? I said.

"His big fucken chance to do crowd control or whatever."

You're smart, I said.

"I—"

"Did you tell him about the Office and the camera?" Ronrico said.

"Did you fucken hear me tell him? You've been standing here the whole time," said Vincie. To me, he said, "The good news is that Brodsky's office is empty and so is Nurse Clyde's, plus look at all these nibs." He emptied a baggie of nibs on the table. "The bad news is: Some Boystar guy with a camera was walking around and I think he caught us on tape."

"We're all gonna be on tape, anyway," Benji said. "Right?"

Right, I said. I said, It doesn't matter.

"Good," said Ronrico. "Cause I flicked that guy off."

"Also," said Vincie, pulling something from his backpack, "I've been stashing these away for a present for your birthday or Chanukah or something." He dropped a second baggie on the table and the baggie clunked and glinted. It was filled with wingnuts and hexnuts and washers. "I started thinking how if you're saying pennies'll…"

I grabbed his head by the ears. I said, You're smart, Vincie.

"Tch," Vincie said, and tried to shrug from my grasp.

I pulled his head down close so our foreheads touched. No, I said. I said, Listen to me. I'm not trying to have an emotional moment with you here. When we get to the gym, you're gonna be making some decisions and you're not gonna be able to ask me or Benji if they're good decisions. You'll be in charge of people, and if you think you're dumb, you'll second-guess yourself and slow us down, and if we're slow we'll suffer for it. You know what you're doing. You're smart. So be fucken smart.

"I will," he said.

I mashed our foreheads.

"For serious," he said.

I let him go with a backslap and he waved his pennygun. He told me, "I need one for Starla."

I gave him the weapon I'd made for her.

Ronrico asked if he should pass out the nibs.

Just the washers and fasteners, I said. Nibs're for us.

"I'm honored," said Ronrico.

Sorry, I said, I didn't mean you.

Ronrico made a whiny noise.

"We're the best shots," Benji told him. "We've been practicing for months. Here's some coins." He gave Ronrico some coins.

There were thirty nibs. I divided them five ways.

"Who're—" said Benji.

I said, June and Eliyahu.

I swept three portions into my bag.

When I looked up, there was a new pile of give-back coins on the table, and some kids were still digging in their pockets, making it larger.

"Should we go?" asked one of the pocketdiggers.

Not yet, I said. I said, We don't know for sure where Floyd is and we have to stay stealth. I said, Stay here til the attack's in progress, then go out the side entrance.

"How will we know when it's in progress?"

I said, Just wait for the end-of-class tone or the fire alarm—whichever comes first.

Other kids started digging in their pockets.

Last chance to go home, I told everyone.

Another two flopped coins into the pile. And then another three. More were lining up.

I called in a murder, Mangey a flasher, Vincie a bank heist, Benji a crazy-eyed man in a quiet cul-de-sac.

"We're in," Benji told me.

How do you know?

"The dispatcher told me, 'Yeah, yeah, yeah, kid.'"

Good, I said. I said, Keep making calls. If they yeah-yeah-yeah you, act incredulous and tell them you'll sue them if they don't respond. Tell them you know the laws and they're being racists and your dad's a civil rights lawyer and just because you're black doesn't mean they can treat you like a second-class citizen.

"Should I do a gangsta voice or something?"

No, I said. Talk like a news anchor.

"Shouldn't we stop?" Vincie asked us. "Aren't they gonna think we're crying wolf?"

"That's the whole idea," Benji told him.

"No," said Vincie, "that's not what I fucken mean. I mean aren't they gonna start thinking that we're crying wolf on purpose—like for a strategy?"

Yes, I said.

I dialed Information, asked them for the number for Stevenson High School.

□ □ □ □ □ □ □

COACH RONALD DESORMIE
(AT HALF-COURT MICROPHONE, USING OWN
MEGAPHONE)
Co-Captain William "The Co-Captain" Baxter!

10:21 AM: C1 (C3; *C4*; *C6*; C9)

WILLIAM BAXTER
(RISES FROM CHAIR NEAR HALF-COURT, STRAIGHTENS
TIE, SALUTES BLEACHERS)

10:21 AM: C3 (*C1*; C4; C6; *C9*)

BLEACHERS
(FIVE BOYS GRASPING THE SLEEVES AND SHOULDERS
OF A SIXTH BOY IN A BLACK HAT WHO APPEARS TO BE
STRAINING AGAINST THEM; VIRGINIA PINGE, SITTING
BEHIND THE SIX, LEANS IN STERNLY, GESTICULATES
WITH HER ARMS.)

10:21 AM: C1 (C3; *C4*; *C6*; C9)

WILLIAM BAXTER
(BOWS AT WAIST, SITS)

COACH RONALD DESORMIE
(AT HALF-COURT MICROPHONE, USING OWN
MEGAPHONE)
And finally, the best of the best who's been saved for last, and for that very reason. The all-time high-scorer in the Western Division

of the North Shore Conference. Averaging twenty-nine points per game last year, this player had a regular-season high of thirty-six points and a playoff high of forty-three. He triple-doubled in ten of twelve regular season games. He's made team Illinois for two years running and was the first seventh-grader in America to ever start at center on a state team at the junior-high varsity level. He's never flubbed a tip-off. He's never blown a dunk. He's ninety-three percent at the line. When the clutch is on, this one goes to eleven. And that's just the numbers. He's got what's known as touch. He's got what's referred to as drive. Whistle blows, he enters an atemporal and totally nonspatial area that we in the coaching profession like to call the zone. And he stays there. He's an athlete with more gumption than a locomotive, a born leader with more leadership skills than all the Ghandis and Reagans to the millionth power *combined*, and he's a non-parallel natural talent who plays basketball better than eagles fly, better than snakes bite, better than cats land on their feet and dogs are man's best friend. This is the guy you gotta foul to even begin to think about having a prayer to stop him—and even then. This is the guy who is the heart of the team that is the soul of the school that is the one you go to which is Aptakisic. People... I give you Co-Captain Alpha of your very own Indians: BAM. BAMMIN. VON BAMMENSTEIN. SLOKUM!

AUDIENCE (OFFSCREEN)
(CLAPPING AND WHISTLING)

BARNUM SLOKUM
(RISES FROM CHAIR NEAR HALF-COURT)

COACH RONALD DESORMIE
(AT HALF-COURT MICROPHONE, USING OWN
MEGAPHONE)
Behold the man!
(PUMPS FIST IN AIR; WITH FREE HAND, PLAY-PUNCHES
BARNUM SLOKUM'S SHOULDER)

BARNUM SLOKUM
(REMOVES HALF-COURT MICROPHONE FROM CLAMP;

STANDS CONTRAPPOSTO, DANGLING HALF-COURT
MICROPHONE BY CORD AT SIDE, NODDING SLOWLY,
AFFIRMATIVELY)

AUDIENCE (OFFSCREEN)
(CLAPPING AND WHISTLING OVER SWELLING MICRO-
PHONE FEEDBACK FROM HALF-COURT MICROPHONE)

10:24 AM: C6 (*C4*; C3; C6; *C9*)

BLEACHERS
(STUDENTS AND TEACHERS APPLAUDING WILDLY,
WHISTLING)

10:23 AM: C1 (C2; C3; C4; *C6*; C8; C9)

BARNUM SLOKUM
(BRINGS HALF-COURT MICROPHONE TO CHIN)
Will you let me holler at you for a minute.

10:23 AM: C6 (*C1*; *C2*; *C3*; *C4*; *C5*; C7; C8; *C9*)

BLEACHERS (PANNING)
(STUDENTS AND TEACHERS APPLAUDING WILDLY,
WHISTLING, SHOUTING "HOLLER")
(THREE BLONDE GIRLS WITH SIMILAR HAIRCUTS
BLOWING KISSES; THREE OTHERS SHOUTING, "WE
LOVE YOU BAM!")
(RED-HAIRED GIRL, ONE EYE SHUT, SIGHTING
THROUGH IMAGINARY RIFLE)

10:23 AM: C7 (C1; C2; C3; C4; C5; *C6*; C8; C9)

BARNUM SLOKUM
(AT HALF-COURT MICROPHONE; REMOVES BROAD-
SHEET FROM JACKET AND UNFOLDS, HOLDS IT UNDER
EYES)
I'm tall.

AUDIENCE (OFFSCREEN)
(EMITS SHUSHING SOUNDS, GROWS QUIET)

BARNUM SLOKUM
(AT HALF-COURT MICROPHONE, BRANDISHING
BROADSHEET)
According to this I'm tall. The *Twin Groves Weekly Eagle* says I'm
tall and my height lets me to dunk, and it's why I win tip-offs. My
fighter-pilot vision, says the *Weekly Eagle*, grants me access to the
angle of the ball's spin be*fore* it hits the boards, and those needles
I thread when I get in the lane I already spotted from way back
at half-court—according to this. This rag here's sports editor says
"Slokum is Justice of the Peace at the wedding of game-smarts and
preternatural reflexes." Says I make use of the power vested in me
to anticipate blocks I'll put to shots the guy I'm guarding doesn't
yet know he'll take. Says my body's toned in places most people
don't even have musculature, and, paired with my perfect skeletal
symmetry, this allows me to maintain balance amid all kinds of
dirty elbowplay. Says the Indians are unstoppable as long as I'm in
the game. Says the Eagles have to take me out. Well let me tell you
something. Can I tell you something. Can I show you something.
Will you let me holler at you some more.

AUDIENCE (OFFSCREEN)
(SHOUTS OF "HOLLER" FOLLOWED BY SHUSHING
SOUNDS, THEN QUIET)

BARNUM SLOKUM
(SLINGS HALF-COURT MICROPHONE OVER SHOUL-
DER, HALVES BROADSHEET, QUARTERS BROADSHEET,
EIGHTHS BROADSHEET, SIXTEENTHS BROADSHEET,
THROWS BROADSHEET CONFETTI OVER SHOULDER;
BRINGS HALF-COURT MICROPHONE TO CHIN)
Weekly Eagle, regal beagle. We've won all our games since I joined
varsity two years back: that's true. It's true I'm tall, it's true I'm a
serious player, and it's true the Aptakisic Indians are unstoppable.
But no matter what any hack at the enemy school's newspaper writes
or thinks, the Aptakisic Indians aren't unstoppable because I'm tall,

and we're not unstoppable because I'm a serious player. We're not unstoppable because I got backup from my excellent Co-Captain William "The Co-Captain" Baxter or Lonnie "Blonde Lonnie" Boyd either. We're not unstoppable because of any one of the players or even all of the players. The Aptakisic Indians are unstoppable because the Aptakisic Indians are the Aptakisic Indians. And the Aptakisic Indians are the Aptakisic Indians because we go to school with you, understand. With *you*. That's what the enemy doesn't want you to know. And yeah, we'll win this afternoon and you're behind us and all of us know that. And yeah, to some people it might look like you're behind us *because* we'll win this afternoon, but what I'm telling you is we'll win this afternoon because *you're behind us*. That's what we're here for, in this gym. Right now. To get rallied. By you. You're *rallying* us, understand. You're showing us you're behind us. We're *all* Indians here, and even though it's the basketball players who bring the victory and even though it's the basketball players who get the most props for the victory, the basketball players are only the right arm of the entire student body, and an arm, no matter how ripped, no matter how powerful, can't operate independent of the body it's attached to, can it. I'm saying it can't. I'm saying *hell no* it can't. Our strength makes you believe in us, sure, but your belief in us is what makes us strong. Aptakisic's victories on the court are as much your victories as they are mine and the other players'. We are all equally responsible for and deserving of what we have and what we'll get. I want you to understand that. I want you to believe that. And so when you get home tonight and your parents ask you what happened at the Indians-Eagles game, I don't want you to say "Bam was strong and our team was victorious." And I don't want you to say, "Our team was victorious and glory is upon them." I want you to stop being so humble. I want you to say, "I was strong and I was victorious."

AUDIENCE
(RISING APPLAUSE)

BARNUM SLOKUM
(PACING MIDCOURT TO THE LENGTHS THE HALF-COURT MICROPHONE CORD ALLOWS; RAISES VOICE)

I want you to say to your parents: "Tonight, on this bread of victory that I baked, I spread the butter of glory I churned with much dedication and elbow grease. Tonight I sup on my victory, Mom, on my glory, Dad. Would. You. Like. To try a bite?"

AUDIENCE
(ROARING)

BARNUM SLOKUM
(PACING MIDCOURT; VOICE RAISED)
And your parents, believe me—I don't care what kind of relationship you've got with them—they'll take you up on that offer. You share that sandwich with them—are you hearing me?—you share that glory sandwich with them and they'll love you forever. Believe. Believe, believe, believe. (STANDS AT HALFCOURT, GESTURES UNTIL SILENCE COMES.) In closing: you guys are so great. And we on the floor here—we know it. And that's another reason why we do this circus every year. Not just for the team to get rallied, understand, but for the team to show you its appreciation for the way you folks are *always* rallying us. It's a beautiful, mutual thing that way, this pep rally, this school, and we've all had fun, it's true, believe, but we're about to have a lot more. The liontamer's still prepping in the locker-room, so to speak—we'll have to wait a few minutes for him to come out and emotionalize us. But in the meantime, I want you to give it up, and give it up heavy for ten jumping beauties in tiny skirts and tight sweaters. They build our pyramids. They lead our cheers. They really know how to shake it. Put your hands together for Aptakisic Squaw Squad.

□ □ □ □ □ □ □

I had twenty-one soldiers behind me. We divided the surplus ammo twenty-two ways. Then I divided the soldiers into platoons.

Vincie's platoon (six total) would guard the fire alarm by the side-exit (three) and between the locker-room doors inside the gym (three). Ben-Wa's (eight total) would establish three positions: one at the southern border of the B-Hall/Main-Hall junction (three), one across Main Hall along the northern border of the front entrance (three), and a third at the B-Hall fire-alarm near the B-Hall/2-Hall junction (two). Before entering the gym, we'd mug Jerry for his keys and lock all the classrooms in B-Hall. Combined with the efforts of the Ben-Wa platoon, the B-Hall lockdown would ensure that anyone who fled the rally couldn't get to an alarm we didn't have soldiers on—they'd either have to pipeline through one of the gym doorways along the northern wall and go out the front entrance of the school, or go straight outside through the side-exit (pushbar-door) of the gym on the western wall.

The third platoon, Nakamook's (seven), would target the Indians.

My platoon, of indeterminate number (me + June + The Five + Eliyahu + Ally'n'Googy + Berman + all unknown armed Israelites in the gym), would take care of the rest, reinforcing where needed.

I described the plans fast.

Any questions? I said.

"I don't want to sound like a pussy," Mark Dingle said, "and I'm gonna do this anyway—but how we gonna all get away with it, like, after we take the school?"

I said, Hundreds of soldiers are coming here today. We hold the gym til they arrive. Then we turn ourselves in and I take responsibility. Simple as that.

"But we'll be on camera, you said," Forrest Kenilworth said. "They'll have us on tape," said Stevie Loop. And Ansul said, "That's evidence against us."

I said, If we start this off right—if you all do what I tell you—there's gonna be a lot of kids in that gym bringing lots of damage—to us, to each other, to everyone. They'll be on tape, too. It'll look like a riot. Like no one's in control. Like everyone's guilty. And even if we do it wrong—even if no one else rises up—even if we get *crushed*—then, like I said: *Hundreds of soldiers*. On their way here. On their way to see *me*. They're all ditching school, they're all carrying weapons, and they're coming all the way from Chicago. If I can get them to do all of that, I can get you to do this—that's what people will say when they see the tapes. They'll say *I* did this. That I did *all of it*. Do you understand?

"Yes," they all said.

Are there any more questions?

There were no more questions.

You've got three minutes to get to know your weapons, I said. Vincie and Benji'll show you how to use them. Shoot exactly how they show you or your thumbs'll get damaged and you'll never hit your targets.

Vincie and Benji stepped forward to demonstrate.

I entered the bathroom and howled wolf.

"Stevenson High School. Principal Barney's office."

Who's this? I said.

"This is Ms. Sampsel."

Good, I said. We hoped it would be you. You were always kind to us. We always liked you.

"Who is this?" she said.

What's important, Ms. Sampsel, is you deliver our message.

"Who is this?" she said.

We're your savior, Ms. Sampsel, we're the enemy who'll save you, the only one who can. Only the love in the heart of your enemy: only our love can save you.

"Who—"

This is our message, Ms. Sampsel. Don't fuck it up with silly questions, now. It's only the love in the heart of your enemy, not the cops who are busy elsewhere, not the firemen stuck on the other side of town trying to save those who need no saving—you'll see, Ms. Sampsel, you'll call them up and they'll call you a liar, they'll tell you you're pranking, you'll feel like we do, every fucking day, EVERY! FUCKING! DAY! MS. SAMPSEL! It is only our love, the love of your enemy—only your enemy can save you, Ms. Sampsel. Tell it to Barney, tell it to the jocks, tell it to your congressman and President. Today we blow up your school out of love. If things don't change, if you don't love us back, our love dies tomorrow, then you and your students. You've got twenty-one minutes til the first explosion. We love you, Ms. Sampsel, each and every one of you. We love each and every one of you and so you are warned and so you are saved. By us, Ms. Sampsel, not the authorities. As-salamu alaykum, shalom and om. Evacuate now or return to dust.

I hung up on Sampsel and dialed 911. Two more calls to finish hyper-blinkering.

"Emergency Services."

Please help, I whispered, Miles Nolan's got a gun.

"Who is this?"

Matty Manx. Please help. Miles Nolan's got a gun.

"Okay then, 'Matty,' where are you this time?"

I'm under the desk. Oh Jesus. Please.

"Under the—"

I hung up.

I counted to seven and dialed again.

This is Bobby Banks! Matty Manx just got shot! Mr. Abel said call you and I'm callin!

"Who is this?"

Bobby Banks!—hold on! Okay!—We're at Twin Groves junior high. Bolan went toward the gym—Twin Groves Junior High I'm supposed to tell you. Niles Bolan!—Hold on! What?—Send everything you've got I'm supposed to tell you: Jiles Brolan's crazy.

I hung up, left the bathroom, stood on a chair. The Side of Damage stopped shooting their guns.

You *will*, I told them, be asked about what happened, and when you're asked—whether it's by teachers or the cops, reporters or historians, your parents or your children, whether today, tomorrow, or years from now, whether the question's why, how, or who—I want to make this clear—I want you to stay safe. I want you to tell the truth.

"It was Gurion." "Gurion." "Gurion did it."

Good, I said.

□   □   □   □   □   □   □

10:29 AM: C2 (C1; C3; *C4*; *C6*;)

APTAKISIC SQUAW SQUAD
(DISMOUNT PYRAMID; BACKFLIP INTO TWO FACING
LINES {"LEFT" AND "RIGHT"})
(ALL)
And one and two and three and

(LEFT)
Ready?

(RIGHT)
Yeah, go!

(ALL)
We're Bamming!
We're slamming!

B-A-M-M-I-N-G!
We're Bamming!
We're jamming!
B-A-M-M-I-N-G!

(LEFT)

Hey Bam.

(RIGHT)

Yeah Jen?

(LEFT)

Won't you come and do the Bam
With me?

(RIGHT)

Sure Jen,
But first I must go put the Bam to him

(LEFT)

Who's he?

(RIGHT)

Just some guy I'll make my prop er ty!

(LEFT)

Go Bam
We all think that's
H-O-T-T-T!

(RIGHT)

Yo Bam,
Bring that hot
D-A-M-A-G-E

(ALL)

We're bamming!
B-A-M-M-I-N-G!

We're jamming!
We're Bamming!
B-A-M-M-I-N-G!
Bamming! Bamming!
Yay!

▫ ▫ ▫ ▫ ▫ ▫ ▫

In C-Hall, winter thunder rumbled ceiling panels. It was helpful—heightening anticipation, jacking our chemicals up an extra tick—but I worried the weather it indicated would stall the scholars, if not discourage some of them entirely. Without a schoolbus to take them from the Metra station to Aptakisic, they had miles to walk. I knew a storm wouldn't stop the likes of Emmanuel or Shai or Samuel Diamond, but the rest of them... What they would or wouldn't do was no longer up to me, at least not for the moment, and I decided that was a blessing. It had to be. And if they didn't show up, I could still protect the Side. They'd say I did it, and I'd say I did it, and most of the world would be happy to believe it. Fine, I thought. We're fine, I thought.

I wrote Ben-Wa a pass to the Deaf Sentinel.

Tell him he's needed in the Cage, I said.

"What if he asks why? I'm a really bad liar."

"Start crying," Jelly Rothstein told him. "He'll follow you."

"I can't just start. Something needs to make me sad first."

"You're a tiny albino with a stupid name," said Jenny Mangey, "and girls don't think about you sexually."

"I know," Ben-Wa said. "It's true. I know. I hate my name."

He walked away crying.

Three minutes later, they stood at the chain-link gate. We stepped out of doorways and surrounded Jerry.

He said, "Show me your passes." He had no idea. This stitchy-looking vein in his temple was throbbing: once, twice—

I projected a penny at it and he dropped, unconscious.

The soldiers all looked at their weapons, and for the length of a breath the only sound in the hall was the whispery ticking of hailfall on the roof.

Imagine what a quarter'll do, I said.

"We're gonna win," said Christian Yagoda.

"No fucken shit," said Vincie.

I recovered my penny, rolled Jerry for his keys and phone. Nakamook's platoon dragged the body to the Cage.

"What should we tie him to?" Fulton Market asked.

"No time to tie him," said Benji. "He won't be able to break out of here, anyway."

"He'll find the Monitor when he wakes up, and untie *him*," said Ronrico.

"Maybe," Benji said. "Maybe he'll be afraid to. Either way, he'll already know what we're willing to do, and anyone else we lock in here—Jerry'll tell them how lucky they are."

"They'll be way too fucken scared to fuck around with us then," said Vincie.

Or too scared not to, I thought. If I was prisoner to a faction I knew had brutalized my cop, I'd wait beside the door with an improvised weapon: the next member of the faction who walked into my cage would get ambushed hard.

I told the Side of Damage: Remove all the chairs.

While they worked, I got the number off Jerry's phone, saved it into Botha's as "Wolf."

I gave Ben-Wa Jerry's, and called it with Botha's.

It rang.

That's the only number you answer, I said. Save it as "Gurion."

Ben-Wa saved it.

The Flunky came back for more chairs. He tried to grab five and dropped his weapon. Potentials I'd not yet foreseen occurred to me.

Flunky, I said.

The Flunky came over.

I climbed on a chair so he wouldn't have to kneel, then wrote DAMAGE on his forehead in 12-gauge Darker.

"What is it?" he asked.

A blessing on your head.

"What for?" he said.

Protection.

I blessed all the rest of them and Benji blessed me.

The sentinel, blinking, started to mutter. Leevon kicked him. Then he was quiet.

"He wakes up again, he'll pull the alarm," Jelly said.

"The alarm'll get pulled anyway," said the Janitor.

"But maybe not so soon, though," said Jelly.

Jelly was right. We put Jerry in the girls bathroom and closed the door, tore a carrel from the wall, and wedged it under the knob. The part of the wall the carrel'd covered looked naked. The Side began to strip the rest of the Cage.

Don't waste your damage on symbols, I told them.

They followed me out into C-Hall.

□ □ □ □ □ □ □

10:35 AM: C2 (C1; C3; *C4*; C5; *C6*; *C7*; *C8*; *C9*)

CHAZ BLACK
(AT HALF-COURT MICROPHONE)

I'm Chaz Black and I'm happy to be here. I'm happy cause you're here and I'm here at the same time and we're about to hear—are you ready for this?—the *freshest* single in the world right now per-formed live by Boystar and his special guest. Now. When I say the freshest single in the world, how fresh do I mean? I'll tell you. Not including the suits at New Thing for whom I middleman to the talent packager—The Boystar Incorporated's what I mean by the talent packager—except for them, only nine people have ever heard this single. *Nine.* (USES FINGERS TO COUNT OFF) I'm one of them. Boystar's another. His parents. That's four. Two producers—Biz Nagle and Jimmy Mineo. Our very special mystery guest. And then the two guys who wrote the song with Boystar—the brothers Chip and Rafe "I'm telling you it's not a pseudonym!" Hottenstein. You students are privileged. The freshness of a new single—let alone a single that's gonna be a hit—is rarely as fresh as the freshness of the single you're about to hear, which is called "Infantalize," by the way. Believe me. The freshness is overwhelming. It'll make you wanna dance in your seats, which I'll get to in just a minute. Point I'm try-ing to make first is: We at New Thing and The Boystar Incorporated wanted to give this freshness to you—it's a once-in-a-lifetime kinda freshness, unless you're planning on working for a major label, which:

good luck with that dream, you'll need it—we wanted to give you students this once-in-a-lifetime type freshness so bad that during soundcheck, we rehearsed the B-side of the song—not "Infantalize" itself, see, but the B-side, "Your Special"—so as not to pollute the freshness of "Infantalize" any further with the listenings of our four sound technicians. The difference between nine people having heard the song and thirteen people having heard the song—it's a difference of nearly fifty percent in terms of relative freshness, so what we did was: we kept it nearly fifty percent fresher for you than some of the more conservative members of our contingent might've thought wise if we'd told them our plan is what I'm telling you. And I'm not asking you to applaud me. I sense the respect in your silence, and I feel good about it, so just keep on keeping the silence, and I'll tell you what we've got. We've got the album pressed. We've got the singles pressed. We've got the cover art sitting in a factory. We've got the website ready for launch. We've got the tour-dates lined up. We've got the stickers. We've got the flyers. We've got the t-shirts. We've got the street team to distribute all that stuff. But what we don't have is the video. That's why we're doing the video here. Right here in the gym with you. With *you.* And I can see by your smiles that you like that. And I can see by the way you're at the edges of your seats, you're thinking: "Will I be in the video, Chaz? Will I, personally, as an individual student here at Aptakisic Junior High School, be in the video, Chaz?" And the answer is: Maybe. And when I say "Maybe," what I mean is: I sure hope so. In music, there's something called harmony. Maybe you've heard of it. What harmony is is the product of two or more sounds doing what? You guessed it: harmonizing. There's also such a thing as harmony in the world outside of music. You and I, friends: we're in that kind of harmony. You want to be in the video, I want you to be in the video. That's a kind of harmony that we'll call the harmony of our most heartfelt wishes. Yet the question remains: How do we make our most heartfelt and harmonizing wishes come true? How do we get these wishes on tape? How do we get you guys on TV? Here's how: First of all I'll give you second of all, and second of all is: If we decide you should be in the video, you have to get your parents to sign a slip we'll mail to them that says we're allowed to put you in the video. Ask me, that infringes on your rights as individuals, but that's the cost of harmony. And like I said that's second of all, because first of all, as you may or may not have picked up on by now, we at New Thing and The Boystar Incorporated have to decide that you *should* be in the video: Much as right now we're all *wishing* harmonically for you to be in the video, for us to *decide* that you should be in the video depends on how you act once we start shooting. I'm gonna tell you a little about that. As soon as I'm done up here, I'm gonna sit down, and the lights are gonna go off. Boystar's gonna come out of the locker-room with the super special mystery guest. Spotlight's gonna be on Boystar. He's gonna do his shout-outs, and then he's gonna start emotionalizing you. He's gonna start singing "Infantalize." "Infantalize" starts out slow, quiet, smooth—sounds like it's gonna be a ballad. But it's a rocker. A real bootyshaker, if I may. And as soon as "Infantalize" starts rocking, the lights are gonna come up—and there's gonna be our very special mystery guest harmonizing with Boystar, and then who else is there gonna be? You guessed it: You. Rather: Maybe you. For us to decide that you should be in the video, you need to be seriously emotionalized when the lights go up, and since we've got only five cameras here—those other four are for the news—and since of those five cameras, three are gonna be on Boystar, and one on the very special mystery guest, that leaves how many cameras dedicated to shooting the audience? That's right. One camera, exactly. And one camera means what? One camera means that sometimes we'll have some tape of you, and other times we won't. And so: You not only have to be seriously emotionalized when the lights come up, but you have to be seriously emotionalized for all of "Infantalize." Simple way to put it: Dance in your seats, you might make the video. Sit still and be boring and you definitely won't make the video. No one who's seriously emotionalized sits still. Now, that said: being seriously emotionalized is not the same as being a spasticated dork. Don't dork out. We've got expensive equipment here. We've got choreography. We've got one take. Do not come off the bleachers and try to dance with Boystar, no matter how beckoning his star presence seems to you. If you think he wants you to come be the co-star of his video: you're wrong. He's just really sexy and likable—that's why he gets to be Boystar. And neither would you want him to come co-star in your video. Not if you were him and he were you. So if you dork out, you'll be ejected, and you'll ruin a part of the video, and everyone will be angry at you because maybe the part of the video you ruined is a part they would have been in, and suddenly you'll find yourself out of harmony with everyone. You'll find yourself friendless, alone, and in serious need of being emotionalized, but no one's gonna want to emotionalize you because of how you acted like a hyper loo, and all you'll have for solace will be *Emotionalize*, the new album by Boystar, which, since it's such a kickin' album, will work to give you solace, but it will do so in a bittersweet way, because even as it comforts you, you'll know you could have been a part of it if you hadn't screwed up and acted like such a spaz. And what's more: you'll have to buy it. Whereas, if you make it into the video we'll pay you with a free copy. Now who wants a free copy? Who? Who does?... Tell me one more time.

□ □ □ □ □ □ □

We kept sixteen chairs and dumped the rest in the pool. We locked down the B-Hall classrooms, locked down the gates at the B-Hall/2-Hall junction, and set half the chairs side-to-side to make barricades: one along the southern border of the Main Hall/B-Hall junction, another between the northern edge of the front entrance and the facing Main Hall-wall. The remaining eight chairs were to be wielded legs-forward by Ben-Wa's soldiers, three at either barricade, two at the B-Hall fire alarm.

I opened the front doors and clicked out the stoppers. Wind blasted hailstones and rock salt onto the traction rug. The Side of Damage was shivering, big-eyed.

I told them: You'll warm up fast.

"We're not cold. We're ready," Nakamook said. "Listen up," he told the soldiers. "Listen to Gurion."

It was time for the blessing on the Damage Proper. If they were Israelites and I the Cohain Gadol, I would have told them, "Hear O Israel, you are coming near to the battle against your enemies. Let your heart not be faint, do not be afraid, do not panic, and do not break down before them, for Adonai, your God, is the One who goes with you, to fight for you against your enemies, to save you," but they were the Side of Damage and I was Gurion ben-Judah, so I said other things:

Strike all turned cheeks that aren't hustling ass-cheeks. Anyone not with us is part of the Arrangement. Let the runners run, but continue to attack in the face of any retreat less definite. There are far more of them than there are of us, and numbers can embolden cowards. We must overwhelm them with ferocity.

Soldiers at the barricades: remain steadfast. Let no one breach your lines. If someone tries to move you, break him down with your chair. If someone gets past you, shoot him. If you miss, chase him down. Lay him out. Don't miss.

Soldiers on alarms: an alarm will almost definitely be pulled at some point. The later that happens, the better, but once it does happen, there's no need to hold position. If you're in the gym, get behind Vincie and reinforce the frontline. If you're in B-Hall, get with Ben-Wa at the Main Hall junction and hold the lines til further instructed. You'll see more action soon enough.

Ben-Wa had a question: "What about phones? Everyone's got phones."

"Everyone's phones're in their lockers," said Dingle. "That's the rules. And isn't it iron—"

"Not everyone follows the rules," Ben-Wa said. "And those aren't the rules for the teachers, anyway."

Sweat the alarms, I said, don't sweat the phones. Don't get distracted trying to confiscate phones. Someone pulls out a phone: shoot him, hurt him, he's trying to stop us, he has to suffer, but every cop and fireman in the county is over at the high school. One pulled alarm and they're here in five minutes, but it'll take a lot of calls to get any to leave Stevenson, and by the time those get made we'll be ready or done for anyway.

Soldiers coming to the gym: If the lights are still on when we get to the gym, we go quiet through the east doors, get under the bleachers, wait for darkness, then position on my cue. If it's already dark, they'll see hall-light when we enter, so we'll come through the center and rush our locations.

Frontline soldiers: be relentless. Project all you can before the hand-to-hand comes on, and know it'll come on fast. Show them the color of their blood. Teach them the sound of their snapping limbs. Almost anything in the gym you can lift can be a weapon, and almost none of our enemies know that yet. Put the enemies down before they can learn.

All of you: Let no numberdrunk fool believe he can defy *any* of us without suffering. If they pin you at the elbows, put your knee in their sack. If you can't move your knee, remember you can headbutt—go for the nose, the eyes, the mouth. If you can't reach to headbutt, remember your teeth—bite arms, bite wrists, bite fingers, taste bones. If you can't bite, spit. If you can't spit, scream—blow out their eardrums. Bring all the pain you can til one of us rescues you.

One of us will always rescue you.

The Arrangement would grind us fine as salt if it could. Do not forget that, much less forgive it. Do not feel sympathy for those we're attacking. Hear no pleas and look away from any tears that may endear you.

Don't sweat the press—they'll just be making movies. Protect June Watermark at all and any cost. Protect my weaponed brothers as if they were your own. Always protect each other. Last chance for questions.

There weren't any questions. Some of the soldiers were doing the pogo. Others banged fists on their shoulders and thighs.

I strike first, then no more stealth. Damage, damage, and damage, the end. Amen? I said.

"Amen," they said.

PLATOONS

VANGUARD

MACCABEE	NAKAMOOK
Gurion ben-Judah	Benji Nakamook
June Watermark	Jelly Rothstein
Eliyahu of Brooklyn	Leevon Ray
The Five	Mark Dingle
Ally'n'Googy	Salvador Curtis
Josh Berman	Fulton Market
Other armed Aptakisic Israelites	Jerry Throop

REARGUARD

PORTITE	WOLF
Vincie Portite	Ben-Wa Wolf
The Janitor	Chunkstyle
The Flunky	Anna Boshka
Ronrico Asparagus	Forrest Kenilworth
Jennie Mangey	Christian Yagoda
Ansul Entsry	Jesse Ritter
	Stevie Loop
	Cody von Braker

PIPELINE

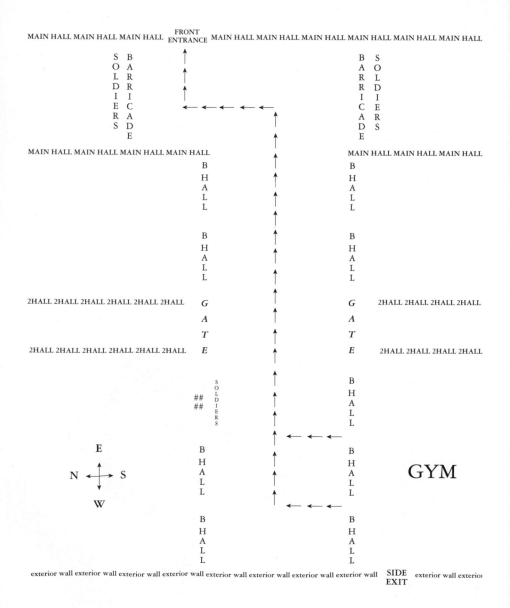

MAIN HALL MAIN HALL MAIN HALL   FRONT ENTRANCE   MAIN HALL MAIN HALL MAIN HALL MAIN HALL MAIN HALL MAIN HALL

SOLDIERS   BARRICADE   BARRICADE   SOLDIERS

MAIN HALL MAIN HALL MAIN HALL MAIN HALL   MAIN HALL MAIN HALL MAIN HALL

B HALL   B HALL

B HALL   B HALL

2HALL 2HALL 2HALL 2HALL 2HALL 2HALL *GATE*   *GATE* 2HALL 2HALL 2HALL 2HALL

2HALL 2HALL 2HALL 2HALL 2HALL 2HALL   2HALL 2HALL 2HALL 2HALL

SOLDIERS   ## ##   B HALL

E   B HALL   B HALL   **GYM**

N ← → S

W   B HALL   B HALL

exterior wall exterior wall exterior wall exterior wall exterior wall exterior wall exterior wall exterior wall **SIDE EXIT** exterior wall exterioı

= ALARM

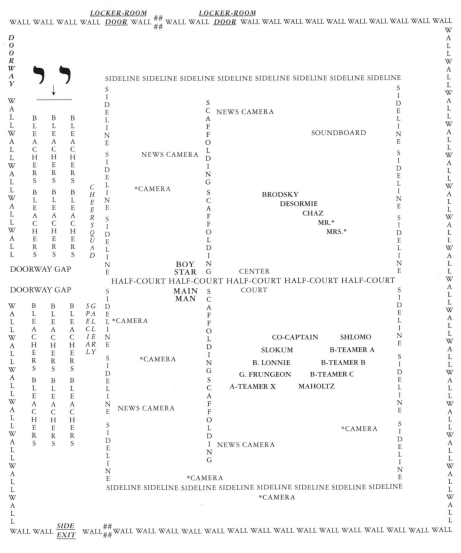

<u>LOCKER-ROOM</u> ## <u>LOCKER-ROOM</u>
WALL WALL WALL WALL <u>*DOOR*</u> WALL ## WALL WALL <u>*DOOR*</u> WALL WALL WALL WALL WALL WALL WALL WALL WALL WALL WALL

D
O
O
R
W
A
Y

↓

W A L L W A L L W A L L W A L L

BLEACHERS BLEACHERS BLEACHERS

SIDELINE SIDELINE SIDELINE SIDELINE SIDELINE SIDELINE SIDELINE SIDELINE

NEWS CAMERA

SOUNDBOARD

NEWS CAMERA

*CAMERA

BRODSKY
DESORMIE
CHAZ
MR.*
MRS.*

C H E E R S Q U A D

BOY STAR

MAIN MAN

CENTER

HALF-COURT HALF-COURT HALF-COURT HALF-COURT HALF-COURT

COURT

DOORWAY GAP

DOORWAY GAP

SCAFFOLDING SCAFFOLDING

SG PA EL CL IE AR LY

*CAMERA

*CAMERA

CO-CAPTAIN   SHLOMO
SLOKUM   B-TEAMER A
B. LONNIE   B-TEAMER B
G. FRUNGEON   B-TEAMER C
A-TEAMER X   MAHOLTZ

NEWS CAMERA

*CAMERA

NEWS CAMERA

*CAMERA

SIDELINE SIDELINE SIDELINE SIDELINE SIDELINE SIDELINE SIDELINE SIDELINE

*CAMERA

<u>SIDE EXIT</u>
WALL WALL ## WALL ## WALL WALL WALL WALL WALL WALL WALL WALL WALL WALL WALL WALL WALL WALL WALL

OUTDOORS

E

N ←→ S

W

ʼʼ =SIDE OF DAMAGE
##
=ALARM

We shut the door behind us and got beneath the bleachers. Chemicals were firing and blood was swelling muscles, lungs and arteries opened wide as runways, our joints and ligaments superelastic. Benji kept whispering, "Do not scream." We pushed on the wall and pounded our fists, twetched ponds of gooze and touched the floor standing, not to let steam off but redistribute it, to stir the snat to delay the flood. Air-seal the spout and flip the boiling kettle. Potentiate, potentiate, potentiate potential.

"I give you… Boystar," announced Chaz Black, and we gathered by the bleachers' easternmost opening.

The gym went dark and I whispered to the soldiers: Wait for my go, then stay to the borders. Look away from the light.

"Do not scream."

Feedback crackled.

Boystar spoke. "Whuddup 'Kisic."

A spotlight revealed him.

He was outside the locker-rooms, tearing off an anorak. He flung it and stood there, touching his headset. Padlock for a buckle, his belt was a tire-chain, the links hanging low between the loops and shining.

We averted our eyes as he dance-walked west, and soon our pupils were the widest in the gym.

Everyone above us stomped and clapped. Shirts came untucked. The floor shook its dust. On its own, the crowd-noise would have zeroed our footfalls, but with the enhancements effected by the man at the sound-board—machine-made enthusiasm booming at his keystrokes—we could have warcried our lungs flat and stayed undetected.

I gave my go.

Half of Portite trailed Nakamook west beneath the bleachers. The rest followed me out the same way we'd entered. We stealthed south and sin-glefile along the eastern border, our left arms brushing the wall.

On his unlit way from the locker-room to centercourt, Main Man tip-toed across our path. If he saw us, he pretended not to.

"Here we all are," said Boystar to the crowd. "At last. Together. Here we are."

The crowd roared more, some still stomping. The man at the board jacked the volume on the synth. Cheerleaders jumped in the darkness, soundless.

By the time that Boystar was halfway to halfcourt, Portite owned both of his zones: Mangey, Ronrico, and the Janitor by the locker-rooms; by the pushbar-door, Vincie, Ansul, and the Flunky. Nakamook assembled near the southwest corner. I stood behind Desormie, searching the bleachers. I bent all my fingers with all of my fingers and none of my fingers would break.

The hundreds I looked on were blind to us.

Hands forward like a boxer, Boystar fancy-footworked. "You ready?" he said. "Are you ready?" Every indicator light in the gym blinked green.

Eliyahu was sitting between the Five and Miss Pinge—western bleachers, middlemost bench. Floyd, eyes hooded, sat low in his chair in the special gallery with four local newsmen, Jelly's sister Ruth, and the New Thing fatcats. I sightlined as obliquely to the spotlight as possible, but some of the photons got in my eyes. I located June—top corner northeast, Starla beside her—then turned away south to recover dilation.

"Are you ready for some of *this?*" said Boystar. The chain around his waist clanked briefly. I didn't have to look to know what he was doing.

Giggles, many ersatz, bounced off the walls.

"Whoa!" Boystar said, hoisting his crotch. "Ha ha!" he said: a hoist for each ha, a clank at each hoist.

"Haha!" added Main Man, unlit beside him. "Ha—" he said, and his mike-feed got cut.

Hoist-clank hoist-clank giggle giggle giggle.

"You guys are crazy, you know that?" said Boystar. "I'm just dancin here. All you guys have dirty minds. E*spec*ially all you Jennys... Now, you Jennys ready to get emotionalized?"

Ecstatic moaning, mostly bogus.

My night-vision maxed.

"You ready. To get. Ro*man*tacized?"

I drew my gun. I loaded a wingnut. Proceeded on my stomach toward the spotlight.

"Are you ready. To get... In*fant*alized?"

The manufactured moans died warmly beneath a sampled orchestra's doleful tuning. The audience grown all hush and tension. A long sighing rustle of fabric, of hundreds leaning forward at once.

The principal squeezed his chin in his fist. I was coming around on his right.

Swelling cellos bled a hesitant pianoline. The lightest of drumrolls, a kind of sated cicada-sound—it murmured near the threshhold, almost subliminal. And then a tweet of birdsong. And then a muted waterfall. Boystar's mom was futzing with her purse-zipper. Nothing got by me. Slokum's popping knuckles. Chaz Black blinking rapidly to unseat a dust-mote. The music got louder, and I could still hear everything. The scratch of Brodsky's mustache against his stroking pointer. Nakamook's pulse. Jelly's kiss on his hand. The tiny suck of disrupted pomade as Boystar's father passed a comb through his hair. All the wet air Desormie pushed through his lips to prove he wasn't gay and had contempt for birds and cellos. Eliza June Watermark whispered my name.

I looked hard inside the spotlit oval, sockets tingling behind my pinned eyes.

Posed and fitted for maximum exaltation—with platforms in his boot-soles to show off his height; his fringeless kneeholes arty-yet-unslovenly; pantslegs symmetrically a-riot with buckles, decorative zippers, glued-on snaps that couldn't unsnap; his pitch-checking finger, bereft of utility, professionally pressed to his headset's earpiece; his tanktop in November attesting to his ruggedness as below it his chain-belt did his streetness; his earstud's gleam bespeaking glamour, its ¼-carat weight counterpointing at humility; his orbits shadowed and his lashes mascaraed, his ecstatic tortured saint's stare, aimed at one o'clock, thus thrown into starkest, most spectacular relief—Boystar opened his mouth to sing a sweet and abdominal measure-spanning nothing of the kind child-pop crooners who fancy themselves "vocal artists" precede all the kicks of their drumtracks with.

Had he oohed, mmmed, or even heyed, I might have targeted a different part of him. The vowel he trilled, though, the second in "robot," required so much maw-gaping I took it for a sign.

And hooded I rose before the spotlight: completely invisible to those behind Boystar; to those in the bleachers but something in the way. A sudden blackness roughly boy-shaped.

I split the penumbra and blasted.

The wingnut ricocheted between his molars. The noise of its impacts, amplified tenfold, blared from the speakers, CHUCKETA-CRACKETA. He dropped looking up and his mouth sprayed particles. A sticky mist of atomized blood, pulverized teeth, spearmint saliva.

Eliyahu was shouting, "Gurion is here!"

I cleared the pink grit from my eyes with a sleeve.

Fifty armed Israelites stood in the bleachers.

20
PROPER

Friday, November 17, 2006
10:41 a.m.–10:49 a.m.

Because otherwise scholars, once they start the next chapter, will wonder to distraction how it is I could have witnessed all that's being described, I'll clarify here: I didn't witness all of it. There's no way I could've. Not firsthand.

Yet it feels like I did. It feels like I did but, just like the rest of you, I've also seen the videos.* I've seen hundreds of the videos, many more than once, and while it's easy to conclude that what I witnessed in the gym and what I've since seen on screens have overlapped in my memory in the six years between the Damage Proper and this writing, it is not at all easy to separate the overlap's components. In fact, it's impossible. I know because I've tried.

Just yesterday, for example, I watched a clip of the Five firing down on Shlomo. It looked like I remembered, *exactly* like I remembered, and I realized my memory must have been of the clip, not the experience.

Except then, just a split-second later, where I expected to see Eliyahu vault the bleachers, the cameraman turned to a wide-eyed Ashley, and this seemed to suggest the memory of Eliyahu was not a memory of something I'd seen onscreen, but of something I'd witnessed firsthand.

Yet on second thought, I thought, it might not have been firsthand. There were, after all, nine cameras in the gym, most of them by that time filming, and Eliyahu's leap may have been recorded with one of the other eight— I might have been remembering that camera's footage from another video.

So I checked the footage and, sure enough, the Fox News cameraman had captured the airborne Eliyahu, and so had the CBS guy. But then again, yet again, that didn't mean I hadn't witnessed it firsthand as well.

I might have witnessed any of it firsthand is the thing. From centercourt you could see anything in the gym. You could see anything in the gym from

---

* Though, unlike most of you, I tend to close my browser the moment any footage of the so-called "11/17 Miracle" intrudes.

nearly anywhere in the gym, just not everything at once. I could have seen any of what I remember, but I could not have seen all of it, yet I remember seeing all of it. At least I seem to.

"But so why, in light of your memory's unreliability," wonder scholars, "why write *any* of the scene, Rabbi? After all, there are, as you've already mentioned, those thousands of videos. Why not just point us toward one or two—even ten—of the best? Certainly most of them are chazerai and narishkeit. Certainly most of them—particularly those second-class mash-ups inspired by the latest in user-friendly software, crafted with mouseclicks and readymade algorithms by spendy technologists who claim to believe that authorship is just a kind of editing, who confuse DIY with owning an iMac, and artfulness for art, and Bal with Adonai: all those rap- and ska- and punk-scored fanvids; all those rapmetal-soundtracked hatervids; those fishlensed and widescreened and retro-black-and-whited; those overdubbed with soundbytes from rabbis and governors; those spliced with your baby pictures and paintings by June, with scenes from Columbine and the Seung-Hui Cho biopic, stills from the Six Day and the Yom Kippur Wars; and the ones with the halos cartooned on your heads, the ones with the halos on the heads of your enemies, those captioned with verses from Ezekiel and Judges, those with their titles atop Israeli flags, the ones that are bordered with stars of David, the Black Power ones that darken your skintone, the Gun Lobby ones that redden all the blood, the ones from the contest held by Al Jazeera, the ones from the festival funded quietly by Marlboro; the splitscreened ones with the footage on the right and the GIDEON MACYNTIRE: COM-ING OF RAGE RPG on the left, their auteurs moving their Gurion-shaped avatars through virtual ballcourts and doorways and bleachers (past bleed-ing STELLARKIDs and spooky LEAVE-OFFs, in the background SLAM HOKUMs cursing BANJO NICKYNACKs, ENDURING JANE PAPER-STAMPs proclaiming love for GIDEONs, JELLO ROSENs biting HEATH-ERs, and so on) in as much the same pattern and at as much the same pace as the filmed you in those filmed settings moves as possible... and all the rest of their ilk—are for the birds. Surely they are. Surely, surely. But what," wonder scholars, "about all the others? like the more straightforward, docu-mentary-type ones? What about the video your father commissioned? What couldn't the right one or few of those show us that a description in here could? Why include the Damage Proper in the scripture at all?"

To all of these questions, the best answer first: Torah is written. The one perfect narrative in the world is written, and not by default—not because

Adonai, Creator of the Universe, lacked the technology it takes to make movies, nor because our ancient Israelite ancestors, for whom He bled rivers, split seas, and made manna, lacked the technology to play them—but because truth is best, if not exclusively, conveyed in writing.

The second best answer (for those with a more Nakamookian bent): Video is the chosen medium of tyrants, and that's not because tyrants lack print technology, but rather because video cannot be examined as rigorously as can the written word. It cannot be as deeply plumbed—at least not yet. The reality a given video does or doesn't convey, even without effects (allowing, hypothetically, that rendering three dimensions as two isn't a host of effects in itself), cannot be fully parsed = The viewer can all too easily mistake realism for reality. E.g., every actor in a movie is wearing makeup, but few of them ever seem to be.

Furthermore, while filmed imagery may very well be possessed of a grammar, that grammar is either mostly unknown to us or changing at a pace with which we can't keep up. It's impossible to tell. Video *may* be like a beautiful girl whose every genuine emotion, thought, and intention gets betrayed by the expressiveness of her brow, but that's of no consequence if we don't look at her brow. And we don't, scholars. Not at all. We can't take our eyes off those fulsome... lips.

I could go on to enumerate video's other problems—the thousands of ways in which the medium starves the muscles off signifiers, draping the bones that remain in sculpted fat—but that would, at this point, be redundant, I think. In any case, it'd be condescending. You're well past page 798 by now. Were you not a scholar when you began this book, you've certainly become one, and you know it in your heart: books are truer than movies; when they are books of scripture, they are truer, even, than what they describe.

So the perspective you'll get in this Damage Proper's telling is that of the first-person-limited omniscient. This is not, of course, because I know everything, but rather because of my particular type of ignorance: because I don't know how I know what I know, and there is no way to figure it out. First-person omniscience plus this disclaimer—it's the only honest option. It's the best I can do.

And lest that last line be read falsely, lest it read humble or apologetic, let me append it:

The best I can do is the best that can be done. I am the author of all of this.

GYMNASIUM at 10:41 AM on 11/17/06

LOCKER-ROOM   *LOCKER-ROOM*
WALL WALL WALL WALL *DOOR* WALL ## WALL WALL *DOOR* WALL WALL WALL WALL WALL WALL WALL WALL WALL
                                  ##

```
D                                                                                    W
O                    ʏʏ ʏʏ    ʏʏ ʏʏ ʏʏ                                                A
O                                                                                    L
R                                                                                    L
W                                                                                    W
A        SIDELINE SIDELINE SIDELINE SIDELINE SIDELINE SIDELINE SIDELINE SIDELINE     A
Y                                                                                    L
                        S                                                    S       L
W                       I             S                                       I      W
A                       D             C   NEWS CAMERA                         D      A
L                       E             A                                       E      L
L                       L             F                           SOUNDBOARD  L      L
W                       I             F                                       I      W
A                       N             O                                       N      A
L                       E             L                                       E      L
L                           NEWS CAMERA  D                                    L      L
W                       S             I                                       S      W
A                       I             N                                       I      A
L                       D             G                                       D      L
L                       E             S                                       E      L
W                       L   *CAMERA   C                                       L      W
A                       I             A        BRODSKY                        I      A
L                       N             F          DESORMIE                     N      L
L                       E             F            CHAZ                        E      L
W       C               S             O             MR.*                       S     W
A       H               I             L               MRS.*                    I     A
L       E               D             D                                        D     L
L       E               E             I                                        E     L
W       R               L             N                                        L     W
A       S               I             G                                        I     A
L       Q               N    ʏʏ  ‐BOY‐  G      CENTER                          N     L
L       U               E        ‐STAR‐                                        E     L
DOORWAY GAP     HALF-COURT HALF-COURT HALF-COURT HALF-COURT HALF-COURT               L
        D               S      MAIN  S      COURT                              S     W
DOORWAY GAP             I      MAN   C                                         I     A
W                       D   L*CAMERA F                                         D     L
A   SG   P              E             O                                        E     L
L   PA   E              L             L   CO-CAPTAIN    SHLOMO                  L     W
L   EL   C              I             D     SLOKUM    B-TEAMER A               I     A
W   CL   L  S           N             I                                        N     L
A   IE   E  I  *CAMERA  E             N   B. LONNIE    B-TEAMER B              E     L
L   AR   A  D           S             G     G. FRUNGEON  B-TEAMER C           S      L
L   LY   C  E           I             S   A-TEAMER X    MAHOLTZ                I      W
W        H  L           D             C                                        D     A
A        E  I           E             A                                        E     L
L        R  N  NEWS CAMERA L          F                                        L     L
L        S  E           I             F                    *CAMERA             I     W
W                       N             O                                        N     A
A                       E             L   NEWS CAMERA                          E     L
L                       S             D                                        S     L
L                       I             I                                        I     W
W                       D             N                                        D     A
A                       E   *CAMERA   G                                        E     L
L        SIDELINE SIDELINE SIDELINE SIDELINE SIDELINE SIDELINE SIDELINE SIDELINE L    L
W                                *CAMERA                              ʏʏ       L      W
A         ʏʏ ʏʏ ʏʏ                                          ʏʏ ʏʏ ʏʏ  ʏʏ       L      A
L                                                                    ʏʏ        L      L
```

WALL WALL *SIDE* ## WALL WALL WALL WALL WALL WALL WALL WALL WALL WALL WALL WALL WALL WALL WALL
        EXIT ##

OUTDOORS

E

N ← | → S

W

ʏʏ = SIDE OF DAMAGE

= ALARM

□   □   □   □   □

Disoriented basketballers cursing in pain, Nakamook's soldiers reloading. The Five plugged Shlomo in the eyes with pennies. Eliyahu of Brooklyn vaulted five bleachers. Desormie mumbling hey-nows ten feet east of me, Main Man two-stepping three feet west of me. Brooklyn landing, scanning for Baxter. June was equipping up in her corner, Israelites all across the bleachers were equipping, and all those around them remained ass-to-bench, the Shovers and bandkids and robots alike, and the Jennys and Ashleys, and the everykid no-ones, immobile as anvils, as hunted opposums, pillars of salt, anonymous animals all gawking courtward: here lay Boystar; there stood Gurion; sillhouettes, stage right, were ducking, scrambling; Brodsky as static as his name on a page.

A switch sent current through a circuit when the drums kicked. Panels of lights strobed. Movement looked gapped.

I fell upon Boystar's chest knees-first, swiping his headset to throw it to Main Man—the rumble of the gooze in Scott's clearing throat failed to boom like it should have; his feed was still dead—but a keyring was streaking, Boystar's mother's, a blur getting thicker in the corner of my eye. I blocked it, just barely, with the hand that held the headset. The ring's junior maglight cracked the mouthpiece on contact. An asterisk of keys splayed on Boystar's chin. Its rabbit's foot, yellow, made his blood look orange. The rape whistle under his nostrils chirped. His mother had the mike by the cord and she swung it. On my knees, I couldn't dodge but wouldn't bow, so I turned. My kidney took the blow. I saw white and she tackled me. Ten seconds in, I was already down.

Co-Captain Baxter was still in his chair, a wide-open target, well within range. Brooklyn, just north of the northern sideline, raised his weapon, pulled the balloon back, shut one eye, and aimed. And aimed.

Nakamook knelt in a V-formation. From its apex, rearmost, Benji yelled, "Barnum!" The rest of the platoon yelled, "Barnum! Barnum!" Slokum extracted a nib from his biceps. Another grazed his cheek and he cupped it and ducked.

Shlomo Cohen: hit multiply, reduced to a speedbump.

"Hey," said Desormie, and then he said, "Hey now!" A nib from above nicked his dextral trapezius. It was meant for the mom, but June's elbow'd got knocked. Some kids in the bleachers had started to jostle, risen robots and Israelites blocking their vistas. Most Israelites weren't bothering to sight. They projected from the hip at Shovers in arm's reach. The Shovers cried out, covered up, got shot more.

The tracers the lightpanels left on your eyeballs were blue and wormy if you looked at the filaments.

Brooklyn kept aiming.

"Barnum!" "Barnum!" "Barnum! Barnum!" "Clear out his lackeys!" Benji ordered his soldiers.

"Excuse me, sir, please, Mr. Mussel, sir, please, but with the height of your stature and the strength of your vision, and this kindness they are speaking every day all the day, all these boys in the band who they play on their horns on my schoolbus to practice to win your fond praise, can you find my good friend who is Beauregard Pate, please, or please to return to a seated position on the bench that you stand so I may see with my own eyes to find my friend Beauregard?"

B-teamers raced for the pushbar-door. Vincie felled the first with a nose-smashing hexnut. The Flunky double-clotheslined the other two.

The gym teacher's soundgun was ten feet away from me, slung from his neck by a thong like a purse. I wanted to get it for Main Man to sing through, but Boystar's mom had me pinned and was biting. Twenty seconds in, I was the only soldier down, and Israelites descending—*from the bleachers*, haters—were finally on their way to help me.

Before you get to the point where you don't know what hit you, you have to know that you've been hit; before knowing you've been hit, you have to know who you are. Some in the gym knew better than others. At one extreme was Boystar's mom, who knew all along she was Boystar's mom: she got shot in the son and she counterattacked. At the other extreme were those Shovers in the bleachers whose bodies had yet to take any punishment: even those who noticed the cries of their fellows—to be sure, many failed to, their attention on the court—didn't yet equate those cries with pain, let alone pain brought on by projectiles sent by Israelites out to end Shovers.

Between these extremes was everyone else who wasn't an Israelite or on the Side. The ones who *did* know that they'd been hit—Slokum, for instance, who couldn't fail to realize his pain originated from external forces (the nibs he plucked from his muscles testified); or any given Shover point-blanked in the face—were, as yet, unaware of what hit them; *what*, in this case, meaning *who*; *who*, in this case, being *we*. And as for how to respond, and whether to respond (which of those decisions gets arrived at first depends less on knowledge than temperament): even for the quickest of those directly stricken, that was still seconds away. For now, they could but duck and cover, or flee their location, or waste some prayers.

The robots, for the most part, knew who they were, and they knew the Arrangement was taking damage. Despite their lack of pain, the damage overwhelmed them, for the hits came from everywhere: kids on the floor who pulled on balloons, kids in the bleachers who pulled on balloons, the mother of a kid who'd been attacked with a balloon, and all those around them jostling and jumping, and the ones who were pushing toward higher ground, who weren't so much looking for a spot to stand safely as searching for a view with a wider sweep.

And they, the vast majority, these everykid no-ones, these X-factors factioning at the simplest level—whether they knew it or not, they were pro or anti, on the Side or against the Side, and in no case merely on the side—they cheered in their hearts, if not yet with their lungs, for victory for this one here and the fall of that one over there, though victory for that one there and the fall of this one over here would certainly do in a pinch. As long as they got to be close to the fight.

They always liked to be close to the fight. They always liked to cheer a side and call that side the underdog; to stand, in their hearts, behind that underdog; to stand, in some cases, on their feet beside him. Yet they stood in most cases *around* all the fighters, siding as much with the fight itself as they sided with their underdog; their bodies bricks in walls they formed to stop robotic interference, to let it be had out.

Of course Jennys and Ashleys had flinched and moaned when Boystar's mouth did its gory explosion. Of course most everyone, and especially the

Shovers, wanted to see Bam Slokum kill Benji, or if they didn't yet see it was Benji who was shooting, then whoever it was who was attacking Slokum. And of course it is possible that I make it too simple, that deep inside all of them were latent desires and motivations that pushed against those which these factions would (or even could) profess—that maybe the Jennys and Ashleys were relieved to see Boystar's face made ugly, that maybe they thought his ugliness would give them a better shot at being loved by him, or maybe the ugliness freed them of their love for him, which, unrequieted, had been causing them pain, and maybe *that's* why they didn't rush the floor, but then again maybe they were just frozen from heartbreak; and maybe the Shovers (like so many others who miss the point of worship) contained in their worship a streak of envy, a desire to discover Slokum wasn't so great as they'd always suspected or feared, and that may be why *they* didn't rush the floor, but then maybe they just thought he could protect himself, just give him a second to get his bearings, Slokum the king, Slokum the beloved— but latent desires and motivations, if they do exist (I suspect they don't, my mother is sure of it, Adonai doesn't care), are, at least in here, inadmissable. Even if they were, in fact, present, they'd be too complicated for me to describe with confidence: I didn't know most of these people at all.

So let it for now suffice to say they'd all been stunned, at least a little; all through the gym the stun wore off in phases, and the velocity at which these phases got passed through varied so widely, person-to-person, and the variance itself did as much in the way of dividing those we'd conquer as the very acts of violence that had at first stunned them. We knew who we were, the Side and the Israelites, and the rest, if not learning, were at least getting taught.

The suckerpunch is not so-named for its puncher.

June spinal-kicked an Ashley in the row below hers. Cameramen parried and panned and zoomed. Boystar's whispers came booming through the speakers—a pre-recorded vocal track to sexy up the verses. "Fan-ta-size, girl, fan-ta-size." Kids avalanched slo-mo under force of the Ashley, laughing as they tumbled, groping and punching, doubling the sightlines available to June. Chaz Black went sprinting to the soundboard for cover. Desormie sat squat near the east leg of scaffolding, calling Floyd's name through the megaphone.

Brodsky pulled Boystar's mom off my body. She kicked at the air and he turned and dropped her. Her husband sprung up, threw a textbook left hook. Brodsky got nose on his chin and cried out. I snicked out the sap and kneecapped the husband. He fell on his ass on his son and thrashed. Israelites got there and shot him til he stopped, Berman among them, and the cousins Kravitz-Segal. The mother, who'd landed with her knee in her sternum, rolled side-to-side to stimulate her lungs. Mustache grisly, auto-tears blinding him, Brodsky walked backwards in half-steps.

Floyd stood his chair and spat through his cone. Out the central exit, swiftly, walked Ruth Rothstein, two of the newsmen, and the New Thing fatcats. Klapper came off the bleachers to follow them, smiling a little, shrugging, amused, and Hector the Janitor followed Mr. Klapper. The other two news-men went looking for their cameramen.

Brooklyn still north of the northern sideline. Brooklyn still aiming, still not shooting. Brooklyn still this, still that, just still. He lowered his weapon, chewed on his lips. He raised it and aimed again, chewing his lips. He threw down his weapon and picked it back up. He pocketed his weapon. His burning eyes burned. No few lines of fire lay between him and Baxter. He covered his eyes and prayed the Sh'ma.

Starla socked the Shover beside her on the ear. The Shover grabbed a neigh-bor and they plummeted in tandem. Two kids they bumped as they fell began to skirmish. Those two bumped three and those three began to skir-mish. Her corner cleared of blockage, June reloaded.

"Barnum!" "Barnum!" "Barnum! Barnum!" Leevon and Jelly broke ranks to flank Main Man, who'd back-pedaled into the Nakamook V. They safed him in the corner and returned to formation, and he kicked off his medley of Marley unamplified.

Brooklyn finished praying and flew between the missiles. Three steps from Baxter, he lowered a shoulder; on impact, he lifted and pushed. They trav-elled a yard, Eliyahu carrying, til Slokum kicked a chair at his knees and he tripped but, holding on tight, brought Baxter down with him. A nib pinned Slokum's tie to his sternum; he took a step back, inhaled, and plucked it. His wince was whole-bodied, but there wasn't much blood. A second nib buzzed his left temple and he ducked. Benji yelled, "Lackeys! Aim at his lackeys! Clear out his lackeys!"

"A hammer, a hammer, a hammer," Scott sang.

Shlomo Cohen: still a speedbump, still getting hit multiply. Frungeon laid a chair on its side to wall him off. Pennies and blows drove Shovers to the floor. "Beauregard!" "Izzy! Izzy! Over here!" "In-fant-a-lize, girl, fan-ta-size." Fifteen people, at most, had fled the gym.

Ally reached a hand down and pulled me to my feet. Googy doffed his ski-cap and did a kind of jig. The Chewer, off his chair now, stepped in our direction.

    The face, I said to the Israelites behind me.

    Three went forward, shot Floyd in the face. He staggered, sat down. Seven more shot him.

    Keys, I said.

    Berman went for the keys.

    "Should I keep them or—"

    No.

    Berman tossed me the keys.

    The principal, waxen, held onto his nose.

The Five shooting Frungeon, Frungeon falling back.

June's avalanche ended remarkably well. Twenty kids formed a pile five-wide by the sideline, the only bones broken a couple of fingers. They rolled over each other, some trying to rise, some crawling to flee, others still having fun, and the Janitor pot-shot the ones who were rising, Ronrico put Chucks to the guts of the crawlers, and Mangey was muttering, "You're the fucker," and firing on fuckers who'd gone off the side.

"I said clear his lackeys! The A-team! The B-team!" "We are!" "We have!" "None of them are running!" "They're sticking by Slokum!" "And you guys keep shooting him!" "We keep shooting all of them!" "It's true, baby, look: we've hit every one of them. We're *hitting* every one of them."

Another twelve Israelites had descended to the floor. Half roved the north sideline, clipping fleeing Shovers. The other half occupied the gap between the bleachers, dropping the Shovers the first half failed to.

Desormie crept westward, a chair in each hand. A cameraman fell, cradling his camera. Salvador Curtis said, "Oopsie," reloaded. "Ori is down," said the cameraman's newsman, who bent over Ori to look in his lens. "Our cameraman's down. We don't know what hit him. Do you have any idea what hit you, Ori?" "Something must have hit me," said Ori. "My dick hurts."

Empty your pockets.
      "Whud?" said Brodsky.

The skirmishes Starla had vectored grew thicker. "Infantalize, you tantalize, undressalize you with my eyes." A cheerleader was chewing on a cheerleader's hand. Next to them, cheerleaders oohed and hugged. Next to them, cheerleaders cheered.

"Why won't they run?" "Cause they're *sticking by Slokum*." "No one's asking you, Dingle." "Mark's right, though, Benji—he makes them feel safe." "Safe?" "Well, safer." "How safer? Why safer?" "He's Slokum," said Jelly.

Brooklyn and Baxter thrashed horizontally, struggling for leverage, squid-shaped, headbutts, gouging, headbutts. Brooklyn rose first, but he took friendly fire—a Dingle-shot quarter, thwack to the ballbag. He dropped to one knee and Maholtz decked him.

Empty your pockets.
      "Emmdy my *poggeds*?"
      A penny struck Brodsky's shin and he hopped.
      Who did that? I said.
      Berman said, "Me."
      He's our prisoner, I said.
      "Okay," said Berman.

There wasn't any action by the push-bar door. The clotheslined B-teamers weren't getting up, the one who took the hexnut in the nose had turned back, and no one in the gym approached the alarm. Vincie told Ansul and the Flunky: "Triangulate." "Don't call me names—we're friends," said the Flunky. "With Benji," Ansul tried to explain. "No, we're *all* friends, Ansul."

"Fucken shoot at the basketballers Nakamook's shooting." "Nakamook the boy or platoon?" said the Flunky. "Same fucken thing, Richard." "Richard's long for Dick, Vincie. Friends call me Flunky."

"Safer cause just cause he's Slokum you're saying." "Yeah," said Jelly, "but except not *just*. Take a look around the court. Take a look at who ran." Jelly pointed north, toward the pushbar-door exit, at the clotheslined B-teamers splayed before the Flunky. "Okay," Benji said. "Fine," Benji said. "Fuck," he said. "So what should we do, baby? Tell us what to do. You want us to charge them?" "I want you to *clear* them so I can charge *him*." "So then we should… what?" "Just keep on—fuck! Keep shooting, I guess. Them, though. Not him. Shoot 'em in the faces, though. Shoot 'em in the eyes. Lay them all out. Get them out of the way."

The guns of Nakamook were obsolescing anyway. For each of their projectiles that hit its mark, four or five went wild. Even twenty seconds earlier—when the Indians, clustered, were still a big static target—this hadn't been much of a problem: the novices' wild shots had often struck lucky. But as the target moved apart, reflexively at first, becoming multiple targets with alleys between them, the currency and fasteners blew through the spaces, failing to damage, and the soldiers, frustrated, aimed worse and worse, and the Indians began to move with more purpose. Slokum flipped a chair and held it like a shield, dragged Baxter by an ankle toward halfcourt. Desormie crossed halfcourt and gave a chair to Lonnie. Maholtz grabbed a chair and they all crouched together, holding their chairs before them by the legs, shouting for their teammates to help form a bulwark. It was half a good strategy and, before it got whole, Benji needed to rush them with all of his soldiers, but he stayed in the corner, married to his strategy.

"A rammer," Scott sang, "a rammer, a rammer."

A misfired wingnut smashed part of a lightpanel, CHUCKETA-CRACK-ETA-CRACKETA-CHUCKETA. Plastic and glass got splintered and whirled. The burst bulbs retarding the stutter of the photons, the strobe effect slackened, devolved to mere flashing. Eliyahu of Brooklyn limped south to the wall, leaned on a gym mat, mumbled in Hebrew. In search of Big Ending's remaining three chubniks, Beauregard and Isadore roamed the west bleachers.

"…and if you end this, now—"

Pockets, Mr. Brodsky.

"…I can tell the police that you saw the error—"

I see no error.

"But if you—"

I see no error and you're wrong either way. Look, I said, at this.

I whipped out Monitor Botha's claw.

In the bleachers, the robots had all come unstunned. Some made attempts to evacuate their students, others cleared paths to get the fallen out first, and others yet shouted for everyone to sit. The few who tried to stop fights took hits. At first, the hits, however predictable—the robots kept stepping between kids who swung blindly—were completely accidental, and for the most part glancing: knees banged shins and elbows grazed asses, not personal at all, no harm no foul. But as the skirmishes spread, the hits came harder and they came more frequently: kids saw kids who hit robots go unstepped, and they began to manufacture their accidents = friends shoving friends so the shoved could bump robots, a tactic inspired by the pervs who pulled sly-gropes on girls in the hallways who didn't like flirting. "I'm sorry, Melissa. I had to hold something. If I didn't hold something, I'd have fallen—John tripped me." "I tripped him, Melissa, and I'm sorry you got held, but you saw how he tripped me when I fell onto Kelly." Actual sly-gropes were happening, too. Big Ending reunited behind the sitting bandkids, exchanging high-fives, and huddling to plot. "I've got to reach Mt. Zion," sang Main Main.

"You fantasize, infantalize, romantacize what I mentalize: it's not your eyes, girl, it's not your eyes." This was the last of Boystar's whispers. Half another measure and the speakers went dead: running from the soundboard to the northeast exit, Chaz Black kicked cords and wires tore out. "Jah put I around," sang Scott. Starla spotted her boyfriend and jumped on a Jenny crushed by the avalanche, ran up the sideline, achieved Western Portite, got pecked on the cheek and pinched and armed. "This thing won't hit who I aim at," said the Flunky. "…what look to be coins," one newsman was saying. "…writing on their foreheads," the other one said. Ori the cameraman: back on his feet.

High-speed currency deflecting off seatpads sounds like knuckles getting cracked through sleeves. In an effort to overcome the bulwark from a distance, Western Portite and Nakamook tilted their weapons like infantry archers so their shots would rain down from above on the Indians, but Benji and Vincie were both out of nibs, and while a few of the fasteners and coins reached their targets, their impact was weak, and the damage inflicted was minor at best, though Maholtz, when crown-struck did yelp "Jeendzus!"

I was brandishing the monitor's claw at the principal. Before understanding, he reached for it—*thwick*—and then he was cradling his wrist.
>   What'd I say?
>   "He's our prisoner,'" Berman said. "And I know, but he was trying—"
>   No he wasn't.
>   "Well he isn't cooperating."
>   He was just about to.
>   "Stop this, Gurion."
>   "See?" said Berman.
>   Don't—
Bad shadow. I grabbed onto Berman and brought us down sideways, twanging my humerus. The base of the mike-stand splintered the hardwood—Boystar's mother, back like a slasher.

Big Ending shoved a teacher and the teacher said, "Careful." They shoved him again, and he told them, "Watch out." Beauregard Pate warned the teacher, "You should fear us," and the teacher turned away, as if he hadn't heard. Big Ending rammed the teacher into another. Both teachers fell on three bandkids and Mussel. All six involved hit the floor in a heap, the clattering instruments bruising their softparts. Next to the heap stood the atheist seventh-grade Shover, Trent Vander. Vander extended his pointer and laughed, and Seamus Fitzsimmons, who played the bassoon, who the Shovers, since the fifth, had called "Faggot Shitzlemons," stood where he'd sat on the bottom bleacher: above moaning friends atop their bent horns, over bandleader Mussel who'd always brought donuts, before the pointing Shover paralytic with mirth. Seamus held his woodwind by the boot-joint and swung it. When he pulled it back to swing again, its reed was chunked with earlobe. Vander blacked out and dropped on the heap. Thirty-odd bandkids understood they held weapons.

The mother hauled back to swing once more, got stopped from above by a

nib through the jaw muscle. Instant bloodstar under the hairline. Holding
her cheek, she began to sit down, and the stand, as she collapsed, dropped
from her grasp, and its base struck the foot of the principal edgewise, right
above the tongue of his shoe. He buckled, went fetal, and let out a choked
sound. Snapped was the tendon connecting his bigtoe. My girlfriend the
deadeye showed me a powerfist. I showed her the palm on the arm that
wasn't fizzing = Stay high, I love you, keep sniping, protect us. Berman
crawled over to see the mother's face.

The untapped rage of the bullied musician, mounting for years, suddenly
loosed.

Seamus Fitzsimmons led his band upward, stalking for Shovers in the
western bleachers, but anyone who stood in their way got clouted, and anyone clouted who dropped got stomped, and anyone stomped who kept laying there... stomped.

Mangey caught an elbow from a runner in the forehead. Ronrico dragged
the runner to the floor by the shirt. A Shover bolted over to help them kick
the runner. They pinned him to the wall between the doors of the locker-
rooms, the lightswitches mounted there got flipped to ON, and the whole
gym was lit by the overhead fixtures. Ronrico cracked the Shover on the eye
while Mangey held him. "Do not try to be us." "Do not try to be us." "Do
not try to be us do not try to be us."

When the lights came up, Seamus and a flautist, atop the western bleachers,
along their eastern edge, held a broken Blake Acer by all four limbs, and
Acer shrieked, "Please!" and he was louder than anyone. Nearly all of the
spectating everykid no-ones[*] revolved to locate the source of the shriek, yet
few of their eyes ever got to Acer; the trail of the stomped left behind by
the bandkids captured their attention first. That trail was becoming wider
and wider, and except for the wealth of bare necks among the stomped (or,
inversely, the scarcity of scarved ones), there was nothing more conspicuous than the spatters of blood that beaded the brass and stained the white
bibbers: nothing more striking than who was stomping except for who it

---

[*] To be clear: such spectators were, as yet, legion. If that's failed to come across, blame Genesis and Exodus
for training my narrative eye on action, for training it away from relative stasis. Despite the avalanche and
the multiplying skirmishes, and despite the attacks on the Shovers by the Israelites, the movement of at least
half the kids in the bleachers—before, that is, the bandkids got their snat up—was still dedicated to blocking robotic interference in the course of manuevering for vistas.

was that was getting stomped. The implications for the everykid no-ones were huge. Under whose gaze hadn't the bandkids suffered the undeserved enmity of Shovers? No one's. Yet who'd ever protected a bandkid from a Shover? Who'd ever defended a bandkid but a bandkid? Who'd ever done other than laugh when one fell, let alone offered a hand to help him up? No one and no one and no one and no one. The everykid no-ones fled the bleachers in droves.

In the meantime, Bam had discovered his advantage. He turned his chair over, legs forward, said, "Guys!" and when the rest of the Indians turned their chairs over, he led them forth crouching in lock-step, a phalanx, and at last Benji Nakamook did what needed doing. The platoon close behind him, their fists at the ready, he pocketed his weapon and charged northeast. Seeing their approach, Bam halted his march and stood higher to strike, to cut Benji down. At three steps distance, Benji sprung. He went horizontal, body turning mid-air, and clipped three Indians at once at the neck. Lonnie and Maholtz, who'd been flanking Bam, hit the floor loud, chairs flying, skidding. Bam dropped his chair and caught Benji on impact. They went down together, a T-shape, Bam-first. Nakamook barrelled through the gap Benji'd opened. Eliyahu came sprinting off the wall to help. Main Man remained in the southwest corner. "Never give the power to the baldhead," he sang. Slokum, half-stunned, still their T's crossbar, groaned beneath Benji, who blindly reached down the length of his torso, feeling around until he found nose, and swatted with the heel of his palm, saying, "Hi!" He swatted twice more—"Hi! Hello!"—and then planted the hand that had done the swatting on the mess of Bam's face, now slick with blood, and started to push, attempting to rise, but Bam turned his head, and Benji's hand slipped, and Salvador Curtis, in the midst of a fists-forward superman dive—the gym teacher's gabardined bulge the bullseye—clipped Benji's temple with the toes of both shoes, and Benji's weight shifted to Slokum's advantage. Bam got an arm free, got leverage, turned sideways, cracked Benji deep in the ribs with an elbow. Benji curled up. Bam flipped himself prostrate, then bucked to all fours. Benji, thrown, hit the floor coughing, and Brooklyn, who was grappling with Co-Captain Baxter, using the kid's own tie to strangle him, took a step back to anchor the choke, landing a heel on Benji's kidney. Benji thrashed and cursed and coughed more. Brooklyn flailed and lost his purchase, used both hands to break his fall. Baxter wheezed and clutched his throat. On Slokum someone dropped a chair. It wasn't the first chair to be mismanaged, nor should that fact come as any surprise. Most people can't make a good fist when the time comes (their snat floods too early, boils them rubbery), let alone apply any kind of strong grip—their barrels wobble, their cudgels slip—and the Aptakisic Indians, in this, were unexceptional. Not even one had swung his chair more than once, let alone aimed for anyone's head. The chairs they didn't drop were pried from their hands or shoved in their guts, the dropped ones pitched from the fray by Jerry Throop while Leevon and Dingle mashed faces with their foreheads, and Jelly bit a B-teamer in the middle of the forehead, and Fulton checked Maholtz, who'd just gotten up, then kneedropped Lonnie, who hadn't gotten up, and Desormie, in child-pose, struggled to recover from Curtis's sackblast, and Curtis came around and kicked him in the crack, and Shlomo Cohen hobbled toward the pushbar door, and Eliyahu, crawling toward Co-Captain Baxter, tripped Gary Frungeon by yanking his ankle, and Frungeon, falling, brought Curtis with him, and Benji and Slokum kept trying to rise.

You'll be okay, I said. I'm not here to hurt you. None of us are, just—
    Brodsky dry-heaved.
    That's nerves, I said. You aren't really sick. You're nothing like dying. You're doing that to yourself. Now I'm just gonna empty your pockets, I said, and I'm gonna be gentle, I know you're in pain, I can see that your foot hurts, but I can also see that your foot will be fine—there isn't any blood there, no bones poking through, you don't have to keep contorting, there's nothing to *see*—but these guys who are standing behind me, watching, they're wound really tight, and they've all got weapons, so please don't make any sudden movements. Please just don't even move at all. If you can just breathe deep and stop with the contortions, you won't get hurt more. You have my word. This isn't about you. This is just how it is. Okay? Okay. I'm reaching in the pocket of your jacket now. You don't have to say bubkes. I'll find what I need.

Seamus and the flautist had thrown Acer on those Israelites who'd gone to the gap to repel fleeing Shovers. Five of the six so dropped upon had crumpled, and just as the two least injured got up, the mob from the bleachers ran them back down. Now robots and kids tripped on robots and kids, and a hill of writhing bodies that was one, then two, then three feet high, grew wide in the gap til it was nearly impassable. Many in the gap continued pushing forward, and a few of them got out, however bruised, to flee the school through the pipeline. Others turned south to escape the bottleneck and go out the northeast- or the pushbar-door-exit, but pressing as they were against those who were northbound, this only caused the bottleneck to clog up more. It is true that some managed to keep reason intact, and they headed sideways, under the bleachers, to proceed toward either of the other two exits, but while many of those who went first escaped, the pushbar-door-exit itself soon bottlenecked. That exit was narrow as a classroom door, and runners on their way to it who didn't get shot or smacked down by Western Portite kept stumbling on the B-teamers who the Flunky had clotheslined, seeding a pileup to rival the gap's. The northeast exit was unobstructed and, despite all the blows Eastern Portite administered, the first hundred who'd initially fled there got out, but by the time that the runners who'd tried the other exits first (roughly four hundred) and could still ambulate (roughly three-hundred-fifty) realized they had to head to the northeast one, the powerdrunk bandkids had descended like berserkers and kids were hitting kids to get out of their way, and those hit hitting back, and robots too, and the throng pushed south toward the least resistance, slowly but steadily, creeping like a honeyspill across a tilted plane, the honey sipped by Samson from the lion's tilted brainpan.

Benji sitting up, Benji holding his ribs. Slokum in a three-point stance, Slokum lunging. Blurring bodies colliding around them.

In a room full of people you've known for a while, when somebody's elbow jams sharp in your sternum, it's hard not to take that personally; it's hard to believe that you could've been anyone. It's harder yet, when you find yourself thrilled by the damage *you're* bringing, to believe you don't have your own good reasons. "Call *me* fat, slut? You ruined third grade." "On the bus with your motherfucken jerkoff spitballs!" "You don't tell girls they can't go to the bathroom!" "Who's crying now, huh? Who's bleeding now?" "I don't show my work cause I do it in my head!" The further south the throng went, the more reasons it discovered. Vendettas once sworn for half-forgotten offenses were remembered and invented with each passing blow. Everyone felt like a conduit of justice.

The Janitor, bashed in the orbit with a trumpet, got dragged from the mob by Mangey and Asparagus.

The Indians/Nakamook ruction had atomized. Mano-a-manos now thrived unimpeded: Baxter/Brooklyn (choking, clawing), Frungeon/Jelly (biting, pleading), Lonnie/Leevon (dukes up, boxing), Maholtz/Dingle (slapping, spitting). Fulton, Throop, and Salvador Curtis divided between them what remained of the B-team (pinning, leglocks, chicken-winging). And Slokum and Benji were tangled again: Benji's thumbs, Slokum's temples; Slokum's forearm, Benji's throat. A-teamer X extended a hand; the gym teacher pulled himself onto his feet.

"*Your* family's ugly." "*Your* brother's gay." "*Your* juicebox, friendo—I'll drink it!"

I found Brodsky's keys and phone in his pockets, put them in mine. He said "Don't" twice, but didn't fight back. Berman, who knelt beside Boystar's mother, was admiring the nib that he'd plucked from her cheek. The Israelites behind us stepped back and stepped back as Ally said my name, then said it again, and the riot of runners-cum-fighters encroached. I ordered the Israelites to move Brodsky south so he wouldn't get trampled, and four came forward and lugged him by the limbs.

Berman, I said.

He didn't seem to hear me, and again I laid hands on Berman to save him. We retreated two yards, got south of the scaffolding. More Israelites slicked through the chaos to join us. A bandkid popped out from the edge of the honeyspill, lunged in my direction, and, raising his sax to deliver his wallop—a wallop I would not have been able to dodge—fell at my feet, a nib in his earhole = June was still safe, her sightlines clear. The Israelites danced on the bandkid's torso. Berman pulled the nib, shot the kid in the guts with it, pulled it again, re-reloaded.

Thirty feet west and ten or so south, Desormie, his back to me, tried to pry Benji off Slokum. I went.

"Teachers are bleeding," a newsman said, "while budding popstar, Boystar, under his father, hasn't moved an iota since this mayhem began."

By the pushbar-door exit, Vincie ordered a retreat before the expanding disarrangement could engulf them. Both halves of Portite had abandoned their posts now, and both the alarms in the gym were accessible.

"A clown who rides to town in a coffin," sang Main Man.

Desormie, on his knees, pulled Benji from Slokum and hurled him toward the throng, bounced him off a speaker. The scaffold trembled.

Eight steps away now, I reached for my sap and my sap wasn't there, it had slipped from my belt during one of my falls, but the twenty-odd feet I'd travelled at topspeed gave me enough momentum, I thought, and the gym teacher, standing now, couldn't see me coming.

Chin tucked low, right shoulder ahead of me, I cannoned at his neck... a step too late. My shoulder met his. The impact barely shook him, but its rebound floored me. I rolled like a pro and leapt back to my feet by the time he revolved, then I lunged again, this time for his throat. He sidestepped and chopped me down solid, mid-air. As I dropped, my arm hooked the megaphone's thong. Its resistance slowed my fall and bent him forward. My shins smacked the floor, but the rest of me didn't. I pulled on the thong to try to climb up him. The thong's clasp snapped and I dropped once more. The megaphone landed just left of my head. He stepped on my wrist as I tried to grab it, and he bounced hard twice before Benji chaired his thighbacks. Slokum tackled Benji, and the two blurred behind me. By my side, on his knees again, Desormie gripped my face by the jaw and started squeezing. I bonked him with the megaphone. He squeezed unfazed. I got the bell to his ear and flipped on the siren. He threw himself backwards and I started getting up, but my hurt wrist kept folding beneath my weight and Desormie returned and he kicked me in the stomach. I came off the ground a little, then met it prone. My lip split wide and my chin felt chipped. My nose was intact. My tongue was intact. The sting that was meanest stabbed from deep in my gums as half of an incisor spilled from my mouth to plop in a puddle of my very own gore. I knew it was over. I had yet to feel the ache from the kick itself: my stomach was a ghost yet, a big bag of numb, my pain receptors still too busy with my facewounds to process its messages properly.

It's over, I thought, and so I turned over, onto my side to see what came next, to see how the end looked, to see what he'd use, the blow that would pull me from out of my chest, if not for good, then forever.

No end was coming, though. No end came. Desormie was sitting. He was sitting right next to me, saying, "Oh no. Wait. Hold on." For a breath I thought: heart-attack. Then: Adonai. And then I saw the blood. It founted in pulses from the nib in his carotid. One... two... three purple bursts, and he kept saying, "Wait now wait now wait," and then the scaffolding was falling and the pain hit my stomach, and a runner running over me tripped on my neck. My trampling was on. It wasn't my brothers. It wasn't, rather, *only* my brothers. Another runner kicked me in the back of the head.

The scaffolding, falling, stopped falling, was fallen. Metal wailed as it bowed. Flooring crunched into tinders. Snapped riggings unwound, buzzing the air, slapping each other while whipping in circles. Lightbulbs exploding inside their bent fixtures. The noise was sufficient to blot out the siren's. Then came the cheers.

All ten of the remaining Jennys and Ashleys, each one of the ambulatory everykid no-ones, every bandkid and Shover who still had his legs: they all saw that the fallen scaffolding was good. Pushing southward to flee from and beat on each other, they'd felled it loudly, and this random outcome—or maybe not random? maybe some of them had actually tried to knock it down?—this outcome, whether random or anything but, clearly struck them all as a kind of achievement, a result which they, whether knowingly or not, had toiled all along to produce, so they cheered.

But on seeing others cheering—their *enemies* cheering—they wondered if their victory wasn't a loss, not exactly pyrrhic, but ironic nonetheless; wondered, each one, if they weren't, after all, like the bumbling protagonist in any of a hundred blockbuster sports-comedies: the running back/power forward/pointguard/striker who moves with all the grace of the athlete unobstructed across the field/court/ice in the wrong direction (unbeknownst to him) to score a touchdown/goal/basket against his own team.

Yet this wasn't like sports, let alone sports movies. The roles weren't fixed, nor the meaning of the scaffolding. It didn't have to be this way. They might have, for instance, all felt stronger. They might have felt stronger and come together. They might have decided that, rather than now, they'd been mistaken *before*: that if their enemies cheered the same damage as they, then they weren't their enemies after all. They might have concluded their interests were mutual, that some other force, earlier—some other enemy—had confused and divided them, and that all those who cheered were thus allies unmasked.

Instead they felt bitter, tricked by each other, last-strawed underdogs, suckers on the mend. Their enmity swelled and they fought even harder. This was, for the robots, none of whom cheered, no unlucky turn. Kids focused their violence exclusively on other kids, in many cases kids who'd been damaging robots.

The force of the push to the south thus dissolved just after the fall of the scaffold.

But that push, however brief, had been a boon for the Indians: to avoid getting crushed, most of Nakamook had scattered, and those of them who hadn't were cleaved from those they'd grappled. Eliyahu'd lost his grip on the Co-Captain's throat. Benji's wristlock on Slokum got broken. Between these combatants, scores wedged at random. Brooklyn was swallowed by a spastic melee, and while he punched his way out, Baxter vanished in the mob. Slokum headed east, in search of a weapon, gathering a comet's tail of Shovers as he went. Nakamook elbowed through the fracas, stalking him.

The damaged near the doorways were rising, clearing out. Except for the people laying trampled on the court—most of whom, by now, had begun to crawl away—the northernmost third of the gym was all clear. Many of the robots, momentarily forgotten, were able to escape, and that's what they did, along with some kids at the edges of the riot, but there were soon as many vectors of attack as aggressors, and there wasn't any shortage of aggressors. By the time most kids who wanted to flee realized the exits were once again passable, the riot, like a mushroom too dense with ballistopores, had launched several mini-riots off of its stem, and those runners who attempted to weave between them were wrangled inside them as often as not.

Desormie, on top of me—the southbound push having tipped him side-ways, opposite the wound from which his blood arcs projected, thinning with each passing spurt—died. No surge of sympathy or sudden sense of loss overcame me as it would have were the world a stage, but it didn't feel much like victory either. Had a dead man I wished alive come alive, it would've been different, but a man I wished dead had merely been made dead. I hoped his final shudder was painful was all, hoped it lasted for years on the astral plane, and I tucked in as close as I could to his body, covered my head and my neck with my arms, let the gym teacher's corpse absorb the horde's footfalls, and that's how I survived getting trampled and piled on.

Most Israelites, meanwhile, had zoned themselves off. After I'd left them to go kill Desormie, they'd retreated southeast, principal in tow. Their zone was a right isosceles triangle, with walls for two borders (the south and the east). Shoulder-to-shoulder, their pennyguns drawn, a line of twelve soldiers spanned the hypotenuse, all of them shooting at passing Shovers, the ex-Shovers among them shooting bandkids as well. An ex-Shover trio, commanded by Berman, held weapons on Brodsky, who was crouched in the corner, while a fourth tied his wrists and legs with cables yanked from the scaffolding's wreckage.

Beneath the west hoop, Shlomo Cohen got cancanned. He couldn't stop coughing. "What happened to your voice?" "Where'd your voice go, Shlomo?" The plasterdust cloud the Five kicked from his cast: it choked him and stuck to his eyeballs and cuts. "Cuh," gacked Shlomo. "Give us a scream." "Where'd your voice go, Shlomo?" "Gack."

Their brass scarred from teeth and their padcups askew, the bandkids were blitzing in squads of fours and fives, walking through the mini-riots, mowing down anyone. Cymbalists alternated neckchops with headclaps. Flautists pulled their flutes apart for double-fisted piking. Tubas and euphoniums remained strapped to players who held them under-arm to ram with like jousters. Splinters poked from fractures in oboes used for skullshots. The buttons jammed forever on trumpets gone knuckleduster.

Once Brodsky was tethered securely to himself, Berman left Cory Goldman—same Cory I'd seen in the Office with Ruth on the previous Tuesday—in charge of the Israelites' triangular zone, and went forth with six others to kick downed Shovers and gather projectiles the Side had fired. "We've got enough coins, so forget about the coins," he said. "Get the nibs and the fasteners—especially the nibs, though. Every single nib that you see. They're the best." "What about the ones that're stuck in people's bodies." "Those too," Berman said. "They'll pull right out. If they're stuck in some meat, you just pull them right out."

His parents still writhing and rolling where they'd dropped and then been trampled (then trampled some more), Boystar stirred, rose, fell. His tire-chain belt failed to clank—it was gone.

It was Vincie who found me, Starla by his side, Ansul trailing. They batted back the swarm with chairs and their belts while the Flunky unpiled me and got me on my feet. Lots of parts of me were throbbing, swelling. Before Desormie'd tipped, I'd taken some stomping.

I reached for the soundgun, lost balance and fell.

The Flunky caught me, put me over his shoulder.

Megaphone, I said.

Vincie picked it up.

Get me to June.

Vincie cleared a way north, soundgun forward, putting sirenblasts into the ears of those who blocked us. Starla, behind him, spun left and right, random-launching fasteners to fend off any flank-assaults. The Flunky, who had me in a fireman's carry, stayed close on her heels, and Ansul, on ours, walked backward to rearguard, twirling his belt like a boat-propeller.

Three everykid no-ones who noticed unbuckled.

The alarms, wide open, remained unpulled. To be near an alarm was to be near an exit, and those near an exit who weren't being damaged were either bringing damage or escaping through the exit.

An everykid, midcourt, was holding the mikestand, lifting it to swing on a Shover with his back turned, when Benji emerged from a nearby skirmish and rabbitpunched the everykid, wrested free the mikestand, swept the Shover's legs with it, and headed, stand-first and vaguely westward, in search of Bam Slokum, who was half the court east of him.

Slokum was the one who'd taken Boystar's belt. With the chain double-knotted around his ropey forearm, the padlock dangled a foot below his fist. He was standing by the east wall, north of the Israelites, catching his breath and panning for Benji and not getting shot or struck by anyone. Maholtz was gathered by his side with some Shovers.

At the corpse of his coach stared Co-Captain Baxter, eyebrows high and mouth agape. He crouched just over the dead man's head and, on a sentimental whim, parted the lips of the dead man's mouth with the whistle that was chained around the dead man's neck, then fixed, by clamping with the fingers of his free hand, the lips around the whistle so the whistle would stay.

When at last he stood up, Eliyahu, before him, face wracked with disgust, said, "Boulders," right crossed, and knocked him out cold.

"Baby!" June said, as we came up the bleachers. The Flunky set me down. June hugged me, I winced. "Does someone have aspirin?"

No one had aspirin.

I'm fine, I said.

I sat by June's feet.

To Vincie and the Flunky, June said, "Nurse Clyde."

"Clyde's gone," said Ansul. "He entered the pipeline as soon as the scaffold fell."

June said, "Fuck."

"Maholtz?" said Vincie.

"Maholtz," June said.

We'll get drugs later, I said. Find Scott.

"Scott's protected," said Vincie. "Look."

Regrouped around Main Man, in the southwest corner, was all of Nakamook, minus Benji. Big Ending was with them, and so was Western Portite. Their zone was arranged the same as the Israelites' (to which Berman, pockets stuffed with nibs, had returned) but half the area and fortified doubly. Big Ending knelt a line holding chairs legs-forward, while half a step behind them all the other soldiers, except for the Janitor, stood a second line shooting whoever Jelly told them to. The Janitor leaned on the walls looking grey, one eye normal, the other like a frog's, and while Ori shot footage from over soldiers' shoulders and while his newsman kept trying to interview anyone, Main Man quit Marley for Radiohead. "Holy Roman Empire," he sang.

"We're winning," said the Flunky.

The Flunky spoke truth—the gym was nearly ours—though you wouldn't have known it if you didn't see the corners, for the bandkids still dominated most of the court. Their dominance no longer owed to their weapons, though: whether chairs, belts, or knuckle-clutched housekeys, nearly all the combatants had improvised weapons. And it didn't owe much to their heartiness, either: anyone who could have run (by then most could've; more than half of the school had done so already) and didn't had heart. They were dominant because, in the midst of 170 other combatants, each of whom attacked anyone within reach, the bandkids would not attack other bandkids = Where the bandkids fought as 30 against 170, each 1 of that 170 fought 199.

The Israelites, Big Ending, and the Side of Damage numbered roughly 80 soldiers in total. Subtracting Main Man, the Janitor, the few downed Israelites, and those manning the pipeline, we had about 60. If 30 could dominate 170, then our 60—assuming that our oneness and superior positioning (6 soldiers on high, 3 of whom were crackshots; the rest in two zones, relatively rested) neutralized the advantage to the Bandkids' of their oneness (a safe assumption)—our 60 could annihilate 200 easy, and 200 diminishing on its own even easier.

"Should we go get Maholtz?" Vincie asked me, and by the time that I answered, 3 more no-ones had already fallen: only 197 were left.

No, I said. We stay here and snipe.

June kissed my cheek. I banged fists with Vincie.

Vincie was low, June was out, but the Flunky and Ansul were flush with projectiles. From my jacket, I pulled three portions of nibs, one portion of fasteners, fifteen coins. "I can't shoot for shit," said the Flunky. "I'll block," and he went to the third lowest bleacher and waited to slow any charge that might come our way. The rest of us split up the coins and fasteners. I doled out the nibs to myself, June, and Vincie.

Eliyahu'd hauled Baxter to a clearing near the southwall. He pulled him up crooked by one lapel, then knuckled his earlobe and jerked. Baxter came to, confused, held his ear. "Fucker," he said to Eliyahu, "you fucker." Brooklyn crowned him, picked him back up. "Now eat this," he said, the earstud gem-forward. "Eat this, you mamzer hat-wrecking bancer. Eat this, you filthy uncircumcized dog."

The Five were fine too; didn't need coverage either. Bored with Shlomo, who no longer convulsed, and glimpsing Eliyahu between heads and shoulders, they gamboled toward the south wall, the better to see, a capering troop that undermined its native cuteness shooting mystified kids in the eyes at close range, stepping on crotches and faces on purpose, vociferating multiple Yiddish vulgarities. On encountering an Ashley weeping into her pom-pons, Shpritzy and Pinker windpiped the Shovers who were squeezing her ass, and Shpritzy kissed her cheek and told her she was gorgeous, and she took Shpritzy's hand and she followed the Five.

Slokum had come off the wall to find Benji, who I kept one eye on, although he was safe, still cutting west through the thinning-out mini-riots.

Vincie quartershot the Shovers who had Slokum's back.

June washered some everykids groping a Jenny.

I'd just smashed a bandkid's nose with a wingnut and was shaking my wrist out—the recoil stung it—when my thigh started humming. Botha's phone.

Ben-Wa, I said. Everyone still standing?

"Cody got whacked by Mr. Novy when it started, but Stevie chaired Novy hard in the face and there was lots of blood, and we kicked him and chaired him because of ferocity until Miss Farmer and that bancer Mr. Bilge got him out, and then anyone else who was trying to fight us ran out of here screaming like you told us they would. Cody lost teeth, but I think they were babyteeth, but maybe they were broken—anyway, everyone's fine except for that. It's the newsguys, though. That's why I called. They're out in the bus circle, setting up cameras and talking to teachers and all these crying kids. What should we do?"

Do you hear any sirens?

"No sirens," he said.

Did the Side evacuate the teachers lounge yet?

"I don't think so," he said. "I wasn't looking. I'm sorry."

It's fine, I said. You're doing good. Give your keys to Anna Boshka and send her to the lounge to evacuate them. Tell her to lock the side-entrance behind them.

"Boshka's on the alarm with Chunkstyle," he said, "but I guess no one's really tried to pull one yet, so..."

No, I said. I said, You're right. Send Jesse Ritter instead.

"Got it."

If any newsguy or anyone tries to get back in, shoot.

"How close should we let them?"

Thirty feet.

"I'm suck at distances, Gurion, I'm sorry."

Don't cry, I said. Distances shmistances. Thirty feet's about a fifth of the way between the door and the bus circle.

"A fifth?" said Ben-Wa.

What's halfway between the door and the parking lot?

"The bikerack."

What's halfway between the door and the bikerack?

"The end of the hedge."

Okay, I said. Three bushes closer than that is how close they can come. Got it?

"Yes."

Now listen, I said. Are you still looking outside?

"Yeah," he said.

In the two-hill field, do you see any kids?

"There's some kids in front of it."

Any you don't know?

"There's that dickhead Ronnie Bascomb and—"

You see any other kids? Maybe behind them? Any kids in black hats?

"No," said Ben-Wa.

Call me when you do. Or if you hear sirens. Now send Jesse Ritter.

I ended the call and looked at the time. Only six minutes since I'd uglied Boystar. I doubted the phonecalls from those who'd escaped had yet convinced dispatch to send in the bulls, but a live broadcast could do so at any second, if it hadn't already. We needed to lock the school down fast. We needed to hold it til the scholars arrived, but in addition to the Israelites and the Side of Damage, some 150 people were left in the gym, roughly 2/3 of them standing up, fighting; 2/3 of those wielding improvised weapons. If we locked down now, we'd have 40 more prisoners than soldiers—no good—and 2/3 would be hostile, hard to manage: they hadn't failed to escape because they loved peace; they weren't still fighting because they feared violence or couldn't take a punch. Other than those on the Side of Damage, these were the hardest hundred kids at Aptakisic.

I said, Give me the soundgun.

Vincie gave me the soundgun.

I turned on the soundgun.

I said, JOSH BERMAN.

Berman and his Israelites looked toward the bleachers.

JELLY, I said.

Jelly and the Side looked up at the bleachers.

ANYONE WITH A PENNYGUN IS MY BROTHER, I said. ANYONE WITH DAMAGE ON HIS HEAD IS MY BROTHER. NO ONE ELSE IN HERE'S ALLOWED TO STAY. MAKE THEM LEAVE. THEIR CHAPTER IS OVER. PUSH THEM OUT. WE'VE GOT YOUR BACK.

And the Side and the Israelites went forth from their corners in two walls of violence with one shared objective, and we in the bleachers shot down at resisters, who after the first thirty seconds were halved, for any fighter in the gym who'd failed to hear me or take my meaning was made by my brothers to understand what I'd said.

And as the mass on the floor moved north toward the exits, Benji found Slokum and Slokum found Benji, and Benji charged Slokum as Slokum charged Benji. They swung on each other with the weapons they'd taken, and each went down, and they blurred and rolled and flew apart, and each rose up, and again they collided, and Benji, whose hand—the weaker, the left—had been, along its chopping-edge, demolished by the padlock, held Slokum, whose chin had been caved by the mikestand, high by the throat, as high as he could reach, in a right-armed impossible, and drove him forward—first slowly and wobbling, then running and steady with the mounting momentum—into the gym's southern wall skullfirst. Slokum went limp, Benji released him, Slokum slipped down the cinderblocks slowly.

"What!" Benji shouted. "What! What!" He slapped Bam's face. Bam's head lolled. He slapped him again. Bam covered his face. "That is *not* fucken it, man! What! Get up! Quit fucken faking! Get the fuck up!"

Knees bent, Benji leaned into Slokum's chest, wrapped an arm around his ribs—just one arm, the right; his left hand was already too swollen to close—and started to hoist him up onto his feet, then suddenly dropped him and stood up straight. A nib was sticking out from his neck, by the spine. He plucked it, revolved, got nibbed in the clavicle, and dove to the floor, behind the scaffold.

To June, Vincie said, "What the fuck?"

"Wasn't me."

It wasn't me either, I said. Just cover him.

But we didn't need to cover him. He had all kinds of coverage. Flanked by three Israelites, Berman went to cover him, threw his body on top of him, knelt on his back, took his hair in his fist, pushed his face in the floor.

We did need to cover him.

Vincie launched a washer, nicked Berman's shoulder, Berman turned around.

I got on the megaphone. BENJI'S WITH US! NAKAMOOK'S US!

"What the fuck!" Vincie said.

They made a mistake.

"What kind—"

Stop shooting. They made a mistake.

And Berman and the Israelites showed us their hands, to shrug or surrender—there was no way to tell. Vincie's gun was still raised and I stepped in front of him, embracing him hard til Berman and his three raced back to the battle and vanished inside it.

A mistake, I said.

"Okay," Vincie said.

Let's end this, I said.

"Okay," Vincie said.

There was little left to end. The Five took turns bracing Baxter and smacking him, while Brooklyn, in front of him, proferred the earstud. Except for that, and Main Man singing, and the prisoners attempting to un-knot their bindings, all action was north of the northern sideline.

I put my last nib inside Seamus's armpit, blew the wire-rimmed specs off a teacher with a nickel, and by the time I reloaded another projectile—a tiny black wingnut—there was no one to shoot.

Israelites cheered, high-fived, banged fists.

Ronrico yelled, "We damage we!" and got echoed.

Fat-lipped and wan, Baxter swallowed the rhinestone.

I aimed at the clock, I fired at the clock.

Jelly found Benji and sat down beside him.

"Eliyahu," the Five said. "Brooklyn." "Hey Brooklyn."

"Yeah?" Brooklyn said.

Chucketa-cracketa, cracketa-chuck. Some glass from the clockface fell to the floor.

"Look." "Brooklyn, look at him."

"What?" Brooklyn said.

You see that? I said.

"Yeah," June said.

I did that for you.

"Thanks," June said.

Jelly cradled Benji's broken hand in her lap.

Something was buzzing.

"Hey," June said. "I think that's your—"

Yeah.

The screen of the buzzing phone read WOLF.

I pressed the green button.

Yeah? I said.

Ben-Wa said, "Gurion."

Yeah? I said.

"Sirens," he said.

21
THE VERBOSITY
OF HOPE

Friday, November 17, 2006
10:49 a.m.–12:09 p.m.

No kids in black hats?
"None," said Ben-Wa.
How loud are the sirens?
"How loud?" he said.
How far away are they?
"They're not in front."
Sirens in the distance, you're saying.
"I am."
Lock down the entrance. No one comes in.

The Side and the Israelites continued to celebrate, blowing out bulbs with projectiles and yelling, lifting our fallen and embracing each other. We in the bleachers went down to the sideline. Thirty-odd bodies were sprawled on the floor. Except for Desormie's, all of them breathed. I ordered the Five to bring Boystar forward, then ordered forward the five remaining camera-men. Three worked for New Thing, two for the news. One of the news ones was wearing a chai.

You get the scoop, I said. Tell me your name.

"Ori," he said.

Ori gets the scoop, I said to the cameramen. Leave us your cameras and you'll get them back later.

One of them hesitated. June shot his lens out.

You've still got the footage. You want to keep the footage?

He laid down his camera. The Flunky took it under the bleachers with the others.

Boystar was saying something. "Please," he was saying, and sniffling blood.

I almost forgot about you, I said.

"Just—"

Pinker shook him and he ceased to speak.

I gave Glassman the nutmeg I'd pocketed earlier.

Feed him, I said.

"Gur—"

The Levinson choked him til he opened his mouth.

I pointed at Desormie and said to the cameramen: Pick up that corpse and bring it to me. Do anything other than what I tell you, and my friends over here will end this kid.

"We'll kill him," said Shpritzy. "We'll kill him with our hands." "His life's in your hands." "We'll kill his whole body." "We'll kill him to death."

His molars destroyed, Boystar chewed like a dog.

I took up the soundgun and made an announcement: EVERYONE LISTEN. THE WAR'S NOT OVER. EVACUATE ANYONE WHO ISN'T MY BROTHER. PUT THEM ALL OUT THROUGH THE PUSHBAR DOOR. VINCIE PORTITE'S IN CHARGE WHILE I'M GONE. NO ONE ELSE.

"Where are you going?" shouted seven random Israelites.

I'M—I turned off the soundgun. I'm going up front, I said.

"Why?" they all said, and just as they said it, the cameramen returned. They dropped Desormie's body on the sideline and stretched.

I'm going up front to protect us, I said. No time for more questions, now.

They stopped asking questions, started clearing the gym out.

I took aside Vincie and gave him the soundgun.

Get this to Scott and stay close to Benji. Don't let him go after Berman.

"Who's Berman?"

The one who accidentally shot him.

"Got it. But I don't think Benji's in shape to fight anyway."

I looked between the shoulders of soldiers at Benji. He was leaning on Jelly and the southwall, sitting, his jawmuscles bulging, his eyes pointed high, his busted hand darkening fast on his lap. Beside himself with pain or anger or both, he seemed to be melting and hardening at once.

I said, Watch Benji. And lock the door when the bodies are cleared.

I gave him Floyd's keyring.

"Don't the firemen have some kind of universal key?"

I don't know, I said. Maybe? Guard the door, too.

"How about I jam it."

With what?

"Cross the mikestand through the pushbar like an X so it wedges and—"

Yeah, I said, do that, that's good, and watch Benji.

Vincie took off.

Desormie's silver whistle was laying on his eyeball.

Pick him back up, I said to the cameramen.

They followed me and June to the northeast exit, and the Five and the Ashley surrounding Boystar—who they clutched at four points: the wrists and the neck and the hair—followed them. Ori walked backwards in front of us, filming. Main Man, finally amplified, sang, "Let's go down the waterfall," and we entered the pipeline and headed east.

As we walked, I gave the Look of The End to Ori's lens, said, Hear O Israel, listen up the rest of you, I'm Gurion ben-Judah and I've got an army. Today's a new holiday. We'll name it later. I've taken prisoners, mostly kids. As a show of good will, in honor of our holiday, I've already released some out the back door. The rest of the prisoners are safe and secure, but there's spotters in here on every entrance, and Adonai is on our side, so don't come within fifty yards of the school, or prisoners will suffer the fate of Desormie, atop whose corpse you've found this recording. My first demand is the last great Jew. I want you to get Philip Roth on the phone. I'll call 911 in thirty minutes. Make sure they can patch me through to Roth. Am Yisrael chai, good yontif, we damage. Cut now, Ori.

Ori turned the camera off.

"You," whispered June, "just sounded like a crazy."

Did I sound sincere?

"That's why you sounded crazy."

Good, I said.

"Who's Philip Roth?"

"The greatest American novelist alive who isn't DeLillo or McCarthy!" said Ori.

How do you spell DeLillo? I said.

Ori spelled DeLillo.

What should I read?

"*End Zone* to start with, then *White Noise*. McCarthy's *Blood Meridian*, though—I'd read that one first. Seems more your style."

I thanked him for the recs and took away his camera, said, Where's the recording?

"On the hard drive," he said.

No backup? I said.

"Auto backup," he said. "There's a flash in that slot."

I ejected the cartridge, put it in his hand.

Mazel tov, I said. I hope they promote you.

We'd arrived at the door.

Two helmeted firemen were retreating toward the bus circle. Ben-Wa was saying, "They told us, 'Open up,' we told them, 'Go away,' and they said they'd come back with the battering ram."

The firemen climbed in the cab of their truck. Another truck and ambulance pulled into the circle. Then a cable newsvan. Then two copcars.

I unlocked the doors and pushed one open.

Put Coach out there, I said to the cameramen. Lay him out flat on his back.

They did what I said, then one of them sprinted away and June drew.

Let him go, I told her.

You guys go, too, I said to the others. Just make sure you run like you're scared, or we'll shoot you.

They ran like they were scared. We didn't shoot them.

Ashley, I said.

Shpritzy's Ashley said, "Yeah?"

Get going, I said.

"She's with me," Shpritzy said.

"I'm with him," said the Ashley.

"She's with Shpritzy," June said. "It's settled. That's that."

It's settled then, I said.

"Thanks, June," said Shpritzy.

I set Ori's camera atop Desormie's chest, then stepped back inside and locked both doors.

Bring him, I said.

The Five brought Boystar before the left door. I stood before the right with my hands in my pockets.

Guns on the Ashley, I said to Wolf.

Behind me, Wolf aimed their guns at the Ashley.

Act threatened, I told her.

The Ashley raised her hands above her head and frowned.

Returning with their ram, the firemen—six of them—slowed at the sight of those we'd let go; they stopped completely when they got to Desormie. Two shorter ones knelt to check his vitals, and a tall one stepped over the gym teacher's body, then rapped on the glass as if testing its thickness, as if seeing killed men laid out in front of schools with holes in their throats and cameras on their chests and blood crusting blackly all over their collars was business as usual for a suburban fireman. Pursing his lips, he rapped on the doorframe, then again on the glass, then went back to the doorframe, squinting and nodding, rapping and tapping, brow all furrowed now, faking unfazedness, pantomiming thinking, the act of calculation, the act of determining ideal points of impact, battering-ramming a science of precision. Throughout this peformance, he threw furtive glances, trying to guage the effect of his poise on us. Pinker said, "He doesn't want to use that ram." And Shpritzy said, "He's scared." "You're scared!" yelled The Levinson. The fireman heard him. He looked at Ben-Wa, the one he'd spoken to earlier, said, "Enough with the bullshit now. Open this door."

Tell *me* what to do, I said. I'm the leader.

"Open this door or we'll break it in."

I spun and cracked Boystar so hard in the nose that it spattered my sleeve all the way to the shoulder. The Five lost their grip and he crumpled up fetal. I kicked him straight, set my heel on his throat.

Tell me again, I said to the fireman.

"Easy," he said. "Easy."

Take that camera and take away the corpse. Get fifty yards back on all sides of the school or I'll kill this kid and then I'll kill some other ones. Everything else you need to know's on the camera.

The fireman stood there, looking down at Desormie.

That's right, I said. Big guy, I said. Thirty pounds on you easy. And that was just me. I did *that* alone. And I've got a whole army and we're armed to the teeth. Get out of here now. Get back to your truck.

I split Wolf up. The four in front—Ben-Wa, Jesse Ritter, Stevie Loop, and Christian Yagoda—would stand at the doors pointing weapons at Boystar, who we tied to a chair with his bootlaces. I gave Cody von Braker Brodsky's phone and posted him and Forrest Kenilworth over at the side entrance. If anyone came at the school from the side, Cody'd call Ben-Wa. If anyone came at the school from the front, Ben-Wa would see it himself. In either case, he and Jesse and Stevie and Christian would whale on Boystar with their weapons and their fists until all comers retreated.

Boshka and Chunkstyle I sent to the library to get a TV so we could watch the news. It was a one-person job, but they were kissing when I found them, pressed against the wall, and it didn't look gross.

□ □ □ □ □ □ □

The gym had been cleared of fallen enemies. The pushbar door was jammed with the mikestand. I headed up halfcourt holding June's hand, the Five and the Ashley walking behind us. The rest of the Israelites were standing in the bleachers, except for Jelly and Eliyahu, who sat with Big Ending and the Side of Damage atop the fallen scaffolding's crossbar.

Vincie and Berman met us at centercourt.

How many soldiers do we have? I said.

"I don't know," Vincie said.

"Fifty?" said Berman.

Let's count, I said.

We all started counting.

I had 43 Israelites up in the bleachers—12 of them ex-Shovers—and then another 19 soldiers sitting on the scaffolding—14 Side of Damage, 5 Big Ending—plus me plus June plus Vincie and Berman and the Five and the Ashley = 72 soldiers in total in the gym. Add the 8 of Wolf platoon, and that gave us 80 soldiers all told.

Vincie and Berman confirmed my count.

I said, What about injured? How many are injured?

Vincie said, "Two."

"Three," Berman said.

Is it two or is it three? I said.

"Five," said Berman. "They've got two, and we've got three."

How bad? I said.

"Benji's hand looks fucked, and the Janitor's ugly, but I asked them if they wanted to leave," Vincie said, "and they gave me the stinkeye, so they can't be that bad."

"Our guys are fine," Berman assured me. "Minor contusions."

"Contusions?" said Vincie.

"Cuts," Berman said.

Wait, I said. They're cut or they're bruised?

"Both," Berman said.

Something started banging. It came from the bleachers. Ex-Shovers parted and I saw Brodsky's head. He was laying in the space between the bottom two benches, bound at the ankles and wrists with cables, gagged with a sock, thrashing around.

Help him sit up! I yelled. Take out that gag!

A pair of ex-Shovers did as I'd ordered. Brodsky sat slumped, chest heaving, scalp red.

What is he doing here? I said to Vincie.

Vincie chinned air at Berman and told me, "He told me you told him to keep Brodsky hostage."

I didn't, I said.

"I told you he was lying," Benji told Vincie. He and Jelly were coming over from the scaffold. His left hand was twice as thick as his right, a big purple pillow.

"Fuck *you*, you told me," Vincie said to Benji. "He's on our side. Why would he lie to us?"

"I didn't," Berman said. "I didn't lie to you."

I didn't tell you to take any hostages, Berman.

"I thought that you... well... I mean I guess you didn't say 'hostage,' but you told us to drag him back into the corner, and then you ran off—to go, like, I don't know, kill Desormie, I think, and—"

I wanted you to protect him from getting trampled, I said.

"Well, we misunderstood. Or I misunderstood. It's probably my fault. But I thought that's what you meant—to take him hostage, I mean. I think the rest of us did, too. Thought that's what you meant, I mean."

In the bleachers, they nodded and mumbled their assent, and a few stood up, started heading for centercourt.

Berman said, "I'm sorry. The way things were happening—"

Fine, I said. It's fine. You misunderstood. Now we have another prisoner.

I didn't want another prisoner. We didn't need another prisoner. We didn't need anything more to control. But it was, like I'd just said to everyone, fine. I didn't like that they'd gagged him and made him uncomfortable—that hadn't been called for; it seemed thoughtless at best, potentially malicious— but that part was over. We'd take him to the Cage, where no one could hurt him, the scholars would arrive, and all would be well.

"We were just trying to do what we were supposed to," said Berman. "If you want us to put him out now, no one's gonna argue with you. I mean—obviously. Right guys?"

The Israelites behind him said, "Right." They said, "Yeah."

"Just tell us and we'll do it," Berman said. "Hand me the key and we'll put him out the door."

That door stays locked. We don't know who's behind it.

"We could put him out the front or the side, then," said Berman.

We can't put him out. It'll look like it means something—like we're bargaining or something. That's not our next move, I said.

"So what's our next move?" an ex-Shover said.

"We should get him some aspirins from the Nurse's," Brooklyn said, "and put him in the Cage with Botha—problem solved."

Exactly, I said. That's what we're doing.

By then, most of the Side had come over from the scaffold. They stood in a semicircle to my left with the Five and Vincie. To my right, right of June, stood twenty-odd Israelites. The suckness of this arrangement wasn't entirely lost on me, scholars—I hadn't failed to notice where they'd been sitting when I'd returned, nor failed to hear Berman's us's and them's—but it seemed to me an outcome of friendship, not animosity. Rather than staying *away* from those he didn't like, each soldier, I'd assumed, was staying *near* those he did like. If that sounds dim, well—maybe it was. At the time, I was filled with all kinds of hope—we'd taken the school together, I'd scared off the firemen—and hope can confuse you as easy as fear. But I thought of it this way: If I'd entered the cafeteria at Lunch one day to find June at one table and, say, Chunkstyle at another, I'd sit next to June because I preferred June's company, not because I abhorred Chunkstyle's, and if Chunkstyle then left his table join us, I'd have certainly welcomed it. And I figured the same would've gone for the soldiers; that the only suck thing was that none had behaved like their Chunkstyle analogue—that no Israelite who wasn't Jelly or Eliyahu moved to my left to be nearer the Side; that no soldier on the Side had moved to my right to be nearer the Israelites. This seemed like a fairly easy thing to repair and I was planning on doing just that in a moment, but standing where I was, amid this thick huddle, I started feeling warm—too warm, too crowded, all too breathed on—and I found myself looking through a gap between torsos to get some relief, some sense of greater space, and my eyes fell on Main Man, sitting on the floor, alone with no soundgun.

I said, Where's Scott's megaphone?

"Exactly," said Nakamook.

Immediately I saw that I'd made a mistake.

"One of them has it," Jelly said, chinning air at the Israelites.

"Them?" came a voice from among the ex-Shovers. "Who's this *them?*" another voice said. "One of *us* says *them!*" "Well look who she's dating." "What's one of us doing with someone like *him?*"

"Come again?" Benji said.

No *don't* come again, I said. *Don't* come again. First thing's first: whoever has the megaphone—

Ally handed it over. I brandished it at Main Man. He wouldn't come and take it.

"He insulted him," Jelly said.

"I didn't mean to insult him!" protested Berman. "I just didn't think he should sing what he was singing."

You didn't think he should—

"No one did, Gurion. None of us, at least. He was singing some slow thing by Radiohead. That's no kind of Israelite victory music."

So you took his megaphone?

"He *gave* it to us."

"*After* you insulted him," Nakamook said.

Eliyahu put a hand on Benji's shoulder. "In fairness," he said to me, "I don't think Aleph meant to insult Main Man. He said he didn't like the songs and, yes, it's true, he might have been a little nicer about it, but—"

Wait, I said.

At least I thought I'd said it. Maybe I hadn't. If I had, no one heard me; no one was waiting.

"Who's Aleph?" said Berman.

"You," said Eliyahu.

"My name's Josh Berman."

"You want me to call you Josh Berman, it's done—calm down. Calm down, Josh Berman."

"What's Aleph mean, though?" Josh Berman said.

"Yeah, what the hell's it mean?" voices on my right said. "What's it mean?" "What's it mean?"

Wait, I said.

"What's it *mean?*" said Eliyahu. "It's a letter. First letter of the Hebrew alphabet, the aleph-bet—like an A, but silent."

"That wasn't my question."

"That wasn't his question." "Answer his question." "Don't dodge the question."

"Pipe the fuck down," Vincie Portite told them. "He was trying to explain," another voice to my left said. "Just let him talk."

Wait wait, I said.

"Why'd you call me Aleph?" Berman said to Brooklyn.

"Josh Berman, please. Don't be so testy. I'm not your enemy. Prior to this I've only seen you in the hallways, maybe once or twice on the late-bus too. I didn't even know you were an Israelite, you know? Let alone a Josh Berman. So I called you Aleph. Like an A. Like a variable. That's all," he said.

"Oh," Berman said. "Like an alpha," he said.

"Sure. Like alpha," Eliyahu told him.

"You know? I like that," Berman said. "I like it a lot. Sorry I got all—"

"No, forget it," Eliyahu said. "We just took the school down together, yes? Anything lousy between any of us here—it needs," he said, "to be forgiven."

And at the sound of those words, *to be forgiven,* nearly every single person in our fifty-head huddle grew visibly relaxed—shoulders falling, face muscles slackening, bodies leaning forward, *toward* each other... there'd even been an audible collective sigh. And I, to my own great surprise, sighed along. Finding out that Berman—ex-Shover leader, June's ex-boyfriend, maker of nasty remarks to Jelly's sister, shooter of nibs into Nakamook's neck, basher into floors of Nakamook's face, inadvertant insulter of Main Man's repertoire... The information that Berman was the same boy as Aleph had performed on me in ways that I couldn't have predicted. I pictured the following in rapid succession: Berman watching Baxter knock Brooklyn's hat off; Berman crawling the floor beneath Benji's legs. But then, instead of thinking: Here's the mouse who stood by doing nothing while his brother got humiliated, or, Here's the coward who'd rather crawl on his belly than stand up and fight, what I thought was: Poor Berman, poor Josh Berman. Not poor *Aleph*—Poor Josh Berman. Coward Aleph had been faceless, scholars. Poor Josh Berman had Berman's face. And maybe it was just as simple as that: his having a face. Or maybe it was even simpler than that: poor Josh Berman's face wasn't just any face; poor Josh Berman's was an Israelite face. Here the face of an Israelite crawling on his belly, there the face of an Israelite avenging himself. I'd've probably done the same, had I been him. Had I crawled on my belly before Benji or anyone, I'd avenge myself too—take the first shot I could, and the second, the third. And I saw that what I'd done was forgiven him. I'd forgiven Berman for having been Aleph and forgiven Aleph for having been Berman. Just like that. And I saw it was good.

And it was true that Benji had long been despised by most of Aptakisic, and that Vincie had long been despised as well, and the others on the Side by association, and true the ex-Shovers hadn't themselves been so beloved either, neither by their fellow Israelites nor by the Side, and it was true, finally, that I had been wrong—that there *was*, at present, animosity here, enmity even— but I nonetheless believed what Eliyahu believed: Because all those soldiers on the Side were my brothers, and because all the Israelite soldiers were my brothers, and because I had led them and because I was leading them, and because we had, all of us, fought together, I believed that they could— I believed that *we* could—dissolve any and all enmity between us.

And I saw that the others believed it too. Brooklyn had said, "To be forgiven," and all of us leaned and slackened and sighed.

All except for Benji, who made the noise "Tch."

To which Josh Berman responded with "Tch."

And everyone stiffened, postures adversarial, their collective intake of breath a long hiss.

And I saw that one of them had to be removed. It didn't matter which—at least it didn't seem to. I watched Berman's eyes go to Nakamook's hand, which was visibly throbbing. Berman, no doubt, saw an exploitable weakness. I saw my out: Nurse Clyde's Office to get fixed up. Benji'd go quiet. He'd lose no face, nor would the Side—no one would.

Yet I couldn't take Benji away just yet—he'd see right through me if I just said: Benji, your hand needs attention. I needed a spoon to replace the baby's knife. Something needed to happen to change the subject. Something relevant, preferably urgent. An act of God. The ceiling falling in. An earth-quake. A fire. Something that didn't emanate from me.

Brooklyn, baruch Hashem, was aware of this.

"Gurion," he said. "Any word from the scholars?"

"What scholars?" said Berman, eyes off Benji's hand now.

And I realized the Israelites didn't know about the scholars—I hadn't told them. They'd helped attack the school without any assurance they'd get away with it. And then they must have become afraid, and gathered together on the bleachers afraid, which must have made the Side afraid of *them*—for the Side was greatly outnumbered by them—and sensing the Side was afraid of them, the Israelites must have grown afraid of the Side, and by the time I'd returned from the firemen to the gym, the 64 I'd left behind were but 44 and 20.

That the Israelites didn't know about the scholars—this was a good thing. A great thing, even. For not only *could* I tell them, which would quell their fears, but I *needed* to tell them. It was urgent I tell them. And anyone could see that, Benji included.

"What scholars?" they said. "Which scholars?" "Who scholars?"

An army of scholars is coming, I said.

"When?" they said.

Soon, I said. They're supposed to arrive at eleven o'clock, but the el's moving slow and the weather's probably delaying them, too, plus they might have missed all the rush-hour Metras. They'll get here, though, they'll take us out of here, you'll all be safe, and you'll blame this on me.

"Who will believe us?"

Who *won't* believe you? Isn't it true?

"In a *way* it's true."

A way that everyone'll want to believe, I told them. It's never the rioters who go to prison—it's only the guy with the megaphone inciting them. Who's got the megaphone?

"You've got the megaphone."

All of your parents will be dying to believe you. All of our teachers will be dying to believe you. Nobody will want to believe anything else. Not even Brodsky, who's sitting there, bound, hearing us conspire.

"All due respect," an ex-Shover said. "How do we know that you'll fess up to everything?"

You don't, I said, but that doesn't matter. I don't need to fess up to anything to protect you. There's seventy-nine of you and one of me. What's anyone's word against ten contradictions, let alone nearly eighty? This school is dead, I said, and we're the ones who deaded it. Now we just have to hold it til the scholars arrive. Do what I say, and that won't be a problem, but we have to move fast, and we can't fight each other. We are, every one of us, brothers.

No one disagreed, at least not aloud, and Josh Berman said, "So what should we do?"

First of all, I said, you should give me some room here. I'm breathing more brotherly breath than I'd like to.

Laughing much harder than the comment warranted, the soldiers all back-stepped and opened up the huddle. They stretched and they yawned and they cracked their knuckles.

I asked which ones had their cellies on them. Seven Israelites raised their hands. I told six of them to call their mothers and repeat the following: "Mom, this is [insert soldier's name]. I'm calling to tell you two things. First of all, I'm safe. Secondly, Gurion ben-Judah says to tell you we'll all be safe as long as the authorities stay fifty yards back. I have to go now." I programmed Botha's number into the seventh soldier's phone and handed the phone to Eliyahu.

That's the only number you answer, I told him. And that's the only number you call, okay?

"Okay," he said. "Look." He pointed over my shoulder.

Boshka and Chunkstyle were entering the gym, pushing television carts.

"Where's the outlets?" said Chunkstyle.

Find them, I said.

Once the callers finished calling, I had them turn off their phones. I gave the phones to June and she put them in her bag.

"Hi," June said.

Hi, June, I said.

She leaned in close. "I'm worried," she whispered.

We'll be fine now, I said.

She squeezed my hand.

A phone started ringing.

"That's mine," said an Israelite. "The power button's jiggly."

I took out its battery.

"But what if that was my mom calling back?"

"What *if?*" said Eliyahu.

"She's worried," said the kid.

And the rest of the callers said the same of their own moms, and many of the non-callers asked why they couldn't call their moms.

I said, There's no way to make it so your mothers don't worry. *All* of your mothers. We'll be on TV soon if we aren't already. Word will spread. They'll be worried either way.

"That is suck."

Less suck, I said, than if the cops come in here. You've called your moms, you haven't told them any lies: you're safe and you'll stay safe as long as the cops stay back. Your moms will make it known to the cops that you're safe.

Your moms will make it known that your safety's conditional, and your moms and the cops will think you're hostages. With me so far?

They all seemed to be with me.

Soon, I told them, the cops'll get their numbers straight. They'll figure out exactly how many people are in here. If I let everyone call and you all talk like hostages, the cops will come to suspect we have a lot fewer soldiers than we want them to think. They'll be quicker to enter. That's why the rest of you can't call your moms.

"When do we get our phones back?" said the callers.

Later, I said.

"What if we promise—"

"Enough already!" Eliyahu shouted. "You believe in Gurion, or you—"

And Berman cut him off, shouting even louder, and although he spoke toward the same end as Eliyahu, Eliyahu's eyes flashed, burning for a second. "Are you nice little Jewish boys missing your mothers, or soldiers of Israel!?" Berman yelled.

They said they were soldiers and stopped asking questions, and they even seemed to forget about the phones, but Chunkstyle and Boshka had turned on the news, and what passed for their forgetting was at least as much caused by that.

"All we get is NBC," Anna Boshka announced. "Everything else is the snow of purest static." No one seemed to mind. Each screen was split between footage of the battle, and a shot of the bus circle filled with flashing lights. Along the bottom, crawled STUDENT UPRISING CLAIMS AT LEAST ONE LIFE... HOSTAGE CRISIS OUTSIDE CHICAGO. Off screen, the studio anchor was saying, "...quasi-proto-terrorist youth group—"

I punched both MUTE buttons, and said to the soldiers: Watch TV all you want, but stay on your feet, keep an eye on the door, and always keep a soldier next to it, listening. I'm gonna go take Brodsky to the Cage and check on the soldiers at the other entrances. I'll be back soon. In the meantime, if you hear anything funny coming from the other side of that door, tell Eliyahu immediately, and he'll call me. I'll come back fast and I'll handle it.

"I wanna watch cable," the Flunky said.

"Flunky," said Vincie, "calm down and watch. You're just about to clothesline a couple of Indians."

"I seen that already," the Flunky said.

☐   ☐   ☐   ☐   ☐   ☐   ☐

Brodsky couldn't walk. The foot on which Boystar's mother had dropped the mikestand caused him too much pain to even take his shoe off. I decided to requisition some soldiers to carry him. Though my talk of the scholars had gone a long way toward quelling the fears of most Israelites, it hadn't done nearly as much for the Side and Big Ending. Even as the television showed him shooting Indians, Vincie turned his head at every small noise— I'd thought I'd even seen his hand jump once—and Ronrico and Leevon and Jelly and Mangey all kept not one but two hands on their guns. I fig- ured this had to do with the numbers: the 44 and 20 (now 50 and 20, or 44 and 26, depending who the Five and the Ashley counted for). Scholars coming or no, the Side/Big Ending was still well outnumbered, and I was about to take off with Benji. I didn't believe they had anything to fear, but that didn't matter: fear engendered more fear, and I wanted less fear. So the soldiers I picked to carry Brodsky to the Cage were Israelites, five of them, non-ex-Shovers: Israelites so as not to reduce the Side's numbers further, non-ex-Shovers because the ex-Shovers were the ones who'd been rough with Brodsky earlier. When the five I picked lifted him, he started to argue and I told him I'd gag him and he ceased to argue.

Halfway up B-hall, they had to put him down.

I called Eliyahu, had him send five more Israelites, again non-ex-Shovers. The two crews of five carried Brodsky in shifts, fifteen to twenty-five feet at a time. I told Benji and June to keep them all moving, and I fell back behind them, just out of earshot—I needed some privacy.

It had been nineteen minutes since I'd said to have Roth on the line in thirty. If they couldn't or didn't have Roth on the line in thirty, I'd have to have Wolf brutalize Boystar, and/or the cops might feel compelled to rush the school in reaction to or in fear of my doing so. If they did have Roth on the line in thirty and the scholars weren't there yet, I'd need to come up with another demand, or make some concession, probably both. I didn't want any of that. I just wanted stasis til the scholars arrived. But what if it took them more than eleven minutes? The hail had stopped hailing, but it had hailed for a while and the el was moving slow. I needed to give the cops more time without seeming too reasonable. I called 911, hoping they hadn't found Roth yet.

This is Gurion ben-Judah, connect me to Roth.

"Hold on, sir," said a female dispatcher.

A click, then a man's voice.

"How do we know that you're Gurion ben-Judah?"

Because I'm calling for Roth.

"That doesn't prove anything. Anyone—" he said. "Please hold on, sir," he said.

And as I held I understood. It didn't prove anything because they must have already played Ori's tape on TV and any prankster would know the demand that I'd made. Whether I'd seen it but was too stupid to figure that out, or I hadn't yet thought to turn on the television, or I *was* a prankster, the guy on the other end of the line wasn't sure.

Another click. "Sir?" said the man.

Get me Roth.

"How do we know that you are who you say?"

Forty-some minutes ago, we phoned in a bunch of fake emergencies to distract you guys, I said. The first one was about an incident at the Frontier Motel. Would I know that if I wasn't Gurion? I said.

The guy hesitated. They must have said something about that on television, too.

"We need to further authenticate."

How about this: For the Frontier Motel one, I used the same phone as I'm using now, but not for the fire in the Nakamooks' basement, and not for the gunmen at the mall. You can check your logs against your caller ID.

"Hold on, sir," he said.

A click.

Now they'd know I wasn't stupid and they'd know I was Gurion; they'd assume, now, that none of us were watching TV. I saw that was good, especially the last part: now, if they decided to raid us, they might not spend manpower preventing live cameras from shooting the raid. We'd be that much more likely to see them coming.

Another click, and then a different man's voice, a Texan-sounding one.

"Wayne Persphere, crisis negotiator," he said. "I'm speaking to Gurion?"

You're not Roth.

"You said thirty minutes. It's hardly been twenty."

My call-waiting beeped—Eliyahu.

Hold on, Wayne Persphere.

I clicked over. Eliyahu? I said.

"The Levinson went to the bathroom," he said. "He heard someone breathing in one of the stalls, and came back into the gym and told me.

Long made short, BryGuy Maholtz now lays at my feet, here in the bathroom, head and shoulders sopping wet from the multiple swirlies the Five, after binding his arms and legs, administered."

Did he call anybody?

"He said he called the police, but they were already here, and he wasn't able to tell them anything that they wanted to know. He said they asked about numbers, but he didn't know the numbers—he'd been hiding in here since before we cleared the gym. He says so, at least."

You believe him? I said.

"I do," said Eliyahu. "He's too scared to lie. He's crying his face off, begging we don't kill him. Should we keep him here, or—"

No, I said. I know something we can do with him. We're on our way to the Cage—tell the Five to bring him. Right now I have to go, though. I'm talking to the cops.

I took a deep breath, and clicked back over.

Roth? I said.

"Wayne Persphere," said Persphere.

Wayne Persphere, I said. Wayne Persphere, I said. Wayne Persphere, I said, you are not Philip Roth. I want to talk to Roth. Put Roth on the phone.

"You said thirty min—"

How long does it take to get a man on the phone?

"I think you can imagine. He's not just some man. He's a great American novelist. Some say the greatest. You yourself called him 'the last great—'"

Don't ever put quotes around my words again, Persphere.

"I'm not trying to upset you. Kindly hear me out. I'm just trying to tell you that it's no easy thing. We rustled up his number from the telephone company, but it turns out he writes in a barn this time of day. A barn in Connecticut. It's a big ole barn, that, with a bathroom and wiring, but a barn nonetheless. The barn's behind his house and he doesn't have a phone there, for reasons, I reckon, of concentration. After we tried him and got no answer, we rung up his publisher and got to his editor, who told us what was and then told us what wasn't."

And?

"And now we're sending some good local lawfolks who live there to talk to him. It might take us a little more than seven minutes, though."

Six.

"Right," he said, "six. We'd like some more time."

How much?

"We'd like ninety minutes—he's really out in the sticks."

You've got one hour.

"Much appreciated. Can we talk about something else now?"

The prisoners?

"Yes," he said. "Well—prisoners. Wait. Are they hostages or prisoners?"

Get Roth on the line and they'll stay safe, Wayne.

"Can we call you back on this line to talk?"

You can call me back as soon as you've got Roth. No concessions before then. And you can tell your boss I don't much take a shine to fake Texans and their like. In your accents I hear deeply harbored contempt.

"Contempt for whom?"

For real Texans, Wayne.

"I rightly must say—"

Rightly come real or pick another accent. And use a better name. No one's ever been a Persphere.

"We'll—"

I punched END.

□ □ □ □ □ □ □

RICK STEVENS, NBC NEWSANCHOR: Sorry to interrupt you, Bob, but we have an important update: we've just received confirmation that Gurion Maccabee had indeed attended two of those schools we reported on earlier. I repeat, he *had* attended two of them. Now on the line with us from Chicago, we have Rabbi Lionel Unger, headmaster of the Solomon Schechter School, where the young terrorist was in attendance from 2001 til just this past May.

Rabbi Unger, a great number of your male students failed to show up to school today, and I take it this isn't any kind of ditch-day prank.

UNGER: No sir, it isn't. Jewish students do not engage in ditch-days, at least they didn't used to, though frankly, we can't yet say for sure why they failed to show up—no one knows. I, for one, suspect that they were told by Gurion of his plans to commit this act of terrorism and they all went somewhere to watch it on television.

STEVENS: Where might they have gone?

UNGER: Maybe to the home of a student with two working parents, maybe to a pizza parlor, it's hard to say.

STEVENS: A pizza parlor.

UNGER: That is correct, sir. They aren't aliens, these boys, but Americans. Like so many young American boys, ours enjoy pizza, and frisbee as well, even black dance music. They play yo-yo and ping-pong and wear denim jeans on casual occasions when slacks aren't called for. Ice cream is something they find delicious. If you prick them, they bleed, sir. Like any American.

STEVENS: I wasn't trying to— Just how many students, in total, are missing, Rabbi Unger?

UNGER: Two-hundred twelve, though three are legitimately ill with strept throat.

STEVENS: Two-hundred twelve from your school alone.

UNGER: Yes, from Schechter Chicago. That's all our boys, grades five through eight, and a smattering of our lower-schoolers.

STEVENS: That's a lot of young boys to congregate in a pizza parlor, let alone a living room.

UNGER: I see your point, and will consider its merits.

STEVENS: In the meantime, can you tell us what kind of student Gurion was?

UNGER: I can't speak of his record. That's private information, pro-tected by the law. I can tell you, however, that I always suspected he was dangerous, violent, too big for his britches, and swollen-headed. He confirmed this for me last May in my office, when in the middle of a quiet conversation we were having, he physically assaulted me on the face with a stapler.

STEVENS: A stapler.

UNGER: My own stapler. He threw it at my face.

STEVENS: May I ask what the conversation was about?

UNGER: Is that important, sir? Is that really important? I tell you that during a quiet conversation in my office, this boy holding hostages, who was, I assure you, the one who murdered the poor murdered gym teacher, threw a stapler at my face—at my *eye*, which *bled*—and you search for motives in our *conversation* to justify the violence? No wonder, sir. No wonder things like this happen, sir.

STEVENS: Thank you for speaking to us, Rabbi Unger.

UNGER: My pleasure.

STEVENS: Now let's go back to Bob Brians at Aptakisic Junior High.

BOB BRIANS, CORRESPONDENT: Thanks, Rick. As you can see behind me, the police and emergency services personnel are establishing a perimeter fifty yards east of the school, in accordance with demands made by the terrorists, demands caught on that exclusive NBC tape that we played for you just a few minutes back. I'm here with the cameraman who captured that footage, NBC's own Ori Gold. Ori, it's a privilege to meet you. You were sent here by NBC to tape the filming of a music video by up-and-coming popstar Boystar currently one of an unknown number of hostages being held inside the school. For viewers just tuning in, that's him—Boystar—tied to that chair just inside the front entrance of the school. Now, Ori, can you tell us—

STEVENS: Sorry to interrupt you Bob, Ori, but we're being asked to play Ori's tape again for those viewers who are just tuning in. Here it is.

□ □ □ □ □ □ □

Neither Botha nor Jerry had broken out of the bathrooms, but both of them were conscious and they shouted for help as we entered the Cage. Benji shouted back so they'd know we weren't saviors, and all shouting stopped.

We sat Brodsky down on the desk of a carrel on the Cage's east wall—the wall opposite the bathrooms—with his wrists tied together behind his back.

Are you comfortable? I said.

"Tch," Brodsky said.

I want you to be as comfortable as possible, I said. That's why we put you on this desk—you've got three walls to lean on. If you'd rather lean on one of the carrel walls, we'll tilt you. Just say so. The main thing is I don't want you to hurt yourself. Those idiots in the bathroom—as soon as we leave, they'll try to convince you to squirm off this carrel, crawl over, free them. Don't try it, Mr. Brodsky. You'll end up hurt. The way you're tied, if you go face-first, you'll knock yourself out when you hit the floor, maybe break your neck. Hurl yourself sideways so your shoulder takes the impact, and that shoulder will break, and maybe your clavicle. Go legs-first with that foot—you can imagine the pain. You can't walk as it is. But say I'm wrong. Say you squirm off, land lucky, undo your bindings, drag yourself across the floor, get the bathroom doors open—you're still locked in here, and you won't get out til I say you get out, and that won't even be that long from now, so—

"None of this is solving your problems," Brodsky said.

I have no intention of killing you, I said. I'm not planning to do you any more harm. I've brought you to the Cage to keep you out of harm's way. No one who'd hurt you has keys to this Cage. Understand me, though: If one of you somehow does get mobile enough and pulls that alarm on the wall—and I don't see why you would, since you looked outside when we passed the front entrance, saw that the cops have already arrived, and you'll be happy to share that information with the idiots in the bathroom—if, though, for some reason you pull the alarm anyway, it will give me a headache, and we *will* kill Boystar. *I'll* kill Boystar, then I'll kill BryGuy. Right, BryGuy? I said.

While I was speaking to Brodsky, the Five and the Ashley had gotten there with Maholtz.

"Please, Mr. Brondsky," Maholtz said.

"Show some mercy," said Brodsky. "You're better than this."

You guys get his phone? I said to the Five.

"Eliyahu's got it," The Levinson said. "We got something else, too," Glassman said. "Show him, Mr. Goldblum," Pinker said. And chinning air at Shpritzy, Mr. Goldblum told me, "The loverboy's got it."

Shpritzy had his hands in the Ashley's back pockets. He took one out, reached into his own back pocket, and produced a mint-tin. I opened it up. It was jammed with pills. One kind was small footballs, orange-flavor-Pez-colored; another was generic Adderall caplets; the third kind was horsey and white with a split.

What are these pills? I said to Maholtz. He could barely stand up. His knees kept touching.

"Which pillns?" he said.

All of them, I said.

"The white one's a paindkiller—hydrocodone. The caplets, Adderall, are speend. The footballs're Xanax. You take those for paningc."

He wasn't lying about the Adderall.

How strong is the first one?

"Four'll knock you out."

Knock who out?

"Anyone," he said.

There were twenty in the tin.

How many you want? I said to Mr. Brodsky.

"Three," he said.

Atop Botha's blotter, next to a coffee-mug—koalas playing tennis, Australian flag background—a bottle of water was sitting unopened. I brought it to Brodsky and, one at a time, I fed him the pills. The third time, I spilled a little water on his shirt.

Sorry, I said.

"It's okay," Brodsky said.

We left the Cage with Maholtz and locked it down.

How about one? I asked Maholtz in C-Hall.

"How about one what?"

Pinker socked his shoulder.

Hydrocodone, I said.

"One's pretty strong."

"*How* strong?" said The Levinson.

"It'll make you feeln happier."

What about pain?

"It depends on the pain."

Shpritzy smashed him on the cheek.

"What?" he whined. "What do you want to know?"

Look at Benji's hand.

Maholtz looked. All of us looked. The hand was so swollen, the pinky-
and the ringfinger-knucks were lineless.

"Stop looking," Benji told us.

"Take four," Maholtz said.

Four'll knock him out, I said.

Glassman hit him.

"You're right! It will! What can I tell you? It's not my faulnt!"

Pinker socked him again.

"Maybe take the Xanax? It makes you not care much. Your pain seems
dindstant; you don't really mind it; take one for 'a feeling of warmth and
well-being'; the pain's still there though... If he can stand *some* pain, and
doesn't want to be too happy, I'd take two hydrocodone instead."

If he passes out...

"I understand," said Maholtz.

It'll hurt a lot before you die.

"I know," he said. "It hurts a lot now."

You want some of these drugs?

"Please," he said.

No, I said.

I held the open tin out to Benji.

"Maybe later," Benji said. "I'm too dry to swallow."

"You can chew them," said Maholtz. "Or crush 'em and snornt 'em
would be evend better. Either way'll taste bintter, but they'll work a lot
faster, hit a lot harnder."

"So helpful all of a sudden."

I told a soldier called Feld to fish a chair from the pool and bring it to
Cody at the Side Entrance.

Feld said, "Thank you for the mission, Rabbi."

June bit my shoulder to keep herself from giggling.

You're welcome, I said.

Feld wanted high fives. We gave him high-fives. He ran to the pool. We
continued up C-Hall.

Maholtz asked me, "Why do you hate me?"

I said, Everyone hates you.

"I know," he said. "I know that," he said, "but they hate me cause I scarend them or had what they wanted. You weren't ever scarend of me. You never wanted what I had. Except for the sap. And then you took it, and now I don't have it, so why do you hate me?"

Maybe it's your accent.

"I'm from Pinttsburgh," he said.

Maybe you shouldn't be.

"I can't help where I'm from."

We turned at Main Hall. Feld was talking to Forrest Kenilworth and Cody. The chair sat dripping in front of the door.

So maybe it's your face. The way you look at girls like you're scheming to corner them.

"I was borng this way, though. I can't help how my face loonks."

So maybe it's all the banced things that you say.

"They just come out of me. I'm hated, I feel it. I say those things without thinking, from hurnt. I can't help that either. It's not my faulnt."

I guess, then, I hate you for being so helpless.

The Five tied him to the chair with his belt and his laces.

"What now?" said The Levinson.

Head back to the gym, I said. Stick by Eliyahu.

The Five took off with the Ashley.

"Should we follow them?" Feld said.

No, I told him. I've got more work for you.

"Yes!" Feld said. "You hear that, guys?" he asked the other nine Israelites who'd helped carry Brodsky. "There's more work to do!"

"Calm down," Benji told him.

"Sorry," Feld said. "I'm sorry. I'm sorry."

"It's okay," Benji said. "I'm just saying: stay stealth."

"Stealth," Feld said.

"Stealth," June whispered.

"Stealth," whispered Feld.

Maholtz twisted in his chair to see me. "Goo-ree-ing," he said. "I'm the same as you, Goo-ree-ing. I've acted real bandly, I know I've acted bandly, but I'm the same as you. We're all the same as eanch other. Hating me's the same as hating yourself. Look in my eyends."

I looked in his eyes. In his eyes I saw irises, pupils, red whites.

You're an object, I told him. We determine your purpose.

"I'm a persond," he said.

You're part of a weapon.

Understand what we're doing? I said to Forrest.

"Cops come we hurt him, call you on the celly. He's our side-entrance Boystar."

Right, I said. I'm leaving three more of these guys here for presence.

I told Feld he should stay and picked two more soldiers.

Listen to Forrest, I told them. He's in charge of you. Ben-Wa by the front door's in charge of all of you.

"We can't watch TV?" "We want to watch TV."

"TV-shmeevee!" Feld shout-whispered. "This job's important."

I'll rotate you back to the gym soon, I said, but we need to be more visible or the cops might get ballsy, so don't leave this post til I send three more soldiers.

"Just two," Feld told me. "I'm here for the long-haul. I'm here to do a job."

☐ ☐ ☐ ☐ ☐ ☐ ☐

RICK STEVENS: This just in from our Milwaukee bureau: Iris Fine, the grandmother of a boy in Kenosha who used to go to school with Maccabee, claims to have discovered an email that was sent last night to her grandson Sandford in which Maccabee allegedly invites his former schoolmates to come to Aptakisic Junior High School to perform some kind of unspecified religious ritual. We're currently working on acquiring a copy of that email from Ms. Fine. Right now, we have her on the line from Kenosha. Ms. Fine, this must be trying for you.

FINE: You don't know the half, Mr. Stevens. Sandy is a good boy, and he's been through so much, and done some not so nice things since his parents were divorced, but he always loved his bubbie, which is to say me, and since he's moved in here we haven't had an incident, not even one, and then I see your program, and you talk about this Maccabee with the self-hating father who's apparently too busy making the world safe for antisemites to teach his son not to murder Gym teachers and torture young singers, and I get a sinking feeling that Sandy is involved, for when Sandy lived in Chicago he used to talk of this Maccabee with so much affection, with the affection of a son for his father he spoke of him, and I call up his school and they condescend to so-called remind me, old lady I am, that I called my grandson in sick just two hours earlier. I did no such thing, Mr. Stevens. No such thing. And now? Where is he? On his way to this suburb by train is my guess. In a different *state*. Likely already he's gotten off the train and is walking alone through suburban Chicago, and it has been hailing, I see, and by the parkas of the policeman, I can tell it's very cold there, and here in Kenosha it's not so bad, an otherwise pleasant autumn morning, and Sandy he left home in a hooded fleece sweatshirt, and his parka is hanging on the coat-tree by the door. My grandson should get pneumonia for this? And you, Mr. Stevens, should question my integrity? I heard what you said. I *claim* this about *alleged* that. I'd like to speak to your manager, Mr. Stevens. I *told* him I couldn't find my glasses.

STEVENS: Your glasses, Ms. Fine?

FINE: Do not take that tone with me unless you want I hang up and call ABC News instead, and forward *them* the email when I find my glasses. Where did I put them? When I read the email, I was wearing them... Then. Then I arose, verklempt, from my chair... I paced around the kitchen... I called the police and was put on hold... I had a butterscotch from the cupboard—

STEVENS: Did you leave them in the cupboard?

FINE: You think I haven't checked the cupboard? Wait! Here they are.

STEVENS: You found them? Where?

FINE: I'd rather not say. What I would like to say is what I called to say to my Sandy: Sandy, if you're watching, and I sincerely hope you are because that would mean that you're somewhere inside and warm where you should stay and call us from and we'll send your uncle to pick you up and feed you and bring you back here, you're a good boy, a nice boy, a boy who loves his bubbie, and this Gurion Maccabee is bad, Sandy. He's troubled, I'm sure, I'm sure he's had his share of troubles, but he's murdering people, and maybe to you this seems like Cowboys and Indians or Cops and Robbers, but if you behave like he does, you will be considered a terrorist. You should have heard the tone the policeman used when I called to help him. Like *we* were the criminals. That's how bad this is. I will love you either way because that is how strong my love is for you, Sandy, but I will be very, very disappointed and even ashamed if you become a terrorist. It's not nice at all. It's just not nice.

STEVENS: Any chance you'd be willing to forward us that email now, Ms. Fine?

FINE: Did you broadcast what I said? My message to Sandy?

STEVENS: Yes, Ms. Fine.

FINE: I've just put the little arrow on the the SEND button and I clicked.

☐ ☐ ☐ ☐ ☐ ☐ ☐

So far so good: both entrances covered; Benji at my side, soon to go to the nurse's; June at my side, forever in love with me; seven Israelites behind us because I was their leader; a less-outnumbered Side of Damage in the gym; scholars presumably approaching the school. What else needed doing? Those seven Israelites were standing there, about to start playing slapslap. I could send them back to the gym to watch TV and potentially cause the Side to feel smaller, or, better yet, I could beef up security.

I sent two of the seven to bolster Ben-Wa's crew, and the last five I took to the library. The library's east wall had a giant picture window, highly visible to the cops and the media outside. It was just the right spot to display another hostage—a fake one this time. Even if the cops got desperate enough to convince themselves that they could lightning-strike Forrest's or Ben-Wa's crew before Maholtz or Boystar could be done deadly harm, this third displayed hostage—too far from either entrance to be gotten to quickly—would keep them in check.

I halted our march just outside of the library, and I said to the smallest, most nervous-looking soldier, who said his name was Fox, though (he told me as quickly as he possibly could) he spelled it Focks when he signed his poems, which were "poems about the difference between language and noise, which all poems are, just not so overtly, not that I'm an expert, I'm really an amateur, but that's my project, which I can only hope is better than me, something to grow into, something to master before I die, I hope": You're the prisoner, Fox. They'll bring you in with your hands behind your back and sit you in a chair in front of the big window. Keep your hands behind you the entire time, and look as scared as you possibly can.

"What if I itch?"

Tell the others in a crying voice, as if you're in pain, and they'll pretend to rough you up, but really they'll scratch you wherever you itch.

"What if I itch on the wang?"

On the wang?

"The wang," said Fox.

Try scratching with your thighs.

"That never works."

I—

"I'm just kidding, Gurion. I can handle a wang-itch. The secret is to picture a nice blue stream full of fishes who are friendly except when there's heat, which makes them grow fangs and try to eat the hot thing."

Okay, I said.

"Really," he said. "Because an itch is heat, so you cool the itch down so the fishes don't tear off your itchy-hot penis."

That works?

"Always works."

I guess that's smart, then. Why don't you just scratch, though?

"I thought I was the prisoner."

I mean in the past—when have you had a wang-itch that you couldn't just scratch?

"If you scratch and someone sees you, they think you're playing with yourself."

Who does?

"Girls?"

I don't think that's true. Why do you think that's true?

Fox blushed.

Anyway, I said, in the future don't sweat that. Just scratch your wang.

"Okay," he said. "Are you really the messiah?"

I might be, I said.

"I hope so," he said, "but if you're not, then I guess that's still okay."

Good, I said. Now—

"Because all these motherfuckers," Fox continued, "used to laugh off their motherfucking heads at me is why, all because I have the soul of a poet, a delicate soul, even in torment. They'd laugh at me to see the faces I'd make and it made me make faces I didn't want to make, then they'd laugh even more at those faces when I made them. I don't think they'll do that anymore, though," he said. "I really fucked them up back there, really tore 'em a new one. I broke someone's nose, I think, fucked him right up, and I'm sure I shot at least two guys down. No one outfoxed me, that's for certain. If they tried to outfox me I'd fuck them up. And then, near the end, I found Blonde Lonnie, funny Lonnie friend, who he thought he was so funny, fucking with Focks when he focksed around, always laughing his head off on the bus with everyone. I found him and I kicked him in the ear and he wiggled. That's a good thing, right? I know that it's good. I feel very good about it. I don't feel bad."

Good, I said. Don't feel bad.

"I don't and I won't. I totally refuse to. Fuck those motherfuckers. No skin off my nose. They had it coming and I really gave it to them. All of us did. Our souls are all delicate. All of us are poets inside of ourselves. Focks those motherfuckers. Laughing motherfocksers. Atheists in foxholes. Fuck them all to hell in motherfucking fur handbags…"

Benji put his good arm around Fox's shoulder.

"Hey," Benji told him. "They got what was coming. They got what they should've."

"They got what I fucking gave them, Benji Nakamook. *I* was what was coming. Focks was. Me."

"That's right," said Benji.

"Now you're this hugger, but you used to be like them."

"I didn't," Benji said.

"You think you're a poet because you hate Slokum and protect Scott Mookus, but you don't have the delicate soul of a poet, you're a killer who hugs me but still a fucking killer. You would have been an Indian if you didn't burn a house."

"You don't know me," Benji told him. "Don't say that."

And just as if Benji had moved to strike him, Fox flinched his shoulders and told him, "I'm shook. Don't hit me, just shook. I'm talking this way because I'm shook and weird. If you say your soul's delicate, I'll try to believe you."

June took the kid's hands between both of hers. "You're fine," she said. "You just got shook."

"You're right," he said. "I'm shook. I'm Fox. We're poets, right?"

"Maybe Fox here should return to the gym," Benji said.

"No," Fox said, "it was just a weird moment. I was shook and I'm weird, now I'm steady again."

You sure? I said.

"Positron Milosevich. Yes sir Arafat. Fucken A Humperdink. Focksen A right."

June seemed to agree.

The others had started to simple slapslap. I told them to stop. Listen, I said, when you enter the library, brandish your weapons and keep on brandishing. Once Fox is sitting, two of you point them unloaded at him, and scratch him if he itches, but make it look violent. The other two stand lookout, right up at the window, making faces like killers—they'll be watching you zoomed.

"What if they shoot us?"

They won't shoot kids. Anyone approaches, three of you shoot Fox with unloaded weapons til the approachers back off, and one of you calls me.

"Which one?" said one of them.

You, I said, and gave him a phone and programmed the number.

"Will you rotate us out like the others?" they said.

Yes, I said.

"What about Fox? They'll know we're faking if you rotate Fox."

You're right, I said. I said, Fox has to stay.

"That's okay," Fox said. "There's no cable anyway."

"They're watching the news in there."

"That's the worst kind of all of the kinds of no cable."

"But *we're* on the news, Fox."

"I *am* the Fox News."

"You're really weird, Fox."

"So I'm weird," Fox said. "I'm the first to admit it. I even said it first. At the same time as Focks. I was shook and I was weird. Now I'm steady and weird. The prisoner is weird. A weird steady prisoner who doesn't feel bad."

□ □ □ □ □ □ □

Benji and June and I went to Nurse Clyde's. In a big metal cabinet, I found gauze and tape, then a box of tongue-depressors in a drawer in Clyde's desk. I sat across from Benji, who sat in Clyde's chair, quietly watching his hand change color. June brought us water in paper cups. I wrapped my wrist first, tight in the gauze, so I wouldn't hurt it worse when I took care of Benji.

"You said you'd replace the guys guarding the hostages," he said.

Those guys can wait.

"I can go to the gym and recruit," said June.

Stay here with us. With me, I said.

"You shouldn't make them wait."

I said, I'll call Eliyahu and tell him what to do.

"You don't want him leaving the gym," Benji said.

He doesn't need to leave, I said. He can just—

"You don't want him just sending them, either," June said. "What if they're scared like they were before? They might run or screw up. Someone needs to go with them and be in charge."

Are you scared? I said.

"No," June said. "Not while I'm with you. But they're not with you."

You won't be either if I send you, I said.

"True," she said, "and I might get scared, but I'd be more scared of what would happen if I abandoned you."

So would I.

"Good," she said. "So I'll go and recruit."

No, I said. I'll have Eliyahu send Vincie to be in charge.

"You don't want Vincie leaving the gym, either," Benji said.

This was true.

Don't recruit, I said to June. *Assign*, I said. Assign on my *orders*; and only use Israelites, and no ex-Shovers. Five to the library, two to Ben-Wa, and three to Cody. *Tell* them who's in charge, and if they ask where I am, just tell them I'm protecting them.

"I'll see you in the gym," she said. She kissed me on the cheek and then she was gone.

When I finished my wrist, I told Benji to lay his hand on the blotter, palm facing up.

He winced when he did it, brought his hand to his chest.

Sorry, I said.

I went to the Quiet Room, got a pillow off a cot. While in there, I found aspirins on a shelf above the sink and swallowed three with water from the tap. I returned to the desk, set the pillow on the blotter.

Lay your hand on the pillow.

"Do you know what you're doing?"

A little, I said.

My mom had shown me movies. I did the best I could. The bad hand was nearly twice the size of the good one. The redder parts were hardening and growing purpler. Black blood beneath the nails pushed up on the enamel in oval formations. I broke in half one of the tongue depressors and taped it tight to the back of his pinky. Then I taped another to the back of his ringfinger. Those were the darkest parts; the ones that the padlock had made direct contact with. The rest of the hand was busted up too, though. Lots of small fractured bones in too small a space. The best I could do was to cushion it. I wrapped the gauze thick as a boxing glove.

"Stupid," Benji muttered, as I started on the wrapping.

I said, Don't call me stupid.

He hadn't and I knew it and he knew I knew it and he showed me by ignoring the statement.

"I knew the lock broke my hand," he said. "Anyone would've known. What do I do, though? As soon as we go down, I hit him square on the jaw with the broken hand. *On purpose* with the broken hand. I had time to think about it: Which should I hit him with?... Hit him with the broken one— that's what I decided."

Why? I said.

"Guy in juvie who taught me how to fight always said to use the blow that got used on you—that right after you block something, the part of your body you blocked with numbs out and the endorphins or whatever rush there to numb it out more, to protect and strengthen it. I don't even know if that's true about the chemicals, but the guy had me throwing knees and elbows against the bedposts for training, and after the first one it always got easier, I could always strike harder, at least that's how it felt. I never did it with a broken bone, though, and if you'd asked me before, I'd've told you it would be a fucken stupid thing to try. If you'd asked me in that split-second when I decided to cave Bam's jaw with this broken hand, I'd've said the same thing. But I did it anyway."

But why? I said.

"Cause I knew it would work. And it did. It worked. I hit that kid harder than I've ever hit anyone—no doubt about it. With my left hand, too, my weak hand. The give of his jaw when I landed the punch was—it was something. I heard things, like, de*tach*ing... except now I've got this mangled hand. Fucken stupid. Kinda thing that's gonna hurt for the rest of my life. It'll rain and I'll whine. I guess at least it's my weak hand. How's your wrist, though? How's that extra half-lip growing off your bottom one, handsome?"

I'll be fine, I said. My chin hurts the most, but whatever. It's fine.

"So why are we still here?"

Where? I said.

"The nurse's," he said. "I'm fine, you're fine..."

We're getting fixed up, I said.

"We're already fixed up. Splinted and wrapped. Ready to fight."

Here. Take these, I said.

I put two Xanaxes next to his watercup.

"Warmth and well-being? Pain without care?"

Yeah, I said.

"Why would I want that?"

You want the other kind instead?

"Four to pass out?"

What's the tone? I said.

"Maybe I want the SpEdspeed."

You don't, I said.

"You know that how?"

What's your problem, Benji?

Benji said "Tch," and dropped the pills in his mouth. He chewed them, wincing, chugged both our waters. "So let's go," he said.

I futzed with my bandage and tried to look purposeful.

⊡　⊡　⊡　⊡　⊡　⊡　⊡

STEVENS: Thanks again, Bob. Indeed, the number of onlookers outside of the Aptakisic Junior High School building in Deerbrook Park does appear to be doubling by the minute. The police have asked us at NBC to ask you folks at home in the Chicagoland area to *not*, I repeat, to *not* make your way to Aptakisic. Three concerned parents of boys believed by police to be members of Maccabee's allegedly Zionist terror organization, the Side of Damage, have already been taken into custody for crossing the cordon in the parking lot. In the meantime, the Chicago Transit Authority just released the following statement: "Between aproximately 8:30 and 9:15 this morning, CTA received four reports from Red and Brown Line operators stating that at least two hundred middle-school-aged boys had boarded their trains without any apparent supervision. As per protocol, CTA sent word of these reports to the Chicago Police. CTA cannot conjecture on how the police responded, but CTA did its part by the book, according to the rules, and as per protocol." We go live now to a press conference outside of police headquarters in Chicago's Rogers Park district, the police district that is home to both of those Jewish parochial schools formerly attended by the terrorist Gurion Maccabee.

SEAN O'MALLEY, POLICE SPOKESPERSON: Now I'll take a couple questions.

REPORTER: We've just learned that the Chicago police received word of a mass migration of students on the Red and the Brown Line el-trains as early as 8:30 this morning. That seems to contradict the statement you made just minutes ago.

O'MALLEY: As far as I know, the first we heard of any of this was 9 a.m. We sent truancy cruisers and graffiti-buster squads to the el stations at which both groups of kids had boarded. There wasn't any graffiti. There weren't any kids.

REPORTER: You said "both groups," but you—or at least the CTA—received four calls. What about the other two groups?

O'MALLEY: Right. We believe this was two groups of kids. Each orginated at red-line stations; each transferred to the Brown Line.

REPORTER: But how can you be sure of that?

O'MALLEY: Go back to New York, funnyguy. Go back to Boston. Wherever you're from.

REPORTERS: (UPROAR OF QUESTIONS)

O'MALLEY: What's wrong with you guys, huh? You're the ones show-ing emails on the television before you show 'em to the police. Thing is, you should have this part cracked already, but you're numbskulls and douchebags. And just to be clear: I don't speak for the mayor here, when I suggest that you're numbskulls, and I don't speak for the city when I call you douchebags, but I am nonetheless in earnest, you lot of pantywaist hacks. Why don't you khaki-clad yokels take a walk to any el station in the city and have a look at a map on the wall before you try to question the authority of the Chicago PD? Course I'm not really asking you take a walk on those spindly legs. And I'm not even suggesting you use one of your handy PDAs there to Google an el map because if you're too numbskull to think of that yourself it's cause you don't know how to use those things to begin with is what I'm saying. Or maybe you're so good at using 'em you forgot about maps because you're all GPS now. I don't know what your problem is, actually. I'm just sayin, here. No more hostility from youse. I'm two days from retirement, I got racquetball with Richie Daley at 1:00, and I will not abide it. This hostility being what I mean by "it." So look: That email's addressed to kids from two schools. You got the Solomon Whoever and the Northside Whatsit. They're going north to the suburbs, these kids, right? They're going north to the suburbs from Rogers Park, right? What do you think? They have to get on the Red Line, and then they gotta get on the Brown Line. And oh, take a look at the attachment that came attached to that email you showed on TV before you showed it to the police. Oh dearie me! In the email there, it says: Take the Red Line to Howard. Transfer to the Brown Line. Now. That latter transfer? That was almost two hours ago when they did it, and the trains have had some slowdowns, sure, but they ain't *that* slow. All of which is to say those kids are not in Chicago anymore. Those kids are in the suburbs and have been for a while. You're bothering the wrong cops, fellas, and in my closing statement, on this, what is certain to be my last press conference before retire-ment, I, with rapidly blossoming flowers of joy in my old Irish heart, would, on behalf of myself, like to say, just one last time, to you, my spindly-legged semi-literate douchebag pantywaist hackish yokel reporter friends: No. Further. Fucken. Comment.

STEVENS: Well, a little comic relief in the midst of tragic events never hurt anyone, I suppose. Here with me in the NBC studios is our Middle East consultant, Allie Momad. Allie, in your opinion, is the terrorist Gurion Maccabee, as has been alleged, a Zionist?

MOMAD: Well, Rick, the long answer is: Who can say for sure? He's a ten-year-old boy, certainly a boy who's been through Jewish schools, certainly an exceptionally violent boy, certainly a boy who invokes the Jewish God in emails that appear to be some kind of coded call-to-arms, certainly someone demanding to speak to Philip Roth, certainly the type of violent Jewish person that both the Eastern and the Western world have been certain would arise soon enough given the Jewish occupation of Palestine, the Israeli apartheid, the war crimes committed daily by the State of Israel, and the rhetoric used by Israeli and American Jewish progagandists to defend the apartheid and the war crimes and the hideous nature of the Israeli occupation of the Palestinean lands and people, not just men and women, Rick, but children, too. Children.

STEVENS: And the short answer, Allie?

MOMAD: Probably a Zionist.

STEVENS: Thank you, Allie. That was Allie Momad, our Middle East Consultant. Now we go to some new exclusive footage NBC has just acquired from another of the five cameras that were in the Aptakisic Junior High School gym at the time of the terrorist attack. I'm told we're about to see the gym teacher, Ronald Desormie, just as—there. Oh my. Oh my, that's vivid. Can we rewind that and slow—thank you, Mark. Yes, it looks, from the way he's holding his neck, and from the angle at which the projectile seems to have pierced him, as though the fatal shot could not have possibly been fired by Gurion Maccabee, who you can see laying on his stomach on the floor before the unfortunate gym teacher. It looks like the shot was fired from on-high. Can we roll that again?

☐ ☐ ☐ ☐ ☐ ☐ ☐

"Unless you're thinking maybe I shouldn't go back into the gym with this… hand like this?"

Yeah, I said.

"Come on, man," said Benji. "Admit what you're doing."

What am I doing?

"You're keeping me away from that dentist Berman and all of his buddies. I make them all nervous, so you're keeping me away."

You both—

"Like the Cage," he said.

That's—

"I'm being dramatic. That was dramatic. Overdramatical. Still, I'm right. And look: I understand. I mean, Berman's got more people behind him than I do. It would've been harder to get him out of there. Plus he's not injured. There'd be no reason to keep him somewhere else. He'd have lost face if you removed him, there could have been a fight, or—"

I'm sorry, I said. I just thought that after—

"I'm not asking for an apology, Gurion. You made the move you had to make, and I've taken the drugs—I'm being cooperative. This is what I want to tell you, though. Jelly is in there. In the gym. With that snake. She's in there with that snake, and so are all our other friends, and you need to watch out because you're acting snakey yourself—for good reason maybe, sure— but you're acting snakey yourself, and all those snakes can see right through you. Some of them at least. Snakes understand snakiness."

I don't think Berman's a snake, I said. Maybe he was, but he's not anymore, none of them are, and everything's gonna be fine, alright? This'll be over soon. The scholars—

"I don't need reassurance. *False* reassurance. *You* need to hear me."

Okay, I said. Fine. So what is it I'm missing? What's the big secret? What did Berman do to you, you hate him so much? Before today, I mean.

"I can't believe you're still— Look. Berman didn't do shit to me. He's just a snake. He's always been a snake. Same way Desormie's always been— same way Desormie *had* always been a scumbomb. He was born that way. Born a snake. All those ex-Shovers. And everyone knows this. June knows it. Vincie knows it. Brooklyn knows it. *You* know it. I know you know it. So let's not pretend. It's just you and me here, two best friends, and you've snaked me a little, but I'm forgiving you for snaking me, okay? So believe me, okay? Stop making that face. You need to believe me. I'm not trying to fuck with you. I'm forgiving you because you waited to bring me here til no one was around to see where you put me. I appreciate that. That you're trying to protect me. So I forgive you for snaking me, so now it's time you stop snaking me—I'm trying to help you out. Those guys are snakes. Especially Berman. And my girlfriend's in there with them, all of our friends are—did I say this part already? I did. These drugs are quick. BryGuy must have himself some serious… *tol*erance. But what I'm saying is you don't have to convince me to stay here. I came here willingly, I took the drugs—I'm on your side is what I'm trying to say. So just be straight with me. Be honest with your friend. Admit you know they're snakes and we can talk about some strategy for when you go back in there."

I'm being completely honest with you, I said.

"Gurion! Bullshit! You took their phones cause you knew they were snakes."

I took their phones cause I knew they were afraid. I didn't want them to freak out while I was gone and call the—

"You thinned their numbers," Nakamook said. "You could've sent someone to get a fucken wheely chair—this very fucken wheely chair into which my ass is melting—and sat Brodsky on it and wheeled him to the Cage. You and June could've done it. You didn't, though, right? Instead you got five, then ten of them to carry him because you wanted to thin their numbers because you knew they were snakes, and you wanted to give the Side a fighting chance in case the snakes attacked."

I thinned their numbers because I thought their numbers were making the Side nervous, Benji. Nervous is contagious, and— What you're saying's not true. I didn't think anyone would attack anyone, and I don't think that now. I just thought that the Side was worried about what would happen if they were attacked, so—

"You thought that because *you* were worried about it yourself! Stop lying to me! I don't see why you're lying. There's no one to protect here."

If I was really worried about the Side getting attacked, I said, I'd've thinned the *ex-Shovers'* numbers, not the other Israelites'.

"Wow," Benji said. "Wow!"

Wow what? I said.

"Wow."

Wow *what?*

"Wow I believe you."

Good, I said. I told you I wasn't—

"No," he said. "No it's not good. Wake the… Wake the fuck up, man."

Good elbow on the desk, Benji had propped his chin on his fist at about the same time as he'd said his first wow. He smiled now, and his chin slipped down, so his cheek was on the heel of his hand. The smile went away in the course of the slip, but had come back harder once the cheek was situated.

"Tchhhhhhhhhhh," he said, and got his face off his hand. He shook his head, as if to clear it out, but it didn't seem to work—his face was all slack. "Fucken," he said. Or maybe, "Fuck it." The end of the utterance got snapped by a yawn he fought to suppress. When the yawning passed, he thumb-flicked the pointer of his broken hand, let out a muffled throatmoan, flicked again, and seemed, by that second pained jolt, to be driven back into his body.

Benji, I said. I'm sorry I acted shady about bringing you here. I should have told you what I was doing, but I didn't think… I don't know.

Again he'd set his chin on his good fist and again it slipped, and again he flicked his wounds, made pained noises, and returned to his body, though his eyes this time weren't as popping. He tried to stand up, and then he stopped trying.

"Okay say that again," he said. "I didn't understand."

I was saying how I know it was hard for you not to retaliate against Berman to begin with, I said, but especially after he insulted Main Man's singing, and whatever else happened between you guys while I was out front with the firemen—I should have told you what I was doing, taking you here, but I didn't think you'd be willing to back down any further.

"I don't— What? What else would I retaliate for?" he said.

What do you mean? I said.

"What do *you* mean?" he said.

And I saw what he meant—or hadn't meant: He didn't know Berman was the one who'd brought him down at the end of the battle. I bit my lip hard, exercised a fantasy of retroactivation.

"'To begin with,'" he said. "You said 'to begin with.' What'd I have to retaliate to begin with for? I mean… I mean what—what'd Berman do before you went out front?"

I said, You should lay down, Benji. Seriously. You're barely awake.

"You're fucken doing it again—but you're doing it… worse. That fuck—" Benji'd made a move as if to flick himself again, but this time I grabbed the offending hand and held it down flat on the table. "Berman shot me, didn't he? Let go, now. On purpose. Let go of me. He shot me's what you're saying, on purpose. I thought that was friendly, like accidental crossfire. He shot me, that fuck *on purpose* shot me. And then it was *him* who jumped on me."

He didn't know you were with us, I said. He thought you weren't supposed to be there. You need to lay down.

"No no. No. You said—I heard you. On the megaphone—let go of my hand—you said we're brothers. Everyone with Damage on his head is brothers. What's on my head? On my head is Damage. Let go of my hand. You're the one who wrote it there. I did the same to you. It didn't wash off. It didn't sweat off. It didn't come off." He struggled to get his hand free of mine, but he didn't seem to know how to—he kept wiggling his shoulder. "I see it right now," he said. "Right in front of me, there on your head. Yours didn't come off, so mine didn't come off. You said we were brothers."

He must not have heard me.

"Bull. Shit," said Benji. "I am *so* fucked up right now, that lucky fucker. I sound like fucken Vincie I'm so fucked up. And he's in there with Jelly. I want to see Jelly."

I'll tell Jelly to come in here.

"Yeah, you do that, you fucken do that, you tell her you fuck, you fucken liar, Gurion. You're a fucken liar. Trying to make me feel paranoid… wrong… fucken…"

I said, You can't be angry at me like this. I said, I'm the one who got him off of you.

"I could've done that myself. I would've done that myself. You think fucken *Berman*… Another ten seconds… Another ten seconds, I'd've killed that kid. You did *him* the favor. You saved *his* ass. Not mine. Even *now* you fuck with me." Now Benji was crying. I'd never seen it, only heard of it once—the day before as I laid on my back in the field beneath yud-clouds, ashamed in front of June. I couldn't help but wonder if he knew he was doing it. There wasn't any sniffling and there wasn't any gasping. There wasn't a glug or whimper. He was about to pass out, face slipping on his fist, his lids nearly shut, but that should have, I thought, had the opposite effect—should have *lessened* his control over how he cried. Maybe it did. Scholars might wish to suggest that it did. They might wish to suggest that this orderly, dignified way of weeping—even the tears themselves were subdued, crawling from his eyes just one at a time, waterpark-goers in line for a slide, each waiting to climb from the squeeze of the duct til the one just ahead had safely cleared chin—was, in fact, for a soldier like Nakamook, as close to a demonstration of the chaos inside him as could be expressed without his resorting to the usual violence, of which, sedated, he was not capable. Whatever it was, this Nakamookian weeping, a show of strength or a show of weakness, an act of restraint or a loss of restraint, I didn't like to see it, and I didn't think that he'd like me to see it, and so I looked away, looked down at my hands, and let Benji finish berating and threatening me, cursing and hurting til he fell asleep, telling myself we'd patch it up later, outside the school. Safe among brothers. Surrounded and protected. The scholars would arrive and all would be well. I looked down at my hands and waited him out.

"Fucken liar," he said. "What a fucken even now a fucken miserable dissembling fucken liar you are, man. Treat me like you're Botha. Manage me like I'm just some dumbfuck SpEd to manage. Made a mistake... I'll fucken... *kill* that fucker. I'll fucken burn your... you fucken lie... liar. Like a... God! Fucking SpEd... I'll fucken burn down *both* your houses."

□   □   □   □   □   □   □

"...to the right of your screen," the anchor was saying.

The photo to the right was from the fall before. It was cropped from a two-pager in the Schechter yearbook which showed me leading a discussion in Torah Study. In the original, ten scholars sit around an oval table, all of us using our hands to gesticulate, and we appear to be having the best conversation. Magnified, though, and with the others cropped out, I looked psychotic—my eyebrows straining to meet at my nosebridge, my pointer extending from a fist toward the viewer—a darker, beardless Uncle Sam in a yarmulke.

Both TVs were still tuned to NBC, both pictures snowy, both volume levels cranked. One sat in front of the eastern bleachers, which, except for June and Jelly and Brooklyn and the Five, were occupied by all the Israelites in the gym. The other sat in front of the western bleachers where everybody else was but Vincie and Starla, who each pressed an ear to the pushbar door.

I had entered the gym through the central door, and now I was standing before them all, between the TVs, where the noise was most blurred. Few of the soldiers seemed to notice my entrance. Some were crying, others shaking their heads, most leaning forward and hugging themselves or stretching their arms, balling their fists, blinking hard, jaw muscles bulging.

June and Jelly and Eliyahu approached to my left, and Berman was descending from the bleachers to my right, the ex-Shover Cory Goldman trailing just behind him. I couldn't hear anything.

I sirened the megaphone and held the trigger til the TVs were muted by Googy and Main Man, who held the remotes. June, by my side now, whispered, "Be careful," and Jelly said, "Where's—"

I said, Go to Nurse Clyde's.

Jelly cut out.

"Where's she going?" said Berman.

"They were saying on the news," Eliyahu said, "that hundreds of scholars from your former schools got emails from you with directions to Aptakisic, and then they were saying they were spotted on trains, and now they're saying hundreds more scholars from other Israelite schools in the suburbs and the city are missing as well."

I strained to keep the relief off my face: I was supposed to have been certain all along that the scholars would show.

So why's it so somber in here? I said.

"Because they're also saying," said Berman, "that cops have blocked the roads off to stop your friends before they get here."

"But," said Eliyahu, "that's not the end of the world. I gave the Five the phone and they called their friend Feingold to warn him that the cops had seen the email with the directions to Aptakisic, and this Feingold said it didn't matter. He said there were two groups of at least two hundred scholars from the suburbs, each heading south along the lakeshore—Feingold was with one group, and he could see the other one a quarter mile up the beach—and since your directions were for the scholars of Chicago, the cops didn't know the route that the lakeshore groups were taking, so there won't be any kind of roadblock to stop them, right?"

"Except," said Berman, "we're a mile east of the lakeshore, so even if they were *directly* east of us, they'd still have about a mile to go, and they're *not* directly east of us—they're still heading south—so we're talking about at least another twenty minutes til they get here."

"At *least*," said Cory. "And that's a while. And you sound crazy on TV."

"Enough of that," said Eliyahu.

"Yeah, enough!" said Pinker. "Cut that shit out!" The Levinson said.

By this point, both sets of bleachers were empty. Much as the last time

I'd returned to the gym, the Side and Big Ending and the Five and their Ashley mobbed up to my left behind June and Eliyahu, while the rest of the Israelites were mobbed to my right behind Cory and Berman.

"What Cory means is Philip Roth," Berman said. "That stuff you said to the camera about talking to Philip Roth... It's..."

"It's weird!" an ex-Shover said. "I thought we were waiting for scholars, not an author." "And what's this stuff about a holiday that doesn't have a name?" said another ex-Shover. "I think you should call it Last Day of School Day," said the Flunky. "That's completely dumb!" an Israelite yelled. "It's *completely* dumb and it doesn't sound Israelite!" "Who cares if it sounds—" "Fuck you who cares! *We* care." "Who's Philip Roth?" "How about Shut the Fuck Up You Fucken Coward Day!" "How about you fucken idiots don't even know who Philip Roth is!" "And the way you keep sending Israelites out to guard the doors!" "Yeah! Why don't you send any of *them*, you know?" "It's like you're trying—" "He's not trying anything! You just want to watch TV and bitch and moan!" "We have to get out of here. Gurion. Baby." "You're supposed to be the messiah, but you're sending Israelites into danger!" "What's the messiah?" "You should send them instead!" "Did that dumbfuck just ask *what's the messiah?*" "*Is* he the messiah?" "*Are* you the messiah?" "What's the messiah?" "And where's that bully?" "The messiah's a who!" "Where'd they hide Nakamook?" "Why's he friends with that kid?!" "He might be the messiah and he might not be the messiah!" "There is no might! He is or he isn't!" "What the fuck do you know? You dropped out of Hebrew School!" "He's our leader!" "Why, though? Why's he our leader if he isn't the messiah?" "He *might* be the messiah!" "Why's he leading *them* if he's our messiah?" "He might *not* be the messiah!" "He is or he isn't! He can't have his cake and eat it too!" "His *cake?*" "Our cake!" "*Our* cake?" "Cake?" "Our who?" "He's our leader!" "Where's he fucken leading us!?" "He's protecting us!" "You feel protected?!"

And I stood there, scholars, listening and listening, trying to get a handle on what needed settling first, til finally I judged that none of it did. These arguers didn't care about what they were arguing. They were all just afraid. In my absence, as before, they'd all grown afraid, and to combat their fears, they argued with each other. It shouldn't have surprised me. In war it's necessary to fill up with enmity—it's even good—but when under siege, you feel out of control, you become afraid, and you wedge that enmity between yourself and your brothers, who you see before you, who you can reach out and strike: if you can't attack the one you want to, you attack the one you're with. It's a way to forget the siege a little, a way to regain some sense of control. It's the wrong way, true, one of the wrongest, but it's still an act of hope, at least inasmuch as it isn't surrender, and these soldiers before me—they weren't surrendering. I saw they had hope yet.

I sirened the megaphone. Their mouths stopped moving.

Brothers, I said, you are wasting your enmity, wasting your strength. You're all just afraid of what might happen next, not in the school, but outside the school; not between one another, but between now and then; us in here and them out—

"It's them!" someone shouted from the edge of the mob. "Look! Come quick! It's them! It's them!"

June grabbed my hand as the mob dispersed. I led her to a spot before the eastern bleachers. Ex-Shovers low-voiced some hey's and what-the's. I sat us on the floor to unblock their sightlines, not even thinking to address them directly.

Emmanuel Liebman was live on TV.

□   □   □   □   □   □   □

The cameraman was shooting from the side of Rand Road, so Emmanuel, in profile, as he pressed forward, was moving from the right of our screens toward the left. Behind him, in columns, scholars were emerging from the edge of the frame. Their pennyguns were drawn, but pointed at the ground. Their columns spanned the asphalt between the road's shoulders.

At the screen's extreme left were a pair of squadcars, parked nose-to-nose to block both lanes, their blue lights rotating lazily. Three of four cops who'd been leaning on the doors straightened their postures and crossed their arms. The fourth reached inside of the car he'd been leaning on, grabbed the PA mike and said, "STAND DOWN." It sounded fizzy.

Emmanuel stopped moving. The scholars stopped moving.

The soldiers in the gym stifled groans, then didn't.

Samuel was heading the centermost column. Emmanuel revolved, said something in his ear. Samuel said something back to Emmanuel. Emmanuel nodded, revolved, went forward. The rest of the scholars followed his lead.

When the gap between Emmanuel and the cross-armed cops, which was roughly forty yards at the sound of "STAND DOWN," shrunk to thirty-five, another order came.

"HALT," said the cop on the microphone.

The scholars pressed forward, filling more of the frame. Nine columns eight-deep to the edge of the screen; now nine-, now ten-, now eleven-deep.

"CEASE. HALT. STAND DOWN," squawked the mike-cop. The others unholstered batons.

As the scholars closed in, not missing a beat, the PA continued to fizzily squawk. Fifteen yards from the cops, they were all onscreen; another couple yards and Emmanuel stopped them. Soldiers in the gym started groaning a little. I tried to count the rows but the camera zoomed in. I'd counted almost halfway and gotten to twenty. Nine columns by forty-odd rows plus flankers (there were flankers picking rocks from the gravel shoulders, handing them in to be passed across the rows) = roughly four hundred scholars in all. Zoomed-in, I was able to make out more faces: the columns switched off between Schechter and Northside, five of the former and four of the latter.

Emmanuel revolved, said something to Samuel. Samuel said something back to Emmanuel.

How far away are they? I said to the soldiers.

"I think those houses are, like, six blocks away." "More like two." "They're nowhere near us." "There's that one with the Santa, though. The year-round Santa one." "The year-round Santa one's minutes away." "Minutes exactly." "Minutes *by bus*, dude." "*Two* minutes by bus when you catch all the reds." "Where is it you think you see a Santa, anyway?" "There at the edge." "That isn't a Santa." "It's the side of a Santa." "It's the side of a whatsit—the water thing." "A hydrant." "You're crazy." "You're blind. That Santa's a hydrant."

"Why don't you call them?" asked Ally Kravitz.

NoJacks, I said.

Onscreen, Emmanuel was addressing the scholars. He pointed east, then pointed north. Samuel leaned, seeming to protest. Emmanuel shrugged. The cops hadn't moved.

"They've *all* got NoJacks?" Josh Berman said.

The ones who I know, I said.

"I fucken hate NoJacks." "I hate NoJacks, too." In the gym, we cursed NoJacks til Emmanuel revolved again.

Hands cupped at his mouthsides, he hollered to the cops. The mike on the camera barely picked it up; what it did get got garbled into frying sounds.

"STAND DOWN," said the mike-cop, when Emmanuel finished.

Emmanuel hollered: more hisses and hums. This time the cops, when Emmanuel was finished, started to argue among themselves.

Emmanuel raised his hand, waiting for something.

The cameraman started to speak in a whisper: "The studio's telling us that our microphone's failing. The network apologizes... To catch you up: The boy at the front yelled out to officers that he intended to 'lead his friends to the two-hill field' and he asked that the officers please get out of his way so that 'we won't have to walk on your cars and dent them.' Some ten seconds later, he seemed to change his mind, and he told the officers that because they 'seem like nice men who probably have families and need to keep your jobs, which maybe you'll lose if you don't stand your ground, we'll just walk around you while you stand your ground, and your cars won't get—' There they go."

Emmanuel turned right and the scholars turned with him, and as all of them headed toward the top of the screen, away from the camera. The cops stayed still, slouching in the street, and one of them was actually scratching his head. They continued like that for about twenty seconds, til the cop who'd manned the mike turned and looked in the camera, then pointed it out for the others to see, and they all came charging, batons still gripped, bigger and bigger.

The camera angled downward, 90 degrees, and evergreen needles, tinily icicled, filled the whole frame before the screen blacked.

Cut to newsroom.

The pursed-lipped anchor, caught offguard, eyes squinted to papercuts, straightened his face out and started to talk. Who knows what he said? The scholars beat the cops, we were cheering our heads off, jumping up and down, cheering so loud that I could barely feel Botha's celly vibrate, let alone hear it. Its screen read: UNKNOWN.

I hit the green button, shouted, Hold on!

I ran out to B-Hall to pretend to negotiate.

◻ ◻ ◻ ◻ ◻ ◻ ◻

Persphere? I said.

"This is Roth," said a man.

Really, I said.

"We exchanged letters, you and I, a little over a year ago."

What did mine say? I said.

"Yours?" he said. He said, "Mostly, it talked about *Operation Shylock*—nice things—and then went on to tell a story about some boys who were sexually obsessed with Natalie Portman."

What else did it say?

"Is this how you want to spend our three minutes? Verifying?"

I wrote an essay for class once where I talked about our letters, I said. Maybe the cops got hold of it and read it. And don't sweat the three minutes: I'm the one who decides how long we talk—not the cops.

"No," Roth said, "I decide. Two more minutes, I'm hanging up."

You sure you're Roth? You sound a little more patrician—a *lot* more patrician than—

"Patrician, he says, the boy who thinks cops want to read his essays."

I didn't mean it mean.

"Boychic, we've got very little time here, and what I want to tell you is you should let these kids go. This stunt you're pulling's sealed fame for you forever, or at least a few years, and now it's time to give up peacefully. Everyone knows someone else killed the gym teacher—they're playing that video left and right—so you won't get pegged for anyone's murder, and on top of that, they're telling me you have ADHD, and I'm sure a good lawyer like your father can spin that into something bigger—temporary insanity, something like that; maybe the school nurse forgot to give you your meds, who knows? You're not a hard case, though, not by any means, so even if they lock you up, it'll be somewhere safe, and you'll write your books, and hopefully they'll outshine this moment and you'll live it down. If you can't live it down, you can always grow a beard and use a pseudonym. It'll all work out if you end this now."

Do you think you're bad for the Jews? I said.

"*This* conversation? Really? *This* one?"

Okay, I said.

"Okay what?"

I'm starting to think you're actually Roth.

"So what do you want from me?"

Nothing, I said.

"So why'd you want to talk to me? Surely not just to hear what you already know, let alone in so dismayingly patrician a baritone. There must be something you'd like to discuss in the remaining ten seconds you've been alotted. Unless maybe you're a stalker? I hope you're not. I didn't take you for a stalker when you sent me that letter—I wouldn't have responded if I—"

I said, I'm really sorry I bothered you, Mr. Roth. I *didn't* want to talk to you. I like your books too much to want to talk to you, and you have my word that I'll do everything I can to forget what you sound like when you're speaking.

"You didn't want to talk to me."

You're hard to get a hold of. You bought me fifty-something minutes.

"You're being serious, now."

If I didn't have a girlfriend who might have taken it wrong, I'd have asked them to get Natalie Portman on the phone.

"So I bought you some time. So what happens next?"

We're past three minutes.

"Don't be a wiseass. What happens next?"

Next I'll talk to Persphere, or whatever he's calling himself. Do you think his accent's real?

"You're asking the patrician-sounding Jew about accents?"

That was just an observation I made—I didn't mean it mean.

"You said that already."

Well it's true, I said. I just thought you'd sound different, like…

"Like?"

It's hard to describe now. Like Groucho Marx, I guess, but not as fast.

"Like a first-generation American Jew. Not shtetl, but tenement."

Maybe, I said.

"Like my parents instead of 'what' said 'vot.'"

That's taking it too far. Forget Groucho Marx. I thought you'd sound hairier.

"Hairier?"

Much, much hairier. And more verklempt. Less amused and more will-ing to attack, less concerned about what he sounds like than what he says—like those guys with hairy shoulders who wear U-shirts cause it's hot out and function trumps form.

"U-shirts," he said.

Dago-T's, I said.

"I know what a U-shirt is."

Please stop being offended, Mr. Roth. You're my favorite writer and what I'm telling you is I thought you'd sound like my father, who doesn't, by the way, have hairy shoulders, but does wear U-shirts when it's really muggy, and would wear them when it was muggy if he *did* have hairy shoulders. I thought you'd sound like my father, who I love, is what I'm saying.

"This being the lawyer, Judah Maccabee, goes to bat for civil liberties." Him.

"Who I *don't* in fact—you're telling me now—sound like."

Not on the phone, but who cares, Mr. Roth? Who cares what you sound like on the phone? Who cares about anything you do off the page? You're a writer.

"You're a writer, too. Obviously you want us to care what you're doing. The taking of hostages, if nothing else, demands that others care about what you're doing."

I write scripture, I said. It's different than fiction. You have to read it different. It matters what I do.

"And what will you do now? Will you do the right thing?"

What disappointing questions, Mr. Roth. Really.

"Disappointing how?"

You're not taking me seriously. You were faking umbrage to get information.

"I *was* faking umbrage to get information, but only because I do take you seriously. Everyone does. The question was serious. Will you do the right thing?"

Whatever seems proper in my eyes is right. There's no king in Israel. Thanks for your time. Good Shabbos, Philip Roth.

"Wait," Roth said. "Let's not end like this. Let's not end with ugliness."

I told you 'Good Shabbos.'

"You *said* 'Good Shabbos.' You told me 'Fuck you.'"

Good Shabbos, fuck you, but good Shabbos nonetheless because you wrote all those books. Good Shabbos, really. Okay? Good Shabbos.

"Backatcha, I guess."

Some silence. I waited. I looked at the screen; the call hadn't ended.

Persphere, I said, I know you're listening.

"I'm here," said Persphere.

The prisoners are safe.

"Prove it," he said.

When my friends get here, you let them inside. I'll come out with the prisoners and surrender myself.

"Can't do it," said Persphere. "I can't let civilians—*kid* civilians...

You've gotta be kidding me. No fucken way, kid."

I'm not asking, I said, and you're suck at bluffing—probably you should have kept that accent for cover. You'll let them in, we'll come out and surrender.

"Have you looked outside?"

Have I what? I said.

I said it to stall, and raced up toward the junction.

"Have you looked outside?"

A line of cops in riotgear were standing the perimeter.

I said, A line of cops in riotgear are standing the perimeter.

"A line of a hundred," he said. "Now listen."

I listened; heard chopping.

A helicopter? You brought in a helicopter? You're cracking me up.

"Come again?" said Persphere.

This is overkill, Persphere. Too asymmetrical. You've got an advantage that's too big to use. To tell you the truth, I've been a little scared of what you might do, but now? A hundred cops in riotgear—them just out front—and a *helicopter*? You're stuck. You could've, thirty minutes ago, raided the school with five or six cops and hurt us a little in the process of saving us, maybe gotten some of the prisoners killed while saving the others—true—and then later made a convincing argument that it was crazy in here, that I was crazy, and that you did the only thing you could have. It would've been hinky, but you probably could've managed it. Now, though, you're live on television everywhere, a helicopter chopping and plexiglass shields, not to mention, I'm sure, the requisite snipers and reinforced vehicles, and even if your cops *are* willing to shoot at or teargas or beat on some kids—and probably some are, but certainly not most of them… You know what a Chow is? Chow's a big, mean guard-dog from China that a fascist I know's mother keeps as a pet. You're a Chow and we're a lapdog. One offhanded swipe on your part and we're dead, no doubt about it, but as soon as you kill us, every neighbor on the block'll demand you put down. And there's lots of good neighbors in that parking lot, there. Lots of good parents behind that cordon who might want to put you down themselves, so listen up: I appreciate the complexity of your position—I'm the one, after all, who put you in your position—and even knowing that you've got nothing, I'm telling you that all you have to do is let my friends in when they get here, and this will all end without any more bloodshed. I'm telling you I'm your only hope.

"So you're saying you're angry at Philip Roth for the way he spoke to you, and now—"

What? I said.

"You're saying you're angry at Philip Roth for the way he spoke to you, and now you're gonna start executing hostages, one every five minutes, til we get you a plane with a pilot you're saying, like in—what did you say? Like in *Dog Day Afternoon*? Your parents let you watch that? I'm expressing surprise here. You want a plane like Pacino, except you also want a Nintendo on board? And Natalie Portman? Is that what I heard you say? You want Portman to do you 'favors' on the plane? If that's what I heard you say, please say it again so that I can record it in order to justify the raid we're about to bring down on your arrogant, terrorist head, because I just realized that—check this out—I just realized that, all along, though I thought I was recording this conversation, what I was actually doing was erasing our earlier conversation, and no one except you and I's ever gonna know what got said here."

You've got that gluggy Biggie Smalls thing in your voice, I said. You're obese, right? You're a fatguy with facial flush, drymouth, and perpetually sweaty nosewings, and the one thing you're *not* gonna do, Wayne, after threatening such an over-the-top deception, is use that deception. Nice last desperate try, though. Goodbye now, to you, and to all you good neighbors listening in, as—

"Gurion, you must kill no one," my mother said.

Ema? I said.

"I want you to listen to me, Gurion. I want you to stop talking and listen to me very, very closely. Your father and I love you. We know that you were already upset about what happened to your father last night and we are sorry that—"

Ema, you don't have to—

"Listen. Closely. Please. Gurion. Please do not interrupt me again."

Okay, I said.

"I do not like to discuss these kinds of things when other people are listening either, but it is important we discuss this right now: We are, first of all, sorry, very sorry that it took us so long to get in contact with you today. Despite your father's injuries, we did end up meeting with our lawyers this morning, and our phones were turned off. We did not know about any of this until only fifteen minutes ago. We are even more sorry, your father and I both, that we chose last night to tell you about the divorce. We are sorry that we did not take into account how upset you already were about what happened to your father at the courthouse, and we are sorry that we did not take your feelings into account regarding where you would live. As a mental health professional, I of all people should have known that you would want to live with me, your mother, even though I am the one at whose feet lay the blame for our marriage's disintegration. Our only excuse for our rash behavior, and it is not a very good one, for you are our son who we need to put before ourselves and protect at all costs—our only excuse is that we were upset, ourselves, and we were being selfish. Me especially. It is not a good excuse, but it is the truth. And you do *not* have to live with your father, not if you don't want to. You can live with Yakov and me and all of Yakov's children at Yakov's house, just as long as you don't kill anyone. Are you listening? This is important."

I said, Ema, I feel like I'm going crazy.

"You have my word, Gurion, that you are *not* going crazy. You just need to pause for a moment and *think clearly* about what I have told you, and you will see that everything, though it will be different from now on, will be nonetheless fine, at least eventually, just as long as you do not kill anyone. Yakov is a kind, forgiving man, and just as soon as this is all over, and just as long as you do not kill anyone—Yakov cannot be expected to abide killers in his house, not with all his children, all your new brothers and sisters—he will treat you as his own son. I am assured of this. He has assured me. He knows who I am and he knows that you are special. Do you understand?"

Yes? I said = I don't know what the fuck you're talking about, but I understand I'm supposed to pretend you're getting a divorce because people are listening and you're speaking in code, some kind of code that I'll decipher any minute now; you're offering me a carrot called "live in Yakov's house," and warning with a stick called "don't live in Yakov's house."

"Now I want you, in English," she said in Hebrew—why in Hebrew? not because she believed there wasn't a Hebrew speaker listening; she had to believe that, or else she would have used Hebrew all along instead of code; rather, she spoke, now, in Hebrew, to clarify that she was no longer speaking in code—"I want you, in English, to tell me you will not kill anyone, and I want that to be the truth. And then I want you to surrender to the police."

June stuck her head out the gym's central exit, started to approach me.

I won't surrender to the police, I said in English. Not before my friends get here. And if I tell you I won't kill anyone, then Persphere's gonna raid.

"That may be so," my mother said in Hebrew. Then back to English:

"But if you surrender now and you don't kill anyone, you will be able to live with me in Yakov's house, and I know that's what you've wanted all along."

All along? What was she talking about, *all along?* What had I wanted *all along?* To write immortal scripture? To ensure my father's safety? To study Torah with my peers? To be married to June by an Orthodox rabbi? Which *all along? All along* starting from when, exactly? And if I didn't know what I'd wanted all along, how could she know what I wanted all along? Yes, she was my mother, and she knew me very well, but she couldn't know me better than I knew myself. No one could. No one can know anyone better than one knows oneself. All I could make of what my mother was telling me was that she believed there was some reason to have hope, and that it was a real reason; that the reason wasn't "one *should have* hope" or "hope will provide," but some actual, tactical-type, on-the-ground reason. Either that or she was, with the best of intentions, lying to me, colluding with the cops to ensure her son's safety; i.e., she knew I would *not* get what I wanted all along—whatever that was—if I promised not to kill and surrendered to the cops, but she knew that if I surrendered and promised not to kill, I wouldn't, myself, get killed, which because she was my mother was her primary concern.

In either case, it wasn't enough.

And here was June, taking hold of my hand in both of hers, shaking it around, widening her eyes.

I said to my mom and to anyone else listening: I love you, Ema, but I've said all I'll say. Persphere lets my friends in and no one gets killed. After that I surrender. Now I have to go.

I turned off the phone.

"Who's this 'Ema'?" June said.

I said, Ema means mom.

June kissed my mouth, and then she stopped. I tried to re-start, but she ducked away.

Hey, I said.

"I have something to tell you that you don't want to hear, and you're not allowed to think I'm a bad Israelite."

I won't, I said.

"Because Eliyahu and the Five think the same thing as me, Gurion."

I like to hear you say my name.

She said, "Berman is bad."

He isn't, I said. He's just been afraid.

"No. You're wrong. All those ex-Shovers are bad, Gurion, and everyone else in their bleachers is with them. On TV they started showing the front of the school again, and there's all these cops in a line, and a helicopter, and everyone got freaked out all over again, and the Israelites started whispering in circles, back and forth. I tried to listen in to what they were saying, but they'd stop the second I was close enough. Eliyahu tried, too, and the Five. Same thing, though. I think they're plotting against you. I don't think you should go back in there. I think you should send *me* back in there and I'll say you ordered that I bring the Side of Damage out for guard duty, and we'll all go somewhere else in the school where you'll be safe, and wait there for the scholars. Vincie thinks so, too. And so does Eliyahu."

I said, The Israelites are with us. They're just afraid.

She said, "Every time you leave, they start acting shady."

I said, Every time I come back, they stop acting shady.

She said, "They're whispering, though, Gurion. If they were shouting, that would be one thing—but whispering…"

I said, We're whispering right now. And so were you and Eliyahu and Vincie.

"And in all those cases, something was being plotted."

And this plot, like that one, is being shot down. I'm shooting it down.

"Please?" June said, "Please just listen to me? I've got a really bad feeling. Let's go somewhere else."

I can't, I said.

"Well I won't go back in with you."

Okay, I said. I understand. Just go wait at the nurse's with Jelly and Benji. No one but us knows that's where they are. As soon as the scholars come in, I'll come get you.

"No," June said. "I'm leaving. I'm going outside."

Okay, I said. Okay, I said. I said, I wish you'd stay, but I guess I understand, or that I will understand. Or no, actually. I mean I don't understand at all, but I should because I love you, so I will, I think, eventually, but… Come on, June, I love you. The hardest part's over. Just stick around. We have to do what's dangerous, remember?

"If you go back in the gym, I'm leaving," she said.

I need to go back in, I said. I wish you wouldn't leave, but if you have to, I guess let me tie up your wrists, and I'll take you out the front.

"No wrists," June said. "I wasn't a prisoner. I'm not gonna pretend I was a prisoner."

Please let me tie your wrists, I said.

"You're missing the point!" she said, and she punched me in the chest, and grabbed my hand, and grabbed my other one, and we didn't go anywhere, but swayed there and hugged and arm-pulled a little. It wasn't exactly dancing.

□   □   □   □   □   □   □

Berman and Cory were waiting in the bleachers-gap. From behind them came the voice of the network anchor, enumerating "non-lethal assets." Tear gas. Pepper spray. Billyclubs. Tazers. I squeezed June's hand, said, I need to talk to Aleph and his boy here, okay? Please tell the Side I'll be there in a minute.

Berman leaned close, checked over his shoulder. When June turned right at the edge of the bleachers, he told me, "We're done for if we don't surrender."

No one's done for, I said. You're all just afraid. I need you to act like a leader, Berman. The scholars are coming. They'll get here soon. I need you to keep the soldiers cool in the meantime. They're looking to you.

Ally Kravitz turned the corner into the gap.

"Listen," Berman said. "There's no way this is gonna work. It's one thing for your friends to get past four cops. I was as happy to see that as the next guy, okay? But there's a hundred cops out front. And a helicopter. And snipers, and—"

"We want to tie up the Side and surrender," Cory said. "We want to tell the cops the Side made us do this, but we overcame them."

And which 'we' is this?

"The Israelites," said Berman.

Which ones? I said to Berman. Eliyahu? The Five? June? Jelly?

"I don't want to be a rat."

That's a funny thing to say.

Berman looked at his feet.

Are you including me in this 'we'?

"Of course," Berman said, hope aflicker. "You're our leader, right?"

Right, I said, I'm your leader. Exactly. And we're not tying anyone up, I said. And what I'm gonna do is tell myself that you're just really scared, and you don't really know what you're saying. You didn't really make the suggestion I thought I just heard. It was a scared little thought you had and you spoke too soon—you're not even thinking it anymore, right? Because the scholars are on their way, and after they get here, we'll all go out, prisoners in tow, and I'll surrender, and all of you will say that I did this, and I will say that I did this, and everyone will believe that I did this, and you will all be fine.

"Okay," Berman said. "Okay. I get it. You don't want the Cage kids to get in trouble either. You're gonna take responsibility for all of us, right? So, like, what about this? We could tie *you* up, and then all of us could walk out of here, the Israelites *and* the Cage kids."

I said, We're waiting for the scholars, Berman.

"But the scholars can't get in here," Ally said. "There's too many cops."

They've gotten past cops. They're coming, I said.

"*Four*," Ally said. "They got past four in regular cop-clothes. Now there's a hundred dressed up in riotgear."

And there's a hundred cameras, too, I said. Plus how many parents in the parking lot? They're not tazing kids or gassing kids or clubbing kids on live TV in front of anyone's parents.

"Maybe they will, maybe they won't," Berman said.

I said, Everything I've said has come true so far.

"You don't know," Berman said. "All due respect. You don't know what they'll do. You can't see the future. It's a risk, Gurion, and all due respect, we don't know these scholars. What difference does it make if they get here or not? To us, I mean. What difference?"

If I can get hundreds of scholars to come here to see me, then it helps to make the case that I got all of you to attack the school, kill Desormie, and take prisoners.

"There's enough of us already, though, right? You said so yourself. If we all say you did this, they'll believe us anyway, scholars or not."

"Maybe they will, maybe they won't," said Vincie, who'd entered the gap without my having noticed. "It's a fucken risk, you respectful fuck."

Vincie, I said, we're all cool here. Go back to the bleachers.

Vincie made the noise "Tch," and walked away.

"They're already on their way—the scholars," Ally Kravitz said. "They don't need to get in the building for your plan to work, Gurion. They've already come all this way to see you. It doesn't really matter if they get inside the school or not—they've come as far as they have because you told them to. No one doubts that, and no one will—there's all those emails. And it's not just us who're taking a risk here if you insist they come inside the school—there's them. They could get hurt, too."

But they're not gonna get hurt, and neither are we.

"You can't possibly know that!" Berman said.

We're going in circles, I said. Now listen to me. I think I know what the problem is here. You're confused because of the pennyguns. All of you are. Your weapons gave you confidence and made you stronger, okay? But they didn't make you strong enough to take the school, despite what you think. We were able to take the school because we protected each other. In protecting each other, we did what Adonai wants us to do. We did what He has always told us to do, and were strengthened. Our victory owes to *that*. Now you see cops outside with superior weapons, and you forget about protection, and you forget Adonai. You think only of weapons. You think that because they have better weapons, they'll defeat us. I'm telling you they won't, not as long as we protect each other. I'm telling you: don't be confused by your weapons.

"Tying you up, now," said Ally, "and surrendering—that's a way to protect each other."

My chemicals were starting to fire a little. Why couldn't they hear me?

I said, Why can't you hear me? Why don't you trust me? Why can't you see what's before your eyes? Everything that is good for me is good for the Israelites.

"So you're saying you *are* the messiah, then," Berman said.

No, I said.

"You're not the messiah?"

I might be, I said.

"You are or you aren't."

That's not how it works.

"That *is* how it works. You can't have it both ways. We can't take it both ways."

I'm not even asking you to, I said. Even if I am the messiah, what good would it do you to hear me say I was? You'd only doubt it like everything else. Forget about the messiah—no, don't forget about the messiah… It's just it doesn't matter if I'm the messiah. Not here, it doesn't. I need to give *myself* up to the cops, or the whole plan crumbles. If I'm tied up, they're only gonna wonder why you didn't tie me up earlier. They're gonna wonder why it took so long.

"We'll come up with a story." "We can come up with a story." "Your back was turned so your swirly pinwheel eyes couldn't cast their crazy spells on us." "Your eyes were on the television and you were distracted." "We came to our senses when you started to—"

Those stories aren't true, though, and plus you'll screw them up. You won't get them straight. You need one story and it needs to be simple. 'It was Gurion.' 'Gurion.' 'Gurion did it.'

"He's right," said Ally. "You're right," he said. "It needs to be simple and it needs to be true. You need to turn yourself in of your own volition. So do it. Do it right now, though, before we get hurt."

I've already made my demands, I said.

"Back off your demands," Ally said. "Say you got scared. That's a simple story for *you* to tell, then we'll tell *our* simple one, and everyone will be believed."

Ally was right. Rather, Ally was correct. His way would work too. If my only concern were the safety of the Aptakisic Israelites and the Side. His solution was the safest, most practical solution. But I had the scholars to think about: delivering them the damage prayer, their public acceptance of June as an Israelite, and the protection of my father. And why didn't I explain that? Why *hadn't* I explained it? Why hadn't I, at any point prior to this one, told them about my plans regarding June, the delivery of the prayer, the protection of my father? Why hadn't I told them at the first opportune moment? It was, after all, the truth. And yet it hadn't even occurred to me to tell them. Rather, it had never occurred to me that it would be a good idea to tell them. But why not? Because I feared they'd suspect me of being blinded by personal motivations? Yes. Because I thought they would, owing to those suspicions, cease to obey me, screwing everything up for themselves and the rest of us? Yes and yes and yes. Because I feared that I was, in fact, blinded by personal motivations?

Curiously or not, scholars: no.

Emphatically no.

I believed what I'd told them with all of my heart. Whether or not I was the potential messiah—and make no mistake; the likelihood that I was seemed to me to be increasing by the second—I believed that what was good for me, in this case at least, was good for the Israelites, and I believed that what was bad for me was bad for the Israelites, and I didn't see any reason to reveal information to them that might put what was good for us at risk. Some scholars may wish to cast this as a failure on my part to trust my brothers in the Aptakisic gym. Fair enough. It was a failure of trust. But it was just as much a success of mistrust. I knew our limitations, at least a few of them.

And beyond that, I wasn't scared. Not of being raided. Not of the cops attacking the scholars outside. Not anymore. I wasn't. They wouldn't. At least I didn't think they would. At least not just yet. And if I was my generation's potential messiah, then to act scared when I wasn't scared, to give up before I wanted to give up, before I thought I had to give up, let alone *to lie* about being scared—no messiah would do that, and any potential messiah who did that would, no doubt about it, be squandering his potential. What was bad for me was bad for the Israelites.

At least potentially. In the ideal.

"Come on," Ally said. "What do you say? You just say you got scared and we'll say you did all of this. Same outcome as if we wait, but less risky. It's elegant," he said. "There's no room to screw up."

No, I said.

"Why not?" said Berman.

I brushed past him and Cory and Ally, out of the gap. June was waiting there for me. I went to the TV in front of the Israelites and muted it, and Main Man muted the Side's TV.

All whispering stopped.

There weren't any new arguments left to make; they'd all been made, I'd made them all. So I made them again, only louder this time, and with more gesticulations, as if I were inspired anew by the truth; as if, as they had, I'd forgotten the truth, and the truth remembered—the truth itself—would somehow unite us, would somehow protect us, save us.

This is what I said: Earlier, you thought I was wrong, and I was right. I'm still right. The cops haven't got you, and they'll never get you. The scholars are coming and they always were. We will wait for them as we always have been, and they will arrive, as they were always meant to. I am, as always, on the side of the Israelites. I am, as always, on the Side of Damage. I have fought, as always, on both of our sides, and both of our sides will always fight for each other. The Israelites will always protect the Side of Damage, and the Side of Damage will always protect the Israelites.

And I stood there before them, meeting their stares, grabbing hold of June's hand, and here's what's crazy, this is what haunts me even today: By the time I'd gotten two sentences in, I *was* inspired anew. My gesticulations *weren't* forced. By the time I'd finished speaking, I was so intoxicated by my own verbosity, I expected a defeaning group amen. And when, instead of that deafening amen, the last thing I wanted to hear got spoken, it took me whole seconds to understand.

"Israelites like her?" someone said. The question came from among the ex-Shovers, and wasn't a question at all.

Who's *her*? I thought.

She was squeezing my hand.

Who said that? I said.

No one would say.

"Doesn't matter," June said.

Berman, I said, tell me who said that.

"Said what?" Berman said.

"It's okay," June said.

Who said it? I said.

"I didn't see," said Berman. "I don't know who said it."

Said *what* then? I said.

"I don't know!" said Berman.

I spun to my right and dumped the TV. It didn't explode, so I lifted the cart, started hacking away, and at last there came a flash and a pop, and some glass shot high and cut me on the cheek, just beneath the eye, the tiniest sting. It wasn't enough, though. I didn't feel better. I wanted the cart in pieces now, too. And I whaled on the floor, and I whaled on the scaffold, but the cart was steel and it barely bent, and Eliyahu touched my shoulder, and June grabbed my other one. I let the cart go and stood up straight. A busted-off casterwheel did clumsy, humming circles and came to a stop at my heel with a buzz. I slipped the glass sliver from my flesh and dropped it. The Israelites stared, watching my face bleed.

I stared back and bled, the opposite of speechless—I just didn't know where to start. There is damage? There is snat and there's face? You'll be stronger tomorrow than you are today? A thin kid wearing tzitzit and a black fedora? To strap down a chicken and pluck it while it's living? A potential messiah's born once a generation? Verbosity is like the iniquity of idolatry? We damage we, a kid who tells, Benji Nakamook thought we should, I pray that we are just, they all called her June, Adonai will kill you and your family anyway?

Leevon yelled, "Look!" Mookus pointed the remote. The Aptakisic Israelites craned their necks westward and June and Eliyahu led me toward the Side. The celly buzzed my thigh as Rick Stevens gabbed. Ben-Wa was calling. Black hats on the high hill, pennyguns forward. I knew. I could see now. All of us saw.

□ □ □ □ □ □ □

Emmanuel stayed on the high hill's summit, the front row of scholars two steps behind him, hidden below the knees by the rise. I pulled out a celly, tossed it to Shpritzy, said, Call your boy Feingold—find out where he is.

"Why'd they stop?" said an Israelite. "Why are they just standing there?"

I told them I'd meet them in the two-hill-field, I said.

"You can't, though." "They can see that." "The blockade's bigger—"

They've been travelling since 8:00 and haven't seen a TV. They don't know what's happening. They're waiting for me to do what I said I would.

The Israelites grumbled some more and whispered. Let them, I thought. They're with me or they're not.

Botha's celly buzzed. I didn't check the screen, assumed it was Persphere. What? I said.

"Two cops dressed in black just rushed at the side door." It was Cody von Braker.

How close did they get?

"Fifteen, twenty steps? But we smacked up Maholtz like you told us we should, and they all fell back."

How far? I said.

"Back to the perimeter," Cody said. "Now they're talking to each other, with all these hand-movements. They're pointing this way, pointing that way, making fists—shit like that. They want us to see them."

You think so? I said.

"Yeah," Cody said. "But I don't know why. Forrest says he thinks they're just trying to scare us by making it seem like they have a plan, but I'm thinking what if they *do* have a plan, and they're trying to distract us from what the real plan is?"

You're doing good, I said. You're doing everything right. Stay in touch. Keep Maholtz visible and don't knock him out.

Four hundred still kids in hats on a hillside does not for great television imagery make, so the anchor, offscreen, as breathlessly as possible, kept saying "new development" and "possible outcomes" and "powderkeg" and "spark" to ramp up the tension, while the helicopter camera zoomed in and out and panned at high speed so the facts on the ground would appear more kinetic. The anchor's voice softened and the camera got steady as soon as two cops left the parking lot cordon and crossed Rand Road to parley with Emmanuel. Reporters and cameramen followed ten steps behind them, waving white handkerchiefs and foam-topped mikes. When the cops got halfway up the slope of the high hill, the scholars at the front of the columns stepped forward, pulled back on their balloons, and the cops stopped coming. The newsmen caught up. A cop spoke to the scholars. The camera-feed switched as Emmanuel responded.

"We're staying where we are," he said to the cops. "Come no closer, and keep off our backs."

"Why?" said a newsguy.

"Cause we're armed and we said so," said Samuel Diamond.

"I meant why are you staying where you are?" said the newsguy.

"We're armed and we say so," Samuel said.

"We've seen emails that speak of a sudden holiday. Could you say something about that? You're live on TV."

"Armed," said Samuel.

"Could you tell us about Maccabee?"

"You mean Rabbi Gurion ben-Judah Maccabee?"

"Him. Yes."

"Gurion's armed."

Alternately craning their necks and whispering, the Aptakisic Israelites remained on their bleachers. I was on the Side's now; they'd formed a circle around me. Shpritzy climbed over, returned me the celly, said, "Feingold's scholars are still on the lakeshore. He says they'll turn west in another couple miles, then they've got another mile to Aptakisic, but they'll walk that a lot faster cause they won't be on sand. So fifty-something minutes is what Nathan's guessing, but the good news is I told him what happened with the scholars from your schools—how they went around the roadblock without getting shot—and Nathan said they'd do the same if they came across a roadblock."

Will they? I said.

"Yeah," Shpritzy said. "No doubt in my mind. Nathan's so religious. He prays for us on Saturdays to protect us from God because of how we go to Cubs games in cars and spend money, and he says you're the messiah, and he's coming to daven, so I don't think he's gonna let some roadblock scare him."

Good, I said.

I started heading down the bleachers. Shpritzy followed.

"Are you the messiah?"

What do you think?

"I don't know, Gurion, but if you are, Ashley here's not an Israelite, and I think I'm in love with her."

It's good to be in love.

"Even though she's not an Israelite?"

Yeah, I said. Of course, I said. It's just she should convert before you guys have babies.

"Babies!" said Shpritzy. "We're too young for babies."

Then there's no need to worry about Ashley converting yet.

"Okay," said Shpritzy. "I hope you're the messiah."

Me too, I said.

We were standing by the television. I reached over Shpritzy and muted the news.

Everyone listen, I said to everyone.

All eyes on me.

I said, Four hundred of our brothers await us on the high hill. Five hundred-some more are on their way. The stakes are up and the cops are getting bold. They rushed the side entrance, and the guards scared them back. They might have been testing us or they might have been trying to distract us—who knows? We don't. We can't. We have to act now. One third of you will play hostages, the rest will play terrorists. We'll all go out front, where the cameras can see us, holding the hostages at gunpoint. I'll call in the scholars and they'll come down the hill and the barricade will part. As soon as they're close enough, we'll rush into the middle of them. We'll all then head east to meet the other five hundred. Once we're all together, I'll say a few words, and then I'll surrender, and this will all be over, and we will have won. Do you have any questions?

"What if they come through the side entrance?" said Salvador. "Or what if they come through the pushbar door? They could sneak up behind us from inside the school, then."

The guards will stay on the side entrance holding Maholtz hostage until the scholars have gotten close enough. Then I'll call Cody and those guards will come running and get in the mass with us. The same will go for those soldiers in the library. The pushbar door is no sweat at all: that's a serious door, and even if the cops can jimmy the lock, the mikestand'll hold for at least a few minutes, and that's all that we'll need. Any more questions?

Berman said, "Do you really need all of us to go outside with you?"

That's not a real question. It only sounds like one.

"What I'm saying," Berman said, "is there doesn't seem like there's any good reason for all of us to go outside with you. The cops, like you said, are getting bold—what if they decide to start shooting or use tear gas?"

They're not gonna do that.

"But what if they do?"

Then we'll bleed and we'll cry.

"And we'll lose, Gurion. Is what I'm saying. I know you're angry at us, but we're still your brothers, right? And wouldn't it be better if as few of your brothers as possible suffered? What I'm saying is that it doesn't seem like you need all of us outside for your hostage-terrorist scheme to work. It seems like maybe you need only five, six hostages at most—it seems like if the cops are willing to move on you when you have five hostages, they'll be willing to move on you with twenty hostages. There's no greater line to cross with twenty than five—they're either willing to endanger hostages or they aren't."

So you want to stay here, watching the television, until the scholars break through the copline, and when you see it happen, you'll all rush outside to join us.

"Right," Berman said.

And if the plan fails, and the cops do attack us, not only will you avoid getting tear-gassed and shot, but you'll bind yourselves, to the scaffold, say, and when the cops come in, you'll say you came to understand that following Gurion was wrong, that Gurion was a terrorist, and you opened your eyes to it right at the end of the battle, which was crazy, you'll say, just watch the tapes. The whole school was fighting, you'll tell the cops, and you lost track of right and wrong—like everyone else—but at the end of the battle, when things calmed down, you came to your senses, and you tried to rise up and overthrow Gurion and turn him in, along with your-selves, but Gurion and the Side of Damage weren't done yet, and they beat you into submission, bound you to the scaffold, called you cowards, held you hostage.

"Yes," Berman said.

Not a bad idea, but I might have a better one. Why don't we just take you all outside like hostages and offer you up as trades? We can trade you to the cops in return for their opening up their barricade, and you can get out now, and tell the same story.

"But what if you win?"

What do you mean?

"I mean what if you win? We want you to win. It'll be better for us if everything works out the way you said you want it to. We'll be more feared. We don't want to be left out of that," Berman said. "It makes the most sense for us to just wait in here to see if you'll win, cause then if you *do* win, we can win with you."

You're right, I said, we'll do it like that. Do you have a source of fire?

"Fire?" Berman said.

Fire, you know—like a lighter. Do you have a lighter?

None of the Israelites had a lighter.

I took out the cracktorch I had in my pocket, handed it to Berman.

Take that, I said, and while we're gone, and you're waiting to see what happens to us, you can build a fire and melt down your ammo.

"Why should we do that?" Berman said.

"You should stop with the mouth," Eliyahu said, "and get to work."

"On what?" Berman said.

"Whatever you want. A calf? A fish? A dog-headed bird? Sculpt *something*, though, and do it fast, lest your Jewish foolishness become unforgettable by dint of its dull aesthetic's salience."

"I don't know what you mean."

"So what else is new?"

□ □ □ □ □ □ □

In B-Hall, way back, where no zoom lens or scope could angle to probe, the Side of Damage, the Five, and Big Ending chose roles. I called up Ben-Wa and told him to be ready to unlock the doors and unchair Boystar as soon as he saw us at the Main Hall junction. I called Cody von Braker and told him the plan. I called the guards in the library and told them the plan. I checked the soundgun. The soundgun still worked. I gave it to June.

Twenty-five soldiers in B-hall, plus us two. Jerry Throop, Salvador, Ansul, the Janitor, Isadore, Mangey, Boshka, and the Ashley would each play hostage to a pair of terrorists. Beauregard Pate was the odd man out. He's who I sent to get Benji and Jelly.

"Now?" he said.

Now, I said. But do it calm. Once you get to the junction, the cops'll be able to see you through the window. Just act like you're going to the bathroom or something.

"When should I bring them out?" he said.

I said, Once you get Benji onto his feet, come out to Main Hall and wait with Ben-Wa. He'll be watching us outside, and as soon as the line breaks he'll call up Cody and the soldiers in the library, and all of you will head out to join us together.

Pate looked worried.

What? I said.

"His feet?" said Pate.

Whose feet? I said.

"Nakamook's, Gurion. You said I have to get him onto his feet?"

He's passed out on drugs.

"And *I'm* supposed to wake him?"

So what? I said.

"What if I say, 'Benji, wake up,' and he doesn't wake up?"

Shake him, I said.

"Shake *Nakamook*?" he said.

You're right, I said. I said, Don't shake Nakamook. Have Jelly shake Nakamook. And here, I said.

"Here?" said Pate.

Hold on, I said.

I was searching my pockets for the mint-tin of pills. I searched three times and couldn't find it.

I said, Somewhere in the nurse's, probably on the desk, there's a mint-tin of pills. The blue ones are spedspeed. If Benji needs shaking, he'll be really groggy. Crush two with the mint-tin and make him snort the powder.

"Make him?" said Pate.

Tell Jelly I said to make him snort the powder.

Pate went calmly, just like I'd told him, and I turned to the soldiers, ready to go, to lead them out, when Vincie said, "Aren't you getting behind us?" and suddenly a portion of Berman's logic, despite its cowardly origins, rang sound:

The cops would endanger hostages or wouldn't, and though I was all but certain they wouldn't, on the off-chance they would, it wouldn't matter how many hostages were present, so there wasn't any need to bring so many out front. I could knock out Boystar, drop him outside the door, set my foot above his throat as I had done earlier, and raise the soundgun, and call the scholars forward. The Side could wait in B-Hall, west of the junction, til the scholars got close, and Ben-Wa could shout out when the copline broke. There wasn't any reason to endanger them at all.

I explained the change of plans.

Vincie said, "Fuck that."

June yanked my hood.

My head jerked back.

Vincie said, "I'll go—you stay here."

They won't listen to you, I said.

"They might listen to me," Eliyahu said. "I'm convincing."

You are, I said, but they're not gonna listen to anyone else. Not when there's that many cops to walk through.

"Listen," said Vincie. "There's snipers out there. We saw on TV. They've got at least two. If you go out there and the cops decide to shoot you—"

They're not gonna shoot me live on TV.

"You don't know that, Gurion. Just please fucken listen." His volume kept lowering. "I'm not playing the dumb one. You're the leader, and they know you're the leader, and they keep on saying 'the terrorist, Maccabee.' You're the one person they can shoot and stay goodguys. Even if it means risking Boystar's life."

They haven't taken a single shot at me yet.

"They might just not have had any clear shots to take."

I've been in front of a million different windows. Not a single shot.

"You haven't been near a window in at least twenty minutes, and you don't know you were clear. Anyway, the stakes, like you said, are much higher now. Those kids on the hill change everything. You need us to go out there to flank you at least."

I can't die, Vincie.

"No you can't," Vincie said, "or we'll all be fucked."

That's not what I meant.

"I know what you meant, and it's as fucken crazy a thing to say now as it's always been, so I'm ignoring it like always, for the same reason as always, because you're my friend and it doesn't matter anyway—You don't have to die to fuck this up, anyway. They don't have to kill you. They just have to—what's the word?"

"Neutralize," Starla said—she'd come up next to June.

"Neutralize. Thank you. All they have to do is get you all neutralized. That's all it'll take. Shoot you in the leg, and you're down, and we're fucked.

We go back inside that gym?—Those kids fucken hate us. You heard fucken Berman. They want to be *feared*. They'll tie us up and say that they overcame us at the last minute or something, all badass heroic and—"

Okay, I said.

"Okay what?"

Okay, you're right.

And he was. Maybe not about the Israelites waiting in the gym—who knew what they would do if they saw me go down?—but about the rest. My kidness, to the cops, probably *was* eclipsed by my ringleaderness, my terroristness, and if any one of us could be shot with impunity, that one was me, and the fewer kids available to take a stray bullet, the greater the odds that the cops would shoot. Above all, he was right that I didn't need to die in order to fail. My father, June, maybe all the world's Israelites—I could fail them just fine if I got shot in the leg. Neutralized, I couldn't deliver the prayer.

I instructed the soldiers to form two lines.

The hostages stood with their hands behind their backs, their wrists tied loosely with shoelaces. Each was held by the hair and the shirt by a terrorist behind him, and to each one's right stood a second terrorist aiming an unloaded gun at his carotid.

The cops will shoot me or they won't, I told them. If they shoot me, you immediately surrender. You drop your weapons and raise your hands high and sob if you can, smile if you can't—you act full of gratitude, full of relief. If I don't get shot, you don't break formation. Not for anything. The cops might give orders and they might make gestures, but they probably won't shoot if we stay close together. After the scholars break through the copline, we'll rush their center and we'll all head east. I don't know exactly how far we'll be going. It might take a while, might start to feel safe. Don't get bold, though—stay to the center and stay right behind me. Do not stray.

"What about teargas?" Chunkstyle said.

You saw the way the hail was slanting before. It's windy outside and the parking lot's packed. Too many civilians in breathing range.

"What about tazers?" Salvador said.

By the time they'd be close enough to use their tazers, the scholars'll already be on their heels. Someone gets tazed, we pick him up and continue. I'm telling you, though: they're either gonna shoot me or part for the scholars. Those are the only two moves that make sense.

"What if they shoot and they miss you?" said Boshka.

That's a good question.

"Thank you," said Boshka. "What is the answer?"

It all depends on how close the scholars are, what the copline's doing, if the shot hits someone else... we'll have to see. I'll tell you when it happens, if it happens, so if it does happen, be ready to listen. We ready? I said.

"Do you think that they'll shoot?" Main Man said.

Do you? I said.

It was Scott I was asking, but they all answered: "No."

I believe you, I said, cause I don't either. I think we'll be safe as long as we're dangerous. I think God will protect us as long as we're dangerous. I think we'll forget that one day when we're old—the second we forget it, we'll be old, I said. We might even be right when we're old, I said, but we can't know now, and we won't know then. Do you understand me?

"We might get shot."

Right, I said.

"But we shouldn't get shot."

Right, I said.

And we all went east.

HOS TER	HOS TER	HOS TER	HOS TER	GURION	HOS TER	HOS TER	HOS TER	HOS TER
TER	TER	TER	TER	JUNE	TER	TER	TER	TER

We entered Main Hall slow and steady, June and I the center of both of the lines, and as Ben-Wa Wolf unlocked the doors, Boystar was yanked to his feet and held by an Israelite guard at each of his elbows. From over his shoulder, he showed us a face no language I know has a word for. The hyper-dilated eyes were full of black wonder, the battered lips twisted as if in disgust, one eyebrow was skeptical, the other determined, and the nostrils were contracted so hard that the nosetip, diagonally gashed by the keys of his mother, bent itself low enough to touch the swollen philtrum. It wasn't a face that signified anything other than a random set of malfunctions. Maybe he was trying to express some feeling, or maybe he was trying to hide some feeling, or maybe he was feeling contradictory feelings, one of which he was trying to hide beneath an expression that signified the other. But nutmeg, nerve-damage, or the combination had made of him a kind of shadow-world Slokum whose visage, for all that was scrawled on its features, was so illegible it might as well have been blank. Boystar was broken and Boystar was crazy. The rubber robot had popped.

At two steps' distance, his legs gave out

and, on his knees, still gripped at the elbows, still showing us the face, he said, "Protect me."

He was talking to June.

She stepped up beside me.

"I love you," he said.

She looked away.

"I love you," he said. "Remember?" he said. "I know you," he said. "I know you and love you."

She caught him on the chin with the bell of the soundgun, an over-handed blow. He collapsed, knocked out. June got behind me.

I said, Wake him up. He can't look dead.

The guards started slapping him. Boystar came to. Botha's phone buzzed. Persphere's number. I let it buzz twice, hit TALK, then END.

Tighten his bindings and stand him up.

They tightened the bindings at his wrists and his ankles. The phone buzzed again.

TALK. END.

Boystar was vertical.

Again the phone buzzed.

This time I answered.

You can see us, I said, and you want us to stop. You're calling to warn us to stop, I said. So what? I said. I'm warning *you* to stop.

I ended the call, took two steps forward, and the soldiers followed. With my right arm, I reached around Boystar's right shoulder. I seized him by the throat and pulled him against me, dug the thumb of my left hand deep in his armpit. His knees went weak, and he began to get lower. I clawed his throat hard and he rose.

You stay on your feet, I said. We're taking this slow. You walk when I push you, stop when I don't. Do anything other than what I want, and I'll tear your windpipe clear off its moorings. Even if they save you, you'll never sing again.

"I'll do what you say," he said, vocal cords grinding.

Now, I told the soldiers.

They opened the doors.

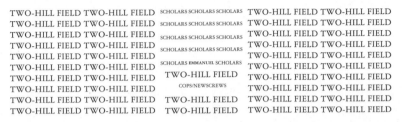

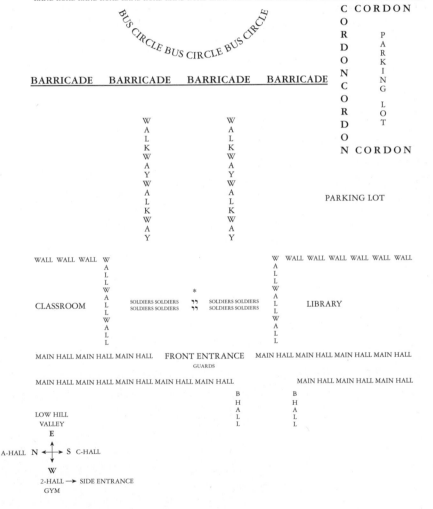

Outside was near freezing, but the wind blew warmer. The sky hung low and greenish. Ten scholars stood the hillcrest, Emmanuel foremost, the others out of sight in the valley behind them, four cops and five news crews on the slope before them. Midway between the front entrance and the scholars, the hundred-cop barricade, facing the field, stretched north-to-south in two even rows. To the barricade's south was the parking lot cordon; thirty cops strong, ten to a side, bracketing off two-hundred-some people—evacuated students and staff and faculty, Aptakisic parents and Stevenson truants, a few jobless locals and newspaper journalists. West of the cordon, where the lot got wider, cruisers and firetrucks, strobing blue and red, were jammed fender to fender with hospital-, news-, and armored police-vans.

The hailstones we stepped on squeaked as they crunched. The rock salt skittered and pecked at our ankles, caught in our treads, jumped into our shoes. We'd traveled a yard when the scholars started shouting, and the cops of the barricade's west row revolved, nightsticks drawn, faces obscured—the spinners on the cruisers glaring their visors. Boystar's face was dripping on my knuckles. A helicopter, white, hovered high above the high hill, its flank stenciled black with a stylized eye; it wasn't police but the CBS News. A magnifed voice that might have been Persphere's crackled from a speaker on one of the cruisers, giving orders in a code that didn't sound real: "BLUE ALPHA BLUNTBACK DOMINO CANOPY." A mom behind the cordon wailed, "Please don't shoot!" Other parents in the parking lot took up the cry. No one seemed sure who was being addressed.

We stopped moving forward three yards out the door. All the scholars in the field were shouting my name. Emmanuel revolved and quieted them.

Resting her elbow on the edge of my shoulder, chest pressed to my back, her breath on my ear, June held the soundgun in front of my head.

Trigger, I said.

She triggered the soundgun.

GOOD YONTIF, I said. PUT YOUR WEAPONS AWAY.

"Good yontif!" yelled the scholars, and they pocketed their weapons. Rather, those on the crest did; those in the valley weren't able to hear me. Emmanuel turned and relayed my instruction.

"Good yontif!" the scholars in the valley all shouted.

I NEED YOU TO HELP ME PERFORM A GREAT MITZVAH. I NEED YOU TO HELP ME PROTECT US, I said.

"We will!" said the scholars atop the hill.

Emmanuel turned, relayed what I'd said.

"We'll help!" shouted those in the valley.

KEEP YOUR HANDS IN PLAIN VIEW AND COME DOWN THE HILL. STOP WHEN EMMANUEL GETS TO THE ROAD.

Emmanuel turned, performed one last relay. The cops on the hillside unholstered their clubs. In columns, the scholars descended the slope, their hands at their sides, palms bare as newborns. The hillside cops backpedaled, kept shouting, "Halt!" til one of them stumbled, another one caught him, and all four fled west to the road's farther shoulder. The newsmen tread slower, continuing to report, aiming mikes at Emmanuel, getting no comment.

"TEACUP NINER WINE NIGHTINGALE CRAYON," came the voice through the speaker that was mounted on the cruiser. The code incited nothing from the cops of the barricade; nothing, at least, that was visible.

As the news crews backed up into Rand's middle lanes, the cops from the hillside—now on the shoulder farther from Emmanuel—ordered them south to the cordon. The news crews faked deafness, or were slow to react, or weren't slow to react and didn't fake deafness, but were slow *enough* to react, or deaf-seeming enough, for the cops on the shoulder to vacate the path between the scholars and the barricade to enforce their orders without looking as if they were running away, or so they must have thought, for that's what they did. They escorted the news crews over to the cordon, and once that was finished, they didn't return.

"FIVE-TEN FORTY-NINE BALSAM CLANDESTINE."

The barricade held. It didn't even twitch.

Emmanuel arrived at the side of the road. The scholars stretched back past the high hill's west foot. The columns were three rows deep up the incline.

PERSPHERE, I said, OR WHOEVER'S IN CHARGE: THIS IS NO KIND OF SHOWDOWN. ELOHEINU IS WITH US. YOU'VE GOT THIRTY SECONDS OF VOLITION REMAINING. PART THE BARRICADE AND NO ONE GETS HURT.

"COLD RUN REDNINE GANGSTAND GANGSTAND."

SCHOLARS, I said, THE ROMANS CAN SEE YOU. IT ISN'T ENOUGH. PRAY THE SH'MA AT THE TOPS OF YOUR LUNGS.

Mournful-sounding Hebrew arose from the field. A second white helicopter chopped overhead; this one's flank bore the NBC peacock.

Five seconds passed and the barricade held.

"Please don't shoot!" scores of parents were chanting. To whom didn't matter. Kids' lives were at stake if anyone fired. The cops wouldn't fire in this current arrangement; if they were willing to fire, they'd have shot me already, or tried to negotiate and then tried to shoot me. They weren't even trying to negotiate, though; we'd been out there two minutes and they'd only made code-noise and postured with clubs. They hadn't even told us to drop our weapons. They thought they could freeze us out til we surrendered.

"They're fronting," said Vincie behind me, just to my left, gripping the Janitor's hair and sweater. "Half those fuckers don't even have masks. They're fucken fronting." Vincie was right. Or somewhat right. All the gear in the department—department*s* by that point; the cruisers that were block-ing off Rand Road's traffic were Glenfield- and Bolling- and Lake County-marked—all the gear they could get must have been on display, but they couldn't use gas when so many lacked masks, and on one hand this meant that a part of their costumes was there just to scare us; on the other hand, though, they all had batons and tazers and mace. They all wore helmets. They were all behind shields. They weren't *just* fronting.

"Please! Don't! Shoot! Please! Don't! Shoot!"

The cops held their ground. The scholars finished praying.

"Hurt him," Vincie said, the him being Boystar.

"Please no!" said Boystar.

I knuckled his armpit. He stopped making noise.

"What're you waiting for? Show them already."

"He's a shield," June said. "He isn't a sword."

That explained it in a poem as elegant as any.

The couplet that followed was even more deft.

Vincie: "What's our sword, then?"

June: "We don't *have* one."

Trigger, I said.

June triggered the soundgun.

SCHOLARS, I said, I'M ABOUT TO ASK YOU TO PUT YOUR LIVES AT RISK. IF YOU WON'T, THEN GO: HEAD BACK UP THE HIGH HILL AND OVER THE CREST. NO ONE WILL SAY YOU WERE COWARDS. THEY WILL SAY THAT YOU KNEW YOUR OWN LIMI-TATIONS. I WILL SAY THE SAME, AND OTHERS WILL LISTEN. WE WILL MEET YOU SHORTLY, AND WE WILL EMBRACE YOU. GO NOW IF YOU'LL GO, THOUGH—GOING LATER WILL HURT US, ALL OF OUR BROTHERS.

I waited out a three-count. No scholar moved.

The barricade's west row revolved to face east.

THESE COPS, I said, WEAR VESTS AND HELMETS. NOTHING YOU COULD LOAD IN YOUR PENNYGUNS COULD DAMAGE THEM. THESE COPS ARE MEN AND WE ARE BOYS. THEIR BODIES ARE STRONGER—THERE'S NO WAY AROUND THAT. THEY HAVE TAZERS AND PISTOLS, CLUBS AND MACE. SOME HAVE SHIELDS, WHICH, LIKE THEIR HELMETS, EVEN BULLETS CAN'T GET THROUGH.

"VAGABOND HELIUM EIGHTBALL TRANSUM."

WHAT WE HAVE IS NUMBERS, AND OUR NUMBERS ARE GREATER. YET OUR NUMBERS, THOUGH GREATER, AREN'T GREATER ENOUGH. AND WE HAVE ELOHEINU, ELOHEINU IS WITH US—ELOHEINU ON HIS OWN, THOUGH, IS NEVER ENOUGH. TOGETHER THEY'RE HELPFUL, ELOHEINU AND OUR NUMBERS, BUT EVEN TOGETHER THEY AREN'T ENOUGH. WE NEED BETTER TECH. WE NEED BETTER TECH!

"We need better tech!"

WE NEED BETTER TECH!

"We need better tech!"

WE NEED BETTER TECH AND WE NEED BETTER TECH. WITH ELOHEINU AND OUR NUMBERS, WE CAN GET BETTER TECH. SO YOU AND ELOHEINU WILL GET US BETTER TECH. ON MY GO, YOU WILL FOLLOW EMMANUEL LIEBMAN. YOU WILL WALK TOWARD THE BARRICADE BEHIND EMMANUEL. IF THE COPS DON'T PART, HE'LL LEAD YOU TO ONE OF THEM. EVERY LAST ONE OF YOU, CONVERGE ON THAT ONE. KNOCK HIM OFF HIS FEET. STRIP HIM OF HIS PISTOL. PULL OFF HIS HELMET AND BLOW OUT HIS BRAINS. THEN CHOOSE ANOTHER ONE AND DO THE SAME. CONTINUE—

"DROP YOUR WEAPONS."

Behind the cordon, a commotion had erupted. People running south, running over each other, getting as far away as they could. Something behind me had started changing, too. Heat on my ear, on the back of my neck.

CONTINUE UNTIL THE BARRICADE PARTS.

Heat from the school on the back of my neck; it came and went. The doors of the entrance had opened and closed. I thought it was Benji. I didn't turn to see. I couldn't take my eyes off the scholars til I finished, and I wasn't yet finished—I hadn't even blessed them. A group behind the cordon refused to flee south; teenagers mostly, ten or twenty. The cops were pushing, the teens going limp; lead-bodied resistance, they'd have to be dragged.

"FREE YOUR HOSTAGES."

LET NOTHING STOP YOU.

I thought he'd forgiven me and come outside; I thought he'd come out to stand behind me, to stand before everyone standing behind me, to be the first person I'd see when I turned: Benji Nakamook, still my friend. I don't know why I thought that, not exactly. I know I was happy, and I remember I was thinking that; thinking I was happy. Thinking: You're happy, Nakamook's your friend. And it didn't cross my mind that that's what I was thinking *because* I was happy; that because when you're happy, what you hope for seems likely, sometimes so likely it even seems real. It didn't cross my mind because I wasn't *that* happy. At least I didn't think I was. Nor do I now. "DROP YOUR WEAPONS. FREE YOUR HOSTAGES." You're happy, you're happy, you're happy, I thought. It stood out right then, that moment of happiness, not for being the happiest of my life, not by a longshot; in the last four days I'd had happier moments, like when June raised her fists when I first said I loved her or Momo said "neepo" to Lonnie by the pool. The Side getting born at the end of Group. Getting hold of the passpad. My hoodie being stolen. EVEN IF I FALL—ESPECIALLY IF I FALL—LET NOTHING STOP YOU. I WILL BE STRENGTHENED. I'LL GET BACK UP. De-sapping Maholtz. Ending Vincie's hand-twitch. Any of the hyperscoots, especially the first. Kissing June onstage. Kissing by her locker. Kissing in the field. Learning from the Five that they'd received *Ulpan*. Eliyahu with the leaf, at the fountain, chasing Baxter. Leevon's broken silence after Slokum held me up. The scholars in my kitchen, believing all I told them. "DOWN ON THE GROUND WITH YOUR HANDS IN PLAIN SIGHT." The Side rising up to protect me from Botha. Getting called a tzadik by Emmanuel on the platform. My father Thursday morning telling jokes about goyim, singing punk in the car, inviting June to join us. Samuel Diamond holding 37 high. My mother saying June should be whatever I determined. Flowers's exegesis of Lauryn Hill's cursing. Rabbi Salt telling me he had to drink coffee. The Cage-wide petition delivered by Chunkstyle. BARNUM on the juice machine. "Gurion's my boy!"

BE STRONG! BE STRONG! I shouted to the scholars.

"Chazak! Chazak!" the scholars roared back.

Though that very morning I'd been much happier, I had not been truly happy since the battle in the gym—in the best moments after, I'd been merely relieved—and this moment stood out at the time for that reason; for being my first happy moment since the battle. It stands out now because it was my last. If I seem to belabor it, it's for that reason. I haven't had a moment of happiness since.

"DROP YOUR WEAPONS! DOWN ON THE GROUND! FREE THE HOSTAGES! COMPLY AT ONCE!"

BE STRONG! BE STRONG! AND MAY WE BE STRENGTH-ENED!

"Chazak! Chazak! Venizschazeik!"

The scholars walked west behind Emmanuel.

And lest they be forced to massacre children, the cops of the barricade fled north and south.

As soon as I revolved, the moment was over.

22
CONTROL

Friday, November 17, 2006
12:09 p.m.–1:01 p.m.

```
DOOR DOOR DOOR DOOR   DOOR DOOR DOOR DOOR
D                 D   D                 D
O                 O   O                 O
O                 O   O                 O
R                 R   R                 R
D                 D   D                 D
O                 O   O                 O
O                 O   O                 O
R                 R   R                 R
D     PUSHBAR     D   D     PUSHBAR     D
O                 O   O                 O
O                 O   O                 O
R                 R   R                 R
D                 D   D                 D
O                 O   O                 O
O                 O   O                 O
R                 R   R                 R
DOOR DOOR DOOR DOOR   DOOR DOOR DOOR DOOR
```

A bubble of curls behind a thick smear of blood: Googy Segal's face, mashed flat against glass. Our guards had him pinned chest-first to the jamb. He struggled against them, slicking the blood around, pressing his forehead to the window for leverage. Suddenly he slipped, or someone lost their grip, and his face slid down and the door wedged open. Palms on the pavement, he donkey-kicked blindly; Stevie Loop dropped. Googy lurched a yard, then crawled for another, but out came Ben-Wa, who fell knees-first on his back and stayed him.

Googy made pleading sounds, looked in my eyes.

Let him up! I said.

Ben-Wa climbed off. "He wouldn't say anything. He just rushed the door. We—"

Googy interrupted. He was up on his elbows, choking on phonemes. Even if I'd been able to make out what he was saying, transcribing it here would be useless. The speech disorders of which Googy was a victim battered his utterances beyond the furthest reaches of any single alphabet's powers of description—of any three alphabets' powers of description. There were Chinesey catsounds and Xhosa-like clicks, Tourrettic stammerings and Afrikaaner diphthongs, W's that might have been L's or R's, Hebraic velar fricatives, a storm of whistled sibilants.

I thought I heard "Ally." I thought I heard "knock." I thought I heard "knock" somewhat proximal to "mook."

Benji? I said. Is Benji with your cousin?

Googy just wailed.

Where's Beauregard Pate?

"He never came back from Nurse Clyde's," Ben-Wa said.

Then Googy, though his stammer made it last five syllables, definitely said the word "gym."

"Benji's in the *gym* you're saying?" Ben-Wa said. "Why's he—"

Vincie vaulted Googy, into the school. June took his spot, grabbed the Janitor's collar.

Emmanuel: approaching the edge of the bus circle.

Brooklyn's in charge, I said. Stay in formation. Follow the plan.

I spun clutching Boystar, hurled him into Main Hall. Jesse Ritter grabbed him. By then I was running.

At the gym's northeast entrance, I pushed on the doors. The doors pushed back.

"They're here!" someone shouted.

I reared up and charged. The doors blew open. I stumbled on the kid I'd downed, struggled for balance, got slammed against the wall between the locker-room doors. Three ex-Shovers had my wrists and my elbows. I lifted my knee, got one in the nutsack—the one in front of me—he sat down hard. Vincie, at centercourt, was facing away from me, swinging a chair. Kids lay at his feet, clutching their struck parts, crawling away. Beyond them, Benji was draped on the scaffold, and Berman was moving cautiously forward, holding the mikestand lancelike. I couldn't squirm free of the guys on my arms; I went whole-body limp, and they had to lean in. The one on my left wasn't all that tall. I smashed his nose flat with the side of my head. On the snapback, my temple met with an edge—the upper southern corner of the fire-alarm—and everything tilted, whited, dissolved.

Some seconds later, I began to come to, aware I was being handled. I couldn't, for the moment, recall what was happening; I only knew I should resist it. I tried to resist it, but nothing responded. My arms wouldn't lift. My legs wouldn't bend. "Tighter," a kid said. I panicked, inhaled, and my eyes popped open. My chin was on my chest. I was looking at my hands being bound at my waist. Beyond them my legs, being bound at the ankles.

I raised my eyes and I saw Berman swinging. He got Vincie's chair with the tip of the mikestand. The chair went flying, and Vincie retreated, ran in my direction, a hand in his pocket, looking at something up near the ceiling. He stopped at the free-throw line, hauled back and launched, sending Floyd's keyring along a broad arc that ended inside of the scoreboard. Berman brought the mikestand down on his shoulder. Vincie half-knelt, popped back up, took another shot to the flank with the mikestand.

Something to the right of me banged at weird intervals—the northeast doors. I heard the Five cursing, Eliyahu pleading, June shouting my name; for once I was grateful to have been disobeyed. Two ex-Shovers were digging in my pockets, three ex-Shovers dragging Vincie to the scaffold, five ex-Shovers shouldering the doors so one could knot multiple cords between the handles. The doors creaked open for an inch, slammed shut. I tried to roll free; I could roll, but not free.

"Stand him up," Berman said.

They brought me to my feet, leaned me back on the wall, hands gripping my hoodie. Berman was close now; I couldn't see past him. His shirt was torn open from neck to navel. His throat looked freshly slapped and kneaded. A bruise had begun to assemble on his ribcage. The kid who I'd nutshot handed him a keyring. Another one handed him a fuller keyring. The first one was Botha's and the second was Brodsky's.

Untie me, I said.

"Which one of these keys gets us out of here?" he said.

The scholars are coming.

I could hear Vincie panting, trying not to cry. Banging noise came from the central door now—it was also tied shut. Soon June and Eliyahu would know what to do: they'd get Ben-Wa, who had Jerry's keys, and they'd come through a locker-room. The locker-room doors were one-way doors; they opened *into* the locker-rooms and didn't have handles on their gym-facing sides, so they couldn't be stopped from inside the gym.

"Which key?" Berman said.

Untie me, I said.

Berman said, "Cory!" and tossed him the keys. Cory's mouth was bleeding. "Try them all," Berman told him, and Cory limped over to the pushbar door.

Someone said, "Berman, what should we do?"

"Tie him to the scaffold."

The him was me. Inasmuch as it was possible, I lunged at Berman's throat. He stepped to the left and I hit the floor sideways.

They dragged me by the hood toward the back of the gym. Berman followed close, examining my face. Eleven Israelites sitting the bleachers were wet-eyed.

Help me! I said.

They all looked away.

The scholars are coming!

"We know," Berman said. "Any minute now, they'll come through the locker-rooms. We're not worried about that."

What you're doing—

"I'm protecting us."

I can protect us.

"There's more than one us."

I'll protect us all.

"Not anymore you won't. Not after this. You won't forgive this."

I will, I said. Just untie us, Berman.

"It's not even our fault, you know—*he* came *here*. But there was never any way to protect us all anyway—that's your whole problem. Cause what? We'd get out of here, you'd take all the blame, we'd say 'Gurion did it,' and… what? *Then what?*"

You'd go free, I said. You *will* go free. You're talking in circles. You're—

"We'd go free, and then what? Where would that have left us? Everything would've just gone back to normal. No one would fear us. We'd say, 'Gurion did it,' and we'd go free, and you'd be in jail, unable to protect us even if you wanted to. We'd be treated like always, they'd treat us like always, make us crawl on our bellies through filth before them. Better for us we say we overthrew you. Better for us we say we escaped. We didn't plan it this way, but this way is better."

It doesn't have to—

"It *does*. How can't you see that? We didn't go get him. We were *following* your plan. And then the second your back was turned—the very fucken second—*he* came *here*."

Vincie'd stopped panting. His eyes were shut hard. They sat me on the floor between him and Benji and leashed me to the scaffold by the bindings at my wrists. Vincie, on his back, was tied by the throat and one of his legs. Nakamook was silent, face-down and limp, an upside-down U, held to the scaffold by nothing but gravity. The side of his face I was able to see pulsed blood from a swollen gouge above his cheekbone. His entire flank was soaked with blood, shot through with nibs, and the splints I'd taped to his fingers were cracked.

Benji, I said.

"He's out," Vincie said. "And now they're gonna kill him."

"Shut your mouth, Portite," an ex-Shover said.

I said, No one's killing anyone. The scholars are coming.

"I barely stopped them," said Vincie. "They're gonna kill me too, now. They'll have to. They'll—"

The toe of Berman's shoe blurred across Vincie's jaw.

"Nakamook came in here," Berman said, "screaming and shouting and swinging a chair, powder-blue gooze pouring out from his nostrils. He knocked me down and got on top of me. The Israelites—our brothers—seven of them, Gurion—it took fucking seven of them, even with his hand—the Israelites finally pulled him off of me. We beat him til he dropped, though, and look at him now."

Okay, I said. I believe you, I said. But you need to calm down. This is happening too fast. Tell me what you want, and we'll work this out.

"We've *worked it out*," Berman said, his voice now public. "The bully has to die. Look what we did to him. He'll never forgive it. He'll haunt us forever."

He won't, I said. I'll make him forgive it.

"You'll *make* him?" said Berman. "You have no control of him! *He* came here! *You're* going to prison! And if you're really on our side, you'll tell the cops, for whatever your word's worth, that the two of them died trying to stop us from escaping."

The two of— No. Josh. I won't. This doesn't have to—

"So you're *not* on our side, then. You never really were."

I *am*, but look— All of you. Listen to me.

"Lucky for us he's the criminal here," Berman said to the Israelites. "Lucky for us, it's him who they'll blame for—"

"Berman," Cory said. He'd returned from the door. "These keys don't work."

"One of them has to. Try them upside-down."

"I did," Cory said. "I tried them twice both ways."

"Floyd's is in the scoreboard," Vincie told Berman. "Jerry's isn't in here, and that's all there fucken is, you walking fucken deadman. You stuck-ass deadman murderous fucker."

Cory raised a chair as if to smash Vincie.

"No, wait," said Berman. Cory lowered the chair. "Is he telling us the truth?" Berman said to me. "About the keys?"

Yes, I said. So, look—

"Okay," Berman said. "Okay... okay."

The doors were still banging. Muffled shouting behind them. Berman no longer faced me. He was talking low to Cory—I couldn't hear what he was saying. I kept saying his name, keeping my voice calm, but he wouldn't turn around. They flipped Benji over, onto his back, pulled the nibs from his body. Benji groaned softly.

You guys, I said to the Israelites nearest me. Listen. It's gonna be fine. The scholars are coming. We've got other keys. We can work something out. I'm your brother, okay? I'm not your enemy. You have to stop this.

One mumbled something about burning down houses, another something else about crawling on bellies. All of the rest of them pretended not to hear me. Berman jumped the scaffold, took my sap from his pocket. He was standing over Benji.

I said, Don't do this.

"I won't," he said. "We will. *Gurion* did it."

Cory and three other ex-Shovers grabbed chairs. The four encircled Benji and raised the chairs high, saying, "Gurion." "Gurion." "Gurion did it."

"On 'Go,'" Berman said.

Berman! I said.

"He'll *kill* us if we don't."

"*I'll* fucken kill you!" Vincie screamed.

Shut up, Vincie! It isn't true! He's barely alive, Josh. I'm talking to you. I'm talking to you, Josh. He can't lift his arms. He can't kill anyone. No one'll kill anyone. I will protect you. I promise you, Josh. I can still forgive you for what you've done. I understand, okay? I understand why!

"He's lying," Berman said, "and he'll be gone, anyway."

I yelled, Someone stop them! I'm the messiah!

Then Aleph said "Go," and brought down his sap, and the others their chairs, and Benji was gone.

□ □ □ □ □ □ □

Sent: March 16, 2013, 5:56 AM Greenwich Mean Time (UTC +2)
Subject: RE: PLEASE, JELLY (version 18)
From: anrothstein@uchicago.edu (Jelly Rothstein)
To: Gurionforever@yahoo.com

The account is attached.

11-17.doc
29.5K View Download

----Original Message Follows----
From: Gurionforever@yahoo.com
To: anrothstein@uchicago.edu
Subject: Re: PLEASE, JELLY (version 18)
Date: March 10, 2013, 7:22 AM GMT (UTC +2)

Dear Jelly,

I'm too afraid to tell you how grateful I am; afraid you'll regret the kindness you're showing me... I'll meet your terms. You know how to reach me if you ever change your mind. I hope you'll change your mind.

A blessing on your head,

Gurion

PS Whoever you think I've got in your classes—I didn't send him. Probably it's just some nice Orthodox boy with a crush. My dad was one of those once.

----Original Message Follows----
From: anrothstein@uchicago.edu
To: Gurionforever@yahoo.com
Subject: Re: PLEASE, JELLY (version 18)
Date: March 9, 2013, 3:07 AM GMT (UTC +2)

Gurion:

I've been trying to forgive you for over six years. I keep almost writing back to you, but something always stops me. Sometimes it's a call or a visit from June, who you've ruined, who you keep on ruining. She sings me your praises with such desperation—forget the ugly headscarf and all the baggy clothing, forget her far-off gazing and tic-like eruptions of "Baruch Hashem, Jelly! Baruch Hashem!"; her stunted voice alone, stuck fast in croaky girlhood, breaks my heart bad enough—I can't even squint, much less protest, for fear that she'll jump off a building.

Other times what stops me is your emails themselves. When my hatred burns its brightest, they often cooled it off a little, true enough, but the times the hate's ebbing, they get it to flow. The times the hate's ebbing, I find myself thinking: Gurion was only a little boy then, a smart boy, sure, but a boy nonetheless; little boys are bastards, little girls too, they don't know any better, no matter how smart; you can't hate a young man for what he did as a boy, he didn't know what he was doing, he couldn't help but make mistakes; I'll respond when he sends his next email. But then I get your next email, and it reads no different than the ones from six years ago, and you say the same things you were saying six years ago. And you CAN hate a little boy for what he's done as a little boy, and you CAN hate a young man for what he's done as a young man. Whether you're still a little boy, or were always a young man (or maybe an old man, born fully formed), I have no idea, but you are who you were; you were who you are. You're the same exact person I hated six years ago, the same exact person I've hated six years.

Still, hatred's no picnic. I don't like to hate you. It rips at my stomach, my mouth tastes like pennies. I don't want to keep doing it. I'm writing you back now not because I forgive you, but because maybe writing back will help me forgive you. It's just about the only thing I haven't tried; that, and giving you what you think you want. And I WILL give you what you think you want, Gurion—I will go for broke here—but you have to agree to my terms first. My terms are simple.

You get my account if you leave me alone. No more emails. No more sending June here to talk to me. No more Scholars Fund goons sitting near me in class, haunting me at yoga, or standing on the corner "watching over" me. Nothing. You give me your word and I'll take you at your word—you were never a liar.

And just for the record, and your own edification: You went way over the line in that last one. You have no right whatsoever to make me feel guilty, even if that seems to you to be what it's taken to get me to respond to you. ESPECIALLY if that seems to you to be what it's taken. You're a fucked up, terrible, impossible person. Fuck you. Fuck you. Fuck you. Fuck you.

I still don't feel better. I hate you even more now than before I typed "Gurion." Maybe I need to actually send this first.

Sending this,
Angelica Rothstein

----Original Message Follows----
From: Gurionforever@yahoo.com
To: anrothstein@uchicago.edu
Subject: PLEASE, JELLY (version 18)
Date: March 8, 2013, 7:56 AM GMT (UTC +2)

Dear Jelly,

Do you remember when you told me that I shouldn't love June because she drew "crazy things"? We were in the Cage, at the teacher cluster, eating our lunches, and Benji told you it didn't matter what she drew. Then he went on to say, in so many words, that he loved you, even though YOU were crazy, you who bit people. Anything I've done to make you hate me, Jelly, it wasn't to make you hate me, Jelly: I was only just biting people, drawing crazy things. I'm not asking you to love me. I'm asking you to remember that Benji did, at least for a while. And I'm asking you to honor that for long enough to really hear me out this time. The Benji I knew, regardless of what he might've thought of me at the very end of his life—he'd at least have wanted you to hear me out.

The problem is that he was life-size, Jelly. Do you remember he was life-size? The problem is that he had crazy long arms, and he was tougher than anyone, and sad, and smart, and too romantic, but still he was life-size, when he was alive, and I just can't get that to come across on the page. All that he is now's "Nakamook" or "Benji" or "Benji Nakamook," larger than life or smaller than life, overly petty or overly noble, overly thoughtful or overly driven, not quite human or all too human, destined by his current state of representation to provide shallow lessons, to suffer shallow ironies, to die as an algo-rithm, wholly comprehensible, a Goliath of Gath where should be a David, a figure where should stand a boy.

And maybe that'll still be the case if you tell me what happened once you got to the Nurse's—I don't know what happened, you're the only one who knows, and my problem, in the end, might have nothing to do with my lack of information, and everything to do with my limited skills as an author—but *The Instructions* is finished, or nearly finished—I can't do it much longer, it's turning me ugly (or I guess, from where you stand: uglier)—and Benji's last best shot at being remembered properly—my last best shot at rendering him accurately, as the person we loved... I won't even be able to take that shot if you decide not to help me. And all the readers of *The Instructions*, of whom there'll be millions, will proceed to make total, simple sense of our friend.

> On bruised, purple knees,
> Gurion ben-Judah

□ □ □ □ □ □ □

11-17

When I entered the nurse's office, Benji was half-asleep at the desk, trying and failing to open a mint-tin. I said his name.

He said, "You're a dream."

I said, "*You're* a dream, baby."

"Don't fuck with me," he said.

I kissed his ear.

"Dreaming," he said.

I pinched the ear.

"Okay," he said.

I sat across the desk from him and opened the tin. The tin contained pills. I asked him what he wanted. He told me the spedspeed, the blue ones: crush them. I pushed aside the blotter to expose the steel desk and turned the pills to powder under the tin. From the powder, I cut lines with the edge of a postcard advertising flu-shots. I cut them the size I'd seen in the movies; the length of a cigarette, thick as a bicpen. "What is a *chazer?*" Benji said, like Tony Montana, and made a cough-laugh noise.

I halved the lines.

"Say goodnight to the bad guy."

I halved them again, and rolled up a dollar, and helped him to hold it. He snorted two lines, took a breath, swallowed hard, did another two lines, took hold of my hand with his good one and frowned. I went around the desk and we started making out, but his mouth was bitter and he wouldn't let me kiss it, so I did some lines and we were even and kissed.

A few minutes later, we were both a little sweaty, and our skin was tingling. The air tasted sweet.

"We're fine," I said.

Benji told me the nurse smoked; he'd seen him sneak out to the lot with Miss Pinge. I rifled through Clyde's desk, found a fresh pack of menthols inside a first-aid kit inside of a file-drawer. Matches in the cellophane. We ashed in a watercup.

"We're fine," I said again.

"Right now," Benji said. "Right this minute we're fine. It's not gonna last. We'll get sent to different schools. We'll never see each other. It'll sound a lot worse when we're done being high."

"We'll see each other sometimes."

"Your mom won't let you."

"I can sneak away sometimes."

"It won't be enough. It's not enough now."

"Isn't that good? To be enough would mean we—"

"But there shouldn't be obstacles. It should fail to be enough despite a *lack* of obstacles. That's the happy ending. Don't get confused. This one's fucked. Why did we do this?"

"Boystar hurt Main Man. Botha grabbed Gurion. Slokum had it coming for years. Once we rodneyed Botha, we were already fucked. All we could lose was the chance to act without anything to lose. Aren't you glad we hurt the right people? And orange you glad I didn't say banana?"

Benji didn't smile. "There's always something to lose," he said. "There's always something left to get damaged."

He lit two more cigarettes, handed one over, said, "I'm finished with Gurion. Over him. Done."

"He's your closest friend."

"You're my closest friend."

"Except for me," I said.

He told me about the conversation you'd had. He said you'd betrayed him to protect Josh Berman, then lied about it.

I defended you. I said you loved him and you did what you thought you had to do at the time. (I don't doubt that, even now, but your love back then, as now—though I didn't know it then—was irrelevant.) I made a point of telling him you sent me, too. I told him the first thing you did when you returned to the gym was send me to him, and now we were there, high and smoking in school in love. Who else had ever gotten to be where we were?

He said that he wished we could run away together. It wasn't a proposal; he said it wistfully. We'd already talked about running away, and why it wouldn't work. Just the day before, we'd had the conversation. Benji'd stabbed himself with a pen and I'd passed out. Botha'd sent us to the Nurse's; we'd dawdled in the hallway, discussed the possibility, the impossibility. We didn't have money or transportation or places to stay, though it wasn't finally those things which kept us from doing it: those things, with luck, could be overcome. We could have, for example, learned to be pickpockets or, failing that, conned or mugged people—Benji was strong and both of us tricky. And once we had money, we could stay at motels, pay the right people to get us our rooms, and sleep all day and steal all night, DO NOT DISTURB cards hanging on our doorknobs, sneaking in and out to avoid the manager, ordering our pizzas in deep parental voices, telling the delivery guys that mom was in the shower.

What stopped us was the likelihood that we'd get caught eventually, that we'd have to last seven years on the run, til I was eighteen; once we got caught, there was no way my parents would let us near each other. Better to stay in the Cage, we'd decided; tossing notes, stealing glances, hanging out alone fifteen minutes a day between the end-of-school tone and start of detention. Plus there were weekends. Plus after school sometimes. My parents were nice, just loud and spastic and a little bit paranoid; they'd like Benji when they met him; I'd convince Ruth to tell them he shouldn't be in the Cage; I'd tell them *I* was in the Cage, what was wrong with the Cage? did they think I was hateful for being in the Cage? And I'd stop with the biting and the mouthing off; they'd let us hang out. They would. It wasn't bad. It wasn't bad at all. Not only couldn't we run away and make it, but there was no good reason to run away, it turned out. So we went to Nurse Clyde's, he sprayed Benji's wound, covered it in gauze, and gave me some orange juice. He sent us back to the Cage with a pass we didn't need, and we went to the gym, out the pushbar door, and we killed what remained of the schoolday outside, walking to the beach and kissing in the sand, getting too cold and un-tarping a boat that was up on a trailer parked in the lot, crawling inside, kissing some more, smoking stolen cigarettes to catch our breaths, and a round or two of slapslap we each tried to lose.

That's why Benji said he wished we could run, there in Nurse

Clyde's. Because none of that could ever happen again. Even if Aptakisic stayed open, we'd be expelled, sent to different schools, and nothing would be able to convince my parents that Benji was okay to hang out with after that. That's what he was saying.

I told him that your plan might work, though. To be clear: I was sure that your plan would work. I completely believed in you, but I told Benji "might" instead of "would" because I didn't want to argue; I felt too good. I said, "We'll all just say that Gurion did it, and Gurion will say that Gurion did it, and we'll all get a pass."

"The ex-Shovers'll ruin it," Benji said.

"How?" I said.

"Like snakes," said Benji.

"How like snakes?"

"I don't know," he admitted.

"So how can you be sure?"

"They're snakes," he said, "and they're following a snake. Can you hand me that postcard?"

I handed him the postcard. "They're following Gurion."

"No," Benji said, cutting lines from the pile. "They're just scared of Gurion. The second he can't hurt them, they'll fuck him over. Berman'll find a way."

"It's better for them to do what Gurion says."

"Maybe, maybe not. Either way, I doubt they'll see that— Dollar?" he said. I gave him the dollar. His eyes were so shiny. "They're too fucking stupid. It doesn't matter anyway." He snorted a line. "I don't give a fuck anyway. Not about them. Not about Gurion. I'm not following him anywhere. I haven't been following him. You want one?... You sure?" He snorted another. "Cause the thing is he *didn't* 'do it.' All of us 'did it.' At least I did. And I won't—glah! This tastes bad." He showed me a finger, leaned to the side, spit into the wastebasket next to the desk. "I'm sorry. That was gross. Are you icked?"

"I'm not icked," I said. "What were you just saying, though? All of us did it and you won't what?"

"I won't rat him out. That's all I was saying. Not to save myself. I did what I did because I wanted to do it, and that's what I'll say to the cops."

"You don't have to say anything."

"I do," Benji said. "Of course I do. If I don't say anything, and everyone else says 'Gurion did it,' staying silent's the same as backing their word, and I'll profit like them. I'm not gonna owe Gurion anything."

"You're not gonna save him from anything, either."

"I said, 'Fuck him,'" he said. "I don't care about him. I don't, Jelly. Or at least I shouldn't. I know that much."

"You'll hurt yourself for no good reason."

"I'll owe nothing to anyone. That's a good reason. I'm done owing people for shit I didn't ask for."

"What about me?"

"I was just about to say—"

"You're making me cry."

He wasn't exactly. I felt like I was crying, but I wasn't really crying. I wasn't gasping, there weren't any tears, my nose didn't run. Just this tension inside of my temples. A pressure. It hurt.

"I was just about to say that I've got an idea."

His idea was that since we couldn't run away, we should stay where we were for as long as we could. He said we should get in the Quiet Room and hide inside the big cabinet. He painted this whole fantasy about the school being shut down. He said that once you'd surrendered, the cops would sweep the school, and after that, the school would be shut down, at least for a little while. He said that if we could manage to stay hidden til the sweep was over, the school would be ours to roam around and make out in. There was food in the cafeteria, cigarettes on the desk, and surely more to be plundered in the desk of Pinge, in the lockers of skids whose combos we'd find— Benji'd seen the binder—in the vaunted hutch of Hector. He said that he thought we could last for weeks, unless they re-opened the school, in which case we could give running away a shot, since maybe—if we were lucky—we'd already be presumed dead, so no one would look for us, and staying on the run would be that much easier.

It sounded great. Not just great, but perfect, really. It sounded like a pipedream. I didn't believe that Benji believed it was possible. I thought he was just trying to get me to stop non-crying, to press up against me inside of a cabinet, and maybe to work a hide-from-the-cops-type seduction. I saw nothing wrong with any of that. I wanted to feel better, wanted to be romanced into pressing against him, had wanted to press against him even without such romancing, and above all, I saw that it would buy us some time in which I could convince him not to incriminate himself. I was sure I could convince him.

Even better than that, when we finally came out, I'd tell my parents a story about Benji having protected me from all the craziness going down in the school. I'd tell them that as soon as Benji saw that things were getting dangerous, he brought me to the Nurse's and put me in the cabinet, and got inside the cabinet and didn't lay a hand on me, but stood at the ready to protect me from attackers. They'd know he was noble; they'd be endlessly grateful. We'd be allowed to see each other.

"I love your idea," I told him. "Let's go."

He said, "Ladies first," swept his arm at the Quiet Room.

I called him a dork, but stood up, started going.

That's when Beauregard came in from Main Hall. "Gurion says to bring you," Beauregard said.

"Where?" Benji said. He sat back down.

"Up by the entrance. The scholars are here."

"So what?" Benji said.

"They'll come through the barricade and we'll join into them. Then we're gonna walk to meet some other ones."

"Who's we?"

"What do you mean?"

"Is Berman going?"

"I don't know," Pate said. "He stayed in the gym with the other Shovers. He said they'll join us once the scholars break the barricade, but they keep backing out of plans, so who knows?"

Benji said, "What do you think?" to me.

"I think I want to hide," I said.

"Maybe it's better if you don't," he said. "If it's gonna work out, I mean."

"If you're gonna get in trouble, I want to hide. I want more time with you."

"Maybe I'll stay quiet."

"Maybe?" I said. "Maybe's not good enough."

"I know," he said. "Let me think," he said. He coughed, grabbed his throat. It was totally fake. I remember what it looked like, the color of his tongue, the back of his tongue, blue from the spedspeed—he stuck out his tongue. It was totally fake. If I knew it then, though,

I didn't suspect what he was up to. Sometimes things like that—they look so fake, you assume they must be real.

"Would you get me a water?" he asked me. "I just want to think a second."

I took his glass off the desk and went to the Quiet Room, turned on the tap, heard Pate shout, "Don't!" and the door shut behind me. Benji leaned against it. I couldn't get out. Through the safetyglass I watched him reach for a chair, wedge it under the knob, then go toward Pate, who was lying on the floor, clutching at his knees. Benji said he was sorry—I saw his mouth form the words—and then he turned to me, told me, "I'm coming back," and I remember the sound, though I couldn't have heard it, not through the glass, and Benji grabbed a chair and threw it into Main Hall, and then he grabbed another chair and went out the door. One chair he wedged beneath the knob in Main Hall, the other he brought to the gym as a weapon. You already know that. There isn't much else I can tell you.

Sometimes I don't like him for having said he'd come back; sometimes it seems to make him a liar. It doesn't, of course—he had no idea, he was no more clairvoyant than he was suicidal—but that's how it seems sometimes. Plus he does keep coming back, though, doesn't he, Gurion? Sometimes I even like that. Mostly I don't. I can't fall in love. All the boys who remain in the world are so weak.

I certainly can't tell you what finally provoked him. Even ignoring that he was high on two drugs, Benji had always been a complicated boy. On reflection it seems that he might have been planning to lock me in the Quiet Room before Pate got there, but maybe he hadn't been; maybe the news of what was happening outside led him to believe that your plan could work if he could stop Berman from somehow thwarting it. Or maybe the opposite; maybe he thought that your plan wouldn't work if he attacked Berman, and he wanted it to fail. Or it could be that he wanted you to succeed, but he wanted to keep Berman from being a part of that success. Or maybe it had nothing to do with you at all, and he took what he saw to be his last chance to exact his vengeance on a snake who'd shot him and jumped on his back at the end of the battle.

What's weird is I don't even know what you'd prefer to believe. If you were a normal human being, you'd feel vindicated thinking that Benji's last gesture might have been born of something other than hate for you. But through it all, and after all, you've been and remained the same Gurion Maccabee, enmity's most religious celebrant. The possibility that your best friend's dying wish might *not* have been to damage you—might even have been to protect you— probably wrecks you inside just as well as the others.

At least one can hope.

☐ ☐ ☐ ☐ ☐ ☐ ☐

The first time you finish any truly great book that isn't the Torah, you remember the end the best.* You remember that event Y followed event X. You recall Y followed X because Y, though unpredictable, was also inevitable, given X's nature, and given the patterns established by the author (between A and B, J and K, R and S...).** You may even remember the sweep of the book; how A, itself, led eventually to Y, how each of the interceding events (B through X), if not wholly necessary to give rise to Y, worked to grant Y the resonance sufficient to cause you to supply the book its (unwritten) Z, which must not only follow as inevitably from Y as did B from A, or R from Q, but must, paradoxically, *un*make sense (if the book is to be other than moralist preaching) of all the above-described causal relations, revealing they weren't inevitable at all.

All great books command re-reading, but you can't ever read the same book twice. Knowing, as you do, from the second reading forward, that A will lead to B, to Y to Z, your post-first readings are far more concerned with what exactly happens *between* those events, far more concerned with those parts you scanned (or even skipped) the first go-round in your rush to discover what would happen next. You look closely at the details—the wordplay, the rhythms, all the "minor" activity—and generate hypotheses as to why they are there, what purpose they serve in the cause of moving you, what they point at, where and to where they misdirect you. This act of analysis creates a sense of distance.***

---

* In Torah, you remember the opening the best, and the events described—on their first reading—often seem fractured, hard to connect, rarely emotional, *until* you subject them to serious analysis.

** If you don't remember these things, you can't possibly believe the book is good, let alone great; you must believe that someone has failed; whether you or the author depends on your temperament.

*** The act of analysis can't help but create a sense of distance between you and what's analyzed. This seems much stranger than it actually is. It seems strange because not only does analysis require you to get up close to a thing, but analysis is undertaken (at least in the case of re-reading great books) with the overt desire

When, for example, you already know that Holden Caulfield will run from his teacher who pet him on the forehead as he slept, you read *Catcher* looking for signs the petting's coming; you read to determine if Holden's right or wrong to assume the teacher's perved. You read this way in order to determine exactly why it was that the scene made you sad: Was it because a man the boy trusted acted like a perv, or was it because the man *didn't?* Soon you realize it could've been either—there's no way to know, each option's supportable—and you attempt to determine which is sadder: for Holden to have been taken advantage of (or to have been on the verge of being taken advantage of) by a man that he trusted, or for Holden to have been so damaged by earlier experiences that innocent (however seemingly inappropriate) affection from a man he *should* trust gets misconstrued (misread by Holden as inappropriate) and sends him running out the door. It's finally impossible to determine which is sadder; not even a hybrid of *both* is sadder.* And eventually you come to see that the saddest option is the one that J.D. Salinger exercised: the one that resists disambiguation.

By now, though, the scene doesn't make you sad; at least not as sad as it did on the first read, when you knew much less about the way it worked. Now, when you read *Catcher in the Rye*, you observe the scene *working* to make you sad, and you appreciate those workings (unless you're a fool), and you examine further subtleties, tinier machines, the sprockets on the cogs behind the wheels behind the wheels. You can't see the time, though, from inside a clock. You know it, of course—at least you know what it *was*; after

---

to get up close to that thing. The resultant sense of distance thus seems to suggest that to get up close to something is to get away from it, to push it away or be pushed away by it.

That suggestion is false. That suggestion is nonsense.

To get up close to something is to get up close to something; to push something away is to push something away; to be pushed is to be pushed. The sense of distance created by the act of analysis indicates only that one shouldn't trust his emotions to measure proximity (or, alternately, that one should not use metaphors of proximity to describe one's emotional states). All that it means to have "a sense of distance" from something is that the emotions which that thing has provoked are less intense than one initially believed they should be. Yet when one acquires a sense of distance from something by way of analysis, instead of concluding that one was in error to believe that one's emotions should be more intense, one believes that the thing that is under analysis has failed to provoke emotion as intensely as it should have; one believes the act of analysis has somehow ruined the thing's ability to properly provoke (or, alternately, one's capacity to be properly provoked).

At least *I* believe that, even when, as now, I would seem to know better. And if this has begun to sound apologetic, or defensive, probably it is—if not one, then the other, depending on your temperament.

* I.e., that the teacher intended to molest Holden *and* Holden had suffered molestation earlier in life: If the teacher *was* about to molest Holden, then while it's still sad for the petting to have happened, and while it's also still sad that Holden ever had to suffer experiences prior to this one which allowed him the certainty to run from his teacher, Holden's seeing the petting for what it is and getting out before it goes any further isn't sad at all; it's a kind of victory.

all, you stopped the clock before climbing inside—but you just can't see it.

And all of this to say that I remember Benji's murder and what happened thereafter on 11/17 the same way I remember great books I've re-read. I know what I thought and why I thought it, and I know what I said and why I said it, but I don't remember thinking or saying any of it. I can't seem to remember *the experience* of any of it.

What's left is fractured, gapped, full of empty. Whether that's because *I* was, or because—through having gone over it again and again—I have since become so, I cannot say with any measure of authority. Nor can I say which I'd prefer to believe. I don't even know which I'd prefer *you* to believe. What's left, however, is all I've got left. It will, eventually, suffice.

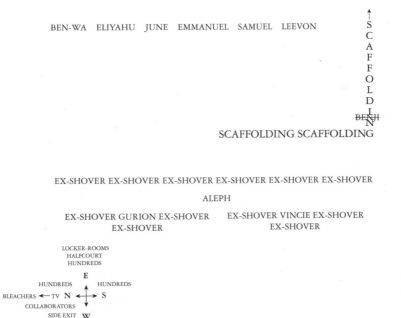

The scholars were coming. Aleph gave orders. Vincie and I were untied from the scaffold and stood at the top of the western key. Two ex-Shover pennyguns, loaded with nibs, were aimed at my throat, two others at Vincie's, both of us held from behind by the hair. Six ex-Shovers stood shoulder-to-shoulder, facing away from us, weapons trained east. Aleph was standing between us and them. The rest of the insurgents crowded the exit.

From the Side and the scholars, they'd demand Jerry's keys in trade for our lives, Aleph explained. He said once they'd all made it safely outside, they'd free us and say that they'd barely escaped from Gurion ben-Judah. That part was a lie, I knew it was a lie—a lie that was told because I was listening. If the insurgents escaped, Vincie and I would be turned over to the cops, the better to bolster Aleph's claims to heroism.

My army came through the boys locker-room door sooner and faster than Aleph expected. They barrelled topspeed at the line of ex-Shovers, which was all they could see til Aleph said "Down," and the ex-Shovers knelt to reveal our tableau.

The frontmost row was six soldiers wide: Ben-Wa and Brooklyn flanked June on the right, Leevon and Samuel Emmanuel on the left. As soon as they saw us, they began slowing down, but the soldiers behind them were all pushing forward, and they couldn't slow much without getting trampled.

Attack! I shouted, but to no effect, except to incite the kid on my left to sock me in the beauty, leaving me muted, bent at the waist, sucking for wind.

June, then Emmanuel, ordered a halt. The soldiers who were still in the locker-room, however, couldn't hear the orders, much less see the leaders, and the Five, who'd been assigned to head up the rearguard, urged them all forward, pushing and shouting, and the drive, though slowing, did not fully stop til the vanguard was three or four feet beyond halfcourt and three hundred scholars were inside the gym.

Sap in his fist, pacing north-south, Aleph presented his single demand.

June refused to hand over the keys, told him he'd have to free us first.

Aleph revolved, sapped Vincie's ribs, spun back around to check June's reaction.

June kept the keys.

I was fighting for breath still, chasing my voice down. Even if I could die (by then I didn't know or care if I could die), if Aleph had me murdered, he wouldn't have anything left with which to bargain; my army would attack and destroy the insurgents. That much had to have been obvious to everyone, and its obviousness to everyone equally obvious = To have me murdered would be irrational.

Aleph wasn't irrational. Aleph was sly: he was sly enough to see that he seemed too rational. That's why he'd rib-sapped Vincie to begin with. It failed to convince, though; it blinkered desperation, but not irrationality. Maybe if he'd sapped my ribs instead of Vincie's, June would've handed over the keys. Or maybe she'd've seen the move for what it was and stood as defiant as she had to Vincie's sapping. It was, however, the third possible outcome that prevented sly Aleph from sapping me: June and the scholars might've attacked, believing he was actually trying to kill me.

Now he was pointing at Benji, saying, "We're already killers. You don't want to test us."

Leevon Ray twetched. Ben-Wa stopped his crying. Emmanuel and Samuel were looking to June, and June put the keys in her pocket and stared.

Apart from backing down, Aleph only had one or two moves left to make, one or two sly moves left to escalate his threat. He could run the above-described risks and sap me, or he could have Vincie Portite murdered. If the action he took—whichever it was—failed to produce a final outcome, then he'd perform the one that remained.

He wasn't backing down and he wasn't walking over, but even if he did walk over and sap me, it might not work—it probably wouldn't work; June didn't look scared—and the scholars might *not* attack, and then Aleph would kill Vincie to see if *that* worked, and though my lungs did hold some air now, it was only a little, and even if I had the breath to explain the entire dynamic to June and the scholars, and even if the kid who'd muted me once failed to do so again before I could finish, Aleph would hear the explanation as well, and he'd only act faster, he'd act more determined, he'd kill Vincie Portite and say, "So what? Attack us and find out how crazy I am," thus no explanation I could give could change anything, and as for a simple command to attack: they'd already disobeyed one of those.

So I said the only thing I could say that might work, and I said it to the one most desperate to believe it, the one who was looking straight into my eyes.

I said to Eliyahu, I do not die.

And Eliyahu went forward to free the messiah, and all of the scholars followed him.

□   □   □   □   □   □   □

A panic-shot nib missed Vincie's carotid. I let my legs fold beneath all my weight. As my knees hit the floor, hair ripped off my head. The ex-Shover holding the hair-chunk was shot—blinded with pennies—and Berman was shot. The rest of the insurgents dropped their guns. They were lined up, as ordered by Samuel Diamond, against the west wall, their hands in the air.

June untied me, and Starla Vincie, and Googy Ally, who'd been under the bleachers, gagged with a sock.

No one saw Jelly come into the gym.

Gaze fixed on my feet, his mouth a bloody donut, Ally approached me and spoke uncued. "It's true that I helped bring him down," he told me. "He was trying to kill Berman—at least that's what it looked like—and I didn't want anyone to die, okay? But then he was out, he wasn't even moving, and they kept kicking and shooting, and they said they would kill him and tell you they'd had to in self-defense, and I *did* try to stop that. I tried to argue, but they wouldn't listen, they said he'd burn down their houses and kill them all, and then I tried to fight them, but I'm—I'm nothing. I'm weak, and I know it's not enough, and—"

What did he say?

"Nothing," Ally said. "He wasn't there, and then he was there. On top of Berman. He didn't say anything. I know I'm in trouble, okay? I know. Leave Googy alone, though. He wouldn't hurt anyone. He does what I tell him. That's all that he does."

Never come near me again, I said.

Ally went east, Googy in tow.

Brooklyn and Emmanuel brought me the sap.

"We've figured out a way to exit," said Brooklyn.

Sitting next to Benji, Jelly chewed her sleeves. June went over, whispered something from behind her. Jelly pressed her face to June's hip and shook.

I gave the sap to Vincie, who was limping beside me.

Below the neck, I said. I want him awake.

Vincie nodded, caved in a rib.

Aleph hit the floor on his side and squirmed. I went through his pockets til I found the cracktorch, straddled his torso, choked him left-handed, and branded his temples, each with a six, and branded a vav on his forehead.

I slackened the choke and set aside the lighter, twetched on the vav to hear it crackle and speed up the scarification. Vincie put the sap in my hand and stepped back. I raised the sap high, and was grasped at the elbow.

"We have to get to work," Emmanuel said. "We're thinking we've got a good plan."

I said, First we kill all these Goddamned Jews.

"Anything, Rabbi," said Emmanuel, "but that. We aren't murderers."

They murdered my friend.

"We aren't killers."

You could be, I said.

"That's not why we came here," Emmanuel said. "Don't stain our hands."

Just mine, I said.

"There's no such thing."

No? I said. We'll see, I said. Hold his wrists to the floor.

"I'm not an executioner."

I know, I said.

"I won't help you kill him."

You won't, I said, just hold down his wrists.

Emmanuel crouched behind Aleph and did it.

I brought the sap down, and again, and again, til the impacts ceased to make breaking sounds.

We did the left hand the same as the right.

I stood before those being held to the wall.

The scarfless insurgents were all crying out: "It was them!" "The ex-Shovers!" "The ex-Shovers did it!"

And the ex-Shovers: "Berman!" "It was Berman who did it!"

Kneel, I said. Kneel before us in awe.

They all knelt before us.

In *awe*! I said. Like *this*! I said.

They pressed their hands like pagans in prayer.

Harder, I said. Harder and harder. Finger to finger and thumb to thumb. Bend til they break. Breaks can be set. Bones can heal, I said. Dust only clumps, deforming the flesh. It settles wherever it's pushed to, I said. Any digit remaining intact I'll make dust.

And they pressed all their fingers against all their fingers til each one had fingers unhinged at his palms. A few got all of them, even the thumbs. Some got one or two, most between three and six.

No discernable pattern of damage emerged; no sense of justice arose from the arithmetic. The number of digits ill-cocked on the hands of any given insurgent was determined, it seemed, by factors that should have been arbitrary: his panic threshold, his tolerance for pain, his ligamental and ten-dinous elasticities, the strength of his muscles versus that of his bones.

All the screaming, say the poets of the Gurionic War, was heard by Hashem, Who led me toward mercy.

But there wasn't any screaming and there wasn't any mercy. Just gasping and groaning and bottomless contempt.

Love one another, I told them.

□ □ □ □ □ □ □

Because the lot had been cleared of civilians and news crews, and every cop manning the ressurected barricade was strapped with a gasmask and little silver canisters, and after the way the first army had entered, the second and third, if they got to the school, would be teargassed on sight, no question.

And because the new barricade was half its former size and we couldn't locate the fifty missing cops, despite all the live footage being shot from choppers. And because the cops had not cut our power, which suggested they wanted us to see what we were seeing on live TV. And because what we saw on live TV, despite being birdseyed, didn't include any part of the sky, and the ceiling of the school was free of skylights. And because what we saw didn't include what lay west of the school, and the school's west wall was entirely windowless.

And because what we saw and what we didn't see—because what they showed us and what they wouldn't show us—seemed to indicate, when added together, that the fifty missing cops were west of the school and/or in choppers high above the roof, poising to raid us.

And because a willingness to raid us entailed, by necessity, a willingness to risk the lives of prisoners and a willingness to use deadly force against us.

And because everything has to come to an end, and shy of immediate surrender on our part, a raid was the end that the cops preferred most—even if they didn't quite know it yet—because no news crews were inside of the school, and the story of what happened inside of the school would belong to the cops once they raided the school.

And because there were news crews outside of the school.

And because the other armies, through sleet and through hail, had traveled all morning because I had asked them to.

And because the second army was still no less than a mile away from us, and the third army—Feingold's—further than that.

And because it is better, all else being equal, to be a moving target than it is to be a static one.

All told, there were, depending how you parse them, between nine and twelve reasons I agreed to the plan Emmanuel described to me, none of which included "to perform a miracle," none of which included "to pray for a miracle," none of which included "to witness a miracle," none of which had fuck-all to do with any miracle.

▫ ▫ ▫ ▫ ▫ ▫ ▫

OFFICERS:

SHORTLY WE WILL EXIT THE SCHOOL, HEADING EAST. WE WILL LEAVE BEHIND SOME PRISONERS AND TAKE OTHERS WITH US. SOME OF THOSE WE TAKE WILL BE HELD ON OUR BORDERS AND RELEASED IN WAVES AS WE GO, FROM ALL SIDES OF US. OTHERS I WILL KEEP FOR A LITTLE WHILE LONGER. THESE OTHERS WILL MARCH WITH OUR COLUMNS, UNBOUND, SPREAD EVENLY AMONG US. YOU WILL NOT BE ABLE TO TELL THEM FROM THE REST OF US.

NOR WILL YOU COME WITHIN THIRTY YARDS OF US. NOR WILL THE DIN THAT YOUR CHOPPERS EMIT SOUND IN OUR EARS ANY LOUDER THAN WHISPERS.

ONCE WE HAVE MET UP WITH ALL OF OUR BROTHERS AND I HAVE SAID WHAT IT IS THAT I HAVE TO SAY TO THEM, I WILL FREE THE REMAINING PRISONERS AND SURRENDER.

NO CALLS WILL BE TAKEN, AND NO COUNTER-OFFERS. THIS NOTE IS A BINDING CONTRACT. FREEING THE MAMZER TO WHOM IT IS AFFIXED IS A GOODWILL GESTURE IN YOUR DIRECTION. SINCE YOU LACK THE OPPORTUNITY TO RESPOND IN KIND, WE HAVE DONE SO OURSELVES, ON YOUR BEHALF: COPIES OF THIS NOTE HAVE BEEN EMAILED TO THE PRESS, ENSURING THAT IF YOU DECIDE TO DOUBLE-DEAL US, THE WORLD WILL KNOW ON WHOM TO PLACE THE BLAME FOR ALL ENSUING TRAGEDIES.

YOUR SIGNATURE IS IMPLICIT.
HERE IS MINE:

Emmanuel gave me the note and I signed it. Brooklyn went to scan it in the library with Shai, after which Shai took it up to the front, where Samuel had gone with the insurgent, Cory. While Brooklyn sent the scan from my gmail account, Shai pinned the note onto Boystar's shirt, and Boystar was launched out the door by the guards. Four cops came forward from amidst the barricade and carried Boystar east to safety. Cory was tied to the vacated chair.

We waited for news of the note to break.

I was sitting next to Benji. June held my hand. Jelly wouldn't look at me, let alone speak. I told her if she wanted I'd change my mind back again, dust all their digits, even the broken ones. I told her she could do it herself if she wanted. She pulled on her hair. She tore at her shirt. I handed her the sap and she flung it blindly. The coat that covered Benji got jarred, and slipped. I tried to fix it. Jelly said, "Don't," and slapped at the air. June led me away.

The scholars, by then, had imprisoned the insurgents inside the boys locker-room, and posted replacements for the guards at the entrances. The ones without duties leaned on the walls and spoke in hushed tones, throwing me and June glances at regular intervals, chinning the air whenever our eyes met. The Side and Big Ending were gathered on the bleachers. Shpritzy approached as we made our way over there.

"I'm scared," said his Ashley, her arm around his waist.

"She's scared," he said. "We were thinking that maybe—"

"No," said Emmanuel. He and Samuel had come up behind the two. "Don't bother Gurion. We told you: No. We need her," he said to me. "We're short as it is. His friend Mr. Goldblum just talked to this Feingold who says they have yet to get off of the beach."

"Can you take an ex-Shover instead?" Shpritzy said.

"What's an ex-Shover?"

"The Jews with the scarves."

"No," said Emmanuel. "No real hostages. They might be resistant. It might cause a ruckus. This needs to go smoothly. We can't invite fire."

"She won't get hurt," said Samuel to Shpritzy. "You won't get hurt," he said to the Ashley. "We'll make you Wave 1. You'll be the first freed. Put out your wrists and let your boyfriend tie them."

Shpritzy looked my way.

You'll see her tomorrow, I said. She'll be fine.

He bent to the floor and unlaced a shoe.

Solly came over, chinned air at Jelly. "She says she's staying and she won't leave the body."

She's staying then, June said. She won't leave the body.

"She's an Israelite, no?"

She's staying, I said.

We went up the bleachers.

Vincie was tying Starla's wrists with a cord while Leevon tied Main Man's, Ben-Wa tied Ansul's, the Flunky the Janitor's, Salvador Dingle's, Chunkstyle Boshka's, Mangey Ronrico's, Fulton Jerry's, Forrest Christian's, Jesse Stevie's, Cody Beauregard's, Chubnik 1 Momo's, and Chubnik 2 3's.

Then Vincie tied Leevon's, Ben-Wa the Flunky's, Salvador Chunkstyle's, Mangey Fulton's, Forrest Jesse's, and Cody Chubnik 1's and 2's the both.

And Vincie tied Salvador's, Ben-Wa Forrest's, and Mangey Cody's.

And then Vincie tied Mangey's and Ben-Wa's the both.

And Vincie revolved and he gave me a cord.

"Not too tight."

A choked sound escaped me.

"Fuck that," said Vincie, leaning in close. "Don't fuck us up. We're holding it down here. Main Main's watching and Main Man's fine. He says you'll raise Benji right after you walk through the Michigan Valley, which I think is in Kansas. The nutmeg—fuck it—God bless the Boystar. Just don't unconfuse him. Don't fuck us up. We don't want to see it. We're not Call-Me-Sandy. Get your eyes sleepy. Slacken the cramp. Good, that's good. It works, I know. I don't know why. It does though. It works. So remember who showed you and leave it at that, and that's the goodbye, the big stupid cheezy fucken cornball goodbye, the what-Vincie-taught-me you've so long awaited, the time that you'll fondly recall forever, when your this was still that, and your that was a something, and that something wasn't jaded by X or Y, or clouded by A or B or C, and the difference between P and Q was still clear, and kenobi kenobi kenobi, okay? Now reach in my pocket. This part's important. This part's more important than keep your eyes sleepy. That doesn't mean stop. Keep your eyes sleepy while you reach in my pocket— not that one, the other one. That one. Good. That's our friend's lighter. He had a whole bunch so it's only one of many and there's nothing at all to get leaky and gooze about. Just some lighter. Keep your eyes sleepy. It's my lighter, now. Don't fuck us up. It's not even the one you burnt that fuck's head with. It's just one I took when our friend wasn't looking. He'd never even used it. Don't fuck us up. It still had the sticker on the back with the warning. It's only a lighter. Last week we sparred and he got me in a hold and I brought us to the ground and was still in the hold, but this lighter was peaking outside of his pocket. My hand was right there. Keep your eyes sleepy. My arm wouldn't move, but my fingers were mine and I reached out my fingers and plucked out the lighter. I said I submitted, and as we got up, our friend started telling me what I'd done wrong, how I got in a position that forced me to submit, what I could've done different to avoid that position, all in that way-of-the-fucken-samurai voice, and I told him fuck off and showed him his lighter. I told him, 'Fuck off, man, I got your fucken lighter,' and he told me who cares, the lighter was mine, I could keep the fucken lighter, he had hundreds more lighters and lighters were free if you had baggy pockets and command of two hands, so stick the fucken lighter in my baggy fucken pocket and shut the fuck up and learn how to fight. 'Whatever,' I said, 'I got your fucken lighter. You took your baggy pockets and commanded your hands and you know how to fight, but the lighter's not yours, it's mine,' I told him. He winked to distract me, and he shot out his freak-arm, snatched the fucken lighter straight out of my fist, then lit it one time so I could see that it worked, then he threw it in the street, and it fell in the sewer, so actually, I'm wrong, this lighter isn't that one, it's a whole nother lighter I stole from his bag when he went to take a piss, or another one I got from his coat when I borrowed it—doesn't matter anyway. That's all I'm saying. The lighter's a lighter that belonged to our friend, one of twenty or thirty I stole this year from the hundreds he took from the thousands on the counters of ten or so local minimarts. If I had another lighter instead of this lighter, we'd use the one I had, and nothing would be different, not even if our friend wasn't dead it wouldn't. We'd do the same thing we're about to do. You'd reach in the hole in the lining of your jacket—we know about the hole, we just never risked it, you're weird about that jacket, really fucken sentimental, and we worried we'd tear the hole bigger if we invaded—he's here or he's not, you'd still reach in the hole, just like you're doing—right, that's good—and you'd pull out the treasure you keep so well hidden—just like that, exactly like that—and you'd do the next thing, the obvious thing—see, you're already doing it—and pass me mine first, cause you like me the best and our time's running out and here comes your—thanks, man—here comes your boy, with news of the news, and you'd tell him five minutes, tell him wait til we're finished, til we burn past the letters—you heard what he said, kid, back the fuck off, I don't know your name even, none of us do—Emmanuel Liebman, that's a lot of fucken name, I'm Vincie Portite and I've never even heard of you, none of us have, so go line your friends up and leave us alone til we burn past the letters—tell him, insist, yeah, just like that—no, Brooklyn, not you, you stick around here—and three at a time now, you'd light one for June and one for Starla and one for Leevon and pass them along, just like that, and two at a time you'd light one for Wolf, who's decided in a rush of blood to the head to take up the habit, the best cure for crying, it always works—you cannot fucken sob while sucking on smoke, make sure to inhale, Wolf—and the other for Brooklyn, who's that kind of kid now, he knows it or not—you are, now you know—and light one for you now and pass the pack down with our dead friend's lighter for whoever I've forgotten, they can light up in pairs, one holding the box and the other takes out from it—takes *two* out, Flunky—and the first one lights them, passes down the goods to the next pair in line, and so on and so on and—don't gank the lighter, Dingle, you bancer, I'll cover your face in a brown paper bag and kill you six times, fucken wager on *that*—and now we're all smoking in the Aptakisic bleachers in the middle of the schoolday, and now we can talk, let's talk, can we talk? I'll start us off. This is how I'll start: It's the middle of the schoolday. We're smoking in the bleachers. To smoke in the bleachers in the middle of the schoolday—it's fucken good. Anyone who says different isn't really a human. Even Brodsky, the cops, even fucken Botha—they know in their fuckfaced hearts this is good. They wish they were us, smoking up here. They wish they were us and we don't have to wish. Now you. It's your turn. Say something smart. No? Not yet? I'll go again: Haven't you always wanted to do this? It turns out I've always wanted to do this. This part's fucken good, right? This part is good. Now give us a blessing. I'm nearly past the letters. Don't fuck me up here. Say something smart. Keep your fucken eyes sleepy, Gurion, and speak."

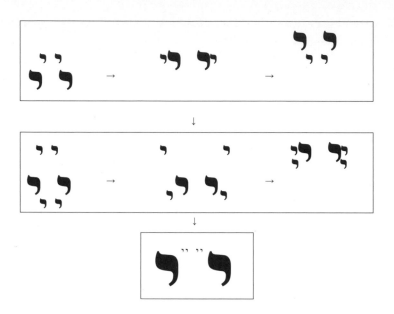

The news broke the note and the barricade parted. Samuel assigned each hostage a number, one through seven, four to a wave, and Cory and Maholtz were locked in Nurse Clyde's. We gathered in columns outside the front entrance. Hands tied before them, their sleeves gripped by scholars, seven hostages—one from each wave—slouched to look captured on each of our borders. Emmanuel and Samuel headed up columns adjacent to the central one, headed by Brooklyn, who carried the megaphone, calling out orders. June and I marched northwest of the middle—columns twelve and thirteen, row eleven—so we couldn't be seen by the cops who were flanking us, nor by those who, eventually, trailed us. Those in the choppers, of course, could see us, but from that point of view we could not be distinguished from any other soldiers, not with our hoods on; not unless they knew we'd hold hands—they didn't.

The march proceeded as seen on TV.

As we crossed Rand Road, Brooklyn ordered the first wave of hostages freed, then freed a wave for each block we traversed. In crocodile tears, the freed hostages ran all thirty-plus yards to the news crews and cops to the west, north, and south of us.

Three blocks east of the two-hill field we met the second army, led by Itzik Leslie Bienstein-Pikowitz, a seventh-grade boy from Hillel Torah Day who Shai Bar-Sholem used to bunk with at camp. At Brooklyn's command, this Itzik halted and parted his army. We got in front of them, returned their Good Yontifs as they lined up behind us, and the hostages on what had been our rear border were passed back westward, to our new rear border. We picked up the march til Sheridan Road.

A ravine divided the road from the beach, and the third army's front-line—Feingold foremost—was in the ravine, their rearguard's heels a yard from the water. Eliyahu ordered them to halt and part, then ordered the second army part and flank us. We freed the last wave and crossed the ravine, advancing eastward til we all stood on sand, a thousand soldiers in forty columns, and June and I went to the front, the shoreline.

Eliyahu of Brooklyn gave me the soundgun. I unfolded my scripture and gave it to June. We revolved to face the soldiers, our backs to the lake. A chopper overhead, helped out by a cloud, was blocking the sun. The sun was descending. The sabbath was coming. In Israel, the sabbath was already there. I knew that I'd spend the next sabbath in Israel, that that's what it was that my mom thought I wanted. I'd known for some minutes, ten or fifteen. The house of Yakov. It was no kind of code. It was barely a metaphor. My mother'd arranged us a haven in Israel on the single condition that no one else died. Someone else died, though. Nakamook died. They would let me stay anyway. Of course they would let me. Of course they would let me, and my mother would make me. All of this occurred to me right around the time the army crested the high hill.

I'm going away for sure, I'd told June.

"I know," she'd said, "but it'll be fine. We'll miss each other, but we already do that. We already miss each other more than we don't, right? It's not like we're used to seeing each other. And you're not the kind of boy who other boys mess with, so we don't have to worry that that'll happen. You'll read a lot of books and write me letters. I'll write you back, and read the books you read, and try to learn Hebrew, and visit you every time I can. The juvie's in Bolling. It isn't that far. And I know my mom'll drive me, I've figured it out: if my boyfriend's in juvie, he's a criminal, true, but I'm not having sex. I won't even have to say that—that's just how she thinks. Gurion. Gurion. Hey. Gurion. Hey Gurion—what? Don't. Not Benji. You have to wait to think about Benji. You'll ruin him forever if you do it right now. Trust me. I know. You know that I know. You'll ruin everything. You're ruining everything."

I—

"No. Listen. You have to listen. If you think about him now, you'll make him one way. You'll make him simple. You'll make him a story. His death will be the climax. You'll bend who he was to make sense of his death. You'll have to edit most of him out to do that. You'll forget he was a bully, or forget he was your friend. You'll forget he was a dickhead a lot of the time, or you'll forget there was kindness in his dickhead heart. And that's not the worst part. It's not even close. The worst part's the story you'll make of the world. If you make him a story right now, Jellybean, right now when its fresh, when his death seems the climax, you'll bend the whole world so it fits that story. It'll be unavoidable. You'll make the world a story that's able to contain him, your edited version, your Nakamook story. His death will be the climax of the story of *everything*. The scholars will be secondary. The Side will be secondary. I will, too. The purpose of the world will be to kill Benji Nakamook, and you will be reduced to a witness, Gurion. Don't do that to us. Don't make this a lie. It isn't a lie I'll agree to tell. You're going away. You'll be locked up. Think about that. How that is suck. That's what you were thinking about before I tried to comfort you with the story of what it would actually be like—the letters and the books and the visits and baked goods. Did I mention the baked goods? I'll bring you baked goods. I'll learn how to bake. I'll listen to Hebrew on tape while I bake. But take my whole story with a grain of salt. Doubt what I'm saying. Doubt what I said. Worry about that. Go back to that. Don't think about Benji. Think about us. Tell yourself I'm probably living in a fantasy. Tell yourself that June, even though she means well, won't follow through, or at least that she might not—that June, herself, the first time you met her, told you that no one could promise forever, and despite what it looks like, she probably hasn't revised her opinion. Can you do that? Do that. Do that, okay? Doubt me a little and we'll be alright."

Okay, I'd said.

"Good," she'd said.

"There is damage," I said to the thousand soldiers.

The ones who'd been jumping to get a better look at me settled on their tiptoes, quiet, listening.

A gust off the lake blew a hiss through the soundgun and flapped my scripture, which June held high, and water crept up and splashed at our ankles. Our hands, abiding the shiver, squeezed, and we took a step forward—that's all there was room for; the beach was packed tight—and got splashed again.

"There was always damage," I said to the soldiers, as the cloud and the chopper that were blocking the sun began drifting apart, "and there will be more damage," I said to the soldiers, as a ray from the sun touched a chink in June's retina, and she, refusing to lower my scripture, let go of my hand to cover her face in order to avoid misting gooze on the soldiers, and proceeded to sneeze a sneeze no one heard, for the noise of the lake being riven was deafening.

No one quite saw what they thought they were seeing, and to this day few see what's truly before them as they marvel at the footage the helicopters shot and choke on huzzahs or cry out, "The horror!" or cry out, "Moshiach!" or postulate U.S. government conspiracies or Hollywood-Zionist-Media ploys or remark with false calm on aberrant tectonics, lunar events, ano-molous plate-shifts, barometric hyperflux, electomagnetic energy bursts, non-contiguous molecular planes, destabilized particles, rogue nuclear states, comets, sunspots, or paratidal deviance.

It's true that a valley had formed in the lake, that the valley was the width of our forty columns, and its miles-high walls, half a foot thick, occluded by foam and sand and stones and baffled fish and swaying vegeta-tion, were smooth as glass on their valley-facing sides, and it's true that the walls cast all their spray outward, and its floor was level and as smooth as the walls, and it's true that the valley, from its moment of creation, stretched east through the lake past the vanishing point, and it's true that the soldiers marched into the valley while I remained standing just east of its mouth watching my east-marching army recede, and true June was standing just southwest of me, and it's true I reached back and took hold of June's hand, goozed though it was, and true that as soon as our palms pressed together the walls of the valley began to splash down on the heads of the soldiers, threatening to drown them, and true that I then let go of June's hand and all the falling water and debris it contained once again became walls, and it's true June thought I'd been icked by the gooze and she wiped off her hand before grabbing mine again, and true that, again, the walls began to splash down, and that this time I didn't let go of June's hand, but that all that was falling again became walls. It's also true, how-ever, that I'd moved my feet. I'd moved my feet just a couple inches west, a couple inches outside the mouth of the valley. That's something nearly everybody fails to see.

And it's true we held hands for the next few minutes, standing in place while the scholars pressed east, deeper and deeper into the valley, and true that what we said was not prolific. The lipreader-dictated subtitles are true. It's true June said, "You have to go."

It's true I responded, Fuck Him, I don't.

It's true she said, "Please."

It's true I said, No. Enough is enough.

It's true that I tried, one last time, in hopes He was bluffing, to enter the valley holding June's hand, and it's true that the walls began to splash down, and it's true I removed my foot from the valley and that all that was falling again became walls.

And it's true the police, some fifty police, had, by then, begun to close in. It's true that I told them, as they've faithfully reported, that if they came any closer I'd stop what I was doing.

I'll stop what I'm doing is exactly what I said.

And they came no closer; that is true.

And it's true the implications of what I'd said were that I was holding the valley open, and that the valley would close and drown all the scholars if I were to cease to hold it open—it's true I implied I was performing a miracle. And it's true I knew that's what I implied, and true that's what I intended to imply. It's also true my implications were false, and true I knew my implications were false, and true as well, and finally true, that there wasn't any miracle—a feat of God certainly, a spectacle stinking of divine interference, a holy stunt sure, but not a miracle. Only a test.

"Please go," June said. "This isn't a test. I mean it," she said. "It's not like when I kicked you and made you bring my sketchbook. I won't love you less if you go," she said.

I said, 'Fuck Him,' I said.

I raised the soundgun.

"Wait," she said. "Let's wait then," she said. "This part we don't have to rush, okay? Let's wait here a minute and look at the valley."

And it's true we waited and looked at the valley, and it's true it was more a chasm than a valley—a *valley* a space between graded planes, between hills or mountains that might be worth trying to climb if you wanted—but still it was less a defile than a valley—a *defile* a thin breach through which only one person could pass at a time, a space that an army would have to break ranks in order to trek—and yet I'd been thinking, before June said *valley*, that it was a defile, and that seems important, how I'd formerly thought of it, especially in light of how I came to think of it, and maybe it is, except not like you think, but only because I'd decided to call it whatever June Watermark thought we should call it.

We looked at the valley, looked into the valley, and all of the soldiers, some hundred yards east, forty columns of soldiers, twenty-five deep, were looking at us, and soon Eliyahu walked up to the mouth and said, "Nu? Are you coming?"

I told him we weren't.

"I'll tell them," he said, and returned to the soldiers.

As soon as they were all within range of the soundgun, I delivered them the blessings of the Gurionic War and the blessings of what would become *The Instructions*.

The soldiers, in their columns, then followed us west, and once the last row had emerged from the valley, the walls of the valley buckled and plunged.

Coda

And men of conspicuous height and fitness popped out of a window-blackened SUV in the evergreen copse inside the ravine into which I had walked hand-in-hand with June and forced on me and another scholar who was roughly my shape (or, in one version, a lookalike boy they'd brought along with them) a clothing switcheroonie to misdirect the cameras. Or else they were barrel-chested, thin-haired men in rumpled khakis and schlubby parkas who looked like dads in their late-model Dodge or Ford sedan, and they offered either bribes too big to refuse, or grave, fascistic threats that, however cartoonish, cowed each and every member of the on-site media into shooting all that footage of the scholars being boarded onto the buses and taken to the commandeered gym at the J to be processed and questioned and retrieved by their parents.

Then a chloroformed handkerchief or tranquilizer dart or a video on a laptop- or PDA-screen showing both of my parents or one of my parents chained to a rail and held at gunpoint, or a gun put to June right there in the ravine (or in the SUV or late-model Dodge or Ford sedan), or promises of protection and pleas for cooperation uttered in fluent, even beautiful Hebrew, after or instead of the threats to my parent(s) or June, in the ravine or the pertinent vehicle (in the trunk or backseat of which—behind tinted windows—my mom was or wasn't hidden or hiding, handcuffed and bound at the ankles or not).

And a million-dollar chamber in an undisclosed locale in a secret facility somewhere out west where my brain was examined with a billion-dollar scanner while a holodeck-quality VR-device worth seventeen billion ran me through a set of provocative scenarios and found that, under battlestress, as well as in the throes of sexual pleasure, I emitted a stream of "omega wave packets" at the same exact frequency—according to the U.S. President's coterie of mystics, who'd discovered said frequency via numerological analyses of ancient scripture—as Yeshua had or Cain or

Esau, or that I didn't emit any such packets, as Yeshua hadn't nor Cain nor Esau, or that unlike Yeshua or Cain or Esau, I did or didn't emit such packets. Or a magnetized "theta-blocking" rubberwalled cell in a secret brig underneath the Pentagon where the U.S. President, through shatterproof glass, looked in my eyes, saw my soul in my eyes, and saw that the soul in my eyes was good. Or a torture chamber in the Air Force Two cargo-hold where the U.S. Vice President himself tazed my nutsack and told me that if I didn't "play the game right" he would "personally gut every single little person [I] care[d] for in America." Or a feast in my honor on the cruiseship owned by the Elders of Zion where we hogtied blue-eyed Christian infants and held them over pans to bleed thick streams from their tiny throats on fine white flour that we baked into matzo and then ate the matzo and danced a wild hora.

Then bewigged and bespectacled and in a pink dress, or shorn-headed and neck-clocked and in a black track-suit, or smallfroed and hoodied and buttonfly bluejeaned, I entered the State of Israel through the port of Haifa or Jaffa or Ashdod or Eilat by cruiseship or carrier or speedboat or yacht or sailboat or paddleboat or catamaran, or I entered the State of Israel via Ben-Gurion International or Haifa Airport or Ramat David Airfield by an El Al Boeing 747 or an American Airlines Boeing 767 or an Air France Airbus A340 or Air Force 1 or Air Force 2 or a USAF C-130 Hercules or an IDF Air Corps Boeing 707, or I entered the state of Israel via teleportation booth which caused one of three brownouts that week in Virginia (the other two, in this version, having been manufactured to throw Russian or Iranian or Chinese enemies off my trail), and my mother went with me or was there to greet me or came the next day, and I made aliya and was immediately arrested and taken into custody or was immediately arrested and taken into custody and then made aliya or made aliya and was immediately fake-arrested and taken into custody slash-vice-versa.

And then I did or didn't try to die by hanging from a noose I made of the sheet on my bunk or the string in my hoodie or I used my belt, or did or didn't open my wrists with a ripped-open Coke can, or I punctured my carotid with a ballpoint or didn't, or climbed my cell's bars and dove at the floor to snap my neck but had second thoughts and turned midair and broke my shoulder or turned midair and didn't even break my shoulder or had no second thoughts but wasn't high up enough to get the job done or was high up enough but somehow survived because I can't die or I never climbed the bars of my cell to begin with.

And had I left June behind to enter the valley, I would not have been able to lead my army to the State of Israel, for Adonai is elegant, and the Great Lake is landlocked, and in order for us to have made it to Israel we'd have needed any number of additional miracles—miracles to sustain us and take us over land, to the ocean, and through the ocean—and because He could have, from the very beginning, just constructed a bridge of reinforced manna to span the sky from Deerbrook Park to the State of Israel or dug a manna-lined tunnel from Deerbrook Park to the State of Israel, it would not have been elegant of Adonai to provide multiple miracles to get us to Israel, and so it can easily be deduced that He created the valley for another reason, and it can just as easily be deduced that this other reason was to trick the watching world into thinking it was me who created the valley, and it can also just as easily be deduced that the reason that He wanted to trick the world was that He didn't want the soldiers to face prosecution for crimes related to the Damage Proper and that He knew that the world wouldn't prosecute the soldiers if the world were to believe I was solely responsible for all that had happened on 11-17 and that He saw that the most elegant way to foment the belief that I was solely responsible for all that had happened on 11/17 was to convince the world that I was capable of miracles. Or Adonai is inelegant, even clumsy, and there would have been more miracles to take us to the ocean and through the ocean and sustain us until we got to Israel. Or Adonai is elegant and would have liked to build a bridge or dig a tunnel to Israel, but He knew that elegance, though impressive to scholars, was less impressive to the rest of the world, and He wanted to impress the rest of the world, and thus He would have provided multiple miracles to get us to Israel, for He knew that scholars would come to understand that His reasons for appearing inelegant to them (the scholars) were elegant reasons and that the rest of the world, lacking any sense of what elegance entailed, wouldn't question Him anyway.

Or none of the above. Adonai was just winging it. Or Adonai is as elegant as first suggested and when He opened the valley He intended me to lead my army through the valley to the State of Indiana (if the valley, as some have insisted, juked a bit south just beyond its vanishing point) or the State of Michigan (if the valley, as others say, proceeded as eastwardly as it appeared to from the shore), certain as He was that by the time we arrived there, the entire world would be in awe of the valley and in awe of me and in awe of the soldiers, and that airplanes would, owing to the awe, be put at our disposal to get us to Israel, and believing as He did that our getting to

Israel in state-sanctioned airplanes would be better for the world (one love, unity) than our getting to Israel strictly via miracle.

And as we came off the beach, all of the cops were just scared and confused, and all the cameras on the ground and in the sky got thrown off when (with or without guile) I entered the copse inside the ravine, and all the TSA workers at O'Hare or Midway were wholly incompetent and the Feds were too busy to watch the news or they watched the news but didn't think the boy who split the lake could be a weapon or didn't think it quick enough or thought they'd get me later out of sight of the cameras, or did come get me later out of sight of the cameras after the cops brought me into the station or the commandeered gym, or got to the beach as fast as they could but as fast as they could was way too slow or nearly but not quite fast enough, unless it was faster than you'd ever imagine in which case the cops who were stationed on Sheridan didn't at first believe that the g-men were g-men because the g-men didn't carry any badges or because their badges were unconvincing and the cops were suspicious and slowed down the g-men, or the g-men did have convincing badges but they spoke to the local cops like schmucks which led to a fistfight with slapstick dynamics involving mud and puddles and small icy inclines and one Fed got gang-stomped and the other was his lover and he sacrificed the mission to get him an ambulance and that's why that ambulance screamed onto Sheridan just minutes after I entered the copse, or there wasn't any fight but there was some condescension on the part of the Feds toward the local cop at whom their badges were flashed who was thereby incited to passively agress and thus took extra-long to examine the badges and meanwhile my mom or Israeli agents took advantage of the distraction and snuck past the barricade and into the ravine and stealthed me for miles through the ravine and put me in a car or a boat or hovercraft that got me to a plane that brought me to Israel or to a car that got me to a(nother) boat that brought me to Israel. Or everyone involved did their jobs right and well but my mother was smarter and stealther than all of them or was owed many favors by the State of Israel by virtue of her service in the IDF or by virtue of my grandfather's service in the IDF or by virtue of her having always been Mossad, and/or because the State of Israel thought I might be a weapon and, having already—nearly two hours before they came to suspect that I was a weapon—arranged my escape at my mother's behest, needed only to modify their plans by a modicum, and so they did. Or the g-men or the cops did come get me under shadow of the copse inside of the ravine, but on our way to the station or the commandeered gym or FBI headquarters or NSA headquarters or the Freemason Lodge in the White House basement, we came across my mom or agents of Mossad who blocked the road with a semi or Humvee or tricked-out Jeep or Ford Excursion and shot my captors or knocked them out or tied them up and then brought me to Israel. Or Gnostic or Papal or Evangelical Christian assassins brought me to Israel. Or Southside Chicago Black Hebrew assassins commanded in secret by Illinois's junior U.S. Senator brought me to Israel and held me in Dimona til the special forces team that my zadie'd once commanded stormed their stronghold and brought me to Jerusalem or Tel Aviv. Or the Evangelicals didn't have assassins but they pressured the President, who sent me to Israel in hopes of apocalypse, or the Secretary of Defense did it, or aliens beamed me, and because June Watermark was so far away or Benji was gone or Berman was wicked or my parents' American lives were ruined or for all of those reasons or for some of those reasons or none of those reasons I did or didn't try to die five times or three or two times or one time or none (never four, for some reason) or it looked like I tried because a hostile faction had attempted to end me and make it look like suicide or because one of the however many times it looked like I'd attempted suicide a hostile faction had tried to end me but not the other time(s) or no one was trying to end me to begin with or no one who tried to end me could get to me or it never looked like attempted suicide because there was no *it* to look like anything or there was an it but the it was what Call-Me-Sandy would call "a cry for help" or the it was intended to engender pity from the judge or the it was staged to help bolster my pleas of insanity which I changed last minute to pleas of guilty because I didn't want to go out like that or it was staged to get me removed from the cell to a nutward, McMurphy-style, or none of it was staged or what was ostensibly staged never happened to begin with.

And Emmanuel Liebman and Eliyahu of Brooklyn were kidnapped by the State of Israel and brought here because I'd threatened to send my secret army to blow up Al Aqsa if they weren't brought here or because I'd threatened to prevent my secret army from *ever* blowing up Al Aqsa if they weren't brought here, or radical Gurionites or Scholars Fund agents or Scholars Fund scholars or Scholars Fund terrorists kidnapped the both of them because I asked them to or because they thought I'd asked them to when in fact I hadn't, or Emmanuel was kidnapped but not Eliyahu, for Eliyahu's aunt and uncle became afraid of Eliyahu and they pawned him off on West Coast cousins from whom Eliyahu kept running away til my mother reached out and offered to adopt him but then my father made it clear that he would be leaving her as soon as all of my trials concluded and my mother thought Eliyahu needed a father and so she arranged for him to stay with the Forems on the Tzur Shalem outpost of the Karmei Tzur settlement because Yuval's house was armed and kosher and he only had daughters but wanted a son and I wanted Eliyahu to get to know some settlers, or Emmanuel wasn't kidnapped either but sent to Sderot to stay with his uncle because that's what he wanted and his parents believed in him or they feared bloody vengeance from Chicago's anti-Gurionites.

And my father did leave my mother for a year or he left for two years or three years or a day or an hour or he left for good or he never left at all but they had or adopted a little girl who I'm not allowed to meet or even see pictures of, let alone hold to my chest and tell stories to, or my mother will allow me some of these things or all of these things but my father won't allow me any of these things or my father on occasion (usually just before Yom Kippur) shows me some pity and lets me see my sister but he acts so nervous whenever they bring her that I don't tell her anything I wish I could tell her for fear that I'll say the wrong thing and they'll leave even sooner than I know they're already going to leave and I come off cold and my sister is afraid of me because no one else comes off cold to my sister because she's so warm and pretty and small and she says funny things when she's not inside a prison or my sister is afraid of me because of what they tell her at school or because she's just been frisked by a polite man with a machine gun and she's surrounded by other polite men with machine guns and the smile on the face of her brother seems just as forced as the smiles on the faces of the other polite men or it doesn't seem forced but she imagines it does and refuses to look at my face for fear that it does and therefore persists in her delusion that it does or my sister is afraid of me because my father is afraid of me because of my size or because a couple years back when we got in a fight over something he thought I'd caused in Judea that I hadn't caused but might have caused had I thought to cause it he put his hands on me and I took his hands off me and held them away from me until the guards rushed us or til my mother said my name or until my mother slapped me or no one interfered but I held his hands away from me for longer than was necessary or longer than I should have or longer than I would have had I *thought* for a second or it's all the same thing, or I don't have a sister but I might as well have a sister because I wouldn't be allowed to see my sister anyway, or I don't have a sister and that is too bad because I would, if I had one, be allowed to see her because everything between my parents and me is the same as always and nothing will change.

And I broke off all manner of contact with June at the age of thirteen or eleven or the moment I arrived here because knowing her was killing me and yet I wouldn't die or because I was "selfless" and couldn't stand to make her wait or because I needed to write this scripture and I couldn't write this scripture with hope in my heart and June gave me hope, relentless hope, or I didn't break contact but bound June to me with romance and guilt and sly manipulations typical of sociopaths, or it was June who did all the contact-breaking, and any which way it was all for the best, or no one broke contact or manipulated anyone and any which way it was all for the best, or it was all for the worst, and June underwent a ceremonial conversion out of love for me or spite for me or because she'd been an Israelite all along or all of the above and she saw it was easier to just do the ceremony, or she didn't participate in any type of ceremony but she lives by the Law and she lives as if married because she is insane and she thinks we are married or because we are in fact married or will be a few months from now when June turns eighteen and makes aliya or because she believes that that's what will happen when she turns eighteen and makes aliya but that won't be what happens because I'll be dead because this scripture isn't really scripture at all but the single longest suicide note in history or because although it's scripture it's also that note or because I no longer believe she's an Israelite because Adonai wouldn't let her into the valley, or we will be married despite what He thinks or because of what He thinks or despite and because or regardless of what He thinks.

. Choose your own adventure. Keep on blogging. Just leave June alone and stay away from my brothers. Those are my instructions for all you wicked sons. What you write matters little, your scholarship is nothing, it will die as soon as you.

For those sons among you who don't know how to ask: I don't know what would have happened had I entered the valley, no one knows what would have happened had I entered the valley, and the details of what happened between the time that it closed and the news of my presence in Israel went public just aren't germane to the scripture at hand. Even if they were, there were friends who helped me, enemies who didn't, and to fink out the enemies would compromise the friends. I arrived here between November 18 and November 25, 2006, was guilty of everything with which I was charged, pled guilty to everything with which I was charged, was found guilty of everything with which I was charged, and the rest, insasmuch as it concerns you—the rest is minutiae, Moshe's shoe size.

Same with name you give to the holiday. Last Day of School Day, Day of Damage, Yom Nezek—I prefer the Hebrew, but call it what you want.

And whether or not I think I'm the messiah, or the potential messiah, or ever thought I was one or thought I was both and now think I'm neither—that's minutiae, too.

Whether I daven, and where I daven, if I don't just stand here—at six-foot-three and one-buck-ninety or six-foot-six and two-bucks-thirty or five-foot-nine and thirteen stones—in my digitally tricked-out nine-by-nine cell. What I'll do when they release me in 2017. Whether or not I'll join the IDF. Whether or not I'll go into hiding. Whether or not I'll attend yeshiva. Whether or not I'll open a yeshiva. Whether or not I'll lead my own army or enter Shin Bet or run for office for Shas or Labor or start my own party. None of it matters. You don't need to know it. It is all minutiae. Quit with the minutiae. Become the wise son. Isn't that what you want? That should be what you want.

Become the wise son and instruct your simple brothers: "The Temple is not descending from the sky. The Side of Damage was good and the underdog is good. Fear Adonai and look after June."

And instruct those brothers who don't know how to ask yet: "The Temple never would have descended from the sky. The Side of Damage was complicated, Adonai is fearsome, and anyone can tell his own underdog story. Be wary of underdogs. Look after June."

Recognize your wicked brothers are beyond all instruction, that that's why they're wicked, but keep your eyes sleepy and instruct them nonetheless: "Stay away from our brothers and leave June alone."

He thought we should fucken waterboard each other. How can you protect somebody like that?

You'll know when the Gurionic War is over. Every day is Yom Nezek except for Shabbat. Observe Yom Nezek. Celebrate and celebrate. Adonai is damaged. Look after June. I led the Side of Damage before I led you. Doubt your underdog story no less than any other. I'm an Israeli, Chicago born. There will be more damage, I'm the end of the Jews, and the Temple will never descend from the sky.

Damage, damage, and damage, the end.

ACKNOWLEDGEMENTS

Thank you, Lanny and Atara Levin, for pretty much everything, especially the sisters.

Thank you, Rachel and Paula Levin, for always showing up, all funny and kind, and for allowing me to be your older brother all these years.

Thank you, Leslie Lockett, for always being Leslie Lockett, for every last thing your being her entails.

Thank you, Susan Golomb, for your acts of agency.

Thank you, Summer Literary Seminars, for the white nights and boat rides.

Thank you, Sid Feldman, for introducing me, way back when, to the work of Philip Roth and Charlie Chaplin and the Marx Brothers, and for then, not so way-back-when at all, inviting me over for home-cooked meals—scores of home-cooked meals—to which I couldn't bring wine or dessert or even a sixpack, and for never making me feel like a shnorer. You too, Renee Feldman.

Thank you, Adam Novy, Arthur Flowers, Christopher Kennedy, Daniel Torday, Eric Rosenblum, Rachael Rosenblum, Jeff Parker, Kathryn TeBordo, Mary Gaitskill, Mary Karr, Mikhail Iossel, Phil LaMarche, Sophie Caird, and Thomas Yagoda, for your counsel and encouragement and hospitality.

Thank you, Christian TeBordo, for reading this book before anyone else, before it was even a tenth of this book, and then when it was more than ten tenths of this book, for keeping me sane for the past nine years, and for never turning down a single invitation to go outside in the cold and smoke.

Thank you, Salvador Plascencia, for your early reads and provisions of sanity, and for coming out to smoke even though you never smoked, except for once or twice, for three or four drags, or maybe five or six, on a snowy porch, late in the night, which was thrilling and weird and made me feel strangely guilty, and Christian too, I bet.

Thank you, George Saunders, for teaching the unteachable, and for letting me into the Syracuse University Creative Writing Program, where I met half the people named on this page.

And thank you, Eli Horowitz, for keeping the faith, for doing this right, for being the kind of reader and editor the doomsayers tell us no longer exists.

ABOUT THE AUTHOR

Adam Levin's stories have appeared in *Tin House*, *McSweeney's*, and *Esquire*. Winner of the 2003 Summer Literary Seminars Fiction Contest and the 2004 Joyce Carol Oates Fiction Prize, Levin holds an MA in Clinical Social Work from the University of Chicago and an MFA in Creative Writing from Syracuse University. His collection of short stories, *Hot Pink*, will be published by McSweeney's Books in 2011. He lives in Chicago, where he teaches Creative Writing at Roosevelt University and the School of the Art Institute. *The Instructions* is his first novel.